Library of America, a nonprofit organization,
champions our nation's cultural heritage
by publishing America's greatest writing in
authoritative new editions and providing resources
for readers to explore this rich, living legacy.

JEAN STAFFORD

JEAN STAFFORD

COMPLETE STORIES
& OTHER WRITINGS

The Collected Stories of Jean Stafford
Other Stories
A Mother in History
Selected Essays

Kathryn Davis, *editor*

THE LIBRARY OF AMERICA

Contents

SELECTED ESSAYS

THE COLLECTED STORIES
OF JEAN STAFFORD

For Katharine S. White

Author's note

By the time I knew him, my father was writing Western stories under the *nom de plume* Jack Wonder or, occasionally, Ben Delight. But before that, before I was born, he wrote under his own name and he published a novel called *When Cattle Kingdom Fell.* The other principal book in my family (the rest were memory books and albums of scenic postal cards) was by my first cousin once removed on my mother's side, Margaret Lynn, and this was *A Stepdaughter of the Prairie,* a reminiscence of her girlhood in frontier days in Kansas. To my regret, I have read neither of these books, so I cannot say that they influenced me. However, their *titles* influenced me when my cacoëthes scribendi set in and I wrote about twisters on the plains, stampedes when herds of longhorns were being driven up from the Panhandle to Dodge, and bloody incidents south of the border. All the foremen of all the ranches had steely blue eyes to match the barrels of their Colt .45's. With this kind of heritage and early practice I might have been expected to become a regional writer, but my father's wicked West and Cousin Margaret's noble West existed only in memory, and I could not wait to quit my tamed-down native grounds. As soon as I could, I hotfooted it across the Rocky Mountains and across the Atlantic Ocean. I have been back to the West, since then, only for short periods of time, but my roots remain in the semi-fictitious town of Adams, Colorado, although the rest of me may abide in the South or the Midwest or New England or New York. Most of the people in these stories are away from home, too, and while they are probably homesick, they won't go back. In a sense, then, the geographical grouping I have chosen for the stories is arbitrary. I have borrowed titles from Mark Twain and Henry James (I am a great one for appropriating other people's titles), who are two of my favorite American writers and to whose dislocation and whose sense of place I feel allied.

J. S.

THE INNOCENTS ABROAD

Maggie Meriwether's Rich Experience

THERE was a hole so neat that it looked tailored in the dead center of the large round beige velours mat that had been thrown on the grass in the shade of the venerable sycamore, and through it protruded a clump of mint, so chic in its air of casualness, so piquant in its fragrance in the heat of mid-July, that Mme Floquet, a brisk Greek in middle life, suggested, speaking in French with a commandingly eccentric accent, that her host, Karl von Bubnoff, M. le Baron, had contrived it all with shears and a trowel before his Sunday guests arrived at his manorial house, Magnamont, in Chantilly. It was quite too accidental to *be* accidental, she declared; it was quite too Surrealist to be a happenstance. Mme Floquet had the look and the deportment of a dark wasp; her thin, sharp fingers, crimson-tipped, fiddled with her bracelets, made of rare old coins ("Oh, Byzantine, I daresay, or something of the sort," she had said carelessly to someone who had admired them; one knew that she knew perfectly well the pedigree and the value of each of them), and through smoked glasses of a rosy cast she gave her lightning-paced regard to a compact that had cunningly been made from a tiger cowrie shell and given by M. le Baron to Mrs. Preston, whose birthday it was today. Mrs. Preston, a Russian, was as Amazonian and fair as Mme Floquet was elfin and swart, and she was the beneficiary of so large a fortune, left to her by an American husband (he had manufactured pills), that in certain quarters she was adored. (Mme Floquet, who was dependent for her livelihood on the largess of a moody Danish lover, had been heard to remark, "I can't say that Tanya carries her money as well as she might, but that sort of thing—money, I mean—can't be ignored. I'd not refuse the offer of the Koh-i-noor, even though it wouldn't be my style." Because of this forbearance on the part of Mme Floquet, she and Mrs. Preston were the best of friends, and the little Greek had frequently accepted presents of slightly worn sables and the use of second-best motorcars.)

It was Mme Floquet's chaffing tone that was immediately adopted by the whole party. The conceit of their host's rising before the dew was dry and arranging this neat tatter and its rural adornment amused them, and, to his delight, they ragged him; someone proposed that he had really done it the night before by moonlight and had recited incantations that would endow this particular herb with magic properties—black or benign, the speaker would not care to guess. Rejoicing in his witty nature, they recalled the Baron's *fête champêtre* of the summer before, when there had actually been jousting and tilting, the knights being jockeys from Longchamp in papier-mâché armor executed by Christian Dior. Someone else, returning to the present joke, said, "If this were Tennessee, we could have mint juleps." But Mme Floquet, who tended to be tutorial, replied to this, "Those, I believe, are made with Bourbon whiskey, and the taste of that, I assure you, is insupportable. I had some one day in America by mistake." She shuddered and her bracelets sang.

Maggie Meriwether, who was from Nashville and was the only American present, and who was abroad for the first time in her young life, blushed at this mention of her native state and country as if someone had cast an aspersion on her secret lover; she was gravely, cruelly homesick. Her French, acquired easily and then polished painstakingly at Sweet Briar, had forsaken her absolutely the very moment the Channel boat docked in Calais, and while, to her regret and often to her bitter abasement, she had understood almost everything she had heard since she had been in France, she had not been able to utter a word. Not so much as "*Merci*" and certainly not so much as "*Merci beaucoup.*" She had been sure that if she did, she would be greeted with rude laughter (not loud but penetrating), cool looks of disdain, or simply incomprehension, as if she were speaking a Finnish dialect. Her parents, who had had to be cajoled for a year into letting her go to Europe alone, had imagined innumerable dreadful disasters—the theft of her passport or purse, ravishment on the Orient Express, amoebic dysentery, abduction into East Berlin—but it had never occurred to them that their high-spirited, self-confident, happy daughter would be bamboozled into muteness by the language of France. Her itinerary provided for two weeks in Paris, and she had suffered through one week of it when, like an angel from heaven, an Englishman called Tippy Akenside showed up at her hotel at the very moment when she was about to dissolve in tears and book passage home. She had met Tippy in London at a dinner party—the English ate awful food and drank awful drinks, but they surely did speak a nice language—and had liked him, and she would have been pleased to see him again anywhere; seeing him in Paris at the crucial moment had almost caused her to fall in love with him, though young men with wavy black hair and bad teeth had never appealed to her. He had been wonderfully understanding of her dilemma (he had had a similar experience in Germany when he had gone there for a holiday from Eton), and the evening before, which had begun at Maxim's and ended at Le Grand Seigneur with rivers of champagne, he had proposed this day in the country as a cheerful relaxation. He was a friend of the Baron and knew most of the people who were to be at the party, and he assured her that all of them spoke English. He had promised on his word of honor that he would manage cleverly to make everyone speak it—English was ever so smart these days, he said—and do so without embarrassing her. Tippy's word of honor had proved to be no longer than a nonsense syllable, and his cleverness as a social arbiter evidently existed only in his mind. For English was not being spoken, not even by—especially not by—Tippy. Not one of the company was French, although they looked it; as for their host, M. le Baron was the son of a Viennese father and a half-French, half-Irish mother.

Maggie had loathed Tippy Akenside from the moment they got out of his Renault. Looking back, she saw that he was a poor driver—not reckless but gawky—so that they had made the trip in fits and starts, and he had not paid any attention at all to her except for making introductions.

Not only was she miserable over the death grip in which the cat had got her tongue; she was feeling very country-looking, although she had thought she looked quite smart when she set out from Paris. The other ladies had all brought a change of clothes, had taken off their city dresses and their city shoes and were wearing stunning linen shorts and shirts and Italian sandals. They had not, however, removed their jewels; rubies and emeralds and diamonds were visible at the open necks of their informal shirts; fashionably crude-cut gems of inestimable worth glittered at their wrists and ears; Mrs. Preston wore an ankle bracelet of star sapphires. Maggie, in a tie-silk print and high-heeled shoes (and, oh, lackamercy on us, *stockings!*) and a choker of cultured pearls, could not tell whether they were all really not aware that she was there or whether they thought that Tippy, who was descended from a long line of eccentrics (and, thought Maggie, of traitors), had brought along his mother's tweeny for some sort of awful joke. She did not know, that is, whether she was invisible or whether she was an eyesore too excruciating to look at. Certainly they were managing marvelously to rise above her presence.

Maggie was sorry that she was not enjoying her experience, because she was sure it was a rich one for a simple country-club girl from Tennessee. M. le Baron was a handsome, sparkling man whom many women, according to Tippy, wished to marry. All but a few diehards, mainly girls of a greedy and romantic age, had sensibly faced up to the fact that he would remain a bachelor forever, because he basked in a perfectly rapturously happy marriage to his demesne, this superb Palladian house that confronted a pool filled with blue water hyacinths—a pool that adroitly became a broad and gracefully meandering stream where black swans rode and charming bridges arched to debouch into charming paths, through acres and acres of classical gardens and orchards, up into vineyards, down into cow pastures and paddocks. At some distance behind the house, within a grove of oaks that dated back to Charlemagne, there was a famous, ancient abbey, inhabited now not by clericals—except for the household priest—but by the Baron's aged French-Irish mother, her aged brother, his aged manservant, and a bevy of aged handmaidens. The valet sometimes played the fiddle—badly but with heart—and the maids beautifully crocheted; the brother and sister, who doted on each other, played backgammon almost unceasingly, and both of them cheated without a prick of conscience. It was a supremely contented community. The servants of Magnamont were happy; the tenants were prosperous and exceptionally fecund; the livestock was stalwart; the fruit of the land was unparalleled. And all of this harmony came about because M. le Baron was so faithful to his husbandry.

What he loved best in the world next to grooming and burnishing Magnamont was showing off Magnamont to visitors, but he was so sensitive to any slight upon his true love that he never forced her on anyone. This reluctance dated from two episodes, occurring within a month of each other: Someone had made a stupid joke about the sheep that were wisely and thriftily used to keep down the grass of the far lawns, and someone else, who had had an excess of drink, had gone a little too far about the topiary garden, which, while admittedly absurd, was heirloom and sacrosanct. These boors, needless to say, had never been asked back. If an invitation to look at his dovecotes or his asparagus beds had been received with indifference, M. le Baron's heart would have bled, so he had to be asked—he sometimes even had to be coaxed—to conduct a tour of the grounds.

Maggie had momentarily warmed to this man, for when Tippy introduced them he had smiled in the friendliest possible way and had said, in English, "How nice of you to come," but then, when rotten Tippy said, "Miss Meriwether is the American girl I told you about on the phone," the Baron thereafter addressed her in highly idiomatic French until, encountering nothing but silence and the headshakes and cryptic groans that escaped her involuntarily, he began to pretend, as the others had done from the start, that she wasn't there.

They had had a long ramble, for these guests knew the way to their host's heart; they had seen everything, including the bees, including the Baron's mother and uncle, who were swindling each other and drinking Jamaica rum out of minute silver goblets. Maggie had not minded the excursion, tiring and baffling as it had been, half as much as she did this present situation, when they all sat in a circle on the mat as if they were about to play spin-the-plate and aim for the clump of mint. They were drinking martinis made with a European and abominable exorbitance of vermouth. They were drinking martinis, that is, with the exception of the Contessa Giovennazzo, who, with enormous originality, had asked for iced *tilleul*. This woman, a vision in shocking pink and violet and with phosphorescent streaks of platinum in her black hair, discomfited Maggie almost more than any of the others, for she talked so much and so knowingly about the United States; she had a great deal to say about the United Nations and about Hollywood, and she told a significant anecdote about a senator of whom Maggie had never heard.

From time to time, Maggie tried to catch Tippy's shifty eye, and she unremittingly sent him an SOS by telepathy. But he was engaged in a preposterous recapitulation of scenes of W. C. Fields movies with a Heer Dokter van Lennep, a psychoanalyst who had emigrated from Amsterdam to practice on Park Avenue, and with a man whose name Maggie had not caught and whose nationality or occupation or age she could not begin to determine; he was rather fat and rather fair and rather seedy and rather melancholy of countenance (he was not enjoying the conversation about W. C. Fields at all), but since all these things were only *rather* true of him, their opposites could just as easily have obtained. She had never seen anyone so nondescript; he looked like a bundle that might have contained anything on earth. Because of his very lack of definition, she pinned her hopes on him. At least, he wasn't elegant; he did not look rich; he did not look well-connected; not a single scintilla burst from his soggy, shaggy person. And she began, parenthetically, to send him a distress signal.

The gossip, over these many, many bad martinis, was global. The jokes (they laughed like mad and had to wipe the corners of their eyes with their monogrammed handkerchiefs) presupposed a knowledge of the early peccadilloes of papal princesses and of deposed kings and demoted Prussian generals, the sharp wit of footmen in embassies in Africa, the gaucherie of certain spies and the high style of certain others, the moral turpitude— ghastly, really, but screamingly funny—of a choreographer in Berlin, the lineage of a positively fascinating band of juvenile delinquents that were terrorizing Neuilly-sur-Seine.

Maggie grew hotter and larger.

The interminable day progressed from one disgrace to another, and Maggie Meriwether, who once upon a time had been considered something of a belle, became more and more bedraggled. Her stem, that green and golden tie-silk print, began to look as if it had been dragged in by the same cat that had hold of her tongue; her roots were swollen (looked like potatoes, to tell the truth, thought Maggie wretchedly) in too new shoes; and her hair, which was thick and red-gold (once called "strictly Maggie's crowning glory"), got stringy with the heat and with her emotion and looked, she knew, exactly like a dying dandelion. What a wallflower! The more she drank, the more trembly she got, and she was obliged to refuse several courses at lunch because she could not possibly have handled the serving spoons; she fancied that the butler divined her difficulty and despised her, and she wished that she could say in withering French that where she came from horsewhips were still widely used on uppity servants.

Lunch, which was long, was served at a semicircular table on the veranda, so that the party had a view of the pool and the avenues of lime trees that flanked it. They started with cold sorrel soup and went on to salmon in mayonnaise and capers, to a capon stuffed with truffles and the bottoms of artichokes; they had asparagus; they had salad; they had melon; they had Brie. They toasted the birthday girl in sweet wine, dry wine, champagne; with their coffee, they drank cassis. Everything, except for the coffee beans, had been grown at Magnamont. There were two subjects of conversation; one was the food they were eating and the other was the food they had eaten at other times at Magnamont. The nondescript man, who was sitting at Maggie's right, recalled, or failed to recall, past entrees, in mutters. Mme Floquet chided him for his mood with such intimate ill-humor that Maggie concluded they were related; the others ignored him much as they ignored Maggie. M. le Baron spoke to her once. In English, he said "Do you fly?," and when she said that she did, he grew cordial until, on further inquiry, he learned that she had often been a passenger on commercial airplanes, that she was not a pilot. He said, "Too bad. You might have enjoyed flying one of my gliders later on." At this hideous proposal, poor Maggie's butterfingers dropped the glass they were holding and wine went all over the priceless damask; the accident was Olympianly disregarded except by the butler, who scowled blackly. The Baron turned to Mrs. Preston and asked her to recollect the menu he and she had planned together for the christening party of his godson; it had included a roebuck shot in Bavaria.

After Mme Floquet had smoked a small cigar, the ladies retired into the house, to a boudoir that contained so many mirrors telling the unvarnished truth that Maggie seriously thought she might have a fit. To add to her concern about herself, the ladies discussed their hairdressers and their dressmakers and admired one another's shorts and cuffs and cuff links. Mme Floquet took a bath in the Lucullan chamber that adjoined this one; Mrs. Preston lay down on a chaise with belladonna packs on her eyes; the Contessa removed her maquillage and put on fresh—she was as deft and as thorough as a topflight surgeon. Maggie—poor kid, she thought of herself—applied new lipstick, realizing that it was the wrong color for her scarecrow duds, and ran a comb through her hopeless hair, and observed through tears that her nail polish was chipping squalidly, and then she sat down as far from the others as possible and looked at a copy of *Country Life*, although she had lost her eyesight as well as her power of speech. For a very long time indeed she glared blindly at a photograph entitled "May on the Westmorland fells," in whose foreground there were daffodils the size of umbrellas, sheep the size of buffaloes, and lambs as big as rams, and in whose background there was a Hop-o'-My-Thumb shepherd and a dog to match. She memorized, as she had once memorized the oath of allegiance, the following: "The fellside Herdwick strain is believed to have been introduced by the Norse settlers of a thousand years ago."

When they had completed the reclamation of their pre-lunch faces, had examined one another's jewels, and had finished off some scandal of a dangerous turn, they went outside again and climbed a flight of sturdy steps into a tree house in a massive oak that grew beside the pool. Maggie Meriwether tagged behind like a tug in the wake of an imperial armada. Here, in the tree house, they sat on brocaded poufs around a low, round table on which stood a narghile; they thought about smoking it but decided it was too much trouble. From time to time they glanced casually down at the men, who, in bathing trunks, were practicing tightrope walking, perilously, along a rope strung across the pool. The rope was low, and a good thing it was, since none of them except the Baron had even a rudimentary skill at this extraordinary Sunday sport. (On seeing the ladies, he had called up that he had decided against the gliders today because the wind was wrong.) They fell into the water frequently and came up splotched with slime, looking as if they were wearing camouflage.

The narghile had led the ladies to a discussion of which narcotics they enjoyed the most, and for some time they vivaciously exchanged memories of their sensations. The Contessa had found her nirvana on the shores of Lago di Garda when she had combined smoking marijuana with drinking champagne and eating apricots. Mme Floquet used Demerol occasionally and achieved noteworthy effects; it tampered in the most bizarre way imaginable with her sense of time, so that she had once arrived for a cocktail party at six o'clock in the morning, thinking it was six in the afternoon, and found no one, of course, but a flabbergasted housemaid—people had dined out on that story for months. Mrs. Preston liked everything; if she had a slight preference, it was for chloral hydrate followed by vodka; whenever she gave herself one of these "Meeky Feens" she had a maid in waiting to remove all matches from her immediate environs, since she had an understandable horror of lighting a cigarette in her delicious coma and setting herself on fire.

All of a sudden the cat turned loose Maggie's tongue, and it behaved like a jack-in-the-box. It said, in English, "Have you-all ever tried snuff? You can lip it or dip it or sniff it. It's mighty good with sour mash and potato chips."

Luckily for her, the tightrope broke just then and there was a good-natured uproar from below, which caused the ladies in the tree house to clap their hands girlishly. The indeterminate man without a name had been halfway across it, and when he came spluttering up out of the water of the pool, he was wearing a hyacinth exactly on top of his head, like a calotte. Mme Floquet exclaimed, "What an oaf! What an ox!" Mrs. Preston said, "He is really a dog in every way," and the Contessa observed, "What bad manners he has to spoil Karl's tightrope." The stumblebum, shaking himself and clawing the flower off his head, wore a look of unspeakable boredom, and Maggie loved him, whoever he was. She even felt a little better off than he; at least she had not excited these recherché dragons to call her names. Who on earth could he be? He looked like a nearly penniless schoolmaster with dyspepsia and a tendency to catarrh, and Maggie resolved, if this day went on much longer, to make friends with him—in sign language, if necessary.

After the men had changed and a great many more people had arrived, from neighboring estates (some bicycled, some came on horseback, a duchess carrying a blue silk parasol arrived in a pony cart, and two beautiful princesses came on motor bikes), the guests returned to the house to sit down for tea around the largest dining table in the largest dining room Maggie had ever seen. A vast three-tiered turntable slowly and automatically revolved, offering a staggering profusion of pastries, fruits, cheese, sandwiches, candies, nuts, hors d'oeuvres; there were tea and coffee and lemonade and orangeade and vinous and spirituous liquors. There must have been twenty-five people at that regal table, and all of them were talking. Though the din was monolingual, it was that of Babel; the laughter was plentiful and it was French; the spoons made a French clatter in the saucers; the bell in the abbey rang *cinq heures*; the Dutch psychoanalyst from New York subjected the duchess, by whom he was impressed, to a Gallic scrutiny through his thick glasses; Tippy Akenside, flanked by the princesses, analyzed Proust.

Not by accident, Maggie found herself next to her shabby counterpart; she had made a beeline for the area in which he was hovering like a rain cloud, and when everyone sat down, she sat beside him. Nearby were her enemies from the tree house. The Contessa, who refused both food and drink, had added a Japanese fan to her costume and oscillated it before her face; it did not disturb a hair of her head. Mrs. Preston fed ravenously and drank deeply. Mme Floquet ate enough to keep a bird alive. And all the time they indulged or abstained, the three of them kept their eyes glued on Maggie's next-door neighbor as if they were waiting to catch him out in some egregious breach of etiquette. They talked of other matters, to be sure, but they plainly had their minds on this poor, dim stick; he appeared to be impervious to their dagger looks, but Maggie suspected that he was only putting up a front, and finally, summoning her courage, she asked him in English, with great compassion, if he had enjoyed the tightrope walking.

"Filthy waste of time," he said, giving her a quick look out of bleary eyes. "I say, are you an American?" Maggie took his accent to be Scotch. Suddenly he looked very Scotch, and she was much comforted, since her maternal grandmother had come from Aberdeen.

Although his question had required a simple yes or no for an answer, Maggie replied at an uncontrolled length, so happy was she to be reunited with her mother tongue, so grateful was she to have her existence acknowledged. She was afterward never able to explain satisfactorily to herself why she had bragged so feelingly about the medical school of Vanderbilt University or why she had delivered a short lecture on the survival of ballad-making among the mountain people in the Cumberland Plateau—nerves, she supposed, a logorrhea coming as the natural result of long privation. The watchful ladies gazed at her as if she were dancing a hula on the tabletop, and this further agitated her compulsive tongue. She talked and talked.

The man did not seem to be terribly interested, but neither did he look away. His tumescent lips were slack and mauve; his pink-rimmed eyes bespoke astigmatism and gin; his skin was dingy, as if he spent much of his time in dingy places—the public bars of railway stations, for example; his fingernails were square and very dirty; he had a huge wart under his left ear; his cheap jacket pinched him under the arms; his shirt was limp and the Kelly-green knit necktie he wore was a disgrace. He was the most unprepossessing of men. Fit company for Maggie in her present condition: Ladies, she implored them silently, please look away.

"I fancy the Civil War," he said when Maggie had finished her recital. And after he had made this surprising statement, not designating what aspect of the Civil War he fancied—whether its literature or its strategy, its ideology or its outcome—he went on to talk volubly about himself, as if, like her, he had discovered that his vocal cords were, after all, not totally paralyzed.

What Maggie learned dumfounded her.

First of all, he was a student at Harrow (she had thought him to be no less than thirty and probably closer to forty), but before Harrow he had flown in the war and had got his "ration of Jerrys." Evidently he had fancied this war, too—had found "mucking up their damned munitions plants not half-bad fun," and had had some "damned good whing-dings with your Commando chaps." He asked her if she knew a damned good cove from Montreal named Agnew MacPherson—they had kicked up one hell of a shindy together in Oxford once, when they were both on leave. Schooling was a bloody bore and he would far rather spend all his time, and not just his hols, in Africa; he made a vague joke about the sport of kings being that of hunting down the king of beasts instead of those tuppenny-ha'penny grouse on the Scottish moors. Give him a safari and then another safari and after that one more safari and then give him a fortnight in Algiers in which to get as drunk as a fiddler and pub-crawl in the Casbah. What could be the possible use of all this damned footling Greek and algebra? The only bearable part of school was going up to town—he had a highly modified Bentley and it was fairly good fun to give the peasants on the road a run for their money. But London was bloody sad; the bottle clubs were mostly a bloody bore and closed too damned early. The floor shows were bloody awful and there were all those damned orchids around.

Orchids were this man's subject. He might be a student of the Civil War, he might be fulfilled by hunting big game, he might like racing cars, he might have all sorts of deep-felt predilections. But what inspired him to oratory was his rabid aversion to orchids, and as he was delivering his vehement tirade against them, he paused once to point his spoon at Mme Floquet as if he were going to shoot her.

"They're not so bad growing in Africa; but they're not my cup of tea even there," he said. "Anyhow, I'm a fauna man, not a flora man—give me a tiger sooner than a tiger lily." He seemed gloomily addicted to this kind of play on words. "And when you have to pay a quid for the damned beastly things for a girl to wear on her dress, it's too thick. They're not worth a bob, let alone a quid. A quid! But do you know there are some women who want you to send them a dozen at once?"

"Serge!" remonstrated Mme Floquet sharply, and tried to sting him with a look.

But his violence had by no means spent itself and he continued, his gray skin taking on an ominous mottle. "I *hate* women who want you to send them orchids," he declared, and savagely devoured the last of his napoleon. "I hate them the most, but I also hate women who drink cold tea in the middle of the night."

"Don't be such an ass, Serge," said the Contessa Giovennazzo calmly. "You'll make yourself ill." She was not as insouciant as she wanted to be thought; Maggie, fascinated, saw that her hand trembled as she fitted a cigarette into a gold holder, and that with one brilliant eye she demolished Serge while with the other she did Mme Floquet in.

"Same to you with nobs on," said Serge, whose face now

looked like a garish batik. A vein stood out, thumping, on his temple. Everyone, except a very hungry and very old man, who was interested only in his food, looked at him; all conversation ceased. As if he had been waiting for this, Serge now stood up, arms akimbo. He said, "And I hate women who gorge themselves on fish."

Mrs. Preston, whose plate was littered with the heads and tails of sardines and the rejected portions of eel, touched her low, Slavic forehead with her fingertips; Maggie had failed to notice before that her nails were painted gold.

M. le Baron, directly across the table from Serge, also rose, and faced his guest with a smile of the utmost tolerance and affection. The genial host, the perfect host of this mad tea party, he said, "I wish to propose a toast." A mob of minions materialized to fill glasses with champagne.

"To Serge," said M. le Baron sonorously. "Our beloved prince among princes."

Tippy Akenside uttered his first words of English. He said, "Hear! Hear!" The company drank and cheered, and Serge let his arms fall to his sides; he paled, and his three ladies beamed at him.

"To Sunday at Magnamont!" cried Heer Dokter van Lennep. The exuberant chorus was deafening.

There were further toasts: to Tanya Preston, because of her birthday; to the duchess, because of a fabulous race horse she had just bought; to the doctor, because he had once insulted Jung; to M. le Baron, and to his mother, his uncle, his table, his cellar, his roses; to Mme Floquet, a love; to the Contessa, a beauty; to the princesses and the princesses' fiancés. Throughout this, Serge stood at Maggie's side like a bump on a log except that he was weeping.

Abruptly, it was all over, and Maggie, having no idea how she had accomplished it, found herself beside Tippy Akenside in his car. One of the straps of her slip was hanging halfway down her arm and it terminated in a small gold safety pin. She did not look back and she did not look at her companion. Exhausted, she wondered how on earth the young set of Nashville could have imagined they were lively and original.

Tippy was laughing hard. "Just as well you don't work for the Marshall Plan people, what?" he said.

"It most certainly is," said Maggie, prim inside despite her outward dishevelment. "Who was that man?"

"Serge? Poor Serge. Simply a balmy Georgian prince, only the difference between him and most of them is that he has pots of money. Everyone wants to marry him and *he* wants to marry the Duchess of Kent."

"He must be thirty-five—and still at Harrow!"

"He's thirty-three," said Tippy. "He was held back by the war, and then he went crackers after it and was in the bin for years—harmless but completely ga-ga. How did you like the orchids speech?"

"Oh, it was grand," said Maggie.

Tippy could hardly drive for laughing. "I've heard him give philippics on everything. You should hear him do bubble-and-squeak."

"I liked him," said Maggie.

"Of course you liked him," said Tippy. "Everyone's mad for mad old Serge."

"I liked him because he spoke English to me," said Maggie. Now that she was safely away from those international clothes-horses and had only to contend with a rather puny Englishman whose cuffs, she observed with pleasure, were none too clean, she allowed her dander to get up. "I think you are a stinker."

"Good Lord! Didn't you like it?"

"Drive fast," commanded Miss Meriwether. "Be as compe-tent as you can but drive fast."

"I *am* sorry, Maggie," he said, and he sounded it. "I thought you were having a good time. And you weren't?"

All the way back to Paris, she cried with her face in her hands. "They treated me like an I don't know what," she blubbered, "except for the nutty prince."

"*Noblesse oblige*," said Tippy, with a nervous laugh, and, realizing that he had put his foot in his mouth, nearly came a cropper with a poultry van.

She bade him goodbye, not *au revoir,* at the door of her hotel.

This appalling day, unlike so many appalling days, had a happy ending. There was a huge bouquet of sumptuous summer flow-ers in Maggie's room, and under the vase was a *pneumatique* from Roger Carrithers, who was the older brother of Maggie's roommate at Sweet Briar; it asked her to dine that night with him and friends. She leaped to the telephone, which heretofore she had avoided like an instrument of darkness, and in rapid, rebellious French got through to the Meurice and then to Roger's kind Tidewater voice.

The group of six who had dinner together that night were all Americans, and they loved Maggie's story, requiring her to repeat parts of it over again, denying that she had looked the ragamuffin she claimed ("Unthinkable," said Roger Carrithers, who had been brought up properly. "You put them in the shade and they were jealous"), and wholeheartedly sympathizing with her predicament.

Taking the cue from that eccentric Baron, they, too, had toasts. They toasted the tree house and the narghile, the tightrope and the hyacinth on top of Serge's head. And they toasted Maggie Meriwether, the most sophisticated, the most cosmopolitan, the prettiest raconteur of middle Tennessee.

The Children's Game

THE wide hanging lamps with beaded fringe and shades of ecru silk cast an unwholesome, joyless light on the watchful countenances of the croupiers and the gamblers at the tables of roulette and *chemin de fer*. Smoke, in this lackluster, was green, not blue, as if it partook of the color of the felt on the tables and it hovered, a sweet effluvium, over the heads that were bent to the study of wheels and cards.

Everyone in the warm, bland, airless room—the tall windows were closed and snuff-brown mohair draperies were drawn over them—looked chronically ill and engrossed with his symptoms. And while the symptoms might vary, the malady was the same in a young Chinese woman, as neat as a cat, who never raised her eyes from a notebook in which she was keeping a system of probabilities; in an aging, florid German whose face was as scarred as the moon, and who wore his monocle like a reprimand; in a cool, queenly Scandinavian whose coronet of golden braids was intertwined with pearls. The common denominator for all of these—and for the rajah in a diapered turban and the two Scots in kilts, for the burghers from Brussels and the wattled old dowagers frothing with native lace and paved with diamonds from Antwerp—was that of the invalid concentrating on the tides of his pain, a look necessarily unsociable.

Indeed, such was the air of apprehension and constraint that the casino could have been a hospital ward save that the uniform was dinner dress, not *déshabillé*. Over the whole Saturday-night throng—five hundred or more, so that the players stood six deep—there was a hush of desperate tension; there was no laughter, there was a little murmured conversation, and except for this, there were only the sounds of the croupiers' muted exclamation, "*Messieurs, mesdames, faites vos jeux!*" and the spinning of the wheels, and the croupiers' further admonition, "*Rien ne va plus,*" and a communal sigh as the balls fell into their final, fateful compartments.

Abby Reynolds had left her escort, Hugh Nicholson, playing at the table nearest the bar. Conscientious cicerone that he was, he had offered to wander about with her, but she had replied that she wanted to observe this phenomenon without a guide, and he had not protested, but had at once addressed himself to the wheel. Abby's preconception of gambling derived from scenes in movies, and as she moved from table to table, endeavoring to understand the games, she realized that either her memory was at fault or Hollywood had carelessly added an apocryphal glitter and subtracted an essential gloom. She had expected rich chandeliers, not these morose and fungoid lamps, and the carpet was not dense and darkly red, but was thin, and it bore upon its lugubrious puce background a vapid pattern of flaxen parallelograms.

Vaguely she had imagined balconies, beset with the branches of flowering trees, where, looking down to a moonlit sea littered with the yachts of millionaires, chic lovers confronted the tortures and the consolations of their love. She thought that in the movies there had been the poignant music of stringed instruments, bittersweet, oblique. The bar should have offered a sprightlier aspect: this one, not altogether clean, presided over by two phlegmatic Walloons, looked rather like something to be found in a railway terminal or on a Channel boat. She reflected that probably the gaming rooms of Monte Carlo (or those of cosmopolitan South American cities) had been the ones that she had seen on the screen and that the beatifying lights and airs and blossoms of the Mediterranean (or of the Atlantic in its Southern countenance) had caused her to misconstrue. Here, in Belgium, in Knokke-le-Zoute, the casino perhaps had borrowed its somber look from the dun North Sea, where the skies were low and heavy and the melancholy dunes were gray.

Nor was the clientele what she had anticipated; their tragedy —or their headlong, suicidal folly—if it existed, was masked by that look of malaise, by that look of removal, of being, somehow, behind clouded glass. There was contagion in the atmosphere, and after an hour's roaming, Abby began to feel edgy and glum, although when she had first entered the room she had been exuberant. She and Hugh Nicholson had won handsomely at the races at Ostend that afternoon and had congratulated themselves at length with champagne, and at the height of their gaiety they had decided to hire a car to drive on here. Now the glow of the champagne had been usurped by a headache and Abby's eyes stung with the smoke and the languid light and all her elation had withered away in the silence of this dedicated and unhappy horde and under the practiced, appraising eyes of the croupiers and the officials on their high chairs who could accurately read the physiognomies of knaves and addicts and tenderfeet. Not only did these men stare and classify; so did the players, implacably hostile as if they resented being caught out at their secret vice which they could indulge only in the most public way.

An ancient woman with a cockled, whiskery face, dressed in purple crepe and wearing a purple toque, gazed long at Abby through a jewel-encrusted lorgnette, and Abby, challenged, gazed back, but stage fright overtook her and she lost the battle and moved on to another table where she was once again stared out of countenance by another beldam whose boa of monkey fur was the same texture and color as her poorly dyed hair. Both pairs of eyes had reviled her, had plainly said, "Tripper! Spectator! Who are you to sit in judgment?" And she felt as she did when someone jostled her in a crowd and then gratuitously scolded her for being in the way.

Suddenly, feeling lost, she was assailed by a wild wind of homesickness and she went into the bar, almost weeping, where she ordered a glass of lemonade.

For nearly a year, ever since her husband's death, Abby Reynolds had lived in Europe, moving from a Florentine *pensione* for bereft or virginal gentlewomen to the same kind of asylum in Rome; she had dwelt in rooms in the flats of respectable elderly couples in Vienna and Munich, and she had lived in a borrowed apartment in Paris with a borrowed maid and a borrowed black cat. Although she was only in her early forties, she had begun to feel quaint and wan. She felt that she had become indistinguishable from the thousands and thousands of lonesome American ladies who lived abroad because a foreign address, however modest, had a cachet that a New York or a Boston apartment hotel had not; the cachet was necessary so that they would not be pitied, and their daughters and nephews, their sisters and friends said of them, "Isn't it peppy of So-and-So to go gallivanting off by herself?" Sometimes their excuse for living abroad was that they did not want to interfere in the lives of their married children and for the children of these children they shopped until they were faint and went through horrifying ordeals with the international mails.

Thus, Abby had come to belong to that group who have spent their lives leaning on someone—or being leaned on by—a father, a mother, a husband; and who, when the casket is closed or the divorce decree is final, find that they are waifs. They hide their humiliating condition—for they tend to look on loneliness as inadmissible and a little disgraceful, they tend to regard themselves as wallflowers—by playing bridge on the breezy piazzas of seaside hotels, and writing multitudinous letters, and going to lectures on the excavations of mounds and ruins in Jericho, and applying themselves with assiduity and dismay to the language of the country in which, at the moment, they find themselves.

For years Abby and her husband, whenever they traveled abroad, had seen and grieved for these forlorn, brave orphans, and Abby knew that John would be appalled to see that she had joined their ranks. She did not really know how it had happened; she was by nature gregarious, sanguine and resilient; but she had been so stricken by John's terribly surprising death that she had moved like a sleepwalker and had taken the easiest course. And despite the pleas of her relatives and friends, despite her own judgment, she had rented her apartment in New York and had withdrawn to Europe, following the pattern of cousins and aunts (sometimes, traveling in pairs, they had taken courses at the Sorbonne) and of her own mother, who had faded away on a balcony in Rome as she was painting a water-color of the Spanish Steps.

One warm melodious evening about a month before, when Abby was still in Paris, her inertia had been replaced by an abrupt restiveness, brought on by the sounds of amorous laughter and fragments of song that were borne, together with flowery smells, on the mild wind through her windows, open to a garden. She was playing Canfield—that old-lady game, that game for septuagenarians to whom dusk is the sympathetic time of day—and as she played, the black cat watched her from where he sat on an ottoman beside her so that he had a clear view of the cards. Scornful, chic and French, hugely self-respecting, the cat embarrassed her and made her feel badly dressed and out of place and timid. She really was badly dressed, and she had no need to be since she had flair and enough money, but along with sad looks, she had put on sad clothes; and she really was out of place, and found that she longed to be in her own apartment on the East River.

When the game was finished—she did not win—and she looked up, the black French cat yawned as if the tedium of her sentimental brown study had been unbearable. Unmoved by her predicament, he washed behind his ears. She was aware at last that she despised the flaccid life she was living and that she wanted to be back in the thick of things, among her innumerable energetic friends, in the familiar and surprising streets of New York; she wanted to give and go to parties; she wanted to sit in a box at the Metropolitan and never again go to La Scala alone; she wanted to be back at Bellevue as a volunteer, counting sponges in the operating rooms and, extravagant now, she told herself that she would rather smell ether than all these dense Parisian flowers. To the cat, defiantly, as if he had contradicted her, she said aloud, "I will go home. I shall simply book passage and I'll do it tomorrow."

The following morning, early, she went to a travel agent and took the first passage she could get, two weeks hence, and now, reborn, impatient to be off, the two weeks of waiting that stretched before her seemed an affront. How on earth would she live through them, being eyed by that uncharitable cat? But providence had taken up Abby's cause and the afternoon's post brought her an agreeable reason to leave Paris and leave the cat in the custody of the maid. There was a letter from Hugh Nicholson, a man she had known for many years and had seen from time to time in the course of her recent traveling. He was a Canadian who had lived most of his life in London and he was associated at various times and in various ways with films. He had written and he had directed and he had occasionally acted. When his fortunes rose, he dressed like a peer and lived at Albany in Regency splendor; and when they descended, he moved into obscure bed-and-breakfast establishments and sang for his supper and for weekends in the country.

There was a wife, estranged, who lived in the north of England and bred Kerry blues, and there were two sons at school whom each summer he took to Scotland for a fortnight of bicycling. Abby and John had never met the wife, and Hugh never spoke of her. Once there had reached their ears some nebulous rumor of a scandal, but their affection for Hugh had safeguarded them against investigating its nature or its truth.

They had met him first in New York during one of his prosperous seasons and had been attracted by his warmth and his ebullient appreciation of America, the novelty of which, throughout succeeding visits, never wore off for him. They had seen him, as well, in London both when he was affluent and when he was poor. When he was on his uppers and his shirts did not look fresh, he was understandably less good fun, but he was never pitiable and he was endlessly optimistic: around any corner at any moment, he might stub his toe on the pot of gold at the end of the rainbow.

Hugh's wonderfully opportune letter this morning invited Abby to be his vis-à-vis at a house party in Sussex. The house, he wrote, was enormous and full of history and ghosts, and the gardens had everything Americans expected English gardens to have—"pleasances, ha-has and gazebos and spinneys." The hostess went in for séances, claiming to converse with the shades of Norman ancestors and with Titus Oates.

Abby, charmed with the invitation, did not deliberate for a moment, but at once wrote back to accept. And then, in a burst of euphoria, she went shopping and bought presents and dresses and some superb hats and some marvelous shoes. She packed and two days later left Paris in its August lull and went to London, where, except for the week in Sussex, she meant to stay until she sailed for home.

So she had spent that week in the sweet, misty English country in a house crowded with treasures and white elephants and dogs, and surrounded by gardens and parks and copses of larches where nightingales sang and she began to redeem her spirit, that had so long been mislaid. Hugh had just finished directing a film that was bound to be a smashing success and he was, in consequence, at the top of his form. He and Abby enjoyed each other enormously; they shone at croquet on the luminous lawns and they shone at darts in the murk of pubs, they found that they were perfectly matched at the bridge table, and Hugh surprised and impressed Abby with his bucolic knowledge of mushrooms and sheep. Lady Caroline was a delight; eloquently attired, looking like a Romney, she rode sidesaddle on a gray cob and at every meal she was served a small onion on a Sèvres plate, which she peeled and sliced to eat with apples or muffins or cheese.

Now and then, when they were walking through a meadow or through a tunnel of dark trees on a back lane, Abby and Hugh spoke nostalgically of gala times they had had when John was alive, and one afternoon, as they were drinking bitter in an empty pub, in the midst of a reminiscence that touched her particularly, Abby realized that it was the removal from her life of John's energy that had enervated her, and energy was what she admired and, moreover, required as dearly as food and drink and air. She could burn, that is, with her own flame, but she must be rekindled; she must be complemented so that she could maintain her poise and pride. She was not the sort of woman who could live alone satisfactorily.

She raised her eyes from the dark ale and looked at Hugh, who was looking at her with a questioning and a solicitous expression. The pub had begun to fill and they talked lightly of other matters. But that night when the last rubber of bridge was over and Lady Caroline, with a sigh, had given up trying to get through to her spooks and everyone prepared to go to bed, Hugh asked Abby to go out with him for a breath of air. "Watch out for bats," said Lady Caroline; "they teem in Leo, I can't think why."

There were no bats, but the romantic air quivered with fire-flies and smelled of roses, and far away a bewitched owl warned. Beneath a pergola where the purple grapes were ripe, Hugh kissed her and Abby felt as young and tremulous as a schoolgirl. But she was not demanding and she was not headlong and she counseled herself to look on this tenuous, auroral experience as one that would last only so long as she remained in England, a handful of days before the boat took her home. Like the cat in Paris whose contempt for her negative life had urged her to repudiate it for a positive one, so Hugh was the agent that reminded her that she must seek a husband. His kiss was no more than a symbol, for Hugh was no more than a friend.

When the house party was over, Hugh and Abby were re-luctant to quit their fun and games and so, with the abandon of leisured youth, they did not drive back to London, but they went instead to Folkestone and took the Channel boat to Ostend; there were two French fillies running there that Hugh wanted to see.

For three days, in that dowdy harbor, alternately sun-baked and sodden with rain, they went to race meetings at the Hippo-drome and rode in hansoms along the *digue* and ate cockles and mussels on the quays as they contemplated the bright shrimpers and the fishwives' bright sunshades and the children's bright balloons that sometimes escaped and went to sea, bobbing along in the wakes of boats.

The kiss in the garden had not been repeated, but their concord had deepened and their joy in each other's society had been so accelerated that Abby lived in a state of heady exultation. She was, indeed, so happy that there came moments when she regretted that the time was running out and she must leave.

And now here they were in this brown and sullen den of dismal, dogged greed, and Abby, drinking warm, sweet lemon-ade, could not remember any of the fun at all. The whole fabric of the heyday had been riddled and stained and frayed within less than two hours' time. She tried sensibly to attribute her desolation to her headache, tried to think that she was coming down with flu. But her uneasiness was more than physical, and she was frightened by some alien distemper that she could not understand. Why on earth had they come here instead of going, as she had wanted to do, to Bruges?

Repelled by the lemonade, she returned to the gaming room and paused, irresolute, beside a table near the cashier's room. One of the croupiers, a youngish man with a mouth like a knife and eyes like awls, stared at her across the table as he was raking in the profits for the house, and there was in his regard such cynicism that Abby felt contaminated, besmirched with venality, and she fled, looking for Hugh in the hope that he had played enough and that they could go to some cheerful bar and have a drink and recapture their earlier mood.

When she had threaded her way through the quiet jungle (but *this* quiet snarled), she found him just where she had left him, beside the croupier at the left of the wheel. She had the feeling that he had not moved at all except to lean forward through the thicket of people to place his bets. Though she stood so close to him that their arms touched, he was unaware of her and instinct warned her not to call attention to herself. He lost steadily and losing angered him, as she could tell by the flush of his face and the set of his mouth.

Observing him and observing the other players, she began to take in the deadly seriousness of their business here; this was no game, but was a combat in which the enemy was the wheel, as capricious as a windmill.

This kind of betting, she saw, was *sui generis*; in bridge, there were partners, there was an interplay of memory and judgment and intuition; in horse betting there were any number of elements to make up the equations and the permutations, just as there were in playing the stock market. But she could not think of any other kind of gambling—or any addiction—that hadn't a social or at least an organic side to it. In roulette, intelligence was no weapon against the solitary element of random chance. As she thus analyzed, in another part of her mind she recognized a paradoxical circumstance: although Hugh was so remote that he might have been only an apparitional representation of the man she knew, she believed that she had fallen in love with him and, in love, that she was jealous. But of whom?

Rashly she took him by the arm and he wheeled with a mutter of exasperation and then, seeing her, smiled with an effort. It was apparent that he did not want to leave, that he wanted to be here and not with her; and when she said she had a headache and wanted to go back to the hotel, said he need not go with her since it was not far and the beach was well lit, he, usually so well-mannered, agreed too readily, with too perfunctory an apology, and told her good night and turned back to the table.

Abby's room, overlooking the sea and receiving the sea winds and therefore airborne sand, was papered with something nondescript, nubby and bilious, and the linoleum had been designed in the same mean-minded way. There was a varnished wardrobe, too short and shallow to hang clothes in, a wicker table with a crippled leg and a scuffed brown blotting pad and a rusty pen. The bed, with its tumid featherbed and its log of a bolster, was low, although its topography was mountainous. She tossed from peak to valley, invaded by the sound of the

sea and distant foghorns and the voices of Flemish revelers and
excited dogs loitering on the beach. It was not only the bed and
the noises—someone in the next room intermittently snored
violently and upstairs a baby howled about a pin or a pain—that
kept her awake. It was Hugh's mood and her own perverseness
that had caused her to fall in love with him at the very moment
she saw that a future for them was plainly impossible, for she
knew that the remoteness she had seen tonight was, though
sporadic, constitutional, and looking back she remembered that
often he had seemed suddenly to disappear, although his flesh
remained, in the middle of a conversation, in the middle of a
dance.

At last she gave up trying to sleep, turned on the lamp, no
brighter than a flashlight, and went to the windows to look out
at the sea and the *plage* where the tall cabañas stood as thick
as gravestones; the air was damp and still and the moon was
hidden and then revealed by dire, swift clouds. One by one the
dogs and people left the beach. In the windowsill, on a couch of
sand, there were two tiny starfish, left behind, Abby supposed,
by some forgetful collector of relics and souvenirs. In the poor
light, she studied their fastidious shape and thinking of all the
beguilements of the world, starfish and the English countryside
and Lady Caroline's idiosyncratic clothes, she recovered from
her disaffection and saw that she had been absurd to be upset by
Hugh's behavior. At peace with him and with herself again, she
allowed sleepiness to overtake her and she left the windows and
shut her eyes against the ominous clouds that beset the moon
and just before she went to sleep she wished on a non-existent
star that Hugh would want her to postpone her voyage home.
    On the next day, he was very much with her. Belabored by
a cold and sandy wind, they explored the town with the same
conjugation of reaction that had made their Roman holiday a
supreme contentment. It was a monstrous town. It possessed
houses that looked like buses threatening to run them down
and houses that looked like faces with bulbous noses and brutish eyes. They wandered, amazed, through street after street of
these teratoid villas and they concluded that the architecture
of Knokke-le-Zoute was unique and far more disrespectful to
the eye than that of any other maritime settlement they had

ever seen, worse, by far, than Brighton or Atlantic City. The principal building material seemed to be cobblestones, but they discovered a number of houses that appeared to be made of cast iron. In gardens there were topiary trees in the shape of Morris chairs and some that seemed to represent washing machines. The hotels along the sea were bedizened with every whimsy on earth, with derby-shaped domes and kidney-shaped balconies, with crenellations that looked like vertebrae and machiolations that looked like teeth, with turrets, bow-windows, dormers and gables, with fenestrations hemstitched in brick or bordered with granite point lace. Some of the chimneys were like church steeples and some were like Happy Hooligan's hat. The cabañas, in the hot, dark haze, appeared to be public telephone booths. Even the flowers dissembled and the hydrangeas looked like utensils that belonged in the kitchen and the geraniums looked like comestibles, not altogether savory. The plazas were treeless plains of concrete where big babies sunned and schipperkes patrolled. The kiosks were the size of round-houses; the trolleys, manned by garrulous grouches, made a deafening hullabaloo that was augmented by pneumatic drills which, inexplicably, were drilling in the sand. There was an enormous smell of fish.

They stopped for tea at a pavilion on the beach where the stinging wind was so strong that, as Abby was pouring, a gale redirected the scalding stream and it gushed painfully over Hugh's hand. If the accident had not been so grotesque, he might have felt it more and Abby might have been more compassionate. As it was, they laughed helplessly and Hugh said, "Oh, don't go back to America. This is too much fun."

A sourceless sorrow overcame her and she said nothing. For a while, then, they were silent. The bathers, emerging from their cabañas like troglodytes from caves, furled their umbrellas, collected their hampers and began to leave. The babies were wheeled home, convoyed by little schipperkes. No landscape could have been less pastoral, and Abby was cold and there was sand in her shoes and her ambiguous feeling of love was like sand in her mouth.

"It's too late to get the Channel boat now," Hugh said at length. "Can you endure another night here or should we go back to Ostend?"

She was too listless to care and she said, "Why did we come here in the first place?"

"I got a sudden hankering for roulette, as I do periodically," he said and then, musing, detached, he told her his gambling history.

When he was a student at Cambridge, he had sometimes gone to Monte Carlo; but he had played only casually until twelve years ago when, being in much need of rest and sun after arduous months of making a historical film, he had gone without his wife to the south of France for a long holiday. He had got no rest and he had got no sun because, during that time, he had become altogether obsessed with roulette. At first he had won and had lost equally and, whether he was victorious or was undone, he was obliged to prove himself again and again, to demonstrate that fate could neither coddle nor outwit him.

He said that he had felt like one of those white rats that don't know whether they are going to get the shock of their life or a piece of cheese. In the end he was wiped out altogether; in one night he was reduced to absolute penury and he had to pawn his watch for his fare home. His marriage at its best had been thin and wavering, and when he had got back from France that time and he had told his wife that all his money was gone, they had had their final row and she had left in a glacial rage. It was not only the grievous loss of money, though; it was, he said, "the unfaithfulness to reality."

"Eventually the only need you have in the world is the need to win. You don't need food or drink or sleep or sex—gamblers don't sleep with their wives after they've been gambling, they sleep with numbers."

For some years now he had not gone to Monte Carlo, but had come here because the very grubbiness of the place seemed to him appropriate. "My masochism is extensive," he said, "and I brought you here—you asked me why I did—because I love you and I want to marry you and I know I can't, we can't. But I wanted you to understand."

"I don't understand," she said, close to tears.

"Try it tonight," he said. "I don't mean to proselytize you. I just want you to see what it's like. Do play for an hour or so, just as a clinician."

She could not decide whether he was the cruelest man she had ever known—how cynical, how basely frivolous to state a love in terms of its impossibility—or the most pathetic; but she concluded that she did want to understand him in order more easily to accept the futility of their situation, and so she said that she would play.

It was Sunday and the gaming-room was less crowded than it had been the night before, so that Hugh was able to find a chair for Abby. She sat, shy and self-conscious, beside a croupier at the end of the table, placing her bets where Hugh indicated. At first, confused by the board, she was inattentive and covertly she studied the other players who overtly studied her. They were the same as the ones last night—those hard-faced witches with their beaded bags; those prosperous, stern-visaged merchants with their big cigars and signet rings; those thin men with mustaches whose dinner jackets were well cut but whose cuffs were worn. The Chinese woman was in the same place she had been the night before, still jotting down figures in her notebook; the rajah, in an even more splendid turban, was betting heavily and, when he lost, he was shaken with sighs. There was again that restive silence.

Presently Abby grasped the mechanics of the game and began to situate her counters for herself. Her interest was at last aroused and when, three times in succession, she won, she felt an extraordinary elation and wanted to cry out in triumph, but any display of emotion here would be *outré* and she allowed her face to demonstrate nothing, although she knew her cheeks were pink.

At some point she realized that Hugh was no longer standing behind her, and at another point she was emboldened to pick up a *râteau* that some bankrupt player had relinquished, and with it she arranged her chips and drew in her winnings, afire with defiance; against what, she was not sure. She had beginner's luck and presently she dared to play for the highest stakes; twice she played *en plein*, and won thirty-five to one; it seemed to her, though she was not certain, that the croupier gave her a faint, congratulatory smile, the smile of a veteran to a lucky greenhorn.

Abby was tired, but nonetheless she was animated and she wished this tonic tension could go on forever; the wheel became her quixotic lover, now scornfully rejecting her and now lavishly rewarding her; it became, as well, her ambition, and while she splurged and then economized, rejoiced or lamented, she knew what Hugh had tried to tell her. The faces that had frightened her receded in the miasma of green smoke; the warmth of the room was oppressive, but she did not care; her mouth was parched, but she was too preoccupied to consider how she might slake her thirst. Eventually, as it grew near closing time, the crowd began to thin; the tables of *chemin de fer* were closed and one by one the roulette croupiers collected their gear and disappeared. At last the table where Abby was playing was the only one open and it was with genuine frenzy that she saw her game was nearly over.

She was still ahead when the wheel was spun for the last time; and when everything was finished she was giddy as she struggled out of her cocoonlike trance. The croupiers' fatigue humanized them; they rubbed their eyes and stretched their legs and their agile hands went limp. Abby was a little dashed and melancholy, let down and drained; she was, even though she had won, inconsolable because now the table, stripped of its seductions, was only a table. And the croupiers were only exhausted workingmen going home to bed.

For a long while Abby and Hugh sat on the veranda of the hotel, silent and unmoving, staring at the sea and the overpopulation of the cabañas on the beach. The moon shone palely through the heavy haze; there was no horizon and a slow ship passing by looked like a smudge on a wall.

"Well, you saw what it was like," said Hugh.

"Yes," she said and, reluctant to discuss her sensations which on reflection seemed squalid, she asked him to arrange for a car to take her to Ostend and the Channel boat. There was no mention of what Hugh was going to do or where he was going. Abby had an image of him here, going back night after night to that joyless brown room.

"Would you like me to go along to Ostend with you?" he asked.

"No," she said and, mustering all the gaiety she could, she said, "I think it's vastly more memorable to say goodbye in

Knokke-le-Zoute. Besides, partings at boats make me sad. Knokke-le-Zoute—it sounds like a children's game."

They rose and in the ugly, awful dawn Hugh kissed her goodbye; kissed her in the good friend's way, and he said, "I wish it hadn't been a children's game."

She would not have given up so easily; she would have died hard; would, out of vanity and love, said that she could, somehow, save him; she would have staked everything on him if she had not so fully understood him. Sensibly, to comfort herself, she thought of how lovely it would be to see the clean September light on the East River. She told herself that, happy as the interlude had been up until last night, it had been an aberration and that she belonged where she had originated; in alien corn, it was imprudent to run risks. Guiltily, because she was fortunate and he was not, she was now anxious to be away from the spectacle of him. "Goodbye, Hugh; goodbye, I must go and pack," she said.

He was a shadow no more palpable than the phantom ships on the dim North Sea, and his voice, when he echoed her, came from an incommensurable distance.

The Echo and the Nemesis

S UE Ledbetter and Ramona Dunn became friends through the commonplace accident of their sitting side by side in a philosophy lecture three afternoons a week. There were many other American students at Heidelberg University that winter—the last before the war—but neither Sue nor Ramona had taken up with them. Ramona had not because she scorned them; in her opinion, they were Philistines, concerned only with drinking beer, singing German songs, and making spectacles of themselves on their bicycles and in their little rented cars. And Sue had not because she was self-conscious and introverted and did not make friends easily. In Ramona's presence, she pretended to deplore her compatriots' escapades, which actually she envied desperately. Sometimes on Saturday nights she lay on her bed unable to read or daydream and in an agony of frustration as she listened to her fellow-lodgers at the Pension Kirchenheim laughing and teasing and sometimes bursting into song as they played bridge and Monopoly in the cozy veranda café downstairs.

Soon after the semester opened in October, the two girls fell into the habit of drinking their afternoon coffee together on the days they met in class. Neither of them especially enjoyed the other's company, but in their different ways they were lonely, and as Ramona once remarked, in her highfalutin way, "From time to time, I need a rest from the exercitation of my intellect." She was very vain of her intellect, which she had directed to the study of philology, to the exclusion of almost everything else in the world. Sue, while she had always taken her work seriously, longed also for beaux and parties, and conversation about them, and she was often bored by Ramona's talk, obscurely gossipy, of the vagaries of certain Old High Franconian verbs when they encountered the High German consonant shift, or of the variant readings of passages in Layamon's *Brut*, or the linguistic influence Eleanor of Aquitaine had exerted on the English court. But because she was well-mannered she listened politely and even appeared to follow Ramona's exuberant elucidation of Sanskrit "a"-stem declensions and her ardent plan

to write a monograph on the word "ahoy." They drank their
coffee in the Konditorei Luitpold, a very noisy café on a street
bent like an elbow, down behind the cathedral. The din of its
two small rooms was aggravated by the peripheral racket that
came from the kitchen and from the outer shop, where the
cakes were kept. The waiters, all of whom looked cross, hustled
about at a great rate, slamming down trays and glasses and
cups any which way before the many customers, who gabbled
and rattled newspapers and pounded on the table for more
of something. Over all the to-do was the blare of the radio,
with its dial set permanently at a station that played nothing
but stormy choruses from *Wilhelm Tell*. Ramona, an invincible
expositor, had to shout, but shout she did as she traced words
like "rope" and "calf" through dozens of languages back to
their Indo-Germanic source. Sometimes Sue, befuddled by the
uproar, wanted by turns to laugh and to cry with disappointment, for this was not at all the way she had imagined that she
would live in Europe. Half incredulously and half irritably, she
would stare at Ramona as if in some way she were to blame.

Ramona Dunn was fat to the point of parody. Her obesity
fitted her badly, like extra clothing put on in the wintertime, for
her embedded bones were very small and she was very short,
and she had a foolish gait, which, however, was swift, as if she
were a mechanical doll whose engine raced. Her face was rather
pretty, but its features were so small that it was all but lost in
its billowing surroundings, and it was covered by a thin, fair
skin that was subject to disfiguring affections, now hives, now
eczema, now impetigo, and the whole was framed by fine, pale
hair that was abused once a week by a *Friseur* who baked it
with an iron into dozens of horrid little snails. She habitually
wore a crimson tam-o'-shanter with a sportive spray of artificial
edelweiss pinned to the very top of it. For so determined a bluestocking, her eccentric and extensive wardrobe was a surprise;
nothing was ever completely clean or completely whole, and
nothing ever matched anything else, but it was apparent that
all these odd and often ugly clothes had been expensive. She
had a long, fur-lined cape, and men's tweed jackets with leather
patches on the elbows, and flannel shirts designed for hunters
in the state of Maine, and high-necked jerseys, and a waistcoat made of unborn gazelle, dyed Kelly green. She attended

particularly to the dressing of her tiny hands and feet, and she had gloves and mittens of every color and every material, and innumerable pairs of extraordinary shoes, made for her by a Roman bootmaker. She always carried a pair of field glasses, in a brassbound leather case that hung over her shoulder by a plaited strap of rawhide; she looked through the wrong end of them, liking, for some reason that she did not disclose, to diminish the world she surveyed. Wherever she went, she took a locked pigskin satchel, in which she carried her grammars and lexicons and the many drafts of the many articles she was writing in the hope that they would be published in learned journals. One day in the café, soon after the girls became acquainted, she opened up the satchel, and Sue was shocked at the helter-skelter arrangement of the papers, all mussed and frayed, and stained with coffee and ink. But, even more, she was dumfounded to see a clear-green all-day sucker stuck like a bookmark between the pages of a glossary to *Beowulf.*

Sue knew that Ramona was rich, and that for the last ten years her family had lived in Italy, and that before that they had lived in New York. But this was all she knew about her friend; she did not even know where she lived in Heidelberg. She believed that Ramona, in her boundless erudition, was truly consecrated to her studies and that she truly had no other desire than to impress the subscribers to *Speculum* and the *Publications of the Modern Language Association.* She was the sort of person who seemed, at twenty-one, to have fought all her battles and survived to enjoy the quiet of her unendangered ivory tower. She did not seem to mind at all that she was so absurd to look at, and Sue, who was afire with ambitions and sick with conflict, admired her arrogant self-possession.

The two girls had been going to the Konditorei Luitpold three times a week for a month or more, and all these meetings had been alike; Ramona had talked and Sue had contributed expressions of surprise (who would have dreamed that "bolster" and "poltroon" derived from the same parent?), or murmurs of acquiescence (she agreed there might be something in the discreet rumor that the Gothic language had been made up by nineteenth-century scholars to answer riddles that could not otherwise be solved), or laughter, when it seemed becoming. The meetings were neither rewarding nor entirely uninteresting to Sue, and she came to look upon them as a part of the week's schedule, like the philosophy lectures and the seminar in Schiller.

And then, one afternoon, just as the weary, mean-mouthed waiter set their cake down before them, the radio departed from its custom and over it came the "Minuet in G," so neat and winning and surprising that for a moment there was a general lull in the café, and even the misanthropic waiter paid the girls the honor, in his short-lived delight, of not slopping their coffee. As if they all shared the same memories that the little sentimental piece of music awoke in her, Sue glanced around smiling at her fellows and tried to believe that all of them—even the old men with Hindenburg mustaches and palsied wattles, and even the Brown Shirts fiercely playing chess—had been children like herself and had stumbled in buckled pumps through the simple steps of the minuet at the military command of a dancing teacher, Miss Conklin, who had bared her sinewy legs to the thigh. In some public presentation of Miss Conklin's class, Sue had worn a yellow bodice with a lacing of black velvet ribbon, a bouffant skirt of chintz covered all over with daffodils, and a cotton-batting wig that smelled of stale talcum powder. Even though her partner had been a sissy boy with nastily damp hands and white eyelashes, and though she had been grave with stage fright, she had had moments of most thrilling expectation, as if this were only the dress rehearsal of the grown-up ball to come.

If she had expected all the strangers in the café to be transported by the "Minuet" to a sweet and distant time, she had not expected Ramona Dunn to be, and she was astonished and oddly frightened to see the fat girl gazing with a sad, reflective smile into her water glass. When the music stopped and the familiar hullabaloo was reestablished in the room, Ramona said, "Oh, I don't know of anything that makes me more nostalgic than that tinny little tune! It makes me think of Valentine parties before my sister Martha died."

It took Sue a minute to rearrange her family portrait of the Dunns, which heretofore had included, besides Ramona, only a mother and a father and three brothers. Because this was by far the simplest way, she had seen them in her mind's eye as five stout, scholarly extensions of Ramona, grouped together against the background of Vesuvius. She had imagined that they spent their time examining papyri and writing Latin verses, and she regretted admitting sorrow into their lives, as she had to do when she saw Ramona's eyes grow vague and saw her, quite unlike her naturally greedy self, push her cake aside, untouched. For a moment or two, the fat girl was still and blank, as if she were waiting for a pain to go away, and then she poured the milk into her coffee, replaced her cake, and began to talk about her family, who, it seemed, were not in the least as Sue had pictured them.

Ramona said that she alone of them was fat and ill-favored, and the worst of it was that Martha, the most beautiful girl who ever lived, had been her twin. Sue could not imagine, she declared, how frightfully good-looking all the Dunns were—except herself, of course: tall and dark-eyed and oval-faced, and tanned from the hours they spent on their father's boat, the *San Filippo*. And they were terribly gay and venturesome; they were the despair of the croupiers at the tables on the Riviera, the envy of the skiers at San Bernardino and of the yachtsmen on the Mediterranean. Their balls and their musicales and their dinner parties were famous. All the brothers had unusual artistic gifts, and there was so much money in the family that they did not have to do anything but work for their own pleasure in their studios. They were forever involved in scandals with their mistresses, who were either married noblewomen or notorious dancing girls, and forever turning over a new leaf and getting themselves engaged to lovely, convent-bred princesses, whom, however, they did not marry; the young ladies were too submissively Catholic, or too stupid, or their taste in painting was vulgar.

Of all this charming, carefree brood, Martha, five years dead, had been the most splendid, Ramona said, a creature so slight and delicate that one wanted to put her under a glass bell to protect her. Painters were captivated by the elegant shape of her head, around which she wore her chestnut hair in a coronet, and there were a dozen portraits of her, and hundreds of drawings hanging in the big bedroom where she had died and which now had been made into a sort of shrine for her. If the Dunns were odd in any way, it was in this devotion to their dead darling; twice a year Mrs. Dunn changed the nibs in Martha's pens, and in one garden there grew nothing but anemones, Martha's favorite flower. She had ailed from birth, pursued malevolently by the disease that had melted her away to the wick finally when she was sixteen. The family had come to Italy in the beginning of her mortal languor in the hope that the warmth and novelty would revive her, and for a while it did, but the wasting poison continued to devour her slowly, and for years she lay, a touching invalid, on a balcony overlooking the Bay of Naples. She lay on a blond satin chaise longue, in a quaint peignoir made of leaf-green velvet, and sometimes, as she regarded her prospect of sloops and valiant skiffs on the turbulent waves, the cypress trees, white villas in the midst of olive groves, and the intransigent smoldering of Vesuvius, she sang old English airs and Irish songs as she accompanied herself on a lute. If, in the erratic course of her illness, she got a little stronger, she asked for extra cushions at her back and half sat up at a small easel to paint in water-colors, liking the volcano as a subject, trite as it was, and the comic tourist boats that romped over the bay from Naples to Capri. If she was very unwell, she simply lay smiling while her parents and her sister and her brothers attended her, trying to seduce her back to health with their futile offerings of plums and tangerines and gilt-stemmed glasses of Rhine wine and nosegays bought from the urchins who bargained on the carriage roads.

When Martha died, Ramona's own grief was despair, because the death of a twin is a foretaste of one's own death, and for months she had been harried with premonitions and prophetic dreams, and often she awoke to find that she had strayed from her bed, for what awful purpose she did not know, and was walking barefoot, like a pilgrim, down the pitch-black road. But the acute phase of her mourning had passed, and now, although sorrow was always with her, like an alter ego, she had got over the worst of it.

She paused in her narrative and unexpectedly laughed. "What a gloom I'm being!" she said, and resumed her monologue at once but in a lighter tone, this time to recount the drubbing her brother Justin had given someone when he was defending the honor of a dishonorable soprano, and to suggest, in tantalizing innuendoes, that her parents were not faithful to each other.

Sue, whose dead father had been an upright, pessimistic clergyman and whose mother had never given voice to an impure thought, was bewitched by every word Ramona said. It occurred to her once to wonder why Ramona so frowned upon the frolics of the other American students when her beloved relatives were so worldly, but then she realized that the manners of the *haut monde* were one thing and those of undergraduates another. How queer, Sue thought, must seem this freakish bookworm in the midst of it all! And yet such was the ease with which Ramona talked, so exquisitely placed were her fillips of French, so intimate and casual her allusions to the rich and celebrated figures of international society, that Ramona changed before Sue's eyes; from the envelope of fat emerged a personality as *spirituelle* and knowing as any practicing sophisticate's. When, in the course of describing a distiller from Milan who was probably her mother's lover, she broke off and pressingly issued Sue an invitation to go with her a month from then, at the Christmas holiday, to San Bernardino to meet her brothers for a fortnight of skiing, Sue accepted immediately, not stopping to think, in the heady pleasure of the moment, that the proposal was unduly sudden, considering the sketchy nature of their friendship. "My brothers will adore you," she said, giving Sue a look of calm appraisal. "They are eclectic and they'll find your red hair and brown eyes irresistibly naïve." As if the plan had long been in her mind, Ramona named the date they would leave Heidelberg; she begged permission, in the most gracious and the subtlest possible way, to let Sue be her guest, even to the extent of supplying her with ski equipment. When the details were settled—a little urgently, she made Sue promise "on her word of honor" that she would not default—she again took up her report on Signor da Gama, the distiller, who was related by blood to the Pope and had other distinctions of breeding as well to recommend him to her mother, who was, she confessed, something of a snob. "Mama," she said, accenting the ultima, "thinks it is unnecessary for anyone to be badly born."

The Konditorei Luitpold was frequented by teachers from the Translators' Institute, and usually Ramona rejoiced in listening to them chattering and expostulating, in half a dozen European languages, for she prided herself on her gift of tongues. But today her heart was in Sorrento, and she paid no attention to them, not even to two vociferous young Russians at a table nearby. She disposed of the roué from Milan (Sue had read Catullus? Signor da Gama had a cottage at Sirmio not far from his reputed grave) and seemed to be on the point of disclosing her father's delinquencies when she was checked by a new mood, which made her lower her head, flush, and, through a long moment of silence, study the greasy hoops the rancid milk had made on the surface of her coffee.

Sue felt as if she had inadvertently stumbled upon a scene of deepest privacy, which, if she were not careful, she would violate, and, pretending that she had not observed the hiatus at all, she asked, conversationally, the names of Ramona's brothers besides Justin.

The two others were called Daniel and Robert, but it was not of them, or of her parents, or of Martha, that Ramona now wanted to speak but of herself, and haltingly she said that the "Minuet in G" had deranged her poise because it had made her think of the days of her childhood in New York, when she had been no bigger than her twin and they had danced the minuet together, Ramona taking the dandy's part. A friend of the family had predicted that though they were then almost identical, Ramona was going to be the prettier of the two. Now Sue was shocked, for she had thought that Ramona must always have been fat, and she was nearly moved to tears to know that the poor girl had been changed from a swan into an ugly duckling and that it was improbable, from the looks of her, that she would ever be changed back again. But Sue was so young and so badly equipped to console someone so beset that she could not utter a word, and she wished she could go home.

Ramona summoned the waiter and ordered her third piece of cake, saying nervously, after she had done so, "I'm sorry. When I get upset, I have to eat to calm myself. I'm awful! I ought to kill myself for eating so much." She began to devour the cake obsessively, and when she had finished it down to the last crumb, and the last fragment of frosting, she said, with shimmering eyes, "Please let me tell you what it is that makes me the unhappiest girl in the world, and maybe you can help me." Did Sue have any idea what it was like to be ruled by food and half driven out of one's mind until one dreamed of it and had at last no other ambition but to eat incessantly with an appetite that grew and grew until one saw oneself, in nightmares, as nothing but an enormous mouth and a tongue, trembling lasciviously? Did she know the terror and the remorse that followed on the heels of it when one slyly sneaked the lion's share of buttered toast at tea? Had she ever desired the whole of a pudding meant for twelve and hated with all her heart the others at the dinner table? Sue could not hide her blushing face or put her fingers in her ears or close her eyes against the tortured countenance of that wretched butterball, who declared that she had often come within an ace of doing away with herself because she was so fat.

Leaning across the table, almost whispering, Ramona went on, "I didn't come to Heidelberg for its philologists—they don't know any more than I do. I have exiled myself. I would not any longer offend that long-suffering family of mine with the sight of me." It had been her aim to fast throughout this year, she continued, and return to them transformed, and she had hoped to be thinner by many pounds when she joined her brothers at Christmastime. But she had at once run into difficulties, because, since she was not altogether well (she did not specify her illness and Sue would not have asked its name for anything), she had to be under the supervision of a doctor. And the doctor in Heidelberg, like the doctor in Naples, would not take her seriously when she said her fatness was ruining her life; they had both gone so far as to say that she was *meant* to be like this and that it would be imprudent of her to diet. Who was bold enough to fly in the face of medical authority? Not she, certainly.

It appeared, did it not, to be a dilemma past solution, Ramona asked. And yet this afternoon she had begun to see a way out, if Sue would pledge herself to help. Sue did not reply at once, sensing an involvement, but then she thought of Ramona's brothers, whom she was going to please, and she said she would do what she could.

"You're not just saying that? You are my friend? You know, of course, that you'll be repaid a hundredfold." Ramona subjected Sue's sincerity to some minutes of investigation and then outlined her plan, which seemed very tame to Sue after all these preparations, for it consisted only of Ramona's defying Dr. Freudenburg and of Sue's becoming a sort of unofficial censor and confessor. Sue was to have lunch with her each day, at Ramona's expense, and was to remind her, by a nudge or a word now and again, not to eat more than was really necessary to keep alive. If at any time Sue suspected that she was eating between meals or late at night, she was to come out flatly with an accusation and so shame Ramona that it would never happen again. The weekends were particularly difficult, since there were no lectures to go to and it was tempting not to stir out of her room at all but to gorge throughout the day on delicacies out of tins and boxes that she had sent to herself from shops in Strasbourg and Berlin. And since, in addition to fasting, she needed exercise, she hoped that Sue would agree to go walking with her on Saturdays and Sundays, a routine that could be varied from time to time by a weekend trip to some neighboring town of interest.

When Sue protested mildly that Ramona had contradicted her earlier assertion that she would not dare dispute her doctor's word, Ramona grinned roguishly and said only, "Don't be nosy."

Ramona had found an old ladies' home, called the Gerstnerheim, which, being always in need of funds, welcomed paying guests at the midday meal, whom they fed for an unimaginably low price. Ramona did not patronize it out of miserliness, however, but because the food was nearly inedible. And it was here that the girls daily took their Spartan lunch. It was quite the worst food that Sue had ever eaten anywhere, for it was cooked to pallor and flaccidity and then was seasoned with unheard-of condiments, which sometimes made her sick. The bread was sour and the soup was full of pasty clots; the potatoes were waterlogged and the old red cabbage was boiled until it was blue. The dessert was always a basin of molded farina with a sauce of gray jelly that had a gray taste. The aged ladies sat at one enormously long table, preserving an institutional silence until the farina was handed around, and, as if this were an alarm, all the withered lips began to move simultaneously and from them issued high squawks of protest against the dreary lot of being old and homeless and underfed. Sue could not help admiring Ramona, who ate her plate of eel and celeriac as if she really preferred it to tuna broiled with black olives and who talked all the while of things quite other than food—of Walther von der Vogelweide's eccentric syntax, of a new French

novel that had come in the mail that morning, and of their trip
to Switzerland.

Justin and Daniel and Robert were delighted that Sue was
coming, Ramona said, and arrangements were being made in a
voluminous correspondence through the air over the Alps. Sue
had never been on skis in her life, but she did not allow this to
deflate her high hopes. She thought only of evenings of lieder
(needless to say, the accomplished Dunns sang splendidly) and
hot spiced wine before a dancing fire, of late breakfasts in the
white sun and brilliant conversation. And of what was coming
afterward! The later holidays (Ramona called them *villeggiatura*), spent in Sorrento! The countesses' garden parties in
Amalfi and the cruises on the Adriatic, the visits to Greece, the
balls in the princely houses of Naples! Ramona could not decide which of her brothers Sue would elect to marry. Probably
Robert, she thought, since he was the youngest and the most
affectionate.

It was true that Sue did not quite believe all she was told, but
she knew that the ways of the rich are strange, and while she did
not allow her fantasies to invade the hours assigned to classes
and study, she did not rebuff them when they came at moments
of leisure. From time to time, she suddenly remembered that
she was required to give something in return for Ramona's largess, and then she would say how proud she was of her friend's
self-discipline or would ask her, like a frank and compassionate
doctor, if she had strayed at all from her intention (she always
had; she always immediately admitted it and Sue always put
on a show of disappointment), and once in a while she said
that Ramona was looking much thinner, although this was
absolutely untrue. Sometimes they took the electric tram to
Neckargemünd, where they split a bottle of sweet Greek wine.
Occasionally they went to Mannheim, to the opera, but they
never stayed for a full performance; Ramona said that later in
the year Signor da Gama would invite them to his house in
Milan and then they could go to La Scala every night. Once
they went for a weekend to Rothenburg, where Ramona, in an
uncontrollable holiday mood, ate twelve cherry tarts in a single
day. She was tearful for a week afterward, and to show Sue how
sorry she was, she ground out a cigarette on one of her downy
wrists. This dreadful incident took place in the Luitpold and

was witnessed by several patrons, who could not conceal their alarm. Sue thought to herself, Maybe she's cuckoo, and while she did not relinquish any of her daydreams of the festivities in Italy, she began to observe Ramona more closely.

She could feel the turmoil in her when they went past bake-shop windows full of cream puffs and cheesecake and petits fours. Ramona, furtively glancing at the goodies out of the corner of her eye, would begin a passionate and long-winded speech on the present-day use of Latin in Iceland. When, on a special occasion, they dined together at the Ritterhalle, she did not even look at the menu but lionheartedly ordered a single dropped egg and a cup of tea and resolutely kept her eyes away from Sue's boiled beef and fritters. When drinking cocktails in the American bar at the Europäischer Hof, she shook her head as the waiter passed a tray of canapés made of caviar, anchovy, lobster, foie gras, and Camembert, ranged fanwise around a little bowl of ivory almonds. But sometimes she did capitulate, with a piteous rationalization—that she had not eaten any breakfast or that she had barely touched her soup at the Gerstnerheim and that therefore there would be nothing wrong in her having two or perhaps three or four of these tiny little sandwiches. One time Sue saw her take several more than she had said she would and hide them under the rim of her plate.

As the date set for their departure for Switzerland drew nearer, Ramona grew unaccountable. Several times she failed to appear at lunch, and when Sue, in a friendly way, asked for an explana-tion, she snapped, "None of your business. What do you think you are? My nurse?" She was full of peevishness, complaining of the smell of senility in the Gerstnerheim, of students who sucked the shells of pistachio nuts in the library, of her land-lady's young son, who she was sure rummaged through her bureau drawers when she was not at home. Once she and Sue had a fearful row when Sue, keeping up her end of the bargain, although she really did not care a pin, told her not to buy a bag of chestnuts from a vendor on a street corner. Ramona shouted, for all the world to hear, "You are sadly mistaken, Miss Ledbetter, if you think you know more than Dr. Augustus Freudenburg, of the Otto-Ludwigs Clinic!" And a little after that she acquired the notion that people were staring at her, and she carried an umbrella, rain or shine, to hide herself from them. But, oddest of all, when the skis and boots and poles that she had ordered for Sue arrived, and Sue thanked her for them, she said, "I can't think what use they'll be. Obviously there never is any snow in this ghastly, godforsaken place."

There was an awful afternoon when Ramona was convinced that the waiter at the Luitpold had impugned her German, and Sue found herself in the unhappy role of intermediary in a preposterous altercation so bitter that it stopped just short of a bodily engagement. When the girls left the café—at the insistence of the management—they were silent all the way to the cathedral, which was the place where they usually took leave of each other to go their separate ways home. They paused a moment there in the growing dark, and suddenly Ramona said, "Look at me!" Sue looked at her. "I say!" said Ramona. "In this light you look exactly like my sister. How astonishing! Turn a little to the left, there's a dear." And when Sue had turned as she directed, a whole minute—but it seemed an hour to Sue—passed before Ramona broke from her trance to cry, "How blind I've been! My brothers would be shocked to death if they should see you. It would kill them!"

She put out her hands, on which she wore white leather mittens, and held Sue's face between them and studied it, half closing her eyes and murmuring her amazement, her delight, her perplexity at her failure until now to see this marvelous resemblance. Once, as her brown eyes nimbly catechized the face before her, she took off her right mitten and ran her index finger down Sue's nose, as if she had even learned her sister's bones by heart, while Sue, unable to speak, could only think in panic, What does she mean *if* they should see me?

Ramona carried on as if she were moon-struck, making fresh discoveries until not only were Sue's and Martha's faces identical but so were their voices and their carriage and the shape of their hands and feet. She said, "You must come to my room and see a picture of Martha right now. It's desperately weird."

Fascinated, Sue nodded, and they moved on through the quiet street. Ramona paused to look at her each time they went under a street light, touched her hair, begged leave to take her arm, and called her Martha, Sister, Twin, and sometimes caught her breath in an abortive sob. They went past the lighted windows of the *Bierstuben*, where the shadows of young men loomed and waved, and then turned at the Kornmarkt and began to climb the steep, moss-slick steps that led to the castle garden. As they went through the avenue of trees that lay between the casino and the castle, Ramona, peering at Sue through the spooky mist, said, "They would have been much quicker to see it than I," so Sue knew, miserably and for sure, that something had gone wrong with their plans to go to San Bernardino. And then Ramona laughed and broke away and took off her tam-o'-shanter, which she hurled toward the hedge of yew, where it rested tipsily.

"I could vomit," she said, standing absolutely still.

There was a long pause. Finally, Sue could no longer bear the suspense, and she asked Ramona if her brothers knew that she and Ramona were not coming.

"Of course they know. They've known for two weeks, but you're crazy if you think the reason we're not going is that you look like Martha. How beastly vain you are!" She was so angry and she trembled so with her rage that Sue did not dare say another word. "It was Freudenburg who said I couldn't go," she howled. "He has found out that I have lost ten pounds."

Sue had no conscious motive in asking her, idly and not really caring, where Dr. Freudenburg's office was; she had meant the guileless question to be no more than a show of noncommittal and courteous interest, and she was badly frightened when, in reply, Ramona turned on her and slapped her hard on either cheek, and then opened her mouth to emit one hideous, protracted scream. Sue started instinctively to run away, but Ramona seized and held her arms, and began to talk in a lunatic, fast monotone, threatening her with lawsuits and public exposure if she ever mentioned the name Freudenburg again *or* her brothers *or* her mother and father *or* Martha, that ghastly, puling, pampered hypochondriac who had totally wrecked her life.

Sue felt that the racket of her heart and her hot, prancing brain would drown out Ramona's voice, but it did nothing of the kind, and they stood there, rocking in their absurd attitude, while the fit continued. Sue was sure that the police and the townsfolk would come running at any moment and an alarm would be sounded and they would be arrested for disturbing the peace. But if anyone heard them, it was only the shades of the princes in the castle.

It was difficult for Sue to sort out the heroes and the villains in this diatribe. Sometimes it appeared that Ramona's brothers and her parents hated her, sometimes she thought they had been glad when Martha died; sometimes Dr. Freudenburg seemed to be the cause of everything. She had the impression that he was an alienist, and she wondered if now he would send his patient to an institution; at other times she thought the doctor did not exist at all. She did not know whom to hate or whom to trust, for the characters in this *Walpurgisnacht* changed shape by the minute and not a one was left out—not Signor da Gama or the ballet girls in Naples or the old ladies at the Gerstnerheim or the prehistoric figures of a sadistic nurse, a base German governess, and a nefarious boy cousin who had invited Ramona to misbehave when she was barely eight years old. Once she said that to escape Dr. Freudenburg she meant to order her father to take her cruising on the *San Filippo*; a minute later she said that that loathsome fool Justin had wrecked the boat on the coast of Yugoslavia. She would go home to the villa in Sorrento and be comforted by her brothers who had always preferred her to everyone else in the world—except that they hadn't! They had always despised her. Freudenburg would write to her father and he would come to fetch her back to that vulgar, parvenu house, and there, in spite of all her efforts to outwit them, they would make her eat and eat until she was the laughing stock of the entire world. What *were* they after? Did they want to indenture her to a sideshow?

She stopped, trailed off, turned loose Sue's arm, and stood crestfallen, like a child who realizes that no one is listening to his tantrum. Tears, terribly silent, streamed down her round cheeks.

Then, "It isn't true, you know. They aren't like that, they're good and kind. The only thing that's true is that I eat all the time," and softly, to herself, she repeated, "All the time." In a mixture of self-hatred and abstracted bravado, she said that she had supplemented all her lunches at the Gerstnerheim and had nibbled constantly, alone in her room; that Dr. Freudenburg's recommendation had been just the opposite of what she had been saying all along.

Unconsolable, Ramona moved on along the path, and Sue followed, honoring her tragedy but struck dumb by it. On the way through the courtyard and down the street, Ramona told her, in a restrained and rational voice, that her father was coming the next day to take her back to Italy, since the experiment of her being here alone had not worked. Her parents, at the counsel of Dr. Freudenburg, were prepared to take drastic measures, involving, if need be, a hospital, the very thought of which made her blood run cold. "Forgive me for that scene back there," she said. "You grow wild in loneliness like mine. It would have been lovely if it had all worked out the way I wanted and we had gone to Switzerland."

"Oh, that's all right," said Sue, whose heart was broken. "I don't know how to ski anyway."

"Really? What crust! I'd never have bought you all that gear if I had known." Ramona laughed lightly. They approached the garden gate of a tall yellow house, and she said, "This is where I live. Want to come in and have a glass of kirsch?"

Sue did not want the kirsch and she knew she should be on her way home if she were to get anything hot for supper, but she was curious to see the photograph of Martha, and since Ramona seemed herself again, she followed her down the path. Ramona had two little rooms, as clean and orderly as cells. In the one where she studied, there was no furniture except a long desk with deep drawers and a straight varnished chair and a listing bookcase. She had very few books, really, for one so learned—not more than fifty altogether—and every one of them was dull: grammars, dictionaries, readers, monographs reprinted from scholarly journals, and treatises on semantics, etymology, and phonetics. Her pens and pencils lay straight in a lacquered tray, and a pile of notebooks sat neatly at the right of the blotter, and at the left there was a book open to a homily in Anglo-Saxon which, evidently, she had been translating. As soon as they had taken off their coats, Ramona went into the bedroom and closed the door; from beyond it Sue could hear drawers being opened and quickly closed, metal clashing, and paper rustling, and she imagined that the bureaus were stocked with contraband—with sweets and sausages and cheese. For the last time, she thought of Daniel and Justin and Robert, of whom she was to be forever deprived because their sister could not curb her brutish appetite.

She wandered around the room and presently her eye fell on a photograph in a silver frame standing in a half-empty shelf of the bookcase. It could only be Martha. The dead girl did not look in the least like Sue but was certainly as pretty as she had been described, and as Sue looked at the pensive eyes and the thoughtful lips, she was visited by a fugitive feeling that this was really Ramona's face at which she looked and that it had been refined and made immaculate by an artful photographer who did not scruple to help his clients deceive themselves. For Martha wore a look of lovely wonder and remoteness, as if she were all disconnected spirit, and it was the same as a look that sometimes came to Ramona's eyes and lips just as she lifted her binoculars to contemplate the world through the belittling lenses.

Sue turned the photograph around, and on the back she read the penned inscription "Martha Ramona Dunn at sixteen, Sorrento." She looked at that ethereal face again, and this time had no doubt that it had once belonged to Ramona. No wonder the loss of it had left her heartbroken! She sighed to think of her friend's desperate fabrication. In a sense, she supposed the Martha side of Ramona Dunn *was* dead, dead and buried under layers and layers of fat. Just as she guiltily returned the picture to its place, the door to the bedroom opened and Ramona, grandly gesturing toward her dressing table, cried, "Come in! Come in! Enter the banquet hall!" She had emptied the drawers of all their forbidden fruits, and arrayed on the dressing table, in front of her bottles of cologne and medicine, were cheeses and tinned fish and pickles and pressed meat and cakes, candies, nuts, olives, sausages, buns, apples, raisins, figs, prunes, dates, and jars of pâté and glasses of jelly and little pots of caviar, as black as ink. "Don't stint!" she shouted, and she bounded forward and began to eat as if she had not had a meal in weeks.

"All evidence must be removed by morning! What a close shave! What if my father had come without telling me and had found it all!" Shamelessly, she ranged up and down the table, cropping and lowing like a cow in a pasture. There were droplets of sweat on her forehead and her hands were shaking, but nothing else about her showed that she had gone to pieces earlier or that she was deep, deeper by far than anyone else Sue had ever known.

Sucking a rind of citron, Ramona said, "You must realize that our friendship is over, but not through any fault of yours. When I went off and turned on you that way, it had nothing to do with you at all, for of course you don't look any more like Martha than the man in the moon."

"It's all right, Ramona," said Sue politely. She stayed close to the door, although the food looked very good. "I'll still be your friend."

"Oh, no, no, there would be nothing in it for you," Ramona said, and her eyes narrowed ever so slightly. "Thank you just the same. I am exceptionally ill." She spoke with pride, as if she were really saying "I am exceptionally talented" or "I am exceptionally attractive."

"I didn't know you were," said Sue. "I'm sorry."

"*I'm* not sorry. It is for yourself that you should be sorry. You have such a trivial little life, poor girl. It's not your fault. Most people do."

"I'd better go," said Sue.

"Go! Go!" cried Ramona, with a gesture of grand benediction. "I weep not."

Sue's hand was on the knob of the outer door, but she hesitated to leave a scene so inconclusive. Ramona watched her as she lingered; her mouth was so full that her cheeks were stretched out as if in mumps, and through the food and through a devilish, mad grin she said, "Of *course* you could never know the divine joy of being twins, provincial one! Do you know what he said the last night when my name was Martha? The night he came into that room where the anemones were? He pretended that he was looking for a sheet of music. Specifically for a sonata for the harpsichord by Wilhelm Friedrich Bach."

But Sue did not wait to hear what he, whoever he was, had said; she ran down the brown-smelling stairs and out into the cold street with the feeling that Ramona was still standing there before the food, as if she were serving herself at an altar, still talking, though there was no one to listen. She wondered if she ought to summon Dr. Freudenburg, and then decided that, in the end, it was none of her business. She caught a trolley that took her near her pension, and was just in time to get some hot soup and a plate of cold meats and salad before the kitchen closed. But when the food came, she found that she had no appetite at all. "What's the matter?" asked Herr Sachs, the fresh young waiter. "Are you afraid to get fat?" And he looked absolutely flabbergasted when, at this, she fled from the café without a word.

The Maiden

"I BOUGHT the pair of them in Berlin for forty marks," Mrs. Andreas was saying to Dr. Reinmuth, who had admired the twin decanters on her dinner table. "It sickens me, the way they must let their treasures go for nothing. I can take no pride in having got a bargain when I feel like a pirate." Evan Leckie, an American journalist who was the extra man at the party, turned away from the woman on his right to glance at his hostess to see if her face revealed the hypocrisy he had heard, ever so faintly, in her voice, but he could read nothing in her bland eyes, nor could he discover the reaction of her interlocutor, who slightly inclined his head in acknowledgment of her sympathy for his mortified compatriots but said nothing and resumed his affectionate scrutiny of the decanters as Mrs. Andreas went on to enumerate other instances of the victors' gains through the Germans' losses. Evan, just transferred to Heidelberg from the squalor and perdition of Nuremberg, joined in the German's contemplation of these relics of more handsome times. One of the bottles was filled with red wine, which gleamed darkly through the lustrous, sculptured glass, chased with silver, and the other with pale, sunny Chablis. The candlelight invested the wines with a property beyond taste and fluidity, a subtile grace belonging to a world almost imaginary in its elegance, and for a moment Evan warmed toward Mrs. Andreas, who had tried to resuscitate this charming world for her guests by putting the decanters in the becoming company of heavy, florid silverware and Dresden fruit plates and a bowl of immaculate white roses, and by dressing herself, a plump and unexceptional person, in an opulent frock of gold brocade and a little queenly crown of amethysts for her curly, graying hair.

The double doors to the garden were open to admit the moonlight and the summer breeze, and now and again, in the course of the meal, Evan had glanced out and had seen luminous nicotiana and delphiniums growing profusely beside a high stone wall. Here, in the hilly section of the city, it was as quiet as in the country; there was not a sound of jeeps or drunken G.I.s to disturb the light and general conversation of

Americans breaking bread with Germans. Only by implication and indirection were the war and the Occupation spoken of, and in this abandonment of the contemporary, the vanquished, these charming Reinmuths, save by their dress and their speech, could not be distinguished from the conquerors. If chivalry, thought Evan, were ever to return to the world, peace would come with it, but evenings like this were isolated, were all but lost in the vast, arid wastes of the present hour within the present decade. And the pity that Mrs. Andreas bestowed upon her German guests would not return to them the decanters they had forfeited, nor would her hospitality obliterate from their hearts the knowledge of their immense dilemma. Paradoxically, it was only upon the highest possible level that Germans and Americans these days could communicate with one another; only a past that was now irretrievable could bring them into harmony.

For the past month in Nuremberg, ever since Evan's wife, Virginia, had left him—left him, as she had put it in a shout, "to stew in his own juice"—Evan had spent his evenings in the bar of his hotel, drinking by himself and listening, in a trance of boredom, to the conversations of the Americans about him. The mirrored walls and mirrored ceilings had cast back the manifold reflections of able-bodied WACs in summer uniforms, who talked of their baseball teams (once he had seen a phalanx of them in the lobby, armed with bats and catchers' mitts, looking no less manly than the Brooklyn Dodgers) and of posts where they had been stationed and of itineraries, past and future. "Where were you in '45?" he had heard one of them cry. "New Caledonia! My God! So was I. Isn't it a riot to think we were both in New Caledonia in '45 and now are here in the Theater?" Things had come to a pretty pass, thought Evan, when *this* was the theater of a young girl's dreams. They did not talk like women and they did not look like women but like a modern mutation, a revision, perhaps more efficient and sturdier, of an old model. Half hypnotized by the signs of the times, he had come almost to believe that the days of men and women were over and that the world had moved into a new era dominated by a neuter body called Personnel, whose only concerns were to make history and to snub the history that had already been made. Miss Sally Dean, who sat across from him tonight, had pleased him at first glance with her bright-blond hair and her alabaster shoulders and the fine length of her legs, but over the cocktails his delight departed when, in the accents of West Los Angeles, she had said she wished General MacArthur were in Germany, since he was, in her opinion, a "real glamour puss." The woman on his right, Mrs. Crowell, the wife of a judge from Ohio in the judiciary of the Occupation, was obsessively loquacious; for a very long time she had been delivering to him a self-sustaining monologue on the effronteries of German servants, announcing once, with all the authority of an anthropologist, that "the Baden mind is *consecrated* to dishonesty." He could not put his finger on it, but, in spite of her familiar housewife's complaints, she did not sound at all like his mother and his aunts in Charlottesville, whose lives, spun out in loving domesticity, would lose their pungency if cooks kept civil tongues in their heads and if upstairs maids were not light-fingered. Mrs. Crowell brought to her house-keeping problems a modern and impersonal intellect. "The Baden mind," "the Franconian mind," "the German character" were phrases that came forth irrefutably. And the bluestocking wife of a Captain McNaughton, who sat on Evan's left and who taught library science to the wives of other Army officers, had all evening lectured Dr. Reinmuth on the faults (remediable, in her opinion) of his generation that had forced the world into war. Dr. Reinmuth was a lawyer. She was herself a warrior; she argued hotly, although the German did not oppose her, and sometimes she threatened him with her spoon.

It was the German woman, Frau Reinmuth, who, although her gray dress was modest and although she wore no jewels and little rouge, captivated Evan with her ineffable femininity; she, of all the women there, had been challenged by violence and she had ignored it, had firmly and with great poise set it aside. To look at her, no one would know that the slightest alteration had taken place in the dignified modus vivendi she must have known all her life. The serenity she emanated touched him so warmly and so deeply that he almost loved her, and upon the recognition of his feeling he was seized with loneliness and with a sort of homesickness that he felt sure she would understand—a longing, it was, for the places that *she* would remember. Suddenly it occurred to him that the only other time he had been in Heidelberg, he had been here with his wife, two years before, and they had gone one afternoon by trolley to Schwetzingen to see the palace gardens. Virginia had always hated history and that day she had looked at a cool Louis Quatorze summerhouse, designed for witty persiflage and premeditated kisses, and had said, "It's so chichi it makes me sick." And she had meant it. How she had prided herself on despising everything that had been made before 1920, the year of her birth! Staring at the wines aglow in their fine vessels, Evan recaptured exactly the feeling he had had that day in Schwetzingen when, very abruptly, he had realized that he was only technically bound for life to this fretful iconoclast; for a short while, there beside the playing fountains, he had made her vanish and in her place there stood a quiet woman, rich in meditations and in fancies. If he had known Frau Reinmuth then, she might have been the one he thought of.

Evan watched Dr. Reinmuth as he poured the gold and garnet liquids, first one and then the other, into the glasses before his plate. The little lawyer closely attended the surge of color behind the radiant crystal and he murmured, in a soft Bavarian voice, "Lovely, lovely. Look, Liselotte, how beautiful Mrs. Andreas' *Karaffen* are!" Frau Reinmuth, wide-faced, twice his size, turned from her talk of the Salzburg Festival with Mr. Andreas and cherished both her husband and the decanters with her broad gray eyes, in whose depths love lay limitlessly. When she praised the design of the cut glass, and the etching of the silver, and the shape of the stoppers, like enormous diamonds, she managed somehow, through the timbre of her voice or its cadences or through the way she looked at him, to proclaim that she loved her husband and that the beauty of the bottles was rivaled and surpassed by the nature of this little man of hers, who, still fascinated, moved his handsome head this way and that, the better to see the prismatic green and violet beams that burst from the shelves and crannies of the glass. His movements were quick and delicately articulated, like a small animal's, and his slender fingers touched and traced the glass as if he were playing a musical instrument that only his ears could hear. He must have been in his middle forties, but he looked like a nervous, gifted boy not twenty yet, he was so slight, his hair was so black and curly, his brown face was so lineless, and there was such candor and curiosity in his dark eyes. He seemed now to want to carry his visual and tactile encounter with the decanters to a further point, to a completion, to bliss. And Evan, arrested by the man's absorption (if it was not that of a child, it was that of an artist bent on abstracting meanings from all the data presented to his senses), found it hard to imagine him arguing in a court of law, where the materials, no matter how one elevated and embellished justice, were not poetry. Equally difficult was it to see him as he had been during the war, in his role of interpreter for the German Army in Italy. Like every German one met in a polite American house, Dr. Reinmuth had been an enemy of the Third Reich; he had escaped concentration camp only because his languages were useful to the Nazis. While Evan, for the most part, was suspicious of these self-named martyrs who seemed always to have fetched up in gentlemanly jobs where their lives were not in the least imperiled, he did believe in Dr. Reinmuth, and was certain that a belligerent ideology could not enlist the tender creature so unaffectedly playing with Mrs. Andreas' toys, so obviously well beloved by his benevolent wife. Everyone, even Mrs. Crowell, paused a second to look from the man to the woman and to esteem their concord.

Frau Reinmuth then returned to Mr. Andreas, but it was plain to see that her mind was only half with him. She said, "I envy you to hear Flagstad. Our pain is that there is no music now," and in a lower voice she added, "I have seen August bite his lip for sorrow when he goes past the opera house in Mannheim. It's nothing now, you know, but a ruin, like everything." Glancing at her, Evan wondered whether she were older than her husband or if this marriage had been entered upon late, and he concluded that perhaps the second was true, for they were childless—the downright Mrs. McNaughton had determined that before the canapés were passed—and Frau Reinmuth looked born to motherhood. But even more telling was the honeymoon inflection in her voice, as if she were still marveling now to say the name "August" as easily as she said "I" and to be able to bestow these limnings of her dearest possession generously on the members of a dinner party. It was not that she spoke of him as if he were a child, as some women do who marry late or marry men younger than themselves,

but as if he were a paragon with whom she had the remarkable
honor to be associated. She, in her boundless patience, could
endure being deprived of music and it was not for herself that
she complained, but she could not bear to see August's grief
over the hush that lay upon their singing country; she lived
not only for, she lived *in*, him. She wore her yellow hair in
Germanic braids that coiled around her head, sitting too low
to be smart; her hands were soft and large, honestly meriting
the wide wedding band on the right one. She was as completely
a woman as Virginia, in spite of a kind of ravening femaleness
and piquant good looks, had never been one. He shuddered to
think how she must be maligning him in Nevada to the other
angry petitioners, and then he tried to imagine how Frau Reinmuth would behave under similar circumstances. But it was
unthinkable that she should ever be a divorcée; no matter what
sort of man she married, this wifely woman would somehow,
he was sure, quell all disorder. Again he felt a wave of affection
for her; he fancied drinking tea with her in a little crowded
drawing room at the end of one of these warm days, and he
saw himself walking with both the Reinmuths up through the
hills behind the Philosophenweg, proving to the world by their
compassionate amity that there was no longer a state of war
between their country and his.

But he was prevented from spinning out his fantasy of a
friendship with the Reinmuths because Mrs. Crowell was
demanding his attention. Her present servant, she told him,
was an aristocrat ("as aristocratic as a German can be," she said
sotto voce, "which isn't saying much") and might therefore be
expected not to steal the spoons; now, having brought him up
to date on her belowstairs problems, she changed the subject
and drew him into the orbit of her bright-eyed, pervasive bustling. She understood that he had just come from Nuremberg,
where she and the Judge had lived for two years. "Isn't it too
profoundly *triste*?" she cried. "Where did they billet you, poor
thing?"

"At the Grand Hotel," said Evan, recollecting the WACs with
their mustaches and their soldierly patois.

"Oh, no!" protested Mrs. Crowell. "But it's simply *overrun*
with awful Army children! Not children—brats. Brats, I'm sorry
to say, is the only word for them. They actually roller-skate

through the lobby, you know, to say nothing of the *ghastly* noise they make. I used to go to the hairdresser there and finally had to give up because of the hullabaloo."

At the mention of Nuremberg, Dr. Reinmuth had pivoted around toward them and now, speaking across Mrs. McNaughton, he said dreamily, "Once it was a lovely town. We lived there, my wife and I, all our lives until the war. I understand there is now a French orchestra in the opera house that plays calypso for your soldiers." There sounded in his voice the same note of wonder that he had used when he acclaimed the decanters that he could not own; neither could he again possess the beauties of his birthplace. And Evan Leckie, to whom the genesis of war had always been incomprehensible, looked with astonishment at these two pacific Germans and pondered how the whole hideous mistake had come about, what Eumenides had driven this pair to hardship, humiliation, and exile. Whatever else they were, however alien their values might be, these enemies were, *sub specie aeternitatis,* of incalculable worth if for no other reason than that, in an unloving world, they loved.

Mrs. Andreas, tactfully refusing Dr. Reinmuth's gambit, since she knew that the deterioration of the Nuremberg Opera House into a night club must be a painful subject to him, maneuvered her guests until the talk at the table became general. They all continued the exchange that had begun with Frau Reinmuth and Mr. Andreas on the Salzburg Festival; they went on to speak of Edinburgh, of the *Salome* that someone had heard at La Scala, of a coloratura who had delighted the Reinmuths in Weimar. Dr. Reinmuth then told the story of his having once defended a pianist who had been sued for slander by a violinist; the defendant had been accused of saying publicly that the plaintiff played Mozart as if the music had been written for the barrel organ and that the only thing missing was a monkey to take up a collection. This anecdote, coinciding with the arrival of the dessert, diverted the stream of talk, and Judge Crowell, whose interest in music was perfunctory and social, revived and took the floor. He told of a murder case he had tried the week before in Frankfurt and of a rape case on the docket in Stuttgart. Dr. Reinmuth countered with cases he was pleading; they matched their legal wits, made Latin puns, and so enjoyed their game that the others laughed, although they barely understood the meanings of the words.

Dr. Reinmuth, who was again fondling the decanters, said, "I suppose every lawyer is fond of telling the story of his first case. May I tell mine?" He besought his hostess with an endearing smile, and his wife, forever at his side, pleaded for him, "Oh, do!" and she explained, "It's such an extraordinary story of a young lawyer's first case."

He poured himself a little more Chablis and smiled and began. When he was twenty-three, in Nuremberg, just down from Bonn, with no practice at all, he had one day been called upon by the state to defend a man who had confessed to murdering an old woman and robbing her of sixty pfennig. The defense, of course, was purely a convention, and the man was immediately sentenced to death, since there was no question of his guilt or of the enormity of his crime. Some few days after the trial, Dr. Reinmuth had received an elaborate engraved invitation to the execution by guillotine, which was to be carried out in the courtyard of the Justizpalast one morning a day or so later, punctually at seven o'clock. He was instructed, in an accompanying letter, to wear a Prince Albert and a top hat.

Mrs. Andreas was shocked. "Guillotine? Did you *have* to go?"

Dr. Reinmuth smiled and bowed to her. "No, I was not required. It was, you see, my *right* to go, as the advocate of the prisoner."

Judge Crowell laughed deeply. "Your first case, eh, Reinmuth?" And Dr. Reinmuth spread out his hands in a mock gesture of deprecation.

"My fellow-spectators were three judges from the bench," he continued, "who were dressed, like myself, in Prince Alberts and cylinders. We were a little early when we got to the courtyard, so that we saw the last-minute preparations of the stage before the play began. Near the guillotine, with its great knife—that blade, my God in Heaven!—there stood a man in uniform with a drum, ready to drown out the sound if my client should yell."

The dimmest of frowns had gathered on Judge Crowell's forehead. "All this pomp and circumstance for sixty pfennigs?" he said.

"Right you are, sir," replied Dr. Reinmuth. "That is the irony of my story." He paused to eat a strawberry and to take a sip of wine. "Next we watched them test the machine to make sure it was in proper—shall I say decapitating?—condition. When they released it, the cleaver came down with such stupendous force that the earth beneath our feet vibrated and my brains buzzed like a bee.

"As the bells began to ring for seven, Herr Murderer was led out by two executioners, dressed as we were dressed. Their white gloves were spotless! It was a glorious morning in May. The flowers were out, the birds were singing, the sky had not a cloud. To have your head cut off on such a day!"

"For sixty pfennigs!" persisted the judge from Ohio. And Miss Dean, paling, stopped eating her dessert.

"Mein Herr had been confessed and anointed. You could fairly see the holy oil on his forehead as his keepers led him across the paving to the guillotine. The drummer was ready. As the fourth note of the seven struck in the church towers, they persuaded him to take the position necessary to the success of Dr. Guillotin's invention. One, he was horizontal! Two, the blade descended! Three, the head was off the carcass and the blood shot out from the neck like a volcano, a geyser, the flame from an explosion. No sight I saw in the war was worse. The last stroke of seven sounded. There had been no need for the drum."

"Great Scott!" said Mr. Andreas, and flushed.

Captain McNaughton stared at Dr. Reinmuth and said, "You chaps don't do things by halves, do you?"

Mrs. Andreas, frantic at the dangerous note that had sounded, menacing her party, put her hand lightly on the lawyer's and said, "I know that then you must have fainted."

Dr. Reinmuth tilted back his head and smiled at the ceiling. "No. No, I did not faint. You remember that this was a beautiful day in spring? And that I was a young man, all dressed up at seven in the morning?" He lowered his head and gave his smile to the whole company. "Faint! Dear lady, no! I took the tram back to Fürth and I called my sweetheart on the telephone." He gazed at his wife. "Liselotte was surprised, considering the hour. 'What are you thinking of? It's not eight o'clock,' she said. I flustered her then. I said, 'I know it's an unusual time

of day to call, but I have something unusual to say. Will you
marry me?'"

He clasped his hands together and exchanged with his wife
a look as exuberant and shy as if they were in the first rapture
of their romance, and, bewitched, she said, "Twenty years ago
next May."

A silence settled on the room. Whether Evan Leckie was
the more dumfounded by Dr. Reinmuth's story of a majestic
penalty to fit a sordid crime or by his ostentatious hinting at his
connubial delights, he did not know. Evan sought the stunned
faces of his countrymen and could not tell in them, either, what
feeling was the uppermost. The party suddenly was no longer
a whole; it consisted of two parts, the Americans and the Germans, and while the former outnumbered them, the Germans,
in a deeper sense, had triumphed. They had joyfully danced
a *Totentanz*, had implied all the details of their sixty-pfennig
marriage, and they were still, even now, smiling at each other as
if there had never been anything untoward in their lives.

"I could take a wife then, you see," said Dr. Reinmuth, by
way of a dénouement, "since I was a full-fledged lawyer. And
she could not resist me in that finery, which, as a matter of fact,
I had had to hire for the occasion."

Judge Crowell lighted a cigarette, and, snatching at the
externals of the tale, he said, "Didn't know you fellows used
the guillotine as late as that. I've never seen one except that
one they've got in the antiquarian place in Edinburgh. They
call it the Maiden."

Dr. Reinmuth poured the very last of the Chablis into his
glass, and, turning to Mrs. Andreas, he said, "It was nectar and
I've drunk it all. *Sic transit gloria mundi*."

A Modest Proposal

THE celebrated trade winds of the Caribbean had, unsea-
sonably, ceased to blow, and over the island a horrid stillness tarried. The ships in the glassy harbor appeared becalmed,
and nothing moved except the golden lizards slipping over the
pink walls and scuttering through the purple bougainvillaea,
whose burdened branches touched the borders of the patio.
The puny cats that ate the lizards slept stupefied under the hibiscus hedges. Once, a man-o'-war bird sailed across the yellow
sky; once, a bushy burro strayed up the hill through the tall,
hissing guinea grass and, pausing, gazed aloft with an expression of babyish melancholy; now and then, the wood doves
sang sadly in the turpentine trees behind Captain Sundstrom's
house.

The Captain's guests, who had been swimming and sunning
all morning at his beach below and then had eaten his protracted
Danish lunch of multitudinous hors d'oeuvres and an aspic of
fish and a ragout of kid and salads and pancakes, now sat on the
gallery drinking gin-and-Schweppes. Their conversation dealt
largely with the extraordinary weather, and the residents of the
island were at pains to assure the visitors that this unwholesome, breathless pause did not presage a hurricane, for it was
far too early in the year. Their host predicted that a rain would
follow on the heels of the calm and fill the cisterns to the brim.
At times, the tone of the talk was chauvinistic; the islanders
asked the outlanders to agree with them that, unpleasant as
this might be, it was nothing like the villainous summer heat
of Washington or New York. Here, at any rate, one dressed
in sensible décolletage—the Captain's eyes browsed over the
bare shoulders of his ladies—and did not shorten one's life by
keeping up the winter's fidgets in the summertime. Why people
who were not obliged to live in the North did, he could not
understand. It was a form of masochism, was it not, frankly,
to condemn oneself needlessly to the tantrums of a capricious
climate? Temperate Zone, indeed! There was no temperance
north of Key West. The visitors civilly granted that their lives
were not ideal, they were politely envious of the calm and

leisure here, and some of them committed themselves to the extent of asking about the prices of real estate.

If the talk digressed from the weather, it went to other local matters: to the municipal politics, which were forever a bear garden; to the dear or the damnable peccadilloes of absent friends; to servant-robbers from the States; to the revenue the merchants and restaurateurs had acquired in their shops and bars when the last cruise ship was in, full to her gunwales of spendthrift boobs. And they talked of the divorcées-to-be who littered the terraces and lounges of the hotels, idling through their six weeks' quarantine, with nothing in the world to do but bathe in the sun and the sea, and drink, and haunt the shops for tax-free bargains in French perfume. They were spoken of as invalids; they were said to be here for "the cure." Some of them did look ill and shocked, as if, at times, they could not remember why they had come.

It was made plain that the divorcées who were among the gathering today were different from the rest; *they* were not bores about the husbands they were chucking; they did not flirt with married men, or get too drunk, or try anything fancy with the natives (a noteworthy woman from Utica, some months before, had brought a station wagon with her and daily could be seen driving along the country roads with a high-school boy as black as your hat beside her); and they fitted so well into the life of the island that the islanders would like to have them settle here or, at least, come back to pay a visit. Mrs. Baumgartner, a delicious blonde whose husband had beaten her with a ski pole in the railroad station at Boise, Idaho (she told the story very amusingly but it was evident that the man had been a beast), and who meant to marry again the moment she legally could, announced that she intended to return here for her honeymoon. Captain Sundstrom reasonably proposed that she not go back to the States at all but wait here until the proper time had passed and then send for her new husband. It would be droll if the same judge who had set her free performed the ceremony. Crowing concupiscently, the Captain invited her to be his house guest until that time. A lumbering fourth-generation Dane, and now an American citizen, he had a face like a boar; the nares of his snout were as broad as a native's and his lips were as thick and as smooth. By his own profession to every woman he met, he was a gourmet and a sybarite. He liked the flavor of colonial argot and would tell her, "My bed and board are first-chop," as he slowly winked a humid blue eye. He had never married, because he had known that his would be the experience of his charming guests; it was a nuisance, wasn't it, to assign six weeks of one's life to the correction of a damn-fool mistake? Who could fail to agree that his was the perfect life, here on a hillside out of the town, with so magnificent a view that it was no trouble at all to lure the beauties to enjoy his hospitality. Mufti for the Captain today consisted solely of linen trunks with a print of crimson salamanders; below them and above them his furred flesh wrapped his mammoth bones in coils. At the beach that morning, he had endlessly regretted that there were no French bathing suits, and privily he had told Sophie Otis that he hoped that before she left, he would have the opportunity of seeing her in high-heeled shoes and black stockings.

To Mrs. Otis, who had left the rest of the party and was sitting just below the gallery on a stone bench in the garden in front of the house, this two-dimensional and too pellucid world seemed all the world; it was not possible to envisage another landscape, even when she closed her eyes and called to mind the sober countryside of Massachusetts under snow, for the tropics trespassed, overran, and spoiled the image with their heavy, heady smells and their wanton colors. She could not gain the decorous smell of pine forests when the smell of night-blooming cereus was so arrogant in her memory; it had clung and cloyed since the evening before, like a mouthful of bad candy. Nor was it possible to imagine another time than this very afternoon, and it was as if the clocks, like the winds, had been arrested, and all endeavor were ended and all passion were a *fait accompli*, for nothing could strive or love in a torpor so insentient. She found it hard to understand Mrs. Baumgartner's energy, which could perpetrate a plan so involving of the heart. She herself was nearly at the end of her exile and in another week would go, but while she had counted the days like a child before Christmas, now she could not project herself beyond the present anesthesia and felt that the exile had only just begun and that she was doomed forever to remain within the immobile upheaval of this hot, lonesome Sunday sleep, with the voices of strangers thrumming behind her and no other living thing visible or audible in the expanse of arid hills and in the reach of bright-blue sea. It was fitting, she concluded, that one come to such a place as this to repudiate struggle and to resume the earlier, easier indolence of lovelessness.

On the ground beside her lay, face down, a ruined head of Pan, knocked off its pedestal by a storm that had passed here long ago. A bay leaf was impaled on one of the horns and part of the randy, sinful grin was visible, but the eyes addressed the ground and the scattered blue blossoms from the lignum vitae tree above. Prurient and impotent, immortalized in its romantically promiscuous corruption, the shard was like the signature of the garden's owner, who now, sprawled in a long planter's chair, was telling those who had not heard of it the grisly little contretemps that had taken place the night before aboard the Danish freighter that still lay in the harbor. Twelve hours before she entered, a member of her crew, a Liberian, had fallen from the mast he was painting and had died at once, of a fractured skull. Although it was the custom of the island to bury the dead, untreated, within twenty-four hours, the health authorities, under pressure from the ship's captain, agreed, at last, to embalm the body, to be shipped back to Africa by plane.

"But then they found," said Captain Sundstrom, "that the nigger's head was such a mess that the embalming fluid wouldn't stay in, so they had to plant the bugger, after all. We haven't got enough of our own coons, we have to take care of this stray jigaboo from Liberia, what?" He appealed to little Mrs. Fairweather, a high-principled girl in her middle twenties, who had fanatically learned tolerance in college, and who now rose to his bait, as she could always be counted on to do, and all but screamed her protest at his use of the words "nigger" and "coon" and "jigaboo."

"Now, now," said the Captain, taking her small ringless hand, "you're much too pretty to preachify." She snatched away her hand and glared at him with hatred and misery; she was the most unhappy of all the divorcées, because it had been her husband's idea, and not hers, that she come here. She spent most of her time knitting Argyle socks for him, in spite of everything, the tears falling among the network of bobbins. She took the current pair out of her straw beach bag now, and her needles began to set up a quiet, desperate racket. Half pitying, half amused, the company glanced at her a moment and then began their talk again, going on to other cases of emergency burials and other cases of violent death on these high seas.

Mrs. Otis had brought the Captain's binoculars to the garden with her, and she turned away from the people on the porch to survey the hills, where nothing grew but bush and, here and there, a grove of the gray, leafless trees they called cedars, whose pink blossoms were shaped like horns and smelled like nutmeg; they did what they could, the cedar flowers, to animate the terrain, but it was little enough, although sometimes, from a distance, they looked beautifully like a shower of apple blossoms. She peered beyond the termination of the land, toward the countless islands and cays of the Atlantic, crouching like cats on the unnatural sea. They were intractably dry, and yet there was a sense everywhere of lives gathering fleshily and quietly, of an incessant, somnolent feeding, of a brutish instinct cleverer than any human thought. Some weeks before, from a high elevation on another island, through another pair of glasses, she had found the great mound of the island of Jost Van Dykes and had just made out its two settlements and its long, thin beaches, and she had found, as well, a separate house, halfway up the island's steep ascent, set in a waste as sheer as a rain catchment, where only one tree grew. And the tree was as neat and simple as a child's drawing. She had quickly put the glasses down, feeling almost faint at the thought of the terrible and absolute simplicity with which a life would have to be led in a place so wanting in shadow and in hiding places, fixed so nakedly to the old, juiceless, unloving land. Remembering that strident nightmare, she turned now to the evidences on the gallery of the prudent tricks and the solacing subterfuges of civilization; even here, as in the cities of their former days, the expatriates had managed to escape the aged, wickedly sagacious earth. See how, with optimism, gin, jokes, and lechery, they could deny even this satanic calm and heat!

Mr. Robertson, the liquor merchant, was explaining the activities of the peacetime Army here to a Coca-Cola salesman who had stopped off for a few days on the island en route from Haiti to the Argentine. Robertson, a former rumrunner and Captain Sundstrom's best friend, was as skinny as one of the island cats, and his skeleton was crooked and his flesh was cold. His eyes, through inappropriate pince-nez, mirrored no intellect at all but only a nasty appetite. He was a heliophobe and could never let the sun touch him anywhere, and so, in this country of brown skins and black ones, he always looked like a newcomer from the North and, with that fungous flesh, like an invalid who had left his hospital bed too soon. On the beach that morning, he had worn a hat with a visor and had sat under an enormous umbrella and had further fended off the sun by holding before his face a partially eviscerated copy of *Esquire*. In spite of his looks, he was a spark as ardent as the Captain, and lately, while his wife had been ailing, he had cut rather a wide swath, he claimed; all day he had giggled gratefully at his friends' charges that he had been stalking the native Negro women and the pert little French tarts from Cha Cha Town.

Rumor had it, he told the salesman, that a laboratory was presently to be set up on an outlying cay for the investigation of the possible values of biological warfare. The noxious vapors would be carried out to sea. (To kill the fancy, flashy fish weaving through the coral reefs, wondered Mrs. Otis, half listening.) Captain Sundstrom, who was connected with the project, turned again to Mrs. Fairweather, a born victim, and prefacing his sally with a long chuckle, he said, "We're hunting for a virus that will kill off the niggers but won't hurt anybody else. We call it 'coon bane.'" One of the kitchen boys had just come out onto the gallery with a fresh bucket of ice, but there was no expression at all on his long, incurious face, not even when Mrs. Fairweather, actually crying now, sobbed, "Hush!" The Coca-Cola man, in violent embarrassment, began at once to tell the company the story of an encounter he had had in Port-au-Prince with an octoroon midget from North Carolina named Sells Floto, but his heart was not in it, and it was clear that his garrulity was tolerated only out of good manners.

Mrs. Otis picked up the binoculars again and found the beach. For some time, she watched a pair of pelicans that sat on the tideless water, preposterously permanent, like buoys, until their greed came on them and they rose heavily, flapped seaward for a while, then dived, like people, with an inexpert splash, and came up with a fish to fling into their ridiculous beaks. The wide-leaved sea grapes along the ivory shingle were turning brown and yellow, a note of impossible autumn beside that bay, where the shimmer of summer was everlasting. Mrs. Otis shifted her focus to the grove of coconut palms that grew to the north of the curve of the ocean, and almost at once, as if they had been waiting for her, there appeared, at the debouchment of one of the avenues, a parade of five naked Negro children leading a little horse exactly the color of themselves. The smallest child walked at the head of the line and the tallest held the bridle. But a middle-sized one was in command, and when they had gained the beach, he broke the orderly procession and himself took the bridle and led the horse right up to Captain Sundstrom's blue cabaña. If her ears had not been aided by her eyes, Mrs. Otis thought she would not have heard the distant cries and the distant neigh, but the sounds came to her clearly and softly across the stunted trees. The children reconnoitered for a while, looking this way and that, now stepping off the distance between the cabaña and the water, now running like sandpipers toward the coconut grove and back again. Then the smallest and the tallest, helped by the others, mounted the horse; it was a lengthy process, because the helpers had to spin and prance about to relieve their excitement, and sometimes they forgot themselves altogether for an absent-minded minute and ran to peer through the cracks of the closed-up cabaña; then they returned to the business at hand with refreshed attention. When the riders were seated, one of the smaller children ran back to the grove and returned with a switch, which he handed up to the tall child. The horse, at the touch of the goad, lifted his head and whinnied and then charged into the water, spilling his cargo, only to be caught promptly and mounted by two others who had run out in his wake. They, in their turn, were thrown. Again and again, they tried and failed to ride him more than a few yards, until, at last, the middle-sized ruler managed to stick and to ride out all the way to the reef and back again. The cheers were like the cries of sea birds. The champion rested, lying flat on the sand before the cabaña, and for a while the others lay around him like the spokes of a wheel, while the horse shuddered and stomped.

On the gallery, the Captain had noticed the children. "Cheeky little beggars, muckering around on my beach, but

I'll let them have it. I'm a freethinker, what?" he said; then, turning to Mrs. Fairweather, "I'm going to give you a fat little blackamoor to take back with you, to remind you of our island paradise, what?"

Mr. Robertson said, "Don't let him ride you, honey. For all his big talk, he's softer about them than you are." He leaned over to sink his fist into the Captain's thigh. "Get me?" he cried.

The Captain laughed and slapped his leg. "The whole thing's a lie, that's what it is, you outlaw!"

"It's a lie if the gospel truth's a lie," said Robertson. Mrs. Fairweather did not look up from her knitting, even though he was as close to her as if he meant to bite or kiss her. "Listen, kiddo, when I first knew him, he used to be all the time saying what he wanted most of all in the world to do was eat broiled pickaninny. All the time thinking of his stomach. So one day I said to him, 'All right, damn it, you damned well *will* one of these fine days!'"

Mrs. Baumgartner gasped, and one of the other women said, "Oh, really, Rob, you're such a fool. Everyone knows that our slogan here is 'Live and let live.'"

But Robertson wanted to tell his story and went on despite them. He said, "Well, sir, a little while after I made that historic declaration, there was a fire in Pollyberg, just below my house, and I moseyed down to have a look-see."

"Let's not talk about fires!" cried Mrs. Baumgartner. "I was in a most frightful one in Albany and had to go down a ladder in my nightie."

Captain Sundstrom whistled and blew her a noisy kiss.

"They had got it under control by the time I got there, and everyone had left," pursued the liquor merchant. "I took a look in the front door and I smelled the best goddamned smell I ever smelled in my life, just possibly barring the smell of roasting duck. 'Here's Sundstrom's dinner,' I said to myself, and, sure enough, I poked around a little and found a perfectly cooked baby—around ten and a half pounds, I'd say."

The Coca-Cola salesman, who, all along, had kept a worried eye on Mrs. Fairweather, leaped into Robertson's pause for breath and announced that he knew a man who had his shoes made of alligator wallets from Rio.

Robertson glanced at him coldly, ignored the interruption,

and went on speaking directly to Mrs. Fairweather. "It was charred on the outside, naturally, but I knew it was bound to be sweet and tender inside. So I took him home and called up this soldier of fortune here and told him to come along for dinner. I heated the toddler up and put him on a platter and garnished him with parsley and one thing or another, and you never saw a tastier dish in your life."

The Coca-Cola man, turning pale, stood up and said, "What's the matter with you people here? You ought to shoot yourself for telling a story like that."

But Robertson said to Mrs. Fairweather, "And what do you think he did after all the trouble I'd gone to? Refused to eat any of it, the sentimentalist! And *he* called *me* a cannibal!"

Robertson and the Captain lay back in their chairs and laughed until they coughed, but there was not a sound from anyone else and the islanders looked uneasily from one visitor to another; when their reproachful eyes fell on their host or on his friend, their look said, "There are limits."

Suddenly, Mrs. Fairweather threw a glass on the stone floor and it exploded like a shot. Somewhere in the house, a dog let out a howl of terror at the sound, and the kitchen boy came running. He ran, cringing, sidewise like a land crab, and the Captain, seeing him, hollered, "Now, damn you, what do *you* want? Have you been eavesdropping?"

"No, mon," said the boy, flinching. There was no way of knowing by his illegible face whether he told the truth or not. He ran back faster than he had come, as if he were pursued. The Captain stood up to make a new drink for Mrs. Fairweather, to whom speech and mobility seemed unlikely ever to return; she sat staring at the fragments of glass glinting at her feet, as if she had reached the climax of some terrible pain.

"Oh, this heat!" said Mrs. Baumgartner, and fanned herself gracefully with her straw hat.

Something had alarmed the children on the beach below, and Mrs. Otis, turning to look at them again, saw them abruptly immobilized; then, as silently and as swiftly as sharks, they led the horse away and disappeared into the palm grove, leaving no traces of themselves behind. Until she saw them go, she had not been aware that the skies were darkening, and she wondered how long ago the transformation had begun. Now, from miles away, there rolled up a thunderclap, and, as always in the tropics, the rain came abruptly, battling the trees and lashing the vines, beheading the flowers, crashing onto the tin roofs, and belaboring the jalousies of Captain Sundstrom's pretty house. Blue blossoms showered the head of Pan. Wrapping the field glasses in her sash to protect them from the rain, Mrs. Otis returned to the gallery, and when the boy brought out a towel to her—for in those few minutes she had got soaked to the skin—she observed that he wore a miraculous medal under his open shirt. She looked into his eyes and thought, Angels and ministers of grace defend you. The gaze she met humbled her, for its sagacious patience showed that he knew his amulet protected him against an improbable world. His was all the sufferance and suffering of little children. In his ambiguous tribulation, he sympathized with her, and with great dignity he received the towel, heavy with rain, when she had dried herself.

"See?" said Captain Sundstrom to his guests, with a gesture toward the storm. "We told you this heat was only an interlude." And feeling that the long drinks were beginning to pall, he set about making a shaker of martinis.

Caveat Emptor

MALCOLM and Victoria agreed that if they had not discovered each other at the beginning of the fall term at the Alma Hettrick College for Girls, where they taught, they would have lost their minds or, short of that, would have gone into silent religious orders. He was twenty-three and she was twenty-two and they were both immediately out of graduate school with brand-new Master's degrees, whose coruscations they fondly imagined illumined them and dazed the Philistine. Malcolm had studied philosophy and the title of his thesis had been *A Literary Evaluation of Sören Kierkegaard and a Note on His Relation to Mediaeval Christian Dialectic.* Victoria, who had specialized in the sixteenth century, had written on *Some Late Borrowings from Provençal* fin amour *in Elizabethan Miscellanies and Songbooks.*

The altitude of their academic ideals had not begun to dwindle yet and they shivered and shook in the alien air that hovered over the pretty campus of this finishing school, whose frankly stated aim was "to turn out the wives and mothers of tomorrow." These nubile girls, all of them dumb and nearly all beautiful, knitted in class (that is how they would occupy themselves in their later lives when they attended lectures, said the dean when Malcolm complained of the clack of needles and the subordination of the concept of doubt to purling); they wrote term papers on the advisability of a long engagement and on the history of fingernail polish; they tap-danced or interpretive-danced their way to classes on walks between signs that read: *Don't hurt me. I'll be beautiful grass in the spring if you'll give me a chance.*

Pale from their ivory towers, myopic from reading footnotes in the oblique light of library stacks, Malcolm and Victoria had met on the day of their arrival in September. The heaviness and wetness of the day, smelling of mildew, had drawn them together first; both, being punctilious, had got to the Geneva S. Bigelow Memorial Library too early for the first convocation of the faculty and so, having introduced themselves, they had gone across the street to drink lemonade in a bake oven that called itself the Blue Rose and that smelled loathsomely of pork. Here, in a quarter of an hour, facing each other across a copse of catchup bottles and vinegar cruets and A-1 sauce, they found out that they had in common their advanced degrees, a dread of teaching and no experience of this kind of heat, since Malcolm came from the Rockies and Victoria came from Maine. Each divined accurately that the other was penniless and that it was this condition rather than a desire to impart what they had learned to girls that had brought them to this town, Victoria on a Greyhound bus and Malcolm in a tall, archaic Buick touring car.

At the faculty meeting that morning and at all subsequent meetings they sat side by side. Their dismay, from which they were never to recover, began with the opening address by President Harvey, a chubby, happy man who liked to have the students call him Butch—the title was optional but the girls who could not bring themselves to use it were few and far between. He began his immensely long speech with a brief account of his own life: he had been born without advantages in a one-room cabin in the Ozarks and had had, in much of his youth, the companionship only of a blind aunt and an exceptionally intelligent hound, both of whom, in their different ways, had taught him values that he would not part with for all the tea in China; from the aunt he had learned how to smile when the sledding was tough and from the dog he had learned how to relax. His transition from this affecting homily to the history of Alma Hettrick was an obscure accomplishment. He described the rise of the college from a small female seminary with twenty students to the great plant of national importance it now was. Year by year Alma Hettrick had grown with the times, adding something different here, cutting out something passé there, its goal being always that of preparing these young women for the real job of the real woman, that is, homemaking. They had dropped Elocution from the curriculum (the president smiled and his audience smiled back at him) and no longer taught how to use a fan, how to tat or how to communicate with a suitor in the language of flowers (the teachers laughed out loud and someone at the back of the room clapped his hands); nevertheless the emphasis was still on those articles of instruction particularly suited to the needs of a woman:

Marriage and the Family, Child Care, Home Ec, Ballet for grace, French for elegance.

Beaming like Kriss Kringle, the president concluded his speech with a timely observation: "It may be novel but I don't think it's iconoclastic to liken education to business. We are here to sell our girls Shakespeare and French and Home Economics and Ballet. They're consumers in a manner of speaking. I don't mean that a student consumes Shakespeare in the sense that the supply of Shakespeare is decreased but that she can assimilate his work just as her body would assimilate meat or any other food. Let's each and every one of us sell ourselves to these girls and then sell our commodity, whether it's those grand old plays or how to run a sewing machine. Good luck!"

Two new programs had been added this year to help the consumer become a well-rounded woman and these were now briefly described by their directors. There was the Personality Clinic, headed by a stern-visaged Miss Firebaugh, who, with her staff, would counsel the girls on the hair styles and nail-polish shades that would highlight their best features. And there was the Voice Clinic, where, presumably, harsh neighs and twangs and whines would be wheedled into the register of a lady. This clinic was under the direction of an ebullient Mr. Sprackling, who was as pink as a rose and had a shock of orange hair and sideburns to match and a fierce exophthalmic green eye. He had the air of a surgeon about him: one saw him cleaving tongues that were tied, excising lisps, loosening glottal stops, skillfully curing girls from Oklahoma who tended to diphthongize their vowels.

At the back of the dais, where several deans and heads of departments sat, there was an arrangement of leaves and maidenhair ferns designed by the joint efforts of the Botany Club and the Flower Arrangement Hobby Group and made known as such by a large placard attached to a basket of sumac. It seemed to Victoria a setting more appropriate to a xylophonist or a bird imitator than to a college faculty. This, however, was less unusual than the housing of the general assembly, a week later, of the staff and the students: because of the greatly increased student body, they could not meet in the auditorium or in the gymnasium and they convened, instead, in a circus tent pitched on the quadrangle; the endorsement of its owner was printed boldly in red on the side: *Jim Sloat Carnival Shows.*

Malcolm and Victoria became inseparable. Under other circumstances they might not have known each other or they might have known each other in a more recreational way. But these singular circumstances produced an infrangible bond; they clung tottering together like unarmed travelers, lost from their party, in a trackless jungle inhabited by anthropophagists. Or they were like soldiers whose paths would never have crossed in civilian life but who stood shoulder to shoulder in profound fraternity in time of war. Their enemy, the entire faculty and all the students, down to the last instructor of cosmetics in the Personality Clinic, down to the last ambulatory patient in Mr. Sprackling's infirmary, was not aware of the hostilities that were being waged against him by these two or the plans that were being laid for sabotage: Victoria was thinking of requiring all her classes in Freshman English to read *Finnegans Wake* and Malcolm was considering delivering a series of twelve diatribes against Edward Bok, whose *Americanization of* he was obliged to teach in his course called "Philosophy of Life."

On the contrary, the enemy found the newcomers shy but cooperative and never dreamed that instead of being shy they were sulky and that they were obedient only because they had both hands tied behind their backs. So the enemy (in the persons of Rosemary Carriage, a great maudlin donkey of a senior; Miss Goss, secretary to the Dean of Extracurricular Activities; Mr. Borglund, who taught Marriage and the Family; and Sally-Daniel Gallagher, who ran the faculty coffee shop) observed with—depending on their ruling humor—complacence, with malice, with a vicarious thrill, that the fall term had started exactly as it should, with a love-at-first-sight romance between the two youngest teachers. These detectives and publicists who presented their data and then their exegesis in the dining rooms knew that each day after their last classes Miss Pinckney and Mr. Kirk went driving through the country in Mr. Kirk's car, that almost every night they dined at the Chicken-in-a-Basket at the edge of town, that they graded their papers together in a tavern on the highway to the city.

What the voyeurs did not know, because they were not close enough to be eavesdroppers as well, was that the exchange, over the drumsticks in the Chicken-in-a-Basket, over the beer and cheese popcorn at the Red Coach Inn, over the final cigarettes in front of Victoria's rooming house, that this exchange, which ran the gamut from gravity to helpless laughter, had nothing whatsoever to do with love. It might occasionally have to do with medieval prose or with symptoms (both of them thought they were starting ulcers), but for the most part what they talked about were the indignities that were being perpetrated against their principles by Butch Harvey's pedagogical fiddlesticks. For they were far too young and their principles were far too vernal for them to rise above their circumstance; their laughter was not very mirthful but was, really, reflexive: now and again they were whacked on the crazy bone. They did not really believe that Alma Hettrick was an actuality, although, as they often said, they couldn't possibly have made it up. Whoever heard of anything so fictitious as the production of *Lohengrin* that was currently under way with an all-girl cast, directed by an Estonian diva, Mongolian of countenance and warlike of disposition? "An Estonian diva has no provable substance," said Malcolm categorically. "Such a figment belongs to the same genus as the unicorn, the gryphon and the Loch Ness Monster."

Victoria, demure and honey-haired, and Malcolm, a black-haired, blue-eyed Scot, muscular and six-foot-four, were, said the vigilant campus, made for each other. The fact was, however, that they had assigned to each other no more of sex than the apparel. And such was the monomania of their interlocution that they had never happened to mention that they were engaged to be married to two other people to whom they wrote frequent letters, often by special delivery.

Besides their fidgets of outrage and unrest, besides their fits of ferocious giggles, Malcolm and Victoria had another mood, an extemporaneous mood of melancholy that immediate time and place determined. By the languid St. Martin River, on whose banks the bracken was turning brown and on whose sallow surface gold leaves rode, they often sat in the triste dusk of autumn, talking with rue of the waste of their lucubrations. Their woe betook them too on Sunday evenings when they were driving back to the college after spending a long and private day in a little town they had discovered early in the term. On Sunday, until the sun went down, they were in a world that was separate and far and they were serene; but when the docile Buick headed home, wrath rose and set their jaws.

Built on the crest of a kind, green hill so that its inhabitants could look far up the river and far down, this town, Georges Duval's Mill, was scarcely more credible than the Estonian diva, but unlike the other chimeras of their lives it was endearing and they loved it dearly.

The twentieth century had barely touched Georges Duval's Mill and, indeed, the nineteenth had not obliterated altogether the looks and the speech of the original settlers of the region, who had been French. There was a Gallic look in the faces of the townspeople, their cuisine was peasant French and most of them were bilingual, speaking a Cajun-like patois. Some, better educated, like the mayor and the priest, spoke as befitted their station. And there were, as well, the Parisian formalities and fillips and the niceties of syntax used by two aged maiden sisters, the Mlles Geneviève and Mathilde Papin, who once, scores of years before, had gone to school in France and who now ran L'Hôtel Dauphin and were persuaded that at some time the luckless son of Louis XVI had lived in the town.

Chickens and geese, ducks and goats and sometimes cattle and swine roved and waddled and mooed and quacked through the cobbled main street. The cats were fat and were collared with smart ribbons and bows and they sat imperiously on sunny sills, festooning themselves with their congratulatory tails. There was a public well—there was little plumbing—in the middle of a green, and here the gawky adolescents flirted, shyer than violets and bolder than brass. Through open windows came the smell of choucroute garnie and pot-au-feu. The children were verminous and out at the elbows; all the women save those over seventy were pregnant. The priest was lymphatic; the mayor was driven by cupidity and hindered by gout; the doctor was as deaf as a post; the town crier was also the village idiot; and the teacher was usually drunk.

It was not the quaintness of Georges Duval's Mill that attracted Malcolm and Victoria, for neither of them had a drop of sightseer's blood. In passing, to be sure, they were pleased by the surprising survival and supremacy of a foreign language spang in the middle of the Middle West. And they enjoyed the rituals: the mannered courtship by the well in which the buckets seemed to play a part; the entourage of children that followed the priest from the church to the rectory, led by two altar boys who carried the chalice and the ciborium in string shopping bags; the countless alarms and excursions of indeterminate origin that would suddenly catapult the whole populace into the street, still wearing their dinner napkins tucked into their collars, still holding a fork or a mug. They liked all this and they liked it, too, that there was a practicing witch at the edge of town who had been seen in the shape of a wolf tearing sheep by the light of the full moon.

But what made the village really precious to them, really indispensable, was that in almost every particular they could name it was the antithesis of Alma Hettrick. Looking at the candles and the gaslights in L'Hôtel Dauphin (the old ladies disapproved of electricity and spoke cattily of their neighbors who had it), seeing roosters emerge from parlors, seeing toddlers being given vin ordinaire to drink, the teachers were oblivious to modern times and modern education and modern girls. They basked in backwardness.

Apparently they were the only visitors who ever came to Georges Duval's Mill. They had not been able to find it on any map and they were sure that none of their colleagues, especially in the Social Studies Division, knew of it or they would have come armed cap-a-pie with questionnaires and Kodachrome and Binet-Simon testing equipment.

When they arrived at about noon on Sunday, Malcolm parked his car (it had a klaxon and from the front it looked like Barney Google) under a vast copper beech in a sylvan dingle behind the green, and then they walked through mud and over the cobblestones to the hotel, where Mlle Mathilde, having seen them coming, was already pouring the water into two glasses of Pernod that stood in saucers on a round marble-topped table in one of two oriels in the dining room. The other oriel was occupied by the mayor, a widower, whose poor gouty foot was propped up on a stool and was being daily worsened by piquant sauces and rich wines. After they had drunk a good deal of Pernod and could feel that they were on the mend, Malcolm and Victoria had a subtle meal. The cook's daughter, Emma, put a white cloth on their table and a Benares vase of carnations made of crinoline and wire, a pepper mill and a salt mill and a carafe of white wine. Sometimes the soup was onion and sometimes it was leek and potato and once—and they would never forget it—it was chestnuts and cress; and then they had an omelet made with mushrooms, with delicious chanterelles that Mlle Geneviève had gathered in the summertime and had dried. With the omelet they had a salad with chervil in it, brioche, sweet butter and Brie. Their dessert was crème brûlée. And then they had coffee and with the coffee, brandy.

By now they were sleepy—the mayor was more than that, he was asleep among his chins—and they moved in a haze of contentment into the parlor, where they gradually woke up under the influences of the disciplinary horsehair sofa and the further coffee and the perky gossip of the old sisters in their nice black silk dresses trimmed with passementerie braid. While they excavated the doctor's secrets and explored the garden paths down which the grocer had led many a girl, the ladies worked at gros point, very fast. They were witty and spry and their eyes were clear but they were, as they admitted, extremely old and after a little while they excused themselves to go and take their naps. Now Victoria stretched out full length on the narrow sofa with a mass of round pillows at her shoulders and Malcolm established himself in a Morris chair. For several hours they read and smoked and drank the cool, strong coffee in the china pot. On Sundays Victoria liked to read *The Canterbury Tales*, while Malcolm, mindful of the Ph.D. he longed to get, worked away at the Whitehead-Russell *Principia Mathematica*, sometimes sighing and at other times nodding in discernment and saying quite spontaneously to himself, "Oh, I see. Oh, of course."

At half past four the innkeepers reappeared, wearing small velvet hats, for after tea they would go to benediction. They had tea and petits fours and fruit and then in the twilight they all left the hotel and shook hands and said goodbye on the steps. The ladies went quickly downhill toward the church, whose bell was ringing, and Malcolm and Victoria made their way much more slowly back to the dell and the Buick, which loomed up in the gathering dark like a moose in a rock garden. They were so heavy-hearted that they had to stop on their way home at the Red Coach and buck themselves up with whiskey at the bar.

One Sunday early in November when the first snow was flying

in great melting stars against the windowpanes in L'Hôtel Dauphin and the mayor was sitting with his back to Malcolm and Victoria, toasting his swollen foot before the fire in the hearth, they fell in love. Their hearts had evidently been synchronized precisely because at the same moment they both stopped eating and met each other's astonished gaze. The hands that a moment before had been spooning up crème brûlée reached across the table and clasped; Victoria quaked from head to foot and Malcolm's mouth went dry. What had led up to it? They could not remember. They were never able to recall what they had been saying just before: had they been discussing St. Augustine as a heretic? Or had they been voicing their essential indifference to the Orient? They could not say. It was like a concussion with amnesia covering all events immediately preceding the blow.

"Vicky," murmured Malcolm. The diminutive announced his state of mind. "Why, Vicky, why, my God, Victoria!"

He clapped his free hand to his forehead and in doing so he knocked over the brass vase of artificial flowers. He is very awkward, thought Victoria, how I love him! The mayor, disturbed by the noise of the vase clattering to the floor, turned around and disapproved of them with his moist, alcoholic eyes and said fretfully, "*Quel tapage.*"

"Do you know what I mean, Vicky?" said Malcolm, leaning over to pick up the scattered flowers but keeping his eyes on her. "Do you know what has happened to me . . . darling?" She nodded, scarlet.

It was difficult for them that day to follow the adventures of Mlle Mathilde's octoroon governess; they could not tell whether she had run away with a pirate or a forger and whether she had stolen a cabochon brooch or had kept a capuchin as a pet. They thought the old ladies would never leave, but at last they put their tapestry needles back into their strawberry emeries and left in a swish of silk and a zephyr of sachet, and Malcolm and Victoria began to kiss.

Of course it could not have happened like this: falling in love is not an abrupt plunge; it is a gradual descent, seldom in a straight line, rather like the floating downward of a parachute. And the expression is imperfect because while one may fall one also levitates. Nevertheless, Malcolm and Victoria enjoyed the conceit of suddenness. Forgetting all that had drawn them together, ignoring the fact that they were uncommonly attractive and intelligent (for all their schoolishness) and humorous and good-humored (for all their jeers), they pretended that at one certain moment they had been knocked galley-west by this thunderbolt out of the blue; they pretended that they had seen stars; they behaved as if there were balloons over their heads containing the word "Zowie!" And in their delirium they gave the whole credit to Georges Duval's Mill, which they personified as a matchmaker. It never in the world occurred to them that Alma Hettrick's machinations long antedated those of the town.

If they had been asked (as they might well have been if a pollster from the Alma Hettrick Social Studies Division had been around), "Which in your opinion is more important, the reading and consumption of hard books, such as *Principia Mathematica*, or the direct observation of behavior patterns in college females?" they would have replied, "Neither amounts to a hill of beans. It's love that makes the world go around."

That night they did not need to stop at the Red Coach but went directly home. A few days later a fiancée in Denver and a fiancé in Bath got airmail letters containing regretful, remorseful, ashamed, confused, but positive and unconditional goodbyes.

In the next weeks the partisans of the attachment between Miss Pinckney and Mr. Kirk were worried and the critics of it said: "I told you so. That much propinquity will willy-nilly breed contempt." For Malcolm and Victoria were seldom seen together. They quit the Chicken-in-a-Basket; Victoria ate at the Faculty Club and Malcolm ate alone in the Blue Rose. The eccentric Buick now was never parked in the cinder drive of the Red Coach and those afternoon rides were apparently a thing of the past. Miss Goss, who had mothered her three motherless sisters and had got them married off and who, through habit, was doomed to mother and marry off everyone, said in the faculty coffee shop: "What *can* have happened? They were so well-suited." Sally-Daniel Gallagher, at the cashier's desk, said: "If you ask me, it's just as well. With those kind of carrying-ons day in and day out, to say nothing of night in and night out, something is bound to happen and it wouldn't do to have it happen on campus." Ray (Marriage and the Family) Borglund, saddened but ever constructive, was moved to give an open lecture on "Snags in Courtship and How to Avoid Them."

Puzzled and disappointed, or smug and malign, the campus watched the estranged couple out of the corner of its eye.

The couple, so afflicted with delight, so feverish and crazy with bliss, had agreed at the start that they did not want their treasure to be public property. On the evening they had opened their oyster and had found therein the pearl of great price, Malcolm had said to Victoria when he took her home: "This is one commodity that's not going on the market. Let's keep this luxury item under our hats." And Victoria, fingering the leather patch on his elbow as if it were the most beloved object in the world, replied: "I don't think it has any consumer value at all."

While Alma Hettrick speculated, the Papin sisters were overjoyed that their young patrons now came to L'Hôtel Dauphin for the whole weekend. They were as sly as foxes in their departure from the college town. Victoria took a cab to the bus station and Malcolm picked her up there; and then they took a circuitous route to Georges Duval's Mill. Victoria wore dark glasses and a hat.

Alma Hettrick, however, was slyer than they were and on a Saturday morning one of its agents, Miss Peppertree of the Art Department, who was catching a bus to Chicago, saw Victoria in her thin disguise get into the Buick carrying a suitcase. She just had time to call Miss Goss before her bus left. By noon the word had spread through all the college personnel who had not gone away for the weekend. Mr. Borglund frankly did not like the sneaky looks of it at all; the word "strait-laced" could never be applied to the policy at Alma Hettrick but *propriety* was mandatory. Sally-Daniel Gallagher said "Aha!" Miss Goss said "Oh, no!" But Mr. Borglund, rallying after his initial shock, said: "We'll set things straight in a jiffy."

It took longer than a jiffy even though Mr. Borglund applied himself to the problem assiduously. On telephoning the mis-creants' landladies, he learned that their lodgers always went away for the weekend but had never named their destinations. Throughout the next week, although he watched them and tried to trick them out individually with leading questions, he accomplished nothing. Both of them seemed preoccupied and a little drowsy, as if they were coming down with colds. On Saturday morning he was at the bus depot at eight o'clock, hoping that like laboratory white rats they had acquired conditioned reflexes. He parked in ambush across the street in an alley; he wore a cap, a large one, and looked a good deal like Mr. Toad. He had to wait two hours in the cold and several times he wondered how reliable Amelia Peppertree was; she was inclined to be flighty and, as a Life Drawing teacher, bohemian. All the same, at ten o'clock he was rewarded for his patience. He saw what Miss Peppertree had reported she had seen and he followed the jade and her reprobate.

He followed them over roads he had never traveled or had known existed, through country so wild and forlorn that he felt he had left his own dimension and was traversing the moon; they would go along the river for a while and then they would strike out cross-country over faint lanes through the middle of tobacco fields.

Malcolm and Victoria, half-frozen, were warming their hands around glasses of mulled claret before the fire when Ray Borglund came into the dining room of the hotel. They gasped and gaped when they saw the civic-minded Swede and sotto voce Malcolm said: "I'll kill him."

"My stars!" cried the sociologist. "Of all places to run into a couple of people I *know*! I got so cold I had to stop—I was on my way to Lakeville." Since Georges Duval's Mill was off all beaten tracks and since Lakeville was in exactly the opposite direction, he made his point very clear whether he meant to or not. He rubbed his hands gleefully and came up to the fire. "Mind?" he said and, leaning down to sniff at Victoria's glass, he went on, "Mmm, that smells good. May I join you in a glass of it? That is, if I'm not interrupting something?"

He joined them in two glasses of hot wine and he joined them at lunch and, because they were in so ticklish a spot, they spilled all the beans about Georges Duval's Mill, cravenly giving him to understand that they were collaborating on a historical-ethnic-anthropological-ideological-linguistic study of this perfectly preserved fossil town. They did not need to go into so much detail (needn't, for example, have mentioned the witch) but out of embarrassment they did and, appalled, they watched Mr. Borglund's interest rise and inundate them.

First of all, he was obviously persuaded of the asexual nature of their collusion and obviously relieved, and then he was drawn to their facts; next he was fascinated and finally he became so fanatic that he blew scalding coffee into his face.

"I don't know what's the matter with us vets at Alma Hettrick. I thought we were on our toes, but it takes you newcomers to show us what's been under our noses the whole time," he said. "Why, we never thought of this town as anything but a wide space in the road. Oh, maybe a little French still used but that's not uncommon along the river. But now I see it's a real find. Why, right here in this one area we've got material for a school-wide project. Why, good Lord, I can see how there could be a tie-in of all the divisions. Maybe not the Personality Clinic—but maybe so. Maybe they have some interesting native costumes. Maybe they still use old-time recipes for hand lotion." He went on in this fashion until the sun began to set, and when at last he left them he did so only because, as he said, he wanted to "contact President Harvey at once so that we won't waste a moment's time in setting up the Georges Duval's Mill Project."

The Papin sisters had not liked Mr. Borglund and the grouchy mayor had hated him. Malcolm and Victoria wanted to explain and apologize and enjoin the town crier to broadcast a warning that snoops were planning an invasion of these innocent precincts. But they did not know how to go about it. And they were so sick at heart at the threat to their bower that momentarily they forgot they were in love. After dinner, unable to speak, they started to read, but Malcolm suddenly threw his big book to the floor and said: "I don't know what they're talking about, this A. N. Whitehead and this Bertrand Russell." Later, they remembered that they were in love and they were happy, but the edge was off and that Sunday they stopped at the Red Coach and drank boilermakers and fell in with a Fuller Brush man who gave Victoria a free-sample whisk broom.

Now at Alma Hettrick a new attitude developed toward them. Their claque applauded the seriousness with which they had undertaken their investigations of this dodo of a town, while their detractors called them selfish and said that as members of the Alma Hettrick crowd they had no right to stake a claim on such a gold mine. The former were sorry that their earlier surmise had been wrong (that Malcolm and Victoria were in love) and glad that their second had been wrong (that they had had a quarrel) and proud that they had such trail blazers in their midst. The opposition said they were grinds and prudes and had no red blood in them.

On two successive Saturdays the Alma Hettrick station wagon and three other cars followed Malcolm's Buick to the hamlet on the hill and delegates from the faculty and from the student body swarmed through the streets and lanes, declaring and querying in restaurant French. Most of the residents were apathetic; some were amazed just as the unready must have been when the Visigoths arrived. Miss Firebaugh of the Personality Clinic went into raptures over the costumes of the Mlles Papin; she asked them to turn around slowly; she exclaimed over gussets and tucks; she took photographs of them using flash bulbs and the mayor winced and said, "*Allons donc! Quelle sottise!*" But this was the only jewel Miss Firebaugh found; the rest of the clothes in the town had come from Sears, Roebuck.

The Child Study Group, working with Marriage and the Family representatives, made gruesome discoveries: intermarriage and rampant disease had lowered the average intelligence quotient to cretinism; incest was prevalent and was not denied. The American History people came up against a blank wall: the only thing anyone knew about Georges Duval's Mill was that a miller named Georges Duval had once owned this land but they did not know when, not even roughly when, and they did not know what had become of him or of his descendants. The only information to be had about the Dauphin was the sentimental testimony of the old sisters, who simply said that he had been there—else, they inquired, why would the hotel be named for him? There were no annals, no pictorial artifacts, nothing but oral and exceedingly uninteresting legends. There were no indigenous arts and crafts. Though urged and bribed, the villagers flatly refused to sing. One idiot child did a dance on the green but the priest explained, tapping his forehead, that she was making it up as she went along and there was no tradition behind it. The Political Scientists found an unparalleled dearth of politics. The Appreciation of Art people found that in Georges Duval's Mill there was no appreciation of art.

As for the deputies from the Community Health class, they wanted to report the town to Federal authorities: the lice in the children's hair were fabulous, the barnyard filth in the streets was unspeakable, there was a public drinking cup at the well and the doctor still practiced phlebotomy.

In the end, the only one who really profited was Mr. Sprackling. He hit upon an excellent formula for his students who mumbled or slurred. "We enunciate when we are not lazy," said he, a man with a nimble tongue and an alert soft palate. "There is all the difference in the world between the way you young ladies say, 'I doan know,' and the way the poorest peasant of Georges Duval's Mill says, '*Je ne sais pas.*'" What made him think the poor peasants were not lazy Malcolm and Victoria could not guess, for in point of fact they were largely loafers and spent most of their time staring at their shoes.

In short order the project was abandoned. Mr. Borglund heartily said in the men's room to Malcolm: "Well, all is not gold that glitters and one man's meat is another man's poison. It wasn't a question of missing the boat—the boat wasn't there. Say, Kirk, are you and Miss Pinckney going on with your study of this place?"

Malcolm said that they were; he said that Victoria, who was very keen on philology, was preparing a paper for *Speculum* on "The Survival of Old French Modal Auxiliaries in One Fluviatile American Town" and that he himself was working on a monograph to be called "The Periodicity of Diabolism in Georges Duval's Mill."

Mr. Borglund gave him a searching look and blinked uneasily. "That seems a little overspecialized, if you don't mind my saying so."

The news of their true, dull nature leaked out and permeated the student body. A mature Georgia peach with a provocative scolding look said to Malcolm, "Is it true that you and Miss Pinckney are all-out intellectuals?" and Malcolm, who had heretofore been intimidated by this girl's voracious flirtatiousness, said, "You bet your boots it's true, Miss Ryder."

Found out, they were pitied or despised. The waste! The waste to themselves and the waste to Alma Hettrick! Here they were, *so* good-looking, the pair of them, so young, so well equipped to put a sparkle into Freshman English and

Philosophy, so well qualified for fun. And how did they spend their weekends? Grubbing away in that more than useless town, that ignorant, unsanitary, stupid town which wasn't even picturesque. And what for? For Victoria to browse about among antediluvian subjunctives and for Malcolm to concentrate on a Halloween witch.

All right: if they wanted to live in the Dark Ages, let them go ahead. But one thing was sure, their contracts would never be renewed, for Alma Hettrick was in tune with the times and that went for everyone on the staff, for every last Tom and every last Dick and every last Harry. Alma Hettrick didn't have time to fool with your reactionary and your dry-as-dust. Right now, anyhow, they were all preoccupied: *Lohengrin* was in rehearsal and the Estonian had proved to be a whiz.

Gradually Malcolm and Victoria became invisible to everyone except themselves and their aloof, accepting friends in Georges Duval's Mill.

"How I love the Dark Ages," said Victoria.

"How I love *you*," said Malcolm, and they smiled in the gloom of the shabby parlor of L'Hôtel Dauphin as, their learning forgotten, their wisdom rose to the ascendancy.

THE BOSTONIANS,
AND OTHER MANIFESTATIONS
OF THE AMERICAN SCENE

Life Is No Abyss

L ILY, who was twenty, was here in this hot, bare-boned room on a luminous winter Saturday, doing poor Cousin Will's penance by proxy, for poor Cousin Will, old and fragile and unstrung, was sick in bed with bronchitis. And his housekeeper, fuming and whistling in an impersonation of his electric croup kettle, had firmly refused to let him disobey his doctor's orders. Lily was Cousin Will's ward and secretary and she loved him and was grateful to him and she had come, will willing and flesh weak, for his sake though it had meant giving up her skating date with Tucky Havemeyer, an exacting beau, who had refused point-blank to understand.

She was in the poorhouse, visiting old Cousin Isobel Carpenter, a self-appointed martyr whom Cousin Will, the worst and most ingratiating investment broker who had ever lived, had ruined. Out of some grand caprice—the Carpenters had always done everything grandly—Cousin Isobel had turned the whole of her fortune over to Cousin Will, who had put it all, she malevolently declared, into banana plantations in Winnipeg. In the pride of the absolute destitution he had brought her to, she had declined the offers of house room from him and all her other cousins, had peremptorily rolled herself to the poorhouse in her old-fashioned caned wheelchair to remain, a fixed and furious reproach to the whole family, loving every moment of her hardship, which hurt them far more than it did her. The cousins (Lily was related to no one but cousins, once and twice removed and even, in their labyrinthine crisscrossings, more distant than that—what kin Cousin Will and Cousin Isobel were to each other could only have been figured on a slide rule) came in droves on visiting days to plead with her to come away with them in their snug cars back to their big, snug houses, but she was unyielding. She was also extraordinarily clever with the authorities because, in view of all the luxury she could have had for the asking, she had no right to be here. "Will put me in the poorhouse," she said with a suicidal gloat, and having a strong strain of literal-mindedness, she was not content to use the term figuratively. She had been here eighteen months now and was, as Cousin Augusta Shephard said, as happy as the day is long. Poor Cousin Will! When he came home on Saturday after one of his visits, he could not eat his dinner but went straight up to bed with a bottle of whiskey and a triple bromide and a volume of Wilkie Collins, who was the only writer that could take his mind off Cousin Isobel. Lily, on this first visit (Cousin Will had vowed he would never expose her, in her youth and innocence, to what he always called "my problem"), had already begun to feel the malaise that glazed the old man's eyes and addled him, and she hoped that other cousins presently would come.

Cousin Isobel, after untangling the cousinly reticulum (it was a spidery family, unbosomy) and establishing to her own satisfaction that Will Hamilton's representative was the product of a man so far out on the limb of her own tree that the name "cousin" was little more than a courtesy title, now began a speech, so carefully syntactical, punctuated so accurately that Lily would not have been surprised to see her referring to a card of notes.

"The whole place is a scandal. It is a public shame. If they would give me pen and paper—don't ask me why they won't, for their regulations are quite incomprehensible to my poor brain—I would write to people in high places, where I daresay the name Judge James Carpenter has not been forgotten. I have never gone in for séances; I have never been taken in by the supernatural; if she telephoned me personally, I would not believe that Mary Baker Eddy was ringing up from her tomb in Mount Auburn Cemetery. *But* I swear I know that that good man, the august Judge, turns in his grave when his immortal soul considers where I am. He never liked Will Hamilton. Small men are shifty." Before arthritis had shortened her, Cousin Isobel had stood six foot in military heels.

Her eighty-year-old voice faltered but it persevered, climbing resolutely over the surge and recession of the boogie-woogie that came from the radio across the three-bed ward; before it, in an engulfing Morris chair, a small woman sat beating her temples in time to the music with forefingers as thin and bent as the twigs that scratched the windows when the wind aroused the trees.

"Yes, to be sure, all right, I grant, concede, accept the fact that this is a public eleemosynary institution." Attorney for the prosecution, she articulated each resounding syllable over the bullfrog voices of the bass fiddles and leaned forward affirmatively in her wheelchair. "But are the public to be treated like so much flotsam and jetsam? Derelict, am I? Guilty of leprosy or vagabondage? I should like to know—and this is a question I regularly put to the so-called doctor who deigns to visit me once a month, to him I say, 'Just what are the torts and misdemeanors listed on my chart for which I am being punished by having a dinner of pap at four in the afternoon and being forbidden to go outdoors from Thanksgiving until Patriots' Day?' This Dr. Merrill has no answer. He bears a most remarkable resemblance to a chore man I once had on Newberry Street."

For a moment she closed her eyes and rocked her head slowly from side to side, thinking, perhaps, of the house on Newberry Street, a tenebrous square of brick and grilles and protuberant oriels, full of marble and chinoiserie and stalactitic chandeliers, a house that before the Judge's death and Cousin Isobel's Ruin had been the meeting place of Cantabrigian luminaries and was now a residence for working girls. But the present clearly held more interest for her than the past and she continued, "If the food and the want of air were all, one might endure: endurance has always been a trait prominent in the Carpenters. But it's not alone the lack of creature comforts that makes my father's bones waltz, it's even more the company I have to keep. For instance, Cousin Lily Holmes (I'm beginning to remember you a little better), it's only by the grace of God that screams aren't coming from that bed there. Last week, three in a row died screaming. Mad at the end, you know. The undertaker came to lay the first one out here, in front of me if you please, and he did not see fit to pull the curtains until I told him to in no uncertain terms. Will Hamilton may have made ducks and drakes of my lares and penates, but I haven't lost my ginger, what?"

One yellow eye, coral-ringed and sparsely lashed, winked at Lily and then it impaled the image of the barbarous mortician as Cousin Isobel glared at the empty hospital bed where the offenders had howled and died. Above it, stuck with strips of adhesive tape to the scuffed wall, was a picture, torn from a magazine, of Franklin Roosevelt, his hand lightly resting on Fala's neck. The thought of sick old people screaming squeezed Lily's insides like an unkind hand and in her heart she called to a vision of Tucky as he wheeled round and round Jamaica Pond, "Help! Tucky, I'm drowning!"

"But depend upon it, this peace won't last," declared Miss Carpenter. "You'll see. They'll bring another lunatic to thrash about and yell, using the kind of language that I do not choose to understand. It doesn't matter to *her* . . ." She aimed a nodulous finger like a pistol at the woman by the radio. "She's blind, blind from birth. And mental. She never seemed to hear the ruckus, just went on listening to that ragtime. Tum-ti-tum, tum-ti-*ta*. I say the whole of it cries to heaven for vengeance."

She described an uneven arc with her trembling hand to include the room and the larger ward beyond it and the other rusty buildings of the quadrangle visible through tall, uncurtained windows. She caught sight of two old men moving along the walk painfully as if they trod on broken glass and her head jerked alertly forward. "My dear Cousin Lily, the discrimination that goes on here beggars description," she said. "Pray tell why should those old codgers who can barely creep be allowed outdoor privileges when I, who can go like the wind in this contraption, must be confined till April?"

She wheeled herself rapidly forward to demonstrate her skill and then wheeled back. Triumphantly she gave her visitor a long, commanding look and Lily monosyllabically applauded her and murmured her regret and her perplexity that Cousin Isobel was not allowed the same freedom as the old (and, Miss Carpenter's look implied, badly born) men.

Just then, providentially for Lily, Cousin Augusta Shephard came into the ward like a garden on wings. Her mink was permanently imbued with Fleurs de Rocaille and she was beautiful, intelligent, fortunate in her husband (if no one else at all had come, Reno could have made a comfortable living on boarding Lily's family) and was by far the happiest of all the cousins. Now she kissed Lily and inquired for Cousin Will, but before Lily could answer, Cousin Isobel said, "He sent me word—oral word, would not even set his hand to paper—that he had the sniffles."

"The doctor said . . ." Lily began possessively.

"The doctor said!" mocked Cousin Isobel. "Will Hamilton said, 'I cannot face the music.' Men of slight stature have slight character."

"Dry up, Izzy," said Cousin Augusta cheerfully and began undoing the paper around a bunch of freesias. "Have you been bending Lily's ear? Complaining when all you have to do is say 'knife' to be whisked off to the lap of luxury and pampered within an inch of your life?"

"Fork!" said Cousin Isobel spitefully, but she smiled a little, for she admired Cousin Augusta's forthright teasing.

"Pretty Lily! She ought to be out with her best beau this afternoon. How you do try us! Roger said for me to tell you, 'For God's sake, dear, enough is enough. It's high time to cut the comedy.' We've done the whole third floor over for you in the most heavenly moss green and plum."

"You always did have taste, Augusta," said Cousin Isobel, pleased. "Will hired a decorator who did *his* third floor over in off-white and rose, which certainly never was my style. However, though I thank you kindly, ma'am, I won't come. Will Hamilton put me in the poorhouse."

Cousin Augusta began, with gentle ragging, to cajole. She spoke of the kitchen they had installed so that Cousin Isobel could have her meals alone if she preferred to be conventual; she said it was simply a question of dialing a number to have at Cousin Isobel's beck and call an educated Swedish woman who was equally adept at cooking and massage; Easter was coming . . . would Cousin Isobel not *please* get out of the trenches before then?

Midway through the futile wheedling (for Cousin Isobel was clearly bent on prolonging her tantrum for some time to come and she stuck out her tongue at each goody dangled before it, said she mistrusted Swedes and that Easter had had no meaning since the year one) an attendant came in to give the old woman a pill and in the interruption Cousin Augusta leaned over to whisper to Lily, "Darling, you shouldn't be here! Darling, promise you won't be traumatized." Lily did not know the word but she nodded reassuringly to her cousin, whose pellucid blue eyes were grave. She suddenly felt much younger than she was and her whisper was a whimper when she said, "May I go when you do?" Cousin Augusta nodded and then turned back to Cousin Isobel, saying, "Why must you be so medieval?"

"I want you to know, Augusta . . ." Cousin Isobel's whole

twisted carcass canted over the side of her chair as she began
a low and sibilant monologue, her hand almost completely
covering her mouth so that Lily could hear nothing of what
she said.

Now that the heavy, mottled, whiskered face was turned
away and she was mercifully excluded from this part of the
visit, Lily looked out the window and tried to think her own
thoughts, of how she would make it up to Tucky Havemeyer,
with whom she was in love to the point of torment. The things
he had said on the telephone! At first he had pleaded and then
he had abused, "You're soft. Or else you're lying. An old sick
cousin is the corniest excuse I ever heard of. Besides, I know
all your cousins and they're no more sick than my aunt's cat."

It was amazing how adroitly Cousin Isobel had kept her
being in the poorhouse a secret; she was believed to be abroad,
sunning in a nursing home in Switzerland, and, caught in her
passion for masochism and intrigue, had made Cousin Will
hire someone to dispatch letters and picture postal cards for
her from Vevey. Lily was in no position to let the family cat
out of its bag; if she did convince Tucky that she had broken
their engagement out of necessity and not whim, and told him
why, he would as likely as not end up by despising her whole
clan. For Tucky was high-minded, rather socialist and rather
poor, and undoubtedly his whole heart would go out to this
mischievous old poseur.

In her imagination she argued with Tucky but she lost, and
hopelessly she tried to become engrossed in the bustle of some
sparrows to whom one of the old men had thrown what looked
to be part of a graham cracker. But she could not pay attention.
She was embarrassed half to death.

She was embarrassed remembering Cousin Isobel before
she came here, remembering the North Shore summer house
and the lawns that had sloped down to the sumptuous sea,
remembering the figure of her father, who had died at the age
of a hundred and three, the Judge, Cousin Jamie, a learned,
tart-tongued wisp, six and a half feet high in a Palm Beach suit,
who delighted, while he excoriated them, the people who came
to pay him homage as he held court on August afternoons
beneath a huge umbrella. The house had been superbly elegant
and Cousin Augusta had said of the Judge and of Cousin Isobel,

"They're probably the greatest swells you'll ever know, Lily, so have yourself a good look." They had been, indeed, so much sweller, so much richer, so much more imperious than anyone else that no compromise had ever been possible for them: they never went in for repairs but always for replacement. After the Judge's death, Cousin Isobel had invited Cousin Will "to play a game of exchequers" with her—she knew better; at the time everyone told her she was out of her mind; his harum-scarum business methods were axiomatic and no other member of the family would have touched the doorknob of his brokerage office with a ten-foot pole although they all adored him. And he had madly and instantly thrown her whole fortune to the four winds. The Judge, a little queer when he had reached the hundred mark, had left no part of it in trust. And thus Cousin Isobel, penniless and untrained, was not equipped to modify her way of life at all: she could not and she would not substitute, she could only and she would only lose. Her descent to threadbare penury had been lightning-paced, so fast that it had had in itself a kind of theatrical splendor. When he heard that she was down to her last sou, Cousin Roger Shephard, troubled as he was, nevertheless had been unable to suppress a smile as he said, "No half measures for *them.*"

Eighteen months, a year and a half now, she had been living in the poorhouse, growing progressively more helpless with arthritis and progressively more cunning in the tortures she contrived for poor Uncle Will. She refused, sarcastically, to eat the edibles he sent her, saying that he had ruined her but he was not going to poison her; she wrote diabolical replies to his letters, threw away the flowers he sent her and his presents of books and magazines and seedless grapes. Someone had said, "The only thing that will dislodge her will be the promise that she can eat poor Will Hamilton alive."

Cousin Augusta, still captive to the whispered diatribe, had closed her eyes and Lily knew that she was suffering, as Cousin Isobel made everybody suffer, a mixture of pity and rage. But after the visit Cousin Augusta would be free to return to the absorbing gaiety of her life, to a charming cocktail party, probably, or to drinks at the Ritz bar with one of the innumerable men she claimed she loved and meant to marry the moment Roger was in his grave. But Lily could only go back to an empty evening and the smell of benzoin in the house and the memory of *this*! This ghastly place! She looked around, resentful and appalled.

It would have been hard to find a place barer than this three-bed ward or one that smelled more dismally, of institutional soup, of sodden mops and iodoform and sweating plaster walls. A steadfast winter sunlight further warmed the overheated room and searched its disheartening appointments of three thin beds, furnished with flat pillows and graying counterpanes, three metal commodes whose paint was chipped and whose delinquent doors sagged open, showing, in the blind woman's, nothing, in Cousin Isobel's, a red, heart-shaped candy box and a pile of cotton handkerchiefs. On top of it there was a listing heap of miscellany, a box of Kleenex and a copy of *McCall's* (sheer fraud! Cousin Isobel never read anything but Pliny and Gibbon), a packet of Christmas cards tied with a string, a distempered batik scarf and, crowning the whole, a lifelike armadillo basket containing a bottle of hand lotion from the five-and-ten, a box of cough drops and a frayed, brown photograph, bound in passe partout, of Miss Carpenter and the Judge, taken sixty years before as they sat in an imposing brougham drawn up before a house swaddled to its chimneys in wistaria. In addition to this array, each item of which had the look of having been salvaged from a wastepaper basket or borrowed from a family pensioner of low rank, there was Cousin Augusta's offering of freesias, crushed into a water glass, their fragrance angelically struggling against the rude smells. Confronting Lily, in one of the windowsills, there was an African violet whose limp leaves languished over the sides of a white pot; not quite dead but in its mortal coma, it looked as if it had been struck down by a virulent and rapid disease and yet, such was the quality of the soil it had been planted in, that robust green weeds were sprouting up among its purulent, disintegrating stems.

Lily hunted cautiously for some sign of vitality or of joy upon this melancholy scene. It was not to be found within the faces or the effects of the two inmates, but the attendants appeared healthy and lively, almost impertinent—impertinence in such a place was macabre; it was like a songbird singing in a cage in a prison. The matron at her desk beside the door was chewing gum and reading a book that made her laugh; and at a long counter against the far wall of Cousin Isobel's ward, beyond the blind woman, several girls in bright blue, dirty uniforms were folding hospital gowns and unironed sheets and were good-humoredly arguing over what was included in the term "cake," which all of them, it appeared, had given up for Lent. The liberal camp maintained that layer cake and éclairs and the like were all they must deny themselves, but two purists, who were older than the others and thinner, said that it was their intention, personally, to abstain as well from corn-meal muffins and raisin bread.

Beyond this hearty band and beyond the laughing matron, Lily could see into the large ward, where every bed—and there were four long rows of them—was occupied by an ancient, twisted woman; the humps of their withered bodies under the seersucker coverlets looked truncated and deformed like amputated limbs or mounds of broken bones, and the wintry faces that stared from the stingy pillows had lost particularity: among them it would have been impossible to determine which was primarily bleak or mean or brave or imbecile, for age and humiliation had blurred the predominant humor and had all but erased the countenance. A few of the women had visitors and the tops of their commodes were littered with purses and hats and gloves; those who were alone glared greedily at their luckier neighbors and, like crones in a comic strip, cupped their ears to eavesdrop. A constant, female babble came from the room, and though they were immobile, the bedridden seemed to bustle and flit; they gave the impression of housewives hurriedly setting things to rights as they saw unexpected callers coming up the drive; the impression came solely from their voices, in which there was neither resonance nor modulation; they chirped like crickets, dry and shrill.

"Why will they not allow me to have my own clothes?" said Cousin Isobel as, shifting in her chair, she briefly took her hand away from her mouth. Cousin Augusta shot back her eyelids to full attention, and Cousin Isobel once again muzzled herself.

Half the size that Lily remembered her to have been (according to a legend, Cousin Isobel, as a tall and stalwart and facetious girl, had been the founder of a society called The Amazonic Sisterhood of Langdon Shore, whose members had been whizzes with the Indian club), she wore a printed cotton dress, bound at the round neck and kimono sleeves with bias tape; tan cotton stockings wrapped her shrunken legs like puttees sizes too big and fell in folds over the tops of her men's high shoes. But around her scaly neck she wore a string of artificial pearls and pinned askew near her shoulder was a brooch of fire opals, surely bought for next to nothing in a curio shop on Revere Beach and surely never bought by Miss Carpenter. A hair net caged her shingled white hair, which she had worn, when it was thick, in a shining chignon. What a show-off she was! How wicked was her squalor! Her fingernails were filthy and Lily knew that her hair would have a rancid smell. She is mad, thought Lily, why can't they see that and commit her to a mental sanitarium?

Oblivious to Lily's inspection, Cousin Isobel went on with her hushed and dogged philippic and Lily was about to turn away again when suddenly her mind registered the nature of the print of her cousin's dress: it was a frieze of children rolling hoops, repeated endlessly, round and round the narrow, brittle torso. Aghast at this unwitting humor, she quickly averted her eyes, but her mood was bitter now and instead of watching the sparrows as they fussed and hopped, causing the easily pleased old men to cheer, she turned to see how the blind woman was dressed.

Similarly, she wore this jocose goods, five-year-olds on a playing field of daisy-scattered blue, and around her shoulders had been thrown a tousled pillowcase that fitted in the back like a cowl. Out of the careless hole that made the neck of the dress, the woman's neck rose long and limber and blue-white, a neck of pre-Raphaelite dimensions that oscillated gently with an untutored, noble grace, its perfect rhythm inspired by but in no way related to the deep-throated piano which, in a distant radio station, played "Hold 'em Hootie." The woman, Lily realized, was not old. Her hair was gray but it was cut short in a youthful style; a demure bang lay on her forehead; and her skin, though here and there it was flecked with blemishes that probably came from some dietary outrage, was smooth and delicately pink. She had a small, straight nose and a firm chin, and though Lily saw only her profile, she was sure that the smile on the lips was broad and genuine. But still, the hands uninterruptedly thumping the temples—in a rhythm independent both of the piano and of the waving neck—were old; heavily veined, dappled with liver spots, they looked ice-cold and nearly mortified and the fingertips were needle-sharp.

The boogie-woogie record ended and a drawling voice with bogus Southern diphthongs and blotted consonants joshed the unseen audience. "What' y'all doin' settin' by the raddio when y'all oughta be washin' the dishes? Wa-el, since you're daid set on loafin', le's take a look in*to* the old ma-el bag and see who'm wantum whatum." The pleasant Irish Catholics laughed and a plump, red-haired girl said, "Those disc jockeys! They're so informal, you know what I mean? It's sort of cute the way they act, telling you they've got a hangover or something."

"Dog mah cats, wha' in the worl' is this?" said the voice and Lily imagined a bored and puffy-faced young man scratching his head and strangling a yawn as he laboriously ad-libbed. "Hy-ear's somebody from way down yonder in Braintree that asks me to play 'Bluebird of Happiness' boogie style. Honey-chile, Miz Edna Murphy of 109 Van Buren Street, there just ain't no sich animal. But I'll tell you what, I'm gonna play it ole style for ole times' sake."

In the brief backstage silence as the new record was being readied, the blind woman was seized with a surprising and irrelevant animation; her hands left her forehead and she clapped them silently and spastically and then she held them, palms together, under her chin like a child saying bedtime prayers, but even in this attitude they were not still; they jerked and crooked and wriggled in a dreadful excitement and Lily became aware that the woman was simultaneously stamping her feet. Though Lily could not see them, since her bed impeded her view, she could hear them, ploddingly and erratically marking time on the linoleum-covered floor; the movement of the columnar neck also grew more pronounced and abruptly the small cropped head began to rotate quickly on its beautiful stem. All these calisthenics were performed at a different pace; she was like someone successfully patting her stomach and rubbing her head at the same time and the effect was dizzying.

At the very moment that the music began again, the blind woman completed the half circle with her head and faced Lily fully. The dead, wide-open eyes lay in deep violet craters; the skeleton was obvious under the nacreous skin, and to complete this imitation of a death's-head, the mouth, thin-lipped and altogether toothless, was open in a permanent, unfeeling grin. For perhaps half a minute, she was motionless, seeming to stare at Lily, and then, with the chin-up non-sequitur of the song,

> Just remember this,
> Life is no abyss,
> Somewhere you'll find the bluebird of happiness

she was momentarily galvanized again. She clasped her hands together on her shallow breast in an onrush of delight and she sighed, embedding in her inspiration a little cry. Her head then resumed its former position, her forefingers returned to the edges of her piquant bangs, and Lily Holmes, stricken and sickened and stunned, closed her eyes.

The generic face had seemed to be no more than a clever armature to support the promontories, apertures and embellishments because neither knowledge nor experience was written on it; its only signature was that of absolute and monstrous poverty. It was a parody, the scaffolding of ageless bone; it was an illustration, a paradigm of total, lifelong want. Because there had been no progress in the life (unless the fleet stirrings of the *déjà vu* could be called progress), there could be no retrogression, so that this woman could not say—if, indeed, she could speak at all—as Cousin Isobel could, "Once I was that and now I am this. Once I dwelt in marble halls and now I live in quarters that the least of my serfs would have scorned," and take from the contrast a certain satisfaction, galling as it might be. To descend, however ignobly, was, nevertheless, to participate. In speaking of Cousin Isobel's tribulations, it was possible to use verbs: she had lost her money, she had been ruined, she had plunged from the highest heights to the lowest depths. But to the woman who had been born without the most important sense and, as Cousin Isobel had implied, been born witless, only adjectives were applicable: she was blind, alone, animal. In that hideous grin and that convulsive dance and that moan of bliss, she had demonstrated something sheer and inhuman and unnamable, and by the very virtue of its limitation, her joy in the puling song was rhapsodic and superlative. There had been no mistaking it: the look on the thinly covered skull had been one of white-hot transport, but what emotions had generated it? Hope? Gratitude for the heartening assurance that life was no abyss? A desire for love? Could there be in that travailing length of blue flesh and devious bone a longing, like Lily's own longing to be with Tucky? If there was, it was too terrible to contemplate. She felt a painful woe rising through the center of her being, inundating her lungs and lashing the tears to her eyes. Help, Tucky! But she knew that nothing he could ever do could efface her memory of that empty ecstasy.

Cousin Isobel altered her position and in the process removed her hand from her mouth; in concluding tones, she said, "Never learned to read Braille because, as I understand it, there was a marked deficiency in gray matter. I meant to inquire of this same well-informed social worker where the radio came from, for not a soul has come to see her in the eighteen months we have shared this cubbyhole. It simply materalized one day last fall. In one way it was a blessing because until it came she had nothing to do but sit and make peculiar noises. She did something with her back teeth that sounded like a hornet."

"I know," said Cousin Augusta with a sigh. "It's pitiful."

"Yes, pitiful," said Cousin Isobel. "I say it's pitiful, but I also say, is it right for me to be imprisoned with an incontinent cretin and her radio, playing that confounded rubbish from matins until vespers? I say damn."

She now looked straight ahead and gave a lecture on the food, which was, she said, without a doubt the very worst in Christendom. She was certain that an East German was in charge of the kitchen.

"Will Hamilton put me in the poorhouse," her quarrelsome voice went on. "This building is known as 'the death house,' but I have given Will to understand that my ghost is all I have left to give up and I'm not parting with it yet. I say damn and double damn." She fell silent, preparing a new deviltry, and she twisted a narrow silver ring on her finger as she gazed with a contemptuous smile out the window at the pampered old men who had now been joined by a fat, lame woman who pointed to the sparrows with her cane and roared with laughter.

"For the last time, Isobel," said Cousin Augusta, "at least for the last time this afternoon, *will* you come live with Roger and me?"

"Why, Gusta," said Cousin Isobel with hateful waggishness, "what would Will say? After all the trouble he went to with his old-rose and off-white? *He* offered me a Finn who would belabor me with birch twigs."

"Poor Will!" cried Cousin Augusta and raised her eyes to heaven. "*Poor* Will!"

Cousin Isobel, ignoring her, wheeled her patrician head slowly around to give Lily a penetrating look. "I hope your father left your money in trust, because if he didn't, Will Hamilton will ruin you. I liked your father," she said and factually she added, "His name was Matthew Holmes."

Lily could think of no rejoinder to this, but there was no need of one, for Cousin Isobel ground on, "I liked Matt Holmes. He was a first-rate sailor, as Judge Carpenter many times remarked. I'm sorry that he's dead. He would still be young, which is more than you can say for most people. Most people are dead by now. Eva Tuckerman's funeral was Thursday. Did a Kingsolving officiate?"

"Yes," said Cousin Augusta. "It was a lovely funeral. Your flowers, cabled from Vevey, were much admired."

"I shall be buried in potter's field," exulted Cousin Isobel. "You didn't answer my question, Cousin Lily. Did your father leave your wherewithal in trust?"

"My father left nothing," said Lily, and this, substantially, was true. A trifling sum, to cover Christmas shopping and hairdressing, would come to her in the next year, but she was now wholly dependent on Cousin Will, who gave her, in addition to a pretty suite of rooms and three agreeable meals a day, a small salary for typing the letters in which he was forever trying to extricate himself from some financial bear-garden.

"Nothing!" howled Cousin Isobel. "What do you mean by 'nothing'?"

"No money," said Lily and felt an inexplicable warm rush of pride.

"Stop joking," said Cousin Isobel sharply. "I've never heard of such a thing. Is she telling the truth, Augusta?"

Cousin Augusta, embarrassed, nodded and said, "You remember that Matt and Laura put everything into that flying school of theirs in Arizona and it all went smash after they were

. . . you know, dear, after the accident. It didn't leave Lily much, but damn it, Izzy, Lily knows how to make do."

Old Cousin Isobel looked from one cousin to the other like a planning rat. "Are you edging up to a sermon on imponderabilia?" she demanded. "It's the prerogative of an antique to speak what's on its mind and I want to warn you that in this place we inmates do not speak in terms of 'spiritual wealth.'" Now she reached out her hand to take between her fingers a pinch of Cousin Augusta's broadcloth sleeve and she said, "Excellent cloth. You had that sent from England at a king's ransom. Roger Shephard is beautifully rich."

"He's rich," said Cousin Augusta, "and he's got a heart of gold. He wants you, *I* want you, everybody wants you to come to us. Roger made me bring you something today to tempt you to rejoin the world," and out of her purse she brought a photograph of two young women in ball gowns and two young men in swallow-tails.

"That's me," said Cousin Isobel, smiling, "and this is Susie Holmes. There's Don Tucker standing behind me, and this, of course, is Stevie Holmes. Will you look at those trains and those pompadours? What made us think we needed ostrich-feather fans two feet wide? And tiaras no less! Mine, I recall, was emeralds." She gazed in fascination at the picture, holding it close to her nose, then moving it away, exclaiming derisively, as pleased as Punch.

The girl attendants had finished with the last of the sheets and gowns and they quit the room, except for one who was pretty and petite and amiably cross-eyed. She came to pull the window shade against the sun, which, beginning to set, was blinding now, and she said, "Time's up, ladies. It's suppertime, Miss Carpenter."

"Suppertime! It's barely time for tea."

"Shall it be the silver service, Moddom?" asked the girl pertly. "Or shall Moddom want the Spode?" But this was a joke, for the girl patted Cousin Isobel affectionately on the shoulder and said, "What you got there, honey? A picture postal?"

"Bernice, this is a picture of me dressed for the Charity Ball. Just look at me."

"The Charity Ball! Oh, Miss Carpenter, you're a caution!

Sometimes she puts me in stitches with her sarcastic sayings."
The girl appealed genially to Cousin Augusta and to Lily and
then, marveling, she studied the photograph. "Tell me about
them all, hey, Miss Carpenter? You were kidding, weren't you,
about it being you and you going to the Charity Ball?"

"I tell you, Bernice, that's *me* arrayed in all my glory. My visitors will bear witness. Have you observed, ladies, the costume I
wear to my daily Charity Ball? Do you like these rambunctious
babies playing on the ground? They upset Will. Will seems to
have lost his sense of humor."

"The ground is too damp for arthritis patients to go out of
doors."

Uttered like a slogan, the words hung over the voices and
the radio. It was the blind woman who had spoken, briskly
and loud, and Lily, turning, saw that her profile, as shallow as
a bas-relief, was pulled upward in a vicious sneer. An attendant
was sitting on the arm of the Morris chair, trying to feed her
cereal with a wooden spoon, but the woman's flailing hands
continually thwarted the service and the attendant muttered
and sighed and impatiently cried out, "Oh, come *on,* it's not
roach poison."

"Don't mind Viola," said Bernice to the visitors. "Viola hates
to eat."

"Who wouldn't?" demanded Miss Carpenter, grimacing as
her own tray was brought to her. This afternoon she was to
eat a bowl of cream-of-wheat and a salad of shredded carrot
and raisins; for dessert she was to have a wedge of pound cake
smudged here and there with dark and glutinous jam. Lily
wondered what she would do after the tray had gone back to
the kitchen and when the winter night set in and she looked to
see whether there were a suitable bedside lamp by which to read
the copy of *McCall's.* But there were no lamps at all in the room
except one small, bare bulb in the center of the ceiling, and as
she stared, dismayed, at this, Cousin Isobel read her mind and
said, "The nights here are more than twice as long as the days.
Tell me, if you can, a Chinese torture worse than mine: that
radio goes on till ten o'clock in the dark. And I can do nothing
but sit in this chair or lie on that bed and sew a fine seam. Sew!
With these hands rendered totally useless by arthritis deformans,
for which there is no known cure? Don't make me laugh!"

"You could have cortisone," said Cousin Augusta wearily, "if you only *would*."

Bernice was urging her food on Cousin Isobel. "Take your nourishment like a good girl, hon," she said kindly. "Here's a lovely oyster stew for you. What's in a name? Just use your imagination, hon, and pretend it's an oyster stew."

"Yum," said Cousin Isobel sourly.

It was clear that the food was far more than physical sustenance for her. As she began to spoon up the cereal, her eyes lighted with rage and Lily thought she would probably not have traded the white mush for all the succulent oysters in the world. Her wrath animated and rejuvenated her; she fed avidly.

"Miss Carpenter, why didn't you ever get married if that was really you in the picture?" asked Bernice. "A pretty young girl like you?"

"I was too good to get married," said the old woman, winking evilly. "I was too good and too rich."

"Only the good die young," announced the blind woman.

"That's all *you* know, Viola," retorted Miss Carpenter and, facing Viola, lectured her, "You do not know the meaning of half the things you say. You cannot think, you can only imitate like a monkey. You might be an interesting case if one happened to be interested in that sort of thing. I am not."

"'Just remember this, life is no abyss,'" screamed Viola over a tinkling cascade of Hawaiian ukuleles, and with amorous despair she put her brittle hands on her small, adolescent breasts.

"Go away, dears," said Cousin Isobel. "Poor little Lily will be here to stay soon enough."

"Now that's the limit!" cried Cousin Augusta. She was really angry and her cheeks flamed as she swirled herself into her coat and drew Lily to her feet. "You leave this child alone! Money *isn't* everything!"

"The lack of money is everything," said Cousin Isobel, smirking, indomitable. "The lack of money is the eternal punishment."

"Don't lie! You love it here! It's not your punishment, it's poor Will Hamilton's."

"And why not, may I ask?" Never had wickedness been more serene. Lily, whose physical demonstrations were limited to the patterned motions of dancing and skating and giving and receiving kisses, wanted to slap Cousin Isobel's face and pull her short hair and pinch her twisted fingers. Such passion as she had never known before in all her life, greater even than the grief she had known when her parents died violently in a plane crash, rose like a second person inside her and in this manifestation she towered above her cousin and she accused, "You are a vulture! You haven't got a drop of love in you! Viola has!" And not wishing to at all, she burst into tears.

For a moment Cousin Isobel was taken aback, but only for a moment, and then she said, "Viola has nothing. Viola is the embodiment of what Will Hamilton has brought me to." Her eyes grew vague, she gestured her cousins away like a distracted dowager queen, and Cousin Augusta led Lily weeping from the room. They went out through the large ward, and in spite of her tears, Lily smiled back at the senile bed patients who smiled patronizingly at her. One of them quaveringly said, "I'm glad *I* don't have to go out on a nasty day like this," and she burrowed into her harsh gray blankets.

The abyss of winter twilight opened like a huge mouth before them and a crude wind scraped their cheeks. Cousin Augusta, hurrying along, scolded like a mother bird, "Will shouldn't have let you come. He must be very low, poor Will, to have let you come."

"I *wanted* to come," sobbed Lily. "I mean, I wanted to do it for Cousin Will."

"You're a loyal little girl. You're a good girl. I know, I know positively in my bones that you had to give up something to come here today. You did, didn't you, darling?"

Now they were in the soft, sweet depths of Cousin Augusta's Cadillac and Lily, putting her head on her relative's shoulder, allowed her tears to peter out before she tried to speak. She said, "I was only going skating on Jamaica Pond. But we had a row. Tucky Havemeyer and I, I mean. He didn't believe I was going to see a sick cousin."

Cousin Augusta took her hand, and looking straight ahead at her chauffeur's neck, she said, "Sweet Lily. I feel awful. I don't know whether to drink champagne with gold leaf floating in it or go sell pencils in the Common. It's an abyss any way you look at it."

Because she was young, and optimistic, and did not, in her

heart of hearts, believe that all was over and done for her and
Tucky Havemeyer, Lily, in direct proportion to Cousin Augusta's collapse, began to be restored. She watched the draggled
purlieus of the city replace the open countryside and for no
reason at all rejoiced to see the ugly, nervous neon advertising
beer and drugs and double-decker sandwiches and all the
other palliatives and excesses available in this non-abysmal life.
Adult—though still she teetered—and consoling, she said to
Cousin Augusta, "Do you know what I'd do if I were you or
Cousin Roger or Cousin Will? I'd send her to an insane asylum.
One for the criminally insane."

"But, Lily!" Cousin Augusta turned to face her, wide-eyed.
"But, Lily, don't you understand that we all love Cousin Isobel?"

Until the car dropped Lily at Cousin Will's door, they said
not another word. Cousin Augusta was too horrified to speak
and Lily was too baffled. Love Cousin Isobel! How was it possible to love what was so intransigently unloving? She felt outside
her family and betrayed by her own betrayal of convention,
which, through some oversight, she had never learned. Did this
mean that poor Cousin Will, too, loved Cousin Isobel, who was
killing him, murdering him as surely as if she had her hands on
his throat? If they did love her, then Lily did not love them.
In deep repugnance she withdrew from the woman beside her,
in anger watched the distance lessen between herself and her
guardian, who was in love with his destruction, and turned,
without reward or comfort, to the thought of Tucky Havemeyer. There's only one person who has love, she thought, and
that's Viola, who can't take anything and can't give anything.
The rest of them are flirts.

Lily grappled with her paradox and, clutched in its Laocoön
embrace, felt ancient. And when the car drew into Brimmer
Street and she saw her blond, scowling, hunter-capped and
booted boy ringing the bell at the Hamilton house, she bridled
at her pleasure, repudiated her hypocritical family blood, cast
one last intellectual look at Viola in her state of grace, and catapulted from the car to cry, "Oh, Tucky! Isn't this well timed?"

The Hope Chest

MISS BELLAMY was old and cold and she lay quaking under an eiderdown which her mother had given her when she was a girl of seventeen. It had been for her hope chest. Though damask tablecloths and Irish linen tea napkins, Florentine bureau runners and China silk blanket covers, point-lace doilies and hemstitched hand towels had gone into that long carved cherry chest (her father had brought it all the way from Sicily and, presenting it to her, had said, "Nothing is too good for my Rhoda girl"), she had never married. The chest now stood at the foot of her bed, and the maid put the tea napkins on her breakfast tray.

It was just before Belle knocked on her door in the gray dawn of winter with the tray that Miss Bellamy quaked so much, as if nothing on earth could ever warm her up again. This unkind light made her remember how old she was and how, in a few minutes when Belle came in, she would be cantankerous; no matter how hard she tried, she could never be pleasant to a servant, black or white, a failing for which her father had once rebuked her, declaring that she behaved like a parvenu. He had scolded her thus when he finally had to admit to himself the fact that she would never marry. There had not, in the history of Boston society, been a greater fiasco than Rhoda Bellamy's debut. It had, indeed, been a miscarriage so sensational that she had forced her parents to move north, into Maine, where her mother soon had died and where she and her father dwelt together in their angry disappointment. *Well, Papa, the laugh's on you. Here I am, thirty-five years old, and in the eighteen years since I came out, I have had no beau but my dear papa. No, I will not go to the concert at Bowdoin College. No, I do not want to join you in a glass of claret. I shall return to my bedroom and read Mrs. Gaskell, thanking you every time I turn a page for giving me so expensive a copy of* Cranford.

This was the Christmas morning of her eighty-second year and she steadfastly held her eyes closed, resisting the daylight. She had been like that as a child, she had loved sleep better than eating or playing. She was not sure whether she had had a dream just now or whether there was something she had meant to remember or to think about that was troubling her aged mind like a rat in a wall. At last, vexed and murmuring, she opened her eyes and what did she see hanging upon the wall (very probably staining the hand-blocked French paper with a design of pastoral sweethearts) but a scraggly Christmas wreath to which had been wired three pine cones, one gilded, one silvered, one painted scarlet. At first she was half out of her mind with exasperation and she reached out her hand for her stick to rap tyrannically for Belle. How *dare* she desecrate this, of all rooms, which, as any fool should know, was not to be changed in any way! But memory stayed her hand: it all came back.

Yesterday, when she was sitting on the lounge in the drawing room, making spills out of last year's Christmas wrappings and sipping hot milk, she heard a timid knocking at the door. She had no intention of answering it, although Belle had gone out to shop and the by-the-day girl had gone home. But she said to herself, "Who is it? Who are they they can't knock out loud like a Christian? If they want something, why don't they try the doorknob? They'll find it locked, but if they had any gumption, they'd try." She slowly made a spill.

It went on, this gentle, disheartened knocking. Was it a squirrel, she wondered, playing with a nut somewhere? *If there is a destructive squirrel in my house, I shall give Belle her walking papers at once.* She did not find the creatures cunning as some people did: they were as wicked as any other rodent and the tail, so greatly admired in some quarters, was by no means a disguise that could not be seen through: essentially they were rats. Perhaps it was not a squirrel but was a loose branch blowing in the wind: *I shall speak severely to Homer. If he calls himself my yard-man, he can attend to these details.* Perhaps it was a dog of the neighborhood, foolishly thumping his tail against the door. *People should keep their dogs at home, tied up if necessary. If they are not kept at home, they come rummaging in my refuse containers and defiling my lawn and littering the garden with things I do not like to know exist.* Aloud in the long drawing room, she said, knowing that she smiled cleverly in her lean lips and in her small eyes, "If you want to come in, knock loud enough so that I shall hear you. Call out your name, confound you. Do you think I receive just anyone?"

She slopped her milk and it made a row of buttons down the front of her challis guimpe. Outraged, she threw the spill she was making into the fire and then she hobbled to the door, saying under her breath, "Whoever you are, I will frighten the living daylights out of you. If you are an animal, I will beat you with my stick; if you are a human being, I will scare you out of ten years' growth. I will say the worst thing you have ever had said to you in your life."

In the winter she had a green baize door and a storm door sandwiching the regular door to keep out any possible draft. She pulled open the green baize one and unlocked the wooden one with a long iron key and she opened it the merest bit, pushing it with the silver ferrule of her blackthorn stick. Through the glass of the storm door, she saw a child standing there in the snow, holding a spruce wreath in his hands. He had come across the lawn, making his own path, deliberately to spoil the looks of the clean, unmarked snow, when he could *much more easily* have walked in Belle's footprints.

He opened the storm door without asking leave and he said, "Will you buy this?"

She prided herself on never having been tricked by anyone. She investigated first and bought afterward. She, Rhoda Bellamy, would be the last to be taken in by a child, and she did not, of course, answer his question. She pushed the door open a little farther and said, "Who are you? What is your name?"

His teeth, she saw, were short and crooked and a nasty yellow color. She supposed he came from one of those indigent families who clustered together, squalidly and odoriferously, on the banks of the Sheepscot. He was not decently shy and he spoke up immediately: "My name is Ernest Leonard McCammon. Will you buy this wreath?"

The spinster said, "Well, Ernest Leonard, you may wipe your feet on my *Welcome* mat and step into the entry, but I am not promising to buy your wreath. We'll see about that later on."

(The sycamores before Miss Bellamy's windows creaked in the cold: *Where is my breakfast? Where is Belle? Why did I invite Ernest Leonard McCammon to cross my threshold in his snowy galoshes, puddling the Tabriz Father bought half price in Belgrade?* She creaked, too, like a tree, and a feather from the eiderdown walked on her ear like a summer fly.)

The child stood before her, small and ambitious, bundled to his ears in a blue plaid mackintosh which was patched with leather at the elbows. He wore blue jeans and in his mittenless hands he carried now, besides the wreath, the purple stocking cap he had taken off before he came through the door. He bore a faint, unpleasant smell of mud. *I will eat you, little boy, because once upon a time I, too, had pink cheeks and a fair skin and clear eyes. And don't you deny it.*

Ernest Leonard McCammon looked at the Adam hall chair, looked at the portrait of Mr. Bellamy, looked at the priceless Florentine coffer, looked at the luster pitchers in which stood cattails ten years old; she had had a man come down from Portland one year to oil the books and at the same time had had him shellac the cattails, although he protested a little, declaring that this was not in his line. No workman ever got anywhere protesting with her. She had simply said, "I don't know what you're talking about, sir. My father picked these cattails by the Jordan." This did not happen to be true, as her father had been dead for twenty years and she had gathered them herself in her own meadow beside the local river.

The rag-tag-and-bobtail boy looked at her father's treasures as if he had seen such things every day of his life. *Do you know who I am, you smelly scrap? Does the name Bellamy mean anything to you, you wool-bound baggage?*

(How the wind was blowing! Where was Belle? Where was her breakfast? Where was her stick? Where was her wrapper? Why did no one come to wish her a merry Christmas?)

He said, "Miss Bellamy, will you buy my wreath?"

"What do you want for it, McCammon?"

"A quarter."

"A quarter! Twenty-five cents for a bit of evergreen you more than likely stole off one of my trees!"

His pink cheeks paled under her shrewd gaze and his blue eyes clouded. "I never stole 'um off your tree, Miss Bellamy.

I went to the woods, I did, and I got 'um there off nobody's tree."

She said, not giving in, "Perhaps so, perhaps not. All the same, a quarter is too much."

"But I painted the pine cones, Miss Bellamy! I had to buy the gold and the silver. Daddy gave me the red."

"And who is this Daddy?"

"The chimney cleaner. We are the ones with the mule. Maybe you have seen our house with the mule in the yard? My daddy's name is Robert John McCammon."

I will blow your brains out with the bellows Father brought from Dresden. I will lay your slender little body on Cousin Anne's andirons that came from the Trianon, and burn you up like a paper spill.

"Come, come, Ernest Leonard," she said, "I don't care what your daddy's middle name is and I have certainly not seen your mule. I will give you fifteen cents for your wreath."

"No, ma'am," he said. "If you don't buy it, some other lady will."

"Some *other* lady? What do you mean, McCammon?"

"Well, Mrs. Wagner would buy it or Mrs. Saunders or Mrs. Hugh Morris, I reckon. Anyways, somebody."

"I will give you fifteen cents for the wreath alone. You can take off the pine cones."

"No, ma'am. That would spoil it."

She fixed him with a severe aristocratic eye, determined now to resolve this impasse to her own liking and not to his. She said slowly, "If I decided to buy your wreath and paid you the absurd king's ransom of twenty-five cents, would you do a favor for me?"

"Yes, Miss Bellamy."

(Belle! Belle! Where is my breakfast? Come before I die of loneliness. Come before the sycamores break at the top and crush the roof over my head!)

"Do you promise, Ernest Leonard?"

"I promise, Miss Bellamy," he said and moved a step away from her.

She took a twenty-five-cent piece out of the purse she carried strapped to her belt and, bending down, took the wreath, which she placed on the coffer. Now Ernest Leonard clutched the stocking cap in both hands. His aplomb had left him; she could tell that he wanted to run away.

"You must give me a kiss, Master McCammon," she said and, leaning heavily upon her stick, stooped toward that small face with pursed lips, coral-colored. They touched her bone-dry cheek and then the boy was gone, and through the door he had left open in his headlong flight there came a blast of cold December. But for a moment she did not move and stared at a clot of snow upon the rug. *I told you, Ernest Leonard, to wipe your feet carefully on my Welcome mat.*

Belle's big country feet were on the stairs. Miss Bellamy trembled for her knock. *Wait a minute, Belle, I have not yet thought out what I am going to say to you.* Had she left any stray spruce needles on the coffer? Had any fallen as she climbed the stairs, breathless with recollection? Belle was at the door. She knocked and entered with the tray.

"Explain that monstrosity," said Miss Bellamy, pointing to the Christmas wreath she had hung last night at the stroke of midnight. *Merry Christmas, Papa dear. Oh, how cunning of you to hang up mistletoe! What girl in the world would want more than a beau like you? Can I have my presents now? It's one past midnight, Papa! Oh, Papa, darling, you have given me a brass fender for my fireplace! Oh, Papa, a medallioned sewing drum! An emerald ring! A purple velvet peignoir! I wish you a very merry Christmas, Papa.*

"Don't pretend you know nothing about it, my good woman. Why did you do it, Belle? Have you no respect for other people's property? Do you think I can have my bedroom repapered every week or so merely for the sake of your vulgar whims?"

Kind, stupid Belle shook out the napkin and she said, as she sprinkled a little salt on the lightly boiled egg, "I'm sorry, Miss Rhoda, that I never seem to do what's right. I thought you'd like the wreath."

The old lady cackled hideously and screamed, "You goose! You namby-pamby! I hung it there myself!"

The maid, unruffled, smiled and said, "Merry Christmas, Miss Rhoda." When she had gone, the spinster closed her eyes against Ernest Leonard's painted pine cones, but she nursed her hurt like a baby at a milkless breast, with tearless eyes.

Polite Conversation

"IT is so good in you to come to tea," said Mrs. Wainright-Lowe as she plucked one last weed beside a petunia that grew out of a crack in the flagstoned terrace. "I have seen so little of you lately."

"I know," said Mrs. Heath, casting about for a new excuse for her unneighborliness, but the effort, on this New England summer afternoon, was too great, and she said only, "It is good in you to let me come," and she wondered how it had been possible to fall so quickly into this habit of saying "in you" instead of "of you." It was but one of the many concessions she had made to the culture of her hostess during the year she had known her, the greatest of all being her frequent attendance at this prolonged alfresco meal. Mrs. Wainright-Lowe, small and brown, like a larger rendering of the nuthatch that nervously regarded her from a shrub of Japanese quince, made a purling sound of understanding or of deprecation—it was not possible to tell which—and felt the belly of the teapot to test its warmth.

One of the Wainright-Lowe daughters, the only one at home today, came through the kitchen door to the terrace bearing a tea cozy appliquéd with Scotties. She had turned on the phonograph, and the first movement of the "Jupiter" soon burst surprisingly upon them, with a blast that sent the nuthatch whirring off to the pine woods. So displeasing was the tone of all the music one heard in this house that one imagined the family often attacked the records with steel wool or pumice stone, or that they used them as properties in the rambunctious charades it was the nightly custom of this high-spirited brood to play.

Mrs. Wainright-Lowe said, "The music is intended to distract your attention from the barn," and she pointed toward the lopped-off elm branches that the tree men had been accumulating for some days past and that were piled now in lavish disorder in the doorway of the barn, the scene of weekly square-dancing parties. The Heaths were bidden to the dances every Saturday by one or by all of the eleven Wainright-Lowe children, not one of whom had ever, under any circumstances, taken no for an answer. For the eleven Wainright-Lowes were seldom idle when they came home from school and college, or from jobs at schools and colleges (they revered education and, even when married, even when pregnant, took graduate courses in political science and Eastern philosophy), to spend the summer with their mother. Their notions of entertainment were on a scale so grand that it was necessary for them to recruit far and wide throughout the county in order to fill the large house and the larger barn with tireless merry-makers. Day after day and night after night, the buildings bulged and burst with nonalcoholic jollifications, with laughing, singing, whistling, with the imitations of birds and beasts, with the spasms of accordions and the yammer of fiddles playing jigs, with the shooting of bottles and the chopping of trees and the repairing of boats and the ringing of old cowbells bought at auctions for next to nothing. The Heaths, who were writers and did not look on the summertime as all beer and skittles, accepted all the invitations but did not appear at any of these shindigs. Indeed, they seldom stirred farther than the lake behind their house, or the general store, and the gentry (and especially the Wainright-Lowes), who had done so much to make them feel "at home" in the town, did not know whether they were abnormal or stuck-up.

It was quiet today; all the children but Eva had gone to the seashore to fly some kites belonging to a house guest and to dig for clams, to swim, to sail, to consume cases of Moxie and pounds of frankfurters, and, in general, to occupy themselves every moment of the radiant day. Eva had not gone with them because, through some unheard-of phenomenon, she was tired.

She put the cozy on the teapot beside her mother and said to Mrs. Heath, "But where is Tommy?"

Margaret Heath told them that her husband was working, and Mrs. Wainright-Lowe, giving her a swift appraisal out of eyes that did not believe her for a minute, said, "He works *all* the time, Eva. That's the first thing you must learn about Tommy Heath." Her voice and her manner implied much more, and she smiled with mild, motherly derision as she bent her attention to a tin of foie gras. Margaret bristled at this devious criticism of her husband (she could never be sure exactly what the implication was, but it was clear that the Wainright-Lowes looked on

writing as something that could be taken or left alone), even
though, half an hour before, she had all but exhausted herself
in a polemic addressed to him on why he should go across
the road with her to tea at the Bishop's widow's house. Her
arguments had been unspeakable; she had sounded like Mrs.
Wainright-Lowe herself—had spoken of their need to become
a part of the citizenry, had said they would soon be hated by
everyone if they did not occasionally accept an invitation; he
had irrefutably replied that he would not go today or any other
day, because he was an eccentric.

There was an abundant tea. There were lettuce sandwiches and
cheese sandwiches, peanut-butter sandwiches and tomato sandwiches, crackers spread with pâté. There was a cake, and there
were brownies, and there was a plate of candy made by Eva
Wainright-Lowe. And the hostess said sweetly, with ineffable
forgiveness, "We had expected Tommy, you see. I had told Eva
that he eats like a proper man. I simply cannot bear men who
have poor appetites, can you?"

"No," said Tommy's wife, although she had never pondered
this question before and could not feel that she had an opinion
on it at all; she had not, until this moment, ever considered
her husband's feeding habits, and she wondered, quite un-
emotionally, if she gave him enough to eat. She supposed that
the departed Bishop had been very much up to snuff in this
particular, for in an august portrait in the library he looked a
thorough trencherman about the jowls and the satisfied eyes.

"Perhaps Tommy would change his mind?" said Eva, a large
girl, eagerly. "If I went and yodeled under his window, do you
think he might succumb?"

The odious image made Margaret's "Oh, no!" come out like
a petition. She said, "He must get this off in the mail tomorrow." She hoped they would not ask what "this" was, but they
did, and she said, "His proofs," although the last of the proofs
had gone off days before.

"His proofs?" said Mrs. Wainright-Lowe. "What are those?
Are those the suggestions the publishers have made to him?"

"Well, no, Mrs. Wainright-Lowe," she said, aimlessly displeased, as she had always been since she had known these pious
people, at their failure to understand that her husband was not

receiving a favor from his publishers but that it was the other way around. And she explained what proofs were.

"Ah, then," said Mrs. Wainright-Lowe craftily, "then after this he *will* be free to come to tea."

Eva said, "Oh, to be a writer!"

Her mother said, "Eva has written some very clever things herself, you know, Margaret. Such a cunning poem it was you wrote on Bishop Masterman's Christmas present when we were in Toledo, Eva!"

"Oh, sweetie," said Eva, "don't tell Margaret about *that*! My goodness, Tommy and Margaret are *real* writers!"

Happily—because, clearly, Mrs. Wainright-Lowe was on the very point of telling Margaret about it—the record ended, and Eva galloped across the terrace to the house, hollering good-humoredly, "That's the trouble with a Vic."

"I wish you would get her to show you some of her writing, Margaret," Eva's mother said. "You've no idea how much my children *respect* you Heaths. On every postal card, Martin sends his love to you and Tommy." She referred to her boarding-school son, an indefatigable youth who, during his vacations, liked to lurk in the shrubbery of the Heaths' yard, waiting until he heard the sound of a typewriter; then he would pounce, hammering madly on the door and entering to cry, "I heard the typewriter, so I knew you were at home! May I come and bother you for half an hour or so?" And bother he did, but who could refuse the red-cheeked, fair-haired lad when he was so exuberant, so full to overflowing with long school-pranks and headmaster anecdotes, through the narration of which he gulped with a glee that was a kind of seizure, sometimes sending his voice wailing into the octaves of his infancy?

Eva, returning, said, "He's in St. Louis now. He says St. Louis isn't what it's cracked up to be."

Mrs. Wainright-Lowe seemed to be eyeing Margaret narrowly, for what dark purpose she could not guess. She said, "You can't think what a delight it is for Martin to have a young man in the neighborhood. He has so many sisters. When he comes back, I hope he and Tommy will often go sailing and fishing together." She paused, and Margaret, sighing for her husband, who was thus to be beset, blew her tea into her face. But the incident went unnoticed, and Mrs. Wainright-Lowe continued, "And skiing at the Christmas holiday and all sorts of things!"

They talked graciously of Martin's three-week tour with a band of schoolfellows, and of Mrs. Wainright-Lowe's snapdragons, and of the wickedly ribald postmaster, who made everyone— not only women—blush, and of the plumber, who had recently adopted the pubescent daughter of a murderer father and a diabetic mother. Midway through tea, they were joined by Sister Evelyn, an Anglican nun of the neighborhood, who, belonging to some order of surpassing liberality, spent long furloughs away from her convent with her truculently unwell mother in an ancestral dwelling here at the top of the hill. She liked to read the Office of the Day with Mrs. Wainright-Lowe in the dead Bishop's study. This evening, she came across the broad and brilliant lawn gently, like a gull, her habit drifting on the early-evening breeze. She came straight to Margaret and shook her hand, an unusual gesture for her and a painful one for Margaret, who had, the day before, dislocated her thumb while she was stacking firewood. Sister Evelyn said, "I hope you are better." Margaret recalled no recent illness, so she said, "Oh, thank you, yes, it's much better. I had it X-rayed and nothing is broken."

The nun looked puzzled, and then she said, "Oh, I was speaking of your being ill on the day of Cousin Peggy's swimming party," and Margaret said "Yes," and was unable to say more. "I thought you must be very low," continued the truth-lover, giving her a straight look, "since you had not come to pick the lettuce."

Although the Heaths had quite adequate lettuce of their own, and although Margaret knew that Sister Evelyn and her mother wanted them to pick theirs only so that it would not go to seed and be a mess all over their kitchen garden, she said docilely, "If I may, I will come tomorrow."

"Do," said the nun. "Come in the late afternoon and have a cup of tea. Mama will be so pleased. She was saying only the other day she did wish the young Heaths would feel more free to call."

It struck Margaret that the word "free" in this sense was the antonym of "free" in all others, for to enter Mrs. Yeoman's house was to consign oneself to a period of imprisonment, to be turned to stone by the hostess's self-supporting and infuriated monologue on the way the times had changed.

Mrs. Wainright-Lowe, with the sure insinuations of a lifelong habit of self-defeat, said, "It is a rare thing to get the Heaths to drink a cup of tea. And almost never does one get both of them together. Now and again, Margaret will come, and once in a blue moon Tommy will."

"Perhaps they don't like tea," said Sister Evelyn.

"Perhaps they don't like the institution of tea," said Eva, going again across the terrace to attend to the phonograph. Everyone laughed at the implausibility of this last suggestion, and Margaret laughed the hardest of all.

Sister Evelyn had brought a slip of pink paper with her, and when Eva, who taught school in Salt Lake and perfectly adored the West, even though she was still a dude, came back and poured herself another cup of tea, the nun said to her, "Now, here are the names of the teachers. I found them out from Audrey. There is a Mrs. Robertson, a Mrs. Pinkham, and someone who was née Kendricks but Audrey didn't know who she had married."

"Audrey is slipping!" cried Eva with a kind of guttural, barroom laugh.

"Isn't she, just?" said Sister Evelyn. "Well, anyhow, we can start out on this. I think we should ask them all to the first meeting, don't you?"

Mrs. Wainright-Lowe, tucking an overlapping bit of lettuce into her sandwich, explained to Margaret, "We are starting some young people's activities in the village. You and Tommy need not think you can get out of helping us! You evaded us in the winter, but we forgave you, since it was your first year here. But now we have you!"

Margaret vividly recalled the scenes of January, when she and Tommy had been made to feel irresponsible and stonehearted because they would not give up their Saturdays to direct the games of sullen children who wholly hated this Christian intrusion upon their privacy. She said hopefully, "Are the activities to be under the auspices of your church?"

"I suppose that, technically, they are, aren't they, Sister?"

And the Sister, glancing at Mrs. Wainright-Lowe's lettuce

and thinking, no doubt, of Margaret's negligence in other quarters, said, "I should think so, certainly. We appear to be the only enterprising group in the county."

"Then, in that case," said Margaret, looking at no one lest her relief show too plainly, "we can't, you know. It's the same as it was last winter. The priest we wrote to said we could not possibly have anything to do with a movement outside our church."

"It's not a movement," said Eva, again with that peculiar, beerhouse laugh.

"I think it's too tiresome," said her mother peckishly. "We are all Catholics, whether we are Romans or Anglicans."

Sister said, with a laugh, with a look of disdain for the Romans on her aristocratic, wimple-bound face, "I don't think Rome would quite accept that dictum, my dear," and Mrs. Wainright-Lowe, pouting, said, "Well, I don't care. I think it's tiresome to deprive these underprivileged youngsters of the writing instruction Margaret and Tommy could give them."

The ladies went on with their plans, and presently it was forgotten that Margaret and Tommy had not "fallen in" with the life that centered around Mrs. Wainright-Lowe's house. Margaret envied Tommy, alone in his study; she looked across the road at their house and at the broad, heart-shaped leaves of the Dutchman's pipe that encroached upon his windows, and she knew that he was as happy as a lark there, lying on his couch reading either the memoirs of Saint-Simon or the New English Dictionary, while she, poor martyr, listened to these hell-for-leather crusaders scheming and facetiously arguing.

Mrs. Wainright-Lowe finally included her and said, "You don't think we're asking too much of the teachers, do you? If you were a teacher, wouldn't your interest in your pupils carry through the summer?"

"Well, I doubt if it would," replied Margaret, astonished at her forthrightness, and then she mellowed it: "But, of course, I'm not a teacher."

"By the way," said Sister Evelyn to Mrs. Wainright-Lowe, "has your *Atlantic* come?"

"Why, no, has yours?" said Mrs. Wainright-Lowe, full of zeal, for upon the *Atlantic* hung these gentlewomen's hopes and fears.

"It came this morning, and I do hope yours will arrive soon, because there is a most interesting article in it by Sir Evanston Marks. It is one of a series of lectures he gave at McGill. He suggests that education is, after all, nothing more than character-building."

"That's just what the Bishop always said," cried the Bishop's loyal widow, spilling her tea in her excitement.

"Besides being ever so original in his ideas, Sir Evanston *does* know his Scripture. He begins with a verse from Jeremiah and scatters bits of the Psalms throughout, and ends up with a passage from Our Lord."

"That is the trouble with us these days," said Mrs. Wainright-Lowe. "We do not read the Bible. Sakes! When I was a child, we read a chapter every night, and we read all sorts of other people, like Newman. Who reads Newman now? Or anyone *like* Newman?"

"That makes me think of *A Tree Grows in Brooklyn*," said Eva, laughing in her private saloon. "Because, don't you remember, it says they read a chapter of the Bible and a page of Shakespeare every night, so that when they went to school, they knew more than anyone else? Did you read the book, Margaret?"

"No," said Margaret.

"Wasn't that girl terribly young to write a novel?" said Mrs. Wainright-Lowe, who had sent over a cake the week before, on Margaret's thirtieth birthday, and seemed, in her rapt glare, to be counting the wrinkles in her neighbor's face. "Wasn't she only twenty-four?"

"I'm sure I don't know," said Margaret coldly, and Sister Evelyn, who had no idea what they were talking about, said, "My soul! That *is* young!"

Mrs. Wainright-Lowe said, "Later, I believe the book was made into a movie. I heard the author on 'Town Meeting of the Air' and did not think she was very quick. Do you ever listen to 'Town Meeting,' Sister?"

"Is that one of those breakfast clubs?"

"Not exactly," said Mrs. Wainright-Lowe. "It's in the evening, but it's the same idea."

"Oh, it isn't at all," cried Eva, and started to explain, but Sister went on, "Our children at the orphanage adored those breakfast clubs. They had guests, you see. They would introduce someone and say, 'Here's Jim, just back from Tokyo,' and then everyone would begin to tease Jim. The children loved them, I think, because there was so much laughing. Do you listen to them, Margaret?"

Wonders followed wonders today. Margaret said, as courteously as she could, that she did not; then, feeling that perhaps she had gone too far in her apathy to this conversation, she said, "But I did hear an amusing thing on the radio the other day when I was trying to get the news. I tuned in to a children's quiz program—"

"Oh, the 'Quiz Kids'!" shouted Eva.

"No, no, it wasn't that," said Margaret, already bored with her contribution. "It was something else entirely. Anyhow, the announcer asked one child what he wanted to be when he grew up, and he said, 'A dry cleaner.'"

They all smiled, but it was not their sort of thing. Sister Evelyn said, "That reminds me of the child who told me he wanted to be a mortician, just like his Uncle George, whom he admired."

"A mortician!" gasped Mrs. Wainright-Lowe. "Sakes!"

"And I was afraid he had learned some of the tricks of his Uncle George's business before he came to us," said the nun, "although he did not seem to be a morbid child."

"Oh, well," said Eva, "kids will be kids."

Sister Evelyn patted her knee, for Eva's love of children was well known. "You ought to know." And Eva gurgled like a stomach.

After a moment's silence, it was announced that the gardener's mother, who had died at noon the day before, was ninety. Mrs. Wainright-Lowe said, "Bishop Masterman spoke once of going to a party for a woman who was a hundred and eight years old, and she remembered that in her childhood General Washington and his staff had often stopped at her father's house on the upper Hudson. All the women of the neighborhood came to help cook for the General. It makes one feel it is just a step from our times to those, doesn't it?"

"It does," said Sister Evelyn. "The sheriff was telling me a similar story the other day. About some old lady in Saco who had memories of the same kind. George Washington, or something of that sort."

"Yes, yes," said Mrs. Wainright-Lowe, sighing to think of the proximity of history. "Bishop Masterman was so clever when he taught children. I remember, on this same occasion, he explained to mine that although the Year One seemed a long time ago, it would only be back twenty lifetimes. Twenty men, that is, living to be a hundred and overlapping one another would be all that would be necessary to go back to the Year One."

"That's awfully good," said Eva, "but I don't remember his telling *me* that."

"You have a good forgetter," said her mother.

"But I do remember that house he took us to see in England. Do you remember the cobblestone court, and how the chapel entry was right under a cherry tree?"

"Such a lovely house!" said Mrs. Wainright-Lowe. "The best sitting room was on the third floor."

"They were always on the second or third floor," said Sister Evelyn. "Even in my mother's day, there was always a 'best' parlor on the second floor. And the ballroom, of course, at the top of the house."

Now Mrs. Wainright-Lowe turned directly to Margaret and said, "I forgot to ask you, what did your architect friend say about your house? Sister, Margaret has an architect friend who is spending the summer in West Bath, and we are both so keen to have him advise us about our kitchens."

Margaret said, "I'm afraid he's not really interested in old houses."

A veil of disapproval came down over the widowed eyes, and she said evenly, "Oh. He's from New York, isn't he?"

"New York," said Sister Evelyn, stating a regrettable fact.

"Yes," said Margaret, and, probing the ugly, public wound, she added, "As a matter of fact, he was born there."

The lacuna hovered like a leaf about to fall. The teacups somehow did not reach their saucers but stayed still in midair. Mrs. Heath's manners and her friend's character would get their due at future teas.

Suddenly, Mrs. Wainright-Lowe sat up straight, in an inexplicable little tantrum, and said, "I think Tommy is gravely mistaken if he thinks one can live by art alone. But I daresay he would call *me* bourgeois for posing that question!"

Eva popped a pâté cracker into her big mouth and said, "Oh, dry up, Mother! Did you knit that sweater yourself, Margaret?"

"No, my mother-in-law did."

Sister Evelyn said, "Mama was so disappointed that your mother-in-law did not come to call when she visited you."

"We didn't like to disturb her, since we knew she'd been ill, and we knew what a time you were having getting servants." This was not exactly true. Margaret's mother-in-law, after hearing the Heaths' description of their neighbor, had said, "I think it's lovely to have her next door, and I'm sure it must be relaxing for you and Tommy to go there to tea after a hard day's work. But don't let's go."

Sister Evelyn, riding the crest of this earthly life, said severely, "She might at least have come to see the woodwork in the library."

Mrs. Wainright-Lowe said, "What *is* your servant situation these days, Sister?"

"The handmaiden arrived from Rockland yesterday. But she will not sleep in. She is staying with her aunt in the village, and the aunt delivers her a little before seven and comes to fetch her a little after seven."

"Who is the aunt?" asked Mrs. Wainright-Lowe.

Sister Evelyn laughed. "It's very intricate. Her name is Annie Bedlow, and she was—I found out all this from Audrey—Annie Cashman before she was married, and her mother, Nellie Cashman, used to live in Arthur Rutherford's house, on the Pond Road, the house that now belongs to the Misses Archer. And these Misses Archer are first cousins, once removed, to Annie Cashman Bedlow, and our child—Betty Temple, her name is—will divide her time between her aunt and these cousins, who are her second cousins. Second?" she asked herself. "Yes, that's right, second cousins."

"Whoop-de-doo!" cried Eva, lying down flat on her back on the lawn. "I vote you get A for recitation, Sister."

The sun was beginning to set. Margaret fixed her eye on Sister Evelyn's broad cuff, and when the nun raised her hand with the teacup, she saw with relief that the hands of the big, efficient watch stood at half past six. She returned her cup to the tray and said, "I must go get dinner."

"You've just had tea," said Mrs. Wainright-Lowe.

"But Tommy hasn't."

"Not because he wasn't *asked* to have it. I do declare, I shall have His Lordship here tomorrow at tea and I shan't take no for an answer. You tell him that for me, Margaret—I shan't take no for an answer. With his thingumbobs off in the mail, he'll have no excuse."

"None," said Sister Evelyn firmly.

"Won't you take some roses to adorn his dinner table?" said the invincible widow.

And Margaret was obliged to wait while Eva went to fetch the shears, while Mrs. Wainright-Lowe, obsessed, donned her thornproof gloves and meticulously and maliciously selected the handsomest of all her flowers, handling each as if it were an inestimably precious chalice, full of hemlock, and, giving them to Margaret, she said, "Thank you for coming. It was so good in you to come to tea."

At that moment, a car came racing down the road, burgeoning with Wainright-Lowes home from the beach, and against this racket Sister Evelyn, who would wait just a moment before she, too, left, said, with a dim, tea-party smile, "And tomorrow, while Tommy is here, you will come and visit with Mama, won't you? So glad you are going to be in residence the year around."

A Country Love Story

An antique sleigh stood in the yard, snow after snow banked up against its eroded runners. Here and there upon the bleached and splintery seat were wisps of horsehair and scraps of the black leather that had once upholstered it. It bore, with all its jovial curves, an air not so much of desuetude as of slowed-down dash, as if weary horses, unable to go another step, had at last stopped here. The sleigh had come with the house. The former owner, a gifted businesswoman from Castine who bought old houses and sold them again with all their pitfalls still intact, had said when she was showing them the place, "A picturesque detail, I think," and, waving it away, had turned to the well, which, with enthusiasm and at considerable length, she said had never gone dry. Actually, May and Daniel had found the detail more distracting than picturesque, so nearly kin was it to outdoor arts and crafts, and when the woman, as they departed in her car, gestured toward it again and said, "Paint that up a bit with something cheery and it will really add no end to your yard," simultaneous shudders coursed them. They had planned to remove the sleigh before they did anything else.

But partly because there were more important things to be done, and partly because they did not know where to put it (a sleigh could not, in the usual sense of the words, be thrown away), and partly because it seemed defiantly a part of the yard, as entitled to be there permanently as the trees, they did nothing about it. Throughout the summer, they saw birds briefly pause on its rakish front and saw the fresh rains wash its runners; in the autumn they watched the golden leaves fill the seat and nestle dryly down; and now, with the snow, they watched this new accumulation.

The sleigh was visible from the windows of the big, bright kitchen where they ate all their meals and, sometimes too bemused with country solitude to talk, they gazed out at it, forgetting their food in speculating on its history. It could have been driven cavalierly by the scion of some sea captain's family, or it could have been used soberly to haul the household's Unitarians to church or to take the womenfolk around the countryside on errands of good will. They did not speak of what its office might have been, and the fact of their silence was often nettlesome to May, for she felt they were silent too much of the time; a little morosely, she thought, If something as absurd and as provocative as this at which we look together—and which is, even though we didn't want it, our own property—cannot bring us to talk, what can? But she did not disturb Daniel in his private musings; she held her tongue, and out of the corner of her eye she watched him watch the winter cloak the sleigh, and, as if she were computing a difficult sum in her head, she tried to puzzle out what it was that had stilled tongues that earlier, before Daniel's illness, had found the days too short to communicate all they were eager to say.

It had been Daniel's doctor's idea, not theirs, that had brought them to the solemn hinterland to stay after all the summer gentry had departed in their beach wagons. The Northern sun, the pristine air, the rural walks and soundless nights, said Dr. Tellenbach, perhaps pining for his native Switzerland, would do more for the "Professor's" convalescent lung than all the doctors and clinics in the world. Privately he had added to May that after so long a season in the sanitarium (Daniel had been there a year), where everything was tuned to a low pitch, it would be difficult and it might be shattering for "the boy" (not now the "Professor," although Daniel, nearly fifty, was his wife's senior by twenty years and Dr. Tellenbach's by ten) to go back at once to the excitements and the intrigues of the university, to what, with finicking humor, the Doctor called "the omnium-gatherum of the schoolmaster's life." The rigors of a country winter would be as nothing, he insisted, when compared to the strain of feuds and cocktail parties. All professors wanted to write books, didn't they? Surely Daniel, a historian with all the material in the world at his fingertips, must have something up his sleeve that could be the *raison d'être* for this year away? May said she supposed he had, she was not sure. She could hear the reluctance in her voice as she escaped the Doctor's eyes and gazed through his windows at the mountains behind the sanitarium. In the dragging months Daniel had been gone, she had taken solace in imagining the time when they *would* return to just that pandemonium the Doctor so deplored, and because it had been pandemonium on the smallest and most discreet scale, she smiled through her disappointment at the little man's Swiss innocence and explained that they had always lived quietly, seldom dining out or entertaining more than twice a week.

"Twice a week!" He was appalled.

"But I'm afraid," she had protested, "that he would find a second year of inactivity intolerable. He does intend to write a book, but he means to write it in England, and we can't go to England now."

"England!" Dr. Tellenbach threw up his hands. "Good *air* is my recommendation for your husband. Good air and little talk."

She said, "It's talk he needs, I should think, after all this time of communing only with himself except when I came to visit."

He had looked at her with exaggerated patience, and then, courtly but authoritative, he said, "I hope you will not think I importune when I tell you that I am very well acquainted with your husband, and, as his physician, I order this retreat. *He* quite agrees."

Stung to see that there was a greater degree of understanding between Daniel and Dr. Tellenbach than between Daniel and herself, May had objected further, citing an occasion when her husband had put his head in his hands and mourned, "I hear talk of nothing but sputum cups and X-rays. Aren't people interested in the state of the world any more?"

But Dr. Tellenbach had been adamant, and at the end, when she had risen to go, he said, "You are bound to find him changed a little. A long illness removes a thoughtful man from his fellow beings. It is like living with an exacting mistress who is not content with half a man's attention but must claim it all." She had thought his figure of speech absurd and disdained to ask him what he meant.

Actually, when the time came for them to move into the new house and she found no alterations in her husband but found, on the other hand, much pleasure in their country life, she began to forgive Dr. Tellenbach. In the beginning, it was like a second honeymoon, for they had moved to a part of the North where they had never been and they explored it together, sharing its charming sights and sounds. Moreover, they had never owned a house before but had always lived in city apartments, and though the house they bought was old and derelict, its lines and doors and window lights were beautiful, and they were possessed by it. All through the summer, they reiterated, "To think that we own all of this! That it actually belongs to us!" And they wandered from room to room marveling at their windows, from none of which was it possible to see an ugly sight. They looked to the south upon a river, to the north upon a lake; to the west of them were pine woods where the wind forever sighed, voicing a vain entreaty; and to the east a rich man's long meadow that ran down a hill to his old, magisterial house. It was true, even in those bewitched days, that there were times on the lake, when May was gathering water lilies as Daniel slowly rowed, that she had seen on his face a look of abstraction and she had known that he was worlds away, in his memories, perhaps, of his illness and the sanitarium (of which he would never speak) or in the thought of the book he was going to write as soon, he said, as the winter set in and there was nothing to do but work. Momentarily the look frightened her and she remembered the Doctor's words, but then, immediately herself again in the security of married love, she caught at another water lily and pulled at its long stem. Companionably, they gardened, taking special pride in the nicotiana that sent its nighttime fragrance into their bedroom. Together, and with fascination, they consulted carpenters, plasterers, and chimney sweeps. In the blue evenings they read at ease, hearing no sound but that of the night birds—the loons on the lake and the owls in the tops of trees. When the days began to cool and shorten, a cricket came to bless their house, nightly singing behind the kitchen stove. They got two fat and idle tabby cats, who lay insensible beside the fireplace and only stirred themselves to purr perfunctorily.

Because they had not moved in until July and by that time the workmen of the region were already engaged, most of the major repairs of the house were to be postponed until the spring, and in October, when May and Daniel had done all they could by themselves and Daniel had begun his own work, May suddenly found herself without occupation. Whole days might pass when she did nothing more than cook three meals and walk a little in the autumn mist and pet the cats and wait for Daniel to come down from his upstairs study to talk to her. She began to think with longing of the crowded days in Boston before Daniel was sick, and even in the year past, when he had been away and she had gone to concerts and recitals and had done good deeds for crippled children and had endlessly shopped for presents to lighten the tedium of her husband's unwilling exile. And, longing, she was remorseful, as if by desiring another she betrayed this life, and, remorseful, she hid away in sleep. Sometimes she slept for hours in the daytime, imitating the cats, and when at last she got up, she had to push away the dense sleep as if it were a door.

One day at lunch, she asked Daniel to take a long walk with her that afternoon to a farm where the owner smoked his own sausages.

"You never go outdoors," she said, "and Dr. Tellenbach said you must. Besides, it's a lovely day."

"I can't," he said. "I'd like to, but I can't. I'm busy. You go alone."

Overtaken by a gust of loneliness, she cried, "Oh, Daniel, I have nothing to *do*!"

A moment's silence fell, and then he said, "I'm sorry to put you through this, my dear, but you must surely admit that it's not my fault I got sick."

In her shame, her rapid, overdone apologies, her insistence that nothing mattered in the world except his health and peace of mind, she made everything worse, and at last he said shortly to her, "Stop being a child, May. Let's just leave each other alone."

This outbreak, the very first in their marriage of five years, was the beginning of a series. Hardly a day passed that they did not bicker over something; they might dispute a question of fact, argue a matter of taste, catch each other out in an inaccuracy, and every quarrel ended with Daniel's saying to her, "Why don't you leave me alone?" Once he said, "I've been sick and now I'm busy and I'm no longer young enough to shift the focus of my mind each time it suits your whim." Afterward, there were always apologies, and then Daniel went back to his study and did not open the door of it again until the next meal. Finally, it seemed to her that love, the very center of their being, was choked off, overgrown, invisible. And silent with hostility or voluble with trivial reproach, they tried to dig it out impulsively and could not—could only maul it in its unkempt grave. Daniel, in his withdrawal from her and from the house, was preoccupied with his research, of which he never spoke except to say that it would bore her, and most of the time, so it appeared to May, he did not worry over what was happening to them. She felt the cold old house somehow enveloping her as if it were their common enemy, maliciously bent on bringing them to disaster. Sunken in faithlessness, they stared, at mealtimes, atrophied within the present hour, at the irrelevant and whimsical sleigh that stood abandoned in the mammoth winter.

May found herself thinking, If we redeemed it and painted it, our house would have something in common with Henry Ford's Wayside Inn. And I might make this very observation to him and he might greet it with disdain and we might once again be able to talk to each other. Perhaps we could talk of Williamsburg and how we disapproved of it. Her mind went toiling on. Williamsburg was part of our honeymoon trip; somewhere our feet were entangled in suckers as we stood kissing under a willow tree. Soon she found that she did not care for this line of thought, nor did she care what his response to it might be. In her imagined conversations with Daniel, she never spoke of the sleigh. To the thin, ill scholar whose scholarship and illness had usurped her place, she had gradually taken a weighty but unviolent dislike.

The discovery of this came, not surprising her, on Christmas Day. The knowledge sank like a plummet, and at the same time she was thinking about the sleigh, connecting it with the smell of the barn on damp days, and she thought perhaps it had been drawn by the very animals who had been stabled there and had pervaded the timbers with their odor. There must have been much life within this house once—but long ago. The earth immediately behind the barn was said by everyone to be extremely rich because of the horses, although there had been none there for over fifty years. Thinking of this soil, which earlier she had eagerly sifted through her fingers, May now realized that she had no wish for the spring to come, no wish to plant a garden, and, branching out at random, she found she had no wish to see the sea again, or children, or favorite pictures, or even her own face on a happy day. For a minute or two, she was almost enraptured in this state of no desire, but then, purged swiftly of her cynicism, she knew it to be false, knew that actually she did have a desire—the desire for a desire. And now she felt that she was stationary in a whirlpool, and at the very moment she conceived the notion a bit of wind brought to the seat of the sleigh the final leaf from the elm tree that stood beside it. It crossed her mind that she might consider the wood of the sleigh in its juxtaposition to the living tree and to the horses, who, although they were long since dead, reminded her of their passionate, sweating, running life every time she went to the barn for firewood.

They sat this morning in the kitchen full of sun, and, speaking not to him but to the sleigh, to icicles, to the dark, motionless pine woods, she said, "I wonder if on a day like this they used to take the pastor home after lunch." Daniel gazed abstractedly at the bright-silver drifts beside the well and said nothing. Presently a wagon went past hauled by two oxen with bells on their yoke. This was the hour they always passed, taking to an unknown destination an aged man in a fur hat and an aged woman in a shawl. May and Daniel listened.

Suddenly, with impromptu anger, Daniel said, "What did you just say?"

"Nothing," she said. And then, after a pause, "It would be lovely at Jamaica Pond today."

He wheeled on her and pounded the table with his fist. "I did not ask for this!" The color rose feverishly to his thin cheeks and his breath was agitated. "You are trying to make me sick again. It was wonderful, wasn't it, for you while I was gone?"

"Oh, no, no! Oh, no, Daniel, it was hell!"

"Then, by the same token, this must be heaven." He smiled, the professor catching out a student in a fallacy.

"Heaven." She said the word bitterly.

"Then why do you stay here?" he cried.

It was a cheap impasse, desolate, true, unfair. She did not answer him.

After a while he said, "I almost believe there's something you haven't told me."

She began to cry at once, blubbering across the table at him.

"You have said that before. What am I to say? What have I done?"

He looked at her, impervious to her tears, without mercy and yet without contempt. "I don't know. But you've done something."

It was as if she were looking through someone else's scrambled closets and bureau drawers for an object that had not been named to her, but nowhere could she find her gross offense.

Domestically she asked him if he would have more coffee and he peremptorily refused and demanded, "Will you tell me why it is you must badger me? Is it a compulsion? Can't you control it? Are you going mad?"

From that day onward, May felt a certain stirring of life within her solitude, and now and again, looking up from a book to see if the damper on the stove was right, to listen to a rat renovating its house-within-a-house, to watch the belled oxen pass, she nursed her wound, hugged it, repeated his awful words exactly as he had said them, reproduced the way his wasted lips had looked and his bright, farsighted eyes. She could not read for long at any time, nor could she sew. She cared little now for planning changes in her house; she had meant to sand the painted floors to uncover the wood of the wide boards and she had imagined how the long, paneled windows of the drawing room would look when yellow velvet curtains hung there in the spring. Now, schooled by silence and indifference, she was immune to disrepair and to the damage done by the wind and snow, and she looked, as Daniel did, without dislike upon the old and nasty wallpaper and upon the shabby kitchen floor. One day, she knew that the sleigh would stay where it was so long as they stayed there. From every thought, she returned to her deep, bleeding injury. He had asked her if she were going mad.

She repaid him in the dark afternoons while he was closeted away in his study, hardly making a sound save when he added wood to his fire or paced a little, deep in thought. She sat at the kitchen table looking at the sleigh, and she gave Daniel insult for his injury by imagining a lover. She did not imagine his face, but she imagined his clothing, which would be costly and in the best of taste, and his manner, which would be urbane and anticipatory of her least whim, and his clever speech, and his adept courtship that would begin the moment he looked at the sleigh and said, "I must get rid of that for you at once." She might be a widow, she might be divorced, she might be committing adultery. Certainly there was no need to specify in an affair so securely legal. There was no need, that is, up to a point, and then the point came when she took in the fact that she not only believed in this lover but loved him and depended wholly on his companionship. She complained to him of Daniel and he consoled her; she told him stories of her girlhood, when she had gaily gone to parties, squired by boys her own age; she dazzled him sometimes with the wise comments she made on the books she read. It came to be true that if she so much as looked at the sleigh, she was weakened, failing with starvation.

Often, about her daily tasks of cooking food and washing dishes and tending the fires and shopping in the general store of the village, she thought she should watch her step, that it was this sort of thing that *did* make one go mad; for a while, then, she went back to Daniel's question, sharpening its razor edge. But she could not corral her alien thoughts and she trembled as she bought split peas, fearful that the old men loafing by the stove could see the incubus of her sins beside her. She could not avert such thoughts when they rushed upon her sometimes at tea with one of the old religious ladies of the neighborhood, so that, in the middle of a conversation about a deaconess in Bath, she retired from them, seeking her lover, who came, faceless, with his arms outstretched, even as she sat up straight in a Boston rocker, even as she accepted another cup of tea. She lingered over the cake plates and the simple talk, postponing her return to her own house and to Daniel, whom she continually betrayed.

It was not long after she recognized her love that she began to wake up even before the dawn and to be all day quick to everything, observant of all the signs of age and eccentricity in her husband, and she compared him in every particular—to his humiliation, in her eyes—with the man whom now it seemed to her she had always loved at fever pitch.

Once when Daniel, in a rare mood, kissed her, she drew back involuntarily and he said gently, "I wish I knew what you had done, poor dear." He looked as if for written words in her face.

"You said you knew," she said, terrified.

"I do."

"Then why do you wish you knew?" Her baffled voice was high and frantic. "You don't talk sense!"

"I do," he said sedately. "I talk sense always. It is you who are oblique." Her eyes stole like a sneak to the sleigh. "But I wish I knew your motive," he said impartially.

For a minute, she felt that they were two maniacs answering each other questions that had not been asked, never touching the matter at hand because they did not know what the matter was. But in the next moment, when he turned back to her spontaneously and clasped her head between his hands and said, like a tolerant father, "I forgive you, darling, because you don't know how you persecute me. No one knows except the sufferer what this sickness is," she knew again, helplessly, that they were not harmonious even in their aberrations.

These days of winter came and went, and on each of them, after breakfast and as the oxen passed, he accused her of her concealed misdeed. She could no longer truthfully deny that she was guilty, for she was in love, and she heard the subterfuge in her own voice and felt the guilty fever in her veins. Daniel knew it, too, and watched her. When she was alone, she felt her lover's presence protecting her—when she walked past the stiff spiraea, with icy cobwebs hung between its twigs, down to the lake, where the black, unmeasured water was hidden beneath a lid of ice; when she walked, instead, to the salt river to see the tar-paper shacks where the men caught smelt through the ice; when she walked in the dead dusk up the hill from the store, catching her breath the moment she saw the sleigh. But sometimes this splendid being mocked her when, freezing with fear of the consequences of her sin, she ran up the stairs to Daniel's room and burrowed her head in his shoulder and cried, "Come downstairs! I'm lonely, please come down!" But he would never come, and at last, bitterly, calmed by his calmly inquisitive regard, she went back alone and stood at the kitchen window, coyly half hidden behind the curtains.

For months she lived with her daily dishonor, rattled, ashamed, stubbornly clinging to her secret. But she grew more and more afraid when, oftener and oftener, Daniel said, "Why do you lie to me? What does this mood of yours mean?" and she could no longer sleep. In the raw nights, she lay straight beside him as he slept, and she stared at the ceiling, as bright as the snow it reflected, and tried not to think of the sleigh out there under the elm tree but could think only of it and of the man, her lover, who was connected with it somehow. She said to herself, as she listened to his breathing, "If I confessed to Daniel, he would understand that I was lonely and he would comfort me, saying, 'I am here, May. I shall never let you be lonely again.'" At these times, she was so separated from the world, so far removed from his touch and his voice, so solitary, that she would have sued a stranger for companionship. Daniel slept deeply, having no guilt to make him toss. He slept, indeed, so well that he never even heard the ditcher on snowy nights rising with a groan over the hill, flinging the snow from the road and warning of its approach by lights that first flashed red, then blue. As it passed their house, the hurled snow swashed like flames. All night she heard the squirrels adding up their nuts in the walls and heard the spirit of the house creaking and softly clicking upon the stairs and in the attics.

In early spring, when the whippoorwills begged in the cattails and the marsh reeds, and the northern lights patinated the lake and the tidal river, and the stars were large, and the huge vine of Dutchman's-pipe had started to leaf out, May went to bed late. Each night she sat on the back steps waiting, hearing the snuffling of a dog as it hightailed it for home, the single cry of a loon. Night after night, she waited for the advent of her rebirth while upstairs Daniel, who had spoken tolerantly of her vigils, slept, keeping his knowledge of her to himself. "A symptom," he had said, scowling in concentration, as he remarked upon her new habit. "Let it run its course. Perhaps when this is over, you will know the reason why you torture me with these obsessions and will stop. You know, you may really have a slight disorder of the mind. It would be nothing to be ashamed of; you could go to a sanitarium."

One night, looking out the window, she clearly saw her lover sitting in the sleigh. His hand was over his eyes and his chin was covered by a red silk scarf. He wore no hat and his hair was fair. He was tall and his long legs stretched indolently along the floorboard. He was younger than she had imagined him to be and he seemed rather frail, for there was a delicate pallor on his high, intelligent forehead and there was an invalid's languor in his whole attitude. He wore a white blazer and gray flannels and there was a yellow rosebud in his lapel. Young as he was, he did not, even so, seem to belong to her generation; rather, he seemed to be the reincarnation of someone's uncle as he had been fifty years before. May did not move until he vanished, and then, even though she knew now that she was truly bedeviled, the only emotion she had was bashfulness, mingled with doubt; she was not sure, that is, that he loved her.

That night, she slept a while. She lay near to Daniel, who was smiling in the moonlight. She could tell that the sleep she would have tonight would be as heavy as a coma, and she was aware of the moment she was overtaken.

She was in a canoe in a meadow of water lilies and her lover was tranquilly taking the shell off a hard-boiled egg. "How intimate," he said, "to eat an egg with you." She was nervous lest the canoe tip over, but at the same time she was charmed by his wit and by the way he lightly touched her shoulder with the varnished paddle.

"May? May? I love you, May."

"Oh!" enchanted, she heard her voice replying. "Oh, I love you, too!"

"The winter is over, May. You must forgive the hallucinations of a sick man."

She woke to see Daniel's fair, pale head bending toward her. "He is old! He is ill!" she thought, but through her tears, to deceive him one last time, she cried, "Oh, thank God, Daniel!"

He was feeling cold and wakeful and he asked her to make him a cup of tea; before she left the room, he kissed her hands and arms and said, "If I am ever sick again, don't leave me, May."

Downstairs, in the kitchen, cold with shadows and with the obtrusion of dawn, she was belabored by a chill. "What time is it?" she said aloud, although she did not care. She remembered, not for any reason, a day when she and Daniel had stood in the yard last October wondering whether they should cover the chimneys that would not be used and he decided that they should not, but he had said, "I hope no birds get trapped." She had replied, "I thought they all left at about this time for the

South," and he had answered, with an unintelligible reproach in his voice, "The starlings stay." And she remembered, again for no reason, a day when, in pride and excitement, she had burst into the house crying, "I saw an ermine. It was terribly poised and let me watch it quite a while." He had said categorically, "There are no ermines here."

She had not protested; she had sighed as she sighed now and turned to the window. The sleigh was livid in this light and no one was in it; nor had anyone been in it for many years. But at that moment the blacksmith's cat came guardedly across the dewy field and climbed into it, as if by careful plan, and curled up on the seat. May prodded the clinkers in the stove and started to the barn for kindling. But she thought of the cold and the damp and the smell of the horses, and she did not go but stood there, holding the poker and leaning upon it as if it were an umbrella. There was no place warm to go. "What time is it?" she whimpered, heartbroken, and moved the poker, stroking the lion foot of the fireless stove.

She knew now that no change would come, and that she would never see her lover again. Confounded utterly, like an orphan in solitary confinement, she went outdoors and got into the sleigh. The blacksmith's imperturbable cat stretched and rearranged his position, and May sat beside him with her hands locked tightly in her lap, rapidly wondering over and over again how she would live the rest of her life.

The Bleeding Heart

E VERY morning and on alternate afternoons, Rose Fabrizio, a Mexican girl from the West, worked at a discreet girls' boarding school as secretary to the headmistress, a Miss Talmadge, who had a sweet voice. It was sweet even when she was dictating a warm comeuppance to the laundry about its mistreatment of the school's counterpanes and bureau runners; and sweet when she was explaining the value of physical education to a recalcitrant pupil who declared that she loathed volleyball. Every day when she arrived shortly after Rose had unlocked the office and uncovered her typewriter, Miss Talmadge cried "Good morning" twice and then she said with a lilt, "How is our Westerner? Acclimated? Finding the charm of New England both within and without?" She then stepped briskly into her own office and made a great clatter with the files, rudely flung up the window no matter what the thermometer said and set to work like a whirlwind. At first Rose, who was twenty-one and uncommonly sensitive, bridled at this greeting, which she believed to be subtly derisive, but now after two months she knew that there was no feeling behind it at all; Miss Talmadge inquired, in the same sweet rapid way, quite indifferent to the answers, about the parlormaid's fiancé and the French teacher's needlepoint and the riding master's brother's greenhouse. But even now, this reminder of her origin (vague as it must be in Miss Talmadge's mind, for if she imagined anything at all, she probably imagined cigar-store Indians and clumps of sage) sometimes brought on a subcutaneous prickle and distracted Rose from her shorthand so that on occasion she had fetched up with sentences that could not possibly be parsed.

Except in the vocal presence of Miss Talmadge, she *was* acclimated and she *did* find New England charming, although she was not quite sure that she had found it so both within and without, having no idea what the headmistress meant. She rejoiced in the abundance of imposing trees, in the pure style of the houses and the churches, in the venerable graveyards and in the unobtrusive shops. One was not conscious of any of the working parts of the town, not of the railroad or of the filling stations or of the water towers and the light-plants. Her own town, out West, had next to no trees and those were puny and half bald. The main street there was a row of dirty doorways which led into the dirtier interiors of pool halls, drugstores where even the soda-fountain bar had a flaccid look, and small restaurants and beer parlors and hotels whose windows were decorated sometimes with sweet-potato vines growing out of jam cans painted red, and sometimes with a prospector's pick-ax and some spurious gold ore, and sometimes with nothing more than the concupiscent but pessimistic legend that ladies were invited or that there were booths for them. The people here in this dignified New England town, shabby as they might be, wore hats and gloves at all hours and on all days and they appeared moral, self-controlled, well-bathed, and literate. The population of her own town was largely Mexican and was therefore, by turns, criminally quarrelsome or grossly stupefied so that when they were not beating one another up they stared into dusty space or lounged in various comatose attitudes against the stock properties of the main street: the telephone poles and fire hydrants and hitching posts. They were swarthy and they tended, on the whole, to be fat and to wear bright, juvenile colors. Repudiating all that, she greatly admired the pallor of the people here and their dun dress and their accent so that the merest soda-jerk sounded as if he had gone to Harvard.

In this atmosphere of good breeding and adulthood, Rose was happy half the time and altogether miserable the rest of it, miserable, that is, with envy of the people who had been born here of upright gentlefolk and had been reared in mannerly calm. And Rose, although she was full-grown and had a Bachelor of Arts degree (to be sure, she had not gone to Radcliffe and her education had been a shabby, uninteresting affair), longed to be adopted by a New Englander. Sometimes this longing coupled with her loneliness—it was not to its detriment that the town was unfriendly but quite the contrary—fretted her so that she could neither read nor play Canfield and she sat idle and unhappy in her bed-sitting room where the wind came down the chimney like a failing voice and now and then caused the long-handled bed-warmer to stir on its hook, chiming against the bricks.

She had selected the very person she wished to become her foster-father, a man about sixty whom she saw on Tuesday and Thursday and Saturday afternoons in the town library, an incongruously modern building dedicated to the memory of Samuel Sewall. Here Rose read books on psychology in a western room where the sun came amply through the windows; in this room, besides herself, there always sat a thoughtful gentleman, wearing a lemon-yellow ascot and a sober dark blue suit. The ascot alone would have set him down as a person of prominence, for no one unimportant, she reasoned, could afford to be so boldly eccentric. She did not know what he read through the scholarly Oxford glasses which perfectly fitted on his stately nose and were anchored to his lapel by a black ribbon ending in a silver button. The books were big, she knew that much, and their bindings were a usual maroon. He did not take any notes (as she did voluminously, having been so recently graduated) and he read quite slowly. He did not move all afternoon save that at half past three he went outside and stood on the steps to smoke a cigarette; she could see him clearly through the window beside which she sat reading of Pavlov's submissive dog. Either he stood still, leaning against a half pillar of the half-Ionic façade with his eyes closed and his lips moving a little, or he took a turn around the little triangular yard, holding his hatless white head at a dignified backward angle. Occasionally he paused under a tree and there, ankle deep in fallen leaves from the wine-glass elm, he was lost impressively in speculation. She thought he might be a mathematician or a novelist. Often when he returned, bringing with him a final remnant of the autumn air, he looked over at Rose across the tables and gave her an amiable, perfunctory nod as if he were her busy employer passing through the office of his underlings. Once he said something to her but in so low a voice and with so noncommittal an expression on his face that she did not understand and only smiled.

Despite a heritage of headlong impulse and her practice of setting forth before the signal was given, Rose made no move to further her acquaintance with the man and, indeed, she took pains never to see him out of his context. She always left the library before he did so that she would be tempted neither to find out what he was reading, since this would give a clue to his profession, nor to discover the direction he took to go home. Earlier in the fall, before she was aware that her library habits coincided with his and before she wanted to be adopted by him, she had enjoyed walking through the woods and over the hills and beside the river. On Sundays she had always gone to the largest and the oldest cemetery and there, upon a crest of rocks which overlooked the thin, ungarnished headstones, she had thoroughly read the literary supplement of *The New York Times* and had absently considered the hedge of barberry that flourished every which way beside a brook. She had liked to imagine the furnishings of the houses she could just see opposite and to wonder what scions of *Mayflower* families lived in them and were about to order tea. But now on Sunday she stayed in her room, long as the day seemed, for it would in no way serve her purpose, she thought sensibly, to be caught spying on the library man if he should come some time to pay his respects to someone's bones, those of his wife, perhaps, or a beloved daughter dead in early womanhood.

And before this, she had gone to dinner once or twice a week to an inn a mile out of the town on a byroad. This inn had the mark of Henry Ford upon it and so had the diners who disputed facts to do with the American Revolution and who exclaimed over the hasty-pudding. The landlord, a lethargic man from Bangor, sat in a chimney corner smoking an authentic pipe and the cook was said to be descended from King Philip on the maternal side. Rose did not think it probable that the man in the yellow ascot would ever come to a place like this since the atmosphere of his own dining room would be, if anything, even more bona fide. But she did not wish to run any risk, for, just as she did not want to know what books he read (he might be proved by them to be in his second childhood) and did not want to see him laying flowers upon his daughter's grave (for it might not be a daughter at all but only some old aunt by marriage), so she did not want to see him eating lest she discover that he followed an idiosyncratic diet and therefore had a constitutional disease.

All this abstention and the restiveness that accompanied it made her days and evenings monotonous and she became very much aware of the drawbacks of her room, which until now she had found—at least by comparison with the room at home which she shared with two younger sisters, both of whom walked in their sleep and one of whom gnashed her teeth—ideal. She lived on the ground floor of a double house that stood on a corner and was shaped like a wedge so that the front doors were on different streets. Her room, at Number 8 Patriot Road, was flush with what she thought must be the parlor at Number 6 Faneuil Lane and through the wood and plaster she sometimes heard throttled voices, heavy footsteps, and the indignant squawk of a mistuned radio. But she never heard a sound in Number 8. She was the only lodger on the first floor, but upstairs there were several meek and apparitional figures whom she met in the mildewed hall as she went to and from the bathroom. The landlady lived across the entryway from Rose and was visible only on Wednesday evening when she came to collect the rent and present the clean towels. Generally this transaction was performed as a dumb show and without smiles. The telephone seldom rang and the doorbell never. Besides this rather sepulchral air, the house was chilly and the lamps in Rose's room were poor.

Her feeling toward the silence of Number 8 and the sounds, low and distorted as they were, of Number 6, passed through several stages between the middle of October and the Thanksgiving holiday. At first the quiet of her own house pleased her because she could read with such concentration, and the noises of 6 irritated her when they were loud enough to intrude upon her page, yet not quite loud enough to be properly identified. Then she was disturbed and next annoyed by the silence and felt that it was unnatural, while she was grateful for the indications through the wall that there was life just yonder. And, again, she would be strained and unsettled, waiting for the noises and unable to make use of the interstices of silence between them. She never saw the tenants of the other house, but she had an idea what sort they might be, for frequently there was an electric car in front, looking like a large, abandoned toy. The driver of it, she was certain, would be a brisk old lady with no nonsense about her, and she came to believe, groundlessly, that there were two such old ladies, sisters, perhaps, or friends since boarding-school days at Lausanne. One must be either rather fat or else somewhat lame and wear special shoes, for nothing else could account for the heavy tread Rose sometimes heard. Once, on a Sunday afternoon, out of a clear blue sky she wondered if the man in the yellow ascot ever called at Number 6 and she snubbed the thought, snubbed the peculiarly awful possibility that he might be there at this very moment.

On Thanksgiving Day, she went to the inn outside the town for midday dinner. The library man was there and the moment she saw him, dressed as usual, she knew that she had secretly expected him, for she was not at all surprised. He was sitting at a table near the fireplace, engaged in conversation with the landlord and simultaneously reading the menu. A bright fire burned in the hearth and his fresh skin shone in the light like a leaf turned golden and it appeared to have a leaf's smooth texture. He sat very straight in his chair and while he waited for the soup he closed his eyes and calmly smiled as he listened to the landlord, who was apparently telling a long joke. He looked as if he might be sitting for his portrait and, indeed, he would have been a distinguished subject for a painter who did accurate "likenesses" of college presidents and notable physicians, for his face had admirable qualities of mellowness and deep, pacific wisdom and irony and casualness. He was in no hurry. He waited for his dinner with his eyes closed, not having to be occupied with looking round the room at the other diners and at the Currier and Ives prints on the walls and all the antique furniture which one might buy if one were able. Rose's own young and impatient mind immediately pranced away from him and dwelt, in quick succession, upon the brindle cat who was balancing for no earthly reason on the newel post; upon the lemon tree in the bay window, fed like an animal to produce fruit of a dreadful size; two quiet brown-eyed children who sat silent at a table with two thin old women, holding their hands between courses in an attitude of prayer. Fleetly it struck her that these two might be her neighbors and at that very moment, as if she had been directed by a voice, she looked out the window at the far driveway and saw the electric car, its square top grizzled with frost. It must be that the children were with their aged great-aunts for the day and she thought it must be a doubtful pleasure to them all since the four mute mouths bore an illegible expression.

Rose did not look at her foster-father save when her eyes fell on him by accident. Once she caught him looking at her over a piled fork and in his surprise he let some of the stuffing fall off. Every inch of her skin felt roasted and her hands shook so that for a moment she dared not try to lift her water glass although her mouth was dry. And later when his salad came she looked again and he distinctly winked at her as he tossed the cloves of tomato and the water cress. It was not a plain-spoken wink at all and it made her nervous. She hurried through her meal in order that she might leave before he did because, besides the ambiguous gambit of his eye, she was inadmissibly afraid that *he*, not the old ladies, might enter the electric car. She grappled hard with her suspicions about him and imperatively pointed out to herself that this stately aristocrat lived in a handsome house and that he had naturally given his housekeeper and his cook the day off and, because the air was fine and sharp, had liked to walk a mile to his dinner. She could not help feeling that it was strange he had not been invited anywhere, for surely a man of his position, whatever it was, would have friends in the town. Perhaps he despised the sentimental fanfare of holidays. Next year, after his adoption of her was a legal fact, she imagined that on Thanksgiving, Christmas, and Easter they would dine alone and afterward would play backgammon. Yet already she was visited with a nettlesome problem: should she play badly so that he would have the pleasure of winning or cleverly so that he would praise her? She rather hoped that he did not have a violin or any whimsical hobbies like collecting Revolutionary artifacts or taking bird-walks.

Rose did not wait for her dessert and on her way out she glanced quickly at the coats hung on the pegs in the hall. She recognized his immediately; it was black with a beaver lining, and although it was quite worn, it still was very rich and serviceable. His derby was there too and a tartan muffler. Fearing the road along which, at any moment, the electric car might pass, she struck into the woods and walked home along the pale, thick river. She found a nickel and a fresh-water mussel shell and she came upon a beached canoe, withering in the dry fall. She passed behind the girls' school and glanced at the windows of the dormitory with their starched dimity curtains. The little girls had all gone home to their fathers for the holiday. She was very lonely here beside the river and she began to walk fast, counting her footsteps to forestall her melancholy, but then she slowed down again as she realized that she would be just as lonely in her room. Until now she had been content with seeing the man in the library and had even been a little proud in a queer way that he had a life quite secret, quite independent of the alternate afternoons in the reading room and that what she did at other times was equally unimaginable to him. But now beside the woeful river, she was almost frightened to think of him just as she had almost been frightened as a child when everyone had left the church after the last mass and she had wondered what happened then, whether the plaster saints came to life and if God emerged, full-bodied, from the wafers in the ciborium.

Rose did not know, until she was actually within her room again, shadowy with dusk and musty with the old upholstery of the buckling wicker chairs, that there had been another reason why she had not liked to come back: now she was face to face with the knowledge that she had seen the driver of the electric car, who was, therefore, one of the authors of the noises in the other house. The car had got there before she did. The very moment she stepped across her threshold onto the distempered carpet with its muddy oak leaves, the sounds came, feebly ill-natured, straight to her anticipating ears. There were no new sounds, no children's voices.

All that afternoon, while she was thinking of the man as he sat in his own library (the Samuel Sewall was closed today) in one of the white clapboard houses in the side streets of the town, the dulled hubbub went on beyond the wall. At first she paid little heed; she was thinking of the chintz wing chair he might be sitting in with his feet on a brass fender before a fire. And at first the sounds were unobtrusive. But toward dark they became more insistent and she grew fully conscious of them. Although she could not hear words nor could she tell what sort of movements were being made, she was entirely alert, straining to read this trifling mystery. After a little, she was able to separate some of the noises and she heard a door open and close and a telephone ring and a clock strike and outside, in the street, she heard a boy irrelevantly cry, "Richard?" and she heard something bump over an uncarpeted floor. But above— or rather beneath, for it was little more than a jerky hum—the other sounds, there was a voice complaining, directly on the other side of the wall; it was a venomous and senile whimper which went on and on. It seemed to be uttering short curses with just time for a breath in between the tenth, perhaps, and the eleventh. Presently there was another opening and closing of the door and a second voice, a man's voice, spoke. There was, as well, a rattle of metal and now Rose constructed a picture: someone was ill and someone else was bringing a tray to the sickbed. But the important fact was that she must revise her general notion of the household: it included a man. Yet why could it not be a doctor, summoned hastily because one of the old ladies had eaten unwisely at the inn? She regretted that she had not scrutinized her neighbors more closely to see if they bore any marks of frailty in the color of the skin or the look about the nose. She sighed and went to the window to pull down the shade, for it had grown dark, and once again the electric car served her, for here it came, a silent, absurd box, round the corner and on its way toward the Mill Dam. "They have gone for the prescription," she said happily, and she saw a peaked spinster lying in a bed, another peaked one operating the simple machinery of the car. And she assured herself that the driver must, indeed must, be one of the children's great-aunts, for no man in his right mind would be seen in such a thing in this day and age.

When she had pulled the bottle-green blinds and turned on her two lamps, no brighter than candle flames, she was momentarily disgusted with herself for spending so much time conjecturing on unseen and unknown people. She was as bad as her mother, who could search a whole evening through for the inner meanings of a neighbor's greeting when they had not been on speaking terms for weeks or the impertinence of a salesgirl in the five-and-ten. So she tried to forget about the other house and to go back to the man in the yellow ascot but he was suddenly gone altogether and instead of him she could only see her real father, Joseph Fabrizio, who would be having a holiday today like everyone else and who, stupid and cynical, would be shambling about the house out West where even the hopvines at the windows were limp and unclean. Her father wore a black coat-sweater from J. C. Penney's and a spotty gray cap and Army store pants and miner's shoes studded with cleats that tore up the linoleum and made a brash racket. The putrefied smell of sugar beets clung to him constantly even after a bath, which he took only once in a month of Sundays. She did not know one good thing about her father except when she was very small she had been delighted to hear him sing "Juanita" and "Valencia" in a tenor voice for which he was admired by two or three people in the town; and one time when he must have been as drunk as a monkey, he brought her a box of Cheese-bits and a copy of *Sweetheart Stories* when she had the pinkeye. Although as far back as she could remember, she had been driven to get away, far away, and never go home again, she was often resentful that he never wrote to her and that he had not been at all sorry when she had gone away. As a matter of fact, he had not even seen her off on the bus and her mother did not know where he was. Her mother said, looking vaguely up and down the street and nodding to several acquaintances, "Well, I'll tell him goodbye for you," and handed her a lunch in a Honey Kist bread wrapper. The simple and humiliating fact was that he cared so little that he had clean forgotten.

The memories of her father, each one of which was uglier than the one before, made her so cross and jumpy that she knew she must quiet herself and she sat down to read *Self Reliance* which she had always found very soothing because it was so sedately dull. But she could pay attention to it even less than usual and the pattern of sounds next door presently was repeated: the telephone, the opening and closing of the door, the sound of china and silver on a tray. She was irritated and when she returned to Emerson, exhorting him to lull her, the voice would give her no peace but went on in its protracted peeve, hovering like a gnat over every word on the page. Finally she grew really angry and she knocked sharply on the wall. There was an immediate silence and then a most terrible and much louder sound: it was a laugh! And such a laugh as she had never heard in her life, for it was as thin as a needle and, unlike the speech, it did not quaver. For a moment she was afraid and she stepped away as if there were real danger, and then she was even angrier than before and her thoughts went quickly down this ladder of unreason, "If my father had not been a low person and if he had loved me, I would not have grown up in poverty and I would not have hated him so much that I had to go away from home to the first job that came along, this mean one that pays so little that I must live in a dark, depressing room where the walls are so thin that the sound of sickness comes through and for no reason at all I am laughed at by a cruel person who does not even know me." And she envisaged her father as he had probably been that day she had boarded the orange bus; fat and foul-tongued, he would have been shooting Cowboy at the pool hall, where they had spittoons since most of the patrons, including (God damn him) her father, chewed tobacco.

It was no longer possible for Rose to stay in her room in the evenings because of the busy personalities so near, and after dinner she went back to the Samuel Sewall. The overhead light was poor and made her eyes smart and she missed not sitting in her wrapper and her slippers. She was impatient with the spinster's prolonged illness and she saw no reason why she was not taken to the hospital. Sometimes they went on for years that way, just clinging to the ragged edge of nothing, getting more and more querulous and bothersome. Miss Talmadge noticed that Rose was distraught and when she asked and Rose said that she was dissatisfied with her room, Miss Talmadge objected with vehement sweetness, "But it is a quaint room! It is a lovely, lovely, lovely room!" and began instantly to dictate a stunning letter to the parent of a pupil who, in a tantrum over nothing at all, had deliberately broken a hockey stick belonging to the school.

One morning just before the Christmas holiday, Miss Talmadge asked, in her pink voice, if Rose would run an errand for her in the afternoon. The girls of the fourth form wished to send a potted plant to someone who was ill, a former matron. Rose was not surprised at all when she heard that the address was Number 6 Fanueil Lane. So important was this illness with which she lived that it did not occur to her that there was another invalid in the town and Miss Talmadge, never dreaming that the retired matron was the reason she did not like her room, said, with pointless cheer, "It will be so handy for you."

She accepted the commission with the greatest reluctance, not only because she wanted the occupants of the other house to remain anonymous but because, as well, she had a horror of being near old people and she remembered a time when the fifth grade had gone to sing Christmas carols at the old people's home. There had been a smell of senility in the long room with its glaring linoleum and Mission benches where the old people sat fiddling with their neckties or with pieces of holly purloined from the dining-room decorations. The last song was "We Three Kings" and by this time Rose was so sick that she only moved her lips, not making any sound. When it was over and they stood for a moment, dumb and immobile, until the teacher came to herd them away, a terribly, terribly old man rose to his feet and cried, "Damned brats! Clear them damned brats out p.d.q." He had bicycle clips on his eleemosynary plus-fours.

She had never actually passed the other house and she was surprised to find that its façade was altogether different from that of Number 8 Patriot Road. The paint was a darker shade of red and instead of two bay windows it had only one, just to the right of the off-center door. In the windows at Number 8, the landlady kept ferns and cactuses, but there was nothing at all alive in those of Number 6 and there were no curtains. There was only a solitary tuberculosis seal from the year before pasted in the lowest middle pane. Instead of a neat brass letter slot, there was a raveling raffia basket which hung on a hammock hook to hold the mail and there was no knocker but a bell instead, the kind you rang by turning an embossed iron handle. She turned it and heard a tinkle and instantly a voice very near her cried thinly, "Just a minute!" Rose could not tell where it came from but she waited in discomfort, feeling that she was being looked at from some vantage point no more than a foot away. Still, no one came. It was snowing and the big soft flakes dissolved in beautiful splashes on the glazed green paper that wrapped the bleeding heart. She rang again, and again, immediately, the voice encouragingly said, "Just a minute!" It was a high and genderless voice and was, she thought, the same one that had laughed at her when she had knocked on the wall. She was despondent here in the twilight snowstorm and her fingers clutching the pot were growing numb. The voice broke its promise for the second time; several minutes passed and nothing happened. She would try once more and if still no one came she would leave the plant on the doorstep even though it might freeze. Each moment she hated her role more, no matter what its outcome was to be. It would be worse than ever now to hear the sounds through the wall if she had the misfortune actually to see the interior of the house (how dreadful if she had to go into the sickroom itself!) and it would be almost as bad if the door was never opened and whoever it was that bade her wait a minute saw her leave and enter Number 8. Her comings and goings would thereafter be observed; or, even if they weren't, she would think they were and now, besides the sounds, she would be rattled by hypothetical eyes spying upon her.

She was about to ring for the last time when out of the corner of her eye she saw the electric car coming cautiously down the gentle slope of the street. Now there was no escaping. The great-aunt driving the car and the bodiless procrastinator behind the door would catch her there with the bleeding heart and make her explain herself. "Just a minute!" The voice, speaking this time of its own accord and not in answer to the bell, startled her and the plant slipped in her hands. The car disappeared in a driveway behind the house and in a little while a distant door opened and closed and Rose firmly rang the bell. This time the voice laughed mockingly up and down an untrue scale and she was in no doubt at all that it was the same one that had sneered at her knock.

The mysterious house behind the black door was seized with spasms. Someone screamed, "Tea!" and a stove was madly shaken down. Heavy footsteps crossed a room and a man's voice roared, "What? What do you say?" "Tea! Toast!" the screamed reply rang clear and the "s" in the toast was prolonged with hatred. "Give a person a chance to turn around, Mother!" said the man and the laughing voice near Rose chuckled high in its throat and mimicked itself, "Just a minute!" and then mimicked the deep voice of the man, "Just a minute!" She would have set the present down and run for dear life, but she was too late, for a light came dimly on in the front hall and feet approached the door.

"Well!" said the man in the yellow ascot with the same comforting smile he gave her in the library when he came in from smoking. He held the door wide open so that she saw a tall spooky staircase and a room to the right where chairs were arranged in a circle as if for a funeral or a clergyman's tea. Rose took a step forward and held out the bleeding heart to him, unable to say a word.

"Well!" he said again. "What's this? A posy for my poor sick mother?" He, for his part, was not in the least discomfited by this meeting. It was clear that he recognized her but he was not surprised; it was almost as if he had expected her all along. Now that she was up close, she saw that the ascot was made of diapered foulard but she saw, as well, that it was not clean and had the uncleanliness that accumulates over a period of weeks. She wondered if it hid something repulsive like a goiter or a birthmark or if it were some sort of fascist insignia and he was cat's-paw to a band of crooks.

"Yes," she said, as bashful as a child. "It is a plant from the school."

From the left came the scream again, beside itself with rage, "Tea! Toast! Me!" The man, as if to himself, said, "Bring my tea and toast to me," and then smiling and looking directly at Rose with active brown eyes, he explained, "My mother has lost her verbs and adjectives. In fact, she has lost all parts of speech except her nouns and pronouns, a very interesting phenomenon. Come in, please," and he put his hand under her elbow with gallant pressure. There was nothing she could do and she stepped inside the vestibule, which had a sweet smell like the taste of Neccos.

"Where shall I put it?" Rose asked.

"Oh, we'll take it right in to Mother, don't you think? What kind is it? A geranium, I hope."

"A bleeding heart."

"Oh," he said, scowling. "Well, we'll have to make the best of it." He tucked her arm in his and bent down toward her. "She likes either geraniums or cut flowers. She has forgotten the names of all the others."

Now that she was so close to him she discovered that it was he who smelled of Neccos and that actually the hall smelled of ordure. There was a rustling like that of stiff silk and the man said, "Excuse me just a minute," and right beside them but still invisible the voice malevolently aped him. He shut the door and there she saw a parrot in a cage on a marble-topped bureau. It regarded her with wicked eyes like a patient maniac.

"I'll bet Waldo here had you buffaloed, didn't he?" said the man with a laugh as he opened the cage and the parrot stepped out on to his wrist with a haughty mutter. "He's a great old bird."

"Hours!" shrieked the voice of the invalid and the man translated for the smug bird, "You have been gone for hours."

Rose, while she could not claim to be really surprised herself, could not adjust herself to the man's unhesitating acceptance of the situation as if they had planned it together some days before. He indicated that she was to precede him down the corridor as if this were the most natural thing in the world, and they went, all three of them, down the slightly veering hall where ghostly pictures hung, and on the way the man said, like a guide, "As you see, we live very simply, Mother and I. The room to your right is the parlor, which we seldom use in winter. Perhaps you observed the portrait on the far wall of that room? An illustrious ancestor. Upstairs there are four bedrooms besides yours truly's. Linen closet, of course, and ample attic space." They paused at a door and he said, secretly as if the parrot were eavesdropping, "I have seen you in the library, you know, Rose." He said her name in a way that the greenest schoolgirl could not have misconstrued and she trembled from head to foot and had to grasp the plant tightly or it would have fallen. His breathing was a little heavy and the parrot, eyeing Rose in the twilight of the hall, gave forth a glottal giggle full of wisdom.

All the low furniture in the invalid woman's room was painted white except for the narrow bed, which was blackish-brown and looked like a catafalque. The bones of the flagging body on it jutted up under a royal purple counterpane. At first only the head and shoulders of the ancient woman showed, but when the small red eyes, witlessly mean with age, saw the parrot, she drew forth a huge piebald hand and her tongue labored on her lip as she said, "Him me."

"Quite like a child," said her son tolerantly as he handed over the parrot, which settled down on her wrist. "The young lady here, Miss Rose, has brought you a plant, Mother. She says it's from the school."

The old woman's fingernails were painted a morbid red and

one of the fingers stroked the parrot's stout yellow talons. Although the woman did not look at her, she said, "Roses. Gratitude."

"No, Mother, not roses. I said this young lady's name was Miss Rose. She has brought a bleeding heart." He added in an exasperated aside, "Not that it matters a hoot in hell what kind of any old thing it is."

The invalid covered Rose with an ambiguous glance and said, "I her."

"I her," repeated her son. "I don't know what she means." He began to take the paper off the plant and growled, "I surely hope she likes it. She surely should. Very thoughtful of the school, to my way of thinking."

"I her," repeated the old woman in a louder voice and the man flushed. Obviously this could signify anything: "I hate her," "I want her to go," or "I have never seen her before." It was a cul-de-sac that could not very well be ignored because she said it over and over and presently Waldo joined with his one sentence and they chanted antiphonally, "I her," "Just a minute," "I her," "Just a minute." While these two obscene creatures on the bed were making a spectacle of themselves, the man was clumsily trying to get the string off the flowerpot and nudging Rose every now and again although he did not need to. There was an awful odor in the room, both medicinal and decayed, and everything looked soiled and moist. The shape of the room and the situation of the furniture were the same as in Rose's room as if in a planned parody.

The man got the knot untied and slipped the paper off and his mother said to the parrot, "Silence," and to her son, "I her bell."

"Of course!" cried the man with relief. "I heard her ring the bell?" And the woman nodded her head up and down with a delighted smile on the thin crescent of her mouth.

He put the bleeding heart on the low white table beside the bed where a Bible lay, conventional and new, and some sticky bottles of medicine and some revolting gobbets of cotton. The other old hand with veins as thick as pencils came staggering out of the bed to pluck a blossom from the plant which it held out for the parrot. The fingernails were the same color as the little flower which disappeared in Waldo's greedy bill.

"Roses. Waldo."

"Yes, Mother," said the man soothingly, "Roses for Waldo." On the wall over the bed hung a sampler that said, "LOOK UPWARD NOT DOWN."

Rose finally found her voice and she said urgently, "I must go." But the man detained her with a soft pat on her arm. "But you haven't had your tea. You must have tea with Mother." Mother was plucking the flowers and feeding them to Waldo very rapidly for one of her years and debility. After each gobble, Waldo ducked his head with villainous coquetry.

"I'm sorry," said Rose, "but I really must go."

He was looking with some consternation at his mother. "I say, you don't think a bleeding heart is toxic, do you? I wouldn't like anything to happen to Waldo."

"I don't know," she said miserably, and to the woman on the bed she said, "Goodbye. I am glad to have met you," although this was a double lie, for she was not glad and there had been no proper meeting.

"Oh, you must have tea!" cried the man and he fingered his yellow ascot nervously as if he could not bear to have her leave. "You must! It isn't often that Mother and I have such a pretty guest." She shivered and buttoned the top button of her coat. "It will only take a minute," he wheedled. "It's on the tray and I just plug in the electric kettle thing and we're all set." He gave himself a private smile and said, "All set and rarin' to go."

She was about to be very firm and cutting if necessary to this tiresome old child by whom she had been so foolishly taken in at the library, but she thought of Miss Talmadge and was afraid if she were discourteous there might be trouble. It could not last long and he could not do anything improper to her in front of his mother and the parrot whose sagacious gaze missed nothing. So she gave in and he drew a rocking chair to the center of the room and beside it he put a bench. "The tray goes here," he said, "and you can pour." And then he left the room, walking out backwards to unnerve her all the more.

The ten minutes he was gone were for Rose a bizarre and separate experience. The old woman and the parrot clucked at one another over the sinister meal of bleeding hearts and but for this there was silence in the darkening room. She was forced to accept the reality of the afternoon, that the man in the yellow ascot lived here and that he drove the electric car and that in no particular did he resemble her image of her foster-father. And it was quite possible to accept it now, but she was apprehensive of the evening to come and the next afternoon when she would meet him again in the Samuel Sewall. There were only two flowers left on the plant and for some reason she hoped that tea would be here before they were gone. She glanced toward the bed; the headboard was just opposite her desk and she knew that she could never again write there with the picture in her mind of the old woman feeding the evil bird. A good deal in her quiet life would be changed. She doubted if she would ever go again to the library on the customary afternoons, for example. She would be free, it is true, to walk once again in the parts of the town and the country she had enjoyed before but this gain was offset by the knowledge that there was no mystery left: she knew exactly where the man lived and, moreover, to her regret, she knew *how* he lived.

The next to the last blossom was gone and then the last was gone and the feeding hand retired under the covers. The old woman looked at Waldo and at Rose and said, "You him." She pretended neither to hear nor to see but stared at the sampler, which had a border of pine cones. A foot surreptitiously moved under the counterpane and Waldo walked off his mistress' hand so that Rose, nauseated, saw that he had not eaten the bleeding hearts at all, but had only mauled them and then had dropped them onto the bed, where they lay in a heap like bloody matter. The command was repeated but she heard her host coming back and she got up to open the door for him. She said, "I think your mother wanted me to take the parrot."

"Oh, did she?" he asked with interest. "That shows she likes you. Yes, sir, that shows you've made a big hit with Mother."

"But I don't like birds," she said.

"Really? How extraordinary! I had a very charming Brazilian oriole to whom I was much attached. Waldo killed her, I never was just sure how."

On the tray were a plate of English muffins and a jar of peanut butter and one of marmalade and a store-bought pound cake and a dish of pickled peaches. There were a can of evaporated milk and a tin of bouillon cubes. This last he picked up, mouthing the words, "This is what she thinks is tea. Isn't allowed tea. A stimulant." Waldo laughed.

It took a long time to prepare the meal. A good deal of furniture had to be moved before the kettle could be plugged in; then he had to go back to the kitchen for spoons which he had forgotten and then for some plates for the pickled peaches. Then he stopped everything when he saw the mess Waldo had made with the flowers and for a moment Rose thought he was going to lose his temper. "Pest!" he said sharply and gave Waldo a baleful look. When everything was ready, the old woman said "Radio," so the lamp had to be unplugged and the radio plugged in and candles had to be lit. The kettle made the radio splutter and creak and Waldo, the everlasting Mr. Fixit, stared at the box and said patiently, "Just a minute." But at last everything was ready and Rose began to pour the tea while the man spread peanut butter on the English muffins. The old woman sucked the bouillon and gave a sip to Waldo now and then.

"I wish she wouldn't do that," said the man, preoccupied with the muffins. "It gives him an intestinal condition."

Rose said politely, "How old is Waldo?"

"Forty-eight," he said. "Quite a character. He used to say some other things. 'I think you're rather foolish' was one and 'Go by-by, Aunt Louisa' was another, but he's lost everything but 'Just a minute.'"

"It is remarkable," said Rose, referring to the habit in this household of mislaying language.

"Yes," he mused, giving her a muffin in his hand. "Yes, Waldo's quite a character. He keeps Mother company. If it weren't for Waldo, I'd never get to have my little afternoons off at the library."

Because there was something in his voice that was not altogether trustworthy, she said, "What does he eat?"

"A special food for parrots," he said. "Called 'Polly's Perfect Preparation.' But he likes fruit too. The trouble with fruit, though, is that it gives him that intestinal condition I alluded to."

Mother finished her bouillon with a hoarse swallow and said, "Time toast."

"Right you are, Mother. Time for toast," and handed her a muffin with marmalade. Returning, he said *sotto voce*, "Time for toast and tea for two, what? Do you often eat at the inn?"

"Oh, no, almost never. Do you?"

"No. Thanksgiving, Christmas, Easter, Patriots' Day, that's all. Not that the cuisine is not to my liking. But I am rather tied here to my poor sick mother. That is to say, I generally dine *en famille*." A note of woe came into his voice: "*En famille* with Waldo."

She could not think of any comment to make on this very sad state of affairs and so she said, "What delicious peanut butter." In point of fact, it was dry and tasteless and the muffin was cold and rubbery. As for the tea, *it* could not be described. She promised herself that she would eat the whole muffin and drink the whole cup of tea and then she would go even if it meant being rude.

"*Is* it delicious peanut butter? Oh, thank you," he said joyfully and from the bed the old woman clamored, "Gratitude!"

The man asked her how she liked Miss Talmadge and if she were ever homesick for the West and if she did not find her room at Number 8 rather chilly when the wind came off the river. He said he imagined she found the fare at the Minute Man café pretty much the same old thing from day to day: swordfish, canned peas, boiled potatoes. It was a little cold for sitting in the cemetery on Sunday afternoon nowadays, wasn't it?

"Lonesome, aren't you, little lady?" he said and Waldo warned from the footboard of the bed, "Just a minute."

She drank the last of the sour tea and returned the cup to the tray. She drew on her gloves and stood up. "Thank you so much for the tea," she said. "It was most kind of you."

The old woman beckoned to her and said, "Time."

"Yes, I know. It's time for me to go." She tried to smile warmly.

"No, no," cried her son anxiously, "she means there's plenty of time."

But Rose would not be detained any longer and she moved toward the door. He was immediately beside her, following her down the hall as long and as dark as a tunnel. Halfway down Waldo came bustling after them and walked between them, laughing busily. The man held Rose's elbow tightly as if by the pressure of his fingers he could communicate the desperate state of his loneliness. "You can't imagine how awful it is," he confided urgently. "Today you only saw her company manners, but you should hear the things she says to me when we're alone." His voice was full of tears. "Rose! Rose, we're near neighbors. Strictly speaking we live in the same house, Rose. Won't you come again?"

"I'll try," she said without any pity at all.

"When?"

"I don't know."

"Tomorrow? Oh, no, tomorrow we meet in the library, don't we? What do you read there?"

She was remote and academic. "I am doing some research work."

"That's wonderful. I knew you were cultured. I went to Harvard. I daresay you've heard of that little old college down Cambridge way?"

He was such a terrible mixture of unattractive qualities that she did not know how his face managed to be so aristocratically handsome. They were at the door now and she put her hand out toward the knob, but he was ahead of her. "Permit me, Rose," he said. "Please greet Miss Talmadge for my mother and me, but don't tell her what happened to the bleeding heart." He grasped her hand in both of his and squeezed it warmly and looking deep into her eyes he whispered, "The Samuel Sewall tomorrow."

She ran down the steps and he called after her, "Rose! My name is Mr. Benson!"

She heard him close the door and at the corner she paused in the snowfall, senseless with misery. She could *not* sleep another night in that room but she had nowhere to go. Tears for her homeless self went down her cheeks with the snowflakes and she let a little sound escape her, the murmur of an unhappy child. And then, because there was nothing else to do, she opened the front door of Number 8 and went into her room. She turned the radio on very loud and got a program of jazz played on an organ and, deafened to any other possible sound, she began to play solitaire, violently slapping the cards down on the table. In this futile tantrum with the cards, she bent a corner of the Queen of Hearts and this reminded her of her father's custom of spending whole winter evenings cleaning a deck of cards with a jackknife. A jackknife which he used, as well, to slice off a plug of chewing tobacco, to trim his fingernails and, in the spring, to dig embedded woodticks out of his skin.

When she came back from her dinner of swordfish at the Minute Man, she found a note on the rug just inside the door which said:

> My dear Rose,
>   If you would care to go to the picture show tonight in Acton, I am at your disposal and wish you would telephone me. My name is in the book. I could come to your door or you could come to mine. Mrs. Morton Ripley is coming to call on Mother. I do not know when another opportunity will offer so hope you will not refuse.
>   Awaiting your communication via telephone,
> I am,
Lucius Benson

There was no sound from the room beyond the wall but the silence was an uneasy one and she shuddered thinking of what might be going on in there. Waldo and his mistress were capable of any sort of monstrous tableau if the demonstration this afternoon with the bleeding heart had not been unusual. She thought of going to the priest to ask for his advice or to the policeman for his protection. In any case, she could not stay here and after a minute of debate she let herself out quietly and went down the street and into the Mill Dam on her way to the library. But she had only just got to the square of lawn in front of it when the electric car eased up alongside her and Mr. Benson leaned across and opened the door.

"Here, here," he gaily cried. "This is no way to treat your Dutch uncle. Climb in! Hop right in, Rosie O'Grady, and off we'll go to the picture show."

"Mr. Benson," she began, giving his derby a hard look, "I can't go to the movies with you tonight."

"Nonsense," he said. "Stuff and nonsense. Hop in, dear, we'll be in time for the newsreel. Good gracious, Rosie, what are you afraid of? Do you mean to say that you're afraid of a harmless old codger, old enough to be your father?"

"No, Mr. Benson," she said, "I'm not afraid of you." And

it was true, she was not afraid, she was only displeased. "But I won't go to the movies."

"Just think of me as your father," he said. "Why don't you call me that as a matter of fact? I mean, not 'Father' but one of the more familiar things like 'Daddy'?"

It was not at all likely, she thought, that this was taking place. It was much too improbable that she was talking under an arc lamp in a snowfall to an elderly roué in an electric car who had invited her to call him Daddy.

"If you won't come with me," he said rather testily, "then I will come into the library and read."

She was at the end of her tether. No longer scared, certainly not respectful of his age, no longer polite for Miss Talmadge's sake, she burst out, "Oh, go to grass," and she scuffled up the snowy path.

"Let me tell you about my Brazilian oriole," he called desperately through the quiet storm. "Waldo killed it out of pure spite! I preferred it to Waldo and Waldo killed it out of spite!"

Rose went on up the path.

"Rose!"

She heard him come running after her but she was not afraid, for the library was brightly lighted. She stopped when he was abreast of her and stamped her foot. "Go away, Mr. Benson," she said.

His head fell forward dejectedly and his beaver-lined coat which was not buttoned hung loosely on him as if he had suddenly shriveled. He was a die-hard. "Oh, Rose," he said, "I assure you I mean no harm." He touched the yellow ascot with the palm of his hand and said, "The most unsightly wen you ever saw. All I am asking is a little pity." He began to undo the scarf as she mounted the steps. When she was within the storm doors, she looked back and saw him standing there in the snow with his neck bare and his arms spread out, his palms upward in supplication. He had flung his head back and his derby had fallen to the ground; he wore the yellow ascot on his left arm like a maniple. Just behind him, the electric car cast an absolutely square shadow on the white ground.

The Lippia Lawn

ALTHOUGH its roots are clever, the trailing arbutus at Deer Lick had been wrenched out by the hogs. Only a few bruised and muddied blossoms still clung to the disordered stems. The old man and I, baskets over our arms, had come looking for good specimens to transplant. It had been a long walk, and Mr. Oliphant was fatigued. Oppressed also with his disappointment, he lowered himself carefully to the ground and sighed.

"They're carnivorous, you know," he said, speaking of the hogs. "They're looking for worms." Everywhere about us, the cloven hoofprints had bitten into the soil, and it was easy to imagine the sow and her retinue lumbering to this place on their preposterously shapely legs, huffing and puffing with incessant appetite. Mr. Oliphant, a man who loved nature in an immense yet ungenerous way, complained as he lay there, shading his eyes against the sunlight that was finely sifted through the hemlock above us. "In town the chickens come to spoil my jonquils, and here the hogs tear up the arbutus. But what good would it do to beg the mountain people to keep their stock at home?"

He was such a spirited and able man that he never seemed old until he commenced to fret, and then, when his deliberate voice became sibilant, I saw how white his hair was and how the flesh of his brown face had been twilled into hundreds of tiny pleats. His large hands, stained with the grime of garden earth, simultaneously became the uncertain, misshapen hands of an aged person. I stopped listening to him and plucked a cluster of trampled blossoms from among the leaves, hoping that my idle twirling of it would make him think I was following what he said. The unvarying tone of his voice made time seem absolute, and absolute, too, became my contemplation of the flower. Once I realized that he had paused. I found myself wanting him to continue, for I was distracted by the ragged petals which, in their revolutions between my fingers, assumed many shapes.

He had only stopped to choose a word, and, having found it, resumed his tirade. I ceased the flower's rotations, and abruptly my rambling daydreams were arrested as the arbutus began to resemble something I had seen before. Although I knew that Mr. Oliphant, a devout horticulturalist, could help me name its cousin, I hesitated to interrupt him lest I interrupt also my own tranquillity. The tenuous memory wove in and out of my thoughts, always tantalizingly just ahead of me. Like the butterfly whose yellow wings are camouflaged to look like sunlight, the flower I could not remember masqueraded as arbutus whenever I had almost discovered it in its native habitat. As I pursued it in the places where I had lived, a voice came back to me. It was not so elusive. Its unique timbre and its accent established it in a particular time, and with only a little research, I found its owner, Fräulein Ströck, my landlady in Heidelberg. She gave me German lessons in exchange for English, and afterward she served me coffee. Of a once fine set, all that remained was the tall pot of white china scattered with pink flowers and minute heart-shaped leaves. I must have complimented her on it, for I recalled her strenuous, elevated reply in English: "No, it makes me very sorry that I do not know the name of the bloom."

Slowly, like a shadow, the past seeped back. A wise scout was reconnoitering for me and at last led me to a place where I never would have looked. The arbutus was larger, pinker, but was something like the lippia that had grown on the lawn when I was a child in California. It was as thick and close to the ground as clover, and it looked like a head of cropped and decorated hair. Under an umbrella tree, I used to sit waiting for the school bus bringing my sisters and my brothers and pretend that the lawn was the ocean at Redondo Beach, and that I could see them coming through the breakers after a long swim. Once, as I ran toward them, the springy earth cool to my feet, I was stung on the ankle by a bee at work in the brilliant sunlight.

Because I was only five years old when we went away, I have never been able to remember much about our ranch. Whenever I think of California, my impressions are confused and ramified with later ones apprehended in Santa Fe, Denver, Chicago, Toledo, and New Orleans. Only a few of my early memories are pure. I can still summon up the taste of oxalis, but whether I ate the stem or the leaf, I cannot say. I remember the day my grandmother came from Santa Barbara, bringing me a pink tatted handbag to carry to Sunday School, but beyond that, all I can reconstruct of my grandmother is her blackthorn walking stick which had belonged to my grandfather, an Irishman. Now and again a random recollection will swim vaguely across my mind, a wisp too ephemeral to detain: a dairy in Covina where we bought Schmierkäse from a German who frightened me by saying that the Bolsheviks would get me because bright red ribbons streamed from my sailor hat; a Mexican's house with a dried mud floor where a girl named Fuchsia made drawn-work doilies and where my brother and I went one Sunday afternoon, instructed by our mother, to say, "Muchas gracias, señorita," for she had sent us a lemon pie. Sometimes I think of a dream I often had of a thousand new pennies heaped up beneath a fig tree. The more I picked up, the more there were, and I cried with impatience because the skirt of my dress was not big enough to hold them all. Sometimes I can see a green glass pig which my brother kept in the china closet, forbidding anyone to touch it. Or suddenly I am standing beside Hana, the Japanese washerwoman, as she lifts the lid of a trunk: the smell of camphor balls is strong as she holds up my mother's pin-striped hobble skirt.

But I remember nothing of the house. From photographs and conversation, I know that my father's den was hung with serapes from Tía Juana and that the floor was covered with deerskins. I know that at the back of the house the grove stretched for eighty acres and that within a south field of chrysanthemums there was a frog pond. But I cannot recall how the fruit looks on an English walnut tree, and the feel and color of those chrysanthemums are spurious, come from later ones I bought or gathered. I can accomplish only a partial reconstruction even of the umbrella tree.

That day in the woods of the Cumberland plateau, the lippia returned unaltered. Tender, fragrant, lavender and white, it extended across a flat and limitless terrain upon which the tree and I, the only altitudes, cast our brief shadows.

"The ground was carpeted with it," said Mr. Oliphant. "Literally carpeted with it, before the mountaineers started digging it up to send off to New York. There used to be a place in the gorge where it grew right out of the rock, but I suppose that's gone too."

He grumbled on as monotonously as the waterfall to our right, reviewing the mountaineers' past offenses and those they would perpetrate in the future. He said it would be his bad luck to come after they had stripped the laurel thicket. They had no respect for nature, he declared, no desire to conserve the beauty of the woods. Why, they were as ruthless as the Visigoths and it was unimaginable to Mr. Oliphant that they should devastate their native soil. "It is my native soil too!" he cried passionately. "They have no right to hurt my share of it!"

He came from city stock, but he had been born here in the mountains. Off and on for seventy years, with an occasional winter in Florida or France, he had lived alone in the flimsy yellow house in the summer resort where he had been born. From September until late May nearly every year, his was the only chimney in the grounds that regularly sent up a tendril of smoke. The village and houses of the mountain people were a mile away, and sometimes, for as long as a week, the only face he saw was his own reflected in the mirror as he shaved. This winter I had shared the settlement of empty cottages with him, but my house was so far from his that even on a clear day he could not hear my radio. Occasionally, he rambled up my front walk, bringing a packet of *tilleul* which he brewed himself on my electric plate.

Mr. Oliphant was not pitiful as friendless old bachelors often are. His innumerable interests and projects kept him perpetually busy. I had encountered him first in the autumn in the woods, where he was gathering mushrooms to dry for winter use. I joined him in the hunt and, as we scrambled over fallen trees and under low branches, he gave me a receipt for making mead and told me how he canned peas in long-necked wine bottles. A few weeks later he summoned me formally through the mail to dine with him. It was late in September and already so cold that we ate beside the fireplace in his cluttered sitting room. He painted in oils and water-colors for his own amusement, and canvases were stacked against every wall, and the room smelled of turpentine and the wood fire. He pointed out his pleasant, untalented pictures of grape hyacinth and wild azalea, and a wavering, ectoplasmic landscape in fog. A gourmet of sorts, he had such reverence for the broiled beefsteak mushrooms, the curried veal and the avocado salad and the home-made sauterne, that we ate in silence. Afterward, he addressed a fluent monologue to me on the repairs he planned for his flagstone walk, his summer house, his roofs and floors. And finally, he took me to his conservatory, as fragrant and luxuriant as a jungle, where all through the winter he nursed his plants. Just as I left the house, he gave me a tin of mingled herbs which he had taken from his glass-windowed cabinet, allowing the smell of basil and thyme to hover in the air a moment.

All winter I saw him roving through the grounds collecting kindling after a wind or an ice storm. Or I saw him, armed with shears and a basket, going to the woods for holly. On fine days, if I called on him, usually I found him working in the pit, fitted with a glass door, where he kept his hydrangeas through the cold months. Early in February he informed me that he had begun negotiating with the mountaineers for fertilizer and that his seed catalogues had arrived. In March, he heard the first flock of wild geese honking over his house, and knowing by this sign that spring was here to stay, he began to get up earlier in the mornings, making use of every hour of daylight to work in his garden.

Nevertheless, people often asked Mr. Oliphant how he put in his time. A look of bewilderment would invade his face and his lips would curve in a tentative smile like that of a child who does not know for a moment whether to laugh or cry. Once he had replied, "Why, I don't know. Seems like there never *is* enough time."

His character was not arresting, and his continual murmuring, which amounted to a persecution mania, was tedious. He had done nothing noteworthy in his life; his religion was of the scantiest and most sentimental. He was not charming, and his information, beyond flowers and food and weather, was banal. But I admired him, for there was something deep about him, a subtle vitality that resided in his fingertips and his eyes which enabled him to make anything flourish in the sour mountain soil and to detect to the hour the coming of frost or rain or wind. I had wondered why he chose to live in a place so inimical to gardening, and he had replied, "If I moved, I'd lose all the years I've spent learning my land."

He was saying, "You might make out that I had no room to talk the way I dig up flowers myself to put in my garden. But

I maintain there's a world of difference between transplanting something and uprooting it to send off to New York City. I don't know what gets into people to make them take and tear things up."

I had been silent for so long that I felt obliged to speak, and I said, "Mr. Oliphant, this trailing arbutus reminds me of a flower I used to know as a child. Have you ever seen lippia?"

"Lippia? No'm, I've never heard of it." He allowed his eyes to rest on my face for the briefest moment as though a sudden curiosity about me had stirred in him. But he immediately looked away. "I reckon a hundred and fifty years ago my kin were coming here for salt."

On our walk, he had told me that the deer, the Indians and the pioneers had been drawn here by the excrescences of salt in the gorge, from which the name, Deer Lick, had been taken. To our right, the chasm dropped a hundred feet. At the head of it, to our left, the waterfall, almost as high, crashed down, furious and swollen with heavy spring rains. We were on a triangular promontory halfway between the walls. Mr. Oliphant had said that here had been found the thighbone of a prehistoric animal that had been big enough to be used as a tent pole. Colossal, aged hemlocks crowded the wild slopes.

I would have asked the old man about his pioneer ancestors, but he had already reverted to the arbutus. "Hard as it is to get it to grow, I just had the feeling this spring I'd succeed. If I was younger, I'd look for that other patch I was telling you about."

His voice was so senile that, although I knew he was as nimble almost as I, I got to my feet and said, "If you'll tell me the way, I'll try to find it for you, Mr. Oliphant."

"That's mighty obliging of you," he said with a smile. "You follow the path through the laurel and go a little beyond a big flat rock. You start going down there, and that arbutus used to grow under a ledge just beyond the first hemlock."

I took the knife and trowel he offered me and set out. Long thorny vines clutched at my dress and stockings and the laurel branches whipped my face. The path was obscure and, though it was only March, the brush was green enough for midsummer. But the autumn leaves, blackened by the winter's wetness, were still deep. I found the flat rock, surrounded by blueberry bushes on which the last year's fruit was dry and rusty. From here, the roar of the waterfall was thunderous, and from here I could see far down into the lower chasm. A straight wall of gray and pinkish rock rose sheer to the cloudless sky, and against it were patterned the blue-green feathers of the hemlocks.

After the rock, the going was difficult, and twice I slipped on the wet leaves and only kept my balance by seizing old roots and rocks. Mr. Oliphant's directions had been precise. I stooped under the low-hanging branch of the first hemlock and, when I straightened up again, I saw the arbutus growing in a shelf, shadowed by a roof of violet stone. The fragile flowers, nudging clean dark leaves, were refined, like something painted on china.

When I knelt down to uproot the plant, though, I found I was dealing with nothing frail. Its long, tough sinews branched under the ground far in every direction, grasping the earth so tightly that when I tugged at the main root, no more than the subsidiary tentacles came loose, and with them came great clods of black earth, leaving triangular gouges in the ground. The root did not go deep; instead, it crept just under the surface, but it was so long that my fingertips could not even guess where it ended, and the vine was confused with fern and low weeds, making it impossible to trace the stubborn filament so as to dig around it with the knife and trowel. I pulled again. It was as though the root was instinct with will. There was something so monstrous in its determination to remain where it grew that sweat, not from exertion but from alarm, streamed from my face, and the broken leaves were pasted to my wet fingers. Something prevented me from cutting it, not only my fear that this was the incorrect procedure, but a sort of inexplicable revulsion at the thought that the knife might not cleave through.

My labor was barely visible when I stood up. I knew that when I told Mr. Oliphant it was gone, I should be obliged to hear his droning tantrum all the way home. But I neither could nor would carry back to him that violent artery and its deceptively dainty flowers.

It was a little cooler now, and the sun was beginning to go down. Narrowing my eyes to shut out from their corners the chasm and the trees, I had a last look at the trailing arbutus and saw that it hardly resembled the lippia at all, or rather, that the lippia had faded away so completely that its name was all I could remember. As though I were being watched, as though some alert ear were cocked to the slightest noise I should make, swiftly, as quietly as possible, I ascended the path. When I had passed the rock, I ran through the blueberries. Halfway through the laurel thicket I stopped and rested, then went slowly so that Mr. Oliphant would not see I was out of breath.

He was lying where I had left him. His wiry old legs in blue jeans were set on the needle-littered ground, bent at the knee, with the long feet in sneakers resting firmly in the pockets he had scooped out for them. Although his eyes were closed, his face wore an attentive look as if all his other senses were still active. As I stepped forward into the clearing, he at once sprang up, not at the sound of my footfall but at the low grunting of a lubberly black boar that came trotting along the path, its snout close to the ground. Mr. Oliphant flung up his arms and screamed imprecations at the creature that came on, oblivious. He reached down and picked up a stone, hurled it, and the hog, clipped on the shoulder, turned and ran squealing, its coiled tail bobbing.

The rout, though it was complete, did not satisfy the old man, and for some minutes he gesticulated and cried out, seemed actually to dance with rage. My gaze descended to his feet. They had not moved from the holds prepared for them, as if they shared the zealous intelligence of their master and of the trailing arbutus and of all beings that resist upheaval and defy invasion. Flushed and shaking, he cried out to me, "It's a crime, I tell you! When I was a boy this place was Eden!"

With quick, juvenile blue eyes he glanced around, and I knew that in that moment he was seeing the place as it had been when he first came here, sixty years ago. I envied him the clarity of his vision. I envied him his past when, pacified for a moment, he said gently, "Anyhow, a man can call the old things to mind."

He turned and led the way down the path. In the silence that had fallen upon us, his words repeated themselves to my disquieted mind, like a phrase of music once admired and now detested.

The Interior Castle

P ANSY Vanneman, injured in an automobile accident, often
woke up before dawn when the night noises of the hospital
still came, in hushed hurry, through her half-open door. By
day, when the nurses talked audibly with the internes, laughed
without inhibition, and took no pains to soften their footsteps
on the resounding composition floors, the routine of the hospital seemed as bland and commonplace as that of a bank or a
factory. But in the dark hours, the whispering and the quickly
stilled clatter of glasses and basins, the moans of patients whose
morphine was wearing off, the soft squeak of a stretcher as it
rolled past on its way from the emergency ward—these suggested agony and death. Thus, on the first morning, Pansy had
faltered to consciousness long before daylight and had found
herself in a ward from every bed of which, it seemed to her,
came the bewildered protest of someone about to die. A caged
light burned on the floor beside the bed next to hers. Her
neighbor was dying and a priest was administering Extreme
Unction. He was stout and elderly and he suffered from asthma
so that the struggle of his breathing, so close to her, was the
basic pattern and all the other sounds were superimposed upon
it. Two middle-aged men in overcoats knelt on the floor beside
the high bed. In a foreign tongue, the half-gone woman bab-
bled against the hissing and sighing of the Latin prayers. She
played with her rosary as if it were a toy: she tried, and failed,
to put it into her mouth.

Pansy felt horror, but she felt no pity. An hour or so later,
when the white ceiling lights were turned on and everything—faces, counterpanes, and the hands that groped upon
them—was transformed into a uniform gray sordor, the woman
was wheeled away in her bed to die somewhere else, in privacy.
Pansy did not quite take this in, although she stared for a long
time at the new, empty bed that had replaced the other.

The next morning, when she again woke up before the light,
this time in a private room, she recalled the woman with such
sorrow that she might have been a friend. Simultaneously,
she mourned the driver of the taxicab in which she had been

injured, for he had died at about noon the day before. She had been told this as she lay on a stretcher in the corridor, waiting to be taken to the X-ray room; an interne, passing by, had paused and smiled down at her and had said, "Your cab driver is dead. You were lucky."

Six weeks after the accident, she woke one morning just as daylight was showing on the windows as a murky smear. It was a minute or two before she realized why she was so reluctant to be awake, why her uneasiness amounted almost to alarm. Then she remembered that her nose was to be operated on today. She lay straight and motionless under the seersucker counterpane. Her blood-red eyes in her darned face stared through the window and saw a frozen river and leafless elm trees and a grizzled esplanade where dogs danced on the ends of leashes, their bundled-up owners stumbling after them, half blind with sleepiness and cold. Warm as the hospital room was, it did not prevent Pansy from knowing, as keenly as though she were one of the walkers, how very cold it was outside. Each twig of a nearby tree was stark. Cold red brick buildings nudged the low-lying sky which was pale and inert like a punctured sac.

In six weeks, the scene had varied little: there was promise in the skies neither of sun nor of snow; no red sunsets marked these days. The trees could neither die nor leaf out again. Pansy could not remember another season in her life so constant, when the very minutes themselves were suffused with the winter pallor as they dropped from the moon-faced clock in the corridor. In the same way, her room accomplished no alterations from day to day. On the glass-topped bureau stood two potted plants telegraphed by faraway well-wishers. They did not fade, and if a leaf turned brown and fell, it soon was replaced; so did the blossoms renew themselves. The roots, like the skies and like the bare trees, seemed zealously determined to maintain a status quo. The bedside table, covered every day with a clean white towel, though the one removed was always immaculate, was furnished sparsely with a water glass, a bent drinking tube, a sweating pitcher, and a stack of paper handkerchiefs. There were a few letters in the drawer, a hairbrush, a pencil, and some postal cards on which, from time to time, she wrote brief messages to relatives and friends: "Dr. Nash says that my reflexes are shipshape (*sic*) and Dr. Rivers says the frontal fracture has all but healed and that the occipital is coming along nicely. Dr. Nicholas, the nose doctor, promises to operate as soon as Dr. Rivers gives him the go-ahead sign (*sic*)."

The bed itself was never rumpled. Once fretful and now convalescent, Miss Vanneman might have been expected to toss or to turn the pillows or to unmoor the counterpane; but hour after hour and day after day she lay at full length and would not even suffer the nurses to raise the headpiece of the adjustable bed. So perfect and stubborn was her body's immobility that it was as if the room and the landscape, mortified by the ice, were extensions of herself. Her resolute quiescence and her disinclination to talk, the one seeming somehow to proceed from the other, resembled, so the nurses said, a final coma. And they observed, in pitying indignation, that she might as *well* be dead for all the interest she took in life. Among themselves they scolded her for what they thought a moral weakness: an automobile accident, no matter how serious, was not reason enough for anyone to give up the will to live or to be happy. She had not—to come down bluntly to the facts—had the decency to be grateful that it was the driver of the cab and not she who had died. (And how dreadfully the man had died!) She was twenty-five years old and she came from a distant city. These were really the only facts known about her. Evidently she had not been here long, for she had no visitors, a lack which was at first sadly moving to the nurses but which became to them a source of unreasonable annoyance: had anyone the right to live so one-dimensionally? It was impossible to laugh at her, for she said nothing absurd; her demands could not be complained of because they did not exist; she could not be hated for a sharp tongue nor for a supercilious one; she could not be admired for bravery or for wit or for interest in her fellow creatures. She was believed to be a frightful snob.

Pansy, for her part, took a secret and mischievous pleasure in the bewilderment of her attendants and the more they courted her with offers of magazines, crossword puzzles, and a radio that she could rent from the hospital, the farther she retired from them into herself and into the world which she had created in her long hours here and which no one could ever penetrate nor imagine. Sometimes she did not even answer the nurses' questions; as they rubbed her back with alcohol and steadily discoursed, she was as remote from them as if she were miles away. She did not think that she lived on a higher plane than that of the nurses and the doctors but that she lived on a different one and that at this particular time—this time of exploration and habituation—she had no extra strength to spend on making herself known to them. All she had been before and all the memories she might have brought out to disturb the monotony of, say, the morning bath, and all that the past meant to the future when she would leave the hospital, were of no present consequence to her. Not even in her thoughts did she employ more than a minimum of memory. And when she did remember, it was in flat pictures, rigorously independent of one another: she saw her thin, poetic mother who grew thinner and more poetic in her canvas deck chair at Saranac reading *Lalla Rookh*. She saw herself in an inappropriate pink hat drinking iced tea in a garden so oppressive with the smell of phlox that the tea itself tasted of it. She recalled an afternoon in autumn in Vermont when she had heard three dogs' voices in the north woods and she could tell, by the characteristic minor key struck three times at intervals, like bells from several churches, that they had treed something: the eastern sky was pink and the trees on the horizon looked like some eccentric vascular system meticulously drawn on colored paper.

What Pansy thought of all the time was her own brain. Not only the brain as the seat of consciousness, but the physical organ itself which she envisaged, romantically, now as a jewel, now as a flower, now as a light in a glass, now as an envelope of rosy vellum containing other envelopes, one within the other, diminishing infinitely. It was always pink and always fragile, always deeply interior and invaluable. She believed that she had reached the innermost chamber of knowledge and that perhaps her knowledge was the same as the saint's achievement of pure love. It was only convention, she thought, that made one say "sacred heart" and not "sacred brain."

Often, but never articulately, the color pink troubled her and the picture of herself in the wrong hat hung steadfastly before her mind's eye. None of the other girls had worn hats, and since autumn had come early that year, they were dressed in green and rusty brown and dark yellow. Poor Pansy wore a white eyelet frock with a lacing of black ribbon around the square neck.

When she came through the arch, overhung with bittersweet, and saw that they had not yet heard her, she almost turned back, but Mr. Oliver was there and she was in love with him. She was in love with him though he was ten years older than she and had never shown any interest in her beyond asking her once, quite fatuously but in an intimate voice, if the yodeling of the little boy who peddled clams did not make her wish to visit Switzerland. Actually, there was more to this question than met the eye, for some days later Pansy learned that Mr. Oliver, who was immensely rich, kept an apartment in Geneva. In the garden that day, he spoke to her only once. He said, "My dear, you look exactly like something out of Katherine Mansfield," and immediately turned and within her hearing asked Beatrice Sherburne to dine with him that night at the Country Club. Afterward, Pansy went down to the sea and threw the beautiful hat onto the full tide and saw it vanish in the wake of a trawler. Thereafter, when she heard the clam boy coming down the road, she locked the door and when the knocking had stopped and her mother called down from her chaise longue, "Who was it, dearie?" she replied, "A salesman."

It was only the fact that the hat had been pink that worried her. The rest of the memory was trivial, for she knew that she could never again love anything as ecstatically as she loved the spirit of Pansy Vanneman, enclosed within her head.

But her study was not without distraction, and she fought two adversaries: pain and Dr. Nicholas. Against Dr. Nicholas, she defended herself valorously and in fear; but pain, the pain, that is, that was independent of his instruments, she sometimes forced upon herself adventurously like a child scaring himself in a graveyard.

Dr. Nicholas greatly admired her crushed and splintered nose which he daily probed and peered at, exclaiming that he had never seen anything like it. His shapely hands ached for their knives; he was impatient with the skull-fracture man's cautious delay. He spoke of "our" nose and said "we" would be a new person when we could breathe again. His own nose was magnificent. Not even his own brilliant surgery could have improved upon it nor could a first-rate sculptor have duplicated its direct downward line which permitted only the least curvature inward toward the end; or the delicately rounded lateral declivities; or the thin-walled, perfectly matched nostrils.

Miss Vanneman did not doubt his humaneness or his talent—he was a celebrated man—but she questioned whether he had imagination. Immediately beyond the prongs of his speculum lay her treasure whose price he, no more than the nurses, could estimate. She believed he could not destroy it, but she feared that he might maim it: might leave a scratch on one of the brilliant facets of the jewel, bruise a petal of the flower, smudge the glass where the light burned, blot the envelopes, and that then she would die or would go mad. While she did not question that in either eventuality her brain would after a time redeem its original impeccability, she did not quite yet wish to enter upon either kind of eternity, for she was not certain that she could carry with her her knowledge as well as its receptacle.

Blunderer that he was, Dr. Nicholas was an honorable enemy, not like the demon, pain, which skulked in a thousand guises within her head, and which often she recklessly willed to attack her and then drove back in terror. After the rout, sweat streamed from her face and soaked the neck of the coarse hospital shirt. To be sure, it came usually of its own accord, running like a wild fire through all the convolutions to fill with flame the small sockets and ravines and then, at last, to withdraw, leaving behind a throbbing and an echo. On these occasions, she was as helpless as a tree in a wind. But at the other times when, by closing her eyes and rolling up the eyeballs in such a way that she fancied she looked directly on the place where her brain was, the pain woke sluggishly and came toward her at a snail's pace. Then, bit by bit, it gained speed. Sometimes it faltered back, subsided altogether, and then it rushed like a tidal wave driven by a hurricane, lashing and roaring until she lifted her hands from the counterpane, crushed her broken teeth into her swollen lip, stared in panic at the soothing walls with her ruby eyes, stretched out her legs until she felt their bones must snap. Each cove, each narrow inlet, every living bay was flooded and the frail brain, a little hat-shaped boat, was washed from its mooring and set adrift. The skull was as vast as the world and the brain was as small as a seashell.

Then came calm weather and the safe journey home. She kept vigil for a while, though, and did not close her eyes, but gazing serenely at the trees, conceived of the pain as the guardian of her treasure who would not let her see it; that was why she was handled so savagely whenever she turned her eyes inward. Once this watch was interrupted: by chance she looked into the corridor and saw a shaggy mop slink past the door, followed by a senile porter. A pair of ancient eyes, as rheumy as an old dog's, stared uncritically in at her and a toothless mouth formed a brutish word. She was so surprised that she immediately closed her eyes to shut out the shape of the word and the pain dug up the unmapped regions of her head with mattocks, ludicrously huge. It was the familiar pain, but this time, even as she endured it, she observed with detachment that its effect upon her was less than that of its contents, the by-products, for example, of temporal confusion and the bizarre misapplication of the style of one sensation to another. At the moment, for example, although her brain reiterated to her that *it* was being assailed, she was stroking her right wrist with her left hand as though to assuage the ache, long since dispelled, of the sprain in the joint. Some minutes after she had opened her eyes and left off soothing her wrist, she lay rigid, experiencing the sequel to the pain, an ideal terror. For, as before on several occasions, she was overwhelmed with the knowledge that the pain had been consummated in the vessel of her mind and for the moment the vessel was unbeautiful: she thought, quailing, of those plastic folds as palpable as the fingers of locked hands containing in their very cells, their fissures, their repulsive hemispheres, the mind, the soul, the inscrutable intelligence.

The porter, then, like the pink hat and like her mother and the hounds' voices, loitered with her.

Dr. Nicholas came at nine o'clock to prepare her for the operation. With him came an entourage of white-frocked acolytes, and one of them wheeled in a wagon on which lay knives and scissors and pincers, cans of swabs and gauze. In the midst of these was a bowl of liquid whose rich purple color made it seem strange like the brew of an alchemist.

"All set?" the surgeon asked her, smiling. "A little nervous, what? I don't blame you. I've often said I'd rather break a leg than have a submucous resection." Pansy thought for a moment he was going to touch his nose. His approach to her was roundabout. He moved through the yellow light shed by the globe in the ceiling which gave his forehead a liquid gloss; he paused by the bureau and touched a blossom of the cyclamen; he looked out the window and said, to no one and to all, "I couldn't start my car this morning. Came in a cab." Then he came forward. As he came, he removed a speculum from the pocket of his short-sleeved coat and like a cat, inquiring of the nature of a surface with its paws, he put out his hand toward her and drew it back, gently murmuring, "You must not be afraid, my dear. There is no danger, you know. Do you think for a minute I would operate if there were?"

Dr. Nicholas, young, brilliant, and handsome, was an aristocrat, a husband, a father, a clubman, a Christian, a kind counselor, and a trustee of his preparatory school. Like many of the medical profession, even those whose specialty was centered on the organ of the basest sense, he interested himself in the psychology of his patients: in several instances, for example, he had found that severe attacks of sinusitis were coincident with emotional crises. Miss Vanneman more than ordinarily captured his fancy since her skull had been fractured and her behavior throughout had been so extraordinary that he felt he was observing at first hand some of the results of shock, that incommensurable element, which frequently were too subtle to see. There was, for example, the matter of her complete passivity during a lumbar puncture, reports of which were written down in her history and were enlarged upon for him by Dr. Rivers' interne who had been in charge. Except for a tremor in her throat and a deepening of pallor, there were no signs at all that she was aware of what was happening to her. She made no sound, did not close her eyes nor clench her fists. She had had several punctures; her only reaction had been to the very first one, the morning after she had been brought in. When the interne explained to her that he was going to drain off cerebrospinal fluid which was pressing against her brain, she exclaimed, "My God!" but it was not an exclamation of fear. The young man had been unable to name what it was he had heard in her voice; he could only say that it had not been fear as he had observed it in other patients.

Dr. Nicholas wondered about her. There was no way of guessing whether she had always had a nature of so tolerant and undemanding a complexion. It gave him a melancholy pleasure to think that before her accident she had been high-spirited and loquacious; he was moved to think that perhaps she had been a beauty and that when she had first seen her face in the looking glass she had lost all joy in herself. It was very difficult to tell what the face had been, for it was so bruised and swollen, so hacked-up and lopsided. The black stitches the length of the nose, across the saddle, across the cheekbone, showed that there would be unsightly scars. He had ventured once to give her the name of a plastic surgeon but she had only replied with a vague, refusing smile. He had hoisted a manly shoulder and said, "You're the doctor."

Much as he pondered, coming to no conclusions, about what went on inside that pitiable skull, he was, of course, far more interested in the nose, deranged so badly that it would require his topmost skill to restore its functions to it. He would be obliged not only to make a submucous resection, a simple run-of-the-mill operation, but to remove the vomer, always a delicate task but further complicated in this case by the proximity of the bone to the frontal fracture line which conceivably was not entirely closed. If it were not and he operated too soon and if a cold germ then found its way into the opening, his patient would be carried off by meningitis in the twinkling of an eye. He wondered if she knew in what potential danger she lay; he desired to assure her that he had brought his craft to its nearest perfection and that she had nothing to fear of him, but feeling that she was perhaps both ignorant and unimaginative and that such consolation would create a fear rather than dispel one, he held his tongue and came nearer to the bed.

Watching him, Pansy could already feel the prongs of his pliers opening her nostrils for the insertion of his fine probers. The pain he caused her with his instruments was of a different kind from that she felt unaided: it was a naked, clean, and vivid pain that made her faint and ill and made her wish to die. Once she had fainted as he ruthlessly explored and after she was brought around, he continued until he had finished his investigation. The memory of this outrage had afterward several times made her cry.

This morning she looked at him and listened to him with hatred. Fixing her eyes upon the middle of his high, protuberant brow, she imagined the clutter behind it and she despised its obtuse imperfection. In his bland unawareness, this nobody, this nose-bigot, was about to play with fire and she wished him ill.

He said, "I can't blame you. No, I expect you're not looking forward to our little party. But you'll be glad to be able to breathe again."

He stationed his lieutenants. The interne stood opposite him on the left side of the bed. The surgical nurse wheeled the wagon within easy reach of his hands and stood beside it. Another nurse stood at the foot of the bed. A third drew the shades at the windows and attached a blinding light that shone down on the patient hotly, and then she left the room, softly closing the door. Pansy stared at the silver ribbon tied in a great bow round the green crepe paper of one of the flowerpots. It made her realize for the first time that one of the days she had lain here had been Christmas, but she had no time to consider this strange and thrilling fact, for Dr. Nicholas was genially explaining his anesthetic. He would soak packs of gauze in the purple fluid, a cocaine solution, and he would place them then in her nostrils, leaving them there for an hour. He warned her that the packing would be disagreeable (he did not say "painful") but that it would be well worth a few minutes of discomfort not to be in the least sick after the operation. He asked her if she were ready and when she nodded her head, he adjusted the mirror on his forehead and began.

At the first touch of his speculum, Pansy's fingers mechanically bent to the palms of her hands and she stiffened. He said, "A pack, Miss Kennedy," and Pansy closed her eyes. There was a rush of plunging pain as he drove the sodden gobbet of gauze high up into her nose and something bitter burned in her throat so that she retched. The doctor paused a moment and the surgical nurse wiped Pansy's mouth. He returned to her with another pack, pushing it with his bodkin doggedly until it lodged against the first. Stop! Stop! cried all her nerves, wailing along the surface of her skin. The coats that covered them were torn off and they shuddered like naked people screaming, Stop! Stop! But Dr. Nicholas did not hear. Time and again he came back with a fresh pack and did not pause at all until one nostril was finished. She opened her eyes and saw him wipe the sweat off his forehead and saw the dark interne bending over her, fascinated. Miss Kennedy bathed her temples in ice water and Dr. Nicholas said, "There. It won't be much longer. I'll tell them to send you some coffee, though I'm afraid you won't be able to taste it. Ever drink coffee with chicory in it? I have no use for it."

She snatched at his irrelevancy and, though she had never tasted chicory, she said severely, "I love it."

Dr. Nicholas chuckled. "De gustibus. Ready? A pack, Miss Kennedy."

The second nostril was harder to pack since the other side was now distended and this passage was anyhow much narrower, as narrow, he had once remarked, as that in the nose of an infant. In such pain as passed all language and even the farthest fetched analogies, she turned her eyes inward, thinking that under the obscuring cloak of the surgeon's pain she could see her brain without the knowledge of its keeper. But Dr. Nicholas and his aides would give her no peace. They surrounded her with their murmuring and their foot-shuffling and the rustling of their starched uniforms, and her eyelids continually flew back in embarrassment and mistrust. She was claimed entirely by this present, meaningless pain and suddenly and sharply she forgot what she had meant to do. She was aware of nothing but her ascent to the summit of something; what it was she did not know, whether it was a tower or a peak or Jacob's ladder. Now she was an abstract word, now she was a theorem of geometry, now she was a kite flying, a top spinning, a prism flashing, a kaleidoscope turning.

But none of the others in the room could see inside and when the surgeon was finished, the nurse at the foot of the bed said, "Now you must take a look in the mirror. It's simply too comical." And they all laughed intimately like old, fast friends. She smiled politely and looked at her reflection: over the gruesomely fattened snout, her scarlet eyes stared in fixed reproach upon her upturned lips, gray with bruises. But even in its smile of betrayal, the mouth itself was puzzled: it reminded her that something had been left behind, but she could not recall what it was. She was hollowed out and was as dry as a white bone.

They strapped her ankles to the operating table and put leather nooses round her wrists. Over her head was a mirror with a thousand facets in which she saw a thousand travesties of her face. At her right side was the table, shrouded in white, where lay the glittering blades of the many knives, thrusting out fitful rays of light. All the cloth was frosty; everything was white or silver and as cold as snow. Dr. Nicholas, a tall snowman with silver eyes and silver fingernails, came into the room soundlessly, for he walked on layers and layers of snow that deadened his footsteps; behind him came the interne, a smaller snowman, less impressively proportioned. At the foot of the table, a snow figure put her frozen hands upon Pansy's helpless feet. The doctor plucked the packs from the cold, numb nose. His laugh was like a cry on a bitter, still night: "I will show you now," he called across the expanse of snow, "that you can feel nothing." The pincers bit at nothing, snapped at the air and cracked a nerveless icicle. Pansy called back and heard her own voice echo: "I feel nothing."

Here the walls were gray, not tan. Suddenly the face of the nurse at the foot of the table broke apart and Pansy first thought it was in grief. But it was a smile and she said, "Did you enjoy your coffee?" Down the gray corridors of the maze, the words rippled, ran like mice, birds, broken beads: Did you enjoy your coffee? your coffee? your coffee? Similarly once in another room that also had gray walls, the same voice had said, "Shall I give her some whisky?" She was overcome with gratitude that this young woman (how pretty she was with her white hair and her white face and her china-blue eyes!) had been with her that first night and was with her now.

In the great stillness of the winter, the operation began. The knives carved snow. Pansy was happy. She had been given a hypnotic just before they came to fetch her and she would have gone to sleep had she not enjoyed so much this trickery of Dr. Nicholas' whom now she tenderly loved.

There was a clock in the operating room and from time to time she looked at it. An hour passed. The snowman's face was melting; drops of water hung from his fine nose, but his silver eyes were as bright as ever. Her love was returned, she knew: he loved her nose exactly as she loved his knives. She looked at her face in the domed mirror and saw how the blood had streaked

her lily-white cheeks and had stained her shroud. She returned
to the private song: Did you enjoy your coffee? your coffee?

At the half-hour, a murmur, anguine and slumbrous, came to
her and only when she had repeated the words twice did they
engrave their meaning upon her. Dr. Nicholas said, "Stand back
now, nurse. I'm at this girl's brain and I don't want my elbow
jogged." Instantly Pansy was alive. Her strapped ankles arched
angrily; her wrists strained against their bracelets. She jerked
her head and she felt the pain flare; she had made the knife slip.

"Be still!" cried the surgeon. "Be quiet, please!"

He had made her remember what it was she had lost when
he had rammed his gauze into her nose: she bustled like a
housewife to shut the door. She thought, I must hurry before
the robbers come. It would be like the time Mother left the
cellar door open and the robber came and took, of all things,
the terrarium.

Dr. Nicholas was whispering to her. He said, in the voice of
a lover, "If you can stand it five minutes more, I can perform
the second operation now and you won't have to go through
this again. What do you say?"

She did not reply. It took her several seconds to remember
why it was her mother had set such store by the terrarium and
then it came to her that the bishop's widow had brought her
an herb from Palestine to put in it.

The interne said, "You don't want to have your nose packed
again, do you?"

The surgical nurse said, "She's a good patient, isn't she, sir?"

"Never had a better," replied Dr. Nicholas. "But don't call
me 'sir.' You must be a Canadian to call me 'sir.'"

The nurse at the foot of the bed said, "I'll order some more
coffee for you."

"How about it, Miss Vanneman?" said the doctor. "Shall I
go ahead?"

She debated. Once she had finally fled the hospital and fled
Dr. Nicholas, nothing could compel her to come back. Still,
she knew that the time would come when she could no longer
live in seclusion, she must go into the world again and must be
equipped to live in it; she banally acknowledged that she must
be able to breathe. And finally, though the world to which

she would return remained unreal, she gave the surgeon her permission.

He had now to penetrate regions that were not anesthetized and this he told her frankly, but he said that there was no danger at all. He apologized for the slip of the tongue he had made: in point of fact, he had not been near her brain, it was only a figure of speech. He began. The knives ground and carved and curried and scoured the wounds they made; the scissors clipped hard gristle and the scalpels chipped off bone. It was as if a tangle of tiny nerves were being cut dexterously, one by one; the pain writhed spirally and came to her who was a pink bird and sat on the top of a cone. The pain was a pyramid made of a diamond; it was an intense light; it was the hottest fire, the coldest chill, the highest peak, the fastest force, the furthest reach, the newest time. It possessed nothing of her but its one infinitesimal scene: beyond the screen as thin as gossamer, the brain trembled for its life, hearing the knives hunting like wolves outside, sniffing and snapping. Mercy! Mercy! cried the scalped nerves.

At last, miraculously, she turned her eyes inward tranquilly. Dr. Nicholas had said, "The worst is over. I am going to work on the floor of your nose," and at his signal she closed her eyes and this time and this time alone she saw her brain lying in a shell-pink satin case. It was a pink pearl, no bigger than a needle's eye, but it was so beautiful and so pure that its smallness made no difference. Anyhow, as she watched, it grew. It grew larger and larger until it was an enormous bubble that contained the surgeon and the whole room within its rosy luster. In a long-ago summer, she had often been absorbed by the spectacle of flocks of yellow birds that visited a cedar tree and she remembered that everything that summer had been some shade of yellow. One year of childhood, her mother had frequently taken her to have tea with an aged schoolmistress upon whose mantelpiece there was a herd of ivory elephants; that had been the white year. There was a green spring when early in April she had seen a grass snake on a boulder, but the very summer that followed was violet, for vetch took her mother's garden. She saw a swatch of blue tulle lying in a raffia basket on the front porch of Uncle Marion's brown house. Never before had the world been pink, whatever else it had

been. Or had it been, one other time? She could not be sure
and she did not care. Of one thing she was certain: never had
the world enclosed her before and never had the quiet been so
smooth.

For only a moment the busybodies left her to her ecstasy
and then, impatient and gossiping, they forced their way inside,
slashed at her resisting trance with questions and congratulations, with statements of fact and jokes. "Later," she said to
them dumbly. "Later on, perhaps. I am busy now." But their
voices would not go away. They touched her, too, washing her
face with cloths so cold they stung, stroking her wrists with
firm, antiseptic fingers. The surgeon, squeezing her arm with
avuncular pride, said, "Good girl," as if she were a bright dog
that had retrieved a bone. Her silent mind abused him: "You
are a thief," it said, "you are heartless and you should be put
to death." But he was leaving, adjusting his coat with an air of
vainglory, and the interne, abject with admiration, followed
him from the operating room, smiling like a silly boy.

Shortly after they took her back to her room, the weather
changed, not for the better. Momentarily the sun emerged
from its concealing murk, but in a few minutes the snow came
with a wind that promised a blizzard. There was great pain, but
since it could not serve her, she rejected it and she lay as if in a
hammock in a pause of bitterness. She closed her eyes, shutting
herself up within her treasureless head.

COWBOYS AND INDIANS,
AND MAGIC MOUNTAINS

The Healthiest Girl in Town

IN 1924, when I was eight years old, my father died and my mother and I moved from Ohio to a high Western town, which, because of its salubrious sun and its astringent air, was inhabited principally by tuberculars who had come there from the East and the South in the hope of cure, or at least of a little prolongation of their static, cautious lives. And those of the town who were not invalids, or the wives, husbands, or children of invalids, were, even so, involved in this general state of things and conversant with its lore. Some of them ran boarding houses for the ambulatory invalids ("the walkers," as we called them) and many were in the employ of the sanitarium which was the *raison d'être* of the community, while others were hired privately as cooks, chauffeurs, or secretaries by people who preferred to rent houses rather than submit to the regulations of an institutional life. My mother was a practical nurse and had come there because there were enough people to need her services and therefore to keep a roof over our heads and shoes on our feet.

My contemporaries took for granted all the sickness and dying that surrounded us—most of them had had a first-hand acquaintance with it—but I did not get used to these people who carried the badge of their doom in their pink cheeks as a blind man carries his white stick in his hand. I continued to be fearful and fascinated each time I met a walker in the streets or on the mountain trails and each time some friend's father, half gone in the lungs, watched me from where he sat in enforced ease on the veranda as other girls and I played pom-pom-pulla-way in his front yard. Once Dotty MacKensie's father, who was soon to die, laughed when I, showing off, turned a cartwheel, and he cried, "Well done, Jessie!" and was taken thereupon with the last awful cough that finally was to undo and kill him. I did not trust their specious look of health and their look of immoderate cleanliness. At the same time, I was unduly drawn to them in the knowledge that a mystery encased them delicately; their death was an interior integument that seemed to lie just under their sun-tanned skin. They spoke softly and their manners were courteous and kind, as if they must live hushed and on tiptoe, lest the bacilli awaken and muster for the kill. Occasionally, my mother was summoned in the middle of the night to attend someone in his final hemorrhage; at times, these climactic spasms were so violent, she had once told me, that blood splattered the ceiling, a hideous thought and one that wickedly beguiled me. I would lie awake in the cold house long after she had left and would try to imagine such an explosion in myself, until finally I could all but see the girandole of my bright blood mount through the air. Alone in the malevolent midnight darkness, I was possessed with the facts of dying and of death, and I would often turn, heartless and bewitched, to the memory of my father, killed by gangrene, who had lain for weeks in his hospital bed, wasted and hot-eyed and delirious, until, one day as I watched, the poisonous tide deluged him and, as limp as a drowned man, he died. The process had been so snail-paced and then the end of it so fleet that in my surprise I had been unable to cry out and had stood for several minutes, blissful with terror, until my mother came back into the room with a doctor and a nurse. I had longed to discuss with her what I had seen, but her grief—she had loved him deeply—inhibited me, and not until we had come West did I ask her any questions about death, and when I did, I appeared to be asking about her patients, although it was really about my father.

The richer of the tuberculars, especially those who had left their families behind, were billeted in the sanitarium, an aggregate of Swiss chalets that crested the western of our twin hills. If they were not bedridden, they lived much as they might have done at a resort, playing a great deal of bridge, mah-jongg, and cowboy pool, learning to typewrite, photographing our declamatory mountain range. Often in the early evening, from the main lodge there came piano music, neither passionate nor complicated, and once, as I was passing by, I heard a flute, sweet and single in the dusk. On walks, the patients slowly ranged the mesas, gathering pasque-flowers in the spring and Mariposa lilies in the summer, and in the winter, when the snow was on the ground, they brought back kinnikinnick, red-berried and bronze-leaved. These pastimes were a meager fare and they were bored, but they were sustained by their stubborn conviction that this way of life was only temporary. Faithfully, winter and summer, spring and fall, they went abroad each day at noon to get the high sun, and because the sanitarium was near my school, I used to see them at the lunch recess, whole phalanxes of them, indulging sometimes in temperate horseplay and always in the interchange of cynical witticisms that banded them together in an esoteric fellowship. In the winter—and our winters were so long and cruel that the sick compared this region to Siberia and their residence there to exile—their eyes and noses alone were visible through their caparisons of sweaters, mufflers, greatcoats, but their sanguine, muted voices came out clearly in the thin air. Like all committed people, whether they are committed to school or to jail, to war or to disease, there was among them a good-natured camaraderie that arose out of a need to vary the tedium of a life circumscribed by rules. I would hear them maligning and imitating the doctors and the nurses, and laying plans to outwit them in matters to do with rest periods and cigarettes, exactly as my schoolmates and I planned to perpetrate mischief in geography class or study hall. I heard them banteringly compare X-rays and temperatures, speak, in a tone half humorous and half apprehensive, of a confederate who had been suspended temporarily (it was hoped) from the fraternity by a sudden onslaught of fever. They were urbane, resigned, and tart. Once, I recall, I met two chattering walkers on a path in the foothills and I heard one of them say, "All the same, it's not the bore a nervous breakdown is. We're not locked in, at any rate," and his companion amiably answered, "Oh, but we are. They've locked us into these ratty mountains. They've 'arrested' us, as they say."

This colony was tragic, but all the same I found it rather grand, for most of the sanitarium patients had the solaces of money and of education (I was sure they all had degrees from Eastern universities) and could hire cars to go driving in the mountains and could buy books in quantity at Miss Marshall's snobbish shop, the Book End, where they could also drink tea in an Old Englishy atmosphere in the back room. I did not feel sorry for them as I did for the indigent tuberculars, who lived in a settlement of low, mean cottages on the outskirts of the town. Here I saw sputum cups on windowsills and here I heard, from every side, the prolonged and patient coughing, its dull tone unvarying except when a little respite came and its servant sighed or groaned or said, "Oh, God Almighty," as if he were unspeakably tired of this and of everything else in the world. There were different textures and velocities to the coughing, but whether it was dry or brassy or bubbling, there was in it always that undertone of monotony.

It was neither the rich nor the poor that my mother nursed but those in between, who rented solid houses and lived—or tried to live—as they had in Virginia or in Connecticut. Whole families had uprooted themselves for the sake of one member; mothers had come out of devotion to a favorite son. There were isolated individuals as well, men with valets and motorcars and dogs (I thought that the bandy-legged basset belonging to the very rich Mr. Woodham, of Baltimore, was named Lousy Cur, because that was how I always heard Mr. Woodham's man address him), and women who were invariably called grass widows whether they were spinsters or divorcées or had left a loving husband and family behind. Grass widows, walkers, lungers—what a calm argot it was! Many of them were not so much ill as bored and restive—lonely and homesick for the friends and relatives and for the landscapes they had left behind. Ma was a valiant, pretty woman and she was engaged more, really, as a companion than as a nurse. She read aloud to her charges or played Russian bank with them or took them for slow walks. Above all, she listened to their jeremiads, half doleful, half ironic, and tried, with kindly derision, to steer them away from their doldrums. It was this attitude of "You're not alone, everyone is in the same boat" that kept them from, as Ma said, "going mental." A few times, solitary gentlemen fell in love with her, and once she accepted a proposal—from a Mr. Millard, a cheerful banker from Providence, but he died a week before they were to be married. I was relieved, for I had not liked to think of living with a stepfather riddled with bugs.

Soon after Mr. Millard died, Ma went to work for a family named Butler, who had come West from Massachusetts, re-sentfully but in resignation, bringing their lares in crates and barrels, leaving behind only the Reverend Mr. Butler, who, feeling that he could never duplicate his enlightened congre-gation, remained in Newton to propagate the Low Church faith. Mrs. Butler, a stout, stern woman who had an advanced degree from Radcliffe, had been promised that here her life, threatened twice by hemorrhages, would be extended to its normal span and that the "tendency" demonstrated by all three of her children would perhaps be permanently checked. Besides the mother and the children, there was a grandmother, not tubercular but senile and helplessly arthritic, and it was for her that Ma had been hired. It was the hardest job she had had, because the old woman, in constant pain, was spiteful and peckish, and several times she reduced my intrepid mother to tears. But this was also the best-paid job she had had, and we were better dressed and better fed than we had been since we left Ohio. We ate butter now instead of margarine and there was even money enough for me to take dancing lessons.

Two of the Butler children, Laura and Ada, were in my grade at school. There was a year's difference between them but the elder, Laura, had been retarded by a six-month session in a hospital. They were the same size and they looked almost exactly alike; they dressed alike, in dark-blue serge jumpers and pale-blue flannelette guimpes and low black boots. They were sickly and abnormally small, and their spectacles pinched their Roman noses. All of us pitied them on their first day at school, because they were so frightened that they would not sit in separate seats, and when Miss Farley asked one of them to sing a scale, she laid her head down on her desk and cried. But we did not waste our sympathy on them long, because after their first show of vulnerability we found them to be haughty and acidulous, and they let it be known that they were not accustomed to going to a public school and associating with just anyone. Nancy Hildreth, whose father was a junkman, excited their especial scorn, and though I had always hated Nancy before, I took her side against them and one day helped her write a poison-pen letter full of vituperative fabrication and threats. We promised that if they did not leave town at once, we would burn their house down. In the end, the letter was too dangerous to send, but its composition had given us great pleasure.

After about a month, Laura and Ada, to my bewilderment and discomfort, began to seek me out at recess, acknowledging in their highhanded way that they knew my mother. They did not use the word "servant" in speaking of her but their tone

patronized her and their faint smiles put her in her place. At
first, I rebuffed them, for they were too timid to play as I
played; they would never pump up in the swings but would
only sit on the seats, dangling their feet in their *outré* boots,
trying to pretend that they were not afraid but were superior
to our lively games. They would not go near the parallel bars
or the teeter-totter, and when the rest of us played crack-the-
whip, they cowered, aghast, against the storm doors of the
grammar school. But when I complained to Ma of how they
tagged after me and tried to make me play their boring guessing
games, she asked me, for her sake, to be nice to them, since
our livelihood depended on their mother, a possessive woman
who would ferociously defend her young. It was hardly fair
of Ma to say to me, "Just remember, it's Laura and Ada who
give you your dancing lessons," but all the same, because she
looked so worried and, even more, because I could not bear to
think of not going to my lessons, I obeyed her, and the next
day grudgingly agreed to play twenty questions while, out of
the corner of my eye, I enviously watched the other children
organizing a relay race.

Not long after I had made this filial compromise, Laura and
Ada began asking me to come home with them after school,
and though my friends glared at me as we left the playground
together, I never dared refuse. Anyhow, the Butlers' house
enchanted me.

It smelled of witch hazel. As soon as we entered the cool and
formal vestibule, where a gilded convex mirror hung above a
polished console table on which there stood a silver tray for
calling cards, the old-fashioned and vaguely medicinal fragrance
came to meet me, and I envisaged cut-glass bottles filled with
it on the marble tops of bureaus in the bedrooms I had never
seen. It made me think of one particular autumn afternoon,
in the Ohio woods, when my father and I went for a walk in a
clean, soft mist and he cut me a witch-hazel wand, with which
I touched a young orange salamander orphaned in the road.
As palpable and constant as the smell in the house was the
hush of an impending death; somewhere, hidden away in such
isolation that I could not even guess where she was, whether
upstairs or in a room behind the parlor, lay the grandmother,

gradually growing feebler, slowly petering out as my mother spooned up medicine for her and rubbed her ancient back with alcohol. There was hardly a sound in that tomb-still house save for the girls' voices and mine, or the footsteps of their older brother, Lawrence, moving about in his chemical laboratory in the basement.

Again, as vivid as the fragrance and the portentous quiet was the sense of oldness in this house, coming partly from the well-kept antique furniture, the precious Oriental rugs, the Hitchcock settles that formed an inglenook beside the hearth, the quaint photographs hung in deep ovals of rich-brown wood (there was a square piano, and a grandfather clock that told the time as if it knelled a death), but coming even more from the Boston accents and the adult vocabularies and the wise, small eyes of my two playmates. I did not think of them as children my own age but rather as dwarfed grownups, and when I walked along between them, towering over their heads, my own stature seemed eccentric, and in my self-consciousness I would stub my toe or list against one of the little girls (who did not fail to call me awkward). Probably they had never been children; if they had, it had only been for a short time and they had long since cast off the customs and the culture of that season of life. They would not stoop to paper dolls, to pig Latin, to riddles, to practical jokes on the telephone, and in their aloofness from all that concerned me and my fellows they made me feel loutish, noisy, and, above all, stupid.

At other houses, visitors were entertained outside in good weather. In the spring and fall, my friends and I roller-skated or stood on our heads and only looked in at the back door to ask for graham crackers or peanut-butter sandwiches; in the winter we coasted down the hills and occasionally made snow ice cream in some tolerant mother's kitchen. If rain or wind quarantined us, we rowdily played jacks with a golf ball or danced to the music of a Victrola. Whatever we did, we were abandoned to our present pleasure.

But at the Butlers' house the only divertissements were Authors and I Spy, and it was only once in a blue moon that we played those. Usually we sat primly, Laura and Ada and I, in the parlor in three wing chairs, and conversed—it is essential to use that stilted word—of books and of our teachers. The

Butler girls were dauntlessly opinionated and called the tune
to me, who supinely took it up; I would not defend a teacher
I had theretofore admired if they ridiculed her; I listened
meekly when they said that *Rebecca of Sunnybrook Farm* was
silly. Sometimes they told me their dreams, every one of which
was a nightmare worse than the one before; they dreamed of
alligators and gargantuan cats, of snakes, ogres, and quicksand.
I would never tell my vague and harmless dreams, feeling that
they would arouse the Butlers' disdain, and once, after they had
asked me to and I had refused, Ada said, "It's obvious Jessie
doesn't have any dreams, Laura. Didn't Father say that people
who sleep soundly have inferior intellects?"

Those long words! They angered and they charmed me, and I
listened, wide-eyed, trying to remember them to use them myself—"obvious," "intellect," "logical," "literally." On one of my
first visits, Ada, picking up a faded daguerreotype of a bearded
man, said, "This is my great-grandfather, Mr. Hartford, whom
my brother intends to emulate. Great-grandfather Hartford
was a celebrated corporation lawyer." My astonishment at her
language must have shown in my face, for she laughed rather
unkindly, and, in shocking vernacular, she added, "That is,
Larry will be a lawyer *if* he doesn't turn into a lunger first." The
Butlers, like the patients at the sanitarium, had their intramural
jokes.

Laura and Ada told me anecdotes of Lawrence, who went
to high school and was at the head of his class and contributed
regularly to the *Scholastic* magazine. They adored him and
looked on every word of his as oracular. He was a youth of
many parts, dedicated equally to the Muses (he was writing
an epic on Governor Bradford, from whom the family was
obliquely descended) and to the study of chemistry, and often,
commingled with the witch hazel, there was a faint odor of
hydrogen sulfide wafted up through the hot-air registers from
his basement laboratory. "Lawrence is a genius," said Laura
once, stating a fact. "Think of a genius having to live *here* all
his life! But, of course, he's stoical."

They told me, also, of incidents in the brilliant university
career of their mother, who wore her Phi Beta Kappa key as
a lavaliere. They spoke of her having studied under Professor

Kittredge, as if this were equivalent to having been presented at court. The formidable bluestocking, Mrs. Butler, seldom came into the parlor, for usually she was out shopping or doctoring or was upstairs writing a play based on the life of Carlyle. But when she did make one of her rare appearances, she took no cognizance of me, although it seemed to me that her discerning eyes, small, like her daughters', and monkey-brown, like theirs, discovered my innermost and frivolous thoughts and read them all with disapproval. She would come in only to remind the girls that that night they must write their weekly letters to their father or to remark indignantly that it was difficult to shop when one was nudged and elbowed by barbarians. For Mrs. Butler had an orthodox aversion to the West, and although almost no one was native to our town, she looked down her pointed nose at the entire population, as if it consisted of nothing but rubes.

After we had talked for half an hour, Laura would go out of the room and come back after a while with a tole tray on which stood a china cocoa set and a plate of Huntley & Palmers sweet biscuits, ordered from S. S. Pierce. We would drink in sips and eat in nibbles and continue our solemn discourse. Often, during this unsatisfying meal (the cookies were dry and the cocoa was never sweet enough for me), the talk became medical, and these sophisticated valetudinarians, nine and ten years old, informed me of extraordinary facts relating to the ills that beset the human flesh and especially those rare and serious ones that victimized them. They took such pride in being hostesses to infirmity that I was ashamed of never having suffered from anything graver than pinkeye, and so light a case of that that Ma had cured it in a day with boric acid. The Butlers, besides being prey to every known respiratory disorder, had other troubles: Laura had brittle bones that could be fractured by the slightest blow, and Ada had a rheumatic heart, a cross she would bear, she said, until the day she died. They had had quinsy, pleurisy, appendicitis; they were anemic, myopic, asthmatic; and they were subject to hives. They started off the morning by eating yeast cakes, and throughout the day popped pellets and capsules into their mouths; at recess, I would see them at the drinking fountain, gorging on pills. Their brother was a little less frail, but he, too, was often ill. The atmosphere of the house was that of a nursing home, and Ma told me that the whole family lived on invalid fare, on custards and broths and arrowroot pudding. The medicine chest, she said, looked like a pharmacy.

I never stayed long at the Butlers' house, for Laura and Ada had to go upstairs to rest. I stayed only until Lawrence came up from the basement, and as I closed the storm door, I saw, through the side lights, the three of them, weak, intellectual, and Lilliputian, carefully climbing the stairs in single file on their way up to their bedrooms, where they would lie motionless until their dinner of soft white food.

I had had friends before Laura and Ada whose lives were far more overcast by tuberculosis than theirs—children born in the same month and the same year as myself who had already spat out blood, children whose mothers had died in the dead of night, whose fathers would never rise from their beds again. But never before had I been made to feel that my health was a disgrace. Now, under the clever tuition of the Butlers, I began to look upon myself as a pariah and to be ashamed not only of myself but of my mother, who was crassly impervious to disease, although she exposed herself to it constantly. I felt left out, not only in the Butlers' house but in this town of consumptive confederates. I began to have fantasies in which both Ma and I contracted mortal illnesses; in my daydreams, Laura and Ada ate crow, admitting that they had never had anything half so bad and praising my bravery. Whenever I sneezed, my heart leapt for joy, and each time my mother told me she was tired or that her head ached, I hoped for her collapse, anxious for even a vicarious distinction. I stood before the open window after a hot bath in the hope of getting pneumonia. Whenever I was alone in the house, I looked at the pictures in a book of Ma's called *Diagnostics of Internal Medicine* and studied representations of infantile spinal paralysis, of sporadic cretinism, of unilateral atrophy of the tongue. Such was my depravity that when I considered the photograph of a naked, obscenely fat woman who was suffering, so the caption read, from "adiposis dolorosa," I thought I could endure even that disfigurement to best the Butlers.

Because my mother valued health above all else (she was not a prig about it, she was only levelheaded), I knew that these of mine were vicious thoughts and deeds, but I could not help myself, for while I hated the sisters deeply and with integrity, I yearned for their approbation. I wanted most desperately to be a part of this ailing citizenry, to be able casually to say, "I can't come to your house this afternoon. I have to have an X-ray." If I had known about such things when I was nine, I might have been able to see the reasons for my misery, but at nine one has not yet taken in so much as the meaning of the words "happy" and "unhappy," and I knew only that I was beyond the pale, bovine in the midst of nymphs. Epidemics of scarlet fever and diphtheria passed me by. Other children were bitten by rabid dogs and their names were printed in the paper, but the only dogs I met greeted me affably and trotted along beside me if the notion took them to. My classmates broke their collarbones and had their tonsils taken out. But nothing happened to me that Unguentine or iodine would not cure, and all the while the Butlers' pallor seemed to me to deepen and their malicious egotism to grow and spread.

I do not think that Laura and Ada despised me more than they did anyone else, but I was the only one they could force to come home with them. "Who wants to be healthy if being healthy means being a cow?" said Ada one day, looking at me as I reached for a third insipid cooky. I withdrew my hand and blushed so hotly in my humiliation that Laura screamed with laughter and cried, "The friendly cow all red and white, we give her biscuits with all our might."

Oh, I hated them! I ground my anklebones together, I clenched my fists, I set my jaw, but I could not talk back—not here in this elegiac house where my poor ma was probably simultaneously being insulted by the querulous octogenarian. I could do no more than change the subject, and so I did, but my choice was infelicitous, for, without thinking and with a kind of self-defeating desperation which I saw to be calamitous even before the words were finished, I asked Laura and Ada if they did not like the tumbling we were having in gym, and Ada, horrified, appealed to her sister (she rarely spoke directly to me but through Laura, as if she spoke a separate language that must be translated)—"Oh, tell her that we don't *tumble*"—and her sister went on, "While the rest of you tumble, we write essays." Who could scale this Parnassus? On the flatlands of Philistia, I held my tongue, and I endured, for the sake of learning how to execute a *tour jeté* in Miss Jorene Roy's dance salon.

And then, one day, at the height of my tribulation, Ada, quite by accident, provided me with the means to petrify them for an hour with curiosity and awe. It was nearing Christmas, and the parlor was pranked out with holly wreaths in the windows and a tree in the bay window and early greeting cards lined up in military ranks on the mantel. The girls had been uncommonly animated lately, for their father was coming from Boston to spend two weeks with his brood. I would have the privilege, as would everyone else in town, of hearing him deliver a sermon as the guest preacher at St. John's; the girls' implication was that his erudition was so great that not a soul in this benighted place would understand a word he said. That day, in the dark room—a beautiful, obscuring snow was falling and the heavy branches of the cedar trees leaned against the windows—I envied them this tribal holiday, envied them their peopled house, and pitied myself for being a fatherless and only child. I thought I would have given anything at this moment for a brother, even for Lawrence Butler, with his peaked, mean face and the supercilious way he had of greeting me by saying, "How *do* you do?" Ada, as if she had read my melancholy thoughts and wished to twist the knife, said complacently, "What a shame she doesn't have a father, isn't it, Laura? Laura, ask her what her father died of."

My brilliant answer sprang instantly to my lips without rehearsal or embellishment. "Leprosy," I said, and watched the Bostonians freeze in their attitude as if they were playing Statues. I had learned of leprosy some weeks before from the older sister of a friend, who had held me spellbound. The belief that was soon to be current among my friends and me when the movie *Ben Hur* was to enthrall us all was that lepers slowly vanished, through the rotting away of their fingers and toes, and then of their hands and feet, and then of their arms and legs, and that all exterior appointments, as ears and noses, hair and eyes, fell off like decayed vegetables finally falling from the vine. If this had been my first impression of leprosy, I doubt whether I would, even in this emergency, have thus dispatched my father to his grave, but at the time, thanks to the quixotic older sister, who had got her information in some byway trod by no one but herself, I was under the impression that leprosy was a kind of sleeping sickness brought on by the bite of a lion. This intelligence I passed on to Laura and Ada, glib crocodile tears gathering in the corners of my eyes, and never dreamed, as I pursued my monologue, that they had a Biblical acquaintance with leprosy and that what rooted them to the spot was the revelation that I was the daughter of an unclean man.

Before I could finish my story or make the most of its picturesque details, Laura gasped, "He was unclean!"

"Unclean?" I was incensed. "He was *not* unclean! He washed himself exactly like a cat!" I screamed.

"She said he was asleep for thirty months," said Ada. "Ask her how he could wash in his sleep."

"Well, he did, anyway," I said, flummoxed at being caught out. "I don't know how, but he did. He didn't have fleas, if that's what you mean."

"Unclean," repeated Ada, savoring the word. "Tell her to stay where she is until we get out of the room and tell her never to come back to this house again."

"She never will," said Laura. "She'll be sent to the Fiji Islands or someplace. Lepers can't run around loose."

"Oh, Laura, do you think she has it? Do you think we'll get it?" moaned Ada. "Where is Mother? We must tell her *now*!"

"Be careful, Ada," said Laura. "Go out of the room backwards and keep your eye on her, and if she starts to move, scream. We'll be all right as long as she doesn't touch us."

"Poor Grandmother!" wailed Ada. "Did you think of Grandmother being *touched* all this time by that unclean woman?" She backed to the door, her eyes fixed on me, who could not have moved for anything.

"It's awful!" said Laura, following her sidewise, like a crab. "Of all days for Mother to be at the osteopath! Still, Larry will have an idea."

"Yes," said Ada from the doorway. "Probably Lawrence will send for the Black Maria."

My many selves, all bedlamites, clamored in my faint, sick heart. I wished to tell them on the spot that the whole thing had been a lie. I wished to say it had been a joke. "I was only kidding," I would say. But how heartless that would make me!

To jest about my dead father, whom I had loved. Still, I must say something, must in some way exonerate myself and my mother and him. But when I opened my mouth to speak, a throttled sound came out, as surprising to my ears as to theirs, and before I had a chance to find my voice, the girls, appalled, had shut the door. I heard them slowly mount the stairs—even in their alarm they were protective of themselves—and I waited, frozen, for the sound of their avenging brother's footsteps up the stairs from the basement that entered into the front hall. When, at last, mobility returned to me, I slipped out of the parlor and made my way down the corridor to the back of the house, fearful of meeting him in the vestibule. I think I had half expected to encounter my mother in these precincts, but the passage I walked along was doorless until I came to the kitchen, a still, enormous room where there was a soft, sporadic hissing from the banked coal fire in the hooded Glenwood range. Against the varnished wainscoting stood ladder-back chairs, demanding perfect posture of their occupants, and on the trestle table there was a fruit bowl full of wholesome prunes. I knew without looking that there would be nothing good to eat in the cupboards—no brown sugar, no mayonnaise, nothing but those corky cookies. Within the pantry was a deer mouse hunched in death in a trap, and the only ray of light coming through the curtained window made an aura around its freckled fur. I bent to look more closely at the pathetic corpse, and as I did so, I heard, from directly overhead, the sound of Laura and Ada Butler giggling. *At what?* It was a high, aquatic giggle that came in antiphonal wavelets, and then one of the girls began to cough. I fled, mystified, and let myself out into the snow that whirlingly embraced me as I ran blindly home. A block from home, I began wildly to call my cat. "Kitty, kitty, kitty, *kitty*!" I shrieked, to drown out the remembered sound of my terrible lies, and Mr. Woodham's valet, passing me with Lousy Cur on a leash, said, "Whoa, there! Hold on! Where's the fire?" Pretending, with great effort, that I was the same person I had been an hour ago, I stopped and forced myself to grin and to stoop down and lightly pat the sad-eyed dog, and when this amenity was done, I continued on the double-quick.

Mine was a desperate dilemma, for I must either stick to my story and force my mother to confirm it, with the inevitable loss of her job and our probable deportation to the Fiji Islands, or grovel before the girls and admit that I had told a lie. I had told many lies before but I had never told one that involved the far future as well as the near. The consequences of telling my mother that, for example, I had been at the public library when in fact I had been prowling on the dump, hunting for colored bottles, were not serious. I might smart under her disapproval and disappointment (I was not forbidden to go to the dump and the needlessness of the lie made her feel, I suppose, that my character, in general, was devious) but I recovered as soon as her reproach was over. But this one, involving everyone—my father, whom I had, it seemed, maligned (although the concept of uncleanness still puzzled me); my mother, whose job and, indeed, whose whole life I had jeopardized; myself, who could never face the world again and must either wear the mark of the beast forever or spend the rest of my days under a banana tree—this lie was calamity. I thought of stowing away on the interurban to the city, there to lose myself forever in the dark alleys under the viaducts or in the Greek Revival comfort stations at the zoo. I thought of setting fire to the Butlers' house, as Nancy Hildreth and I had threatened to do, and burning them all to death. I thought, more immediately, of shaving off my hair by way of expiation.

When I got to the house, I scooped up Bow, the cat, from the rocking chair where she was sleeping, and went to my bedroom. Without taking off my coat, or even my galoshes, I lay down on my bed, my head beneath two pillows, the outraged and struggling cat clutched in my arms. But before I had time to collect my wits to formulate a plan of action (my disappearance in the city had its attractions), the telephone screamed its two hysterical notes, one short, one long, and I catapulted down the stairs to answer it. Bow trotted after me, resumed her place in the rocking chair, and went instantly to sleep.

It was Laura Butler, who, in a muffled voice, as if she did not want to be overheard by someone nearby, said, "Larry has arranged everything. He knows how we can cure you, and no one will ever know. So you come here tomorrow afternoon on the dot of three o'clock."

The next day was Saturday, and at three o'clock on Saturdays I went to Miss Roy's, and so dear to my heart was dancing class that even in this crisis I protested. "Can't I come at four instead?"

"Why should you come at four?" asked Laura imperiously.

"Because I'm the prince in 'The Cameo Girl.'"

"The *what* in the *what*?"

"I mean I go to dancing class at three," I said. "You know? My fancy-dancing class?"

"Dancing will do you very little good, my dear girl, if your legs fall off," Laura said severely.

"If my legs fall off?" I cried. "What has that got to do with it?"

"Larry says that your legs will undoubtedly fall off if you don't come here at three o'clock tomorrow." There was a slight pause; I felt she was conferring with someone, and she said, "By the bye, your mother doesn't have to have the cure, because she was too old to get leprosy, but of course if you don't have the cure, she'll have to go to the Fiji Islands with you. Larry says that's the law."

"Laura?" My voice explored the tiny tunnel of space between our telephones. Shall I tell her now, I thought. "Laura?" I asked again.

"You know it's Laura," she said, so briskly, so contemptuously that on the instant I was stubborn.

"I can't come," I said.

Aside—to Ada or to Lawrence, I presumed—she said, "We may have to take steps after all. Larry says—"

"Wait!" I cried. "Hey, Laura, are you still there? Laura, listen, let me come right now!" For I was thinking of the *entrechat* I had almost perfected, and more than anything else in the world I wanted Miss Roy to tell me, in her jazzy way, that it was "a lulu." But I knew that until my mind lay at rest, I could not dance a single step.

I could hear whispers at the other end, and finally Laura said, "Very well, although it will inconvenience us," and then she warned, "If you are late, my mother will come home. I suppose you don't want *her* to know?"

I sighed deeply into the telephone and heard the other

receiver being returned to its hook. Immediately the bell rang again, and Laura said, "Come in ten minutes. We have to get things ready."

The stillness of the house unnerved me as I waited those ten minutes, and, perversely, I frightened myself still more by speaking aloud and hearing my voice come hollowly back to me. "What are they going to do to me, Bow? What *things* have they got to get ready?"

It occurred to me to kill myself. I heard the interurban going out and thought again of skipping town. *Cure* me. What did that mean? I picked up Bow and carried her to the window with me and stood there with her face against mine, watching the storm. She was tense, watching Lousy Cur as he trotted home. "Shall I take the cure, Bow?" I said, and she growled deep in her gentle white belly. "Does that mean yes, Bowcat? Or shall I tell them it was a lie?" She growled again, for Lousy Cur was opposite our house, and, as if he sensed her being there, he paused, one foot uplifted, and gazed with interest at our front door. "Which?" I asked her, and in answer she writhed with a howl from my arms, furious at this double invasion of her privacy. She forgot us both and abruptly took a bath.

My hands were so damp that I could hardly peel my mittens off when I got to the Butlers' front door, and there was a severe pain in my stomach that made me think I had probably got cancer in punishment for my sin (not, as I might have hoped earlier, as a reward for my virtue). Planless still, my parched lips mouthed my alternative opening speeches: "It was a lie" and "I am ready for the cure." The door opened the moment I rang the bell, and Laura and Ada stood waiting for me in the vestibule, ceremonious in odd brown flannel wrappers with peaked hoods attached at the back of the neck. Gnomelike and leering, they ushered me into the parlor, where they had set up a card table and had covered it with a white cloth. On it stood a group of odd-shaped bottles, which, they explained to me, Larry, the chemist, had lent to them. Did they mean to burn me with acids? To sprinkle me with lye? There was also a covered willowware tureen on the table, and an open Bible.

"Ask her if she believes in God," said Ada.

"Yes," I said quickly, although I was by no means sure. "Listen, Laura—" What if I said the joke was on them? What if I said I'd planned this hoodwink for weeks? The worst they could do was get angry. But I knew I could not convince them, and I floundered, stuttering, beginning, stopping dead.

"The prisoner at the dock wishes to speak," said Ada. "Hear ye! Hear ye!"

"Yes?" said Laura, preoccupied. She had lifted the lid of the tureen and to her sister said, "Do you think the insides of one bird will do?"

Ada, looking into the dish, grimaced. "It will simply have to. There's only one to be had. Larry said it would be all right."

"Do you mind asking him again, just to make sure?"

"I wouldn't dream of disturbing him," said Ada. "He's in his laboratory, boiling his spittle. He can make it turn purple and he can make it turn green."

It made me even more uneasy to know that Lawrence was in the house, and again I started to speak. "Laura, listen to me—" But Laura had picked up the Bible now, and she read, "'Two birds alive and clean, and cedar wood'"—she held up a beaker half full of cedar berries—"'and scarlet, and hyssop.'" And her sister pointed to two test tubes, which appeared to be filled, one with red ink and the other with blue.

"Laura—"

"One moment. Be quiet, please." She continued to read, "'And the priest shall command that one of the birds be killed in an earthen vessel over running water.'" She opened the tureen again and poured out water from a cream pitcher while Ada murmured doubtfully, "Of course, it's already dead."

"A very good thing it is that she believes in God, or the cure would never work," said Laura and went on reading. "'As for the living bird, he shall take it, and the cedar wood, and the scarlet, and the hyssop, and shall dip them and the living bird in the blood of the bird that was killed over the running water.'" With this, she put into the bowl the picture of an eagle, which she had probably cut out of a magazine, and she poured in the red ink, the blue ink, and the cedar berries. Then, bearing the vessel in both hands, she came to where I stood and allowed me to look into a dreadful mess of ink and feathers and the entrails of the chicken that they were doubtless going to have that night for dinner. She dipped her fingers into the stew, and though she shuddered and made a face, she persevered, and before my nose she dangled a bit of dripping innards.

This was enough for me. I would not be touched by those slithering, opalescent intestines, and I shrank back and I cried out, "Will you listen to me? I told a lie!"

Laura's look roasted and froze me, sent me to jail, to hell; it drew and quartered me. "A lie!" she exclaimed, as if I had confessed to murder. Ada turned to her sister with a pout and said crossly, "I *told* you it would never work."

Laura continued to look hard at me, but at last her face relaxed and, patronizing, like a minister, speciously kind, like a schoolteacher, she said, "Now, what's all this about a lie?"

"He didn't die of leprosy," I said. I looked at my feet and moved them slightly, so that the toes of my shoes pointed to the hearts of two roses in the carpet.

"Why did you say that he did?"

"Because—"

"It's more important, I should think," said Ada sulkily, "to find out what he *did* die of. It's quite possible that he died of something worse."

"Why did you say that he did?" said Laura, ignoring her.

"Because it was a joke."

"A joke? I thought you said you had told a lie. There is a world of difference between the two, Jessie. Well, which was it, a joke or a lie?"

"A joke!" I cried, almost in tears.

"Do you hear that, Laura?" said Ada. "She tells a *joke* about the deceased."

"I mean it was a lie," I said. I was on the verge of a fearful sobbing. "A lie, and I am sorry." The smell of witch hazel was inordinately dense. In the silence, I heard the click of a ball on the Christmas tree. Suddenly, my ignorance of where my mother was in this unhealthy house terrified me, and I loudly said, "How is your grandmother today?"

"Stick to the subject," said Laura.

But Ada was glad to tell me. "Grandmother is not well at all today. She had a bilious attack this morning. So did I."

She smiled smugly at me, and I, magically emboldened by my distaste, moved to the door, and as I went, I said, "*I* am never sick. I have never been sick in my life."

"Lucky you," gloated Ada.

"What did he die of?" persisted Laura.

"He got shot out hunting, if you want to know," I told them. "My father was as tall as this room. The district nurse told Ma that I am the healthiest girl in town. Also I have the best teeth."

Across those small, old faces there flickered a ray of curiosity to know, perhaps, how the other half lived, and for just that split second I pitied them. My mind cleared and I realized that all this torment had been for nothing. If the Butlers had tried to blacken my name for telling a lie, no one would have believed them, for they had no friends, and, by the same token, if they had noised it about that my father had died of leprosy, I could have said *they* were telling lies. Now I was exalted and hungry and clean, and when I had put on my coat and opened the door, I cried exuberantly, "So long, kids, see you in church!"—a flippancy I would not have dared utter in that house two hours before. By way of reply, Ada coughed pitifully, professionally.

Until the grandmother died, in April, and Ma took another job, I went two or three afternoons a week to the Butlers' house, and over our light collation, as Laura and Ada called it, we talked steadily and solely of the girls' grave illnesses. But as I left, I always said, with snide solicitude, "Take care of yourselves." They were unshakable; they had the final word: "We will. We have to, you know." My vanity, however, was now quite equal to theirs. Feeling myself to be immortal and knowing myself to be the healthiest girl in town, I invariably cut an affronting caper on the Butlers' lawn and ran off fast, letting the good mountain air plunge deep into my sterling lungs.

The Tea Time of Stouthearted Ladies

"As I tell Kitty, this summer job of hers is really more a vacation with pay than work. What wouldn't *I* give to be up there in the mountains away from the hurly-burly of this town! They have a lake right there below the main lodge where the girls can cool off after they serve lunch. And quite often they can have the horses to trot off here, there, and the other place—go down to Brophy, for instance, and have a Coke. They can help themselves to the books in the lounge, play the Victrola, sit in the sun and get a good tan. They go to the square dances and dance with the dudes as if they were dudes themselves, and if there's a home movie they're invited to come and view. Mrs. Bell and Miss Skeen are very democratic along those lines and when they first hired Kitty, when she was just fourteen, they told me they didn't look on their employees as servants but as a part of the family."

"Not my idea of work," agreed Mrs. Ewing, and made a hybrid sound, half deprecating giggle, half longing sigh. "Some different from *our* summers, what with those scorching days in August and no let-up in the way of a breeze. Oh, I'm by no means partial to summer on the plains. And all those pesky grasshoppers spitting tobacco juice through the screens onto your clean glass curtains, to say nothing of the fuss-budget old schoolmarms—give me a dude any day of the week sooner than Miss Prunes and Prisms from Glenwood Springs still plugging away at her M.A. after fifteen years. Kitty's in luck all right."

Lucky Kitty Winstanley, home from her last class for the day at Nevilles College, stood in the middle of her small, shadowy bedroom, her arms still full of books, and listened to the voices in the kitchen below her. She visualized her mother and the turnip-shaped, bearded neighbor as they lingered in the bright hollow of the dying May afternoon. Their ration of icebox cookies eaten, their pale, scalding coffee drunk, they would be sitting in the breakfast nook, facing each other through spotless, rimless spectacles. Their tumid hands mutilated by work would be clasped loosely on the tulip-patterned oilcloth and their swollen feet would be demurely crossed as they glibly evaluated the silver lining of the cloud beneath which they and their families lived, gasping for every breath. It was out of habit, not curiosity, that Kitty listened; she knew all their themes by heart and all of them embarrassed her. She listened with revulsion, with boredom, pity, outrage, and she moved stealthily so that they would not know she had come home.

Each afternoon, in one house or another along this broad, graveled street, there was such an imitation tea party in such a fiercely clean kitchen as Mrs. Winstanley's when two women or more established themselves in speckless cotton dresses in the breakfast nooks for a snack and a confab. United in their profession, that of running boarding houses for college students, and united more deeply but less admissibly in hardship and fatigue and in eternal worry over "making ends meet," they behaved, at this hour of day that lay tranquilly between the toasted peanut-butter sandwiches of lunch and the Swedish meatballs of dinner, like urban ladies of leisure gossiping after a matinee. Formal, fearful of intimacy lest the full confrontation with reality shatter them to smithereens, they did not use each other's first names, asked no leading questions; it was surprising that they did not wear gloves and hats. They did not refer, even by indirection, to personal matters, not to the monotonous terror of debt that kept them wakeful at night despite the weariness that was their incessant condition, or to the aching disappointment to which they daily rose, or to their hopeless, helpless contempt for their unemployed husbands who spent their days in the public park, clustering to curse the national dilemma or scattering to brood alone upon their individual despair.

Valorously, the landladies kept their chins up, rationalized; they "saw the funny side of things," they never said die. One would not guess, to listen to their light palaver, that they had been reduced to tears that same morning by the dunning of the grocer and the coal man and had seen themselves flung into debtors' prison for life. To hear their interchange of news and commentary on their lodgers, one might have thought they were the hostesses of prolonged, frolicsome houseparties. The cancer was invisible, deep in their broken, bleeding hearts.

They sat at the social hour of four to five in the kitchens because their parlors were either rented out or were used as a common room by the lodgers, but even in this circumstance they contrived to find expansive consolation. Often Mrs. Winstanley, sitting at attention on the stark bench, had said, "I can relax so much better in a kitchen." Did she think, her daughter wondered, that the repetition of this humbug was one day going to make it true? She sometimes went on from there to say, "When I was a girl back home in Missouri, we used to call our kitchen 'the snuggery,' and we used it more than any other room in the house." As she complacently glanced around, her manner invited her caller to believe that she saw a Boston rocker and braided rugs, copper spiders hanging on whitewashed walls, a fireplace with a Dutch oven and cherry settles in the inglenooks, and a mantel crowded with pewter tankards and historic guns. In fact, the caller looked on a room all skin and bones: a coal-oil range with gaunt Queen Anne legs, a Hoosier cabinet ready to shudder into pieces, a linoleum rug worn down to gummy blackness save in the places that were inaccessible to feet and still showed forth its pattern of glossy bruises—a room, in short, in which there was nothing to recommend itself to the eye except the marmalade cat and the sunshine on the windowsill in which he slept.

But the neighbor conspiratorially played the game with her hostess, gladly breathed in these palliative fibs without which the ladies would have spent their days in tears. In one way or another, they had all "come down in the world," but they had descended from a stratum so middling, so snobbish, and so uncertain of itself that it had looked on penury as a disgrace and to have joked about it would have been as alien to their upright natures as it would have been to say aloud the name of a venereal disease. They had come to Adams, this college town in the Rocky Mountains, from the South and the Midwest and New England, most of them driven there by tuberculosis in one member of the family, and now that the depression had slid to its nadir and there were no jobs for their husbands, they had taken up this hard, respectable work.

They bore their shame by refusing to acknowledge its existence: except in the bitter caverns of the night when they reproached their husbands in unflagging whispers, too soft for the boarders to hear but not too soft for their own sons and daughters. For years, Kitty had heard these static diatribes coming up through the hot-air register from her parents' bed-room off the kitchen; sometimes they lasted until the coyotes howled at sunup in the foothills. Rarely did her ruined father answer back; all the charges were true, brutally unfair as they were, and he had nothing to say for himself. He was a builder, but no one was building houses these days; he had only one lung and so he could not work in the mines. The oppressive facts of the depression and of his illness testified to his innocence, but his misery, so long drawn out and so unrelieved, had confused him until he was persuaded that he was jobless because he was no good at his work and he believed his wife when she, cruel out of fear, told him that if he had a little more gumption they would not have to live this way, hand to mouth, one jump ahead of the sheriff. Kitty hated her father's unmanliness (once she had seen him cry when a small roof-repairing job that he had counted on was given to someone else, and she had wanted to die for disgust) and she equally hated her mother for her injustice; and she hated herself for hating in them what they could not help.

In the daytime, the woe and bile were buried, and to her lodgers Mrs. Winstanley was a cheery, cherry-cheeked little red hen who was not too strict about quiet hours (their portable phonographs and radios drove Kitty nightly to the library) or about late dates.

With her friends, she liked to talk of her lodgers and of theirs: of their academic failures and successes ("I wasn't a bit surprised when Dolores got a con in psych," Kitty once heard Mrs. Ewing say, using the patois as self-confidently as if it were her own. "She told me herself that she hadn't cracked a book all term," and Mrs. Winstanley, au courant and really interested, replied, "But won't those A's in oral interp and business English bring her average up?"); they talked of the girls' love affairs, their plans for holidays, their clothes, their double dates. Gravely and with selfless affection, they told each other facts and sometimes mildly looked for overtones and meanings. Once, Kitty heard her mother say, "Helen went to the Phi Delt tea dance on Thursday with the boy in Mrs. McInerney's single front, but she didn't have a good time at all. She said afterward she was sorry that she had turned down an invitation to go to the show at the Tivoli, even though everyone said it was punk. Of course,

I didn't ask any questions, but between you and me and the gatepost I think she was simply cutting off her nose to spite her face by going to the dance instead of keeping her regular date with her steady. Jerry Williams, that is, that big tall engineer with the Studebaker."

They liked to speculate on the sort of homes their students came from; someone's mother's diabetes, someone's younger brother's practical jokes, someone else's widowed father's trip to Mexico were matters that mattered to them. They counted it an equal—and often thrilling—trade if one landlady, offering to her interlocutor the information that one of her girls or boys had been elected to Phi Beta Kappa, got in return the news that Helen or Joyce or Marie had been "pinned" with his Chi Psi pin by a prominent member of the football team.

It was not often that they discussed their own sons and daughters who were working their way through college, but when they did their applause was warm. They were, said the landladies, a happy-go-lucky bunch of kids (though serious in their studies) despite the fact that they did not belong to fraternities and sororities (and were known, therefore, as Barbarians) and could not have exactly the clothes they wanted ("But they keep warm!" the ladies cried. "And when you come right down to it, what else are clothes for?") and had to think twice about spending a nickel on a Coca-Cola. They mouthed their sweet clichés like caramels: "Anything you work hard for means so much more than something just handed to you on a silver platter." "Our children's characters will be all the better for their having gone to the School of Hard Knocks." "For these youngsters of ours, Mrs. Ewing, the depression is a blessing in disguise."

With this honorable, aggressive, friendly mendacity, they armed themselves against the twilight return of their gray-faced husbands from the park and of their edgy children, exhausted from classes and study and part-time jobs and perpetually starved for status (they loathed the School of Hard Knocks, they hated being Barbarians) and clothes (a good deal of the time they were *not* warm) and fun. The husbands ate early, fed like dogs in the kitchen, and then, like dogs, they disappeared. Kitty's father spent his evenings in the furnace room where, under a weak light, he whittled napkin rings. But the landladies' sons and daughters, at the end of the day, became maids or footmen to the students whom they had earlier sat next to in Latin class or worked with on an experiment in chemistry. Kitty Winstanley, setting a plate of lamb stew in front of Miss Shirley Rogers, rejoiced that the girl had flubbed her translation in French and had got a scathing jeer from the instructor, but it was cold comfort because this did not detract at all from the professional set of Miss Rogers' fine blond hair or the chic of her flannel skirt and her English sweater on which, over her heart, was pinned the insignia of her current fiancé. Sometimes in the kitchen, as Kitty brought out dirty dishes or refilled the platter of meat, her mother whispered angrily, "Don't look so down in the mouth! They'll go eat some place where they can find a cheerful smile and then what will we do?" Blackmailed, Kitty set her lips in a murderous grin.

A little work never hurt anyone, the landladies assured each other, and if it was not Mrs. Winstanley yearning to trade places with Kitty in the debonair life she led as waitress and chambermaid at the Caribou Ranch, it was Mrs. Ewing, similarly self-hypnotized, enumerating the advantages that accrued to her asthmatic son in nightly setting up pins in a bowling alley. What a lark she made of it! And what a solemn opportunity. It was a liberal education in itself, according to his mother, for Harry Ewing to mingle until one in the morning with coal miners and fraternity boys, a contrast of class and privilege she found profoundly instructive. A cricket match on the playing fields of Eton would not seem to offer more in the demonstration of sportsmanship than a bowling tournament between the Betas and the ATOs at the Pay Dirt Entertainment Hall. And, again, a stranger might have thought that Harry was only slumming when Mrs. Ewing spoke, with a sociologist's objectivity, of the low mentality and lower morality of the men from the mines and the scandalous girls they brought with them on Ladies' Night. She never touched upon the sleep that Harry lost or on those occasions when a doctor had to be summoned on the double to give the pin boy an injection of adrenalin. "I do believe Harry's outgrowing his asthma," she said once, although that very morning Kitty had seen him across the hall in modern European history buffeted suddenly by an attack so debilitating that he had had to be led out by a monitor.

Kitty sat down at her study table and opened her Renaissance survey book to Donne, shutting her ears against the voices of the heroines below. But she was distracted and disconsolate, and the *Divine Poems* fled from her eyes before her mind could detain them. She turned to stare out of her narrow window at the sweet peas that her father's green thumb had coaxed to espalier the wall of the garage. Somewhere in the neighborhood, a music student was phrenetically practicing a polonaise, making villainous mistakes, and somewhere nearer a phonograph was playing "I Wonder Who's Kissing Her Now," the singer's tribulation throbbing luxuriously in the light spring air. Beyond the garage, over the tops of the mongrel houses and through the feathery branches of mountain ash trees, Kitty could see the red rock terraces of the foothills and the mass of the range beyond where, in a high, wild, emerald and azure and bloodstone park, she would spend her summer.

She would not spend it exactly as her mother imagined. She thought of that lake Mrs. Winstanley so much admired, sight unseen, where the girls could swim after lunch if they were not repelled by the mud puppies that abounded in the icy water; and then she thought of the lambent green pool in the main lodge for the exclusive use of the dudes. She thought of the one spooked and spavined old cow pony the kitchen help could ride if they wanted to go where he contrarily wanted to take them, up in the hot sage where the rattlers were or through thick copses of scratchy chokecherry or over sterile, stubbly fields pitted with gopher holes into which he maliciously stumbled when there was no need; and then she saw in her mind's eye the lively blooded bays and palominos that the dudes rode, never failing, as they mounted, to make some stale, soft-boiled joke about Western saddles. It was true, just as her mother said, that the help was asked to the square dances, only "asked" was not the right word; they had to go to show the Easterners the steps, and there could not have been any dances at all if Wylie, the horse-wrangler, had not been there to call the turns. And it was hardly like going to Paris to go down to Brophy, all but a ghost town, where the only buildings that were not boarded up were a drugstore, a grocery, the post office, a filling station, and a barbershop that was open on Tuesday and Saturday when an itinerant barber came to town. A handful of backward people, most of them named Brophy, lived in battered cabins in the shadows of the ore dumps of extinguished gold mines. In the wintertime, the story was, they often killed each other because they had nothing else to do.

The help at the Caribou blundered out of bed at five o'clock before the sun came up to begin a day that did not end until after nine at night, a day filled, besides work, with the fussy complaints about their cabins and their food from the older guests, pinches and propositions from the randy younger ones (who were not that young). There was ceaseless bickering among the staff who, xenophobic, despised the dudes and, misanthropic, despised each other. The kitchen was ruled by a fat red cook and a thin yellow pantry girl who did not speak to each other although they glared verbosely across the room, the cook from under the lowering hood of her enormous stove, the pantry girl over the counter of her bailiwick, where the smell of rancid butter was everlasting.

Every morning, as the girls and the wranglers drowsed through their breakfast of flapjacks and side meat, Miss Skeen appeared in the outer doorway of the kitchen, a homicidal German shepherd at her side (his name was Thor and he lived up to it; he had bitten many ankles and had abraded countless others), and boomed through the screen, "Howdy, pardners!" Miss Skeen, a tall and manly woman, combined in her costume the cork helmet of the pukka sahib, the tweed jacket of the Cotswold squire, the close-fitting Levi's and the French-heeled boots of the wry American cowboy, and the silver and turquoise jewelry of the colorful Southwestern aborigine. Her hair was short, her face was made of crags, she spoke in a Long Island basso profundo.

While Miss Skeen gave the men their orders for the day, her partner, Mrs. Bell, entered the kitchen to chirp admonitions to the female servants. Mrs. Bell was stout, small-mouthed, doggishly dewlapped, and she wore the khaki uniform of a Red Cross ambulance driver; her contribution to the Great War still gave her great satisfaction, and her memories of France, which were extensive and fresh, were ever on the tip of her tongue. Quite often she lapsed from Western into Army lingo, called the dining room "the mess hall," asked a guest how he liked his billet, spoke of the wranglers as "noncoms." Her awful greeting was, "Cheerio, boys and girls! Everybody get out of the right side of bed this morning, I hope, I hope?"

The five waitress-chambermaids lived a mile from the main lodge down in a pine-darkened gulch in what had once been a chicken coop and what now Mrs. Bell archly called "the girls' dorm." The door still latched on the outside and the ceilings were so low that no one taller than a child could stand up straight in any of the three small rooms. There was an outhouse, vile and distant; they were so plagued by trade rats that they had to keep everything they could in tin boxes if they did not want to find their money or their letters stolen and replaced by twigs or bluejay feathers. At that altitude it was freezing cold at night, and the laundry stove in which they burned pine knots could not be regulated, so that they had the choice of shivering or being roasted alive. They had a little time off in the afternoon, but, as often as not, Mrs. Bell would dream up some task for them that she tried to make out was a game: they would have to go gather columbines for the tables in the dining room or look for puffballs to put in the pot roast. It was exhausting work; sometimes, after a thronged weekend or a holiday, Kitty's arms ached so much from carrying burdened trays that she could not sleep, and through the long night listened anxiously to the animals gliding and rustling like footpads through the trees.

But, all the same, each spring for the past four years Kitty had been wild with impatience to get to the Caribou, to get away from home, from the spectacle of her eaten father and from her mother's bright-eyed lies, from all the maniacal respectability with which the landladies strait-jacketed the life of the town. The chicken coop was filthy and alarming, but it was not this genteel, hygienic house in which she was forced to live a double life. At the Caribou, she was a servant and she enjoyed a servant's prerogative of keeping her distance; for instance, to the rich and lascivious dude, Mr. Kopf, a painter, she had been respectful but very firm in refusing to pose for him (he wanted to paint her as Hebe), had said, in a way that left no room for argument, "I have to rest in my time off, sir." But, at home, what could she do if a boarder, valuable to her mother for the rent she paid, asked for help with a translation or the loan of lecture notes? She could not put the girl, her contemporary and classmate, in her place by calling her "ma'am," she could do nothing but supinely deliver the lecture notes together with the dumplings or lend a hand with *De Amicitia* after she had taken to the various rooms the underwear and blouses her mother had washed and ironed.

At the Caribou, there was no one she knew in any other context. Her fellow waitresses were local mountain girls, so chastely green that they were not really sure what a college was and certainly did not care. They never read, but it did not embarrass them that Kitty did. At Christmas she exchanged cards with them but they did not exist for her, or she for them, before the first of June or after Labor Day. And the dudes whose bathtubs she scoured and whose dietary idiosyncrasies she catered to came from a milieu so rich and foreign and Eastern that she could not even imagine it and therefore did not envy it.

Friendless, silent, long and exasperating, the summers, indeed, were no holiday. But she lived them in pride and without woe and with a physical intelligence that she did not exercise in the winter; there in the mountains, she observed the world acutely and with love—at dusk, the saddle horses grazing in the meadow were joined by deer seeking the salt lick; by day the firmament was cloudless and blinding and across the blue of it chicken hawks and eagles soared and banked in perpetual reconnaissance; by night the stars were near, and the mountains on the moon, when it was full, seemed to have actual altitude. On these wonders, Kitty mused, absorbed.

The voices downstairs invaded her trance. She began to calculate in pencil on the margin to the left of "If poisonous minerals . . ." how many more hours there were to come before she got into the rattletrap mail coach that would take her, coughing spastically in its decrepitude, up the rivered canyons and over the quiet passes to her asylum. Her arithmetic did not deafen her. She heard:

"I grant you that the hours are long and the pay is low," her mother said, "but the Caribou attracts big spenders from the East and the tips more than make up for the poor wages. I don't mean your flashy tourists and I don't mean your snobby new rich but simply your settled, well-to-do people, mostly middle-aged and older. Mrs. Bell and Miss Skeen are cultured—went to boarding school in Switzerland as I understand it—and they are ladies and, as a result, they are particular about their clientele—

absolutely will not tolerate anything in the least out-of-the-way. For one thing, they don't allow drinking on the premises, and anyone who breaks the rule is given his walking papers without any further ado, I don't care if his name is Astor or John Doe. And with all the beer-drinking and what-not going on down here when those fast boys come flocking to town from heaven knows where in those convertible roadsters with the cut-outs open and those horns that play a tune, it's a comfort to me to know that my daughter is out of the way of loose living."

"Oh, I agree," said Mrs. Ewing, and Kitty could imagine her nodding her head spiritedly and shaking loose the bone hairpins that held her gray braids in place. "I happen to know that the drinking that goes on in this town is decidedly on the upgrade. In these bowling alleys and so on, they spike the three point two with grain alcohol. And that's the very least of it. There are many, many ether addicts in the frat houses. Oh, I'm telling you, there are plenty of statistics that would make your hair stand on end. D.T.s and so on among the young."

For a few minutes then the ladies lowered their voices and Kitty could not hear what they said, but she knew the bypath they were joyfully ambling down; they were expounding the theory that beer-drinking led to dope and dope to free love and free love to hydrocephalic, albino, club-footed bastard babies or else to death by abortion.

The fact was that both Mrs. Bell and Miss Skeen were lushes, and they fooled nobody with their high and mighty teetotal rule and their aura of Sen-Sen. The rule was at first a puzzle and a bore to the dudes, but then it became a source of surreptitious fun: outwitting the old girls became as much a part of the routine as fishing or hunting for arrowheads. For the last two years, Kitty Winstanley had acted as middleman between the guests and the bootlegger, Ratty Carmichael. There was local option in the state, but in Meade County where the Caribou lay there was nothing legal to drink but three point two. In an obscure, dry gully back of the cow pasture, Kitty kept her trysts with Ratty (his eyes were feral and his twitching nose was criminal) and gave him handfuls of money and orders for bottles of atrocious brown booze and demijohns of Dago Red. These he delivered at dinnertime when Miss Skeen and Mrs. Bell were in their cabin, The Bonanza, oblivious to everything but their own elation, for which excellent Canadian whisky, bought honorably in Denver, was responsible. Kitty had no taste for this assignment of hers—she was not an adventurous girl—but she was generously tipped by the dudes for running their shady errands and for that reason she put up with the risks of it—being fired, being caught by the revenue officers and charged with collusion.

She smiled, finishing her multiplication. In 283 more hours, immediately after her last examination in final week, she would be putting her suitcase into the mail truck parked behind the post office. And a good many of those hours would be blessedly spent in sleep. Then she'd be gone from this charmless town on the singed plains where the cottonwoods were dusty and the lawns were straw. She'd be gone from the French dolls and baby pillows in the lodgers' rooms. And, in being gone, she would give her mother a golden opportunity to brag to the summer roomers: "Kitty has the time of her life," she could hear her mother say to some wispy, downtrodden schoolteacher waif, "up there where the ozone is as good as a drink, as they say."

Now the light was paling on the summit snows. Kitty heard her father's soft-footed, apologetic tread on the back porch and heard Mrs. Ewing brightly say, "Well, I must toddle along now and thanks a million for the treat. My turn next time."

The music student was at work on *The Well-Tempered Clavichord* and the phonograph was playing "The Object of My Affection" as fast as merry-go-round music. And down in the kitchen, as she clattered and banged her pots and pans, Mother Pollyana began to sing "The Stein Song."

The Mountain Day

WHEN I woke up that morning, in the fallow light before the sunrise, and remembered that the night before I had got engaged to Rod Stephansson, I could feel my blue eyes growing bluer; I could feel them becoming the color of the harebells that were blooming now in August all through the pasture beneath my window, and I thought, Will Rod notice this change and how will he speak of it? For weeks, like a leaf turning constantly to the sun for its sustenance, so my whole existence had leaned toward Rod's recognition and approval of me, as if without them I would fade and wither. When I was alone and he was miles away from me, not thinking of me at all, probably, as he catalogued botanical specimens at the Science Lodge, I nevertheless caused his eyes to take in the way I brushed my hair or mounted my horse or paddled my little brother Davy across our lake and back in the canoe. And going further, I would project us into the autumn, when our Western holiday would be over and he would come down from Harvard for a weekend in New York. I would, in my daydreams, receive him in a dozen different dresses and a dozen different countenances: now I was shy, now I was *soignée*, now unassailably cool and pure; sometimes I was talking in sparkling repartee on the telephone when he arrived, and sometimes I was listening to phonograph records; depending on my costume and my coiffure, the music was Honegger or Louis Armstrong or plainsong. Often, in the self-conceit of my love, I was so intent upon his image of me that I could not, for a moment, summon up an image of *him*. How was that possible! The mountain sun had turned him amber and had lightened his leonine hair; he was tall and lithe and sculptured and violet-eyed, and the bones of his intelligent face were molded perfectly. My sister Camilla, two years older than I and engaged to be married to a brilliant but distinctly batrachian Yale man, had, on first seeing Rod, said, "If he's really going to be a doctor, the girl that marries him is in for trouble. What a practice he's going to have among women! Brother!"

I think I got this pressing need for high opinion from my

father, who was a rich man of intellect and education but one of no vocation. Our life was sumptuous and orderly, and we lived it, in the winter, in New York and, in the summer, in the mountains of Colorado. The Grayson fortune, three generations old, founded on such tangibles as cattle, land, and cargo vessels, was now a complex of financial abstractions, the manipulation of which my father had turned over to bankers and brokers, since money, as a science, did not interest him. He had zeals and specialties, but I think he spent his whole life worrying about what people thought of him; a man of leisure had become an anachronism. One time, when he came to visit me at college and I had been telling him about a close friend of mine who was going on to study law after she finished at Bryn Mawr, he said, "D'you know, Judy, if I hadn't been rich, I'd have been a bum." He was not ashamed of his millions—they were no fault of his—but he *was* ashamed that his life was not consecrated; he had no fixed orbit. And, in a different way, this unease of his had come down to me, his middle child.

But I wasn't thinking of Daddy that morning—it was only years later that I was able to arrive at this analysis—and when I thought of Camilla's reaction to Rod, I went back to the first time I had met him and reviewed all the stages of growth that had culminated the night before in his asking me to marry him. I lay straight and still and smiling, my eyes wide open, hearing the pristine song of the first meadow larks on the fence posts, and hearing the famished, self-pitying coyotes wailing up in the sage.

One day late in June, soon after our arrival in Colorado, Daddy and Mother and Camilla and I had ridden our horses over to the Science Lodge to have lunch with a friend of Daddy's—Dr. Menzies, a geophysicist from Columbia, who taught there in the summers. It was an annual expedition, like the trip to the glacier, and the regatta at Grand Lake, and opening night at Central City; Daddy was a ritualist—each year, for example, he had the same four seats at Carnegie Hall for the Boston Symphony—and whether we liked it or not, we participated in his ceremonies. It had always bored Camilla and me terribly to go to the Science Lodge. The place was a dismal aggregate of log cabins, some of which were laboratories and lecture rooms and others Spartan living quarters for the faculty and for the dozen or so students—solemn, silent, myopic youths, who, we decided, must be even more solemn in the winter, at college, since coming to the Lodge to study high-altitude vegetation and the mineralogy of moraines was their notion of a holiday; the boys we knew bicycled through France or fooled around on boats off Martha's Vineyard. Everyone, staff and students and guests, sat at one long table in the mess hall and ate fried beefsteak, dehydrated potatoes, canned peas, and canned Kadota figs, and drank sallow coffee with canned milk. Daddy and Dr. Menzies would fervently discuss some such thing as the wisdoms and the follies of foundations. Mother, who was a beauty and had no intellectual class consciousness, would try to talk about flower arrangement with the ecologists and the systematic botanists, who blushed and addressed their eyes to their food. And Camilla and I would flounder through the maneuvers of "Do you know So-and-So at Dartmouth?" or "Have you been up to Troublesome Falls yet?," and, for our pains, got monosyllabic replies, usually in the negative. Not one time, until this summer, had she and I found any of these young men worthy of comment; they were, indeed, so much of a kind and so stunningly dull that in our private language we had a generic term, "a Science Lodge type," to designate nonentities we got stuck with at parties.

And then, this year, sitting directly across the table from me was Rod Stephansson, so sudden, somehow, so surprising, that I averted my eyes, as if his radiance would blind me. He was as serious as the other boys, but he was not solemn, and he and Mother, in a conversation about Boston, which she knew from visits to our aunts and cousins there and he knew because he went to Harvard, so charmed each other that long before we had reached the Nabiscos and the viscous figs, she had invited him to our house for Sunday supper. He was sophisticated and funny and acute, but he was gentle, too, and mannerly. His smile, in which the responsive eyes played the leading role, made me giddy, but I wanted, nevertheless, to remain within its sphere.

As soon as lunch was over, the scientists and their apprentices bolted for their microscopes and samples of pyrites—all except Dr. Menzies and Rod, who came with us to the hitching post where we had left the horses. As we sauntered through the red dust under the amazing alpine sky, I was breathless, filled with trepidation that I was going to do something clumsy and cause this paragon, who had not once looked in my direction, to despise me. So emphatic had been his immediate effect on me that, as if I had already committed the blunder and excited his disdain, I angrily shrugged my shoulders and said to myself, "Oh, to hell with him! He's nothing but a Science Lodge grind." But something quite else happened; when I had mounted Chiquita, my squatty little pinto cow pony, Rod took a blue bandanna handkerchief out of his pocket and, as if this were the most natural thing in the world, began to wipe the red dust off my boot and the edge of my jodhpurs, and when he was through—in my heady reveries later on I was to find it significant that he cleaned only *one* boot, so that my horse concealed him from the rest of the party—he looked up and gave me that inebriating smile and, in a secret voice, for my ears only, he said, "You'll be there on Sunday, won't you? You won't go off to Denver, or anything like that?" It never occurred to me to give him a flirtatious reply; I realized, with awe and with self-consciousness, that Rod had outgrown boyhood and the games of boyhood.

On the five-mile ride home, I was glad that Camilla and Daddy questioned Mother about him, because my voice would have come out as a croak or a squeak. Mother said he had told her that he was of Norwegian descent and came from Buffalo, and that he was going into his second year at Harvard Medical School. His family for generations had been landscape gardeners and horticulturists, and he had come out to the Science Lodge because, through his father, he had become interested in plant pathology ("He's very keen on viruses," said Mother), and Dr. Miles Houghton, eminent in the field, was on the staff this year. It was then that Camilla expressed her pity for the girl who married him, but Mother said, "I don't think he's in the least like that. His looks wouldn't mean a blessed thing if he weren't so awfully bright and nice. I think his character is very well put together."

It was a storybook summertime romance, woven in the mountain sun and mountain moonlight, beginning that first Sunday when he came to supper and delighted everyone. All my senses were heightened, as if I had been inoculated with some powerful, sybaritic drug: the aspen leaves were more brilliant than they had ever been before, the upland snow was purer, the pinewoods were more redolent, and the gentle winds in them were more mellifluous; the berries I ate for breakfast came from the bushes of Eden. In love with Rod, I seemed to love my parents more than ever, and Camilla and Davy, and my grandmother, who summered in a house across the lake from us; I adored the horses and the dogs and the barn cats and the wary deer that sometimes came at dusk down to the salt lick after the cows had been taken in.

Rod had never been West before, and because I had been coming here in the summer ever since my infancy, I was his cicerone, and took him to beaver dams and hidden waterfalls and natural castles of red rock, and to isolated, unmarked tombstones where God knew what murdered prospectors or starved babies were buried. We sifted the fool's gold of the cold streams through our fingers and we ate sweet piñon nuts; we rowed and rode and climbed and fished, and played doubles with Daddy and Camilla. No other young man—not even Camilla's Fritzie Lloyd, whom Daddy liked enormously—had ever evoked from Daddy so much esteem, and once he said, "He plays at everything so well and handsomely, *besides* having medicine and virtue."

Rod rose at dawn to study ergot and potato blight, but in midafternoon he walked over to our house, in long, easy strides. When he got to the foot of the broad steps that led up to the veranda, he was not out of breath or hot or exhausted. I, trembling inwardly and greeting him with a falsely cool "Hey, Rod," would think, If I tell him I have been reading *War and Peace,* will he respect me?

For it was his respect, I suppose, that I wanted as much as I wanted his love. I wanted him to honor my judgments and my abilities as much as I honored his, but through some fortunate poise, inherited from my mother to counterbalance the doubt I had got from Daddy, I was not compelled to compete with him, as I often had to compete, to my grief, with boys whose unsureness of themselves made me arrogant. I must complement, not equal, Rod. Actually, I was not so uneasy with him as I sound; in his presence I was simply and naturally happy, and it was only when we were apart that I tried on different attitudes and opinions in search of the one he would like in me the best.

When August came and the holiday began to wane, I grew restive. In two weeks more, Rod would go back to Buffalo and I would go back to New York with my family, and soon after that we would be separated—we who had been inseparable since June—by a million light-years, he in Cambridge and I at Bryn Mawr. The night before, I had thought that if he did not speak in some way of the future, I would get sick. But I had set my sights so low that the most I had hoped for was an invitation to the Yale-Harvard game, and instead of that he had asked me to marry him! Is there anything on earth more unearthly than to be in love at eighteen? It is like an abundant spring garden. My heart was the Orient, and the sun rose from it; I could have picked the stars from the sky.

The evening had started out badly. Fritzie Lloyd had come on from St. Louis for a week's visit, and at dinner he and Daddy had had an argument about Truman's foreign policy that had unsettled everyone. My father was, except in one particular, the very mildest of men: politically, he was a mad dog, and someone who disagreed with him became, temporarily, his mortal enemy. As I have said, he was very fond of Fritzie and highly approved of him for Camilla, but that night, over the Nesselrode, when Fritzie suggested, at considerable length, that the British attitude toward Communist China was more realistic than ours, Daddy protested so violently that you would have thought he might at any moment go and get a gun and shoot to kill. Everyone, and Fritzie most of all, was frightened by his fuming, stuttering rage, and after dinner Mother, to get us out of the house and calm Daddy down with a game of cribbage, proposed that Camilla and Fritzie and Rod and I take the station wagon and go somewhere to dance.

The only place within miles was a squalid, dusty honky-tonk in Puma, patronized by subhuman ne'er-do-wells and old wattled trollops who glared hostilely at us when we went in; at the bar an ugly customer, very drunk, spat on the floor as we walked by, and with feral hatred said, "Goddam yearling dudes!" The reek of beer and green moonshine and nasty perfume, together with my grief that the summer was almost gone, harried me and made me hot and weak, and I was silent. Fritzie was morose and kept saying things like "I *know* which way the land lies with your old man, so why do I have to make him sore? Damn it, I like him so, what makes me pick the one thing that's going to make him take a scunner to me?" And Camilla kept stroking the back of his hand and consoling him, telling him that of *course* he didn't have to go back to Missouri the next day, and that while she knew it had been an awful experience, she was awfully proud of his sticking to his guns, and he must stop fretting, because Daddy honestly was probably dying of remorse this minute and was the *original* hatchet-burier. Rod and I danced once—speechless, except at the very end of the jukebox record, when he said, his lips in my hair, "I wish when we went out it would be snowing." Snowing! He wanted the winter to come? I gasped and whispered back, "Oh, no! I love the summer," and he replied, "I know, but I love the snow. I love the Public Garden in the snow. The swan-boat pond, those trees . . ." And he drifted off into a musing reverie that excluded me. Soon after that, we went back home, in melancholy silence.

Mother and Daddy had gone to see Grandmother, and Camilla and Fritzie, cheered by Daddy's absence, went into the house to drink Jack Daniels, which they had just discovered, and which they talked about as if their drinks of it, on the rocks, were the insignia of a particularly lofty secret society. Rod wanted to go out on the lake, and as I was helping him put the red canoe into the water, my mood of sorrow left, and I was abruptly dreadfully excited and felt that all my nerves were pulsing.

At its widest, Daddy's lake was just under a mile, and it was so deep in places that whenever I took Davy out on it, I put him in a Mae West. It was a wonderful lake—limpid, blue, shaped like a heart. Daddy stocked it each year, and the rainbow trout that came from it were so beautiful they looked like idealized paintings of trout. Not far from the pier at Grandmother's house, there was a dense meadow of water lilies, and in the shallows near the shores tall cattails grew. But there were some horrid inhabitants of that lovely water, too—huge turtles and hellbenders, about which Davy sometimes had screaming nightmares. Rod and I paddled smoothly and languidly across to Grandmother's shore, and when we turned back, he said,

"Let's sprint." The speed, our harmony, our skill, the spicy smell of the serviceberry bushes blooming along the bank, the stars, the lost, lorn, glamorous admonitions of far-off owls—these, and my love for Rod, required of me some articulation, for I could not bear the pressure and the tension of my experience. I might have screamed, I might have cried, but instead I began uncontrollably to laugh. It was my nervous system, not my mind at all, that initiated this uproarious giggling, which was immediately communicated to Rod. The lake had an echo, and we could hear our gagging, pealing ha-ha's coming back to us from all sides, but we managed, crippled as we were—aching, undone—to continue at the speed we had set and, still laughing, get the canoe to shore and up into the reeds and grass. We were spent. There had been no joke and I was a burst balloon. Now, in me, there was nothing but dejection, like a burden on my bones, and I lay down on the grass with my arms straight at my sides, as if I were lying in my casket.

And it was then, in the vast mountain hush, after our meaningless, visceral bout of mirth, that Rod asked me to marry him. Oh, the originality of my sensation! The uniqueness of this circumstance!

We heard Camilla and Fritzie talking on the veranda, and after a while we went up to join them, and to tell them that we were engaged They seemed immeasurably old to me, for they had been through this delirious distemper so long ago, and they seemed kind and staid, as if they were our aunt and uncle, when, soothingly, they said that in this case we must have champagne.

Now, the next morning, the household was sleeping late, for it was Sunday, and there wasn't a sound except for the birds and an occasional moo or whinny; the sun had risen, and the derelict coyotes had slunk away, still hungry and pessimistic. While I was bewitched with my treasures—my memories were as new and crisp and astonishing as Christmas presents—I grew restless and could not wait for everyone to get up. I wanted to talk to Camilla and Mother, I wanted to hug Davy, I wanted to rush across the lake in the outboard to embrace my acerb, Dresden-doll grandmother and tell her what had happened to me; she would quiz me and tease me and insult me for being so young, and in the end she would rummage through the bottle-green velvet reticule she always carried and give me something antique and precious—a tiny perfume flask or a set of German-silver buttons.

Rod was coming over at eleven, and he and Fritzie and Camilla and I were going up to the glacier. We would ride as far as the ruin of the Bonanza silver mine, and go the rest of the way on foot and have our lunch on the summit of McFarland's Peak, above the mammoth slope of ice. But that was eleven and it was only six! Is he awake, I thought. Is he trying to imagine what I'm doing? With his eyes following me, I got up and put on my pink quilted peignoir and went to the window to see what sort of day we would have for our excursion. It was going to be perfect; it was what my father called "a mountain day." The air was so clear and rarefied it seemed to be an element superior to anything terrestrial—an unnamable essence that had somehow made its way to our valley and our range from another hemisphere. The violent violet peaks stood out against a sky of cruel, infuriated blue, and the snows at timberline shone like sun-struck mirrors. There was no wind; the field of harebells was motionless; the dark-blue lake was calm, and the red canoe, bottom up in the reeds, gleamed in the pure light like a bright, immaculate wound.

I dressed at last, changing a dozen times, trying first slacks, then Levi's, then khaki frontier pants, then jodhpurs, next a red shirt, a blue pullover, a black turtleneck, a striped apache jersey; I did my hair in a ponytail, in a pompadour, in pigtails, and finally I brushed it out straight and let it hang loose to my shoulders.

As soon as I decently could, I went across to Grandmother's and had breakfast with her and told her about Rod. She was pleased; she said that Rod was an Adonis and that she saw no point in marrying if one couldn't marry a handsome man. She opened up that vast, obsolete bag of hers and gave me a gold pin in the shape of two clasped hands.

My grandmother's house was, in these wildwoods of Colorado, a remarkable incongruity, for while she loved the West—she and my grandfather, who died when I was six, had started coming out here when my father, their son, was a baby, suffering from asthma—she despised roughing it. She could

not bear crudity or imperfection, and she constantly implored
Mother and Daddy to get rid of our cowhide rugs and our
flawed, bubbly Mexican glassware and our redwood furniture.
Her own house, though its exterior was the same as ours—rambling and made of logs—was furnished much as her apartment
in New York was; the Oriental rugs were second-best and some
of the tapestry chair-seat covers were machine-made, but the
total effect, nonetheless, was that of an oasis of civilization in a
barbaric waste. Each year she brought her maids with her, and
for the past two or three summers they had been two red-haired
Irish girls, Mary and Eileen, who looked down their pretty
noses at Mother's servants—local mountain girls who wore
ankle socks and cardigans when they served dinner.

Grandmother was not a snob. It was simply that her nature
demanded continuity. Her maids today were going to Mass
in Peaceful Glen, twenty miles away, and were to be driven
there by Bandy, our horse-wrangler and general handyman.
Mass was celebrated at the Glen only once a month, by an
itinerant priest, who toured continually through the mountains
and the plains to the sparse and widely separated settlements of
Catholics. Like all such Sundays, it was a red-letter day for Mary
and Eileen, and I could hear them in the kitchen, chattering
as excitedly as girls going to a dance. Grandmother, a benign
and understanding mistress, always gave them the day off after
breakfast until it was time for them to prepare her tea, and
she came to our house for lunch. After church, if the weather
was good, the girls had a picnic beside the lake—an endearing,
old-fashioned picnic, with a tablecloth and a wicker hamper.
They were planning one for today, Mary said when she came
in to clear away the breakfast things.

Grandmother told her that I was going to marry Rod. "That
Viking lad," said Grandmother, and Mary, transfigured with
happiness for anyone else's happiness, said, with her habitual
lavish sentimentality, "It's as if it was my own wedding day. Oh,
Miss Judy! May every saint and angel bless you!"

The rest of the morning somehow passed. Daddy had
completely forgotten his wrath of the evening before and was
talking baseball with Fritzie on the veranda while Mother and
Camilla and I sat in Mother's bedroom and talked about en-

gagements and marriage, and about Rod. Mother said, "What good girls I have, to pick out such extremely agreeable young men!" Finally, the last drop of the coffee in the pot on Mother's breakfast tray was gone, and she got up and went to the window and exclaimed, "What a day, what a day! How I envy you pretty girls going off up to McFarland's with your beaux! Do you realize how *important* love is at this time of your lives?" She was ragging us, of course, as Grandmother always did, but she partly meant what she said, for there was the faintest note of the disappointment of maturity in her voice. "What a mushy woman you are!" said Camilla affectionately, and Mother said, "And what a cold, critical woman you are! Now run, the pair of you, and have the grandest skylark ever."

Camilla and Fritzie rode ahead and carried on an enthusiastic conversation. Fritzie was studying architecture at Yale, and Camilla was studying art at Vassar, and they were both extremely ardent and in the know; they were, besides, after nearly a year of being engaged, so comfortable with each other that their relationship was no longer an *idée fixe*. But Rod and I were shy and strained, and, I suppose, in a sense we were wretched. These early stages of love are an egg-treading performance, and one is stiff and scared; the day after betrothal is made up almost equally of hell and heaven. He told me at length and feelingly, as if he were talking about the death of beloved kinsmen, how blight had all but obliterated the chestnut trees in the Northeast; so earnestly did I seek to maintain our concord of the night before that I nearly moaned to hear his facts, and languished with the roots of those afflicted trees, and turned my face away from the disease spores disseminated by the wind, and with my whole heart hoped that the attempt to cross the American species of chestnut with the blight-resistant Asiatic would be successful. After this, a leaden silence fell. But gradually, as we ascended the faint trail through Indian paintbrush and columbines, and the air began to make us drunk, we were infected by the glory and the grace of the day and we relaxed a little. I had, indeed, been so rigidly controlled that I had got cramps in the calves of both legs. Finally, ready to cry out with pain, I told Rod, who at once became my doctor and my protector. We dismounted in a field of volunteer timothy, and he massaged my legs until the knots were gone; the gesture, in itself utilitarian, served to return us to our rapture of the night before, and we were able to meet each other's eyes.

And now, much happier, we spurred our horses and came abreast of Camilla and Fritzie, and all the rest of the way to the mine the four of us had a general, factual conversation about New York restaurants, and Broadway musicals we had seen. To the unspoken relief of both Camilla and me, Rod and Fritzie obviously liked each other, and when they were hobbling the horses, we stood aside, praising them. Camilla said, "Rod really is a pet," and I said, "Fritzie grows on one. Last night when Daddy was being such a pain in the neck, I decided he was made of *steel*."

We had our lunch at the top of the world, sitting on saddle blankets spread out upon waxy yellow glacier lilies, which grew beside a snowdrift that some exotic bacteria had made the color of raspberry sherbet. We had cold fried chicken and tomato sandwiches and melon balls and lemony iced tea; it was unquestionably the best meal I had ever eaten in my life. I suddenly remembered Mary and Eileen and their picnic; they would be sitting among the wildflowers, eating dainty nasturtium sandwiches and telling each other spooky ghost stories in their delicious Dublin voices, and I thought, Everyone is happy today; this is the happiest day in the history of the world.

We dozed a little, all four of us, and drowsily watched an eagle banking and wheeling overhead as he scanned the earth for a jack rabbit for his lunch. We remained in this golden somnolence until a sharp wind riffled our hair and warned us that not long from now the sun would start going down. We gathered some of the lilies to decorate our bridles, and then we went slowly back to the horses, all of us quiet from our tranquil cat naps and our fulfillment and our unshakable faith in our future lives.

In Colorado, almost every afternoon in the summertime the Devil briefly beat his wife; the skies never darken but there is a short, prodigal fall of crystal rain. When it came today, we made for shelter in a stand of spruce, and when it was over, in only a few minutes, and we emerged, we found a vivid rainbow arched over the eastern sky. The pot of gold must be in the middle of our lake, I thought, exactly where my paroxysmal laughter had begun last night.

"This is too much," said Fritzie. "This is overdoing things. It's a cheap Chamber of Commerce trick."

"I know," said Camilla. "This is the most embarrassing, show-off place in the world. It's like advertisements for summer resorts. Strictly corn."

By the time we came in sight of the clearing where Grandmother's house stood, the shadows were beginning to lengthen and the air was turning cold. Camilla, shivering, said, "Let's stop at Grandmother's for tea. If we play our cards right, she'll give us rum in it."

"I want Jack Daniels," said Fritzie. "I feel so good I want to get loaded."

"You can't get loaded in my well-bred grandmother's drawing room," said Camilla. "She loathes oafs. But she won't mind if you get *comfy* with booze."

I was hesitant. "Grandmother won't like us to be dressed this way for tea," I said, but Camilla overrode my finicking objection, and we followed her lead, going the rest of the way at a lope and enthusiastically agreeing that we were hungry and that we wanted the indoor amenities of a hearth fire and soft sofas. After we had dismounted, leaving the horses free to crop the grass, and were walking up the path to the house, I heard, from our house, across the broad expanse of water, the sound of the phonograph playing Daddy's favorite Mozart quintet; every stimulus that my senses received intensified the enraptured condition of my heart, which was palpitating now in anticipation of Grandmother's regal greeting to Rod.

Tousled and dusty, we tramped through the foyer, where stood a venerable grandfather clock and two ponderous Spanish chairs, and into the long, generous drawing room, where vases of columbines were everywhere. But there was no fire burning and the tea table had not been laid, and Grandmother, dressed in Sunday-afternoon taffeta, with a fichu at her throat, was pacing up and down, Grandfather's thin gold pocket watch in her hand. She turned to us with a look of consternation and appeal, and, forgetting, in her engrossing worry, to be a hostess, she said, "Did you come round the lake? Did you see Mary and Eileen? They were due back long ago!"

"No, we didn't come that way," said Camilla. "We've come down from the glacier. Don't you suppose they're just off looking for puffballs? They so love the nasty things."

Grandmother shook her head. "They're the most punctilious servants I've ever had. They wouldn't go roaming off without letting me know. I was taking a nap, but all the same they would have left a note."

"Maybe they went to sleep after their picnic," I said. "We did."

"Oh, I don't think they'd do a thing like that," said Grandmother. "Still . . ."

"Bandy brought them home all right?" I said, and when Grandmother nodded, Rod said, "Then they can't be far."

"We'll go and see if they went to sleep," said Camilla. "We'll find them, darling, never you fear. They've got to make us an enormous tea, because we're absolutely ravenous."

"We'll find them," echoed Rod reassuringly, and Fritzie said, "Don't worry, Mrs. Grayson. We'll be back with your girls in a minute."

"Good children," said Grandmother, and smiled at us, but then she looked fearfully out the window, where vermilion had begun to tinge the western sky. "Hurry, my dears, it'll soon be dark."

My grandmother's anxiety had not really infected us, partly because, being fearless ourselves, we were not afraid for anyone else, and partly because we were unwilling to relinquish our earlier carefree mood, and we started our walk around the lake in a spirit of sport, affectionately making fun of Grandmother for sending us out as a posse, as if the West were still wild and her maids had been scalped by Indians or were being held as hostages by road agents. We took the trail around the lake that was the longest way to our house, for Camilla and I knew that it was on this side, on a favorite plot of grass, that the girls always had their picnic; we had often seen them there. After they had come back from Mass, they would take off their perky, beflowered, beribboned hats and their white cotton gloves and their good shoes, but they would keep on their Sunday-best dresses for their light and ladylike collation. To Camilla and me, whenever we spied on them, they looked like an illustration in an old-fashioned romantic novel.

As we walked along, in single file, we discussed the many places they might be, safe and innocent, if we did not—as we were sure we would—find them snoozing in the dying day. Perhaps, all unknown to Grandmother, they had beaux, who had flattered and cajoled them into being late; perhaps they were bird watchers and could not tear themselves away from some fascinating rite of magpies; perhaps they had strolled over to the dude camp nearby and were watching an amateur rodeo; perhaps a dozen things. Punctilious as Grandmother said they were, they were bound to lapse at least once in a blue moon.

Presently, halfway around the lake, we came to that favorite plot of grass, where, sure enough, the Irish girls had spread out their picnic. Its corners neatly held down with rocks, the tablecloth with a pattern of tulips was neatly set for two with blue willowware plates and kitchen silver and jelly glasses; in the middle of the tablecloth there was a Dundee marmalade jar filled with Mariposa lilies. But the embossed-paper napkins had not been unfolded, the glasses had not been filled from the thermos, and the hamper had not been opened.

Perplexed and at last alarmed, we stood silent and unmoving for a minute, pointlessly scanning the immediate neighborhood, as if the maids were going to materialize before our eyes. It was Rod who spoke first.

"It does look queer," he said. "If they'd gone for a swim, they'd have come back by now. They'd have been starved after fasting for so long."

"Anyhow, they don't know how to swim," I said. "Neither one of them. Not a stroke."

"Then the lake's out, thank God," said Fritzie. "Or— They never use the boats, I suppose?"

Camilla and I exchanged a look of horror. Mary and Eileen were forbidden to use the canoe, but, out of their ignorance, they could not, would not, believe in the perils of the lake, and over and over again someone would catch them paddling, grotesquely maladroit, through the shallow water under the willow trees that lined the shore on this side.

"Oh, God!" cried Camilla, and she and I, with the boys at our heels, plunged down through the bushes that hid the water from us here, stumbling over the rocks and the willow suckers. When we got to the lake's edge, we saw the canoe immediately, away to our right, riding upside down in the mild wind over a deep spot in the lake, not far from shore.

"Where do you keep the outboard?" asked Rod. His voice, though it was urgent, was controlled.

"There's one at Grandmother's," I said. "That's nearest."

"Then come on!" he said.

As Grandmother and Camilla and I stood by the dock watching the boys get into the outboard, it occurred to me suddenly that there was just possibly a chance that the poor, dear, clumsy girls had let the canoe go adrift after their guilty outing in it, and that—first debating for a while, dreading the scolding Daddy would give them for their carelessness—they had decided to go to our house to get help. Galvanized by this wild, ingenious hope, I ran off, saying nothing to the others, and this time I took the shorter path, on the other side of the lake. As I ran, I could hear the bee-buzz of the outboard and, faintly, from our house, the promise of peace of Bach's "Sheep May Safely Graze." Daddy seemed to be having a Roman holiday this afternoon, with all the music he fancied most. And as I ran, my mouth dry and my heart hurting, through the wavering, leafy patterns of sun and shade, my obsessed and egocentric mind began, in this crisis, to seek Rod's admiration, and I thought, What will he think of this practical, intelligent, well-thought-out act of mine? Dear God, let Mary and Eileen be there! Let nothing have happened to them but Daddy's dressing down! Just then I tripped and twisted my ankle, and the pain was so sharp that it took my breath away, and, pausing for a moment in my surprise and shock, I was seized with a passion of self-loathing for wanting the girls to be alive chiefly because their being so would set me up in Rod's eyes. I began to cry for the fair-skinned, green-eyed Dublin girls, and then I faltered on.

"Sheep May Safely Graze" still floated out serenely from our house, and a peaceful tower of smoke rose from our chimney. I prayed that in a minute I was going to see Mary and Eileen. But, instead, I saw Mother standing at our dock, and Daddy and Bandy starting out in our boat. The living-room windows of our house commanded a comprehensive view of the lake, as did Grandmother's, directly opposite, and Mother told me later that she had seen Rod and Fritzie in the outboard by chance as she was watering the terrarium she kept on the sill; she had gazed at them idly for some time before she sensed that something was wrong and called my father. He had gone immediately down to the shore and shouted at the boys, who shouted back what they were doing.

"Have they—" I began, out of breath.

"They've found them, yes," said Mother. Out on the lake, I could see Rod and Fritzie diving from the boat. "Come, Judy, we must go and break the news to your grandmother. They're going to bring the bod— They're going to come back to this shore."

"Where's Davy?" I said. "Davy mustn't see!"

"Davy's all right. Luella will keep him busy. Come now." And Mother and I started out briskly, our eyes on the ground, not looking again, lest we see the boys bring two pitiful burdens to the surface of the water.

When we got to Grandmother's, we found Camilla and Grandmother in the drawing room. Even before the boys had sighted the bodies, Camilla had gone back there, to comfort Grandmother and to take her inside and persuade her not to look at the lake. We found them both in front of the fire, which Camilla had lit, Grandmother huddled in a big chair, looking terribly old and enervated. None of us could think of a word to say; we kept warming our hands at the fire and listening to the loud ticking of the grandfather clock. An age went by before we finally heard both outboards coming to this shore.

When the three men came into this silent room, their faces were stricken and sickened. My father went to his mother and put his arm around her shoulder, and she looked up at him imploringly and said, "How ever shall I tell their poor families? Ah, Samuel, we should have destroyed that canoe." My father bent down and whispered something in her ear, and she got up, weakly, and went with him into the next room. Daddy had taken her away to tell her, as gently as he could, what Fritzie told us now. Mary and Eileen could not have been in the water for more than a few hours, but in that time the hellbenders and the ravenous turtles had eaten their lovely faces and their work-swollen hands; no one, certainly no kinsman, must see them.

A heavy hush and torpor fell on all of us after we had heard this new piece of frightful intelligence. I wanted to busy myself—to turn on the lamps and dispel the murk of twilight, to straighten a stalk of yucca that was leaning gracelessly out of a vase, to prod the logs and make the sparks scintillate and snap. But my flesh was leaden, and I sat still. Once, I looked at my mother, sagging in her chair as inertly as the rest of us, and I thought, with a rush of sympathy, that living did not insulate one against shock. What must my gentle, humane grandmother be going through there in the library! How was she going to write to the girls' distant families of their death? And how, without going into the ghastly details, could she enjoin them not to open the coffins?

After a long time, Grandmother came back into the room and, mistress of her house again (though the bright unshed tears in her eyes and the quivering of her thin old hands showed that she was not yet mistress of herself), flicked the master light switch and went to draw the curtains, saying, as she did so, "By this time of day, I have had enough of the wonders of Colorado." Strengthened by her example, I got up now and attended to the listing yucca. There was a general stir in the room, and our voices were restored to us. Fritzie asked Camilla if she thought our horses would be all right, and she assured him that by this time they would have gone back to the barn and one of the men would have unsaddled them; Mother, going to the fireplace, asked Rod to help her return to its proper place one of the andirons that had shifted. My grandmother came at last to the windows that gave on the lake, and she pulled the curtains shut quickly; she shuddered and for a moment stood still, confronting the blank expanse of wine-red velours. As if she were alone, as if she were speaking to herself or to God, she murmured, "I won't come here again with innocents."

She turned around then and said to my mother, "Samuel and I have agreed that under the circumstances someone should personally explain to the girls' families what happened—Samuel will go to Ireland at once."

My mother said only, "He'll have no trouble booking at this time of year," and my grandmother nodded, closing the subject of the sudden voyage.

My father came into the room carrying a tray of drinks, and Grandmother said, "It's cold; there's autumn in the air. Samuel and I decided that we all needed something to warm us on the inside."

It was the first time I had ever been given a real drink, and as Daddy handed me the glass, I thought, Is he being absent-minded or does this mean I'm accepted as grown up? I didn't know which it was—the symbol of the whiskey, or my family's love for me and my love for them and my recognition of my security (I was thinking simultaneously of Mary's family and Eileen's, still ignorant of the crumbling of *their* solidarity as they lived through an ordinary day in Dublin), or whether it was my grandmother's moral majesty, which I saw for the first time and wanted to emulate. Whatever it was, I found myself just then standing firmly on my own, and I was able to see everyone clearly—even myself. Earlier, in my blinding cocoon, when I had thought so constantly about Rod's respect for me, I had lost, in a sense, my respect for myself, but now, at last, I was able to think of *him* and not of his opinion of *me*. Bedraggled, my hair all wild, beggar's-lice on my sweater and my trousers, I did not care at all how I looked. I cared only, looking at the green pallor of his face, that he had suffered. I wanted him to be as happy as he had been before we had started our search for the girls, and I thought, Love, real love, is just that: it is wanting the beloved to be happy. The simplicity of the equation surprised me, but only for a moment and then it was incorporated into me as naturally as if it had been there all along.

The Darkening Moon

THERE was not a star in the sky, scarcely a sound in the air except for the soft gabbling of the creek. The little girl, when she had shut the kitchen door behind her and so shut in the yellow light, stood for a moment in the yard, taking her breath in sharply as though to suck in the mysterious element that had abruptly transformed day into dark. She was alone beneath the black firmament and between the blacker mountains that loomed up to the right and to the left of her like the blurred figures of fantastic beasts. She stepped forward, round the corner of the house where her brother's horse was tied. Before her lay the town with its long, glittering serpentine line of lights leading down from the mine, the double line marking the main street, and the helter-skelter porch lights of the miners' cabins. She heard the children tumbling out screen doors, calling, "One, two, three, four, five, six, Red Light!" before they had swallowed the last mouthful of their suppers. And the jukeboxes at The Silver Slipper and Uncle Joe's commenced to play conflicting tunes.

Ella was glad that tonight she was going to take a ride on Squaw, who, impatiently stamping one foot, gave voice to a muted whinny as if to show that she, too, was ready for adventure. Ella slipped the loose knot of the reins and turned the mare to mount. As she threw her leg over the saddle, her brother Fred opened the front door and called, "Wait a shake, sister." Without turning, he reached back to the table in the center of the room. His bare arm, against the glare of the lamp, was enormously magnified and knotted like the branch of a tree. He came out, leaving the door open, hesitated on the porch, and closed it just as their mother's voice came from the back of the house, "Fred! You see that stuff is tied on good and tell her not to waste no time." Ella was taking ten pounds of elk steak, tied on behind her saddle under a tarp, Fred's payment to Mr. Temple for the use of his gun sight and hackamore on the hunting trip he had just made. Her mother, who never knew a moment's peace when game was in the house, was afraid that the warden, Mr. Flint, would come by before Ella was out of the yard.

As Fred slipped the hackamore over the pommel, his sister laughed, "Golly, she's a big crybaby."

"Well! If it ain't Grandma!" he replied, and although she could not see his face for the shadows, she knew by the tone of his voice that there was a long grin on his face under the scanty blond mustache and a spiteful glint in his narrow blue eyes. Suddenly, she was spoiling for a fight. Instead of riding through the gate which he had opened for her, she lingered in the yard, waiting for an excuse to start a quarrel. But when he spoke again, it was in a different voice, the one he used when he remembered that their father's death, a year ago, had made him the head of the house.

"You shove. What do you think the Temples pay you for?" He reproduced their father's inflections so well that had she not seen his tow head, hung like a ball of mist in the darkness, she would have thought the speaker was red-haired and gray-eyed. He had perfected the imitation only in the last month: at first, his voice would break and his peremptory tone would then be merely absurd. The sound of his voice did not inspire her to obey now. Rather, it made her turn her head as though from some intolerable sight and slowly relax the reins, though she still held her feet quiet in the stirrups.

Fred slapped Squaw on the rump and the mare leaped forward violently, flinging back her head. "Looky here, when I say shove, I mean shove."

Ella did not reply, but she spurred sharply and galloped through the gate. Her brother's voice pursued her, "If you run my horse on the highway, I'll beat the living hell out of you." As she went up the steep gravel road that led to the highway, the wind whistling in her ears, she knew that he was waiting in the yard, listening to see what change in the sound of the hoofs there would be when she turned off onto the macadam. As soon as he could hear nothing more, he would turn toward the house next door and, making a megaphone of his hands, would bellow, "Harold! Oh, Harold!" Fred and Harold Bowman, who was only a senior in high school, went to Uncle Joe's about this time every night. She had heard them make the engagement this afternoon as they squatted on their haunches on either side of the fence, boasting at cross-purposes. "Yessir," Fred had been saying, "I got me a six-point buck in the flattops and it took some huntin' to get him." "Uh-huh," said his friend, "I know where there's a beaver must weigh sixty pounds."

As soon as the town was behind her, her skin stopped tingling and she gave herself up to enjoying the ride. Sometimes she dreaded this trip down to the Temple ranch to keep the children. When there was a moon or when snow had fallen, the glowing bluffs on the right side of the highway, just out of town, alarmed Squaw and she would wheel and rear, trying to throw her rider. Once, on the way home, after a heavy snow, Ella had been tossed as lightly as though she had been a pillow to the side of the road just as the big one o'clock Sante Fe Trailways went past. The bus, with its popeyes on a blunt snout, had swerved and missed her and sped on. She had had to walk the rest of the way, a mile and a half, numb with cold.

Tonight she had no trouble with the horse until she left the highway and took the Snake River road. At John Perkins' head gate, the beavers were at work in their lodge, and at the sound of them tamping the mud with their tails or dropping a stone from their forepaws, Squaw shied and it was all Ella could do to keep her from pivoting round toward home. Farther on, Squaw was startled when, coming round a bend in the narrow road, they were confronted by a grove of sarvis berry bushes, phosphorescent in the darkness. And then, when they had reached the crest of the first hill, a splash of something in the river made her rise on her hind legs, a trembling column of terror. But these antics did not disquiet Ella, for the road was only dirt and was infrequently traveled so that a fall would not amount to much. For the last mile, up and down five low hills, the horse behaved herself and Ella slowed her to an easy trot, for, although she was late, she wanted to postpone as long as possible the moment when she would go into the house.

So long as she was outdoors, she was not afraid at night. Her father had taught her that, long ago, when she was only a little girl of five and he had taken her and Fred fishing one night when the grayling were spawning. They had left her alone at the riverbank for half an hour while they went upstream through brush that would have cut her bare legs. Before they left, her father had said, "There ain't nothing to harm you, sister. The animals is all there is and they won't be looking you up." She had never been frightened by the coyotes lamenting in the sage or the bobcats howling in the woods. But if she heard them when she was alone in the Temples' house, she fancied them closing in, sobbing and whining for fresh meat, peering through the windows at her with their sulphur-colored eyes. Nor did the owls dismay her if she heard them while she was riding, but when their smug prophecies of doom were sifted through distance and closed windows, she trembled, for they seemed to speak directly to her, to say, "Look out! Look out!" Even the rats, frolicking through the walls, and even the old collie making his rounds hinted at danger. Afraid to move lest by moving she make a noise that would obscure another noise, like a footstep in the yard, she would sit motionless all evening in a big pink wing chair, staring at the wall opposite her where hung an oil painting of Mr. Temple's prize bull, Beau Mischief. By midnight, she would be wringing wet with sweat, although it was cold and she had let the fire go out. And yet, as soon as she had mounted for the ride back, her fear changed its focus and she was not anxious to get home, but only to get Squaw safely past the bluff.

One night, her foot had gone to sleep, and though it hurt enough to make her sick, she was too frightened to stamp it or even to change its position. Early in the evening, she had heard a cowbell tinkling nearby the house. None of Mr. Temple's stock wore bells. She knew she should chase away the intruder, but before she had risen to her feet, it occurred to her that perhaps it was a gypsy with a tambourine, or it might be a cow with her owner, one of those half-crazy men from Oklahoma who came to Colorado to get away from the dust and went around the country with all they owned in the world slung over their backs, sometimes leading an emaciated animal. Long after the bell had stopped, she continued to hear its echo, and dared look nowhere but at the copper ring in Beau Mischief's nose, for a straying glance might discover a sly and bitter face in the deep shadows of the open dining-room door.

She had reached the Temples' lane. In the wide hollow, the

farmhouse was so brilliantly illuminated that it seemed twice its natural size. There were lamps only on the lower floor, but over the windows of the upper story there was cast a smoky shimmer of reflected light. Two pointed chimneys at opposite ends of the roof were clearly outlined, like a bear's wide-set ears. Mr. Temple always said that if you left your house well-lighted there was less danger of being robbed, but Ella took little stock in the argument, for she reasoned that a dark house, on a dark night, was hard to see.

The children were already asleep when Ella came in, and the Temples were putting on their coats. Mr. Temple thanked her for the meat and said, "Ella, there's a cow down to the corral that's crying for her calf I butchered today. She'll carry on all night, I reckon, but don't you pay her no mind."

"Pshaw, Milton. Ella's not afraid, are you, Ella? A big girl going on twelve."

"No, ma'am, I'm not afraid," Ella said, but she clasped her hands nervously and looked down at the scuffed toes of her moccasins.

"Well, I guess a person that'll pack ten pounds of San Quentin bacon behind her saddle ain't going to be rattled by a dairy cow." Mr. Temple laughed. His wife, to urge him on, put her plump, smooth hand on his massive shoulder and, as she did so, the light caught her diamond ring, which shot forth swift filaments of green and purple. Mr. Temple, in his store clothes, would have looked like a city man if it had not been for his sunburned face and his bowlegs. But Mrs. Temple, in spite of her permanent wave and her high-heeled shoes and her georgette redingote, would always look like a farmer's wife.

Mr. Temple asked Ella if she would like to put Squaw in the east pasture by the house with the team and the boys' ponies since Squaw was clever at getting loose from a hitching post. When they started, she followed the car up the lane and turned in at the gate by the slough. The six dark forms in the field, standing in an almost perfect semicircle, did not move as the newcomer trotted toward them, but when she had taken her place, all, with one accord, lowered their massive heads and began rhythmically to crop the invisible grass.

The Temples waited until she got back to the house and shouted, "All right!" She watched the car go over the hill and listened until its diminishing snore was absorbed. In the silence that followed, the mourning cow moaned deeply; an owl gave forth one loitering, melancholy note. As she turned the door-knob, she heard, close by, a splash in the river, the second one tonight, and thought that it was either a trout leaping or an aspen sapling falling after the beavers had gnawed it down. But as she closed the door and stepped onto the shining hardwood floor, it seemed to her that the tone of the disturbed water had not been true and therefore had not been made by an animal. She stopped short, wondering what it was.

Was it one of the Negroes from the mine fishing? Often, when they did not go to The Silver Slipper on a Saturday night after they had been paid, they went to the river, taking their liquor with them. You could see them starting out about five in the afternoon. A battered, protesting old Dodge sedan would be full of black figures, so many that, although there appeared to be seven or eight in the driver's seat, no one seemed to be in charge, and the car would careen in every direction like a chicken with its head cut off. Later on, from the highway, their fires would be visible along the banks, and on a clear night, rich, imploring songs would wind through the weeping-willow trees. Ella knew what she would do if one of them came to the house. She would say, "Mr. Temple's asleep, but I'll call him," and then she would go to the back bedroom and take a .22 out of the gun cabinet and, pointing it at the man's heart, she would say, "Mr. Temple says for you to clear out."

In three long, stealthy steps she crossed the room and slipped so far back into the pink chair that her feet did not touch the floor, and then began counting by ones, calculating that when she had reached a hundred, five minutes would have passed. The clock was in the kitchen, but she had not the courage to go through the dining room, across the creaking floor of the pan-try, into the spacious kitchen, where not even bright daylight dispelled the gloomy shadows cast by large cabinets and by the many chaps hanging along one wall. Mrs. Temple, knowing that she always spent the evening in the pink chair, had put some jigsaw puzzles, *Good Housekeeping,* and the Montgomery Ward midsummer sale catalogue on a little table beside it, but Ella disliked the rustle the leaves made. She preferred to count. Sometimes, if she felt that she had gone too fast through the last decade, she made herself go back the way a teacher made a child start at the beginning again if he made a mistake in something he had memorized. It didn't pay to think it was nine o'clock when it was only a quarter to.

When she was in the eighties of her ninth hundred, so that she knew it must be around nine-thirty, she was suddenly frozen to the bone by the abrupt trotting of a horse, so near that it seemed to be halfway past the slough. Immediately, she heard another horse then another and another until it sounded like a dozen, trotting abreast. At first she thought they were on the road and would presently turn into the lane. But she did not hear the hoofs on the bridge over the slough and the sound did not come any closer. Yet it did not recede, and directly the pace speeded up to a gallop and then to a full run, and one of the creatures neighed crazily. At once, as if this had been a signal, there was a dead silence. In a moment came the epilogue: the cow's heartbreaking moo. Ella tried to go on with her counting, but she could not remember if she had left off at eighty-five or sixty-five and no sooner did she get her bearings than the horses began again: first just one trotting, then two, and so on until they had all joined in the race. The lunatic neigh was repeated; once more there was a pause, but this time it lasted only a second or two and was followed by a different sound, that of hoofs stamping on the soft sod.

"Squaw!" Ella cried the name aloud and sprang to her feet. For she knew now that Mr. Temple's Steamboat was kicking her horse. He was a big, mean, ball-faced black, sixteen hands high, and if he took a dislike to another horse, went crazy mad. He had once attacked a fine, blooded palomino that belonged to a dude from Boston who was boarding with the Temples. Steamboat had backed him up against a barbed-wire fence, and there had been a ten-inch tear in the creamy withers, and for months tufts of the white tail had stuck like feathers to the barbs.

She ran out of the house and down the lane, calling, but uselessly, for the little mare never knew her name. As she stumbled across the fields, pitted with gopher holes, she could just make out the four team horses running after her paint, and when she was halfway there, she saw the largest of them get Squaw cornered by the branding corral and start to kick, while the others stood at attention, watching respectfully. She edged along the board fence and, when she was face to face with Steamboat, flapped her arms and shouted, "Whoosh!" And the big black horse, as though he had had nothing to do with the rumpus, turned disdainfully and gave his tail an impudent flick.

As she led Squaw back to the hitching post, she looked up into the sky and, to her amazement, saw that there was a full moon overhead. It was as large as a harvest moon, as pale as lard. There had been no moon when she rode down, nor even moon sign. It was as though it had not risen, but had been slid along to cover a round hole in the sky, the way a plate with a picture on it was sometimes put over the place in a wall where a stovepipe had been.

"Ah, hell," she thought. "She'll try to buck me sure, bright as that is."

It could not have taken her more than two or three minutes to tie the horse, but when she looked up again, it seemed to her that the moon was a little smaller than it had been. It was not hidden behind a cloud, for no cloud she had ever seen could cut so clean a line. It looked as though Fred's curved butcher knife had been laid over the top part; around the curve was a narrow rim of red, not bright and barely luminous, but a rusty, burnt-out color. The immense moon had little light. The team and ponies were invisible; a faint sheen lay on the south pasture but only as far as the first irrigation ditch, and the river bridge, ten yards away, was only a black square.

The timothy had been cut two weeks before and the smell came strong and sweet. She heard the animals in the woods telling her where they were and, surveying the line of trees along the river, she saw there were no fires tonight. She gave the horse a last caress with the tips of her fingers and started back to the house. At the porch, she looked over her shoulder at the moon. At least an eighth of it was gone! The red rim glowed now and the circumference of the rest of the orb had shrunk. Her sharp eyes sought clouds to explain the phenomenon; they found nothing but the moon in the black vault.

The numbers twisted in her head. She seemed unable to get past the sixties and kept repeating herself: sixty-nine, sixty-two, sixty. It was odd, but the cow did not moo again. Usually they were inconsolable all the first night. And the owls were still. The rats traveled so lightly that they sounded more like moth millers flapping against the walls. She began counting again; she would get to fifty and then strain her ears for sounds. Once, she thought she heard a bobcat, but it was only the loose door to the bunkhouse wailing in a gust of wind. Another time, the distant drone of a truck on the highway made her think for a second that the cow had tuned up again. She counted another fifty, slipping backward, going forward two at a time, and listened. But everything was quiet. At the end of each five hundred, she went on tiptoe to the front window and knelt down, fitting her hands to her temples like blinders to look out at the moon. Each time she looked, a little more had dwindled away and the red girdle gleamed brighter. Her mouth was dry and she sucked the sides of her cheeks to moisten her throat with saliva.

Perhaps the owls and the coyotes and the beavers were still busy, quieter than usual for their own reasons. She would be able to hear them if she went outside. She could lean up against one of the porch pillars and, when she heard the car, could slip back into the house and no one would be any the wiser. And yet, when she tried to get up, her legs were wooden and she was so cold that a shiver went the length of her. The four Coleman lamps, placed at regular intervals about the long room, no longer seemed so garish; they cast a warm, saffron glow over the curly cowhide rugs and the serapes on the davenports. For the first time, she reflected that it was an elegant room. She had never before noticed the tasseled velvet runner on the library table.

Crouching on the top step, her head resting against the banister, she did not allow herself to look up into the sky for a few minutes, but instead gazed directly in front of her, making out the contours of the horse across the yard. It was motionless between the two tall leaning posts and seemed un- naturally large. At last, she admitted to herself that there were no sounds out here either. A deep silence had settled down over the sage-covered hills to the left, over the east pasture where the horses were, over the timothy and the fields beyond it. She would have been glad to hear the cow again, or the measly whine of a mosquito, or to hear . . . even a footstep! But there was nothing.

At last she looked at the sky. Less than a sixth of the moon was left, and beyond that one livid slice of light, the heavens stretched blacker than a mine shaft. As she watched, it seemed to her that the darkness, bit by bit, encroached upon the last thin rind.

Were all the creatures waiting, like her, for the final disappearance of the moon and the disaster that would follow it? Was the owl in its treetop staring upward with its yellow, impassive spectacles? Were the ravenous eyes of the quivering coyotes fixed on the moon? Perhaps the beavers had stopped in their housebuilding to keep a horrified vigil, and the cow was upturning her velvety gaze to the mortal moon. Ella could not tell precisely when the last scrap of the moon had been covered over. In a moment, even the red ring was gone, and then there was no evidence of any kind that in the sky there had hung that great white disk.

She whimpered without volition and instantly an owl in the cottonwood grove warned her, "Look out! Look out!" Holding her hands clasped over her rowdy heart, she leaped across the porch, through the door, and into the living room. One of the lamps was going out. The mantel spit forth a final spark and upon the wall above it was thrown an oblong shadow where before had been the pale green kalsomine. All the other lamps seemed mellower than usual, and she knew that any moment they, too, would use the last drop of their fuel. As though to fend off the sight of this second catastrophe, she lifted her arm, and, as she did so, saw that, just as Fred's had been, its size was doubled and its joints were caricatured.

A second lamp went out, and at once a grove of shadows shot up beside the bookshelves. They looked like cattails and made her think of the place in the river where they had gone to catch the grayling. The water had been cold and once she had slipped and fallen in up to her waist. The fish were so thick that they swarmed slimily over her and she had nearly gagged at the smell. "Bring me them on the bank there," her father had said and she had had to pick up the fat slithering blobs in her bare hands. Her father, reaching out to take them, had smeared her wrist with fish's blood which dripped in gouts from his fingertips as if it were his own. Even if he were still alive and asked her, she would not go there again! The memory for some reason, though it was only a memory of a time long ago, made her start to cry. She bent her head and crossed her arms on her chest and allowed the tears to stream down her face. She could not drive away the horror of the reptilian odor, nor could she summon her father's good-natured face. When she tried and said to herself the word "Daddy," the fruitless effort made her sob aloud and her lips lifted in the grin that accompanies the misery of weeping.

After one sob that made her rock with pain, she heard a car slowing at the water gap, picking up speed, going up the hill, and coming down it. It turned into the lane before she had wiped her eyes. So that they would not see her swollen face, she ran out and stood beside the gate.

"Why, Ella!" cried Mrs. Temple getting out of the car.

"I come out to get my horse," she said. "Your Steamboat was kicking at her and I thought I better get her out. I was just going in the house."

"Well, that ornery old bench," said Mr. Temple. "I'll straighten him out. I thought maybe my cow spooked you."

"No, sir. She never scared me. She never bellowed only once or twice."

"You're shaking, Ella," said Mrs. Temple and took her by the elbow. So that she would not see the tears, Ella turned her face away. Mrs. Temple was saying, "Maybe we oughtn't to make a little girl stay here all by her lonesome."

"Why, Opal! You're the one always says Ella don't get scared."

"I know, Milton. But it's a funny thing. Works backward with some people, you might say. Some way, as you get older . . . I don't know. I'm just thinking the way I used to be. Until I was fifteen, wasn't a living thing could give me a turn. And then, later on. . . ."

She turned away meditatively. Mr. Temple said, "Well, Ella, would you like me to take you home in the car?"

"No, sir," she replied. "I can make it."

He untied Squaw and held her steady for Ella to mount. When she had her seat, he handed her a fifty-cent piece. As she put it in the money pocket of her Levi's, Mrs. Temple called from the gate, "Oh, Ella, did you see the eclipse? The earth's shadow passed right over the moon . . . we heard about it on the radio."

"Go on, Opal," said Mr. Temple. "Ella wasn't stargazing. She was too busy looking at the pretties in the catalogue."

Ella moistened her lips with the tip of her tongue. She said, "I seen it."

"It'll come out again, you know, Ella," cried Mrs. Temple. "It'll be a full moon again by the time you get to the highway!"

Ella did not answer, for Squaw, eager to be off now that her nose was pointed toward home, pranced and whinnied so that her flanks rippled like a hard, fast pulse, and at the touch of the lines on her neck, she bounded forward at a gallop. Steamboat's long head was hung over the fence and they passed so close to him that Ella could see how his lip was hooked up, showing his grass-stained teeth. For a moment, it looked as though Squaw were going straight into the sage-covered hill and that both of them would be flattened against the boulders at the base. But the horse was no lunatic. She took the turn without slackening her pace and up and down the hills, between the scrub oak and the sarvis berry, she skimmed the air, while her dry-mouthed rider sat in the saddle with her eyes closed, certain of the animal's sagacity. A world slipped past her blinded eyes as she traversed a road she would not recognize again, beneath the full, unfaithful moon.

Bad Characters

Up until I learned my lesson in a very bitter way, I never had more than one friend at a time, and my friendships, though ardent, were short. When they ended and I was sent packing in unforgetting indignation, it was always my fault; I would swear vilely in front of a girl I knew to be pious and prim (by the time I was eight, the most grandiloquent gangster could have added nothing to my vocabulary—I had an awful tongue), or I would call a Tenderfoot Scout a sissy or make fun of athletics to the daughter of the high-school coach. These outbursts came without plan; I would simply one day, in the middle of a game of Russian bank or a hike or a conversation, be possessed with a passion to be by myself, and my lips instantly and without warning would accommodate me. My friend was never more surprised than I was when this irrevocable slander, this terrible, talented invective, came boiling out of my mouth.

Afterward, when I had got the solitude I had wanted, I was dismayed, for I did not like it. Then I would sadly finish the game of cards as if someone were still across the table from me; I would sit down on the mesa and through a glaze of tears would watch my friend departing with outraged strides; mournfully, I would talk to myself. Because I had already alienated everyone I knew, I then had nowhere to turn, so a famine set in and I would have no companion but Muff, the cat, who loathed all human beings except, significantly, me—truly. She bit and scratched the hands that fed her, she arched her back like a Halloween cat if someone kindly tried to pet her, she hissed, laid her ears flat to her skull, growled, fluffed up her tail into a great bush and flailed it like a bullwhack. But she purred for me, she patted me with her paws, keeping her claws in their velvet scabbards. She was not only an ill-natured cat, she was also badly dressed. She was a calico, and the distribution of her colors was a mess; she looked as if she had been left out in the rain and her paint had run. She had a Roman nose as the result of some early injury, her tail was skinny, she had a perfectly venomous look in her eye. My family said—my family discriminated against me—that I was much closer kin to Muff than I was to any of them.

To tease me into a tantrum, my brother Jack and my sister Stella often called me Kitty instead of Emily. Little Tess did not dare, because she knew I'd chloroform her if she did. Jack, the meanest boy I have ever known in my life, called me Polecat and talked about my mania for fish, which, it so happened, I despised. The name would have been far more appropriate for *him*, since he trapped skunks up in the foothills—we lived in Adams, Colorado—and quite often, because he was careless and foolhardy, his clothes had to be buried, and even when that was done, he sometimes was sent home from school on the complaint of girls sitting next to him.

Along about Christmastime when I was eleven, I was making a snowman with Virgil Meade in his back yard, and all of a sudden, just as we had got around to the right arm, I had to be alone. So I called him a son of a sea cook, said it was common knowledge that his mother had bedbugs and that his father, a dentist and the deputy marshal, was a bootlegger on the side. For a moment, Virgil was too aghast to speak—a little earlier we had agreed to marry someday and become millionaires—and then, with a bellow of fury, he knocked me down and washed my face in snow. I saw stars, and black balls bounced before my eyes. When finally he let me up, we were both crying, and he hollered that if I didn't get off his property that instant, his father would arrest me and send me to Canon City. I trudged slowly home, half frozen, critically sick at heart. So it was old Muff again for me for quite some time. Old Muff, that is, until I met Lottie Jump, although "met" is a euphemism for the way I first encountered her.

I saw Lottie for the first time one afternoon in our own kitchen, stealing a chocolate cake. Stella and Jack had not come home from school yet—not having my difficult disposition, they were popular, and they were at their friends' houses, pulling taffy, I suppose, making popcorn balls, playing casino, having fun—and my mother had taken Tess with her to visit a friend in one of the T.B. sanitariums. I was alone in the house, and making a funny-looking Christmas card, although I had no one to send it to. When I heard someone in the kitchen, I thought it was Mother home early, and I went out to ask her why the green pine tree I had pasted on a square of red paper looked as if it were falling down. And there, instead of Mother and my baby sister, was this pale, conspicuous child in the act of lifting the glass cover from the devil's-food my mother had taken out of the oven an hour before and set on the plant shelf by the window. The child had her back to me, and when she heard my footfall, she wheeled with an amazing look of fear and hatred on her pinched and pasty face. Simultaneously, she put the cover over the cake again, and then she stood motionless as if she were under a spell.

I was scared, for I was not sure what was happening, and anyhow it gives you a turn to find a stranger in the kitchen in the middle of the afternoon, even if the stranger is only a skinny child in a moldy coat and sopping-wet basketball shoes. Between us there was a lengthy silence, but there was a great deal of noise in the room: the alarm clock ticked smugly; the teakettle simmered patiently on the back of the stove; Muff, cross at having been waked up, thumped her tail against the side of the flower box in the window where she had been sleeping—contrary to orders—among the geraniums. This went on, it seemed to me, for hours and hours while that tall, sickly girl and I confronted each other. When, after a long time, she did open her mouth, it was to tell a prodigious lie. "I came to see if you'd like to play with me," she said. I think she sighed and stole a sidelong and regretful glance at the cake.

Beggars cannot be choosers, and I had been missing Virgil so sorely, as well as all those other dear friends forever lost to me, that in spite of her flagrance (she had never clapped eyes on me before, she had had no way of knowing there was a creature of my age in the house—she had come in like a hobo to steal my mother's cake), I was flattered and consoled. I asked her name and, learning it, believed my ears no better than my eyes: Lottie Jump. What on earth! What on earth—you surely will agree with me—and yet when I told her mine, Emily Vanderpool, she laughed until she coughed and gasped. "Beg pardon," she said. "Names like them always hit my funny bone. There was this towhead boy in school named Delbert Saxonfield." I saw no connection and I was insulted (what's so funny about Vanderpool, I'd like to know), but Lottie Jump was, technically, my guest and I *was* lonesome, so I asked her, since she had spoken of playing with me, if she knew how to play Andy-I-Over. She said "Naw." It turned out that she did not know how to play any games at all; she couldn't do anything and didn't want to do anything; her only recreation and her only gift was, and always had been, stealing. But this I did not know at the time.

As it happened, it was too cold and snowy to play outdoors that day anyhow, and after I had run through my list of indoor games and Lottie had shaken her head at all of them (when I spoke of Parcheesi, she went "Ugh!" and pretended to be sick), she suggested that we look through my mother's bureau drawers. This did not strike me as strange at all, for it was one of my favorite things to do, and I led the way to Mother's bedroom without a moment's hesitation. I loved the smell of the lavender she kept in gauze bags among her chamois gloves and linen handkerchiefs and filmy scarves; there was a pink fascinator knitted of something as fine as spider's thread, and it made me go quite soft—I wasn't soft as a rule, I was as hard as nails and I gave my mother a rough time—to think of her wearing it around her head as she waltzed on the ice in the bygone days. We examined stockings, nightgowns, camisoles, strings of beads, and mosaic pins, keepsake buttons from dresses worn on memorial occasions, tortoiseshell combs, and a transformation made from Aunt Joey's hair when she had racily had it bobbed. Lottie admired particularly a blue cloisonné perfume flask with ferns and peacocks on it. "Hey," she said, "this sure is cute. I like thing-daddies like this here." But very abruptly she got bored and said, "Let's talk instead. In the front room." I agreed, a little perplexed this time, because I had been about to show her a remarkable powder box that played "The Blue Danube." We went into the parlor, where Lottie looked at her image in the pier glass for quite a while and with great absorption, as if she had never seen herself before. Then she moved over to the window seat and knelt on it, looking out at the front walk. She kept her hands in the pockets of her thin dark-red coat; once she took out one of her dirty paws to rub her nose for a minute and I saw a bulge in that pocket, like a bunch of jackstones. I know now that it wasn't jackstones, it was my mother's perfume flask; I thought at the time her hands were cold and that that was why she kept them put away, for I had noticed that she had no mittens.

Lottie did most of the talking, and while she talked, she never once looked at me but kept her eyes fixed on the approach to our house. She told me that her family had come to Adams a month before from Muskogee, Oklahoma, where her father, before he got tuberculosis, had been a brakeman on the Frisco. Now they lived down by Arapahoe Creek, on the west side of town, in one of the cottages of a wretched settlement made up of people so poor and so sick—for in nearly every ramshackle house someone was coughing himself to death—that each time I went past I blushed with guilt because my shoes were sound and my coat was warm and I was well. I wished that Lottie had not told me where she lived, but she was not aware of any pathos in her family's situation, and, indeed, it was with a certain boastfulness that she told me her mother was the short-order cook at the Comanche Café (she pronounced this word in one syllable), which I knew was the dirtiest, darkest, smelliest place in town, patronized by coal miners who never washed their faces and sometimes had such dangerous fights after drinking dago red that the sheriff had to come. Laughing, Lottie told me that her mother was half Indian, and, laughing even harder, she said that her brother didn't have any brains and had never been to school. She herself was eleven years old, but she was only in the third grade, because teachers had always had it in for her—making her go to the blackboard and all like that when she was tired. She hated school—she went to Ashton, on North Hill, and that was why I had never seen her, for I went to Carlyle Hill—and she especially hated the teacher, Miss Cudahy, who had a head shaped like a pine cone and who had killed several people with her ruler. Lottie loved the movies ("Not them Western ones or the ones with apes in," she said. "Ones about hugging and kissing. I love it when they die in that big old soft bed with the curtains up top, and he comes in and says 'Don't leave me, Marguerite de la Mar'"), and she loved to ride in cars. She loved Mr. Goodbars, and if there was one thing she despised worse than another it was tapioca. ("Pa calls it fish eyes. He calls floating island horse spit. He's a big piece of cheese. I hate him.") She did not like cats (Muff was now sitting on the mantelpiece, glaring like an owl); she kind of liked snakes—except cottonmouths and rattlers—because she found them kind of funny; she had once seen a goat eat a tin can. She said that one of these days she would take me downtown—it was a slowpoke town, she said, a one-horse burg

(I had never heard such gaudy, cynical talk and was trying to memorize it all)—if I would get some money for the trolley fare; she hated to walk, and I ought to be proud that she had walked all the way from Arapahoe Creek today for the sole solitary purpose of seeing me.

Seeing our freshly baked dessert in the window was a more likely story, but I did not care, for I was deeply impressed by this bold, sassy girl from Oklahoma and greatly admired the poise with which she aired her prejudices. Lottie Jump was certainly nothing to look at. She was tall and made of skin and bones; she was evilly ugly, and her clothes were a disgrace, not just ill-fitting and old and ragged but dirty, unmentionably so; clearly she did not wash much or brush her teeth, which were notched like a saw, and small and brown (it crossed my mind that perhaps she chewed tobacco); her long, lank hair looked as if it might have nits. But she had personality. She made me think of one of those self-contained dogs whose home is where his handout is and who travels alone but, if it suits him to, will become the leader of a pack. She was aloof, never looking at me, but amiable in the way she kept calling me "kid." I liked her enormously, and presently I told her so.

At this, she turned around and smiled at me. Her smile was the smile of a jack-o'-lantern—high, wide, and handsome. When it was over, no trace of it remained. "Well, that's keen, kid, and I like you, too," she said in her downright Muskogee accent. She gave me a long, appraising look. Her eyes were the color of mud. "Listen, kid, how much do you like me?"

"I like you loads, Lottie," I said. "Better than anybody else, and I'm not kidding."

"You want to be pals?"

"Do I!" I cried. So *there,* Virgil Meade, you big fat hoot-nanny, I thought.

"All right, kid, we'll be pals." And she held out her hand for me to shake. I had to go and get it, for she did not alter her position on the window seat. It was a dry, cold hand, and the grip was severe, with more a feeling of bones in it than friendliness.

Lottie turned and scanned our path and scanned the sidewalk beyond, and then she said, in a lower voice, "Do you know how to lift?"

"Lift?" I wondered if she meant to lift *her*. I was sure I could do it, since she was so skinny, but I couldn't imagine why she would want me to.

"Shoplift, I mean. Like in the five-and-dime."

I did not know the term, and Lottie scowled at my stupidity.

"*Steal*, for crying in the beer!" she said impatiently. This she said so loudly that Muff jumped down from the mantel and left the room in contempt.

I was thrilled to death and shocked to pieces. "Stealing is a sin," I said. "You get put in jail for it."

"Ish ka bibble! I should worry if it's a sin or not," said Lottie, with a shrug. "And they'll never put a smart old whatsis like *me* in jail. It's fun, stealing is—it's a picnic. I'll teach you if you want to learn, kid." Shamelessly she winked at me and grinned again. (That grin! She could have taken it off her face and put it on the table.) And she added, "If you don't, we can't be pals, because lifting is the only kind of playing I like. I hate those dumb games like Statues. Kick-the-Can—phooey!"

I was torn between agitation (I went to Sunday School and knew already about morality; Judge Bay, a crabby old man who loved to punish sinners, was a friend of my father's and once had given Jack a lecture on the criminal mind when he came to call and found Jack looking up an answer in his arithmetic book) and excitement over the daring invitation to misconduct myself in so perilous a way. My life, on reflection, looked deadly prim; all I'd ever done to vary the monotony of it was to swear. I knew that Lottie Jump meant what she said—that I could have her friendship only on her terms (plainly, she had gone it alone for a long time and could go it alone for the rest of her life)—and although I trembled like an aspen and my heart went pita-pat, I said, "I want to be pals with you, Lottie."

"All right, Vanderpool," said Lottie, and got off the window seat. "I wouldn't go braggin' about it if I was you. I wouldn't go telling my ma and pa and the next-door neighbor that you and Lottie Jump are going down to the five-and-dime next Saturday aft and lift us some nice rings and garters and things like that. I mean it, kid." And she drew the back of her forefinger across her throat and made a dire face.

"I won't. I promise I won't. My *gosh*, why would I?"

"That's the ticket," said Lottie, with a grin. "I'll meet you at the trolley shelter at two o'clock. You have the money. For both down and up. I ain't going to climb up that ornery hill after I've had my fun."

"Yes, Lottie," I said. Where was I going to get twenty cents? I was going to have to start stealing before she even taught me how. Lottie was facing the center of the room, but she had eyes in the back of her head, and she whirled around back to the window; my mother and Tess were turning in our front path.

"Back way," I whispered, and in a moment Lottie was gone; the swinging door that usually squeaked did not make a sound as she vanished through it. I listened and I never heard the back door open and close. Nor did I hear her, in a split second, lift the glass cover and remove that cake designed to feed six people.

I was restless and snappish between Wednesday afternoon and Saturday. When Mother found the cake was gone, she scolded me for not keeping my ears cocked. She assumed, naturally, that a tramp had taken it, for she knew I hadn't eaten it; I never ate anything if I could help it (except for raw potatoes, which I loved) and had been known as a problem feeder from the beginning of my life. At first it occurred to me to have a tantrum and bring her around to my point of view: my tantrums scared the living daylights out of her because my veins stood out and I turned blue and couldn't get my breath. But I rejected this for a more sensible plan. I said, "It just so happens I didn't hear anything. But if I had, I suppose you wish I had gone out in the kitchen and let the robber cut me up into a million little tiny pieces with his sword. You wouldn't even bury me. You'd just put me on the dump. *I* know who's wanted in this family and who isn't." Tears of sorrow, not of anger, came in powerful tides and I groped blindly to the bedroom I shared with Stella, where I lay on my bed and shook with big, silent *weltschmerzlich* sobs. Mother followed me immediately, and so did Tess, and both of them comforted me and told me how much they loved me. I said they didn't; they said they did. Presently, I got a headache, as I always did when I cried, so I got to have an aspirin and a cold cloth on my head, and when Jack and Stella came home, they had to be quiet. I heard Jack say, "Emily Vanderpool is the biggest polecat in the U.S.A. Whyn't she go in the kitchen

and say, 'Hands up'? He woulda lit out." And Mother said,
"Sh-h-h! You don't want your sister to be sick, do you?" Muff,
not realizing that Lottie had replaced her, came in and curled
up at my thigh, purring lustily; I found myself glad that she had
left the room before Lottie Jump made her proposition to me,
and in gratitude I stroked her unattractive head.

Other things happened. Mother discovered the loss of
her perfume flask and talked about nothing else at meals for
two whole days. Luckily, it did not occur to her that it had
been stolen—she simply thought she had mislaid it—but her
monomania got on my father's nerves and he lashed out at
her and at the rest of us. And because I was the cause of it all
and my conscience was after me with red-hot pokers, I finally
had to have a tantrum. I slammed my fork down in the middle
of supper on the second day and yelled, "If you don't stop
fighting, I'm going to kill myself. Yammer, yammer, nag, nag!"
And I put my fingers in my ears and squeezed my eyes tight
shut and screamed so the whole county could hear, "Shut *up*!"
And then I lost my breath and began to turn blue. Daddy hastily apologized to everyone, and Mother said she was sorry for
carrying on so about a trinket that had nothing but sentimental
value—she was just vexed with herself for being careless, that
was all, and she wasn't going to say another word about it.

I never heard so many references to stealing and cake, and
even to Oklahoma (ordinarily no one mentioned Oklahoma
once in a month of Sundays) and the ten-cent store as I did
throughout those next days. I myself once made a ghastly slip
and said something to Stella about "the five-and-dime." "The
five-and-*dime*!" she exclaimed. "Where'd you get *that* kind of
talk? Do you by any chance have reference to the *ten-cent store*?"

The worst of all was Friday night—the very night before
I was to meet Lottie Jump—when Judge Bay came to play
two-handed pinochle with Daddy. The Judge, a giant in intim-
idating haberdashery—for some reason, the white piping on
his vest bespoke, for me, handcuffs and prison bars—and with
an aura of disapproval for almost everything on earth except
what pertained directly to himself, was telling Daddy, before
they began their game, about the infamous vandalism that had
been going on among the college students. "I have reason to
believe that there are girls in this gang as well as boys," he said.

"They ransack vacant houses and take everything. In one house on Pleasant Street, up there by the Catholic Church, there wasn't anything to take, so they took the kitchen sink. Wasn't a question of taking everything *but*—they took the kitchen sink."

"What ever would they want with a kitchen sink?" asked my mother.

"Mischief," replied the Judge. "If we ever catch them and if they come within my jurisdiction, I can tell you I will give them no quarter. A thief, in my opinion, is the lowest of the low."

Mother told about the chocolate cake. By now, the fiction was so factual in my mind that each time I thought of it I saw a funny-paper bum in baggy pants held up by rope, a hat with holes through which tufts of hair stuck up, shoes from which his toes protruded, a disreputable stubble on his face; he came up beneath the open window where the devil's food was cooling and he stole it and hotfooted it for the woods, where his companion was frying a small fish in a beat-up skillet. It never crossed my mind any longer that Lottie Jump had hooked that delicious cake.

Judge Bay was properly impressed. "If you will steal a chocolate cake, if you will steal a kitchen sink, you will steal diamonds and money. The small child who pilfers a penny from his mother's pocketbook has started down a path that may lead him to holding up a bank."

It was a good thing I had no homework that night, for I could not possibly have concentrated. We were all sent to our rooms, because the pinochle players had to have absolute quiet. I spent the evening doing cross-stitch. I was making a bureau runner for a Christmas present; as in the case of the Christmas card, I had no one to give it to, but now I decided to give it to Lottie Jump's mother. Stella was reading *Black Beauty*, crying. It was an interminable evening. Stella went to bed first; I saw to that, because I didn't want her lying there awake listening to me talking in my sleep. Besides, I didn't want her to see me tearing open the cardboard box—the one in the shape of a church, which held my Christmas Sunday School offering. Over the door of the church was this shaming legend: "My mite for the poor widow." When Stella had begun to grind her teeth in her first deep sleep, I took twenty cents away from the poor widow, whoever she was (the owner of the kitchen sink, no doubt), for the trolley fare, and secreted it and the remaining three pennies in the pocket of my middy. I wrapped the money well in a handkerchief and buttoned the pocket and hung my skirt over the middy. And then I tore the paper church into bits—the heavens opened and Judge Bay came toward me with a double-barreled shotgun—and hid the bits under a pile of pajamas. I did not sleep one wink. Except that I must have, because of the stupendous nightmares that kept wrenching the flesh off my skeleton and caused me to come close to perishing of thirst; once I fell out of bed and hit my head on Stella's ice skates. I would have waked her up and given her a piece of my mind for leaving them in such a lousy place, but then I remembered: I wanted *no* commotion of any kind.

I couldn't eat breakfast and I couldn't eat lunch. Old Johnny-on-the-spot Jack kept saying, "*Poor* Polecat. Polecat wants her fish for dinner." Mother made an abortive attempt to take my temperature. And when all that hullabaloo subsided, I was nearly in the soup because Mother asked me to mind Tess while she went to the sanitarium to see Mrs. Rogers, who, all of a sudden, was too sick to have anyone but grownups near her. Stella couldn't stay with the baby, because she had to go to ballet, and Jack couldn't, because he had to go up to the mesa and empty his traps. ("No, they *can't* wait. You want my skins to rot in this hot-one-day-cold-the-next weather?") I was arguing and whining when the telephone rang. Mother went to answer it and came back with a look of great sadness; Mrs. Rogers, she had learned, had had another hemorrhage. So Mother would not be going to the sanitarium after all and I needn't stay with Tess.

By the time I left the house, I was as cross as a bear. I felt awful about the widow's mite and I felt awful for being mean about staying with Tess, for Mrs. Rogers was a kind old lady, in a cozy blue hug-me-tight and an old-fangled boudoir cap, dying here all alone; she was a friend of Grandma's and had lived just down the street from her in Missouri, and all in the world Mrs. Rogers wanted to do was go back home and lie down in her own big bedroom in her own big, high-ceilinged house and have Grandma and other members of the Eastern Star come in from time to time to say hello. But they wouldn't let her go home; they were going to kill or cure her. I could not help feeling that my hardness of heart and evil of intention had had a good deal to do with her new crisis; right at the very same minute I had been saying "Does that old Mrs. Methuselah *always* have to spoil my fun?" the poor wasted thing was probably coughing up her blood and saying to the nurse, "Tell Emily Vanderpool not to mind me, she can run and play."

I had a bad character, I know that, but my badness never gave me half the enjoyment Jack and Stella thought it did. A good deal of the time I wanted to eat lye. I was certainly having no fun now, thinking of Mrs. Rogers and of depriving that poor widow of bread and milk; what if this penniless woman without a husband had a dog to feed, too? Or a baby? And besides, I didn't want to go downtown to steal anything from the ten-cent store; I didn't want to see Lottie Jump again—not really, for I knew in my bones that that girl was trouble with a capital T. And still, in our short meeting she had mesmerized me; I would think about her style of talking and the expert way she had made off with the perfume flask and the cake (how had she carried the cake through the streets without being noticed?) and be bowled over, for the part of me that did not love God was a black-hearted villain. And apart from these considerations, I had some sort of idea that if I did not keep my appointment with Lottie Jump, she would somehow get revenge; she had seemed a girl of purpose. So, revolted and fascinated, brave and lily-livered, I plodded along through the snow in my flopping galoshes up toward the Chautauqua, where the trolley stop was. On my way, I passed Virgil Meade's house; there was not just a snowman, there was a whole snow family in the back yard, and Virgil himself was throwing a stick for his dog. I was delighted to see that he was alone.

Lottie, who was sitting on a bench in the shelter eating a Mr. Goodbar, looked the same as she had the other time except that she was wearing an amazing hat. I think I had expected her to have a black handkerchief over the lower part of her face or to be wearing a Jesse James waistcoat. But I had never thought of a hat. It was felt; it was the color of cooked meat; it had some flowers appliquéd on the front of it; it had no brim, but rose straight up to a very considerable height, like a monument. It sat so low on her forehead and it was so tight that it looked, in a way, like part of her.

"How's every little thing, bub?" she said, licking her candy wrapper.

"Fine, Lottie," I said, freshly awed.

A silence fell. I drank some water from the drinking fountain, sat down, fastened my galoshes, and unfastened them again.

"My mother's teeth grow wrong way to," said Lottie, and showed me what she meant: the lower teeth were in front of the upper ones. "That so-called trolley car takes its own sweet time. This town is blah."

To save the honor of my home town, the trolley came scraping and groaning up the hill just then, its bell clanging with an idiotic frenzy, and ground to a stop. Its broad, proud cowcatcher was filled with dirty snow, in the middle of which rested a tomato can, put there, probably, by somebody who was bored to death and couldn't think of anything else to do—I did a lot of pointless things like that on lonesome Saturday afternoons. It was the custom of this trolley car, a rather mysterious one, to pause at the shelter for five minutes while the conductor, who was either Mr. Jansen or Mr. Peck, depending on whether it was the A.M. run or the P.M., got out and stretched and smoked and spit. Sometimes the passengers got out, too, acting like sightseers whose destination was this sturdy stucco gazebo instead of, as it really was, the Piggly Wiggly or the Nelson Dry. You expected them to take snapshots of the drinking fountain or of the Chautauqua meeting house up on the hill. And when they all got back in the car, you expected them to exchange intelligent observations on the aborigines and the ruins they had seen.

Today there were no passengers, and as soon as Mr. Peck got out and began staring at the mountains as if he had never seen them before while he made himself a cigarette, Lottie, in her tall hat (was it something like the Inspector's hat in the Katzenjammer Kids?), got into the car, motioning me to follow. I put our nickels in the empty box and joined her on the very last double seat. It was only then that she mapped out the plan for the afternoon, in a low but still insouciant voice. The hat—she did not apologize for it, she simply referred to it as "my hat"—was to be the repository of whatever we stole. In the future, it would be advisable for me to have one like it. (How? Surely it was unique. The flowers, I saw on closer examination, were tulips, but they were blue, and a very unsettling shade of blue.) I was to engage a clerk on one side of the counter, asking her the price of, let's say, a tube of Daggett & Ramsdell vanishing cream, while Lottie would lift a round comb or a barrette or a hair net or whatever on the other side. Then, at a signal, I would decide against the vanishing cream and would move on to the next counter that she indicated. The signal was interesting; it was to be the raising of her hat from the rear—"like I've got the itch and gotta scratch," she said. I was relieved that I was to have no part in the actual stealing, and I was touched that Lottie, who was going to do all the work, said we would "go halvers" on the take. She asked me if there was anything in particular I wanted—she herself had nothing special in mind and was going to shop around first—and I said I would like some rubber gloves. This request was entirely spontaneous; I had never before in my life thought of rubber gloves in one way or another, but a psychologist—or Judge Bay—might have said that this was most significant and that I was planning at that moment to go on from petty larceny to bigger game, armed with a weapon on which I wished to leave no fingerprints.

On the way downtown, quite a few people got on the trolley, and they all gave us such peculiar looks that I was chicken-hearted until I realized it must be Lottie's hat they were looking at. No wonder. I kept looking at it myself out of the corner of my eye; it was like a watermelon standing on end. No, it was like a tremendous test tube. On this trip—a slow one, for the trolley pottered through that part of town in a desultory, neighborly way, even going into areas where no one lived—Lottie told me some of the things she had stolen in Muskogee and here in Adams. They included a white satin prayer book (think of it!), Mr. Goodbars by the thousands (she had probably never paid for a Mr. Goodbar in her life), a dinner ring valued at two dollars, a strawberry emery, several cans of corn, some shoelaces, a set of poker chips, countless pencils, four spark plugs ("Pa had this old car, see, and it was broke, so we took 'er to get fixed; I'll build me a radio with 'em

sometime—you know? Listen in on them ear muffs to Tulsa?"),
a Boy Scout knife, and a Girl Scout folding cup. She made a
regular practice of going through the pockets of the coats in
the cloakroom every day at recess, but she had never found
anything there worth a red cent and was about to give that up.
Once, she had taken a gold pencil from a teacher's desk and
had got caught—she was sure that this was one of the reasons
she was only in the third grade. Of this unjust experience, she
said, "The old hoot owl! If I was drivin' in a car on a lonesome
stretch and she was settin' beside me, I'd wait till we got to a
pile of gravel and then I'd stop and say, 'Git out, Miss Priss.'
She'd git out, all right."

Since Lottie was so frank, I was emboldened at last to ask her
what she had done with the cake. She faced me with her grin;
this grin, in combination with the hat, gave me a surprise from
which I have never recovered. "I ate it up," she said. "I went
in your garage and sat on your daddy's old tires and ate it. It
was pretty good."

There were two ten-cent stores side by side in our town, Kresge's and Woolworth's, and as we walked down the main street
toward them, Lottie played with a Yo-Yo. Since the street was
thronged with Christmas shoppers and farmers in for Saturday,
this was no ordinary accomplishment; all in all, Lottie Jump was
someone to be reckoned with. I cannot say that I was proud
to be seen with her; the fact is that I hoped I would not meet
anyone I knew, and I thanked my lucky stars that Jack was up
in the hills with his dead skunks, because if he had seen her
with that lid and that Yo-Yo, I would never have heard the
last of it. But in another way I *was* proud to be with her; in a
smaller hemisphere, in one that included only her and me, I
was swaggering—I felt like Somebody, marching along beside
this lofty Somebody from Oklahoma who was going to hold
up the dime store.

There is nothing like Woolworth's at Christmastime. It smells
of peanut brittle and terrible chocolate candy, Djer-Kiss talcum
powder and Ben Hur Perfume—smells sourly of tinsel and wax-
ily of artificial poinsettias. The crowds are made up largely of
children and women, with here and there a deliberative old man;

the women are buying ribbons and wrappings and Christmas cards, and the children are buying asbestos pot holders for their mothers and, for their fathers, suède bookmarks with a burnt-in design that says "A good book is a good friend" or "Souvenir from the Garden of the Gods." It is very noisy. The salesgirls are forever ringing their bells and asking the floorwalker to bring them change for a five; babies in go-carts are screaming as parcels fall on their heads; the women, waving rolls of red tissue paper, try to attract the attention of the harried girl behind the counter. ("Miss! All I want is this one batch of the red. Can't I just give you the dime?" And the girl, beside herself, mottled with vexation, cries back, "Has to be rung up, Moddom, that's the rule.") There is pandemonium at the toy counter, where things are being tested by the customers—wound up, set off, tooted, pounded, made to say "Maaaah-Maaaah!" There is very little gaiety in the scene and, in fact, those baffled old men look as if they were walking over their own dead bodies, but there is an atmosphere of carnival, nevertheless, and as soon as Lottie and I entered the doors of Woolworth's golden-and-vermilion bedlam, I grew giddy and hot—not pleasantly so. The feeling, indeed, was distinctly disagreeable, like the beginning of a stomach upset.

Lottie gave me a nudge and said softly, "Go look at the envelopes. I want some rubber bands."

This counter was relatively uncrowded (the seasonal stationery supplies—the Christmas cards and wrapping paper and stickers—were at a separate counter), and I went around to examine some very beautiful letter paper; it was pale pink and it had a border of roses all around it. The clerk here was a cheerful middle-aged woman wearing an apron, and she was giving all her attention to a seedy old man who could not make up his mind between mucilage and paste. "Take your time, Dad," she said. "Compared to the rest of the girls, I'm on my vacation." The old man, holding a tube in one hand and a bottle in the other, looked at her vaguely and said, "I want it for stamps. Sometimes I write a letter and stamp it and then don't mail it and steam the stamp off. Must have ninety cents' worth of stamps like that." The woman laughed. "I know what you mean," she said. "I get mad and write a letter and then I tear it up." The old man gave her a condescending look and said, "That so? But I don't suppose yours are of a political nature." He bent his gaze again to the choice of adhesives.

This first undertaking was duck soup for Lottie. I did not even have to exchange a word with the woman; I saw Miss Fagin lift up *that hat* and give me the high sign, and we moved away, she down one aisle and I down the other, now and again catching a glimpse of each other through the throngs. We met at the foot of the second counter, where notions were sold.

"Fun, huh?" said Lottie, and I nodded, although I felt wholly dreary. "I want some crochet hooks," she said. "Price the rickrack."

This time the clerk was adding up her receipts and did not even look at me or at a woman who was angrily and in vain trying to buy a paper of pins. Out went Lottie's scrawny hand, up went her domed chimney. In this way for some time she bagged sitting birds: a tea strainer (there was no one at all at that counter), a box of Mrs. Carpenter's All Purpose Nails, the rubber gloves I had said I wanted, and four packages of mixed seeds. Now you have some idea of the size of Lottie Jump's hat.

I was nervous, not from being her accomplice but from being in this crowd on an empty stomach, and I was getting tired—we had been in the store for at least an hour—and the whole enterprise seemed pointless. There wasn't a thing in her hat I wanted—not even the rubber gloves. But in exact proportion as my spirits descended, Lottie's rose; clearly she had only been target-practicing and now she was moving in for the kill.

We met beside the books of paper dolls, for reconnaissance. "I'm gonna get me a pair of pearl beads," said Lottie. "You go fuss with the hairpins, hear?"

Luck, combined with her skill, would have stayed with Lottie, and her hat would have been a cornucopia by the end of the afternoon if, at the very moment her hand went out for the string of beads, that idiosyncrasy of mine had not struck me full force. I had never known it to come with so few preliminaries; probably this was so because I was oppressed by all the masses of bodies poking and pushing me, and all the open mouths breathing in my face. Anyhow, right then, at the crucial time, I *had to be alone.*

I stood staring down at the bone hairpins for a moment,

and when the girl behind the counter said, "What kind does Mother want, hon? What color is Mother's hair?" I looked past her and across at Lottie and I said, "Your brother isn't the only one in your family that doesn't have any brains." The clerk, astonished, turned to look where I was looking and caught Lottie in the act of lifting up her hat to put the pearls inside. She had unwisely chosen a long strand and was having a little trouble; I had the nasty thought that it looked as if her brains were leaking out.

The clerk, not able to deal with this emergency herself, frantically punched her bell and cried, "Floorwalker! Mr. Bellamy! I've caught a thief!"

Momentarily there was a violent hush—then such a clamor as you have never heard. Bells rang, babies howled, crockery crashed to the floor as people stumbled in their rush to the arena.

Mr. Bellamy, nineteen years old but broad of shoulder and jaw, was instantly standing beside Lottie, holding her arm with one hand while with the other he removed her hat to reveal to the overjoyed audience that incredible array of merchandise. Her hair was wild, her face a mask of innocent bewilderment, Lottie Jump, the scurvy thing, pretended to be deaf and dumb. She pointed at the rubber gloves and then she pointed at me, and Mr. Bellamy, able at last to prove his mettle, said "Aha!" and, still holding Lottie, moved around the counter to me and grabbed *my* arm. He gave the hat to the clerk and asked her kindly to accompany him and his redhanded catch to the manager's office.

I don't know where Lottie is now—whether she is on the stage or in jail. If her performance after our arrest meant anything, the first is quite as likely as the second. (I never saw her again, and for all I know she lit out of town that night on a freight train. Or perhaps her whole family decamped as suddenly as they had arrived; ours was a most transient population. You can be sure I made no attempt to find her again, and for months I avoided going anywhere near Arapahoe Creek or North Hill.) She never said a word but kept making signs with her fingers, ad-libbing the whole thing. They tested her hearing by shooting off a popgun right in her ear and she never batted an eyelid.

They called up my father, and he came over from the Safeway on the double. I heard very little of what he said because I was crying so hard, but one thing I did hear him say was, "Well, young lady, I guess you've seen to it that I'll have to part company with my good friend Judge Bay." I tried to defend myself, but it was useless. The manager, Mr. Bellamy, the clerk, and my father patted Lottie on the shoulder, and the clerk said, "Poor, afflicted child." For being a poor, afflicted child, they gave her a bag of hard candy, and she gave them the most fraudulent smile of gratitude, and slobbered a little, and shuffled out, holding her empty hat in front of her like a beggar-man. I hate Lottie Jump to this day, but I have to hand it to her—she was a genius.

The floorwalker would have liked to see me sentenced to the reform school for life, I am sure, but the manager said that, considering this was my first offense, he would let my father attend to my punishment. The old-maid clerk, who looked precisely like Emmy Schmaltz, clucked her tongue and shook her head at me. My father hustled me out of the office and out of the store and into the car and home, muttering the entire time; now and again I'd hear the words "morals" and "nowadays."

What's the use of telling you the rest? You know what happened. Daddy on second thoughts decided not to hang his head in front of Judge Bay but to make use of his friendship in this time of need, and he took me to see the scary old curmudgeon at his house. All I remember of that long declamation, during which the Judge sat behind his desk never taking his eyes off me, was the warning: "I want you to give this a great deal of thought, miss. I want you to search and seek in the innermost corners of your conscience and root out every bit of badness." Oh, *him*! Why, listen, if I'd rooted out all the badness in me, there wouldn't have been anything left of me. My mother cried for days because she had nurtured an outlaw and was ashamed to show her face at the neighborhood store; my father was silent, and he often looked at me. Stella, who was a prig, said, "And to think you did it at *Christmas*time!" As for Jack—well, Jack a couple of times did not know how close he came to seeing glory when I had a butcher knife in my hand. It was Polecat this and Polecat that until I nearly went off my rocker. Tess, of course, didn't know what was going on and asked so many questions that finally I told her to go to Helen Hunt Jackson in a savage tone of voice.

Good old Muff.

It is not true that you don't learn by experience. At any rate, I did that time. I began immediately to have two or three friends at a time—to be sure, because of the stigma on me, they were by no means the elite of Carlyle Hill Grade—and never again when that terrible need to be alone arose did I let fly. I would say, instead, "I've got a headache. I'll have to go home and take an aspirin," or "Gosh all hemlocks, I forgot—I've got to go to the dentist."

After the scandal died down, I got into the Camp Fire Girls. It was through pull, of course, since Stella had been a respected member for two years and my mother was a friend of the leader. But it turned out all right. Even Muff did not miss our periods of companionship, because about that time she grew up and started having literally millions of kittens.

In the Zoo

KEENING harshly in his senility, the blind polar bear slowly and ceaselessly shakes his head in the stark heat of the July and mountain noon. His open eyes are blue. No one stops to look at him; an old farmer, in passing, sums up the old bear's situation by observing, with a ruthless chuckle, that he is a "back number." Patient and despairing, he sits on his yellowed haunches on the central rock of his pool, his huge toy paws wearing short boots of mud.

The grizzlies to the right of him, a conventional family of father and mother and two spring cubs, alternately play the clown and sleep. There is a blustery, scoundrelly, half-likable bravado in the manner of the black bear on the polar's left; his name, according to the legend on his cage, is Clancy, and he is a rough-and-tumble, brawling blowhard, thundering continually as he paces back and forth, or pauses to face his audience of children and mothers and release from his great, gray-tongued mouth a perfectly Vesuvian roar. If he were to be reincarnated in human form, he would be a man of action, possibly a football coach, probably a politician. One expects to see his black hat hanging from a branch of one of his trees; at any moment he will light a cigar.

The polar bear's next-door neighbors are not the only ones who offer so sharp and sad a contrast to him. Across a reach of scrappy grass and litter is the convocation of conceited monkeys, burrowing into each other's necks and chests for fleas, picking their noses with their long, black, finicky fingers, swinging by their gifted tails on the flying trapeze, screaming bloody murder. Even when they mourn—one would think the male orangutan was on the very brink of suicide—they are comedians; they only fake depression, for they are firmly secure in their rambunctious tribalism and in their appalling insight and contempt. Their flibbertigibbet gamboling is a sham, and, stealthily and shiftily, they are really watching the pitiful polar bear ("Back number," they quote the farmer. "That's *his* number all right," they snigger), and the windy black bear ("Life of the party. Gasbag. Low I.Q.," they note scornfully on his

276

dossier), and the stupid, bourgeois grizzlies ("It's feed the face and hit the sack for them," the monkeys say). And they are watching my sister and me, two middle-aged women, as we sit on a bench between the exhibits, eating popcorn, growing thirsty. We are thoughtful.

A chance remark of Daisy's a few minutes before has turned us to memory and meditation. "I don't know why," she said, "but that poor blind bear reminds me of Mr. Murphy." The name "Mr. Murphy" at once returned us both to childhood, and we were floated far and fast, our later lives diminished. So now we eat our popcorn in silence with the ritualistic appetite of childhood, which has little to do with hunger; it is not so much food as a sacrament, and in tribute to our sisterliness and our friendliness I break the silence to say that this is the best popcorn I have ever eaten in my life. The extravagance of my statement instantly makes me feel self-indulgent, and for some time I uneasily avoid looking at the blind bear. My sister does not agree or disagree; she simply says that popcorn is the only food she has ever really liked. For a long time, then, we eat without a word, but I know, because I know her well and know her similarity to me, that Daisy is thinking what I am thinking; both of us are mournfully remembering Mr. Murphy, who, at one time in our lives, was our only friend.

This zoo is in Denver, a city that means nothing to my sister and me except as a place to take or meet trains. Daisy lives two hundred miles farther west, and it is her custom, when my every-other-year visit with her is over, to come across the mountains to see me off on my eastbound train. We know almost no one here, and because our stays are short, we have never bothered to learn the town in more than the most desultory way. We know the Burlington uptown office and the respectable hotels, a restaurant or two, the Union Station, and, beginning today, the zoo in the city park.

But since the moment that Daisy named Mr. Murphy by name our situation in Denver has been only corporeal; our minds and our hearts are in Adams, fifty miles north, and we are seeing, under the white sun at its pitiless meridian, the streets of that ugly town, its parks and trees and bridges, the bandstand in its dreary park, the roads that lead away from it, west to the mountains and east to the plains, its mongrel and multitudinous churches, its high school shaped like a loaf of bread, the campus of its college, an oasis of which we had no experience except to walk through it now and then, eyeing the woodbine on the impressive buildings. These things are engraved forever on our minds with a legibility so insistent that you have only to say the name of the town aloud to us to rip the rinds from our nerves and leave us exposed in terror and humiliation.

We have supposed in later years that Adams was not so bad as all that, and we know that we magnified its ugliness because we looked upon it as the extension of the possessive, unloving, scornful, complacent foster mother, Mrs. Placer, to whom, at the death of our parents within a month of each other, we were sent like Dickensian grotesqueries—cowardly, weak-stomached, given to tears, backward in school. Daisy was ten and I was eight when, unaccompanied, we made the long trip from Marblehead to our benefactress, whom we had never seen and, indeed, never heard of until the pastor of our church came to tell us of the arrangement our father had made on his deathbed, seconded by our mother on hers. This man, whose name and face I have forgotten and whose parting speeches to us I have not forgiven, tried to dry our tears with talk of Indians and of buffaloes; he spoke, however, at much greater length, and in preaching cadences, of the Christian goodness of Mrs. Placer. She was, he said, childless and fond of children, and for many years she had been a widow, after the lingering demise of her tubercular husband, for whose sake she had moved to the Rocky Mountains. For his support and costly medical care, she had run a boarding house, and after his death, since he had left her nothing, she was obliged to continue running it. She had been a girlhood friend of our paternal grandmother, and our father, in the absence of responsible relatives, had made her the beneficiary of his life insurance on the condition that she lodge and rear us. The pastor, with a frankness remarkable considering that he was talking to children, explained to us that our father had left little more than a drop in the bucket for our care, and he enjoined us to give Mrs. Placer, in return for her hospitality and sacrifice, courteous help and eternal thanks. "Sacrifice" was a word we were never allowed to forget.

And thus it was, in grief for our parents, that we came cringing to the dry Western town and to the house where Mrs. Placer lived, a house in which the square, uncushioned furniture was cruel and the pictures on the walls were either dour or dire and the lodgers, who lived in the upper floors among shadowy wardrobes and chiffoniers, had come through the years to resemble their landlady in appearance as well as in deportment.

After their ugly-colored evening meal, Gran—as she bade us call her—and her paying guests would sit, rangy and aquiline, rocking on the front porch on spring and summer and autumn nights, tasting their delicious grievances: those slights delivered by ungrateful sons and daughters, those impudences committed by trolley-car conductors and uppity salesgirls in the ready-to-wear, all those slurs and calculated elbow-jostlings that were their daily crucifixion and their staff of life. We little girls, washing the dishes in the cavernous kitchen, listened to their even, martyred voices, fixed like leeches to their solitary subject and their solitary creed—that life was essentially a matter of being done in, let down, and swindled.

At regular intervals, Mrs. Placer, chairwoman of the victims, would say, "Of course, I don't care; I just have to laugh," and then would tell a shocking tale of an intricate piece of skullduggery perpetrated against her by someone she did not even know. Sometimes, with her avid, partial jury sitting there on the porch behind the bitter hopvines in the heady mountain air, the cases she tried involved Daisy and me, and, listening, we travailed, hugging each other, whispering, "I wish she wouldn't! Oh, how did she find out?" How *did* she? Certainly we never told her when we were snubbed or chosen last on teams, never admitted to a teacher's scolding or to the hoots of laughter that greeted us when we bit on silly, unfair jokes. But she knew. She knew about the slumber parties we were not invited to, the beefsteak fries at which we were pointedly left out; she knew that the singing teacher had said in so many words that I could not carry a tune in a basket and that the sewing superintendent had said that Daisy's fingers were all thumbs. With our teeth chattering in the cold of our isolation, we would hear her protestant, litigious voice defending our right to be orphans, paupers, wholly dependent on her—except for the really ridiculous pittance from our father's life insurance—when it was all she could do to make ends meet. She did not care, but she had to laugh that people in general were so small-minded that they looked down on fatherless, motherless waifs like us and, by association, looked down on her. It seemed funny to her that people gave her no credit for taking on these sickly youngsters who were not even kin but only the grandchildren of a friend.

If a child with braces on her teeth came to play with us, she was, according to Gran, slyly lording it over us because our teeth were crooked but there was no money to have them straightened. And what could be the meaning of our being asked to come for supper at the doctor's house? Were the doctor and his la-di-da New York wife and those pert girls with their solid-gold barrettes and their Shetland pony going to shame her poor darlings? Or shame their poor Gran by making them sorry to come home to the plain but honest life that was all she could provide for them?

There was no stratum of society not reeking with the effluvium of fraud and pettifoggery. And the school system was almost the worst of all: if we could not understand fractions, was that not our teacher's fault? And therefore what right had she to give us F? It was as plain as a pikestaff to Gran that the teacher was only covering up her own inability to teach. It was unlikely, too—highly unlikely—that it was by accident that time and time again the free medical clinic was closed for the day just as our names were about to be called out, so that nothing was done about our bad tonsils, which meant that we were repeatedly sick in the winter, with Gran fetching and carrying for us, climbing those stairs a jillion times a day with her game leg and her heart that was none too strong.

Steeped in these mists of accusation and hidden plots and double meanings, Daisy and I grew up like worms. I think no one could have withstood the atmosphere in that house where everyone trod on eggs that a little bird had told them were bad. They spied on one another, whispered behind doors, conjectured, drew parallels beginning "With all due respect . . ." or "It is a matter of indifference to *me* but . . ." The vigilantes patrolled our town by day, and by night returned to lay their goodies at their priestess's feet and wait for her oracular interpretation of the innards of the butcher, the baker, the candlestick maker, the soda jerk's girl, and the barber's unnatural deaf white cat.

Consequently, Daisy and I also became suspicious. But it

was suspicion of ourselves that made us mope and weep and grimace with self-judgment. Why were we not happy when Gran had sacrificed herself to the bone for us? Why did we not cut dead the paper boy who had called her a filthy name? Why did we persist in our willful friendliness with the grocer who had tried, unsuccessfully, to overcharge her on a case of pork and beans?

Our friendships were nervous and surreptitious; we sneaked and lied, and as our hungers sharpened, our debasement deepened; we were pitied; we were shifty-eyed, always on the lookout for Mrs. Placer or one of her tattletale lodgers; we were hypocrites.

Nevertheless, one thin filament of instinct survived, and Daisy and I in time found asylum in a small menagerie down by the railroad tracks. It belonged to a gentle alcoholic ne'er-do-well, who did nothing all day long but drink bathtub gin in rickeys and play solitaire and smile to himself and talk to his animals. He had a little, stunted red vixen and a deodorized skunk, a parrot from Tahiti that spoke Parisian French, a woebegone coyote, and two capuchin monkeys, so serious and humanized, so small and sad and sweet, and so religious-looking with their tonsured heads that it was impossible not to think their gibberish was really an ordered language with a grammar that some day some philologist would understand.

Gran knew about our visits to Mr. Murphy and she did not object, for it gave her keen pleasure to excoriate him when we came home. His vice was not a matter of guesswork; it was an established fact that he was half-seas over from dawn till midnight. "With the black Irish," said Gran, "the taste for drink is taken in with the mother's milk and is never mastered. Oh, I know all about those promises to join the temperance movement and not to touch another drop. The way to hell is paved with good intentions."

We were still little girls when we discovered Mr. Murphy, before the shattering disease of adolescence was to make our bones and brains ache even more painfully than before, and we loved him and we hoped to marry him when we grew up. We loved him, and we loved his monkeys to exactly the same degree and in exactly the same way; they were husbands and fathers and brothers, these three little, ugly, dark, secret men who minded their own business and let us mind ours. If we stuck our fingers through the bars of the cage, the monkeys would sometimes take them in their tight, tiny hands and look into our faces with a tentative, somehow absent-minded sorrow, as if they terribly regretted that they could not place us but were glad to see us all the same. Mr. Murphy, playing a solitaire game of cards called "once in a blue moon" on a kitchen table in his back yard beside the pens, would occasionally look up and blink his beautiful blue eyes and say, "You're peaches to make over my wee friends. I love you for it." There was nothing demanding in his voice, and nothing sticky; on his lips the word "love" was jocose and forthright, it had no strings attached. We would sit on either side of him and watch him regiment his ranks of cards and stop to drink as deeply as if he were dying of thirst and wave to his animals and say to them, "Yes, lads, you're dandies."

Because Mr. Murphy was as reserved with us as the capuchins were, as courteously noncommittal, we were surprised one spring day when he told us that he had a present for us, which he hoped Mrs. Placer would let us keep; it was a puppy, for whom the owner had asked him to find a home—half collie and half Labrador retriever, blue-blooded on both sides.

"You might tell Mrs. Placer—" he said, smiling at the name, for Gran was famous in the town. "You might tell Mrs. Placer," said Mr. Murphy, "that this lad will make a fine watchdog. She'll never have to fear for her spoons again. Or her honor." The last he said to himself, not laughing but tucking his chin into his collar; lines sprang to the corners of his eyes. He would not let us see the dog, whom we could hear yipping and squealing inside his shanty, for he said that our disappointment would weigh on his conscience if we lost our hearts to the fellow and then could not have him for our own.

That evening at supper, we told Gran about Mr. Murphy's present. A dog? In the first place, why a dog? Was it possible that the news had reached Mr. Murphy's ears that Gran had just this very day finished planting her spring garden, the very thing that a rampageous dog would have in his mind to destroy? What sex was it? A male! Females, she had heard, were more trustworthy; males roved and came home smelling of skunk;

such a consideration as this, of course, would not have crossed Mr. Murphy's fuddled mind. Was this young male dog house-broken? We had not asked? That was the limit!

Gran appealed to her followers, too raptly fascinated by Mr. Murphy's machinations to eat their Harvard beets. "Am I being farfetched or does it strike you as decidedly queer that Mr. Murphy is trying to fob off on my little girls a young cur that has not been trained?" she asked them. "If it were housebro-ken, he would have said so, so I feel it is safe to assume that it is not. Perhaps cannot *be* housebroken. I've heard of such cases."

The fantasy spun on, richly and rapidly, with all the skilled helping hands at work at once. The dog was tangibly in the room with us, shedding his hair, scratching his fleas, shaking rain off himself to splatter the walls, dragging some dreadful carcass across the floor, chewing up slippers, knocking over chairs with his tail, gobbling the chops from the platter, barking, biting, fathering, fighting, smelling to high heaven of carrion, staining the rug with his muddy feet, scratching the floor with his claws. He developed rabies; he bit a child, two children! Three! Everyone in town! And Gran and her poor darlings went to jail for harboring this murderous, odoriferous, drunk, Roman Catholic dog.

And yet, astoundingly enough, she came around to agreeing to let us have the dog. It was, as Mr. Murphy had predicted, the word "watchdog" that deflected the course of the trial. The moment Daisy uttered it, Gran halted, marshaling her reverse march; while she rallied and tacked and reconnoitered, she sent us to the kitchen for the dessert. And by the time this course was under way, the uses of a dog, the enormous potentialities for investigation and law enforcement in a dog trained by Mrs. Placer, were being minutely and passionately scrutinized by the eight upright bloodhounds sitting at the table wolfing their brown Betty as if it were fresh-killed rabbit. The dog now sat at attention beside his mistress, fiercely alert, ears cocked, nose aquiver, the protector of widows, of orphans, of lonely people who had no homes. He made short shrift of burglars, homicidal maniacs, Peeping Toms, gypsies, bogus missionaries, Fuller Brush men with a risqué spiel. He went to the store and brought back groceries, retrieved the evening paper from the awkward place the boy had meanly thrown it, rescued cripples from burning houses, saved children from drowning, heeled at command, begged, lay down, stood up, sat, jumped through a hoop, ratted.

Both times—when he was a ruffian of the blackest delinquency and then a pillar of society—he was full-grown in his prefiguration, and when Laddy appeared on the following day, small, unsteady, and whimpering lonesomely, Gran and her lodgers were taken aback; his infant, clumsy paws embarrassed them, his melting eyes were unapropos. But it could never be said of Mrs. Placer, as Mrs. Placer her own self said, that she was a woman who went back on her word, and her darlings were going to have their dog, softheaded and feckless as he might be. All the first night, in his carton in the kitchen, he wailed for his mother, and in the morning, it was true, he had made a shambles of the room—fouled the floor, and pulled off the tablecloth together with a ketchup bottle, so that thick gore lay everywhere. At breakfast, the lodgers confessed they had had a most amusing night, for it had actually been funny the way the dog had been determined not to let anyone get a wink of sleep. After that first night, Laddy slept in our room, receiving from us, all through our delighted, sleepless nights, pats and embraces and kisses and whispers. He was our baby, our best friend, the smartest, prettiest, nicest dog in the entire wide world. Our soft and rapid blandishments excited him to yelp at us in pleased bewilderment, and then we would playfully grasp his muzzle, so that he would snarl, deep in his throat like an adult dog, and shake his head violently, and, when we freed him, nip us smartly with great good will.

He was an intelligent and genial dog and we trained him quickly. He steered clear of Gran's radishes and lettuce after she had several times given him a brisk comeuppance with a strap across the rump, and he soon left off chewing shoes and the laundry on the line, and he outgrew his babyish whining. He grew like a weed; he lost his spherical softness, and his coat, which had been sooty fluff, came in stiff and rusty black; his nose grew aristocratically long, and his clever, pointed ears stood at attention. He was all bronzy, lustrous black except for an Elizabethan ruff of white and a tip of white at the end of his perky tail. No one could deny that he was exceptionally handsome and that he had, as well, great personal charm and style. He escorted Daisy and me to school in the morning, laughing interiorly out of the enormous pleasure of his life as he gracefully cantered ahead of us, distracted occasionally by his private interest in smells or unfamiliar beings in the grass but, on the whole, engrossed in his role of chaperon. He made friends easily with other dogs, and sometimes he went for a long hunting weekend into the mountains with a huge and bossy old red hound named Mess, who had been on the county most of his life and had made a good thing of it, particularly at the fire station.

It was after one of these three-day excursions into the high country that Gran took Laddy in hand. He had come back spent and filthy, his coat a mass of cockleburs and ticks, his eyes bloodshot, loud *râles* in his chest; for half a day he lay motionless before the front door like someone in a hangover, his groaning eyes explicitly saying "Oh, for God's sake, leave me be" when we offered him food or bowls of water. Gran was disapproving, then affronted, and finally furious. Not, of course, with Laddy, since all inmates of her house enjoyed immunity, but with Mess, whose caddish character, together with that of his nominal masters, the firemen, she examined closely under a strong light, with an air of detachment, with her not caring but her having, all the same, to laugh. A lodger who occupied the back west room had something to say about the fire chief and his nocturnal visits to a certain house occupied by a certain group of young women, too near the same age to be sisters and too old to be the daughters of the woman who claimed to be their mother. What a story! The exophthalmic librarian—she lived in one of the front rooms—had some interesting insinuations to make about the deputy marshal, who had borrowed, significantly, she thought, a book on hypnotism. She also knew—she was, of course, in a most useful position in the town, and from her authoritative pen in the middle of the library her mammiform and azure eyes and her eager ears missed nothing—that the fire chief's wife was not as scrupulous as she might be when she was keeping score on bridge night at the Sorosis.

There was little at the moment that Mrs. Placer and her disciples could do to save the souls of the Fire Department and their families, and therefore save the town from holocaust (a very timid boarder—a Mr. Beaver, a newcomer who was not to linger long—had sniffed throughout this recitative as if he were smelling burning flesh), but at least the unwholesome bond between Mess and Laddy could and would be served once and for all. Gran looked across the porch at Laddy, who lay stretched at full length in the darkest corner, shuddering and baying abortively in his throat as he chased jack rabbits in his dreams, and she said, "A dog can have morals like a human." With this declaration Laddy's randy, manly holidays were finished. It may have been telepathy that woke him; he lifted his heavy head from his paws, laboriously got up, hesitated for a moment, and then padded languidly across the porch to Gran. He stood docilely beside her chair, head down, tail drooping as if to say, "O.K., Mrs. Placer, show me how and I'll walk the straight and narrow."

The very next day, Gran changed Laddy's name to Caesar, as being more dignified, and a joke was made at the supper table that he had come, seen, and conquered Mrs. Placer's heart—for within her circle, where the magnanimity she lavished upon her orphans was daily demonstrated, Mrs. Placer's heart was highly thought of. On that day also, although we did not know it yet, Laddy ceased to be our dog. Before many weeks passed, indeed, he ceased to be anyone we had ever known. A week or so after he became Caesar, he took up residence in her room, sleeping alongside her bed. She broke him of the habit of taking us to school (temptation to low living was rife along those streets; there was a chow—well, never mind) by the simple expedient of chaining him to a tree as soon as she got up in the morning. This discipline, together with the stamina-building cuffs she gave his sensitive ears from time to time, gradually but certainly remade his character. From a sanguine, affectionate, easygoing Gael (with the fits of melancholy that alternated with the larkiness), he turned into an overbearing, military, efficient, loud-voiced Teuton. His bark, once wide of range, narrowed to one dark, glottal tone.

Soon the paper boy flatly refused to serve our house after Caesar efficiently removed the bicycle clip from his pants leg; the skin was not broken, or even bruised, but it was a matter of principle with the boy. The milkman approached the back door in a seizure of shakes like St. Vitus's dance. The metermen, the coal men, and the garbage collector crossed themselves if they were Catholics and, if they were not, tried whistling in the dark. "Good boy, good Caesar," they caroled, and, unctuously lying, they said they knew his bark was worse than his bite, knowing full well that it was not, considering the very nasty nip, requiring stitches, he had given a representative of the Olson Rug Company, who had had the folly to pat him on the head. Caesar did not molest the lodgers, but he disdained them and he did not brook being personally addressed by anyone except Gran. One night, he wandered into the dining room, appearing to be in search of something he had mislaid, and, for some reason that no one was ever able to divine, suddenly stood stock-still and gave the easily upset Mr. Beaver a long and penetrating look. Mr. Beaver, trembling from head to toe, stammered, "Why—er, hello there, Caesar, old boy, old boy," and Caesar charged. For a moment, it was touch and go, but Gran saved Mr. Beaver, only to lose him an hour later when he departed, bag and baggage, for the Y.M.C.A. This rout and the consequent loss of revenue would more than likely have meant Caesar's downfall and his deportation to the pound if it had not been that a newly widowed druggist, very irascible and very much Gran's style, had applied for a room in her house a week or so before, and now he moved in delightedly, as if he were coming home.

Finally, the police demanded that Caesar be muzzled and they warned that if he committed any major crime again—they cited the case of the Olson man—he would be shot on sight. Mrs. Placer, although she had no respect for the law, knowing as much as she did about its agents, obeyed. She obeyed, that is, in part; she put the muzzle on Caesar for a few hours a day, usually early in the morning when the traffic was light and before the deliveries had started, but the rest of the time his powerful jaws and dazzling white saber teeth were free and snapping. There was between these two such preternatural rapport, such an impressive conjugation of suspicion, that he, sensing the approach of a policeman, could convey instantly to her the immediate necessity of clapping his nose cage on. And the policeman, sent out on the complaint of a terrorized neighbor, would be greeted by this law-abiding pair at the door.

Daisy and I wished we were dead. We were divided between

hating Caesar and loving Laddy, and we could not give up the hope that something, some day, would change him back into the loving animal he had been before he was appointed vice-president of the Placerites. Now at the meetings after supper on the porch he took an active part, standing rigidly at Gran's side except when she sent him on an errand. He carried out these assignments not with the air of a servant but with that of an accomplice. "Get me the paper, Caesar," she would say to him, and he, dismayingly intelligent and a shade smart-alecky, would open the screen door by himself and in a minute come back with the *Bulletin,* from which Mrs. Placer would then read an item, like the Gospel of the day, and then read between the lines of it, scandalized.

In the deepening of our woe and our bereavement and humiliation, we mutely appealed to Mr. Murphy. We did not speak outright to him, for Mr. Murphy lived in a state of indirection, and often when he used the pronoun "I," he seemed to be speaking of someone standing a little to the left of him, but we went to see him and his animals each day during the sad summer, taking what comfort we could from the cozy, quiet indolence of his back yard, where small black eyes encountered ours politely and everyone was half asleep. When Mr. Murphy inquired about Laddy in his bland, inattentive way, looking for a stratagem whereby to shift the queen of hearts into position by the king, we would say, "Oh, he's fine," or "Laddy is a nifty dog." And Mr. Murphy, reverently slaking the thirst that was his talent and his concubine, would murmur, "I'm glad."

We wanted to tell him, we wanted his help, or at least his sympathy, but how could we cloud his sunny world? It was awful to see Mr. Murphy ruffled. Up in the calm clouds as he generally was, he could occasionally be brought to earth with a thud, as we had seen and heard one day. Not far from his house, there lived a bad, troublemaking boy of twelve, who was forever hanging over the fence trying to teach the parrot obscene words. He got nowhere, for she spoke no English and she would flabbergast him with her cold eye and sneer, "*Tant pis.*" One day, this boorish fellow went too far; he suddenly shot his head over the fence like a jack-in-the-box and aimed a water pistol at the skunk's face. Mr. Murphy leaped to his feet in a scarlet rage; he picked up a stone and threw it accurately, hitting the boy square in the back, so hard that he fell right down in a mud puddle and lay there kicking and squalling and, as it turned out, quite badly hurt. "If you ever come back here again, I'll kill you!" roared Mr. Murphy. I think he meant it, for I have seldom seen an anger so resolute, so brilliant, and so voluble. "How dared he!" he cried, scrambling into Mallow's cage to hug and pet and soothe her. "He must be absolutely mad! He must be the Devil!" He did not go back to his game after that but paced the yard, swearing a blue streak and only pausing to croon to his animals, now as frightened by him as they had been by the intruder, and to drink straight from the bottle, not bothering with fixings. We were fascinated by this unfamiliar side of Mr. Murphy, but we did not want to see it ever again, for his face had grown so dangerously purple and the veins of his forehead seemed ready to burst and his eyes looked scorched. He was the closest thing to a maniac we had ever seen. So we did not tell him about Laddy; what he did not know would not hurt him, although it was hurting us, throbbing in us like a great, bleating wound.

But eventually Mr. Murphy heard about our dog's conversion, one night at the pool hall, which he visited from time to time when he was seized with a rare but compelling garrulity, and the next afternoon when he asked us how Laddy was and we replied that he was fine, he tranquilly told us, as he deliberated whether to move the jack of clubs now or to bide his time, that we were sweet girls but we were lying in our teeth. He did not seem at all angry but only interested, and all the while he questioned us, he went on about his business with the gin and the hearts and spades and diamonds and clubs. It rarely happened that he won the particular game he was playing, but that day he did, and when he saw all the cards laid out in their ideal pattern, he leaned back, looking disappointed, and he said, "I'm damned." He then scooped up the cards, in a gesture unusually quick and tidy for him, stacked them together, and bound them with a rubber band. Then he began to tell us what he thought of Gran. He grew as loud and apoplectic as he had been that other time, and though he kept repeating that he knew *we* were innocent and he put not a shred of the blame on us, we were afraid he might suddenly change his mind, and, speechless, we cowered against the monkeys' cage. In dread, the monkeys clutched the fingers we offered to them and made soft, protesting noises, as if to say, "Oh, stop it, Murphy! Our nerves!"

As quickly as it had started, the tantrum ended. Mr. Murphy paled to his normal complexion and said calmly that the only practical thing was to go and have it out with Mrs. Placer. "At once," he added, although he said he bitterly feared that it was too late and there would be no exorcising the fiend from Laddy's misused spirit. And because he had given the dog to us and not to her, he required that we go along with him, stick up for our rights, stand on our own mettle, get up our Irish, and give the old bitch something to put in her pipe and smoke.

Oh, it was hot that day! We walked in a kind of delirium through the simmer, where only the grasshoppers had the energy to move, and I remember wondering if ether smelled like the gin on Mr. Murphy's breath. Daisy and I, in one way or another, were going to have our gizzards cut out along with our hearts and our souls and our pride, and I wished I were as drunk as Mr. Murphy, who swam effortlessly through the heat, his lips parted comfortably, his eyes half closed. When we turned in to the path at Gran's house, my blood began to scald my veins. It was so futile and so dangerous and so absurd. Here we were on a high moral mission, two draggletailed, gumptionless little girls and a toper whom no one could take seriously, partly because he was little more than a gurgling bottle of booze and partly because of the clothes he wore. He was a sight, as he always was when he was out of his own yard. There, somehow, in the carefree disorder, his clothes did not look especially strange, but on the streets of the town, in the barbershop or the post office or on Gran's path, they were fantastic. He wore a pair of hound's-tooth pants, old but maintaining a vehement pattern, and with them he wore a collarless blue flannelette shirt. His hat was the silliest of all, because it was a derby three sizes too big. And as if Shannon, too, was a part of his funny-paper costume, the elder capuchin rode on his shoulder, tightly embracing his thin red neck.

Gran and Caesar were standing side by side behind the screen door, looking as if they had been expecting us all along. For a moment, Gran and Mr. Murphy faced each other across the length of weedy brick between the gate and the front porch, and no one spoke. Gran took no notice at all of Daisy and me. She adjusted her eyeglasses, using both hands, and then looked down at Caesar and matter-of-factly asked, "Do you want out?"

Caesar flung himself full-length upon the screen and it sprang open like a jaw. I ran to meet him and head him off, and Daisy threw a library book at his head, but he was on Mr. Murphy in one split second and had his monkey off his shoulder and had broken Shannon's neck in two shakes. He would have gone on nuzzling and mauling and growling over the corpse for hours if Gran had not marched out of the house and down the path and slapped him lightly on the flank and said, in a voice that could not have deceived an idiot, "Why, Caesar, you scamp! You've hurt Mr. Murphy's monkey! Aren't you ashamed!"

Hurt the monkey! In one final, apologetic shudder, the life was extinguished from the little fellow. Bloody and covered with slather, Shannon lay with his arms suppliantly stretched over his head, his leather fingers curled into loose, helpless fists. His hind legs and his tail lay limp and helter-skelter on the path. And Mr. Murphy, all of a sudden reeling drunk, burst into the kind of tears that Daisy and I knew well—the kind that time alone could stop. We stood aghast in the dark-red sunset, killed by our horror and our grief for Shannon and our unforgivable disgrace. We stood upright in a dead faint, and an eon passed before Mr. Murphy picked up Shannon's body and wove away, sobbing, "I don't believe it! I don't *believe it!*"

The very next day, again at morbid, heavy sunset, Caesar died in violent convulsions, knocking down two tall hollyhocks in his throes. Long after his heart had stopped, his right hind leg continued to jerk in aimless reflex. Madly methodical, Mr. Murphy had poisoned some meat for him, had thoroughly envenomed a whole pound of hamburger, and early in the morning, before sunup, when he must have been near collapse with his hangover, he had stolen up to Mrs. Placer's house and put it by the kitchen door. He was so stealthy that Caesar never stirred in his fool's paradise there on the floor by Gran. We knew these to be the facts, for Mr. Murphy made no bones about them. Afterward, he had gone home and said a solemn Requiem for Shannon in so loud a voice that someone sent for the police, and they took him away in the Black Maria to

sober him up on strong green tea. By the time he was in the
lockup and had confessed what he had done, it was far too late,
for Caesar had already gulped down the meat. He suffered an
undreamed-of agony in Gran's flower garden, and Daisy and
I, unable to bear the sight of it, hiked up to the red rocks and
shook there, wretchedly ripping to shreds the sand lilies that
grew in the cracks. Flight was the only thing we could think
of, but where could we go? We stared west at the mountains
and quailed at the look of the stern white glacier; we wildly
scanned the prairies for escape. "If only we were something
besides kids! Besides girls!" mourned Daisy. I could not speak
at all; I huddled in a niche of the rocks and cried.

No one in town, except, of course, her lodgers, had the
slightest sympathy for Gran. The townsfolk allowed that Mr.
Murphy was a drunk and was fighting Irish, but he had a heart
and this was something that could never be said of Mrs. Placer.
The neighbor who had called the police when he was chanting
the *Dies Irae* before breakfast in that deafening monotone had
said, "The poor guy is having some kind of a spell, so don't be
rough on him, hear?" Mr. Murphy became, in fact, a kind of
hero; some people, stretching a point, said he was a saint for
the way that every day and twice on Sunday he sang a memorial
Mass over Shannon's grave, now marked with a chipped, cheap
plaster figure of Saint Francis. He withdrew from the world
more and more, seldom venturing into the streets at all, except
when he went to the bootlegger to get a new bottle to snuggle
into. All summer, all fall, we saw him as we passed by his yard,
sitting at his dilapidated table, enfeebled with gin, graying,
withering, turning his head ever and ever more slowly as he
maneuvered the protocol of the kings and the queens and the
knaves. Daisy and I could never stop to visit him again.

It went on like this, year after year. Daisy and I lived in a mesh
of lies and evasions, baffled and mean, like rats in a maze. When
we were old enough for beaux, we connived like sluts to see
them, but we would never admit to their existence until Gran
caught us out by some trick. Like this one, for example: Once,
at the end of a long interrogation, she said to me, "I'm more
relieved than I can tell you that you *don't* have anything to

do with Jimmy Gilmore, because I happen to know that he is after only one thing in a girl," and then, off guard in the loving memory of sitting in the movies the night before with Jimmy, not even holding hands, I defended him and defeated myself, and Gran, smiling with success, said, "I *thought* you knew him. It's a pretty safe rule of thumb that where there's smoke there's fire." That finished Jimmy and me, for afterward I was nervous with him and I confounded and alarmed and finally bored him by trying to convince him, although the subject had not come up, that I did not doubt his good intentions.

Daisy and I would come home from school, or, later, from our jobs, with a small triumph or an interesting piece of news, and if we forgot ourselves and, in our exuberance, told Gran, we were hustled into court at once for cross-examination. Once, I remember, while I was still in high school, I told her about getting a part in a play. How very nice for me, she said, if that kind of make-believe seemed to me worth while. But what was my role? An old woman! A widow woman believed to be a witch? She did not care a red cent, but she did have to laugh in view of the fact that Miss Eccles, in charge of dramatics, had almost run her down in her car. And I would forgive her, would I not, if she did not come to see the play, and would not think her eccentric for not wanting to see herself ridiculed in public?

My pleasure strangled, I crawled, joy-killed, to our third-floor room. The room was small and its monstrous furniture was too big and the rag rugs were repulsive, but it was bright. We would not hang a blind at the window, and on this day I stood there staring into the mountains that burned with the sun. I feared the mountains, but at times like this their massiveness consoled me; they, at least, could not be gossiped about.

Why did we stay until we were grown? Daisy and I ask ourselves this question as we sit here on the bench in the municipal zoo, reminded of Mr. Murphy by the polar bear, reminded by the monkeys not of Shannon but of Mrs. Placer's insatiable gossips at their post-prandial feast.

"But how could we have left?" says Daisy, wringing her buttery hands. "It was the depression. We had no money. We had nowhere to go."

"All the same, we could have gone," I say, resentful still of the waste of all those years. "We could have come here and got jobs as waitresses. Or prostitutes, for that matter."

"I wouldn't have wanted to be a prostitute," says Daisy.

We agree that under the circumstances it would have been impossible for us to run away. The physical act would have been simple, for the city was not far and we could have stolen the bus fare or hitched a ride. Later, when we began to work as salesgirls in Kress's, it would have been no trick at all to vanish one Saturday afternoon with our week's pay, without so much as going home to say goodbye. But it had been infinitely harder than that, for Gran, as we now see, held us trapped by our sense of guilt. We were vitiated, and we had no choice but to wait, flaccidly, for her to die.

You may be sure we did not unlearn those years as soon as we put her out of sight in the cemetery and sold her house for a song to the first boob who would buy it. Nor did we forget when we left the town for another one, where we had jobs at a dude camp—the town where Daisy now lives with a happy husband and two happy sons. The succubus did not relent for years, and I can still remember, in the beginning of our days at the Lazy S 3, overhearing an edgy millionaire say to his wife, naming my name, "That girl gives me the cold shivers. One would think she had just seen a murder." Well, I had. For years, whenever I woke in the night in fear or pain or loneliness, I would increase my suffering by the memory of Shannon, and my tears were as bitter as poor Mr. Murphy's.

We have never been back to Adams. But we see that house plainly, with the hopvines straggling over the porch. The windows are hung with the cheapest grade of marquisette, dipped into coffee to impart to it an unwilling color, neither white nor tan but individual and spitefully unattractive. We see the wicker rockers and the swing, and through the screen door we dimly make out the slightly veering corridor, along one wall of which stands a glass-doored bookcase; when we were children, it had contained not books but stale old cardboard boxes filled with such things as W.C.T.U. tracts and anti-cigarette literature and newspaper clippings relating to sexual sin in the Christianized islands of the Pacific.

Even if we were able to close our minds' eyes to the past,

Mr. Murphy would still be before us in the apotheosis of the polar bear. My pain becomes intolerable, and I am relieved when Daisy rescues us. "We've got to go," she says in a sudden panic. "I've got asthma coming on." We rush to the nearest exit of the city park and hail a cab, and, once inside it, Daisy gives herself an injection of adrenalin and then leans back. We are heartbroken and infuriated, and we cannot speak.

Two hours later, beside my train, we clutch each other as if we were drowning. We ought to go out to the nearest police-man and say, "We are not responsible women. You will have to take care of us because we cannot take care of ourselves." But gradually the storm begins to lull.

"You're sure you've got your ticket?" says Daisy. "You'll surely be able to get a roomette once you're on."

"I don't know about that," I say. "If there are any V.I.P.s on board, I won't have a chance. 'Spinsters and Orphans Last' is the motto of this line."

Daisy smiles. "I didn't care," she says, "but I had to laugh when I saw that woman nab the redcap you had signaled to. I had a good notion to give her a piece of my mind."

"It will be a miracle if I ever see my bags again," I say, mount-ing the steps of the train. "Do you suppose that blackguardly porter knows about the twenty-dollar gold piece in my little suitcase?"

"Anything's possible!" cries Daisy, and begins to laugh. She is so pretty, standing there in her bright-red linen suit and her black velvet hat. A solitary ray of sunshine comes through a broken pane in the domed vault of the train shed and lies on her shoulder like a silver arrow.

"So long, Daisy!" I call as the train begins to move.

She walks quickly along beside the train. "Watch out for pickpockets!" she calls.

"You, too!" My voice is thin and lost in the increasing noise of the speeding train wheels. "Goodbye, old dear!"

I go at once to the club car and I appropriate the writing table, to the vexation of a harried priest, who snatches up the telegraph pad and gives me a sharp look. I write Daisy approx-imately the same letter I always write her under this particular set of circumstances, the burden of which is that nothing for either of us can ever be as bad as the past before Gran mercifully died. In a postscript I add: "There is a Roman Catholic priest (that is to say, he is *dressed* like one) sitting behind me although all the chairs on the opposite side of the car are empty. I can only conclude that he is looking over my shoulder, and while I do not want to cause you any alarm, I think you would be advised to be on the lookout for any appearance of miraculous medals, scapulars, papist booklets, etc., in the shops of your town. It really makes me laugh to see the way he is pretending that all he wants is for me to finish this letter so that he can have the table."

I sign my name and address the envelope, and I give up my place to the priest, who smiles nicely at me, and then I move across the car to watch the fields as they slip by. They are alfalfa fields, but you can bet your bottom dollar that they are chockablock with marijuana.

I begin to laugh. The fit is silent but it is devastating; it surges and rattles in my rib cage, and I turn my face to the window to avoid the narrow gaze of the Filipino bar boy. I must think of something sad to stop this unholy giggle, and I think of the polar bear. But even his bleak tragedy does not sober me. Wildly I fling open the newspaper I have brought and I pretend to be reading something screamingly funny. The words I see are in a Hollywood gossip column: "How a well-known starlet can get a divorce in Nevada without her crooner husband's consent, nobody knows. It won't be worth a plugged nickel here."

The Liberation

ON the day Polly Bay decided to tell her Uncle Francis and his sister, her Aunt Jane, that in a week's time she was leaving their house and was going East to be married and to live in Boston, she walked very slowly home from Nevilles College, where she taught, dreading the startled look in their eyes and the woe and the indignation with which they would take her news. Hating any derangement of the status quo, her uncle, once a judge, was bound to cross-examine her intensively, and Aunt Jane, his perfect complement, would bolster him and baffle her. It was going to be an emotional and argumentative scene; her hands, which now were damp, would presently be dripping. She shivered with apprehension, fearing her aunt's asthma and her uncle's polemic, and she shook with rebellion, knowing how they would succeed in making her feel a traitor to her family, to the town, and to Colorado, and, obscurely, to her country.

Uncle Francis and Aunt Jane, like their dead kinsmen, Polly's father and her grandfather and her great-grandmother, had a vehement family and regional pride, and they counted it virtue in themselves that they had never been east of the Mississippi. They had looked on the departures of Polly's sisters and her cousins as acts of betrayal and even of disobedience. They had been distressed particularly by removals to the East, which were, they felt, iconoclastic and, worse, rude; how, they marveled, could this new generation be so ungrateful to those intrepid early Bays who in the forties had toiled in such peril and with such fortitude across the plains in a covered wagon and who with such perseverance had put down the roots for their traditions in this town that they had virtually made? Uncle Francis and Aunt Jane had done all in their power—through threats and sudden illnesses and cries of "Shame!"—to prevent these desertions, but, nevertheless, one by one, the members of the scapegrace generation had managed to fly, cut off without a penny, scolded to death, and spoken of thereafter as if they were unredeemed, treasonous, and debauched. Polly was the last, and her position, therefore, was the most uncomfortable of all; she and her aunt and uncle were the only Bays left in Adams, and she knew that because she was nearly thirty they had long ago stopped fearing that she, too, might go. As they frequently told her, in their candid way, they felt she had reached "a sensible age"—it was a struggle for them not to use the word "spinster" when they paid her this devious and crushing compliment. She knew perfectly well, because this, too, they spoke of, that they imagined she would still be teaching *Immensee* in German I years after they were dead, and would return each evening to the big, drafty house where they were born, and from which they expected to be carried in coffins ordered for them by Polly from Leonard Harper, the undertaker, whose mealy mouth and shifty eye they often talked about with detestation as they rocked and rocked through their long afternoons.

Polly had been engaged to Robert Fair for five months now and had kept his pretty ring in the desk in her office at college; she had not breathed a word to a soul. If she had spoken out when she came back from the Christmas holidays in her sister's Boston house, her uncle and aunt, with a margin of so much time for their forensic pleas before the college year was over, might have driven her to desperate measures; she might have had to flee, without baggage, in the middle of the night on a bus. Not wanting to begin her new life so haphazardly, she had guarded her secret, and had felt a hypocrite.

But she could not keep silent any longer; she had to tell them and start to pack her bags. She did not know how to present her announcement—whether to disarm them with joy or to stun them with a voice of adamant intention. Resenting the predicament, which so occupied her that her love was brusquely pushed aside, and feeling years younger than she was—an irritable adolescent, nerve-racked by growing pains—she now snatched leaves from the springtime bushes and tore them into shreds. It was late May and the purple lilacs were densely in blossom, offering their virtuous fragrance on the wind; the sun was tender on the yellow willow trees; the mountain range was blue and fair and free of haze. But Polly's senses were not at liberty today to take in these demure delights; she could not respond today at all to the flattering fortune that was to make her a June bride; she could not remember of her fiancé anything beyond his name, and, a little ruefully and a little cynically, she wondered if it was love of him or boredom with freshmen and with her aunt and uncle that had caused her to get engaged to him.

Although she loitered like a school child, she had at last to confront the house behind whose drawn blinds her aunt and uncle awaited her return, innocent of the scare they were presently to get and anticipating the modest academic news she brought each day to serve them with their tea. She was so unwilling that when she came in sight of the house she sat down on a bench at a trolley stop, under the dragging branches of a spruce tree, and opened the book her uncle had asked her to bring from the library. It was *The Heart of Midlothian*. She read with distaste; her uncle's pleasures were different from her own.

Neither the book, though, nor the green needles could hide from her interior eye that house where she had lived for seven years, since her father had died; her mother had been dead for many years and her sisters had long been gone—Fanny to Washington and Mary to Boston—but she had stayed on, quiet and unquestioning. Polly was an undemanding girl and she liked to teach and she had not been inspired to escape; she had had, until now, no reason to go elsewhere although, to be sure, these years had not been exclusively agreeable. For a short time, she had lived happily in an apartment by herself, waking each morning to the charming novelty of being her own mistress. But Uncle Francis and Aunt Jane, both widowed and both bereft of their heartless children, had cajoled her and played tricks upon her will until she had consented to go and live with them. It was not so much because she was weak as it was because they were so extremely strong that she had at last capitulated out of fatigue and had brought her things in a van to unpack them, sighing, in two wallpapered rooms at the top of the stout brown house. This odious house, her grandfather's, was covered with broad, unkempt shingles; it had a turret, and two bow windows within which begonia and heliotrope fed on the powerful mountain sun. Its rooms were huge, but since they were gorged with furniture and with garnishments and clumps and hoards of artifacts of Bays, you had no sense of space in them and, on the contrary, felt cornered and nudged and threatened by hanging lamps with dangerous dependencies and by the dark, bucolic pictures of Polly's fore-bears that leaned forward from the walls in their insculptured brassy frames.

The house stood at the corner of Oxford Street and Pine, and at the opposite end of the block, at the corner of Pine and Plato (the college had sponsored the brainy place names), there was another one exactly like it. It had been built as a wedding present for Uncle Francis by Polly's grandfather, and here Uncle Francis and his wife, Aunt Lacy, had reared an unnatural daughter and two unnatural sons, who had flown the coop, as he crossly said, the moment they legally could; there was in his tone the implication that if they had gone before they had come of age, he would have haled them back, calling on the police if they offered to resist. Uncle Francis had been born litigious; he had been predestined to arraign and complain, to sue and sentence.

Aunt Jane and Uncle Richard had lived in Grandpa's house, and their two cowed, effeminate sons had likewise vanished when they reached the age of franchise. When both Uncle Richard and Aunt Lacy had been sealed into the Bay plot, Uncle Francis had moved down the street to be with his sister for the sake of economy and company, taking with him his legal library, which, to this day, was still in boxes in the back hall, in spite of the protests of Mildred, their truculent housekeeper. Uncle Francis had then, at little cost, converted his own house into four inconvenient apartments, from which he derived a shockingly high income. A sign over the front door read, "The Bay Arms."

Polly's parents' red brick house, across the street from Uncle Francis's—not built but bought for them, also as a wedding present—had been torn down. And behind the trolley bench on which she sat there was the biggest and oldest family house of all, the original Bay residence, a vast grotesquerie of native stone, and in it, in the beginning of Polly's life, Great-grandmother had imperiously lived, with huge, sharp diamonds on her fichus and her velvet, talking without pause of red Indians and storms on the plains, because she could remember nothing else. The house was now a historical museum; it was called, not surprisingly, the Bay. Polly never looked at it without immediately remembering the intricate smell of the parlor, which had in it moss, must, belladonna, dry leaves, wet dust, oil of peppermint, and something that bound them all together—a smell of tribal history, perhaps, or the smell of a house where lived a half-cracked and haughty old woman who had come to the end of the line.

In those early days, there had been no other houses in this block, and the Bay children had had no playmates except each other. Four generations sat down to Sunday midday dinner every week at Great-grandmother's enormous table; the Presbyterian grace was half as long as a sermon; the fried rabbit was dry. On Christmas Eve, beneath a towering tree in Grandpa's house, sheepish Uncle Richard, as Santa Claus, handed round the presents while Grandpa sat in a central chair like a king on a throne and stroked his proud goatee. They ate turkey on Thanksgiving with Uncle Francis and Aunt Lacy, shot rockets and pinwheels off on the Fourth of July in Polly's family's back yard. Even now, though one of the houses was gone and another was given over to the display of minerals and wagon wheels, and though pressed-brick bungalows had sprung up all along the block, Polly never entered the street without the feeling that she came into a zone restricted for the use of her blood kin, for there lingered in it some energy, some air, some admonition that this was the territory of Bays and that Bays and ghosts of Bays were, and forever would be, in residence. It was easy for her to vest the wind in the spruce tree with her great-grandmother's voice and to hear it say, "Not a one of you knows the sensation of having a red Indian arrow whiz by your sunbonnet with wind enough to make the ribbons wave." On reflection, she understood the claustrophobia that had sent her sisters and cousins all but screaming out of town; horrified, she felt that her own life had been like a dream of smothering.

She was only pretending to read Walter Scott and the sun was setting and she was growing cold. She could not postpone any longer the discharge of the thunderbolt, and at last she weakly rose and crossed the street, feeling a convulsion of panic grind in her throat like a hard sob. Besides the panic, there was a heavy depression, an ebbing away of self-respect, a regret for the waste of so many years. Generations should not be mingled for daily fare, she thought; they are really contemptuous of one another, and the strong individuals, whether they belong to the older or the younger, impose on the meek their creeds and opinions, and, if they are strong enough, brook no dissent. Nothing can more totally subdue the passions than familial piety. Now, Polly saw, appalled and miserably ashamed of herself, that she had never once insisted on her own identity in this house. She had dishonestly, supinely (thinking, however, that she was only being polite), allowed her aunt and uncle to believe that she was contented in their house, in sympathy with them, and keenly interested in the minutiae that preoccupied them: their ossifying arteries and their weakening eyes, their dizzy spells and migrant pains, their thrice-daily eucharist of pills and chops, the twinges in their old, uncovered bones. She had never disagreed with them, so how could they know that she did not, as they did, hate the weather? They assumed that she was as scandalized as they by Uncle Francis's tenants' dogs and children. They had no way of knowing that she was bored nearly to frenzy by their vicious quarrels with Mildred over the way she cooked their food.

In the tenebrous hall lined with closed doors, she took off her gloves and coat, and, squinting through the shadows, saw in the mirror that her wretchedness was plain in her drooping lips and her frowning forehead; certainly there was no sign at all upon her face that she was in love. She fixed her mouth into a bogus smile of courage, she straightened out her brow; with the faintest heart in the world she entered the dark front parlor, where the windows were always closed and the shades drawn nearly to the sill. A coal fire on this mild May day burned hot and blue in the grate.

They sat opposite each other at a round, splayfooted table under a dim lamp with a beaded fringe. On the table, amid the tea things, there was a little mahogany casket containing the props with which, each day, they documented their reminiscences of murders, fires, marriages, bankruptcies, and of the triumphs and the rewards of the departed Bays. It was open, showing cracked photographs, letters sallow-inked with age, flaccid and furry newspaper clippings, souvenir spoons flecked with venomous green, little white boxes holding petrified mor-

sels of wedding cake. As Polly came into the room, Aunt Jane
reached out her hand and, as if she were pulling a chance from
a hat, she picked a newspaper clipping out of the box and said,
"I don't think you have ever told Polly the story of the time you
were in that train accident in the Royal Gorge. It's such a yarn."

Her uncle heard Polly then and chivalrously half rose from
his chair; tall and white-haired, he was distinguished, in a dour
way, and dapper in his stiff collar and his waistcoat piped with
white. He said, "At last our strayed lamb is back in the fold."
The figure made Polly shiver.

"How late you are!" cried Aunt Jane, thrilled at this small
deviation from routine. "A department meeting?" If there had
been a department meeting, the wreck in the Royal Gorge
might be saved for another day.

But they did not wait for her answer. They were impelled,
egocentrically and at length, to tell their own news, to explain
why it was that they had not waited for her but had begun their
tea. Uncle Francis had been hungry, not having felt quite himself
earlier in the day and having, therefore, eaten next to nothing at
lunch, although the soufflé that Mildred had made was far more
edible than customary. He had several new symptoms and was
going to the doctor tomorrow; he spoke with infinite peace of
mind. Painstakingly then, between themselves, they discussed
the advisability of Aunt Jane's making an appointment at the
beauty parlor for the same hour Uncle Francis was seeing Dr.
Wilder; they could in this way share a taxi. And what was the
name of that fellow who drove the Town Taxi whom they both
found so cautious and well-mannered? Bradley, was it? They
might have him drive them up a little way into the mountains
for the view; but, no, Francis might have got a bad report and
Jane might be tired after her baking under the dryer. It would
be better if they came straight home. Sometimes they went on
in this way for hours.

Polly poured herself a cup of tea, and Aunt Jane said, as she
had said probably three thousand times in the past seven years,
"You may say what you like, there is simply nothing to take the
place of a cup of tea at the end of the day."

Uncle Francis reached across the table and took the newspaper clipping from under his sister's hand. He adjusted his

glasses and glanced at the headlines, smiling. "There was a great deal of comedy in that tragedy," he said.

"Tell Polly about it," said Aunt Jane. Polly knew the details of this story by heart—the number of the locomotive and the name of the engineer and the passengers' injuries, particularly her uncle's, which, though minor, had been multitudinous.

Amazing herself, Polly said, "Don't!" And, amazed by her, they stared.

"Why, Polly, what an odd thing to say!" exclaimed Aunt Jane. "My dear, is something wrong?"

She decided to take them aback without preamble—it was the only way—and so she said, "Nothing's wrong. Everything's right at last. I am going to be married ten days from today to a teacher at Harvard and I am going to Boston to live."

They behaved like people on a stage; Aunt Jane put her teacup down, rattling her spoon, and began to wring her hands; Uncle Francis, holding his butter knife as if it were a gavel, glared.

"What are you talking about, darling?" he cried. "Married? What do you mean?"

Aunt Jane wheezed, signaling her useful asthma, which, however, did not oblige her. "Boston!" she gasped. "What ever for?"

Polly returned her uncle's magisterial look, but she did so obliquely, and she spoke to her cuffs when she said, "I mean 'married,' the way you were married to Aunt Lacy and the way Aunt Jane was married to Uncle Richard. I am in love with a man named Robert Fair and *he* is with *me* and we're going to be married."

"How lovely," said Aunt Jane, who, sight unseen, hated Robert Fair.

"Lovely perhaps," said Uncle Francis the magistrate, "and perhaps not. You might, if you please, do us the honor of enlightening us as to the qualifications of Mr. Fair to marry and export you. To the best of my knowledge, I have never heard of him."

"I'm quite sure we don't know him," said Aunt Jane; she coughed experimentally, but her asthma was still in hiding.

"No, you don't know him," Polly said. "He has never been in the West." She wished she could serenely drink her tea while she talked, but she did not trust her hand. Fixing her eyes on a maidenhair fern in a brass jardiniere on the floor, she told them how she had first met Robert Fair at her sister Mary's cottage in Edgartown the summer before.

"You never told us," said Uncle Francis reprovingly. "I thought you said the summer had been a mistake. Too expensive. Too hot. I thought you agreed with Jane and me that summer in the East was hard on the constitution." (She had; out of habit she had let them deprecate the East, which she had loved at first sight, had allowed them to tell her that she had had a poor time when, in truth, she had never been so happy.)

Shocked by her duplicity, Aunt Jane said, "We ought to have suspected something when you went back to Boston for Christmas with Mary instead of resting here beside your own hearth fire."

Ignoring this sanctimonius accusation, Polly continued, and told them as much of Robert Fair as she thought they deserved to know, eliding some of his history—for there was a divorce in it—but as she spoke, she could not conjure his voice or his face, and he remained as hypothetical to her as to them, a circumstance that alarmed her and one that her astute uncle sensed.

"You don't seem head over heels about this Boston fellow," he said.

"I'm nearly thirty," replied his niece. "I'm not sixteen. Wouldn't it be unbecoming at my age if I *were* lovesick?" She was by no means convinced of her argument, for her uncle had that effect on her; he could make her doubt anything—the testimony of her own eyes, the judgments of her own intellect. Again, and in vain, she called on Robert Fair to materialize in this room that was so hostile to him and, through his affection, bring a persuasive color to her cheeks. She did not question the power of love nor did she question, specifically, the steadfastness of her own love, but she did observe, with some dismay, that, far from conquering all, love lazily sidestepped practical problems; it was no help in this interview; it seemed not to cease but to be temporarily at a standstill.

Her uncle said, "Sixteen, thirty, sixty, it makes no difference. It's true I wouldn't like it if you were wearing your heart on your sleeve, but, my Lord, dear, I don't see the semblance of a light in your eye. You look quite sad. Doesn't Polly strike you as looking downright blue, Jane? If Mr. Fair makes you so doleful, it seems to me you're better off with us."

"It's not a laughing matter," snapped Aunt Jane, for Uncle Francis, maddeningly, had chuckled. It was a way he had in disputation; it was intended to enrage and thereby rattle his adversary. He kept his smile, but for a moment he held his tongue while his sister tried a different tack. "What I don't see is why you have to go to Boston, Polly," she said. "Couldn't he teach Italian at Nevilles just as well as at Harvard?"

Their chauvinism was really staggering. When Roddy, Uncle Francis's son, went off to take a glittering job in Brazil, Aunt Jane and his father had nearly reduced this stalwart boy to kicks and tears by reiterating that if there had been anything of worth or virtue in South America, the grandparent Bays would have settled there instead of in the Rocky Mountains.

"I don't think Robert would like it here," said Polly.

"What wouldn't he like about it?" Aunt Jane bridled. "I thought our college had a distinguished reputation. Your great-grandfather, one of the leading founders of it, was a man of culture, and unless I am sadly misinformed, his humanistic spirit is still felt on the campus. Did you know that his critical study of Isocrates is *highly* esteemed among classical scholars?"

"I mean I don't think he would like the West," said Polly, rash in her frustration.

She could have bitten her tongue out for the indiscretion, because her jingoistic uncle reddened instantly and menacingly, and he banged on the table and shouted, "How does he know he doesn't like the West? You've just told us he's never been farther west than Ohio. How does he dare to presume to damn what he doesn't know?"

"I didn't say he damned the West. I didn't even say he didn't like it. I said *I* thought he wouldn't."

"Then *you* are presuming," he scolded. "I am impatient with Easterners who look down their noses at the West and call us crude and barbaric. But Westerners who renounce and denounce and derogate their native ground are worse."

"Far worse," agreed Aunt Jane. "What can have come over you to turn the man you intend to marry against the land of your forebears?"

Polly had heard it all before. She wanted to clutch her head in her hands and groan with helplessness; even more, she wished that this were the middle of next week.

"We three are the last left of the Bays in Adams," pursued Aunt Jane, insinuating a quaver into her firm, stern voice. "And Francis and I will not last long. You'll only be burdened and bored with us a little while longer."

"We have meant to reward you liberally for your loyalty," said her uncle. "The houses will be yours when we join our ancestors."

In the dark parlor, they leaned toward her over their cups of cold tea, so tireless in their fusillade that she had no chance to deny them or to defend herself. Was there to be, they mourned, at last not one Bay left to lend his name and presence to municipal celebrations, to the laying of cornerstones and the opening of fairs? Polly thought they were probably already fretting over who would see that the grass between the family graves was mown.

Panicked, she tried to recall how other members of her family had extricated themselves from these webs of casuistry. Now she wished that she had more fully explained her circumstances to Robert Fair and had told him to come and fetch her away, for he, uninvolved, could afford to pay the ransom more easily than she. But she had wanted to spare him such a scene as this; they would not have been any more reticent with him; they would have, with this same arrogance—and this underhandedness— used their advanced age and family honor to twist the argument away from its premise.

Darkness had shrunk the room to the small circle where they sat in the thin light of the lamp; it seemed to her that their reproaches and their jeremiads took hours before they recommenced the bargaining Aunt Jane had started.

Reasonably, in a judicious voice, Uncle Francis said, "There is no reason at all, if Mr. Fair's attainments are as you describe, that he can't be got an appointment to our Romance Language Department. What is the good of my being a trustee if I can't render such a service once in a way?"

As if this were a perfectly wonderful and perfectly surprising solution, Aunt Jane enthusiastically cried, "But of course you can! That would settle everything. Polly can eat her cake and have it, too. Wouldn't you give them your house, Francis?"

"I'd propose an even better arrangement. Alone here, Jane, you and I would rattle. Perhaps we would move into one of my apartments and the Robert Fairs could have this house. Would that suit you?"

"It would, indeed it would," said Aunt Jane. "I have been noticing the drafts here more and more."

"I don't ask you to agree today, Polly," said Uncle Francis. "But think it over. Write your boy a letter tonight and tell him what your aunt and I are willing to do for him. The gift of a house, as big a house as this, is not to be scoffed at by young people just starting out."

Her "boy," Robert, had a tall son who in the autumn would enter Harvard. "Robert has a house," said Polly, and she thought of its dark-green front door with the brilliant brass trimmings; on Brimmer Street, at the foot of Beacon Hill, its garden faced the Charles. Nothing made her feel more safe and more mature than the image of that old and handsome house.

"He could sell it," said her indomitable aunt.

"He could rent it," said her practical uncle. "That would give you additional revenue."

The air was close; it was like the dead of night in a sealed room and Polly wanted to cry for help. She had not hated the West till now, she had not hated her relatives till now; indeed, till now she had had no experience of hate at all. Surprising as the emotion was—for it came swiftly and authoritatively—it nevertheless cleared her mind and, outraged, she got up and flicked the master switch to light up the chandelier. Her aunt and uncle blinked. She did not sit down again but stood in the doorway to deliver her valediction. "I don't want Robert to come here because I don't want to live here any longer. I want to live my own life."

"Being married is hardly living one's own life," said Aunt Jane.

At the end of her tether now, Polly all but screamed at them, "We *won't* live here and that's that! You talk of my presuming, but how can *you* presume to boss not only me but a man you've never even seen? I don't want your houses! I hate these houses! It's true—I hate, I despise, I abominate the West!"

So new to the articulation of anger, she did it badly and, ashamed to death, began to cry. Though they were hurt, they were forgiving, and both of them rose and came across the room, and Aunt Jane, taking her in a spidery embrace, said, "There. You go upstairs and have a bath and rest and we'll discuss it later. Couldn't we have some sherry, Francis? It seems to me that all our nerves are unstrung."

Polly's breath toiled against her sobs. but all the same she took her life in her hands and she said, "There's nothing further to discuss. I am leaving. I am not coming back."

Now, for the first time, the old brother and sister exchanged a look of real anxiety; they seemed, at last, to take her seriously; each waited for the other to speak. It was Aunt Jane who hit upon the new gambit. "I mean, dear, that we will discuss the wedding. You have given us very short notice but I daresay we can manage."

"There is to be no wedding," said Polly. "We are just going to be married at Mary's house. Fanny is coming up to Boston."

"Fanny has known all along?" Aunt Jane was insulted. "And all this time you've lived under our roof and sat at our table and never told *us* but told your sisters, who abandoned you?"

"Abandoned me? For God's sake, Aunt Jane, they had their lives to lead!"

"Don't use that sort of language in this house, young lady," said Uncle Francis.

"I apologize. I'm sorry. I am just so sick and tired of—"

"Of course you're sick and tired," said the adroit old woman. "You've had a heavy schedule this semester. No wonder you're all nerves and tears."

"Oh, it isn't that! Oh, leave me alone!"

And, unable to withstand a fresh onslaught of tears, she rushed to the door. When she had closed it upon them, she heard her aunt say, "I simply can't believe it. There must be some way out. Why, Francis, we would be left altogether *alone*," and there was real terror in her voice.

Polly locked the door to her bedroom and dried her eyes and bathed their lids with witch hazel, the odor of which made her think of her Aunt Lacy, who, poor simple creature, had had to die to escape this family. Polly remembered that every autumn Aunt Lacy had petitioned Uncle Francis to let her take her children home for a visit to her native Vermont, but she had never been allowed to go. Grandpa, roaring, thumping his stick, Uncle Francis bombarding her with rhetoric and using the word "duty" repeatedly, Polly's father scathing her with sarcasm, Aunt Jane slyly confusing her with red herrings had kept her an exhausted prisoner. Her children, as a result, had scorned their passive mother and had wounded her, and once they finally escaped, they had not come back—not for so much as a visit. Aunt Lacy had died not having seen any of her grandchildren; in the last years of her life she did nothing but cry. Polly's heart ached for the plight of that gentle, frightened woman. How lucky *she* was that the means of escape had come to her before it was too late! In her sister's Boston drawing room, in a snowy twilight, Robert Fair's proposal of marriage had seemed to release in her an inexhaustible wellspring of life; until that moment she had not known that she was dying, that she was being killed—by inches, but surely killed—by her aunt and uncle and by the green yearlings in her German classes and by the dogmatic monotony of the town's provincialism. She shuddered to think of her narrow escape from wasting away in these arid foothills, never knowing the cause or the name of her disease.

Quiet, herself again, Polly sat beside the window and looked out at the early stars and the crescent moon. Now that she had finally taken her stand, she was invulnerable, even though she knew that the brown sherry was being put ceremoniously on a tray, together with ancestral Waterford glasses, and though she knew that her aunt and uncle had not given up—that they had, on the contrary, just begun. And though she knew that for the last seven days of her life in this house she would be bludgeoned with the most splenetic and most defacing of emotions, she knew that the worst was over; she knew that she would survive, as her sisters and her cousins had survived. In the end, her aunt and uncle only *seemed* to survive; dead on their feet for most of their lives, they had no personal history; their genesis had not been individual—it had only been a part of a dull and factual plan. And they had been too busy honoring their family to love it, too busy defending the West even to look at it. For all their pride in their surroundings, they had never contemplated them at all but had sat with the shades drawn, huddled under the steel engravings. They and her father had lived their whole lives on the laurels of their grandparents; their goal had already been reached long before their birth.

The mountains had never looked so superb to her. She imagined a time, after Uncle Francis and Aunt Jane were dead, when the young Bays and their wives and husbands might come back, free at last to admire the landscape, free to go swiftly through the town in the foothills without so much as a glance at the family memorials and to gain the high passes and the peaks and the glaciers. They would breathe in the thin, lovely air of summits, and in their mouths there would not be a trace of the dust of the prairies where, as on a treadmill, Great-grandfather Bay's oxen plodded on and on into eternity.

The next days were for Polly at once harrowing and delightful. She suffered at the twilight hour (the brown sherry had become a daily custom, and she wondered if her aunt and uncle naïvely considered getting her drunk and, in this condition, persuading her to sign an unconditional indenture) and all through dinner as, by turns self-pitying and contentious, they sought to make her change her mind. Or, as they put it, "come to her senses." At no time did they accept the fact that she was going. They wrangled over summer plans in which she was included; they plotted anniversary speeches in the Bay museum; one afternoon Aunt Jane even started making a list of miners' families among whom Polly was to distribute Christmas baskets.

But when they were out of her sight and their nagging voices were out of her hearing, they were out of her mind, and in it, instead, was Robert Fair, in his rightful place. She graded examination papers tolerantly, through a haze; she packed her new clothes into her new suitcases and emptied her writing desk completely. On these starry, handsome nights, her dreams were charming, although, to be sure, she sometimes woke from them to hear the shuffle of carpet slippers on the floor below her as her insomniac aunt or uncle paced. But before sadness or rue could overtake her, she burrowed into the memory of her late dream.

The strain of her euphoria and her aunt's and uncle's antipodean gloom began at last to make her edgy, and she commenced to mark the days off on her calendar and even to reckon the hours. On the day she met her classes for the last time and told her colleagues goodbye and quit the campus forever, she did not stop on the first floor of the house but went directly to her room, only pausing at the parlor door to tell Aunt Jane and Uncle Francis that she had a letter to get off. Fraudulently humble, sighing, they begged her to join them later on for sherry. "The days are growing longer," said Aunt Jane plaintively, "but they are growing fewer."

Polly had no letter to write. She had a letter from Robert Fair to read, and although she knew it by heart already, she read it again several times. He shared her impatience; his students bored him, too; he said he had tried to envision her uncle's house, so that he could imagine her in a specific place, but he had not been able to succeed, even with the help of her sister. He wrote, "The house your malicious sister Mary describes could not exist. Does Aunt Jane *really* read Ouida?"

She laughed aloud. She felt light and purged, as if she had finished a fever. She went to her dressing table and began to brush her hair and to gaze, comforted, upon her young and loving face. She was so lost in her relief that she was pretty, and that she was going to be married and was going away, that she heard neither the telephone nor Mildred's feet upon the stairs, and the housekeeper was in the room before Polly had turned from her pool.

"It's your sister calling you from Boston," said Mildred with ice-cold contempt; she mirrored her employers. "I heard those operators back East giving themselves *some* airs with their la-di-da way of talking."

Clumsy with surprise and confusion (Mary's calls to her were rare and never frivolous), and sorry that exigency and not calm plan took her downstairs again, she reeled into that smothering front hall where hat trees and cane stands stood like people. The door to the parlor was closed, but she knew that behind it Aunt Jane and Uncle Francis were listening.

When Mary's far-off, mourning voice broke to Polly the awful, the impossible, the unbelievable news that Robert Fair had died that morning of the heart disease from which he had intermittently suffered for some years, Polly, wordless and dry-eyed, contracted into a nonsensical, contorted position and gripped the telephone as if this alone could keep her from drowning in the savage flood that had come from nowhere.

"Are you there, Polly? Can you hear me, darling?" Mary's anxious voice came louder and faster. "Do you want me to come out to you? Or can you come on here now?"

"I can't come now," said Polly. "There's nothing you can do for me." There had always been rapport between these sisters, and it had been deeper in the months since Robert Fair had appeared upon the scene to rescue and reward the younger woman. But it was shattered; the bearer of ill tidings is seldom thanked. "How can you help me?" Polly demanded, shocked and furious. "You can't bring him back to life."

"I can help bring you back to life," her sister said. "You must get out of *there*, Polly. It's more important now than ever."

"Do you think that was why I was going to marry him? Just to escape this house and this town?"

"No, no! Control yourself! We'd better not try to talk any more now—you call me when you can."

The parlor door opened, revealing Uncle Francis with a glass of sherry in his hand.

"Wait, Mary! Don't hang up!" Polly cried. There was a facetious air about her uncle; there was something smug. "I'll get the sleeper from Denver tonight," she said.

When she hung up, her uncle opened the door wider to welcome her to bad brown sherry; they had not turned on the lights, and Aunt Jane, in the twilight, sat in her accustomed place.

"Poor angel," said Uncle Francis.

"I am so sorry, so very sorry," said Aunt Jane.

When Polly said nothing but simply stared at their impassive faces, Uncle Francis said, "I think I'd better call up Wilder. You ought to have a sedative and go straight to bed."

"I'm going straight to Boston," said Polly.

"But why?" said Aunt Jane.

"Because he's there. I love him and he's there."

They tried to detain her; they tried to force the sherry down her throat; they told her she must be calm and they asked her to remember that at times like this one needed the love and the support of one's blood kin.

"I am going straight to Boston," she repeated, and turned and went quickly up the stairs. They stood at the bottom, calling to her: "You haven't settled your affairs. What about the bank?" "Polly, get hold of yourself! It's terrible, I'm heartbroken for you, but it's not the end of the world."

She packed nothing; she wanted nothing here—not even the new clothes she had bought in which to be a bride. She put on a coat and a hat and gloves and a scarf and put all the money she had in her purse and went downstairs again. Stricken but die-hard, they were beside the front door.

"Don't go!" implored Aunt Jane.

"You need us now more than ever!" her uncle cried.

"And we need you. Does that make no impression on you, Polly? Is your heart that cold?"

She paid no attention to them at all and pushed them aside and left the house. She ran to the station to get the last train to Denver, and once she had boarded it, she allowed her grief to overwhelm her. She felt chewed and mauled by the niggling hypochondriacs she had left behind, who had fussily tried to appropriate even her own tragedy. She felt sullied by their disrespect and greed.

How lonely I have been, she thought. And then, not fully knowing what she meant by it but believing in it faithfully, she said half aloud, "I am not lonely now."

A Reading Problem

O NE of the great hardships of my childhood—and there were many, as many, I suppose, as have ever plagued a living creature—was that I could never find a decent place to read. If I tried to read at home in the living room, I was constantly pestered by someone saying, "For goodness' sake, Emily, move where it's light. You're going to ruin your eyes and no two ways about it," or "You ought to be outdoors with the other youngsters getting some roses in your cheeks." Of course, I knew how to reply to these kill-joy injunctions; to the first I said, "They're *my* eyes," and to the second, "Getting some brains in my head is more important than getting any so-called roses in my cheeks." But even when I had settled the hash of that Paul Pry—Mother, usually, but sometimes a visiting aunt, or even a bossy neighbor—I was cross and could no longer concentrate. The bedroom I shared with my sister Stella was even worse, because Stella was always in it, making an inventory of her free samples out loud, singing Camp Fire Girl songs, practicing ballet steps and giggling whenever she made a mistake; she was one of the most vacant people I have ever known.

At one certain time of year, I could read up in the mountains, in any number of clearings and dingles and amphitheaters, and that was in the fall. But in the winter it was too cold, and in the spring there were wood ticks, and in the summer there were snakes. I had tried a pinewoods I was very fond of for several weeks one summer, but it was no good, because at the end of every paragraph I had to get up and stamp my feet and shout and describe an agitated circle on the ground with a stick to warn the rattlers to stay away from me.

The public library was better, but not much. The librarian, Mrs. Looby, a fussbudgety old thing in a yellow wig and a hat planted with nasturtiums, was so strict about the silent rule that she evicted children who popped their gum or cracked their knuckles, and I was a child who did both as a matter of course and constantly. Besides, she was forever coming into the children's section like a principal making rounds, and leaning over you to see what you were reading; half the time she disapproved

315

and recommended something else, something either so dry you'd go to sleep reading it or so mushy you'd throw up. Moreover, our dog, Reddie, loved to follow me to the library, and quite often, instead of waiting outside under the lilac bush, as he was supposed to do, he would manage to get in when someone opened the door. He didn't come to see me; he came to tease Mrs. Looby, who abominated anything that walked on four legs. He would sit on his haunches in front of her desk, wagging his tail and laughing, with his long pink tongue hanging out. "Shoo!" Mrs. Looby would scream, waving her hands at him. "Emily Vanderpool, you get this pesky dog of yours out of here this minute! The very idea! Quick, Emily, or I'll call the dogcatcher! I'll call the dogcatcher. I will positively call the dogcatcher if a dog ever comes into my library again." I had to give up the library altogether after one unlucky occasion when Reddie stood on his hind legs and put his paws on top of her high desk. She had had her back to him, and, thinking she heard a customer, she turned, saying in her library whisper, "Good afternoon, and what may I do for you this afternoon?" and faced the grinning countenance of my dog. That time, in her wrath and dismay, she clutched her head in her hands and dislodged her hat and then her wig, so that a wide expanse of baldness showed, and everyone in the children's section dived into the stacks and went all to pieces.

For a while after that, I tried the lobby of the downtown hotel, the Goldmoor, where the permanent residents, who were all old men, sat in long-waisted rocking chairs, rocking and spitting tobacco juice into embossed cuspidors and talking in high, offended, lonesome voices about their stomach-aches and their insomnia and how the times had changed. All in the world the old duffers had left was time, which, hour after hour, they had to kill. People like that, who are bored almost to extinction, think that everyone else is, too, and if they see someone reading a book, they say to themselves, "I declare, here's somebody worse off than I am. The poor soul's really hard up to have to depend on a book, and it's my bounden Christian duty to help him pass the time," and they start talking to you. If you want company on the streetcar or the bus or the interurban, open a book and you're all set. At first, the old men didn't spot me, because I always sat in one of the two bow windows in a chair that was half hidden by a potted sweet-potato plant, which, according to local legend, dated from the nineteenth century—and well it might have, since it was the size of a small-size tree. My chair was crowded in between this and a table on which was a clutter of seedy Western souvenirs—a rusted, beat-up placer pan with samples of ore in it, some fossils and some arrowheads, a tomahawk, a powder horn, and the shellacked tail of a beaver that was supposed to have been trapped by a desperado named Mountain Jim Nugent, who had lived in Estes Park in the seventies. It was this tabletop historical museum that made me have to give up the hotel, for one day, when I was spang in the middle of *Hans Brinker,* two of the old men came over to it to have a whining, cantankerous argument about one of the rocks in the placer pan, which one maintained was pyrites and the other maintained was not. (That was about as interesting as their conversations ever got.) They were so angry that if they hadn't been so feeble I think they would have thrown the rocks at each other. And then one of them caught sight of me and commenced to cackle. "Lookit what we got here," he said. "A little old kid in a middy reading windies all by her lonesome."

I had been taught to be courteous to my elders, so I looked up and gave the speaker a sickly smile and returned to my book, which now, of course, I could not follow. His disputant became his ally, and they carried on, laughing and teasing me as if I were a monkey that had suddenly entered their precincts for the sole purpose of amusing them. They asked me why I wasn't at the movies with my sweetheart, they asked me how I'd like to be paddled with that stiff old beaver tail of Mountain Jim's, and they asked me to sing them a song. All the other old men, delighted at this small interruption in their routine of spitting and complaining, started rubbernecking in my direction, grinning and chuckling, and a couple of them came shuffling over to watch the fun. I felt as if I had a fever of a hundred and five, because of the blush that spread over my entire person, including my insides. I was not only embarrassed, I was as mad as anything to be hemmed in by this phalanx of giggling old geezers who looked like a flock of turkey gobblers. "Maybe she ran away from home," said one of them. "Hasn't been any transients in this hotel since that last Watkins fella. Fella by the name of Fletcher. Is your name Fletcher, Missy?" Another said,

"I think it's mighty nice of her to come and pay us a call instead of going to the show with her best beau," and when a third said, "I bet I know where there's a Hershey bar not a thousand miles from here," I got up and, in a panic, ducked through the lines and fled; taking candy from a strange old man was the quickest way to die like a dog from poison.

So the hotel after that was out. Then I tried the depot, but it was too dirty and noisy; a couple of times I went and sat in the back of the Catholic church, but it was dark there, and besides I didn't feel right about it, because I was a United Presbyterian in good standing. Once, I went into the women's smoking room in the library at the college, but it was full of worried-looking old-maid summer-school students who came back year after year to work on their Master's degrees in Education, and they asked me a lot of solemn questions, raising their voices as if I were deaf. Besides, it was embarrassing to watch them smoke; they were furtive and affected, and they coughed a good deal. I could smoke better than that and I was only ten; I mean the one time I had smoked I did it better—a friend and I each smoked a cubeb she had pinched from her tubercular father.

But at last I found a peachy place—the visitors' waiting room outside the jail in the basement of the courthouse. There were seldom any visitors, because there were seldom any prisoners, and when, on rare occasions, there were, the visitors were too edgy or too morose to pay any heed to me. The big, cool room had nothing in it but two long benches and a wicker table, on which was spread out free Christian Science literature. The sheriff, Mr. Starbird, was very sympathetic with me, for he liked to read himself and that's what he did most of the time (his job was a snap; Adams was, on the whole, a law-abiding town) in his office that adjoined the waiting room; he read and read, not lifting his eyes from Sax Rohmer even when he was rolling a cigarette. Once, he said he wished his own daughters, Laverne, thirteen, and Ida, sixteen, would follow my example, instead of, as he put it, "rimfirin' around the county with paint on their faces and spikes on their heels and not caring two hoots for anything on God's green earth except what's got on pants." Mr. Starbird and I became good friends, although we did not talk much, since we were busy reading. One time, when we were both feeling restless, he locked me up in a cell so I could see how it felt; I kind of liked it. And another time he put handcuffs on me, but they were too big.

At the time I discovered the jail, in the first hot days in June, I was trying to memorize the books of the Bible. If I got them by heart and could name them off in proper order and without hesitating or mispronouncing, I would be eligible to receive an award of a New Testament at Sunday School, and if there was one thing I liked, it was prizes. So every day for several weeks I spent the whole afternoon more or less in jail, reading whatever fun thing I had brought along (*Rebecca of Sunnybrook Farm, Misunderstood Betsy, Trudy Goes to Boarding School*) and then working away at I Samuel, II Samuel, I Kings, II Kings, whispering so as not to disturb Mr. Starbird. Sometimes, on a really hot day, he would send out for two bottles of Dr. Pepper.

One blistering Saturday, when I was as limp as a rag after walking through the sun down the hill and into the hot valley where the courthouse was, I got to the stairs leading to the waiting room and was met by the most deafening din of men yelling and bars rattling and Mr. Starbird hollering "Quiet there, you bastards!" at the top of his voice. I was shocked and scared but very curious, and I went on down the steps, hearing the vilest imaginable language spewing out from the direction of the cells. I had just sat down on the edge of one of the benches and was opening *Tom Sawyer Abroad* when Mr. Starbird, bright red in the face, came in, brushing his hands. Two sweating deputies followed him. "Not today, Emily," said Mr. Starbird when he saw me. "We got some tough customers today, worse luck. And me with a new Fu."

The prisoners were moonshiners, he told me as he led me by the arm to the stairs, whose still up in the mountains had been discovered, because they had drunk too much of their own rot-gut and had got loose-tongued and had gone around bragging at the amusement park up at the head of the canyon. There were five of them, and they had had to be disarmed of sawed-off shotguns, although, as Mr. Starbird modestly pointed out, this wasn't much of a job, since they had been three sheets in the wind. "Whew!" said the sheriff. "They got a breath on 'em like the whole shootin' match of St. Louis before the Volstead Act." I told him I didn't mind (it would give me considerable prestige with my brother and my friends to be on hand if one of them should try to make a break, and I would undoubtedly get my name in the paper: "Emily Vanderpool, daughter of Mr. and Mrs. Peter Vanderpool, witnessed the attempted escape of the desperate criminals. Emily is to receive an award at the United Presbyterian Church on July 29th"), but Mr. Starbird told me, a little sharply, to go on now, and I had no choice but to go.

Go where? I had exhausted every possibility in town. I thought of going to the Safeway, where my father was the manager, and asking him if I could read in his office, but I knew how that would go over on a busy Saturday when the farmers and the mountain people were in town buying potatoes and side meat; my father didn't have Mr. Starbird's temperament. Then, vaguely, I considered the front porch of a haunted house at the top of Carlyle Hill but rejected it when I remembered a recent rumor that there was a nest of bats under the eaves; I didn't want them in my hair, using my pigtails to swing on. I wasn't too sure I could read anyhow, because I was so excited over the prisoners, but it was far too hot to roller-skate, too hot to explore the dump—too hot, indeed, for anything but sitting quietly beside the lockup.

I started in the direction of home in a desultory way, stopping at every drinking fountain, window-shopping, going methodically through the ten-cent stores, looking for money in the gutters. I walked down the length of the main street, going toward the mountains, over whose summits hung a pale heat haze; the pavement was soft, and when it and the shimmering sidewalk ended, I had to walk in the red dirt road, which was so dusty that after a few steps my legs, above the tops of my socks, looked burned—not sunburned, *burned*.

At the outskirts of town, beside the creek, there was a tourist camp where funny-looking people pitched tents and filled up the wire trash baskets with tin cans; sometimes, on a still night, you could hear them singing state songs, and now and again there was the sound of an accordion or a harmonica playing a jig. Today there was only one tent up in the grounds, a sagging, ragged white one, and it looked forlorn, like something left behind. Nearby was parked a Model T, dark red with rust where its sky-blue paint had worn off, and to it was attached a trailer; I knew how hot the leather seat of that car would be and I could all but hear the sun beating on the top of it like hailstones. There wasn't a soul in sight, and there wasn't a sound nearby except for a couple of magpies ranting at each other in the trees and the occasional digestive croak of a bullfrog. Along the creek, there was a line of shady cottonwoods, and I decided to rest there for a while and cool off my feet in the water.

After I had washed as well as I could, I leaned back against the tree trunk, my feet still in the water, and opened the Bible to the table of contents, and then I closed my eyes so that I wouldn't cheat; I started reciting, softly and clearly and proud of myself. I had just got to Ezra, having gone so far very fast without a hitch, when a noise caused me to fling back my eyelids and to discover that a man's big foot in a high buttoned shoe had materialized on the ground beside me. Startled, I looked up into the bearded face of a tall man in black clothes (black suit, black string tie, black-rimmed eyeglasses, black hat—the hat was dented in such a way that it looked like a gravy boat) and into the small brown eyes of a girl about Stella's age, who wore a tennis visor and a long, dirty white thing that looked like her nightgown.

"Greetings, Christian soldier," said the man, in a deep, rich Southern accent, and he offered me a large, warty hand. "Evangelist Gerlash is the name, and this is my girl, Opal."

Opal put her hand on my head and said, "Peace."

"Same to you," I said awkwardly, and took my feet out of the water. "You can have this tree if you want. I was just leaving."

I started to get up, but Evangelist Gerlash motioned me to stay where I was, and he said, "It uplifts my heavy heart and it uplifts Opal's to find a believer in our wanderings through this godless world. All too seldom do we find a person applying themself to the Book. Oh, sister, keep to this path your youthful feet have started on and shun the Sodoms *and* the Gomorrahs *and* the Babylons!"

My youthful feet were so wet I was having a struggle to put on my socks, and I thought, Peace! That's all he knows about it. There's not an inch of peace or privacy in this whole town.

"Seek truth and *not* the fleshpots!" said the man. "Know light, *not* license! 'A little child shall lead them,' says the Book you hold in your small hands, as yet unused to woman's work. Perhaps *you* are that very child."

"Amen," said Opal, and with this they both sat down, tailor-fashion, on the bank of the stream. For some time, nothing more was said. The Gerlashes complacently scrutinized me, as if I were the very thing they had been looking for, and then they looked at each other in a congratulatory way, while I, breaking out in an itching rash of embarrassment, tried to think of an urgent bit of business that would excuse me from their company without being impolite. I could think only of the dentist or of a dancing class, but I was dressed for neither; some weeks before, my Uncle Will M'Kerrow, who lived in Ridley, Missouri, had gone to a sale at the Army and Navy store in St. Joe and had bought presents for me and my brother and my two sisters, and today I was wearing mine—khaki knickers and a khaki shirt and a cavalry hat. I had perked up the hat by twining a multicolored shoelace around the band; the other shoelace I had cut in two to tie the ends of my pigtails; over my heart was sewn a red "C," a school letter that I had got in the spring for collateral reading. The dentist, Dr. Skeen, a humorist, would have died laughing if he had seen me in these A.E.F. regimentals, and Miss Jorene Roy, the dancing teacher, would have had kittens. Although the Gerlashes had no way of knowing the personality of either of them, I was so unskillful at useful lies, and believed so firmly that my mind could be read, that I did not dare pretend I was going to have a cavity filled or to assume the five ballet positions. I said nothing and waited for an inspiration to set me free. People who talked Bible talk like this made me ashamed for them.

Evangelist Gerlash was immensely tall, and his bones had only the barest wrapper of flesh; he made me think of a tree with the leaves off, he was so angular and gnarled, and even his skin was something like bark, rough and pitted and scarred. His wild beard was the color of a sorrel horse, but his long hair was black, and so were the whiskers on the backs of his hands that imperfectly concealed, on the right one, a tattoo of a peacock. His intense and watchful brown eyes were flecked with green, and so were Opal's. Opal's hair was the color of her father's beard and it fell ropily to her shoulders; it needed a good brushing, and probably a fine comb wouldn't have done it any harm.

Presently, the evangelist took his beard between his hands and squeezed as if he were strangling it, and he said, "We have had a weary journey, sister."

"You said a mouthful," said Opal, and hugely yawned.

"We come all the way from Arkansas this trip," said her father. "We been comin' since May."

"I liked it better last summer," said Opal, "up in Missouri and Iowa. I don't like this dry. Mountains give me the fantods." She looked over her shoulder up at the heat-hidden range and shuddered violently.

"We been roving like gypsies of the Lord, warning the wicked and helping the sick," her father went on. "We are pleased to meet up with a person who goes to the source of goodness and spiritual health. In other words, we are glad to make the acquaintance of a *friend*." And, still wringing his beard, he gave me an alarming smile that showed a set of sharp, efficient teeth. "Yes, sir, it gladdens me right down to the marrowbone to see a little girl on a summer day reading the word of God instead of messing with the vanities of this world *or* robbing the honest farmer of his watermelon *or* sassing her Christian mother."

"We stopped in nineteen towns and preached up a storm," said Opal. "You got any gum on you?"

Fascinated by the Gerlashes, although the piety the evangelist assigned to me discomforted me, since I was no more reading the Bible than your cat, I took a package of Beech-Nut out of the pocket of my knickers, and along with it came my hand-me-down Ingersoll that hadn't run for two years. Opal took a stick of gum, and her father, with his eye on my watch, said, "Don't mind if I do," and also took a stick. "That's a dandy timepiece you got there. Remember that nice old gold turnip I used to have, Opie?"

"Yeah," said Opal scornfully. "I remember you hocked that nice old gold turnip."

"Possessions are a woe and a heavy load of sin," said her father, and reached out for my watch. But after he had held it to his ear and fiddled with the stem for a while, he gave it back, saying, "*Was* a dandy timepiece. Ain't nothing now but a piece of tin and isinglass." Then he returned to his thesis. "I reckon this is the one and only time I or Opal has come across a person, let alone a child, drinking at the wellspring of enlightenment." And he gave me his hand to shake again.

"Amen," said Opal.

There followed a drawling antiphonal recitative that related the Gerlash situation. In the winter, they lived in a town called Hoxie, Arkansas, where Evangelist Gerlash clerked in the Buttorf drugstore and preached and baptized on the side. ("Hoxie may be only a wide space in the road," said Opal, "but she don't have any homely mountains.") Mrs. Gerlash, whom Abraham had untimely gathered to his bosom the winter before, had been a hymn singer and an organ player and had done a little preaching herself. Opal, here, had got the word the day she was born, and by the time she was five and a half years old she could preach to a fare-thee-well against the Catholics and the Wets. She was also an A-1 dowser and was renowned throughout the Wonder State. In the summer, they took to the road as soon as Opal was out of school, and went camping and preaching and praying (and dowsing if there was a call for it) and spreading the truth all over the country. Last year, they had gone through the Middle West up as far as Chicago (here Opal, somewhat to her father's impatience, digressed to tell me the story of Mrs. O'Leary's cow), and the year before they had gone through New England; on earlier trips they had covered Florida and Georgia. One of these days, they were going to set up shop in New York City, though they understood the tourist-camp situation there was poor. Sometimes they found hospitality and sometimes they didn't, depending on the heathens per capita. Sometimes the Christian citizens lent them a hall, and they put up a sign on the front door saying, "The Bible Tabernacle." Often, in such a receptive community, they were invited to supper and given groceries by the believers. But sometimes they had to do their saving of souls in a public park or in a tourist camp. ("Not much business in this one," said Opal, gazing ruefully at their solitary tent.) Mr. Buttorf, the druggist in Hoxie, always said he wasn't going to keep Gerlash one more day if he didn't quit this traipsing around three months of the year, but the Lord saw to it that right after Labor Day Buttorf came to his senses and hired him again. They had arrived in Adams this morning, and if they found fertile ground, they meant to stay a week, sowing the seeds of righteousness. Evangelist Gerlash would be much obliged to learn from me what sort of town this was; he said he guessed nobody could give him the lay of the land—spiritually speaking—any better than a Bible-reading girl like me.

"But first," he said, "tell Opal and I a little something about yourself, sister." He took a black notebook out of the pocket of his black coat and took a stubby pencil out of his hatband, licked it, and began to ask me questions. All the time he was taking down my dossier, Opal rocked gently back and forth, hugging herself and humming "Holy, Holy, Holy." I was much impressed by her, because her jaws, as she diligently chewed her gum, were moving in the opposite direction to her trunk; I was sure she would be able to pat her head and rub her stomach at the same time.

It never occurred to me that I didn't have to answer questions put to me by adults (except for the old men in the Goldmoor, who were not serious)—even strange ones who had dropped out of nowhere. Besides, I was always as cooperative as possible with clergymen, not knowing when my number might come up. The evangelist's questions were harmless enough, but some of them were exceedingly strange. In between asking my name and my age and my father's occupation, he would say, "Which do you think is the Bible Sabbath—Saturday or Sunday?" and "Do you know if the Devil is a bachelor or is he a married man?" When to these hard, interesting questions I replied that I did not know, Opal left off her humming and said, "Amen."

When he had got from me all the data he wanted, he said, "I bet you this here town is a candidate for brimstone. I bet you it's every bit as bad as that one out on the plains we were at for two weeks in a hall. Heathens they were, but *scared*, so they give us a hall. That Mangol."

"Mudhole is what I call it," said Opal.

Her father chuckled. "Opal makes jokes," he explained. Then he said, "That was the worst town we come across in all our travels, sister, and somewheres on me I've got a clipping from the Mangol daily showing what I told the folks down there. I wouldn't be surprised if the same situation was here in Adams, being in the same state with Mangol and not any too far away from Mangol and having that college that is bound to sow freethinking. Forewarned is forearmed is what I always say. I may have a good deal of hard work to do here." He began to fish things out of his pockets, and you never saw such a mess—a knife, a plug of chewing tobacco, a thin bar of soap, envelopes with arithmetic on them, a handkerchief I am not going to describe, any number of small pamphlets and folded-up handbills. Finally, he handed me a clipping. It said,

ANOTHER SOUR, GASSY STOMACH
VICTIM SAYS GASTRO-PEP
GAVE RELIEF

There was a picture of an indignant-looking man with a pointed head and beetling brows and a clenched jaw, who testified:

"For 3 years I had been a Great Victim of stomach gas and indigestion," said Mr. Homer Wagman, prominent Oklahoma citizen of 238 Taos Street, Muskogee. "My liver was sluggish, I would get bloated up and painful and had that tired dragged out feeling all the time. Recently a friend told me about Gastro-Pep so I decided to give it a trial. After taking 3 bottles of this medicine my WHOLE SYSTEM has gone through such a change that I can hardly believe it! Now my gas and stomach discomfort are relieved and I can eat my meals without suffering. I sleep like a schoolboy." Advt.

I did not know what I was reading, but I didn't like it anyway, since it had so nasty a sound; I didn't mind hearing about broken legs or diphtheria, but I hated any mention of anyone's insides. I started to read it for the second time, trying to think of something intelligent or complimentary to say to Evangelist Gerlash, and I must have made a face, because he leaned over me, adjusting his glasses, and said, "Oops! Hold on! Wrong write-up," and snatched the clipping out of my hand. I'm not absolutely sure, but I think Opal winked at me. Her father shuffled through his trash again and finally handed me another clipping, which, this time, was not an advertisement. The headline was

GERLASH LOCATES HELL IN
HEART OF CITY OF MANGOL

and the story beneath it ran:

"Hell is located right in the heart of the city of Mangol but will not
be in operation until God sets up His Kingdom here in the earth,"
declared Evangelist Gerlash last night to another capacity crowd in
the Bible Tabernacle.

"There are some very bad trouble spots in the city of Mangol
that no doubt would be subjects of Hell right now," continued the
evangelist and said, "but there are so many good people and places
in this city that overshadow the bad that God has decided to postpone Hell in Mangol until the time of the harvest and the harvest,
God says, 'is the end of the world' (Matthew 13:39).

"Hell, when started by God with eternal fire that comes from
God out of Heaven and ignites the entire world, including this city,
will be an interesting place. It will be a real play of fireworks, so
hot that all the elements of earth will melt; too hot all over to find
a place for any human creature to live. God is not arranging this
fireworks for any human creature and therefore, if you or I ever land
in this place, it is because we choose to go there."

Evangelist Gerlash and his daughter, Opal Gerlash, 12, of Hoxie,
Arkansas, have been preaching on alternate nights for the last week
at the Bible Tabernacle, formerly the Alvarez Feed and Grain store,
at 1919 Prospect Street. Tonight Opal Gerlash will lecture on the
subject, "Are You Born Again by Jumping, Rolling, Shouting, or
Dancing?"

I read this with a good deal more interest than I had read
of Mr. Wagman's renascence, although as Evangelist Gerlash's
qualifications multiplied, my emotion waned. I had assumed
from the headline, which made the back of my neck prickle,
that he had some hot tips on the iniquities of that flat, dull little
prairie town of Mangol that now and again we drove through
when we were taking a trip to the southwest; the only thing
I had ever noticed about it was that I had to hold my nose
as we went through it, because the smell of sugar beets was
so powerfully putrid. The city of Mangol had a population of
about six hundred.

Nevertheless, though the evangelist did not scare or awe me,
I had to be polite, and so, handing back the clipping, I said,

"When do you think the end of the world is apt to be?" Opal had stopped her humming and swaying, and both she and her father were staring at me with those fierce brown eyes.

"In the autumn of the world," said Evangelist Gerlash sepulchrally, and Opal said, as she could be counted on to do, "Amen."

"Yeah, I know," I said. "But what autumn? What year?" He and Opal simultaneously bowed their heads in silent prayer. Both of them thoughtfully chewed gum.

Then Opal made a speech. "The answer to this and many other questions will be found in Evangelist Gerlash's inspirational hundred-and-twelve-page book entitled *Gerlash on the Bible*. Each and every one of you will want to read about the seven great plagues to smite the people of the world just before the end. Upon who will they fall? Have they begun? What will it mean to the world? In this book, on sale for the nominal sum of fifty cents or a half dollar, Evangelist Gerlash lets the people in on the ground floor regarding the law of God." From one of the deep sleeves of her kimono—for that was what that grimy garment was—Opal withdrew a paper-bound book with a picture of her father on the front of it, pointing his finger at me.

"Fifty cents, a half dollar," said the author, "which is to say virtually free, gratis, and for nothing."

Up the creek a way, a bullfrog made a noise that sounded distinctly like "Ger-lash."

"What makes Mangol so much worse than any place else?" I asked, growing more and more suspicious now that the conversation had taken so mercantile a turn.

But the Gerlashes were not giving out information free. "You will find the answer to this and many other questions in the book," said Opal. "Such as 'Can Wall Street run God's Business?'"

"Why does the Devil go on a sit-down strike for a thousand years?" said her father.

"*What*?" said I.

"Who will receive the mark of the beast?" said Opal.

"Repent!" commanded Evangelist Gerlash. "Watch! Hearken!"

"Ger-lash," went the bullfrog.

"Will hell burn forever?" cried Opal. "Be saved from the boiling pits! Take out insurance against spending eternity on a griddle!"

"Thy days are numbered," declared her father.

Opal said, "Major Hagedorn, editor of the Markston *Standard*, in his editorial said, 'This man Gerlash is as smart as chain lightning and seems to know his Bible forwards and backwards.'" All this time, she was holding up the book, and her father, on the cover of it, was threatening to impale me on his accusing finger.

"Perhaps our sister doesn't have the wherewithal to purchase this valuable book, or in other words the means to her salvation," he said, at last, and gave me a look of profound sadness, as if he had never been so sorry for anyone in his life. I said it was true I didn't have fifty cents (who ever heard of anyone ten years old going around with that kind of money?), and I offered to trade my Bible for *Gerlash on the Bible*, since I was interested in finding out whether the Devil was a bachelor or had a wife. But he shook his head. He began to throttle his beard again, and he said, "Does a dove need a kite? Does a giraffe need a neck? Does an Eskimo need a fur coat? Does Gerlash need a Bible?"

"Gerlash is a regular walking encyclopedia on the Bible," said Opal.

"One of the biggest trouble spots in the world is Mangol, Colorado," said Evangelist Gerlash. "No reason to think for a minute the contamination won't spread up here like a plague of locusts. Don't you think you had ought to be armed, Christian soldier?"

"Yes, I do," I said, for I had grown more and more curious. "But I don't have fifty cents."

"Considering that you are a Christian girl and a Bible reader," said the man, "I think we could make a special price for you. I reckon we could let you have it for twenty-five cents. O.K., Opal?"

Opal said rapidly, "Gastro-Pep contains over thirty ingredients. So it is like taking several medicines at once. And due to the immense volume in which it sells, the price of Gastro-Pep is reasonable, so get it now. Tonight!"

Evangelist Gerlash gave his daughter a sharp look. And,

flustered, she stammered, "I mean, owing to the outstanding nature of Gerlash's information, the price of this *in*valuable book is a mere nothing. The truth in this book will stick and mark you forever."

"You want this book bad, don't you, sister Emily Vanderpool?" asked her father. "You are a good girl, and good girls are entitled to have this book, which is jam-packed with answers to the questions that have troubled you for years. You can't tell me your mammy and pappy are so mean that they wouldn't give their little girl a quarter for *Gerlash on the Bible*. Why don't you skedaddle over to home and get the small sum of twenty-five cents off your Christian ma?" He opened his notebook and checked my address. "Over to 125 Belleview Avenue."

"I'm hungry," said Opal. "I could eat me a horse."

"Never mind you being hungry," said her father, with a note of asperity in his mushy voice. "Don't you doubt me, sister Vanderpool," he went on, "when I tell you your innocent life is in danger. Looky here, when I got a call to go and enlighten the children of darkness in Mangol, just down the line from here, I got that call like a clap of thunder and I knew I couldn't waste no time. I went and I studied every den of vice in the city limits and some outside the city limits. It's bad, sister. For twenty-five cents, you and your folks can be prepared for when the Mangolites come a-swarming into this town." He glanced again at his notebook. "While you're getting the purchase price of my book, please ask your pure-hearted mother if I might have the loan of her garage to preach the word of God in. Are you folks centrally located?"

"My brother's got his skunk skins drying in it," I said. "You couldn't stand the smell."

"Rats!" said Evangelist Gerlash crossly, and then sternly he said, "You better shake a leg, sister. This book is offered for a limited time only."

"I can't get a quarter," I said. "I already owe her twenty cents."

"What're you going to have for supper?" asked Opal avidly. "I could eat a bushel of roasting ears. We ain't had a meal in a dog's age—not since that old handout in Niwot."

"Alas, too true," said her father. "Do you hear that, my sister Emily? You look upon a hungry holy man of God and his girl who give to the poor and save no crust for himself. Fainting for the want of but a crumb from the rich man's groaning board, we drive ourself onwards, bringing light where there is darkness and comfort where there is woe. Perhaps your good Christian mother and father would give us an invite to their supper tonight, in exchange for which they and theirs would gladly be given this priceless book, free of charge, signed by hand."

"Well, gosh," I said, working my tennis shoes on over my wet socks, "I mean . . . Well, I mean I don't know."

"Don't know what?" said that great big man, glowering at me over the tops of his severe spectacles. "Don't you go and tell me that a good Bible-reading girl like you has got kin which are evolutionists and agnostics and infidels who would turn two needy ministers of God away from their door. To those who are nourished by the Law of the Lord, a crust now and then is sufficient to keep body and soul together. I don't suppose Opal and I have had hot victuals for a good ten days, two weeks." A piteous note crept into his versatile voice, and his brown eyes and his daughter's begot a film of tears. They did look awfully hungry, and I felt guilty the way I did when I was eating a sandwich and Reddie was looking up at me like a martyr of old.

"Didn't she say her daddy ran a grocery store?" asked Opal, and her father, consulting my vital statistics, smiled broadly.

"There's nothing the matter with *your* ears, Opie," he said. And then, to me, "How's about it, sister? How's about you going down to this Safeway store and getting Opal and I some bread and some pork chops and like that?"

"Roasting ears," said Opal. "And a mushmelon."

It had suddenly occurred to me that if I could just get up and run away, the incident would be finished, but Evangelist Gerlash was clairvoyant, and, putting two firmly restraining hands on my shoulders and glaring at me straight in the eye, he said, "We don't have a thing in the world tonight to do but show up at 125 Belleview Avenue round about suppertime."

"I'd rather cook out," said Opal. "I'd rather she brought the groceries." Her father bent his head into his hands, and there was a great sob in his voice when he said, "I have suffered many a bitter disappointment in this vale of tears, but I suppose the bitterest is right now here in Adams, Colorado, where, thinking I had found a child of light, she turned out to be a mocker, grinding under her heel shod in gold the poor and the halt. Oh, sister, may you be forgiven on the Day of Judgment!"

"Whyn't you go get us some eats?" said Opal, cajoling. "If you get us some eats, we won't come calling. If we come calling, like as not we'll spend the night."

"Haven't slept in a bed since May," said her father, snuffling.

"We don't shake easy," said Opal, with an absolutely shameless grin.

My mother had a heart made of butter, and our spare room was forever occupied by strays, causing my father to scold her to pieces after they'd gone, and I knew that if the Gerlashes showed up at our house (and plainly they would) with their hard-luck story and their hard-luck looks and all their devices for saving souls, she would give them houseroom and urge them to stay as long as they liked, and my father would not simmer down for a month of Sundays.

So I got up and I said, "All right, I'll go get you a sack of groceries." I had a nebulous idea that my father might let me buy them on time or might give me a job as a delivery boy until I had paid for them.

To my distress, the Gerlashes got up, too, and the evangelist said, "We'll drive you down to Main Street, sister, and sit outside, so there won't be no slip-up."

"It's Saturday!" I cried. "You can't find a place to park."

"Then we'll just circle round and round the block."

"But I can't get into a car with strangers," I protested.

"Strangers!" exclaimed Evangelist Gerlash. "Why, sister, we're friends now. Don't you know all about Opal and I? Didn't we lay every last one of our cards on the table right off the bat?" He took my arm in his big, bony hand and started to propel me in the direction of the Ford, and just then, like the Mounties to the rescue, up came Mr. Starbird's official car, tearing into the campgrounds and stopping, with a scream from the brakes, right in front of me and the Gerlashes. A man in a deputy's uniform was in the front seat beside him.

"Why, Emily," said Mr. Starbird as he got out of the car and pushed his hat back from his forehead. "I thought you went on home after that ruckus we had. You'll be glad to hear those scalawags are going off to the pen tomorrow, so you can come back to jail any time after 10 A.M."

Opal giggled, but her father shivered and looked as if a rabbit had just run over his grave. "We're getting outa here," he said to her under his breath, and started at a lope toward his car.

"That's them all right," said the man in the deputy's uniform. "They set up shop in the feed store, and when they wasn't passing out mumbo-jumbo about the world going up in firecrackers, they was selling that medicine. Medicine! Ninety percent wood alcohol and ninety percent fusel oil. Three cases of jake-leg and God knows how many workers passed out in the fields."

Mr. Starbird and the deputy had closed in on the Gerlashes. Mr. Starbird said, "I don't want any trouble with you, mister. I just want you to get out of Adams before I run you out on a rail. We got plenty of our own preachers and plenty of our own bootleggers, and we don't need any extra of either one. Just kindly allow me to impound this so-called medicine and then you shove. What kind of a bill of goods were they trying to sell you, Emily, kid?"

The deputy said, "That's another of their lines. We checked on them after they left Mangol, checked all the way back to Arkansas. They get some sucker like a kid or an idiot and give them this spiel and promise they'll go to heaven if they'll just get them some grub or some money or my Aunt Geraldine's diamond engagement ring or whatever."

I said nothing. I was thrilled, and at the same time I was mortally embarrassed for the Gerlashes. I was sorry for them, too, because, in spite of their predicament, they looked more hungry than anything else.

Opal said, "If we went to jail, we could eat," but her father gave her a whack on the seat and told her, "Hush up, you," and the procession, including myself, clutching my Bible and *Tom Sawyer Abroad*, moved toward the tent and the Model T. The sheriff took two cases of medicine out of the tent and put them in his car, and then we stood there watching the Gerlashes strike camp and put all their bivouac gear into the trailer. They worked swiftly and competently, as if they were accustomed to sudden removals. When they were finished, Opal got into the front seat and started to cry. "God damn it to hell," said the child preacher. "Whyn't we ever have something to eat?"

Mr. Starbird, abashed by the dirty girl's tears, took out his wallet and gave her a dollar. "Don't you spend a red cent of it in Adams," he said. "You go on and get out of town and then get some food."

Evangelist Gerlash, having cranked the car, making a noise like a collision, climbed into the driver's seat, and grinned at the sight of the dollar. "I have cast my bread upon the waters and I am repaid one hundredfold," he said. "And you, in casting your bread upon the waters, you, too, will be repaid one hundredfold."

"Amen," said Opal, herself again, no longer crying.

"Now beat it," said Mr. Starbird.

"And give Mangol a wide berth," said the deputy.

The car shook as if it were shaking itself to death, and it coughed convulsively, and then it started up with a series of jerks and detonations, and disappeared in a screen of dust and black smoke.

Mr. Starbird offered to give me a lift home, and I got into the front seat beside him while the deputy from Mangol got in the back. On the way up the hill, Mr. Starbird kept glancing at me and then smiling.

"I've never known a girl quite like you, Emily," he said. "Memorizing the books of the Bible in the hoosegow, wearing a buck-private hat."

I blushed darkly and felt like crying, but I was pleased when Mr. Starbird went on to say, "Yes, sir, Emily, you're going to go places. What was the book you were reading down at my place when you were wearing your father's Masonic fez?" I grew prouder and prouder. "It isn't every girl of ten years of age who brushes up against some moonshiners with a record as long as your arm in the very same day that a couple of hillbilly fakers try to take her for a ride. Why, Emily, do you realize that if it hadn't of been for you, we might not have got rid of those birds till they'd set up shop and done a whole lot of mischief?"

"Really?" I said, not quite sure whether he was teasing me,

and grinned, but did so looking out the window, so Mr. Star-bird wouldn't see me.

Was I lucky that day! On the way home, I saw about ten people I knew, and waved and yelled at them, and when I was getting out in front of my house, Virgil Meade, with whom I had had an on-again off-again romance for some time and to whom I was not currently speaking, was passing by and he heard the sheriff say, "Come on down to jail tomorrow and we'll get some Dr. Pepper."

The sheriff's invitation gave me great prestige in the neigh-borhood, but it also put an end to my use of the jail as a library, because copycats began swarming to the courthouse and making so much racket in the waiting room that Mr. Starbird couldn't hear himself think, let alone follow Fu Manchu. And after a few weeks he had to post a notice forbidding anyone in the room except on business. Privately, he told me that he would just as lief let me read in one of the cells, but he was afraid word would leak out and it might be bad for my reputation. He was as sorry, he said, as he could be.

He wasn't half as sorry as I was. The snake season was still on in the mountain; Mrs. Looby hated me; Aunt Joey was visiting, and she and Mother were using the living room to cut out Butterick patterns in; Stella had just got on to pig Latin and never shut her mouth for a minute. All the same, I memorized the books of the Bible and I won the New Testament, and I'll tell you where I did my work—in the cemetery, under a shady tree, sitting beside the grave of an infant kinswoman of the sheriff, a late-nineteenth-century baby called Primrose Starbird.

A Summer Day

HE wore hot blue serge knickerbockers and a striped green shirt, but he had no shoes and he had no hat and the only things in his pants pockets were a handkerchief that was dirty now, and a white pencil from the Matchless Lumber Company, and a card with Mr. Wilkins' name printed on it and his own, Jim Littlefield, written on below the printing, and a little aspirin box. In the aspirin box were two of his teeth and the scab from his vaccination. He had come on the train barefoot all the way from Missouri to Oklahoma, because his grandmother had died and Mr. Wilkins, the preacher, had said it would be nice out here with other Indian boys and girls. Mr. Wilkins had put him on the through train and given the nigger man in the coach half a dollar to keep an eye on him, explaining that he was an orphan and only eight years old. Now he stood on the crinkled cinders beside the tracks and saw the train moving away like a fast little fly, and although Mr. Wilkins had promised on his word of honor, there was no one to meet him.

There was no one anywhere. He looked in the windows of the yellow depot, where there was nothing but a fat stove and a bench and a tarnished spittoon and a small office where a telegraph machine nervously ticked to itself. A freshly painted handcar stood on a side track near the water tower, looking as if no one were ever going to get into it again. There wasn't a sound, there wasn't even a dog or a bee, and there was nothing to look at except the bare blue sky and, across the tracks, a field of stubble that stretched as far as year after next beyond a rusty barbed-wire fence. Right by the door of the depot, there was an oblong piece of tin, which, shining in the sun, looked cool, although, of course, Jim knew it would be hot enough to bite your foot. It looked cool because it made him think of how the rain water used to shine in the washtubs in Grandma's back yard. On washday, when he had drawn buckets of it for her, it would sometimes splash over on his feet with a wonderful sound and a wonderful feeling. After the washing was on the line, she would black the stove and scrub the kitchen floor, and then she would take her ease, drinking a drink of blood-red sassafras as she sat rocking on the porch, shaded with wisteria. At times like that, on a hot summer day, she used to smell as cool as the underside of a leaf.

There was nothing cool here, so far as you could see. The paint on the depot was so bright you could read the newspaper by it in the dark. Jim could not see any trees save one, way yonder in the stubble field, and it looked poor and lean. In Missouri, there were big trees, as shady as a parasol. He remembered how he had sat on the cement steps of the mortuary parlor in the shade of the acacias, crying for his grandmother, whom he had seen in her cat-gray coffin. Mr. Wilkins had lipped some snuff and consoled him, talking through his nose, which looked like an unripe strawberry. "I don't want to be no orphan," Jim had cried, thinking of the asylum out by the fairground, where the kids wore gray cotton uniforms and came to town once a week on the trolley car to go to the library. Many of them wore glasses and some of them were lame. Mr. Wilkins had said, "Landagoshen, Jim boy, didn't I say you were going to be Uncle Sam's boy? Uncle Sam don't fool with orphans, he only takes care of *citizens*." On the train, a fat man had asked him what he was going to be when he grew up and Jim had said, "An aborigine." The man had laughed until he'd had to wipe his round face with a blue bandanna, and the little girl who was with him had said crossly, "What's funny, Daddy? What did the child say?" It had been cool before that, when he and Mr. Wilkins were waiting under the tall maple trees that grew beside the depot in Missouri and Mr. Marvin Dannenbaum's old white horse was drinking water out of the moss-lined trough. And just behind them, on Linden Street, Miss Bessie Ryder had been out in her yard picking a little mess of red raspberries for her breakfast. The dew would have still been on them when she doused them good with cream. Over the front of her little house there was a lattice where English ivy grew and her well was surrounded by periwinkle.

But Jim could not remember any of that coolness when he went out of the shade of the maples into the coach. Mrs. Wilkins had put up a lunch for him; when he ate it later, he found a dead ant on one of the peanut-butter sandwiches and the Baby Ruth had run all over the knobby apple. His nose had felt swollen and he'd got a headache and the green seat was as scratchy as a brush when he lay down and put his cheek on it. The train had smelled like the Fourth of July, like punk and lady crackers, and when it stopped in little towns, its rest was uneasy, for it throbbed and jerked and hissed like an old dog too feeble to get out of the sun. Once, the nigger man had taken him into the baggage car to look at some kind of big, expensive collie in a cage, muzzled and glaring fiercely through the screen; there were trunks and boxes of every shape, including one large, round one that the nigger man said held nothing but one enormous cheese from Michigan. When Jim got back to his seat, the fat man with the little girl had bought a box lunch that was put on the train at Sedalia, and Jim had watched them eat fried chicken and mustard greens and beet pickles and pone. The next time the train stopped, the nigger man had collected the plates and the silverware and had taken them into the station.

Jim had made the train wheels say "Uncle Sam, Uncle Sam," and then he hadn't been able to make them stop, even when he was half asleep. Mr. Wilkins had said that Uncle Sam wasn't one of your fair-weather friends that would let a Cherokee down when all his kin were dead. It was a blessing to be an Indian, the preacher had said, and Mrs. Wilkins had said, "It surely is, Jim boy. I'd give anything to be an Indian, just anything you can name." She had been stringing wax beans when she'd said that, and the ham hock she would cook with them had already been simmering on the back of the stove. Jim had wanted to ask her why she would like to be an Indian, but she'd seemed to have her mind on the beans, so he'd said nothing and stroked the turkey wing she used for brushing the stove.

It was hot enough to make a boy sick here in this cinder place, and Jim did not know what he would do if someone did not come. He could not walk barefoot all the way back to Missouri; he would get lost if he did not follow the tracks, and if he did follow them and a train came when he was drowsy, he might get scooped up by the cowcatcher and be hurled to kingdom come. He sat on his heels and waited, feeling the gray clinkers pressing into his feet, listening to the noontime sleep. Heat waves trembled between him and the depot and for a long time there was no sound save for the anxious telegraph machine, which was saying something important, although no one would heed. Perhaps it was about him—Jim! It could be a telegram from Mr. Wilkins saying for them to send him back. The preacher might have found a relation that Jim could live with. The boy saw, suddenly, the tall, white colonnade of a rich man's house by the Missouri River; he had gone there often to take the brown bread and the chili sauce Grandma used to make, and the yellow-haired lady at the back door of the big house had always said, "Don't you want to rest a spell, Jimmy, here where it's cool?" He would sit on a bench at the long table and pet the mother cat who slept on the windowsill and the lady would say, "You like my old puss-in-boots, don't you? Maybe you'd best come and live with me and her, seeing that she's already got your tongue." Sometimes this lady wore a lace boudoir cap with a blue silk bow on the front, and once she had given him a button with a pin that said, "LET'S CRACK THE VOLSTEAD ACT." The stubborn stutter of the machine could be a message from her, or maybe it was from Miss Bessie Ryder, who once had told his fortune with cards in a little room with pictures of Napoleon everywhere; the English ivy growing just outside made patterns on Napoleon's face, and in the little silver pitcher in the shape of Napoleon's head there was a blue anemone. Or it could be the Wilkinses themselves sending for him to come and live in the attic room, where there was the old cradle their baby had died in and a pink quilt on the bed with six-pointed stars.

Jim cried, catching his tears with his gentle tongue. Then, a long way off, a bell began to ring slowly and sweetly, and when it stopped, he heard an automobile coming with its bumptious cutout open. He went on crying, but in a different way, and his stomach thumped with excitement, for he knew it would be the people from the school, and suddenly he could not bear to have them find him. He ran the length of the depot and then ran back again, and then he hopped on one foot to the door and hopped on the piece of tin. He screamed with the awful, surprising pain. He sat down and seized his burned foot with both hands, and through his sobs he said, "Oh, hell on you, oh, Judas Priest!" He heard the car stop and the doors slam and he heard a lady say, "Wait a minute. Oh, it's all right." Jim shut his eyes as feet munched the cinders, closer and closer to him.

"Don't touch me!" he shrieked, not opening his eyes, and

there was a silence like the silence after the district nurse in Missouri had looked down his throat. They did not touch him, so he stopped crying, and the lady said, "Why, the train must have come *long ago*! I will positively give that stationmaster a piece of my mind."

Jim opened his eyes. There was a big man, with very black hair, which fell into his face, wearing a spotted tan suit and a ring with a turquoise the size of a quarter. The woman had gold earrings and gold teeth, which she showed in a mechanical smile, and she wore a blue silk dress with white embroidery on the bertha. They both smelled of medicine. The man touched Jim on the arm where he had been vaccinated; baffled by everything in the world, he cried wildly. The woman bent down and said, "Well, well, well, there, there, there." Jim was half suffocated by the smell of medicine and of her buttery black hair. The man and woman looked at each other, and Jim's skin prickled because he knew they were wondering why he had not brought anything. Mr. Wilkins had said you didn't need to, not even shoes.

"Well, honey," said the lady, taking his hand, "we've come a long way all by our lonesome, haven't we?"

"A *mighty* long way," said the man, laughing heartily to make a joke of it. He took Jim's other hand and made him stand up, and then they started down the cinder path and around the corner of the depot to a tall, black touring car, which said on the door:

DEPARTMENT OF THE INTERIOR
INDIAN SERVICE

In the back seat there were two huge empty demijohns and a brand-new hoe.

"Hop in front, sonny," said the man. The black leather seat scorched Jim's legs, and he put his hand over his eyes to shut out the dazzle of the windshield.

"No shoes," said the woman, getting in beside him.

"Already noted," said the man. He got in, too, and his fat thigh was dampish at Jim's elbow.

Jim worried about the telegraph machine. Would it go on until someone came to listen to it or would it stop after a while like a telephone? It must be about him, because he was the only one who had got off the train here, and it must be from someone saying to send him back, because there was nothing else it could be about. His heart went as fast as a bobbin being filled and he wanted to throw up and to hide and to cram a million grapes into his mouth and to chase a scared girl with a garter snake, all at once. He thought of screaming bloody murder so that they would let him get out of the car, but they might just whip him for that, whip him with an inner tube or beat him over the head with the new hoe. But he wouldn't stay at the school! If there was no other way, he would ride home on a freight car, like a hobo, and sleep in the belfry of the church under the crazy bell. He would escape tonight, he told himself, and he pressed his hand on his heart to make it quiet down.

From the other side of the depot, you could see the town. A wide street went straight through the level middle of it, and it had the same kind of stores and houses and lampposts that any other town had. The trees looked like leftovers, and the peaked brown dogs slinked behind the trash cans in an ornery way. The man started the car, and as they drove up the main street, Jim could tell that the men sitting on the curb were Indians, for they had long pigtails and closed-up faces. They sat in a crouch, with their big heads hanging forward and their flat-fingered hands motionless between their knees. The women who were not fat were as lean and spry as katydids, and all of them walked up and down the main street with baskets full of roasting ears on one arm and babies on the other. The wooden cupola on the red brick courthouse was painted yellow-green and in the yard men lay with their hats over their eyes or sat limply on the iron benches under the runty trees, whose leaves were gray with dust or lice. A few children with ice-cream cones skulked in the doorways, like abused cats. Everyone looked ailing.

The man from the school gestured with the hand that wore the heavy turquoise, and he said, "Son, this is your ancestors' town. This here is the capital of the Cherokee nation."

"You aren't forgetting the water, are you, Billings?" said the woman in a distracted way, and when the man said he was not, she said to Jim, "Do you know what 'Cherokee' means?"

"No," said Jim.

The woman looked over his head at the man. "Goodness

knows, we earn our bread. What can you do with Indians if they don't know they're Indians?"

"I always knew I was an Indian," said the man.

"And so did I," said the woman. "Always."

Jim sat, in this terrible heat and terrible lack of privacy, between their mature bodies and dared not even change the position of his legs, lest he hit the gearshift. He felt that they were both looking at him as if a rash were coming out on his face and he wished they would hurry and get to the school, so that he could start escaping. At the thought of running away after the sun was down and the animals and robbers started creeping in the dark, his heart started up again, like an engine with no one in charge.

The car stopped at a drugstore, and the man got out and heaved the demijohns onto the sidewalk. In the window of the store was a vast pink foot with two corn plasters and a bunion plaster. Next door was an empty building and on its window lights were pasted signs for J. M. Barclay's Carnival Show and for Copenhagen snuff and for Clabber Girl baking powder. The carnival sign was torn and faded, the way such signs always are, and the leg of a red-haired bareback rider was tattered shabbily. How hot a carnival would be, with the smell of dung and popcorn! Even a Ferris wheel on a day like this would be no fun. Awful as it was here, where the sun made a sound on the roof of the car, it would be even worse to be stuck in the highest seat of a Ferris wheel when something went wrong below. A boy would die of the heat and the fear and the sickness as he looked down at the distant ground, littered with disintegrated popcorn balls.

The lady beside Jim took a handkerchief out of her white linen purse, and as she wiped the sweat away from her upper lip, he caught a delicate fragrance that made him think of the yellow-haired lady in Missouri and he said, "I want to write a letter as soon as I get there."

"Well, we'll see," the woman said. "Who do you want to write to?" But the man came back, so Jim did not have to answer. The man staggered, with his stomach pushed out, under the weight of the demijohn, and as he put it in the back seat, he said savagely, "I wish one of those fellers in Washington would have to do this a couple, three times. Then maybe the Department would get down to brass tacks about that septic tank."

"The Department!" ejaculated the woman bitterly.

The man brought the other jug of water, and they drove off again, coming presently to a highway that stretched out long and white, and as shining as the piece of tin at the depot. They passed an old farm wagon with a rocking chair in the back, in which a woman smaller and more withered than Jim's grandmother sat, smoking a corncob pipe. Three dark little children were sitting at her feet, lined up along one edge of the wagon with their chins on the sideboard, and they stared hard at the Indian Service car. The one in the middle waved timidly and then hid his head in his shoulder, like a bird, and giggled.

"Creeks!" cried the woman angrily. "Everywhere we see Creeks these days! What will become of the Cherokees?"

"Ask the boy what his blood is," said the man.

"Well, Jim," said the woman, "did you hear what Mr. Standing-Deer said?"

"What?" said Jim and turned convulsively to look at the man with that peculiar name.

"Do you remember your mother and father?" said the woman.

"No, they were dead."

"How did they die?"

"I don't know. Of the ague, maybe."

"He says they may have died of the ague," said the woman to Mr. Standing-Deer, as if he were deaf. "I haven't heard that word 'ague' for years. Probably he means flu. Do you think perhaps this archaism is an index to the culture pattern from which he comes?"

Mr. Standing-Deer made a doglike sound in his throat. "Ask me another," he said. "I don't care about his speech at this stage of the game—it's the blood I'm talking about."

"Were Mama and Daddy both Indians?" asked the woman kindly.

"I don't care!" Jim said. He had meant to say "I don't know," but he could not change it afterward, because he commenced to cry again so hard that the woman patted his shoulder and did not ask him any more questions. She told him that her name was Miss Hornet and that she had been born in Chickasha and that she was the little boys' dormitory matron and that Mr. Standing-Deer was the boys' counselor. She said she was sure Jim would like it at the school. "Uncle Sam takes care of us all just as well as he can, so we should be polite to him and not let him see that we are homesick," she said, and Jim, thinking of his getaway this night, said softly, "Yes'm, Mr. Wilkins already told me."

After a time they turned into a drive, at the end of which was a big, white gate. Beyond it lay terraced lawns, where trees grew beside a group of buildings. It was hushed here, too. In spots, the grass was yellow, and the water in the ditch beyond the gate was slow. There was a gravelly space for kids to play in, but there were no kids there. There were a slide and some swings and a teeter-totter, but they looked as deserted as bones, and over the whole place there hung a tight feeling, as if a twister were coming. Once, when a twister had come at home, all the windows in Mr. Dannenbaum's house had been blown out, and it had taken the dinner off some old folks' table, and when Jim and his grandmother went out to look, there was the gravy bowl sitting on top of a fence post without a drop gone out of it.

Jim meant to be meek and mild until the sun went down, so that they would not suspect, and when Mr. Standing-Deer got out to open the gate, he said quietly to Miss Hornet, "Are the children all asleep now?"

"Yes, we are all asleep now," she said. "Some of us aren't feeling any too well these hot days." Jim stole an anxious glance at her to see if she were sick with something catching, but he could tell nothing from her smooth brown face.

The buildings were big and were made of dark stone, and because the shades were down in most of the windows, they looked cool, and Jim thought comfortably of how he would spend this little time before nightfall and of all the cool things there would be inside—a drink of water and some potted ferns and cold white busts of Abraham Lincoln and George Washington and rubber treads on the stairs, like those in the public school back in Missouri. Mr. Standing-Deer stopped the car by one of the smaller buildings, whose walls were covered with trumpet creeper. There had been trumpet creeper at Grandma's, too, growing over the backhouse, and a silly little girl named Lady had thought the blossoms were really trumpets and said the fairies could hear her playing "The Battle Hymn of the Republic" on them. She was the girl who had said she had found a worm in a chocolate bar and a tack in a cracker. With Lady, Jim used to float nasturtium leaves on the rain water in the tubs, and then they would eat them as they sat in the string hammock under the shade of the sycamores.

It was true that there were ferns in the hall of the small building, and Jim looked at them greedily, though they were pale and juiceless-looking and grew out of a sagging wicker-covered box. To the left of the door was an office, and in it, behind a desk, sat a big Indian woman who was lacing the fingers of one hand with a rubber band. She was wearing a man's white shirt and a necktie with an opal stickpin, and around her fat waist she wore a broad beaded belt. Her hair was braided around her head, and right at the top there was a trumpet flower, looking perfectly natural, as if it grew there.

"Is this the new boy?" she said to Miss Hornet.

"Who else would it be, pray tell?" said Miss Hornet crossly.

"My name is Miss Dreadfulwater," said the woman at the desk in an awful, roaring voice, and then she laughed and grabbed Jim's hand and shouted, "And you'd better watch your step or I'll dreadfulwater *you*."

Jim shivered and turned his eyes away from this crazy woman, and he heard his distant voice say, "Did you get Mr. Wilkins' telegram?"

"Telegram?" boomed Miss Dreadfulwater, and laughed uproariously. "Oh, sure, we got his telegram. Telegram and long-distance telephone call. Didn't you come in a de-luxe Pullman drawing room? And didn't Uncle Sam his own self meet you in the company limousine? Why, yes, sir, Mr. Wilkins, and Uncle Sam and Honest Harold in Washington, and all of us here have just been thinking about hardly anything else but Jim Littlefield."

Mr. Standing-Deer said wearily, "For Christ's sake, Sally, turn on the soft music. The kid's dead beat."

"I'm dead beat, too, Mr. Lying-Moose and Miss Yellow-Jacket, and I say it's too much. It's too much, I say. There are six more down in this dormitory alone, and that leaves, altogether, eight well ones. And the well ones are half dead on their feet at that, the poor little old buzzards."

There was something wrong with Miss Dreadfulwater that Jim could not quite understand. He would have said she was drunk if she hadn't been a woman and a sort of teacher. She took a card out of the desk and asked him how old he was and if he had been vaccinated and what his parents' names were. He wanted a drink of water, or wanted at least to go and smell the ferns, but he dared not ask and stood before the desk feeling that he was already sick with whatever it was the others were sick with. Mr. Standing-Deer took a gun out of his coat pocket and put it on the desk and then he went down the hall, saying over his shoulder, "I guess they're all too sick to try and fly the coop for a while."

"How old was your mother when she died?" said Miss Dreadfulwater.

"Eighteen and a half," said Jim.

"How do you know?" she said.

"Grandma told me. Besides, I knew."

"You *knew*? You remember your mother?"

"Yes," said Jim. "She was a Bolshevik."

Miss Dreadfulwater put down her Eversharp and looked straight into his eyes. "Are you crazy with the heat or am I?" she said.

He rather liked her, after all, and so he smiled until Miss Hornet said, "Hurry along, Sally, I haven't got all day."

"O.K., O.K., Queenie. I just wanted to straighten out this about the Bolshevik."

"Oh, do it later," said Miss Hornet. "You know he's just making up a story. They all do when they first come."

Miss Dreadfulwater asked some more questions—whether his tonsils were out, who Mr. Wilkins was, whether Jim thought he was a full-blood or a half-breed or what. She finished finally and put the card back in the drawer, and then Miss Hornet said to Jim, "What would you like to do now? You're free to do whatever you like till suppertime. It's perfectly clear that you have no unpacking to do."

"Did he come just like this?" said Miss Dreadfulwater, as-tonished. "Really?"

Miss Hornet ignored her and said, "What would you like to do?"

"I don't know," Jim said.

"Of course you do," she said sharply. "Do you want to play on the slide? Or the swings? None of the other children are out, but I should think a boy of eight could find plenty of ways to amuse himself."

"I can," he said. "I'll go outside."

"He ought to go to bed," said Miss Dreadfulwater. "You ought to put him to bed right now if you don't want him to come down with it."

"Be still, Sally," said Miss Hornet. "You run along now, Jim."

Although Jim was terribly thirsty, he did not stop to look for a drinking fountain or even to glance at the ferns. The composition floor was cool to his feet, but when he went out the door the heat came at him like a slapping hand. He did not mind it, because he would soon escape. The word "escape" itself refreshed him and he said it twice under his breath as he walked across the lawn.

In back of the building, there was a good-sized tree and a boy was sitting in the shade of it. He wore a green visor, and he was reading a book and chewing gum like sixty.

Jim walked up to him and said, "Do you know where any water is?"

The boy took off the visor, and Jim saw that his eyes were bright red. They were so startling that he could not help staring. The boy said, "The water's poisonous. There's an epidemic here."

Jim connected the poisonous water and the sickness in the dormitory with the boy's red eyes, and he was motionless with fear. The boy put his gum on his lower lip and clamped it there with his upper teeth, which were striped with gray and were finely notched, like a bread knife. "One died," he said, and laughed and rolled over on his stomach.

At the edge of the lawn beyond all the buildings, Jim saw a line of trees, the sort that follow a riverbank, and he thought that when it got dark, that was where he would go. But he was afraid, and even though it was hot and still here and he was thirsty, he did not want the day to end soon, and he said to the ugly, laughing boy, "Isn't there any good water at all?"

"There is," said the boy, sitting up again and putting his visor on, "but not for Indians. I'm going to run away." He popped his gum twice and then he pulled it out of his mouth for a full foot and swung it gently, like a skipping rope.

Jim said, "When?"

"When my plans are laid," said the boy, showing all his strange teeth in a smile that was not the least friendly. "You know whose hangout is over there past the trees?"

"No, whose?"

"Clyde Barrow's," whispered the boy. "Not long ago, they came and smoked him out with tommy guns. That's where I'm going when I leave here."

For the first time, Jim noticed the boy's clothes. He wore blue denim trousers and a blue shirt to match, and instead of a belt, he wore a bright-red sash, about the color of his eyes. It was certainly not anything Jim had ever seen any other boy wear, and he said, pointing to it, "Is that a flag or something?"

"It's the red sash," replied the boy. "It's a penalty. You aren't supposed to be talking to me when I have it on." He gave Jim a nasty, secret smile and took his gum out of his mouth and rolled it between his thumb and forefinger. "What's your name, anyway?" he asked.

"Jim Littlefield."

"That's not Indian. My name is Rock Forward Mankiller. My father's name is Son-of-the-Man-Who-Looked-Like-a-Bunch-of-Rags-Thrown-Down. It's not that long in Navajo."

"Navajo?" asked Jim.

"Hell, yes. I'm not no Cherokee," said the boy.

"What did you do to make them put the red sash on you?" Jim asked, wishing to know, yet not wanting to hear.

"Wouldn't you like to know?" said Rock Forward and started to chew his gum again. Jim sat down in the shade beside him and looked at his burned foot. There was no blister, but it was red and the skin felt drawn. His head ached and his throat was sore, and he wanted to lie down on his stomach and go to sleep, but he dared not, lest he be sleeping when the night came. He felt again the burden of the waiting silence; once a fool blue jay started to raise the roof in Clyde Barrow's woods and a couple of times he heard a cow moo, but the rest of the time there was only this hot stillness in which the red-eyed boy stared at him calmly.

"What do they do if you escape and they catch you?" Jim asked, trembling and giving himself away.

"Standing-Deer comes after you with his six-gun, and then you get the red sash," said Rock Forward, eyeing him closely. "You can't get far unless you lay your plans. I know what you're thinking about, Littlefield. All new kids do. I'm wise to it." He giggled and stretched his arms out wide, and once again he showed his sickening teeth.

The desire to sleep was so strong that Jim was not even angry with Rock Forward, and he swayed to and fro, half dozing, longing to lie full length on a bed and dimly to hear the sounds the awake people made through a half-open door. Little, bright-colored memories came to him pleasantly, like the smallest valentines. The reason he knew that his mother had been a Bolshevik was that she'd had a pair of crimson satin slippers, which Grandma had kept in a drawer, along with her best crocheted pot holders and an album of picture postal cards from Gettysburg. The lovely shoes were made of satin and the heels were covered with rhinestones. The shiny cloth, roughened in places, was the color of Rock Forward's eyes and of his sash. Jim said, "No kidding, why do you have to wear the red sash?"

"I stole Standing-Deer's gun, if you want to know, and I said, 'To hell with Uncle Sam.'"

Jim heard what the boy said but he paid no mind, and he said, not to the boy or to anyone, "I'll wait till tomorrow. I'm too sleepy now."

Nor did Rock Forward pay any heed to Jim. Instead, he said, turning his head away and talking in the direction of the outlaw's hangout, "If I get sick with the epidemic and die, I'll kill them all. Standing-Deer first and Dreadfulwater second and Hornet third. I'll burn the whole place up and I'll spit everywhere."

"Do you have a father?" said Jim, scarcely able to get the words out.

"Of course I have a father," said Rock Forward in a sudden rage. "Didn't I just tell you his name? Didn't you know he was in jail for killing a well-known attorney in Del Rio, Texas? If he knew I was here, he'd kill them all. He'd take this red sash and tear it to smithereens. I'm no orphan and I'm not a Cherokee like the rest of you either, and when I get out of here, Standing-Deer had just better watch out. He'd just better watch his p's and q's when I get a six-gun of my own." Passionately, he tore off his visor and bent it double, cracking it smack down the middle of the isinglass, and then, without another word, he went running off in the direction of the line of trees, the ends of the red sash flapping at his side.

Jim was too sleepy to care about anything now—now that he had decided to wait until tomorrow. He did not even care that it was hot. He lay down on the sickly grass, and for a while he watched a lonesome leaf-cutter bee easing a little piece of plantain into its hole. He hoped they would not wake him up and make him walk into the dormitory; he hoped that Mr. Standing-Deer would come and carry him, and he could see himself with his head resting on that massive shoulder in the spotted coat. He saw himself growing smaller and smaller and lying in a bureau drawer, like Kayo in the funny papers. He rustled in his sleep, moving away from the sharp heels of the red shoes, and something as soft and deep and safe as fur held him in a still joy.

The Philosophy Lesson

CORA SAVAGE watched the first real snowfall of the year through the long, trefoiled windows of the studio where the Life Class met. It was a high, somber room in one of the two square towers of the auditorium, which, because of some personal proclivity of the donor, were exorbitantly Gothic and had nothing to do with the other buildings on the campus, which were serene and low and Italian Renaissance. Here, in this chilly room, three mornings a week from nine until twelve, twenty-seven students met in smocks to render Cora, naked, on canvases in oil, and on sheets of coarse-grained paper in charcoal, seriously applying those principles of drawing they had learned, in slide talks, in their lecture classes. But just as Cora had predicted to her anxious United Presbyterian mother, the students took no more account of Cora than if she had been a plaster cast or an assemblage of apples and lemons for a still-life study. At first, the class had been disquieted by her inhuman ability to remain motionless so long, and they chattered about it among themselves as if she had no ears to hear. Their instructor, Mr. Steele, a fat and comfort-loving man who spent a good part of the three hours seated on a padded bench, reading and, from time to time, brewing coffee for himself on a hot plate behind a screen, told them bluffly that since this talent of hers could not possibly last, they should take advantage of it while it did. Thereafter, they ceased to speak of her except in the argot of their craft. Mr. Steele, deep in Trollope, was polite if they sought him out for help, and, once an hour, he made a tour of the room, going from easel to easel commenting kindly but perfunctorily.

Cora rested only twice in the three hours. After she struck the pose at nine, she waited, in heavy pain, for the deep bell to ring in the chapel tower, signaling the passage of fifty minutes. When she stepped off the dais with the first peal and came to recognizable life again by putting on her blue flannel wrapper, a tide of comfort immediately and completely washed away the cramps and tingles in her arms and legs. For ten minutes, then, she sat on the edge of her platform, smoking cigarettes, which, because of her fatigue, made her agreeably dizzy and affected her eyes so that the light altered, shifting, like the light on the prairies, from sage-green to a submarine violet, to saffron, to the color of a Seckel pear. When the bell rang again, on the hour, she turned herself to stone. She did not talk to the students, unless they spoke first to her, nor did she look at their drawings and paintings until afterward, when everyone was gone and she stepped out from behind her screen, fully dressed. Then she wandered about through the thicket of easels and saw the travesties of herself, grown fat, grown shriveled, grown horsefaced, turned into Clara Bow. The representations of her face were, nearly invariably, the faces of the authors of the work. Her complete anonymity to them at once enraged and fascinated her.

As she posed, she stared through those high, romantic windows at the sky and the top of a cottonwood tree. Usually, because the tension of her muscles would not allow her to think or to pursue a fantasy to its happy ending, she counted slowly by ones, to a hundred, and she had become so precise in her timing that five minutes passed in each counting: ten hundreds, a thousand, and then the bell commenced to ring. Often she felt she must now surely faint or cry out against the pain that began midway through the first hour, began as an itching and a stinging in the part of her body that bore the most weight and then gradually overran her like a disease until the whole configuration of bone and muscle dilated and all her pulses throbbed. Nerves jerked in her neck and a random shudder seized her shoulder blades and sometimes, although it was cold in the studio, all her skin was hot and her blood roared; her heart deafened her. If she had closed her eyes, she would have fallen down—nothing held her to her position except the scene through the windows, an abridgment of the branches of the cottonwood tree whose every twig and half-dead leaf she knew by heart so that she still saw it, if her mind's eye wandered. She knew the differences of the sheen on its bark in rain and in sun and how the dancing of the branches varied with the winds; she waited for birds and squirrels, and if they came, she lost track of her numbers and the time went quickly. She had grown fond of the tree through knowledge of it and at noon, when she left the building—this beautiful release was like the first day after an illness and all the world was fresh—she greeted it as if it were her possession, and she thought how pleasant it would look when its leaves came back to it in April.

Thus, while she recognized the chills and fevers and the pins and needles that bedeviled her, she remained detached from them as if their connection with her was adventitious and the real business at hand was the thorough study of her prospect of bits of wood and bits of cloud, and counting to tell the hours.

On the day of the first snowfall, though, she did not deny her discomfort, she simply and truly did not feel it and, although she was pinioned, she drifted in a charming ease, a floating, as if she hovered, slowly winding, like the flakes themselves. The snow began in the second hour, just as she resumed her pose, one in which she held a pole upright like a soldier with a spear. It was the most unmerciful attitude she had yet held, for all her weight lay on her right heel, which seemed to seek a grafting with the dais, and the arm that held the pole swelled until she imagined in time it would be so bellied out that her vaccination scar would appear as an umbilical indentation. For the first time she had felt put upon, and during her first rest she had been angry with the students and with Mr. Steele, who took it for granted that she was made of a substance different from theirs. And, when a girl in Oxford glasses and a spotless green linen smock, radiating good will, came to sit for a moment on the dais and said admiringly, "That would *kill* me! Are you going to do this professionally?" she was the more affronted; the servant whose ambitions go beyond his present status does not wish to be complimented on the way he polishes the silver.

When the snow came, the studio was dematerialized. The storm began so suddenly, with so little warning from the skies, that for a moment Cora doubted its existence, whirling there in the cottonwood, and thought that her eyes had invented it out of a need to vary their view. She loved the snow. When she had first heard of heaven, she had thought it would be a place where snow was forever falling and forever concealing the harshness of the world. And she had never remembered, when she was a child, from one year to the next how cold snow was; always, when the first flakes flew, she had run out in her bare feet, expecting the miraculous purity to be as soft as a cat, and then she ran back into the house to lie on the floor in the front hall, giggling with surprise.

In Missouri, by the river, the snow was as hard as a floor, but now and then a soft place would take her unawares and she would go in up to the top of her galoshes, and then she was a mess, her astrakhan coat covered with snow, her tasseled yellow mittens soaking wet. They went, she and her father and her brother Randall, for the Christmas greens each year, for holly and ground hemlock and partridge berry to put in the long, cold summer parlor where a green carpet spread like a lawn. The purple light of early Christmas morning came through the scrim curtains as the Savage children, Cora and Randall, Abigail and Evangeline, opened their presents. Often snow fell on Christmas day, shutting them in, protecting them, putting a spell on them. The little girls, wearing new tam-o'-shanters, wearing the bracelets and rings and fake wrist watches sent by cousins, surrounded by double-jointed dolls and sets of colored pencils, pig banks, patent-leather pocketbooks, jackstones, changeable taffeta hair ribbons, teased their poor brother with his ungainly boy's things—tool chests, fishing gear, the year he was eight, a .22.

The snow had been best, perhaps, most elegant there in Missouri. There had been times when Grandmother Savage had driven over from Kavanagh to call; she had an old-fashioned sleigh with rakish curled runners. In the little parlor, what Mr. Savage derisively called "the pastor's parlor," they drank hot cocoa from fat, hand-painted cups, bordered with a frieze of asters. And all the while the snow was coming down.

More elegant in Missouri, but it had been more keenly exciting here in Adams. Randall and Cora (by now Cora was a tomboy and disdained her older sisters) often took their sleds over the practice ski jumps in the foothills behind the college. The wind was knocked out of them as they hit the ground and once Cora lost control and went hurtling into a barbed-wire fence. It seemed to her, on reflection, that she had slowly revolved on her head, like a top, for a long time before the impact. Then, too frightened to move lest she find she could not, she had lain there waiting for her brother. Blood, in niggardly drops, from the wounds in her forehead stained the snow. Afterward, she had been afraid of the ski jumps and had only coasted down a steep hill that terminated in a cemetery; but this was dangerous enough, and reckless children sometimes crashed into the spiked palings of the iron fence and broke their heads wide open. There were so many of these accidents and the injuries were often so nearly serious that a city ordinance was passed, forbidding anyone to slide down that street. Then, added to the danger, there was the additional thrill of possibly being caught by the police and put into jail. One hid oneself and one's sled behind the spooky little stone house at the graveyard's edge, where the caretaker kept his lawn mower and gardening tools, and waited for the Black Maria. But it never came.

Cora was pleased today that probably she alone in the studio had seen what was happening outside. The students were intent on their work, applying to each other for criticism or for palette knives, measuring parts of Cora with pencils held at arm's length as they squinted and grimaced; sometimes, to her mistrust, they came quite close to examine the shape of a muscle or the color of a shadow on her skin. For the time being, the snow was a private experience; perhaps everything at this moment proceeded from her own mind, even this grubby room with its forest of apparatus and its smell of banana oil, even all these people. She thought of Bishop Berkeley, whom Dr. Bosch had assigned to the class in Introduction to Philosophy; she thought of the way Berkeley had dismantled the world of its own reality and had made each idiom of it into an idea in the mind of God. "Or in his own mind," said Dr. Bosch dryly, for he had no use for the Bishop. This morning, Cora had much use for him, and she concluded that she would be at peace forever if she could believe that she existed only for herself and possibly for a superior intelligence and that no one existed for her save when he was tangibly present.

As she pondered this quieting phenomenon (it just might work, she just might tutor herself to believe in such sublimity), the door to the studio opened and she turned away from the window. A latecomer entered, a boy in a sheep-lined mackinaw and a freshman beanie; his ashen corduroy trousers, freckled with oil paint, were tucked into the tops of his yellow field boots. His name was Ernie Wharton and he had been in high school with Cora; in the beginning, she had resented him and had disliked hearing that familiar voice she had heard the year before in Spanish II. Once she had even been in a play with him and on several evenings after rehearsal he had walked her home and they had talked at length at the foot of the steps on Benedict Street, where the smell of lilacs nearly led her to infatuation. But they had only gone on talking learnedly of *The Ode on Intimations of Immortality*, which both of them admired. On the first day of the Life Class, he, too, had been embarrassed, and had looked only at the model's feet and at her face, but in time he merged into the general background and was no more specific to her than any of the others.

Panting, as if he had been running, red from the cold, his canine face (the face of an amiable dog, a border collie) wore a look of befuddlement and at first Cora thought it stemmed from worry over his being so late, but she knew this could not be true, for Mr. Steele paid no heed at all to the arrival and departure of his students. Indeed, he did not so much as look up from *Framley Parsonage* when the outside air came rushing through the door, up the spiral staircase. No one gave Ernie's entrance more than passing recognition, no one but Cora, at whom he looked directly and whom he seemed to address, as if he had come to bring this news exclusively to her. "Somebody just committed suicide on the Base Line," he said.

In their incredulity, the class fell over itself, dropped pencils, splashed turpentine, tore paper, catapulted against their easels, said, "Oh, damn it." Then they surrounded Ernie, who stood against the door as if he did not mean to stay but was only a courier stopping at one of the many stations on his route. Although no one was looking at her, Cora continued to hold her pose and to look at the snow in her tree, but she listened and, now and then, stole a glance at the narrator's face, awry with dismay and with a sort of excruciated pleasure in the violent finality of the act he described. A second-year pre-medical student, two hours before, had been run over by the morning mail train coming from Denver. He had driven his car to the outskirts of town and there it had been found at a crossing, its motor still running. The engineer had seen the body on the tracks but he had had no time to stop the train, and the man had been broken to pieces. Wharton had gone out there (they were fraternity brothers; the president had called him just as he was leaving for class) and had seen the butchered mess, the head cut loose, the legs shivered, one hand, perched like a bird, on a scrub oak. His name was Bernard Allen, said Ernie, and he had been one prince of a fellow.

Bernard Allen!

The girl in Oxford glasses went pale and said, "My godfather, I knew *him*! I went to the Phi Gam tea dance with him Friday."

(Friday? thought Cora. But that was the night he and Maisie Perrine went horseback riding. That was the night I saw his white hair shining like this snow as I looked out my bedroom window toward the boarding house where Maisie lives next door to us. I, spying at all hours of the day and night, spying and tortured at what I saw, saw Bernard Allen's blue Cord town car draw up to Mrs. Mullen's house at midnight last Friday. Bernard and Maisie must have been to a dance, for Maisie was wearing a long dress of gold lamé and her sable coat. "I'll be waiting on the porch. Don't be long," said Maisie. They kissed connubially. "I hate to have you take off that gorgeous dress," said Bernard, and she replied, "I'd look good riding a horse in this, wouldn't I?" He let her out of the car and took her to the door and then he drove away. Half an hour later he was back and Maisie, in riding clothes, ran down the sagging steps of Mrs. Mullen's front porch. Where would they find a stable open at this time of night? They could. They would. For they had claimed the pot of gold and were spending it all on everything their hearts desired, on clothes and cars and bootleg whiskey. Probably one of them kept a string of blooded horses somewhere with a stableman so highly paid that he did not mind being waked up in the middle of the night. "Why didn't you bring Luster?" asked Maisie. "Because he doesn't like the moon." Luster was his dog, a golden retriever. They drove away then in the direction of Left Hand Canyon. I suppose eventually I went to sleep.)

Forgetting now that Ernie Wharton's facts were immediate and that, because he had been united with the dead boy in a secret order, his was the right to tell the tale and to lead the speculation—forgetting this, the art students shrilly turned to the girl in Oxford glasses. Had he been strange, they asked her, had he seemed cracked?

"He was like everybody else," she said, "like all pre-meds.

You know, a little high-hat the way they all are because they know those six-dollar words."

She did not like to speak ill of the dead, she said, but, frankly, Bernard had been the world's worst dancer and, as she looked back on it, she thought he had probably been tight. Not that that made any difference, she quickly added, because she was broad-minded, but it might throw some light on his suicide. Maybe he was drunk this morning. It was unlikely, she supposed, that he would have been drinking at eight-thirty in the morning. Still, you never could tell. She could not think of anything else about him. Except that he had this pure white hair—not blond, not towheaded; he had had a grandfather's white hair. It had been a blind date and a very short one, for they'd only gone to the dance and that was over at six and then she had gone right home to dress for the SAE formal. It had been just one of those dates that fills an afternoon and comes to nothing, when you get along all right, but you aren't much interested. Christmas, though, it gave her the creeps.

All the time the girl talked, Ernie stared at her, dumbstruck with rage. How *dare* she be so flip, said his frosty eyes. Presently, because her facts were thin, the students returned to him and they interrogated him closely as if he were a witness in a court of law. What had they done with the car? How long was it before the police arrived? Where did the guy come from? Had his family been told? At first, Ernie answered factually but abstractedly and then, hectored by a repetition of the same questions, he grew impatient and, turning wrathfully on the girl in the green smock, he shouted, "I'm not sure you knew him at all. He was engaged. He was engaged to be married to Maisie Perrine, and they announced it at the Chi Psi dance about three hours after you claim to have been at a tea dance with him."

The girl laughed lightly. "Keep your shirt on, sonny. That doesn't cut any ice. Can't you be engaged to somebody and take somebody else to a tea dance?"

Ernie said, "Not if you're so deep you end up by killing yourself."

"Oh, bushwa," said the girl and went back to her easel, but she was the only one who did, and among the others a moral debate began: whether suicide did demonstrate depth, whether suicide was an act of cowardice or of bravery.

Cora no longer listened. She was thinking of Maisie Perrine and wondering whether her yellow Cadillac roadster was there now at the crossing, its top whitened with snow, the windshield wipers going. Maybe she did not know yet and was still in class, still undisheveled in her orderly, expensive clothes, her sumptuous red hair shining, her fine hand taking down notes on Middle English marketplace romances. What would happen when she heard? And where was Luster, where was Bernard Allen's fond golden dog?

And what was the misery that had brought the boy to suicide? Rich, privileged, in love, he and his girl had seemed the very paradigm of joy. Why had he done it? And yet, why not? Why did not she, who was seldom happy, do it herself? A darkness beat her like the wings of an enormous bird and frantic terror of the ultimate hopelessness shook her until the staff she held slipped and her heart seemed for a moment to fail. She began to sweat and could feel the drops creeping down her legs. The bell rang and her pole went clattering to the floor, knocking over a portrait on an easel nearby, and all the students, still talking of the death that morning, looked up with exclamations of shock, but she could tell by their faces that none of them had been thinking her thoughts, that she alone, silent and stationary there on the dais, had shared Bernard Allen's experience and had plunged with him into sightlessness. No. No, wait a minute. Each mortal in the room must, momentarily, have died. But just as the fledgling artists put their own faces on their canvases, so they had perished in their own particular ways.

The snow was a benison. It forgave them all.

MANHATTAN ISLAND

Children Are Bored on Sunday

THROUGH the wide doorway between two of the painting galleries, Emma saw Alfred Eisenburg standing before "The Three Miracles of Zenobius," his lean, equine face ashen and sorrowing, his gaunt frame looking undernourished, and dressed in a way that showed he was poorer this year than he had been last. Emma herself had been hunting for the Botticelli all afternoon, sidetracked first by a Mantegna she had forgotten, and then by a follower of Hieronymus Bosch, and distracted, in an English room as she was passing through, by the hot invective of two ladies who were lodged (so they bitterly reminded one another) in an outrageous and expensive mare's-nest at a hotel on Madison. Emma liked Alfred, and once, at a party in some other year, she had flirted with him slightly for seven or eight minutes. It had been spring, and even into that modern apartment, wherever it had been, while the cunning guests, on their guard and highly civilized, learnedly disputed on aesthetic and political subjects, the feeling of spring had boldly invaded, adding its nameless, sentimental sensations to all the others of the buffeted heart; one did not know and never had, even in the devouring raptures of adolescence, whether this was a feeling of tension or of solution—whether one flew or drowned.

In another year, she would have been pleased to run into Alfred here in the Metropolitan on a cold Sunday, when the galleries were thronged with out-of-towners and with people who dutifully did something self-educating on the day of rest. But this year she was hiding from just such people as Alfred Eisenburg, and she turned quickly to go back the way she had come, past the Constables and Raeburns. As she turned, she came face to face with Salvador Dali, whose sudden countenance, with its unlikely mustache and its histrionic eyes, familiar from the photographs in public places, momentarily stopped her dead, for she did not immediately recognize him and, still surprised by seeing Eisenburg, took him also to be someone she knew. She shuddered and then realized that he was merely famous, and she penetrated the heart of a guided tour and proceeded safely through the rooms until she came to the balcony that overlooks the medieval armor, and there she paused, watching two youths of high-school age examine the joints of an equestrian's shell.

She paused because she could not decide what to look at now that she had been denied the Botticelli. She wondered, rather crossly, why Alfred Eisenburg was looking at it and why, indeed, he was here at all. She feared that her afternoon, begun in such a burst of courage, would not be what it might have been; for this second's glimpse of him—who had no bearing on her life—might very well divert her from the pictures, not only because she was reminded of her ignorance of painting by the presence of someone who was (she assumed) versed in it but because her eyesight was now bound to be impaired by memory and conjecture, by the irrelevant mind-portraits of innumerable people who belonged to Eisenburg's milieu. And almost at once, as she had predicted, the air separating her from the schoolboys below was populated with the images of composers, of painters, of writers who pronounced judgments, in their individual argot, on Hindemith, Ernst, Sartre, on Beethoven, Rubens, Baudelaire, on Stalin and Freud and Kierkegaard, on Toynbee, Frazer, Thoreau, Franco, Salazar, Roosevelt, Maimonides, Racine, Wallace, Picasso, Henry Luce, Monsignor Sheen, the Atomic Energy Commission, and the movie industry. And she saw herself moving, shaky with apprehensions and martinis, and with the belligerence of a child who feels himself laughed at, through the apartments of Alfred Eisenburg's friends, where the shelves were filled with everyone from Aristophanes to Ring Lardner, where the walls were hung with reproductions of Seurat, Titian, Vermeer, and Klee, and where the record cabinets began with Palestrina and ended with Copland.

These cocktail parties were a modus vivendi in themselves for which a new philosophy, a new ethic, and a new etiquette had had to be devised. They were neither work nor play, and yet they were not at all beside the point but were, on the contrary, quite indispensable to the spiritual life of the artists who went to them. It was possible for Emma to see these occasions objectively, after these many months of abstention from them, but it was still not possible to understand them, for they were so special a case, and so unlike any parties she had known at home. The gossip was different, for one thing, because it was stylized, creative (integrating the whole of the garrotted, absent friend), and all its details were precise and all its conceits were Jamesian, and all its practitioners sorrowfully saw themselves in the role of Pontius Pilate, that hero of the untoward circumstance. (It has to be done, though we don't want to do it; 'tis a pity she's a whore, when no one writes more intelligent verse than she.) There was, too, the matter of the drinks, which were much worse than those served by anyone else, and much more plentiful. They dispensed with the fripperies of olives in martinis and cherries in manhattans (God forbid! They had no sweet teeth), and half the time there was no ice, and when there was, it was as likely as not to be suspect shavings got from a bed for shad at the corner fish store. Other species, so one heard, went off to dinner after cocktail parties certainly no later than half past eight, but no one ever left a party given by an Olympian until ten, at the earliest, and then groups went out together, stalling and squabbling at the door, angrily unable to come to a decision about where to eat, although they seldom ate once they got there but, with the greatest formality imaginable, ordered several rounds of cocktails, as if they had not had a drink in a month of Sundays. But the most surprising thing of all about these parties was that every now and again, in the middle of the urgent, general conversation, this cream of the enlightened was horribly curdled, and an argument would end, quite literally, in a bloody nose or a black eye. Emma was always astounded when this happened and continued to think that these outbursts did not arise out of hatred or jealousy but out of some quite unaccountable quirk, almost a reflex, almost something physical. She never quite believed her eyes—that is, was never altogether convinced that they were really beating one another up. It seemed, rather, that this was only a deliberate and perfectly honest demonstration of what might have happened often if they had not so diligently dedicated themselves to their intellects. Although she had seen them do it, she did not and could not believe that city people clipped each other's jaws, for, to Emma, urban equaled urbane, and ichor ran in these Augustans' veins.

As she looked down now from her balcony at the atrocious iron clothes below, it occurred to her that Alfred Eisenburg had been just such a first-generation metropolitan boy as these two who half knelt in lithe and eager attitudes to study the glittering splints of a knight's skirt. It was a kind of childhood she could not imagine and from the thought of which she turned away in secret, shameful pity. She had been really stunned when she first came to New York to find that almost no one she met had gluttonously read Dickens, as she had, beginning at the age of ten, and because she was only twenty when she arrived in the city and unacquainted with the varieties of cultural experience, she had acquired the idea, which she was never able to shake entirely loose, that these New York natives had been deprived of this and many other innocent pleasures because they had lived in apartments and not in two- or three-story houses. (In the early years in New York, she had known someone who had not heard a cat purr until he was twenty-five and went to a houseparty on Fire Island.) They had played hide-and-seek dodging behind ash cans instead of lilac bushes and in and out of the entries of apartment houses instead of up alleys densely lined with hollyhocks. But who was she to patronize and pity them? Her own childhood, rich as it seemed to her on reflection, had not equipped her to read, or to see, or to listen, as theirs had done; she envied them and despised them at the same time, and at the same time she feared and admired them. As their attitude implicitly accused her, before she beat her retreat, she never looked for meanings, she never saw the literary-historical symbolism of the cocktail party but went on, despite all testimony to the contrary, believing it to be an occasion for getting drunk. She never listened, their manner delicately explained, and when she talked she was always lamentably off key; often and often she had been stared at and had been told, "It's not the same thing at all."

Emma shuddered, scrutinizing this nature of hers, which they all had scorned, as if it were some harmless but sickening reptile. Noticing how cold the marble railing was under her hands, she felt that her self-blame was surely justified; she came to the Metropolitan Museum not to attend to the masterpieces but to remember cocktail parties where she had drunk too much and had seen Alfred Eisenburg, and to watch schoolboys, and to make experience out of the accidental contact of the palms of her hands with a cold bit of marble. What was there to do? One thing, anyhow, was clear and that was that today's excursion into the world had been premature; her solitude must continue for a while, and perhaps it would never end. If the sight of someone so peripheral, so uninvolving, as Alfred Eisenburg could scare her so badly, what would a cocktail party do? She almost fainted at the thought of it, she almost fell headlong, and the boys, abandoning the coat of mail, dizzied her by their progress toward an emblazoned tabard.

In so many words, she wasn't fit to be seen. Although she was no longer mutilated, she was still unkempt; her pretensions needed brushing; her ambiguities needed to be cleaned; her evasions would have to be completely overhauled before she could face again the terrifying learning of someone like Alfred Eisenburg, a learning whose components cohered into a central personality that was called "intellectual." She imagined that even the boys down there had opinions on everything political and artistic and metaphysical and scientific, and because she remained, in spite of all her opportunities, as green as grass, she was certain they had got their head start because they had grown up in apartments, where there was nothing else to do but educate themselves. This being an intellectual was not the same thing as dilettantism; it was a calling in itself. For example, Emma did not even know whether Eisenburg was a painter, a writer, a composer, a sculptor, or something entirely different. When, seeing him with the composers, she had thought he was one of them; when, the next time she met him, at a studio party, she decided he must be a painter; and when, on subsequent occasions, everything had pointed toward his being a writer, she had relied altogether on circumstantial evidence and not on anything he had said or done. There was no reason to suppose that he had not looked upon her as the same sort of variable and it made their anonymity to one another complete. Without the testimony of an impartial third person, neither she nor Eisenburg would ever know the other's actual trade. But his specialty did not matter, for his larger designation was that of "the intellectual," just as the man who confines his talents to the nose and throat is still a doctor. It was, in the light of this, all the more extraordinary that they had had that lightning-paced flirtation at a party.

Extraordinary, because Emma could not look upon herself as an intellectual. Her private antonym of this noun was "rube," and to her regret—the regret that had caused her finally to disappear from Alfred's group—she was not even a bona-fide rube. In her store clothes, so to speak, she was often taken for an intellectual, for she had, poor girl, gone to college and had never been quite the same since. She would not dare, for instance, go up to Eisenburg now and say that what she most liked in the Botticelli were the human and compassionate eyes of the centurions' horses, which reminded her of the eyes of her own Great-uncle Graham, whom she had adored as a child. Nor would she admit that she was delighted with a Crivelli Madonna because the peaches in the background looked exactly like marzipan, or that Goya's little red boy inspired in her only the pressing desire to go out immediately in search of a plump cat to stroke. While she knew that feelings like these were not really punishable, she had not perfected the art of tossing them off; she was no flirt. She was a bounty jumper in the war between Great-uncle Graham's farm and New York City, and liable to court-martial on one side and death on the other. Neither staunchly primitive nor confidently *au courant*, she rarely knew where she was at. And this was her Achilles' heel: her identity was always mistaken, and she was thought to be an intellectual who, however, had not made the grade. It was no use now to cry that she was not, that she was a simon-pure rube; not a soul would believe her. She knew, deeply and with horror, that she was thought merely stupid.

It was possible to be highly successful as a rube among the Olympians, and she had seen it done. Someone calling himself Nahum Mothersill had done it brilliantly, but she often wondered whether his name had not helped him, and, in fact, she had sometimes wondered whether that had been his real name. If she had been called, let us say, Hyacinth Derryberry, she believed she might have been able, as Mothersill had been, to ask who Ezra Pound was. (This struck her suddenly as a very important point; it was endearing, really, not to know who Pound was, but it was only embarrassing to know who he was but not to have read the "Cantos.") How different it would have been if education had not meddled with her rustic nature! Her education had never dissuaded her from her convictions, but certainly it had ruined the looks of her mind—painted the poor thing up until it looked like a mean, hypocritical, promiscuous malcontent, a craven and apologetic fancy woman. Thus she continued secretly to believe (but *never* to confess) that the apple Eve had eaten tasted exactly like those she had eaten when she was a child visiting on her Great-uncle Graham's farm, and that Newton's observation was no news in spite of all the hue and cry. Half the apples she had eaten had fallen out of the tree, whose branches she had shaken for this very purpose, and the Apple Experience included both the descent of the fruit and the consumption of it, and Eve and Newton and Emma understood one another perfectly in this particular of reality.

Emma started. The Metropolitan boys, who, however bright they were, would be boys, now caused some steely article of dress to clank, and she instantly quit the balcony, as if this unseemly noise would attract the crowd's attention and bring everyone, including Eisenburg, to see what had happened. She scuttered like a quarry through the sightseers until she found an empty seat in front of Rembrandt's famous frump, "The Noble Slav"—it was this kind of thing, this fundamental apathy to most of Rembrandt, that made life in New York such hell for Emma—and there, upon the plum velours, she realized with surprise that Alfred Eisenburg's had been the last familiar face she had seen before she had closed the door of her tomb.

In September, it had been her custom to spend several hours of each day walking in a straight line, stopping only for traffic lights and outlaw taxicabs, in the hope that she would be tired enough to sleep at night. At five o'clock—and gradually it became more often four o'clock and then half past three—she would go into a bar, where, while she drank, she seemed to be reading the information offered by the *Sun* on "Where to Dine." Actually she had ceased to dine long since; every few days, with effort, she inserted thin wafers of food into her repelled mouth, flushing the frightful stuff down with enormous drafts of magical, purifying, fulfilling applejack diluted with tepid water from the tap. One weighty day, under a sky that grimly withheld the

rain, as if to punish the whole city, she had started out from
Ninetieth Street and had kept going down Madison and was
thinking, as she passed the chancery of St. Patrick's, that it
must be nearly time and that she needed only to turn east on
Fiftieth Street to the New Weston, where the bar was cool, and
dark to an almost absurd degree. And then she was hailed. She
turned quickly, looking in all directions until she saw Eisenburg
approaching, removing a gray pellet of gum from his mouth as
he came. They were both remarkably shy and, at the time, she
had thought they were so because this was the first time they
had met since their brief and blameless flirtation. (How curious
it was that she could scrape off the accretions of the months
that had followed and could remember how she had felt on that
spring night—as trembling, as expectant, as altogether young
as if they had sat together underneath a blooming apple tree.)
But now, knowing that her own embarrassment had come from
something else, she thought that perhaps his had, too, and she
connected his awkwardness on that September day with a report
she had had, embedded in a bulletin on everyone, from her sole
communicant, since her retreat, with the Olympian world. This
informant had run into Alfred at a party and had said that he
was having a very bad time of it with a divorce, with poverty,
with a tempest that had carried off his job, and, at last, with a
psychoanalyst, whose fees he could not possibly afford. Perhaps
the nightmare had been well under way when they had met
beside the chancery. Without alcohol and without the company
of other people, they had had to be shy or their suffering would
have shown in all its humiliating dishabille. Would it be true
still if they should inescapably meet this afternoon in an Early
Flemish room?

Suddenly, on this common level, in this state of social dis-
placement, Emma wished to hunt for Alfred and urgently tell
him that she hoped it had not been as bad for him as it had
been for her. But naturally she was not so naïve, and she got up
and went purposefully to look at two Holbeins. They pleased
her, as Holbeins always did. The damage, though, was done,
and she did not really see the pictures; Eisenburg's hypothetical
suffering and her own real suffering blurred the clean lines and
muddied the lucid colors. Between herself and the canvases
swam the months of spreading, cancerous distrust, of anger

that made her seasick, of grief that shook her like an influenza chill, of the physical afflictions by which the poor victimized spirit sought vainly to wreck the arrogantly healthy flesh.

Even that one glance at his face, seen from a distance through the lowing crowd, told her, now that she had repeated it to her mind's eye, that his cheeks were drawn and his skin was gray (no soap and water can ever clean away the grimy look of the sick at heart) and his stance was tired. She wanted them to go together to some hopelessly disreputable bar and to console one another in the most maudlin fashion over a lengthy succession of powerful drinks of whisky, to compare their illnesses, to marry their invalid souls for these few hours of painful communion, and to babble with rapture that they were at last, for a little while, no longer alone. Only thus, as sick people, could they marry. In any other terms, it would be a *mésalliance*, doomed to divorce from the start, for rubes and intellectuals must stick to their own class. If only it could take place—this honeymoon of the cripples, this nuptial consummation of the abandoned—while drinking the delicious amber whisky in a joint with a jukebox, a stout barkeep, and a handful of tottering derelicts; if it could take place, would it be possible to prevent him from marring it all by talking of secondary matters? That is, of art and neurosis, art and politics, art and science, art and religion? Could he lay off the fashions of the day and leave his learning in his private entrepôt? Could he, that is, see the apple fall and not run madly to break the news to Newton and ask him what on earth it was all about? Could he, for her sake (for the sake of this pathetic rube all but weeping for her own pathos in the Metropolitan Museum), forget the whole dispute and, believing his eyes for a change, admit that the earth was flat?

It was useless for her now to try to see the paintings. She went, full of intentions, to the Van Eyck diptych and looked for a long time at the souls in Hell, kept there by the implacable, indifferent, and genderless angel who stood upon its closing mouth. She looked, in renewed astonishment, at Jo Davidson's pink, wrinkled, embalmed head of Jules Bache, which sat, a trinket on a fluted pedestal, before a Flemish tapestry. But she was really conscious of nothing but her desire to leave the museum in the company of Alfred Eisenburg, her cousin-german in the territory of despair.

So she had to give up, two hours before the closing time, although she had meant to stay until the end, and she made her way to the central stairs, which she descended slowly, in disappointment, enviously observing the people who were going up, carrying collapsible canvas stools on which they would sit, losing themselves in their contemplation of the pictures. Salvador Dali passed her, going quickly down. At the telephone booths, she hesitated, so sharply lonely that she almost looked for her address book, and she did take out a coin, but she put it back and pressed forlornly forward against the incoming tide. Suddenly, at the storm doors, she heard a whistle and she turned sharply, knowing that it would be Eisenburg, as, of course, it was, and he wore an incongruous smile upon his long, El Greco face. He took her hand and gravely asked her where she had been all this year and how she happened to be here, of all places, of all days. Emma replied distractedly, looking at his seedy clothes, his shaggy hair, the green cast of his white skin, his deep black eyes, in which all the feelings were disheveled, tattered, and held together only by the merest faith that change *had* to come. His hand was warm and her own seemed to cling to it and all their mutual necessity seemed centered here in their clasped hands. And there was no doubt about it; he had heard of her collapse and he saw in her face that she had heard of his. Their recognition of each other was instantaneous and absolute, for they cunningly saw that they were children and that, if they wished, they were free for the rest of this winter Sunday to play together, quite naked, quite innocent. "What a day it is! What a place!" said Alfred Eisenburg. "Can I buy you a drink, Emma? Have you time?"

She did not accept at once; she guardedly inquired where they could go from here, for it was an unlikely neighborhood for the sort of place she wanted. But they were *en rapport*, and he, wanting to avoid the grownups as much as she, said they would go across to Lexington. He needed a drink after an afternoon like this—didn't she? Oh, Lord, yes, she did, and she did not question what he meant by "an afternoon like this" but said that she would be delighted to go, even though they would have to walk on eggs all the way from the Museum to the place where the bottle was, the peace pipe on Lexington. Actually, there was nothing to fear; even if they had heard catcalls, or if someone had hooted at them, "Intellectual loves Rube!" they would have been impervious, for the heart carved in the bark of the apple tree would contain the names Emma and Alfred, and there were no perquisites to such a conjugation. To her own heart, which was shaped exactly like a valentine, there came a winglike palpitation, a delicate exigency, and all the fragrance of all the flowery springtime love affairs that ever were seemed waiting for them in the whisky bottle. To mingle their pain, their handshake had promised them, was to produce a separate entity, like a child that could shift for itself, and they scrambled hastily toward this profound and pastoral experience.

Beatrice Trueblood's Story

WHEN Beatrice Trueblood was in her middle thirties and on the very eve of her second marriage, to a rich and reliable man—when, that is, she was in the prime of life and on the threshold of a rosier phase of it than she had ever known before—she overnight was stricken with total deafness.

"The vile unkindness of fate!" cried Mrs. Onslager, the hostess on whose royal Newport lawn, on a summer day at lunchtime, poor Beatrice had made her awful discovery. Mrs. Onslager was addressing a group of house guests a few weeks after the catastrophe and after the departure of its victim—or, more properly, of its victims, since Marten ten Brink, Mrs. Trueblood's fiancé, had been there, too. The guests were sitting on the same lawn on the same sort of dapper afternoon, and if the attitudes of some of Mrs. Onslager's audience seemed to be somnolent, they were so because the sun was so taming and the sound of the waves was a glamorous lullaby as the Atlantic kneaded the rocks toward which the lawn sloped down. They were by no means indifferent to this sad story; a few of them knew Marten ten Brink, and all of them knew Beatrice Trueblood, who had been Mrs. Onslager's best friend since their girlhood in St. Louis.

"I'm obliged to call it fate," continued Mrs. Onslager. "Because there's nothing wrong with her. All the doctors have reported the same thing to us, and she's been to a battalion of them. At first she refused to go to anyone on the ground that it would be a waste of money, of which she has next to none, but Jack and I finally persuaded her that if she didn't see the best men in the country and let us foot the bills, we'd look on it as unfriendliness. So, from Johns Hopkins, New York Hospital, the Presbyterian, the Lahey Clinic, and God knows where, the same account comes back: there's nothing physical to explain it, no disease, no lesion, there's been no shock, there were no hints of any kind beforehand. And *I'll* not allow the word 'psychosomatic' to be uttered in my presence—not in this connection, at any rate—because I know Bea as well as I know myself and she is not hysterical. Therefore, it has to be fate. And there's a particularly spiteful irony in it if you take a backward glance at her life. If ever a woman deserved a holiday from tribulation, it's Bea. There was first of all a positively hideous childhood. The classic roles were reversed in the family, and it was the mother who drank and the father who nagged. Her brother took to low life like a duck to water and was a juvenile delinquent before he was out of knickers—I'm sure he must have ended up in Alcatraz. They were unspeakably poor, and Bea's aunts dressed her in their hand-me-downs. It was a house of the most humiliating squalor, all terribly genteel. You know what I mean—the mother prettying up her drunkenness by those transparent dodges like 'Two's my limit,' and keeping the gin in a Waterford decanter, and the father looking as if butter wouldn't melt in his mouth when they were out together publicly, although everyone knew that he was a perfectly ferocious tartar. Perhaps it isn't true that he threw things at his wife and children and whipped them with a razor strop—he didn't have to, because he could use his tongue like a bludgeon. And then after all that horror, Bea married Tom Trueblood—really to escape her family, I think, because she couldn't possibly have loved him. I mean it isn't possible to love a man who is both a beast and a fool. *He* was drunker than her mother ever thought of being; he was obscene, he was raucous, his infidelities to that good, beautiful girl were of a vulgarity that caused the mind to boggle. I'll never know how she managed to live with him for seven mortal years. And then at last, after all those tempests, came Marten ten Brink, like redemption itself. There's nothing sensational in Marten, I'll admit. He's rather a stick, he was born rather old, he's rather jokeless and bossy. But, oh, Lord, he's so *safe*, he was so protective of her, and he is so scrumptiously rich! And two months before the wedding *this* thunderbolt comes out of nowhere. It's indecent! It makes me so angry!" And this faithful friend shook her pretty red head rapidly in indignation, as if she were about to hunt down fate with a posse and hale it into court.

"Are you saying that the engagement has been broken?" asked Jennie Fowler, who had just got back from Europe and to whom all this was news.

Mrs. Onslager nodded, closing her eyes as if the pain she suffered were unbearable. "They'd been here for a week, Marten and Bea, and we were making the wedding plans, since they were to be married from my house. And the very day after this gruesome thing happened, she broke the engagement. She wrote him a note and sent it in to his room by one of the maids. I don't know what she said in it, though I suppose she told him she didn't want to be a burden, something like that—much more gracefully, of course, since Bea *is* the soul of courtesy. But whatever it was, it must have been absolutely unconditional, because he went back to town before dinner the same night. The letter I got from him afterward scarcely mentioned it—he only said he was sorry his visit here had ended on 'an unsettling note.' I daresay he was still too shocked to say more."

"Hard lines on ten Brink," said Harry McEvoy, who had never married.

"What do you mean, 'hard lines on *ten Brink*'?" cried Mrs. Fowler, who had married often, and equally often had gone, livid with rage, to Nevada.

"Well, if he was in love with her, if he counted on this . . . Not much fun to have everything blow up in your face. Lucky in a way, I suppose, that it happened before, and not afterward."

The whole party glowered at McEvoy, but he was entirely innocent of their disapproval and of his stupidity that had provoked it, since he was looking through a pair of binoculars at a catboat that seemed to be in trouble.

"If he was in love with her," preached Mrs. Fowler rabidly, "he would have stuck by her. He would have refused to let her break the engagement. He would have been the one to insist on the specialists, he would have moved heaven and *earth*, instead of which he fled like a scared rabbit at the first sign of bad luck. I thought he was only a bore—I didn't know he was such a venomous pill."

"No, dear, he isn't that," said Priscilla Onslager. "Not the most sensitive man alive, but I'd never call him a venomous pill. After all, remember it was *she* who dismissed *him*."

"Yes, but if he'd had an ounce of manliness in him, he would have put up a fight. No decent man, no manly man, would abandon ship at a time like that." Mrs. Fowler hated men so passionately that no one could dream why she married so many of them.

"Has it occurred to any of you that she sent him packing

because she didn't want to marry him?" The question came from Douglas Clyde, a former clergyman, whose worldliness, though it was very wise, had cost him his parish and his cloth.

"Certainly not," said Priscilla. "I tell you, Doug, I know Bea. But at the moment the important thing isn't the engagement, because I'm sure it could be salvaged if she could be cured. And how's she to be cured if nothing's wrong? I'd gladly have the Eumenides chase me for a while if they'd only give her a rest."

Jack Onslager gazed through half-closed eyes at his wholesome, gabbling wife—he loved her very much, but her public dicta were always overwrought and nearly always wrong—and then he closed his eyes tight against the cluster of his guests, and he thought how blessed it would be if with the same kind of simple physical gesture one could also temporarily close one's ears. One could decline to touch, to taste, to see, but it required a skill he had not mastered to govern the ears. Those stopples made of wax and cotton would be insulting at a party; besides, they made him claustrophobic, and when he used them, he could hear the interior workings of his skull, the boiling of his brains in his brainpan, a rustling behind his jaws. He would not like to go so far as Beatrice had gone, but he would give ten years of his life (he had been about to say he would give his eyes and changed it) to be able, when he wanted, to seal himself into an impenetrable silence.

To a certain extent, however, one could insulate the mind against the invasion of voices by an act of will, by causing them to blur together into a general hubbub. And this is what he did now; in order to consider Mrs. Trueblood's deafness, he deafened himself to the people who were talking about it. He thought of the day in the early summer when the extraordinary thing had taken place.

It had been Sunday. The night before, the Onslagers and their houseparty—the young Allinghams, Mary and Leon Herbert, Beatrice and ten Brink—had gone to a ball. It was the kind of party to which Onslager had never got used, although he had been a multimillionaire for twenty years and not only had danced through many such evenings but had been the host at many more, in his own houses or in blazoned halls that he had hired. He was used to opulence in other ways, and took for granted his boats and horses and foreign cars. He also took for granted, and was bored by, most of the rites of the rich: the formal dinner parties at which the protocol was flawlessly maneuvered and conversation moved on stilts and the food was platitudinous; evenings of music to benefit a worthy cause (How papery the turkey always was at the buffet supper after the Grieg!); the tea parties to which one went obediently to placate old belles who had lost their looks and their husbands and the roles that, at their first assembly, they had assumed they would play forever. Well-mannered and patient, Onslager did his duty suavely, and he was seldom thrilled.

But these lavish, enormous midsummer dancing parties in the fabulous, foolish villas on Bellevue Avenue and along the Ocean Drive did make his backbone tingle, did make him glow. Even when he was dancing, or proposing a toast, or fetching a wrap for a woman who had found the garden air too cool, he always felt on these occasions that he was static, looking at a colossal *tableau vivant* that would vanish at the wave of a magic golden wand. He was bewitched by the women, by all those *soignée* or demure or jubilant or saucy or dreaming creatures in their caressing, airy dresses and their jewels whose priceless hearts flashed in the light from superb chandeliers. They seemed, these dancing, laughing, incandescent goddesses, to move in inaccessible spheres; indeed, his wife, Priscilla, was transfigured, and, dancing with her, he was moon-struck. No matter how much he drank (the champagne of those evenings was invested with a special property—one tasted the grapes, and the grapes had come from celestial vineyards), he remained sober and amazed and, in spite of his amazement, so alert that he missed nothing and recorded everything. He did not fail to see, in looks and shrugs and the clicking of glasses, the genesis of certain adulteries, and the demise of others in a glance of contempt or an arrogant withdrawal. With the accuracy of the uninvolved bystander, he heard and saw among these incredible women moving in the aura of their heady perfume their majestic passions—tragic heartbreak, sublime fulfillment, dangerous jealousy, the desire to murder. When, on the next day, he had come back to earth, he would reason that his senses had devised a fiction to amuse his mind, and that in fact he had witnessed nothing grander than flirtations and impromptu pangs as ephemeral as the flowers in the supper room.

So, at the Paines' vast marble house that night, Onslager, aloof and beguiled as always, had found himself watching Beatrice Trueblood and Marten ten Brink with so much interest that whenever he could he guided his dancing partner near them, and if they left the ballroom for a breath of air on a bench beside a playing fountain, or for a glass of champagne, he managed, if he could do so without being uncivil to his interlocutor and without being observed by them, to excuse himself and follow. If he had stopped to think, this merciful and moral man would have been ashamed of his spying and eavesdropping, but morality was irrelevant to the spell that enveloped him. Besides, he felt invisible.

Consequently, he knew something about that evening that Priscilla did not know and that he had no intention of telling her, partly because she would not believe him, partly because she would be displeased at the schoolboyish (and parvenu) way he put in his time at balls. The fact was that the betrothed were having a quarrel. He heard not a word of it—not at the dance, that is—and he saw not a gesture or a grimace of anger, but he nevertheless knew surely, as he watched them dance together, that ten Brink was using every ounce of his strength not to shout, and to keep in check a whole menagerie of passions—fire-breathing dragons and bone-crushing serpents and sabertoothed tigers—and he knew also that Beatrice was running for dear life against the moment when they would be unleashed, ready to gobble her up. Her broad, wide-eyed, gentle face was so still it could have been a painting of a face that had been left behind when the woman who owned it had faded from view, and Bea's golden hand lay on ten Brink's white sleeve as tentatively as a butterfly. Her lover's face, on the other hand, was—Onslager wanted to say "writhing," and the long fingers of the hand that pressed against her back were splayed out and rigid, looking grafted onto the sunny flesh beneath the diaphanous blue stuff of her dress. He supposed that another observer might with justification have said that the man was animated and that his fiancée was becomingly engrossed in all he said, that ten Brink was in a state of euphoria as his wedding approached, while Beatrice moved in a wordless haze of happiness. He heard people admiringly remark on the compatibility of their good looks; they were said to look as if they were "dancing on air"; women thanked goodness that Mrs. Trueblood had come at last into a safe harbor, and men said that ten Brink was in luck.

As soon as the Onslagers and their guests had driven away from the ball and the last echo of the music had perished and the smell of roses had been drowned by the smell of the sea and the magic had started to wane from Onslager's blood, he began to doubt his observations. He was prepared to elide and then forget his heightened insights, as he had always done in the past. The group had come in two cars, and the Allinghams were with him and Priscilla on the short ride home. Lucy Allingham, whose own honeymoon was of late and blushing memory, said, with mock petulance, 'I thought *young* love was supposed to be what caught the eye. But I never saw anything half so grand and wonderful as the looks of those two." And Priscilla said, "How true! How magnificently right you are, Lucy! They were radiant, both of them."

Late as it was, Priscilla proposed a last drink and a recapitulation of the party—everyone had found it a joy—but ten Brink said, "Beatrice and I want to go down and have a look at the waves, if you don't mind," and when no one minded but, on the contrary, fondly sped them on their pastoral way, the two walked down across the lawn and presently were gone from sight in the romantic mist. Their friends watched them and sighed, charmed, and went inside to drink a substitute for nectar.

Hours later (he looked at his watch and saw that it was close on five o'clock), Jack woke, made restless by something he had sensed or dreamed, and, going to the east windows of his bedroom to look at the water and see what the sailing would be like that day, he was arrested by the sight of Beatrice and Marten standing on the broad front steps below. They were still in their evening clothes. Beatrice's stance was tired; she looked bedraggled. They stood confronting each other beside the balustrade; ten Brink held her shoulders tightly, his sharp, handsome (but, thought Onslager suddenly, Mephistophelean) face bent down to hers.

"You mustn't think you can shut your mind to these things," he said. "You can't shut your ears to them." Their voices were clear in the hush of the last of the night.

"I am exhausted with talk, Marten," said Beatrice softly. "I will not hear another word."

An hour afterward, the fairest of days dawned on Newport, and Jack Onslager took out his sloop by himself in a perfect breeze, so that he saw none of his guests until just before lunch, when he joined them for cocktails on the lawn. Everyone was there except Beatrice Trueblood, who had slept straight through the morning but a moment before had called down from her windows that she was nearly ready. It was a flawless day to spend beside the sea: the chiaroscuro of the elm trees and the sun on the broad, buoyant lawn shifted as the sea winds disarrayed the leaves, and yonder, on the hyacinthine water, the whitecaps shuddered and the white sails swelled; to the left of the archipelago of chairs and tables where they sat, Mrs. Onslager's famous rosary was heavily in bloom with every shade of red there was and the subtlest hues of yellow, and her equally famous blue hydrangeas were at their zenith against the house, exactly the color of this holiday sky, so large they nodded on their stems like drowsing heads.

The Allinghams, newly out of their families' comfortable houses in St. Louis and now living impecuniously in a railroad flat in New York that they found both adventurous and odious, took in the lawn and seascape with a look of real greed, and even of guile, on their faces, as if they planned to steal something or eat forbidden fruit.

In its pleasurable fatigue from the evening before and too much sleep this morning, the gathering was momentarily disinclined to conversation, and they all sat with faces uplifted and eyes closed against the sun. They listened to the gulls and terns shrieking with their evergreen gluttony; they heard the buzz-saw rasp of outboard motors and the quick, cleaving roar of an invisible jet; they heard automobiles on the Ocean Drive, a power mower nasally shearing the grass at the house next door, and from that house they heard, as well, the wail of an infant and the panicky barking of an infant dog.

"I wish this day would never end," said Lucy Allingham.

"This is the kind of day when you want to kiss the earth. You want to have an affair with the sky."

"Don't be maudlin, Lucy," said her husband. "And above all, don't be inaccurate." He was a finicking young cub who had been saying things like this all weekend.

Onslager's own wife, just as foolishly given to such figures of speech but with a good deal more style, simply through being older, said, "Look, here comes Beatrice. She looks as if her eyes were fixed on the Garden of Eden before the Fall and as if she were being serenaded by angels."

Marten ten Brink, an empiricist not given to flights of fancy, said, "Is that a depth bomb I hear?"

No one answered him, for everyone was watching Beatrice as she came slowly, smiling, down the stone steps from the terrace and across the lawn, dulcifying the very ground she walked upon. She was accompanied by Mrs. Onslager's two Siamese cats, who cantered ahead of her, then stopped, forgetful of their intention, and closely observed the life among the blades of grass, then frolicked on, from time to time emitting that ugly parody of a human cry that is one of the many facets of the Siamese cat's scornful nature. But the insouciant woman paid no attention to them, even when they stopped to fight each other, briefly, with noises straight from Hell.

"You look as fresh as dew, dear," said Priscilla. "Did you simply sleep and sleep?"

"Where on earth did you get that fabric?" asked Mrs. Herbert. "Surely not here. It must have come from Paris. Bea, I do declare your clothes are always the ones I want for myself."

"Sit here, Beatrice," said ten Brink, who had stood up and was indicating the chair next to himself. But Beatrice, ignoring him, chose another chair. The cats, still flirting with her, romped at her feet; one of them pretended to find a sporting prey between her instep and her heel, and he pounced and buck-jumped silently, his tail a fast, fierce whip. Beatrice, who delighted in these animals, bent down to stroke the lean flanks of the other one, momentarily quiescent in a glade of sunshine.

"What do you think of the pathetic fallacy, Mrs. Trueblood?" said Peter Allingham, addressing her averted head. "Don't you think it's pathetic?" By now, Onslager was wishing to do him bodily harm for his schoolmasterish teasing of Lucy.

"Monkeys," murmured Beatrice to the cats. "Darlings."

"Beatrice!" said Marten ten Brink sharply, and strode across to whisper something in her ear. She brushed him away as if he were a fly, and she straightened up and said to Priscilla Onslager, "Why is everyone so solemn? Are you doing a charade of a Quaker meeting?"

"Solemn?" said Priscilla, with a laugh. "If we seem solemn, it's because we're all smitten with this day. Isn't it supreme? Heaven can't possibly be nicer."

"Is this a new game?" asked Beatrice, puzzled, her kind eyes on her hostess's face.

"Is what a new game, dear?"

"What *is* going on?" She had begun to be ever so slightly annoyed. "Is it some sort of silence test? We're to see if we can keep still till teatime? Is it that? I'd be delighted—only, for pity's sake, tell me the rules and the object."

"Silence test! Sweetheart, you're still asleep. Give her a martini, Jack," said Priscilla nervously, and to divert the attention of the company from her friend's quixotic mood she turned to ten Brink. "I believe you're right," she said, "I believe they're detonating depth bombs. Why on Sunday? I thought sailors got a day of rest like everybody else."

A deep, rumbling subterranean thunder rolled, it seemed, beneath the chairs they sat on.

"It sounds like ninepins in the Catskills," said Priscilla.

"I never could abide that story," said Mary Herbert. "Or the Ichabod Crane one, either."

Jack Onslager, his back toward the others as he poured a drink for Beatrice, observed to himself that the trying thing about these weekends was not the late hours, not the overeating and the overdrinking and the excessive batting of tennis balls and shuttlecocks; it was, instead, this kind of aimless prattle that never ceased. There seemed to exist, on weekends in the country, a universal terror of pauses in conversation, so that it was imperative for Mary Herbert to drag in Washington Irving by the hair of his irrelevant head. Beatrice Trueblood, however, was not addicted to prattle, and he silently congratulated her on the way, in the last few minutes, she had risen above their fatuous questions and compliments. That woman was as peaceful as a pool in the heart of a forest. He turned to her, handing her the drink and looking directly into her eyes (blue and green, like an elegant tropic sea), and he said, "I have never seen you looking prettier."

For just a second, a look of alarm usurped her native and perpetual calm, but then she said, "So you're playing it, too. I don't think it's fair not to tell me—unless this is a joke on me. Am I 'it'?"

At last, Jack was unsettled; Priscilla was really scared; ten Brink was angry, and, getting up again to stand over her like a prosecuting attorney interrogating a witness of bad character, he said, "You're not being droll, Beatrice, you're being tiresome."

Mrs. Onslager said, "Did you go swimming this morning, lamb? Perhaps you got water in your ears. Lean over—see, like this," and she bent her head low to the left and then to the right while Beatrice, to whom these calisthenics were inexplicable, watched her, baffled.

Beatrice put her drink on the coffee table, and she ran her forefingers around the shells of her ears. What was the look that came into her face, spreading over it as tangibly as a blush? Onslager afterward could not be sure. At the time he had thought it was terror; he had thought this because, in the confusion that ensued, he had followed, sheeplike with the others, in his wife's lead. But later, when he recaptured it for long reflection, he thought that it had not been terror, but rather that Priscilla in naming it that later was actually speaking of the high color of her own state of mind, and that the look in Beatrice's eyes and on her mouth had been one of revelation, as if she had opened a door and had found behind it a new world so strange, so foreign to all her knowledge and her experience and the history of her senses, that she had spoken only approximately when, in a far, soft, modest voice, she said, "I am deaf. That explains it."

When Onslager had come to the end of his review of those hours of that other weekend and had returned to the present one, he discovered that he had so effectively obliterated the voices around him that he now could not recall a single word of any of the talk, although he had been conscious of it, just as some part of his mind was always conscious of the tension and solution of the tides.

"But you haven't told us yet how she's taking it now," Mrs. Fowler was saying.

"I can't really tell," replied Priscilla. "I haven't been able to go to town to see her, and she refuses to come up here—the place probably has bad associations for her now. And I'm no good at reading between the lines of her letters. She has adjusted to it, I'll say that." Priscilla was thoughtful, and her silence commanded her guests to be silent. After a time, she went on, "I'll say more than that. I'll say she has adjusted too well for my liking. There is a note of gaiety in her letters—she is almost jocose. For example, in the last one she said that although she had lost Handel and music boxes and the purring of my Siamese, she had gained a valuable immunity to the voices of professional Irishmen."

"Does she mention ten Brink?" asked someone.

"Never," said Priscilla. "It's as if he had never existed. There's more in her letters than the joking tone. I wish I could put my finger on it. The closest I can come is to say she sounds *bemused*."

"Do you think she's given up?" asked Jennie Fowler. "Or has she done everything there is to be done?"

"The doctors recommended psychiatry, of course," said Priscilla, with distaste. "It's a dreary, ghastly, humiliating thought, but I suppose—"

"I should think you *would* suppose!" cried Mrs. Fowler. "You shouldn't leave a stone unturned. Plainly someone's got to *make* her go to an analyst. They're not that dire, Priscilla. I've heard some very decent things about several of them."

"It won't be I who'll make her go," said Priscilla, sighing. "I disapprove too much."

"But you don't disapprove of the medical people," persisted Jennie. "Why fly in the face of their prescription?"

"Because . . . I *couldn't* do it. Propose to Beatrice that she is mental? I can't support the thought of it."

"Then Jack must do it," said the managerial divorcée. "Jack must go straight down to town and get her to a good man and then patch up things with Marten ten Brink. I still detest the sound of him, but *de gustibus*, and I think she ought to have a husband."

The whole gathering—even the cynical ex-pastor—agreed that this proposal made sense, and Onslager, while he doubted his right to invade Bea's soft and secret and eccentric world, found himself so curious to see her again to learn whether some of his conjectures were right that he fell in with the plan and agreed to go to New York in the course of the week. As, after lunch, they dispersed, some going off for *boccie* and others to improve their shining skin with sun, Douglas Clyde said sotto voce to Onslager, "Why doesn't it occur to anyone but you and me that perhaps she doesn't *want* to hear?"

Startled, the host turned to his guest. "How did you know I thought that?"

"I watched you imitating deafness just now," said the other. "You looked beatific. But if I were you, I wouldn't go too far."

"Then you believe . . . contrary to Priscilla and her Eumenides . . . ?"

"I believe what you believe—that the will is free and very strong," Clyde answered, and he added, "I believe further that it can cease to be an agent and become a despot. I suspect hers *has*."

Mrs. Trueblood lived in the East Seventies, in the kind of apartment building that Jack Onslager found infinitely more melancholy than the slum tenements that flanked and faced it in the sultry city murk of August. It was large and new and commonplace and jerry-built, although it strove to look as solid as Gibraltar. Its brick façade was an odious mustardy brown. The doorman was fat and choleric, and when Onslager descended from his cab, he was engaged in scolding a band of vile-looking little boys who stood on the curb doubled up with giggles, now and again screaming out an unbelievable obscenity when the pain of their wicked glee abated for a moment. A bum was lying spread-eagled on the sidewalk a few doors down; his face was bloody but he was not dead, for he was snoring fearsomely. Across the street, a brindle boxer leaned out a window, his forepaws sedately crossed on the sill in a parody of the folded arms of the many women who were situated in other windows, irascibly agreeing with one another at the tops of their voices that the heat was hell.

But the builders of the house where Mrs. Trueblood lived

had pretended that none of this was so; they had pretended that the neighborhood was bourgeois and there was no seamy side, and they had commemorated their swindle in a big facsimile of rectitude. Its square foyer was papered with a design of sanitary ferns upon a field of hygienic beige; two untruthful mirrors mirrored each other upon either lateral wall, and beneath them stood love seats with aseptic green plastic cushions and straight blond legs. The slow self-service elevator was an asphyxiating chamber with a fan that blew a withering sirocco; its tinny walls were embossed with a meaningless pattern of fleurs-de-lis; light, dim and reluctant, came through a fixture with a shade of some ersatz material made esoterically in the form of a starfish. As Onslager ascended to the sixth floor at a hot snail's pace, hearing alarming *râles* and exhalations in the machinery, he was fretful with his discomfort and fretful with snobbishness. He deplored the circumstances that required Beatrice, who was so openhearted a woman, to live in surroundings so mean-minded; he could not help thinking sorrowfully that the ideal place for her was Marten ten Brink's house on Fifty-fifth Street, with all its depths of richness and its sophisticated planes. The bastard, he thought, taking Jennie Fowler's line—why did he let her down? And then he shook his head, because, of course, he knew it hadn't been like that.

This was not his first visit to Beatrice. He and Priscilla had been here often to cocktail parties since she had lived in New York, but the place had made no impression on him; he liked cocktail parties so little that he went to them with blinders on and looked at nothing except, furtively, his watch. But today, in the middle of a hostile heat wave and straight from the felicities of Newport, he was heavyhearted thinking how her apartment was going to look; he dreaded it; he wished he had not come. He was struck suddenly with the importunity of his mission. How had they *dared* be so possessive and dictatorial? And why had *he* been delegated to urge her to go to a psychiatrist? To be sure, his letter to her had said only that since he was going to be in the city, he would like to call on her, but she was wise and sensitive and she was bound to know that he had come to snoop and recommend. He was so embarrassed that he considered going right down again and sending her some flowers and a note of apology for failing to show up. She could not know he was on his way, for it had not been possible to announce himself over the house telephone—and how, indeed, he wondered, would she know when her doorbell rang?

But when the doors of the elevator slid open, he found her standing in the entrance of her apartment. She looked at her watch and said, "You're punctual." Her smiling, welcoming face was cool and tranquil; unsmirched by the heat and the dreariness of the corridor and, so far as he could judge, by the upheaval of her life, she was as proud and secret-living as a flower. He admired her and he dearly loved her. He cherished her as one of life's most beautiful appointments.

"That you should have to come to town on such a day!" she exclaimed. "I'm terribly touched that you fitted me in."

He started to speak; he was on the point of showering on her a cornucopia of praise and love, and then he remembered that she would not hear. So, instead, he kissed her on either cheek and hoped the gesture, mild and partial, obscured his turmoil. She smelled of roses; she seemed the embodiment of everything most pricelessly feminine, and he felt as diffident as he did at those lovely summer balls.

Her darkened, pretty sitting room—he should not have been so fearful, he should have had more faith in her—smelled of roses, too, for everywhere there were bowls of them from Priscilla's garden, brought down by the last weekend's guests.

"I'm terribly glad you fitted me in," repeated Beatrice when she had given him a drink, and a pad of paper and a pencil, by means of which he was to communicate with her (she did this serenely and without explanation, as if it were the most natural thing in the world), "because yesterday my bravura began to peter out. In fact, I'm scared to death."

He wrote, "You shouldn't be alone. Why not come back to us? You know nothing would please us more." How asinine, he thought. What a worthless sop.

She laughed. "Priscilla couldn't bear it. Disaster makes her cry, good soul that she is. No, company wouldn't make me less scared."

"Tell me about it," he wrote, and again he felt like a fool.

It was not the deafness itself that scared her, she said—not the fear of being run down by an automobile she had not heard or violated by an intruder whose footfall had escaped her. These anxieties, which beset Priscilla, did not touch Beatrice. Nor had she yet begun so very much to miss voices or other sounds she liked; it was a little unnerving, she said, never to know if the telephone was ringing, and it was strange to go into the streets and see the fast commotion and hear not a sound, but it had its comic side and it had its compensations—it amused her to see the peevish snapping of a dog whose bark her deafness had forever silenced, she was happy to be spared her neighbors' vociferous television sets. But she was scared all the same. What had begun to harry her was that her wish to be deaf had been granted. This was exactly how she put it, and Onslager received her secret uneasily. She had not bargained for banishment, she said; she had only wanted a holiday. Now, though, she felt that the Devil lived with her, eternally wearing a self-congratulatory smile.

"You are being fanciful," Onslager wrote, although he did not think she was at all fanciful. "You can't wish yourself deaf."

But Beatrice insisted that she *had* done just that.

She emphasized that she had *elected* to hear no more, would not permit of accident, and ridiculed the doting Priscilla's sentimental fate. She had done it suddenly and out of despair, and she was sorry now. "I am ashamed. It was an act of cowardice," she said.

"How cowardice?" wrote Onslager.

"I could have broken with Marten in a franker way. I could simply have told him I had changed my mind. I didn't have to make him mute by making myself deaf."

"Was there a quarrel?" he wrote, knowing already the question was superfluous.

"Not *a* quarrel. An incessant wrangle. Marten is jealous and he is indefatigably vocal. I wanted terribly to marry him—I don't suppose I loved him very much but he seemed good, seemed safe. But all of a sudden I thought, I cannot and I will not listen to another word. And now I'm sorry because I'm so lonely here, inside my skull. Not hearing makes one helplessly egocentric."

She hated any kind of quarrel, she said—she shuddered at raised voices and quailed before looks of hate—but she could better endure a howling brawl among vicious hoodlums, a shrill squabble of shrews, a degrading jangle between servant and mistress, than she could the least altercation between a man and a woman whose conjunction had had as its origin tenderness and a concord of desire. A relationship that was predicated upon love was far too delicate of composition to be threatened by cross-purposes. There were houses where she would never visit again because she had seen a husband and wife in ugly battle dress; there were restaurants she went to unwillingly because in them she had seen lovers in harsh dispute. How could things ever be the same between them again? How could two people possibly continue to associate with each other after such humiliating, disrobing displays?

As Beatrice talked in discreet and general terms and candidly met Jack Onslager's eyes, in another part of her mind she was looking down the shadowy avenue of all the years of her life. As a girl and, before that, as a child, in the rambling, shambling house in St. Louis, Beatrice in her bedroom doing her lessons would hear a rocking chair on a squeaking board two flights down; this was the chair in which her tipsy mother seesawed, dressed for the street and wearing a hat, drinking gin and humming a Venetian barcarole to which she had forgotten the words. Her mother drank from noon, when, with lamentations, she got up, till midnight, when, the bottle dry, she fell into a groaning, nightmare-ridden unconsciousness that resembled the condition immediately preceding death. This mortal sickness was terrifying; her removal from reality was an ordeal for everyone, but not even the frequent and flamboyant threats of suicide, the sobbed proclamations that she was the chief of sinners, not all the excruciating embarrassments that were created by that interminable and joyless spree, were a fraction as painful as the daily quarrels that commenced as soon as Beatrice's father came home, just before six, and continued, unmitigated, until he—a methodical man, despite his unfathomable spleen—went to bed, at ten. Dinner, nightly, was a hideous experience for a child, since the parents were not inhibited by their children or the maid and went on heaping atrocious abuse upon each other, using sarcasm, threats, lies—every imaginable expression of loathing and contempt. They swam in their own blood, but it was an ocean that seemed to foster and nourish them; their awful wounds were their necessities. Freshly appalled each evening, unforgiving, disgraced, Beatrice miserably pushed her food about on her plate, never hungry, and often she imagined herself alone on a desert, far away from any human voice. The moment the meal was finished, she fled to her schoolbooks, but even when she put her fingers in her ears, she could hear her parents raving, whining, bullying, laughing horrible, malign laughs. Sometimes, in counterpoint to this vendetta, another would start in the kitchen, where the impudent and slatternly maid and one of her lovers would ask *their* cross questions and give crooked answers.

In spite of all this hatefulness, Beatrice did not mistrust marriage, and, moreover, she had faith in her own even temper. She was certain that sweetness could put an end to strife; she believed that her tolerance was limitless, and she vowed that when she married there would be no quarrels.

But there were. The dew in her eyes as a bride gave way nearly at once to a glaze when she was a wife. She left home at twenty, and at twenty-one married Tom Trueblood, who scolded her for seven years. Since she maintained that it took two to make a quarrel, she tried in the beginning, with all the cleverness and fortitude she had, to refuse to be a party to the storms that rocked her house and left it a squalid shambles, but her silence only made her husband more passionately angry, and at last, ripped and raw, she had to defend herself. Her dignity trampled to death, her honor mutilated, she fought back, and felt estranged from the very principles of her being. Like her parents, Tom Trueblood was sustained by rancor and contentiousness; he really seemed to love these malevolent collisions which made her faint and hot and ill, and he seemed, moreover, to regard them as essential to the married state, and so, needing them, he would not let Beatrice go but tricked and snared her and strewed her path with obstacles, until finally she had been obliged to run away and melodramatically leave behind a note.

Beatrice was a reticent woman and had too much taste to bare all these grubby secret details, but she limned a general picture for Onslager and, when she had finished, she said, "Was it any wonder, then, that when the first blush wore off and Marten showed himself to be cantankerous my heart sank?"

Onslager had listened to her with dismay. He and Priscilla were not blameless of the sin she so deplored—no married people were—but their differences were minor and rare and guarded, their sulks were short-lived. Poor, poor Beatrice, he thought. Poor lamb.

He wrote, "Have you heard from Marten?"

She nodded, and closed her eyes in a dragging weariness. "He has written me volumes," she said. "In the first place, he doesn't believe that I am deaf but thinks it's an act. He says I am indulging myself, but he is willing to forgive me if I will only come to my senses. Coming to my senses involves, among other things, obliterating the seven years I lived with Tom—I told you he was madly jealous? But how do you amputate experience? How do you eliminate what intransigently *was*?"

"If that's Marten's line," wrote Onslager, revolted by such childishness, "obviously you can't give him a second thought. The question is what's to be done about *you*?"

"Oh, I don't know, I *do* not know!" There were tears in her voice, and she clasped her hands to hide their trembling. "I am afraid that I am too afraid ever to hear again. And you see how I speak as if I had a choice?"

Now she was frankly wringing her hands, and the terror in her face was sheer. "My God, the mind is diabolical!" she cried. "Even in someone as simple as I."

The stifling day was advancing into the stifling evening, and Jack Onslager, wilted by heat and unmanned by his futile pity, wanted, though he admired and loved her, to leave her. There was nothing he could do.

She saw this, and said, "You must go. Tomorrow I am starting with an analyst. Reassure Priscilla. Tell her I know that everything is going to be all right. I know it not because I am naïve but because I *still* have faith in the kindness of life." He could not help thinking that it was will instead of faith that put these words in her mouth.

And, exteriorly, everything was all right for Beatrice. Almost at once, when she began treatment with a celebrated man, her friends began to worry less, and to marvel more at her strength and the wholeness of her worthy soul and the diligence with which she and the remarkable doctor hunted down her troublesome quarry. During this time, she went about socially, lent herself to conversation by reading lips, grew even prettier. Her analysis was a dramatic success, and after a little more than a year she regained her hearing. Some months later, she married a man, Arthur Talbot, who was far gayer than Marten ten Brink and far less rich; indeed, a research chemist, he was poor. Priscilla deplored this aspect of him, but she was carried away by the romance (he looked like a poet, he adored Beatrice) and at last found it in her heart to forgive him for being penniless.

When the Talbots came to Newport for a long weekend not long after they had married, Jack Onslager watched them both with care. No mention had ever been made by either Jack or Beatrice of their conversation on that summer afternoon, and when his wife, who had now become a fervent supporter of psychiatry, exclaimed after the second evening that she had never seen Beatrice so radiant, Onslager agreed with her. Why not? There would be no sense in quarreling with his happy wife. He himself had never seen a face so drained of joy, or even of the memory of joy; he had not been able to meet Bea's eyes.

That Sunday—it was again a summer day beside the sea— Jack Onslager came to join his two guests, who were sitting alone on the lawn. Their backs were to him and they did not hear his approach, so Talbot did not lower his voice when he said to his wife, "I have told you a thousand times that my life has to be exactly as I want it. So stop these hints. *Any* dedicated scientist worth his salt is bad-tempered."

Beatrice saw that her host had heard him; she and Onslager travailed in the brief look they exchanged. It was again an enrapturing day. The weather overhead was fair and bland, but the water was a mass of little wrathful whitecaps.

Between the Porch and the Altar

At five in the morning in February, it is darker than at midnight. The streets are empty of automobiles; the latest readers have gone to bed and the earliest risers are only just opening their eyes. The few people abroad are swift and furtive, like creatures who must quit a place before the sun shines forth. At that hour, their business seems mysterious and even shady, although they are not cutthroats or thieves but only watchmen and charwomen and night waitresses on their way home to dine at sunrise. So uncluttered are the streets, so starkly direct is the walk of the people that anyone whose custom it is to get up much later, at the normal hour, feels when he goes out that he intrudes upon a scene of bare but important privacy. And a light, springing on abruptly to make a staring eye in a blackened building, may stir him with embarrassment and wonder as if this were an alarm or an esoteric signal of hostility.

It was cold and the girl was hungry. She paused in the vestibule of the apartment building and half turned to unlock the outer door again and go back to her warm bed. But as she lingered, she observed a bright blue star high over the houses opposite and the sight inexplicably gave her resolution, even though its color was so pure and frigid that it made her all the more conscious of the cold. She drew on her gloves and went out, shocked by a biting gust of wind which passed her by like a big rapid bird. She turned the corner and hurried along Sixth Avenue on her way to the first mass.

Although the star, which was now behind her, had had a decisive effect on her, it had not dispelled her apprehension and her distrust of the unfamiliar streets. While her feet were steady enough, her breath was erratic and her ears were fanciful, making her think she heard sinister noises behind the blank faces of the buildings. She looked straight ahead, fearful of what she might see in the dark doorways and even in the interiors of delicatessens and bakery shops whose cheerless windows were dimly silvered by the street lights. And still, discomforting as it was, she took a certain pleasure in her uneasiness, feeling that even the most accidental castigation was excellent at the beginning of Lent.

On the corner of Thirteenth Street, there was a large second-hand shop whose windows she had many times studied with an incredulous amusement, so dreadful were the objects shown there: funeral wreaths made of human hair, armadillo baskets, back-scratchers that looked like sets of bad teeth, ceramic vessels of an unimaginable function. The antelope with eaten ears and rubbed-off hide, the alabaster boar and the complacent Chinese philosopher made of porcelain stared out, looking, even at five in the morning, for someone to adopt them and give them a good home.

Within the doorway of the shop, a drunken beggar sprawled like a lumpy rug, his feet in ruptured tennis shoes thrust out onto the sidewalk. He was not asleep. Under a cap set raffishly at an angle on his head, he regarded the girl's approach with an eye made visible to her by the arc light at the intersection. Paradoxically, her pace slowed down as her terror rose, and the man had risen to his feet before she was abreast of him. The smell of whisky was so strong that it was like a taste in her mouth. He stretched forth his hand and whined, "Lady, I'm hungry, lady."

She did not carry a purse, but in her pocket were two dimes and a quarter. She intended to put the quarter into the poor box and the dimes in the candle offering, for she wished to light a candle for the repose of her mother's soul and another for the safe-keeping of two friends, captive in China by the Japanese. Although it was only a fraction of a minute that she debated, a succession of images with an individual emotion attending each revolved through her mind. She saw the poor box in the dim vestibule of the lower church and heard her quarter click upon the other coins. This box was stationed beside the holy-water font, near the statue of Our Lord between whose palely gleaming feet someone placed fresh flowers each day. Then she saw her mother lying in the limbo of her last hours, unsightly, unconsoled, and heard the sonorous matter-of-factness of her Protestant relatives to whom this transformation, so unbearable to her, was neither strange nor dreadful. It was not that they did not grieve their kinswoman, but it was that they had many

times before known death and had learned, through its reiteration, that it was no wonder. She, still bedewed with baptism,
had knelt and the blue beads of her rosary slipped through her
fingers until her mother's soul abandoned its wrecked flesh. She
had been, she remembered, in the middle of the fourth decade
when her aunt, vigilant at the bedside, had whispered, "She is
gone now." And she remembered how the odor of belladonna
had obtruded so in her devotions that part of her mind pronounced the word over and over as if it belonged to a litany.

Then she tried to fancy her friends as they might be in prison
and could not, could only see them before their fireplace on
a winter day of the year before. She had come to tea and had
stayed on for sherry. She sat on a maroon sofa; a little dog
slept with his chin on her arm, whimpering once in a dream.
There was shortbread to go with the wine and as she ate a piece
she realized that it was the texture rather than the taste that
made it her favorite pastry. In an easy silence that came in the
conversation, she saw her reflection in the brass bedwarmer that
hung beside the fireplace, and this blurred travesty of her face
had the power, as the star had done this morning, to make her
suddenly purposeful, and she told her friends goodbye that day,
although they did not leave for another week.

In the early desolation of this present year, she felt tenderness
muffling her like smoke and smaller, general pictures showed
themselves to her: a clean room, a forced branch of apple
blossoms, her mother's silver-backed hairbrush, her friends'
passport pictures.

No time at all had passed. She saw the beggar's lips part again.
She could not find her voice, and one bold self chided her for
her nervousness, for this was no extraordinary occurrence. On
the contrary, the rarest day in New York was the one on which
one was not asked for money by a fellow like this or by a senile
tart or by a belligerent child. She could pass by, or she could say
she had no money. But mechanically she had paused—she was
not yet a craftsman in the selection of experience and her days
were often a chain of pauses—and the man took advantage of
her hesitance, saying, with his vague face close to hers, "Lady,
was you ever hungry?" Her fear of him was obliterated by an
abstract but brilliant anger, for his question was beside the point,
unfair, a contemptible trick. She almost spoke her indignation

aloud and then her anger burnt itself out; she controlled herself stiffly like a soldier: on this grave day she should not presume to judge. And into the cold hand, she put the quarter and one of the dimes. The man muttered something but she did not hear what he said and she went on hastily. In the windows of a flower shop, she saw her shadow drift through pots of white azaleas. When she turned the corner at Sixteenth Street, she slowed down, for two nuns walked slowly ahead of her. Her hunger returned with savage force.

The entrance to the Jesuits' church was dark. Its black iron gates were open only a crack. A nightlike and velvety blackness stood solidly between the columns on the porch of the upper church. The stone steps leading downward seemed colder than the sidewalks, and the holy water was cold. It teemed with the ripples of fingers that had been dipped there before her own, and the touch of it on her forehead was icy. Today, between the wounded feet, were dark roses. One of the sisters touched the feet and then pressed her fingers to her lips.

The mass had not begun. The girl said her prayers, but she could not concentrate, for her mind was occupied with what she would do with her last dime. Who was the neediest, she questioned: the poor, the dead, or the oppressed? Truly, she had to admit that she loved the poor less than her mother and her friends, and yet, for this very reason—for a willful sacrifice—should she not put the dime into the poor box? Then she thought, but I have given already to the poor. Lout, wastrel that he was, he was poor and it is not the duty, nor even the right, of the almsgiver to distinguish between degrees of poverty. But between her mother and her friends, how should she choose? Should one pray for someone's long life here or for someone else's shortened term in Purgatory? It occurred to her to offer her mass for her mother and light the candle for the prisoners. This seemed like a compromise and did not satisfy her, yet there was no alternative.

Four nuns were in the pew ahead of her and, finishing their prayers, they sat back and simultaneously opened their missals. On the right hand of one, she saw a wedding ring. She had never before been close enough to a nun to notice this, and she wondered when it was that the badge of their eternal marriage was placed upon them and if they really did feel unity with God at that moment or felt, instead, hushed isolation. The words of the Gospel today were: *Lay up to yourselves treasures in heaven: where neither the rust nor the moth doth consume, and where thieves do not break through nor steal. For where thy treasure is, there is thy heart also.* The words, now that she had seen the wedding ring, seemed richer and more profoundly exciting than they had done before, and for a moment she was almost idolatrous, worshipful, almost, of the fair-skinned sisters in their tower of ivory and their house of gold. And then she recoiled, for under the coif of one she saw black stubble.

The church was full, principally of old people who slept so little that rising for the earliest mass on Ash Wednesday was no great hardship. Most of them were telling their beads and only a few had missals. An aged man behind her said his Aves aloud in a harsh, sibilant voice and his false teeth clicked on one another in counterpoint to the measured whispers of his wooden beads. A bald young seminarian entered the sanctuary to light the candles on the altar. He genuflected gracefully and liquidly like a dancer, and the hand with which he crossed himself was as long and white and as shapely as one painted by El Greco. He was incongruously beautiful in his surroundings, for the lower church was ugly and in bad taste. The statues were gaudy, even in this shadowy light, and the crucifix was sentimental. In all the accouterments of the sanctuary, there was a mixture of modern leanness and Victorian laciness. The seminarian alone seemed a product of inspiration.

At last the bell rang and the celebrant with his altar boys entered the sanctuary. The girl prayed that nothing would mar the spirit of penance which she carried like a fragile light; she closed her eyes to the nun's neck and begged forgiveness for her fault-finding. All through the mass, while she fixed her attention on her mother—imagining her face, disembodied, hovering in a crowd of other faces in Purgatory, which she saw as an echoing marble hall—she wondered if she had not committed an act of betrayal, both to the beggar to whom she gave unwillingly and to the parish poor, deprived of her offering through her cowardice. Although she knew that her confusion would be understood and unraveled by the counsel of a confessor, she went, half dazed, to the communion rail and received, she felt, with an imperfect heart. Afterwards, her thanksgiving was more full of petition than of gratitude: I humbly beseech guidance and my whole heart desires wisdom and stern purpose. Reason reiterated to her that she had properly allocated her good will: money to the poor, a mass for the dead, a candle for the oppressed. Yet she was not assured in her heart and she prayed with a dry compulsion.

When she had received the cross of ashes on her forehead, she went directly to the altar of St. Francis Xavier at the back of the church. The cups for the candles were blood-red; the flames cast a sheen on the closed tabernacle. She knelt down to pray the saint to watch over her friends. As she stood up to take the taper to light her candle, she saw an old woman coming from the vestibule. She pretended not to see, for she recognized the old crone who was always there before the sun and the Jesuits discovered her. At later masses she begged on the sidewalk. The girl had already lighted the taper and was looking for a fresh cup when the woman reached the altar.

Blear-eyed, unctuous, crafty, she slithered to her knees. "God bless you, dearie," she began, her face touching the skirt of the girl's coat. The dime was in the pocket on that side, and it was as if the woman smelled it with her long nose or heard it with her ear beneath her sour gray hair or felt it on her furrowed cheek. It was impossible to ignore her, and the girl could think of no way to resolve this preposterous dilemma. Her hand still held the taper and her eyes still roved the tiers of candles seeking an unlighted one.

It seemed some time before the old woman spoke again. Behind them, people were moving about, unconcerned with anything but the small devotional tasks they had set themselves. Some were making the stations of the cross, some prayed at the Lady altar, others gazed meditatively at the crucifix. The bald young beadle had come again into the sanctuary and was preparing the altar for the next mass. Everything happening in the church was pious and usual, save for the squalid commerce at St. Francis' altar. The ceiling seemed oppressively low; she was reminded of a dreary train shed.

When the woman spoke again, her voice was more eager and hopeful. She nodded toward the candles and said, "They're every one of them lit already and they won't bring the new ones round till after the eight o'clock." How well she knew the habits of this church's servants! She had probably studied them for months, huddling in shadows behind the grating that enclosed the baptismal font or in the corner where the statue of St. Ignatius stood. The girl saw that what she said was true and she blew out the taper and replaced it. But she was determined to make the offering and she stepped down to go to another altar. The old woman took hold of her coat and peered straight into her face, shamelessly. She said, "You're young and pretty, girlie." The oblique entreaty weakened her, embarrassed her movement like a web, and finally she put her hand into her pocket and took out the dime. Before the clever, metropolitan fingers had enclosed the alms, the girl had gone, running down Sixteenth Street to the corner of Sixth Avenue. The streets were lighter now, and the big star had begun to pale. Shopkeepers were putting trash on the sidewalks; news vendors were cutting the ropes that bound the morning papers; a melancholy white horse ambled down the street dragging a milk truck after him.

When the coffee was nearly ready and her rooms were full of its fragrance, the girl looked at her forehead in the bathroom mirror and saw that the Jesuit had marked her clearly. She washed away the ashes, leaving herself alone possessed of the knowledge of her penance.

I Love Someone

M Y friends have gone now, abandoning me to the particular pallor of summer twilight in the city. How long the daytime loiters, how noisily the children loiter with it! I hear their reedy voices splintering like glass in the streets as they tell their mothers no, they *won't* come in, and call up to the filmed windows of the tenements on the avenue, "Marian!" or "Harold!" dropping, invariably, the final consonant. Abashed by my own indolence, I wish to scold them for theirs, to ask them sharply, as if I were their teacher, "Who on earth is Harol?" I hear their baseballs thudding against the walls of shops, hear their feet adroitly skipping rope, hear them singing songs from *South Pacific*, hear a sudden, solo scream for which there is neither overture nor finale: the moment it is formed, it is finished like a soap bubble. Listening to them half against my will, I think how strong a breed they are, how esoteric a society with their shrouded totems and taboos. What is the meaning of this statement I hear, shouted in singsong suddenly, "My mother is in the bathroom shooting dice"? Or ponder this: a day or so ago, I saw a legend on the sidewalk that haunts me; within a fat, lopsided heart were chalked the words "I LOVE SOMEONE." I thought at the time how artful this confession was that concealed the identity both of the lover and of the beloved. In an adult (in myself, say) it would have been a boast or a nervous lie, but in the child who wrote the words, it was no more than an ironic temporizing.

My impatience with the children tonight is not real; I am lorn for other reasons as I sit here in the heat and in the mauve light, facing an empty evening, realizing too late that I should have provided myself with company and something to do. It has been a melancholy day and the events of it have enervated me: I simply sit, I simply stare at a bowl of extraordinary roses. Harriet Perrine and Nancy Lang and Mady Hemingway and I went this afternoon to the funeral of our dear friend, Marigold Trask. Famously beautiful, illustrious for her charm and her stylish wit, inspired with joy, Marigold killed herself with sodium amytal last Thursday night, leaving bereft a husband

and two young sons. The five of us had been fast friends since school days and the death has shocked us badly; in an odd way, it has also humiliated us and when we lunched today before the service (held in a non-religious "chapel" fitted out with an electric organ and bogus Queen Anne chairs) we did not speak of Marigold at all but talked as we had talked before, when she was alive and with us. We talked of plays and clothes and we plumbed the depths of the scandals that deluged the world outside our circle. We behaved, even now that it had happened, as if nothing unsightly would ever happen to any of us. But afterward, after we had seen the gray-gloved lackeys close her casket and carry her out to the hearse, we came up here to my apartment and with our drinks we did discuss at length the waste and the folly and the squalor of her suicide. There was a note of exasperation in the tone of all our voices. "If people would only wait!" cried Nancy Lang. "Everything changes in time."

"If it was Morton, she could have divorced him," said Mady. " *We* would have stuck by."

"I don't think it was Morton," said Harriet and we all nodded. Morton was a stick and none of us liked him, but he was not at all the sort of man who would drive a woman to *that*. To lovers, yes, and trips alone, but not to *that*. Then Harriet proposed, "It could have been the Hungarian."

"Oh, but that's been over for months," said Mady. "Besides, *she* chucked *him*." Mady is an orthodox woman. Her mind is as literal as her modern house.

Nancy said, "It must have been something much deeper. If it wasn't, then it was simply beastly of her to do this to the boys."

We talked then of the effects of such catastrophes on children, and though we spoke wholly in banalities (we are not women with original minds; we "keep up" and that's the most that can be said of us) and were objective, I could not help thinking that the others felt it would have been better if, assuming that one of us had had to take the overdose of sleeping pills, it had been I. For I have never married and my death would discommode no one. My friends would miss me, it is true: to put it bluntly, they would have no one to coddle and champion in a world unfit for solitary living. They are devoted to me, I am sure, and in their way they love me, but they are not *concerned*. They cannot be, for there is no possible way for them really to know me now; it would embarrass them, as married women, to confront the heart of a spinster which is at once impoverished and prodigal, at once unloving and lavishly soft. Therefore, out of necessity, they have invented their own image of me, and I fancy that if I tried to disabuse them of their notions, they would think I was hallucinated; in alarm they would get me to a really good doctor as quickly as possible.

Harriet, who is a tireless and faulty analyst of character, often explains in my presence that I am "one of those beings whom nothing, but nothing, can bring down to earth." Does she mean by this that I am involved in nothing? Or does she derive her ethereal vision of me from the fact that I never appear to change? My moods don't show and perhaps this gives me a blandness that, for some reason, she associates with the upper air. I never make drastic changes in my life; I seldom rearrange my furniture; I have worn the same hairdress for twenty years. Harriet lives in a state of daily surprise but surprise only for things and scenes and people that do not alter in the least. She begins her day by marveling that her egg is, in color and constituents, exactly the same as the egg of yesterday and of the day before and that tomorrow the same phenomenon will greet her happy, natural eyes. Whenever she goes into the Frick to look at her favorite pictures, she stands awed before the El Greco "St. Jerome," her hands clasped rapturously, her whole being seeming to cry out in astonishment, "Why, it's still here!"

But I am grateful that Harriet and Nancy and Mady have embedded me in a myth. This sedative conviction of theirs, that ichor runs in my veins and that mine is an operating principle of the most vestal kind, has kept me all these years (I am forty-three) from going into hysteria or morbidity or hypochondria or any other sort of beggary by which even the most circumspect spinster of means is tempted. I have no entourage of coat-carrying young men and drink is not a problem; the causes I take up are time-honored and uncontroversial: I read aloud to crippled children but I do not embroil myself in anything remotely ideological. I know that my friends have persuaded themselves that I once had a love affair that turned out badly—upon this universal hypothesis rests perhaps as much as half the appeal of unmarried women who show no signs of discontent, and there is no tact more beatifying than that which protects a grief that is never discussed. Now and again it amuses me to wonder what their conjectures are. I daresay that when they speculate, they kill off my lover in splendor, in a war, perhaps, or in a tuberculosis sanitarium. I can all but hear them forearming their dinner guests before I arrive: "Jenny Peck has never married, you know. She had one of those really tragic things when she was very young, so totally devastating that she has never said a word about it even to her closest friends."

But the fact is that there has been nothing in my life. I have lived the whole of it in the half-world of brief flirtations (some that have lasted no longer than the time it takes to smoke a cigarette under the marquee of a theater between the acts), of friendships that have perished of the cold or have hung on, desiccated, outliving their meaning and never once realizing the possibility of love. I have dwelt with daydreams that through the years have become less and less high-reaching, so apathetic, indeed, that now I would rather recite the names of the forty-eight states to myself than review one of those skimpy fictions. From childhood I have unfailingly taken all the detours around passion and dedication; or say it this way, I have been a pilgrim without faith, traveling in an anticipation of loss, certain that the grail will have been spirited away by the time I have reached my journey's end. If I did not see in myself this skepticism, this unconditional refusal, this—I admit it—contempt, I would find it degrading that no one has ever proposed marriage to me. I do not wish to refuse but I do not know how to accept. In my ungivingness, I am more dead now, this evening, than Marigold Trask in her suburban cemetery.

But my reflexes are still lively and my nerves are spry, and sometimes I can feel the pain through the anesthetic. Then it is on certain mornings I will not wake, although my dreams, abstract and horrible, pester me relentlessly and raucously. The sarcasm of my dreams! All night long my secret mind derides and crucifies me, "Touché!" All the same, I do not consciously nurse the wound. Be caught red-eyed by my friends? It would never do, for their delusion is my occupation: *cogitant, ergo sum*. Unlike Marigold, I will never unsettle these affectionate women, for whatever would I do without them? I would not know how to order my existence if they did not drop in on me after a gallery or a matinee, have me to dine when the extra man is either "interesting" or "important" (the Egyptologists I have listened to! The liberals with missions! Shall I forget until my dying day the herpetologist that Mady once produced who talked to me of cobras throughout the fish?), have me to come for long weekends in the summer, send me flowers and presents of perfume in clever bottles, lend me their husbands for lunch, treat me, in general, like someone of royal blood suspended in an incurable but unblemishing disease.

Thus it is I sit and meditate in the ambiguous light while beyond me and below me the city children vehemently play at stick-ball, postponing their supper hour just as I postpone mine. I know that I should stir. I must take the glasses and the ashtrays to the kitchen and rinse them out because my silent and fastidious maid, who comes to me by the day, would be alarmed if I departed from my custom. I must eat what she has prepared for me, I must read, must bathe, must read again, and finally turn off my light and commence my nightmares in the heat that lies like jelly on the city. But thinking of myself, of Marigold (how secretly she did it!), of the anonymous child who told the world he loved someone, I am becalmed and linger exactly where I am, unable to give myself a purpose for doing anything.

By now my friends are at home in Fairfield County. All three of them are ardent gardeners, and presently they will be minding their tomato vines and weeding between their rows of corn. I imagine their cool, rose-laden drawing rooms where, later, they will join their husbands for cocktails. Is it too late for me to ring up someone and propose dinner and an air-conditioned movie? Much too late. Much too late. Idiotically, I say the phrase aloud, compulsively repeat it several times and try to think how my lips look as I protract the word "much."

Gradually the words lose their meaning and I am speaking gibberish. *Now* what would they think of me, babbling like a cretin? I have just set my tongue against the roof of my mouth to say "late" for the dozenth time when a bumble of voices invades my open windows. The clamor, as of an angry, lowing multitude, is closer than the street sounds and I sit up, startled. Perhaps it is a party in the garden next door; but the voices are harsh and there is no laughter. The sound echoes as if a mass of people were snarling at the bottom of a pit; muted, they are nevertheless loud—and loud, the words are nevertheless indistinguishable. For a minute I remain, true to my character, remote from the tumult; but then, because there is neither pause nor change and because the sound is so close at hand, I grow ever so slightly afraid. Still, I do not move, not even to switch on a light, until suddenly, like the report of a gun, an obscenity explodes in the hot dusk. The voice that projects it is an adolescent boy's and it is high and helpless with outrage. I rise and stand quivering before my chair and then I move across the carpet and open the door to my bedroom.

As I hesitate, I once again take note of the glasses and the ashtrays. And once again, although my heart is pounding rapidly now with a fear that is gathering itself into a shape, I think, quite separately, of Marigold and I wonder if she knew when it was coming. *It!* Shocked at my circumvention, I revise: when *death* was coming. But does that improve the sentence? *It* means as much to me as *death* does—or, for that matter, life. I go further and I say, "I wonder if she finally knew why she wanted nothing else?" For I, you see, dwelling upon the rim of life, see everyone in the arena as acting blindly. I would know, but did Marigold? Does the bullfighter know, until he is actually in danger, that the danger itself is his master? Not the glory, not the ladies' roses, or the pageant, or the accolades, but the flashing glimpse of the evil and the random and the unknown? Far from the stage and safe, I, who never act on impulse, know nearly precisely the outcome of my always rational behavior. It makes me a woman without hope; but since there is no hope there is also no despair.

I lean from my bedroom window and discover the source of the noises in the courtyard of this respectable apartment house: a huddle of boys stands in the service entry where the gate has not yet been locked. They are of all sizes and all shapes and colors, and I recognize them at once as a roving band of youthful hoodlums whose viciousness I have read about in the tabloids. All their faces wear the same expression of mingled rage and fascination, and all their eyes are fixed on something I cannot see. There are twenty-odd of them and it is from them that comes this steady snarl. I lean out farther and at my end of the areaway I see a pair of boys fighting. The fight is far advanced, for one of them, big and black-haired, has the other down on the cement. Blood comes from his wide mouth, open in a gasp, and his hands flutter weakly against his assailant's shoulders. The engagement is silent. Stunned by its cynicism, I try to pity the loser but I cannot, for his defeat has made him hideous. Strands of his brown hair lie like scattered rags on the cement in a parody of a halo.

Now other tenants are aroused and come to their windows to look in revulsion and indignation. Above me a man shouts down, "I am going to call the police!" But the fight continues, silently and maliciously, and the boys in the gateway ignore my neighbor, who grows very angry and cries, "Get out of this court! I have a gun here!"

But still they pay no attention. At last the boy on his back closes his eyes and utters some soft sentence that is evidently his surrender, for the other, giving him one last brutish punch in the ribs, gets up, staggering a little. Now that the excitement is over, the audience instantly quits the gateway; they vanish swiftly in a body, every man jack of them, and do not even glance back. But the victor lingers like an actor on a stage as if he were expecting applause, and seeing that the boys are gone, he looks up at the windows of the apartments. Perhaps he is seeking the man who threatened him with the law; perhaps he wants to challenge *him*. But he finds, instead, myself and as he looks at me, his feral face breaks into a shameless smile. I suppose he is eighteen or nineteen, but the wickedness in his little black eyes and his scarlet mouth is as old as the hills. He wears a thin mustache, so well groomed and theatrical that it appears to adhere to his lip with gum. He looks at me and then looks down at the other boy, who is just now getting to his feet, and then looks up at me again and shrugs his shoulders. Is he asking me to confirm the justice of his violence? Or the beauty of it? Or the passion?

The blood is driven crudely to my face and I turn from the window. It is my intention at first to lie down on my bed and, if I can, to close my inner eye to what I have just seen. But instead, as will-less as a somnambulist, I go to my door and take the elevator down and let myself out into the street where there is no longer any tumult but, rather, a palpable and sneaky hush. I feel watched and mind-read. With no conscious plan,

I walk quickly down the street past the dull buildings with their mongrel doors and their minuscule plots of gritty privet, walking toward the avenue where I reason the boys have gone. A squad car drives slowly by and a bored policeman throws his cigarette stub from the window.

My aim is now articulate. I realize that I want to see the ruffians face to face, both the undefeated and the overthrown, to see if I can penetrate at last the mysterious energy that animates everyone in the world except myself.

But I do not reach the avenue. Halfway there, I glance down at the sidewalk and I see that swollen heart with its fading proclamation, I LOVE SOMEONE. As easily it could read, beneath a skull and crossbones, I HATE SOMEONE. Now there is no need to investigate further; the answer is here in the obvious, trumpery scrawl, and I go back to my apartment and gather up the glasses and the ashtrays.

My friends and I have managed my life with the best of taste and all that is lacking at this banquet where the appointments are so elegant is something to eat.

Cops and Robbers

THE child, Hannah, sitting hidden on the attic steps, listened as her mother talked on the telephone to Aunt Louise.

"Oh, there's no whitewashing the incident. The child's hair is a sight, and it will be many moons, I can tell you, before I'll forgive Hugh Talmadge. But listen to me. The worst of it is that this baby of five has gone into a decline like a grown woman—like you or me, dear, at our most hysterical. Sudden fits of tears for no apparent reason and then simply hours of brooding. She won't eat, she probably doesn't sleep. I can't stand it if she's turning mental."

The door to the bedroom, across the hall, was half open, and through the crack of the door at the foot of the attic steps Hannah saw that in the course of the night her parents had disarrayed the pale-green blanket cover and now, half off the bed, drooping and askew, it looked like a great crumpled new leaf, pulled back here and there to show the rosy blankets underneath. In the bedroom it is spring, thought Hannah, and outdoors it is snowing on the Christmas trees; that is a riddle.

Her mother lay in the center of the big bed, which was as soft and fat as the gelded white Persian cat who dozed at her side, his scornful head erect, as if he were arrested not so much by sleep as by a coma of boredom and disgust. A little earlier, before he struck this pose, he had sniffed and disdained the bowl of cream on his mistress's breakfast tray, and when she had tried to cajole him into drinking it, he had coolly thrashed his tail at her. In the darkness of her enclosure, Hannah yearned, imagining herself in the privileged cat's place beside her mother, watching the mellowing, pillowing, billowing snow as it whorled down to meet the high tips of the pine trees that bordered the frozen formal garden. If she were Nephew, the cat, she would burrow into the silky depths of the bed up to her eyes and rejoice that she was not outside like a winter bird coming to peck at suet and snowy crumbs at the feeding station.

It was ugly and ungenerous here where she was, on the narrow, splintery stairs, and up in the attic a mouse or a rat scampered on lightly clicking claws between the trunks; some hibernating bees buzzed peevishly in their insomnia. Stingy and lonesome like old people, the shut-ins worried their grievances stealthily. And Hannah, spying and eavesdropping (a sin and she knew it), felt the ends of her cropped hair and ran a forefinger over her freshly combed boy's cut—the subject of her mother's conversation. Something like sleep touched her eyeballs, though this was early morning and she had not been awake longer than an hour. But it was tears, not drowsiness, that came. They fell without any help from her; her cheeks did not rise up as they usually did when she cried, to squeeze themselves into puckers like old apples, her mouth did not open in a rent of woe, no part of her body was affected at all except the eyes themselves, from which streamed down these mothering runnels.

"Why did he do it?" Her mother's question into the telephone was an impatient scream. "Why do men do half the things they do? Why does Arthur treat you in public as if you were an enlisted man? I swear I'll someday kill your rear admiral for you. Why does Eliot brag to Frances that he's unfaithful? Because they're sadists, every last one of them. I am very anti-man today."

"What is anti-man?" whispered Hannah.

The stools on either side of the fireplace in the den were ottomans, and sometimes Hannah and her mother sat on them in the late afternoon, with a low table between them on which were set a Chinese pot of verbena tisane, two cups, and a plate of candied orange rind. At the thought of her mother's golden hair in the firelight, and the smell of her perfume in the intimate warmth, and the sound of her voice saying, "Isn't this gay, Miss Baby?" the tears came faster, for in her heavy heart Hannah felt certain that now her hair was cut off, her mother would never want to sit so close to her again. Unable to see through the narrow opening of the door any longer, she leaned her face against the wall and felt her full tears moistening the beaverboard as she listened to her mother's recital of Saturday's catastrophe.

"On the face of it, the facts are innocent enough. He took her to town on Saturday to buy her a pair of shoes, having decided for his own reasons that I have no respect for my children's feet—the shoes he got are too odious, but that's another story. Then when he brought her back, here she was, cropped, looking like a rag doll. He said she'd begged to have it done. Of course she'd done nothing of the kind. To put the most charitable construction on the whole affair, I *could* say that when he went into the barbershop to have his own hair cut, he'd had a seizure of amnesia and thought he had Andy with him, or Johnny, or Hughie, and decided to kill two birds with one stone. And then afterward he was afraid of what I'd say and so cooked up this canard—and more than likely bribed her to bear him out. The way men will weasel out of their missteps! It isn't moral. It shocks me."

He did *not* think I was Andy or Johnny or Hughie, Hannah said to herself. In the barbershop at her father's club there had been no one but grown men and a fat stuffed skunk that stood in front of the mirror between two bottles of bay rum, its leathery nose pointed upward as if it were trying to see the underside of its chin in the looking glass. Through a steaming towel, her father had muttered, "Just do as I say, Homer, cut it off," and the barber, a lean man with a worried look on his red face, flinched, then shrugged his shoulders and began to snip off Hannah's heavy curls, frowning with disapproval and remarking once under his breath that women, even though they were five years old, were strictly forbidden on these premises. On the drive home, her peeled head had felt cold and wet, and she had not liked the smell that gauzily hovered around her, growing more cloying as the heater in the car warmed up. At a red light, her father had turned to her and, patting her on the knee, had said, "You look as cute as a button, young fellow." He had not seemed to hear her when she said, "I do not. I'm not a young fellow," nor had he noticed when she moved over against the door, as far away from him as she could get, hating him bitterly and hating her nakedness. Presently, he'd turned on the radio to a news broadcast and disputed out loud with the commentator. Hannah, left all alone, had stared out the window at the wolfish winter. In one snow-flattened field she saw tall flames arising from a huge wire trash basket, making the rest of the world look even colder and whiter and more unkind. Her father scowled, giving the radio what for, swearing at the slippery roads—carrying on an absent-minded tantrum all by himself. Once, halted by a woman driver whose engine was stalled, he'd said, "Serves her right. She ought to be home at this time of day tending to business." As they turned in their own drive, he said a lie: "That was a fine idea of yours to have your hair cut off." She had never said any such thing; all she had said, when they were having lunch in a brown, cloudy restaurant, was that she would rather go to the barbershop with him than wait at Grandma's. But she had not contradicted him, for he did not countenance contradiction from his children. "I'm an old-fashioned man," he announced every morning to his three sons and his two daughters. "I am the autocrat of this breakfast table." And though he said it with a wink and a chuckle, it was clear that he meant business. Johnny, who was intellectual, had told the other children that an autocrat was a person like Hitler, and he had added sarcastically, "That sure is something to brag about, I must say."

The voice speaking into the phone took on a new tone, and Hannah, noticing this, looked out through the crack again. "What? Oh, please don't change the subject, pet, I really want your help. It isn't a trifle, it's terribly important, I really think it is the *final* effrontery. . . . All right, then, if you promise that we can come back to it." With her free hand, Hannah's mother lightly stroked the cat, who did not heed, and she lay back among her many pillows, listening to her sister but letting her eyes rove the room as if she were planning changes in its decoration. "Yes, I did hear it but I can't remember where," she said inattentively. Then, smiling in the pleasure of gossip, forgetting herself for a moment, she went on, "Perhaps I heard it from Peggy the night she came to dinner with that frightful new man of hers. That's it—it was from *him* I heard it, and automatically discounted it for no other reason than that I took an instantaneous dislike to him. If he is typical of his department, the C.I.A. must be nothing more or less than the Gestapo."

Hannah's head began to ache and she rolled it slowly, looking up the steep, ladderlike steps into the shadowy attic. She was bored now that the talk was not of her, and she only half heard her mother's agile voice rising, descending, laughing quickly, pleading, "Oh, no! It's not *pos*sible!" and she sucked her fingers, one by one. Her tears had stopped and she missed them as she might have missed something she had lost. Like her hair, like all her golden princess curls that the barber had gazed at sadly as they lay dead and ruined on the tiled floor.

Now that Hannah's hair was short, her days were long: it was a million hours between breakfast and lunch, and before, it had been no time at all, because her mother, still lying in her oceanic bed, had every morning made Hannah's curls, taking her time, telling anyone who telephoned that she would call back, that just now she was busy "playing with this angel's hair."

Today was Wednesday, and Hannah had lived four lifetimes since Saturday afternoon. Sunday had been endless, even though her brothers and her sister had been as exciting as ever, with their jokes and contests and their acrobatics and their game of cops-and-robbers that had set the servants wild. But even in their mad preoccupation it had been evident that the sight of Hannah embarrassed them. "The baby looks like a skinned cat," said Andy, and Hughie said, "It was a dopey thing to do. The poor little old baby looks like a mushroom." The parents did nothing to stop this talk, for all day long they were fighting behind the closed door of the den, not even coming out for meals, their voices growing slower and more sibilant as they drank more. "I hate them," Johnny had said in the middle of the long, musty afternoon, when the cops were spent and the robbers were sick of water-pistol fights. "When they get stinking, I hate them," said Johnny. "I bet a thousand dollars he had had a couple when he had them cut the baby's hair." Janie shouted, "Oh, that baby, baby, baby, baby! Is that goofy baby the only pebble on the beach? Why do they have to mess up Sunday fighting over her? I'm going crazy!" And she ran around in a circle like a dog, pulling at her hair with both hands.

On Monday morning, when Hannah's father took the older children off to Marion Country Day School on his way to the city, she had nearly cried herself sick, feeling that this Monday the pain of their desertion was more than she could bear. She would not let go of Janie's hand, and she cried, "You'll be sorry if you come back and find I'm dead!" Janie, who was ten and hot-blooded—she took after Daddy, who had Huguenot blood—had slapped Hannah's hand and said, "The nerve of some people's children!" Hannah had stood under the porte-cochere, shivering in her wrapper and slippers, until the car went out the driveway between the tulip trees; she had waved and called, "Goodbye, dearest Janie and Johnny and Andy and Hughie!" Only Johnny had looked back; he rolled down the window and leaned out and called, "Ta-ta, half pint." They were all too old and busy to pay much attention to her, though often they brought her presents from school—a jawbreaker or a necklace made of paper clips. The four older children were a year apart, starting with John, who was thirteen, and ending with Janie, and when family photographs were taken, they were sometimes lined up according to height; these were called "stairstep portraits," and while Hannah, of course, was included, she was so much smaller than Janie that she spoiled the design, and one time Uncle Harry, looking at a picture taken on Palm Sunday when all five children were sternly holding their palms like spears, had said, pointing to Hannah, "Is that the runt of the litter or is it a toy breed?" Andy, who was Uncle Harry's pet, said, "We just keep it around the house for its hair. It's made of spun gold, you know, and very invaluable." This evidently was something the barber had not known, for he had swept the curls into a dustpan and thrown them into a chute marked "Waste." She wondered how long they would keep her now that her sole reason for existence was gone.

In other days, after Daddy and the children left and the maids began their panicky, silent cleaning, flinging open all the windows to chill the house to its heart, Hannah would run upstairs to the big bedroom to sit on the foot of the bosomy bed and wait while her mother drank her third cup of coffee and did the crossword puzzle in the *Tribune*. When she was stuck for a definition, she would put down her pencil and thoughtfully twist the diamond ring on her finger; if it caught the sun, Hannah would close her eyes and try to retain the flashing swords of green and purple, just as she unconsciously tried to seal forever in her memory the smell of the strong Italian coffee coming in a thin black stream out of the silver pot. Hannah remembered one day when her mother said to the cat, "What is that wretched four-letter word that means 'allowance for waste,' Nephew? We had it just the other day." Finally, when the puzzle was done and Edna had taken away the tray, she stretched out her arms to Hannah, who scrambled into her embrace, and she said, "I suppose you want your tawny tresses curled," and held her at arm's length and gazed at her hair with disbelieving eyes. "Bring us the brush, baby." All the while she brushed, then combed, then made long, old-fashioned sausage curls, turning and molding them on her index finger, she talked lightly and secretly about the dreams she had had and Christmas plans and what went on inside Nephew's head and why it was that she respected but could not bear Andy's violin teacher. She included Hannah, as if she were thirty years old, asking for her opinion or her corroboration of something. "Do you agree with me that Nephew is the very soul of Egypt? Or do you think there are Chinese overtones in his style?" After telling a dream (her dreams were full of voyages; one time she sailed into Oslo in Noah's ark and another time she went on the *Queen Mary* to Southampton in her night clothes without either luggage or a passport), she said, "What on earth do you suppose that means, Hannah? My id doesn't seem to know where it is at." Bewitching, indecipherable, she always dulcified this hour with her smoky, loving voice and her loving fingers that sometimes could not resist meandering over Hannah's head, ruining a curl by cleaving through it as she exclaimed, "Dear Lord, I never saw such stuff as this!" Actually, her own hair was the same vivacious color and the same gentle texture as Hannah's, and sometimes her hands would leave the child's head and go to her own, to stroke it slowly.

Lately now, for this last month, when the afternoons were snug and short and the lamps were turned on early and the hearth fires smelled of nuts, there had been another hour as well when Hannah and her hair had been the center of attention. Every day at half past two, she and her mother drove in the toylike English car over to Mr. Robinson Fowler's house, three miles away, on the top of a bald and beautiful hill from which it was possible, on a clear day, to see the beaches of Long Island. In a big, dirty studio, jammed with plaster casts and tin cans full of turpentine and stacked-up canvases and nameless metal odds and ends, Mr. Fowler, a large, quiet man who mumbled when he talked, was painting a life-size portrait of Hannah and her mother. Her mother, wearing a full skirt of scarlet felt and a starched white Gibson-girl shirt and a black ribbon in her hair, sat on a purple Victorian sofa, and Hannah, in a blue velvet jacket trimmed with black frogs and a paler-blue accordion-pleated skirt, stood leaning against her knee. In the picture, these colors were all different, all smudgy and gray, and the point of this, said Mr. Fowler, was to accent the lambencies of the hair. Before they took their pose, all the morning's careful curls were combed out, for Mr. Fowler wanted to paint Hannah's hair, he murmured in his closed mouth, "in a state of nature." Occasionally, he emerged from behind his easel and came across to them with his shambling, easygoing, friendly gait, to push back a lock of hair that had fallen over Hannah's forehead, and the touch of his fingers, huge as they were, was as light as her mother's.

Hannah liked the heat of the studio, and the smell of the tea perpetually brewing on an electric grill, and the sight of the enormous world of hills and trees and farms and rivers through the enormous windows, and she liked the quiet, which was broken only once or twice in the course of the hour's sitting by an exchange of a casual question and answer between Mr. Fowler and her mother, half the time about her hair. "It must never be cut," said the painter one day. "Not a single strand of it." After the sitting was over and Hannah and her mother had changed back into their regular clothes, Mr. Fowler drew the burlap curtains at the windows and turned on the soft lamps. Then he and her mother sat back in two scuffed leather armchairs drinking whisky and talking in a leisurely way, as if all the rest of the time in the world were theirs to enjoy in this relaxed geniality. Hannah did not listen to them. With her cup of mild, lemony tea, she sat on a high stool before a blackboard at the opposite end of the room and drew spider webs with a nubbin of pink chalk. Mr. Fowler and her mother never raised their voices or threw things at each other or stormed out of the room, banging doors and Hannah was sorry when it was time to go home where that kind of thing went on all the time, horrifying the housemaids, who never stayed longer than two months at the most, although the cook, who had a vicious tongue herself, had been with them ever since Johnny could remember.

The picture, when it was finished, was going to hang in the drawing room over an heirloom lowboy, where now there hung a pair of crossed épées, used by Hannah's father and his adversary in a jaunty, bloody *Studentenmensur* at Freiburg the year he went abroad to learn German. The lilac scar from the duel was a half moon on his round right cheek.

Now the picture would never be finished, since Hannah's corntassel hair was gone, and the sunny hour at the start of the day and the teatime one at the end were gone with it.

Hannah, sitting on the attic stairs, began to cry again as she thought of the closed circle of her days. Even her sister's and her brothers' return from school was not the fun it had been before; her haircut had become a household issue over which all of them squabbled, taking sides belligerently. Janie and Andy maintained it did not matter; all right, they said, what if the baby did look silly? After all, she didn't go to school and nobody saw her. Johnny and Hughie and the cook and the maids said that it did matter, and Johnny, the spokesman for that camp, railed at his father behind his back and called him a dastard. But all the same, no one paid any attention to Hannah; when they spoke of "the baby," they might have been speaking of the car or a piece of furniture; one would never have known that she was in the room, for even when they looked directly at her, their eyes seemed to take in something other than Hannah. She felt that she was already shrinking and fading, that all her rights of being seen and listened to and caressed were ebbing away. Chilled and exposed as she was, she was becoming, nonetheless, invisible.

The tears came less fast now, and she heard her mother say, "How can I *help* looking at it closely? I shall eventually have to go to an analyst, as you perfectly well know, if I am to continue this marriage until the children are reasonably grown. But in the meantime, until I get my doctor, who can I talk to but you? I wouldn't talk to you if you weren't my sister, because I don't think you're discreet at all." Sad, in her covert, Hannah saw that her mother was now sitting up straight against the headboard and was smoking a cigarette in long, meditative puffs; the smoke befogged her frowning forehead.

"Forget it, darling," she continued. "I know you are a tomb of silence. Look, do let me spill the beans and get it over with. It will put me into a swivet, I daresay, and I'll have to have a drink in my bath, but the way I feel, after these nights I've had, that's in the cards anyhow. . . . Oh, Christ, Louise, don't preach to me!"

Briefly, she put down the telephone and dragged Nephew to her side. Then she resumed, "Excuse me. I was adjusting my cat. Now, dear, right now, you can forget my 'charitable construction' because, of course, that's rot. At this juncture, neither one of us does anything by accident. I cannot believe that criminals are any more ingenious than wives and husbands when their marriages are turning sour. Do you remember how fiendish the Irelands were?

"Well, the night before the haircutting, we had a row that lasted until four, starting with Rob and going on from him to all the other men I know—he thinks it's bad form (and that's exactly how he puts it) that I still speak fondly of old beaux. He suspects me of the direst things with that poor pansy the decorators sent out to do the carpets on the stairs, and he's got it firmly rooted in his mind that Rob and I are in the middle of a red-hot affair. He doesn't know the meaning of friendship. He's got a sand dune for a soul. He suggested loathsomely that Rob and I were using Hannah as a blind—oh, his implications were too cynical to repeat.

"All this went on and on until I said that I would leave him. You know *that* old blind alley where any feint is useless because when five children are involved, one's hands are tied. Unless one can be proved mad. If only I could be! I would give my eyes to be sent away for a while to some insane asylum like that one Elizabeth loved so.

"It was hideous—the whole battle. We were so squalid with drink. We drink prodigiously these days. The ice ran out and we didn't even take time to go get more, so we drank whisky and tap water as if we were in a cheap hotel, and I kept think-ing, How lowering this is. But I couldn't stop. This was the worst quarrel we've ever had—by far the most fundamental. The things we said! We could have killed each other. In the morning, not even our hangovers could bring us together. And let me tell you, they were shattering. If I hadn't known I had a hangover, I would have sent for an ambulance without thinking twice. Hugh sidled around like a wounded land crab and swore he had fractured his skull. Fortunately, the children, all except the baby, had been asked to the Fosters' to skate, so at least we didn't have to put up appearances—we do that less and less as it is. But finally we began to pull ourselves together about noon with Bloody Marys, and when he proposed that he take Hannah into town and buy her lunch and some shoes, I almost forgave him everything. I was so delighted to have the house to myself. I would not rise to that bait about my neglecting the welfare of my children's feet. All I could think of was just being alone.

"I should have known. I think I might have sensed what was up if I hadn't been so sick, because as they were about to leave, the baby asked why I hadn't curled her hair and Hugh said, 'You leave that to me today.' Now, looking back on it, I can see that he rolled his eyes in that baleful, planning way of his and licked one corner of his mouth. But even if I had noticed, I still would never have dreamed he would be so vile.

"It goes without saying that we have been at swords' points ever since, and it doesn't help matters to see the child so woe-begone, wearing this look of 'What did I do to deserve this?' How can one explain it away as an accident to a child when one perfectly knows that accident is not involved? Her misery makes me feel guilty. I am as shy of her as if I had been an accessory. I can't console her without spilling all the beans about Hugh. Besides, you can't say to a child, 'Darling, you are only a symbol. It was really *my* beautiful hair that was cut off, not yours.' . . .

"Rob *crushed*? Oh, for God's sake, no, not crushed—that's not Rob's style. He's outraged. His reaction, as a matter of fact, annoys me terribly, for he takes the whole thing as a personal affront and says that if Hugh had wanted to make an issue of my afternoons in his studio, he should have challenged him to a duel with the Freiburg swords. His theory, you see, is that Hugh has been smoldering at the thought of these testimonials of his manliness being replaced by the portrait. Rob claims that Hugh hates art—as of course he does—and that it's the artist in him, Rob, not the potential rival, that he is attacking. Needless to say, this gives him a heaven-sent opportunity to berate me for living in the camp of the enemy. He was horrid on Monday. He called me an opportunist and a brood mare. It depresses me that Rob, who is so intuitive about most things, can't see that

I am the victim, that *my* values have been impugned. Today I hate all men.

"What am I going to do? What can I do? I'm taking her this afternoon to Angelo to see what he can salvage out of the scraps that are left. I'll get her a new doll—one with short hair. That's all I can do now. The picture will never be finished, so the dueling swords will stay where they are. And I will stay where I am— Oh, there's no end! Why on earth does one have children?"

For a minute or two her mother was silent, leaning back with her eyes closed, listening to Aunt Louise. Hannah no longer envied the cat curled into her mother's arm; she hated his smug white face and she hated her mother's sorrowful smile. Hot and desolate and half suffocated, she wished she were one of the angry bees. If she were a bee, she would fly through the crack of the attic door and sting Nephew and her mother and her father and Janie and Andy and Mr. Fowler. "Zzzzzzz," buzzed the child to herself.

After the telephone conversation was over and her mother had got up and gone to run her bath, Hannah let herself silently out the door into the hall and went downstairs to the kitchen. The cook was dicing onions, weeping. "There's my baby," she said as Hannah came to stand beside her, "my very own baby." She put down her knife and wiped her hands and her eyes on her apron and scooped Hannah up in a bear hug.

"I love you, Mattie," said Hannah.

The cook's teary face looked surprised and she put the child down and said, "Run along now, kiddikins—Mattie's got work to do."

Hannah went into the den and kneeled on the window seat to watch the snow settling deeply on the branches of the trees. "I love you, snow," she said. It fell like sleep.

The Captain's Gift

THOUGH it is wartime, it is spring, so there are boys down in the street playing catch. Babies and dogs are sunning in the square and here and there among them, on green iron benches under the trees, rabbis sit reading newspapers. Some stout women and some thin little girls have brought crusts of bread in paper bags and are casting crumbs to the pigeons. There is a fire in one of the wire trash baskets and bits of black ash fly upward, but there is no wind at all to carry them off and they slowly descend again. Out of the windows of the maternity hospital, new mothers, convalescent, wearing flowered wrappers, lean to call to their friends who stand in little clumps on the sidewalk, waving their arms and shouting up pleasantries and private jokes in Yiddish. They are loath to end the visit, but finally they must, for unseen nurses speak to the women at the windows and they retire, crying good-humored farewells and naming each friend by name: Goodbye, Uncle Nathan! Goodbye, Mama! Goodbye, Isabel! Goodbye, Mrs. Leibowitz! Goodbye! In the pushcarts at the curbstone are lilacs and mountain laurel, pots of grape hyacinth and petunias for window boxes; between sales the venders rearrange their buckets and talk with the superintendents of the apartment buildings who idle, smoking, in the cellar entries where they lean against the tall ash cans. Six blocks away, the clock at St. Marks-in-the-Bouwerie strikes four.

Mrs. Chester Ramsey, the widow of the general, has one of the very few private houses in the neighborhood. At the window of her drawing room on the second floor, she is writing letters at a little desk that looks like a spinet. Now and then, pausing for a word, she glances through the marquisette curtains that blur the scene below and impart to it a quality she cannot name but which bewitches her at this time of day, especially in the spring. It separates her while it does not take her quite away; she becomes of and not of the spectacle. And then, too, it makes her nostalgic for the days, long ago, when young matrons, her friends, strolled through the square under their parasols, when trim French nursemaids wheeled babies, whose names she knew, in English prams; and little girls in sailor hats walked briskly with their governesses to confirmation class; when she herself was well-known there and was greeted and detained innumerable times in her passage through the flower-lined walks.

But there is no bitterness at all in her reflection; indeed, she enjoys the lazy turmoil of the anonymous crowd below. Often, on a nice day like this if no one is coming in to tea, she goes out to sit on one of the benches, and it is always thrillingly strange to her that no one notices her, even though she wears the sort of clothes her mother might have done when she was an old lady: a black taffeta dress with a long skirt and a tightly buttoned, high-necked jacket with a garnet brooch at the throat, a small velvet hat, black silk gloves. She is not in the least unconscious of her appearance, but she does not hope to be greeted with a flurry of surprise; rather, its absence is what she looks forward to, and she is like a child, who, dressed in her mother's clothes, is accepted as a grown-up. She is no more eccentric than the bearded rabbis or the brown gypsy women who occasionally waddle along the paths with their greasy striped skirts and their waist-long strings of beads. Sometimes, sitting there, she feels that she is invisible. Surely, she thinks, the people would remark on her if they could see her; they would certainly realize that in her reside memories of this square and this neighborhood older than some of the plane trees. She is surprised and not resentful that none of them knows that she alone belongs here.

The lady's friends and relatives, who live uptown, year after year try to dislodge her from her old and inconvenient house. It is, they feel nervously, much too close to Third Avenue with its swarming, staggering riffraff, and living alone as she does with only two faithful maids (one of whom is deaf) and a choreman, she would be quite defenseless if burglars came. Moreover, the fire department has condemned her house as well as many others in the block, and they shudder to think of Mrs. Ramsey's being trapped in her bedroom at the back of the second floor, far from help. There is no question about it: she would be burned in her bed. But she baffles them with what they say is a paradox. She says, "I have never liked change, and now I am too old for it." They protest, unable sometimes to keep the note of exasperation out of their voices, that change is exactly what they want to preserve her from. They predict, with statistics to back them up, that the neighborhood will go still further downhill and soon will be another Delancey Street. She returns that, while she is touched by their solicitude, she has no wish to move. She is, she thanks them, quite at home. Finally they have to give up and when they have accepted defeat with a sigh, they begin to admire her stubbornness all over again, and to say it is really heroic the way she has refused to acknowledge the death of the past. The ivory tower in which she lives is impregnable to the ill-smelling, rude-sounding, squalid-looking world which through the years has moved in closer and closer and now surrounds her on all sides. Incredibly, she has not been swallowed up. She has not gone out of her way to keep the streets in their place, but the streets have simply not dared to encroach upon her dignity. Take the matter of the smells, for example. Her visitors, stepping out of their taxis before her door, are almost overpowered by the rank, unidentifiable emanations from cellars and open windows: food smells (these people think of nothing but food) that are so strong and so foreign and so sickening that they call to mind the worst quarters of the worst Near Eastern cities. And yet, the moment the door of Mrs. Ramsey's house closes upon them, shutting out the laden atmosphere, they have forgotten the stink which a moment before they had thought unforgettable, and are aware only of aged potpourri, of lemon oil, and of desiccated lavender in linen closets.

Despite her refusal to leave her inaccessible slums, Mrs. Ramsey passes hardly a day without at least one caller, for she remains altogether charming, preserving the grace of manner and the wit that marked her at her first Assembly almost sixty years ago. She has not, that is, kept even a suggestion of her beauty. The flesh has worn away from her crooked bones and her white hair is yellowish and rather thin; she has a filmy cataract over one eye, and in her skinny little face, her large nose has an Hebraic look. Indeed, though she was famous for her looks, no one on first meeting her ever says, "She must have been a beauty in her day." It is quite impossible to reconstruct her as she might have been since there is nothing to go on; the skeleton seems quite a badly botched job, and the face has no reminder in it of a single good feature. One supposes, in the end, that she was one of those girls whose details are not independently beautiful, but who are, nevertheless, a lovely composition. General Ramsey, on the other hand, five years dead, was a handsome man at the very end of his life, and the portrait painted just before his final illness shows him to be keen-eyed, imposing, with a long, aristocratic head on a pair of military shoulders, heavily adorned.

A stranger, having heard of Mrs. Ramsey's charm, thinks when he first sees her that it must lie in a tart wit since she looks too droll, too much like a piquant chipmunk, to have a more expansive feminine elegance. But while the wit is there, bright and Edwardian, this is not the chief of her gifts. Rather, it is her tenderness and pity, her delicate and imaginative love, her purity that make her always say the right thing. She is so wise a husbandman, so economical, that her smallest dispensations and her briefest words are treasure. She has neither enemies nor critics, so that like an angel she is unendangered by brutality or by "difficult situations." Even her sorrow at her husband's death and her loneliness afterward seemed only to make sweeter her sweet life. She is an innocent child of seventy-five.

Among her friends, Mrs. Ramsey numbers many well-bred young men who, before the war, came to her house for tea or for lunch on Sunday. Now they are all in uniform and many of them are overseas, but they write to her frequently and she replies, in a wavy old-fashioned hand, on V-mail blanks. In spite of this substitution of the blanks for her own monogrammed letter paper, in spite of the military titles and the serial numbers which she copies down in the little box at the top of the page, in spite of the uniforms which she cannot help seeing in the square, and the newspapers and the War Bond drives, the blackout curtains at her windows and the buckets of sand in her fourth-floor corridor and the ration books, Mrs. Ramsey is the one person, her friends say, to whom the cliché may accurately be applied: "She does not know there is a war on." Her daughter, who is a Red Cross supervisor and who comes in uniform once a week to dine with her mother, says she is "too good to be true," that she is a perfect asylum, that in her house one can quite delude oneself into believing that this tranquillity extends far beyond her doorstep, beyond the city, throughout the world itself, and that the catastrophes of our times are only

THE CAPTAIN'S GIFT

hypothetical horrors. Her granddaughters, who are Waves, her grandson Ramsey who is an instructor in a pre-flight school, her son who manufactures precision instruments and has bought fifty thousand dollars' worth of bonds, her son-in-law, the military attaché, her daughter-in-law who works at the blood bank, all say the same thing of her. They say they frightfully pity people who cannot have a holiday from the war in her house. She continues to speak of Paris as if the only reason she does not go there is that she is too old and her health is too unsteady; she hopes that one of her favorite young men, wounded at Anzio, will enjoy Easter in Italy and she assumes that he will go to Rome to hear the Pope. She speaks of Germany and Japan as if they were still nothing more than two foreign countries of which she has affectionate memories. It is true that at times her blandness becomes trying. For example, if someone speaks of the mistakes of Versailles, she quite genuinely believes he refers to the way the flower beds are laid out in the palace gardens and she agrees warmly that they could have been ever so much nicer. But one has no business to be annoyed with her. Since there are so few years left to her (and since there is now no danger of our being bombed) it would be an unkind and playful sacrilege to destroy her illusion that the world is still good and beautiful and harmonious in all its parts. She need never know how barbarically civilization has been betrayed.

How refreshing must be her letters to the soldiers! She neither complains of their hardships nor gushes over their bravery. It must be marvelous, indeed, to know that there is someone across whose lips the phrase "the four freedoms" has never passed, someone whose vocabulary is innocent of "fascism," someone who writes calm reminiscences in her letters (even so! on the printed V-mail form!) of summer band concerts in Saratoga Springs, of winter dinner parties at the Murray Hill, which, in reality as fusty as an old trunk, she thinks is still the smartest hotel in town. Mothers of the soldiers are overjoyed: she is their link with the courtly past, she is Mrs. Wharton at first hand.

Mrs. Ramsey has written five letters to soldiers and sailors and a sixth is begun. But her eyes have started to burn, and since it is anyhow nearly time for tea, she rises from her desk and prepares to go to her bedroom to freshen up for her guests, who today will be one of her granddaughters and the fiancée of one of her young admirers. She looks down once more into the little park and thinks that it is the loveliest in the city. It reminds her of Bloomsbury Square. There she used to sit waiting for her husband while he copied out notes and lists of things in the British Museum whenever they visited London. One of his avocations, perhaps the mildest of them all, had been a study of English ballads and he kept notebooks full of their variants. Great as was her delight in his society, she was always glad when he stayed away a long time, for she loved sitting there alone, heedless of anything but the simple fact of her being there. Perhaps it is the memory of those days that now motivates her occasional afternoon in the square, for the atmosphere is just as foreign and her presence seems just as unusual as it used to be in London. The difference is that in London she had been a visitor from a distant country while here she is a visitor from a distant time. As she looks down she sees a little boy in a beret like a French sailor's. He is carrying a string shopping bag with a long loaf of bread sticking out of it. He walks beside his enormous mother who wears a red snood over a bun of hair as big as the loaf of bread in the bag. Mrs. Ramsey, for no reason, thinks how dearly she loves Europe and how sorry she is that there is no time left for her to go abroad again. If she were just a few years younger, she would be envious of the boys to whom she has been writing her letters.

She has just turned toward the door when she hears, far off, the bell at the street entrance and she makes a convulsive little gesture with her hand, afraid that the girls have come already and she is not prepared. She opens the door and waits beside it, listening, and then, hearing Elizabeth coming up the stairs alone, she steps out into the hall and calls down, "I am just going to dress, Elizabeth. Who was at the door?"

The plump middle-aged maid is deaf and she has not heard. She comes into sight on the stairs; she is carrying a parcel and, seeing her mistress, she says, "The special-delivery man brought it, Mrs. Ramsey, and I thought you would like to have it at once since it comes from overseas." She hands over the package, adding, "From Captain Cousins."

Mrs. Ramsey returns to the drawing room, saying to the

maid, "Oh, I shan't wait to open *this*! If I am late and don't have time to dress, I am sure the young ladies won't mind." The maid beams, delighted with the look of pleasure in Mrs. Ramsey's face, and retires quietly as though she were leaving a girl to read her sweetheart's letter.

The little old lady sits down on a yellow and pink striped love seat, holding the box in her hands, but she does not immediately open it. She sits remembering her grandson, Arthur Cousins, of all the young men, her favorite. He looks much as the General did as a youth and it is this resemblance, probably, that so endears him to her. She recalls him in exquisite detail and his image takes her breath away. He is as tall, as fair, as red-cheeked as a Swede. Before he went away, when he used to come to see her, he always seemed sudden and exotic, making her drawing room look dusky. Whenever she saw him and now whenever she thinks of him, she remembers, rapturously, the hot beaches of Naples, the blinding winter sun at Saint Moritz, the waves of heat rising from the gravel slope before the Pitti Palace. The sunlight he calls up is not parching but wonderfully rich and heady. His mind is as luminous as his skin and his hair; and he is so happy! She thinks of him leaning forward in his chair at a recital to watch a woman playing a lute, bending her head down to look at it with love, as if she were looking into a child's face; his lips are parted and his eyes shine. She sees him sitting beside her in church and she remembers the days when he was an altar boy. The very package that she holds seems to give off a warmth of summertime and she touches it lightly here and there with her fingertips.

Arthur, first in England, then in France and then in Italy, has sent not only countless letters to his grandmother, but presents as well. Under the General's portrait, in a Chinese chest to which she wears the key on a gold chain round her neck, the letters lie in ribbon-bound packets and so do the gifts, still in their tissue-paper wrappings. From London, he sent Irish linen handkerchiefs and heliotrope sachets and a small pink marble shepherdess; from Paris, gloves and a silver box for oddments; from Italy, a leather writing case and two paste-studded shell combs. His affectionate letters, which she reads and rereads through a magnifying glass on a mother-of-pearl handle, tell of his homesickness, of his unwillingness to be so far away from her. He writes that, on his return, they must go again, as they did on the last day of his last furlough, round Central Park in a carriage. "Only with you, my darling Grandma, is this not just a stunt," he writes. They must, he goes on, dine at the Lafayette where the *moules marinières* have been celebrated from her day until his; she must allow him to come every day to tea and must tell him stories of her girlhood. He knows that he will find her exactly the same as she was when he told her goodbye.

On the last little square photograph headed "Somewhere in Germany" he had written, "I am sending you the best present that I have found for you yet. It is something that Helena Rubinstein (as if you knew who she is!) would give a fortune for, but I'm not going to tell you what it is. I like thinking of you trying to guess as you sit there among all your lares and penates and your fresh flowers."

Mrs. Ramsey, repeating to herself the phrase "fresh flowers," regrets that she has not sent out for some lilacs, for the only things in bloom are two white African violets on the sideboard. She feels a little guilty as though she has betrayed Arthur's picture of her and she thinks of what her daughter, Arthur's mother, said at dinner last night, "With you, Arthur will not change because you are unchangeable. But in his letters to me, he is becoming more and more unrecognizable."

She had forbidden her daughter to pursue this subject: there was a hint of disloyalty in her voice, or was it a hint of fear? The whole last sentence of Arthur's letter now reechoes in her mind and a slight cloud comes over her face. She feels a touch of cold and decides that she must tell Elizabeth to lay a fire after all. When one is very old and fleshless, one is like a thermometer, registering the least change in temperature.

But the fire must wait until she has opened her present. She smiles. She knows who Helena Rubinstein is, but it pleases her that Arthur thinks she does not. Perhaps it is a bottle of some rare scent that would so much gratify both of them. The clock at St. Mark's strikes the quarter hour and she goes to her desk and brings back a pair of scissors. She is so happy that she does not any longer try to imagine what is inside; she rather hopes she has not guessed rightly, that it is not scent, that it will take her completely by surprise.

Under the outer wrappings there is a shoe box, and in the

box, a parcel in tissue paper, tied with a piece of string. It is something shapeless and, even when she has taken it out and has held it a moment in her old wrinkled hands, she cannot tell what it is. It is not a bottle and not a box or a case; it is rather heavy but its heaviness is of a curious kind: it seems to be a mass of something. She delays no longer and snips the string. There in her lap lies a braid of golden hair. At the top it is ruffled a little as though a girl, just fallen asleep, had tossed once or twice on her pillow; the rest of it is smooth, down to the end, which is tied with a little pink bow. It has been cut off cleanly at the nape of the neck, and it is so long that it must have hung below her waist. It is thick and it seems still so vital in the light that streams through the windows that Mrs. Ramsey feels its owner is concealed from her only by a vapor, that her head is here beside her on the love seat: she is hidden from Mrs. Ramsey just as Mrs. Ramsey is hidden from the people in the square.

She pushes the tissue paper with the handle of the scissors and the braid slips to the gray carpet and lies there shining like a living snake. Now the old lady clasps her hands together to end their trembling, and looking at the African violets she admits to some distant compartment of her mind the fact that they are dying and must be removed tomorrow. She speaks aloud in the empty room. "How unfriendly, Arthur!" she says. "How unkind!" And as if there were a voice in the hair at her feet, she distinctly hears him saying, "There's a war on, hadn't you heard?"

The End of a Career

B Y those of Angelica Early's friends who were given to hyperbole, she was called, throughout her life, one of the most beautiful women in the world's history. And those of more restraint left history out of their appraisal but said that Mrs. Early was certainly one of the most beautiful of living women. She had been, the legend was, a nymph in her cradle (a doting, bibulous aunt was fond, over cocktails, of describing the queenly baby's pretty bed—gilded and swan-shaped, lined with China silk of a blue that matched the infant eyes, and festooned with Mechlin caught into loops with rosettes), and in her silvery coffin she was a goddess. At her funeral, her friends mourned with as much bitterness as sorrow that such a treasure should be consigned to the eyeless and impartial earth; they felt robbed; they felt as if one of the wonders of the world had been demolished by wanton marauders. "It's wrong of God to bury His own masterpiece," said the tipsy aunt, "and if that's blasphemy, I'll take the consequences, for I'm not at all sure I want to go on living in a world that doesn't contain Angelica."

Between her alpha and omega, a span of fifty years, Mrs. Early enjoyed a shimmering international fame that derived almost entirely from the inspired and faultless *esprit de corps* of her flesh and her bones and her blood; never were the features and the colors of a face in such serene and unassailable agreement, never had a skeleton been more singularly honored by the integument it wore. And Angelica, aware of her responsibility to her beholders, dedicated herself to the cultivation of her gift and the maintenance of her role in life with the same chastity and discipline that guide a girl who has been called to the service of God.

Angelica's marriage, entered upon when she was twenty-two and her husband was ten years older, puzzled everyone, for Major Clayton Early was not a connoisseur of the complex civilization that had produced his wife's sterling beauty but was, instead, concerned with low forms of plant life, with primitive societies, and with big game. He was an accomplished

430

huntsman—alarming heads and horns and hides covered the walls of his den, together with enlarged photographs of himself standing with his right foot planted firmly upon the neck of a dead beast—and an uneducated but passionate explorer, and he was away most of the time, shooting cats in Africa or making and recording observations in the miasmas of Matto Grosso and the mephitic verdure of the Malay Peninsula. While he was away, Angelica, too, was away a good deal of the time—on islands, in Europe, upstate, down South—and for only a few months of the year were they simultaneously in residence in a professionally and pompously decorated maisonette that overlooked Central Park. When Major Early was in town, he enjoyed being host to large dinner parties, at which, more often than not, he ran off reels on reels of crepuscular and agitated movies that showed savages eating from communal pots, savages dancing and drumming, savages in council, savages accepting the white man's offerings of chewing gum and mechanical toys; there were, as well, many feet of film devoted to tarantulas, apes, termite mounds, and orchidaceous plants. His commentary was obscure, for his vocabulary was bestrewn with crossword-puzzle words. Those evenings were so awful that no one would have come to them if it had not been for Angelica; the eye could stray from a loathsome witch doctor on the screen and rest in comfort and joy on her.

Some people said that Early was a cynic and some said that he was a fool to leave Angelica unguarded, without children and without responsibility, and they all said it would serve him right if he returned from one of his safaris to find himself replaced. Why did a man so antisocial marry at all, or, if he must marry, why not take as his wife some stalwart and thick-legged woman who would share his pedantic adventures—a champion skeet shooter, perhaps, or a descendant of Western pioneers? But then, on the other hand, why had Angelica married *him*? She never spoke of him, never quoted from his letters—if there were any letters—and if she was asked where he was currently traveling, she often could not answer. The speculation upon this vacant alliance ceased as soon as Early had left town to go and join his guides, for once he was out of sight, no one could remember much about him beyond a Gallic mustache and his ponderous jokes as his movies jerked on. Indeed, so completely

was his existence forgotten that matchmakers set to work as if
Angelica were a widow.

They did not get far, the matchmakers, because, apart from
her beauty, there was not a good deal to be said about Angelica.
She had some money—her parents had left her ample provision,
and Early's money came from a reliable soap—but it was not
enough to be of interest to the extremely rich people whose
yachts and châteaux and boxes at the opera she embellished.
She dressed well, but she lacked the exclusive chic, the unique
fillip, that would have caused her style in clothes to be called *sui
generis* and, as such, to be mentioned by the press. Angelica was
hardly literate; the impressions her girlish mind had received
at Miss Hewitt's classes had been sketched rather than etched,
but she was not stupid and she had an appealing, if small and
intermittent, humor. She was not wanting in heart and she was
quick to commiserate and give alms to the halt and the lame
and the poor, and if ugliness had been a disease or a social
evil, she would, counting her blessings, have lent herself to its
extirpation. She wasn't a cat, she wasn't a flirt or a cheat, wasn't
an imbecile, didn't make *gaffes*; neither, however, alas, was she
a wit, or a catalyst, or a transgressor to be scolded and punished
and then forgiven and loved afresh. She was simply and solely
a beautiful woman.

Women, on first confronting Angelica Early, took a backward
step in alarm and instinctively diverted the attention of their
husbands or lovers to something at the opposite end of the
room. But their first impression was false, for Angelica's beauty
was an end in itself and she was the least predatory of women.
The consequence of this was that she had many women
friends, or at any rate she had many hostesses, for there was no
more splendid and no safer ornament for a dinner table than
Angelica. The appointments of these tables were often planned
round her, the cynosure, and women lunching together had
been known to debate (with their practical tongues in their
cheeks but without malice) whether Waterford or Venetian
glass went better with her and whether white roses or red
were more appropriate in juxtaposition to her creamy skin and
her luminous ash-blond hair. She was forever in demand; for
weeks before parties and benefit balls hostesses contended for

her presence; her status—next to the host—in protocol was permanent; little zephyrs of excitement and small calms of awe followed her entrance into a drawing room. She was like royalty, she was a public personage, or she was, as the aunt was to observe at her funeral, like the masterpiece of a great master. Queens and pictures may not, in the ordinary sense, have friends, but if they live up to their reputations, they will not want for an entourage, and only the cranks and the sightless will be their foes. There were some skeptics in Angelica's circle, but there were no cranks, and in speaking of her, using the superlatives that composed their native tongue, they called her adorable and indispensable, and they said that when she left them, the sun went down.

Men, on first gazing into those fabulous eyes, whose whites had retained the pale, melting blue of infancy, were dizzied, and sometimes they saw stars. But their vertigo passed soon, often immediately, although sometimes not until after a second encounter, planned in palpitations and bouts of fever, had proved flat and inconsequential. For a tête-à-tête with Angelica was marked by immediacy; she did not half disclose a sweet and sad and twilit history, did not make half promises about a future, implied the barest minimum of flattery and none at all of amorousness, and spoke factually, in a pleasant voice, without nuance and within the present tense. Someone had said that she was *sec*—a quality praiseworthy in certain wines but distinctly not delicious in so beautiful a woman. All the same, just as she had many hostesses, so she had many escorts, for her presence at a man's side gave him a feeling of achievement.

Angelica was not, that is, all façade—her eyes themselves testified to the existence of airy apartments and charming gardens behind them—but she was consecrated to her vocation and she had been obliged to pass up much of the miscellany of life that irritates but also brings about the evolution of personality; the unmolested oyster creates no pearl. Her heart might be shivered, she might be inwardly scorched with desire or mangled with jealousy and greed, she might be benumbed by loneliness and doubt, but she was so unswerving in her trusteeship of her perfection that she could not allow anxiety to pleat her immaculate brow or anger to discolor her damask cheeks or tears to deflower her eyes. Perhaps, like an artist, she was not always grateful for this talent of beauty that destiny had imposed upon her without asking leave, but, like the artist, she knew where her duty lay; the languishing and death of her genius would be the languishing and death of herself, and suicide, though it is often understandable, is almost never moral.

The world kindly imagined that Mrs. Early's beauty was deathless and that it lived its charmed life without support. If the world could have seen the contents of her dressing table and her bathroom shelves! If the world could have known the hours devoured by the matutinal ritual! Angelica and her reverent English maid, Dora, were dressed like surgeons in those morning hours, and they worked painstakingly, talking little, under lights whose purpose was to cast on the mirrors an image of ruthless veracity. The slightest alteration in the color of a strand of hair caused Angelica to cancel all engagements for a day or two, during which time a hairdresser was in attendance, treating the lady with dyes and allaying her fears. A Finn daily belabored her with bundles of birch fagots to enliven her circulation; at night she wore mud on her face and creamed gloves on her hands; her hair was treated with olive oil, lemon juice, egg white, and beer; she was massaged, she was vibrated, she was steamed into lassitude and then stung back to life by astringents; she was brushed and creamed and salted and powdered. All this took time, and, more than time, it took undying patience. So what the world did not know but what Angelica and her maid and her curators knew was that the blood that ever so subtly clouded her cheeks with pink and lay pale green in that admirable vein in her throat was kept in motion by a rapid pulse whose author was a fearful heart: If my talent goes, I'm done for, says the artist, and Angelica said, if I lose my looks, I'm lost.

So, even as she attentively lent the exquisite shell of her ear to her dinner partner, who was telling her about his visit to Samothrace or was bidding her examine with him his political views, even as she returned the gaze of a newcomer whose head was over his heels, even as she contributed to the talk about couturiers after the ladies had withdrawn, Angelica was thinking, in panic and obsession, of the innumerable details she was obliged to juggle to sustain the continuity of her performance.

Modern science has provided handsome women—and especially blondes, who are the most vulnerable—with defenses against many of their natural enemies: the sun, coarsening winds, the rude and hostile properties of foreign waters and foreign airs. But there has not yet been devised a way to bring to his knees the archfiend Time, and when Angelica began to age, in her middle forties, she went to bed.

Her reduction of the world to the size of her bedroom was a gradual process, for her wilting and fading was so slow that it was really imperceptible except to her unflinching eyes, and to Dora's, and to those of an adroit plastic surgeon to whose unadvertised sanitarium, tucked away in a rural nook in Normandy, she had retreated each summer since she was forty to be delivered of those infinitesimal lines and spots in her cheeks and her throat that her well-lighted mirror told her were exclamatory and shameful disfigurements. Such was the mystery that shrouded these trips to France that everyone thought she must surely be going abroad to establish a romantic ménage, and when she paused in Paris on her return to New York, she was always so resplendent that the guesses seemed to be incontrovertibly confirmed; nothing but some sort of delicious fulfillment could account for her subtlety, her lovely, tremulous, youthful air of secret memories. Some of her friends in idle moments went so far as to clothe this lover with a fleshy vestment and a personality and a nationality, and one of the slowly evolved myths, which was eventually stated as fact, was that he was a soul of simple origin and primal magnetism—someone, indeed, like Lady Chatterley's lover.

Angelica would suddenly appear in Paris at the beginning of September with no explanation of the summer or of that happy condition of her heart that was all but audible as a carol, and certainly was visible in her shimmering eyes and her glowing skin. She lingered in Paris only long enough to buy her winter wardrobe, to upset the metabolism of the men she met, to be, momentarily, the principal gem in the diadem of the international set, and to promise faithfully that next year she would join houseparties and cruises to Greece, would dance till dawn at *fêtes champêtres*, and would, between bullfights, tour the caves of Spain. She did not, of course, keep her promises, and the fact is that she would have disappointed her friends if she had. At these times, on the wing, it was as if she had been inoculated with the distillation of every fair treasure on earth and in heaven, with the moon and the stars, with the seas and the flowers, and the rainbow and the morning dew. Angelica was no longer *sec*, they said; they said a new dimension had brought her to life. Heretofore she had been a painted ship upon a painted ocean and now she was sailing the crests and the depths, and if her adventurous voyage away from the doldrums had come late in life, it had not come too late; the prime of life, they said, savoring their philosophy and refurbishing their cliché, was a relative season. They loved to speculate on why her lover was unpresentable. Wiseacres proposed, not meaning it, that he was a fugitive from the Ile du Diable; others agreed that if he was not Neanderthal (in one way or another) or so ignobly born that not even democracy could receive him into its generous maw—if he was not any of these things, he must be intransigently married. Or could he perhaps be one of those glittering Eastern rulers who contrived to take an incognito holiday from their riches and their dominions but could not, because of law and tradition, ever introduce Angelica into their courts? Once or twice it was proposed that Angelica was exercising scruples because of her husband, but this seemed unlikely; the man was too dense to see beyond his marriage feasts of Indians and his courtship of birds.

Who ever the lover was and whatever were the terms of their liaison, Angelica was plainly engaged upon a major passion whose momentum each summer was so forcefully recharged that it did not dwindle at all during the rest of the year. Now she began to be known not only as the most beautiful but as one of the most dynamic of women as well, and such was the general enthusiasm for her that she was credited with *mots justes* and insights and ingenious benevolences that perhaps existed only in the infatuated imaginations of her claque. How amazingly Angelica had changed! And how amazingly wrong they all were! For *not* changing had been her lifelong specialty, and she was the same as ever, only more so. Nevertheless, the sort of men who theretofore had cooled after their second meeting with her and had called her pedestrian or impervious or hollow now continued to fever and fruitlessly but breathlessly to pursue her. Often they truly fell in love with her and bitterly hated that anonymous fellow who had found the wellspring of her being.

Inevitably the news of her friends' speculations drifted back to her in hints and slips of the tongue. Angelica's humor had grown no more buxom with the passage of the years, and she was not amused at the enigma she had given birth to by immaculate conception. She took herself seriously. She was a good creature, a moral and polite woman, but she was hindered by unworldliness, and she was ashamed to be living a fiction. She was actually guilt-ridden because her summertime friend was not an Adonis from the Orient or a charming and ignorant workingman but was, instead, Dr. Fleege-Althoff, a monstrous little man, with a flat head on which not one hair grew and with the visage of a thief—a narrow, feral nose, a pair of pale and shifty and omniscient eyes, a mouth that forever faintly smiled at some cryptic, wicked jest. There was no help for it, but she was ashamed all the same that it was pain and humiliation, not bliss and glorification, that kept her occupied during her annual retreat. The fact was that she earned her reputation and her undiminishing applause and kept fresh the myth in which she moved by suffering the surface skin of her face to be planed away by a steel-wire brush, electrically propelled; the drastic pain was sickening and it lasted long, and for days—sometimes weeks—after the operation she was so unsightly that her looking glass, which, morbidly, she could not resist, broke her heart. She lay on a chaise in a darkened bedroom of that quiet, discreet sanitarium, waiting, counting the hours until the scabs that encrusted her flensed skin should disappear. But even when this dreadful mask was gone, she was still hideous, and her eyes and her mouth, alone untouched, seemed to reproach her when she confronted her reflection, as red and shining as if she had been boiled almost to death. Eight weeks later, though, she was as beautiful as she had been at her zenith, and the doctor, that ugly man, did not fail, in bidding her goodbye, to accord himself only a fraction of the credit and assign the rest to her Heavenly Father. Once, he had made her shiver when, giving her the grin of a gargoyle, he said, "What a face! Flower of the world! Of all my patients, you are the one I do not like to flail." Flail! The word almost made her retch, and she envisioned him lashing her with little metal whips, and smiling.

During the time she was at the sanitarium (a tasteful and pleasant place, but a far cry from the pastoral bower her friends imagined), she communicated with no one except her maid and with the staff, who knew her, as they knew all the other ladies, by an alias. She called herself Mrs. London, and while there was no need to go so far, she said she came from California. It was a long and trying time. Angelica had always read with difficulty and without much pleasure, and she inevitably brought with her the wrong books, in the hope, which she should long since have abandoned, that she might improve her mind; she could not pay attention to Proust, she was baffled by the Russians, and poetry (one year she brought "The Faerie Queene"!) caused her despair. So, for two and a half months, she worked at needlepoint and played a good deal of solitaire and talked to Dora, who was the only confidante she had ever had, and really the only friend. They had few subjects and most of them were solemn—the philosophy of cosmetics, the fleetingness of life. The maid, if she had a life of her own, never revealed it. Sometimes Angelica, unbearably sad that she had been obliged to tread a straight-and-narrow path with not a primrose on it, would sigh and nearly cry and say, "What have I done with my life?" And Dora, assistant guardian of the wonder, would reply, "You have worked hard, madame. Being beautiful is no easy matter." This woman was highly paid, but she was a kind woman, too, and she meant what she said.

It was Angelica's hands that at last, inexorably, began to tell the time. It seemed to her that their transfiguration came overnight, but of course what came overnight was her realization that the veins had grown too vivid and that here and there in the interstices of the blue-green, upraised network there had appeared pale freckles, which darkened and broadened and multiplied; the skin was still silken and ivory, but it was redundant and lay too loosely on her fingers. That year, when she got to the sanitarium, she was in great distress, but she had confidence in her doctor.

Dr. Fleege-Althoff, however, though he was sincerely sorry, told her there was nothing he could do. Hands and legs, he said, could not be benefited by the waters of the fountain of youth. Sardonically, he recommended gloves, and, taking him literally, she was aghast. How could one wear gloves at a dinner table? What could be more parvenu, more telltale, than to lunch in gloves at a restaurant? Teasing her further, the vile little man proposed that she revive the style of wearing mitts, and tears of pain sprang to Angelica's eyes. Her voice was almost petulant when she protested against these grotesque prescriptions. The doctor, nasty as he was, was wise, and in his unkind wisdom, accumulated through a lifetime of dealing with appearances, said, "Forgive my waggery. I'm tired today. Go get yourself loved, Mrs. London. I've dealt with women so many years that I can tell which of my patients have lovers or loving husbands and which have not—perhaps it will surprise you to know that very few of them have. Most have lost their men and come to me in the hope that the excision of crow's-feet will bring back the wanderers." He was sitting at his desk, facing her, his glasses hugely magnifying his intelligent, bitter eyes. "There is an aesthetic principle," he pursued, "that says beauty is the objectification of love. To be loved is to be beautiful, but to be beautiful is not necessarily to be loved. Imagine that, Mrs. London! Go and find a lover and obfuscate his senses; give him a pair of rose-colored glasses and he'll see your hands as superb—or, even better, he won't see your hands at all. Get loved by somebody—it doesn't matter who—and you'll get well."

"Get well?" said Angelica, amazed. "Am I ill?"

"If you are not ill, why have you come to me? I am a doctor," he said, and with a sigh he gestured toward the testimonials of his medical training that hung on the walls. The doctor's fatigue gave him an air of melancholy that humanized him, despite his derisive voice, and momentarily Angelica pitied him in his ineluctable ugliness. Still, he was no more solitary in his hemisphere than she was in hers, and quickly she slipped away from her consideration of him to her own woe.

"But even if I weren't married, how could I find a lover at my age?" she cried.

He shook his head wearily and said, "Like most of your countrywomen, you confound youth with value, with beauty, with courage—with everything. To you, youth and age are at the two poles, one positive, the other negative. I cannot tell you what to do. I am only an engineer—I am not the inventor of female beauty. I am a plastic surgeon—I am not God. All you can do now is cover your imperfections with *amour-propre*. You are a greedy woman, Mrs. London—a few spots appear on your hands and you throw them up and say 'This is the end.' What egotism!"

Angelica understood none of this, and her innocent and humble mind went round and round among his paradoxes, so savagely delivered. How could she achieve *amour-propre* when what she had most respected in herself was now irretrievably lost? And if she had not *amour-propre*, how could she possibly find anyone else to love her? Were not these the things she should have been told when she was a girl growing up? Why had no one, in this long life of hers, which had been peopled by such a multitude, warned her to lay up a store of good things against the famine of old age? Now, too late, she wrung her old-woman hands, and from the bottom of her simple heart she lamented, weeping and caring nothing that her famous eyes were smeared and their lids swollen.

At last the doctor took pity on her. He came around to her side of the desk and put his hands kindly on her shaking shoulders. "Come, Mrs. London, life's not over," he said. "I've scheduled your planing for tomorrow morning at nine. Will you go through with it or do you want to cancel?"

She told him, through her tears, that she would go through with the operation, and he congratulated her. "You'll rise from these depths," he said. "You'll learn, as we all learn, that there are substantial rewards in age."

That summer, Dr. Fleege-Althoff, who had grave problems of his own (he had a nagging wife; his only child, a son, was schizophrenic) and whose understanding was deep, did what he could to lighten Angelica's depression. He found that she felt obscurely disgraced and ashamed, as if she had committed a breach of faith, had broken a sacred trust, and could not expect anything but public dishonor. She had never been a happy woman, but until now she had been too diligent to be unhappy; the experience of unhappiness for the first time when one is growing old is one of the most malignant diseases of the heart. Poor soul! Her person was her personality. Often, when the doctor had finished his rounds, he took Angelica driving in the pretty countryside; she was veiled against the ravages of the sun and, he observed, she wore gloves. As they drove, he talked to her and endeavored to persuade her that for each of the crucifixions of life there is a solace. Sometimes she seemed to believe him.

Sometimes, believing him, she took heart simply through the look of the trees and the feel of the air, but when they had returned to the sanitarium and the sun had gone down and she was alone with her crumpled hands—with her crumpled hands and her compassionate but helpless maid—she could not remember any of the reasons for being alive. She would think of what she had seen on their drive: children playing with boisterous dogs; girls and young men on horses or bicycles, riding along the back roads; peasant women in their gardens tending their cabbages and tending their sunning babies at the same time. The earth, in the ebullience of summertime, seemed more resplendent and refreshed than she could ever remember it. Finally, she could not bear to look at it or at all those exuberant young human beings living on it, and began to refuse the doctor's invitations.

You might think that she would have taken to drink or to drugs, but she went on in her dogtrot way, taking care of her looks, remembering how drink hardens the skin and how drugs etiolate it.

That year, when Angelica arrived in Paris on her way back to New York, she was dealt an adventitious but crippling blow of mischance from which she never really recovered. She had arrived in midafternoon, and the lift in her hotel was crowded with people going up to their rooms after lunch. She had been one of the first to enter the car and she was standing at the back. At the front, separated from her by ten people or more, were two young men who had been standing in the lobby when she came into the hotel. They were Americans, effeminate and a little drunk, and one of them said to the other, "She must have been sixty—why, she could have been seventy!" His companion replied, "Twenty-eight. Thirty at the most." His friend said, "You didn't see her hands when she took off her gloves to register. They were old, I tell you. You can always tell by the hands."

Luckily for Angelica and luckily for them, the cruel, green boys got off first; as she rode up the remaining way to her floor, she felt dizzy and hot. Unused as she had been most of her life to emotion, she was embraced like a serpent by the desire to die (that affliction that most of us have learned to cope with through its reiteration), and she struggled for breath. She walked down the corridor to her room jerkily; all her resilience was gone. Immediately she telephoned the steamship line and booked the first passage home she could get. For two days, until the boat sailed, she lay motionless on her bed, with the curtains drawn, or she paced the floor, or sat and stared at her culprit hands. She saw no one and she spoke to no one except Dora, who told all the friends who called that her mistress was ill.

When these friends returned from Europe, and others from the country, they learned, to their distress and puzzlement, that Angelica was not going out at all, nor was she receiving anyone. The fiction of her illness, begun in Paris, gained documentation and became fact, until at last no one was in doubt: she had cancer, far too advanced for cure or palliation; they assumed she was attended by nurses. Poor darling, they said, to have her love affair end this way! They showered her with roses, telephoning their florists before they went out to lunch; they wrote her tactful notes of sympathy, and it was through reading these that she guessed what they thought was the reason for her retirement.

The maisonette seemed huge to her, and full of echoes; for the first time since she had married, she began to think about her husband and, though he was a stranger, to long for his return. Perhaps he could become the savior Fleege-Althoff had told her to seek. But she was not strong enough to wait for him. The drawing room was still in its summer shrouds; the umbrageous dining room was closed. At first, she dined in the library, and then she began to have dinner on a tray in her bedroom, sitting before the fire. Soon after this, she started keeping to her bedroom and, at last, to her bed, never rising from it except for her twice-daily ritualistic baths. Her nightdresses and bed jackets were made by the dressmaker she had always used to supplement her Paris wardrobe; she wore her jewels for the eyes of her maid and her masseuse—that is, she wore earrings and necklaces, but she never adorned her hands. And, as if she were dying in the way they thought, she wrote brave letters to her friends, and sometimes, when her loneliness became unbearable, she telephoned them and inquired in the voice of an invalid about their parties and about the theater, though she did not want to hear, but she refused all their kind invitations to come and visit, and she rang off saying, "Do keep in touch."

For a while, they did keep in touch, and then the flowers came less and less often and her mail dwindled away. Her panic gave way to inertia. If she had been able to rise from her bed, she would have run crying to them, saying, "I was faithful to your conception of me for all those years. Now take pity on me—reward me for my singleness of purpose." They would have been quick to console her and to laugh away her sense of failure. (She could all but hear them saying, "But my dear, how absurd! Look at your figure! Look at your face and your hair! What on earth do you mean by killing yourself simply because of your hands?") But she had not the strength to go to them and receive their mercy. They did not know and she could not tell them. They thought it was cancer. They would never have dreamed it was despair that she groped through sightlessly, in a vacuum everlasting and black. Their flowers and their letters and their telephone calls did not stop out of unkindness but out of forgetfulness; they were busy, they were living their lives.

Angelica began to sleep. She slept all night and all day, like a cat. Dreams became her companions and sleep became her food. She ate very little, but she did not waste away, although she was weakened—so weakened, indeed, that sometimes in her bath she had attacks of vertigo and was obliged to ring for Dora. She could not keep her mind on anything. The simplest words in the simplest book bewildered her, and she let her eyes wander drowsily from the page; before she could close the book and set it aside, she was asleep.

Just before Christmas, the drunken aunt, Angelica's only relative, came back to town after a lengthy visit to California. She had not heard from Angelica in months, but she had not been alarmed, for neither of them was a letter writer. The first evening she was back, she dined with friends and learned from them of her niece's illness; she was shocked into sobriety and bitterly excoriated herself for being so lazy that she had not bothered to write. She telephoned the doctor who had taken care of Angelica all her life and surprised him by repeating what she had heard—that the affliction had been diagnosed as cancer. At first, the doctor was offended that he had not been called in, and then, on second thought, he was suspicious, and he urged the aunt to go around as soon as she could and make a report to him.

The aunt did not warn Angelica that she was coming. She arrived late the next afternoon, with flowers and champagne and, by ill chance, a handsome pair of crocheted gloves she had picked up in a shop in San Francisco. She brought, as well, a bottle of Scotch, for her own amusement. The apartment was dark and silent, and in the wan light the servants looked spectral. The aunt, by nature a jovial woman—she drank for the fun of it—was oppressed by the gloom and went so quickly through the shadowy foyer and so quickly up the stairs that she was out of breath when she got to the door of Angelica's room. Dora, who had come more and more to have the deportment of a nurse, opened the door with nurselike gentleness and, seeing that her patient was, for a change, awake, said with nurselike cheer, "You have company, madame! Just look at what Mrs. Armstrong has brought!" She took the flowers to put in water and the champagne to put on ice, and silently left the room.

The moment Angelica saw her aunt, she burst into tears and held out her arms, like a child, to be embraced, and Mrs. Armstrong began also to cry, holding the unhappy younger woman in her arms. When the hurricane was spent and the ladies had regained their voices, the aunt said, "You must tell me the whole story, my pet, but before you do, you must give me a drink and open your present. I do pray you're going to like them—they are so much *you*."

Angelica rang for glasses and ice, for the Scotch, and then she undid the ribbon around the long box. When she saw what was inside, all the blood left her face. "Get out!" she said to her aunt, full of cold hatred. "Is that why you came—to taunt me?"

Amazed, Mrs. Armstrong turned away from a book she had

been examining on a table in the window and met her niece's angry gaze.

"*I* taunt you?" she cried. "Why, darling, are you out of your mind? If you don't like the gloves, I'll give them to someone else, but don't—"

"Yes, do that! Give them to some young beautiful girl whose hands don't need to be hidden." And she flung the box and the gloves to the floor in an infantile fury. Twisting, she bent herself into her pillows and wept again, heartbrokenly.

By the end of the afternoon, Mrs. Armstrong's heart was also broken. She managed, with taste and tact, aided by a good deal of whisky, to ferret out the whole story, and, as she said to her dinner companion later on, it was unquestionably the saddest she had ever heard. She blamed herself for her obtuseness and she blamed Major Early for his, and, to a lesser extent, she blamed Angelica's friends for never realizing that they, with their constant and superlative praise of her looks, had added to her burden, had forced her into so conventual a life that she had been removed from most of experience. "The child has no memories!" exclaimed Mrs. Armstrong, appalled. "She wouldn't know danger if she met it head on, and she certainly wouldn't know joy. We virtually said to her, 'Don't tire your pretty eyes with looking at anything, don't let emotion harm a hair of your lovely head.' We simply worshipped and said, 'Let us look at you, but don't you look at us, for we are toads.' The ghastly thing is that there's nothing to be salvaged, and even if some miracle of surgery could restore her hands to her, it would do no good, for her disillusion is complete. I think if she could love anyone, if that talent were suddenly to come to her at this point in her life, she would love her ugly man in Normandy, and would love him *because* he was ugly."

When Angelica had apologized to her aunt for her tantrum over the gloves, she had then got out of bed and retrieved them and, in the course of her soliloquy, had put them on and had constantly smoothed them over each finger in turn as she talked.

She was still wearing the gloves when Dora came in to run her evening bath and found that her heart, past mending, had stopped.

OTHER STORIES

And Lots of Solid Color

THE blessed night had passed and it was once more cool, hazy morning. Marie woke slowly and peacefully. As usual, she thought of staying there, sleeping all day long, half conscious of the smell of the lily field next door, drowsily aware only of the cool blue daylight, flowers, trees, the sound of the neighbor's mother cat as she mewed softly at the admirers of her kittens. If she stayed in bed she could avoid the endless hours of anxiety, of waiting for the Western Union messenger who had no reason whatever to come, of waiting for a telephone call although no one on the whole of the Pacific coast knew her, of trying in vain to make a new, clean daydream out of the few desiccated hopes she had left. But though these daily expectations were plucked out of nothing or out of the nebulous belief that "this can't go on forever, something has to happen, either good or bad" and from them she could extract no sure hopes but only the feeling of continual waiting, waiting, waiting, until she wanted to scream, still there was one sure thing: the mail delivery at nine. Today something might come. It was Saturday. If there were nothing, then it might mean that the letters would accumulate over Sunday during which time one was suspended, not really waiting, hardly breathing, just suspended, and that on Monday morning there would be a neat little pile of fat envelopes before her coffee cup.

Against her will, she listened, straining, to the sound in the other part of the house. Presently the clock struck nine. That was a good sign. Her father would just be going for the mail now. If it had struck ten, it would have meant that he had gone and had come back with nothing because if ever there were a letter and she was sleeping too long, her mother came in and sat on the edge of the bed saying brightly, "You have some mail, baby." And then she would read the return addresses. One from Harry, one from the agency, one from the school in Galveston. *Thank you for letting us consider you. Your qualifications are excellent but we have chosen a young woman from Cornell who has specialized in speech. I sincerely hope that you will soon find a position which will do justice to your record.*

There were still four schools to be heard from and in addition there was the job as photographer's model she had applied for through the want-ad section of the newspaper. Surely that would bring an answer. It must bring an answer. It has to, God, Mary, Jesus, all of you. Somehow a Hail Mary seemed silly in the morning when you were so conscious of your body—the foul taste in your mouth, the need for coffee, the sleepiness of your muscles, and the tangles in your hair. At night, though, after you got through the "Star light, star bright," the black magic part, then a Hail Mary seemed perfectly reasonable. Oh, tower of ivory, Mary most bountiful, house of divine love, intercede with thy son, the blessed fruit of thy womb. But maybe the "star light, star bright," pagan as it was, counteracted the prayer. These days she walked in fear and doubt. Her old sins, her lies, her blasphemies flowed back upon her and reminded her that she was the chief of sinners, and it was fatuous to suppose for one moment that Mary, most chaste, would be interested.

She heard the front door. Her father returning? About this time special delivery letters might come . . . Quickly she got up and put on her huaraches. The leather on the inside was cool and smooth. She thought of the day she had bought them in the market place in Mexico City and her sister had held her nose when they got back to the hotel because the leather smelled like very strong cheese.

The door to the bathroom that opened into the dining room was ajar. She walked across the floor softly and looked out. There was nothing on the dining room table but an open book and her breakfast dishes. Her father was reading the newspaper in the living room. He had gone and had come back and *there was no mail*. Her heart that had been beating violently thudded dully once and then resumed its normal pulse. She brushed her teeth, busied herself for a long time so that her father would be gone when she came out. This morning she could not hear it if he said, "Well, we'll be riding in a Packard pretty soon if I sell this article. I'll buy a farm and then we won't have to worry about teaching jobs. You can just read and write all the time." All my life, all my life, all my life I've heard those same words, *well, pretty soon we'll be riding in a Packard*.

Johnny would have been gone to the paper mill for hours.

She paused in brushing her hair, remembering the time he had come back, almost crying from the lime-burns on his hands and face. If you stop whatever you are doing for one intense second, then the pain goes and afterward you can think about your own troubles. It is too much to think about the whole family at once: Evelyn gradually losing her job in the Indian service. *Honest Harold says we must be replaced by Indians,* Martha not being able to afford a cook for the haying season, baking bread in the hot mornings . . . *oh, I would love to live on a western ranch. Your sister is so fortunate.*

Her mother and aunt sat down at the table for a second cup of coffee. She looked through the want-ads. The same ones as every other day: stenographer, cook, beauty operator. Nothing for a college graduate, no food for them, hell, no, they could eat their education, live on words as her father had done all his life. *As long as I have Mommsen's History of Rome to read, I don't have to give way to lugubrious worry.* In the section "Unclaimed Answers to Want-Ads" there was her letter listed about the posing job. Unclaimed. Not even a consideration. She was too sick to say anything, but there was no need. She knew her mother had already seen, knew that the whole household had been watching that section furtively all week. But there were still those four schools. The third week in August and she still hoped! Knowing that appointments must have been made, knowing everything, *but still hoping!*

As if she were merely making small talk, as if it didn't really matter, as if there were no emotion behind it and no last minute daydreams, she said, "Mother, if I should get the job in El Paso, I'd probably have to have bedding. They usually don't furnish it in dormitories."

Her mother did not change expression. She did not laugh and did not wince. Perceptibly, at least, she didn't. Out of the corner of her eye, Marie looked at her aunt, the dried old spinster who could talk only of the people back home in Nebraska where she had lived all her life taking care of Grandmother and now that Grandmother was dead, she had come to complicate everything even further. There was nothing left in that old body, nothing beautiful in the old mind, nothing ugly either, just something that was old and crippled and pathetic. Marie told herself that she should be glad at least that she was young and firm and whole. She told herself that it was wrong to talk of Berlin and Paris and New York in front of Aunt Eva who had nothing but her dreadful complexes about snakes and water and fires to talk about. She looked full at her fat, rosy mother who could live in Berlin with her because they were of a piece, and even though her mother yearned, still she was not really envious, not really sickened.

"Well, you could borrow some money before you went down. Somewhere, you certainly could. With a salary like that you could have everything. Oh, I hope you get it!"

"If I get it, I'm going to make El Paso the place where I live always. I'm tired of moving around. It's a nice town."

"Marie and Evelyn went down there one summer," explained her mother to Aunt Eva. "They went on down into the interior of Mexico. That's where my mesquite-wood bread plate came from."

Aunt Eva smiled wanly and drank some more coffee.

"I loved Mexico," said Marie.

"So did I. When your father and I went down there, I smuggled a serape out on my bustle. Have I told you about that?"

It was merely a rhetorical question. The story was one of the oldest in the family tradition. She did not tell it over again. Marie was aware that she and her mother must seem, to Aunt Eva, to be children of fortune because they had been outside of America, to Canada and Mexico and Europe, and it sounded wonderful to say, "My sister Evelyn teaches in Alaska." It *sounded* lovely if you didn't know about what she did besides teaching . . . acting as midwife to the natives, helping to build coffins, de-lousing the heads of the children.

"If I should get it, I would buy a piece of land in Mexico. I'd have an adobe house like that one we had in Santa Fe, Mother, with lots of solid color pottery dishes and Mexican blue glassware."

But the day went on. The clock struck as the slow hours crawled past into the nomailatall territory of Sunday. *I would have an adobe house like the one we had in Santa Fe.* All day she heard her father at his typewriter in the basement. *I think I'll write a review of Das Kapital for the Saturday Review of Literature.* But, Dad, they don't take things like that. *How about the New Yorker?* What can I say, Mother, when he makes such statements? *We'll be riding in a Packard pretty soon now.* For fifteen years (or was it fifty?) they had been hearing that. *The trouble with these damned editors is that they are afraid of new ideas. Vague? I'm vague, am I? They're afraid of new ideas, that's it. They won't take the penalty imposed on them by accepting real thought. Hell, yes, it's hard to get. Vague. Hell.* His flesh was melting away as he sat hour after hour at his typewriter quarrelling with Marx and Roosevelt, Christ and hundreds of others grouped into the general category of "abstractionists." His eyes were red from strain behind glasses that were wrong and could not be replaced.

She read the newspaper, wondering idly how much longer America would be able to get along with Miss Shirley Temple as dictator of the nation's culture. She listened to the radio, walked around the house and spoke to the white cat next door. The cat was not interested. At first it was skittish, then bored, then it stalked off, oblivious of her cooing which she had thought was positively hypnotic. Aunt Eva came out to hang up her corset on the clothesline.

"Don't the cat like you?"

"I guess not."

"Just like the colleges, ain't it?"

She laughed with her little withered face not showing any sign. Gaunt and stoop-shouldered she stood by the post and looked down at Marie sitting on the grass. Whatever it was, that brutal disappointment, that dryness coming from restricted experience, whatever it was that at the breakfast table had seemed old and pathetic now seemed old and unkind, envious and mean. *I would have an adobe house where my friends could come to stay for months and months and we would drink wine and laugh and we would have the kind of potatoes that are mentioned in* The Past Recaptured, *"as firm as Japanese ivory buttons" in solid color pottery dishes. My beautiful friends, happy and rich, not worried.*

In the afternoon she sat at the dining room table playing solitaire. *Passing the time, passing the time, for what, for what. Red jack on the black queen, maybe I will win it this time, if I win all kinds maybe it will mean that I will get a letter tonight. Not tonight. Nothing comes at night but Pacific coast mail. Air mail, yes, that comes too. Yesterday there was an airmail from*

Harry. *Father had a cocktail party at the club yesterday for my cousin who is leaving for London. I was very nostalgic for England . . . I hope your complacence continues . . .* As black is never white, so am I never complacent. What did he mean? Complacence? Ace of hearts and the deuce is in the deck. Seven of clubs, nine of diamonds, here it is, deuce of hearts. Yes, no, a letter, oh, please, please, I want the adobe house so much. Aunt Eva sat down opposite her and began to play. The game did not come out. It was perhaps the presence of someone else. You couldn't be too careful about the little things, the particular tone in which you said Star light, star bright, the particular position of humility you assumed for the Hail Mary, the perfect circumstances for playing solitaire. She went into the living room and sat on the floor playing again. Over the radio came the crisp voice of a Washington news commentator, "European diplomats expressed the belief that if Europe can get through the month of August, there will not be a general war for at least another year." The news commentator was unaware that he spoke in symbols. "If Marie Charles gets through the month of August and gets a job, there will not be a repetition of this distress for at least another year." It is always the nation that seems to be poor or unhappy, never the people in the nation. That is why there are so many communists. There are a lot in Harvard. Oh, hell, Harvard! It costs, God, let me see, how much does it cost to go to Harvard? An enormous sum. Yes, I went to the University of Berlin for one year. I was in Italy for five weeks, staying at the best hotels. How nice. How interesting. If you can go to Europe you must have some money somewhere. *Dear Marie, it is not that we are asking for the money you borrowed, but we feel that you ought to be financially independent. Can't you get a job, just any kind? You are such an impractical dreamer.* Her mother had said, "Once I asked Johnny if he had ever gone hungry when he came out here before we did, and he said, 'oh, I missed a few meals now and then.'" As I was riding in a gondola, my brother was going hungry in Portland. Did he stay in a flop house, Mother? I guess so, what's a flop house? I don't know exactly, it's horrible, it's where you get a bed for a dime or something like that. Yes, he stayed in those places. It would have been better if he had gone on and got his master's degree. Oh, I don't know, Mother, look at me. But he loved working in the seed laboratory. I know. There isn't anything I don't know, Mother, except how to get a job. But you wait. When I get the adobe house, we'll all be happy there and we'll build a laboratory for Johnny . . . lime-burns on his face and arms and hands and he used to wear a white laboratory coat.

Aunt Eva went into her bedroom and closed the door sharply. Marie went back to the table. Then she heard the bathroom doors closing. Why are there three? If you're in a hurry, her mother had said, you won't want to stop to lock three doors. It seems so silly. It won't be like that in my adobe house. And there will be lots of bathrooms and bright solid color bathtowels. Don't you like solid colors, orange and yellow and red and blue? Oh, I love them!

Aunt Eva thrust her head out the door. "Tell your mother she'll have to come fix the toilet, will you, Marie? It's stuck again." She was conscious of those little old eyes watching her. What was she looking at this time? She went out to the porch where her mother was peeling the potatoes. *Your hair is so white, Mother, let me brush it sometime.* Then she went back to the table and started her game over again. There was a long, hushed conference in the bathroom. The door to Aunt Eva's room shut again. Her mother came out.

"Aunt Eva says you don't like to sit at the same table with her."

"Oh, Mother! That's not true. I went in there to listen to the radio."

"I know. She's so sensitive. I told her it was just silly. She was crying the other night about the same thing. It's ridiculous. I told her she was just silly."

"What else did she say?"

"Oh, nothing. She's so afraid of being alone, though. She says if you get that adobe house then you won't want her. She's afraid she won't have any home."

"It's not that. Oh, Lord, I'm not going to get the house *ever.* You can tell her that if it'll make her feel any better."

"She's never had anything. It's hard for her to listen to you talk about New York and everything. But don't you worry."

"Oh, I *know.*"

Sunday passed. She read *Vincent Van Gogh* and when she came to the part about the yellow house in Arles, she closed her eyes for a while and thought about the Mexican blue glassware on the orange linen table cloth, the little firm potatoes, her friends laughing over their wine and saying, "Marie, tell us about the time you didn't get met in Paris. We love that story." A little adobe house, long and low and bright. Orange teacups in blue saucers and red candlewick spreads for the beds.

On Monday she woke early. It was the fourth week in August. On Monday usually there was something, sometimes just a card from Jane in Europe or Harry writing about whom he had seen at what Chicago bar. Not that she was envious of that, no, bars were just dull and stupid now, but if you could go around to them, it meant that you had some money and you could be carefree about spending it. She lay wide awake for a few minutes, waiting for the clock to strike. Then she felt drowsy again and went back to sleep and dreamed that Harry was waiting for her in the living room and saying, darling, the velvet cape is lovely.

"It's something from El Paso." Her mother sat down on the bed.

Marie's hands fumbled as she opened the envelope. "Pray, Mother, pray *hard*."

"We are sorry to inform you . . ."

She lay back and closed her eyes.

"I think I'll stay in bed for a while. I'm not hungry yet."

The door closed. She heard Aunt Eva come into the kitchen. "Any luck?"

"Shh!" said her mother, "No."

Aunt Eva laughed, a little tight silly giggle. She wouldn't be opening her mouth. "Sometimes it don't pay to have a college education after all," she said, "what'll she do now? That velvet cape she got in Paris on her borrowed money ain't going to do her much good. She can't *milk* it!" The giggle was louder this time, exultant in a way. "I feel so good this morning. I can be content with just having some place to stay. I don't have to have a velvet cape and a trip to Europe to be happy. No, I don't."

Oh, God, I would have let her stay in the adobe house. Didn't you understand?

A Reunion

L IKE cooled-off lovers meeting again after a long separation, we were excessively courteous. We plied our interrogations with a well-bred inattention to their answers and we diligently observed all those amenities which are calculated to tame a difficult encounter. My father's letter (his calligraphy, I had noted, had neither become less neat nor more mature) had not stated his reason for inviting me to visit him. Moreover, in my reply, I had not told him why I was accepting, and I concluded that we were each activated by no more than curiosity, as the lovers would be, to know what alterations the years had accomplished in the other.

I learned that for seven years my father had, as usual, done a little reading, been occasionally ill, entertained a few guests, and had largely spent his time gardening. He learned that I had had an equal share of bad and good luck. Throughout the first hour of our reunion, coinciding happily (and by no means accidentally) with dinner, we exchanged, like the calling cards of strangers, the names of his guests and the names of the places where I had lived. We pursued the recent tributaries of our lives and never once returned to seek the old meanderings of our mutual experience.

Proud of his garden and because there was a full moon that night, my father took me out after our coffee to show me the gladiolas and the dahlias which had commenced to bloom a week or so before. As he stooped amongst them to caress their petals, I noticed for the first time that he was an old man. Livid and sharp as one of his trees in winter, his large and noble nose and his insistent cheekbones had been uncovered nearly to the skeleton, yet, elsewhere, particularly in the hands that quivered as they reached toward the flowers, the skin was too ample an integument and stood up in limp ridges over the bones. He was a small man. Now he seemed even smaller, and he had dried up everywhere save in his brown eyes. He was like one of the bearded weeds that every summer invaded his garden; had I touched his skin, I thought, I would have found it harsh like the hollyhock leaf. Into his voice, which had always been half an octave higher than a man's should be, there had crept the note of senility's sour protestations. Yet, in a sense, he looked exactly as he had when I last saw him: his seven static years had done no more than reinforce what had been there all along.

It was here that I had seen him last. I had told him goodbye while he pruned the rhododendrons. Then, I had longed to confirm our kinship by some gesture which, no matter how brief, would unite us for its duration: a look, perceiving me at last from the eyes that benevolently studied the shrub and shears, a clasp of the hands that tenderly ministered to the leaves and blossoms, or a word from the mouth that an hour ago had elegantly and incisively said, "Of course you may stay as long as you like. It is your privilege." I had come out to him, believing that the crisis had not been reached yet, that there was still time to deflect the catastrophe. But he did not look up, and the stretch of grass between us seemed unnavigable. As I stared at him stupidly, a naive tear in either eye, I realized that my misery was gauche for I knew that my father did not see our estrangement in the heroic dimensions that I did. And so I had turned at last and facing the house, my back to him, had said, "Well, goodbye." Before he echoed me, I heard, several times, the snip of his shears and the rustling of the rhododendron leaves.

We moved tonight from shrub to shrub and from the bed of zinnias to the rose-bushes, and he murmured that he hoped I was not bored, although he knew I was not interested in flowers ("something, as you remember," he said, "I never understood in you"), but that it was his habit to spend half an hour in the garden every evening after dinner. An abrupt movement in the grass unnerved my citied feet and I asked my father if there were snakes here still.

"Of course," he laughed. "One wouldn't want one's garden to be incomplete. Besides, they kill the spiders."

We slowly approached the far end of the garden where his splendid azaleas were planted and the japonica and where three mountain ash trees dropped their scarlet globules on to my mother's grave. Our advance, deliberate and silent like that of acolytes toward the sanctuary, enclosed us in a parenthesis whose solemnity, for me, was trumped-up, and I, to demolish the ambiguity of my role, said lightly, "How the ash trees have flourished."

"Yes. The soil here welcomes anything. John Stuart, whom you may remember, was surprised when he came to visit me some years ago, at my choice of decoration for this part of the garden. 'Red?' says he. 'And something so foreign to us? I'd thought you would plant junipers.' And still, when I had explained my reason to him, he had to agree that I'd been right. You recall the reason? That she loved this special red? I have no doubt other friends of mine have wondered, but they've been too tactful to enquire."

"Too tactful?"

"Why, yes, to be sure. Isn't that a kind of tact? To speak as little as possible of the dead to the bereft?"

He had stopped some paces from the gravestone and had turned away from me to pluck a dying leaf from an azalea plant, but I knew that his face, in spite of the changes of age, wore an expression of anger and yet of satisfaction that I had seen so often from the earliest days of my childhood. For, adroitly, he had trapped me into revealing for the millionth time, my ignorance (he had, seven years ago, called it my "willful ignorance") of his grief which, like a precious flower, had under his care become immortal, as fresh, as faultless as on the day she died and I was born. And yet, he liked to coax a canker to its immaculate petals to cherish them the more when he had cleansed them. Just as he was pulling off the limp yellowing leaf from the azalea, gently, so as not to disturb the delicate living tissues of the plant, so he was removing my careless blight from his heart's rose.

He was reluctant to leave the garden and in that hallowed place—for every flower and tree and bush was dedicated like the appointments of an altar—we would not quarrel, not even in lowered voices and not even in the language so shrewdly civil we had used, on the other occasion, to deceive the servants who might be eavesdropping. It occurred to me, seeing him delay our return to the house by examining the soil about the olean-ders and rambling thoughtfully about the lily pond, consuming more than half an hour in an aimless survey of his consecrated grove, that if he were able to predict me better, he would like to prolong my stay; for who but I could so often and yet so

impotently threaten his exquisite obsession? Whose guilt was so
ineradicable? And I wondered if this was why he had written me
after so many years: a curiosity to know if I *had* become more
predictable, and if he could now check me before I had gone
too far. He had been careful to name no term for my visit. At
any moment, he might say, as he had done before, "Of course
you may stay as long as you like, but surely you are intelligent
enough to see that we can never be at peace with one another."

"I have put a new floor in the summer house," he said. "Perhaps you would like to see it. If I remember rightly, the summer
house was all you really cared about in my little garden." He
smiled beseechingly at me like the great lady deprecating her
"little house" to her poor cousins. Indeed, I had liked the summer house and had often played there, for it was the only place
in the garden where I was not haunted by my mother's ghost
and by the slumbrous fragrance of my father's offerings to her.
One day I had marked with brilliant blue paint the diamonds
patterned on the floor by the sunlight coming through the
lattice work. Now my marks, made with an enamel advertised
as indelible, were gone.

We sat down on the circular bench, my father gazing out the
doorway in the direction of the gravestone, a slab of marble beneath whose ivory surface a clouded rosiness showed through.
He spoke almost to himself, "No, of course you wouldn't
remember John Stuart." I did not contradict him, though I
perfectly recalled his gaunt and sentimental friend who had
come, fifteen years before, at the time my mother's skeleton
was transferred from the graveyard to the garden. Evening after
evening, I heard their low voices behind the closed door of the
library. One night, they walked along the terrace below my
windows and I heard John Stuart say, "What a saint you are!"
And once, when, at my father's request, I had set out before
them glasses and a decanter of brandy, he said, "She is the
image of her mother." There was a precise moment of silence,
and then my father said, "I am thinking of hiring a tutor. Her
Latin is very bad." His voice was even and remote with distaste.

"I noticed this evening at dinner," he said, "that your hair
seems a little darker." I did not miss the satisfaction in his
words. Anything that made me unlike my mother called forth
his secret admiration. As always before, I blushed and quickly

diverted his attention from my appearance. "Your new floor is handsome," I said.

"Oh, yes," he said starting. "Yes, it will do very well." As he bent over to look at it, a large black bug scuttled across the floor and stopped near his foot. I saw him shudder and lift his foot to crush it, but he did not. "A spider," he said. "We have a great many of them at this time of year. Some are poisonous." He continued to gaze at it and in a moment slowly lifted his foot again and brought it down lightly, "Not to make a mess," he whispered. I heard a brittle cracking and my father said, "Oh, what a pity. It wasn't a spider, only a harmless beetle."

He had not killed it. The creature struggled with a frenzied energy and worked itself onto its back, then tossed and labored to right itself, waving weary legs, straightening and flexing them, pausing and wildly fluttering them again. It gained a little and lay upon its side, shuttered a mangled wing, and helplessly rolled over on its back.

"It's not dead," I said. "Hadn't you better kill it?"

His smile was mutilated by the moonlight. It was at once inquiring and patronizing. He said, "Why?"

"I don't know. Only perhaps it's suffering."

"Let me allow you to complete the murder," he said, and as I stood up and started to move towards the dying bug, he added, "I couldn't step on it again myself. The shell cracking under my foot gave me a horrible feeling that I was breaking human bones."

"Then I can't *now*!" I cried. I returned to my place. For some time we remained there, watching the beetle's noiseless fit; it seemed hours later that a sudden darkness passed over the floor of the summer house and my father sprang to his feet with a cry. But immediately himself again, as though he had not uttered it, as though the sound were as unconnected with us as the distant hoot of an owl, he said, "You must excuse me. I go to bed early, though I don't sleep. Feel free to stay as long as you like. I can send a lantern out to you."

He lighted a lantern he had taken down from the shelf above the bench and his face, illumined briefly, revealed no more than had his voice, the dismay that had made him cry out.

"No, thank you," I said. "The moon will come out again. I can see without it anyhow."

I followed him out the door and lay down upon the grass. I leaned on my elbow and watched him pass through the opening in the hedge. His lantern's arc caricatured him as a ghost out-of-joint; his head was peaked by the phenomenon of the light and in place of arms, two narrow wings listlessly swung while the fattened torso wambled. The sad light diminished and was absorbed. The moon shone forth again and in its light, as I turned and leaned upon the other elbow, I could see the beetle on the floor of the summer house still pitching in its morbid dance. I lay back upon the grass and seemed to fall into the depths of the earth with a forcible weariness and closed my eyes and, perhaps for a few minutes, dozed. Then, suddenly confused as one whose dream of last night contradicts or corresponds to today's facts, it occurred to me that the beetle actually was dead and had been from the first and that the changeable moon's ruffling chiaroscuro had misled us. I went into the summer house and stooping down, saw that some time since, its life arrested, death had chosen for its final attitude that of a human foetus with curved thorax protected by the folded, tattered wings. I left it in its desolate repose and as I passed through the garden on my way to the house, I shook the lowest branch of the middle mountain ash tree so that in the silence, the crimson fruit, soft as it was, made a faint sound as it fell on the gravestone.

The Home Front

IN the back yard of the lodging house, in the top of a dead tree, glib blackbirds swung in the wind on their individual twigs. Now and again, at some signal, they dropped to the ground but presently returned in a flutter of wings. Then the fancy would strike them to clear the tree, every man jack of them and off they would go like a whole company of hysterical busybodies. All the while they were fussing, big silver gulls sailed at their ease, high above them, descending occasionally to sit on the edge of a moored fishing boat that slowly turned round and round at the head of the little harbor. Some of the gulls set out to sea, as straight and sure in their flight as though a great hand carried them out beyond the causeway to the Sound. A savage sunset ignited the windows of defense plants across the water, caused derelict heaps of rubbish to glitter blindingly, smote the khaki wings of helicopters which all day long gyrated over the disheveled land.

Although it was late in April and the day had been warm, the room was chilly and the stout doctor, shivering, drew the heavy Paisley shawl closer about his shoulders, sighed, and settled more firmly into the rocking chair by the window. Steadfastly he stared out. It would be self-indulgent to turn away in displeasure from all the symbols he read in his prospect, unprofitable to admit the intrusion of homesickness or vexation. (He had, of necessity, come to this twilight discipline; in days past he had been so imprudent in his revery that he had often lost all perspective and had thought of the war as a deliberate insult to himself.) And, indeed, it was not so much sad or vexing as it was puzzling that he, a homeless man, native of a distant country, was willy-nilly a part of the "home front," sharing richly in the spoils. As he followed the ascent of a helicopter, he marveled as frequently he did at the wonderful aptness of the phrase, "the home front." Here people lived as headily and impermanently as soldiers on battlefields. There seemed to be no natives unless the babies born here during this long pause could be called such. No indigenous architecture was visible. Probably it existed but it was hidden away behind blocks of temporary structures, by barrack-like apartment houses, sprawling into the yards of churches, huddling in the sulphurous shadows of factories. And although everything was new, made freshly for this especial period in the world's history, it had a second-hand look. Houses, oil drums, buses, people seemed to have been got at a fire sale.

There was a perpetual stirring in the lodging house. All the other tenants were defense workers, and the walls of the corridors were hung with warning pennants: "QUIET! BULLARD WORKER! HELP HIM HELP WIN THE WAR!" At the most unseemly hours—eleven at night, four in the morning—alarm clocks shrieked, taps gushed, feet crunched over the gravel of the driveway to the never ending stream of buses. The lodgers ranged from late adolescence to early senility and they came from all over the country, from Harrisburg, Pennsylvania; Pueblo, Colorado; Mobile; Galveston; Wilmington, Delaware. They lived three to a room and six to a bathroom and because there were so many of them and their existence was so migratory, it was impossible to tell them apart, to give them more specific designations than "old" and "young," "male" and "female." Dr. Pakheiser from time to time received bits of information about them from the Hungarian manageress, Mrs. Horvath. She tossed them to him, dry and meatless, and did so without the least good humor. On the first floor there was (or had been) a Sikorsky worker who owned a fishing boat and on Sundays went to the Sound for bass. A lady accountant at Remington Arms had left her electric grill on for six hours and the pan that had been on it melted down to nothing, creating a fearful stink. A foreman at the Brunner Ritter plant had been rejected by the Army for ulcers of the stomach. A girl at Chance Vought had, returning from a weekend in Massachusetts, seen a trainload of prisoners of war passing through the station in Providence and she had reported that they grinned shamelessly as if they were on a holiday. But the doctor did not know whether these adventures belonged to current tenants or to former ones, and if he had inquired further and had correctly assigned the histories to the right names and faces, it would have served no purpose; by the time he was sure of his ground, they would have packed up their suitcases and moved away and immediately been replaced.

He was sympathetic with their restlessness but sternly held himself detached from it. Had he not done so, he, too, probably would have wandered from one boarding house to the next like a sick person constantly shifting about in his bed trying to find a comfortable position for his aching bones. Refusing to think of himself as a "transient," pretending that there would never be an end to the war or to this exile, he had put up with the chilliness of the house, the unpleasant manner of the manageress, the excessive rent, and had furthermore doggedly transformed the room into *his* room as if he were going to live in it the rest of his life. It was the first time in his three years of residence in America that he had accomplished the transformation, and it had not been easy. In former rooms, though, it had been impossible. This was like one in a hotel which defied any eccentric impress, and in the beginning he had almost despaired, had been convinced that like all the others, it would remain inviolably and complacently itself and that when he finally went away, if his signature were there at all, it would be nothing more characteristic of him than of the tenants before him or the ones to follow: a half-used box of toothpowder and a rusted razor blade in the medicine chest, or on the desk a bottle of ink or a glass ashtray bought for a dime. There was, upon everything, the mark of an absolute and wholly impersonal vulgarity. The furniture was mongrel. The walls were cream-colored plaster that could offend no one; fastened to them here and there were besilvered lamps containing bulbs shaped like fat candleflames that shed a pale and genteel light. The rugs were scrupulously unobtrusive. The sturdy column of the standing lamp was embellished with twists of iron that represented nothing on earth, and the shade, seemingly designed to diminish illumination by exactly half, was silk of a color that could not be named, a color like one acquired by an amateur chemist or by a child experimenting with crayons. The ample bed (too ample for his understanding. It was called a "three-quarter" bed and he wondered whether it was meant for two children or for someone prodigiously obese) was covered with a faded counterpane made of two Indian prints sewn together.

But the room had its virtues. The rocking chair was comfortable, the table was steady, and there were plenty of clothes hangers in the closet. And Mrs. Horvath kept everything clean. Aside from the fireplace which he had been requested not to use, and the only mirror which was hopelessly defective, and the writing desk which had a limping leg, everything was in "good working order."

The exterior of the house was equally noncommittal. It was large, shapeless and built of yellow stone. It stood behind a high brick wall, its back windows overlooking an arm of the sea which, at low tide, was a black and stinking mud-flat. A dump had been made at the end of the water and here was heaped all the frightful refuse of the city, the high-heeled shoes and the rotten carrots and the abused insides of automobiles; when the wind blew, the odor from the dump was so putrid in so individual a way that it was quite impossible to describe. But on a clear day, the doctor could look the other way and see, far off, the live blue Sound and the silhouettes of white sailboats and gray battleships. And while the plants, their windows ghastly blue all night, their noises constant every hour of every day, were almost within a stone's throw of his window, he had at least the illusion of being in the country. For the lawns in front and in back were healthy, the trees were abundant, and forsythia was blooming now along the wall. He had pondered often in the year he had lived here why so expensive a house (for clearly it was that; its plate glass and the intricate furbelows of its façade testified to suddenly acquired money) had been built on so unprepossessing a site, and at last he learned from a taxi-driver that the original owner had been a rum-runner who had brought his boats up the narrow neck of water and had unloaded them at the cottage in the back yard where now the Horvath family lived. While he was unable to find more than a humorous token in it, he thought with certain pleasure of the interview in which the house had changed hands and become the property of the present landlord, a Roman Catholic priest.

Sometimes, too, he wondered how the bootlegger would regard the changes he had made in his room, a room which perhaps had formerly been the office for the transaction of his illegal business. And how, for that matter, the priest did when he came on his monthly tour of inspection. Very likely both of them would find it prissy and impractical. He had taken down the pictures he found there: a tinted photograph of the Grand

Canyon (which he thought must be the most dreadful sight in the world), a subdued study of an English cottage and one of a vase of asters. In their place he had hung a print of "The Siege of Toledo" and one of "The Fall of Icarus" and a photograph of the bridge in Würzburg. On top of the bookcase were three decanters, for kümmel, brandy and Dubonnet, a little white pot of philodendron, and a pewter tray on which stood two heavy wine glasses and a curious pipe. In the shelves were the few books he had brought with him from Ludwigshafen: Dante, Rilke, Plato, some medical books, *Buddenbrooks, Crime and Punishment, The Charterhouse of Parma,* and those he had bought here, in the hope, never realized, of learning to read English easily. Those were *For Whom the Bell Tolls, The Late George Apley, The Golden Treasury* and *The Story of San Michele.* A cuckoo clock hung on the wall over the bed and on the bureau a large wooden nutcracker lay amongst big pecans in a polished lemonwood bowl. On the bedside table were an ashtray he had bought in Milan, a brown earthenware carafe, a diary bound in green leather, and a silver letter opener.

When, at nightfall, he drew the windowblinds against industrial America, it was not hard to imagine himself in his student room at Heidelberg. He had never been rich enough to eat at the town restaurants and he had disliked the tepid white food at the Mensa of the University, and so he had made little suppers for himself at his desk. And while now he was quite able to afford four-course dinners (the dearth of doctors for civilians had contrived for him a flourishing and gainful practice amongst Hungarian defense workers and their pregnant wives) he preferred to remain in his room and eat the sort of food he had done when he was a young man. Upon the table he would place the parcels he had brought from the delicatessen: a little sausage and a loaf of bread, a bottle of pickled tomatoes, a carton of Schmierkäse, perhaps a jar of marinated herring. Then, his meal ready, he would pour himself a glass of Dubonnet, light an Egyptian Prettiest cigarette and sit for a while in the chair by the window, staring now at the dark green blind that was punctured here and there, admitting star-like bits of light.

During the day, Dr. Pakheiser smoked American cigarettes, but he had found that nothing so completely and happily restored his student days to him as the smell of Oriental tobacco, and because he was so busy until he left his office, he could not afford time for the nostalgic meditations it brought. Closing his eyes, he would fancy himself twenty years younger, not yet fat, but even now near-sighted, eating ham and bread and drinking *Rotwein* in the narrow room of Frau Jost's flat. Frau Jost was a pretty, friendly young widow about whom he sometimes had romantic daydreams, and she had a daughter of four, a jolly little girl named Greta. Every morning, as Alfred left the house, Greta came to wish him good-by. She clutched in her arms a black cat who wore a red ribbon about its neck. And as he ran down the stairs, she always said, "Please look up at the window, Herr Pakheiser, and I will wave." Outside, in the steep street, he had to hold his head far back so that he could see the top window, and there she was, on time and faithful every day, to wave her hand and smile at him, still holding her cat.

Although those years at Heidelberg had been rich and full of importance, it was little Greta Jost that the flavor of the cigarette brought back most clearly. While he had had friends with whom he played chess at Burkhardt's *Konditorei* and had drunk with on Saturday nights at the Vater Rhein and while he had even occasionally had a girl, it was his daily encounter with the child that seemed now to fix the days of the past. He had been, even then, a person of strict habit. Once Greta had had chicken-pox and for a week had not appeared at the window, and all that time Alfred had been somewhat inattentive to his lectures and had spent more time at Burkhardt's. But strangely enough, he had not really been fond of Greta—children, in general, made him shy—and he had even found himself wishing that the ritual had never been established since once it had been, it had to be repeated every day without fail for his complete peace of mind. He was even annoyed if the cat did not appear at the window or if it appeared without its ribbon.

But what he would not give for Greta now! With a perversity which he acknowledged frankly, he imagined that he had been devoted to her, that he had called her pet names and had dandled her on his knee. And that his relationship with her mother had been intimate. He could even long for the irascible porter at the medical college, for the torpid *Bademeister* at the public baths who invariably tried to give him a towel which someone else had just finished using. All these people whom he had known slightly or not at all seemed, in his misshapen reflection, to be his friends.

Dr. Pakheiser was not given to self-pity. A scientific man, he looked on facts. He knew that the *Bademeister* had no more been his friend than was Mrs. Horvath and that, in the end, Greta was the only one who had that stature. And just so now, twenty years later, he had again one friend, one companion, a solitary daily relation with a breathing creature. His companion was a gray tom-cat who called on him each evening with the same unswerving regularity that had brought the little girl to the window every morning. The cat came at seven o'clock, announcing himself with a trilling mew outside the door. He drank the heavy cream his host had poured into a bowl for him and then he spent the evening, until about midnight, curled up in the doctor's lap, asleep. Two or three times in the course of the evening, he roused himself to make an excursion round the room, cleverly picking his way through the decanters, patting the trailing leaves of the philodendron to watch them sway. He washed a little and returned and slept again. Half-roused by the turning of a page or the sound of a match being struck, he would briefly purr as if to say that his affection had not lessened, that he was merely preoccupied. At midnight, Dr. Pakheiser took him downstairs, dropped him on the veranda and watched him, revived by the night air, streak across the lawn and disappear over the wall.

The doctor called him Milenka which in Russian, of which he knew a few words, means "darling." He knew too little Russian, even, to affix the masculine diminutive. "Milenka," he would say, "I-yi-yi-yi, bad puss! Bad boy. Ah, Milenka!" Milenka was an ordinary gray cat with white mittens, a white snout and a shell-pink nose. He was rather ugly, for he was underdeveloped and rangy and since he spent a good part of the day in the coal bin, his paws were always smudged. But he had a full, healthy purr and a gentle nature. Rarely did he strop his claws on the carpet, and thanks to the doctor's weekly application of One Spot powder, he had very few fleas.

Dr. Pakheiser realized once with half-ashamed amusement that he had for Milenka a real love, whereas for Greta he had had only a perfunctory gratitude. It was chiefly, he supposed, because he was the cat's protector as well as his friend and had it not been for his suppers of cream and herring, the poor thing would have had to shift for himself on the dump. Indeed, he was quite sure that if he moved away, Mrs. Horvath would have the cat destroyed, for she had not known, she declared cantankerously, when she took over the job, that she would have an animal to care for as well as beds and bathtubs. No one knew where Milenka had come from. The landlord disclaimed all knowledge of him; the former manageress denied that she had ever fed him or invited him in any way to stay.

The doctor neither liked nor disliked animals. He had always been indifferent to them, save for police dogs whom he feared and cocker spaniels whom he scorned for their somehow homosexual softness. He had never known an individual dog or cat well. So this strong feeling about Milenka perplexed him. Was he turning into an old lady? And would he, together with his cat-fancying, get notions before he was fifty? But these speculations did not really worry him; he was sure that his fundamental motive in helping the cat survive was that he did not like Mrs. Horvath and by his lavish purchases of fish and cream, he was deviously repaying her for her impertinences.

Mrs. Horvath was a dirty, dumpy person in a brown coverall and a blue work shirt. She was anti-Semitic in the most extraordinarily forthright way Dr. Pakheiser had ever seen. On the first day of her regime she had been introduced to the doctor by the departing manageress, and she had said, "I think you are Jew, Doctor. But I get rent every Wednesday all same. You don't worry." Each time he recollected this speech (delivered with a smile which could not have disarmed a child) he was so taken aback that he was never able to analyze exactly what she meant. Evidently it was her intention to announce her antipathy to Jews at the very outset so that her tenant would not start off under a misapprehension. It became clear, after a few days, that her rule was firm: she decidedly was not one of those people who say, "Some of my best friends are Jews." On the contrary, she would say, "I hate all Jews." In a way, he preferred her attitude to that, say, of his office girl, Miss Johnson, who, with aggressive piety, often congratulated him on being one of the chosen people. With Mrs. Horvath, he was dealing with an armed enemy and war, with her, was war. Miss Johnson, on the other hand, while less wounding, was more treacherous. She could catch him offguard when he was fatigued and, sympathizing with him for being uprooted from his country, could make him prey to a burning, unobjectified anger on behalf of his whole race, and to a weepy grief for himself. Then he would despise America, Connecticut, his cramped and cluttered office, the strapping great charwoman who cleaned it, the smell of workmen in the waiting room and of workmen's cigarettes, but most of all he would despise Miss Johnson.

Milenka was the immediate cause of war between Mrs. Horvath and Dr. Pakheiser. About two weeks after her arrival, she came one evening to collect the rent. Seeing the cat curled up on the pillow of the bed, she wrinkled her low forehead, bunched up her flat Magyar nose and said, "Cat! I *like* dog. I *like* cat. But outside. Not in the house. In Europe, we have dog, we have cat, but all outside. Inside they make their doing on the carpet and all where. Outside, Doctor, I must ask you." Dr. Pakheiser, unnerved, a man who preferred on all occasions to agree, cried, "I see!" and pretended to himself that this was only a humorous crotchet she was airing conversationally. But she remained firm in the doorway even after he had given her the money and then, so suddenly that he scarcely realized what was happening, she bounded forward toward the bed, shrieking, "Out! Out, you!" and Milenka, his eyes widening with terror, leaped from the bed and ran out the door.

The next evening, though, admitted to the house by the man who left for the graveyard shift at Chance Vought, the cat came back, and the doctor, emboldened by his desire for company and his need for continuing custom, again opened his door. Every night thereafter, except on Wednesday when the rent was due, he came and was not turned away. Mrs. Horvath, to be sure, was aware of what was going on. In the morning when the doctor went downstairs, he usually found her indolently flicking a dust cloth over the newel post or frankly reading the lodgers' postal cards or sitting, sprawled like a big tom-boy, in one of the chairs of the foyer. She would give him a look half scornful, half angry and would say, "I don't know what happen to you when Father come and see those places on the carpet with sausage marks." Or she would tell him, jeeringly, that Father was going to be outraged when he saw the hole in the curtain the cat had clawed. "I tell *you*, Doctor," she would say, "on the grass, okay when they lose their hair. Outside, all right. Inside, on the cushions, hell's bells!" Sometimes she would simply ask him, in the derisive voice of a bad schoolboy, "How you find Milenka last night, Doctor? Plenty good fleas on him, eh?" And once, reaching the limit of her insolence, she followed him out the door and paced up the driveway, calling shrilly, "Milenka! Milenka!"

When he was not in school, the manageress was accompanied by her thirteen-year-old son, a large boy with a malicious face that forever grinned under a sailor cap. Occasionally it was he who came for the rent and Dr. Pakheiser, fumbling in his wallet, felt that the boy with his obscene leer had expected to find dirty French pictures on the wall or a light woman in the bed. "Hey, Doc," he said once, "you like that cat?" And the doctor, laughing violently, replied, "Ach, yes! Very much." Freddie continued. Pretty soon now "that cat" had better watch its step for he was going to trap and tame some birds and if that dope of an old gray dumbbell got one of them, it would be "good-by, cat." Dr. Pakheiser, baffled by the assurance of the outsized youth, cried, "Ach, so!" louder and more amiably than ever.

So far, no birds had been caught, but Freddie, on Saturday and Sunday, worked all day long making his traps out of wooden crates, and in time the back yard was so full of them that it appeared he intended to catch entire flocks. And the doctor had no doubt either that Milenka would chase the birds or that Freddie would cruelly punish him.

II

On this damp April evening, Dr. Pakheiser was about to draw his windowblinds and prepare his supper when he saw Mr. Horvath come out of the cottage bringing a step-ladder which he set up underneath an apple tree. At his approach, the blackbirds all flew off, twittering irritably. Some time before, he had built a bonfire at the water's edge which now was burning brightly, sending up bits of charred paper, like smaller blackbirds. The man called out, "Hey, Freddie, come here a minute." And Freddie came charging through the door, wearing a baseball mitt on one hand. There was a colloquy which the doctor could not hear and then the boy, rushing to the bonfire, hurling his mitt to the ground, cried, "Oh, boy!" He lighted a torch and came back to the step-ladder, sedately so that the flame would not go out, handed it to his father and then climbed up. At the top, he wavered a little and let out an exclamation of fright, but he regained his balance and stooped down to receive the torch. He was just tall enough to reach the puffy white tent of caterpillars in a high crotch of the tree. The doctor watched, sickened, saw yellow flames shoot up as the fat tumor caught fire. Freddie had not thought ahead. A worm fell upon his upturned face and he screamed with revulsion and let the torch drop to the ground where it went on burning and sending up black smoke. The work, though, was done and while his father beat the caterpillars to death with the back of a shovel where they had fallen in the grass, the boy came down the ladder and went toward the cottage, wiping his face with both hands as though it never would be clean again. Mr. Horvath laughed at him and went on killing the pests. Mrs. Horvath came to the screen door and hooted at her son, "Ha! Ha!" she laughed. "You keep the mouth open next time and see what comes in." Restored to his normal spirits, Freddie hooted back, "Yeah, like fun I will! Yeah, in a pig's valise I will!"

There was a miaow at the doctor's door. He drew down the windowblind sharply, shuddering at what he had just seen. There was something primeval in those people; their communal enjoyment of the annihilation of the caterpillars was so stupid and so brutish that the doctor actually retched. Then he let in the refined, soft-moving cat.

"I-yi-yi-yi!" he said, stooping to pick Milenka up. "I-yi-yi-yi, my bad puss, my bad boy." Milenka stretched his head forward and rubbed the top of it against Dr. Pakheiser's chin, purring loudly. "Milenka," murmured the man. "Ah, my good friend, my dearest one." He poured the cream into the cereal bowl, fetched a quart of Irish ale from the window sill and, sitting down, said to his companion, "*Gut' Mahlzeit.*"

When they had both finished and the doctor had put away the food, he settled once more in the rocking chair with the brandy decanter at his elbow. He opened the journal that had come that day and began methodically with the first article, one on the use of sulfa drugs in the treatment of sinusitis. He had read only a few sentences when Milenka leaped to his lap. Dr. Pakheiser ran his fingers under the cat's jaw and around the ears, laid his whole hand on the little gray belly to feel the vibration and read on, at last in repose now that his house was complete. But there was an uneasiness stirring at the back of his mind and although he concentrated and extracted the full meaning from all he read that night, he observed when he rose at twelve to put Milenka out that he had drunk three times as much brandy as was his custom and had made a great inroad into the package of Egyptian Prettiests which he never smoked after supper.

That night he had a strange dream. He dreamed of D-day. He and little Greta Jost had come to wish Mr. Horvath good luck and they had set out to find rooms. The hotels were crowded, for the holiday throngs were tremendous. They sauntered up the boardwalk, admiring the bright tailored shingle where fashionable people were gathered for the start of the regatta. They entered a hotel which was quite deserted save for a man sitting alone on a little mezzanine at one end of the lobby. He sat at a round amethyst-colored glass table, drinking a very pink cocktail, and as they approached, he stood up smiling and cordially extending his hand. They recognized the President and they were gratified when he called them both by name. His address was old-fashioned: he said "Miss Greta" and "Mr. Alfred." Linking arms, the three of them went out. The President said that while he wished the invasion to be as leisurely as possible, it would be folly, would it not, to give the signal too late in the day? Did not his young friends agree that despite our great advances in electricity, there was something essentially *better* about sunlight? Never was there so civilized a man! In the pure, brilliant sky, exquisite airplanes circled and swooped like the loveliest of birds. There was such a profusion of scarlet! In the flags, in the hats of the spectators, on the wings of planes, in colossal bouquets in vases a mile high situated on the beach at intervals of fifteen yards. The yachts were all ready, freshly painted, brightly bannered for the race to Europe.

Alfred and Greta were the first to land. As they walked up the ramp, he noticed the tiny Scotch plaid ribbons that bound her pigtails. Wandering, they could not find the *Konditorei* he had suggested although time and time again they set forth

from the Heiliggeist cathedral and took the familiar street.
Nor was it possible, as formerly, to see the ruined castle from
the bridge, and Greta said, "Herr Pakheiser, I don't believe
this is Heidelberg. Now I am afraid and I want my mother.
I think we have come to Heilbronn by mistake." But Alfred
pointed to the marking that clearly read, "Philosophen Weg,"
and he soothed her, "Don't be frightened, dearest." They were
speeding in a dirty express train through Freiburg, its towers
and steeples flattened out like any corpse, its vineyards wasted
with drought and disease. The Alps diminished as they neared
them. No trees were left. The sun was small and red like an
ember. Alfred, receiving a wicker-covered jug of wine from a
weeping man who shared their compartment, was too touched
and too embarrassed to begin a conversation, but at last he
thought of something. "Sir," he said solemnly, "sir, did you ever
go fishing in the Sound for bass, using a caddis worm as bait?"
The wine in the man's throat gurgled like a death rattle as he
looked out at the leveled mountains. "There was a short notice
in some review or other," he said, "outlined in black. Even so
. . . even so . . ."

In the limbo where he waited a moment before he wakened
fully, he thought he was writing the opening paragraph of a
children's story in which a little boy lay on his stomach drinking
water from a stream. Suddenly his eyes encountered two others,
hooded, sparkling with some horrible intelligence. They belonged to a monstrous caddis worm which advanced through
the water as he withdrew.

He woke violently. He clasped his hands to his forehead and
in the darkness softly moaned. "I must control myself. I must
not perish here."

III

Late in May, Milenka disappeared. Dr. Pakheiser was disturbed
but not really anxious until the fourth night passed and he still
dined alone. On the fifth morning he diffidently asked Mrs.
Horvath if she had seen the cat, and he detected something
doubtful, something covert in her reply. She was not arrogant
and her eyes seemed unable to focus on his face. She said—
uncomfortably, it seemed to him—"No, Doctor. I see him

Sunday. My husband see him Sunday. He come back, don't you worry." Then she looked directly at him and smiled, "He know where his sardine is, I tell you." The doctor was smoking and as he went to the table to drop a long ash into the tray there, his hand abruptly shook and the ashes fell to the carpet. He and the woman both briefly looked at them, dispersed fanwise on the green border. And he knew then that she was hiding something, for she did not reproach him for his clumsiness even though she had just finished using the carpet sweeper. He was so angry that he stumbled to the door and his rage so blinded him that he had to lean against the jamb a moment before he could see the steps. It was not, at this moment, that he was mourning the loss of Milenka; it was that he had sensed, despite her near-civility and his own timorousness, as killing a hatred between them as though they were two jungle beasts, determined to destroy one another. "If she has killed my cat," he brooded as he drove through the gate, "then I . . ." but he could not finish the sentence. He could devise no penalty high enough for such wickedness, no penance sufficiently humiliating.

For two weeks nothing passed between the manageress and her lodger. Nothing, that is, but glances boldly indignant on the doctor's part, guilty on the woman's. It seemed to him that the life of the rest of the house had ceased, that all was at an ominous standstill before a final battle to the death. And then, incredibly, the cat came back. When he first heard the mewing outside his door on the dot of seven, Dr. Pakheiser could not believe his ears. Not until the sound had been repeated two or three times did he open the door. His joy at the reunion was less than his shame for falsely accusing Mrs. Horvath and less than his bewilderment at her shifty-eyed embarrassment. Apparently Milenka had just wandered off somewhere as tom-cats do in the spring. He was thin and mangy and his coat was matted with cockleburs and beggar's-lice. His purr had a bronchial rasp and the doctor made a note on his memorandum pad to bring home a worm pill the next night. Nor had he any appetite for the bit of herring which was all that the doctor had to offer him, and after less than half an hour, he asked to be let out. But this strangeness, under good care, would pass. That night the doctor slept well.

"Good morning," he cried heartily as he met Mrs. Horvath

in the hall the following day. "Have you seen my friend, Mrs. Horvath? He came back for his sardine as you promised me."

The woman's eyes opened from their sleepiness, her lips parted in disbelief, and she said, "Back? That cat back?" Dr. Pakheiser assured her that what he said was true and at that moment, to confirm him, Milenka leaped to the window sill from the veranda and sat there in profile, blinking his eyes. Mrs. Horvath stared, "I do not know," she said. "It is like a dream." The doctor surmised, then, that the cat had been put into a bag and taken into the country somewhere and been abandoned. It was scarcely believable that he could be so gross as to laugh triumphantly and almost to sob his words: "Yes, Mrs. Horvath, my dearest friend is restored to me!"

She looked away from the window. "But, Doctor, I do not know. My son, he catch birds all while now. His school finish pretty soon. I think he don't want that cat here."

"It is cruel to catch birds," he said severely, no longer tyrannized over by her now that he had got his cat back. "And *I* want him here even if that boy doesn't." It gave him pleasure to say "that boy" just as she and her son spoke of "that cat."

"But, Doctor, the cat kill birds. My boy don't kill them. He make them into good pet."

"It is the cat's nature to kill birds. But it is not the nature of man to take prisoners."

"No?" she said. The look of cunning returned to her face. "What we fight war for, then, Doctor?"

"I don't know, Mrs. Horvath, I am sure." He was overpowered with disgust that he should be haggling with this obtuse woman over the life of a diseased cat, and that he should be confronted by so irrelevant a question which he could not answer and which, in spite of its fatuous context, made him feel that because he could only say he did not know, like an unprepared schoolboy, his mind was growing dull. And just as he was preparing to bid the manageress good morning and to hurry to his office to plunge himself into work, she threw out a remark more imbecilic than the first but one that utterly confounded him. She said, "My son protect birds from cats just like America protect Jews from Hitler."

For a moment, before he had collected himself, he read an awful symbolic wisdom into this absurdity. Unhampered by learning, in a country where she could not read the language and could barely speak it, where she could be influenced only by the most basic of national prejudices and loyalties, she was truly a natural enemy. Here was the perfect, the pure hatred; the real thing was in Mrs. Horvath's simple heart. He was not so far gone yet as to think that she was bent on getting rid of the cat out of vengeance. Her reasons were more human than that; she did not like cats and she wanted to indulge her son. But at the same time, there was something so sure in her figure of speech that it was as if, from now on, she would implicitly believe it, would even repeat it in later conversations.

In reply, Dr. Pakheiser only smiled. On his way out, he gave Milenka a pat on the head and said loudly, "I-yi-yi-yi, bad puss!" and walked jauntily round the house to his car, whistling. Whistling, as the phrase went, in the dark.

All spring, Dr. Pakheiser trod on eggs. Each evening when he came home and parked his car in the back yard where Freddie was at work on his bird traps, his heart constricted with apprehension. This would be the night, he thought, when Milenka would not come. The boy, grinning even as he pounded in the nails, looked up with a dispassionate greeting. "Hi, Doc. This is for me to get me an oriole in, see? And that there one is for me to get me a purple grackle in. I lure 'em—I know how they whistle and I whistle and they think I'm a bird—and then they get in this little place here, see, and I pull a string and the door comes down and they can't get out. And then I get 'em so tame they'll eat right out of my hand." Once or twice the doctor inquired about his school with the intention of keeping things running smoothly between them. He went to the nuns to whom he referred collectively as "Sister." "Sister flunked me in Latin but she gave me B in Algebra and D plus in English." But it bored him to talk about the contents of his days; he would break off suddenly and pointing to the blackbirds in the dead tree would say, "See them? I don't want 'em but I could have 'em all if I did." And the doctor would look up at the crowded branches, object of his dreamy contemplation every day. "They're dumb birds," Freddie would say as he threw a pebble into the tree and they all disbanded. "They don't know where they're at." Dr. Pakheiser would reply, "I don't think any birds at all know where they're at." They had come to this conventional rite through a mutual understanding: the doctor disliked birds, the boy disliked cats. Neither spoke of his aversion, but under their banter was the serious warning, "Your pet stays where it belongs, or else."

Milenka was soon prospering. His coat came in soft and shining; his purr cleared and his eyes lost the milkiness that had clouded them when he first came home. He was full grown now and, obliged to assume the responsibilities of a male animal, sometimes missed a meal and spent the time with a plump old tabby who howled for him on the stone wall. But good friend that Milenka was, if he failed to come one evening, he sneaked through the door early the next morning when someone went out to the day-shift. The doctor came to enjoy these morning visits even more than the evening ones. He would go back to bed after he had poured out the cream and lie there watching; when the cat had finished, he would jump to the bed, walk carefully up Dr. Pakheiser's legs to the thigh and there establish himself. But there was one drawback to his coming in the day-time. Ironically, a pair of wrens had built a nest under the eave of the corner window and Milenka, hearing them rustle and chirp, would sit up, his whiskers twitching, his sleek little body poised for a leap. And whenever this happened, Dr. Pakheiser felt a thrill of disquiet, afraid the cat would commit a crime during the day while he was at his office and could not intercede for him.

Just as Milenka thrived, so did Freddie's successes multiply and by the first of June, the clumsy home-made cages in the garage were half full of orioles and robins and finches and flickers which, at feeding time, gave out a dissonant and reedy clamor. One Sunday afternoon, when school was over for him and the skies were full of birds, Freddie stalked a robin in full view of the doctor's windows. He crept across the lawn on his hands and knees toward the large unmoving bird. The advance could either have been for the purpose of murder or for min-istration to an injured wing. It was beautiful to watch. There was no sudden nervous jerking, no change of pace. When he was within two feet of the bird, his hands left the ground and his lips parted in his earnestness. His posture and his skill made the doctor think of a praying mantis, one of those miraculously ugly creatures which he had seen on the road under a tulip tree and had taken at first for withering seed pods. Now, a foot away, the hands parted. He was ready for the capture. Dr. Pakheiser found himself holding his breath and could not tell whether he wanted the bird to foil the boy or wished to see it taken. Directly under the certain hands, the prey was still unaware. Now they descended and gently took the bird. Freddie stroked its head tenderly with his forefinger and when the captive made a movement to escape, he drew it to his chest smiling rapturously. And the doctor might have warmed toward him, seeing the innocent happiness in his face, had he not bawled out, "Hey, Mom! Got me another one. Boy, oh, boy, am I *good*!"

IV

Its head high, its tail feathers trailing the ground, the great cock-pheasant moved with dignity out of the shadow of the apple tree into the light where all the glory of its habiliments shone like a sun-struck diamond. Dr. Pakheiser, who had been roused early by an urgent telephone call, paused in his dressing to watch the wonderful bird. He had never seen one before save in pictures which he had not altogether believed. The japanning of its plumage had been masterful: emerald blazed forth beside gold and gold beside scarlet. There was something about it so rich and unusual that he did not think of it as a bird at all but as a costly ornament for the patch of bright grass where now it stopped, surveying the terrain as if this were its own dominion. But the kingly creature was no wiser than its plebeian brothers, and it began to walk rapidly toward one of Freddie's traps. The doctor immediately flung wide his window, unfastened the screen and leaned out, shouting and waving his arms to scare away the foolish bird. He disturbed the sleeping wrens in the eave and they flew wildly against the screen, then sailed off to the apple tree. But the pheasant was deaf to warnings and walked complacently toward his prison. In a frenzy, Dr. Pakheiser reached back to the bedside table and picked up his metal ashtray from Milan. He hurled it at the pheasant. It fell close to the quick feet and instantly the bird turned, running, this time, back over the grass through the shadow of the apple tree and disappeared in the tall weeds that grew about the abandoned boats. Freddie ran out of the cottage. The doctor fastened his screen and stepped back out of sight behind the drapery at the window, but he watched the boy whose face was contorted with fury and frustration. Tears began as he picked up the ashtray. For a second he stared at it as if he were not sure what to do with it and then, with a bawl, he flung it into the water which was at low tide and, cursing at the top of his voice, went indoors.

Dr. Pakheiser finished dressing. He knew that he was not steady enough to shave, but he washed his face and hands slowly and thoroughly, using the nail brush with unaccustomed vigor. He lighted a cigarette and sat down, aware that his delay was selfish. But his patient seemed remote, the illness unimportant. It was not until the cigarette had burned down to nothing that he got up, found his hat and went out. He stole quietly down the stairs and round the house. There was no sign of life in the back yard. From within the cottage came the sound of Mrs. Horvath's voice; she spoke loudly but in Hungarian and he understood nothing of what she said. He gained his car and he was safe. But he knew that the score was not yet settled, for as he drove away, he saw Freddie's face at the window, the strange Mongolian nose spread out as it pressed against the pane. This, finally, would be the day of reckoning.

When he came home at five that afternoon, Dr. Pakheiser found both Mrs. Horvath and Freddie in the large front bedroom downstairs. Someone had just moved out and they were making it ready for a new tenant. They were turning the mattress, but when they saw the doctor, they stopped, the great thing folded halfway over and held in their strong red hands.

Mrs. Horvath said, "Good night, Doctor. I bring you ashtray tomorrow. You lose your blue one?" He had not anticipated so devious an attack and he was nonplused. Since all three of them knew well enough that the ashtray was lying in the mud, it was absurd to carry on her game, to say, for example, that he had taken it to the office. And so he replied ambiguously, "Oh, thank you. If you have an extra one, I will be glad to have it." He started toward the stairs, but they had not finished with him yet.

Mrs. Horvath said, "Was it a good day, Doctor?"

"A busy day," he said. "But, yes, a good one, I think."

The boy, his chin upon the mound of the mattress, fixed

him with the fearless eye of the insulted child and slowly said, "It wasn't a good day for me, Doctor. It was a bad day for me, wasn't it, Mom?"

His mother giggled and winked at Dr. Pakheiser. "His birds! He think of nothing but his birds. Today he don't catch one big pheasant and this evening another get out of her house and fly away."

"Oh, I'm sorry," said the doctor. "But perhaps your bird will come back. They seem so tame. They eat out of your hand, don't they?"

"That bird won't come back," said the boy. "*I* know what happened to him. That cat got him. You get a bird tame and if it gets out anybody can catch it." The cold, accusing face began to contract in a childish pucker and tears hindered the next words: "That damned cat ate my bird!" He wrenched the mattress out of his mother's hands and flung it back onto the springs and flung himself upon it, sobbing maniacally. "And if I catch that cat, I'll kill it! I'll kill it! I'll kill it!"

The doctor flushed with embarrassment at this display, unchecked by the mother who merely stood smiling beside the bed. In time, the tantrum spent itself and Freddie lay shaking, face down on the naked bed. In the quiet, Mrs. Horvath, deceptively matter-of-fact, said, "Doctor, did you read that book by the doctor of Hitler? He say Hitler don't like women, only men? You think that true, Doctor?"

He could not chart her course, begun so remotely. He stalled, took off his glasses and put them on again. She went on. "I hate Hitler, Doctor. But I do not believe all what they say. This book I buy in the drugstore for one dollar ninety-eight cents. I think a Jew write the book out of madness for what Hitler do to Jews."

If only he could turn his leaden flesh and carry it up the stairs to his own room and lock the door upon these savages! There rest, there drink his Dubonnet, there be at home! But a score of weights held him immobile, facing the barbarous woman and he listened to her: "I hate Hitler," she repeated. "I like Jews. But if you're mad you don't all times tell the truth, isn't it? So this doctor in this book I got say Hitler like men. You know? What you think of that, Doctor?" She went on and on. Unskilled as were her thrusts, they were direct. And when at last she was finished and had dismissed him (did she, he wondered, in her marvelously malicious mind think that perhaps *he* was the "doctor of Hitler"? Or that *he* did not like women, only men?) he felt trampled upon. Actually he ached and when he got to his room, he was sure he was coming down with something. Never in all these three years had his loneliness been so acute. It sprained his whole body, buried his faculties so deeply that sensation, if it came at all, was ambiguous and incomplete. Impassively, he accepted the anonymous voices of machines: radios, motor boats, factory whistles, trains, a random bomber. They came to him thickly insulated so that, shrill or loud as they might really be, they did not penetrate his mind but lay, all of them together, in a humming mass on the threshold. His thoughts faltered like sleep-burdened eyes or attached themselves with imbecilic fixity upon one trivial object. For a long time he studied a minute fissure in the plaster of the wall beside the window. Later, he meditated intently upon the small, dispirited American flag on a pole beside the Sikorsky plant, and when at last he broke from this trance, it was only to become absorbed in the spectacle of a fouled old fish-bucket raffishly perched on a stump at the water's edge. Once, from some remote region of the house, there came the sound of a music box tinkling over a radio and at least a hundred times he stubbornly reiterated the words he knew it heralded: "PEPSI COLA HITS THE SPOT." At last, passing his hand over his cool forehead, he closed his eyes. The sounds cohered as in delirium. He could still visualize the blackbirds and fancied them to be a deathless band of flies which refused to walk upon the glass where they could be swatted. Hearing a train screaming in the station for passengers to Boston, he tried to imagine that he stood in the Bismarckgarten waiting for the yellow tram to Mannheim, but all he could see, in his mind's eye, were the shabby girls at the flowerstall deftly plucking daffodils from the pails of water. Next, he pretended that the train he heard was the express to Munich, and this time the recollections spun out effortlessly. He had gone to Salzburg once for a fortnight at the house of a classmate, a yellow-haired boy named Heine Waffenschmidt. He remembered that in the compartment there had been two soldiers on leave who had played chess the whole journey and had gladly drunk the

wine offered to them by a tipsy letter-carrier on his way to
Garmisch-Partenkirchen to see his tubercular daughter who
was dying. The old man's blue coat glistened with age and the
brass buttons on it were so tarnished that when the light fell on
them they did not shine. "*Danke*, Papa," the soldiers had said.
Once, at the end of a game, they stretched and yawned and
told the old man what they were planning to do. "And Papa,"
said one of them, "what do you think? We have hired a café
and ordered a keg of Löwenbräu and we'll have Scotch whisky
besides." Dr. Pakheiser remembered how whenever the train
stopped at a station, the pause seemed as clearly defined as a
box; his eyes burned now as if he were looking up at the bright
blue ceiling light. It was hard to redeem much of the two weeks
in Salzburg. He had been happy, he was quite sure, and dimly
he recalled a ski tournament after which he and Heine had gone
to a rathskeller for *Glühwein*. There had been a troop of players
on their way to Danzig and one of them, an effeminate young
man, had described the jumpers he had seen that afternoon.
"*Und er geht so und so und so!*" he said, gesturing with his
hands. "*'Swar unglaublich wunderbar.*"

The memory was flat and he rejected it. He tried to think of
his patients, but could think, instead, only of his office where
something was always wrong. The electricity unaccountably
went off or the water ran rusty or the windows got stuck. Today
Miss Johnson had worn an artificial rose in her hair and he had
already been so nervous that the sight of it had nearly sent him
into a tailspin.

He had a glass of brandy which quieted his fidgeting hands.
The smoke from the flat Egyptian Prettiest gave off a fragrance
like sweet wood, but tonight, it did not bring back Greta.
Through the open windows came sharply the sound of Mr.
Horvath's voice warning his son who was clipping the hedge.
"Watch out for snakes, Freddie." The shears clicked steadily;
the boy was a good worker. With his glass in his hand, the
doctor went to the window and stood beside it looking out.
The appalling grin had come back to Freddie's face in which
there were no signs of sorrow or even of anger. Once he stood
up straight to rest his back from its stooping position and the
big clippers dangled by their handle from his little finger.

Dr. Pakheiser went straight through the brandy and even

then had not had enough to drink, so he replaced the empty decanter with the one half full of kümmel. He thought of the supper he soon would eat and he began to wonder what the Horvath family had upon their table. For some reason, he had an idea they were fond of mussels (which made him ill) and he was positive they enjoyed the displeasing flavor of celeriac in their soup. They would have chunks of fat meat; they would especially like rutabaga, watermelon, molasses, pancakes and hot tamales. Again, he wondered if they ever bathed. He had frequently seen Mrs. Horvath's wash hanging on the line in the back yard and had been certain that she used neither soap nor hot water in her laundry. He suspected that they did not brush their teeth which were very long and extremely black. He did not, to tell the truth, altogether understand why the United States had given Mr. Horvath citizenship.

The sun went down and the helicopters left the sky. At a little before seven, the doctor heard a noise in his room and, conscious that he was quite drunk, he allowed his full lips to curl into a smile as he thought of the pleasure Milenka would have if this were a mouse he might catch for his first course. The sound came again, a faint rustling. He thought at first it was in the closet, but then, at its repetition, concluded that it was in the fireplace. Rather slowly, for his hands were awkward, he took away the flowered screen and looked in at the bare, clean hearth. The sound continued, close beside him. He stuck his head in the opening and listened and it came again. There was no doubt about it, something was trapped in the chimney. He returned to his chair in indecision and poured out another glass of kümmel and considered. He knew that it was Freddie's lost bird, beating its wings against the walls.

The boy had left the hedge and his shears lay atop the formal leaves. He would be at his supper now (were they not, at this very moment, spooning up the repellent sauce that surrounded their mussels?) so there was still time in which to choose between an armistice and revenge. For a few minutes the man sat still in his rocking chair, listening tensely to the desperate wings. But presently he could endure the creature's agony no longer and he left his room, having decided to drive a bargain with the boy.

From the top of the stairs, Dr. Pakheiser could see through

the window to the left of the front door. Milenka was sitting
on the wall, looking archly down at the tabby who crouched in
the grass. "I-yi-yi-yi, bad puss," he thought. His feet were slow
on the steps and he clutched the bannister with an unnaturally
moist hand. He was halfway down when Mr. Horvath came
into his ken. The large man moved soundlessly around the
corner of the house and stood at the edge of the lawn under a
young elm tree, and in a moment, Freddie joined him, carrying
a rifle. Dr. Pakheiser hesitated for the length of time it took Mr.
Horvath to aim and fire and then, in order not to see the body
fall off the wall, turned and went back to his room.

Later, after the Chance Vought worker had gone to the
graveyard shift, Dr. Pakheiser opened the damper of the fireplace and a dead oriole fell to the hearth. He gazed abstractedly
at the black and golden feathers and touched the soft body
with the fire tongs. A bright apple leaf was caught under one
wing. He picked the bird up carefully with a piece of newspaper
and put it in a box which he found on the shelf of his closet.
He carried the box downstairs and into the back yard and he
floated it on the water, blue with the lights from the factory
windows. He pondered if it would float to the Sound and if it
did, how far it would go then. A mile on the way to Europe?
Halfway? "Go, Milenka," he addressed the box which already
had drifted several feet from the bank. In the cool air his head
cleared a little and he felt a wonderful exhilaration as if he had
been freed of a persistent pain. He ran like a young man back
to the house, took the stairs two at a time and when he got to
his room, he lay down without undressing and at once was fast
asleep.

A Slight Maneuver

THEY would have preferred to spend their last day in some occupation of their own choosing, but Mrs. Heath, with whom Theo could not dispute because she was a guest, and with whom her nephew found it tiring and profitless to dispute, planned their last hours for them down to the smallest details, designating with ruthless finality the errands and activities that would catapult them toward the hour when the train left. "Activities" was not in the least a vague word as it presented itself in Theo's mind. Her father had said, just before she left for this visit, "Naomi Heath would be a nicer woman if she didn't make everything into a Camp Fire Girl activity. You always imagine at dinner that she has bought the food from a Grange. Not that you get bad things to eat, for you don't; she sets a very good table indeed. But it is all managed, if you get my meaning." She operated a dude camp, and Theo had seen at once upon her arrival what her father had meant, for Clyde's Aunt Naomi, a manly woman, paddled everyone's canoe.

"Since it is Theo's last day, I think it would be nice if you took her through the Caverns, Clyde, for she's certain to be asked if she saw them when she goes home. Besides, she's bound to find them interesting." She stated this, irrefutably, looking up from *The House of Mirth* which she had been reading all summer making very little headway. Theo wondered what sort of tangent the novelist had started that had made Mrs. Heath alight abruptly and firmly upon the Carlsbad Caverns, which she had no desire to see, from the thought of which, indeed, she had turned away in aversion all summer just as, whenever Yellowstone Park was mentioned, she quickly suppressed the recollection of Old Faithful monstrously gushing while an obese male tourist fed a lettuce sandwich to a chained and crippled bear. For Theo, no outdoor girl at best, found the deformities of nature appalling and she shudderingly remembered a climb over the lava fields of Vesuvius, a parched eternity in the Petrified Forest and the sedulous resemblance of Niagara Falls to its likeness on the back of the Shredded Wheat box.

Despite the peevishness in her nephew's voice who said that

if the day were fine, as tonight's sky indicated, it would be a pity not to ride, and despite the stare of vexation on her visitor's face, Mrs. Heath made their plans for them with exactly the same efficiency, the same knowledge of routes, distances and landmarks with which she had arranged the horseback rides of her docile dudes. She would not need the station wagon, she said, and it would be at their disposal. They could put Theo's bags in before they started out and would just make the train nicely after they had done the Caverns. It was a shame they would have to leave before sunset and would therefore miss the exodus of the bats, but a flock of bats, after all, was not hard to imagine. It would be possible to have luncheon in the bowels of the earth, and Theo could dine on the train. There was nothing further to be said.

Returning once more to *The House of Mirth*, Mrs. Heath was unaware that her project, presented with so frequent a repetition of the phrases "her last day," "when she gets home," "her reservations," had been as frightening to the lovers as the appearance of a priest in a sickroom. Left to themselves, they would have let the day pass as all the others had done with no fixed design, no specifically ended hours. Theo had pictured her departure as hasty, leaving no time for prolonged farewells on the platform. She had intended not to pack until it was nearly time to go to the station. But now it would be necessary to pack tonight to begin the ending long ahead. She exchanged with Clyde a look of anguish and when she got up and said good night, she spoke it like a valedictory.

Mrs. Heath closed the book on her thumb and crossing the room with a stride like a big-game hunter's, enveloped Theo in sweatered arms. "But my dear, I wasn't thinking. I shan't see you again since you will leave so early in the morning. Oh, let's not be premature with our farewells. We should have a stirrup cup." And so, although she had pronounced the death sentence, she now allowed a short reprieve, and for another hour the three of them sat in the living-room, drinking excellent Irish whisky. Clearly, Theo saw Aunt Naomi was taking her in for the first time: the last of the dudes had only just gone that afternoon, and she had been much too preoccupied with her paying guests to bother with one who not only did not pay but who had, as well, come for the purposes which were not included in the policy of the Lazy S. K. She directed toward Theo a series of businesslike looks which were annoying but not alarming since they were so impersonal; she might have been judging the depth of a well or the running condition of an outboard motor.

It was apparent, however, that she was not altogether satisfied with what she saw, and Theo had the feeling that there was more imagination than met the eye behind that unimaginative face. She abandoned *The House of Mirth* and devoted herself entirely to her ward and his fiancée, talking obliquely of their marriage and forthrightly of her own, which had ended in a towering rage in Reno. It seemed likely that this rage had included a physical tussle, and there was no doubt in Theo's mind who had been the winner—this virile woman who wore her hair cropped short, who often smoked a pipe, who did not wear skirts or women's blouses, who addressed all humankind and all horseflesh in the same way without regard to age or sex and whose vocabulary compassed such words as ratchet, crupper and turnbuckle. Aunt Naomi's husband, Uncle Matt, had repaired to foreign parts—some thought to the west of China, others to Tibet, still others to one of those Protean Balkans.

At certain times, but not tonight, it had interested Theo to ponder why this self-sufficient woman had concerned herself so greatly with Clyde who really was not her sort at all, being rather submissive and a little bookish and built, in general, upon a mild scale. He had, of course, been her legal ward but now that he had come into his money, it seemed odd that she had not pushed him out of her nest, but odder that he had not flown out of his own accord. Not until tonight, though, when she was being considered by his aunt, did she really consider Clyde. She considered him, that is, not as the person with whom she was in love and who had rarely failed to delight her, but as the person she was going to marry, and while both the Irish and her summerlong delirium obfuscated her thought, she resolved, nevertheless, to prolong her engagement. She realized with surprise and disappointment that his will-lessness with his aunt was transformed, when he was with her, into a firmness which might in time become bullying. Aunt Naomi's mind was impenetrable to his argument, but similarly, his was impenetrable to Theo's, so that she suffered a double defeat.

To the question she often asked him, "If you want to take me to Europe on our honeymoon, why don't you?" he always replied, "You do not understand Aunt Naomi," and the subject was closed.

Clyde and Theo, so enfeebled in their melancholy that they could neither contrive an excuse to take a walk or to go to the patio where they could be alone, smiled and seemed to appreciate Mrs. Heath's monologue, although all the tensility had gone out of them and they felt limp, confronted as they were by the vigor and precision of the woman who, such ages ago, had been stricken like themselves and had recovered so well that she could not now remember what the pain had been like. Or had she been swept off her feet? It was rather hard to imagine because it was so hard to imagine Mr. Heath of whom she knew only this fact, that he had been "a regular fellow but not one a woman like myself could hit it off with."

The hour was one of the longest of Theo's life and during it she made a number of disquieting discoveries: that actually she despised the handicraft of Mexico with which this room was decorated, the orgiastic colors on thick imperfect glass, the rough fabrics, the clumsy pottery, the huge baskets. While Mrs. Heath was planning how she might come to New York at Christmastime to visit Theo's family, she fixed her attention with climactic hatred upon a mesquitewood bowl containing painted gourds. And progressing in a leap from the furnishings to their owner, she lost herself irrevocably in dislike for this future aunt-in-law. At the moment of this acquisition, against which she had successfully held out all summer, she poured herself a double-sized drink out of the horrid blue glass decanter and perceived with vindictive pleasure the startled pause in Mrs. Heath's voice and the look upon her mouth which clearly said, "I knew it all along, she takes after her father, poor fellow," and the smile of triumph which followed upon her nephew's apologetic outcry, "Oh, Theo, I would have fixed it for you."

At last Mrs. Heath put her empty glass on the tray, turned out the lamp by which she had been reading and came to Theo's chair. She stood looking down at her, *The House of Mirth* tucked under one arm, her legs in blue jeans far apart, a sergeant standing at ease. "We have loved having you, Clyde and I, and you must come again one of these days. Have a good trip and when you get home, give your father my love. Have you read this book, by the way? It's a corker." From the doorway then she turned and said to Clyde, "The Sawhills are coming on tomorrow, you know. I expect you'd better get some vermouth on your way home. They drink it with soda—quite a saving when you consider how much Irish costs these days."

When she had gone, there was nothing to say. She had wrapped up the visit and put it away like the slip covers and the summer rugs. The Sawhills, whoever they might be, were clearly the autumn visitors, now that the labors of the summer were past.

Their sorrow at this temporary separation was not to die so quickly. It might die easily, *that* they could not help, but they refused to take the sound of Mrs. Heath's running bath, her last act before she went to bed, as a command that they part now and go to their rooms. Clyde suggested the patio. The certainty of his voice was restorative only for a moment. He was *not* sure: turning at the door, he went back and picked up the tray with the decanter and the siphon and their glasses. Outside, under a perfectly colored and perfectly appointed sky, feeling upon their faces and arms the first rasp of autumn, they loitered futilely.

But Theo felt her resentments flourishing like creatures in a careful culture, multiplying and growing into massed forces. If he had taken a positive stand, she thought, had said sternly, "No, Aunt Naomi, we will not go to the Caverns," she would not have disliked Mrs. Heath nor would she have done to her rapture this small but irreparable damage. Suddenly, overtaken by rage, she said, "She will never finish *The House of Mirth*. Besides being hell on wheels, she is illiterate." And inexplicably, both to herself and to her staggered young man who could not utter a word, she took off her huarachos and padded angrily barefoot across the patio and up the stairs in her room.

In the morning as she dressed, however, it struck Theo that perhaps it had been considerate of Mrs. Heath to arrange the day for them so that they could avoid the Sawhills who were, Clyde had told her, the sort of people who went in for Osage artifacts and jokes about Cal Coolidge. What could prevent them from going somewhere else? And then, to her surprise, she found the thought of the Caverns not half as unappealing as she had last night. It was true, she *would* be asked about them and it would be convenient to have something to say about the summer since she could not possibly describe how it had actually been spent, in a stupefied intoxication so that she had half the time not known what day of the week it was and, though she had been told half a dozen times, had never been able to remember the name of the aged but agile dude, a surgeon from Rochester, who played a steel guitar incompetently and without pleasure at regular intervals throughout the day. She had felt that this was the sort of detail she ought to remember: if she brought home no facts to her fact-loving father, he would be quickly suspicious of her and would say, diagnostically, "I'm afraid I don't like the effect Clyde Tompkins has on you. You don't seem to have your feet on the ground." If she could, on the other hand, go on rather endlessly and boringly about the Carlsbad Caverns, he might picture to himself what she pictured without even having seen them: stalagmites made to be photographed in color for the *National Geographic,* and he would know that at least part of the time she had been an adult pedestrian.

Indeed, that was how she felt as she faced Clyde over the rush mats and the yellow breakfast pottery. She wondered how soon it had been that Uncle Matt had got *his* feet on the ground again. When she said she was quite looking forward to the day, she fancied she caught a look of relief on her fiancés face, as if he had been afraid she might rebel at the last minute and then he would be caught between the two women of his life, unable to be mannerly to the one without offending the other. And observing this, Theo added, "That is, I look forward to having the beach wagon to ourselves. Shan't we go to the slot-machine place? Since it's my last day, I'll play the dollar one." But it seemed not worth while to be difficult and almost at once she gave in, though not without a challenge: she said, "I don't mean it. I particularly want to go to the Caverns." Even so, he was the master, it was his decision.

As they left the house and were getting into the beach wagon,

Mrs. Heath with bedtime hair and a Rogers Peet wrapper for a medium man called down from her window, "Good-by. Do have a good tramp through the Caves. Make it three of the sweet and one of the dry, Clyde, for I shall have to make them Martinis now and again."

In company with a few over a thousand other sight-seers, Theo and Clyde descended for a four-hour ramble through the vast gruesome cavity. It was cool and glimmering; beyond the groves of white and green stalactites patinated with damp and with obscure electric light, was darkness of a hellish impenetrability, a darkness too awful to scream against. It was superlative, like the worst nightmare of one's whole life. Theo, clinging to Clyde's hand, seeking out the park naturalists stationed everywhere with kindly smiles and gentle admonitions to watch one's step or not to touch, walked gingerly as if she trod on something nameless and alive, and when once her shoulder brushed against a horny stalagmite, she exclaimed in horror. They peered into unplumbed pits of the same primeval blackness that lay behind the tusks and fangs and they looked at castles, animals and faces made by an eternity of revision, shaped by a million years. At some times there was the sound of running water, wickedly hidden away.

Theo was weary immediately and though, at this point, Clyde might have given in, there seemed to be no way of turning back; to begin with, it would be impossible to stem the tide of people moving along in Indian file back to the entrance; once there, she imagined she would have to trump up an illness to be let out, for the Federal Government had put its signature on this vagary of the earth and policed it like the Senate House. They began, very soon, to have small fretful misunderstandings. Theo complained, that Mrs. Heath had recommended the wrong kind of shoes; she was quite sure she should have worn sneakers rather than walking shoes, and Clyde, taking this as an attack upon his aunt which indeed it was, said, "For God's sake, Theo, she has been here. She knows what's what."

"Obviously she doesn't," Theo replied, "because my feet hurt."

His jaw solidified with fury, and suddenly he looked exactly like Mrs. Heath. They had never quarreled before and so she had never seen this metamorphosis of his face. In the nasty murk, she watched him, clenched her fists and felt a hard resistance.

Midway through, they entered the largest chamber where a lunch counter had been set up and where one brought ham sandwiches and oranges and cartons of milk. Their fellow pilgrims stood about, bemused, nibbling the dry bread, their faces green in the dim light. Even those who had started out exuberantly were quiet now. Some of them were bored and some were frightened. A boy of ten in horn-rimmed spectacles, who had begun by educating his father in the history of the Caverns, now stood, unable to eat or speak, so close to his mother that he seemed to have been grafted onto her pongee skirt. A fat man yawned, consulted his watch, remarked to his companion that he wanted a smoke and wished they'd move on.

"She was right when she said we would have lunch in the bowels of the earth," said Theo, revolted, smelling the staleness of the bread, fancying that if the light were not so vague she would see mold upon the ham.

Clyde, who distractingly continued to take after his aunt, said sharply, "Why didn't you tell her you didn't want to come?"

"Why didn't *you*?"

This unaffectionate squabbling went on in low voices, although the babble of other quarrels about them made their precaution unnecessary. Mrs. Heath, the target, was like a tackling dummy, permanently resilient. Halfway through her orange (a very effrontery of an orange it was, pachydermatous and dry) Theo realized that she had gone quite beyond vexation, that she was extremely angry, that Clyde was weak and that he valued her happiness less than peace with his aunt. His face, which at one time she had found so beautiful that its image was indispensable to her, contained now the purposeless and unintelligent bullheadedness of Mrs. Heath's; handsome as they both were, will could make them hideous. It was, as she proceeded clove by clove through her orange, impossible to separate Clyde from his awful relative ("My God—she had worn driving gloves with Indian beading on the cuffs!") but she held her tongue, thinking, "I must not throw it all away simply because I should have worn sneakers."

At last they moved on at the invitation, unctuous but Governmental, of a park naturalist, and they left behind them the rinds of a thousand oranges and the crusts of a thousand sandwiches, marks immediately obliterated from the timeless floor by the men employed to keep the Caverns pristine. The ten-year-old, a querulous and intellectual child who was bound to have trouble at his boarding school no matter how progressive it was, plucked Theo's skirt by mistake, and when his mother claimed him, he said furiously, "You said you would be where I said for you to be. Why weren't you there?" His mother answered, "Hush, Brother, I came as soon as I could. The young lady isn't mad." Actually the young lady *was* mad and an interior voice stormed, "If it had not been for Mrs. Heath, this problem child would not have put his orange-juice fingers on my absolutely clean gabardine skirt."

Clyde and Theo did not talk much after the luncheon recess. They were surrounded by people who could overhear, and it seemed impossible to think of anything unquarrelsome in this place. Theo left off snatching at Clyde's hand when she was startled by some particularly improper aspect of the earth's hobby. Parasitically she followed the hushed, metallic alterca-tion between two schoolteachers (they could easily have been mistaken for librarians) over the quality of a pair of sunglasses which one had bought for the other at a rest station on the road from Roswell. Involved, as well, were a shrouded misdeed in Gallup and a person named Grace. Finally, when the vanguard of the mob had paused before a salty, noded palace which only fiends could have inhabited even in the imagination, one of these peckish old maids said to the other, "Estelle, we have come to the parting of the ways. At El Paso, I will quite *finally* say good-by to you at the bus station." The other replied, with keen decision, "Nothing could please me more."

A little after this (the ladies, after their declarations, had maintained a silence and a straight look forward) the entire party halted, ordered by an invisible hand at the very head of the procession, and a voice came booming through the un-healthy twilight, inviting everyone to find a seat in the "natural amphitheatre." There was a general murmur as the thousand reluctantly crouched, not easy in their minds about what they sat upon. The voice announced that they had reached the end of their journey and that now, with their kind permission, they would be bidden farewell by the civil servants who had shown them through. There was a pause and the bodiless voice bantered, "Don't be surprised, folks, keep your seats," and all at once, the lights all over the Caverns went out. A male chorus, made up entirely of baritones, sang *Lead, Kindly Light,* and each note came rumbling back from the echoing walls of the fun house.

The shock was maiming. Theo could see nothing, feel nothing, think nothing, desire nothing. The molehill became a mountain; she so disliked Clyde that she could not remember ever having liked him and she could not imagine what had got into her when she agreed to marry him. Even so, she became conscious of him, and her mind, lagging far behind her physical perceptions, finally understood that he had fumbled over her face with his lips until he found hers; he had planted a kiss upon her absolute void of a mouth, and this kiss was as stupid, as temporary, as messy as the orange rinds on the cavern floor. She was as repelled as if it were Mrs. Heath kissing her, and there was no tapering off: she drew away, the voices died, the lights went on and everyone moved to the elevators. But the time, filling up the vacuum, did not blur the moment of his doglike attempt to fawn away his offenses, and she, looking with willful courage into his eyes as the lift shot upward, knew that he had experienced what she had done, what Mrs. Heath in her brilliant subconscious mind had known they would do, and that the moment, rotten, black and round, ran up and down the channels of his mind, finding no outlet.

The very sharing of their injury made it possible for them, parting at the railroad station, to shake hands warmly, to wish one another a good winter, companionably to poke fun at Mrs. Heath's regret that they had missed the egress of the bats, to go their separate ways like the fed-up schoolteachers after a *final* good-by. And still Theo, who died hard and died always with her boots on, could not help crying from the vestibule of the moving train, "Don't forget the vermouth. Three of the sweet and one of the dry." And Clyde, before he took in the disdain in the concluding voice, nodded, smiled, cried back, "Thanks for reminding me. I had almost forgotten."

The Cavalier

THERE were times, that autumn in Heidelberg, when a sound or a sight made Duane realize that he was in a foreign country, and he might stop dead still for a moment, as he had all the year before at home in Arizona whenever he remembered, in the middle of a humdrum day, that he was in love with Phoebe. He would hear the remote double blast of a river barge as it approached the locks, or the lorn cry of a fish vender in a distant street, or the faraway plock-plock of a horse's hoofs over the cobblestones of the suburb of Handschuhsheim. Or he would be arrested by the spectacle of a flock of starlings flying down from the tops of the lime trees to drink at the old fountain, rusty and blue, that played before the *altes Gebäude* of the University; or of a soldier sitting by himself in an al-fresco café, so bemused by the sun and his thoughts that he had let his beer go flat; or of a salamander slipping through the pleached alley of hornbeam in the castle gardens; or of a *deutsches Mädel* sprawled in a hoydenish attitude against a path marker in the woods, tossing two horse chestnuts into the air as she waited for her companions, whom she had outdistanced.

With the realization, half delight and half despair, there came a growing pain and, after that, a stricture of homesickness, not so much for rooms and faces and familiar streets as for other times, for years when he had still been a school child, shuffling through the lemon-yellow elm leaves in the silent, coppery midafternoon. But the alien, German smells of hand-milled coffee and sweet cigarettes and brine balanced and then, after a while, overcame the remembered smells of new arithmetic books, and apples bruised on the walls of lunchboxes, and gregarious boys who smelled half of leather and half of fish. The schoolroom atmosphere retired then, and so did all the feelings of comfort and surprise that had marked the first week after Labor Day when he was a child. He confronted the facts of his being nineteen, a junior in college, and many miles and many years from those innocent places and those ignorant times (and an ocean and a lifetime away from Phoebe), and he sighed and stirred from his trance and moved on under the

oblique stare of the policeman who had observed him when
he halted.

How happy he had been then, he thought, before they had
pushed him out of the nest! When his shyness had been counted
a sad but understandable and even rather endearing trait. When
neighbor children came to play, Duane, hearing them call his
name in the yard, would run at once to the hall closet and
hide there among the canes and rubbers, every part of him
petrified except his headlong heart; at parties he sat miserably
in corners, ashamed of his solitude and terrified that someone
would benevolently try to deprive him of it. The dentist made
him shy by talking of matters other than his teeth, and if he saw
a teacher or a doctor out of the context of a classroom with a
blackboard or an office where a sterilizer hissed, he ran up alleys
or hid in doorways or boarded trolleys going to the outskirts
of the town. If relatives came to visit or friends of his parents
came to call, he was suddenly overburdened with schoolwork
and stayed in his room with the door bolted, listening enviously
to the soft, mumbling aplomb of their voices downstairs in the
parlor. Later on, when he was in his last years of high school
and his first two at college, his family had got impatient with
him and no longer called his timidity, in indulgent tones,
"Duane's unworldliness" but looked on it as a shameful disease,
nine-tenths egotism, and they crossly enumerated the opportunities he had denied himself, the friendships he had failed to
nurture, the pleasures he had fled, blushing, as if his very life
were threatened. Finally, although they could not afford it after
four years of the depression, they had sent him to Germany to
be cured of it. "If this doesn't turn the trick, when he is really
on his own," they said, throwing up their hands, "nothing on
earth ever will."

But nothing, so far, had been gained, and actually the plan
had been very naïve, since here, where he knew no one, no one
paid any attention to him and he was allowed, day after day,
to sit unmolested in the reading room of the library, under the
regard of Frederick the Great, who lowered in marble over the
doorway. He was not required to give more than a compatri-
otic nod to the other American students, and his professors
were much too much pure scholars to be concerned, as their
American counterparts had been, with the "adjustment" of

their students; their only intention was to disseminate learning. And thus, if Duane was desperately lonely, if he was often so lonely that, without histrionics, he wished he were dead, he *was* left alone; a whole week might pass when, except in recitation classes, he uttered no words beyond those essential to the barest mechanics of existence—the ordering of meals, the request for a towel from the porter at the public bath.

It was in consequence of the eventlessness of Duane's quiet, scholarly existence that he treasured the revelation of his being in a foreign country as if this were the thrilling, inner meaning of his present life. Now and again, after his morning lectures, he walked out along the river, on the highway toward Ziegelhausen, and had lunch at a *pension* called the Haarlass, nearby a monastery. One day, after he had eaten, he walked a little way into the woods, and on a particular rise he stopped to watch the monks below, in their long black skirts, swinging scythes and sowing the winter oats. An agile postulant chased a wayward sheep, tripped, and with a cry fell full length on the field. The monastery dog, a sorrel dachshund, burrowed in the ground at the boundaries, and occasionally ran to one of his masters and leaped into the air like a circus dog, barking madly. On the highway, there was a parade of washerwomen carrying baskets of clean linen to the young University gentlemen in the town; and Reichswehr lorries passed them, full of new recruits, who rattled the women with pleasantries and made them turn away their faces to giggle. The ferryman who rowed his boat between the landing of the Pension Haarlass and the trolley station across the river gathered driftwood and held a shouted conversation with Ernst, the landlord's cretinous son, who stood on the bank, constantly smoothing his scarlet stocking cap down over his shaved skull. And then, when Duane went back to Heidelberg, his joy was renewed as he crossed the Universitätsplatz, threading his way through the students, most of them in uniform, all their faces wearing, to his undiscriminating eye, the same expression of deep dreaminess, as if they stayed up all night at their lucubrations and all day long still listened to the music of the spheres. It pleased him to remember that this noble seat of learning had been established when the first breath of the Renaissance was stirring in Florence and Ferrara, when Chaucer was alive, before Christopher Columbus had been born. For all their badges of the twentieth century, their Brown Shirts and Black Shirts and Army uniforms, and for all their vehement, parochial polemic in the cafés of the town when they had had too much to drink, his fellow-students honored scholarship and pursued it with assiduous dignity.

Only two people in Heidelberg addressed Duane by name, and these were his landlady and the teacher of Anglo-Saxon, Herr Professor Kahler. The Professor was an old, grand man, and the moment he entered the lecture hall, wearing a cape and carrying a gentlemanly stick, Duane was so happy at the sight of him that he forgot how shy and how lonely he was and gave himself over wholly to the present, luminous hour. All the hard lines of youth had disappeared from the old man's face, and his whole appearance was like the raising of a fine hand whose gesture meant "No noise, no disturbance, please. Our concern is with the elevated consolations of philosophy." With his smooth white hair and his smooth white beard and his smooth brown face, he was the very true and perfect image of a German professor. Such was his air of timelessness (Melanchthon could have worn his cape), and so prominent upon him were the marks of humanism, that the S.S. men who littered his class, and the military women, and the salute "*Heil Hitler*!," with which he was obliged by law to open his lecture, seemed as trifling as personal troubles under the aspect of eternity.

Herr Professor Kahler had a love of language as devout as a love of God, and though he deferred to his foreign students, he spoke their languages better than they did, and spoke them in the most mellifluous voice imaginable. Duane was sure that unfastidious grammar caused him actual pain, and was always in dread that some offense would steal into his translations. Professor Kahler's conjugation of Anglo-Saxon verbs was a liturgy, and he sought the Indo-Germanic origin of words they found in "Widsith" as if he sought the Grail. And if Duane's German remained faulty to the end, so that he could not easily ask for thumbtacks in the Woolworth's on the Hauptstrasse, he learned a great deal about the vagaries of old nouns and subjunctives, and he knew Grimm's Law and Verner's Law as well as he knew his prayers.

It was an honor of high degree to be called upon to recite,

and Duane, who had always been an ardent student and whose diffidence vanished in a class, was excited and glad that Professor Kahler called on him so often. And so long as he was in that room, he thought he could not ask any more of life than to have this erudite man smile warmly at him and courteously ask his exegesis of a disputed line in "Beowulf." His manner as he began, "*Bitte, mein Herr,*" as he all but bowed, seemed to say, "Although I am the teacher and you are the pupil, we communicate on the same plane, and my age and your youth and our separate nationalities do not hinder the marriage of our true minds."

But Duane, while he was ambitious to impress Herr Professor Kahler with his high and serious intent, did not, of course, detain him after class with questions, as some of the other students did. And if ever, by chance, he saw the old man on the street, he scuttered quickly into the nearest shop; once, without realizing it, he chose a saddlery, where he stood gaping and being gaped at, and where he could not have explained himself even if he had known the language well. Another time, as he was setting forth to walk up to the Königstuhl, he saw the Professor toiling with an old man's care, supported by his stick, up the serpentine, steep street on his way, Duane supposed, to the café in the castle gardens. As he waited for him to pass out of sight, the boy wondered what the great man drank and whether, while he drank, he thought of the syntactical eccentricities of Walther von der Vogelweide, who had made his poems here in the castle courtyard.

The other American students were having the time of their lives. They did not care a pin that their German was execrable and that they were always overcharged, and, curiously enough, although they were taken in, they were not despised, because their loud, clowning manner was so good-natured and so self-assured. With a kind of mature, objective sorrow for himself, Duane watched the girls and the boys who had come over on the ship with him as, almost at once, they were assimilated into the life of the University. By day, they congregated in the Universitätsplatz with the uniformed autochthons, to jostle and joke and flirt and quarrel and haggle over American cigarettes; and by night they took the *Bierstuben* by storm, to sing interminably and to drink like bottomless fishes and to dance the German waltzes that it had taken them no time at all to learn. Now and again, abandoning his studies for a night, Duane followed a rowdy herd of them to a café, and, irrationally fascinated, he watched them from the darkest corner, where he sat at the smallest table, ostensibly immersed in Amadeus Thing's interpretation of "The Owl and the Nightingale." Often, at these times, the wine he drank and the youth of his quarry (he never felt that he belonged to their generation; sometimes he felt as old as one of the old men reading newspapers, and sometimes he felt like a baby) conspired to bring up Phoebe's image, which unexpectedly effaced his page of print, and made him feel entitled, by reason of his having been in love, to the habits and the pleasures of the revellers across the room from him. But he did not know how to approach them, and the moment that the desire to do so was fully formed, it was shattered and ruined totally by the memory of Phoebe's final laugh of scorn over the telephone and her shamelessly vulgar dismissal, "Go peddle your violets."

He drifted very soon into the routine that he had had at college at home—rising early and studying all the hours when he was not at lectures. As a treat, he would take a walk on Saturday or Sunday through the hills behind the castle. He usually ate his midday meal at the Mensa, the great, barnlike student cafeteria, where the food was certainly not worth more than the sixty pfennigs it cost, for it was cooked to pallor and flaccidity and then was seasoned with unheard-of condiments, which sometimes made him really sick. He went there rather than to a more expensive place, with better things to eat, because, though he was not part of it, he enjoyed the spectacle of the men in uniform, so many and so meticulous in their salutes that the Mensa was something like a barracks, and because deeply, inadmissibly, he had always admired soldiers and had longed for a war.

His breakfast was served to him in his room by his landlady, Fräulein Schmetzer, and he made his own supper, of cheese and *Wurst* and chocolate that he bought in the shop at the foot of his street. His room was not generally a bedroom at all but was a back drawing room Fräulein Schmetzer had let to him because the times were hard. He never entered it without that urgent realization that he was abroad, for it was a very German room. It was dark, and it was clogged like a fruitcake with furniture and garnishings. There were Napoleon and Bismarck Tobies, whose waggishness was damaged and lost by flaws and warts and bubbles; awful little bronze figurines of the Statue of Liberty and the Eiffel Tower and of Saint Sebastian. There were flowered-china slippers and cloisonné stamp boxes and dusty felt posies from discarded Tyrolian suspenders. Everything was missing in one part or broken in another, spotted or faded if it was a fabric, scratched if it was made of wood, chipped if made of marble or porcelain. Stoppers did not match decanters, and the dregs of wine in the decanters were solidified and old: his cup did not match his saucer, and the lid of the sugar bowl had been intended for some quite different purpose. He had to remember to choose his chair carefully, or he would find himself on something with only three legs, or would be impaled on a broken spring. The two front legs of a fusty red settee had been replaced by piles of shaggy old geography books. There were kidney-shaped ottomans and small gilt tables with marble tops, fish bowls, rubbery sofa pillows, tapestries, and lidless boxes containing buttons, Austrian schillings, corks, mutilated hairpins, and the scabby nibs of pens. There was a painting of five wasted cows drinking in a roiled river, and there were numerous photographs of the landlady's obsolete relatives. Hiding a balcony that gave on to a view of the castle was a tall Chinese screen, intricately carved of some hard, dark wood; in a recess in its middle panel stood a silver falcon, with sullen, popping eyes and a ferocious beak. But even worse than the bird were the plants ranged against the windows in majolica pots on wrought-iron stands; their leaves were so hairy and so darkly red, as if with rage, and their stems were so stout and calloused that they struck Duane as carnivorous, not in the subtle way of pitcher plants but boorishly gluttonous, as if they fed on tinned horse meat and bones. But Fräulein Schmetzer loved them, and he could not, therefore, ask her to take them away. She felt of their stems and prodded the earth around them and wiped the dust off their leaves, and sometimes, to make them glisten, she coated them with mineral oil, which she applied with a hygienic swab. All these ministrations she performed while Duane ate his breakfast.

Fräulein Schmetzer was a panicky spinster, who taught at the Volksschule. She was, by her own confession, the wretchedest woman alive, because she had never married and never had children, and all her wasted womanhood came feebly out to Duane in a tearful solicitude over a cold that he had ignored until it turned into a cough, and in a general kind of worrying over him, as if he were not real but were an abstract, generic boy who might have been her son. She had reserved the right to come into his room whenever she liked, and because the drawers and shelves and vessels were full of things for which she often had a sudden need, she did not fail to come at least once a day, and sometimes she came as often as a dozen times. Invariably, on Saturdays, she knocked on the door just as Duane was spreading out his supper, and, on the pretext of inspecting her uncouth plants or of looking for a vital photograph that had mischievously lost itself, so that she had to search all over the room, she stayed until Duane offered her a cup of spearmint infusion, which he brewed over a spirit lamp, thinking it helped his cough. Fräulein Schmetzer never accepted the infusion, which, she said, she associated with childhood illnesses, but she did accept the invitation to sit down that had been implied, and as her lodger ate and drank, she told melancholy tales of cousins who had lost their minds, of friends whose babies had been born dead or monstrous, and of her fiancé, who had been killed in the first year of the war and whose grave, in France, she visited every summer. When she spoke of this, her misery disordered her, and she seemed to disintegrate before Duane's very eyes. Her wan, thin hair slipped loose from its hairpins and wavered down over her freckled cheeks, her skin got duller and more wrinkled, and her eyes, enlarged by thick lenses with a violet cast, took on the look of an invalid in whom the will to live has perished. She was hugely fat, and her deep sighs made the great bulb of her bosom pitch and toss under her quilted foulard vest, while the boneless fingers of her clasped hands kicked hysterically in her lap. Her young man lay in a German graveyard between Amiens and Arras, where seventy-five thousand were buried; once she said—in a voice that was barely audible, as if this were the most distressing part of all—that a certain kind of pallid flower grew there between the painted crosses, but the roots were so frail, because the earth was sandy, that the slightest breeze was apt to pull them up.

The intricate smell of this room, as various and biographical as its litter, and the pitiful, unappealing woman made Duane even more bashful, and he felt so out of place in the ocean of her unhappiness that he spilled his tea or dropped his cigarette, and he could not find anything to say, not even in answer to her unjust accusations that he was too young to understand, and that his country had suffered nothing. She was at once enraged and captivated by this American immunity to misfortune, and she told him categorically, in a mixture of venom and respect, that he would never know what life was but would always live in Elysium, where hunger, cold, disease, and despair were unknown. And although she looked directly at him and saw that his clothes were shabby and had been cheap to begin with, and though she knew how little rent he paid and how little his meals cost, and though, by cleaning his room, she must have known how modest were all his belongings, she took no stock of these symptoms but deliberately assigned him wealth and lofty status and the unclouded happiness of one who does not know what hardship is.

In the beginning, out of his embarrassment at being just a little better off than she, Duane denied this image, but she so *wanted* it, she so persistently *knew*, in spite of all he said, that he had come from America first-class and that his parents drank champagne whenever they liked that gradually he was forced into silence and into an absurdly false position, which, in time, however, against all his private laws of modesty and truthfulness, he came to enjoy. Once, he had occasion to mention his grandmother's death, two years before, and Fräulein Schmetzer immediately described the pomp and ceremony that, she assumed, had preceded the burial in a luxurious tomb, and although everything she said was far from the truth, Duane allowed her to think what she liked. And then, by way of grievous contrast, she once more described those terribly temporary flowers in the soldiers' cemetery. Though Duane could not tell her so, he was reminded of the sand lilies that grew on the mesa behind his grandmother's graveyard, where he had sometimes gone to walk and to meditate on how he should lead his life. One blazing August afternoon, after he had seemed to defy all life by crushing the sand lilies under his moccasins, he had walked down past her grave, and there, upon the flat headstone, a brown snake was sunning, too insensate with its greed for heat to heed his coming. He had never worried the symbolic meanings out of this scene, but he knew they were there, images of evil and of suffering, and, remembering it now, in this room in Heidelberg, he was resentful of his landlady's flat denial that he had had any experience of life.

Because she had dedicated herself to the belief that he was happy, like all rich people, and because she teased him, angrily and affectionately, about the love affairs he must be having and the gay parties he must be going to with other Americans at the Scheffel Haus and the disreputable Vater Rhein, it became necessary in time for Duane to spend several evenings each week out of the house, and although he went only to the library or to the movies or to some quiet café where there was no singing, she was satisfied. She always waited up for him, and the moment she heard his key in the lock, she billowed out of her bedroom to interrogate him. These evenings, which were essential to her peace of mind, were bad for his cough, and often she scolded him absent-mindedly for setting his pleasures above his health. Another might have taken this infirmity as an indication that even the rich may falter in their well-being, but Fräulein Schmetzer, as clever as an alchemist, looked on it, rather, as but one more sign of Duane's good luck; a poor German boy would quickly waste away into tuberculosis and die of neglect, but Duane, she intimated, could go at any time he liked to the most expensive and most fashionable resort in Switzerland.

The truth of it was that he was obliged to economize so strictly that when he finally decided he must do something about the cough, he dared not go to a physician, for fear he would again be thought rich because he was an American and get a huge bill, and he went instead to the clinic of the Medical School, in a distant section of the town, where he was steamed in a box and massaged by a powerful woman and sent home, sometimes in the rain and often in the wind, which, day by day, grew colder as the autumn advanced.

Duane had always had the wisdom of a dumb animal whenever he was sick, and had simply lain motionless until all the pain or the fever was gone, but now, because he felt he could not disappoint his landlady, he did not give up but continued to go to all his classes and to spend long, dreary evenings in crowded, badly ventilated, and ill-lighted places, where he hacked and hacked, to the obvious annoyance of everyone around him. And whenever he came in at night, Fräulein Schmetzer sprang out at him, sometimes in such eagerness that she had failed to set herself to rights and appeared in a semi-dishabille that made him blush. A savage pride, barely distinguishable from the hatred he had begun to have for her, made him now contribute to the picture of the gala evenings that she limned for him, and though he was miserable and had no desire but to go to bed, he suffered her to stay an unconscionable time and, between his paroxysms of coughing, told her lies about the dancing he had done and the bridge he had played and the brandy he had drunk, in the American bar at the Europäischer Hof, in the company of smart travellers en route from Vienna to Paris, whom he had known in Newport, in Charlottesville, in New Orleans, in Bar Harbor. He had not seen So-and-So since her début, at the Boston Ritz, he would say, or Blank since they had cruised together in the Caribbean. If his ignorance and his discomfort led him into discrepancies, Fräulein Schmetzer was never aware of it, and when at last she left him, he fell on his bed, as exhausted from his triumph as from his cough.

Finally, realizing that he had fever, Duane diminished his mythical pace and stopped going out except for one night each week. Fräulein Schmetzer made up the reason for this change in his habits, and since it satisfied her, it also satisfied him; she said that he had had a quarrel with his girl. He selected Saturday as the night to go out, to give the appearance of keeping his hand in with the ladies, despite his rupture with the girl, who, for the sake of convenience, he referred to as Phoebe. Saturday was the traditional night for a gay dog such as himself to go abroad, and besides he could sleep on Sunday. But it was more difficult to find a place to go Saturdays than on other nights, for the library was not open; the movie was crowded, and because the sound track was defective, the audience openly objected to the continual racket he made with his coughing; the cafés, even the smallest ones, were almost as full, and the activity in them harried him like a prolonged and complicated nightmare, until, although he rarely drank anything but tea, he felt unpleasantly giddy and often he found himself on the point of giggling or bursting into tears. His eyes swerved and swagged like wounded birds over the busy scene until they came to rest on the open book he had brought along to cover up his solitude, but the words moved weirdly, sometimes swimming out of his ken and at other times leaping up to fasten themselves tenaciously to his brain, so that he could see no others.

He soon got into the habit of spending these Saturday nights out-of-doors, aimlessly walking through the streets and eventually ending up at the castle, where he stood on the shivered parapet of Otto's Tower, peering down through the river mist at the town below and thinking of the pleasures of his countrymen, which baffled him because he did not really understand why he did not share them. When this melancholy thought came to him, he made an impatient gesture with his hand and petulantly said, "I don't care at all. I came here to study, not to fritter away my time." Like a child, he would kneel down and lay his hot cheek against the stone of the parapet.

But very soon (because he was so ill and yet was so bent on enduring, these days went fast for him, so perhaps it was not soon at all but was a matter of some weeks) his Saturday nights acquired a goal, and instead of dreading them he now looked forward to them all during the week. A little after Fräulein Schmetzer left his room, about half past eight, there always came a queer conglomerate of sounds through the windows. There were fifes, drums, hoofbeats, shouts, and a sudden swell of German song, which sounded like a chorus of many hundred voices, followed by applause. Now and then, a single clear voice called out something and was then enfolded by the general commotion. Gradually the sounds would diminish, but through some acoustical freak, depending probably upon the configuration of the hills and the disposition of the buildings, it seemed, at certain intervals in its recession, to come nearer, like the voice of someone who has gone on talking absent-mindedly when he has left the room and then comes back. There would be a noise in the neighborhood—a group of boys singing, hoofs over the bridge—and Duane would think that he heard a detachment from the main body or its vanguard. He would lean far out the window and hear the boys' voices growing fainter as they descended into the town, and far off he could hear the cocky fifes, made frail and sweet by distance.

It was agreeable to be high up on the hill on these sharp-aired nights and to hear the celebration without being jostled or pushed back with the crowd by brusque policemen, or being offended by displeasing smells and the howls of babies in their mothers' arms. The suggestion of tumult only deepened Duane's desire to stay here, and he remembered the ease and strangeness he had felt as a child when he had lain ailing on the second floor and had heard from below the sounds that the well people made as they went about their business. He heard the noises still when, presently, he went out, and now and again a sharp wind brought them as far as the castle hill, where he homelessly roamed through the yew-bordered gardens.

One Saturday, as Fräulein Schmetzer was tending her plants—she seemed to be paring corns—he asked her where this hubbub came from. "Oh, they are going to the Stadthalle," she said. "It is a way to spend your Saturday night if you can't go to the Europäischer Hof." And without explaining who "they" were or what they did at the Stadthalle, she commenced to tell him a most miserable story she had had in a letter from an aged aunt in Schwetzingen. The old lady had reported that three boys of the town had been killed on maneuvers, although anyone with an ounce of sense could guess that they had really been killed in Spain, and that the supposed bodies that had been sent home in sealed, official caskets were nothing at all but sandbags. Duane did not listen to her but listened instead to the pleasure-seekers who could not afford the rich hotels, and because their general voice was happy and the voice in this room was nocturnal and embittered, he was wild to be off, and it occurred to him, like a stroke of madness, that if he found that boisterous mob, he could mingle with them; for the duration of one Saturday night he might be taken for a German, with his blond hair and his blue eyes, and suddenly there seemed possibilities of joy without end, and he wondered fretfully how long he had been hearing these sounds without recognizing the joy in them.

And still, the moment he left the house, his excitement left and his shyness overcame him, and he remembered how sick he was and how he must spend this night, as all the other Saturdays, coughing by himself in the mangled relics of the castle. But all the same he hunted the owners of the voices, thinking of a future time when he would be well and could join them.

That night and for three succeeding Saturdays, Duane sought the singing Germans and sought the Stadthalle, making it a point of honor not to inquire the way or to consult a map of the town. The voices, he told himself, would guide him, but their owners were all ventriloquists, and once they led him all the way to the freight station, a mile on the road to Mannheim, and another time fetched him up in the street of the brothels, where he was brought to bay by a phalanx of drunk Storm Troopers, who decided, for no reason at all, that he was a pimp and seized him by the arms, demanding his honest estimate of the rank and quality of the ladies in the houses. In this pursuit of phantoms through the streets whose buildings were dematerialized by the mist, he was often unbearably excited, as he had been on Halloween when he was a little boy, and he was sometimes immobilized with fright if he had to stop suddenly to cough beside a thick and ominous shadow.

On the fourth of these expeditions, he described a crescent through the town, going past the lighted windows of the cafés, where the shadows of his contemporaries loomed and waved; past the pawnshops of the Hirschstrasse and the shuttered *Konditoreien* and the dark butcher shops, where whole cow heads lay like sacrifices, their eyes still in their sockets, loose and filmed with a luminous blue. He stumbled, dispossessed of reason with his coughing, through a deformed little street that debouched into the cathedral square, and here he had to stop to let himself be shaken until his very backbone twisted like a snake. Someone, at this unnatural hour, was playing the organ. The crowd's voices were no more now than a pale hum somewhere to the west of him, so that the music, enwrapped by the silence of the empty church, came to him clearly. Whoever he was, this valiant soul braving the ghosts in the enormous church, he was playing a long Kyrie, and he was either an amateur or the music was very difficult, for often he struck a false, braying chord, broke off, and began again at the beginning of the phrase, but his errors did not lessen the richness of the grand voice. Once, a boy came cycling hell-for-leather around the corner of the cathedral, and another time the trolley clanged and careered down the Hauptstrasse. Two children, out on a late errand for their parents, passed him, running like birds; they were dressed alike, in peaked red hats and blue sailor coats, with crocheted shawls about their shoulders; one carried a basket full of parcels and the other carried a pail of beer. They smiled as they ran, not merrily and not really like children but out of some secret and satisfying wisdom. He had got his breath for a moment and he said *"Guten Abend"* to them, and they paused to stare at him, as if he had done some outrage to their privacy, and then he began to cough again, so hard that their eyes widened with indignation and fright, and they ran on without answering.

The protean crowd neared and he took a few steps forward to meet it, and then, coyly, it veered to the right of him, and by the time he had turned around it was miles away and had spun about in a circle, so that now it was in the east. Worn out with disappointment and with sickness, he sank to the paving and leaned his aching back against a closed bookstall between two buttresses. He sat there, half dozing between his attacks of coughing, and rousing himself abruptly when the organist made a rumbling *gaffe* and startled him into the knowledge that he must get up, he must go home, in spite of Fräulein Schmetzer—a knowledge that was annulled by the feeling that he could not carry his burning body a single step. A dozen times, in his imagination, he climbed the steps behind the Kornmarkt and trudged between the beds of daphne in the castle gardens and crossed the courtyard and descended his own street. As often, he drunkenly climbed the stairs to Fräulein Schmetzer's flat and faithfully told his stint of lies. But more than a dozen times—at least a hundred times—he thought of how, after it all was over, he would lie in his bed until morning, as safe, indeed, as any child in his own bed at home. As if from another world, he heard the voices of the natives, a swelling and ebbing stanza from the "Horst Wessel" song, and simultaneously he heard, hard by, the sedate and holy music, which lulled him like a song, and time and again he thought that he *was* in bed and that this whole experience was a vivid and almost reasonable dream.

A policeman crossing the Platz with his dog stopped when he heard Duane coughing, hesitated a moment, and then came briskly across the cobblestones. And the man and the black bitch, which bared her teeth and wanted to tear Duane apart, had exactly those proportions of reality and improbability that some dreams have.

"Good evening. *Heil Hitler!*" said the policeman. He smiled down unsympathetically on the young man sprawled in the shadows, his clothes awry. Clearly, he thought Duane was drunk.

"I'm sick," said Duane, and he tried to get up, but the dog pranced forward at the end of her leash and frightened him so badly that he sank back, his heart going heavily.

"So?" said the policeman, with the tolerant smile of the one in charge. "I don't very often find invalids lying about in the streets. Perhaps you were on your way to the chemist and were overcome?"

"No," said Duane and did not know why he could not stop himself from saying, "I was hunting for the Stadthalle."

The policeman chuckled and his face, which Duane now saw was brutishly handsome, altered a bit, and for a moment in the course of this game, which obviously was the kind he enjoyed, he was almost indulgent, his narrowed eyes seeming to say, "It can happen to anyone, old man, but you'll sleep it off."

He said good-naturedly, "You were hunting for the Stadthalle? At this time of night? In this part of town? I imagine you had some business to transact there? Something so pressing that it couldn't wait until the place was open and the officials were there?" He could hardly keep from laughing as he asked these rhetorical questions, and his dog was beside herself for wanting to fly at Duane's throat. Duane answered him artlessly, "My landlady told me that there's some kind of celebration at the Stadthalle on Saturday nights and that is where all those people go whose voices you hear in the distance." They listened, and the dog cocked her head to one side, but there was no sound at all; even the organ was still.

"Voices?" The policeman came closer to him to stare and judge, and the dog opened her mouth in a dangerous grin. A light on the man's military black helmet, reflected by the arc light, smote Duane's eyes like a small electric shock and made him sneeze, and then he began to cough again, dryly and with absorbing pain. First he stretched his legs straight out, and then he doubled them up and travailed with his head between his knees, and once a sort of wail, of which he could scarcely believe he was the author, escaped him, and it trembled pathetically in the lonely, misty night. When the spell was over and he could make himself heard, the policeman said, "May I see your papers, please? It is only a formality."

Duane gave him his passport and a loan card from the library, which the policeman held for some time, flicking the loose edges of the library stamps with his thumbnail.

"Well," he said at last, "I envy you, young man. If I could have a wish right now, I'd wish to be you—a young, rich, drunk American, as happy as a lark in Heidelberg on a Saturday night. But it is my duty to stop your pleasures. Get up, sir, and go home."

He helped Duane to his feet and, seeing that he was quite weak, steadied him with his capable hand and spoke roughly to the dog, who wanted bloodshed. Something in Duane had taken the man's fancy, and he said, "Perhaps I should see you home. You seem to be having some trouble with your legs." He laughed a little, almost affectionately. They proceeded slowly and silently through the Hauptstrasse and up the hill, and Duane was certain that he was on the point of delirium, for the thoughts he had and the visions that passed rapidly before his eyes were incomplete and unlikely. He imagined the conversation that he felt was inevitable between the policeman and Fräulein Schmetzer, in which, comparing notes with as much justice as possible, they would have to conclude against him and he would be arrested as a liar and a fraud.

Fräulein Schmetzer, wearing a shawl and carrying a basket over her arm, was unlocking the outer gate as Duane and the policeman approached. At first, she saw only her lodger and cried out, "I have been to the Stadthalle. What a time we had!" She smelled sweetly of beer, and her large face, even in this dim light, was orange. Then she saw whom Duane was with, and with bitter satisfaction she cried, "Oh, the gay blade! Now he has done everything! A duel, is it? Now he'll get a scar to take home to America with him and tell them all about avenging his honor in the Fauler Pelz!" And then she turned to the policeman and said, "But he's an angel, you know, in spite of all his money."

"I don't doubt it," said the policeman. "He gave me very little trouble." He said "*Heil Hitler!*" to them, apostolically lifting his white-gloved hand as if in benediction, and moved off with his dog.

Fräulein Schmetzer held the gate open for Duane to pass through. She was trembling with excitement. She said, "I can't wait to hear about it. Was it a quarrel over Phoebe?"

"Yes," said Duane, and his stricken mind, on fire with pain and loneliness, commenced loyally to outline this evening's installment for the obese, dolorous old child.

Old Flaming Youth

W E knew it must have been the Ferguson twins who had stolen Janie's gold bracelet because no one else had been in the house that day except the iceman and he had only come onto the back porch. It was not an expensive bracelet or an heirloom or anything like that, but Janie set great store by it because it was the last birthday present Daddy had given her before he died. We hunted everywhere for it, in every cupboard and closet and in the button box and in the first-aid kit and under rugs and in the rag bag; we even looked in the flower boxes on the front porch that held nothing but frozen dirt and a few stems as hard as wire and one exploded lady cracker. We emptied out the carpet sweeper and Mr. Pendleton, our step-father, even went through the garbage. We hardly spoke as we wandered upstairs and down, rummaging through the same places twenty times: I think I must have looked in the secret drawer of the sewing machine regularly every five minutes.

I don't imagine Daddy had paid more than two-fifty for it—it was just thin little links and probably it wasn't even real gold—but finding the bracelet came to be the most important thing in our lives. Janie wanted to find it for the reason I have said and Mother felt a little that way too, I think, for it had been only three days after that last birthday supper that Daddy had been electrocuted when he was repairing the lines at the depot. Mr. Pendleton wanted to find it because he was a methodical, fussy man and he hated to have things lost or moved or broken. Once he had had a conniption fit when Carrie, our dog, went off for a week, even though he didn't like her at all and called her names when she begged at the supper table. He wanted everything just so. And the reason I hunted so hard for the bracelet was that I didn't want the Fergusons to have stolen it and from the very first I was almost certain that they had.

I did not say so, but I distinctly remembered seeing it lying on the bureau in plain sight the afternoon before when Helen and Grace and Janie and I were all in Janie's room smoking and burning Maine Balsam incense to kill the smell and pushing the smoke out the window with our hands. It was cold and the twins were annoyed that we had to have the window open but we couldn't help that. I remembered seeing it because I had gone to the bureau once, pretending that I wanted to comb my hair but really to see in the mirror how I looked with a cigarette in my mouth. It was just a few minutes after that that Janie and I went down to make peanut butter sandwiches and when we came back we found, a little to our surprise, that the twins had put their coats on; they said they had to leave right away because they had a coke date with some boys from out of town. They each took a sandwich to eat on the way. Janie and I were rather peeved, but just for a second, and I didn't think about it again until we found that the bracelet was gone.

All day I kept my fingers crossed and prayed that it wouldn't occur to Mr. Pendleton to suspect the Fergusons, for he was a great one for calling the police, a fact so well known in town that at school Janie and I sometimes got teased by kids who would say, "Had any Peeping Toms lately?" or "There's a Mexican I know that's got his eye on your henhouse." And besides his liking to ring in the law whenever he got a chance, he did not approve of the Fergusons who peroxided their hair and wore high-heeled shoes and earrings just to go to the store. To keep peace, Mother had tried to get us to break up with them. She thought they were unsuitable too—there was no use denying it, they *did* have bad reputations—but she could see our point: they were the only girls our age in our part of town except for Mary Jo Baxter who was retarded and Ethel Bull who had been to New York and lorded it over us in a way no self-respecting person could stand. She used to call Mr. Ek's big old general store "the corner delicatessen." If you can imagine!

Helen and Grace had quit high school in their sophomore year because they didn't like to get up early in the morning, and nobody lifted a finger to stop them. I can just feature what would have happened if Janie or I had tried that. Wow! During the Christmas rush they worked at the dime store, but the rest of the time they did nothing at all except have a good time and sort of keep house for their mother who was away at work all day and their grandfather who was as old as Methuselah and couldn't do much more than sit in a rocking chair and whimper to himself. He rather cramped their style when boys came to see them, so they would get a couple of the fellows to pick him up, chair and all, and put him out on the back porch. I hated it when they did that because he would look so horribly scared and hang onto the chair arms for dear life and bleat the way Carrie does when I am taking a thorn out of her paw. But they said he didn't mind, that he was really not all there and anyhow he hadn't any right to mind since he was totally dependent on them and didn't have a red cent to call his own.

Mrs. Ferguson was a divorcée, a red-haired woman who had a millinery shop on Opal Street, and Mr. Pendleton, who had it in for milliners, don't ask me why, said she was no better than she should be. One night at supper he said that as he was going past the Fergusons' house on his way home from work he had seen her shimmying (that's what he said, *shimmying,* though when we pinned him down it turned out that she was doing the Hesitation Waltz) on the front porch with one of the twin's boy friends while another boy friend sat on the steps playing the saxophone. Mother, who had not danced a step since Daddy died, said she thought a plucky little woman like Mrs. Ferguson, with two daughters and an old sick father to support, deserved to have a little fun although she, personally, would not have gone about it so publicly. Mr. Pendleton was furious. He banged on the table and he said, "Next you'll be boosting free love."

Janie and I used to stop by their house on our way home from school a little after three, about the time the twins were having lunch. They had two menus, and only two. One was potato chips and Van Camp's pork and beans which they ate cold on paper plates and the other was wienies and canned sweet corn. For dessert they had either a Love Nest or graham crackers spread with Hippolyte. The grandfather cooked for himself; about all he cared for was fried mush. We could smoke freely there; Mrs. Ferguson knew and didn't mind—we were positive she smoked herself—and after the twins had finished eating and had thrown out the cans and paper plates, we would go into the front room and put a record on the Victrola (we were all four of us crazy about St. James Infirmary) and smoke. The square Mission chairs were so hard and slippery that we usually sat on the floor and sometimes, when my mind wandered, I tried to see a design in the blue and mustard linoleum, but there was nothing there except daubs and dots. The room was full of souvenirs from the amusement park up in the mountains, kewpie dolls, leather sofa pillows with burned-in designs of pine trees or Old Faithful, swagger sticks, burros made of lead and cowboys made of straw, presents from their beaux who had won them in the shooting gallery.

We didn't do much of anything there. Whenever Mother told us that she would "just as soon" we didn't see so much of Helen and Grace, we said how on earth could their influence be bad when all we did was play the phonograph and sometimes have a game of cassino? Of course we did not mention the smoking nor the fact that once in a while we had cokes sent in from the drugstore—Mr. Pendleton had convinced her that Coca-Cola was habit forming. But we really didn't do anything more than that; we didn't even talk about things we shouldn't although my sister and I agreed that Helen and Grace could probably have told us plenty if they'd wanted to. They were extremely popular; they went to Cotillion Hall two or three times a week and in the summer they practically lived at the amusement park. They looked exactly alike; they were small and thin and they had big yellow-green eyes and they used orange lipstick on their Cupid's-bow mouths. They dressed alike, too; when they put on their black satin dresses and their opera pumps with rhinestone heels and put artificial roses in their Jean Harlow hair, they looked like a pair of French dolls and Janie and I said it was no wonder they had about a million dates. They had their differences though. Helen was sometimes quiet, but Grace never was; when Grace wasn't telling a joke or singing a song or doing a Spanish dance and snapping her fingers like castanets, she was chewing gum and popping it loud enough to wake the dead. And often she almost but not quite told things she shouldn't have, to Helen's uneasiness. Once I remember Helen's saying quite sharply, "Do you want people to say you kiss and tell?" Another time Grace let slip a remark about wishing she had a bottle of cold beer and although Helen covered up for her by saying she didn't even know what beer looked like, she didn't convince us. It was a well-known fact that two of their boy friends, Arthur Bonelli and Ray Stapleton, were bootleggers and successful too.

But as I say, those afternoons at the Fergusons were as harmless as Girls' Friendly and they were necessary to Janie and me, mainly, I suppose, because we had to have some kind of interval between school, which neither of us liked, and supper, when Mr. Pendleton every single night would fly off the handle about something none of us was to blame for, like a customer who had come into the hardware store that afternoon and had run down his line of monkey wrenches, or the sin and wickedness which he was dead sure was rampant in the peanut gallery at the Rialto. Good gosh! Nobody sat up there but little tiny kids who hissed the villain.

We would get through the evening, though, if we had had that time with Helen and Grace. They were so easy going and good-natured—except, that is, about the grandfather and even so we could see how he was a bother and an embarrassment, being so outstandingly old and just sitting there day after day like a bump on a log and smelling funny, probably of all that mush he ate though sometimes it smelled to me more like coal smoke. We could forget about their meanness to him and their high-handedness with their mother ("I didn't ask to be born," said Grace once, "but since she went and had me anyhow, she can damn well support me.") because they were so casual and nice with us. They liked us and they said so and if it hadn't been for Mr. Pendleton, they would have got us dates. "You poor kids," they would say, "why don't you tell the old prude to go jump in the lake?" They did share with us the boys who came to see them and even bragged about us sometimes. "Did you ever see such long eyelashes as that Janie has?" "Sue is going to knock your eye right out when she gets to be about sixteen." We didn't usually stay long though, after the boys came, because we really hated to see them take the old man out; I think that sometimes that pathetic squawk he made was "Help! Help!"

Well, we hunted for the bracelet all day Sunday and by the time we sat down to supper, we had to accept the fact that it wasn't in the house. And then Mr. Pendleton asked who had been there the day before. I suppose that Mother and Janie had been thinking the same thoughts I had because all three of us together said "The iceman."

"Dude Kennedy?" said Mr. Pendleton. "Rats. Dude wouldn't

know a gold bracelet from a potato worm." And he was probably right because Dude had been simple from birth. "Who
else was here?"

"Was anyone else here, girls?" said Mother as if she honestly
could not remember. Personally, I would have lied and said
no, even if it had been my bracelet and was set with rubies and
pearls. But Janie, either because she hadn't suspected the twins
or because she wanted her bracelet back, no matter what, said,
yes, the Fergusons had been here.

Mr. Pendleton stopped cutting his meat—he has the most
maddening way of cutting it up fine before he eats a bite, exactly as if he were fixing it for a child—and slapping his hands
palm down on the table he said, "Of all the rattlebrained ways
to waste a man's time! Looking through the garbage on my day
of rest for something those flappers stole. Well, it's clear the
Misses Thomas want to make a chump out of me."

It rankles terribly with him that Janie and I have kept Daddy's name and that we've never been able to call him anything
except Mr. Pendleton. Mother did what she could to calm him
down and he agreed not to call the sheriff if Janie and I would
promise to go over to the Fergusons right after school the
next day and demand the bracelet. At first he wanted us to do
it after supper—he said you never could tell with people like
that, they might have skipped town. The way he talked, you'd
have thought the thing came from Tiffany's instead of from the
Nelson Dry. But Mother said we had our homework to do and
finally he dropped the subject.

After we went upstairs I couldn't help telling Janie that I
thought she was a selfish pill but she felt so awful about giving
the twins away that I apologized and we started to lay our plans.
At first we thought we would try to prove to Mr. Pendleton
that they hadn't taken it, although we knew they had, but we
were afraid he wouldn't believe us and might go down there
himself and make a scene. We decided it would be better if we
could go into the house when they weren't there and see if we
could find it. One of them might be wearing it, of course, but
we thought they probably wouldn't dare for a day or so. So it
was agreed that Janie was to go to their house by herself and
say that I was still at school getting help in geometry and she

was to persuade them somehow to go out for a coke. I would be hiding behind the ashpit and as soon as I saw them leave the house, I was to go in the back door which they never kept locked and get the bracelet. If the old grandfather saw me, I would first ask him where the twins were and then I would say that I had left my protractor here somewhere and would he mind if I looked for it. If I found the bracelet, we were going to tell Mr. Pendleton that it had been in Janie's gym locker all the time.

It was a pretty day that Monday, soft and springlike although this was only February, and Janie had no trouble at all getting Helen and Grace to go out with her because the weather had made them restless. That is what they *said*, but of course later on we knew they had another reason for wanting to be away from the house. I was in luck, too, for the grandfather was sitting on the front porch in the creaky old swing they never bothered to take down in the winter. He looked as if he were going somewhere; he had on a pale gray hat which he had dented in a way to make it look like a shovel and he was wearing an old polo coat of Grace's and a pair of galoshes with the buckles gone and one red and black striped mitten. On the swing beside him there was a Boston bag which I remembered to have seen before in the kitchen, full of potatoes. The Fergusons did things like that; for instance, they kept the playing cards in the icebox.

I saw the girls leave. I heard Helen say to the old man, "Now don't you move. You stay right where you are until they come. They're supposed to be here in precisely fifteen minutes."

His thin, wispy voice said, "You coming back?" I realized that it was the very first time I had ever heard him say actual words. Somehow I had thought he was a sort of deaf-mute: not really one, but just so old that he couldn't speak or hear. It gave me a queer feeling to know that all this time he had heard the dreadful things his granddaughters had been saying about him.

Helen said, "We're coming back when we get good and ready. As soon as they get here, you go along with them."

"So long," said Grace. "See you in church."

"Where is Ada?" he said in a little scream.

"At the store. Where did you think?"

The old man lifted the hand that was bare and seemed to wave it. The twins waved back and Grace said, "Go bye-bye?" and laughing they ran down the steps.

I waited for a few minutes and then went into the house. I was scared and I felt guilty, as if I had come here to steal something instead of simply to take back my sister's personal belonging. The water dripping in the kitchen made a loud and lonesome noise and every time I caught a glimpse of the grandfather sitting out there on the porch as I passed by one window or another, my heart did a loop the loop. He sat absolutely still, staring into space. Maybe he was going to visit friends or some other relatives; the Fergusons had some cousins in Nebraska and several times I'd heard them say they didn't see why they didn't take some responsibility for the old man, having a great big farm and plenty of space. It was none of my business, but I hoped that was where he was going and that the cousins would be nicer to him than the twins were.

They had hidden the bracelet well or else, I thought, they had it with them. I hunted everywhere, and though there were about twenty bracelets in all sorts of places—I found a bright green one in a box of nails—Janie's wasn't one of them. The drip in the kitchen and the noisy clock nearly sent me crazy the way they worked together offbeat: drip, tick, drop, tock. I was almost ready to give up and I was almost ready to cry when all of a sudden I saw the clasp hanging down below the orange wig of the kewpie doll on top of the Victrola. The wig came off and showed a round hole in the doll's head and there the bracelet lay like brains.

Everything happened at once then. I heard the girls come up the walk and heard Grace say, "For cat's sake, they haven't come *yet*," and at the same time I heard a car stop outside the house. All the same, I had time to get out the back way and then I walked very slowly around the block and up to the Fergusons' front lawn. The District Council car was there beside the parking and that thick-ankled Mrs. Downes, who is also the chief public nurse, was up on the porch with the grandfather, sitting beside him on the swing and rubbing his ungloved hand between hers as if it were frostbitten. She recognized me as I came up the steps; she ought to know me, I've been in quarantine enough times and she's the one who puts me in and lets me out. "Hello, Sue," she said. "Do you know where the Ferguson girls are?"

There was not a sound from within the house and though I knew they were there, I dared not say so for I was not supposed to know.

"I thought I saw someone going in the house as I drove up, but nobody answered when I rang the bell and the door is locked."

"I think they're at the drugstore with my sister," I said and loudly I added, "I had to stay in this afternoon and work on my geometry."

Mrs. Downes clucked her tongue and said, "What do you think of girls who go to the drugstore when their own grandfather is going to the County Home? I'm surprised that you are friends with girls like that."

County Home! I nearly passed out. That awful poor farm out beyond the city limits where they still didn't have electricity and not a single tree or flower grew for miles around: I mean it, there wasn't a solitary thing to cast a shadow. Once a long time ago we had had more beans in the garden than we could eat or can and Daddy and I had taken a bushel basket of them out there. I had never forgotten the look and the sound and the smell of misery and how everything was gray and damp and weak. They had all looked like rags, those old outcasts, sitting on the piazza on benches with no backs to them, staring at their feet and not even looking up when Daddy cheerily said, "Hello! Anybody home?"

Mrs. Downes stood up and put her arm around the grandfather and eased him to his feet. She took the Boston bag and then she guided Mr. Ferguson down the steps saying, "Careful, dear, step! Now another." She did not turn around but she said, "Tell those girls for me that I hope some day *they* are down and out. Some day soon! And the same goes for their mother. As for you, Sue Thomas, Mr. Pendleton ought to take a hairbrush to you for keeping company like that."

After the car drove off, the front door opened and Grace cautiously peered out. "For Pete's sake, come in," she hissed at me. "What the heck did you say we were at the drugstore for? She might go down there and look for us and then it'll be all over town."

Janie was as white as a sheet but she was smoking and she had a smile on her face, but I knew my sister well enough to know it was a made up one, that she had just put it on the way you put on your hat. The first thing Grace did was to light a cigarette and give it to me and then she tried a riddle on me that they had heard from the soda jerk, a wisecracking boy named Milo Bean. "When a man marries how many wives does he have?" The answer was "Sixteen—four richer, four poorer, four better, four worse." I made the most ridiculous sound when I tried to laugh and Grace said, "What's the matter, kiddo? You're not worried about the old man, are you?"

"Doesn't he have a coat of his own?" I asked.

"Don't be ridick!" Grace blew a perfect smoke ring. "Where would he get the shekels to buy a coat? Listen, hon, don't blame us, it was Ada's idea. We told her it was us or him and naturally she picked us."

"Mrs. Downes is nice," said Helen.

"Nice? Did you hear what she said about us? She's a polecat." Grace's gum exploded like a popgun. She was chewing Tea-berry; I could smell it. "Let's play St. James Infirmary."

She started to the phonograph, stopped short and then went on. I had forgotten to put the wig back on the kewpie doll. We all looked where Grace was looking and Helen said, "St. James Infirmary is too boo-hoo. Why don't you play us something on the uke instead?"

So Grace played "Show Me the Way to Go Home" and "Sleepy Time Gal" on the ukulele and Janie and I stayed until we had each smoked two cigarettes. We left as soon as Arthur Bonelli and Ray Stapleton came. Ray looked at the empty rocking chair and said, "Where's old Flaming Youth? Don't he want his joy ride?"

The girls laughed and Grace said, "He's getting it, big boy!" Ray rumpled her hair.

Mr. Pendleton believed Janie when she said she had found the bracelet in her locker and after he had lectured her on forgetfulness, he stopped talking about it though he never quite forgave her for wasting that Sunday and making him go through the garbage. We never went back to the Fergusons again and Mother, who has a lot of sense, never asked us why. The only time the name was ever mentioned again was when she heard at the store that the grandfather had died in the county home. Of the mumps, if you can believe it.

I'll never forget that afternoon as long as I live and I know that Janie won't either, for she has never worn the bracelet since and if she comes across it when we are cleaning out our bureau drawers. I see her quickly cover it up with a handkerchief or a pair of gloves. Of course we see the Fergusons; we couldn't help it, living only two blocks away. They are always friendly when we meet. "Hey there, Thomases, how's tricks?" they say but we notice that they don't want to stop and talk.

Now what we do to get ready for Mr. Pendleton at supper time is go to the Public Library and read Faith Baldwin's books.

The Violet Rock

ONE day in the early spring when I was eight and my sister Emily was twelve, we went together up into the foothills to look for pasqueflowers. These were the earliest flowers to bloom after our stern Colorado winters, and a reward of a Fabrikoid pencil box with ten pencils in it was given each year to the child who brought the first of them to school. It was as much to have the subtle hints of spring confirmed as it was to win the pencil box that we hunted so hard all afternoon, combing the mesa, rummaging through the gulches, seeking in the greening dell below the beaver dam. We were alternately assiduous and absent-minded in our search, and we were the more impatient since everything indicated that the pasqueflowers must be out by now: In the canyons, the waterfalls, released from the ice, were engorged by the thaw, and they roared and frothed with violent life; on the prairies yonder below us, volunteer timothy was beginning to show in patches in the dun sage; the chokecherries had commenced to bud out rustily; and in the secret forests, where the last of the snows were perishing even in the deepest shadows, we heard the tentative songs of birds just up from the South. More than any of these things, the light and the air of the newborn season animated us, and we were occasionally so headlong that we turned cartwheels and did not even care that the harsh ground skinned the heels of our hands. Emily, an emotional and literary girl, recited "I wandered lonely as a cloud" in a natural amphitheatre nearby the red rocks, and I was profoundly impressed by her loud, heartbroken voice and her tragic gestures. We sang sometimes, and sometimes, in a sheltered place, we screamed and listened to the walls of rock cast back to us a thin and tremulous mimicry.

But we found no pasqueflowers, although we did not give up until after the sun had set and the sky was marble and the light had gone yellow on the far glacier. Nor did we have any adventure to take the edge from our disappointment. We had found no objects to invite our speculation—no empty whiskey bottles, no deer shot out of season, no prospector's warped and rusted pan, no torn-up letters dropped by spurned lovers at their wits' end. Though this was the time of year the sheep started coming up from the plains, heading for the mountain meadows, we had seen no half-cracked Mexicans gibbering to their herds. There had not been a sign of Willy Lathrop, the handsome and swashbuckling forest ranger on his cross black horse; there had not even been a patient from the sanitarium to sneak up on and scare as he smoked a forbidden cigarette.

In fact, we had seen no one at all, and this was odd, for on a fair day like this the mesa was a favorite place for the town's invalids and sweethearts to stroll. Once, I asked myself why there were no other children prowling, like ourselves, upon the broad tableland so high above the town; the announcement of the prize had been made that day in general assembly, and I remembered that in other years my schoolfellows had come up in droves and we had teased and pushed each other and giggled and squabbled, as we would all do a few weeks later on Easter Sunday, when there was a community egg hunt in the park. I nearly spoke to Emily of our unusual solitude, but I held my tongue because I knew that Emily, volatile and clever, would either give me some practical and belittling explanation that would dispel my half-pleasant uneasiness or seize upon the circumstance and magnify it so hugely and embellish it so intricately that she would frighten me half to death and cause me, very probably, to walk in my sleep that night. A part of me wanted to be frightened by Emily, but another part knew that it would be unwise now, when we were still so far from home and the night was coming on. And I certainly did not want to walk in my sleep again—not after the last time, when I had gone right out of the house and down the street to the widowed Mrs. Bradford's, and had, as she said, "petrified" her when she saw me on the front porch, barefooted and in my pajamas and still sound asleep. A fear of bad dreams and a fear of fear began slowly to invade me and to generate hypotheses as dire and as imaginative as Emily's would have been: the mesa that we were traversing now, on our homeward journey, was deserted because everyone in town was dead except the two of us, who had escaped the plague (or the pirates, or the dangerous runaways from the penitentiary in Canon City) purely by accident and who were now returning to a settlement of charnel houses about whose chimneys the scavenger birds were circling already. Or this whole day had been nothing more than a long, logical dream and there really had not been any assembly and I was walking in my sleep right now.

I said nothing, though, lest, by giving voice to these fearful possibilities, they become reality, and I scuffed along quickly, looking neither to the right nor to the left. While I was nervous in the cooling air (behind us, the evening wind was keening in the lodgepole pines), Emily was first bored and then angry. In her frustration, she had suddenly remembered that she despised me because I was a child.

She had come with me this afternoon chiefly because she had nothing better to do (of course, she did want the pencil box, though she would never admit to that, for she pretended that she was above such things—a ridiculous pose, since there had never been a girl so greedy for public distinction), having quarrelled this week with all her friends and most bitterly with our older sister, Stella. Now, grumpy with anger, Emily persuaded herself that she had had a thousand urgent things to do, and she accused me of leading her on a wild-goose chase because I was a scaredy cat, afraid of going up to the mesa alone. I started to remind her that she had *offered*—had very amiably said, as she saw me going through the back yard, "Do you want company, Tess-girl?" Actually, she had sounded rather plaintive—actually, I had been doing *her* the favor—but if I had said so, she would have told me that I was lying like a rug, and anyhow she did not give me a chance to get a word in edgewise. If it had not been for me, she nagged noisily, she could have spent the afternoon doing some collateral reading, for which she would eventually get a school letter to wear on her sweater, like an athlete; or she could have memorized "John Gilpin's Ride," or worked on a raffia basket for which she expected to win a Campcraft merit badge (I happened to know, though I was not at liberty to tell, that there had been some talk of expelling her from the Big Horn Patrol, because of the way she ceaselessly took the Lord's name in vain); or she could have finished making her crossword puzzle, or made divinity. And she knew for a fact, she said, because she knew me and my scurvy ways, that if she had found a pasqueflower, I would have claimed the credit and hogged the pencil box. She called me a cad and a nitwit, a Hottentot and a crook, and she told me that I had been adopted from a home for feeble-minded children whose parents were all in the pen. I had known positively for a year and a half that I was not adopted, but the habit of believing Emily was so ingrained and strong that I shivered with self-pity, and, feeling so lonely anyhow, I nearly cried.

Abruptly, my sister stopped in the middle of the path and doubled up, clutching her stomach and groaning, "I'm starving! I'll be dead before we get home, thanks to you and your damn dumb flowers."

Emily's temper tantrums, like her ghost stories and her tales of mutilation and kidnapping, entranced while they horrified me. They came on with as little warning as an electric storm, and they were as dramatic and incomprehensible. Her whole being participated in them—not just her oratorical big eyes and her lopsided mouth and her rich, wide-ranged voice but her hands and her elbows and her knees and her feet, which articulated just as clearly as any vile words could the fury that had bedevilled her since she was born. (According to our parents, when she was in her cradle she had alternately yelled at the top of her lungs and held her breath till she turned blue, and Mother said that for the first four years of "that girl's" life she had not had a decent night's sleep.) She would do a kind of writhing witch dance, shrieking out the most appalling imprecations against everyone she had ever known or heard about; if she ran out of friends and relatives, teachers and other professional people she personally knew, and still had spleen and energy to spare, she would excoriate the President of the United States. Sometimes, when the rage was spent, she turned grayly pale, and not infrequently she vomited and had to be put to bed in a dark room with a wet washrag over her feverish and aching head. Docile and pathetic then, she would lie there moaning like a dove, but she was never penitent; on the contrary, blaming us all, she'd be forgiving. Her favorite speech after she had upset the whole family was "I forgive you, for you know not what you do." One thrilling night, she was really sick and the doctor had to be sent for; and he took her to the hospital, where her exploded appendix was taken out. Our mother quite seriously thought that now this actual poison was out of her system, her disposition would improve. But it seemed, if anything, to worsen, and our bamboozled, bullied parents enjoined Jack and Stella and me never to cross her and never to bait her and never to disagree; Emily might die of apoplexy, they said. Jack and Stella would not be a party to such contemptible blackmail, and they would tell her to dry up or go peddle her papers. But I did what I was told, because I had a yellow streak, and consequently I was the target of her worst broadsides.

Emily needed only the most tenuous materials with which to build her towering rages—as now, when she had fashioned a passion out of nothing more than her normal suppertime appetite and the tardiness of the pasqueflowers. Her long, skinny arms were flailing in their blue serge middy-blouse sleeves, her pigtails thrashed, her feet stomped out a warpath in the red dust, which rose in clouds to powder her knee socks, and her mouth was a livid cave from which spewed out, like rats and reptiles, the declarations of her hatred of everyone and of her intentions to murder with an axe, to burn up schoolhouses and churches, to blow up the bank, to strangle the cat and poison the dog, to puncture the tires on the cars that belonged to the fathers of the girls with whom she was not on speaking terms. She even, parenthetically, maligned the pasqueflowers and bellowed that their hideous, hairy stems were enough to make a decent person sick.

I had moved out of reach of her dangerous gesticulations, and my view of her, from a few yards down the path, was oblique and weird. Silhouetted against the darkening vast sky toward which the blue teeth of the mountains rose, she was like some huge injured bird of prey, a little fictitious and a little farcical but exciting and resplendent. (Once, Jack had been sincerely carried away by her performance and had cried "Bravo!," and Emily had thrown a lump of coal at him.) She warned me not to move one step toward her or she would beat me within an inch of my life. "You and your foul, goddam, obnoxious pencil box!" she snarled. "You filthy, rotten, dirty, lousy cur!" She never paused for breath, she seldom repeated herself, and her tone ranged from the iciest sarcasm to the fieriest venom.

We were at the entrance to a beggarly public park into which the lower canyon debouched—a rocky tract of land that got its title "park" from nothing but a couple of disreputable picnic

tables and a small pavilion where, in summer, Jack and I operated the popcorn machine for the concessionaire and where
bottles of pop were kept in a barrel with a block of ice, presided
over by Jack's patrol leader. I knew every inch of the park by
heart—each tree and turning, each boulder and minuscule plot
of grass—for it was here that we played run sheep run and
hunted caddis worms in the amber pools of the creek. But this
evening, as I glanced away from Emily, the whole place looked
altogether unfamiliar to me, unnaturally dark, the cottonwoods
immense, and the springtime voice of the creek that bifurcated
it was strange; it clattered over its rocks with a bony sound, and
from time to time I heard a watery chiming that I could neither
identify nor situate.

It was a queer evening, and when I scanned the sky and saw
Venus, huge and single over Blanchard's Peak, I shuddered
and felt the gooseflesh leap out along my arms. From here,
at this declivity, we could not see the lights of the town (If
there were any tonight! If the man in the substation hadn't
died before he turned the switch!), and it seemed to me that
everything human and understandable was far, far off, and that
here at hand and surrounding me were nothing but threats of
cold-blooded murder from the scornful old earth and from
this crazy girl; it would not have surprised me very much if
Emily had taken a gun out of her pocket and shot me through
the heart, nor would it have surprised me to see the evening
star sail across the sky and drop down on top of me. And as
the last of the afterglow began to ebb away behind the range,
I thought again of the buzzards that might well be feeding on
the citizenry. We would have a better chance against them, I
thought, if we were in a house with the doors and windows
locked and the damper of the fireplace closed, and I was at last
so panicky that I interrupted Emily, who was fiercely denouncing the principal, whose hash she meant to settle, whose goose
to cook to a cinder. I said, "Come on, Emily. Please come on.
I think something's wrong."

"Bushwa!" she roared. "Bushwa, I say, ten thousand times!"

But then, all of a sudden, she was absolutely still; it was really
as if she had been paralyzed and struck dumb. Her face, in
which the causeless anger was already obsolescent, took on an
expression that warned me she was going to scare me. For this

was the look she wore in the middle of the night when she crept out onto the sleeping porch and woke me to whisper that the coyotes were closing in upon our house and would not be satisfied with anything to eat but me, or that the Germans were coming to cut off my hands, or that she was no sister, she was no girl—she was a maniac named Jack the Ripper.

After a heavy moment, in which we stared at each other (Emily's talent as Svengali was actually less than mine as Trilby, for I was instantaneously responsive and obedient to all her moods), she spoke. "I'll *say* there's something wrong! Here, Tess. Here, Tess," she said, wheedling as if she were calling a dog, and, holding her hands outstretched, she inched toward me in her soft sneakers. "Don't be scared, Tess-girl," she said. "Just keep cool but move away from it. Don't jump and don't make any noise but move *away*."

"What from?" I cried. I knew it was far too early in the year for snakes, but, even so, I quickly scanned the ground and bounded away at the sight of a long, thin stick. "What *is* it?"

"The Violet Rock," said Emily, in a stage whisper. "It's right behind you. For Pete's sake, *do* move before it's too late."

I wheeled and faced a tall and well-known (and until now nameless) boulder, lichen-covered, girdled rankly with poison ivy in the summer—a convenient promontory on which Jack and I stood when we were reconnoitring as Indian scouts or were giving orders to our troops to go and decimate the Hessians.

"Watch out! Don't even *look* at it!" my sister called, and involuntarily I ran up the path toward her, but, like Orpheus, I could not resist looking back, and as I did so, I saw a massive shadow loom against the face of the rock. It was my own shadow, as I knew, but I was now bewitched, and when Emily put her arms around me and tensely asked if I was hurt, I burst into tears of terror, which became a sort of fit when this bad girl reminded me of the long way we still had to go, with no sun and no moon to light our twisted path through the park ("What's wrong with the crick?" she said, her voice hushed. "It sounds as if something were damming it, up by the bridge. We'd better get out of here—it may be a corpse") and through the outskirts of the town where the miners lived, ready to carve up a girl into pieces if they took a mind to. And past a haunted house, set in a snarled field where, in a long-dead, weed-ravaged garden, there were three flat stones, marking the graves of three horses, whose ghosts were heard trotting through Main Street invariably on a night when someone met a violent death.

"But let's just get past the Violet Rock first," said Emily. "And then we can run." She linked her arm through mine, and with her other arm she fended off the enemies and vampires that I believed were skulking in the rifts of the rock, and as we passed safely by, my sister sighed and said, "Good grief! Was *that* a narrow escape! In another minute, I swear it would have started, and it would have been goodbye Tess."

"Do you mean poison ivy, Emily?" I asked her hopefully, leaning hard against her and remembering a time when my eyes had been swollen shut with poison-ivy blisters. "Do you, Em?"

"No, dear heart," she said sadly. "I wish it were nothing more than that."

My huge heart was in my sandy throat. "What's the Violet Rock?" I bleated.

We had not, as Emily had promised, begun to run. Holding me tight in her stalwart grasp, she made me accommodate my pace to hers, and as we went slowly down through the park, past the bridge where the dead body was turning spongy, past hunchbacked bushes and hiding places for cutthroats and laughing hyenas, she told me, freezing my blood and my bones, the dooming story of the Violet Rock and why it was that I, and I alone, must never go near it after the sun had set. The facts, she said, were known only to herself—never mind how she had found them out. And I must never, never breathe a word of them to a living soul, or something too terrible even to describe would happen to me. Something a thousand times worse than the guillotine.

The rock, Emily said, belonged to Mr. Norman Ferris, the multimillionaire owner of the Gold Palace Hotel, which stood on a high hill at the northern end of our town. Mr. Ferris, I knew, was richer by far than Croesus; he would buy a whole mountain if he liked the looks of it, and build a luxurious shelter house on the summit, which he would then forget about and leave to the pack rats and the tramps; though he himself was a freethinker, he had built a Catholic church for his aunt to worship in when she came to visit him for two weeks each August;

he had bought an elephant for the children of his employees to ride; the floor of his bedroom was paved with twenty-dollar gold pieces. He had the reputation of being philanthropic and democratic, but no one in the town had first-hand knowledge of him, because he and his guests and his employees were a world apart from us; they all came from the East, and, with our Western and small-town xenophobia, we tended to mistrust them and to give them a wide berth. Emily, however, who had ways of finding things out and who was, besides, clairvoyant, happened to know that there were things about Mr. Ferris that did not meet the eye, and the one that was to endanger my whole life was the fact that he bore grudges.

"You remember the day you sassed him?" said Emily.

"I never!" I exclaimed, aghast. "I never did sass Mr. Ferris!"

Well, Emily would help me to remember. I did remember, did I not, that Sunday last September when, hearing that Mr. Ferris and his friends were to play polo on his private polo field, Jack and I, thinking there might be a big crowd there to watch the rich men at their sport, had got permission from the owner of the popcorn stand to wheel it down from the park, through the town, and up the other hill to the grassy grounds beside the hotel?

Did I remember! Jack and I, dreaming of hundreds of dimes, had got up at five o'clock that morning to start our laborious trip, so that we would not be seen and criticized by people going to church. We had no way to brake the machine, and a couple of times, in steep places, it had almost got away from us. There had been times when we thought we would have to abandon it in the middle of the street and get our father to take it back to the pavilion in his pickup, and we were on the verge of collapse from thirst and pain by the time we got to the courthouse and drank from the public fountain there and lay down for a while on the lawn. But we were strong and we needed the money, and though it took us four full hours, we made it, with pounding hearts and blistered hands and aching legs, long before even the Sunday schools began. We were eyed curiously by people reading the *Rocky Mountain News* on their front porches, but no one questioned our right to do so outlandish a thing on a Sunday morning, and the only person who spoke to us was the deputy fire marshal, who warned us to make sure the stoppers for our kerosene cans were in tight and then smiled at us and said, "I hope you strike it rich, you kids."

We were accompanied by our dog, Reddy, half collie and half Saint Bernard, a companionable and fatuous animal, who had been given us, when he was a puppy, by a paroled convict who ran a diner on the road to Canon City. A few weeks earlier, Reddy had come home from a two-day vacation in the mountains so encrusted with burrs and ticks that our father had barbered him like a poodle, leaving only his great, tawny ruff and his foxy tail. Jack and I thought he looked like a lion, but Emily said he looked like a fool and she, personally, was ashamed to be seen with him in public.

We stationed our popcorn stand under a cottonwood tree behind the spectators' bleachers, and then Jack and Reddy and I sat down in the shade to wait for Mr. Ferris and his friends to bring their horses out. The rich people in the hotel must all be late sleepers, we guessed, for we did not see a soul in the patios or on the verandas, or even any of the help, except a couple of grooms by the door of the stable, sitting on their heels for all the world as if they were Westerners. We had read about the polo game in the society column of the paper, and we knew that it was going to start at noon, for the snobbish woman who wrote the column had said that "Mr. Ferris and his socially prominent friends will disport themselves at high noon, after which they will join their ladies at a gala luncheon to close the summer season." So when we heard the bell in Mr. Ferris's aunt's church ring half past eleven, we started our kerosene burners and began to pop the corn and melt the Nucoa.

The day was so pretty, so red-and-gold crisp, and the smell of the popcorn was so delicious, and we were so happy to think of the money we were going to make, so happy to think of school beginning, so pleased with our flattering dog, that it never once occurred to Jack and me that Mr. Ferris might not like our coming here without asking leave. Consequently, we were utterly flabbergasted when a skinny, red-haired man in imitation Levis walked briskly over to us from the stable, where we had seen him talking to the grooms, and shouted, "Clear out, and step on it!"

Reddy wagged his tail, for Reddy was the kind of dog who

would help the burglar find the spoons. But Jack looked this tall Yankee man coolly in the eye and said, "Why should we? It's a free country."

"Not this polo field, it isn't, Buster," said the man, whose bloodshot eyes looked as dry as if he had not been to sleep for a week. "Now, you take the ozone before the big shot finds you here."

"Who said?" asked Jack, his voice still cocky, although I could tell that he was beginning to lose his nerve.

"*I* said," replied the man. "You get this junk off Mr. Ferris's property, starting now."

"Hell's bells," said Jack to me, and we both looked sadly at the glass box where the popcorn was snowily piled up like countless tiny clouds. To the man he said, in a more conciliatory voice, "How do you know the people won't want popcorn while they're watching the game?"

"Look, Skeezix," said the man as he reached in through the glass door of the machine and took a handful of our own popcorn, "somebody must of given you a bum steer. Did you think this game was for the hoi polloi? Did you think Mr. Ferris and his big-shot friends want a lot of local yokels rubbernecking around here eating five-cent popcorn?"

"It costs ten cents," I said.

"The paper said—" Jack began, and then, seeing the man deliberately pour melted margarine over a handful of popcorn, he got sore again. He slammed and latched the door, and he said, "Who are you calling a local yokel? You cheesy dudes, you think you're Mr. God. Whyn't you go back to New York City if you're so stuckup?"

"Like you said, it's a free country." The man was smiling now, with an odious look of superiority on his face, and, glancing down at Reddy, who was still trying to make friends with him, he burst into laughter. "What kind of a dog is that?" he said. "Is that a Colorado lion hound? There's one dog that don't take any pride in his personal appearance."

Our doormat of a dog just stood there, grinning and taking the slander as his just due. I knew that Jack was boiling, but we both knew we were defeated, and, scowling, our lower lips thrust out, we started to roll the machine back the way we had come. Jack growled, "Outa my way, you sissy horse wrangler."

The man chuckled and turned away. At the door of the stable, he rejoined the two grooms and he pointed to Reddy and we heard him say, "It's called a Rocky Mountain stagecoach dog," and all of them laughed. When we got to the end of the hotel driveway and the popcorn stand was on the town road, Jack stopped and ran back a little way, and he shook his fists and yelled, "The only good dude is a dead dude!"

Now that we were almost out of that hostile region, I grew courageous and I piped shrilly, "Dudes! Dudes! You dudes go back to New York City!"

Just then, I saw the sportsmen come around the corner of the stable, Mr. Ferris, a tall, dark man, in the lead. They were all dressed in spotless riding trousers and expensive boots, short-sleeved white shirts, and rakish polo helmets. They looked at Jack and me with a kind of scientific curiosity, and one of them shaded his eyes against the sun to get a better view. Reddy, who would kiss the foot of his worst enemy, ran up to the group of men, and when the horse wrangler repeated his snide joke, they all burst into peals of laughter.

I called to our dumb dog. I cried, "Here, Reddy! Get away from those dudes!" Reddy came running, and the men laughed even harder as Jack and I, our faces burning, started our humiliating retreat.

So in a sense it was true that I had sassed Mr. Ferris, but how did Emily know? Jack and I had been too ashamed and sick at heart to tell anyone what had happened. Had Emily been lurking around somewhere, spying and eavesdropping? For a second, my alarm gave way to indignation. How had Mr. Ferris found out who I was? From that distance, I must have looked like any old town kid; you couldn't even tell, except up close, whether I was a boy or a girl, because my hair was cut short and I wore overalls and one of Jack's outgrown shirts. And why had he taken a scunner to me and not to Jack?

I did not ask Emily any of these questions. When I had admitted that I did remember all about that day, she told me that Mr. Ferris, immediately after the polo game was over, had started laying his nefarious plans. He had set a bunch of private detectives on my trail, and in short order they found that I spent a great deal of time in the vicinity of this particular boulder. "Did you know that simply troops of plainclothesmen have been following you around for months?" asked Emily, and my knees shook so that I would have fallen into the creek if she hadn't been holding me. So then Mr. Ferris bought the rock, and he had his scientists imbue it with gentian violet ("You see now why it's called the Violet Rock?"), which was a special kind of lethal gas that was released only at twilight and would kill only me. The reason for this last was that one of the scientists had come onto the sleeping porch one night and taken a drop of blood out of my finger and had mixed it up with the poisonous things in their laboratory, and the gas, with some sort of magic intelligence, had known thereafter (and would know forever, said Emily) when I was in the neighborhood. It was only by the grace of God that I had not been felled like a rat tonight, she said, and she was, as a matter of fact, quite perplexed (though very *glad*, she assured me, giving me a spuriously loving hug), and imagined that it had something to do with my having just got over chicken pox.

When we got out of the park, I started to cry again, this time with relief at seeing the street lights on and lights in the houses all down through the valley. But I still had many eggs to walk on, for Emily told me that Mr. Ferris had also had the horse tombstones treated in the same way, and actually even more virulently, so that I must hold my breath and keep my eyes closed as we walked the long block where stood the haunted house and its spook-thronged garden.

Oh, I can tell you I was glad to see the smoke of our chimney and the bright windows of our house! My father was reading the paper, and my mother was cooking supper, and Jack and Stella were playing mah-jongg in the living room. "Remember, not a word to anyone," whispered Emily as we came up on the porch and I could see these comforting, humdrum sights through the windows. "And also remember, Tess-doll, don't ever go near the Violet Rock at sundown. As a matter of fact, if I were you, I'd never go near it at any time, because you can't tell what a true-blue scalawag like Mr. Ferris may plan to do next."

The minute I entered the house and fully took in the fact that Jack and Stella were playing a game instead of doing homework, I realized why no other children had been out on the mesa, for today was Friday and no one would want to bring to school pasqueflowers that had been wilting all weekend. And the other people we might have encountered had, I deduced, been occupied downtown, for the headline in the evening paper said, "BIG TURNOUT FOR NATIONAL GUARD PARADE TODAY." But this was thin consolation to me, who had upon my shoulders a terrible worry; all through supper and all through the evening, Emily would catch my eye and put her finger to her lips and solemnly shake her head.

For a week, I did not go near the park, and this abstention was hard to explain to my friends, for the season of outdoor games was in full swing. They were skeptical and then annoyed, feeling that I was giving myself airs when I would not join them after school and said I would rather stay at home and read. My mother, who liked to have the house to herself and who warmly welcomed spring, when we stayed out-of-doors, tried to shoo me off the window seat, but I would not go. I would sit there with a moony look on my face, and whenever she came into the room, I would pretend to be so absorbed in my book that I did not even hear her. I could no longer use the short cut to school through the grounds of the haunted house, and I got three tardy marks on my otherwise perfect attendance record. Two nights in a row, I walked in my sleep. I wanted to consult with Emily, but she had made up with her friends and with Stella again, and they were busy rehearsing for a play that Emily had written and in which she played the role of a gypsy queen. And there was, of course, no one else that I dared talk to, since if I did, that even more hideous thing than the guillotine would happen to me.

My dilemma became desperate, for my parents and Jack and Stella began speaking of my queer behavior. My mother feared that I was sick; the others less charitably suspected that I had stolen something or had cheated in a spelling test.

One night, just a week after I had learned about the curse upon me, I heard my father saying to my mother, "I'm going to get to the bottom of this." I knew from experience that if he set his mind to it, he would worm the whole thing out of me, and then my life would not be worth a red cent.

So I decided that the only thing to do was to go directly

to Mr. Ferris, abase myself, and apologize for calling him a
dude. I had a restless night that night, dreaming fantastically,
and dreaming that I dreamed, and when I finally got up, at
the first light, my bed looked as if a dozen people had slept
in it. Noiselessly I dressed, not in my blue jeans but in a red
tissue-gingham dress trimmed with rickrack, and noiselessly I
let myself out of the house, so stealthily that not even Reddy
heard me. It was the loveliest morning imaginable, which even
I, with my heavy heart, could see. The mountain range was
ruby in the sunrise, and the summit snows were the color of
pale-pink petals; I knew that by now the pasqueflowers were
thick in the foothills (a boy in Stella's grade had won the pencil
box two days before); Jack had already had a wood tick; and
it had said in the paper that the snowdrops were up in the
sanitarium grounds. Soon now, spring housecleaning would
begin all over town and everywhere there would be the sound
of rug beaters.

As I went up the drive of the Gold Palace Hotel, I heard a
meadow lark and I stopped to look around for him. As I did
so, I saw a man leading a palomino out of the stable, and the
beauties of this spring day receded to give way to the maiming
details of that other day in the fall. For the first time, it occurred
to me to wonder how on earth I, a girl in the third grade, could
ever get through his phalanxes of servants to Mr. Ferris. On
the other hand, I was clearly important to him, since he had
gone to so much trouble to put the hex on me. I looked at
the Spanish façade of the hotel, and tried to guess which were
the windows of the laboratory where the scientists had made
the gentian-violet gas; it was possible that at this very moment
they were watching me through spyglasses, and at the thought
I started to turn away. I would write Mr. Ferris a letter instead.

But I did not want to be cross-examined by my father, and,
besides, the Brownies were having a wiener roast in the park
that day and I wanted to go. I walked on up the drive slowly,
and as I went over toward the polo field, I was barely moving;
I meant to give the man with the horse a message to take to
Mr. Ferris, to say that I would like to speak to him about an
urgent matter.

I was concentrating so closely on my speech that I did not
notice until I was upon him that the man was watching my

approach, one hand resting lightly on the saddle, the other fondling an unlighted pipe. When I did look up and did focus on him, I saw that the smiling face belonged to Mr. Ferris himself, and I stubbed my toe on a rock and lunged forward so sharply that the blond mare shied a little.

"Well, good morning," said Mr. Ferris pleasantly. I knew that his manner was hypocritical and that I would have to watch my step. "Since we seem to be the only two early birds around, we'd better introduce ourselves. My name is Ferris, Norman Ferris. What's yours?"

He perfectly well knew my name, but I saw at once that it would be wise to humor him, and so I said, "Tess Vanderpool."

"Vanderpool?" he repeated. "Do we have guests named Vanderpool? Or did you just arrive?"

"I'm not no guest," I said, and blushed hotly at my double negative. "My father runs the Safeway."

"He runs the safe way? Well, there's a prudent man for you!" He laughed out loud, and I could tell, although I did not understand what he meant, that he was ridiculing me. But I swallowed my pride and said nothing. "Doesn't that mean that your father misses much of the richness of life? Doesn't he ever kick over the traces and take a side trip on the dangerous way?"

I was baffled and ready to take to my heels, but I was irritated, too, by his teasing. "Mr. Ferris," I said, licking my papery lips, "I came to apologize."

Mr. Ferris was extremely handsome, I had to admit, much as I hated him. And he was a consummate actor, for now, just after he had so meanly made fun of me with obscure, grown-up words, his face became serious, as if he were an honest man. He took his hand off the saddle and slapped the horse on the rump, sending her away, and then he squatted down on his heels, and as he began to fill his pipe, he looked at me solicitously and he said, "Why, Tess, I really didn't give it a second thought. It *is* to me you want to apologize, isn't it?"

"Oh, yes, Mr. Ferris," I said. I could feel the tears gathering into a clod in my throat. "I wouldn't have called you a dude if you hadn't made fun of Reddy."

"That was pretty low, I admit," said Mr. Ferris, bending intently over his pipe. "How long ago was it that all this happened? I seem to forget."

"It was in September. The Sunday before Labor Day."

"So long ago as that? Good Lord, time flies! Well, Tess, I think it's about time we buried the hatchet, don't you?" He looked me straight in the eye, with such sincerity and friendliness that it was hard to believe he had wanted to asphyxiate me. "I'm sorry I laughed at what-you-may-call-it, and now that you're sorry you called me a dude, we can be friends—what?" He put his pipe in his mouth and stretched out his hand for me to shake.

But he was not going to pull the wool over my eyes with his becks and smiles. "Yes, but will you take the spell off me?"

"Hold on a minute, Tess," said Mr. Ferris. He tried to put his arm around my shoulder, but I slipped away from him. "Who told you about the spell?"

"Emily. My sister Emily Vanderpool."

"Did she have her facts right? I think that to have the record straight you'd better tell me what she said."

I told him. From time to time, he nodded, and occasionally he said, "Right," or "Check." And frequently he coughed, making me wonder if Mr. Ferris, like so many Easterners (not even privately did I use the word "dude" now), had tuberculosis.

When I had finished, he said, "You've been pretty convincing, young lady. I think that in your case I went to extremes out of all proportion to your misdemeanor, and I am going to put a stop to the spell right now. I'm going up to the laboratories and tell my head sorcerer to switch off the gas both at the Violet Rock and at those tombstones."

Now I would shake hands with him and, for a moment, even let him put his arm around me. He gave me a quick hug and then stood up. "I'll just have a ten-minute canter on Pearl, here, and then go in and give the order. O.K.?" He knocked out his pipe, and put his fingers in the corners of his mouth and whistled for the mare, who came as obediently as a dog. "We ought to put a seal on this truce," said Mr. Ferris, and he took a silver dollar out of his pocket. "You keep this as your lucky piece," he told me. "But don't you tell Emily you have it. This is the sign that the Violet Rock is now the safe way for you."

I took the dollar, and Mr. Ferris and I exchanged a warm, new-friends look; then, as he turned to mount his horse, he said, "I'll be interested to know what ever becomes of Emily."

I did not know what he meant and I did not have a chance to ask him, for, waving to me and smiling broadly, he ran the horse into the paddock; under the fresh sun, her golden hide and her silvery mane and tail gleamed like metal, as bright, nearly, as the dollar that already was making the palm of my hand wet.

The Connoisseurs

"STUNNING! But it won't compare with Iceland." The nervous, long-nosed Englishman, busily photographing the banks of Loch Lomond from the deck of a pleasure steamer, the *Princess May*, indicated by his sidelong smile that Mr. and Mrs. Rand were bound to understand exactly what he meant. Mary Rand murmured, "I suppose not," and addressed herself to her guidebook while her husband stared moodily at the retreating pier at Balloch. From the beginning of the excursion, when the trippers had set forth on the first lap by train from Glasgow in a black rain, Mary and Donald Rand, disinclined today to chatter with a stranger, had been endeavoring to defeat this voluble man, but he stanchly stood his ground. Having caught sight of their American passports and being, evidently, of the belief that Americans collected information as they reputedly did French perfume and Venetian glass, he had attached himself firmly to them, as conscientiously as if he were in their employ. He had ingeniously managed to sit between them in the railway carriage and had talked so incessantly and rapidly on such a number of diverse matters that Mary had once or twice thought he might have a disturbance of the mind. And now, on the *Princess May*, which was small and had no private cabins, he was constantly at their side, bristling with tripods and knapsacks and alpenstocks and all the other appurtenances of a professional traveler, and visiting them with avalanches of intelligence on the derivation of Scottish place names, the capers Rob Roy had cut in these regions and the intellectual life of Reykjavik, a city he found far more congenial at the present time than London. When he was not feverishly issuing facts, he inveighed against the Labor Government, beginning each philippic with the statement, "America has been long-suffering," and ending each with the indignant outcry, "Our food is a deadly sin."

Ordinarily the Rands, who were accomplished travelers themselves, could have vanquished him or they might even have found him amusing; but today they were incapable of laughter and the windbag's tyranny was especially oppressive because they could not sympathize with each other in whispers or in signs: they were not on speaking terms. They had not communicated since the evening before when they had had a frightful row in their hotel in Edinburgh, beginning with a debate on the political probity of a writer neither knew personally and neither had read, and going on from there to the acidulous examination of each other's character and opinions. They had disinterred grudges ten years old, had picked every trite old bone in the domestic yard.

Although they knew from past experience that the opposite tended to be true, the Rands held stubbornly to the belief that all difficulties between the married could be unknotted by taking a trip. But on this European tour, their first since the war, planned to cover the same ground they had traversed on their honeymoon, they had been obliged to take so many trips within the trip and trips within trips that at last they had begun to suspect that travel was not a panacea after all. Still, the habit was profound in them and this morning at breakfast, after both had spent a miserable night, pitching in resentment and tossing in remorse, Donald had silently laid on Mary's tray two excursion tickets which he had got up early to buy. And although they did not discuss the matter, both of them thought that "getting away from it all" (although "it" in this case meant only the hotel where they had been for two days) would restore them to a civilized respect for each other. They were (they thought) always much more reasonable when they were actually en route, soothed by locomotion and consoled by the anticipation of a new place, the promise of some cranny of the earth where happiness, already made, awaited them. Each had imagined that aboard the *Princess May*, moving gently over the famously romantic lake they had not seen before, they could calmly talk again and could, with dignity, concede. The solution to everything might lie on the farther bank; there was the possibility that in a tea shop in Inversnaid they might, in sudden revelation, learn how to accept.

But they had failed to reckon on the presence of this generic bore and their frustration only deepened the feelings of the night before. Silence could not rebuff the man and dissent propelled him into rebuttals of parliamentary length. One could either jump overboard, a gesture which Mary and Donald, even though they were unstrung, felt excessive, or endure him and meditate in snatches between onslaughts of data, recall and prophecy. Mute and morose, they watched the mists rise, slowly peeling the grassy head of Ben Lomond, stared at the smooth black water, felt the fresh spray and followed the ambling of blond cows through small pastures at the water's edge.

"If you don't care for a stark landscape, don't go to Iceland," warned the Englishman, taking a fresh roll of film out of a fishing creel he carried on a long strap. "Go to the Lake Country. But I am of a different persuasion. I respect the character of bleak and barren lands. Their natives are hardy. In the environs of Grasmere, on the other hand, there breeds a kind of troglodyte lower, in my opinion, than the worst rascal in the whole of Iceland. Actually, the country has very few rascals."

There followed a soliloquy on the pride and morality of that Lutheran and treeless island and the Rands nodded from time to time. This was enough attention to satisfy him, for clearly the last thing in the world he wanted was to be interrupted. He did not even ask that his audience look at him while he talked, so they continued to gaze at the scraps of ruined castles on diminutive green islands and at their fellow passengers, nearly all of whom looked as melancholy as themselves. A great many of them had defacing colds in the head, deepening the hue of their pink Scotch faces; coughing and sneezing and blowing their noses, they lent to the atmosphere a distracting air of peevishness and Mary, while she was on the edge of despair, was also cross. It was an ignoble state of mind.

Opposite them, leaning against the rail, stood a pair of lovers, hand in hand and dumb with bliss, the only passengers on the boat who looked as if they were glad they had come. Several times the burly, dark young man bent to peer through her spectacles at his sweetheart's pale amber eyes; there was solicitude in his gesture which she received with the mild smile of a woman safe in her harbor. As the bell for lunch sounded and they prepared to go below, the girl said with grave joy, "Traveling is lovely. I could travel for a week."

Mary Rand said to herself, "So I thought once." Out of the corner of her eye, she looked at her husband in whose intelligent, thin face there showed not a hint of amiability. Frowning and with the corners of his mouth drawn down, he looked dour as if he had come at last to a serious and incontrovertible decision. And for a moment she was terrified that even if the oracle did inhabit Inversnaid, he would not listen. Although he maddened her, although she sometimes questioned that she loved him and although she was certain that nothing short of a miracle could bring about the restitution of their concord, the thought of parting stunned her. She reeled back against the railing and felt a headache coming on.

"I advise you not to eat the meal," said the Englishman. "These included-in-the-fare lunches are infamous. I have some passable sausage here and some excellent Icelandic chocolate. Better than steamed cod, what? And their villainous muffins. The oat was meant to be eaten by the horse."

From the pannier-like pockets of his tweed jacket, he drew forth two parcels wrapped in crumpled newspaper and he offered Mary and Donald each an unpleasant slice of salami and a jagged wedge of chocolate, but they had no appetite and they refused. He did not take offense but wolfed down his presents himself and cut off more of both, using a long and dangerous hunting knife that he had extracted, unsheathed, from the rubbishy interior of his knapsack. While he ravenously lunched, he continued to talk, telling them about a cycling trip he had made long years before through the hinterlands of Bulgaria, where for twelve days he had not heard a word of any language intelligible to him except for the short speech of an Arab he had come upon resting against the trunk of a tree beside the road. He had opened one blackguardly eye and had said, "Hell, boy, where are you going?" and had gone back to sleep.

When he had concluded this anecdote which seemed to afford him little pleasure, he returned to his camera assiduously to record the pastoral scenes along the bonny banks and to recite for Mr. and Mrs. Rand several poems by Sigurd of Broadfirth, which he assured them were very pretty. At the end of one, he said irrelevantly, "Did you hear that girl say that she could travel for a week? If I had to be a week *without* traveling, I would be fit for nothing but a nursing home." He then recited another lyric of many stanzas.

Travel, to Mary Rand, had come to be the name of a neurosis, and it was on travel that she blamed the hurricanes that rocked her marriage and seemed at last to have wrecked it. It had been travel that had brought them together in the first place;

travel, she thought bitterly, and absolutely nothing else. Donald from the upper reaches of the Hudson and Mary from the potato lands of Idaho had first met at tiffin in Bombay fourteen years before. The encounter, actually, had not been strikingly auspicious. It had been a humid, buggy day and the meal had been long. Their host, a Canadian professor at the Victoria Jubilee Technical Institute, had been a lecturer similar to to-day's companion. He had been given, by turns, to expounding in a monotone the methods of producing hybrids in a certain greenhouse in Winnipeg, and to telling puzzling stories that presupposed a knowledge of the faculty at the Sir Jamsetjee Jeejeebhoy School of Art. Both Mary and Donald, moreover, had had severe headaches and they had spoken together only in the most perfunctory way, learning that they were of about the same age and were both slowly girdling the globe alone. But little as they had inspired each other at the time, later they liked to reconstruct that day. They were pleased to be asked how they had met and in their reply to juxtapose the exotic and the homely; they said, "We took aspirin tablets together on Malabar Hill."

Mary was peripatetic because she had a fortune, no family and nothing to do in Boise and because, in the absence of "background" and "connections," her demure, millionaire parents had had faith in travel as a means to an obvious end, and on their deathbeds had enjoined her to hunt a husband abroad. Fair and rosy-cheeked, Mary Rand looked like a girl out of *The Shepheardes Calender*, disguised by the modistes of Paris, and the *tabula rasa* of her winning, western mind had been inscribed at eastern finishing schools with a pencil easy to erase: she was more than ordinarily receptive but she was not discriminating at all, and these two qualities adjusted her perfectly to traveling as an occupation. Obedient to her parents' wish, she looked on it only as an interim occupation, but she shied away from involvements and she refused proposals of marriage (which were abundant, considering her youth, her looks and her riches) because the thought of "settling down" made her restless and she felt she could not marry anyone of a sedentary cast. She was, even then, affianced in her imagination to the man who would discover for her that perfect place; she thought of herself not as an aimless traveler but as a pilgrim with a goal. She felt certain that when, with her guide, she entered Eden, she would be content to let her passport molder and her trunk keys rust.

Donald's money was of an older mintage and his *Wander-jahr,* traditional. Like most people with no particular bent, he fancied that he would one day write and from time to time he collated his jottings in the intention of putting them together in a book in order to justify what his mother, a plain-spoken woman, called his "life of vagrancy." Like Mary, he was endowed with an affectionate and outgoing nature that attracted to him innumerable friends; the recipients of letters of introduction never regretted inviting him to tea and, indeed, as often as not ended up by asking him to stay a week. It was a life as rich as a tapestry that he led, and though he said otherwise to his mother, he had no intention of ever leading any other kind. Not until Mary spoke of it had it occurred to him that he might finally find a place from which he would never wish to stir again, but he gracefully accepted the hypothesis.

In the course of a year after their first meeting, the two wanderers met five times by chance in widely separated localities; once, going in opposite directions, they passed in gondolas under the Rialto and another time they collided in the Street of Plenty in Pompeii. The fifth of their meetings took place on a bleak and buffeted channel boat crossing from Ostend to Dover. They discovered each other on deck and, agreeing that this arm of coincidence was too long to be ignored further, they repaired to the damp, brown bar where throughout the voyage, they traded dossiers and talked of scenery and railway systems. They discovered that without knowing it they had often been in the same place at the same time. On the same Tuesday in February, for example, Donald had lost and Mary had won at chemin de fer in Baden-Baden; they had both been present at a dinner party in Chantilly but because the guests had been a multitude, they did not remember having been introduced. In Tangier, Mary had had a sunstroke and two weeks later, in the same hotel, Donald, mysteriously enough, had come down with chicken pox. They exchanged the names of hotels where they had stopped, of restaurants they had esteemed and picture galleries they had visited. They compared the sunsets of Jerusalem and Rome and they applauded the winds and the hills of Rhodes. They reviewed the villages of the Schwarzwald and they agreed that, on the whole, Gothic churches left them cold. By the time they had reached the English shore, they had privately told themselves that they had been made for each other.

Mary Rand, watching the *Princess May* lunge through the black waters of Loch Lomond, thought how much longer and more devious had been the restive journeys of their spirits than had been those of their most indefatigable flesh. For so many years they had—as well as literally, figuratively—sought that secure dingle where they might shed all subterfuge, but the very earnestness of their search had led them astray. Was it that each had demanded that the other be the infallible guide? Or was it a human lack, equivalent to the power of their money, that made them both refuse the responsibility of the search? Setting forth together, she reflected, they had always, always parted at the first fork in the road, refusing, through a sudden petulance (or a contempt), to veer from the direction of their choice; and then had come scrambling back to the point of departure, vociferous with reproach at having been misled. Alas, it had not been thus in the beginning, that hopeful time! For solace, tepid as it was, she turned back to sweet and early recollections, but before she could transport herself, the Englishman's voice came bustling into her reverie again.

"The language is not so formidable as you might suppose," he said, taking a photograph of a trailer camp of blue and red caravans at the foot of Ptarmigan. "*Yes*, for example, is pronounced *yow*. What could be simpler?"

Donald replied that he supposed nothing could and Mary nodded. The Englishman then went into declensions.

The Rands' courtship, lasting several months, had been conducted in all of the British Isles. They had gone to the same house party in Wales and had gone together to see the Botanical Garden in Cheltenham and the Palladian houses in Bath. They had attended the Dublin horse show and had played golf in Ballybunion. They had been guests for a fortnight in a house near Aberdeen which belonged to Donald's aunt by marriage and under her auspices, they had gone to a military ball in Edinburgh and had motored around the coast of Arran. One comely afternoon, on the battlements of Stirling Castle, Donald had proposed and Mary had accepted him. They were married in Aberdeen and went for a month to the Outer Hebrides. From Panama to Donegal, their friends observed that so long as there were booking agents, the Rands' honeymoon would continue.

From time to time they spoke irresolutely of establishing a place of residence somewhere, but while they were agreed on the architecture they wanted, they could not decide on the country of their permanent address. Once in a while, during a rare bout of insomnia, Mary, turning her pillow in Paris or Budapest or Istanbul, thinking about the time when they would stay put, wondered uneasily what they would talk about, for the subjects of their conversation, witty as it might be, weighty as it often was, originated always in their itinerary. If her meditations became too pessimistic, she got up and took a sleeping pill. In the morning, she studied Baedekers and border regulations with renewed enthusiasm, restored to her hope of the *paradisus* that lay just around the next corner, just over the yonder hill, that spot of earth that would itself become the protagonist and the creator of their life together.

For two years they roved, finding few faults in each other and finding, instead, a union of affinities and of prejudices beyond their wildest dreams (in less than a month they were speaking out freely, confident that they would not tread on each other's toes; they were disappointed in the Casbah in exactly the same degree and in the same degree were overwhelmed by the Sphinx); even if there had been differences, they were too busy, too phrenetically galvanized, ever to brood. And then, suddenly, the honeymoon ended for precisely the reason their friends had given: there were no longer booking agents, for the war came and immobilized them. It sent them back to America and it pinioned them, these birds of passage, in the dark and permanent halls and parlors of the elder Mrs. Rand's country house. They concluded against taking a place of their own, saying that they could imagine this was only a long stopover during which they could bone up on Greece which they intended to tour extensively the moment the war was finished.

Sufficiently myopic to be ignored by the armed services, Donald spent four days a week in New York giving his talents as a translator to a worthy cause, and he returned to Vanderhaven for the other three to a wife not altogether able to conceal her boredom and her wanderlust. If not in fact, certainly in feeling, she continued to live out of a suitcase. She was ill at ease with her mother-in-law and with the neighborhood gentry who dropped in for tea and talked of matters so parochial that she could enter into none of their conversation, and she began to feel that her own wide experience of places and of foreign ways was of the least possible interest to anyone in the world except herself and her husband. Furthermore, she suspected, in a heavy foreboding, that she would never be able to adjust to a life of such sameness. Not unless, that is, she found The Place where the status quo would have a meaning beyond mere contentment. With a certain frenzy, she sought the place on maps and, in despair at her limitless choice, she gave the globe an angry whirl and left it spinning in the library while she went to walk rapidly and without purpose along the country roads.

The elder Mrs. Rand was as settled in her habits as her son was nomadic in his. She complained that she could not sleep in hotels and that she was claustrophobic in ships; she believed that the majority of all peoples, except the British (including the Protestant Irish) and the Americans and certain French of her personal acquaintance, were afflicted with communicable diseases and were emotionally unstable. She did not protest her son's penchant but she did not want to hear about it, and talk of travel was forbidden in her presence. "It's as tiresome to me to hear about the bargain rates at the Danieli in the off-season as it is to hear a post-mortem on a bridge game," she said. This basic conflict, seldom as it was aired and then good-naturedly, inhibited Mary and Donald although when they were alone they continued to make plans for their exploration of Greece and for their trips to Egypt and to Norway, and they subsisted for a long time on the memory of places they had been, hotel porters that had interested them, touts they had defeated, friendships struck up in railway stations. But their hostess's indifference to the world beyond Vanderhaven began gradually to infect them and oftener and oftener they carried over from the dinner table the intellectual fare that had sustained them there. Neither was articulate on any subject except travel, but on almost everything they found that they were in obstinate and fundamental disaccord.

It was over music that they had had their first quarrels. In Munich and Milan, where it had only been a part of the rich fabric of an unfamiliar city, they had seemed to enjoy the same music. But now, in Upstate New York, far from La Scala and the Odéon, confined to an umbrageous octagonal music room and offered the restricted choice of Mrs. Rand's phonograph records, they made the disquieting discovery that each keenly disliked the other's favorites. In the beginning, they were bantering in their disputes; then they grew formal and polite and finally, as the winter encircled them and they grew less hopeful of a quick ending to the war, their voices were fretful and accusing. When Donald said that Bach's fugues were nothing more than "strumming," Mary told him sharply that he was a vulgarian. When Mary said that Wagner hurt her ears, her husband said that that particular snobbery was no longer fashionable and he even dragged in by its heels the platitudinous observation that the West—and especially Boise, Idaho—was culturally backward. After some weeks of squabbling, they tacitly arranged never to be in the music room at the same time.

But the library became a battleground equally sanguinary. Mary loathed reading aloud and Donald loved and practiced it. She would be lost in the pages of George Eliot when from across the room Donald would say, "Listen to this," and read aloud a long passage from Toynbee which did not interest her and which, because she did not have an auditory mind, she could not follow. Her protest caused her husband to charge her with frivolousness. She tried twice to retaliate by reading to him a section from *Middlemarch,* but he objected only to George Eliot, not to the interruption. They had had an ugly scene in which Mary said that she had always regarded *Middlemarch* as one of the finest novels of the nineteenth century although, in point of fact, she had never read it before. Donald replied that he had never had any respect at all for any woman novelist.

They were disunited over football games, psychiatry, capital punishment, modern furniture and progressive education. Their religious and political views were diametrically opposed and they were pugnacious when they debated, as masochistically they often did, the Sacco and Vanzetti trial. Hardly a day passed when they did not inflame each other and finally, hoping to be healed, they began to take trips on the weekends, to Boston, to Saratoga Springs or to the Poconos. But these were too short and makeshift; they could not lose themselves and therefore could not find each other. Half the time, their Sunday night partings were glacial and even so, Monday morning found them making promises to each other in avid letters that their equilibrium would be restored when they could go abroad again. Upon this certainty, this absolute conviction that they would once again be enraptured in the capitals of Europe where they had found their initial rapture, they revisited—over the long-distance telephone—their castles in Spain and in their imagination, filled their hotel rooms with regional flowers, as evanescent as their own residence. And obdurately, whenever the wartime restrictions permitted, they took short trips.

As soon as the ocean liners were refurbished and passports were once again available, the Rands set forth to Europe. As faithfully as possible, they had retraced their steps and everywhere, disappointment had stalked them spectrally. They had failed to realize, except in the most intellectual way, that the face of Europe would be changed, that half the hotels where they had been the most in love did not exist or existed now as something else, that travel would be beset by handicaps they had never experienced before. Nor, in spite of the warnings of returning friends, had they fully taken in the fact that they would be called upon to exercise emotions beyond their personal desire and pleasure. Indeed, their pity for the ravished Continent, for the cities' wounds, for all the privation and dismay of the people they saw limping through a day-to-day existence should have brought them together—their hearts were charitable although their charity neither began nor ended at home—and, at moments, it did. But then, back in their costly, uncomfortable hotel suite, attended by shiftless maids, out of sight of all but their own miseries, they quarreled, coldly and acidly. Together with the trunks and hatboxes, the Gladstones and the portable typewriters, they had brought Pandora's box, filled with the handiwork they had created on those paralyzing weekends in Vanderhaven and the awkward, inconvenient ones in Gettysburg, in Lexington, in Lyme.

Nothing had been gained for either of them except a few new impressions. Like this English crank who, pointing out to them that they would dock at Inversnaid in a few minutes, suggested that they climb up the rocks to Rob Roy's cave with himself as their cicerone. His information on Bruce, who had reputedly quartered there, was exhaustive. Mary looked again at her husband, but his expression had not altered and sighing deeply, she turned to watch the shores advance. At Inversnaid, she told herself, there will be a tea shop where Donald and I will begin our lives again. But because she had her moments of practicality, she added the corollary: And if there is none in Inversnaid, we will leave the trippers at Stirling and go back to the castle where he proposed to me. Like a touch of fever, a joy momentarily intruded on her sorrow as she wondered if Donald had all along intended to take her back to Stirling, to that selfsame place. How ecstatic she had been that afternoon! She had flown like a bird upon his beautiful question.

Without volition, she turned to him with a smile. But he was methodically collecting their wraps and cameras and when he spoke, it was to the Englishman. He said, "I think that power line over there might make an interesting photograph," and the Englishman, apprehending no note of derision in his voice, thanked him briskly and immediately took a picture of the ungainly towers. Mary chuckled softly as she leaned toward Donald but he would not meet her eyes and, disheartened, she said nothing.

The mist was dense at Inversnaid and the ice-cold waters of the Arklet stormed down a high and narrow fall. The trippers stationed themselves about the dock in silent groups, awed or bored or chilled, to wait for the bus that would take them to their next voyage, across Loch Katrine. Only the two lovers still smiled. The young man scrambled up the hill and brought back a sheaf of heather which the girl cradled in her arms like a doll. The silent Mr. and Mrs. Rand made their way into the small hotel where the walls were adorned with the pitiful stuffed heads of baby boars. Behind them, prattling still of historic highwaymen, came the monologist, whittling off chunks of chocolate and, in his seizure of talk, failing to mind his lips so that streaks of brown ran nastily down the sides of his mouth. The public room was closed at this hour and all they could have for refreshment was coffee, false and cool, and old buns sliced and filled with flaccid slivers of tomato. Still, Mary pertinaciously thought: Perhaps the magic word awaits us here, even in this dispiriting place with the poor dead pigs glaring at us. And she felt that surely something of the same hope had entered Donald, for he touched her shoulder gently as he seated her at the table in the lobby and he smiled, though not at her, as he sat down himself.

The Englishman, taking for granted that they were now a threesome, sat down too. "The drive to Loch Katrine will be abominable, I can tell you. These Highland drivers have no respect for human life." He tasted his coffee, said, "Pah!" and pushed it away with a fierce grimace. "On the other hand," he said, "the caliber of driving in Iceland is superb. The men who drive the public buses are, in my opinion, unparalleled."

This statement, innocent to the point of idiocy, made Mary begin to laugh helplessly but Donald's frown sobered her at once and to her amazement she heard him say, "Do tell me, how does one go about getting to Iceland?"

Oh, how the disheveled creature cavorted in his element! In a maniacal Oxonian scream he described the exquisite dangers and anguishes of the voyage in a fishing vessel. "The only way to go!" he shrilled. "Don't do this thing by halves. Don't go by air. Go as I did: *in a gale.*" The cold, he told them, had been dreadful, the noise, infernal; the ship had rollicked like a cork, the sailors had been sick and he himself had been knocked unconscious when a hatch had flown open and caught him square in the back of the knees. But once there! Again he warmed to the subject of Reykjavik.

"We think of going there," said Donald, refusing still to give his wife any clue to his extraordinary behavior. "Are the hotels good?"

"Oh, odious!" laughed the Englishman in a delighted memory. "By far the worst I've ever seen. Cheerless. Overheated. Unheard-of bad service."

Mary, bewildered, tried to join them in this absurd conversation. "I shall be so curious to see Iceland. Is the architecture interesting?"

"Hopeless," he replied and tried his coffee again. This time he drank the whole cup down in a gulp and smacked his lips in obvious relish. Hypocrite, thought Mary. "It is, I suppose, the ugliest city I have ever seen including Glasgow which ought to be submerged in the Clyde."

"Good," said Donald with an irony she could not bear. "My wife and I, you see, have never been to an ugly city. Everything we have seen has been beautiful in prospect, nonexistent in reality and beautiful in retrospect. You follow me?"

The Englishman did not choose to follow Donald Rand. Grinning, he turned to Mary and he said, "You will find chastity in Iceland, intellectually, morally, geographically, gastronomically, architecturally. Chastity, as we know, is always ugly, but what a wonder true ugliness is!"

Her husband laughed and Mary, baffled by this game, asked timidly, "Are there flowers in Iceland?"

"Madam, there is nothing in Iceland, nothing at all," replied the man.

A boy came into the lobby with lucky white heather to sell and Mary waited for Donald to buy some for her. But when the boy came to their table, he ignored him and the Englishman said, "Go away, whatever it is, go away," but Mary gave him half a crown and buried her eyes in the brush and would not look up to see the men's reproaches.

"I intended to take my wife to Stirling Castle this afternoon," Donald began.

Interrupting him, the Englishman said, "You'd lose your trip-ticket that way. There are no stopovers."

"All the same, I had intended to do that. But now I've decided on a greater extravagance. We'll go to Iceland, my wife and I." Now for the first time he addressed her. "There we will regain the halcyon time." He spoke weightily, as if he were handing down a verdict of guilty.

Close to tears she said, "And shan't we go to Stirling Castle?"

"*You* can go," he said. "But I am going to Iceland." Then, for no reason, he said, "We met in Bombay."

"Breach Candy is tolerable," said the Englishman. "Otherwise, the place is hell."

"We did not know Breach Candy. Only Malabar," said Donald.

"Poor souls."

"And do you like Venice and are you partial to Pompeii?"

To the double question, their companion only shuddered in reply. And so Donald went through the list of the places they had met by chance and those where they had lived in love. And each name called from the Englishman a glad squawk of scorn. Finally Donald said to him, "Are you married?"

"Married?" His voice sailed high. "Why would a traveler marry? For any reason whatever?"

Bravely, scooping up her strength as if she scooped up fine beach sand, Mary said, "For love perhaps?"

"To a traveler, there is only one love: travel; and only one roosting place: on the wing."

"You see?" said Donald to Mary.

"The traveler is dedicated," said the Englishman, oblivious of innuendoes. "He is dedicated to his own wants which are few. And let me tell you, he can't change."

"What if he should find a perfect place? Wouldn't he then stop traveling?" asked Mary, sincerely wanting an answer.

The man shook his head. "If there were a perfect place, there would be no travelers. But who wants it? Who wants to be *placed*?"

"I do," said Mary. "At last I do." The ardor in her voice was specious for even as she said the words she knew that they were not exactly true; it was that she wished to be *replaced* in an earlier way of life, to be restored to her original heady state. Actually, travel had nothing to do with it and it was ridiculous to imagine that she and Donald could ever achieve their goal in this fashion. They had deceived themselves, had confounded the terms, had put all their eggs in one basket. They had refused to admit that they had long since ceased to love each other and their guilt over their failure, constant and inadmissible, had wedded them far more rigidly than any marriage vows.

"I am off tonight for Stornoway," the Englishman was saying. "I'm told the Minch has been wild this week."

He occupied himself once again with his chocolate and Donald, almost kindly, said to her, "We can stop at Stirling if you like. If you think it would help, although it seems to me it would be rather like trying to capture the Loch Ness monster."

She smiled at the superlative figure and shook her head.

"Then it is agreed that we will go to Iceland where there is nothing?" She nodded and saw the rest of her life stretching out before her like a flat western prairie without a single altitude to vary the monotony.

The bus to Loch Katrine was announced and the Englishman

crossed the lobby in a capable lope in order to get a good seat and called back to them, "If there's an accident, sue."

Sadly Donald said, "What an appalling gasbag. And still, if it hadn't been for him, we would only have added the *Princess May* to the general pretense. It was a good try."

They rose and joined their fellow trippers and they knew that now the end had come, there would be no limit to their civility. Politely on the bus they discussed Reno although, for the sake of the Englishman's *idée fixe,* they called it Reykjavik.

A Winter's Tale

THE long French window of my bedroom frames a scene so stylized that it appears to be deliberately composed like a tasteful view from a false stage window that is meant to be looked at only out of the corner of the eye. There is a church spire toward which four slender, hatted chimneys quizzically list; there are eleven sugar maples whose winter branches seem, from a distance, to twine emotionally together; and there is a neglected clock on a tower whose hands, since Christmas, have stood at twelve. I do not know whether it is forever midnight or forever noon.

At dusk my prospect all is gray, overcast by the film of Cambridge and by the sad lackluster of February; it has an opaline, removed, Whistlerian complexion and it suits the mood that for some days now I have received like a speechless and ghostly visitor whenever I am alone, and especially at this still, personal time of day before the familial facts and courtesies of the nursery and the dining room restore me to the pleasures of my maturity. For what I address so assiduously is a winter of my youth, irrelevant to all my present situations, a half-year so sharply independent of all my later history that I read it like a fiction; or like a dream in which all action is instinctive and none of it has its genesis in a knowledge of right and wrong.

I am at peace with my beyondness and the melancholy that it implies—for these memories are a private affair and I am lonely in my egocentricity—but there do come moments when I wonder if ever again I will prefer the sun of summer to this weary light. Occasionally I am chilled as well as clouded, but I am not quite chilled enough to light a fire on the hearth, although sometimes I pour myself a glass of whiskey and drink it straight, shuddering at the sudden path of heat across my breastbone. I lie in a long chair in the cool half-light, like a convalescent too bemused to read, and perpetually smoke so that the blue vapor further blurs the chimneys and the trees. Solemnly I watch myself as I remove the winding sheets from the dead days, enlarged by time, by desuetude invested with significance and with a leitmotiv. Often I am so beguiled by my

experiments, so far gone in my addiction to discovery, that it is
not easy for me to come fully to life when I have left my room.
It is like emerging slowly and unwillingly from some adventurous, dream-bound anesthetic into a world which, however
pretty and however dear, has no magic and few amazements.

My husband, who is a lawyer and famous for his insight,
and my young son and daughter, gifted with the acuity of the
uninvolved, sense my vagrancy but I ignore the questions in
their faces and bend, instead, to kiss the children, as surprised
as they to smell the whiskey on my breath so long before the
cocktail hour. Once, a few nights ago, Laurence said as he made
our drinks before dinner, "You're not really *drinking*, are you,
Fanny, dear?" And when I told him that I wasn't, I added, to
ward off any other questions, "I'm trying to write something
and I find that whiskey helps." Poor Laurence looked ashamed
and terrified; writing amongst women embarrasses him, for his
mother wrote godly verses and he had a maiden cousin who
perpetrated several novels, long and purple. He did not even
ask me what I was writing but instantly dropped the subject
and told me in detail of the plane and hotel reservations he had
made for our annual visit to Bermuda two weeks from now. I
know that I am safe with my brown studies and my afternoon
whiskey—he'll never ask again.

On one of the last days of January at about this hour, at about
five o'clock in the afternoon, I was up in the attic rummaging
through a trunk full of clothes that have lost their style, thinking that I might find something for my daughter Nan who is at
the age of liking to parody me by dressing in my clothes. At the
bottom of the trunk I found a short quilted jacket with a design
of blue hunters, red horses, and yellow dogs. I have not worn it
since I was twenty, seventeen years ago, when I went to spend
the winter in Heidelberg, sent there by my father in my junior
year at Boston College to learn the language. I put the jacket
on and as I did so, that year, like a garment itself, enclothed
me; and ever since I have moved in its disguising folds. From
one of the shallow pockets I withdrew a small sea shell, a thin
and golden scoop, and immediately I heard Max Rössler's voice
saying to me, "A memento." As if it were yesterday I remember
how I bitterly expanded this to myself into, "*Memento mori*."
We had made an expedition to a beach near Naples and the

day had been a cold fiasco. But I had taken the shell at his bidding and had thought that in later years perhaps, when I saw it again, time would have cultivated my recollection of that day into a pearl of great price. Seventeen years later, when my heart is sedate and my hair is going gray, I recall little but the discomforts of it and our dissatisfaction, so that, in order not to quarrel with each other, we had quarreled with the sea for being so gray and so interminably at low tide. There had been a muddle over the funicular tickets that had disproportionately rubbed us the wrong way; earlier at breakfast in the hotel, a menacing Dane had said in clear, frigid English to his wife, as he stared at us, that he fancied "that chap and girl" were not married. The woman was smoking a thin black cigar. Hating the Dane for the truth of what he said and hating Rössler as the sire of my cheerless, worthless guilt, I told him that I hated Europe. Momentarily it was true; I centralized my disapproval on the limp and cottony tablecloths blotchy with Chianti stains.

In my attic, on looking back, I saw that his giving me the shell—I did not forget that his doing so had made me angry as well as bitter; I thought there should have been some ritual, however small, to mark the beginning of the peremptory end—had been a valiant gesture, really, a stroke of policy as humane as it was clever, for it said, "Remember the moment of this otherwise unmemorable day when I put the sea shell into your hand as a souvenir of our love affair; and remember of it *only* that we were in love." Even so, even after all these years, I stood among the trunks and hampers with a hardened and unforgiving heart, recalling his scornfully bad Italian (he spoke it perfectly as he spoke all languages, but in Italy he was driven, by some obscure caprice, to taunt), remembering his heretofore unknown gluttony for food and drink, his waywardness when we went sailing in the Bay of Naples without a mariner and climbed Vesuvius without a guide. On the Friday of our wretched holiday he had proposed a hideous trip to Sorrento on motor bikes and I had said, "If you must kill yourself, I wish you'd do it alone." He had shrugged and slowly, insouciantly had beheaded the violets he had bought for me.

To say that I have never thought of Heidelberg or of Max Rössler in all these years is not accurate; the town has come back to me when I have smelled certain smells—oriental tobacco returns to me the interior of the Cafe Sö and the American bar at the Europaischer Hof; I see the snug Konditoreien sometimes when I smell coffee in the middle of the afternoon and then I see myself, ashen and enfeebled after a day of lectures, and ravenously hungry, selecting a cake from the glass case in the front of the shop; church bells in the very early morning make me think of the monastery near my pension and of the tranquil Benedictines I sometimes encountered, reading their breviaries as they idled along the Philosophenweg. But until now I have not thought about anything except the data that my senses accepted and recorded; I know that the shock of the rest of it is finished; I'm safe from injury; I can reflect and chronicle. (Surely this rage I feel at the thought of my terror in that little boat on the rabid Bay of Naples is only an echo, is no more than an involuntary reflex that continues briefly after death.) And I *must* look back. I have given myself a deadline: I'll be finished with this recapitulation before our plane takes off for the pink beaches and the southern sun.

2

My father, widowed by my birth, was an ascetic Boston Irishman, austerer and more abstinent than the descendants of Edwards or the Mathers. Wickedness engrossed him and its punishment consoled him; he looked on me, not without satisfaction, as his hair shirt, and my failure to receive a vocation pleased at the same time that it exasperated him. My junior year in college coincided with his sabbatical from the Jesuit school where he taught Latin, and he felt it would be instructive for us both to go abroad. He remained in Paris, brooding darkly on the venality of the French clergy and writing a scandalized account of his impressions of the city, while he sent me on to Germany. He had elected Germany for me instead of France or Italy because, while it was largely Protestant, he admired its thrift and discipline; and he had chosen Heidelberg because he had a friend there who would act as my surrogate parent. This was Persis Galt, a Bostonian and a convert, married to an atheist Scot who taught Anglo-Saxon at the university. I had never seen Frau Professor Galt—for, having been completely Teutonized, this was how she liked to be addressed—but I had heard her legend from my aunts and from their friends who joined them at high, protracted tea. In Boston, Persis Brooks, born well, born rich, presented to society with care by trusting parents, had been a singular failure, and by that I mean she had got no proposals of marriage that had suited her, a situation ceaselessly puzzling to these kind Irish ladies who observed that she had had every qualification necessary to a match with a lawyer from State Street or a doctor from Commonwealth Avenue. They were sorry, my aunts Patty and Eileen and the Mesdames O'Brien, Malloy and Killgallen, that she had given up and gone to Europe to marry this man Galt who was known to be acidulous and cold. Her conversion had come later on, after she had taken up permanent residence in Heidelberg, but Daddy and his sisters and their friends had known her earlier, before her flight, when, perhaps to spite the graduates of Episcopalian boarding schools who had not married her, she attended lectures given by Catholic apologists, went to visit the co-operative society at Antigonish, made retreats, and became a habitual browser in the bookshop of St. Paul's Guild at the top of the Hill. They could never stop regretting that she had not stayed on in Boston to set an example to her dissenting breed.

Daddy praised Frau Professor Galt to me as an exemplary woman with a heavy cross to bear, her burden being her husband who was not only an infidel but was reported to be a scoffer as well and who had, moreover, seduced his children to his own position. On the eve of my first emancipation from Daddy these limnings of the Galt household did not engage me, and I was relieved when she wrote that she regretted she could not lodge me in her own house but that she had found a respectable pension an easy bicycle ride from the university. When Daddy and I parted at the *Gare de l'Est* with a short and manly hand shake, he said, "I am going to be in touch with Persis Galt and if I hear from her that you are drinking whiskey and are falling into the habits that go with it, I warn you I shall take steps. You will go to a Cistercian retreat house for a long, long time, and there won't be any hole-in-corner monkey business there." For, kithless except for Daddy and the spinster aunts and lonely all through childhood, I had recently been consoled and caressed by whiskey given to me by beaux, and often had come home to our flat reeling and reeking and shamelessly gay—at which times Daddy, a teetotaller, deplored the Irish in me as if he himself had not been conceived in County Clare. On the train to Germany I had a compartment to myself and half the night I drank the brandy that I had bought one day on the sly; I nestled and postured in my daydreams until I slid into dense sleep.

Frau Professor Galt met my train and drove me from the station in a miniature automobile so small that I, accustomed only to American cars, did not think at first that it would go. But it went, it went like the wind, careering up the narrow Hauptstrasse, hugging now the blue flanks of the trolley and now the curb where other baby cars like hers were parked together with bicycles and horse-drawn carts. The impetuosity that compelled her to drive in this fashion (we narrowly missed a policeman's dog and once seemed headed for the door of a hairdresser's shop) was nowhere evident in the calm of her person at the helm of this wild machine, nor in her pleasant inquiries about my father and my aunts and my journey. She was in her middle forties and she was firm and ripe like an autumn fruit; her heavy, lustrous hair was sorrel and she wore it in a coronet that further added to her stately altitude. Her pedigree was manifest; it showed forth in her well-made and canine nose, in her high eyes, her long lip, her stalwart Massachusetts jaw. She was plain, but she was constructed on so chivalric, so convincing a scale, she was so shapely and so evidently wrought to last that I could not begin to imagine, just as my aunts had not been able to, why she had come a cropper in Boston; she looked to me exactly like the purposeful matrons in black Persian lamb marching down Beacon Street on their way to lunch at the Chilton Club.

I knew at first glance that Frau Professor Galt had done well at field hockey at the Winsor school and I knew, further, that ever since that time she had kept fit in order to preserve intact the business-like organism into which she had been born; she would be a great walker, she probably skied; she would rise early; she would be intolerant of illness, idleness, or intemperance. She wore good, gloomy tweeds, a stout pair of driving gloves, lisle stockings with a lavender cast and common-sense oxfords with heavy soles. I recalled hearing her spoken of by another of my father's friends—one of the fashionable New York ladies with whom he associated in fashionable apostolates and retreat houses, the ladies who displayed fine editions of Bossuet on the tables in their libraries and rejoiced in quoting the sharp witticisms of Monsignor Ronald Knox—who said, "I'll never forget the day I met Persis Galt in the lobby of the Adlon. She was quite impossible to seize in that doubtful German costume of hers. Her hat, I declare, was an act of treason. She was quite anonymous, quite thoroughly Berlin in the worst sense. I felt I wanted to mark her with a big red crayon so that I wouldn't confuse her with someone else. And at tea, I must have taken leave of my senses for a minute because without thinking, I said, 'Aren't the women of Germany exactly like grouse in their protective coloring? You can't tell where the cobblestones end and their stockings start or find the point at which their collars leave off and their muffinish hats begin.'" The description had been accurate, but I had the feeling that Frau Professor Galt knew what she was up to and that this was not her only style; she had had her reasons for being a frump at the Adlon as she had for giving me this first impression. All the time we were exchanging trifling information we were appraising each other and doing so as if we were contemporaries. I stopped feeling like a girl and felt like a woman; an immediate antipathy between us made me wary and adult. Never before and never since have I known this sheer and feral experience of instantly disliking and being disliked by another woman for no reason more substantial than that we were both women.

I was dry and full of aches from the trip and the brandy's punishments and I was disoriented by having been obliged to change trains before dawn at the border station, so I was downhearted to learn that Frau Professor Galt was not going to take me directly to my pension, but to her house. I would have protested if I had had the chance, but there was no breach in the soliloquy she had begun; she touched upon a multitude of subjects: my father must be induced to come and hike through the Schwarzwald with her; my aunts were dears and she was glad that they were alive and well; Paris was detestable; it was the worst sort of luck that Hitler was not a practicing Christian since there was no denying his qualities; now we were passing the Altesgebäude of the university ("Just a little like S.S. Pierce, don't you think?" I did not but replied that I did); and here was the library on our right where at this very moment her son

August was more than likely studying one of his dry-as-dust books on fertilizer and ensilage for he meant—I was not to ask her why since God alone knew—to be a scientific farmer; it was possible that her daughter Paula was there too, reading something even worse since she was a medical student and had a passion for acquiring information about such things as blood.

We began to ascend a steep hill paved with brick, and the Frau Professor told me that she lived in the house almost at the top, one with a green gambrel roof and iron balconies. As we drew nearer and I caught my first glimpse of the ruined castle through tall trees and saw in the distance the bend in the river, I exclaimed, "What heavenly views you must have!"

Frau Professor Galt replied, "When one views heaven, all views are heavenly," and she gave me a quick, orderly smile.

"I'm so glad you came on the morning train instead of the evening one," she said as we passed through her garden gate where the snobbish legend *Cave Canem* was posted, "for now you will be able to meet my guardian angel at tea this afternoon. My own private monk, my Dom Paternus, my heaven on earth."

"How very nice," I said, and, appalled to think of having to stay through tea time, I added impudently, "I don't believe I've ever known a monk socially before." A cloud of reproach passed over my hostess's face, but she delivered me again that official little smile and said, "Then you have something in store for you. There's far more *mingling* in Europe than in Boston." Thus by opposing a whole continent to a single city she proclaimed herself inalienably Bostonian, however Popish her metaphysics, however Bavarian her walking shoes, however firm her resolution never again to see the swan boats and the public tulips in the Public Garden. She continued, "One of the nicest things about the pension you're going to, by the way, is that it's so near the monastery at Stift Neuburg you'll have no trouble getting to daily mass. And how those Benedictines sing! Dom Paternus's Kyrie is divine."

During this girlish speech (her vocabulary puzzled and even shocked me a little for it seemed profane to call a living monk divine; moreover, her voice altered to accommodate her extravagance in a higher key and one that was not appropriate to her stature and her general design), she had led me across a chilled, bare vestibule, up a flight of stairs carpeted in thick, grim brown and into a room familiar to my imagination; it was a room in any house on Beacon Hill where in the late afternoon a lady would celebrate the ancient rite of tea with silver and Limoges or where, being alone, she might make spills of last year's Christmas wrappings. The brilliant brass hearth accouterments were there, the fender and the Cape Cod lighter and the tools, even though the logs were counterfeit and the fuel was gas; and the *chinoiserie* was all in place, the matching Ming vases and the glass tree *sous cloche,* and Frau Professor Galt told me at once that the painting of a family group over the mantel was a doubtful Copley. But besides these plausible and predictable things (I liked them all and this was the sort of room in which I would have liked to spend *my* afternoons) there were religious objects everywhere, dreadful to the point of disrespect: figurines of St. Sebastian pierced by far too many arrows, of the Little Flower unduly dimpled and unduly vacant, of St. Francis looking like a sissy schoolboy; there was a miniature in polychrome of the grotto at Lourdes, a crucifix of bird's-eye maple with a corpus of aluminum, and a dim, bromidic print of the "Sistine Madonna."

Before the gas fire stood my breakfast table, the food kept warm by quilted cosies. Frau Professor Galt perfunctorily introduced me to my meal and then, pursuing the subject that she had not relinquished, she said, "If I lived at the Pension Haarlass, I'd begin my day with matins." She stood towering above me while I poured pale coffee into my cup and thought with gloom of the dark chapels of priories where, making a retreat, I had knelt beside Daddy at matins, shivering, sick for the sleep from which I had been wrenched. I hesitated, but I did not wish her to be misled and I said, "I'm afraid I don't even go to daily mass." This was not altogether true; I did not go to daily mass except when I was under the same roof with my father.

The Frau Professor chided me flirtatiously, "Oh, you Sabbatarian cradle Catholics! But I should think that *you* with your father and your aunts—dear Fanny, you have disconcerted me."

When I told her I was sorry I partly meant it, for there had come to me the image of my merry, plump-cheeked aunts, busier than belles with their sodalities and their novenas; their pleasure in confession and their homely use of churches as places in which to meet friends before a Wednesday matinee or in which to rest their feet during long shopping trips; their standing jokes with priests. They lived for and they lived in the church, but theirs was a natural condition; they were too secure to care a thing for polemics; they loved embroidering altar cloths, harvesting indulgences, offering prayers for the sick and the dead.

The Frau Professor rose above her disillusion. "I know you'll forgive me for treating you straight off as a member of the family," she said. "You won't think me too beastly for leaving you alone for a bit? I retire now to my chaste cell to read the noon office—for you see, I'm not like you, not born to the purple, not able to take all these riches for granted. I shan't ask you to join me because I know you're tired and you're—we don't really see eye to eye, do we? Would you like a rosary? Or will you simply meditate?"

"I'll meditate," I said, and drank disgusting coffee.

"If you would like to bathe, ring for Erika," she said. "She doesn't speak a word of English, so you must say to her *Ich möchte ein Bad, bitte.*" My German was sparse but it was serviceable and I was offended that it had been impugned. When my overseer was gone and all the doors were closed and I was left to meditate, I stuck out my tongue. And then I began to move restlessly about the room, queerly scared as if I had committed some sin graver than my mild flippancies; it was not agreeable to me to dislike Persis Galt so much after so short a time; certainly it was unreasonable of me to resent her asking me, over her shoulder as she left the room, to call her by her Christian name.

All the curtains in the room were drawn and the lamps were lighted although the sun was high in the vivid sky. One pair of heavy damask draperies, I found, covered a door to a balcony and I drew them aside and stepped out into the comely autumn. On my right rose the castle hill and for the second time I saw the sundered, rosy stronghold through the bruised leaves of the hornbeam and the lime trees that were beginning to turn; momentarily I quickened to its august antiquity and to its romantic biography of ups and downs, and realized that my reluctance to come here (I had longed to go to Florence) had been balanced by fantasies that the savory air revived. I turned from the pretty rubble and looked below at the town of gabled houses, tall and lean, that hugged the steep slopes, their chimneys raffishly askew, their leaded windows burning in the noon. I supposed that the cluster of buildings with mansard roofs would be the university, where my father had enjoined me to keep my nose to the grindstone until my declensions were letter perfect. I watched three barges pass slowly through the locks up the river, their genial flags unfurling in an easy breeze; far off, on the yonder bank, I looked on fields tilled in neat squares of violet and brown; and here and there, at their junctions, like the figures on a chessboard, stood whitewashed cottages. It was a kindly prospect, it was a tender, mothering countryside.

Suddenly, from all quarters of the town, the church bells began to ring the Angelus; echoes loitered in the calm air to perish in a fresh shower of melody; I was charmed by this concert in recognition of high noon. For a few minutes, on the Frau Professor's balcony in Neueschloss Strasse, my senses were infatuated with foreignness and and my antic spirits rose, delighted; to confront the world of possibilities that had opened up before me (they were vague, but my confidence in them was sure) I wanted to look my best and I started to go back into the room to ring for Erika and ask for my bath. But on the threshold I was arrested by the spectacle of a young man in a uniform coming through the door with a muzzled toy Schnauzer in his arms. Simultaneously the maidservant came through another door to greet the dog with gushes, "Ah, the good Herr Rössler brought the good dog home!" She cradled the grizzled creature in her arms. "Shall I tell the Frau Professor you are here?"

Herr Rössler looked at his wrist watch and said solemnly, "By no means. She will be at her orisons. But when she gets off her knees, you can tell her she owes me two marks fifty for the damned dog's bill. He had a tooth pulled."

"Nay, nay!" cried Erika in consternation and kissed the top of the dog's head. "Be kind, Herr Rössler. Remember how you brought him when he was a puppy—oh, so sweet, so sweet," and murmuring, purling, she left the room to warm some milk for the dear good dog. The man looked at himself in an Adam mirror beside the door. "Coat carrier, dog carrier, my very obliging young friend, Herr Rössler," he said. "He flies, he's very charming, he'll be a catechumen yet." Before he left the room, he opened the other door and called, "Hello! Erika! Tell her I'll collect the two marks fifty this afternoon. And Heil Hitler!"

3

Persis Galt was going to greet the monks who stood in the doorway, and so absorbing was her salutation of the short and corpulent man in front, whom she greeted as Dom Paternus, that I got no clear picture of him until, twittering and exclaiming, the singular woman knelt on the floor to receive his blessing while her other guests busied themselves in looking elsewhere. I was as embarrassed as the others and the momentary obliquity of the monk's gaze made me think he shared our discomfort. I had expected Dom Paternus to be a thin and pallid hull for the ascetic spirit of which I had heard so many dithyrambs in the few hours I had been under this roof; far from that, Dom Paternus, by twenty years older than I had imagined, was round and red. His head was perfectly spherical and perfectly bald and his small, winsome ears stood out straight. He had a bright double chin and jocose eyes and a pink nose. He was something like Friar Tuck and something like Father Lynch from St. Anne's parish who often played two-handed pinochle with my Aunt Patty.

I had not been at all surprised that Persis had changed from her tweeds and brogans into a less workaday costume. At lunch time she had emerged from her chaste cell in a black velvet dress with a long skirt and a tight bodice that cherished her small waist; her long arms moved beautifully in narrow sleeves that terminated in pointed cuffs extending halfway down her splendid hands; at her throat (the neck of her dress was low) she wore an ebony cross on a velvet ribbon. I was sure that her intention had been pious, but the result was provocative; her chic and her decolletage at sunny midday had unsettled me; and they unsettled me even more now in her gathering of monks, of shabby students from her husband's Beowulf class, and of bulky Stormtroopers and Blackshirts. After lunch she had invited me to have a look at the room where she prayed and I did not fail to be impressed at the sight of her kneeling at her cherry *prie-dieu*; she was the only decoration in the room; indeed it was chaste and more than chaste, it was sterilized.

Now she got to her feet, warmly clasped the hand of the other monk, and turning to me with her arm outstretched to Dom Paternus as if to a dumb beast, she said, "Here is a pretty American who has come to be your neighbor at the Haarlass. You must take her in hand at once because she says she doesn't go to daily mass." The monk forebore to judge me on these grounds and did no more than affably acknowledge the introduction. The Frau Professor told me—and told the whole room—that I would find my pension absolute heaven. In the beginning, she explained, it had been the house where the oblates had been shorn before they entered the monastery, hence its name. Herr Pirsch, the landlord, was a devout man and the cook, Gerstner, despite a somewhat cretinous look, had the soul of a saint and often took surprises to the monks, surprises, that is, that did not interfere with their laws of fast and abstinence. Dom Paternus and the younger brother, Dom Agatho, listened gravely and with infinite patience like the indulgent husbands of women addicted to telling twice-told tales. She went on to say that I must not get the impression that there was anything worldly about her brothers; on the contrary, they could not be more pious, but there was a heartening liaison between them and a certain section of the Heidelberg laity of which, it was clear to me without being told, Frau Professor Galt was the leader.

There were other conversations in the room and there were, as well, the sounds of spoons on teacups and the gush of fizz water into glasses and a drift of street noise, but these were only a blurred background for the cascade of speeches from the leading lady's lips. She had returned to her tea table and had assumed a presidential posture, erect and magnanimous; she seemed to be bowing to the applause of her constituents when she said, "I should have been born in the middle ages." This was evidently meant for me since the declaration seemed new to no one else. She went on to say that her husband (he was late as usual, the wretch) and her children (late, too; how like *him* they were!) could have lived at no time in history but these very days. "I love them, the darlings," she said, "but alas,

alas, they've missed the whole point of life. My poor abandoned Paula and her awful preoccupation with the pancreas! I'm sure St. Francis never knew about his enzymes—what's the good of all these new acquisitions of the body, I should like to know. August is a little less absurd with his agriculture—one should love the land, but I know that you, Dom Paternus and Dom Agatho, didn't learn your farming in laboratories."

"Speaking of the land," said Dom Paternus, a merciful man, "that gorgeous Spanish chestnut on the Kuehruhweg has begun to turn. I went up this morning to look at it."

"After lauds or before?" She was indefatigable; I thought the Benedictine sighed. He did not answer; he picked up a tea caddy and said, "Your tea is so good." But Frau Galt was not to be put off and she repeated her question. The younger monk answered for Dom Paternus, "Why, afterward. It's too cold and dark nowadays at the hour we get up to go for a botanical ramble. It was bitter this morning. Dom Placid came to breakfast wearing a red sweater—I dared not look below his waist to see if he had decided his rheumatism had entitled him to any other dispensations." Persis frowned, not liking this frivolity—the intramural humor left her out of things—but the monks and I smiled at the mild joke. And she took the conversation back, repeating what she had told me at lunch (an abominable meal of steamed eel and unsalted dumplings), that she and I would bicycle to see the cathedral at Speyer, a building that had always induced in her great peace of mind; since my birthday came on the Dedication of St. Michael the Archangel she would give a lunch party in my honor after the last mass; we would possibly make a pilgrimage on foot to some shrine or other. Then, addressing me, she said, "I forgot to tell you that we play bridge every Tuesday at the Europaischer Hof. I hope you'll join us there as often as you have the inclination."

Having been chilled to the bone by her other plans I accepted this invitation with relief, and even with enthusiasm, although I was afraid that "we" would be the monks (armed with pastoral dispensations to accommodate their secular sister) or members of that top flight laity into which I felt I was being drawn willy-nilly.

Abruptly she stopped talking; I followed her sidelong glance to the door and saw entering it the young man who had been here earlier with the dog; now, though, he was in civilian clothes and he was through with his sulks, smiling agreeably. Persis Galt said, "I am monopolizing my guest of honor. Didn't I introduce you to Mellie Anderson, Fanny? She's that sweet little thing over there by the Schnapps; August's girls always seem to be near the Schnapps. Speak to her, won't you?"

I left her side and so did the friars; we were replaced by Herr Rössler and the Frau Professor's voice ceased to be audible. At the same time the tension in the room relaxed and there was even laughter. On my way to Mellie Anderson I was several times detained, once by a sad, grubby girl in octagonal glasses whose eyes all afternoon had followed Persis worshipfully and who told me that in another year she was going into an order of German-speaking nuns in the Rocky Mountains. "Persis is wonderful," she said reverently. "If I didn't have a vocation, I'd like to be exactly like her." Poor soul! Emotion leaked from her strained eyes; she was the dismalest sight on earth. Again I was halted by a heavily decorated army officer who told me irrefutably that he had met me in Berlin at the Olympics when I was staying with the Gaisenströcks and when I denied this, saying that I had arrived in Europe only ten days before, he asked me if Giselle Gaisenströck had had her baby yet. And Dom Agatho with an ingratiating grin told me that his uncle had been born in Cincinnati.

Mellie Anderson and I had everything in common; she, too, had been sent to Persis Galt, but by a zealous mother instead of father, and she, too, was lodged in the Pension Haarlass. She had been here for a month, the longest month of her life, she said, eyed constantly and chided constantly by Persis Galt, who had spies everywhere, among the servants at the Haarlass and at the Europaischer Hof. Mellie felt sometimes that she was going nutty the way her slightest aberration from the straight and narrow boomeranged; Persis wrote voluminous letters to her mother and her mother wrote back threats—Mrs. Anderson was evidently much like Daddy. Mellie had taken up with August Galt, though she detested him for the rowdy and rambunctious Nazi he was, in the hope that Persis would ease up on her vigilance; the hope was dashed, for Persis openly and even ostentatiously disliked her son and now Mellie was stuck with him. The fact was, she said, that Persis loathed all her family and they all loathed her. Then why didn't they leave one another? I asked.

"She has the money," said Mellie. "She has money enough to buy something better to drink than this peasant slop. Have some?" The smell of the Schnapps was worse than the taste; we drank from wineglasses. Mellie went on, "It all has to do with money. Even in my case it does—and it will in yours too probably. If my mother stopped my allowance, what would I do? So I go to mass at seven every morning no matter what I've been doing the night before—I am sure the chambermaid keeps a report card for me—and come here to let her explain the Epistle of the day and refrain from making irreligious jokes and show up on bridge night—and when I think of how I looked forward to this year! I was naïve enough to think that Mother was giving me a lot of fun and games."

Mellie's grievances were manifold and justified; I liked her and I was listening to her, but at the same time I was watching Persis and Herr Rössler. At the beginning of lunch, Erika had spoken of the two marks fifty that her mistress owed the aviator and Persis said tartly, half to herself, "What an ungraceful thing to speak of. One would think he'd have some affection for the animal he gave me." It occurred to me to ask Mellie to explain Rössler's role in the house, but on second thought, I decided to puzzle it out myself. The man had risen but he lingered beside the tea table as if he were receiving some final instructions and then he made his way towards us. Persis Galt resumed her earlier role; she summoned the monks to return to her; her voice became a carillon: "You must teach me to love Monica's son as much as I love Monica!" she cried. "I've prayed, I've prayed with utmost contrition and my heart is still hard toward St. Augustine."

Softly Mellie said, "Listen, I can't stand another minute of it. I'm going to tell her I'm going to Benediction. Watch out for Max Rössler—he's her Number One spy." She returned her glass to the tray and then she groaned, "Oh, Jesus, here come the atheists." August Galt, so blond and broad and Aryan that he looked more German than any German in the room, and Godfrey Galt, black-haired, beak-nosed, looking clever and cantankerous, saluted Persis as if she were a chance acquaintance, and came to meet me.

My host, casting hard looks everywhere, rubbing his hands together, made me think of a hangman. "My wife knew your father," he said. "In Boston. She has reproduced a Boston drawing room with considerable fidelity, don't you think?" I agreed with him and started to elaborate but he interrupted me. "I live in a hideous house. My wife cannot bear the light of day. She is fond of darkness, inconvenience, bad ventilation, gorgon-headed waste. I myself am by way of being a Bauhaus man." He was building a modern house in the hills above Heidelberg, he told me, and his son said, "There will be nothing for Mutt to do in Vat's house."

"In my house," said the professor, "there will be nothing for a woman to do but sit and stare," and with this he began to stare at his wife's back. He accepted the glass of Schnapps August poured for him, drank it like medicine and took leave of us, saying, "I'll just say hello to the Blackfriars and Blackshirts. Grüss Gott, Heil Hitler, what's the difference?"

Mellie said to August, "I have been waiting for you for an hour. I am leaving *now,* this instant. You meet me and I mean it."

I had never seen so much ill-humor displayed simultaneously by so many people. August, who had not spoken to me at all, snarled like a dog and followed Mellie, who paused beside Persis and curtsied. "I've had a divine time," she said in cheeky burlesque, "but I must run to Benediction. I haven't said a rosary since morning."

"*Aufwiedersehen,* my darling," said Persis. "In Christ!"

"In Christ! Heil Hitler! *Guten Abend! Aufwiedersehen! Danke schön!*"

I had no time to see the effect of this on Persis Galt or on the monks because Max Rössler was at my side and had taken my elbow and was guiding me to the dining room. "I'm to give you a real drink and then I'm to take you to the Haarlass," he said. "My name is Max Rössler, I know yours. Persis apologizes but as you see she can't leave her guests."

Until we had gone into the cold, quiet dining room I had not realized that I was tired to death, and tired in a way that I enjoyed; it was a merited fatigue and it claimed my bones and my blood as well as my muscles. It was a condition in which I was vulnerable to everything, to liquor, to joy, to despair, to love, to quarreling; I might cry or I might be crippled with giggles. I cared nothing at all for Mellie Anderson's warning; I was too grateful for the delicious drink the spy had given me, too happy to be out of earshot of the Frau Professor Galt.

This dark young man was well turned-out; his manners were a second nature and he spoke his perfectly idiomatic English without any accent at all; his laugh was easy and somewhat professional and gave me the feeling that he was peering into the darkness over footlights which at once blinded and reassured him. The smell of his tobacco was as unusual as incense and when he offered me a cigarette I found the taste of it entirely new. He smoked through an amber holder which he bit between his good white teeth. He was very handsome and he looked like the Devil. His forehead was high and his nose was sculptural and all the surfaces of his face were fine; his eyes and his mouth expressed nothing. His upper lip was long and the lower one was full but its fullness did not suggest intemperance or even pleasure; it was the mouth of a child who had been pampered in his sulks which, in adulthood, had become selfish desires, desires for power, perhaps, or for a feudal preservation of the *status quo*. And his eyes, polished and dark like some hard wood, copied and clinched the self-love of the mouth. His face was less a face than a representation of a kind of conduct and it had, therefore, a certain antiquity which made his American slang anachronistic. I, used to simple, noisy boys, not much younger than Max Rössler, was flurried by his sophistication, which I distrusted and admired. We covered some customary topics; we exchanged compliments on each other's countries although I had seen nothing of his and he had never been to mine. We were sure that I would enjoy my winter here although my study of philology depressed us both. I would find the veranda cafe of the Haarlass agreeable, he told me; he often went there on sunny afternoons at this time of year, when it was especially nice to look at the autumn leaves on the Jettenbühel across the river.

"Is there a bar there?" I asked him.

"A bar? You mean do they sell drinks? My God, of course! You are in Europe, Fräulein."

"Then I would rather drink there than here," I said. "I want to go there now."

"At your service," he said and bowed and gave me an ambiguous smile, half seducing and half warning; I felt mocked and as green as grass and needlessly I added, "I don't mean you have to stay. I halfway promised to meet Mellie Anderson."

"Well, they *don't* have a bar at Stift Neuburg where presumably Mellie is telling her beads like a good girl." He smiled warmly, really amused and surely on our side, and he took my hand; the touch of his warm fingers on my cold ones was exciting; he bent toward me as if I were much shorter than I was, as if I were some small woman whom he loved. "We won't go to the Haarlass yet," he said. "We'll go to the Cafe Sö. There won't be anyone there."

4

Persis Galt, a Blackwood specialist, played bridge ferociously on Tuesdays. The salon at the Europaischer Hof which she dominated was a sumptuous room, brightly lighted, thickly carpeted, and full of artificial roses and counterfeit Louis Quatorze. Technically this room could be used by any guest of the hotel or even by a nonresident pleasure seeker who was willing to buy enough drinks at the bar to make his visit worth-while. But Persis had some power over the lackeys so that, at a word from her, anyone could be denied admission. If her bridge nucleus, which numbered twelve with an occasional peripatetic thirteenth, was annoyed by outsiders, they were treated with such snubs and outright discourtesies by the waiters and the bartender that they departed in humiliated silence.

It was my misfortune almost always to draw as partner a Hungarian dipsomaniac called Countess Tisza who for many years had been working on a life of Walther von der Vogelweide. Her bridge, as she steadily drank (her capacity had been likened to that of the Great Tun in the castle which held forty-seven thousand gallons) became so disengaged from any kind of method that I often thought it would be possible to bring legal action against her. The Countess was sometimes in and sometimes out of favor with Persis, but in or out, she was always at the Europaischer Hof on Tuesday evening and each time without fail she asked Max Rössler and she asked me why we were not interested in each other. The question embarrassed me and Rössler seemed not to hear it. It was sometimes for this reason that the Countess fell from our leader's favor, but more often she was sent to Coventry for making a scene with the bartender, whom she suspected of watering her Scotch, or for accusing someone of being homosexual. Whenever she took a false step Persis Galt and her cohorts not only commented devastatingly on her drinking but, as well, attacked her friend von Ribbentrop, who they said was a man no one would want to know, a sycophant and, worse, a bore; although at other times it was because of this friendship that the Countess was looked on respectfully as someone who got about in the most amusing and important places. When she was "in" her boozing was called an eccentricity.

The other players, for the most part, were residents of this hotel; if they had had the money they would have lived at the Ritz in Paris or in London or in New York or Boston. They were chic, uneducated, indolent and discontented; they lived in Heidelberg because this was a good hotel and it was cheap in Germany and they were not far from the casino at Baden-Baden. They were so entirely cosmopolitan that there was no way of telling their nationality save by their surnames.

As I looked back, I realized that I had imagined a much more pastoral way of life in Germany; I had thought of waltzing, wine festivals and pleasure steamers on the Rhine. I had thought of seidels of dark beer and evenings of fraternal song, of Mosel in stemmed glasses for quiet trysts. At the Europaischer Hof the drinks were expensive (we paid for our own), the conversation was tedious, the anecdotes were provincial and obscure, and the evenings ended invariably in a squabble over the score. Frau Galt, an adroit Yankee, generally managed to extort an undue sum from me which I paid without protest when she casually remarked, "I *must* remember to write to your dear father tomorrow."

Sometimes Persis and Max Rössler played against the Countess and me. The combination of the Countess's irresponsibility and my preoccupation with Rössler's hands and with his gentle leaning toward that hypothetical *petite* caused me to play so badly that the Frau Professor caustically observed, "I am sadly enlightened. I thought in America these days one took in bridge with one's mother's milk."

Rössler had never come to the Haarlass. I knew that I had frightened him away from me when we had gone that first afternoon to the Cafe Sö, but still I did not know why. Twice I had terribly disrupted his stagy calm, once when I asked him where he was to be stationed after his three-months' leave was over and again when invasively I told him I had seen him look at himself in the mirror in Persis Galt's drawing room that morning. He did not answer my question and he chose to ignore my other tactlessness by calling for the check.

On the train from Paris I had made no bones to myself about my intention to have a love affair in Heidelberg, and I was not in the least ashamed that the images of my daydreams were largely derived from scenes in *The Student Prince*. I did not mean to love. I meant to be "in love" and to be sorry when it was all over; but because I was a levelheaded girl (my rebellion against Daddy was little more than a convention) I did not wish to be a spendthrift: I expected some time to marry. But my plans had gone amiss, for I was in love with Max Rössler and I loved him. I had neither eyes nor ears for any of the German or American youths from the university with whom I drank beer and danced occasionally, who were accessible, who would gladly have helped me carry out my lighthearted project. Daily I expected Max to come to the Haarlass and daily I waited, watching the road from Heidelberg as I sat on a rock on the hillside behind the inn. In my disappointment I gazed through tears that did not fall at the fields where the Benedictines were swinging scythes or sowing the winter wheat. From the paths in the hills behind me I heard fagot gatherers greeting one another and heard the Hitler Jugend singing on their way home from a hike. Sometimes I waited until the light began to fade, the red softening to the smoky flush of a peach which was then overtaken, at evensong, by a green light that lay over the monks' paradisus. And then when all the light and all my hope were gone, I would return forlornly to the cafe and if I found no one there I knew, I would play a game of solitaire. I did not understand his delay; the days of his furlough were going fast.

It was delay rather than neglect, I thought, for he was not unconscious of me. I could tell that by the way he sometimes looked at me when I cut the cards for his deal, or implied a toast to me as he lifted his glass. Now and again at the end of an evening he saw Mellie Anderson and me into a cab. Dissatisfied, I looked at him standing there on the steps of the hotel, his carnation as white as his starched shirt, and said to myself that I might as well give up, that anyhow he was not worth it, that he looked like the sort who would come a dime a dozen on the Riviera.

One night late in October as we all left the Europaischer Hof Persis observed that the night was much too fine for a cab and she suggested that Max and Mellie and I walk home with her to the Neueschloss Strasse and come back then to the town for a cab to the Haarlass. Mellie, as she often did, pleaded a headache and disappeared, making a beeline for the Roter Ochsen where she would spend the rest of the evening wrangling with August Galt and his Nazi friends who refused, laughing like peasants, to believe that she had been a member of the Young Communist League.

It was a bewitched night, balmy, misty, muting. As we stood chatting a moment before the door of the Galts' house I looked up at the castle, dematerialized by the river mist, and felt stopped dead by the timelessness not only of Heidelberg but also of this false and enigmatic man, the deathless archetype that figured in the dreams of all masochistic schoolgirls. Tonight he was dressed as a man of action, the lieutenant in uniform, and when, after seeing Persis into her vestibule, he proposed that we walk up to the castle I agreed too readily and gaspingly, sounding like Persis or like Mellie's parody of Persis, "Oh, an absolutely heavenly idea!" We climbed the steep street in silence; in the stubbornness of his ideals, Max bent his head downward as if I were three inches shorter than I was.

He asked me if I liked Heidelberg by now and I replied that I did; we brutally ridiculed the Countess; we talked about the weather. When we passed Charlemagne's dry fountain just inside the castle gate it occurred to me that there were probably ghosts here; I earnestly wanted there to be for I wanted an emotion, and terror would be better than none. And all the same in direct denial of my wants and of my intentions, I said, "I can't stay long. I have a lecture in the morning at nine."

"So?" Was he bored or was he a bore? Both, I concluded, and I agreed now with Mellie, who said he was depthless and stupid.

We stood on the parapet of Ottosthur looking down on the

roof tops dimmed by the mist and I found the Haarlass, its
veranda cafe a blurred scar of lights. Rössler said, "Schenck will
be marking the Americans' beer coasters double." It was true;
the head waiter was a thief and a panhandler.

"I thought you often came to the Haarlass," I said.

"I do. I was there last night."

I was quite beside myself, as if I had an intolerable pain but
could not describe it to the doctor. I did not know whether
to be angry that he had come to my pension and had not told
me (last night I had spent the evening in my room writing to
Daddy and translating my *Beowulf*) or to be frenzied with the
suspicion that he had been there with a girl, or to be insulted
that he had so casually told me he had been there at all.

I finally said, "It is often rather fun in the veranda."

He made no reply. He did not speak and he did not look at
me; I found him unforgivable. I wondered whether his privacy
came from shrewdness or if there was not something else
besides, an old confusion or uncertainty. His retirement was
not always the same kind and now, standing beside me on the
parapet, staring down like a general from a reviewing stand,
he withdrew almost perceptibly into some private speculation;
he would not have noticed if I had walked away. Embarrassed
by our silence, even though he had dictated it, I snatched at
straws and caught the memory of having read somewhere of
an English princess named Elizabeth who had married into the
Palatinate and had spent her entire life here in homesickness.
She had had her gardeners plant daphne and hedges of yew to
make her think of England.

I said, "Tell me, do you know anything about the English
princess, Elizabeth, who took being here so hard?"

Instead of answering, he repeated the name Elizabeth with a
loving prolongation of the vowels and in a voice of the greatest
tenderness. I had taken off my gloves and had laid my hands
flat on the chilled stones. He said the name again with as much
affectionate direction as if it belonged to me and he embraced
me, not suddenly but with so sure an art that it was not until
he was about to kiss me that I found my voice, crying out one
of those commonplaces that spring to the lips of a girl taken by
surprise. My gloves fell to the paving. Max dropped his hands.
Indeed, I had been so surprised that I had not realized until I

saw the patience of his smile that the whole sequence of these trivial events was based on the coldest cynicism. For he had not thought of conquest any more than now he thought of defeat. He was neither bewildered nor disappointed, neither humiliated nor angry. He restored my fallen gloves—I fancied that he clicked his heels as he handed them to me—and as if this hiatus had not come he said, "I have no information about the English princess at all. I suggest you try a history of the Heidelbergerschloss."

I put on my gloves and turned to go. "Wait a minute, Fanny," he said. A sixth sense prompted me to move a little farther down the parapet. But he stood absolutely still, wearing a look of grief for which I had no preparation. "Listen," he said, "have you any idea how much I hate Persis Galt?"

"Hate her? Why *hate* her? She's only a goose."

"She is also my mistress," he said. "She has been for five years. For four of them I have hated her."

I was smashed. I put my gloved hands to my cheeks and stretched the skin tight over the bones. Max sat down on the floor of the balcony and leaned his back against the breastwork. This was so out of character, it was a gesture so unmilitary, so pitiful and weak that I could not hold back my tears for him and for myself, but I made no sound and I listened to his stale, sad tale.

At eighteen, five years ago, he had studied under Herr Professor Galt and several times had been to the house on Neueschloss Strasse where he had been charmed by Persis in her medieval costumes, surrounded by her monks and her priests and bishops from Munich and Berlin. She had had an altogether different style in those days, as bogus as her present one but far less foolish. She had seemed the soul of sympathy and of serenity; Rössler, together with half a dozen other students, was in love with her. He sent her flowers with no card, "certain, of course, that she would know who had sent them. I thought so incessantly of her that it seemed impossible for her not to know." He lurked in the doorways of houses and shops next to those he had seen her enter, but he had not the courage to speak to her when she came out. "Anyhow, she would not have recognized me. Even then she and Galt made a point of not knowing each other's friends. I was only one of many supernumeraries who could be told to ring for Erika for more hot water on one of her days." Then one night he had gone to the Europaischer Hof with Liselotte Schmetzer because her husband was ill and she needed a partner and there, to his astonishment, was Persis Galt in a role he had never dreamed. Earlier he had thought of her as unapproachable; it was her piety and her inviolable position as the wife of his professor that had appealed to his romantic nature and he had never had any intention of making an actual overture to her: the hopelessness of his case was the poetry of it. He had known, he thought, exactly how Dante felt when he watched Beatrice at her prayers. But at the Europaischer Hof, he had discovered that she was an accomplished flirt, less shy than the commonest slut on Semmelstrasse. They had left early when she said she felt faint and could not drive herself home, and they went to his rooms straight off.

For the first year Max was unable to see, because he was too enraptured, any discrepancy between Frau Galt's life of devotion and her transgression of the Sixth Commandment. But through growing a year older and through taking Persis for granted as his personal property—of which he began to tire; she was voracious of his time—he saw what she had done, what he had done, what they had done together, and from that time forward the principle of his nature was self-disgust. But he had continued with the affair because he was so deeply enmeshed in it; she had made him grow old too fast; he lived in a kind of connubial sluggishness, convincing himself that by not breaking off he was punishing her in her own terms. He had concluded that she had taken a lover to make up for a lack of talent, a lack of talent which she had deceived herself into thinking was a talent for writing poetry or painting water colors or marrying a Bostonian but was really a lack of talent for being good. In the absence of goodness, she had to have power, and who could be better controlled than an eighteen-year-old weakling? "Because I *am* a weakling," he said urgently as if I must believe in the justification for his self-excoriation. "In every way I am the worst possible coward. I am afraid of the sky so I am an aviator; I am afraid of the sight of blood so I am a soldier. I cancel out a phobia with a mania. I am afraid of Persis so I go on with her, on and on and on—"

"You could leave her," I said. "You don't depend on her for money the way her family does. She can't get your parents to punish you for what she knows about *you*."

"Let me tell you something, Fanny. Sooner or later everyone who crosses that threshold gets blackmailed unless they're too disabled, in one way or another, for her to bother with."

"What's her hold over you?" I said with terrible spontaneous anxiety.

"It doesn't matter. She has one but it doesn't matter. Let's go down to the Roter Ochsen."

At the foot of the stone steps that took us down the castle hill into the Kornmarkt, Max took my face in his hands. "What are you crying for, for God's sake?" he said unkindly. "Didn't you ever hear of adultery before?"

"I wasn't thinking about you."

"You *were* thinking about me. You've thought about me from the beginning. You'd better not, Fanny, I'm a swindler from being swindled. I am sick, I must die, may the Lord have mercy on my soul."

Under the cold searchlight of his eyes I felt like a frangible object that he could take apart or could break or could sell or could take home with him to be used for something or other, altered perhaps, to go with the furniture of his rooms. He took the will out of me as neatly as if he had removed the stone from an apricot, and I received his plausible caresses as gratefully, as obsessively, as if I received the man himself. "I've warned you," he said.

5

It was an intolerable love affair, raddled and strangled with our knowledge of its end. If I had a lecture we met at the Stadtgarten in the town where Persis never went; hurrying from the university, I thought only of the small round table at which I would meet him, and it was as if this meeting were the aspiration toward which my whole existence bent and which receded from me to an incommensurable distance once I had recognized it: I ran in dreadful fear that he would not be there.

Often he went away from Heidelberg for a few days at a time, never saying where nor for what reason or whether he would ever come back, and at these times I went to confession at the monastery, where I chattered like a goose through the wicket to an ancient monk who did not listen because I spoke in English. Hearing the sandaled feet of the friars on the stone stairs somewhere above, I hysterically reiterated *Deus te amo* to myself as if this were a charm to dispel the effluvium of my own grave. Once after this I went across the river in the ferry and climbed the castle hill, and while I stood debating with my soul in the English garden, I allowed my blue rosary to fall from my hand. Some child would find it, although as it slipped from my fingers, its gilt gauds glittering, I wished it would not be found except by the feet of a salamander running across a lichened rock.

Almost immediately Max and I had become inseparable, forcing ourselves through our obsessiveness to ignore all the admonitions we heard and saw. Often I was naïve enough to think it was unsafe only because he was an aviator and there might be a war, but most of the time I knew better than that, I knew that it would have ended with a smash at any time and for any woman. There was no pleasure in it, I suffered perpetually, it was monstrous to live through, but I could not have escaped it, not possibly. We were restive, continually seeking diversion, hiding continually from Persis. We went walking for hours through the blue mist of the forests or we took the tram to Neckar-Gemünd and went on from there into the hills. We sought out shabby Bierstuben in Handschusheim. On Persis Galt's days at home and on bridge nights at the Europaischer Hof we were wild with impatience and frantic with deceit but we stayed until the end. Moving, or when we were surrounded by others, our stubborn hope stayed alive until Max's misery suddenly rose between us and nothing was any more of any use. There was something in him, some prehistoric wound, that made me walk within this love (but it was not love; it was another thing, I don't know what) on tiptoe, thinking only of the split second next to come. I dared not disturb the sleeper whom I often saw in his large, cold eyes, for I did not know his identity although I sometimes thought I almost knew.

The week in Naples had been almost like a week any other two lovers might have spent together and once, as we drank rank Italian beer at a quayside bar, he even asked me to marry him, but the quixotic idéa could not be entertained even in fun and he laughed in his thorough and bitter knowledge of himself—*his* knowledge, not mine, for he would not share it with me. This had been the last week of his leave and he got off the train at Karlsruhe, where he was to be on maneuvers.

The day I got back August Galt and Mellie Anderson and I walked up to Ziegelhausen. On the way August told us he had a bad hang-over acquired the night before at a farewell party for two aviators who were leaving for maneuvers. He was burdened with photographic gear and he asked us, when we got to the village, to pose for a picture. His reason had behind it a lengthy and fuzzy logic; he had no photograph of the aviators, Rüdiger and Barth, but he would remember whenever he looked at our picture why we had been in Ziegelhausen on that particular day. "Why should you care," Mellie asked him, "if they're only going on maneuvers?" He pretended not to hear her, for she was suggesting that perhaps they were on their way to the war in Spain. Just as August snapped the shutter the town crier wheeled slowly by on his bicycle. As if it were a lamentation, this archaic man with his silver bell intoned the announcement that cards for the potato ration would be issued on the next day. Mellie and I, breaking our pose, turned to each other in astonishment. The butter ration, inaugurated a month or so before with fanfare and a slogan, had not seemed extraordinary—but potatoes—that *sine qua non* of every German table!

"I know what you're thinking," said August as if he had only now heard Mellie. "How many times do I have to tell you that Franco is in this thing alone? Are you deaf?"

At this time Persis Galt was blessedly preoccupied with a new project. She was gathering about herself a group who were to prepare themselves for becoming Benedictine oblates, the idea having come to her when Mellie's mother wrote that she was becoming one. Once every two weeks she summoned them all to dine with her at the Europaischer Hof and after the consommé and the pheasant, the artichokes, the Nesselrode and the Mosel and the brandy, they all recited compline. Mellie and I were obliged to attend these dinner parties because Persis, busy as she was, never forgot that she was our proprietor and gave us to understand that she and our parents were in close, indeed it might be said, in quotidian correspondence.

She took us to the high mass at Stift Neuburg where none of us received; she brought us books of sermons and lives of saints and meditations, mawkish verses by ungifted nuns; and she behaved, in general, as if the house were on fire and there was no time to waste. At the same time Daddy was writing me endless letters of instruction and questions. He told me that he planned to come to Heidelberg in January; he expected me to come to Paris at Christmas.

A few days before Christmas there was a Day of Recollection at Stift Neuburg. At an interlude between services the ladies and several of the monks went across the road to the Wirtschaft to have tea before an open fire. Dom Paternus offered me a yellow apple, saying, "May I tempt you?" and everyone laughed but Persis, who turned blue with horror. A chair was drawn into the circle for Countess Tisza, who had just come in from the chapel, and when everyone had made a few minor adjustments and the Countess had declined tea (it was almost possible to hear her thinking, If I can't have whiskey, I don't want anything), the Prior, thinking that we had worn out the conversation we had been having about the spiders and reptiles of the Philippines from which Dom Bardo had recently returned, charmingly inquired of the Countess whether she had liked the new statue of St. Benedict in the entry.

The Countess, fixing him with sincere eyes (one could not help admiring her for the way she carried it off), replied, "Father Prior, explain it to me! Will you forgive me if I say it seems to me the sculptor hasn't captured Benedict at all?"

Dom Bardo, a white-haired urbane old man, chuckled cosily. "Good for you! I have an ally, Dom Prior. The Countess doesn't like it either." The grave face of the little noblewoman did not alter as she reproached the monk. "You are unkind, Father. I have only asked for an explanation."

I had seen the statue; it was roughhewn of quartz, an oddity in itself distracting, and what had struck me at first was that all the saint's appurtenances—the vase from which emerged the dragon's head, the raven at his feet clutching the loaf of bread, the crosier and the halo—were unconnected with the figure as if they had been put there as an afterthought; it was as though St. Benedict had annexed these things but their sponsorship remained that of the sculptor. It had occurred to Dom Prior too who, smiling at Dom Bardo, said, "I find it hideous. It's not only a travesty of Benedict, it's bad art. Michelangelo said that a really good piece of sculpture could be rolled down hill and not be broken in any part."

Persis Galt flushed and swallowed angrily. "The same could be applied to a barrel, Father." She went on to argue that the subject was so sacred that even the worst treatment of it could not be harming, that displeasing as the statue might be, they were bound in conscience to admire and revere it because it represented a saint. Poor Persis! In their own bailiwick the monks defied her and not even Dom Paternus came to her rescue, for it was she who had commissioned the statue and she who had paid its exorbitant price. But he took pity on her presently when it was time to go back to the monastery. "What are your Christmas plans? I hope you will make your duty with us."

She paled a little. "I am so sorry," she cried. "I've contracted to go to Strasbourg."

The monk turned then to me. "And what will you do? Will you go to your father in Paris?"

"I'm going to Freiburg," I said.

"To Freiburg?" demanded Persis. "I heard only yesterday from your father that he was expecting you in Paris."

"I've written him that I don't want to come to Paris until spring."

As we were leaving, and as Mellie and I refused the offer of a lift in Persis' car, she plucked me by the sleeve and said, "If I didn't know you so well, I'd think you were going off to be compromised." And she looked at me sharply, believing the opposite of what she said. "Who do you know in Freiburg?"

I wanted to say, "The same man you think will be in Strasbourg." For I knew that Strasbourg, just over the border from Karlsruhe, was where she and Max had often met in the past. But I said, "Friends from the boat."

6

I saw him for the last time in Freiburg. It began to snow in Baden-Baden, and as the train paused there a well-tailored Englishman passing through the corridor said over his shoulder to his companion, "God, what a beastly country! Have a look-see at that muck out there!" The snow drifting through the rafters of the train shed in the wintry light looked unclean as if it would smudge whatever it fell upon, and for a moment I wished that, like the Englishmen, I were leaving Germany, were leaving all this murkiness for some brilliant southern sky. In a disabling ennui I stared at two lovers who sat opposite me in the carriage, fingering each other's hands and exchanging bashful grins of rapture. I was displeased with the spectacle of them for I felt no rapture myself, and I closed my eyes to the dreary village and to the sweethearts and thought not of Max but of unimportant matters: the error in my week's bath bill, a fish stew at the Haarlass that had poisoned Mellie, a blouse I had seen and liked in a shop on the Hauptstrasse. I had been awake for years and years, I thought; this morning my eyes had opened wildly long before the sun was up when the bells were ringing for prime and, confused, I had thought it was Sunday. Adjusting the eiderdown, I had closed my eyes again and had said to myself, "God does not know I am awake."

A pall of grime hung over the bleak platform in Freiburg as it had hung over Baden-Baden, and because I moved through the station slowly I was too late to get a cab when finally I emerged through the storm doors. The Platz was deserted except for an old policeman who stood with his dog at the main entrance of the station. I advanced through the bountiful snowflakes and asked him the way to the Hotel Salmen.

"Heil Hitler!" he saluted me. "Straight ahead." He pointed down the wide avenue that began at the station yard and when he raised his white-gloved hand once more and we said in unison, "Heil Hitler!" he smiled at me out of some spontaneous happiness, and though I was surprised I smiled back. "The snow!" he exclaimed to me. "So beautiful!"

The air, with this gentle, mothlike snow, was sweet after the close compartment, which had been blue with the smoke of all the cigarettes and sour with the reek of red wine that a sullen soldier had steadily drunk out of his canteen. A little canal ran at the side of the street; but for its soft sound there was an immense quiet in the avenue and nothing seemed to stir within the timbered houses through whose closed shutters came bent shafts of light.

Max was waiting for me in the public bar, sitting at a table drinking a brandy and looking, in his civilian clothes, like all the tall lean sanitary Englishmen sitting at other tables alone or in pairs, also drinking brandy. I had not been prepared for so immediate a meeting in so great a throng and I was upset to see that there was a second glass on the table and that he meant our rendezvous to be begun in this crowded, brightly lighted place full of skiers loquaciously recounting their day's adventures. He did not see me at first. He was fitting a cigarette into his holder and only when he snapped open his lighter did he look up. He rose then and waited for me to cross the room: I thought, he would never come to *meet* me. He drew out a chair for me and he could not help touching my shoulder, lightly and in a way no one could see; and leaning over the table he said, "Ah, I am so eager." Someone was somewhere inexpertly playing Chopin on a piano with a crackly tone, but there was delicacy in the playing, and in the moment between our greeting and our conversation, I listened pleased. Our conversation, when it began at last, was as urgent and shapeless as that of any other lovers who, but for their love, would have remained strangers. There was no point in which we lost ourselves in interest of what we were saying, and the talk around us was as pertinent to us as anything we might whisper to each other.

A very old man with a thick mustache and spectacles sat drinking Glühwein with his wife. He said in a high, peckish voice, "That young woman was unmannerly about my eggs."

His wife tenderly touched his hand. "All the same, Franz, the sun was lovely. You said so yourself."

"Yes, yes, all right," he said irritably. "The sun *was* lovely. I said so then and I say so now. But I repeat, that girl was rude about my eggs."

"Persis knows I'm here," I said to Max. "I told her I was coming."

"It's all right," he said. "She thinks I'm meeting her in Strasbourg tomorrow."

"Is there—" I decided I did not want to ask him a question about the war in Spain just then.

At the table on our left an Englishman and a Frenchman sat together. The Frenchman said, "I have been refreshing my memory of Florence," and withdrew a map from his coat pocket. He added with humble woe, "For I shall not ever see it again."

"What are you talking about?" said his companion.

Max and I waited for the Frenchman's answer as if it had something close to do with us.

"I'm afraid I haven't made myself clear to you, Montgomery," said the Frenchman. "I'm not what you think I am at all. I am no intellectual although at one time in my life it was said by a number of my teachers that I didn't have a half bad brain. My plan to seek culture in the culture centers of Italy was just my little joke, poor as it was. The fact is that I am about to be married to a widow of great respectability who owns a pension in Passy. We met on a bus last summer to Fontainebleau. She is one okay dame."

"Is that the end of the American lesson for today?" asked the bored Englishman. "You ought to take better care of yourself."

"You mean I'm nuts?" The Frenchman laughed. "What a wag I am. Good lord, yes."

The smell of evergreens was as strong as mint in the warm room. Skiers warmed their feet at the fireplace and bragged of the jumps they had made and the climbs so steep they had had to use bearskins on their skis. A heavily pregnant cat sat on the stool beside the fire. If I had not been taught better, I would have thought that all of this belonged to the real world and that we were present in it. But I was not so fooled; what we saw and what we heard, though we received and though we acted with absorption, came adventitiously, did not last, meant nothing.

All my selves but one spoke falsely when I said, "I have never been happier."

Max said, "I shall never be this happy again."

Everyone in the bar was enjoying himself, everyone, that is, but the cross old man, who smoothed the bristles of the goatbeard in his green hat and continued to mope over his eggs. Two pretty blond American girls sat smiling like dummies with two men who were perhaps their fathers or perhaps their sugar-daddies. The men observed mildly that the mark was up, that it was a pleasure to travel in Germany with the present rate of exchange, that there had been a scientist fellow in Cologne who had had some interesting things to say about the pressure at the bottom of the hotel swimming pool.

"If you had come earlier," said Max, "we could have taken the *Bergbahn* to the Schauinsland and had drinks there. I would have managed the *Bergbahn* better than I did the funicular."

"I wish I had. I wish everything bad could be canceled out by something good."

"That's wishing for the moon."

He told me that he had lived three years in Freiburg when he was a child and that he had learned to ski in the mountains that surrounded the town. It was in keeping with the piecemeal nature of our relationship that I knew nothing of his background and that he knew nothing of mine; indeed, it had hardly occurred to me that he had been a child. "I was told that a sort of witch called the Budelfrau lived on the top of the Schlossberg and had marvelous eyes that could see mischief but not good. I thought she lived beside a pathmarker and whenever I went up to ski, I was certain I was going to crash into it and break all my bones. I can't imagine why. I was far too good a child for the Budelfrau to bother with."

"I am sure you were," and I had never been more sure of anything. I could see him, as silent and forbearing as a saint, walking unmolested through all the terrors of childhood, never knowing the need for armor until he was eighteen and it was too late.

We killed another half an hour with another brandy. And then lightly, as if he were offering me another piece of information as casual as that about the Budelfrau, he said, "Did I tell you I am off to Spain?"

"To Spain?" I said, mimicking his grace and calm. "To the war?"

"What else? Would I go to look at pictures at this time of this particular year?"

"I'm sorry," I said.

"I imagine you really are," said Max. "And the pity of it is that I can know and that even so I can't really wish I weren't going. I don't believe in the damned war, but I don't care. I haven't any politics and I haven't any ideals."

I was sure he really did not mind going; in a sense, he had gone already, already he was dead and buried in an unimaginable land, and already he was no more than a memory to me; but a memory indispensable and imprisoning.

"It's too bad you don't care," I said. "I think I would."

"It *is* a waste," he said. "It would be wonderful to be a Christian or entirely to love one's country. Entirely loving oneself would be the best of all."

"Do you have to go? I don't want you to go, Max." In spite of my resolutions, I was dying hard.

"I'm grateful, Fanny, I really am. But, yes, of course I have to go, and I have no intention of coming back. You understand, it is not I do not *hope* to come back but I don't *intend*."

"Oh, think of me! Think for a moment of me!" I really was angry now and I cried, "You're vain and sentimental!"

"Certainly," he said crisply. "I am a German."

"For God's sake tell the waiter to bring us some glasses of a sensible *size*," I said. "And before I forget it, who is Elizabeth?"

He smiled, "My sister. Only my poor sister."

We had dinner in our rooms. As the waiter arranged the table with lobster from Hamburg, figs and oranges from Italy, wine from Alsace, I intently studied a map of the mountains that lay under a glass slab on the desk, making a note of the names: Güntersthal, Schauinsland, Feldberg, as if I were getting them by heart for an examination. I would take with me nothing new except these names. If Max died in Spain, and now I felt sure he would for he had willed himself to die, I thought I would not mourn him very long. It was not at all that I did not love him (Oh, but did I? Oh, it was a dismembering confusion!), was not sunk into this love as permanently as into stone, but that in willing himself to die, he forbade me to interfere with his plans. Turning as the waiter closed the door and Max opened a bottle of champagne, I went to take my glass and across the room, as if from across a field of flowers, I called, "I love you," as if they were the last words I was ever to utter in my life.

It was a long night and this was the only one, for orders had come for the bootleg troops; they were to be sent out on the day after Christmas and all leaves had been curtailed. When it was daylight we went to the windows and looked out at the stiff vineyards on their zigzagged arbors. The bells began to ring for Lord Jesus, their tones commingled and cadenced against one another like a madrigal. I had put on the quilted jacket he had brought for my Christmas present: its design was of blue hunters on red horses with yellow dogs running at their feet.

And I had taken the sea shell from Naples out of my coin purse and put it into one of the pockets. We stood listening to the bells and to the wind's wings beating the branches of the cedar trees against the windowpanes.

"Will Persis go mad at losing you?" I asked.

"She'll find another paschal youth," he said. "But I doubt if she'll find another Jew. There aren't many of us left."

"Max! Oh, Max! Oh, my God!"

"Hush, Fanny. Listen, my sister is taking my rooms for a few weeks until she can get to England, but she won't be there for a day or so. Here is the key. If you want anything, take it." Dressed in his slate blue uniform, his cape loose at his shoulders, he was at the door.

"Persis knows? Is that her blackmail?"

"Hush, Fanny." He opened the door.

"*Aufwiedersehen*, Max," I said.

"*Lebewohl.*"

7

Elizabeth Rössler never came to Heidelberg and I never could bring myself to go to his rooms. I had a letter from her, though, sent from Berlin. It said, coldly and dutifully in perfect English, that Max had been killed "on maneuvers near Karlsruhe" and that he had directed in his last letter that I be notified if anything happened to him. The day I got it I bicycled to Heilbronn with Mellie and two rowdy American boys. We played poker all night long and got drunk on atrocious champagne; I had a wonderful time.

There was a day when Persis Galt came to my room at the Haarlass to say that a friend of Godfrey's had seen Max and me in Freiburg. I was too woebegone to fear her; she was too afraid of me to scold me. She had come, craven, to drive a bargain with me: we would keep each other's secrets. I agreed although I did not give a damn. She was in her masquerade of tweeds and I pitied her immensely.

My father died that May in Paris and I came back to Boston and my aunts.

Soon the scene from my window will begin gradually to change; I find myself reluctant to think that the leaves will presently be coming out. Similarly, I remember, Heidelberg was intolerable to me when the wild plum began to bloom. I hardly dared go into the hills for fear of meeting pairs of sweethearts; I scarcely dared look out the windows of the veranda for fear they would be rowing on the river to Neckar-Gemünd. There had always been the danger that I would mourn Max, that I would miss him, would become inward about him. It had been necessary to get back to America to return to the exterior. And so, until I was summoned to Paris to Daddy dying of a thrombosis, I hid in my Gothic grammar, in the confessional boxes and in my room, half hallucinated by the Haarlass homemade red wine. I never thought of the future and I never thought of the immediate past. I lived in a heavy stupefaction.

It is warm today and the window is open. At half past five I throw the sea shell out and see it caught in the tall privet before my house. I am exalted; I believe that I am altogether purged. I look at the clock that still reads twelve and I say, "Goodbye, then, *lebewohl.*"

When *did* that clock stop? Midnight or noon? Someone has come into my room and I wheel to face my husband. He sees the decanter beside the long chair and he sees the glass in my hand and he sounds like Daddy when he says, "Fanny, I don't like this at all."

"Do like it," I say and laugh and hold out both hands to him. "I've decided to give up trying to write poetry." He really should not look so pleased.

"Well, in that case—" he says and pours a glass for himself. "Isn't that jacket new?"

"No, it's old. It's as old as the hills."

"It's hideous," he says. He is right; perhaps seventeen years ago it was not so coy as it is now. I turn back to the stuck clock for a split second and during it I think, my God, Jew or not he was a Nazi; and then I think, what did Nazi mean when I was twenty? So, finding no reason for preserving my guilt, I watch it give up the ghost. Tomorrow at this time we will be in Bermuda.

"I know it's hideous," I say. "But Nan won't know it is."

The Warlock

THE S.S. Carmelita, a thin merchant vessel painted a withered yellow, was ready to set sail from Brooklyn for the
West Indies on the afternoon of the day before Christmas with
a full cargo of automobiles, beer, Frigidaires, and Mason jars,
and with, as well, a full booking of a hundred and fifty tourists.
On the decks it was cruelly cold, in the cabins it was tropical,
and in the public rooms the fans had already been turned on
to counteract the heating system. Shivering and sweating, don-
ning and doffing cardigans and coats, using bad language, the
passengers were out of sorts; the air of festivity in which they
had embarked had dwindled and had finally died along with
the glow of their lunchtime Martinis, and the whiskey they
were drinking without ice or soda, out of thick tooth glasses,
seemed only to lower their spirits further. Most of them were
tired to begin with after a day of last-minute shopping and
last-minute telephone calls, and now they were overwhelmed
by well-intentioned baskets of farewell fruit ("Exactly *like* that
bird-brained sister of mine," growled an empurpled man to his
wife, "when she knows good and well where we're going the
papayas lay around on the ground") and high poinsettias (more
coals to Newcastle), which crowded them in their cramped and
humid quarters. Those quarters! They were a far cry indeed
from the spacious, airy suites the travel bureaus had described
and, through trickery and optical illusion, had photographed
for their brochures; they were, in point of fact, airless cubicles
in need of paint, not fit for the meanest of the crew. A good
many passengers went straight to the purser to complain. There
was also the problem of communication with the Puerto Rican
stewards, who were at once ubiquitous and migratory; if these
small, slippery souls with the eyes of fawns and the sable hair
of dolls could momentarily be detained, they gestured with
polite regret and helplessness, and in rampageous English they
disclaimed all responsibility for misplaced bags and denied all
knowledge of how to regulate the heat. Cardiac signs appeared
on the faces of middle-aged men who were going south to relax; lone librarians and lonesome secretaries who had hoped for

shipboard adventure were too short-tempered to reconnoitre the field; children whined that the Carmelita was not as big as the Queen Mary and that they had nothing to do. And visitors, seeing off their disgruntled friends, were heard to thank their lucky stars that they were only visitors.

Mrs. Mark Kimball, on her way to the plantation of friends in Antigua for a convalescence in the sun after a long and depressing illness and an operation, began to realize as soon as she was on board and was threading her way through a labyrinth of glowering and expostulating malcontents that she had made a mistake in choosing to travel by boat at this popular time of year. Having refused to allow any member of her family to come down with her from Boston—she had feared that a farewell, especially with her husband, might make her weep—she had been seen to the gangplank by Nancy Jamieson, an old school friend, who had shuddered at the sight of the ship, had kissed her warmly and said goodbye, and now was gone. Now, when it was too late, she reproached herself for having listened to her old-fashioned doctor, stoutly loyal to the august therapeutics of an ocean voyage, instead of to her more travelled and sophisticated family, who had urged her to spend the holidays at home and then go quickly and simply by plane. They had warned her that a cruise was nothing like an Atlantic crossing, when one might have privacy or company as one chose. There would be organized—and perpetual—entertainment, they said; there would be some dreadful romp on Christmas Eve with trick hats and noisemakers and vinous song; they groaned to think of the sociable drunks that were bound to be on board. But Mrs. Kimball had been afraid neither of her isolation in the midst of merrymakers nor of their infringement upon it; it would be obvious, from her pallor and emaciation, that she was in bad health, and she was sure that no one pleasure-bent would pay her court. And the fact was, further, though she was careful to conceal it, that she was glad to be escaping the familial season at home, because, while she loved her husband and her children and her kinsmen dearly, she was tired nearly to death, and even their conversation, considerate as it was, was often a tribulation to her. She could not face them en masse during the galas of the holidays; in secret she confessed to herself that if she was obliged to listen to her sons' anecdotes about life at Groton, she would probably go quite to pieces. Her nerves were fitful, and there was a chill, like the mortal chill of old age, that lay in the marrow of her bones; she wanted to lie, still and warm and silent, by herself and wait, as a patient animal waits, for her renascence.

She had imagined—and so had Dr. Otis—that on the boat she would sleep, without the help of medicine, dreamlessly and deep into every day, pampered by the motion of the monotonous, benevolent waves, her face tenderly bedewed by spray coming through the porthole, and stirring herself at last to eat a light, delicious breakfast brought by a stewardess of quiet, nurselike deportment. She had seen herself sunning on deck (how Dr. Otis had praised the sun, growing lyrical when he said it was no wonder Apollo was the god of healing!), insentient with ease, turning a heavenly color to set off the summery dresses she had bought at Jay's while outside a blizzard rushed against the trees in the Common. She had thought that she would sit long hours in her deck chair, watching the flying fish by day and by night the stars, trying to determine the change from the northern to the southern configuration of the heavens. By the time she got to the Montagues' in Antigua, she would be so warmed and freshened that her visit to these charming friends might well prove to be a holiday instead of a rest cure.

But neither she nor Dr. Otis had ever been on board the Carmelita. And her faith in the boat died instantly and without a struggle as soon as she was confronted by its utilitarian and down-at-heel appointments. It was far from shipshape. Its interior paint, in places, peeled away in curls; in other places, it was liverish with mildew. The whole boat reeked with smells of machinery and fish; it trembled with furious noise. The main saloon, decorated with rubbery Christmas holly and asbestos Christmas bells, was littered already with Lily cups and dishevelled tabloids, like Revere Beach on a Sunday in July. This room and all the passages were thronged, and thunderous with a collectively churlish voice. She had not reckoned on so many people, nor had she ever dreamed that they would be so large and loud and bright. Many of them had already put on descriptive sports shirts and narrative neckties; she even saw a tall fat man wearing a straw hat shaped like a cornucopia. None of these amenities, however, had brought with them a moment of good will, and the man in the hat was himself especially fierce as he gave a steward his comeuppance for the presence, in his cabin, of a cockroach the size of a hen.

Mrs. Kimball was required to revise the most important of her plans—that is, her long slumbers—as soon as, after many wrong turnings and rebuffs, her porter found the hot cranny in which she was to travel, and not by herself, as she had been led to believe, but with a Mrs. McNamara, of Bridgeport, who wore a purple flannel suit and, in her hair, a garland of vast buckram roses. Unlike the other passengers, Mrs. McNamara was cheerful; an inexorable, an undying bonhomie radiated from her like the heat of a summer day. At the moment Mrs. Kimball arrived, the cabin was occupied and overflowing with Mrs. McNamara's large brother, Mr. Weed (the jollity was a family trait, and he performed the introductions with breathless joy, as if Mrs. Kimball's appearance on the scene were the principal reason for their being there), and his two large adolescent daughters, all three of them further magnified by swaddles of camel's hair, in which they suffered with smiles upon their moist, pink faces. Mrs. McNamara, almost as tall as her brother and far fatter, was in the corridor making arrangements to have her breakfast brought each morning at seven, explaining genially to the stewardess that she thought sleep was a downright waste of time. Poor Mrs. Kimball paled at this and only hoped that her companion did not do exercises on arising or greet the sun with song. The stewardess, hard of face and breezy, chewing gum and smelling of some expletive perfume, said, "You're the doctor, dear, but you don't know about the planters' punches on this bucket—they keep a girl up at night and they keep her down in the morning." The glandular group in the cabin were delighted with this naughty sally, and they giggled and turned even redder, and Mrs. McNamara, beaming, said, "Fresh!"

Mrs. McNamara had evidently been in residence for some time, for her bags were unpacked, the open closet revealed a wardrobe of roomy cotton dresses, and her extensive gear was strewn about on her bed and on half of the top of the bureau. She seemed prepared for a long, domestic trip on a houseboat. She had a sewing basket and a loud alarm clock, a hot-water bottle, materials for giving herself a home permanent, for removing spots, for polishing shoes, for stretching gloves; she had a half-worked needle-point pillow cover, a pile of magazines, a knitting bag, a bottle of Scotch and one of brown sherry and one of blond Dubonnet. There were several boxes of chocolates and jars of sour balls standing about, and one of those big girls was hungrily eating salted nuts.

To accommodate the steward who was carrying Mrs. Kimball's bags, the Weeds clambered out of the cabin, and she was able to make a survey of the awful little room. Mrs. McNamara had chosen the bed against the wall, leaving to her the outer one, beneath a louvered window that looked out upon a shuffleboard court; to her alarm, she saw that several of the narrow slats were missing from the blinds, permitting anyone strolling on the deck a clear and comprehensive view inside. The bathroom was shaped like a piece of pie, and in one of its angles there was a dangerous shower stall with a declivitous floor and fungus walls; something in there was hissing ominously, and something else was pounding in a heavy, regular rhythm, like a bared heart.

Mrs. McNamara pointed to a vase of white roses on the writing desk, and she said, "They came for you a while ago and I had the señorita—*señorita*, how do you like that! Before we're even out of Brooklyn! I had her put them in water. I was afraid they'd curl up and die in all this heat."

Mrs. Kimball thanked her and thanked the stewardess, who told Mrs. McNamara rather sharply that she was *not* a señorita and had only joined this staff of spicks because she liked going south; her tone implied that she had refused much better offers from the Cunard line.

The Weeds, joined by Mrs. McNamara, tumbled back into the cabin, and they all stood around Mrs. Kimball like a herd of inquisitive cattle as she glanced at the card that had come with the flowers. Mr. Weed, speaking to his sister, said, "Maybe Mrs. Kimball is going to keep you company for a while, girl," and he cocked his head whimsically to one side, to Mrs. Kimball's bewilderment until Mrs. McNamara enlightened her: "Roy means— Roy, you shouldn't say such things. I *told* you not to have that extra Jack Rose. Roy means since I'm going to the Virgin Islands to get a divorce, maybe you are, too. He's got the most terrible one-track mind! I suppose maybe he means those roses came from— Oh, I'm just getting in deeper! You'll just have to excuse us Weeds, Mrs. Kimball. I'm afraid we're full of the dickens today."

"No offense meant, I'm sure," said Mr. Weed, "and I surely trust none taken."

Hoping that her shock was not audible in her voice, Mrs. Kimball said as amiably as she could that she was not going to be divorced, and that the roses, in fact, were from her husband. She thought that the brother and sister exchanged a wink, and she thought that Mrs. McNamara's voice was heavy with significance when she observed, "It's not much fun to be away from home at Christmas—unless it isn't any fun at home." Mrs. Kimball was on the point of explaining why she happened to be on board the Carmelita, but she decided against it; sickness was far too personal to reveal to strangers.

Mr. Weed said, "You know what they call it down there? Getting your diploma. That's what we said the kid sister was going to do—she was going to St. Thomas College to get her diploma. That's what they call the divorce decree down there. It used to be a six-week cram course but now it's full term, so the girl's going to get herself a job—as a rum-taster maybe—and work her way through college."

"Roy, you stop! You see what I mean by his one-track mind?" Rosy with pleasure, Mrs. McNamara put a hand over her brother's mouth, and her two nieces wailed with laughter; these girls had hair the color of forsythia. Then, soberly, Mrs. McNamara said, "Maybe you think this is a flip way for us to talk, but we Weeds say that if a person has to do something hateful—why, make a joke of it."

Mrs. Kimball felt very feeble and inexperienced, and she knew that her nods and smiles of agreement were not convincing. It was so extremely difficult to reconcile Mrs. McNamara's optimistic air with divorce, which, she had always thought, must sadden any woman; Mrs. McNamara was as carefree as a schoolgirl on an outing. Rather desperately, out of her depth, Mrs. Kimball made her way out of the cabin, treading on Mr. Weed's galoshes and refusing to join them in a toast of sherry by saying that she must send a telegram. As she left, Mr. Weed waved to her as if he were waving bye-bye to a baby, and she heard him say, "She's nice. Plenty of time for you two to get acquainted. You get her to go to that raw-silk place with you in San Juan. You kind of chaperon each other, hear?"

The telegram that Marianne Kimball referred to was not a ruse; she had promised to wire Mark once she was safely (the word was a little euphemistic, she felt) on board, but when she went back into the passage, she was so oppressed by the heat and the rancor of the crowd, which had not abated at all, that she made her way instead to the deck, for air and solitude. She huddled into her collar and leaned against the rail as the whistles, with a tone of outrage, blasted the visitors back to land. Then the Carmelita was eased from her berth by a tug named Dorothy Talbot, onto whose funnel had been lashed an artificial spruce tree, too small for the American flag that, in lieu of a star or a Santa Claus, palpitated at its top in the cold and furious wind.

Mrs. Kimball, watching Brooklyn's rusty shores shrink swiftly as the boat toiled into a beautiful sunset and the open sea, was visited with woe and then with a moment of panic; trapped now, she wildly wished that she could get back to land and take the first train home to see and hear and feel all those comforts and realities that illness had obscured for her. The blithe interchange between Mrs. McNamara and her brother had set in motion her ugliest train of thought, and it came rushing and crushing down on her, forcing the tears to her eyes. For just before her illness, she and Mark Kimball had been on the very brink of divorce, and while they were now at peace and safe again, she felt that never could she be sure whether it had been pity for her in her weakness and fear or the restitution of his married love that had brought him back to her from a long and serious digression. Nor—and this was even worse—could she be sure that her illness, coming at a time so crucial, had not been unconscious blackmail; it was almost, she often thought, as if her body itself had said to Mark, "See, if you leave me for Martha, I will die!" Marianne Kimball, an honest woman, could not bear these days to hear the word "psychosomatic."

Through the flawed windows of her tears, she saw her house peopled with her family, and she was shaken by a wave of homesickness. With pain, as if she were never to see the house again except as a remembered image in her mind's eye, she thought of it as it would be tonight in last night's snow: its white clapboards would gleam more brightly than the snow that lay on the elegant slope of land on which it stood; at the edge of the back lawn the crescent stand of hemlocks would reach into the cleanly winter sky, and starward, too, would rise the smoke from the western chimney. The smoke would mean that within the house, beside the library fire, her husband and her sons and her relatives-in-law were drinking affectionately to her in her absence and drinking to the season, which, out of habit, they kept with all its shining finery—a tree in the corner of the front parlor and red bunting stockings and a burning plum pudding. . . . She would have given her very eyes at this moment to be listening to Tim, in his changing voice that cracked excruciatingly, tell her of the latest prank that had been perpetrated against the guileless Latin master. How fanciful she was! Sensibly, she reminded herself that she was still poisoned with the countless anodynes that had been mingled with her blood, and that this foreboding she felt came from the strange condition of her chemistry; some part of her mind, she was sure, had been awake in the operating room while the rest of her had been killed violently with ether, and this unforgiving and unforgetting self could sometimes prejudice the rest of her and persuade her that she was a scapegoat and a victim.

In the garden that the hemlocks guarded, there grew, in summer, old-fashioned roses of the subtlest colors she had ever seen—saffron, coral, beige, and other colors so tender there were no names for them. Oh, those roses! And the dark French lilacs, and the white peonies stained with one bruise of pink! In May, every vase in the house was full of flowers and every room smelled sweet. What if something *did* happen to prevent her from seeing her garden again? What if she should die at sea among these angry strangers? Would Mark then, after a seemly interval, marry the woman, Martha, who was, as in her honesty she knew, so beautiful with health, so wise and kind, so irreproachable?

This is absurd, she told herself, it is ghoulish, it is a wrong to Mark. Practically, she remembered the telegram, but she rejected it in favor of another errand she must run; she must find the ship's doctor and hand over to him her vials of liquid vitamins for safekeeping in his refrigerator. Shaking herself, as if the gesture could disperse her unwholesome thoughts to the wind, she set forward briskly, having a momentary but infinitely sweet recollection of what it felt like to be altogether well. She smiled, she almost laughed; for a minute or two she was a rosy picture of delight.

Dr. Cortez, in the heart of this shabby boat, lived opulently in a red-carpeted and rococo suite of rooms, so grand by contrast with the rest of the Carmelita, so much a residence, that Marianne felt as if she were calling on a bishop or a minor king. Antique apothecary jars were arranged on the gilded shelves of a slim *étagère*, which faced, on the opposite wall, a full bookcase. In a Chinese bird cage on the top of the bookcase, two exquisite little lovebirds perched on a golden rod. There were no pictures on the walls, but there were two ornate mirrors, one of which was superlatively (superciliously, really) faithful to reality, the other capriciously made to distort. The beautiful desk had been a beautiful spinet; the sofa and the pretty Empire chairs (reproductions, but good ones) were upholstered in rich plum corduroy. The examining room beyond the bookcase, however, appeared properly functional and austere, except for one trinket—a jade tree under a glass bell, which stood on top of the instrument chest. Through another door she saw the corner of a bed and a pair of trousered legs upon it. She hesitated, not sure how to announce herself, and then she saw a sign on the desk, which, in cursive type, declared, "Please ring for the physician." Beside this legend there was a small, exotic bell, chased with an intricate pattern of ferns and peacocks; when Mrs. Kimball rang it, she found its tone unbelievably sweet, like cool bird song in the forest in the spring. The legs upon the bed exuberantly flung themselves over the side, and a man's high voice called out, "One twinkling! While you wait, regard my library, yes?"

Obediently, she crossed the room—never had a rug been so soft and deep; it was like walking on a healthy old lawn—and began to study the surprising titles of Dr. Cortez's books. They did not deal with allergy or circulation or diseases of the heart. There was one full shelf of science fiction; of the rest, roughly half were texts of physics and of mathematics, while the others dealt, in several languages, with yoga, reincarnation, voodoo, telepathy, alchemy, astrology, and obeah. Before she had time to construct an image of the owner of this unmedical scramble, Dr. Cortez came out of his bedroom. He was a neat and tiny man in a green gabardine suit that matched his birds, and a sassy black-and-white bow tie; he wore his bright smile like a piece of jewelry, and his dark eyes were deeper than the sky at night.

"Delighted!" he cried, and passionately bowed to her. "Hopefully you are not ill?"

A little taken aback by his enthusiasm, Mrs. Kimball laughed nervously and explained that she only wanted him to keep her medicines for her, and she took them out of her purse and gave them to him. He looked at the bottles as if they were either gorgeous or priceless, and he exclaimed, "A Boston pharmacist! You are Mrs. Kimball?"

She stared at him, startled, for she knew her name was not on the labels. "Yes," she said, "but how did you know?"

Dr. Cortez clasped his hands silently together and slowly shook his head, as if the wonder of the news had struck him dumb. And then, in a tone of reverence, he said, "Then you will tell me all about the machine at M.I.T.! We will have a drink together in the bar, dear Mrs. Kimball, and you will tell me each detail. We will drink something exceedingly delicious. Champagne, perhaps."

"But I have never been to M.I.T.," said Mrs. Kimball, "and I know nothing of the machines there."

"The one who thinks! That brilliant brain that astronomically computes! Surely you know?"

His voice was plaintive, pleading with her not to disappoint him, but she was no good at make-believe, and regretfully— because he looked so appealing, he was so well-fashioned on a scale so small—she repeated that she did not know the machine. It was as if she had said she had never heard of a dear and famous friend of his. He sighed, his smile vanished and was replaced by a succession of trembles at the corners of his lips.

"I had hoped! I was expecting you, you see," he said, and his smile came on again like sunshine. "Don't fear, Mrs. Kimball. How I know you is not occult—although clairvoyance *is* a gift of mine. I read the passenger list yesterday. You are the only one from Boston. Cleverly, I put you at my table. I'm sad that you cannot tell me about M.I.T., but, after all, there are other

things in the world to talk about, though most of them are not
so interesting."

He went into the examining room, and she heard him open
and close the refrigerator door, chattering on: "Such forceful
vitamins! Poor thing, she is ill. *Was* ill, and now must be built
up."

Returning, he said, "Shall we go up now to the bar?"

"I don't think . . ." She hesitated, completely mystified.

"You scruple, yes? Thinking perhaps such a public appearance with a total stranger would be premature?" He seemed to
be skipping, although actually he was standing still; he looked
to be not more than ten years old. "Then permit me to serve
you here."

"No, really, thank you so much. I can't—I must—"

The Doctor giggled, really amused, and said, "You can't say
you have a previous engagement, Mrs. Kimball. You cannot
plead a headache, for if you do, you will have to let your doctor
cure it. Pray be calm. Sit down on my soft sofa. The door is
open for all the world to see we are merely holding a conversation and having a little glass for Christmas Eve."

Mrs. Kimball was deeply alarmed, but in her confusion she
could think of no way to extricate herself and she suffered him
to lead her to the sofa. Again he left the room, this time disap-
pearing into the bedroom, and presently he came back carrying
a light, low japanned table, which he set down before her; then
he brought a tray, on which stood glasses and a cocktail shaker
and a bowl of pumpkin seeds.

"But you are expecting someone!" cried Mrs. Kimball, with
relief.

"I am expecting you!" He clicked his shiny black heels and
bowed again. "Don't fear, Mrs. Kimball, that is only my joke.
I always hope for someone at this time of day to walk into my
parlor. It is more suave to drink with a companion than alone,
yes? You agree? So I am always prepared—prepared to go to the
bar or stay here. But I would rather stay here, far from the mad-
ding crowd. The Carmelita does not attract the élite. Though
you, Mrs. Kimball of Boston, are clearly blue-blooded."

His looks, not his flattery, continued to disarm her; besides,
she realized that it would be improvident to offend him, since
later on she might need his care and she did not like to think of

a hypodermic needle in the hands of an enemy, so she sat quietly, in a perfect imitation of composure, and accepted the drink
he poured for her. The taste—or, rather, the many tastes—of it
was entirely foreign to her; had he combined rare jungle flowers
with herbs of Araby and spices of Cathay and some ferment
made according to a witch's recipe? It was delicious and red hot
and the strangest flavor her palate had ever known.

"I am designing a genius machine, too," said Dr. Cortez,
nesting himself snugly in the other corner of the sofa. "For my
own pleasure. More modest than the one at M.I.T.—a ship's
doctor is not a millionaire—but with very winning ways. She
will add, subtract, do square root. She is still a blueprint but
she has a name already. I call her 'La Belle Dame Sans Merci.'
Someday she will compose *concerti grossi*!"

The room seemed darker than when Mrs. Kimball had
entered it, and the racket of the boat was muted and far away;
the flavor of the second swallow of her drink was even more unusual than the first, if that was possible, and she became aware
of a mysterious, not unpleasant, smell commingled with the
odors of Turkish tobacco and lemon rind. The ardent Doctor's
soliloquy was long, and it was uttered through his imperishable
smile, his fox eyes prancing. This hypothetical machine was, he
confessed, an *idée fixe*, so much so, indeed, that Mrs. Cortez
had grown quite mental about it; Mrs. Cortez, he hastened
to explain, was a religious woman and seemed to think—the
Doctor laughed—that La Belle Dame was tantamount to a
graven image. But did not Mrs. Kimball agree that disputes
between the married were inevitable—that if it had not been
the plan for the metal brain, they would have found some other
bone to pick? Was there, please to tell him this, such a thing as
a marriage made in Heaven? He seemed to eye her closely, and
then, perhaps apologetically, he changed the subject.

The siring of the mechanical brain, it seemed, was not the
Doctor's only venture into the out-of-the-way. He was much
interested in the use of supersonic wave lengths as a weapon
to destroy the enemy through the collapse of his sympathetic
nervous system. Effective, too, were recorded sound effects
to "scare poor Mr. Enemy to death." Into a camp in the dead
of night there would come—projected from somewhere miles
away—the sound of a rushing wind and, within the wind, a

voice, like the voice of doom, heralding hell and holocaust; so terrible could be the effect of this disembodied basso profundo on soldiers awakened suddenly that mutiny could follow and surrender follow that. Unfortunately, it was not so easy to right a human being after causing him to go berserk as it was to right a robot; indeed, it might be possible to drive half the world permanently stark staring mad with just such simple tools as a tape recorder and a shortwave radio.

Mrs. Kimball looked into her drink for the eyes of newts and the tongues of asps. She was tempted to ask the Doctor what his real name was.

"You do not comment on my experiments, Mrs. Kimball," he said, with a deprecatory laugh. It was not possible to tell whether he was deprecating her or himself. "Perhaps you are a Catholic? A religious lady, like my wife?"

She shook her head but she could not speak.

He sighed. "If I have bored you, I am sorry. You have your own troubles to think about," he said, and looked deeply, like a hypnotist, into her eyes. "I must assume that a lady travelling by herself at Christmastime, a married lady— But perhaps Mr. Kimball is dead?"

Nothing displeased Marianne Kimball more than the intrusiveness of strangers, for not only was she never able to answer a direct question with anything except the direct truth but she was, as well, driven, out of some perverse compulsion, to elaborate. With horror, she heard herself describing Mark, her sons, her house. At least, though, she had the common sense to conceal from this villainous little man the reason she was going to Antigua.

In conclusion, she said firmly, "My destination is Antigua. It is not the Virgin Islands."

Like Mrs. McNamara and Mr. Weed, the Doctor received this cold information doubtfully and let it drift away, as if it had been a lie too obvious to recognize, and returned to the subject of his own marital condition. Mrs. Cortez was a beauty but she had been reared too strictly; perhaps she should have been a nun—perhaps she still might become one. He said this hopefully, and Mrs. Kimball, too vexed and too embarrassed to listen to another word, set her glass down with finality and rose to go. Her leave-taking was prolonged by his insistence that she stay, but finally he consoled himself when he remembered that he would see her soon again, at his table in the dining room.

"So you slip out of my fingers for only a little nonce," he said. "You like ventriloquy?"

Mrs. Kimball, catching sight of her spread-nosed, pig-eyed, squashed-in face in the distorting mirror, gasped, and she shivered in a sudden icy chill. From behind the mirror—or from outer space—came an exact echo of her own voice, saying, "I am Mrs. Kimball."

The lovebirds twittered, and Dr. Cortez laughed madly at his antic. She heard him halfway down the corridor.

The chill that had come over her when she saw that appalling travesty of her face was not imaginary or emotional; it marked the onset of a new affliction, and by dinnertime she was burning with fever. There was a gnawing ache in her legs, her head hurt dully, and she recognized that she had flu. The knowledge made her weep. Was she faltering into permanent invalidism? Was the rest of her life to be a succession of fleshly ills? If it was, she would have no choice but to let Mark go—drive him away if, out of honor, he protested. As if it were borne on one of Dr. Cortez's versatile winds, Martha's clear-eyed, full-lipped fair face hovered over her, four times the size of life, and when it left, it was replaced by the cartoon of her own face in Dr. Cortez's looking glass.

It was thus, in tears and hot to the touch, that Mrs. McNamara found her roommate when she came back to the cabin to dress for dinner. Mrs. Kimball apologized and hoped Mrs. McNamara would not catch the fever, but Mrs. McNamara assured her that not only was she "as tough as a nanny goat" but she was, it just so happened, a trained nurse. Mrs. Kimball, if Mrs. McNamara did say so herself, was in luck. With this, she set efficiently to work, filling her hot-water bottle, and draping a bath towel over the window, so that the deck lights would not shine through the places where the slats were missing; she produced a thermometer and a bottle of rubbing alcohol from a bottomless carpetbag; she summoned the stewardess and ordered tea. But the blessing was a mixed one. Mrs. McNamara's good will toward man was indefatigably vocal, and all the time she was performing her Samaritan acts, she talked;

her monologue was less distressing than the Doctor's, but it was no less voluble and no less self-sustaining. She had struck up a friendship with a Mr. and Mrs. Bauer, from Schenectady, whom she already called Ed and Grace, and the details of whose daughter's September wedding (al fresco, the bridesmaids all in red, like maple leaves—"Cute!" said Mrs. McNamara) she recited for the sick woman as if they both—as if, in fact, the whole world—were personally involved. She had had a planters' punch with the Bauers and had found the drink all the señorita had implied—dynamite, pure and simple. But grand-tasting! She personally saw no reason why she shouldn't cheer herself up if she felt like it, and if the drinks tasted good (and they did) and made her feel good (top of the world!), what was the harm? Later in the evening, perhaps Mrs. Kimball would like one herself; it would chirk her up no end.

She was just as bland and just as fully documented when she talked about her impending divorce as she had been when she described the wedding of the Bauers' daughter and Arthur—no, Arnold—Sloat. As she set about dressing for dinner, in satin and sequins and enormous earrings that resembled egg whisks, she enumerated a score or so of her troubles with Jack McN., but because of the indulgent, even loving, way she laughed, it was hard to know why she had left him; she seemed to find him adorable. There was, in her analysis of his character, a wealth of direct quotation from friends, enemies, and relatives, who thought either that she had been right to forgive him for the last time or that she should have given the poor so-and-so another chance. Someone named Mildred was on her side heart and soul, but Jane Betz wasn't, but, after all, who was Jane Betz to talk about bustups, having had no less than three herself? It went on and on and on; it included descriptions of clothes and interiors, of salad dressings and stuffings for turkey, of operations and automobile accidents, and of public scandals involving movie stars of whom Mrs. Kimball had never heard. Interspersed throughout her catalogue of sins and hats ("Read's, in Bridgeport, has a lovely price range") were axioms and proverbs and jocularities: "They say the first hundred years are the hardest" and "It never rains but it pours" and (mysteriously) "Easy come, easy go." She also had a limitless repertory of shaggy-dog stories.

At last, mercifully, the bell rang for dinner, and Mrs. Mc-Namara prepared to join the Bauers; Ed was going to treat them to champagne, if you please. There followed several recollections of occasions when flying corks had caused near accidents. Before she left, she offered Mrs. Kimball her choice of a jigsaw puzzle, a deck of cards for solitaire, a comic book of "Nancy," or a book of native Caribbean recipes. "I guess I don't have to tell you I like food!" she said. She must have weighed two hundred pounds.

"Toodle-oo, then," she said, finally. "Are you going to be all right, cutie? I'll pop in off and on and see how you're doing. Sure you don't want me to get the Doc? I don't blame you. Ship's doctors stink. It's my opinion they're all disqualified, or something."

After she was gone, Mrs. Kimball found that she was too listless even to cry. She had been on board the Carmelita for less than three hours; Antigua was ten days away.

Mrs. Kimball's Walpurgisnacht lasted for the four days it took the Carmelita to reach San Juan. The shuffleboard court was always in use in the daytime, and the voices of the players, arguing over points and laughing over blunders, seemed magnified a hundredfold in her hot cubbyhole. Then there were the drunks, singing and giggling in the corridors, and the newlyweds, prowling the decks by night, and there were the stewards, who squabbled shrilly amongst themselves, banged mop buckets together, broke the glasses on the breakfast trays, and operated vacuum cleaners that roared like airplanes about to crash. The food deteriorated rapidly. Mrs. McNamara reported that as they moved southward into warm waters, the crew had undergone a marked change: their uniforms were not entirely clean and badly needed pressing; the radio engineer had stopped shaving and he looked a sight; the headwaiter was frequently drunk and, not to put too fine a point on it, risqué. The cruise director had been caught red-handed cheating at canasta. The captain had acquired a blonde. It would be a miracle, said Mrs. McNamara, with her ineffable jocundity, if these good-time Charlies ever got the boat to port. As if she had an inside track on it, she then reported the sinking of the Titanic; this led her to floods, to fires, to hurricanes; eventually, though, she always got back to Jack McN. and to those French poodles whose name was Legion and who ordered Gibsons in cocktail bars.

Mrs. Kimball thought she might have been able to bear all this, and the bizarre, hallucinatory dreams of fever, and the tempests of her chills; she could have put up with the articulate and dipsomaniac poodles, with Jack McN.'s money meanness with Mrs. McNamara and his liberality with—well, frankly, Jane Betz; she could have endured the Bauers (*their* specialty was moron jokes) and the heat and the disgusting food and the smother of fruit flies that hovered over Mr. Weed's *bon-voyage* basket of grapes—she could have risen above it all if only Dr. Cortez had left her alone.

Her absence from his table on Christmas Eve had brought him around the following morning to inquire, and, thereafter his captive, Mrs. Kimball, was forced to submit to his twice-daily professional calls, his stethoscopic examinations, and his injections of penicillin. Moreover, he often sent her little presents—a bottle of Pernod, a book on cannibalism, a hibiscus made of wax. Sometimes when she lay dozing in the early evening, between the last shuffleboard game and the first murmuring of the sweethearts, he came and whispered through her window. "Don't fear, Mrs. Kimball," he would say. "It is only the solicitous Doctor, come to wish you happy dreams."

She was sure that his interest in her was accidental and that he would have attached himself to anyone, man or woman or child or cat, who had strayed into his office on that first afternoon; she suspected that on every voyage he singled out one passenger to receive his odd attentions. There was nothing in the least untoward in the way he examined her; he was very quick and deft with his needle, and she thought he was probably a good doctor. But this only added to her uneasiness, because, if he was, what was he doing on this squalid boat? Mrs. McNamara, uncritical of nearly everyone in the world except Jane Betz, Jack McN., and a member of the boat's steel band who had said something uppity to Mrs. Bauer, could not bear the sight of Dr. Cortez; she stated flatly that he was an abortionist and no two ways about it, and whenever he came to the cabin, she immediately flounced out, her ebullience masked with keen dislike—a dislike reciprocated by Dr. Cortez, who said it was an impudence for any woman to carry on herself an *embonpoint* so flagrant.

Dr. Cortez, sitting on Mrs. McNamara's bed when he had finished with his doctoring, talked unflaggingly of everything on earth that was unearthly. He talked of his machine as if, when it was finally built, it would be his darling daughter; he talked of zombies, rockets to the moon (he wanted to go), ghosts, instances of dreams that had coincided exactly with subsequent events; he was an expert hypnotist, he could cause chairs to levitate, he possessed telepathic powers. And how he liked to talk about those voices in the wind! Once, when the real wind was buffeting the Carmelita, making her timbers groan, he demonstrated the effect for her. "Surrender, Madame Enemy!" His altered voice seemed to originate in a far, weird distance, on a nameless desert island in the middle of the Atlantic. "Give in, or my Belle Dame will carry your husband and all your loves away." Afterward, he said, "You'd do as the voice said, yes?"

She knew he knew he terrified her with his sly, contemptuous talk and pranks, and fretfully she sought his motive, but each time she pondered what it might be, she could come only to the conclusion that he was insane and that it would therefore be futile, and possibly dangerous, to implore him to leave off. Much as she was tempted to, she did not speak to Mrs. McNamara of the Doctor's avocation of riding broomsticks—Mrs. McNamara was so busy and she was so gay. Once or twice, Mrs. Kimball thought of asking to see the captain and tactfully getting from him a dossier on Dr. Cortez, but, according to Mrs. McNamara, who didn't miss a trick, the captain's entanglement with the blonde had become the talk of the boat, and obviously he was far too engrossed to bother his head with complaints about his crew. Having at last accepted the Doctor's radical originality of mind as a disease—for the time being she diagnosed it as advanced and galloping paranoia—she tried to be objective about it, and when he was not actually in her cabin, and especially by day, she was able to bury her horror by playing game after game of Canfield as if her very life depended on beating Sol. She even found herself, as she shuffled to deal again, making of the Doctor an interesting story to entertain the Montagues. But while he was there, practicing his ventriloquy, making her hair stand on end, and when by night she dreamed of him, she believed that he was her murderer, sent by the Devil himself to destroy her when she was far from home. Sometimes, waking in a drenching sweat, she thought she heard that ghastly voice in the wind threatening the very principles of her life; pompously it taunted her and told her that the die was cast already, that even now Mark had returned to Martha, and that she, Marianne Kimball, was presently to perish, be killed in some unimaginably horrible way. Her grave would be this garish emerald sea, and she would be shredded by sharks and scrutinized by octopuses; her skeleton would be a reef for electric eels.

Both Mrs. McNamara and Dr. Cortez, the one jestingly and the other hopefully, believed that Mrs. Kimball was hiding a shattered heart. They could not in any other way account for her being away from home at Christmastime; their questions were loaded with insinuation, and because her answers were evasive (she had developed this talent and was proud of it), the questions were incessant. It might have saved her some vexation if she had told them the whole truth—that she had been ill and was going south simply for the sun—but she knew that they would both be far too fascinated, the Doctor from a professional point of view and the nurse from a social one, and she shrank from the thought of their cross-examinations. She did admit to anemia, but she could tell by their patient smiles that they construed this as the greensickness of the lovelorn. She began to believe that something endlessly repeated would eventually become true, and so she said to herself, over and over, "Mark loves me and what was wrong is now forever right." To the Doctor and to Mrs. McNamara she said, telling her lie with dignity and self-esteem, "My husband is flying down to join me." If only he were! She hungered for the sight of him, she thirsted for the consolation of his voice.

The Carmelita was to lie at the dock in the harbor of San Juan for three days to unload her cargo before proceeding to the southern islands, and Mrs. Kimball learned with relief that Mrs. McNamara was leaving the boat there to make the rest of her journey by plane. On the last night out, as she watched that elephantine soul pack up her big bathing suits and her evening dresses—she had at least seven, and every one of them had either fringe or sequins—and her toys, Mrs. Kimball kept herself from screaming by repeating, "She will be gone in twelve more hours." The subject of that night's discourse, delivered with hoots of laughter, was Roy Weed's practical jokes; he was a great one for fooling people on the telephone.

When Mrs. Kimball woke the following morning, Mrs. Mc-Namara was gone, and the cabin, without her, looked as stern as a convent cell. A lovely peace invaded the room, and Mrs. Kimball discovered that she was much stronger; for the first time in months, she was really hungry. In the early afternoon, she was able to get up and go on deck to sit in the blessed, blazing sun. The unloading, which had begun at dawn, was being conducted with a hue and cry, with raucous bangs and crashes and rasps and savage altercations amongst the stevedores; the city beyond was a pandemonium of horns and sirens and hysterically barking dogs; gulls screamed with greed; even the picture-postcard landscape shouted. Consequently, she did not hear Dr. Cortez come up behind her deck chair, and she thought that the hullabaloo all around her must surely have distorted his words; what she heard him say was "The anopheles has found my Mrs. Kimball sweet. Misfortune dogs my poor Mrs. Kimball."

She looked up at him, blinking against the immoderate tropical sky, and her own voice sounded thin and querulous as she cried above the din, "What? What on earth are you talking about?"

He bent toward her—for a moment she thought he was going to bite her—and he said, "I said that the anopheles has found you sweet. Foolish lady! In San Juan, you must wear an armor of citronella. But never mind, I'm here. Forever at your service."

Oh, that smile! Rosy lips parted slightly to show his snowy, feral teeth; it was an arrangement of the face rather than an expression of the heart.

"But I haven't been bitten!" cried Mrs. Kimball.

Dr. Cortez said nothing, but with his forefinger he pointed to a spot, minute and white, on her wrist and to another, just below the rings on her left hand. The second he actually touched, and she recoiled.

"How do you know what these are?" she demanded, petrified.

"I know so much," he said dreamily. He shut his eyes and turned his face upward to the sun. "Malaria is not so bad, but you are frail—never mind, never mind. The boat is deserted, Mrs. Kimball. Everyone has gone ashore to buy, to drink, to rubberneck. Tourists bore me so, Mrs. Kimball!"

She got up so quickly that she was dizzied, and she staggered a little, black spots before her eyes. "So shall I go ashore," she said. Anything, she thought, to escape this sleek, too well-dressed vampire. She would hire a cab and go sightseeing, like the tourists that bored him, or she would sit in a church and pray to God.

"Goodbye till evening, then," said Dr. Cortez, still letting the sun pour down upon his face, not looking at her. "Take care."

She was so relieved that he made no move to accompany her that she even considered saying something polite to him, but she decided against it and made her way quickly to the gangplank and the quay. The sun, which a little while before had been healing and benign, now smote her brutally, and she felt faint, and a surge of nausea caused her to slow her walk. When she was halfway down the stark, unshaded dock, she heard Dr. Cortez call out to her from the boat, "But you wear no hat, Mrs. Kimball! Beware of sunstroke." She looked back; he was as she had left him, sitting in the deck chair next to hers, his face upturned. When she was out of sight of him, she looked at her hands and found that the white spots had vanished. She almost laughed to see that this particular trick of his had not worked.

Mrs. Kimball had neither the instincts nor the knowledge of a traveller, and once she was on the street that paralleled the waterfront, she was overcome with shyness. She saw nothing that looked like a cab and she saw, certainly, no haven among the shops and saloons across the way, from whose Stygian interiors came cries of laughter and growls of rage and the "St. Louis Blues," which, moving south, had, like the crew of the Carmelita, undergone a change. She had never heard anything so lascivious and at the same time she had never heard lasciviousness so stupid; it was delinquent and ever so juvenile.

She walked slowly and self-consciously beside the piers and came shortly to a sort of park; it was not a park at all, really, but only a little grove of dusty trees on a plot of debris-littered dirt.

In the islands of shade, there were gimcrack stands for the sale of something sticky and pink to drink and of ice-cream cones; the smell of vanilla was so powerful that her mouth tasted as if she had drunk a whole bottle of extract straight. A sign, stuck casually in one of the trees, informed her that every fifteen minutes a ferry left from here for Cataño, and, having nothing better to do and thinking that perhaps there might be a breeze on the water, she joined the crowd waiting for the boat that was approaching on the return trip across the milky, moldy water, cutting its way through fishing boats, through gulls and pelicans. Mrs. Kimball had a moment's misgiving once she was on board, for the ferry had a tippy, untrustworthy feeling, but there was no turning back, and she settled down, surveying her fellow-passengers who flanked or faced her. They were girls dressed in the shimmering green of parakeets or grass snakes, in numbing purple, in scarlet that made the eyes look down; they were men in pastel zoot suits and oxblood shoes, or in incredible rags; they were babies—dozens of babies—their mouths stoppered up with pacifiers, in the arms of mothers so young it was hard not to think they were playing hooky from the seventh grade. Besides these colorful commuters, there was Dr. Cortez.

Although he was sitting directly opposite her and his deadly smile was as fixed as ever, she had failed to see him at first; when she did, a groan involuntarily escaped her. It was, however, a groan principally of boredom, for she was not afraid of him here, surrounded, as she was, by all these people, protected by the brilliant public light of day and by the fact that she was fully dressed and out of bed. It occurred to her that she might ride back and forth on the ferry for the rest of the afternoon, and if he chose to do the same, she would simply snub him. She gazed calmly over the top of his straw-hatted head and watched the slum-bound suburb come to greet the ferry. He made no move to speak to her. He only smiled.

All of that hot, peculiar afternoon, till nearly five o'clock, Mrs. Kimball rode back and forth across this stretch of filthy water, her nose assailed by awful smells, her eardrums vibrating with the racket, her eyes bedazzled by rayon satin and bright-black hair dressed up with frangipani blossoms. She was mesmerized by Dr. Cortez's smile. For he did not leave the boat; he did not speak to her; he did not change his place. She did not enjoy her pastime; she had, in fact, wearied of it after the first round trip, and she longed for her dark cabin and her narrow bed. But she thought of the empty boat and of the Doctor lurking in the passage outside the room where she would lie so terribly alone, she thought of his low voice through the jalousies . . . No, she preferred this.

Of course she wondered why he did not speak to her; she was glad but she was extremely puzzled that he did not come to sit beside her when, between trips, the boat was emptied and there were vacant seats on either side of her. Their dumb show was ridiculous, but she let it play on.

There was an especially crowded trip from Cataño to the mainland a little before five; people were standing up, lurching and jostling, and Mrs. Kimball lost sight of Dr. Cortez altogether. When they reached the pier, she mingled with the throng and made her way with it back to the park. Glancing over her shoulder, she thought she saw the Doctor, still in his accustomed place on the bench of the ferry, and, delighted that she had given him the slip, she returned to the Carmelita, almost running.

The dock was abandoned; the workmen had finished for the day and the hatches of the Carmelita's hold were closed. The boat was so still it could have been a ghost of a boat—the Flying Dutchman, a frigate manned by spectres. The bartender, having no customers, was asleep, his head on the bar among glasses of swizzle sticks and colored straws; the deck chairs were unoccupied, the main saloon was empty, the wickets in the purser's office were drawn down.

As Mrs. Kimball turned in to her own passage, she saw a figure at the end of it advancing at a measured, ecclesiastical gait; it appeared, to further the churchly impression, to be clad in a flowing robe. She stopped and waited, frightened to death.

Dr. Cortez, in a black shantung wrapper that came down to his straw scuffs, covered his yawning mouth with a delicate hand when he stood before her, and then he adjusted the elegant white ascot at his neck.

He clucked his tongue and said, "Have you been out all this time, dear Mrs. Kimball?"

She did not believe her eyes or ears.

"You were there!" she cried, horrified, unable to move past him. "You were on the ferry all afternoon. *Weren't you?*"

"Ferry? Oh dear, oh *dear* Mrs. Kimball, I have been asleep all afternoon in my trundle bed! So tired. In the middle of last night I had to treat a man who had d.t.s. I have been fast asleep. Now I am going to the swimming pool to wake up."

"You're lying!" She wanted to tear out his eyes; she wanted, indeed, to kill him and obliterate that smile forever.

"Poor Mrs. Kimball," he said soothingly. "You have had a touch of sun intoxication, I believe, just as I feared."

Enraged, she fumbled in her purse for her key and brushed past him to the door of her stateroom. A cablegram lay on the sill. Something has happened to Mark! Mark and Martha have run away together to the ends of the earth! My sons are dead! The Christmas tree has caught fire and the house has burned to the ground, and the flames have eaten Mark and Tim and John alive!

Babbling, she stooped down to pick up the envelope while Dr. Cortez, arms folded on his breast, watched her, interested.

It was a long message from Mark; he was worried because she had not sent him a telegram from the Brooklyn pier as she had promised (how could she have forgotten?), and he missed her so sorely that he had decided to fly down to the Montagues and stay there for a week! She realized as she smiled that she had not truly smiled for weeks on end, and she turned, with this grace upon her lips and in her eyes (she could feel it like a kiss, like sunshine, like love), to show the Doctor her transformation. His own smile was extinguished; he made a gesture of defeat and, with a sort of limp, he edged away.

"What did you want of me, Dr. Cortez?" she asked him calmly, mistress of herself once more, her suffering interred now in a past that moved steadily toward oblivion.

He smiled but his smile was sorrowful, and he said, "I follow the pipes of Pan."

At first, she thought that he had said "the pipes of Panic," and then she knew that he had not. He was retreating modestly; his wrapper, she saw, was old and bedraggled and its hem was coming out, and his dandified ascot was sleazy. She felt a clutch of pity and, beginning to doubt herself, she said remorsefully, "I am sorry, Dr. Cortez. I had been ill before I came on board—I was full of drugs."

"Yes, Mrs. Kimball, yes. You do not tell me news." His sleepy voice trailed off and he was gone.

She locked herself into her cabin and looked in the mirror over the chest of drawers. Her flesh was still haggard and her skin was still ashen, but her eyes had lost their hectic glint and her mouth its dolorous look; she was almost recognizable and she was, moreover, almost merry. Mrs. McNamara, kind creature, had left behind her bottle of Scotch, since, because of the Bauers' largess ("That Ed's the limit, absolutely won't hear of me going Dutch"), she had had no need of it. Mrs. Kimball opened it up and poured herself a drink to toast her release from gloomy caverns and her return to the blue-skied world, and to toast the donor of the whiskey and wish her many happy evenings in her spangled dresses. The whiskey dizzied her rapidly, and for a moment she thought she was being sucked back into the maelstrom, but she gentled her nerves by reading the glad tidings of the cable again, and, exhausted suddenly, but in a natural and healthy way, she lay down and closed her eyes in halcyon tranquillity, enjoying everything—even the stridulous cries of the gulls, even the windless heat. When her thoughts strayed to Dr. Cortez, she was partly ashamed and partly puzzled, and she wondered if she would ever be able to separate the facts from her fancies. Had the drink he had given her been, after all, so unusual? Was there perhaps some good reason for his having the falsifying mirror on his wall? It could have had a valuable frame that she had not noticed. She did not, in her reflections, find him nice, for he *was* a tease and a cynic and brimful of guile, and while he had doubtless cured her flu, he had made himself a pest. But he was scarcely a fiend or a lunatic; he was a henpecked little man (she imagined, though she had no reason to, that Mrs. Cortez towered above him) who was glad to escape his cross and pious wife on this seedy boat. If Mrs. Kimball continued to deplore his pastimes, she could no longer take them personally. She nonetheless thanked God she was well and needed his services no further.

Just then she heard the irascible whine of a mosquito, and she leaped up. She thoroughly covered every inch of her exposed skin with oil of citronella, and when she had finished with that, she drank some more of Mrs. McNamara's whiskey. "I will not get malaria," she said, half aloud, and crossed her fingers. And then, with an absolutely steady hand, she wrote at length to Mark, telling him she had never felt so well in all her life and couldn't wait to meet him in Antigua.

My Blithe, Sad Bird

MIRANDA Grierson was looking up the telephone number of a hairdresser who had been recommended to her when a name leaped forth from the dense print of the directory, causing her eyes to widen and a flush of astonishment to visit her cheeks. Aloud, she said, "Ian Ferguson! Can it be possible that that innocent from Texas still lives here?" In her surprise, she forgot how badly she needed a shampoo and a manicure before she proceeded on her way to Paris the next day, and she began to muse in the Indian-summer-morning sunshine that came, together with the songs of boys and birds, through the broad windows of her Heidelberg hotel room. And as she mused, now and again she looked back at that Caledonian name, so tense and sudden there among the Teutonic ones; even the print of it, it seemed to her, looked slightly different, slightly lighter. She was sure that the name could belong to no one but the man she had known; the arm of chance could never reach out far enough and cleverly enough to discover and set down in this particular, out-of-the-way place a second Ian Ferguson.

While she had known of Ian's being in other places, it was with Heidelberg that she associated him, since it was here that they had at one time happened to live in the same house—a square yellow house, with a garden and a pear tree, beside the brown-green Neckar River. Almost twenty years ago this spring, at the opening of the summer term, Miranda, bookish, twenty-one years old, had come from Pennsylvania to learn the German language and to study philosophy on a fellowship at Heidelberg. She had taken a small but pleasing room (the branches of the pear tree brushed her window, and leaf shadows lay on the plump feather bed) in the house of a straitened and widowed Baroness in middle age who offered bed and breakfast to five university students.

The Baroness, whose bright-blue eyes were frantic and whose thin hands trembled in perpetual anxiety, maintained, despite her poverty and humiliation, the manner and tone of a distinguished hostess at a subdued but nonetheless chic houseparty. The morning trays were laid with linen cloths (a little discolored and a little frayed) and Bavarian china (some of it chipped and some of it crazed), although the fare was only rolls and ersatz coffee that tasted, inexplicably, of margarine. And quite often, in the evening, the Baroness invited those of her lodgers who were at home into her shabby, ill-lit drawing room, which served, as well, as her bedroom (the bed, a noble four-poster, stood in an alcove curtained with aged blue velours that was embroidered at the front with her husband's armorial bearings), and there, giving them tisane, which she brewed on a spirit lamp, she showed them sad, fussy mementos of her courtly life when the Baron was still alive and they had waltzed, shot birds and boars, boated on the North Sea, and travelled in Italy with an entourage. The room smelled of obsolete mignonette sachet and it smelled of sorrow—a proper setting for the Baroness, who, to Miranda, was the very crystallization of pathos. Poor woman, her clothes were left over from another time in history; she wore a seedy ermine tippet when she went shopping in the Kornmarkt, and she gardened in a Paisley basque. Her costume in the evening was usually a rusty dark-green satin redingote over a faded violet underdress of peau de soie; the toes of her French-heeled slippers were cruelly pointed; her stockings, khaki-colored, were lisle. The diamonds (of which she spoke, lamenting) were gone from her fingers, and she had neither tiaras nor gem-studded combs for her grayed yellow hair, but she wore a pair of ruby earrings in her pierced ears, and frequently she fingered them, as if to make sure that bad luck had not robbed her of them, too.

Alas, her little soirées were not very well or very enthusiastically attended, and in the same voice she used when she described balls of long ago she spoke to Miranda of how, in earlier years, her guests had called upon her nightly and they had had *such* galas, singing goliardic songs (the naughtiness of the words made only the most erudite Latinists blush), playing charades, telling fortunes, consulting a ouija board, reading Goethe's love songs. She found, she said with a sigh, that the youth of today was too earnest; along with grandeur, gaiety had gone from the world. Herr Winkler, the solemn, top-heavy Brown Shirt who lived on the third floor, rarely accepted her invitations, because when he did not have his vast nose in a lawbook, he was in the town, at the Stadthalle, involved in Party business. Herr Griffiths, the English boy of seventeen, whose room was next to the Nazi's, spent most of his evenings at the kino learning German from the dubbed-in voices of Laurel and Hardy. (The Baroness did not find this droll but, rather, vulgar.) And Fräulein Waldock, who occupied the room next to Miranda's, on the second floor, a girl of Dutch and English descent, from Rhodesia, was assiduously applying herself to the study of biochemistry and had no time for infusions of jasmine and tales from the Vienna woods.

Two or three evenings a week, Miranda, out of politeness and pity, visited the drawing room and listened to the lady's soliloquy, delivered in fluent, faulty English. As she talked, she sewed or embroidered, making pretty dresses for a favorite niece of five, who lived in Stuttgart. And as she sewed and talked, the terror in her eyes gave way to hope and peace; it was as if by remembering the dead days so well she had truly resuscitated them and was living through them again. She clearly heard—and made Miranda hear—the playing of fountains long since gone dry, the neighing of hunters and the baying of hounds long since dead; she plainly saw the *repoussé* ceiling and the superb chandelier of the ballroom where the Baron, as they were dancing, had asked her to marry him; saw the frocks and the furs and the hats and the gloves and the jewels of her friends; tasted marvellous food, drank marvellous wine; laughed at the wit and lived by the wisdom of diplomats, poets, sportsmen, and kings.

Though the Baroness was disappointed in Herren Griffiths and Winkler and Fräulein Waldock, and though Miranda was really not her style, she had cause for rejoicing in the fifth of her lodgers, Ian Ferguson, who came into the drawing room on Thursday evenings and kissed her hand and flattered her, addressing her as "Right Honorable Milady." He came on Thursday, that is, unless he was away on some voluptuous mission—in Paris, going to the theatre, or in London, adding to his sumptuous wardrobe. When he did come, the refreshments were not tisane and pfeffernuesse but aquavit and caviar, which he brought, having, the Baroness declared, paid the earth for them.

Ian Ferguson, much older than the other guests in the house, was a storybook American—a rich and golden man out of the west of Texas. He was long-legged and rangy, red-haired and brown-eyed, and his nice, bony face wore always an expression of boundless amiability. He drove a red Mercedes; his Egyptian cigarettes were monogrammed; he hired halls in Heidelberg in which he entertained at midnight dancing and supper parties; he hunted grouse in Yorkshire and roe deer in Bavaria; he bet on the horses at Ostend, gambled regularly at the Kurhaus in Baden-Baden, and sat in a box at La Scala. The raison d'être of Heidelberg for him was not the august university of Ruprecht-Karl but the city's tradition of romance, of duelling and dancing, of fraternal song in the rowdy *Studentenlokale*, which he frequented when he was in town, staying until closing time at the Roter Ochse, where he played host to everyone and treated the barmaids like queens in disguise. He could not speak a word of German beyond "*Guten Tag*," "*Auf Wiedersehen*," and "*Noch einmal*"; he was politically an abysmal ignoramus: although he had studied four years at Harvard, one would never have known it except for his jocular enmity to Yale and an occasional reference to a debut at the Boston Ritz; he had knocked about South America and the Orient and had travelled widely in Europe, but though he had seen everything, he had regarded little. For example, he had Luxor quite badly confused with Baghdad, since in both places he had been insensibly drunk. But no one cared about these shortcomings of his. His German friends spoke English with him; the Nazis he knew tried to indoctrinate him and so did the anti-Nazi Americans; and all of them drank his Scotch and ate his food. If they thought him a fool, they never showed it.

This agreeable, smiling *bon vivant* lived across the passage from Miranda in a suite that consisted of a bedchamber, dressing room, sitting room, and bath, and there was, besides, a balcony, which commanded a handsome view of the river and of the ruined castle on the opposite hill; here, on bright days, Ian lay in a long chair sunning his lithe, Western legs. In his travels, he had gathered beautiful and curious things, and they were on display in his apartment—paintings, rare books, porcelains, guns, old maps. He had a shortwave radio; on it you could hear Tokyo as clearly as you could hear Berlin. He had a priceless cellar of Mosels and French wines, and priceless glasses to drink them from. Now and again, he gave a small dinner party in his sitting room; the food, ordered from Strasbourg, was prepared by the chef at the Hotel zum Ritter and served by a waiter in tails. Till dawn, on those occasions, much to the vexation of the studious Herr Winkler and Fräulein Waldock, the giggling of girls and drunken choruses of "Gaudeamus Igitur" rang through the house and troubled the air of the quiet valley.

The Baroness was Ian's confidante—a role she dearly loved to play—and it was from her, rather than from him, that Miranda, picking the facts out of the panegyrics, learned his history; it was a pastiche of many American histories. He had not risen from rags to riches, but his father, an illiterate emigrant from Arran, had, and the riches Ian had inherited were so blindingly brand-new that it had taken time and pains to patinate them with good manners and good taste. Now, said the Baroness with the air of an expert, his aura was patrician and he would be accepted and sought after by high society throughout the world. He had been intended to carry on a family tradition of ranching, but he had no bent for stockbreeding or agronomy, and he hated the heat and the arid treelessness of Texas. He had not known what he wanted to do or be, and in his years at Harvard he had sampled one variety of learning after another and had left without taking a degree. And so, not having found himself at one with anything, he had gone back to Texas and, in partnership with his two brothers, had dutifully and unenthusiastically set about raising white-faced cattle. He built a house and married a wife as rich and as restless as himself; their restlessness went hand in hand with apathy, and because they had no reason to go elsewhere, they could not extricate themselves from their parochial existence in those dry lands. This beautiful wife, though she was nearly a decade older than Ian, had not learned calm, and their passion for each other continued to be a thrilling infatuation and did not mature into a nourishing love. She was fragile, and their imprudent, desperately euphoric life with the fast young set of Amarillo put her at last into a tuberculosis sanitarium, where, after a year, she died. Ian, stricken and lost and guilt-ridden, sure he had murdered her with too many parties, which had sometimes lasted through the green Texas dawn into the blazing flood of noon, left Texas immediately after the funeral, selling his land

and his share of the herd to his steady brothers, and selling the house where those phrenetic revelries had taken place. Ian was close to no one in his family except his mother, and he regretted leaving no one but her. She was English, and all the time she had lived in America, she had been homesick for the demure gardens of Surrey. Urged by her loving descriptions of them, Ian, as a child, had imagined the gentle roses and the feathery larches and the sweet songbirds of Abinger, though what he had looked at was yucca and mesquite and what he had heard was the stridulous nagging of magpies.

"Poor lady," said the Baroness, sighing and looking fondly at a vase of roses from her own garden. "Now she has neither summer flowers nor her favorite son. But she told him to go. What she said was poetic—'Go mend your broken heart in a soft land.'"

When Miranda came to live in the Baroness's house, Ian had been there since the previous autumn, and during that time, the landlady breathlessly reported, he had been in London and Paris and Rome and Cairo, spending money, losing money, winning friends. "He goes away from romantic Heidelberg in his *sehr rot* motorcar," said the Baroness, captivated, "but he comes back to my humble villa by the river. What an honor! Thank God!" Her eyes sparkled, bedewed. It did not occur to her, as it did to Miranda, to wonder why, out of all the places in the world, he had picked this town, whose palaces of pleasure were few and for the most part dismal, and whose society was either academic or mercantile; the handful of aristocrats in Heidelberg were, like the Baroness, impoverished, and sustained only by their souvenirs. Miranda thought that he had not lost his heart in Heidelberg but perhaps had found that it beat more calmly there.

Usually when the Baroness spoke of money, there was grief in her voice for the loss of her own, but when she spoke of Ian's it was as if she were commending a shining talent or a sterling virtue. To be sure, because the revenue she got from his rooms was probably what kept her going, because he overtipped her underpaid servants, because he gave her presents of hothouse grapes and hothouse flowers, she was grateful. But besides gratitude there was awe in her voice and awe in her eyes whenever she contemplated the mountain of Texas silver and gold that stood, like a wonder of the world, behind his blessed, beloved checkbook. This woman, with her bourgeois code, would have been shocked if it had been proposed to her that she liked— indeed, all but adored—Ian for his money; she would have protested that character and personality were what counted, and she would have extolled his gallantry, his dash without brag, his *amour-propre* without egotism, his generosity, his way of sowing good will. But the fact was that if she had been pinned down, she might possibly have conceded that the reason she valued her other lodgers less was that they were obliged to make do and do without and eat atrocious sixty-pfennig meals at the Mensa and study hard to prepare themselves to earn a living, and all this hardship and privation removed them to a realm of unworldliness that the once-worldly Baroness confounded with barbarism. Though they were blameless, indigence had placed them beyond the pale, and they depressed and embarrassed her; they would remain forever strangers. In Ian's presence, on the other hand, her animation and her optimism testified to her belief that as long as there were people like him left, there was the possibility that the old, elegant order might one day be restored to the world. And thus, superstitiously, she kept her eye on him, and did not let it stray to the curt and hidebound Nazi, or the grubby English boy, with his gluttony for cheap films, or the serious South African girl, with her mind full of enzymes and yeast.

There existed between Ian and the Baroness such concord that they might have been friends for years. On those jubilee evenings when the well-dressed, well-made millionaire came into the drawing room with his expensive treat, he and his landlady made cryptic references to episodes on drives they had taken on fair spring days, and excused themselves to Miranda for their private laughter but said they couldn't explain; out of context the incident would have no meaning. They would discuss the latest letter from Stuttgart, with its news of Friede the niece, whom Ian knew from a visit she had paid her aunt at Easter. Much at home in the cluttered room, Ian, wandering about, would pinch away a dead leaf from the Jerusalem cherry, straighten a picture (the etching of the gardens at Trier was forever askew), look at a book (though he could not read a word of it), bend down to admire the blue daisies with which the Baroness was deftly bestrewing the skirt of a dress for Friede. Sometimes he wound up the music box; the music box was a gilded cage with a tarnished bird on a perch, which turned its head from left to right as a minuet tinkled and trilled and slowly trailed off. While it played, the Baroness dropped her work, and her head moved with the bird's, and she hummed, eyes closed, remembering—seeing—some immortal loveliness. When it was over, she would clap her hands and cry "Ah, my sweet-bitter linnet! My blithe, sad bird!" and finish off her aquavit and hold out her glass for more. The aquavit and the caviar were mnemonics as urgent as the mechanical bird, and, by now quite tipsy, she would excitedly go off into recollections of visits to cousins in Copenhagen when she was a girl. Ian loved her stories and pressed her for details; he treated her rather like an older sister who brought to him in the nursery news of the world. And, indeed, at these times his naïve and sweet sincerity stripped him of many of his years and he was a touching, beardless boy, as dreamy as he might have been in Texas, stirred by his mother's poignant memories of the gentle English countryside.

Although he shied with a shudder away from any talk of his life before he had left America, Miranda, from bits and pieces he inadvertently let fall, was able to determine that he had been miserable as a child, fearing his dour, money-making father, uneasy with his conventional brothers and his smug sisters, and allied only with his mother, sighing away her days amid the alien corn. Above all, Ian had hated the West, and if in this mild and vacant man there was a passion, it was a passion for the dense, luxuriant landscape of Germany, so sharp a contrast to the sahara where he had been reared. Often, on Sunday, he and the Baroness, in the national tradition, took a long ramble through the hills, and at dusk Miranda would see them coming home with their arms full of ground pine and autumn leaves; sometimes the Baroness carried a basket of mushrooms or nuts that she had gathered in the woods. At these times, in *Lederhosen* and a Tyrolian hat, his face colored by wind and sun and exercise, Ian looked like a part of the bucolic German scene—a far cry from his sleek other self that frequented noisy bars and the tables of *chemin de fer*—and the Baroness, exhilarated by her outing, laughing with happiness, looked many years younger as she waited with feminine dependence for Ian to open her garden gate. Miranda, gazing down on them through the branches of the pear tree, was moved by the man's tender solicitude for the woman bereft of all her privilege.

Except for Thursdays, Miranda seldom had more than a glimpse of Ian. Once in a while, he invited her into his rooms for a drink, but conversation between them was stiff; *her* memories were all American and they were for the most part schoolish, so, without the Baroness to act as catalyst, she felt far more the bluestocking than in fact she was, and, to her horror, she heard herself being pompous or found herself tongue-tied. In their uncomfortable silences, she looked about at his treasures, hunting a source of occupation for him during the day, when all his young friends were at lectures or in laboratories, but she could find none; his rare books were too rare to read. What could Heidelberg's lodestone possibly be for this lazy, hedonistic Texan? A mistress, perhaps? When she asked the Baroness if this was possible, the lady paled, offended, and took a moral tone and said, "A cosmopolitan gentleman of leisure has better things to do than visit the houses of Semmelstrasse." And when Miranda explained that she had not been thinking in such terms at all, had simply wondered if Ian was involved in a genuine affair of the heart, the Baroness prissily pursed her lips and said no more and arranged two sprays of edelweiss in a glass tear jar.

About a month after the fall semester began, there came a day so beautiful that by afternoon Miranda could no longer bear to be indoors; unable to support the thought of Herr Professor Zintgraff's exegesis of Kant's categories of judgments, she cut her last lecture and went for a long, aimless walk in the sun on the Philosophenweg, which wound up the Mönchberg, behind the Baroness's house. High on the hill, she found a fine harvest of chestnuts, and she gathered the nuts in her baize book bag for the Baroness, who would combine them with parsley and onion to make a soup for her lonely dinner. As she descended the opulently arboreal path, passing through sudden misty glades, enjoying the smell of dying, drying leaves, she wondered what the Baroness and Ian talked about when they made their Sunday excursions through romantic ways like these. What a truly curious friendship! When he went away for a weekend of gambling, the Baroness was quiet—almost woebegone—but when he was in residence, she was *spirituelle* and affably loquacious, detaining even the silent Herr Winkler in the foyer to tell him some quaint bit of nonsense perpetrated by the *Dienstmädchen*. Miranda dreaded for her the day when her nomadic millionaire would go off for good in his *sehr rot* motorcar.

That afternoon, when she came up the steps of the yellow brick house, she found the Baroness and Ian sitting on the terrace that overlooked the river. The Baroness, as usual, was at work with her needle and her rainbow of silk threads, and Ian, sprawled in a long chair, was drinking beer from a stein. Because the day was still warm, because a few late roses still bloomed on the garden wall, because exuberant young men and their girls were canoeing on the river, the whole scene wore an air of easy, summery holiday, and Miranda, seduced by the lackadaisical atmosphere, felt as if she were coming to a particularly pleasant party as she joined the smiling man and woman taking their ease in the sun. She gave the chestnuts to the Baroness, who was delighted, and she accepted a stein of Ian's cool, delicious beer, and then the two resumed the conversation that her arrival had interrupted.

There had come that day to Heidelberg an American girl from North Carolina and her brother, whom Ian had met in Berlin in August, at the Olympics, and he and the Baroness were discussing how he should entertain them that evening.

"I might take them up to the castle for a drink before dinner," he said. "Do you think the Tarheels would like the string quartet at the Casino?"

The Baroness cried out in pain. "That ensemble is frightful! It scratches and squeaks like guinea pigs, and the tables there are all grit on top. It is only a place for Hollander tourists."

Ian laughed. "Right Honorable Milady's a snob," he said, and the Baroness, who secretly loved to be called a snob, since she did not understand the word and thought it a compliment, turned pink with pleasure.

They talked of other possibilities. He could drive his friends up to the Molkenkur—but the food there was banal. Perhaps a pub crawl through the *Studentenlokale*? The Baroness thought not; the evening would probably be warm, and those rooms would be uncomfortable, with too many people and too much smoke and noise. Mannheim—but what was there to do in Mannheim? Perhaps he should take his friends to Schwetzingen, then. "Die Entführung aus dem Serail" was being sung there that night, but while the theatre was a love and they would love it, the opera company was indifferent and could not possibly do Mozart justice; the soprano, according to the Baroness, looked like a turtle and sang like an owl.

"It is a lovely day!" said the Baroness, looking up from her work, her happy eyes roving her roses with pride, as if her garden rivalled Versailles. "Why not bring them here to enjoy a *kalte Ente chez moi* in the true German *Abendsonnenschein*. And later we—" But she did not finish, for Ian turned on her a look of terrible embarrassment and profound pity, and it seemed to Miranda that a cloud came down, dark, through the branches of the lime trees.

"I think my friends might rather . . ." he faltered, and then he busied himself with fitting a cigarette into his holder.

The Baroness resumed her work and brightly said, "I was not serious." Yet it was plain, from her sorrowing frown, that she had been.

The shadow continued to enshroud the terrace and fade the crimson rambler on the wall. The three were silent. Miranda, though she desperately tried, could think of nothing to say. The world about them was alive with sound; barges signalled to pass through the locks, the canoeing sweethearts laughed, church bells rang, birds in the high hills sang. With keen concentration, she watched the meaningless meanderings of a rooster and three brown hens on a barge. She could see no coop for them, and wondered if they laid their eggs in the coiled-up hawsers; save for the poultry, there was no sign of life on board, and the vessel drifted downstream on an erratic course. For some time, she looked at a fire in a field across the river, slowly turning the stubble black. She saw a girl herding tall geese along the riverbank; one of them was blue, and his character as well as his plumage was eccentric, for he dawdled and then took it into his head to go swimming, then attended to his person, slapping the waterdrops away with his bill, ignoring the girl's cross outcries, and hissing at her stick.

After a long while, Ian said to the Baroness, "Perhaps I should take them up to Neckargemünd tonight, to the Pfalz."

"The Pfalz—oh, lovely!" said the Baroness. "Because the moon is full!" She was as charmed and charming as if she were to be the guest of honor on whom the orange harvest moon would shine. She had never, it seemed to Miranda, looked so threadbare and so faded and so dreadfully poor, so insecurely held together with pins and patches. But all the same, having regained her poise, she was once more the hostess, gifted with cordiality and small talk, making it gently plain that she was to the manner born. Delicately she caressed the rubies in her ears and smiled, as if to say, "I know what I once was and I shall never forget." Although Ian had earlier rebuffed her in her invitation to bring his friends to her house, he was now as admiring as he was on Thursday evenings, and listened to her tell of an adventure that had befallen her and the Baron one time in Naples; the lighthearted boaters in the bright-colored boats on the Neckar had reminded her of the wild blue southern bay.

Presently, the Baroness got up, saying that she must go into the kitchen to make her chestnut soup; she could not trust the maid to do it, for the girl was gross. When she had wished Miranda and Ian a good appetite and had vanished into the house, Ian said, "I hated to do what I did. But I couldn't have brought those people here; they wouldn't have known from her looks that she's a great lady, and looks is all *they* go on. I won't have her laughed at." He clenched his fist in his friend's defense against her hypothetical assailants.

That evening, although Miranda had planned to come home early to call briefly on the Baroness and then get to her books, she stayed late with friends at a cafe. She remembered Ian's look of pity and embarrassment; it expressed her own feeling when she thought of the needy noblewoman in her murky, musty drawing room that swarmed and echoed with memories. At midnight, when she let herself into the house, she heard faintly, behind the door of the drawing room, the tinkling of the music box.

Throughout the winter, Ian continued to be a carefree, spendthrift, toping, foppish, indolent man of the world, terrorizing the townsfolk with his reckless driving, filling the tills of the *Bierstuben*, bringing girls home with him late at night, dancing attendance on the respectable daughters of professors, occasionally going away. But the rakish side of him was eradicated on Thursday nights, when he came with his eucharist for Right Honorable Milady. And then, in the spring, a change came over him; he went away only once, and that was to drive the Baroness to Stuttgart to visit her sister and niece. While they were gone, the house was as still as a library and as lifeless as a grave. And then, when they came back, he began to show up in the evenings far more often than just on Thursdays, and such now was the wealth of experience common to him and his hostess that Miranda felt intrusive and tended to leave early, if she came at all. They did not press her to stay, for they had taken up mah-jongg, and even before Miranda had left the room, their heads, the red one and the wispy, whitish-yellow one, were together over the pretty tiles. All spring, as the Baroness tended her flowers and planted her kitchen garden and cross-stitched dirndls for Friede, she sang in a thin, true schoolgirl voice.

On the day Miranda left Heidelberg in June, Ian waved goodbye to her from his balcony as she got into her cab; he was wearing a velvet smoking jacket and an ascot, and, fancifully, he was smoking a porcelain pipe; he looked, in a sense, like the man of the house. But despite his smile and his friendly wave, there was something wistful in his voice when he cried down, "*Auf Wiedersehen!*"

From time to time in the next few years, Miranda heard scraps of news of Ian Ferguson. He had stayed in Heidelberg until the war and then had returned to America to continue restlessly to look for the land of Cockaigne, to drink so much that he was often put away in nursing homes, to wreck his cars (in one crash, on Long Island, he lost the sight of an eye, and this, together with a number of serious allergies, eliminated him from the draft), to underwrite businesses that promptly failed, and to have his name linked in the gossip columns with galaxies of starlets and renowned divorcees. A good part of the time, he roved the Caribbean, and Miranda, hearing of him in Haiti and Jamaica, could perfectly see him in this appropriate setting, sunning his golden flesh on pale beaches under garish skies, drinking Daiquiris in the company of people like himself, cosmopolitan and untroubled by any cosmology or any politics, good-looking, charming, disarming, unharming, a useless vestigial appendage of society, but one for which Miranda, despite her moral objection to waste and despite her own dedication to work, had a soft spot in her heart. She had been really fond of Ian and the Baroness, and even when she no longer heard of them, she often thought of their sympathetic affection for each other—those Sunday walks, those mah-jongg games. She remembered the tune the music box had played and remembered the smell of the carnations Ian used to bring as a tribute to Milady's blue blood; the fragrance overcame that other, that pathetic, scent of dead sachet.

Returning to Heidelberg after twenty years had been a strange experience even before she saw Ian's name in the telephone book. Miranda was fond of revisiting scenes to learn what changes history had made in them, and when she found that en route from Italy, where she had been visiting friends, to Paris, where she was to meet her husband, she could stop in Heidelberg for a few days with no great inconvenience, she was delighted. She had found the town unchanged. It was spring, and the same big blond boys had pitched their sleazy pup tents on the grassy esplanade of the river and were engaged in rowdy horseplay, trying to push each other into the oily water, bursting into song, cooking what were bound to be nasty messes in iron pots over smoky fires. The pleasure craft were spry, their paint was fresh, the same heavy-laden barges rode proudly down. The same myopic, ill-dressed students were bicycling through the narrow Hauptstrasse, where the same blue trolleys swayed and clanged. The sun shone brightly on the sweet dark hills, and the gardens, behind their gates, were spruce, and the upriver checkerboard of fields beyond the peaceful Benedictine monastery was thriving in a dozen different hues of green. There was upon this lovely landscape no mark of disaster.

Of course, there were changes—profound ones, which presently she saw. Where once there had been S.S. men, now there were American soldiers, and where once there had been a leanness of purse, now there was immense prosperity. Nevertheless, the experience of Heidelberg—far more than just the memory of it—returned to her, and she lived in it in reflection more intensely than she had originally.

Observing the vividness of her sensations and impressions, she realized that her backward glance had probably increased the rosiness of what she saw. When she wandered the streets that smelled of cheese and wurst, gazed into the shops, with their gimcrack steins and *Lederhosen* for babies and overwrought etchings of the castle, twenty years dropped from her mind and her muscles, and she actually *was* a resilient girl, intoxicated with the headiness of being abroad.

And now, to complete the restoration of that long-ago time, here was Ian Ferguson's name—a name, she thought romantically, to conjure with. At last, her curiosity overcame her reticence, and she picked up the telephone and gave the porter Ian's number; it was only then she noticed that his address was the same as ever—Ziegelhäuser Landstrasse 18, the Baroness's yellow house. As she waited for the telephone to be answered, she heard a hard pulse in her temple and half hoped no one was at home, for she felt like a voyeur. But Ian was at home ("Ferguson here," he said), and when Miranda had established her identity—his vagueness indicated that his recollection of her was uncertain—he invited her to come to tea that afternoon.

A sign under the bell at the derelict and rusted gate of No. 18 warned the visitor to beware of the dog, and when Miranda rang, a ferocious and unkempt young schnauzer tore down from the garden, barking murderously. Immediately a man's voice cried, in English, "Hansel! Shut up, damn you! Shut up, I say!" and the man himself came hurtling down the worn steps to slap the dog and send him off, howling. Because the pales of the grille obscured him, Miranda did not recognize Ian until he had opened the gate. But there was no mistaking him, despite the black patch over his right eye—she recalled hearing of the automobile accident—and a thick and sleek mustache. These two new appurtenances gave him the look of a character actor who had wandered off the set of a melodrama taking place in a British colony; he wanted only a pith helmet and a retinue of blacks. But he was so thin and pale, so hollow-eyed and sunken-cheeked, that on second thought she decided he looked more as if he had just quitted a bed in a tuberculosis sanitarium where he had been gravely ill.

He greeted Miranda hospitably, but she was sure that he did

not really know who she was. "Sorry about that dog," he said. "Come in, come in, what a pleasure! Right Honorable Milady will be delighted."

"The Baroness?" said Miranda, amazed at first, but then realizing that she was not amazed at all.

"Yes, she stayed on. Most of the aristocrats got out in the thirties, bag and baggage, but she stayed. I call that pluck."

"Will she remember me?" asked Miranda.

Ian smiled. "Did you ever know Milady to forget anything? She's a little deaf now, but apart from that I don't think you'll find her changed." And then, fussing with the gate and taking Miranda's elbow, he urged her up the steps, saying, "It's much too hot to stand in the sun. Friede—Milady's niece—has made some refreshments for us. Do you remember the terrace? We'll sit there, in the sun."

The Baroness, as desiccated as a dried leaf or a bug, sat, a tiny huddle of bones, in a cavernous upholstered chair under a Roman-striped umbrella. She extended her hand to Miranda imperiously but hospitably, and grandly indicated a chair where her guest might sit. She said, "How good you are to come to pay your respects to this aged denizen of Heidelberg. When Ian told me you were coming, I said, 'Then, for old time's sake, we must have tisane.' Do you remember those evenings? Lemon verbena was your favorite, I think. But Ian vetoed my proposal. He said it wasn't a properly festive tipple for so unusual a reunion. So we are having a true American cocktail party." And she gestured toward the garden table, where there were glasses and a bowl of ice and two bottles of bourbon and a dish of peanuts. "I remember the first time I ever drank whiskey," she said, and she began, in her familiar, breathless voice, to tell a story Miranda had once known by heart—of a steamer trip down the Danube from Ulm to Brăila. The Baroness was wearing a brown Mother Hubbard and a hat woven like a basket, and though the day was very warm for April, she hugged to her shoulders that bedraggled, yellowed old ermine tippet. All the same, she still played the grand lady, adding to her monologue fillips of French and Italian. Her pride and her hopeless vanity broke Miranda's heart.

In the course of that long afternoon, the whole household broke Miranda's heart. Friede, that beloved niece for whom her aunt had smocked frocks and embellished the collars with forget-me-nots during her happy childhood, was a heavy-legged, round-shouldered young woman with a smooth, unsmiling face, whose expression was forever one of puzzlement, as if she had never got used to being alive. She had been, Miranda learned, orphaned by the war, for her parents, seeking shelter in their cellar during an air raid, drowned in their own wine when the tuns burst; at the time, Friede had been in Heidelberg with her aunt, and she had never left the yellow house on Ziegelhäuser Landstrasse. Ian had come back to Heidelberg at the very beginning of the Occupation, in some minor job with the Information Service. Although Americans were not then allowed to buy property, he had managed, by money paid surreptitiously into the right hands, to purchase the Baroness's house just at the moment the American Army was about to commandeer it for the use of bachelor officers. In the deed, he had stipulated that the Baroness was to live in it until her death. It was the Baroness who told these facts, and, leaning over to pat her benefactor's hand, she said, "There is no greater gentleman in all the world."

To be sure, they had been obliged to billet transient personnel, but they had not felt invaded; they had enjoyed the company of the captains and majors. ("They made me think of the days when dashing young hussars came to call on my sisters and me," said the Baroness, twinkling all over. "I remember one hussar in particular, a Captain Frommel, who went with us when we called on Chancellor von Bismarck at Friedrichsruh in the last years of his life.") Now, just as before the war, the extra rooms were let to students. "It seems only yesterday that Herr Ferguson was my lodger," said the Baroness, "and now he is, so to say, my landlord."

"Not landlord!" protested Ian, and got up to retrieve the gardening gloves she had let fall. "You must not call me that."

"Dear friend, then," said the Baroness, gazing at him with ineffable affection, and to Miranda she said, "You see, there was something about my humble villa by the river that always drew him back."

"It was the noble lady who lived there that drew me back," said Ian, and though he spoke with devotion, Miranda could not help feeling that he spoke by rote—that this was a game they had played over and over, never missing a cue, never fumbling a line.

Ian, drinking straight bourbon rapidly, grew garrulous. "You remember me, I'm sure, as a gay blade who used to go cavorting about from one casino to the next, never giving a thought to tomorrow and never bothering my head about a rainy day," he said to Miranda. "Black sheep of the family, that was Yours Truly, as my brothers rejoice in telling me whenever they deign to write. Oh, they're rich, I can tell you! And sober and God-fearing, and surrounded by offspring who count it a rare privilege to live in the Lone-Star State. But I'm not one to regret that I made ducks and drakes of my money, because I had a hell of a good time doing it. I've seen a lot in my day, and sometime I'm going to write down my experiences."

"He's been everywhere!" exclaimed the Baroness, beaming.

Just for example, he said, he had been here in Germany while the Spanish civil war was going hot and heavy, and it had been as plain as a pikestaff then that a general war was on the way. (It had been plain to almost everyone but Ian, who one time had asked the Baroness what on earth could be the meaning of the words, stamped in his passport, "Not Valid for Travel in Spain." She had not the faintest idea; she had roguishly suggested that he was *persona non grata* in Spain because of some cavalier scandal involving a grandee's daughter, or even a grandee's wife.) His hindsight was astigmatic, and he saw himself as a serious inquirer into political and sociological matters, and also as a dog gayer than Casanova had ever thought of being. Poor man, thought Miranda, he had not even been really gay—he had cut a narrow swath in a fallow field, and his thrills had been ever so tame—but she listened attentively to his romantic exaggerations, as she had once listened to the Baroness's. Gratuitously, and with vehemence, he insisted that he was the happiest of men, and if he had his life to live over again, he would do the same things; he wanted to spend the rest of his days right here on this sunny belvedere, watching the ceaseless change and play of light on the broken turrets of the castle.

The Baroness said, "Sometimes I say to him, 'Why don't you take a trip somewhere? Why don't you go to England and make a pilgrimage to your mama's birthplace?' I say, 'She'd be happy in her grave in Texas if she knew you were looking at the roses in Surrey.' But he's such a stay-at-home!"

"The roses in Surrey can't be any more beautiful than the ones you grow," said Ian, and he gazed out across the river. These lines, too, thought Miranda, were a part of the game.

He went on, meditatively, "I suppose my brothers and sisters are right—that I'm a wastrel. God knows, it's the truth that I'm poor. I never wanted to spend the time with brokers and bankers, so I just spent the money till it was gone. But my tastes are simple now. Do you remember the way I used to have lobster brought down from Hamburg for those dinner parties I threw in my rooms?" He laughed at the memory of his debonair days. "But though I'm poor, I've got what I want. Sometimes I'm not just sure what it is, but I've got it anyway."

"He won't go to England. He won't even go to the Harz, where he used to love to hunt," said the Baroness complacently. "These late afternoons in Heidelberg are so beautiful! Why *should* anyone want to be anywhere else?"

"If my ship comes in, I'll tell you what I'll do, Milady," said Ian. "I'll move my mother's body from Texas to England."

Friede, sitting on a stone bench beside the wall where the rambler grew, had been silent with boredom or with despair, but now she shuddered and got up and said "How morbid you are!" and she went into the house, slamming the door.

"The young are so strict," said the Baroness. "I'm sure I wasn't when I was her age, but then in those days we lived like the lilies of the field."

"My oldest sister came through Heidelberg last year," said Ian, "and came out here for the sole purpose of upbraiding me. She said she wasn't a bit surprised that I had gone to the dogs—that's how she put it—and behaved as if this were Skid Row. She said I'd been spoiled all my life. Oh, Lord, the things she said!"

He was very drunk now; his handsome face fell into pleats and corrugations, his good eye was red and moist, and, in his awful woe and disappointment, he stumbled over to the Baroness and knelt before her on one knee. The Baroness touched him on the shoulder. "I dub thee Sir Ian," she said.

Miranda could no longer watch the creaking antics of this

game, and she asked if she might ring for a cab, but Ian insisted on driving her home, and the Baroness, in her grandest manner, said, "I personally have never ridden in a public vehicle. That is one thing I look on as really infra dig."

Their goodbyes were formal and effusive; it was as if they were taking leave of one another after a ceremony of great importance—a christening party, perhaps, for an infant queen. The Baroness plucked a tulip for Miranda, and stood there in the filtered sunlight in those dilapidated clothes and fingered the rubies in her ears.

Ian drove Miranda back to her hotel in a sudden April shower. He had a Mercedes again, but it was old and halting and its upholstery was scuffed. At the door of the hotel, he stood on the bottom step, unprotected, the rain pouring down his face.

"This time tomorrow you'll be in Paris," he said, and there was anguish in his voice. "I'd like to go to Paris. I'd love to go to England, but Milady is frail—I'd worry if I left her alone." In his reluctant exile in this unlikely place, with his waning, paling ladylove (Or *was* she that, or had she ever been? Probably he no longer knew himself), he envied Miranda, but what he said—and he said it gallantly—was "Don't forget Heidelberg! Come back! You will, you know—you'll be drawn."

"Oh, I'll be back," said Miranda limply, knowing that nothing on earth could drag her here again. There was an awkward pause between them, in the thundering rain, and finally Miranda said, "Well, Ian, *auf Wiedersehen*," although she meant "goodbye."

A Reasonable Facsimile

$\mathbf{F}$AR from withering on the vine from apathy and loneliness after his retirement as chairman of the Philosophy
Department at Nevilles College, Dr. Bohrmann had a second
blooming, and it was observed amongst his colleagues and his
idolatrous students that he would age with gusto and live to be
a hundred. He looked on the end of his academic career—an
impressive one that had earned him an international reputation in scholarly quarters—as simply the end of one phase of
his life, and when he began the new one, he did so with fresh
accoutrements, for, as he had been fond of saying to his students, "Change is the only stimulus." He took up the study of
Japanese (he said with a smile that he would write hokku as
tributes to his friends on stormy days); he took up engraving
and lettering (designed a new bookplate, designed a gravestone
for his dead wife); he began to grow Persian melons under
glass; he took up mycology, and mycophagy as well, sending
his fidgety housekeeper off into shrill protests as he flirted with
death by eating mushrooms gathered in cow pastures and on
golf links. He abandoned chess for bridge, and two evenings a
week played a cutthroat game with Miss Blossom Duveen, the
bursar's blond and bawdy secretary, as his partner and as his
opponents Mr. Street, the logician, and Mr. Street's hopelessly
scatterbrained wife.

But the radical thing about his new life was the house he
had had built for himself in the spring semester of his last year
at the college. It was a house of tomorrow—cantilevered, half
glass—six miles out on the prairies that confronted the mountain range in whose foothills lay Adams, the town where the
college was. The house, though small and narrow, was long,
and it looked like a ship, for there was a deck that went all the
way around it; from certain points Dr. Bohrmann could see
Pikes Peak, a hundred and fifty miles away, and from every
point he could watch the multiform weather: there dark rain,
here blinding sunshine, yonder a sulphurous dust storm, haze
on the summit of one peak, a pillow of cloud concealing a second, hyaline light on the glacier of a third. The house amazed

643

that nondescript, stick-in-the-mud Western town, which, from the day it was founded, had been putting up the worst eyesores it could think of. Whoever on earth would have dreamed that the professor, absent-minded and old, riding a bicycle, wearing oldfangled gaiters and an Old World cape, would make such an angular nest for himself and drastically paint it bright pink? The incongruity between the man and his habitat could not possibly have been greater. He belonged in and had, in fact, spent most of his life in fusty parlors where stout, permanent furniture (bookcases with glass fronts, mahogany secretaries with big claw feet, lounges upholstered in quilted black leather, ottomans, immovable bureaus, round tables as heavy as lead) bulked larger than life in the dim-orange light of hanging lamps with fringe. You could see him cleaving through those portières people used to have that were made of long strands of brown wooden beads; you could see him hanging his hat on a much ramified hatrack. Imagine, then, this character, with his silver beard, wearing a hazel coat-sweater from J. C. Penney, and a mussed green tweed suit, those gaiters, a stiff-collared shirt, a Tyrolian hat—dressed, in general, for an altogether different *mise en scène*—sitting in a black sling chair on the front deck of this gleaming, youthful house, drinking ginger beer out of an earthenware mug and looking through binoculars at eagles and the weather. Or look at him pottering in his pretty Oriental garden (it had a steeply arching bridge over a lily pond and a weeping willow, and a deformed pine tree that he had brought down from up near the timber line), shading himself with the kind of giant black bumbershoot one associates with hotel doormen in a pouring rain. See him in his sleek, slender blond dining room eating a mutton chop or blood pudding with red cabbage, drinking *dunkles Bier* from a stein. No matter where you placed him in that house, he simply would not match. It was the joke of Adams, but a good-natured one, for Dr. Bohrmann was the pet of the town.

Dr. Bohrmann and his wife, who died two years before his retirement, had arrived in Colorado from Freiburg by way of Montreal, where, just as he was beginning to make his presence felt at the university, he was halted in his stride by a sudden, astounding hemorrhage of the lungs. When, after seventeen wan, lengthy months, he was discharged from the sanitarium, not as cured but as arrested, his careful doctors counselled him to go West, to the Rocky Mountains, under whose blue, bright skies he could, in time, rout the last bacterium. On their further recommendation, he applied for an appointment at Nevilles College, since Adams was famous for the particular salubrity of its air. And providence was pleased to accommodate him, having a few months earlier created a vacancy on the staff through the death—from tuberculosis—of a young instructor. Adams was high above sea level and its prospect of soaring palisades and pinnacles of rock was magnificent, if, at first, dismaying to European eyes that had been accustomed to grandeur on a smaller scale. Moreover, the faculty of its college was remarkable—was, in part, illustrious—because so many of its members had come here for Dr. Bohrmann's reason; if their distemper had been of a different nature, they would have lectured in much grander but moister groves—in New Haven or Princeton, in Oxford or Bonn. For the most part, they accepted their predicament with grace—it is no myth that the tubercular is by and large a sanguine fellow—and lived urbanely in rented houses, year by year meaning it less and less when they stated their resolve that as soon as their health was completely restored they would go back to the East or to their foreign fatherlands. Although their New York *Times* came four days late, and although perhaps they were not in the thick of things, neither did their minds abide in Shangri-La. Visiting lecturers and vacationing friends were bound to admit that the insular community was remarkably *au courant* and that within it there was an exchange of ideas as brilliant and constant as the Colorado sun.

At first, when the Bohrmanns came, in 1912, they had no intention of lingering any longer than was absolutely necessary. But after little more than a year, neither of them could imagine living anywhere else; the immaculate air was deliciously inebriating and the sun, in those superlative heavens, fed them with the vibrancy of youth. They daily rejoiced in their physical existence, breathed deeply, and slept like children. They liked to walk on the mesas, gathering kinnikinnick in the winter and pasqueflowers in the spring; sometimes they rented sweet-faced burros and rode up to a waterfall of great temperament and beauty. They admired the turbulent colors of the sunsets, the profound snows of winter, the plangent thunderstorms of summer. There was, they said, some sort of spell upon the place that bound them to it; roving the tablelands, whence one could gaze for miles on miles upon the works of God, they paused in silence, their hands upon their quickened, infatuated hearts. And besides the land, they loved the people of it, both the autochthonous Town and the dislocated Gown; students thronged their house at the *gemütlich* coffee hour, and their coevals and their elders came at night to drink hot wine or beer and, endlessly, in witty, learned periods, to talk.

Sometimes Dr. Bohrmann and Hedda spoke of summering in Europe—in spite of their contentment, they were often grievously homesick for Freiburg—and occasionally they went so far as to book passage, but something always prevented them from going. One year, Wolfgang was engaged in writing a monograph on Maimonides for the *Hibbert Journal,* another year Hedda was bedridden for a long while after a miscarriage that doomed them, to their everlasting sorrow, to childlessness. After the Second World War, they no longer even spoke of going back, for the thought of how Freiburg now must look sickened them.

All in all, they had an uncommonly happy life and they so much enjoyed each other that when Hedda died, with no warning at all, of heart disease, Wolfgang's friends were afraid that he, too, might die, of grief. And, indeed, he asked for a semester's leave and spent the whole of it indoors, seldom answering his doorbell and never answering his telephone. But, at the end of that time, he emerged as companionable and as exuberant as ever, as much at home with life.

It was then, upon his return to the mild and miniature hurly-burly of the campus, that he began to lay in his supplies against the lean times when his rank would be emeritus. He started Japanese with Professor Symington, the historian, who, until he had got tuberculosis, had been an Orientalist resident in Kyoto; he read Goren and Culbertson on bridge; he studied every magazine on architecture that was published, and throughout that winter he worked on designs for his new house. In the beginning, when he went to the builders, they dismissed his plans as the work of a visionary—all that expanse of window, they said, was impractical in a cold climate; they said he would rue the day he put a flat roof over his head. If it had been anyone but Dr. Bohrmann, they probably never would have come round, but Dr. Bohrmann had a way about him that could persuade a river to stand still or a builder to build a pavilion at the North Pole. So, in the end, they took on the job, and they admitted, grudgingly but still with fondness, that he had not faltered in his specifications by so much as a fraction of an inch. While the house was going up, he rode out on his bicycle each afternoon at tremendous speed, his romantic mantle billowing, the brim of his hat standing straight up in the wind, to watch the installation of his windows and the progress of his grass; he was like a mother watching, in pride and fascination, the extraordinary daily changes in her first-born.

In June, after his last Commencement, he moved out of the house in which he and Hedda had lived all those years, and he transferred to the new house his vast polylingual library, his busts of Plato and Lucretius and Aesculapius and Kant, his collection of maps and of antique firearms, and Hedda's pure-linen sheets. He sold or gave away the durable, lubberly furniture he and Hedda had accumulated and all those souvenirs of another time—antimacassars, needlepoint cushions, afghans, porcelain umbrella stands, Lalique bud vases. He transplanted his tuberous begonias to the terrace on the west side of the new house and, at the back, he put in mountain-ash trees, a row of eight Lombardy poplars, and an ambitious kitchen garden, bordered with herbs, pinks, primroses, and bachelor's-buttons.

On the morning he moved, after the vans had gone, Dr. Bohrmann got on his bicycle, with his fiddle strapped in its case behind him and his ginger cat in a basket in front of him, and he pedalled out to the plains, singing "Gaudeamus Igitur" in a rich, if untrue, baritone. Street, the logician, saw him wheeling past his house and later said on the telephone to Symington, the historian, "You should have seen *mein Herr Doktor Professor* this morning, with his cat and his fiddle, singing hi-diddle-diddle, ready to hop right over the moon." Symington, with a laugh, rejoined, "When we're pushing up daisies, he'll be learning jujitsu." Blossom Duveen saw him, too; she drove past him in her brash crimson convertible on her way to Denver and a flicker of interest started a flame in her heart; he was really a dear, she thought, and by no means all that old.

She wouldn't mind in the least little bit going to live in that snappy, streamlined house.

The moving men, aided by Mrs. Pritchard, the housekeeper who had taken care of Dr. Bohrmann since Hedda's death, and by a crew of students who were staying on for the summer term, had everything in place by midday and had even cleared away the excelsior and the cartons and barrels, and, on the dot of noon, the jocund old professor fired a shot into the sky from a harquebus he himself had restored to working order, the boys gave a cheer, and Dr. Bohrmann opened up a keg of beer. To each of his helpers in turn he genially raised his glass and said "*Prosit.*" Momentarily, as he saluted them, he wished he had bedrooms enough to lodge every one of these warmhearted lads who talked like cow hands but whose minds were critical and tough and appreciative of his own appreciations. He was sorry, so very sorry, that he had no sons. But he erased his useless regret by telling himself that the next best thing to a son was a student and the Lord knew he had a host of those.

When the beer was gone, and the last raffish jalopy had roared away, and Mrs. Pritchard was in the kitchen making his lunch, he went into his new library, handsomely appointed in black wood and saffron upholstery, and, sitting before his windows that commanded a view from the plains to the tundra, he smiled on everything as if he were smiling on a gathering of intimate friends. Then his smile ebbed and his eyes grew grave, for he realized that in a year or two there would be no more of his students to come and match wits with him as they ate apples and pecans and fanned the fire on his hearth with bellows. Once they were out in the world, they seldom came back to Adams, and when they did, they were not the same, for they had outgrown their lucubrations; they were no longer so fervent as they had been, and often their eyes strayed to their wristwatches in the midst of a conversation. Dr. Bohrmann sighed at his sad loss of the young, and he sighed again, sorely missing Hedda; she had laughed so charmingly, he had liked her so extremely well. He thought of her sitting opposite him over a backgammon board, her fingers approaching and then withdrawing from the men, and his heart broke with longing for the sweet look of her perplexity. But then he chided himself for his unphilosophical egocentricity, and reminded himself of the marvels that were to emerge in his gardens and of the quotidian pleasure he was to know in this house with its kingly prospects, and, ashamed that he had brooded even for a minute, he resolutely turned to the morning mail, separating the journals and bulletins from the letters.

For many years, Dr. Bohrmann had kept up a prodigious correspondence with all manner of people all over the world—with a handful of relatives scattered by war and pogroms, with the friends he had known at Freiburg and in Montreal, with his fellow-invalids and the doctors in the tuberculosis sanitarium, with philosophers he had argued with at meetings of learned societies. And besides these, he wrote to a great many people he had never met. His was a nature so benign, so full of generous heart, that whenever he read a book he liked, or a short story or a poem in a magazine, whenever he heard on the radio a piece of music by a contemporary composer, he wrote the author a letter of congratulation—a careful, specific letter that showed he had read or listened with diligence and discrimination. More often than not this ingratiating overture led to a lasting friendship by mail, and, through the years, Dr. Bohrmann grew as conversant with these friends' families and pets and illnesses and sorrows and triumphs as if he had frequently dined at their houses. One time, Rosalind Throop, the greatly gifted young woman novelist in Johannesburg, flatteringly asked him to send a photograph of himself, saying, "Since the shape of your heart is now so clear to me, I am impelled to know the shape of your face as well." He sent a snapshot of himself and Hedda, up to their knees in columbines, a grand reach of snowy peaks behind them, and Mrs. Throop wrote by return mail, "What are these flowers you and the *Frau Professor* wade in? Only last night, before the photograph came, I dreamed I met you in a meadow in the Cotswolds abloom with Michaelmas daisies, and you said to me, 'We must gather our daisies quickly, for the snows are on their way.' And here in the picture you stand in flowers and at your back there is snow!" Thereafter, in their letters they made allusions to their pastoral encounter in England, where neither of them had ever been, until it no longer seemed fantasy.

To South Africa and to Japan, to Scotland and France, to

Israel and Germany, he sent presents of books and subscriptions to magazines and CARE packages; to his friends' children he sent arrowheads and feathered Indian headbands. His correspondents sent him presents in return, and now and then someone dedicated a book to him. When he had been obliged to write of Hedda's death, they mourned sincerely and worried over his solitude, but they took heart once again when he started building his house, of which he sent them photographs.

There was another side to the coin, for often an admiring reader wrote him an appreciation of or an objection to an essay of his that had appeared in the *Journal of the History of Ideas* or in *Revue de Métaphysique et de Morale*; he was a prolific writer and, by his own wry, rueful admission, a prolix one. (Once he had written to Mrs. Throop, "I have read your new novel with the monster's green eye. How you write! If I had but a tittle of talent! I have instead a galloping *cacoëthes scribendi* and you don't go to Heaven on the strength of that! May I be summoned by the Gabriel horn when I'm about a modest business—gathering toadstools, e.g., or making Jap squiggles.") But in spite of the turgid vocabulary and the Germanic, backward syntax of his monographs, Dr. Bohrmann had a wide following, and really nothing in the world pleased him more than a letter from someone who had read him through to the end.

At the time he withdrew from society, after Hedda's death, he acquired a new correspondent, a young man named Henry Medley, who taught English at a college in Florida, and who had come across Dr. Bohrmann's "A Reinquiry into Burke's Aesthetic." This princely lad (Dr. Bohrmann did not stint in his use of laudatory adjectives when he described his partisans) had been inspired to look further into the philosopher's work, and painstakingly he compiled a complete bibliography, which included early studies that Dr. Bohrmann had forgotten altogether and, in some cases, would have preferred to disown. Medley's dossier, gradually revealed in the course of a two-year exchange of letters, was this: he came from the upper regions of New York State and he was in his early twenties; he was the only child of a lawyer father, who had been dead for many years, and of a pedigreed but impecunious mother, who had been reduced to the status of paid companion to "a dragon nearly ninety who hurles her hideous taile about a Hudson-River-Bracketed den. It's here I spend my holidays, keeping a civil tongue in my head." He had worked his way through Harvard by tutoring the rich and retarded, and he had caught swift glimpses of Europe one summer when he had escorted a band of adolescents on a bicycle tour. He wrote Miltonic epics and Elizabethan songs which, someday, when the time and the poems were ripe, he hoped to show Dr. Bohrmann.

Medley had apparently read everything and forgotten nothing, and his immense letters, written on onionskin in a hand so fine that it could only be properly seen through a magnifying glass, were the most learned Dr. Bohrmann had ever got from anyone. When he mentioned that he was taking up Japanese, Medley sent him a list of "musts" to read; when he announced that he was going to build a modern house, Medley wrote at length on Frank Lloyd Wright vs. Miës van der Rohe; he knew about opera, medicine (he could quote from Sydenham, Pliny the Elder, René Théophile Hyacinthe Laënnec), painting, horticulture ("You speak of planting peonies and I presume to warn you, lest you don't know, that they are extremely crotchety. They detest any direct contact with manure and they detest being encroached upon by the roots of trees. And plant shallow!"). He knew movies and jazz and Marx and Freud and Catullus and the Koran, military strategy, iconography, geography, geology, anthropology, theology; he was amused by such cryptosciences as phrenology, alchemy, and astrology; he knew about wines and fish and cheese; he read German, French, Italian, Latin, Greek. He played tennis, swam among coral reefs, and during his Christmas vacations in the North he skied; he repaired the dragon's electrical appliances and designed his mother's clothes. Dr. Bohrmann wrote him once that his name was so apt it could have been taken from the dramatis personae of an allegorical play.

Once in a while, when Medley replied in five close-written pages to something that in Dr. Bohrmann's letter had been virtually no more than a parenthetical musing, Dr. Bohrmann was annoyed and brought him to book for his excess. One time he wrote, "I think you have made a Jungfrau out of the hill of a pygmy mole. My reflections don't *all* deserve such attention, dear boy, and I fear I must have expressed myself more abominably than usual to inspire you to this support of my wisecrack about Euripides. I can't possibly agree with you that he has 'the shabbiest mind in history.' My joke was no good to begin with and I am much ashamed." By return post came an apology so abject that Dr. Bohrmann was further ashamed; nevertheless, he continued to scold Medley whenever he committed that sin he so much deplored—of impassioned, uncritical agreement.

It had been a challenging interchange; the chap was brilliant, though undisciplined and incorrigibly highfalutin. "Don't be so hard on the dumb blondes in your classes," Dr. Bohrmann once wrote him. "What sort of world would it be if we didn't have the Philistines to judge ourselves by? God bless 'em." After that, Medley barely mentioned his trials when he confronted girls in his classrooms who had never heard of Aristotle. But while Medley's voracity was greater than his digestion, Dr. Bohrmann was sure that time would balance his chemistry. No one, these days, was mature at twenty-four. Often, after some especially felicitous letter—for when the boy was at his best and dropped his airs, he was a charmer—Dr. Bohrmann was moved to wish that Henry Medley had been his son. What a delight it would have been to nurture and prune a mind like that! To have a son in whose lineaments he could read dear Hedda's face and his own mind—ah, *that* would be a harvest for the autumn of an old philosopher's life!

Today, as if to salute him on his first day in his new house, there was a letter from Medley, as thick as ever, and sent, as always, by airmail. It was posted from the Hudson River town, since his teaching in Florida was over until fall, and he was back with his mother and the dragon, who had got, he wrote, "a barkless dog to match the dummy piano, on which for years she has been playing the Ballades of Chopin. That is, she *says* she is playing Chopin." The first five pages of the letter—there were seven altogether, written in that microscopic hand—gave an account of a few days he had spent in New York on his way up from Florida; he had gone to the museums, and reported his reactions to Matisse and Rembrandt, he had heard some contemporary chamber music, and he had found a set of the eleventh edition of the Encyclopædia Britannica for twenty dollars. He enjoined Dr. Bohrmann to read the article on the alphabet without delay, and from that he went on to say that he had resumed his study of philology and that he found Holthausen's glossary to "Beowulf" far inferior to Klaeber's.

As he read on, Dr. Bohrmann shifted his position from time to time to ease the arthritic pain in his left hip, remembering that in the confusion of moving today, he had forgotten to take his pain-killing pills. He was, on the whole, in remarkably good health for a man of his age, but he was wearing out in the joints and the eyes—not grievously but in a bothersome way. The energy expended on Medley's New York stay made his legs and his heart ache. Page six of the letter began, "Now for the surprise, which I hope you will accept with as much pleasure as I take in the telling of it." We all like surprises and Dr. Bohrmann was no different from the rest of us; hoping for news of the arrival of a box of oranges from Florida perhaps, or something edible that was indigenous to upstate New York, he polished the magnifying glass and read on. He learned that Medley was getting a free automobile ride to the West with some former Harvard classmates who were going out to dig in Arizona, and that he would like to propose himself, "as our English cousins say, for a week or two weeks, or however long you enjoy me as your vis-à-vis. I will come with my own quarters (pup tent), and my own kitchen (portable grill), and hope you will give me houseroom in your back yard, though, should I detract from the aspect, I'll go up to your famous mesa. If my calculations are correct, and if we are not hindered by any act of God, and *if,* etc., I should be on your doorstep, with my camp, my typewriter, a change of shirt, and a sheaf of poems, on the 25th of June." He went on to say that he was anxious to do some mountain climbing and visit a cattle ranch and tour the ghost towns; that he had all sorts of ideas for Dr. Bohrmann's Oriental garden, which he would disclose on his arrival; that he had enough questions to ask, and theories to expound, and half theories to solidify, to last "till two each morning for a lifetime." He added, in a postscript, "Since I'm leaving tomorrow, I'm afraid there will be no way for you to put me off. But the cordiality of your letters, dear sir, gives me confidence in your welcome. I cherish the prospect of your midnight oil."

In all his life, Dr. Bohrmann had never had a house guest (it would, of course, be unthinkably infra dig to let the kid pitch a tent in the yard when there was an unused bedroom), not through any want of hospitality but because it was a matter that had never arisen, and he was so surprised by Medley's precipitous and inexorable assignment to him of the role of host that, while he never drank before five and seldom then drank spirits, he called to Mrs. Pritchard for the whiskey bottle and a glass.

Mrs. Pritchard, who was shaped like a pear and wore a blue mustache under a fleshy and ferocious bill, was punctual to the point of addiction (the professor said that she suffered from "chronic chronomania"), and, moreover, the slightest breach in routine sent her into a flushed and flustered minor nervous breakdown. "Whiskey? In the middle of the day?" she shouted from the kitchen, appalled. "But you've already had your beer, and I'm putting the soufflé in. This nice soufflé with chives in will be a fizzle." But she came bustling into the library anyhow with the whiskey and some ice, and, setting them down beside him, she said, "I declare! Are we going to have meals any which way just because we've moved into a modernistic house?"

"I don't know," said Dr. Bohrmann thoughtfully. "I don't know what our life is going to be from now on, Mrs. Pritchard. We have a guest arriving—a Mr. Henry Medley."

"A guest for lunch? You *might* have told me!"

"No, no. Not a guest for lunch today. On Friday a young man is arriving to spend several days—perhaps weeks. Who knows? He offers to live in a wigwam under the trees. But we'll give him the spare room, Mrs. Pritchard."

Mrs. Pritchard gaped like a landed fish, but all she managed to say was, "He can't come Friday. Friday is your night for bridge, and the Streets and Miss Duveen are coming to dinner. You might have remembered that when you invited him."

"Well, the fact is, I didn't exactly invite him," said Dr. Bohrmann. "He is dropping out of the blue, so to speak. He is springing full grown out of the Hudson River."

"You mean you don't know him? Do you mean to tell me that I am to fetch and carry for a total stranger? A strange *young man*?" Mrs. Pritchard keenly disliked the young, and when students came to call, she was as rude to them as she could possibly be without actually boxing their ears.

Dr. Bohrmann, flinching under his housekeeper's snapping eyes, timorously said, "If we don't like him, we'll turn him out.

But I think we're going to like him. I think we're going to find him a man of parts."

"Then why do you have to have whiskey just the selfsame minute I've put my soufflé in the oven?" Mrs. Pritchard, as she often said of herself, was nobody's fool. With this retort, she went back to the kitchen, and the needless bangings and crashes that came from it indicated plainly that she did not mean to take Medley's intrusion lying down.

As the professor drank, he was in a tumult of emotions, a most uncommon condition for him, a placid man. He was a little uneasy at contemplating a change of pace in his life (the remark about the midnight oil alarmed him; he had gone to bed at ten o'clock ever since he could remember), and he was a little scared of Medley's erudition; part of the pleasure, shameful to be sure, of teaching at Nevilles had been that for the most part his students were as green as grass. But, on the other hand, he was touched to think of having a daily companion of such enthusiasm; they could walk together on the mesas and dispute matters pertaining to God and man and, in lighter moods, they could go to the movies. He began to consider how he might influence and temper his young friend's thought; in his imagination Henry Medley became so malleable that Dr. Bohrmann, with tenderness and tact, molded him into one of the most impressive figures on the intellectual scene of the twentieth century. How about adopting him? He could be a sort of monument to Dr. Bohrmann after Dr. Bohrmann's bones were laid to rest, beside Hedda's.

He caught himself up in the midst of his daydream and said to himself, "Come off it, Bohrmann," and turned aside to read a lighthearted scenic postcard from Mrs. Throop, sent from Durban, where she was having a holiday with her children. "I like gathering sea shells beside the Indian Ocean so very much better than writing novels," she wrote in a relaxed and generous hand, "and I do it so much better. These lovely shells! Jon is making a collection of them, to repay you for the arrowheads. You see, you're a daily part of our life."

Darling Mrs. Throop! He wished he could adopt *her*. He wished that all his distant friends were coming to bless his house.

When Henry Medley arrived, at about dusk, he greeted his host in a torrent of epigrammatic and perfect Hanoverian German, refused the offer of the spare bedroom, and then, cajoled, accepted it. And he began to unload his gear from the taxi that had brought him up from the interurban station. (He had parted with his companions in Denver.) Besides the tent and the portable grill and the sleeping bag, he had brought two bulging Gladstones, a typewriter, a tennis racket, a pair of skis, a rifle, a fishing rod and tackle box, a recorder, a green baize bag full of books, extensive photographic equipment, and two large boxes of cuttings of field flowers from the Hudson Valley. At the sight of the skis, Mrs. Pritchard's eyebrows disappeared into her hair; there would be no skiing near Adams for three months. Before Medley went up to his room, he produced two bottles of Bernkasteler Doktor from the depths of one of the Gladstones and asked Mrs. Pritchard, with ineffable sweetness, to make a *Bowle* (for which he gave her the recipe), so that he could toast "the most distinguished scholar in America." Such was his sweetness and such, also, his air of authority that Mrs. Pritchard, that virago and nobody's fool, was disarmed, and trotted obediently to the kitchen and began to cut up fruit.

Before Dr. Bohrmann had got any real impression of the youth at all—beyond the fact that he lived like a gale—he found himself sitting on the western deck, sipping the wine (how had Medley guessed that this was his favorite of all Mosels—the *Bowle* was delicious), and answering Medley's rapid and knowledgeable questions about the differences between ground and push moraines, about glacier flora, about the mining history of this region. The young man listened to the old man's answers as closely as a doctor listening to a heartbeat through a stethoscope, and Dr. Bohrmann had the feeling that he was indelibly recording every fact and every speculation, however irrelevant or tenuous. It is flattering to be so closely attended and so respected, and Dr. Bohrmann glowed as he talked, slaking this burning student's thirst.

Henry Medley wore glasses and a beard, and a beholder, looking at the two from afar, would have said they bore a close resemblance. Nearer at hand, it would have been observed that the frames of the young man's glasses were of thick tortoise shell and that the old man's were gold, that Medley's curly beard was black and Dr. Bohrmann's was straight and frosty. An eavesdropper would have said their German was the same, but an expert would have heard the academy in Medley's inflections and his stilted usages, and would, in Dr. Bohrmann's accent, have heard a southern softening.

At first, dismissing the beard as an amusing coincidence, Dr. Bohrmann's view of the boy was an agreeable one. Henry Medley was small, constructed thriftily and well, and he emanated indestructibility from the soles of his neat little feet, shod in immaculate white sneakers, to the top of his shapely and close-cropped head. His hands were quick and nervous, and darkly stained with nicotine, for he smoked cigarettes ceaselessly, down to nothing; his clever eyes glinted as they swiftly detached themselves from one focus and fixed upon the next. His voice was high and tended to be phrenetic. Despite the voice, despite the crew cut, despite the lissome limbs, Medley gave the impression of having existed on the earth for much more than twenty-four years, and Dr. Bohrmann was sure that at seventy he would not look much different from the way he did now. He was, thought Dr. Bohrmann as the sun began to set, darkening Henry Medley's face and whitening his perfect teeth, like a spruce, good-looking, ageless imp. He was respectful, responsive, articulate, enthusiastic, astoundingly catholic in his information. Dr. Bohrmann, however, was pleased to note that he wasn't perfect: there was somewhere in him a lack—a lack of a quality an imp did not need but a man could not live without. For example, when Dr. Bohrmann inquired about his journey, really wanting to know, Medley was perfunctory. "The Lincoln Highway is as hot as Tophet, and as ugly as sin—the trip was no Odyssey to put into dactylic hexameters," and then asked Dr. Bohrmann how he would evaluate Croce as a historian. Generally people of this age were so self-centered that one was obliged to defend oneself against autobiography with the greatest diplomacy. But Medley was so unself-centered that Dr. Bohrmann began to wonder if he had a self at all. He would discuss his plans, but not his aspirations; he would talk about his ideas on a subject, but not his feelings on it; he would quote from "Voyage of the 'Beagle,'" but would not say that he longed to go on a voyage himself. It comes from having no father, and only a mother and a dragon and dumb little blondes, said Dr. Bohrmann to himself, and he resolved to rear this orphan imp into a human creature.

That evening, at dinner, Medley was a smashing success. As Mr. Street said afterward, he had never found anyone who had so fully grasped Whitehead and Russell; the ladies were delighted with his droll descriptions of Hudson River Bracketed and his account of a meeting with a manufacturer of embalming supplies. When Medley praised the *coq au vin*, Mrs. Pritchard fell head over heels in love; when he gave a short talk on the viticulture of the Rhine, the Hochheimer in their glasses turned to nectar. After dinner, when the bridge game began, he sat quietly in a distant corner of the library reading the "Diary of William Dunlap" until Blossom Duveen protested and archly told her host that he was rude. Thereafter, at the end of each rubber, someone sat out, and, in the end, as it happened, Medley was always at the table. He played, said the overwhelmed logician Street, like a rattlesnake.

At half past nine, as his elders were yawning, having had enough bridge and having finished the one weak highball they allowed themselves, Medley said, "I don't suppose you'd like me to teach you ombre? I learned it after a close reading of 'The Rape of the Lock.'"

And so, for two more hours, the company spent a stimulating, if puzzling, time with a pack of forty cards, learning—or, rather, failing to learn—such terms as *manille* and *basto*, and being reminded every so often by their teacher that "There is no *ponto* in black trumps, and this is most important to remember."

When the Streets and Miss Duveen departed, they were seen to the door not only by their host but by Medley as well, who warmly shook hands with them all and cordially said he hoped they would meet again soon. Back in the library, he tidied up, emptying ashtrays, putting away the cards, plumping up the cushions. Suddenly, in the midst of his housewifery, his eyes began to water, and then he sneezed explosively and repeatedly; in the lacunae between these detonations, he grimaced painfully and mopped his face and made a sort of moaning sound.

"Poor chap," said Dr. Bohrmann. "I expect it's some pollen or other from the prairie. We've been very dry this year."

"Not pollen," gasped Medley. "That!" And with a quivering forefinger he pointed at Grimalkin, the ginger cat, who had apparently come into the house through his own entrance, which Dr. Bohrmann had had cut into the kitchen door, and was sitting on the window sill, looking with interest at the shaking and sneezing and wheezing stranger.

What a way for the visit to begin and the evening to end! Breathing with difficulty, Medley told Dr. Bohrmann that from earliest childhood, cats had affected him thus. What was there to do? Plainly Grimalkin, an admirable cat and the lord of the manor, would not dream of changing his habits. And Dr. Bohrmann would not dream of Medley's going up to the mesa with his tent or—for Medley, in his discomfort that was mixed with fear, proposed this—of his returning at once to the dragon and her barkless dog.

"But look here," said Dr. Bohrmann. "My beast has never set foot in the spare room—I assure you it's innocent of his dangerous dander. Come along upstairs and let's see if you don't feel better."

Once in his bedroom, Medley gulped down antihistamines of divers colors and did presently feel better. He said he would stay out of the cat's way, and Dr. Bohrmann, very unhappy over the contretemps, said that he and Mrs. Pritchard would do what they could to keep Grimalkin out of the house; at this time of year he had a good deal of business outdoors, what with hunting shrews and smelling flowers. Dr. Bohrmann would board up the cat door first thing the next day.

In the morning, as Dr. Bohrmann was going through the upper hall, he found the corpse of a gopher on the floor in front of Medley's door. In spite of himself he smiled, and when he went into the dining room and found Grimalkin in his accustomed chair, opposite his own, he stroked the tom's big manly head and said, "Rotten cat! Wicked cat! How did you get in?" though he knew perfectly well Grimalkin had got in through his own private door. The cat, according to his lifetime habit, had his breakfast of corn flakes, well saturated with heavy cream. His purr, as he ate, was loud and smug.

Mrs. Pritchard had, since Dr. Bohrmann had known her, loved three creatures: Hedda, himself, and Grimalkin. For the cat she bought toys at the five-and-ten, grew catnip in a flowerpot in the kitchen, made special dishes (he was particularly fond of corn pudding); she brushed him, scratched him behind the ears, petted him, talked to him, suffered him to involve himself in her knitting. And when Dr. Bohrmann, strengthening himself with an unwonted third cup of coffee, announced to her that he was going to board up the cat door, and that Grimalkin must henceforth live outside because of Medley's disaffection, she was outraged.

"What next!" she cried. "I've been giving that boy some second thoughts. For all his kowtowing and his mealy mouth and his 'Sublime chicken, Mrs. Pritchard' and his 'After you, Dr. Bohrmann,' there's something about him that tells me he's sneaky. Put Grimalkin out of the house indeed! And what if milord takes a scunner to me? Will my door be boarded up, too?"

"Oh, come, Mrs. Pritchard," said Dr. Bohrmann. "It's summer and Grimalkin has plenty to do outdoors. He won't mind for a few days."

"A few days! Did you see those skis? Whoever heard of skiing here before October? To my way of thinking, Mr. Henry Medley brought his entire worldly goods with him and means to stay till kingdom come."

"Oh, lady, be good!" said Dr. Bohrmann, and he sighed. He was not used to domestic trouble and it embarrassed him. Moreover, he was not entirely sure that Mrs. Pritchard was wrong about Medley and he found himself hoping that the boy slept late; he did not feel like a deep conversation just now.

"Very well," said Mrs. Pritchard. "But we shall see what we shall see." And she closed her mouth firmly, scooped Grimalkin up in her loving arms, and marched to the kitchen.

Henry Medley stayed with Dr. Bohrmann for three weeks and was, during this lengthy time, the most sedulous of apes. He rented a bicycle and he bought a Tyrolian hat; he appropriated Dr. Bohrmann's politics and his taste in music and food; in company, he quoted his host continually but did not acknowledge his source. On the second day of his visit, Dr. Bohrmann began to tire of him; on the third day he began to avoid him; on the fourth, he begged a ride to Denver with Blossom Duveen, where he went to a double-feature Western while she was shopping. But Henry Medley was not aware that he bored his host; on the contrary, he often observed that their meeting of minds was enough almost to make him believe in a magnanimous God. He was very busy. Besides tirelessly picking Dr. Bohrmann's brains, he gardened ferociously, moved the porch furniture about, played his recorder and Dr. Bohrmann's fiddle, read his poems aloud (they were awful and long), took hundreds of photographs. At the end of the first week, Dr. Bohrmann, worn out with company and conversation, suggested that Medley join an organized tour that was going to the ghost towns, but Medley replied that unless Dr. Bohrmann went with him, he would prefer to stay at home. He did not go fishing, because Dr. Bohrmann did not fish; he did not play tennis, because Dr. Bohrmann was too old for the courts. They were invited out as a pair, and when Dr. Bohrmann had guests, Medley did the honors. "We are giving you a Piesporter tonight," he would say, or, "We prevailed upon Mrs. Pritchard to make cold sorrel soup." It was *us* and *our* and *we* until Dr. Bohrmann began to feel that his identity was ebbing away from him. Or that he had attached to his side an unmovable homunculus, who, by the way, now spoke German with a Breisgau accent and who mimicked his every thought and every gesture. The gratification he had felt on that first afternoon when Medley had seemed to listen so wisely and so well never returned.

Mrs. Pritchard would not speak to Medley. Her hatred was murderous; it was evident that she would have liked to put arsenic in his food. And it was Mrs. Pritchard who in the end—guileful, beloved thing that she was—dislodged him. Mrs. Pritchard, ably assisted by Grimalkin. She accomplished this through the simple expedient of taking away the board that had immobilized the swinging cat door. But she was very sly. Later on, she confessed that each night she waited up until the young man had gone to bed and then she would creep down to the kitchen and take away the board; in the morning, long before either of the men got up, she nailed it on again.

One night, Dr. Bohrmann was in a restive sleep, troubled by his arthritis and wakened often by the brightness of the moon. He was distressed, moreover, about Medley, for this was the first time in his long life that he had ever really disliked anyone; he had come to detest that bearded and permanent fixture almost as keenly as Mrs. Pritchard did. And what was the matter with him, a man full of years and of experience, that he could not gracefully remove himself from this dilemma? He dozed, and woke, and dozed again. He dreamed sadly of Hedda. They were cycling, he and Hedda, through the Schwarzwald, toiling up a hill but talking continually, though they had little breath. "Aunt Gertrude will be cross because we're late for tea and I promised to bring the butter," said Hedda. Her worry at last made her weep, then sob tragically, and Wolfgang comforted her in shouts; he tried to lower his voice but he could not, and he woke himself by yelling, "We're not too late, my darling! We have until the sun goes down." Startled by the sound of his own voice, he switched on the light. Medley was standing in the doorway.

"Is the cat in here?" he said.

"Look here, Medley," said Dr. Bohrmann in an amazing burst of courage. "I don't like having people walk into my bedroom in the middle of the night."

"I'm sorry, sir, I wouldn't have, only—" and he was seized with a violent paroxysm of sneezes. His red eyes streamed and his breathing, after the sneezes, was stertorous. Obviously he was in for an asthma attack.

Dr. Bohrmann sat up in bed and he grasped at a straw. "Poor chap," he said kindly. "I'm afraid my old ginger tomcat has outwitted us. That's the way they are, you know—foxy."

Medley, in a choked voice, said, "I have concealed this from you, sir, but every morning for a week now, that cat has brought some unspeakable piece of carrion to my bedroom door. Tonight, though, it went the limit. It got into my room through some diabolical system of its own, and now the room will be dangerous for me for days."

Dr. Bohrmann smiled behind his concealing hand. "I'm sorry for that," he said, and clucked his tongue.

"I don't suppose you would . . . No, I don't suppose you would."

"Would what, Medley?"

"Would—oh, no, sir, I won't propose it."

"Get rid of Grimalkin? Is that what you're trying to say?"

"Well, in a manner of speaking."

"No, I would not. I've had my handsome ginger tomcat for fifteen years, and I'll have him till he dies."

"Then, if he's to have the run of the house," said Medley, "I'd better move out to the yard."

"Well, I'll tell you, Medley," said Dr. Bohrmann, ashamed of his cunning and pleased as punch with it, "if Grimalkin has got your number, and it's plain that he has, moving outdoors won't do a particle of good. He'll get into your tent and plague you there. No, Medley, my boy, I'm afraid Grimalkin has us over a barrel."

A frenzy of sneezes—the intellectual face turned red and blue. When the storm was over, Medley leaned weakly against the door and groaned. When he spoke again, there was a decided testiness in his voice. "If I had known you had a cat," he said, "I wouldn't have made this trip. Isn't there *anything* we can do?"

"I'm afraid not," said Dr. Bohrmann. "I'm just afraid there isn't a thing we can do."

"I could go up to the mesa, I suppose?"

"I wouldn't recommend that," said Dr. Bohrmann. "It's rattlesnake time."

"Then what *shall* I do?" He was plaintive and pathetic, and for a split second Dr. Bohrmann almost weakened, but he remembered in time the sapping tedium of Medley's monologues and interrogations, and the feeling he had that Medley had robbed him of his own personality, and he said, "It looks like Hudson River Bracketed and the barkless dog for you."

In the morning, when they met at breakfast, Henry Medley was pale and shaky; obviously he had had a very bad night. Dr. Bohrmann, who had slept excellently after his visitor left his room, tried to start a conversation about Spanish cave drawings. But the wind was out of Medley's sails; he smiled wanly and asked to be excused.

The taxi came an hour later, and Medley piled his mountain of belongings into the back seat. Mrs. Pritchard, beaming, brought him a box lunch. Grimalkin, sitting in a lake of sun under the weeping-willow tree, was cleaning a shoulder blade.

"Now you write to me," said Dr. Bohrmann heartily. "Now *auf Wiedersehen*, Medley."

"Goodbye," said Medley sorrowfully. "To think that a cat . . . I might almost think there was a plan behind it."

"Have a good trip, son," said Dr. Bohrmann, and shuddered at the appellation.

At last, sulkily, Medley got into the taxi, and then he rallied and his old self reappeared. He said, in German with a South German accent, "If Grimalkin ever goes to join his ancestors, perhaps you will invite me again? We haven't scratched the surface of our common interests."

But happily the driver started the motor and went off before Dr. Bohrmann was obliged to reply. Mrs. Pritchard had gone into the house and now came out again with a dish of sardines, which, without a word, she handed to Dr. Bohrmann; he received it without a word and took it to the heroic tom, who accepted it with an open diapason of purrs. The old man, squatting on his heels beside the cat, surveyed his pretty garden with delight and looked at his house with amazement. How beautiful and bountiful was life! How charming it was of accident to cause contrast: it was good to be cold, so that one could get warm; it was good to wear out so that one could renew oneself; it was really a lovely thing that Medley had come and had gone. With these heartwarming and reasonable thoughts, Dr. Bohrmann watched his cat finish the last fishtail, and then, fetching his big black umbrella, he began to work in his garden. He uprooted the field flowers Medley had brought from the Hudson Valley, not in anger but because they had never really belonged with the rest of the planting, and just as he threw them into the lily pond, Blossom Duveen drove up.

"Came by to remind you it's bridge night," she called out in her vulgar, brassy voice. "No goulashes tonight, I hope, I hope."

As he strolled over to talk to her, Dr. Bohrmann listed to himself some of the other pleasures of life: this dumb dear, for example, after Medley with his hellbent enlightenment; bridge after ombre; a contented Mrs. Pritchard.

"What gives?" said Miss Duveen. "You look like the cat that swallowed the canary."

"I am," said Dr. Bohrmann, grinning conspiratorially at Grimalkin who was washing the top of his brainy head.

The Scarlet Letter

I KNEW from the beginning that Virgil Meade was crazy, but I didn't know he was a crook until it was too late and he had got me into a fine how-do-you-do that might have altered the whole course of my life. I mean I might have killed him and either gone to the gallows or spent the rest of my natural days in the pen.

Virgil unofficially became my fellow when he put a big valentine in the box for me. At first I was sorely affronted because it was a very insulting comic one he had made himself—when you opened it up, there was the outline of a huge foot on each page and underneath it said: "All policemen have big feet but Emily Vanderpool's got them beat." Moreover, he had signed it so there would be no doubt in my mind who was trying to hurt my feelings. I couldn't decide whether to write him a poison pen letter beginning "Dear (oh yeah?) Four-Eyes" or to beat him on the head with an Indian club. But then I discovered that he had written "S.W.A.K." on the back of the envelope and I knew what that stood for because my sister Stella, who was popular and was therefore up on codes and slang, had told me: "Sealed With a Kiss." Ordinarily such mushiness would have made me go ahead and write the letter or take out after him with the Indian club; but it so happened that at that particular time I didn't have a friend to my name, having fought with everyone I knew, and the painful truth was that Virgil's valentine was positively the only one I got that year except for a dinky little paper doily thing, all bumpy with homemade paste, from my baby sister. Tess. And besides being all alone in the world, I was a good deal impressed by Virgil because he was as clever as a monkey on the parallel bars (the way he skinned the cat was *something*), and I had heard that at the age of eleven he already had a wisdom tooth, a rumor that seemed somehow the more likely because his father was a dentist. And so, on second thought, although he had insulted me and although he wore glasses (a stigma far more damning than the biggest clodhoppers in the world), I decided that he was better than nobody and I looked across the room at him. He was staring

moodily out the window at the icicles, cracking his knuckles
to the tune of "Shave and a haircut." To attract his attention I
cracked mine in harmony, and he turned around and smiled at
me. He had a nice smile, rather crooked and wry, and I liked his
pert pug nose and the way his shiny black hair came to a neat
widow's peak in the exact middle of his forehead.

We kept up our antiphony for about a minute and then Miss
Holderness heard us and looked up from the valentine box she
had been grubbing in. Her snappish brown eyes went darting
around the room as, in her ever irascible voice, she cried: "Valentine's Day or no Valentine's Day, I decidedly will not tolerate
any levity in this class. Who is making that barbarous noise?"
She pushed up the paper cuffs that protected the sleeves of her
tan challis dress and glared. There was one of those weighty,
stifling silences in which everyone held his breath, everyone
feeling accused and everyone feeling guilty. Finally, unable to
single out any faces that looked more blameworthy than any
others, she had to give up with the threat: "If there is ever again
any knuckle-cracking in this class, the miscreant will go straight
to Mr. Colby for his or her punishment. I have reiterated ad
infinitum that levity is out of place in the sixth grade." (Miss
Holderness abhorred children and she loved hard words. Once,
after making me sing a scale by myself, she put her fingers in
her ears and she said: "I have never heard such cacophony.
Try it again, Emily, and this time endeavor not to agonize my
Eustachian tube." To get even with her I read the dictionary
that night and the next day asked her what "palimpsest" meant,
but she outsmarted me by congratulating me on my intellectual
curiosity and asking me to go to the Unabridged and read the
definition out loud to the class. Everyone, including Miss Holderness, was baffled.) Virgil and I looked at each other again
and grinned, and when Miss Holderness had bent her head
once more to the valentine box he stuck out his tongue and
thumbed his nose. This demoralized everybody in his immediate vicinity and a general giggle began like a gale. Luckily, all
the valentines had been handed out and the bell rang and Miss
Holderness dismissed us with a look of hatred. A humorist,
especially an antiteacher one, enjoys great prestige in grammar
school, and the more I thought about it, the more I was sure
I would realize considerable benefit in being associated with

Virgil. My own status was at present so low, by reason of my many quarrels, that I could not possibly elevate it by myself and very quickly I began to look on Virgil as the savior who would raise me from my ignominy. Little did I dream that that wily boy had a long-range plan to ruin me.

As we were putting on our galoshes, Virgil asked if he could walk me home, thereby proving that his intentions were serious. I shrugged my shoulders and said: "Suit yourself. It's a free country." I may have sounded nonchalant, but actually I was already afire with that puzzling, unnamable feeling that had preceded each of my betrothals since the age of five (I was a roughneck, fond of Indian wrestling and addicted to swearing, but I was vulnerable to love and the lacunae between my romances were melancholy); my throat and eyes were hot, my stomach was uneasy, my brains ticktocked like an Ingersoll and some of my bones felt as if they were coming loose. As we were leaving the schoolyard, a two-legged rat, a former friend of mine—in fact, he was Virgil's predecessor, with whom once upon a time I had planned to grow old gracefully—Dicky Scott, saw us and yelled: "Red and yella, kiss your fella! You'll be sorry, Specs! Vanderloop-the-loop's a dizzy old doughhead!" Virgil put his books and his lunch box down on the stone wall and before you could say "Knife" he had made a good hard snowball and caught Dicky on the chin, surprising him so that he just stood there gaping and making no attempt to retaliate. Several other children who had witnessed the episode called, "Atta-boy, Meade!" and "You tell 'em, partner!" Nobody had anything against Dicky—it was simply that in our savage society it was de rigueur to applaud whoever cast the first stone. I was gratified that my honor had been so swiftly and brilliantly defended and I seemed to sense that my stock was going up among the spectators. Indeed, Ruby Miller, who had not spoken to me for two weeks after an altercation over the ownership of a roller-skate key (it belonged to her but I was too proud to admit it when I found that out), came up and said: "Will you come to my birthday party on the twenty-first of July? I'm going to wear silk stockings."

Virgil and I walked home in total silence. Sometimes, in unspoken agreement, we walked stiff-legged; sometimes we left the cleared path and scuffed through the snow up to our knees. In the last block we broad-jumped from crack to crack in the sidewalk. Nobody was home at my house and I was glad of that because I wanted our first interview to be conducted without any interference from Mother (who had some crazy idea that kids liked to be asked such questions as "Have your folks taken up the new contract bridge that's all the rage?" or "What does your mother think about taking off the interurban and running buses to Denver?") or from Jack and Stella, who loved to tease me about my suitors. I made some sandwiches for Virgil and me of peanut butter and piccalilli and mayonnaise and Virgil said it was better than eating a fried chicken dinner. I told him to go on—this was the standard after-school sandwich in every house in Adams I'd ever been in—but he said he'd never eaten one before and he asked if he could have another. "Pardon me for living, girl, but can I have seconds?" He used this expression, "Pardon me for living," to precede almost everything he said, and although I didn't know exactly what it meant, it sounded sporty and I filed it away to spring on my family as soon as I could. When we had eaten we went into the living room and Virgil told me some riddles and jokes he had learned from his father, who was in great demand as the end man for minstrel shows at the B.P.O.E. One riddle was "What's black and white and red all over?" and the answer was *not* "A newspaper" but "A blushing zebra." Another was "Why is the Statue of Liberty's hand eleven inches long?" The answer was that if it were twelve inches it would be a foot. He taught me several Mr. Tambo–Mr. Bones dialogues and we decided that when it got warmer we would put on a show in his father's garage. His father, he said, had the latest thing in make-up kits—grease paint, false noses, funny whiskers.

Then we talked about what we were going to do when we grew up; it was a romantic coincidence that I was going to be an organist in a movie house and Virgil was going to be an usher, and we both planned to follow our calling in a big city, Omaha, perhaps, or Chicago. Virgil and I had a great deal in common; we both walked in our sleep and had often waked up just before we fell out of the window or down the stairs; both of us loved puzzles and card games and the two things in the world we really detested were Sunday school (Virgil said in so many words that he didn't believe in God) and geography homework.

"Down with the blankety-blank principal exports of the Malay Archipelago," said this articulate and forthright boy. "Gutta-percha—don't make me laugh."

"Tell the class all you know about the Hottentots," I said, imitating Miss Holderness, and Virgil got up and stood on his head, putting his feet against the wall. Upside down he said: "The Hottentots eat gutta-percha out of gutta-percha nose bags and they teach their grandmothers how to suck eggs."

Reddie, the dog, came padding in and looked at Virgil for a long time and then he yawned and padded out again. After that, Muff, the cat, came in to give Virgil the once-over. Virgil righted himself and waved his hands madly at Muff, who walked out of the room slowly, twitching her tail with disgust. Virgil said, "If there's one thing I can't stand it's to have an animal rubberneck at me. Especially cows. Pardon me for living, if a cow rubbernecks at me, I sock it right on the snoot," and he went on to tell me how he showed who was boss when he went to visit at his uncle's ranch on the western slope. There was a cow named Hildy that he had pasted in the beezer more than once and there was also a gawking billy goat that he had given a good lesson to. I was thrilled to think of this brave gladiator striding through pastures walloping cows that gave him the eye and when he said, "I'm about the only man in this town that can make those mangy old burros of Mr. Hodge's turn off their headlights," I was bowled over with admiration and I exclaimed, "Boy, you're the only man *I* ever heard of that can do it." Virgil promised that some day soon he would take me up to Mr. Hodge's ratty shack on the mesa and show me how he could make the little donkeys "see stars instead of yours truly." The fact was that I dearly loved those little animals, Pearl and Princess, and whenever Jack and I got a quarter saved up we hired them from Mr. Hodge and rode them all over town. And here, out of blinding rapture, I was accepting an invitation to watch Virgil mistreat them.

He made a general survey of the living room. He picked the Bible up off the library table and said, "Phooey," and then he began to examine the Civil War saber that had belonged to a bounty-jumping relative on my mother's side. He unsheathed it and hefted it and he said thoughtfully: "This may come in handy sometime."

After a pause he said: "Pardon me for living, girl, can I have another one of those keen sandwiches?" While he ate it Reddie came out to the kitchen to watch him with his big heartbroken hungry eyes and Virgil slapped him on the nose. "You heard me, you good-for-nothing scalawag," he said. "Don't you look at me and my sandwich with your googly-googly eyes." Reddie, the meekest thing in the world, looked as if he were going to cry, and when I, disloyal to my nice old dog because I was in love with this bloodthirsty swashbuckler, laughed, he cringed and slunk out of the room, and for the rest of the afternoon he lay under the china closet in the dining room with his head between his paws.

Virgil pardoned himself for living again and again asked for a sandwich. When he was finally satisfied and we went back to the living room he told me a sad story that explained why he was so hungry. He said that at home they had nothing to eat but doughnuts. His mother made about a million of them on Sunday, enough to last a week, and every day they had doughnuts with maple sirup for breakfast. These she called "doughnut waffles"; for supper she put ketchup on them and called them "doughnut meatballs" or "doughnut roast." "Doughnut surprise" had canned salmon and peas in the doughnut hole and it was awful. At one of the sanitariums in our town the food was all made of cereal; the cranky old valetudinarians ate things like "Grape Nut cutlet" and "Corn Flake loaf," a bill of fare that never ceased to amaze and sadden my mother, who occasionally had lunch there with a friend of my grandmother's. So I got the idea that Mrs. Meade was some sort of invalid and I thought it was cruelly unfair that everybody in her family willy-nilly had to follow her diet. But after a while I realized that Virgil was only telling lies because he went on to say that the reason they only had doughnuts was that his mother had bats in the belfry and spent all her time, when she should have been cooking for her growing children, collecting cold cream jars in the alleys and on the dump. She caught the bats in her belfry in the cold cream jars, screwed the lids down tight and sent them by post to her nutty twin sister in Boise who was named Aunt Dandelion.

Aunt Dandelion! Did he really think I was dumb enough to believe a name like that?

This is what I mean about Virgil being crazy. One time he told me that he had been kidnaped by a runaway convict from Canon City named Ben the Red Beard. The desperado, who had murdered hundreds and permanently crippled many more with his six-shooter, handcuffed Virgil and took him up to a shack in the mountains and kept him there for three days. On the third night, after the man was asleep, Virgil managed to crawl over to the grocery supplies and he ate three big onions; then he crawled back to the cot where Ben the Red Beard was snoring away and breathed into his face until the kidnaper, undone by the fumes, took off the handcuffs and Virgil was free. He had walked all the way home in the dark, a distance of twenty-two miles, and it was seventeen below zero. When I asked him why his family hadn't sent out a posse for him, he said: "I go away for three or four days at a time by myself without telling them and they don't mind—I mean, if they did mind, I'd tell them where to get off. I go deer hunting, you see. Last year, I got an eight-point buck up by the glacier but I gave it away to some bootleggers I know. And now and then I hop a rattler and go down to Denver and hang around Larimer Street playing pool for two or three days."

Virgil left long before anyone came home, but there were traces of him everywhere. When he had stood on his head he had left two precise footprints on the white wall; his voracity had done away with most of the bread and all of the peanut butter; Reddie was still grieving and Mother, thinking he was sick, wanted to call the vet. Naturally I couldn't take the blame for all these things and had to let the cat out of the bag. When I told Mother why Reddie was so woebegone, she was at first too shocked to speak and then she said: "Emily, no good will ever come of this friendship, you mark my words." Would that I had! I tried to make up with Reddie but Jack snarled, "You stay away from him," and Stella, weeping, implored Mother to send me away, anywhere, so that she would never again have to lay eyes on a dastardly tormentor of man's best friend.

I was chastened, but I had no intention of giving up Virgil

and thereafter we had our sandwiches at his house. They were usually made of peanut butter, mayonnaise and piccalilli—I never saw a single doughnut in his house and the smells in his mother's kitchen were perfectly delicious. I had been right about one thing: though my family might deplore my new alliance, the other kids looked on it with envy because Virgil and I were always whispering and passing notes in school and we refused to play or even talk with anyone else. Dicky Scott one day offered me an arrowhead and I haughtily refused—I might have accepted it but I happened to know, because Dicky himself had one time unwisely told me, that it was spurious.

Virgil and I were together every afternoon except on ballet day. Sometimes we coasted and sometimes we made lists (of kinds of automobiles, of three-letter words, of the movies we had seen), but usually we just sat in his father's den and talked. I loved this dark and crowded room that smelled of cigars and furniture polish, and I wished that my own father had a room of his own. The walls were hung with all sorts of documents in frames, diplomas, certificates of membership in dental and social and religious societies; there was a serape with a bird and a snake on it; there was a tomahawk, a collection of minerals, an Indian headdress that Virgil said had once belonged to King Philip. On the roll-top desk, whose pigeonholes were so stuffed that nothing could ever be inserted in any of them, there was an enormous typewriter that had eight banks, three for the upper-case letters, three for the lower and two for the characters. When we used it, as we often did (wrote our names, wrote "Down with Miss Holderness"), it sounded like a small tractor and its bell was like one on a trolley car. Here, seated in leather armchairs, we were continually eyed by Virgil's dog, a His Master's Voice dog, who lay on a deerskin rug. We discussed our many projects. For one thing, we planned to make a trip in the summer with a wagon and horses up to a mine where Virgil knew that a lot of pieces of eight were buried; this involved making lists of what we would take and we wrote out a long order to Montgomery Ward—Virgil said the money would turn up somehow. Then there was the minstrel show we were going to put on and we had to rehearse our acts.

More immediately, though, what we talked about was a plan we had to draw up a petition against geography homework,

which was really ruining our lives and the lives of everybody
else in the sixth grade. At least three thousand years ago Miss
Holderness had gone around the world with some other old
maids and she never stopped bragging about rice paddies and
rickshas and the Yangtze and Big Ben. She was forever passing
around pale brown picture post cards that showed camels,
Norwegian fisheries and the Victoria and Albert Museum; she
showed us a little bottle with water from the Jordan and an
ordinary pebble she had picked up in the neighborhood of
the Taj Mahal. Every blessed night of the world we had to
get something by heart—the chief rivers of Asia, the capitals
of the Isles of Greece, European mountain ranges, famous
monuments in Rome—and the next day she would either give
us a paper test or would single out some poor kid to recite, and
it seemed to Virgil and me that the poor kid was always one
of us. We had to make relief maps with salt and flour and each
Friday afternoon during the last period, when we were all wild
with fidgets, she made us draw a map of the United States from
memory; to this day I don't know whether Delaware is on the
left-hand side of Maryland or the right, and I can never find
room for Vermont. Talk about a one-track mind.

One Friday afternoon she told us that by Monday we would
have to know all the counties of England, and Virgil and I
decided that this was the limit and the time had come for us to
act. I had intended to depart from custom that afternoon and
go straight home, because that morning at Assembly I had won
a school letter for collateral reading and I wanted to sew it on
the sleeve of my middy right away, but Virgil said: "Pardon me
for living, girl, haven't you got any class spirit? Do you know
that this geography junk may keep us in the sixth grade for
eighty-nine years?" He said we had no time to lose, that everybody was now so mad at Holderness (hadn't I heard the whole
room groan?) that we'd have no trouble getting signatures for
our petition. We must draw it up this afternoon and then spend
tomorrow going from door to door getting people to sign. "In
ink," said Virgil. "This has gotta be official with no ifs and buts
about it." And so, ever his slave, I went along home with him.

I want to say something about that afternoon that isn't
related to the Mutiny of the Sixth Grade of Carlyle Hill but

will show you the kind of looniness Virgil was capable of. His
mother wasn't home that day so Virgil made the sandwiches.
He couldn't find the peanut butter but he said for me not to
look and he would make a surprise. I'll say he made a surprise.
He made those sandwiches of Campbell's vegetable soup and
I'm not kidding. I was eating this stuff and I couldn't tell for
the life of me what it was; it didn't taste bad but it *felt* funny, so
I surreptitiously turned my back and lifted up the top slice of
bread and there I saw a lima bean. And then I saw the empty
can on the drainboard.

After the soup sandwiches and after one game of Shasta Sam,
we got down to work in the den. Among Dr. Meade's framed
testimonials there was a bounty land grant awarded to Virgil's
Great-Uncle Harry, who had fought at Murfreesboro. It was
signed by Abraham Lincoln, and Virgil, taking it down and
handing it to me, said it was worth several million dollars. (If
all the things in the Meades' house had had the value Virgil
assigned to them, Dr. Meade could have retired and bought
the Teapot Dome.) We would use it, said Virgil, as the model
for our petition because it had a high and mighty tone and
high and mighty was what we were going to be from now on.
Virgil typed while I dictated, paraphrasing the land grant. It
was uphill work because every key stuck and the *s* wouldn't
budge at all so that had to be filled in later with ink. But when
we were finished we were pleased with the results, although
there were mistakes abounding. The petition (more properly,
the declaration) read:

HTE SIXTH GRADEO%F CRaLYLE HILL GRADE SCHOOL
OF ADAMS
TO?ALLT
TO ALL TI WHOM THESE PRESENTS SHALL COME ¼
GREETING WHEREAS, in persuance of the art of Ggeography
Ha Enemys, approved March 2, 1926, entitled aN Act to Stop Ge-
ography Homewoork, the undersigned people will not do any more
Geograph HomeWork because it is not fair to give t so much of it.

We left a space for the signatures and then:

NOW NOW YE, that there is ther3fore granted by the Surveyor
Genersl of this class unto the said undersigned the privelege tto have

and to hold, of NO MORE Geography HOMEWORK AND TO
their heirs the privelege above described with the apuurtenances
thereto.
WHEREOF I,   , have caused these letters to be
made patent and affixed my signature thereto.

Abraham Lincoln's name was after the "WHEREOF I" and we
debated what to write there. We thought it would look wrong
to say "WHEREOF WE" and sign both our names and at last
Virgil gallantly said that my name should be there because I
now had a school letter and this gave me a status he didn't have.
He said I should be the one, too, to hand it to Miss Holderness
and he suggested that on Monday morning I carry Mother's
Civil War saber to school, not to intimidate Miss Holderness
but to carry out the motif of the Civil War. He rather regretfully
rejected King Philip's headdress as an anachronism.

He said: "Boy, oh, boy, can I see old Prune Face when you
march into the room with the sword and say, 'Madam, allow me
to present these presents,' and you hand her this!"

A flicker of trepidation entered my infatuated mind and I
said: "What if she sends me to Mr. Colby and I get expelled?"

"She'd have to send the whole class—everybody's name will
be there. Pardon me for living, girl, you're not by any chance
getting cold feet? Because if you are—well, you know how I feel
about cowards. I wouldn't be seen at a dogfight with a coward."

I blushed and hastily said that of course I wasn't getting cold
feet, what was there to get cold feet about—as he had said, if
anybody had to go to Mr. Colby, we'd all have to go. Anyhow,
Holderness wouldn't have any right to punish us since we were
protected by freedom of speech. Reassured that I was stouthearted, Virgil smiled his crooked smile and began to tinker
with the petition, putting in the absent *s*'s and filling in the
o's. When he had finished he handed me the scratchy pen and
said: "Here, put your John Hancock here on the dotted line."
When I had signed—the pen went through the paper a couple
of times and a big blob of ink floated like a rain cloud over my
surname—I was both scared and proud and had a stomach
sensation that was half-pleasant and half-terrible. I was by no
means sure that freedom of speech would cover our action;
I was by no means sure that a petition of this sort was not

against the law, and to distract my thoughts from the possible
consequences of our daring I took my red felt C out of my book
bag and held it up to my sleeve.

Virgil said: "Listen, Emily, you know what? Why don't you
sew it on someplace else? Someplace different? So you'll be
different from the common herd?"

"Like on my back?" I asked. "You mean like an athlete?"

"No, I was thinking of like on your sock."

"My *sock*!" I yelled. "Have you gone cuckoo?" But I rather
liked the idea and I placed the letter experimentally on the
outside of my right leg about in the middle of my shank. The
bright red looked very striking against my navy blue knee-length
sock, sort of like a cattle brand.

"Higher," said Virgil critically. "Yeah, right there. Hey, that's
the pig's wings."

"Well, I don't know . . ." I began doubtfully, for on re-
consideration it seemed to me that the letter would be more
conspicuous on my sleeve. But Virgil said, "I double dare you,"
and that, of course, was that: I went home and blanket stitched
the scarlet letter on my sock. That evening when I went into
the dining room and my family saw what I had done, they all
began to fuss at me. My mother, who was active in the P.T.A.,
said: "Why, Emily, do you think that's a nice thing to do when
Miss Holderness was so nice to give you that letter?"

"Miss Holderness was so nice! What did that dopey old goop
have to do with it?" I demanded. "I suppose she read all those
books and wrote all those reports. I'll have you know I *earned*
this letter. And anyhow the *school* gave it to me."

"Well, then, the school was nice," said Mother, missing the
point as usual. "Oh, Emily, why must you forever and a day be
so contrary?"

"Because she's a scurvy rapscallion black sheep," said Jack,
who had barely spoken to me since Virgil had upset Reddie.

"Baa, baa, black sheep, Emily's a black sheep," chanted
copycat Tess and began to bubble her milk.

"Shut up, you little wart hog," I said to her and she did,
terrified.

"Miss Holderness is not a dopey old goop," said Stella, who
was sanctimonious and stood up for authority of all kinds.

"She's a lady which is something you're never going to be in a thousand million years."

"Lady! Who wants to be a *lady*?" I said. "You make me sick." I made a sound of intense nausea and then I said: "Hasten, Jason, bring the basin. Ulp! Too late! Bring the mop!"

My father put down his napkin and faced me with his chin outthrust. "Now you listen to me, Emily Vanderpool. I've had just about enough of your shenanigans. I will not have bad language at my supper table and I will not have wrangling, do you hear me? I'm a hard-working man and when I come home at night, I'm tired and I want peace and quiet instead of this eternal confounded trouble you're always stirring up."

The unfairness of his attack brought tears to my eyes. Had anyone in the history of the world ever been so lamentably misunderstood? My voice was quivery as I said: "I didn't start it. Everybody started picking on *me* about my own personal property, damn it to hell!"

"What did I say about bad language?" he shouted, rising menacingly from his chair.

The devil at that moment made a conquest of my tongue and, blue in the face with fury, my eyes screwed shut, my fists clenched, I delivered a malediction in the roughest billingsgate imaginable, vilifying everyone at the table, all the teachers at Carlyle Hill, my uncles and aunts and cousins, my father's best friend, Judge Bay. The reaction was the same as it always was to one of my tantrums: appalled, fascinated, dead silence. When I was finished Jack, awed, said: "Yippy-ki-yi! That was a humdinger of a one!" I threw my glass of water in his face and stamped out of the room.

That was the last that was said at home about my school letter and when Stella came into the room we shared, she was at pains not to cross the chalk line I had drawn down the middle of the floor and not to speak to me: if she had uttered one word, on any subject whatsoever, I would have beaten the hide off her.

The next day a blizzard somewhat hampered Virgil and me in our house-to-house canvass. Most people were at home because the wind made it uncomfortable coasting weather, and though this meant that they were easy to find (and so bored that they were delighted to see us), it also meant that there were a lot of nosy mothers around, asking questions and trying to distract us from our mission by inviting us to make popcorn or taffy. We had very little respect for the intelligence of these snoops, but we didn't want to run the risk of having some one of them call up Miss Holderness and spill the beans, and so we had to dally in a number of houses and pretend we had just come to pay a social call. We got stuck in Valerie Bemis' house for nearly an hour while her mother showed us views of Yellowstone and the Grand Canyon through a stereopticon.

To our considerable surprise and disappointment, we found that several of our classmates were partisans of Miss Holderness' (Estelle Powell, for instance, said she loved our teacher because she smelled so wonderful) and we found, furthermore, that the phobia for geography homework was not, after all, universal. Indeed, six or seven stick-in-the-muds said they liked it better than anything else and they refused to sign the petition. Ruby Miller admitted that she agreed with us, but she had already learned the English counties and didn't want them to go to waste, so she too refused to sign. This schism disturbed us, but all the same, at the end of the day, we had a majority of seventeen names. It was dark by the time we left the last house and the street lights had come on. Under a light beside a mail-box we paused in the whirling snow and Virgil solemnly put the petition in a long envelope, solemnly handed it to me and solemnly said: "Pardon me for living, girl, but this will probably get us into the Hall of Fame. Good luck." And with this he started off in the direction of his house, his dramatic shadow long and lean beside him.

When the sixth grade got into line on Monday morning there was an undercurrent of great excitement and everybody was looking at me: there were gasps from those who caught sight of the honor badge on my leg, there were uneasy whispers about my Civil War saber, which was imperfectly hidden under my coat. Someone murmured in my ear, "Scratch out my name, Emily, please?" and someone else said: "Looky, if you're going to kill her, I don't want to have anything to do with it." I glared fiercely but I didn't feel fierce, I felt foolish and scared because Virgil Meade was nowhere to be seen.

The soft exclamations of incredulity and fear continued as we marched into the building and hung up our wraps, and even after we had said, "Good morning, Miss Holderness," and had sat down there was still a faint buzzing and thrumming like noises in the grass on a summer day.

"Quiet, please!" said Miss Holderness and clapped her hands smartly. "What is the meaning of this deafening pandemonium?"

There was immediate silence and then Johnny Thatcher, who had not signed the petition, held up his hand and giggled and said: "Emily has something to show you, teacher."

"I see Emily's sword," said Miss Holderness. I had tried to put it under my desk but it stuck out into the aisles on each side. "And I think we will simply ignore it. We do not know why she brought it to school and we do not care to know."

Johnny Thatcher said: "No, I don't mean that. She's got something else to show you. Something about geography homework."

"Very well, Emily," said the teacher, snapping her fingers and snapping her eyes. "Show me what it is. We cannot spend the entire day on the subject of Emily Vanderpool's tricks to attract attention to herself. Come along, Emily, quickly, quickly!"

"I haven't got anything," I stammered.

"You have too," said Johnny.

Everyone began to babble at once and Miss Holderness angrily rapped her desk with her ruler. "I have a good mind to punish everyone in this class," she said. "Emily, I want you to show me whatever this is at once."

Reluctant, furious, I stumbled up to the desk and put the petition down in front of her. She gave me a black look and then she opened the envelope; as she read, moving her lips, her color rose until she looked like an apple.

"So!" she cried. "So Miss Emily Vanderpool is now known as 'the surveyor-general of this class.' I was not aware that elections had been held and she had been voted into office."

Everyone tittered.

"I . . ." I began, but Miss Holderness held up her hand for silence.

"Now let me see," she said and began checking the names on the petition against those in the class book. There was a pause and every heart beat wildly. Then she said, "Ruby, Estelle, Homer, Johnny, Marjorie and Virgil—these are the children who are still loyal to Carlyle Hill Grade School and have not kowtowed to this self-styled surveyor-general. Children, I congratulate you."

"Virgil!" I cried. "But Virgil . . ." Then, because I did not want to be a tattletale, even against that foxy fourflusher, I held my peace.

"What about Virgil?" asked Miss Holderness. "I am sorry that Virgil is absent today, for I would like him to know how deeply I appreciate his refusing to affix his signature to this outrageous scrap of paper. Shame on you, Emily Vanderpool, shame on you!"

She looked me up and down with revulsion as if I were a reptile or a skunk and suddenly she saw the school letter on my sock. She gaped, speechless, and then said: "Ruby, I shall leave you in charge of the class. Emily and I have some business to transact in Mr. Colby's office."

That was a long last mile I walked. I thought sadly and enviously of all the children behind the closed doors who would continue their lives of ease and respectability while I was working on a mason gang at the reform school. All my sensations were intense: the smell of cedar shavings was stronger than ever and the smell of wet Mackinaws and overshoes (overshoes are made of gutta-percha, I thought sorrowfully, homesick for the principal exports of the Malay Archipelago), and the sounds of teachers' voices and the thud of feet and balls in the gym below and the piping squeals from the kindergarten room were like a loud song of farewell to me. Miss Holderness' hand, grasping my arm, was a cruel metal claw.

Mr. Colby was an asthmatic old man with a purple-veined nose and a sorrel toupee. He had very short legs but he had strong, broad shoulders and sitting behind his magisterial desk he looked like a giant. His two bluebell blue eyes were on quite different levels, giving him a quizzical and half-amused look as if he were trying to figure out a joke he didn't entirely understand. He was playing with a sharp letter opener when we came into his office, flicking the point with his index finger as he made half-revolutions in his swivel chair. He invited Miss Holderness to sit down and with the letter opener indicated the place where I was to stand, directly in front of his desk.

Several times in the course of my teacher's indignant recital of my felonies he swiveled himself completely around so that his back was to us and he coughed and wheezed—it sounded like strangled laughter. When he leaned over his desk to look at my shameful leg he had such a seizure that he had to bury his face in his handkerchief, and when he read the petition I thought he was going to explode. After the case against me had been stated, Mr. Colby told Miss Holderness to go back to her class and said that he would deal with me himself.

"Now, Emily," he said when she was gone, "there is no doubt about the gravity of your misdemeanors . . . incidentally, why did you bring a sword to school?"

"Well, it's a Civil War one and Vir . . . I mean it's a Civil War one and since the petition was a Civil War thing . . ."

"A Civil War thing? What sort of thing?"

"Just a thing. I don't know what you call it. But where my name is is really Abraham Lincoln's name."

He wheeled his chair around again and he wheezed for quite some time. "The name of Emily Vanderpool has been substituted for that of Honest Abe," he said at length. "The case grows stranger. I confess to a certain amount of confusion. I can't seem to see the tie-in with the sword, the petition and your putting your school letter on your stocking, a gesture tantamount, as Miss Holderness so aptly put it, to dragging the Star-Spangled Banner in the dirt. Can you help me out?"

Mr. Colby's voice, though firm, was kind and his funny eyes were sweet and though my legs were buckling and my heart thundered I longed to tell him the whole truth. But naturally I could not without involving Virgil and I said only, as mad murderers often do: "I don't know why I did it."

He picked up the petition again and this time I thought he was really going to fly apart. He threw back his head so far I thought his toupee would surely fall off and he coughed and wheezed and gurgled fearsomely. "You'll be the death of me!" he howled and I thought I really would be. He groped, blinded with tears, for a bottle of pills and a carafe of water, and when he had dosed himself and straightened his vest and put on a pair of severe spectacles he gave me a sober lecture on the value of geography and the sin of insubordination, the inadvisability of carrying arms, the folly of arrogating power, the extreme impropriety of wearing an honor badge on the leg. Finally he told me to go back to my room and apologize to Miss Holderness and then to go home for the rest of the day and explain to my mother exactly why I was in disgrace. When I had closed the door behind me I heard him having another attack and I knew that it would be the gallows for me if he died.

For the next two weeks I was in double dishonor. Miss Holderness made me stay after school every day and write lists of rivers and cities and principal exports. I had to go home immediately thereafter and stay in my room with the door closed until suppertime. Jack and Stella did not speak one word to me. During those weeks I was not allowed to wear my letter even in its proper place. The sixth grade got more geography homework than ever and consequently I was sent to Coventry by all my classmates. I crept around like a sick dog and wished I were dead.

At first the namby-pamby boobs in my grade took Virgil's side against me even though they knew good and well that I could have got him in Dutch too if I had snitched. They all knew, of course, that he had been just as responsible for the petition as I, but they did not know that he had put me up to sewing the C on my sock and it was this act of insolence to dear old Carlyle Hill that they regarded as my cardinal crime. For the two weeks of my quarantine Virgil enjoyed an immense, ill-gotten popularity, and I heard, with mixed feelings, that he was practically engaged to Ruby Miller. I did not deign to recognize his existence.

And then, on the very day I was first allowed to wear my letter, silly Virgil tipped his hand. Ruby Miller told me during lunch hour. At morning recess she and he had been swapping bird cards out of Arm and Hammer Baking Soda boxes as I passed by. Ruby saw that I was wearing my letter again and asked Virgil why he thought I had done that awful thing. Ruby said, "Who would *think* of doing a thing like that?" and Virgil had said: "I'll tell you somebody who wouldn't and that's Vanderloop-the-loop—she's too dumb. *I* told her to sew it on her leg."

The news spread rapidly, whispered during Palmer Method, written on notes in Current Events, and by the end of the after-noon session I was in and Virgil was out. People came up to me singly and in groups to congratulate me on my nobility; some of them shook my hand. I accepted their acclaim with a wan and martyred smile, thanked them for their many invitations to visit their houses but said that I had to go home because I was reading the Bible.

I remained aloof only that one day and the next day plunged into a social whirl. Virgil, as it was fitting, was totally ostracized. In time I took pity on him; indeed, some months later, we again became boon companions, but I saw to it that he never hoodwinked me again: I ruled him with an iron glove and after he had made one slip he never made another.

The slip was this. We were walking home one day in the spring and he picked a leaf off a lilac bush. He said to me: "If you can divide this exactly in half, I'll give you a quarter." What could be easier than dividing a lilac leaf? The midrib is clear and the flesh is crisp, and I accomplished the feat in a second. "O.K., where's my quarter?" I said and Virgil, tearing one of the halves of the leaf in two, handed me a piece. "Here's your quarter," he said and doubled up with laughter. I simply looked at him and then I turned and walked away. He came running after me, begging for mercy, reminding me of all the good times we'd had together. I marched on for two blocks, ignoring him, but then, at a vacant lot, I stopped, climbed up on top of a boulder and told him to kneel on the ground. Then, like Moses on Mount Sinai, I laid down the law, and ever after that Virgil Meade was the most tractable boon companion I had.

The Ordeal of Conrad Pardee

FIVE days a week until nightfall, for eleven months of the year, Conrad Pardee was the Pardee of Hyde, Pardee, Evans, Parsons and Chapin, a stately brokerage in Wall Street that had numbered a Pardee among its partners for a hundred years. The rest of the time he occupied a misty, Parnassian niche in society in which, according to his own profession, he "cultivated the minor arts." A stranger, talking to him for the first time, would not have guessed that he dwelt by day among the fierce and worldly bulls and bears (and shrewd investing women) in the febrile confusion of the Exchange, but would have thought that he kept the company of serener souls in cool athenaeums and ateliers. It must not be thought that his refusal to admit the Street into the drawing room derived from any disdain of high finance; on the contrary, like his father and his grandfather before him, he was fascinated by the convolutions and permutations of economies that furthered or hindered the careers of Canadian minerals or Australian wool, and the stock market was at times to him the greatest show on earth. He was perspicacious and intuitive and bold, and among his colleagues he was honored as a sage and envied as a wizard.

But the drama of money is esoteric and its language is occult, and Conrad was disinclined to instruct greenhorns at a dinner table, especially since the greenhorns who applied for instruction were in fact applying for a tip on something good, just as the uncouth sometimes seek the counsel of a physician whom they have only just met at a crowded cocktail party. One year, Conrad went abroad to attend a meeting of the World Bank in Istanbul, but, from his conversation on his return, people were led to believe that he had really made the trip for the purpose of photographing Luxor by moonlight and Barbary casbahs in the sun and pausing in London to have the Byzantine coins he had picked up in Turkey appraised at Spink's.

Other brokers did not sit at his table or in his box at the opera; his guests were doctors, scholars, writers, painters, women of beauty or women of influence, prelates of a sophisticated cast of mind.

Conrad's minor arts were social rather than creative. He was not eccentric and he was not effete and he did not play a recorder, make bonsai, or write *pensées*. What he directed his attention to was the appropriate gesture: the *mot juste*, the well-timed and well-turned compliment, the delightful surprise to someone jaded (a jar of fresh caviar, a basket of snow peas), the opportune telephone call to someone in despair. He lived entirely for his friends, and his wife, when she divorced him after a brief marriage, lamented that there had been no room for a planet in the vast galaxy of Conrad's protégés and pals. He took children, just recovered from the mumps, to tea at Rumpelmayer's and enslaved them for life with riddles and eclairs; he was titular uncle to hundreds. He made old ladies' sleepy hearts come wide awake when he took them driving in the country to see the leaves in autumn and the dogwood in the spring. He remembered anniversaries unfailingly and sent to the celebrants their favorite flowers or kinds of oddments or drink, and with the offering a perfect note. He was famous for his letters of condolence on occasions of death and divorce, and for those of congratulations when engagements were announced and when babies got born. He was so considerate and well-mannered, so perpetually calm and genial, so dependably *there* when he was needed that his friend, Doctor Hardesty, a psychoanalyst, was forever puzzled that he had not made use of these humane gifts but had chosen to concern himself with the abstractions of money. He even looked like the benevolent head of a family with his affable Edwardian mustache and his sober clothes—he wore a vest of the same material as his suit, he wore a grandfatherly watch chain, a Chesterfield, a Homburg hat. He was a large and well-constructed man, and he emanated good health and an inviolable *amour-propre*. He was so snugly at home with his condition that simply to look at him was to experience comfort.

Conrad Pardee had no need to be a snob, since fortune had smiled affectionately on him, and he knew whomever he wanted to know. But even in the armor of this gentil, parfit Knyght, there was a chink: He did have one unrealized ambition that nagged and chagrined him, and this was to endear himself to Mrs. James Grant Grace, a daunting woman who ruled society in the New Hampshire community where he owned a house and where he spent his month-long summer holiday. High Hill, in the mountains near Dublin, was far from smart. Its large, dowdy wooden villas, which seemed not so much to have been built as to have been accumulated, had been used by generations of Bostonians in their annual retreat from the heat of Back Bay. They were beset by sprawling, cordial porches that looked on Mount Monadnock and the seas of hills that led to it; they were full of wicker rocking chairs and stuffed screech owls, with albums of scenic postal cards, and cases of butterflies, and tennis rackets, and fishing gear, and hanging lamps with fringe.

The largest of the houses and the one on the highest point of land, directly above Conrad's, which was in a bosky dale, belonged to the gubernatorial Mrs. Grace, blue-stockinged, blue-blooded and somewhat blue-nosed, who had been coming here for nearly all of her seventy years. She was an authority on the lore and the legends of the region; she knew the histories and the pedigrees of every family, native and ultramontane, for miles around; she knew, as well, the trees and the rocks, the birds, the mosses, the fish and the flowers. She had been a horsewoman in her day and she knew the trails by heart; she still played golf and she daily walked two miles and a half from her lofty nest to the post office in the village, where she distributed her greetings and her trade in a grand manner, without favoritism. Her father, the historian Stearns, and her husband, the mathematician, had been prominent members of the Cantabrigian intelligentsia that had coruscated in High Hill and Dublin at the turn of the century. She had met and conversed with Mark Twain when he had summered there, and her father and Winston Churchill had been close friends. Mrs. Grace herself had written a novel, the style of which had been favorably compared to George Eliot's by two or three reviewers, and she and her husband, until his death, had annually played a recital of piano duets in Mrs. Gardner's museum. One of her sons was a teacher of Greek, the other a Sinologue. Her grandchildren, who spent the summer with her, were a severe, accomplished group whose tennis was quite as good as their excellent algebra. The other visitors who came to sleep in her creaking and furbelowed chalet, whose rotting piazzas perilously overhung chasms, were usually illustrious, and a number of them had won the Nobel prize.

One was not really "in" until one had received Mrs. Grace's imprimatur, and Conrad, though he had prayed and connived for five years, could not persuade her to affix her official seal to his brow, which furrowed every time he thought of her. He had not, of course, been denied membership in the Country Club, nor had the other colonists failed to take him up, and he was ashamed of himself for the disproportionate passion of his longing to be asked to her house. He was sure he would not like her—she was craggy and cold like an Alp—and that his communication with her would be imperfect; but nonetheless, he terribly wanted to overcome her archaic, intransigent Bostonian mistrust of people from New York; it would be enough if she gave him no more than a cup of tea and shook his hand as he took his leave. Johnny-come-latelies from Cincinnati and Colorado Springs were bidden to her Thursday teas; transient Texans had dined with her; she played golf with a desiccated politician from Bridgeport. But Conrad had not once walked up her garden path. Mrs. Grace was not uncivil and she did not altogether snub him, but whenever they met in other people's houses and gardens or in the village or on the links, she made him feel like a pushing parvenu, and a silly one at that.

Their first meeting had been unlucky. She had asked him what he did, and he had replied with the gambit that had always served him so well, "I cultivate the minor arts," and knew, the moment the words were out of his mouth, that they had been a mistake. In a dreadful silence this heavily hatted eagle pulled off her white silk gloves inside out, as if preparing for combat, and as she did so, scrutinized Conrad's face and attire (his Abercrombie tweeds felt like something seen in Times Square) with a pair of electric-blue eyes that had never, he knew, been hoodwinked. Then, forthrightly and pedagogically, she cross-examined him, and when she learned that he neither practiced nor patronized any art to which had been assigned a muse, she said, "Young man, you don't mean *minor arts*. You mean *frivolities*." And her sharp tone belied her social smile. She was clearly no better pleased when he admitted, stammering, that he was a stock-broker, and her manner implied that she could not be expected to consort with a person in commerce and that, furthermore, commerce was a barbarism indigenous to New York: money, in Boston, was a different sort of thing. When, delving further, she discovered that he had studied as an undergraduate at Columbia, she could not have looked more pained if he had said he had taken a correspondence course or gone to a normal school in West Virginia. And when he told her that he had been at the Harvard Business School, she said icily and with very little circumlocution that this was not really a part of Harvard but was an unsightly excrescence which she earnestly hoped would one day be excised; his years of residence in Cambridge did not, in her eyes, count, and she had never heard any of the Beacon Hill or Back Bay names he optimistically dropped. He, whose ancestors had fought in the War of Independence, felt like an immigrant newly off a cattle boat, speaking pidgin English, reeking of delousing solution. And ever after that his mournful memory and her keen, disapproving eye so unnerved him that he, the most fastidious man alive, never failed to make some awful *gaffe* in her presence; she exercised over him a spiteful power that caused glasses to leap from his hand, spilling their contents, transformed his agreeable laugh into a high-pitched neigh, made him give voice to absurdities, commonplaces and anecdotes that did not come off. She seemed to think that he was a sort of latter-day Ward McAllister, threatening to sully the decorum of High Hill with tawdry splurges and rampageous romps, and she clung to her belief despite the evidence before her eyes that he was completely domesticated and lived as all the other residents did, golfing, swimming, briskly walking through the green and golden days.

Some of his friends in High Hill told him not to despair, that Mrs. Grace had only put him on probation and that in time she would come around and forgive him for the misfortune of his birthplace, but he doubted them and believed that she would go to her grave convinced that New York was a quagmire of savagery and humbug and that he was one of its most offensive deputies.

In his large, drafty house on Eightieth Street, Conrad entertained extensively and his parties were works of art. Never too large (rarely more than twelve sat down at the two round tables in his dull-gold and dark-red dining room) and never stiff (he required white ties only on even Mondays when he took his guests to the opera), these evenings nearly always marked an occasion; there would be a guest of honor, someone whose book had been published that day, or a visitor from abroad, or a delegate to the U.N. whose country was currently in the headlines. Or there would be no guest of honor but there would be a feast of doves which Conrad had shot in South Carolina or of venison he had brought down from High Hill. Whatever the nature of the ceremony, his guests shone and cohered because he, adroit impresario that he was, knew the sources of their illumination and the stimuli to which they responded with the most contagious enjoyment and the most articulate intelligence. Crows sang like larks for their supper in Conrad's house. Beautiful, bright and incorrigibly difficult Elsie Appleton, a designer of jewelry, who invariably quarreled in other houses, was sugar and spice and everything nice in his, and hostesses, forgetting her wretched past performances in her present behavior, impulsively invited her to their next parties, which she disrupted with unprovoked tantrums over fancied persecutions and with insults that left her victims pale. How Conrad managed her was Conrad's secret and his alone. In other houses Lucia Mabon spoke French when there was no possible need to do so, but in Conrad's she used her mother tongue exclusively. With him they were like certain people who are at their very best when they are abroad.

One winter evening he was entertaining a small group of his closest friends (Harriet Gildersleeve's birthday coincided with her return from Las Vegas where she had divorced a grouchy pinchpenny) and conversation turned, as it often did in this house, to the lamentable passing of the glories of the world. Over their meringues the company regretted that shipboard travel was no longer romantic as it had been when they were young—the moon over the Atlantic had seemed, in recent years, to pale and diminish, tempests had been tamed by stabilizers, the morning bouillon was unseasoned and weak. They regretted that trains had lost their sad, grand voices and had been replaced by diesel honks; they regretted that waltzing was all but obsolete. They were especially sorry that the leisurely house parties of the past had been abandoned for the rushed and nerve-racking weekend visit, when one arrived rumpled by a swarming and gritty train or harassed by a clogged highway, paused only long enough to drink too much in the sun beside a swimming pool and to nap fitfully through a short night and then returned to the city, exhausted and dyspeptic. Mrs. Gildersleeve, recalling a sumptuous house party in Newport when she was seventeen, said, "There were fourteen of us and we stayed ten days and nobody squabbled. It was divine." The Mabons spoke then of rustic fortnights in the Adirondacks when groups convened in autumn in Jason Gould's ample lodge and shot wild geese and fished for bass and watched deer join the cows at the salt lick at dusk. Someone remembered an elegant gathering in Virginia in an elegant house during the elegant hunt, remembered the blessing of the hounds by an Episcopalian clergyman of rank, and the early-morning mint juleps drunk out of ancestral silver goblets and the breakfast of fried chicken and batter bread.

Pensive with nostalgia, they all grew quiet, and then Harriet Gildersleeve, still bewitched with her memories of moonlight sails in Narragansett Bay thirty years ago, said, "But why can't we do it again? What's to prevent us from having a slap-up house party now?"

"This is the age of anxiety," said Joe Sperry, a pessimistic literary critic who was barnacled with phobias. "Besides, these days it always rains. Because of the bombs. And we're too old."

"Oh, rubbish, Joe," said Mrs. Gildersleeve. "And what a thing to say on my birthday—you make me feel mildewed." She appealed to her host for consolation, and Conrad said, "You're sick, Sperry, sick, sick, and do stop looking at your champagne as if there were strontium in it," and then he rose and proposed a toast to Harriet, who would always be "bedewed with youth and never mildewed like Wet Blanket Sperry," and when he sat down, he observed that he himself would be fifty in August. "A nice, neat age, I think," he said, "though when I get there I may find a mare's nest and change my tune." Harriet Gildersleeve, who by now had acquired an exuberant fixed idea, cried, "The perfect excuse for a house party! A smashing jubilee for Conrad for being fifty! I agree—fifty is *very* chic."

"Hear, hear!" said Charley Mabon, a rosy and ebullient man who resembled many of the figures in the sporting prints he sold; and the others, except for Mrs. Sperry, who was as saturnine as her husband, echoed Charley's enthusiasm. No one had made plans for the summer, and August was the month they all took time out, and it seemed reasonable and cheerful that they refresh themselves together for part of the time. The logical *mise en scène* was Conrad's house in High Hill—the others, who were not as rich as he, made do with skimpy summer rentals on the Cape and Martha's Vineyard. Besides, although this was not stated in so many words, Conrad was the only one among them who could possibly manage so elaborate and novel and delicate an undertaking. If feuds began, Conrad would smooth ruffled feathers; if Elsie Appleton became a holy terror, Conrad would cope. Having set the stage, they went on now to plan the action, and they were as excited and loquacious as if they meant to make a long safari. They would address themselves to all the healthful sports, to riding and fishing and golf and tennis and exposing themselves to the nourishing sun; they could have endless evenings of bridge. Doctor Hardesty, by avocation a naturalist, intended to forget human travail by taking bird walks and botanical rambles. John Madigan, the poet, to whom Mrs. Gildersleeve was romantically attached, said they must climb Mount Monadnock and sleep on the summit under the stars—it was possible that he saw himself as Childe Harold in the Juras. Elsie Appleton wanted a picnic every day with old-fashioned hampers of nasturtium sandwiches and Liebfraumilch, and Harriet Gildersleeve said that on Conrad's birthday they must certainly have a masquerade ball, that *sine qua non* of the smart house parties of the past.

"There is a proper Boston lady autocrat up there who will deplore us," said Conrad. "It's hard enough for her to be at peace when there's only me from beyond the pale—an invasion of eight from New York will unseat her altogether," and, far away from Mrs. Grace's censuring eyes, he laughed to think of how she would receive the news of anything so outlandish as a costume ball. He went on to tell his friends about her and about his miserable gaucheries whenever they met, and the friends, hard put to believe that anyone could ever muddle him, resolved that by the end of their stay Mrs. Grace would be persuaded once and for all that High Hill did not belong solely to her. If they could not charm her, they would defeat her.

When Conrad began to make concrete plans for this communal holiday, he found the logistics of the maneuver densely intricate. His path, indeed, was strewn with so many hurdles that a lesser man might have abandoned the project in frustration, but Conrad was fearless, and the difficulties only made him the more ambitious to carry it off and provide for his friends the time of their lives.

First, there was the problem of the servants. His couple in High Hill, Mr. and Mrs. Link, who were accustomed to having no more than two or three in the house at a time and then only for a few days, could not be expected to take care of eight guests for two weeks, and he tried to recruit his cook and butler from Eightieth Street, but Marie, a country woman from Quebec, hated the country and had solemnly vowed when she left St. Jean that her feet would tread asphalt for the rest of her life, and Arthur had such bad hay fever that the very thought of goldenrod brought tears to his eyes. Conrad then called Mrs. Link and asked her to find some local help; their connection was bad and was frequently severed (this was the usual condition of the telephone up there), but it was intermittently sufficiently clear for Conrad to learn that Mrs. Link took a dim view of the neighborhood girls who, in her opinion, were no better than they should be; she told him a long and scandalous story, which he could not follow because of the tumult on the wire, about the recent elopement of a high-school girl with a married man in a stolen pickup truck.

However, a few days later, she rang back to say that she had found a strong and upright, if stupid, girl, one of the Petersons from Keene (she here digressed to distinguish between the Keene Petersons and the Marlboro Petersons) who would help her with the beds and the serving and that the girl's strong, stupid young man would help Mr. Link with the driving and the fireplaces and, she added ominously, "the plumbing breakdowns and whatever are bound to come." A volley of detonations, interspersed with thin, supernatural screams, obscured her final words, but Conrad thought she said that, according to the Farmer's Almanac, August was going to be the rainiest in thirty-five years. Mrs. Link loved detail and she loved disaster and she loved the telephone and, liking to marry her loves whenever she could, she called Conrad nearly every day, to requisition extra blankets and to recommend that he lay in a good supply of citronella, since she had never seen the like, for size and numbers, of this year's mosquitoes. She called once to report that a fox had decimated the chicken flock and that deer had made a shambles of the kitchen garden, that there would be no corn because of the crows and that the power mower was irreparably on the blink. Often Conrad heard not a word she said, but only got sounds of gnawing and cheeps as if mice and small birds were at play. His guests shared Mrs. Link's predilection, and it seemed to him that throughout June and July he was perpetually on the telephone, giving counsel on itineraries for those who were motoring, advising on clothes and gear. The Mabons had to be tactfully persuaded to leave their two unmanageable children at home, and Conrad was obliged to refuse houseroom to the Hardestys' testy Great Dane.

He sent out more than a hundred invitations to the masked ball on his birthday, and the response was gratifying—everyone who would be in High Hill on that day was enchanted to accept, and Jessie Rogers wrote, "What a breath of fresh air you are! Think of a *bal masqué* after all these years of the country-club dances and those dismal buffet suppers beforehand with always, *always coq au vin*." For the occasion he ordered favors for the ladies—pill boxes for their tranquilizers in the shape of a heart—and he and Mrs. Link conferred at length about the menu for the supper, which would not include *coq au vin*. He hired tables and dishes and accommodators from a catering service in Manchester; he arranged for an orchestra to be flown up from New York, he ordered ten cases of champagne. Through the greatest stroke of luck, the moon was to be full that night. Think of it—Harlequins and Columbines eating and festively drinking at tables set up on lawns and terraces in moonglow!

And at last, when New York was languishing in an abominable heat wave, the party headed north to cool breezes and bright skies, to the peaceable sounds of birds and of the wild stream that ran over stones behind Conrad's house, to the smell of resin and the poignant spectacle of birches bending and hummingbirds tilting at flowers in hanging baskets and eloquent sunsets over the evergreen hills.

In the beginning everything went well. In spite of the Farmer's Almanac, it did not rain; in spite of Mrs. Link's predictions, the plumbing remained intact. The Peterson girl was deft and her young man was willing. No one argued over bridge scores and no tempers were lost at croquet. Even the telephone was on its best behavior, and the Mabons had no trouble hearing encouraging reports about their children from the babysitter, and the same clarity prevailed when the Hardestys called the medical student who was sitting with their dog.

To be sure, there were embarrassments and accidents, but none was serious. In the evenings, when they sat in the living room playing bridge and backgammon, the ladies wore hats and kept tennis rackets near at hand because a bat lived in the rafters and often made daring test flights, coming close to coiffures. Jane Hardesty was thrown by a horse, but she fell on soft ground where only a small patch of poison ivy grew. John Madigan, an ophidiophobe, encountered a nest of garter snakes when he was retrieving a golf ball, and he tended to remain indoors thereafter, writing in dimeter.

These traumatic experiences were outweighed by the sunny ones, and Conrad, as the gilded days went by, knew that in all his successful life he had never been so successful as this. The summer people took his guests to their hearts—the younger ones invited them to Bloody Mary parties after golf and the older ones asked them to tea.

And one day, at Captain Codman's garden party, they were presented to Mrs. Grace. Mrs. Grace, as befitted her station, was seated centrally on the central lawn in a circle of chairs that surrounded the sundial. She wore a hat that looked like a taxidermal mounting of a whole Wyandotte, and as Conrad and his party came through the pergola, she lifted a lorgnette, gazed briefly, and resumed her conversation with an old man and three ugly young girls. Elsie Appleton giggled and gasped, "It isn't true! Nobody's looked like that for a hundred years." Conrad begged her to hush, and he begged the gods to treat him kindly. Captain Codman, a bustling and flirtatious man had, quite unlike his second cousin Mrs. Grace, an enraptured infatuation with New York, and he plied the newcomers with drink and plied them with questions about nightclubs and Greenwich Village and he praised the ladies' clothes. The party was large and it was some time before any of Conrad's guests met Mrs. Grace; Conrad himself remained far from her court and got a little drunk.

With amazement and relief, he saw that one by one, as they were introduced, Mrs. Grace accepted them all. With John

Madigan, she talked modern poetry, of which she knew and disliked a great deal; she asked Jack Hardesty to elucidate Freud and, learning that he was fond of botanizing, she offered to go walking with him and identify the flowers that stumped him; she discovered that Lucia Mabon shared her Gallophilia, and they talked of France in French for a quarter of an hour. As Conrad was debating whether to go and speak to her himself, hoping for a reprieve through the accomplishments of his protégés, he saw her, still talking, turn away from Lucia and with her lorgnette make a survey of the guests who chatted and drank beside the oleanders and underneath the willow trees. Her eye fell at last on Conrad and, with her lavender sunshade furled into a slender and commanding wand, she motioned toward him and called out, "There he is now!" This was all she said, and he did not know whether she was summoning him or whether she had been derogating him to Lucia and the statement might be expanded into, "There he is now, the common little man." He smiled—his smile felt fatuous—and quivered and took a provisional step forward and nearly fell headlong into Captain Codman's rock garden that grew in a brusque ravine. Mrs. Grace, not returning his smile, called again as if to a dog that could not put two and two together, "Come, Mr. Pardee, come along!"

His head was bare, but he endeavored to lift a hat as he bowed too low; the sun was warm, but his teeth were chattering.

Mrs. Grace indicated a place for Conrad to sit down. He took it gingerly, salivating, hot. "I believe I have you to thank for a stimulating afternoon," she said. "I like new people when they're likable. I find your poet in the tradition. I think I sense a soul in him. And your psychologist is a brainy fellow. I have a weakness for brains, Mr. Pardee." This she said giving Conrad a hard look as if his own want of brains were the reprehensible concomitant of poor character. "And *this* girl . . ." she turned to Lucia with the smile of a queen conferring an honor of the realm. "We have had a provocative meander through our remembrances of things French."

"How lovely! How lovely!" cried Conrad as if he were rooting for a horse.

"Mrs. Mabon has been telling me that you are having a gala to celebrate your fiftieth birthday," continued Mrs. Grace.

"I would have said you were much younger." (This was not intended as a compliment.)

"Yes, it could be called a sort of gala, I suppose," said Conrad, with the feeling that she really meant "bacchanal." "I daresay it's conceited of me to do such a thing on my own birthday. Rather like having one's own portrait in one's drawing room. Do you think so?"

"You have never been to my house in Mt. Vernon Street," said Mrs. Grace, stating an irrefutable fact. "So you have never seen Harvey Beaver's portrait of me. Harvey Beaver was a brilliant comet who streaked through Singer Sargent's orbit. He died young, I regret to say. My portrait was numbered among his masterpieces. Naturally it hangs in my drawing room."

"Naturally," mourned Conrad.

"You have invited the whole countryside to your party," she told him, "on a night when I meant to have some people in to meet Lovell Ramsgate, who will be staying with me. Lovell Ramsgate has just come back from Africa and will be informative about Zanzibar."

"Oh, I *am* sorry, Mrs. Grace," said Conrad. "If I had known—"

"You could not have known. I didn't know myself. Lovell only rang me up today, but of course I couldn't put him off. It is a rare treat for High Hill to get a visitor of Lovell Ramsgate's stature."

Conrad, who had never heard of Lovell Ramsgate, temporized. "Have you ever been to Beirut? An extraordinary place—turbulent . . . yet not—"

Mrs. Grace interrupted. "Lovell Ramsgate can spare us only two evenings before he goes on to Washington to make his report. The first evening, of course, he will want to be quiet since he will be travel-worn. And on the second evening everyone will be dancing at your house. What are we going to do, Mr. Pardee?"

He knew that if he capitulated, postponed, or cancelled his party, Mrs. Grace out of common decency (that is, if there were a scrap of it in the selfish old beast) would be obliged to show her gratitude by inviting him at least to one of her weekly teas. But his heart was set on his masquerade ball, and he did not intend to yield.

In the silence that fell, Conrad gazed sheepishly at the ground and with uncertain eyes—he was really quite drunk as well as baffled and exasperated—he saw a four-leaf clover. As he bent to pick it, Mrs. Grace said, "Those things are common on Jim Codman's lawn. I'd not advise you to pin your hopes on it."

Tyrant, thought Conrad, bitch. Mrs. Grace, tireless, pursued. "I suppose we must come to some sort of compromise. I suppose that in some sort of slipshod way we must join forces, though how we can combine a colloquium with a cotillion I can't quite see."

"Your guests could come on to me after they have heard about Zanzibar," said Conrad, losing ground.

"It would be odd if they came to meet Lovell Ramsgate in fancy dress," said Mrs. Grace. "That means that they would have to go home and change before they came to you. It would make them very late."

"Oh, that wouldn't matter," said Conrad, "we'll probably go on till morning in any case."

"With the *orchestra* playing the whole time?" said Mrs. Grace, thinking no doubt that her distinguished lion's sleep would be disturbed.

Conrad, spreading out the four-leaf clover in the palm of his hand, took the bull by the horns and said, "Mrs. Grace, why don't *you* come to my party? I have a study upstairs where you and Mr. Ramsgate and the Zanzibar fanciers could talk to your hearts' content."

"Oh, come, Mr. Pardee. Really, Mr. Pardee." She was shocked. She rose to go, and she said, "Somehow our dilemma will be resolved," and he knew, with a sinking heart, that she meant to resolve it to her liking, not to his. In all probability she would commandeer whomever she chose to come and be bored by Ramsgate: nobody would dare refuse. He put his head in his hands, and Lucia Mabon said, "She's a terror. Simply wonderful. Do you know that she asked *me* to meet the Zanzibar man?"

She had, so it appeared, invited all of Conrad's guests to come and meet the Zanzibar man, and the only one who had been bold enough to give her a flat no was Elsie, who had risked her skin and Conrad's by saying, "I put up with world affairs only when there's absolutely nothing else to do."

All that evening and the next morning Conrad was glum and edgy, certain that up on the hill Mrs. Grace was at work on the telephone undermining him. Harriet Gildersleeve was loyally angry; Jane Hardesty, like Lucia Mabon, had been impressed and secretly wanted to meet Lovell Ramsgate, although she had Zanzibar confused with Xanadu. John Madigan, flattered, said the old dame was a treat.

And then the clouds parted and the sun came out. At cocktail time Jack Hardesty returned from a tour of flowery swamps and woodlands and reported that he had met Mrs. Grace halfway up her hill and she had kindly identified *Decodon verticillatus* for him and then had asked him to tea. While he was there a call had come from Lovell Ramsgate, who said that he must proceed at once to Washington, and Mrs. Grace had then declared, "Since all my friends will be at Mr. Pardee's, I shall look in for a while. Will you tell him that?"

Conrad's party sighed with relief and refilled their glasses, and shortly Mrs. Grace rang up. Her voice was remarkably pleasant. "I was wrong about your four-leaf clover, Mr. Pardee," she said. "My loss—what a loss!—is your gain. Is it in accordance with New York customs as it is in Boston that I exercise the prerogative of age and invite myself to toast you on your birthday?"

"But of course, Mrs. Grace! It didn't occur to me that you would stoop to such a frolic or I'd have asked you in the beginning."

"I haven't seen fireworks at a party in years," said Mrs. Grace.

There were to be no fireworks (they were against the law), but Mrs. Grace said that there had always been fireworks at masquerade balls. The party to which Mrs. Grace seemed to plan to come was not the party Conrad planned to give but one she remembered from three quarters of a century before. She appeared to envision phalanxes of servants in ducal livery (they would, in fact, be yokels in white drill monkey jackets) and she assumed that colored lights would play upon the fountains (Conrad had a bird bath).

"Then that's settled," said Mrs. Grace. "Billy Butterfield can pick me up. Lucky Mr. Pardee. I'll not be blasé about an abnormal *Trifolium repens* again."

Conrad had not invited Billy Butterfield for the simple reason that he had never met the daffy old curmudgeon who lived at one end of the lake and wrote irritable pamphlets denouncing Henry Wallace. Dutifully, however, he telephoned. The cross octogenarian bellowed, "Thank you, no. What did you say your name was? I'll have to ring off now. I abhor the telephone." Conrad called Mrs. Grace. She said, "In that case I shall have the poet fetch me. He may call for me at half past six and I shall show him the prothalamium my father wrote for my marriage." Conrad said that the party was to begin at half past nine, and a surprised pause followed. Then Mrs. Grace said, "Very well. Tell him to come and dine with me at seven." John Madigan was amused and cooperative, but Harriet Gildersleeve was displeased, and a noticeable chill settled down on paradise.

Two days before the ball, shortly after noon, the Peterson girl was rushed to the hospital for an emergency appendectomy.

Lunch was delayed, and Elsie Appleton drank too much while they were waiting. During the second course she said to Lucia Mabon, "Will you, for heaven's sake, stop driveling French?" Lucia, without a word, left the table and later quarreled with her husband, who had heartlessly gone on eating steak-and-kidney pie.

That afternoon a sullen rain began to fall, and Mrs. Link said, "I've never known the Almanac to be wrong. We're in for it, all right. Forty days and forty nights of it."

In the evening the bat's wings touched Jane Hardesty's forehead and she screamed just as all the lights went out.

All the same, Conrad's spirits remained high, and he often smiled to think that if he had not brought Mrs. Grace to her knees, he was, at least, bringing her to his house.

The malevolent rain continued on the next day, and the radio, spluttering, reported widespread washouts and promised no relief for several days. The electricity was mercurial; the telephone developed hiccups. The shutins pouted, and the dahlias drowned. The lawns were lakes, and the tables that were to have been set up outside now had to be tucked into awkward nooks and crannies in the house, in halls and under stairs and, as Mrs. Link observed, the place looked like moving day. A new and clumsy Peterson girl, replacing her sick sister, dropped and broke the most important vase in the house, and a tin bucket had to be camouflaged to hold the gladiolus in the center of the buffet table—this was the sort of compromise that set Conrad's teeth on edge. And then, through some wanton error, the orchestra arrived twenty-four hours ahead of time and, at forbidding cost, had to be put up at the village inn and served large quantities of food and drink, since the weather prevented more pastoral activities which, in any event, they would have scorned. They all got drunk and some of them got churlish, and the publican threatened to call in the police if they persisted in playing their bass fiddles and pounding their drums in the cocktail lounge to the annoyance of the Kiwanis Club which was meeting that day in the dining room.

When he was not concerned with one of these predicaments, Conrad was at work trying to restore order among his disgruntled house guests. As if his gesture were motivated by no more than pure generosity, he gave Lucia Mabon a carriage lamp which she had been coveting, and she was so mollified that she forgave both her husband and Elsie. The price of the reconciliation between Harriet and John was Conrad's favorite Audubon, but it was well worth it, and he was comforted to see the truce flags flying.

That afternoon Jessie Rogers telephoned from Marlboro to say that her husband was in agony with bursitis and that they could not possibly come the next evening. Conrad did not really care, but his voice sorrowed and blandished as he said, "We will be devastated, as you know, but not inconvenienced."

There was an intake of breath and then a little cry of delight and Jessie said, "'We will be devastated but not inconvenienced'! What an absolutely bewitching way to accept a cancellation! Conrad Pardee, you are the most civilized man in the world!"

Conrad thought the speech not half bad himself, and he used it, with variations, to several more people who called in the course of the day to regret that they could not come because of illness or because of the weather. To Frances Madison, he said, "We will be heartbroken but not discommoded": to Betty Modell, he said, "Don't give our arrangements another thought, but we will be *triste* without you." And to Mrs. Belknap, he said, "We will be inconsolable but not embarrassed." He was acclaimed by all for his felicity, and his spirits soared. Imitating their host, the others grew vivacious in spite of the rain, and they rose above the darkness and the wet by playing charades and drinking dark rum in tea.

Mrs. Grace telephoned at five o'clock. For some time she and Conrad discussed the rain and Mrs. Grace commiserated with him over the need to abandon the alfresco aspect of his fete; a veritable Mississippi was raging through her meadow, and her upstairs sitting room was littered with pails and pans to catch the water leaking through the ceiling. After a few more minutes of discursive talk—Mrs. Grace had heard about Conrad's musicians and did not find the contretemps droll—she said, "I'm sorry to say that I am calling to tell you that I shan't come tomorrow after all, nor shall I be able to give your poet his dinner. A pity. I have started a sniffle which tomorrow will be a sneeze, so I must sit by my fire in a hug-me-tight and drink bouillon. I do ask to be forgiven for inviting myself and causing you all sorts of botheration and then begging off."

"Oh, sad tidings," said Conrad earnestly, "but do be assured that while we'll be inconvenienced, we'll in no way be heartbroken."

The silence lasted, Conrad calculated, for months, and he knew now what it was like to be condemned to life imprisonment and how much preferable it would be to be shot through the heart. In the mirror over the telephone, he saw that the red of his blush gave way to the blue of cyanosis and then he turned a cadaverous green. He fancied that his hair was standing on end, but this was an optical illusion caused by some bizarre impairment of his burning eyes.

As he was about to give up the ghost, Mrs. Grace, from her throne on high, passed sentence. "Well!" she said. "Well, Mr. Pardee, there you are." The telephone began to ululate and bark and then Mrs. Grace hung up.

There he was indeed, and for a time it seemed to him that he would remain forever rooted to the spot, unable, because of *rigor mortis*, to return the receiver to its cradle. He thought of calling her back to explain, but he knew full well that there was no conceivable explanation. He thought of sending her his first edition of *Pride and Prejudice* or a check for fifteen thousand dollars for her favorite charity. But Mrs. Grace was not a woman to be bribed. He thought of packing up at once and putting his house on the market for sale.

But he liked High Hill and he liked his house and he realized suddenly how much he disliked Mrs. Grace and he resolved to stand his ground against this rude old Boston beldam. When he went back to his friends and told them what had happened, they roared with laughter, they said Conrad had behaved, as usual, with finesse. Then they played "I Packed My Bag for Boston," and into the bag they put vile things and useless things: a gecko, a gibbet, a goat and a gadfly and, when it was bulging, they sent it to Mrs. Grace in Mt. Vernon Street. Lucia Mabon said that Mrs. Grace's French was odious; John Madigan said that her taste in poetry was that of a twelve-year-old; Jack Hardesty impugned her botany. She emerged finally as a boor and a figure of fun, and Broker Pardee resumed his rightful place as the most civilized man in the world.

An Influx of Poets

THAT awful summer! Every poet in America came to stay with us. It was the first summer after the war, when people once again had gasoline and could go where they liked, and all those poets came to our house in Maine and stayed for weeks at a stretch, bringing wives or mistresses with whom they quarrelled, and complaining so vividly about the wives and mistresses they'd left, or had been left by, that the discards were real presences, swelling the ranks, stretching the house, *my* house (my very own, my first and very own), to its seams. At night, after supper, they'd read from their own works until four o'clock in the morning, drinking Cuba Libres. They never listened to one another; they were preoccupied with waiting for their turn. And I'd have to stay up and clear out the living room after they went soddenly to bed—sodden but not too far gone to lose their conceit. And then all day I'd cook and wash the dishes and chop the ice and weed the garden and type my husband's poems and quarrel with him. I had met Theron Maybank in Adams, Colorado, five years earlier at a writers' conference at Neville University, where, as a graduate student, I was serving on the arrangements committee. Theron had left his native Boston for his first trip West in order to meet the famous and reclusive American poet Fitzhugh Burr, who had agreed to make a rare public appearance on the campus. I found Theron's brilliant talk and dark good looks somehow reminiscent of the young Nathaniel Hawthorne. We were married in Adams a few weeks after the conference ended, and left one week later for Baton Rouge.

On the Labor Day weekend the well went dry: a death rattle shook every pipe in the house, there was a kind of bleating sound, and then a sigh. Three poets—one with a wife—were in residence at the time, and so was Minnie Rosoff, just divorced from Jered Zumwalt, the bard of Harvard, Canarsie-born. The well went dry, and Evan and Lucia Bronson left the next day, taking Harry Matthews with them back to Princeton. They had been guests for three full weeks, and the reading of poetry had been perpetual. Lucia and I were kept at our typewriters typing

Evan's and Theron's poems as they wrote them; it seemed to us they wrote at the speed of light, but this was not so. They were snail-paced (oh, I admit they were brilliant poets, if you happen to be interested in that sort of thing), but if they changed an "a" to a "the" the whole sonnet had to be typed over again. And I grant that such a change can make all the difference in the world (if, that is, you happen to be a poet or a lover of poetry), but why couldn't the alteration be made by hand? Meanwhile, down in the finished room in the lower part of the barn, Harry Matthews, whose precocious glitter eventually came to nothing—he was forgotten soon after his first book appeared—really *was* writing like greased lightning.

And then at night the ladies of the house sat in my pretty parlor (*my* parlor! My own! I bought the house, I bought the furniture, the student lamps, the cachepots, the milk-glass bowls I used for water lilies from the lake—Theron and I had got to Maine before the antique dealers, and there were still big old ramshackle firetraps called "secondhand stores," generally owned by men whose real income came from undertaking), listening to the poets listen to themselves and not to one another. What Lucia thought about I couldn't guess; we did not know each other as friends—only as the wives of young poets—but I know that my own mind strayed, browsing in fields far distant from those bounded by the barbed-wire fences (some of them electric) of my marriage. I was a child back in Missouri, in my grandfather's Sunday punishment room, listening to Foxe's "Book of Martyrs," scared and rebellious and disloyally bored. Usually, to be sure, I took a drink as the poetry was read, but drink didn't help; if I'd been out in the kitchen by myself, drinking that emetic compound of rum and Coca-Cola, I would have been at peace, staring into space and dreaming of what my life could have been if I had married someone else, or what it still could be if Theron drowned, perhaps, in the lake behind my house or in the tidal river in front of it. But I was in this throng of litterateurs (three poets in one medium-sized room constitute a multitude), enjoying nothing. I never did, even afterward, know what Lucia was thinking. But Minnie Rosoff was agape, adoring and adorable, loving them all, especially my husband, and, because she was so obvious, mendaciously flattering me.

I had been in Boston the day Minnie came to begin her visit with us; the Bronsons had gone down the coast to stay with friends for a few days. (They came back to us, of course—there was more poetry in *our* house, and they would be there when the well gave up the ghost.) Just back from Nevada, where she had divorced Jerry Zumwalt, Minnie had been moving slowly down the coast of Maine, alighting like a bird to charm and sing in other houses, making her carefree passage in other people's motorcars and other people's boats. She came to us, quixotically and at the expense of her last host, in a Piper Cub, landing on an island in Hawthorne Lake, behind us, flown there by a Seabee so stricken with her that he loitered in the village several days afterward. If I had been there when she came, the outcome of my marriage would, I daresay, have been the same, but the end of it would probably not have come so soon. Certainly it would not have been so humiliating, so banal, so sandy to my teeth. But I was not there on that beautiful afternoon when her blithe plane banked and came bobbing to rest on Loon Islet and she came swimming to our landing.

I'd gone to Boston two days before to try to learn the reason for the headaches that daily harrowed me. I knew they came from something more than rum, and I knew—although I did not want to know—that I could not honestly attribute them to too many iambs and too many dithyrambic self-congratulations by the baby bards. (Though they were no longer enfants terribles, the blood of despots was in their veins and they would very soon usurp their elders' thrones and their dominions.) When I came back to Edwards Mills, depleted by the dark and heavy heat of Boston, dirty from the train, I found Minnie and Theron sitting in the garden in the perishing day like a Watteau summer idyll, already so advanced in their lore (infatuation acquires its history and literature in minutes) that they were beyond the need of language and were listening, as they drank mint juleps from my silver goblets, to the phonograph playing in the living room, playing Scarlatti sonatas, my favorites, which Theron theretofore had barely tolerated, preferring the music of Beethoven, which, he said, showing off, was "impeccably flatulent—all bawdy hoydens and horny knaves," adding, "He's the Bruegel of music."

I did not at that moment apprehend the reason for their

blissful circumstance; I saw only that they *were* blissful, and I envied their simple pleasure in the cool air and the light waning to violet and the smell of the flowers and the feeling of the icy dew on the goblets they held, all bespangled with the wit of the harpsichord. Soon there would be fireflies.

As I paused at the door without their knowledge of my looking at them, I saw Theron not as the husband I loved to despair and hated to the point of murder—the man I wanted to flee because, in failing to commit myself entirely to him, I knew he would not commit himself to me; I saw him only as a thin, dark, tall, large-headed genius, complementing by his differences of stature and structure the pretty, small, dark, *zaftig* girl who was luring and foiling my silver tabby cat with a piece of string to which she had tied a small green pinecone. At first the tableau—except for the gentle swinging of the impromptu toy and the contraction of my cat's withers as she prepared to spring, the scene was motionless—eased me, made me think, "I'm not done for yet if I can still get this far outside myself to be made so happy by so slight a scene," and then, suddenly, I sickened and felt gross and smutted, alien, and I remembered the blunt, brusque doctor, prejudiced against me by my having come to him at the apex of the humid day, saying to me without compassion and without interest, "Considering your symptoms and your history, I can do nothing but advise you to see a psychoanalyst."

I had not expected Minnie until dinnertime. All the way from Boston on the East Wind, steeling myself with drink (and, as I steeled, softening my headlong nerves), I had planned how I would tell Theron of Dr. Lowebridge's recommendation, one that I knew he would greet with an admixture of contempt and complacence, for while he despised psychiatry—he despised medicine in general—he had many times ended our vicious quarrels with the reminder that if what I had told him about my father (whom he had never met) was the truth, my mental heritage was doubtless suspect and I was *immoral* not to be examined by someone competent to navigate the eccentric meanders of my mind. ("What meanders?" I demanded. He would only smile and roll back his eyes, and I would go mad with rage and terror.) I dreaded equally his satisfaction and his indifference: whether he crowed or shrugged, he would

undermine me, he would cripple me and make me mute, for
latterly I had so feared the smile that when I sensed it coming
I would say nothing more and bear his scorn, his lofty, hidebound disapproval, as if I were an uppity field hand getting
what was coming to me.

Dr. Lowebridge's prescription for me was, I thought, appalling; it had taken my breath away. How could these brutish
headaches and this lurching nausea have their genesis in my
mind? It was preposterous. Still, there had been compensations
in the advice—if, that is, I decided to follow it—and I had dimly
seen a way that it might suspend my struggle with Theron for
a while. He was, despite his eccentricities and his rebellion, an
intransigently conventional man; thus his diehard repudiation
of psychiatry as poppycock, a Viennese chicanery devised to
bilk idle women and hypochondriacal men. After accepting Dr.
Lowebridge's diagnosis, Theron was almost bound to send me
to New York lest the news that I was "mental" be noised about
in Boston, and such a separation, justified and temporary, was
what I had prayed for all these stewed and sleeplessly stewing
nights of summer.

I meant (this had been my plan on the train) to come to
him suppliantly with the news, to come in such humility and
courage that he could not fail to console and support me and,
seeing my need, would leave off his snobberies. I had intended
to be wifely and womanly, freshly bathed and wearing my most
floating dress when I appeared, my hair done blamelessly and as
he liked it, in braids around my head, my external integument
past any criticism. I would jocosely take his side against me; I
would seriously assume all responsibility for our antagonisms
and would hold out hope (I had no hope at all) for their extirpation. Simply to be away from him, I thought, would signal
the beginning of the end of my nightmare. I was glad that our
conversation would not be long but must be suspended with
Minnie's arrival and with the proprieties of dinner, to which
I had invited three guests. I had got home in good time, just
after five, for an hour of dress rehearsal, but Minnie's being
there already, and as if she'd been there for weeks, or even years,
deflected the course of my strategy and sent me astray into a
wilderness of confusion and shame and embarrassment.

I stepped down into my own garden as if *I* were a guest,

related only by the kind amenities of my hostess to the cat, to the roses, and to the man—who, barely looking at me, said, "I called off dinner because I knew you'd be tired. Besides, Minnie didn't want to dress."

Perhaps my deepest, longest lingering dismay began then, in that kind of panoramic view of his whole history which is supposed to flash before the eyes of a man drowning or hurtling to his death from a great altitude. I gasped, looking at Minnie Rosoff in her sleek, chic negligee of white linen shorts and a long-sleeved pale-blue shirt with bogus-emerald Chanel cufflinks; my city black was wrinkled, ash-smudged, my hands were swollen and red from the heat and black from the train, too clumsy for the cat's casual and elegant toy (Colette would have devised such a thing) or for the silver goblets. My smile for this woman became a green schoolgirl's grin; I blushed, I stumbled toward a canvas chair, and when Minnie Rosoff said, "Theron, do make a drink for your poor exhausted wife," I felt like a traveller who had just debarked from steerage and who, through some unthinkable mistake, had got into the first-class customs line.

With his back to me, as if he could not bear the sight of me, my husband said, "You don't mind that I called off dinner?"

I minded very much, but I smiled, and, for the sake of our guest, I was polite and thanked him warmly, and I said, "In that case, we can have our supper on trays out here."

"Minnie would like to take a picnic to Loon," he said. "She wants to see the Cub Scout again."

"*Piper Cub*, you goose!" cried Minnie, and laughed the infant, fluting laugh that had heretofore enchanted me as it had everyone she knew. "But Cora doesn't know how I got here! I flew down from Castine in a *wee* plane, like a kite exactly. With such a sweet boy, and the plane is still on that *tiny* island. The moon will be full—it's summertime! Say that you want a picnic, sweetie!"

Theron gave me no chance to sanction or to veto the picnic, which I did not want—which seemed to me unbearably bois-terous. He said, "Cora can't row and can't swim, and she's got a thing about small boats."

"Oh, poor lamb," said Minnie. "But with two of us to save you you'll be perfectly safe." And she tried to persuade me with those arguments, logical and sensible, with which people who are not sufferers themselves try to subdue a phobia in someone else. "But it's only a garter snake," they say. "It can't possibly hurt you." And the ophidiophobe repeats that his horror comes not from the venom or the size of the snake but from the movement and the shape and the especial *essence* of the creature, and that he recognizes but cannot help his irrationality. Thus, my fear of water (not of drowning, not of what the water would do to me, but an aboriginal, a prehistoric fear, but prehistoric in the present tense, of the nature of water and its antiquity and its secrecy) could in no way be diminished by Minnie's assurances that the lake was not deep at our end, that she had had experience in giving artificial respiration, that our dory was as safe as houses (so they'd been rowing earlier among the lily pads?), that she could have the pilot of the Piper Cub bring over a Mae West for me. The more she tried to persuade me, the more stubbornly I resisted, until finally I was angry, protective of this neurosis—which, in point of fact, had been a nuisance and an impediment to me all my life and one I would have given anything to be delivered from.

Theron remained silent, and while once I might have been grateful that he did not add to my discomfort by teasing me, now I was suspicious: his faint smile, the way in which his gaze followed the capers of the cat and never fell on me, although occasionally it did on Minnie, still moving the pinecone like a pendulum, baffled me. I had often thought that when I was out of his sight I was literally out of his mind, that he never imagined me as I might be in a train or in a strange hotel, as I always imagined him when he was away from home. I had never felt myself to be so far away from him—as if we were separated by many actual miles—as I did this early evening when I sat opposite him in the garden, three feet away, conjoined by our house (mine! Remember, Cora Savage, if you forget all else, that this is *your* house), our cat, and the inveigling voice of Minnie Rosoff. I did not understand his silence; I was alarmed, for in my misery I was wholly egocentric and looked on every act as being related in some way to me. What was the motive that caused him to hold his peace instead of bolstering Minnie's arguments with impatient ones of his own? And what on earth possessed him, when at last she gave up and he went in to make me a drink, to make it double strength, when all summer he had denied or rationed me with public frowns and headshakes that had made my blood boil? "What the bleeding hell?" I'd yell at him. "You drink as much as I do. You drink more!" and he'd reply, "A difference of upbringing, dear—no more than that. I learned to drink at home in the drawing room, so I know how. No fault of yours—just bad luck. You don't drink well, dear. Not well at all."

When he gave me my triple hemlock on crushed ice, bedizened with a spray of mint, he said, "Minnie and I will have our picnic. You can stay here. Will you make us some sandwiches, Cozy Cora? Please? Pretty please with sugar on it?"

I put my drink down on the grass beside my chair and stood up and took my cat into my arms and buried my face in her satiny flank. She was bored with the game anyhow, and when I sat down again she curled serenely into my lap.

"You are my cat," I said. "You are my personal cat." At the sound of my voice she looked up and blinked her Mediterranean green-blue eyes. Always literary, Theron had named her Anna Livia Plurabelle, and she was known as Livvy for short. "You are my cat," I repeated, "and from now on your name is Pretty Baby."

After Minnie and Theron had gone down through the meadow with their picnic basket and a bottle of wine I had brought up from the well, I sat for some time in the garden, unthinking, trying to count the short, soft beams of the magic fireflies. (Each Fourth of July night at Granny Savage's house in Missouri, before we moved to Colorado, my father had caught fireflies in one of Mama's hairnets and draped it over my older sister Abigail's head. The green, and sometimes blue and sometimes violet, lights went on and off among her dark-red curls and, to please her idol, she would twirl around, swoop down, and then rise up on her toes. "By George, what's this we have?" exclaimed my father. "Queen Mab herself! Titania!" Mama laughed and clapped, and my younger brother, Randall, giggling and howling like a wolf, would chase her. We'd see them weaving in and out among the willow trees and the acacias. The trapped fireflies attracted others, and my brother and sister were enveloped in a mist of stars. I wanted a halo, too, but there was no other hairnet, and when I stamped my foot and shouted, "It isn't *fair*!" Mama tried to soothe me, saying, "Never mind. You can put it on when Abigail is through.") I postponed going to bed, the more to savor the sleep I knew awaited me. For a long time now, I had not been able really to sleep unless there was a moon. I could not close my eyes until the fallow light overtook the serious country darkness on the windowpanes and consolingly revealed to me familiar objects in the room—my wrapper thrown over the blue velvet slipper chair, the silver-birch logs lying across the andirons on the tiny hearth, the Quimper pitcher on the mantelpiece which I kept full of wild flowers. And then, almost at once, after this last look, my eyelids would close, cherishing the warmth and love of sleep, my breathing would deepen, I could feel myself falling headlong into the most delectable condition on earth. Only thus could I escape Theron the poet, and Theron the poet's poet friends. He was beside me and they were in all the rooms around me and in the barn, but I was dead to their world, and they, thereby, were dead to mine.

Pretty Baby was mewing in the living room and, knowing that she would be moving her kittens and, liking to watch the curious ritual scene-shifting, I went into the house and saw her carrying the runt of the litter, all black, across the carpet from the nest she had made for them behind the sofa to the basket beside the fireplace, where they properly belonged. The other three were there already, and I wondered if she had taken the runt last because she liked him least or because she feared his fat siblings would smother him. They were still blind and she was still proud, cosseting them with her milk and her bright, abrasive tongue and the constant purr into which, now and again, she interjected a little yelp of self-esteem. When she was nestled down, relaxed amongst her produce, I knelt and strongly ran the knuckle of my thumb down the black stripes that began just above her nose and terminated in the wider, blacker bands around her neck, and then I left her to her rapturous business of grooming her kittens, nursing in their blindness and their sleep.

I turned out all the lights but one—one to guide back to shore the Loon Islet revellers who did not fear the water. I did not doubt that Minnie would at some time sing "Over the sea to

Skye," one of her specialities. Her voice was as high and as clear
as a blockflöte. How gifted was this little minx, raven-tressèd,
damask-skinned, by turns so sharp-witted as a critic that critics
cringed when she attacked them in the pages of the leading
intellectual quarterly, *The Divergent*, and as moon-eyed and
adoring as a daft maiden when she was in the presence of a
poet. Still, she was not feared by the poets' wives, because her
unchivalric and murderously moody husband, Jered Zumwalt,
had broadcast wide, in disgraceful but convincing detail, the
news that she was as cold as stone. Theron, respectful of Jerry,
who with much éclat had published several books and was
generally regarded as the most gifted of the young Cambridge
poets (Theron was moving steadily up in the race but he had
not yet published a book), had fretted with Jerry over Minnie's
defection through cases of beer and quarts of blended whiskey
in our apartment on Kirkland Street. Quite often, too drunk to
go home, Jerry spent the night on the sofa in the living room,
where I would find him in the morning on my way to Miss
Heath's School, where I taught English. His ruptured loafers,
bloated and stained with rain and snow and mud, lay always
at some distance from each other—one by the chair where he
had been having his last swallow, the other halfway across the
room where he had walked out of it on his way to the short,
slippery leather sofa on which now he lay as contorted as an
old wind-worn tree, his left hand clenched under his chin, the
right resting on a stiff round pillow atop his head. I had one
time seen a photograph of him and Minnie taken in the early
days of their marriage: so similar were their textures and their
values, so clear their grave innocence and so concealed their
wit and wisdom, that they could have been two star-crossed,
moonstruck lovers—Romeo and Juliet, Aucassin and Nicolette,
Floris and Blanchefleur. Soon those sweet and plaintive images
shattered: Jerry grew generally drunk, maudlin, and bilious by
turns, and Minnie, in Nevada for the divorce, was, we gathered
from letters to us and to other friends, having a ripsnorting
romp, learning to ride a cow pony and to sing cowboy songs
and, most rambunctious of all, working as a shill in a gambling
house. When Jerry told us of this last improbable lark, Theron,
heavily Bostonian in his sarcasm, said, "After the battle royal,
taper off on fun and games, what?," and Jerry, drinking dollar

sherry straight from the bottle, then drawing on his five-cent cigar (his bad habits were so inappropriate to his Donatello looks that I never could take them seriously), said, "The only reason she's a shill in the Big Bonanza is that she didn't happen to think of going to Virginia City to be Lucius Beebe's printer's devil."

Now she was back at her old post, beguiling poets. There was an influx of poets this summer in the state of Maine and ours was only one of many houses where they clustered: farther down the coast and inland all the way to Campobello, singly, in couples, trios, tribes, they were circulating among rich patronesses in ancestral summer shacks of twenty rooms, critics on vacation from universities who roughed it with Coleman lamps and outhouses but sumptuously dined on lobster and blueberry gems, and a couple of novelists who, although they wrote like dogs (according to the poets), had made packets, which, because they were decently (and properly) humble, they were complimented to share with the rarer breed. As Mr. Zumwalt worked his way north, so the former Mrs. Z. was migrating south, and we, the Maybanks, and Eliza and her critic husband, Andrew Brandt, in the middle, had tidings from several longitudes and latitudes. So far, the paths of the disaffected had not crossed, and there were jubilant and studious speculations on what would happen if they did. It was the fashion to use Freud's works as a recipe book and to add garnitures from Henry James and Proust.

Standing still in the dim-lit living room, I shuddered suddenly, aware of my dishevelment and remembering the brusque doctor on Commonwealth Avenue who had made my headaches a disgrace and counselled me to go and be shriven of my mortal sins by a psychoanalyst. How would I tell Theron? And when? The poets Bronson and Matthews and the poem-typist Lucia would soon be back and now that Minnehaha was here, the fly-by-nights who had seen Jerry at Isle au Haut or in Aroostook would come flocking in to spy and gabble and prophesy. I would have a ton of fish to fry and bake and poach, a rod of shoe-peg corn to shuck, a gross bushel of salad to harvest and wash and tear and slice and dress, a floe of ice to chop for Cuba Libres. Although the war was over, we were still rationed; for some while to come, I must postpone my

shameful revelation to my husband while I hatched up means
to disguise horsemeat.

This was not the way I had planned the summer. We had
limped painfully through the fifth year of our marriage, having
changed the scene of our travail each year from the beginning.
Cambridge was no better than New York, New York no better
than Connecticut, Connecticut no better than Louisiana or
the mountains of Tennessee. But we often limped on different
routes, shedding our blood on sand and rocks miles apart.
When we did meet in some kind oasis or quiet glade, we were
at first shy and infatuated and glad, but the reunion did not last,
the shade and water were part of a mirage, lightning smote and
burned the hemlocks of our forest sanctuary.

   Theron, who had found Catholicism shortly after he found
me, ran to Father Bernard—our spiritual adviser in Cambridge—and came back whimpering *"Mea maxima culpa"* so
heartbrokenly that I crept from the hiding shadows to console
him with old running jokes, and for a while we played again,
two precocious, oafish six-year-olds. The blood of the Salem
witch-burners scalded the walls of Theron's veins and so, per-
force, did that of the Salem warlocks; and I was hot to the touch
where I had been scoured and curried with Ayrshire brimstone.
We baffled Father Bernard, who had not been trained to crack
the whip over wayward rowdies. Surely he must have dreaded
Theron's abstruse and convoluted confessions, he must have
longed to shut the wicket against those pedantic admissions of
frailty and pad softly home to tea and a scone.

   Actually, save for the sin of pride, Theron was a blameless
man. I was the lost one, for I did not believe in any of it—not
in the Real Presence, not in the Immaculate Conception, not
in God—and, to compound my perfidy, I received the Host
each Sunday and each day of obligation and did not confess
my infidelity. Not to Father Bernard and no longer to Theron.
In the beginning, I had tried, but he, rapt in his severe belief,
had brushed me aside and called my doubt a temporary matter.
"But it isn't *doubt*! It's positive repudiation!" I'd cry. We talked
like that, in our frustration forgetting to be colloquial, in our
insanity forgetting to be sane. Theron once told me that I
was going through the dark night of the spirit and I should

meditate and read John of the Cross. I did, with a certain kind of recognition, read St. John's friend Teresa's "Interior Castle," and one morning in the shallow sleep just before awakening I dreamed I got a penny postal in the mail which read, "Dear Cora, I keep out. Love, Teresa of Avila." I was fond of my dreams, particularly of brief verbal ones like this, but Theron scorned them and said they had no style.

Long before Theron had thought of Catholicism, long before we had met and I was eighteen, I had been instructed by Father Strittmater in the Sacred Heart Church in Adams, and had been baptized and had once and once only received the wafer. My mission had not been accomplished, despite my fervor and my need. Later on, from time to time, I tried again in different churches of different towns at different seasons of the year and different hours of day and night. But I was God-forsaken; the shepherd could not hear my bleating, for I was miles astray in the cold and the dark and the desert. And at last I vanished without a trace; with a faint shiver and a faint sigh, I gave up the Ghost.

Half a year after we were married, Theron, immersed in the rhythms of Gerard Manley Hopkins the poet, was explosively ignited by Gerard Manley Hopkins the Jesuit, and, as my mother would have said, he was off on a tear. We were in Louisiana then—in steaming, verminous fetor; almost as soon as the set of Cardinal Newman's works arrived from Dauber & Pine, the spines relaxed, for the Deep South cockroaches, the size of larks, relished the seasoned glue of the bindings and banqueted by night. Like Father Strittmater, Theron's instructor was Pennsylvania Dutch—a coincidence that only mildly interested me but one by which my husband set great store: Our Lord (he adopted the address with case) had planned likenesses in our experience. Father Neuscheier wore the miasmas from the bayous like a hair shirt, having chosen Baton Rouge out of many possibilities because it afforded him so excellent a chance to chasten his chaste flesh. Air-conditioning was in its infancy—not even the movie houses had it, or the saloons—but in most buildings of a public nature there were those large, romantic ceiling fans, whirling and whirring quietly, at a slow speed, resembling animated daisies with petals made of wood. But there was no fan in the nave of Our Lady of Pompeii, and

Father Neuscheier must have suffered as the wet air thickened and warmed, but not a bead of sweat shone on his perfectly round face or his perfectly bald head. His austerity was right up Theron's alley, and before I knew what had happened to me, I had been dragged into that alley which was blind.

Theron had promised at the start that he would not impose his old-time religion on me, but within a week after he was confirmed I found myself being remarried in the Catholic Church, and a week after that I was going to daily Mass at seven in the morning, before I taught my first class at eight, and to benediction in the late afternoon; together we told two Rosaries a day, and we replaced our reproductions of "A Little Street in Delft" and "La Grande Jatte" with black-and-white photographs of Bellini's "St. Francis Receiving the Stigmata" and Holbein's "Thomas More." There would be, so did declare the head of the house, no sacrilegious jokes: we did not even laugh one rainy Sunday when Father Neuscheier announced at Mass that if anyone had sneakily or even accidentally caught some raindrops on his tongue, thereby breaking his fast, he would not be eligible to receive Communion.

What had become of the joking lad I'd married? He'd run hellbent for election into that blind alley—that's what had become of him—and yanked me along with him, and there we snarled like hungry, scurvy cats. If I had stubbornly withstood him from the beginning, or if I had left him when he left me for the seraphim and saints—but I had tried to withstand and had got for myself only wrath and disdain. Leaving him had not really occurred to me, for I had married within my tribe, and we were sternly monogamous till death. Supinely I endured and made out lists of things while Mass was being sung—the cities I had traversed by bus on journeys from east to west and west to south, the names of the buildings on Neville's campus, all the people I knew whose given name was John. In each new place we lived and I taught, as soon as I had got my house in order and my schoolwork planned I called at the rectory of the church Theron had selected as home base and, depending on the nature of the man of God I found, humbly declared my doubts or concealed them and invited him to tea.

In Cambridge, Father Bernard, an innocent, tired, and affectionate old man, had befriended me and had done so at a time
when I was needier than I had ever been before. Somewhere—
on a park bench in the Common, in a bar-and-grill in Scollay
Square, on the steps of Widener—Theron had met up one day
with a fanatic who convinced him that the only godly way was
a life of holy poverty, and we were to move to a mission house
in Dorchester and live on turnips and bean soup. We would
sleep on the floor and, I gathered, prowl the slums barefoot in
the snow on the lookout for derelicts sleeping off their Tokay
sprees in sub-zero temperatures. We were to give away our
clothes and furniture—one of the first things to go was my
engagement ring, which had belonged to Theron's great-aunt
Charity Nephews, who had theatrically widowed her husband
when she contracted dengue fever at the opening of the Panama Canal. Although Theron appeared to have repudiated all
the luxuries and the limitations of his Bostonian breeding and
totems, he had not in fact done so at all: he was as vain as a
peacock that Copley had painted his distant Cousin Augustus'
family and that Great-Aunt Charity had died while she was
acting as foreign correspondent for the Boston *Evening Transcript*. (T. S. Eliot, whose poem of that name he would have
liked me to embroider as a sampler, was then one of his muses.)
We were to give away the Nephews diamond, beset with the
palest of pink pearls, and, as well, a silver tea service bought in
Rangoon by Theron's father, the Captain, and disliked by his
mother for its showy bosses of birds and beasts and octopoid
goddesses. But we could not be all spirit (if we were, we would
not have the means to be Lord and Lady Bountiful as well as
Samaritans), so I was not to give up my job of teaching at Miss
Heath's. And while I taught subjunctives to the bonny, snobby
girls, Theron would write psalms and hymns and Christmas
carols. "Quid pro quo," said he, his eyes rolled back so that the
pupils rested on the optic thalamus. "Quid pro quo and tit for
tat," I said to myself, thinking how I might set this to a simple
tune to sing to a friendly cat.

If it had not been for Father Bernard, I am quite sure I would
have taken on this graceless, humbug role of holy poverty. But
Father Bernard, who in looks and in deportment resembled the
dog named after his patron saint, was fond—perhaps profanely

so—of creature comforts, and when one day I went to call on him to tattle on Theron and his latest excess, he took my side. Indeed, although he endeavored to maintain serenity, he showed his consternation—or, rather, his embarrassment—by giving his attention to a jardiniere planted with mosses and small ferns and keeping his back to me. Kind as he was, and affectionate, Father Bernard had not been cut out for the role of spiritual adviser; because he was humorless, he was vulnerable, and complicated emotional troubles upset his bowels. Theron mightily dismayed him, pestering him with abstruse exegeses of the sacraments as they might be applied to the modus vivendi of the New England transcendentalists, complaining of his failure to dislodge his mother from her Unitarianism, demanding that I be brought to book for my failure to obey the letter of the law. (One time I had eaten a Salisbury steak on a Friday when we took the Merchant's Limited from New York to Boston; Theron maintained that the journey was too short to justify such a dispensation.)

I very rarely called on Father Bernard, but because the rectory was on Irving Terrace, nearby our apartment building, on Kirkland, I often ran into him on the street and sometimes at the greengrocer's, where he liked to browse among the lettuces and roots; he loved all vegetables that grew underground, and the closest he ever came to making a joke was when, while fondling a turnip which was especially white and had especially pretty lilac markings, he said, "Do you think I am a *radical*?" Occasionally he would invite me to tea and, snug beside his fire, we talked over our good strong brew and Peek Frean shortbread biscuits. But on the day I sought his counsel on how to avoid a life of evangelical destitution, I made an appointment. I was as shy as he, for I was no better equipped to be the recipient than he to be the donor of marriage guidance. For some minutes he fiddled with his terrarium while I stroked his marmalade tom, whose name, curiously enough, was Moses; this golden robust fellow, gleaming on an ottoman before the hearth, was the extension of his master—well fed and safe, immune to disarray. At last, having waited in vain for the arrival of the tea cart and then remembering that this was Thursday and was therefore the housekeeper's afternoon off, I spoke to Father Bernard's back.

"Oh, my!" said the auntly priest. "Oh dear! I'm all for lay apostolates, you understand. Third orders do grand things with soup kitchens and warm clothes for the poor—I say, Mrs. Maybank, I'm afraid there isn't any tea today. Would you like a glass of sherry? Or of whiskey? I think I may have gin, too."

And so it was that Father Bernard and I, sipping some very old bourbon neat from some very old topaz Sandwich tumblers, came upon a possible solution to my dilemma. I could tell—by the lacunae during which we blew our noses (we both had awful head colds, and our affliction made the prospect of holy poverty the more discomfiting) and by certain near slips of the tongue—that impassioned converts were less to his liking than impenitent thieves. I told him how all my life I had been making houses for myself—in a corner of the attic in my parents' house in Missouri, in clearings among lodgepole pines in the Adams foothills, in offices I shared with other teachers. My nesting and my neatening were compulsions in me that Theron looked on as plebeian, anti-intellectual, lace-curtain Irish; he said I wanted to spend my life in a tub of warm water, forswearing adventure but, worse, forswearing commitment. My pride of house was the sin of pride. I took no stock in this, I knew it to be nonsense, but I did not know how to defend myself against his barbs, the cruellest of which was that I could not sin with style; as my dreams were wanting in vitality, so was my decoration of houses wanting in taste. (God almighty! Never was a man so set on knocking the stuffing out of his bride!)

Blessed Father Bernard pointed out to me and I was to point out to Theron that churches were made magnificent because they were the domiciles of God, and, since the sacrament of Holy Matrimony was exalted by God, it, too, should be enshrined as beautifully as possible. As for holy poverty, well, *that,* in his opinion, was a way of living that required a vocation, a clear call, and he did not think it was one I was likely to receive. I was so happy at that moment that if I had heard not a clear call but a clarion shout from the skies, "Discalce thyself! Be host to lice! Eat maggots without salt!" I would have refused the bidding and dismissed it as a prank of the Auld Clootie.

I wanted to hug and kiss my savior. Instead, I hugged and kissed Moses, who, ruffled by my forward demonstration, left a lawn of tawny fur on my midnight-blue wool skirt. Father Bernard and I were a little snugly tipsy. Or perhaps it was our head colds as much as the whiskey that made us giggle foolishly as we shook hands and said goodbye.

I thought I had won that bout, but by the time I got home my whimsical consort had changed his tack. This time, he'd met some guy on the Pepperpot Bridge while slogging across it in a blizzard (for no good reason that I could see) who was down on cities. They had spent the afternoon in a Scollay Square pub-crawl talking about getting through to reality by means of Nature, and now there was nothing for it but that we move to some remote outpost of the Laurentians or to the nine hundred and ninety-ninth of the Thousand Islands. (This new preacher was himself aiming for Mangareva, a French island in the South Pacific, at the bottom of the world, where a solitary ship called once a year. That was too Spartan even for my poet, who was dependent on the mail, which brought us *The Divergent* and several other quarterlies, as well as letters from poets and from pen pals he had picked up on retreats.) But our move to the wilderness depended on where I could get a job, because except for a trust fund that paid Theron—depending on the welfare of A.T. & T., the Boston & Maine, and other sobersided companies—about thirty-two dollars a month, I was the only means, visible or covert, of our support. I did not wholly rejoice in the thought of rural life (Thoreau had never fully captivated me), but it was so glamorous an alternative to a pious doss house in Dorchester that I set about at once writing letters to boards of education in the province of Quebec.

At Christmastime that year, the only miracle of my life befell me—a miracle so amazing and so magically well timed that I almost came to believe in Heaven as a place whence miracles were sent. My twin aunts Amy and Jane McKinnon had, after the death of my grandfather, fled Missouri and had gone to New South Wales, where both of them almost at once found prospering husbands; both of them were barren and—poor, pretty dears—loved children. Their disappointment led them to good works among the aborigines, but when the chips were down for Aunt Jane and she commenced to die of cancer, loyalty to her own Gaelic clan atavistically returned, and in her will, besides endowments to charitable institutions for the needy of the bush, she remembered her nieces and nephews. She had been widowed for several years by the time she died, and her estate was considerable. Her bequests to my cousins and to Abigail and me (my brother had been killed in the war the year before, in Normandy) vexed my father and mother, because, not to put too fine a point upon it, as they iteratively implied they did not, they were far more sorely pinched than we were and could have used a helping hand. My father, with one of his bootless and wicked tricks of legerdemain, tried to dissuade us from accepting the money, because the individual sums were small—five thousand apiece, but there were nine of us!

Five thousand dollars! The evening of the day I got the news, Theron and I went to Locke-Ober for dinner and, although we both hated it, we drank champagne. We were charming to each other, and when I proposed that with my windfall we buy a simple cabin somewhere near a country public school, Theron was so bowled over with enthusiasm that he ordered another bottle of champagne. The next day we were as sick as dogs, our stomachs churning with simon-pure hydrochloric acid.

And so, when I had taught my last class at Miss Heath's, we rented our apartment and went to Maine for the summer, working our way slowly down the coast from Eastport, looking for a house to buy. We were so happy! We were so fond! Once again in love, we fell in love with Stonington, where we wanted to spin out the rest of our days, Theron as a commercial fisherman and I as a teacher and a respected small-town matron. I saw myself, in the autumn of my life, retired, putting on a pair of white gloves at three o'clock in the afternoon and putting on a hat and going to the public library to borrow a Ouida novel. But there were no houses for sale.

We finished out the summer in Rankin Harbor, and just before Labor Day, too late for me to find a job, we discovered the house—*my* house—in Edwards Mills; I bought it, paying for it with a check.

For a few weeks, back in Cambridge, we remained friendly. I made a trip back to Maine in October and with no trouble at all got a job teaching at the high school beginning the following year. But the delay took the snap out of Theron's fancy for rural rides, and by Christmas of that year (no manna from Aunt

Jane's Heaven this time) I was a witch again, and all day and all night my God-fearing yokemate burned me at the stake in Salem. He was right. I make no plea for myself, for I had the tongue of an adder and my heart was black with rage and hate.

Unpeopled and at peace, my little country drawing room bewitched me because it was part of the house that belonged to me, and while everything in it was a castoff from my Maybank in-laws or something I had bought at a secondhand store or on the cheap at Filene's, and while it was a far cry from being all of a piece, it had for me a flawed and solacing enchantment. I was thirty now, and I had achieved at last what I had striven for from the beginning: a house and a lawn and trees. I had seen Father Bernard more often than before in Cambridge during the winter, and because he, too, was a nester he could revive my flagging spirits simply by asking me if I thought lightning rods would be necessary or if I planned to put a weathervane on the barn that was attached to the house.

On weekends in the spring, I went up to check on the progress of the workmen. Honoring my marriage by making this temple for it, my acolytes—the carpenters and the electricians, the chimney sweep and the plumber—became my friends and allies. We were together in a blameless conspiracy to overwhelm my husband. They worked with uncommon fidelity (the postmistress, who was an outlander like myself, assured me of this), and each time I unlocked my front door and was greeted with the smell of sawdust and of paint and the litter everywhere of tag ends of hardware and snarls of frayed old electric wires and heaps of plaster commingled with bent and rusted nails, I was delirious. For the last week of March and the first of April, I was in residence during the spring holiday from Miss Heath's. Theron was making a retreat with the Trappists in New Jersey, and I was therefore free to be absorbed completely in washing the windows and hanging the Swiss-organdie glass curtains and, beside them in the living room, the red velvet draperies. (Oh, how sumptuous I thought they were, poor skimpy things!) When the mossy carpet came from Boston, I could not sleep at all that night but kept going downstairs, walking on it in my bare feet; in the morning my bed sheets were downy with green lint from my excursions, and they were rumpled from my excited leapings out of bed.

Where now were my beatitudes? From my darkened living room, I could no longer see the sunlight on the hay and lilies and could only sense the folds and the effluvia of night, and instead of birds saw snakes and instead of grass saw pestilential ooze. Supperless and sleepless, I went up to our bedroom, taking a bottle of whiskey and a dagger of ice in a glass; as I chipped it off the block, I thought how proud I had been to find this huge old ice chest for two dollars and a half.

I drank, stared into space, connived. Some accident befell Theron and Minnie on the lake and they never came back; honorably widowed, I was free. Or they fell in love and their adultery exonerated me of all my capital crimes and all my peccadilloes and all my hypocrisies and self-indulgences. I was in love with their sinful love and saw them doomed, like Paolo and Francesca, to an eternity of passion and of loathing. Theron Maybank the watchful, jealous Salem Puritan, the watchful, zealous Roman Catholic catechumen turned overnight into the most banal kind of sinner even before the baptismal water was dry upon his forehead! Dishonored, I would ascend refreshed, putting aside the ruin of this marriage shattered so ignominiously by *the other woman*, by that most unseemly of disgraces, above all by something *not my fault*, giving me the uncontested right to hate him. And I would come eventually into a second marriage: I saw my husband and I saw my sons. But the house I saw was this house, bought with Aunt Jane's legacy; I saw my fireplaces and I saw my barn until my tears erased them and I sobbed into the pillow as if, already deprived and homeless, I lay alone on stones.

At last, dead drunk, I slept.

There is no advice sounder than this, and none, I daresay, so difficult to follow: Be careful what you wish for, be wary of the predicates of your fantasies and lies. So ignorant and sheeplike is my flesh that if, at the eleventh hour, I telephone my hostess to say that I cannot come to her party because I have a headache, at the twelfth hour a fang of pain strikes deep within my skull, and by the time the party is over and the guests are at home in bed asleep, I am haggard with suffering, doomed to twenty hours of the blindness and throbbing of a migraine. It is not prudent to say, "I would rather break an arm than keep this appointment with the dentist." The hyperbolic substitute we devise in this offhand fashion, if it is realized, does not circumvent but only postpones, so we are doubly burdened by the headache or the broken arm and by another party and a later appointment with the dentist. So when I wished that Theron and Minnie Rosoff would enter upon an outrageous affair, I was safeguarded against the calamities it would sow in me because it seemed an impossibility (as does the migraine or the fractured humerus)—something too good to be true, a fictional expedient having its initiation only in my mind. Because it could not happen, it did not occur to me that it *might* happen and that I *would* be dishonored by it, I *would* taste the vilest degradation, the bitterest jealousy, the most scalding and vindictive rancor.

The daydream was still with me in the morning, and it lasted that day and the next and more days thereafter. Blinded by my wish for the farthest-fetched, the most grotesque product of the former Mrs. Zumwalt's visit, I never dreamed, despite the obvious testimony before my eyes, that it had already come true (and that, indeed, at least so far as Theron was concerned, it had come true about the time my train was pulling out of Portland the day I was homeward bound from Boston). In consequence, I urged Minnie to prolong her stay with us, and, until the Bronsons and Harry Matthews came back, I excused myself from their society by saying that I must prepare for my classes at the high school, so that they could be free to go sailing and swimming and fishing without me. I helped in every way to make the match, which was already a fait accompli and which, when I discovered that it was, was to hurtle me off the brink on which I had hovered for so long into a chasm.

It was true that Theron's attendance on Minnie puzzled me a little, for she was not the kind of woman he liked; she was flirtatious, competitive, argumentatively political. Her taste was modern, and he repudiated as soulless or dull or ugly everything that had been built or painted or written (except for certain poetry and the prose of certain contemporary English divines) after 1850. Moreover, he was, by heritage and by instinct, anti-Semitic, and soon after we met Jerry Zumwalt, he dumbfounded me by saying, "I would never have a Jew as a close friend." And they never had been close—not in the way he was close with friends from boarding-school and college days.

The sensible and wifely side of me looked on his games with Minnie with pleasure: I was glad he was having fun, and perhaps his attraction to her meant that he was relaxing his rigidity. The hermit side of me, the secret boozehead side, looked on the alliance with even greater pleasure: I was blissfully addicted to the fantasies the genie of the bottle contrived for me each night they went for a late swim in the lake, each day they went clamming on the mud flats of the tidal river.

Because now there was no longer anything for us to say to each other, we sat in separate cars on the train from Camden to Boston, but we did so with discretion, and with explanations ready on our tongues lest we encounter anyone we knew. We were so in concord in this desire to keep up appearances that it had not been necessary for us to plan our behavior before we boarded the train. Until Wiscasset we sat together in a parlor car, and for the benefit of the ticket-taker and the porter and for the passengers Theron listed again to me (as he had done to everyone in Edwards Mills, down to the cretinous child who peddled his mother's homemade bread) the reasons we had decided, after all, not to live in Maine.

So on the train, among the travellers returning from Mt. Desert and Blue Hill, heedless of everything but the boats they had stored and the pleasures and problems of the city season they were now confronting, my husband, unknown to them, loudly addressed congratulations to us both on our sensible leave-taking. And when the derelict schooner in the Sheepscot at Wiscasset loomed forth, he felt he had said enough, and, turning to me with a perfect imitation of solicitude, even bending forward to look into my face, he said, "You look worn out. Don't you want a drink?"

I nodded, accepting his signal, and gathered together my purse and scarf and book (I had not understood a printed word for months) and, matching my manners to his for the sake of those total strangers, I said, "You needn't come. I know you want to work."

"You're a dear," he said and picked his briefcase up off the floor, opening it to show a Loeb "Confessions of St. Augustine," distended with sheets of onionskin on which for a year or so he had made fine notes, cryptic and self-centered, in black ink, which, however, dried as purple, giving the pages a schoolish look. "I'll join you when I've finished Monica's death."

Liar, I thought. Swindler. Ten minutes before the North Station you'll come into the club car, where you'll find me drunk; the sight of you will drive me wild, for I will know what you have been doing, with your eyes so piously attentive to the Latin of your little book. You will have been dreaming, mooning, delighting yourself with thoughts of your reunion with Minnie, your playmate, this very night. (He had dismissed me with that word. "I don't want a wife," he had said, "I want a playmate.")

I could not help myself. I said, "Where will you have din-din tonight with your playmate?"

My question enraged us both, and I got up before he could answer. As I left the car, I looked back; apparently deep among the Manichees, he was thinking of his doll-sized, doll-dressed doll with her bisque-doll skin.

The bar car was empty except for two Army officers recollecting D Day. It was not necessary for me to be surreptitious as I took a phenobarbital before I started to drink my lulling drink, but even so, having asked the waiter for a glass of water, I explained, with Theron's kind of insistence, that I was taking a headache pill, and I was careful not to say aspirin, fearing he might observe how small the pellet was. Like Theron, I stared at the pages of a book; like his, my mind was far.

We would say goodbye at the North Station and I would then go to the South and take a train for New York, where I had an appointment with a psychoanalyst two days hence.

We had killed Pretty Baby and killed her kittens. Theron himself had put them in a gunnysack and weighted it with stones and had rowed halfway out to Loon Islet and dropped them among the perch and pickerel.

He beached the boat. I was waiting for him on the front stoop; I had already locked the door. The idling of the motor in the waiting taxi was the only sound that broke the silence of that absolutely azure and absolutely golden early autumn day.

Woden's Day

THE Savages had come from Graymoor, Missouri, to Adams, Colorado, in 1925, when Cora was ten. Both parents had known the town at different times and in different ways: Maud, then Miss McKinnon, upon her graduation from Willowbrook Female Seminary—ten miles from Graymoor, where she boarded but at her father's command went home on Sundays lest she stray beyond the United Presbyterian pale and lie abed on the Sabbath or read Zola's brazen novels—had accepted the position of assistant mistress in a small private school in Adams named, remarkably, Summerlid. "What kind was it?" her children, doubled up with laughter, wanted to know. "A leghorn? A Panama? Was it a sunbonnet, Mama? Did it have a mosquito net on it to keep the horseflies off?" Mrs. Savage, who had taken her year-long academic career seriously, was vexed and wounded and tried to put them down by saying, "I have told you and told you that Mr. Summerlid of Grosse Pointe founded it for unfortunate tubercular children. Now stop fashing me." But the rotten children, especially Randall and Cora, helplessly seized with giggles, ran off howling, "Missy Maud McKinnon pounded fractions into the wallydrag noggins of head chiggers in a lousy limey sailor hat!" They'd one time heard Dan (as they called their father) say this as part of one of his long ridiculing, affectionate litanies. They did not know that it had made their mother cry and, if they had, probably would not have cared. Why Dan and Mama did not run away from each other and quit their endless insults, they could not imagine. (Once when they discussed the matter in a tentative and half-fearful way, they ended up by shrugging their shoulders and saying, "Ishkabibble. One of these sunshiny days we'll run away from them.") Miss McKinnon had loved her experience of being away from home out in the wilds that way, and while she was devoted to her family and her friends and sometimes was homesick enough to cry, it had been so nice to meet new people, to be taken into the Sororsis which had supper meetings at a different house each week (oh, those treats of Mexican chili con carne and of creamed sage-hen!). And riding burros!

"We called them 'Rocky Mountain canaries,' you know. What pesky scamps they were! They'd find an appetizing bush and you couldn't budge them till they'd had their fill. We'd whip and kick and scold but it was *no ma'am* as far as they were concerned, and they were so comical about it we nearly fell off laughing. The big its!" She had loved to go on picnics beside waterfalls; they'd sing and gather wildflowers and sometimes pretend they were oreads and go prancing and weaving through the lodgepole pines. During the Easter holiday she had gone to Manitou Springs with some other young ladies from Summerlid and they had had a real lark, but, to tell the truth, they had found the mineral waters disagreeable beyond words: "Pew!" said Mama and held her nose.

Some years before Dan Savage's future wife had wended her slow way west on the Denver & Rio Grande with her trunk and her foulard parasol and her travelling tailormaid of grey De'Beige cloth, Dan had taken it into his quixotic head to go prospecting for gold in the Rockies. Throughout the summer of 1892, he had panned the rivers from the lower canyons to the tundra of the Wilson range and had found long tons of pyrites and his placer pan had brimmed with fool's gold. No, he hadn't made his fortune, but he had had a larruping good time; that had been far and away a summer better than all summers before when he and his older brother, Uncle Jonathan—a year ahead of him at college—had had to drive their father's herd up from the Panhandle to Dodge City through dust storms so bad that when you took a drink of water you had a mouthful of mud. He had graduated from Amity College that spring, *summa cum laude*, and this holiday had been his reward. Mind you, if he had wanted to go to sea or go to New York City to explore the music halls and free-lunch saloons and Turkish baths, his father wouldn't have put up a red cent for a fandango such as that; but while he was a cattle man and a crop man, he had an understanding of gold-fever and he staked his son to fare on the cars to Denver, the price of a horse to ride and a horse to pack with gear and grub. Dan had a companion, a college classmate, Thad McPherson, a fellow so brilliant at Hebrew that to the other students, all Methodist or Presbyterian, he was known as The Jew, and then, because he was so often lost in thought that, strolling by himself, he sometimes got lost in the woods by the

river and missed classes and examinations, he came to be called
The Wandering Jew. And to top it all off, he played a Jew's harp
and played it like a professional, sometimes as rowdy-dowdy as
a showboat skalawag, sometimes as sweet as a Muse. He was a
pretty solemn man, and silent. Yet he had been a good friend
to have along that summer to speculate on matters of geology,
to wonder ("By the Lord Harry!") at the beaver's practicality
and genius, to come, amazed, upon a solid acre of glacier lilies,
to hack away with pick-axes (and find pyrites shining like pure
gold), to pan in the ice-cold amber streams and, along with the
fool's gold, get a mess of caddis worms. Often of an evening
when they were full of trout, fresh-caught, and fried mush
with bacon gravy, they would talk well past moonlight beside
their camp fire about what they had learned at Amity of history
and the literatures of ancient languages: they had learned little
else—some mathematics, some chemistry and physics, some
biology. Thad had a leaning toward The Almighty but Dan
was an up-to-the-minute Darwinian and they had debated on
this ticklish subject until the moon went pale, "I'd try my level
best to rile him, but old Thad was as mild as mother's milk.
His theology had no more brimstone in it than a daisy. I think
that old Wandering Jew was a B.C. pagan, believed in the wee
people, believed in Santy Claus." About once every two years,
Dan got a letter from him, from a different state each time, for
he had turned into a salesman for the Watkins Company that
sold spices and condiments and soap and such like from door
to door. One time he had turned up in Adams, a tall, gaunt
awkward man, as red and yellow as a summer sunset. Mama
saw his sample case and said, as she always said to peddlers,
that the lady of the house was not at home; but he only asked,
gently, to see Dan. The two of them with Oddfellow, the dog,
a border collie, went off towards the mountains and Dan didn't
come home until long after dark. "I declare," Mama was later
and often to say to each child individually and in confidence
as if she had never uttered this dread fear before, "that man
looked like a *ghost* to me! I don't care about that carrot-top or
that red face of his, he *felt* like a ghost, and when he went off
with your father that way, I thought the pair of them would
vanish. Just vanish."

The summer in Adams had been Dan's Wanderjahr, her

nine months there at Summerlid had been Mama's debutante season, and when their life in Graymoor came crashing down upon them in disgrace, they picked this distant hiding place. Cora's last memory of Graymoor was of going to say goodbye to Albert and Heinie, the children of the chicken farmer next door. It was in the morning and Mrs. Himmel was busy with the wash so there was no Kinder Kaffeeklatsch (in the morning, of course, it would have been called Zweites Frühstück, which the Savage children pronounced "Fruit-stick"), but the little boys had taken them into the parlor and ritualistically had wound up the seven music boxes and when the nightingale, *Der Liebling Vogel,* sang to her for the very last time, huge golden globes of tears blinded Cora, but she managed not to let them burst and spill. They all shook hands then and, unsmiling, contrapuntally, the Scotch-Irish children said, "Auf Wiedersehen," and the German children said, "Ta-ta. See you in church."

Grandfather Brian Savage had died of dengue fever in Coffeyville, Kansas, when he and his youngest daughter were almost within hailing distance of home after having gone half way around the world to visit kinsmen in Australia. Aunt Caroline, her father's darling, his blooming emerald-eyed and raven-locked colleen, had been as quirky and as saucy as he and when she was seventeen the two of them took ship at San Francisco to go have a look at kangaroos and stranger, albeit technically human, beasts in the outback. And on the very day that they set sail for that outlandish continent, Granny and Aunt Elizabeth who was twenty, as spirited as the other two but brainier and more domesticated, embarked at New Orleans for a stylish and conventional tour of London and Paris, Vienna and Rome. They all went off at the end of June, the same June that Dan had gone to Colorado.

He would push his hat back, take off his glasses, close his eyes and, remembering, say, "Thad and I would have been about at Loveland when the tugs were toting their ships out to the bounding main, one east, one west; Loveland or a short piece beyond. We'd paid handsomely for those horses in Denver and we treated them like little Lords and Ladies Fauntleroy, not working them hard, keeping them in fettle. Besides, we weren't in any hurry and the weather was fine to mosey through." Then he would laugh his infernal laugh. "I'd lie there under the stars and think about Brother Jonathan with his mouth full of dust and his eyes full of the sweat of his brow, punching cows in Paris, Texas, while our sweet Sister Lizzie was buying kid gloves in Paris, France." But Jonathan had had his summer off the year before when he had gone to Crete to be Sir Arthur Evans' third water-boy's sixth water-boy. And then, almost to himself, with contempt, with pity, with disappointment, Dan mused, "If he wanted to be an archaeologist, why didn't he turn in and be one? Look at him now, tied to the Tammany lion's tail with all the rest of the rag-tag-bobtail tinhorns of New York City." Uncle Jonathan was a lawyer and Dan, despising the profession, looked on his success and his wealth as ill-got; moreover, Jonathan had political ambitions and Dan, schooled by his father and mother, had looked on politicians as scum.

The travellers had been gone for half a year. In the autumn, Uncle Jonathan had entered his second year of law school at the University of Missouri and Dan Savage was left alone in Kavanagh to study over what he wanted to do with the rest of his life. Should he be a scholar? Teach Greek at some high-falutin Eastern college? He read Herodotus, Thucydides, he read Xenophon and Arrian, Hesiod and Homer, Sophocles and Aeschylus. But then, languid in a hammock on an amber day, he'd be seduced by Vergil and he would meditate on vine-yards and bees and growing melons under glass in a pastoral, green land like this thrice-blessed Missouri. He'd had his fill of Longhorn beeves and the crude company of drovers.

He had enjoyed being the boss of the Kavanagh house, being alone. Once in a while, he would invite Thad or some other of his Amity classmates to come and visit for a while and his mother's cook, accustomed to feeding a flock—for when the elder Savages were in residence they and their daughters had guests to dinner four or five times each week—was pleased to serve her Louisiana French specialities to these easygoing young men and to be praised by them. The trouble was that most of them weren't easygoing; they had found jobs and some of them had already married, or, like Jonathan, they had gone on to universities to prepare themselves for medicine or the law. "What's the hurry, boys?" he'd say to them. But their fathers were not rich as Brian Savage's was and their expectations, if there were any, were far in the future. For a few days they would ride and shoot, revel at table, play billiards after dinner ("Most of the poor coots had never seen a billiard table in a private house and, my! how they would carry on") and act the role of carefree young squires but then they would itch to be back in their harnesses: "For what? For *gain*! Aye, God, they were no better than my father's hands, shackled to the land. Pawns in the hands of nature. I recollect the way those bozos used to loaf around the kitchen stove before the sun was up and before the *women* were up to make their breakfast, just purely and simply waiting in their dumb animal way for the sunrise. Like apes. They'd been raised on the precept that a man must get up when the Lord gets up, and out of their abounding self-conceit, they reckoned to do the Lord one better, but it never got them anywhere. And then they took their pay and spent it all on Jamaica rum and the doxies who just *happened* to be ambling by the horse-troughs in town when they were watering their nags before they themselves went into the saloons to wallow. Yes sir, with the exception of Thad, that moon-struck old Wandering Jew, my college classmates were not different by a whit from Pa's help. The early bird catches the worm and it don't matter if the worm sticks in his craw."

One time Randall said to his father, "Sir, why do you get up before the sun?" and Dan replied, "I emulate Frederick the Great." His tone was final; the reminiscence and the metaphor were finished; he was through talking. Randall and Cora had looked up Frederick the Great in the Encyclopedia Britannica, but they could find no mention of his being an early riser. Just as on another occasion, when Dan had bragged for the seven hundred and nineteenth time that his pulse rate was 59, the same as Napoleon's, they had tried and failed to check this arresting detail. If they had persevered in their research and tried to pin Dan down, they would have got nowhere. Instead, they would have got rods and acres, *miles*, of the Seven Years' War and the French Revolution; once Dan started he would never stop. He knew too much for a child, for anybody, to bear.

It was along about Thanksgiving time when Dan had got his sister Caroline's telegram from Coffeyville, saying that his father was gravely ill. The ship bringing them back from Australia

had docked at Galveston, and they had made their way up
through Texas and Oklahoma, changing trains a dozen times
and travelling often by stage from one depot town to the next.
They had been headed for Wichita, whence they could get a
through train to St. Louis, when the fever had laid the old man
so low that they could not go on another mile. He was out of
his head for a week before he died and he died in the evening of
the day Dan got to his bedside in the one antigodlin hotel—the
floors were so slanty that when a man walked through a door
he thought he might pitch right through the window opposite.
It was a hell of a note to meet your maker in that one-horse
burg on the plains where the wind whipped along steady at a
mile a minute and your handkerchief froze to your nose if you
had to blow it. The irony, the almighty irony, of perishing of
tropical breakbone fever in November in Coffeyville, Kansas!
"Your mother's father's Father which art in Heaven every so
often takes it into his cerebellum to play a practical joke and
when he does, lo and behold and *mirabile dictu,* he does it up
to a fare-thee-well. No holds barred when he wants to pull off
a real dandy."

Granny Savage and Aunt Lizzie got to Kavanagh two days
after Dan and Aunt Caroline came back with the coffin from
Coffeyville. (Cora had made up a shameful rhyme, so shameful
she never even told it to Randall: "When they brought the
coffin from Coffeyville/I poured me coffee and drank my fill.")
And so, instead of a grand family reunion with tales to tell of
Europe's wonders and the marvels of the Antipodes, there was a
funeral. "My mother and I mourned the man," said Dan. "The
others . . ." he shooed off his sisters and his brothers with the
back of his hand. Grandfather Savage's will was no surprise to
Dan, his second son and second child: the burden of the estate
was left to the widow and the rest was divided equally among
the four children, but while Jonathan, Caroline and Elizabeth
would receive their share in trust, Dan was given his in capital
since he, according to the flowery testament, was the only
one of the heirs who would know how to manage his money.
The Texas holdings and the Missouri holdings (which Brian
Savage had greatly extended after the War between the States
by buying up bounty grants for next to nothing from veterans

who wanted to join the westward push) and a ninety-thousand-acre tract in Arizona, not stocked or farmed but bought for speculation, were also parcelled out equally.

Dan, in those months alone in Kavanagh, pondering the route he wished to take, had concluded finally against school-mastering; he would be Vergil rather than Aristotle and when he was not upon his rural rides, overseeing his flocks and grain, his apiary and his vineyards, he would write: not idylls, not epic poetry but fiction and meditative essays. In time he would take a wife because he wanted sons, sons to teach, thereby combining all his talents, agrarian, literary, academic. But he was in no hurry.

Jonathan quit Missouri for New York City as soon as he had his law degree; Caroline went back to Australia to marry a sheep-rancher she had fallen in love with when her father had taken her to see the wallabies and kangaroos and her Irish uncles and cousins. You may be sure that one of the early kings of cattledom, Brian Savage, mightily shifted in his grave when this mésalliance took place. He couldn't have known what had been taking place behind his back: else he would have out-witted the Lord and risen from his bed in Coffeyville at least until he'd seen his darling girl-child wedded to a decent man. Sheep! And Lizzie, sap-sweet, sap-silly Lizzie took up with a sap-*sucker* she met during Mardi Gras in New Orleans and with him went off to California to grow oranges. With her money. He was a Lothario was Lizzie's pretty Cajun and after a year and a baby, he vanished, sank plumb out of sight. She married again and married this time sensibly: Uncle Frank Boatright was an engineer, a bridge-builder, a dull, good man and Lizzie had two more children by him. After the birth of the second, Cora's Cousin Lucian, poor headlong Lizzie, feeling her oats, was out riding by herself in wild country beyond the orange grove when her horse was spooked to frenzy by a sidewinder and threw her, breaking her leg so intricately and mangling it so grievously that it had to be amputated just above her knee. ("You recollect that your Dan was thrown from a horse when he was a chap," said Dan and reached for his blackthorn walking stick to illustrate. Usually the stick was not in the room and he would go to look for it; by the time he had come back, his audience had dispersed. They knew what came afterward:

the children's mother's father's Lord had, for once in His life, been just—well, hardly just, but not as ornery as usual—it had been a cruelty to separate a woman from her leg but it would have been a sin crying to Heaven for vengeance if the victim had been a man.)

Dan stayed on in Missouri, lord of the manor, master of the hounds and the hinds, his mother's manager and playmate, her host when she was hostess. And, faithful to his promise to himself, he was a writer. There was a photograph of him sitting at his writing table beside an open and uncurtained window: some flowering tree is in bloom just outside and through its white, enclouded branches, the sun lies full upon a huge dictionary held closed by flanges on a stand; he has only to turn a little to the right to open the book which will lie flat, cleverly supported by the flexible brackets as he looks up a word. The table is square and its narrow aprons are carved with interlocking garlands and they are edged with egg-and-dart. The table is strewn with papers, on one of which Dan is writing with a long-stemmed pen; his other hand is relaxed, the fingers (how filled with ease they seem!) touching another sheet. He is in profile and because his sharply aquiline nose is in shadow, his face looks delicate and young. How young, unlined, how cleanly his high forehead reaches up to meet the dense curls of his dark hair. He has taken off his collar—you can see it lying on top of the bookcase just behind him—and the sleeves of his shirt look uncommonly full, they look as full as bishop sleeves, and the starched cuffs are closed with oval links; his galluses are wide. In the foreground, on the floor or perhaps on some low stool, there is a jardinière of branches bearing flowers. It is a portrait of youth in the youth of a year. You read his mortal vulnerability in his lowered eyes (he does not yet wear thick glasses) and in his bent, clean-shaven neck.

The photograph had been taken to commemorate the sale of his first short story to *Century* magazine and Granny Savage, who prided herself on her lack of pride, had had a man come over from Jefferson City to take it. Ostensibly he was there to photograph the new outbuildings, the new milkhouse and the new silo. At the same time, she and Dan had posed in the lounge where they sat playing war with their lead soldiers, smiling, both of them, Granny's white hair piled up in a pompadour

with a coquettish bow above one ear. And there was another
picture of them on their horses, Dan on his father's favorite, a
strawberry roan named Jack, and Granny on her much smaller
Betsy Ross: Dan wore a hard hat and an ascot and a jacket
belted across the back, and Granny, in a broad-brimmed hat
with an ostrich feather curling down against her cheek, wore a
divided skirt and a pin-tucked shirtwaist beneath her tailored
jacket with a perky peplum.

None of the children ever knew certainly how this loving
son and mother had come to their violent and unconditional
parting. It was not until they were grown that Cora and Randall
understood how weak a man their father was for all his tempests
and his brutality; and, seeing that, saw to their incredulity how
strong their mother was, that often weepy, often quaking
goose. They had been born in Graymoor, they deduced, in the
shadow of the McKinnon house, rather than in Kavanagh near
Granny Savage because Grandfather McKinnon had so willed.
But why? They were only seven miles apart and if Mama had
been dead set on being an obedient Sabbitarian daughter and
bringing up her children in her own image, why could they
not have made the weekly trip by buggy or, a year or so later
by auto, to hear The Word and learn the topography of Hell?
Had the McKinnon clan feared the snows of winter or summer
thunderstorms? But, that aside, why had Dan knuckled under?

Kavanagh was not a town; it was a place, having two blocks of
buildings that housed the barest essentials: a bank, a feed store,
a general store for buttons and baking powder, the sheriff's
office behind which was the jail and above which the doctor
and the lawyer practiced (the doctor was also the dentist, and
the lawyer was also the Justice of the Peace and the Notary
Public and every second election or so, the Mayor), the saloon
and over that the hotel; the post-office and the telegraph office
were combined and so were the livery and the undertaking
parlor. There was a single church, Methodist, and beside it
stood the Manse. There was a barber chair in the pool-hall
and the blacksmith and his sons were also the carpenters, the
chimney-sweeps, the veterinarians and the well-diggers. On
Saturday nights, the one-room schoolhouse was the grange
hall. From this small, trim and modest hub narrow roads radi-

ated out to a baker's dozen or so of large, rich homesteads like the Savage's.

But Graymoor was a town with a Main Street a quarter of a mile long and dozens of other streets named Front Street, Elm, Maple, Miller's Lane, Plainview, Bluff, First, Second, Third and (why on earth?) Lausanne. The McKinnons lived solitary on a hill that rose up from Aberdeen Avenue, and while the Savages were out of town a way so that their address was RFD, their road was known as The High Street. Dan, used to thinking of land in terms of miles, had a mere ten acres. And these adjoining a poultry farm run by a limberger who, never seeing the ring-tailed farce of it, had named one of his kids Heinie!

Graymoor was on the railroad, on a spur of the Missouri Pacific and Santa Fe, and at four o'clock each Monday morning, Grandfather McKinnon swung aboard and from then until late Friday evening he was a conductor, punching tickets and calling "All aboard!" from St. Louis to Los Angeles and back again. By his wife and his sister and his daughters and, until they learned the truth, his grandchildren, he was known as being "in railroads." At one time, thrilled, Cora thought he was the locomotive engineer; later, even more infatuated, she thought he travelled in a private car similar to Theodore Roosevelt's of which she had seen photographs in an old copy of the *National Geographic*.

Despite the fact that they no longer shared the same roof and nightly dined together, the devotion between Dan and Granny did not falter. And then, when Cora was nine years old, they quarreled and quarreled for keeps. Dan had gone to Jefferson City and had stayed there for two nights and when he got back to Graymoor, he came home in the jitney; this in itself had been unusual, for after a visit to the stock exchange, he liked to walk home in his important city clothes, his gray fur fedora at a rakish angle but maintaining its dignity the while, carrying his blackthorn in his suede-gloved hand, smoking a cigar. But on this day, he was in such a tearing rush that he got out of the snorting jitney and straight into the Franklin. Cora and Randall were playing mumblety-peg under the black walnut tree and they heard him call out, "To Kavanagh!" in answer, they supposed, to their mother who must have seen him from the kitchen door. It had been some time in the early spring, for Cora remembered that grape-hyacinths had come up in the lawn.

Afterward, they began to be poor. And never again, not once, did they see Granny Savage, although at Christmastime she always sent them presents, clothes, usually, from Marshall Field's, so grand they made the rest of their duds look like something the cat had dragged in. Their poorness showed itself gradually, so gradually, indeed, that they misconstrued it for something else: when their older sisters, Abigail and Evangeline, had to give up their fancy-dancing class, they thought Dan was only being cranky. For their friends, who were in their second year of ballet and were beginning round-dancing with boys, they invented a yarn that eventually they believed: they said they had no time for they were learning French because they were going to be sent to boarding school in Paris. (Who in all of Graymoor could say more than "Parlez-vous"?) Dan's bilious moods came oftener, his "spells" were terrifying: one time he went into Hubbard's Dry, where both Aunt Jane and Aunt Amy clerked, and inveighed against his father-in-law with such blood-curdling invective, such heart-splitting blasphemy that Mr. Hubbard himself ushered him out of the store like a hobo. And he looked a hobo: barefoot, his long underdrawers showing beneath his unlaced cavalry britches; his hair was as long as William Jennings Bryan's and he hadn't shaved in a week; tobacco juice oozed down his chin from the quid he held in his cheek. Mr. Hubbard sent the mortified McKinnon twin sisters home for the rest of the day, and they sent word to Mama by their hired girl to come right over. The town was appalled and off its head with delight; the school-children imitated Dan's limp and spat imaginary tobacco juice at the Savages' feet and made up tirades with nonsense words to scream at them until Abigail, with mysterious and quietly theatrical power, one day at recess stood on the top step of the stairs leading to the main door and commanded silence. "My father is a genius," she said. "My father is poetically licensed by President Wilson to do anything he likes. Hark to my words and from now on cease and desist this persiflage." It worked, as everything always worked for her when she let out those wondrous words and phrases, as harmless as fireflies but seeming, to her cowed audience, like red-hot buckshot. She must have been as shamed as the others but though she might be put on the rack or pinioned to the Catherine wheel, she was Dan's unflinching martyr.

When he was himself—that other self, the reader of Mommsen and Shakespeare and of Victor Hugo, the writer, the kindly spouse and papa—he would be barbered and shaved; he would whistle arias from *Madame Butterfly* and dance his little jig in front of Mama, sportively untie her apron strings and with it pretend to be a toreador and he would carol, "There's always the land, me bonny! There's always the star in the Lone Star State! The amber waves of grain wave o'er the Show-Me! And my ship, she is a-comin' in, lass o' the braes."

The children could not make head or tail of this impromptu spiel. Later on, they would learn that on those two days in Jefferson City, he had been wiped clean of all his capital and had, as well, made ducks and drakes of Granny's. Granny did not feel the pinch—the money he had hurled to the four winds had been her own, and Grandfather Savage's trust fund allowed her to go on being nearly as rich as she had always been. And he was far from destitute himself because he still shared the revenue from the productive Texas cattle ranches and the Missouri farms scattered all over the state. It was Granny's disgust at Dan's reckless, know-it-all prodigality that had made her send him packing. And there was something else: Granny, that smart, witty, well-read, sure-footed little woman had fallen hook, line and sinker for Mary Baker Eddy, led down the garden path by her daughter Lizzie who, in southern California, was prey to all diseases of the mind. And Granny, indignant over the encroachments of age (her hearing in one ear was much diminished, she had several times felt dizzy when she dismounted Betsy Ross after riding in the sun), was easily persuaded that she could handle her flesh with her mind. In the beginning, she had been skeptical when in the copy of *Science and Health* that Aunt Lizzie had sent her, she had read among the testimonials printed at the back the unequivocal claim of a man that while chopping wood, he had swung his hatchet too high and had deeply gashed his temple, an injury that would most certainly have been fatal had he not immediately requested his wife to read to him from Mrs. Eddy. Within half an hour the Mortal Error was corrected, and where the wound and rushing blood had been there was nothing but a white painless swelling. But while she knew this to be bosh and while some of Mrs. Eddy's God-talk affronted her, she was converted and believed that she could heal her servants and her livestock *in absentia*.

Sometimes, at winter dusk before the open fire in the living room, Dan, reflective as he peeled an apple with his Bowie ("I declare to goodness you're going to cut your fingers off with that desperado weapon!" cried Mama. "For land's sake, use your *pen*knife!" Dan went right on and finally let the whole unbroken dark red spiral skin fall into the kindling hod), would say to whoever was within earshot—Cora was sure that if there were no one in the room, he would address the stuffed golden pheasant on the mantel—"I mourned to see my Ma go daft. I lamented the degeneration of that fine intellect. It riddled her like ergot through a stand of oats. You see there yonder that fair crop shimmering? Now close your eyes and look again and what do you see? Black blight."

Then he would throw his naked apple into the fire and listen to its juices hiss. "But for all of that, it was a joke. A joke! A high larruping opera comique and not unlike the one the Great Lord put on for Job." His laughter strangled him; his eyes screwed up like a bawling baby's and the veins on his forehead swelled and pulsed, a dreadful blue.

Mama no longer had her chafing-dish suppers. Nobody came to call except the aunts. Now and then Aunt Rowena came with the first cousins, Fannie, Faith and Florence, with whom the Savages were instructed to play although the mothers knew that their children hated one another and even such a peaceable game as Statues could end in a nosebleed or a broken collar bone. Florence, the oldest and the biggest, had once clapped a pail on Evangeline's head, jamming it down so hard that it wouldn't come off and Dan had had to cut it with his tin-shears; there wasn't even enough room in there for Evangeline to scream but she hopped around like somebody with St. Vitus dance while Dan crooned softly to her, "Whoa, there, girl. Hold on there, girl. Your old Dan ain't going to cut your ear off." This reassurance sent her hurtling blindly into a cherry tree which she hugged for dear life and while she was thus occupied, Dan got the bucket off.

"It was all her fault," said Florence. "She double-dared me to."

"I never!" sobbed Evangeline, holding her ears. The tin-shears had cut clean through one of her pigtails and about an inch of it was gone. Abigail picked it up from the grass, its blue bow still tightly tied.

"You lie, Florence Sinclair," she said in her coldest, her most authoritative voice. "You lie like a rug. The Savages hate the Sinclairs and will forever and a day. Avaunt, you three witches! Graymalkin calls!" Evangeline was calmed. The Sinclair sisters gingerly backed away. But Dan broke the spell by clapping his hands and crying out, "Bravissima! It'll soon be time for your first buskins, Mamsell Bernhardt!"

Wholly baffled, the three sisters ran to the house. After that, when Aunt Rowena came, the children were put into the dining room to play Twenty Questions or I Spy, and the door to the small parlor was left open so that the mothers could hear if a ruckus broke out. It never did, for the seven children were as quiet as mice, trying to hear what the ladies were saying.

This life in Graymoor might have gone on for years and years, gone on until the last embattled tribesman was six feet under, if Grandfather McKinnon had not died. Or, as for some months afterward, Grandmother, Great Aunt Flora, Aunt Rowena and Mama were to say, been *murdered* by Jane and Amy, always known as "the girls." They ran away from home.

Who did they know in St. Louis high society to get them invitations to the Veiled Prophet's Ball? There were no kinsmen in St. Louis, no collaterals. A drummer come to Hubbard's Dry to sell a bill of goods and, by the way, to vamp those pretty twins with their mournful violet eyes and their perfect laughing lips? Of course not: drummers were not connected to high echelons. The store was closed on Wednesday afternoons as was every other place of business, a practice carried over from New England whence the founding fathers had come. One Wednesday, Jane telephoned home a little after eleven and there was no answer; Grandma and Great Aunt Flora were outside making sure that the men were transplanting that big old box elder to just the place they wanted it, and the hired girl was making soap and was at that tricky point of putting in the lye. But Central (Jessie Lovelady; after five o'clock Belle Bruce came on) said she'd keep on ringing and give the message which was, "Tell her we're going to have ourselves a picnic and won't be home for dinner." Well, Grandma was put out when Jessie Lovelady finally reached her, but she got over her pet—it *was* an awfully bonny autumn day, smelling of nuts. She always liked to have a little treat for dinner on the girls' day off and that day she had planned banana fritters, but never mind, she'd have them for supper instead. It didn't worry her until twilight came and they didn't come home and night came and they didn't come home. About nine o'clock she called Mama and Mama said she knew in her bones that something was *very* rotten in the state of Denmark. If they'd been abducted, they couldn't have telephoned. The picnic sounded to her like a fish-story, because from the year one the girls had been hemstitching linens and painting Haviland for their hope-chests on their free afternoons. (They couldn't let Grandfather know what they were doing so they couldn't sew their dreams on Saturday night. On Saturday night they hemmed didies for the Heathen Chinee.) Mama told Grandma that she'd better call the police and she did. She got the Marshal himself, Mr. Doff, who told her to look in their rooms and see if they had taken any clothes and then to call him back. I say! Their closets and their bureau drawers were as clean as a whistle! She looked in the attic and gone was the trunk Mama had taken to Colorado when she went to teach at Summerlid! Gone were both hat-boxes! And the only umbrellas left in the umbrella stand were Mama's and Aunt Flora's, and the spare one in case it rained as an afternoon caller was saying goodbye. As soon as Marshal Doff heard this, he called Frank Ferguson, the jitney driver. Frank Ferguson knew every bit of everybody's business because he eavesdropped while he drove his high maroon Hupmobile and at the same time spied on pedestrians: if you wanted to know who had stopped using the jakes and moved indoors, ask Frank Ferguson and he would tell you that he had seen Mrs. Cobbett come out of Hubbard's on Tuesday at 11:22 A.M. carrying a sack that unmistakably contained a roll of bathroom paper.

Frank was asleep but he snapped to attention when the police chief called and he was overjoyed to say that why, yes, he had

taken the McKinnon twins to the depot for the 1:45 inter-urban
to Jeff City. Were they carrying any baggage? No, they weren't
but one week ago that day, they had come up to him when he
was parked in front of the P. O. and had asked him to come
to their house at 7 p.m. to take a trunk and two hat-boxes and
check them through to St. Louis. They gave him their tickets
and he returned them the next day at Hubbard's Dry. All they
had with them today was just their pocketbooks and umbrellas
and a book apiece. They didn't do much talking; mainly they
giggled, but they said enough to let him understand that they
were going to the Veiled Prophet's Ball: he had wondered at
the time, pardon him please, how they had managed to get
their father's permission to go. Last Wednesday night at seven.
The pieces were beginning to fit together. That was why those
perfidious minxes, looking as if butter would not melt in their
mouths, had said they were so absolutely, posi*tive*ly fagged out
from unpacking a shipment of winter coats at the store that
morning that they could *not*, absolutely, posi*tive*ly could *not*
go to Prayer Meeting. Grandma and Aunt Flora and the girls
always had supper with the Widow Bird on Wednesday night
at her house (she came to them for "high tea" after Christian
Endeavor on Saturday afternoon) at five o'clock and this gave
them ample time to be leisurely at table and do the washing up
and even crochet for a little while until they went to the church
just across the road on the dot of seven. It was then that Frank
Ferguson had come to pick up their traps. How did he manage
that big trunk all by himself? He didn't. Chub Jackson, Judge
McIntyre's yard man and strong as an ox, had brought it down
the steep brick steps cut into the lawn and he and it and the
hat-boxes and the girls were rowed up there right on Aberdeen
Avenue. Chub was ready with a couple of ropes and he strapped
the trunk on the running board and then rode in the back seat
down to the depot and took it off and put it on the St. Louis
through baggage wagon. One of the twins, it might have been
Jane, it might have been Amy, you couldn't tell them apart, had
given him what Frank was pretty certain was four bits. (And
he himself only charged two bits for the run. Life is like that.)

Mama and Grandma and Great Aunt Flora were terrified
out of their wits. Aunt Rowena, basically a carnal woman,
shrugged her shoulders and laughing meanly said, "I hope they

get themselves some Good-time Charleys. I could put one to use myself." She despised Uncle Hugh who was despicable. And while she was mortified to be Dan's in-law (Catch Hugh Sinclair chewing: Never!), in her heart of hearts she admired his eccentricity. This was a fact known to the children because after school one day, Randall was lying under the bandstand in the Lincoln Park, thinking. All of a sudden he heard Aunt Rowena's voice coming, he thought, from a ringside bench on the northeast side. "My brother-in-law, you know who he is, Dan Savage?" she said to someone. "The writer. He got word yesterday that his novel has been accepted by Dodge and Company, the publishing concern in New York City." Her companion said, "Sakes! My, Maud must be proud." "She is," said Aunt Rowena. And she was. Only, at that time, the jealous sister's statement was not true because her sister had not told *her* the truth. The only one in Graymoor who knew the truth was Dan.

In those dreadful days (The Ordeal as it came to be known) between the twins' disappearance and Grandfather McKinnon's return for the Sabbath bonfire, so much simmered under so many kettle-lids that everybody walked on tippy-toe, including Dan, The Great.

That Sunday, the diminished McKinnon congregation sat in Grandfather's parlor, erect of spine and apparently alert, although a look of languid disease showed forth now and again in all the captives. It seemed to Cora that Grandfather had never read with so much righteous rage as he did this afternoon: his voice rocked the house, its walls were going to tumble down like Jericho. How had Grandma broken the news to him? Poor little tea-cosy of a woman, she must have been scared silly. The clock in the hall chimed four and, at the last sonorous boom, something happened.

Cora and Abigail were sitting side by side on an uncushioned ottoman. Cora was demented with discipline, distempered with swallowed screams and swallowed yawns. Silently she kicked her Mary Janes together; woefully, in the absence of anything else to do, she crossed her eyes. Suddenly, and she did not know why, she turned rogue and tried to tickle Abigail who wrenched away in surprise, almost toppling off the slippery seat. Although they were to one side of Grandfather's ken, he saw the quiet scuffle out of the corner of his eye and he wheeled on them like Wrath.

"Wantons!" and he would have impaled them on his pointing finger if they had not been across the room from him. "Is a man to be made a gowk of in his own castle by the blethering of females?"

Blethering! They had not made a sound.

Abigail hotly declared that Cora was solely to blame for this outrageous impudence, this dangerous breach of decorum on the Good Lord's day. But Grandfather ordered her to be silent and he gave a familiar lecture on the wages of sin, the high price of defiance of authority, the destiny of mockers who misconducted themselves on Sunday. He raved of the cauldrons and the griddles. Weeping, his sister, Great Aunt Flora, hysterically cried, "Don't faunch yourself into a lather! Duncan! Duncan!" and he gored her with a look.

By no means finished with his diatribe, he said, "Hark!" and flicking *The Book of Martyrs* to, he opened the Old Testament to Isaiah and read of the Fall of Babylon. Red in the face with rectitude, veins standing out, dark and vermicular in his neck and on his forehead, as Dan's did when he sneered, he read:

"Therefore the Lord will smite with a scab the crown of the head of the daughters of Zion, and the Lord will discover their secret parts. In that day the Lord will take away the bravery of their tinkling ornaments about their feet, and their cauls, and their round tires like the moon, the chains and the bracelets, and the mufflers, the bonnets and the ornaments of the legs, and the headbands, and the tablets, and the earrings, the rings, and nose jewels, the changeable suits of apparel and the mantles, and the wimples, and the crisping pins, the glasses, the fine linen, and the hoods and the veils. And it shall come to pass that instead of sweet smell, there shall be stink; and instead of a girdle, a tent; and instead of well-set hair, baldness; and instead of a stomacher, a girding of sackcloth; and burning instead of beauty. Thy men . . ."

It was probably the violent, accusing voice (which was really directed at his twins) more than the words that made Cora finally cry out with terror and she ran to hide her face in Mama's lap. She knelt there shuddering and hoarsely babbling, "I don't want to be bald! I don't! I don't!"

Her uproar was contagious and all the other Savage children
and the Sinclairs, in their different ways, turned mutinous.

Abigail cried, "It isn't fair, Grandfather! It was all Cora's
fault!"

Evangeline giggled and squeaked, "Oracay illway avehay otay
earway anay igway!" and Faith Sinclair, a precocious little snit,
said, "Cora Savage is the Whore of Babylon."

"Grandfather McKinnon," said Randall solemnly, standing
up as if he were in school, "is it true that we are descended
from monkeys?"

"Children, children, that's enough!" said Grandma, shaking
her head and clapping for order.

"Monkeys!" little Fannie Sinclair was fascinated. "How
come, Randy? How come *monkeys*?"

The pandemonium lasted only a minute or two and then the
children, realizing what they had done—had headed for the
seething pits and locked themselves on the wrong side of the
pearly gates—froze in their attitudes. But brief as the revolution
had been, it had had a remarkable effect on their grandfather.
He seemed to shrivel and his skin was as gray as the trunk of
a tree. He pounded his craggy fists on the table. "What is the
meaning of this sacrilege and insubordination?" he demanded,
but he was so choked with passion that his voice lost its body
and it came out thick and pallid. "Absconding and tricks and
pranks and now *evolution*!"

Gasping for breath, coughing, alarmingly red again, he railed
like a stark staring crazy man, called them all backsliders, apos-
tates, iconoclasts, the gall and wormwood of his life. His storm
was long but his thunder was a squawk and his thunderbolts
were duds. He had lost his women and he had lost his only lad.

Holy cow! His face was bleeding. A fast red flood was coming
from his beak; bewildered, he did nothing about it. His arms,
too long for his coatsleeves so that his big wrists showed below
the cuffs, hung slack at his sides and he relaxed his hands so that
they were no longer fists. Everyone watched, astonished, as that
red eruption continued to ride down his face. An age went by.

Then Grandma, galvanized at last, went to him, gently pushed
him back into his chair and tried to stanch the nosebleed with a
foolish little handkerchief.

"Send away the bairns," she said. "Maud, get me some ice."

But Mama did not move. No one moved. They sat motionless, witless with astonishment and with a strange, inadmissible embarrassment; the crumbling of the tyrant made them shy.

Grandfather, accepting his wife's ministrations like a dog or a child, put his hand to his forehead. "Giddy," he said. His voice was as far away as if he were in another room. The forehead that he touched above his heavy, raven eyebrows glistened with a morbid sweat. Cora ran from the room, ran from the earthquake, and outdoors hurled herself into a pile of fresh raked maple leaves. But dreadful curiosity drove her back into the house and as she stood in the doorway, she saw Grandfather collapse, fall from the chair dragging the Bible with him. He lay there like a tree hewn down, his branches every whichway; his loud, jerky breathing was a funny wind and his nose kept copiously bleeding, spilling over his beard, staining the pages of the Bible where it had broken open.

"Maud!" said Grandma. "Will you let your father bleed to death for the want of a whang of ice?"

Mama got up then and seeing Cora said sharply, "Scat! You may have killed my father, you bad girl!"

He did not die that day. Dr. Grimes said that he had had a stroke and that he might live for long years yet, but on the other hand, he might go in a second apoplexy or a third, a fourth, a twenty-fifth. He wanted to know what had brought this on and when he heard about Jane and Amy, he, a sour elder of the U.P. church, was scandalized to bits.

The next Wednesday (three momentous Wednesdays in a row!) a postal came from the twins: they had had a tintype made of themselves, probably at an amusement park, posed in a cardboard Pierce Arrow and on the back of it they had written, "Having a wonderful time and never coming back to Graymoor. Love to all." There was a row of hugs and kisses and they had made a grinning face in the last hug.

And they never did come back to Graymoor, never in their lives. The next time they were heard from, more than a year later, they were both in New South Wales and both of them were married. No one ever knew whom they had gone to visit in St. Louis; they never were sure that the girls really had gone to the Veiled Prophet's Ball or had just said that to impress Frank Ferguson.

Grandfather had three more strokes within a month, and each one left him with a fresh derangement. He spent his time in the parlor in his black leather sermonizing chair, his great shoulders hunched together as he hugged Grandma's Paisley shawl to him, for he was always cold. His eyes were bloodshot; they looked sore. He seemed half asleep—his whole life was one long doze and when the grandchildren went to visit him, a different child each day, he paid no heed to them for the five minutes they stood before him. He said nothing but his stomach querulously growled. He withered and dried; sometimes his five wits were altogether lost to him and then he fought and sought tenaciously until he collected them.

He died in his sleep the night before Thanksgiving. Wednesday again. Woden's day. "Woden was the Norsemen's Jehovah," said Dan matter-of-factly. "His familiars were two black ravens named Hugin and Munin." And then, funereally he intoned, "There were twa corbies / Sat in a tree." And laughed his laugh.

Granny Savage had lost her mind; Grandfather McKinnon could no longer shackle Mama and, as soon as school was over in May, the Savages moved west.

A MOTHER IN HISTORY

Sections of this book appeared originally in *McCall's* magazine, and I would like to thank Miss Barbara Lawrence of its staff for her editorial acumen. I am grateful, too, for the contributions of Mr. Lon Tinkle, Mr. Hermes Nye, Mr. Hugh Aynesworth, Mrs. Arch Swank, and Mrs. John Satton.

J. S.

I

IN a tidy, unexceptional little house, on an unexceptional block of similar houses (they were seedy, but they were not squalid, and in some of their front yards roses grew) in Fort Worth, Mrs. Marguerite Oswald received me one steamy May afternoon. Without preambulatory small talk, beyond asking me whether I found the air-conditioning cool or not cool enough (it was exactly right), she plunged straightaway into her memoirs—or rather, into those parts of her memoirs having to do with the arrest and murder of her son Lee Harvey Oswald that catapulted her to international renown. In the recitative of this, President Kennedy was little more than the deus ex machina, essential but never on stage.

Her voice had a considerable histrionic range; in a moment's time, she could shift her tone from resignation to irony, from sonorous patriotism to personal indignation, but at all times a central intelligence was at the controls, regulating the pitch and volume as she entered the successive roles of mother, citizen, widow, public figure. There was a suggestion of elocution lessons, nearly forgotten but learned well, long ago; and there was more than a suggestion of rehearsal and past performance—she spoke almost always in complete sentences, she was never visibly caught off guard.

She declared at the beginning that she was "not a mother defending her son," but was "speaking for history," since history, she is persuaded, has been deformed by the press and by the report of the Warren Commission's inquiry into President Kennedy's assassination, which is "all lies, lies, lies."

I had come to Texas to see Mrs. Oswald because she is, as she was frequently to tell me, "a mother in history," and while she remains peripheral to the immediate events of the Dallas killings, she is inherent to the evolution of the reasons for them. She is inherent, that is, if we accept (as I do) the premise that her son had something to do with the assassination and accept the further premise that the child is father of the man: we need to know the influences and accidents and loves and antipathies and idiosyncrasies that were the ingredients making up the final compound. I hoped that Mrs. Oswald would be able to tell me what these had been.

For all practical purposes, she was her son's only parent, since his father died before he was born and her later marriage lasted too short a time to have much effect on him. Relatives are often (perhaps more often than not) the last people on earth to know anything about each other. Still, there was the possibility, and I had come down from Connecticut to explore it.

Mrs. Oswald, an inactive Lutheran, believes that "if ye seek, ye shall find," that at last "truth will prevail," and to correct the false impressions of her son and herself under which most of the nation and most of the world labor, she is dedicating her life to her own investigation. From morning, when she rises early, until night, she is at work "researching the case," collating newspaper stories, studying theories of conspiracy (right-wing, left-wing, wingless, Catholic, Baptist, Jewish, Black Muslim, anarchist, fascist, federalist, masterminded by the cops, masterminded by the robbers) that have been propounded from Los Angeles to West Berlin; reading between the lines of the Warren Report and scrutinizing the errors of omission in it and those of commission, and the ambiguities and the garbles. She accepts any invitation anywhere to appear on platforms or on television screens to pass on her observations and to interpret them. For several months after the assassination, she was strenuously peripatetic, popping up all over in this country and in Canada. "My theme is the American way of life," she said to me, "and this, of course, is what I talked about."

"I want the truth known," she said, sitting upright on a sofa, her hands crossed at the wrists, palm upward. "I believe the American people are entitled to the truth and I believe they want to know. Now I will agree that immediately after the assassination, and while President Johnson was taking the place of President Kennedy, let me say in all respect that this was not the time to bring these truths before the public. But after his time in office most people think—I don't agree, but that's beside the point—that he is a very powerful President, and the assassination itself has subsided. I think these truths should be leaked now, and if in the leaking they can prove to me that my son was the assassin of President Kennedy, I won't commit suicide or drop dead. I will accept the facts as a good straight human being. But up until this day they have not shown me any proof and I have things in my possession to disprove many things they say. I understand all the testimony off the cuff is in Washington and will be locked up for seventy-five years. Well, I've got news for you. It will not be for seventy-five years, because if today or tomorrow I am dead or killed, what I have in my possession will be known. And I in my lifetime have got to continue what I have been doing, using my emotional stability and speaking out whenever I can. Would you like a cup of coffee?"

Because there was no hiatus between the proclamation of unwavering purpose and the hospitable, colloquial question, and because both were delivered in the same tone and at the same pace, I did not immediately take it in, but in a moment I did and said I would. (The drinking of coffee in Texas is almost as involuntary as respiration. One night I went into a restaurant in Dallas where, on every table, there was a glass pot of coffee kept bubbling over a candle-warmer. One or two of my guests poured out cups for themselves at once, following this aperitif with the Jack Daniel's and Johnnie Walker I had brought in a brown paper bag. I had forgotten, or had never known, that in Texas you produced your own liquor in public places and ordered setups just as in the oldentime.)

While Mrs. Oswald busied herself in the kitchen that abutted on the dinette at the end of the living room, she did not pause in her soliloquy. She asked herself questions and answered them in patient asides: "All the news mediums said he was such a failure in life. A failure in life?" she cried out in stunned disbelief. "He was twenty-four years old when he was murdered! The attorneys that are interviewing these witnesses make a hundred to a hundred and fifty dollars a day and they never lived this type life. Lee Harvey a failure? I am smiling. I think it took courage for a young boy to go to Russia at twenty, for whatever reason he went. I find this a very intelligent boy, and I think he's coming out in history as a very fine person."

Generally dropping the final "g's" of gerunds in a relaxed, rustic way, she spoke in the accent and the cadences of that part of New Orleans to which she was native, an accent that my late husband, A. J. Liebling, once described as "hard to distinguish from the accent of Hoboken, Jersey City, and Astoria, Long Island, where the Al Smith inflection, extinct in Manhattan, has taken refuge." "Point" becomes "pernt," and, conversely, "person" becomes "poyson."

Accustomed as she was to public speaking, Mrs. Oswald did not seem to be addressing me specifically but, rather, a large congregation; this was to be her manner with me on each of the three occasions I saw her. Taking advantage of my anonymity in this quiet crowd and of the fact that her back was turned, I looked around the room in the snoopy way women do when they are in other women's houses, and tried to think what sort of occupant I would assign to it if I did not already know who she was.

The house itself was a white stucco bungalow divided into two apartments, and as I had come up the short path, I had noticed a "For Rent" sign at the approach to the other side. Each apartment consisted of a living room–dining room that then turned a corner and became a kitchen; off the living room there was a small bedroom, and off that, a bath. The two kitchen doors debouched onto a common back porch, screened and looking out to a downward sloping lawn and pleasant shade trees.

The space was limited, but Mrs. Oswald had arranged her furniture adeptly, so that I did not feel nudged or threatened, and the furniture itself, while it was middle-aged and had been nondescript all its life (except for a Danish modern chair up-holstered in carroty polyethylene), was solid and in good repair and comfortable. The armchair I sat in was hard enough and soft enough, and there was an adequate table to the right of it on which stood an ashtray, a small vase of artificial violets, and a copy of *The Wounded Land*, Hans Habe's high-strung book on the American state of mind following the assassination. The walls were that general color that can be called beige or ecru or bone or buff or oatmeal, and hanging on the longest, over a sofa thronged with multiform and multicolored cushions, was a print of Whistler's "Mother." The glass that protected it was spotless and the brass identification plate was smartly burnished. I could not tell whether the picture was a recent acquisition or whether it was daily treated with polish and a chamois skin; clearly, it was cherished. On another wall, but oblique to my line of vision, there hung what seemed to be a copper scroll; I wanted to get up and look at it, but I felt this would be presumptuous, particularly because it was over a writing desk where orderly piles of papers were laid out to which my Paul Pry eye would be bound to stray. Near the television set (it confronted the sofa, and the vantage point from which Ben Casey would be observed was directly under Mrs. Whistler) there was a low tripod on which stood a jardiniere planted with crotons whose patterns were picked out in assertive shades of purple and red and leonine yellow; the health of these leaves was so obviously robust that they testified to a green thumb and made a puzzling contrast to the fake flowers and fake emperor grapes in other parts of the room. I had noticed the same phenomenon in the small front yard, where heather, far from home and made of wax and wire, emerged from a plastic pot toward which a few late tulips leaned their mortal, languid heads.

Mrs. Oswald, pouring hot water over instant coffee, was saying, "I can absolutely prove my son innocent. I can do it any time I want by going to Washington, D.C., with some pictures,[1] but I won't do it that way. I want to get my story before the public, so young and old all over the world will know the truth. Why don't I go to Washington?" With this question, she turned to face me, arms akimbo. Embattled, but at the same time an imperturbable strategist, she answered it: "Because they've been so ugly to me, to me and my boy. I'll write a book and the title of it will be *One and One Make Two* or *This and That*. Oh, I could write three books or five books! I could write books and *books* on what I know and what I have researched."

My own research, this cursory study of her living room, had yielded little more than the evidence that whoever lived here was a good housekeeper of modest means and a mild affection for bric-a-brac, so I gave up my elementary sleuthing and, hoping to set her back in time to the days before the concussion that had stunned the world, I asked her about her early life in New Orleans. But if she had any nostalgia for that most raffish and romantic and sweet and sinful city, she had suppressed it, and she brushed me aside as if there were no time for frivolous parentheses when the business at hand was history.

---

1. See Appendix I, page 809.

"Now maybe Lee Harvey Oswald was the assassin," she pursued, stirring the coffee. "But does that make him a louse? No, no! Killing does not necessarily mean badness. You find killing in some very fine homes for one reason or another. And as we all know, President Kennedy was a dying man. So I say it is possible that my son was chosen to shoot him in a mercy killing for the security of the country. And if this is true, it was a fine thing to do and my son is a hero."

"I had not heard that President Kennedy was dying," I said, staggered by this cluster of fictions stated as irrefutable fact. Some mercy killing! The methods used in this instance must surely be unique in the annals of euthanasia.

"Oh, yes," she went on with authority. My ignorance did not surprise her; she plainly was accustomed to dealing with people who, either through laziness or want of opportunity, did not know the ABC's of the case. "It's been in many articles that President Kennedy was a dying President, that he had At-kinson's disease, which is a disease of the kidney, and we know that he had three operations on his back and that he would have been a lingering President. For security reasons, we could not have a lingering President, because of our conflicts with other nations." She turned to me with her sociable smile and asked, "Do you take cream and sugar, sweetheart?"

Her affable face was round and lineless, and the skin that covered her small bones was delicate; her eyes were clear behind glasses in pale frames; and her clean white hair, only a little smudged with left-over gray, was pulled back straight into a plump and faultless bun. She wore a lime-green sheath that was appropriate to her short stature and her tubular, well-corseted construction. She would, I thought, be called "modish." Her general appearance and her demeanor were consistent with the several roles she has played in her fifty-eight years: insurance agent, saleslady, manageress of lingerie shops, switchboard operator, practical nurse. Terms of endearment came naturally to her lips, as they do to those of many Southern women; she could have been the stand-in and the off-stage voice for the woman from whom I had bought a rain cape in Neiman-Marcus that morning, who rejected the first one I tried on, saying, "No, honey, that just won't do. Your little dress shows." A Northerner is at first taken aback, then is seduced, then realizes—sometimes too late—that these blandishments are unconscious and wholly noncommittal and one need not feel obliged to reciprocate by buying the next rain cape. (In this case I did, and it comes nicely below the hems of all my little dresses.)

Mrs. Oswald, having delivered my creamed and sugared coffee, reestablished herself with her own cup on the sofa beneath her generic sister (fleetingly I wondered how Whistler, a noteworthy scrapper, had got along with Mrs. W.) and continued. "Now it could have been that my son and the Secret Service were all involved in a mercy killing. I have thought about this seriously. We teach our boys to kill in war and we don't think a thing about it, yet if these same boys kill someone on the street they are lawfully put in jail or else electrocuted, which is right. So why wouldn't it be just a normal thing to have a mercy killing of the President?"

She uttered the word "normal" without a suggestion of inverted commas, and I think this is exactly what she meant; as for "mercy killing," she made that sound as commonplace as the use of aspirin to bring down a fever.

"If he was dying of an incurable disease, this would be for the security of our country. Now when President Kennedy came to Fort Worth, Texas, for one night, there was an article in the paper that said the maid at the Hotel Texas had fixed his room for him and had to re-do the bed because he had his own hard mattress. Even for one night! He must have been a very bad man." (I was momentarily startled, but realized that this was merely a slip of the tongue.) "And his rocking chair is still the way it was, with the towel in the back because he was in such pain."

There floated across my mind a cloudy recollection of having heard (after the assassination, I thought) it rumored that the President had Addison's disease, which is not a distemper of the kidneys but a malfunction of the adrenal gland, and which, since the advent of cortisone, has become tractable; a victim of it can, with proper treatment, live out his allotted span of years. I asked Mrs. Oswald if she had meant this when she had spoken of "Atkinson's disease." Once again she found my interruption footling and answered simply, "Whatever," and put me down along with her coffee cup, which she returned to its saucer.

"As I was saying, as we all know, Lee Harvey Oswald, after leaving the Texas Book Depository, got off the bus and got into a taxi. This was right by the Greyhound bus station. Isn't it a strong likelihood that he went into the bus station to make a telephone call to the people he was working with, to say the mercy killing had come off? Maybe he did, maybe he didn't. But if he was guilty, why didn't he get on a bus and get out of Dallas? This theory fits in with the other theory. So were they all subversive and in a plot? Or were they all humanitarian and in a plot? The same people, though."

I wondered if, in my musings on her lares and penates when she was in the kitchen, I had missed the exposition of "this theory" and "the other theory," and rather tentatively, apologetic for my slow-wittedness, I asked, "The same people? Which people were these?"

"*They*," said Mrs. Oswald, and shook hands with herself for emphasis. "When I say *they*, I'm gonna quote Mrs. Kennedy when her husband was killed. She said, '*They* have killed my Jack,' and I say *they* in the same text. *They*, who are *they*? Ah! I have my own theory, and I'm sure everybody else has. There was one or two others that I can't recall at the moment to say '*they*.' I think Governor Connally said, '*They* are going to assassinate us all.' It's always *they*."

My interviews with Mrs. Oswald took place in the third or fourth week of the derangements in the Dominican Republic, and just as, in reading the reports of those, I could not keep the dramatis personae on the proper sides (or on top of) the proper fences, so now "they" swarmed about me like gnats, midges, fruit flies, and sand fleas, impossible to differentiate. I could not find my way out of the buzzing mob, and so I bent my head and drank some coffee and closed my eyes and tried to concentrate.

"If my son was an agent of the United States, this should be known. I wonder why Chief Justice Warren had tears in his eyes when President Johnson asked him to head up this commission? I wonder why?" She meditated, reading her palms. "Did Chief Justice Warren have to whitewash something the public don't know about? Did he know my son was innocent? Who *used* my son? This is the question I must find the answer to. Research and research, until I can bring the truth to light. My son was killed on cue, and this I can prove. The television cameras were ready, and the TV directors gave the order. As I understand it, some very important men in the networks got in trouble, lost their jobs and everything. But that's beside the point. What I want to know is who used Lee Harvey Oswald?"

The question was rhetorical and was put to the audience out there beyond the footlights, but I countered it with another, "Do you have any idea?"

"I don't have an *idea*, I *know*," she said. "And of course when I find out who framed my son, then we can find out who killed Kennedy. I go a little different way than most of the books on who killed Kennedy. My theory is a little different, because *I* know who framed my son and *he* knows I know who framed my son."

"Is 'he' in Texas now?"

"I can divulge nothing on that score," she said brusquely, but screwed up her eyes in a cordial grimace to show that she forgave my intrusion into something that was none of my bees-wax. I backed out of this dead end and returned to the avenue of the past I had tried to guide her down before. I asked what Lee Harvey's hobbies had been as a child.

"He had a stamp collection," she said with a practiced smile, "and he loved to play Monopoly, which is a thinking game. So was stamps. He had a stamp collection. He loved to play chess, he was a very good chess player. And anything like that. So he was really a very busy little boy, and I don't see anything abnormal about any part of his life. He'd climb up on the roof to look at the stars, and I'd have to get the older boys to get him down, because he was interested in astronomy. Now I'm talking about a boy eight, nine, ten years old. And he loved, he just loved to read very deep books. He liked Darwin, Heming-way, Norman Vincent Peale. When he went to visit my sister, all she said she saw him read was comic books, and this is what she said to the Warren Commission. Well, that was true, and he did like comic books. Isn't that normal in a young boy? He loved to read about animals. He knew all about animals. You know they said he played hooky in New York, and he did, and then of course we had to go to the board several times because he was always picked up in the Bronx zoo. We only lived about two blocks from there, and this is where they would always find him, because he loved animals. Someone said, 'Well, at least it was educational.' I have to smile a little bit because boys do play hooky. I don't say it's the right thing to do, and I don't say children should do it, but I certainly don't think it's abnormal. Lee came home one day when we were in New York just about a week or so, and it was exactly the time he was supposed to get home from school and I had given him enough lunch money and always gave a few extra nickels, you know, in case they needed something or got lost on the subway. Now I had never been in the subway—we had been in New York just about one week and I had driven to New York with Lee. So he said, 'Mother, I didn't go to school today.' I said, 'You didn't? Where did you go?' 'Oh,' he said, 'I rode all around. I rode all day on the subway. I rode to Brooklyn, I went to Queens, blah, blah, blah.' Well, I'm smiling to myself because, there again, from Texas if you go a few miles you pay twenty-five cents for bus fare, and if you go a few miles further, you have to pay extra, so I think he's pulling my leg. I'm going along with him, not saying a thing. So that afternoon we're having supper and I said to his brother, John Edward, 'What do you think? Lee didn't go to school today, he rode the subway all day long.' And of course they're grinning because I'm the fool and don't know it, see? And this went on and on and finally John Edward said, 'Mother, he's telling the truth, he can ride the subway all day for the same amount of money.' Well, I didn't know that, but the point is Lee was telling me he didn't go to school. Now, I want to say this in defense of my son—let's have some defense of Lee Harvey Oswald and his mother! How many boys at age thirteen that play hooky from school would come home from school and tell his mother that he did so?

"Well, of course, he played hooky after that and they cautioned me *and* they cautioned me, and finally they brought us into court and Lee was taken from me and he was placed in a children's home. I think he was in the home five or six weeks and that was Warwick—I think that was the name of it, I'd have to check in the Warren Report. In Brooklyn. After the assassination, all of this came out, and that Lee needed psychiatric treatment and so on and so forth, and that I refused and that—well, this was a clue to the assassination. I would have to read you the Warren Commission Report on Lee's psychiatric treatment and tear it apart. Lies! I was never told my son needed psychiatric treatment, believe me. And this man, I forget his name, I stepped on his toes, and sometimes I wonder, did he hold it against me enough to harm my son? By the way, do you know that he is Mayor Wagner's right-handed man? How do you suppose he got from probation officer to an official capacity in New York State?"

This time she really seemed to want an answer, but since I did not know who Mayor Wagner's right-handed man was (didn't know who his southpaw was either), let alone what his credentials were, I had to let her down. In view of the mass of detail she had at her command and the dexterous use she made of it to fit her argument, I felt like a flop on a junior high debating team who hadn't a prayer of reaching the semifinals.

"I find these things very, very interesting," she said, "because as I'm researching Lee's life—and I'm not the only one—it looks as though this boy's life has been supervised. But if I stress this, they say, 'This woman is out of her mind. Let's put her in a mental institution.' Isn't it silly?"

She chuckled at the preposterous way of the world, sipped coffee and, changing from her official to her chatty voice, said, "Lee purely loved animals! With his very first pay he bought a bird and a cage, and I have a picture of it. He bought this bird with a cage that had a planter for ivy, and he took care of that bird and he made the ivy grow. Now, you see, there could be many nice things written about this boy. But, oh, no, no, this boy is supposed to be the assassin of a President of the United States, so he has to be a louse. Sometimes I am very sad."

I started to mouth some safe platitude of sympathy, but I got no further than an introductory mutter. She went right on. "When I think of all the things Lee did!" Her tranquillity was ruffled, and her voice went up a note or two; it was the voice of a woman in altercation with a butcher who had overcharged her or with someone who had jostled her in a bus. "How can you call him a loner or an introvert or whatever they wanted to call him? Of course after they arrested him they had to find an environmental factor, and right away they said we moved around a lot. Well, all right, what if we did? We weren't drifters. This is the twentieth century, and people move around. That's educational, isn't it? No matter where we were, we always had

a decent home. I wouldn't put up with a piece of torn upholstery or something broken or anything like that—I'd go to the
five-and-dime and get something and fix it up. You see how I
live—nothing fancy, but a bright touch, a little decorator piece
here and there." She waved both hands, gesturing toward the
appointments of the room and bestowing her good wishes on
them.

"And I never neglected my children. Oh, yes, we didn't have
steak, but we never even thought about steak—I didn't anyway,
I was always grateful to eat. And the children never really and
truly complained. I know of one or two occasions when the
boys said, 'Mother, why don't you have a platter of chops? I was
at such and such a house yesterday and they served seconds,'
and I said, 'Well, now, honey, this is all Mother can do.' If, say,
three days before payday, I had a dollar and a half to my name,
I would cook up a big pot of beans and cornbread or a big pot
of spaghetti and meatballs and make it last, but I happen to
know some women in that position who would take that dollar
and a half and go to the corner restaurant and come home
with hamburgers and Coke, and there's your difference. I have
always done what I thought was right, and I always did it in a
true Christian way. And even though we were poor and I was
a widow and I did have to support myself and three children,
I always seemed to manage. I have often been complimented
about how I look when I'm dressed up, about my little home
and about the way the children act and so on and so forth.

"Now I'm patting myself on the back as a mother only so
that the people will understand. Why am I so concerned that
the people will understand? It is natural because I am a mother
in history. I am in twenty-six volumes of the Warren Report,
which is all over the world, so I must defend myself and defend
my son Lee."

She altered the position of a green glass ashtray in the shape
of a swan. Then, as if she had given the matter sober thought
and this was her considered opinion, she said, "I would say that
the Oswald family was actually an average American family."

What the components were that made up Mrs. Oswald's
image of "an average American family," I never learned.
I asked, but the answer was apparently self-evident and she
ignored me. Since I do not know either how the sociologists

and statisticians arrive at this denomination, it is quite possible that she and her brood fitted into it. But certain eccentricities of their circumstance had struck me when I had read the acres of newsprint, following the assassination, and I doubted that the word "average" was precise, or even approximate. To begin with, the record of Mrs. Oswald's matrimonial misfortunes shoots off at a forty-five degree angle from the norm. She was abandoned by her first husband, Edward John Pic, when her child by him, John Edward, was an infant; she was widowed by Robert Lee Oswald when her first son by him was a child and Lee Harvey was not yet born. Her third marriage to a Mr. Eckdahl was a hurricane, and while the lull before it was lengthy ("I made him wait a year") and the restoration period afterward was long, the storm itself, which raised the roof under which they dwelt together, was brief. The household, therefore, was only sporadically manned by a man.

The Oswald economy was far from stable. Under the terms of the first divorce, Mr. Pic was required to contribute to the support of his son, and Mr. Oswald had insured his life for a nominal sum. But these were humble funds, and Mrs. Oswald, pressed and proud and energetic, went to work. The boys, in the absence of a full-time caretaker, were sent variously to schools and to church-sponsored children's homes. Lee Harvey joined his older brothers in a Lutheran orphanage when he was three. Sometimes they were at home with their mother, and when they were old enough, they got jobs to pay for their board and keep. (Robert Oswald, at sixteen, had a job as a shoe-stock boy at Everybody's Department Store.)

The family moved with dizzying frequency while they lived in New Orleans, and later on when they lived in and around Fort Worth. Sometimes they rented apartments and sometimes they owned houses; they appear very often to have lived in two-family dwellings; when she was unencumbered, Mrs. Oswald stayed in lodgings. In both cities, their addresses were in similar neighborhoods, and John Edward Pic and Robert Lee Oswald, in their testimony before the Warren Commission, had trouble remembering the names of the streets where they had lived. When I asked Mrs. Oswald where John Edward Pic had lived in New York at the time she and Lee Harvey stayed with him there for a short and troubled interval, she said she did not know, that he and his wife were "somewhere on the East side," giving me a choice ranging from Delancey Street to Spanish Harlem, with Sutton Place and Gracie Square in between. She was an urban product, the kind of person who knows her own neighborhood thoroughly, may know two or three neighborhoods thoroughly, but who has no sense of a city as a whole; the ambience of New York did not differ from that of New Orleans, nor did New Orleans differ from Fort Worth.[2]

Even as she sat in her own parlor with only me to stimulate her, she emanated restlessness; she fairly skipped as she was sitting down. She had handed down her energy and wanderlust to her sons, all of whom joined the Marines as early as they could. ("We are a military family," she said.) However, at the same time, nomadic as she was, her nest-building instinct was steadfast; but it was the instinct of a migratory species that insofar as possible duplicates in successive nests twigs and leaves from the same sorts of trees and swatches of the same kinds of moss and lichen. Nothing in the room appeared to have more than the most ephemeral association of time or place; whenever, in the course of my interviews, I asked where she had got a vase or a bowl or a tray, she said, "Oh, that's just a little decorator thing I picked up to go with the other colors."

Her sons, under her guidance, were upright. "They didn't cuss—of course I don't say they didn't on the outside, but they didn't in front of me. We none of us used obscene language— oh, I might say 'damn,' you know, some time, but none of the boys. And one little thing I did with 'em—but they never did know until later on in life—I never let them have a key to the front door. I remember Robert asking me and I said, 'Oh, no, honey, it's better you wake me up because if I ever heard the front door I would think it was a burglar or something.' But this wasn't the idea. I wanted to be sure that no boy of mine would come into my home drunk. And I can truthfully say not a one of them ever entered my home stinko. They probably had a beer on the outside, for I'm not saying they're perfect. Now I have no objection to social drinking and I've been to cocktail parties myself, but I don't drink, because alcohol doesn't agree with me at all, but I would if I wanted to. And another thing,

2. See Appendix II, page 810.

I never let my boys have my car, 'cause I thought they were too young to use it, and as it was my livelihood, as I was an insurance lady, I couldn't afford to let a teen-ager wreck it. The teen-agers, as we say—I think they're a wonderful bunch, but they were going a little wild, had their own cars and so on and so forth. So I never let my boys have my car, and I can truthfully say, none of my boys ever came into my home drunk. I think this is a very nice thing to say, a woman raising children by herself, particularly boys. I'm gonna give myself credit for this, and I think I deserve it."

The room was still cool, but the air was heavy, imbued with the second-hand mustiness of air-conditioning and the smoke from my cigarettes. I was tired and headachy, but Mrs. Oswald was as fresh and kinetic as she had been when she greeted me, and she persevered like a long-distance runner.

"You know, there was a violent campaign against me as well as my son in magazines, newspapers, and written literature. Most all the papers pictured me in a sort of a bad light, but really I'm not that way at all and never was. I should say I'm very outspoken, I'm aggressive, I'm no dope. Let's face it, if you step on my toes I'm gonna fight back, and I don't apologize for that. This was my training along with Lee's father, who, as we all know, is now deceased."

(Although I should have been used to it by now, I was surprised each time she used the royal or tutorial "we," and only the most tenuous hold on reality kept me from glancing from left to right to see who besides me was attending the lecture.)

"When my older boy first went to school, he came home one day crying that the children had taken his pennies away from him. Mr. Oswald took his little hand and started teaching him how to fight back, and I listened and I thought it was a wonderful thing. I remember him saying 'If you ever start a fight, you're gonna be whipped, but if they ever start a fight with you and you don't fight back, I'm gonna whip *you*.' Let me give you one little instance with Lee and the next-door neighbor boy. They were approximately the same age, and if not, they were the same height, and Lee had a dog. He loved his shepherd collie dog. It was named Sunshine. He used to romp in the back yard with his dog and took him every place he went, and this little boy was throwing rocks over the fence at Lee's dog. Well, my kitchen window had a view to the back yard. And I watched my son Lee for approximately three days telling the little boy over the fence he better stop throwing rocks at his dog. Well, I was amused, and I was just waiting to find out what happened. Finally, one day when I came home from work the father called me on the phone. It seemed his son was very badly beaten up—in a child's way. My son Lee had finally taken upon himself, after much patience, I thought, to confront the little boy enough to fight him, and the father didn't approve. I told the father what happened, and since the boys were approximately the same age and height, let them fight their own battles.

"Now my boys were never tied to my apron strings. And Lee, Lee wanted to know all there was about life. Talking about going to Russia. He never did tell me why he went to Russia. I have my own opinion. He spoke Russian, he wrote Russian, and he read Russian. Why? Because my boy was being trained as an agent, that's why. Another thing I found out in some book where it said he was placed in another hut because he couldn't get along with someone. He was placed with a Cuban, and he was learning Spanish. I think he was spying on that Cuban. It's just so obvious. How many Marines are going around reading Russian and getting Russian newspapers? One and one make two to me. That boy was being trained."

I asked her what she thought Lee would have done with his life if he had not been killed, and she answered at once, as if she had answered the question many times before. "From what I know of my boy, and of course you have to understand that actually the last time I was very close to Lee was before he joined the service in 1956. After that, it was just through correspondence and on his leaves home from the Marines that I knew him. But every time he came home he talked and talked about the Marines and nothing else. I know when he came back from Japan he said, 'Oh, what a wonderful experience, what a wonderful trip!' He said, 'Do you know it cost my government over two thousand dollars to send me there? I could never afford it on my own.' I think he was doing with his life what he wanted to do. And I'm gonna say he was working for his country as an agent. I think that at age sixteen he became involved, that at age sixteen Lee Harvey Oswald was being trained as a government agent. And this brings up Russia and, of course, Marina."

I was glad she had broached the subject of her daughter-in-law. I had been shy of doing so myself because I knew that there was bad blood between the two women.

"Let's have some more coffee before I go into that," she said. "We'll *need* it." She went once again to the kitchen, where, with her back to me as she went about the business of the coffee, she honed her scalpels for the vivisection of Marina.

"Of course I don't know too much about Marina. She lived with me the one month when they came back from Russia. She was a very humble foreign girl, and she never smoked in front of me. Everything was 'Momma' and the baby, and we got along fine. Now this person never smoked in front of me for a reason, because she did smoke, and she smoked in Russia. The testimony of the Presidential report showed that she knew Americans before she knew Lee, and they taught her how to smoke. Now I smoked for twenty years, and Lee never did say a word to me about smoking—maybe he had respect because I was a mother. But he objected to his wife smoking. And she evidently thought I never smoked, because she never smoked in front of me. I didn't know Marina smoked, until the assassination."

(At the moment, like a white rat in some unprecedented experiment, I had a lighted cigarette in my hand, and another was burning in the ashtray.)

"And you see, I wouldn't be that type. I would be natural and do what I have to do, and there again we get into she's not a true person. If I smoke, I smoke in front of everybody. Of course, I would ask permission of an older person."

There was a moment's silence, and I tried to remember if I had minded my manners at the beginning and asked if I could smoke; I thought I had, but at this point I could be sure of nothing except that I was a white rat.

"To me, Marina is not a true person," she said with fair-minded deliberation. "And this is hard to explain. I have to ask myself who Marina Oswald really is. I'd like to see her marriage certificate some time, and I'd like to know more about her. Oh, when Marina went to Washington, Washington fell in love with Marina Oswald, and Chief Justice Warren was her grandfather, but when I went to Washington—'Don't listen to her. Momma hadn't seen Lee in a year, and she doesn't know anything, blah, blah, blah.' Everything was against me. Yet *I* was the mother. Now I don't say that Marina is necessarily guilty of anything, but both she and Mrs. Paine have lied, lied continuously. Maybe they are not guilty, but why is it necessary to lie? When it first happened, Marina did not identify the rifle. She said, 'Yes, Lee had rifle,' but when they showed it to her she said she couldn't say whether that was his. Now this is understandable. If your husband had a rifle, and particularly if he had it as they say he had it, wrapped up in a blanket and never using it, would the wife be able to identify it? Yet a few weeks later, when she had taken oath and been brainwashed by the Secret Service, she identified the rifle as Lee's. And at first she said, 'Lee good man, Lee no shoot anybody.' And then she changed her testimony. Marina seems French to me."

"French!"

"Yes, sweetheart, that's what I said, Marina Oswald seems French to me. Oh, definitely." She came back with our coffee, and as she put it down beside me, she said, "But that will have to be continued in our next. You'll have to drink up, honey, your driver's here."

I had not heard a car, and shrubbery obscured the window that looked onto the street, but when I peered through the interstices of the privet, I saw that she was indeed right and the car to take me back to Dallas, where I was staying, was at the curb. I began to respect the sixth sense she had several times laid claim to. ("I have a very unusual extrasensory perception," she had said once, "so doesn't it stand to reason that if my boy shot the President I would have *known* at the time it happened?") I respected, also, her dramatic sense of timing, and I wondered how I would hang to the cliff until I heard about Marina's French origins.

As I got up to go, I asked if she would object to my bringing a tape recorder the following day; she said that, on the contrary, she would be glad if I did, if, that is, I brought two machines, since she wanted one tape to preserve "for history." She had made many recordings, she told me, for "mass mediums" and for her own purposes; she knew that she spoke at the rate of a hundred and eighty words a minute, and I was to tell that to the man I rented the machines from. An operator would not be necessary, because she knew how "to work 'em all."

I started toward the bedroom to fetch my Neiman-Marcus rain cape, and my eye drifted willy-nilly toward the scroll over the desk. I did not look at it directly but instead at a tempera on wood of a baroque orange and chestnut newel post (a detail from backstairs at Blenheim Castle? from Marion Davies' house?), which she dismissed: "A little decorator thing. I thought it would go with the chair. But now this, this is important, this is what you should see," and she took the scroll down from its hook.

"I was gonna show you this," she said. "Here, the man can wait—I guess he's getting paid, isn't he? You get out your notebook and copy it down, and be sure you get the words right."

The legend, cut into copper, read,

MY SON—

LEE HARVEY OSWALD EVEN AFTER HIS DEATH HAS
DONE MORE FOR HIS COUNTRY THAN ANY OTHER
LIVING HUMAN BEING

MARGUERITE C. OSWALD

As I was writing down this abstruse manifesto (I could not get a purchase on the syntax), Mrs. Oswald brought my things and smiled disarmingly. "Of course, I'm not a writer like you," she said. "But I like how that sounds. That's what I said at the year period when I went to the grave. Newspaper reporters came by the galore and asked if I had anything to say, and I said this. And every word of it is true. I'm proud of my son, and why not? My son is an unsung hero."

I remembered that she had petitioned to have Lee Harvey buried in Arlington Cemetery.

I thanked her for giving me so much of her time, and I thanked her for the coffee. Her handclasp was firm and straightforward, and her eyes shone with zeal and satisfaction and optimism. "We're going to win in the end."

I was not sure whether the "we" was editorial or whether I had now been initiated into a coterie whose adversaries were "they."

On the drive back, I browsed through some matter Mrs. Oswald had lent me. One was a paperback book by Kerry

Thornley, who had known Lee Harvey in the Marines and had dedicated his "iconoclastic critique on how America helped Oswald to become what he did" to "Clint Bolton, who first said to me: 'Go home and write—ya bum!'" I did not get much further than that. The other was a pamphlet proving that it was ballistically impossible for Oswald to have killed Kennedy; this was a compilation of diagrams and of copies of letters that had been sent, accompanying the diagrams, to leading magazines and to people of position—the letters, significantly, had gone unanswered or had been brushed aside; a ferocious admonition in the beginning of the text prevents me from quoting any part of it.

Soon after the assassination, my husband got a good many letters addressed to him in his role as critic of the press; most of them told him how to go about his reporting, and most of them went into the wastepaper basket. He was, as a matter of fact, at work on one of his "Wayward Press" analyses for *The New Yorker* just before he died, a little more than a month after the President was killed. He brought home for me to read one of the letters, whose author implored, "Mr. Liebling, go to Dallas and tell us the truth. You might of course get killed in Texas, but if you get killed, the world shall know that somebody from the right (be it Birchers or Southern Democrats) wants to hide the truth."

Exegetes of the Dallas murders sprang up like mushrooms in a pinewoods after a soaking rain; the mycelium at the round earth's four corners was rich and ready. Many of the toadstools that appeared were harmless but without flavor, some were tasty and even delicious, many more were as noxious as the amanita verna. In the cities, in whose purlieus these mycologists' wonderlands flourished, kangaroo courts met round the clock, and some of the judges and some of the jurors were responsible people, and the opinions they handed down were persuasive. They were shooting in the dark, but they managed to convince themselves and millions of others that their shots dispelled the darkness and everything was limpidly illuminated; theory, creative and flexible, made mincemeat of circumstantial evidence. The name of the prisoner in the dock was legion; he had every pigmentation and every shape of jaw known to anthropology; he was a member of every political organization, every religious fraternity, every business, scientific, criminal, occult conclave of every country on the face of the earth. In some of these courtroom spectaculars (the remarks from the peanut gallery were deafening; the confusion was such that one could not remember which were the good guys and which the bad ones among Mark Lane, Perry Mason, Melvin Belli, and *The Defenders'* man, let alone which belonged to the bar association and which to the American Federation of Radio and Television Artists), Lee Harvey Oswald was convicted of having pulled the trigger, *but* at the instigation of a highly organized and dangerous gang; in other reenactments of the drama, he was not even on the premises, but was under a haystack, fast asleep. In Europe, where there has never been an assassination of a political figure for an apolitical, individual reason, the idea that Oswald, obscure, untutored, could have acted on his own was insupportable, and the most important papers of the most important capitals carried stories categorically proving conspiracy.

As we entered Dallas and drove along the route of the President's caravan, I observed, as I had the other two times I had been over this same ground, that the distance between the sixth-floor window of the Texas Book Depository and the place where the car, slowing for a turn, had been, seemed to be much less than it had appeared in photographs. I was struck, moreover, by the fact that between the window and the target there was no obstruction of any kind to challenge aim or deflect the attention, no eave or overhang or tree. The drop shot, from a steadied rifle, was fired on a day of surpassing clarity; the marksmanship of the gunner did not have to be remarkable.

II

Having taken Mrs. Oswald at her word, I refused the offer of a lesson in manipulation when the man delivered the tape recorders to my hotel. This was unwise; despite her boast that she could work 'em all, Mrs. Oswald couldn't work these, and I had never clapped eyes on a tape recorder before in my life. After a quarter of an hour of bungling experimentation, plugging and unplugging, punching buttons and shifting levers, reversing bobbins, profitlessly studying instructions that might as well have been written in Arabic (and possibly were), we were both exasperated. Sitting on the floor with our hair awry, amid furniture that we had dislodged in our futile fiddling, we were exasperated with the contraptions and with each other. Mrs. Oswald said with some asperity that these were inferior machines, that I should not have cut corners when matters of such importance were at stake (I felt as defensive as if the machines belonged to me; I wanted to invent an affidavit from *Consumer Reports* to fling before her), but, having chosen to do so, I should have learned how to run the trashy thingumbobs. She went to the bedroom to telephone the shop to ask for help, and while she was gone, Lady Luck visited me in a dazzling revelation and piloted my fingers in a virtuoso performance, unique in my experience, so that when she came back with the disgruntling news that since it was Saturday the shop was closed, I was delighted to point to the smoothly revolving wheels. (In that moment I became eight years old, and, having just outwitted one of my smug older sisters, it was all I could do to keep from yammering like a monkey.)

"Well, now! If we just keep at a thing, we'll get it to go in the end, isn't that the truth?" she cried, pleased with her stick-to-itiveness, which had borne practical fruit as well as an opportunity to express an eternal verity. "Oh, I can tell we'll work well together! Right here it's proved that together we're a mechanical genius."

We stationed ourselves, I in the chair where I had sat the day before and Mrs. Oswald beneath Whistler's old lady.

She picked up her microphone and spoke into it clearly. Because she never groped for a word and because her undertones and overtones and rhythms altered at such cleverly strategic times, I, the only visible member of her audience, was caught up and indoctrinated even when I heard grumblings from the back of the house that her arguments were specious, her logic bizarre, and her deductions plucked from the foggy, foggy air.

"Now about Marina being a true or untrue picture," she said, stating the text for the day. "Marina, as I have said, seems French to me. I have researched everything about Marina over and over. When she went to New Orleans, she did not want to live in an apartment with high ceilings. Now where does she know about the high ceilings? There may be a simple answer for this and all the other things, but I don't have it, and I want it. And she complained about the cockroaches, which is all right, but a foreign girl knows how to clean up things. And then, of course, she knew a little French too."

Considering that she was French, the fact that she knew a little French too must have been useful.

"There's one letter in the Warren Report from Russia from Lee that said he married this girl and she spoke a little French. Well, the letters had to be retyped because they didn't photograph well, and they omitted the word French. If you use a magnifying glass and look at Lee's letter, you will see that Marina speaks a little French. Now I ask myself: was this deliberate, or was this just an error? But when you find so many errors and so much coincidence, then you begin to wonder if something's being whitewashed and if there isn't something more to it than meets the eye.

"And Marina knew English. Marina and I conversed. I don't know Russian and this is the part that I was indignant about. Because after she went to live with Mr. Martin in his home with his family they put her on television, and that day she spoke real well broken English. If they said she didn't know English, that's baloney. She could understand, but when she went out any place she didn't open her mouth and she made out she didn't speak or understand English. This is what I mean when I say she is not a true person."

"But why do you think she's French?" I insisted, not at all satisfied with the proposition that an aversion to high ceilings and cockroaches was idiopathically Gallic.

"I wish I could go into this, I truly do, but it's just like 'how do I love you?' It's just something that doesn't make sense, you know, and you know it. I felt this almost when I first met her and saw that she didn't look Russian. She doesn't look Russian at all."

I recalled that when I had seen the first photographs of Marina, I had been reminded of the flawed beauty of the girls in the Soviet films of a few years ago—the imperfections of skin and teeth of Veronica in *The Cranes Are Flying* had been inexplicably touching. Today, Oswald's widow is much different, cropped and kempt and "styled," but at the time no face had looked to me more Chekhovian or Dostoevskian or Pushkinesque—she could have been Lisa in *Pique Dame*, destined to hurl herself into the Neva as the sad snow fell all around her, or Masha, of all the three sisters the one most given to tears.

Mrs. Oswald, however, stated unequivocally, "She looks French," and that was that. "Now the only thing I'm *sure* of is that *I* had nothing to do with the assassination. I'm not sure about anybody else. And because I am looking for the truth, everyone is under suspicion in a way. You see, I don't know who's who. I have to evaluate everybody, and Marina doesn't ring true. Of course, I never hear anybody else say she was French. But I have my reasons for saying this, which will be very delicate. She doesn't ring true, to begin with, in respect to motherhood. Even if she thinks in her mind that Lee was guilty, the thing to do was protect him for her children's sake and for her sake—no, I'm not talking about lying, because I don't believe in lying, but I mean, to give out stories like if she had met him outside Russia she would never have married him, because of the type he was and so on and so forth. That's just downing him more and more, and yet she's the mother of his children. This is not true of motherhood or womanhood. Even if he was a louse, she would defend him to a certain extent. She never goes out to the cemetery. She did in the very beginning. She went out, and everything was fine, and then when she was taken over she started changing. And whether it was for the security of the country, whether this was her role, whether she's being threatened, which is a possibility—whatever reason, it's not a nice reason, and this is why she is not a true person. First she says, 'Lee good man, Lee no shoot anybody,' and

everything was in Lee's favor, and then all of a sudden they get
aholt of her and put her on television and she says she thinks in
her mind her husband is guilty, and from then on her husband's
a louse. These are the things that just don't jive.

"And now another thing, all the witnesses told how she
started complaining about everything as soon as she got here,
how she treated him and how she talked about her sexual life
and how she denounced him and so on and so forth, and taking
up with these Russian people. This is all in black and white. I'm
not imagining these things, and thank God there are other people taking this up. I say thank God because there some people
who would like to think that I have hallucinations—I know it's
already been said in the Warren Report. It was said by some
attorney. Point blank. 'Do you think your sister'—they said this
to my sister—'do you think that your sister has hallucinations?'
Why? Because I notice the inaccuracies and coincidences and
things that don't jive? I know some people who wouldn't hesitate to make a mental case outa me, and believe me, if anybody's
in their right mind, it's Mrs. Marguerite Oswald."

She paused to let this sink in and take root, and, as she did
so, looked me in the eye.

"No matter what Marina does, it's news, but locally I can
show reporters something in black and white and they won't
give me coverage. This is the difference. This is where the human
element comes in. And this is where I have been persecuted and
have suffered just like my son. Oh, I can hear the 'ah's' when
they read this—here is Miz Oswald feeling sorry for herself.
No, no, I'm not feeling sorry for myself, but I know for a fact
that I have been persecuted. What's wrong with Miz Oswald?
Why does she think she's being persecuted? Is she mentally
unbalanced? I have been asked that question publicly. No, no.
Without persecution, there wouldn't be a persecution complex.
This is what Freud[3] said himself. Shut off your tape, dearheart."

I did as I was told, anticipating a confidence too sensitive or
hazardous to national security to be recorded, but all she said
was, "Don't you think it's too hot for coffee today? Let me
make you a glass of iced tea. I've got some nice Indian iced tea
with a kind of a spicy flavor."

3. See Appendix III, page 811.

Today she was wearing a blue denim jumper and a perky red and white striped shirt, and she was shod in sneakers. She looked as carefree and fun-loving as the wife of the man in the ad who has retired to Florida at the age of fifty, thanks to having taken the advice of his farsighted insurance broker. I felt that she should have been telling me more about the iced tea, but even as she emptied ice trays clamorously and rattled spoons, she rode her tempest. "Maybe you saw where Marina was offered ten thousand dollars for the guns? The gun that killed President Kennedy and the telescope sight that went with it and the gun that killed Tippit?"

I said that I had. I had been dumfounded, as a matter of fact, that the weapons had not been acquired by the FBI or by the Smithsonian Institution, but I had been reminded that they belonged to the dead man's estate and were now Marina's to dispose of as she wished. The story I had read said that a "private collector" was negotiating for them, and at the time I had wondered what manner of man he could be.

"Well, now, let me tell you about Marguerite Oswald being a mental case. When I read that, I said to myself, now those guns are worth a great deal more than ten thousand dollars and Marina should get more money for my grandchildren. I am thinking about *my* grandchildren. So I called the Fort Worth *Star Telegram* and told them what I thought. I said, 'Those guns are priceless, but if they're gonna be sold, let's see some justice done to the children of Lee Harvey Oswald.' And just last week there was an item in the Fort Worth *Star Telegram* that said a Frenchman had offered twenty thousand."

(Later on that evening, back in Dallas, a newspaper reporter told me that the second offer had been topped and that Marina had received five thousand on account and that forty thousand more was being held for her in escrow until the estate was settled. Since that time, the picture has changed altogether.)[4]

"So, you see, I do my bit. But nobody knows, and it's a shame they don't. I'm not unhappy. You can see I'm not, can't you? But I'm a mother in history, I'm all over the world. There's two Presidents in my life, and *my* son's the one accused. You know, here is Mrs. Kennedy, a very wealthy woman, Mrs.

4. See Appendix IV, page 811.

Tippit, a very wealthy woman, Marina, very wealthy, but *I* am wondering where my next meal is coming from. It's almost unbelievable, it's sometimes almost like a spiritual."

She brought me a dewy glass of tea with a spray of fresh mint. It was sugary and rather good, and it had no taste of tea.

"Here we are, we four women in history, and yet *I* am the mother. But has anyone come forward to reimburse me for my emotional stability? No, no! And I have given of time and my voice, yet I have twenty-three hundred dollars to my name. I'm not complaining. I have my health. I eat well, I'm not brooding. But isn't it strange? Now I made a television interview with Belli in Los Angeles, and we were so good they wouldn't stop the cameras but wanted us to go on for an hour instead of the half hour. And I got one hundred dollars for that. Yet Richard Burton was on the same program the next night and he got *five thousand* dollars. What do you think he did with it? He gave it to charity. He is not even an American, yet he gave it to charity, and here is Mrs. Oswald, the mother, talking and talking about the American way of life, and where's the rent money coming from? You understand I don't care about money. Money is only good to its use, but I need money to carry on the campaign against the campaign against me, and as a mother, I think I deserve it. I got fired from my job as practical nurse because of the assassination, and it broke my heart. I didn't make only five dollars a week, but I was glad to work for that because I was doing it for humanity."

"Five dollars a week?" I asked, wondering what part of the century she had flashed back to.

"Sometimes five, sometimes twenty-five. Seven days a week helping people. I was fired because of the assassinating, yet I was only the mother. Six months later when I went in the clothes locker I saw my uniform and shoes and everything and I just broke down. It just hit me hard. But now I have accepted this, and I feel like now I would never like to nurse again. I just don't feel like I would like to go into anybody else's sorrow. I have enough of my own. It's a hard life. Why, the very day of the assassination I was nursing and I heard it on the radio, that my son, Lee Harvey Oswald had been taken into custody. I came right home and called the Fort Worth *Star Telegram* and asked them to send over a press car to take me to Dallas. You can push the button on again. We can drink our tea and talk at the same time. Is there anything you want to ask me?"

"Yes, there is," I said. "When did you last see Lee?"

"I saw Lee in the jailhouse after the assassination, and he was all bruised up with black eyes and all and I said, 'Honey, did they beat you?' and he said, 'It isn't anything, Mother. I just got in a scuffle.' Now this is normal, he wouldn't tell his mother if he had been mistreated by the police. But I have my opinion."

"But before the assassination? How long had it been since you'd seen him?"

"I hadn't seen Lee since October, the end of October, 1962. Just about a year, that would make it. I used to do live-ins and sometimes I'd be two hundred miles away, but the truth is, Lee and Marina left Fort Worth and didn't even tell me where they were. I called Robert and he said Lee had a box number on him and I told Robert to make sure he took care of his brother and so on. I was not in a position financially to help, working the way I was. And another thing, I was a little miffed. They left without telling me they were leaving. I was there that afternoon, and they left the next morning, and there's more to it than that, but never mind. And I thought, well, when they get good and ready they'll come and see me. I hadn't seen John Edward for years before, or Robert either, and I felt, well, I'm their mother and when they get ready it's their place to come and see me. I don't worry about them any more. And this was the attitude I took with Lee and Marina. They lived with me for a month and then they moved out. I'm a working person, I have to pay my own rent, make my own living, and I don't have the money or the time to run back and forth and they didn't have a car to come over here. You understand? And, too, I wouldn't have a place to put them up if they came to visit me. Maybe if I had a three-bedroom house. Maybe then they'd take the bus and come over for the weekend, but I never was in that position. I am entirely alone. I do not have even my children to discuss things with. For instance, Lee was left-handed, and right away I realized whoever shot the gun, it would make a difference. So I called Robert and he wouldn't answer these important questions. I have suffered very much."

Although Mrs. Oswald frequently made statements like this,

designed to cause the blood of her interlocutor to run cold with embarrassment and to immobilize the tongue, such was the self-protecting and even complacent nature of her hostility to the world at large and to Washington in particular that she did not urge (indeed, she did not invite) one to enter her Castle Rackrent to view each tribulation separately. Rather, it was as if she had posted a notice on the door that read "Black Death" or "Beware of the Snakes," to indicate that inside there was mortification so monstrous and esoteric and ineradicable, and, paradoxically, so precious, that it could not be taken in by any ordinary intelligence. I was guilty, I had contributed my galling bit to this treasure house of anguish and humiliation, but so had everybody else on earth.

Serenely she spoke to the microphone, smiling now and then in composure as she tallied some of life's ironies, arching her dark eyebrows in astonishment at some of the most "spiritual" aspects of "The Case."

"You know, it's a strange thing, a very interesting thing the way things have happened to me all my life. I said it's sometimes like a spiritual and I say it again. Now ever since right before the Warren Report came out, the Fort Worth *Star Telegram* wrote they would not run a thing on the assassination—they had had a big dose, a big dose of castor oil. I asked why wasn't the *Star Telegram* carrying any of my quotes—the Dallas reporters and everybody else was out at the cemetery for the year period— *they* wanted to hear from me and I was on television and all, but there wasn't a thing said in the local paper about me being out at the cemetery for the year period. And of course there were things said about the Tippits and the Kennedys, and I asked this young reporter, and he said, 'Miz Oswald, they had a big dose here.'

"But let's go back a little bit and I'll give you an example of the way things have always worked against me. I used to work in Algiers, Louisiana, during the war, and that is across the river from New Orleans. I was a switchboard operator. My duty was six o'clock in the morning until three or six-thirty, I forget which. So I rented a room in Algiers, Louisiana, and my sister was taking care of Lee permanently at this particular time. He was about two years old. Every evening I left Algiers and took the ferry and came over and took care of my baby, and would have to leave early enough to get home before dark—after all, I was a woman alone—to be across the river so I could go to work for six-thirty. And the Naval Base personnel used to come with a jeep to pick me up because there was no other way to get to the Naval Base. Well, this was typical of most of my life. It's a little humorous in a way, but it's typical of things that have happened to me right along. I was on this side of New Orleans and this young lady that also roomed where I was rooming had a car and she was coming to New Orleans and she told me that if I would stay over she would take me home. Well, my two nephews had had a tonsillitis operation and I went to the hospital and stayed a little while with them and then I met this young lady and she had a date and they decided that we should go into one of the nightclubs in the Vieux Carré and have a little recreation. Well, now I love to dance and go out to dinner and places like that, and so I said I would.

"And before I knew it, it was two o'clock in the morning. What could I do? I'm with them, they have the car, so I have to wait. So when I did get home I called the other young lady who worked the evening shift for the switchboard and told her I wasn't feeling well and would she take the morning and I would take the evening. She said she would. However, it didn't please her too much. So that afternoon I was called to the Colonel's office and he asked me what happened and I told him I wasn't feeling well, and that I had been up until late and had been to the hospital—that part of course was true—so it was perfectly natural that I call the other young lady and ask her to change with me.

"However, I did dance, you see, with a few of the boys, and they happened to be men from the base, but how was I to know that? And he told me that I was not telling the truth and that I had been seen in a nightclub and I was dancing until two o'clock in the morning when I should have been home in bed resting to be there for the six o'clock shift. And he fired me, right then and there."

She allowed the climax to remain frozen for a moment before she rang the curtain down to point the moral. "This is just a little story that shows what goes on in my life. I was fired right on the spot! When I think of all the things that are being said about me, I think about all these things that have happened, and there must be a simple explanation for them. It is my job to *find* that explanation for all the inaccuracies and distortions and so on and so forth so that the people will understand."

I asked only one more question that day, and I did so with trepidation. I asked if she had voted in the last Presidential election. She bridled, but her outrage was put on like a false nose.

She said, "Why, honey, you know I can't discuss my personal politics. After all, I *am* responsible for two Presidents."

She took off the nose and meandered on. She bemoaned the loss of mementos of Lee. "Lee was a beautiful child, and this is why I gave all the pictures of him to the magazines. I got rooked financially, but that was all right because they showed a nice clean boy and a boy not underfed. But I don't have many mementos for this reason: when Lee and Marina returned from Russia, I did as I did with the other boys as soon as they were married. I gave Lee his baby book and things of that kind, and Marina has them all now and refuses to give them to me. I gave Lee a watch that belonged to his father that was in my possession for years and years and years. It was a pocket watch and my husband was called after the General Robert E. Lee, but he was always called Lee. You see, my first son by Mr. Oswald is named Robert E. Lee and then Lee is called Lee. When Lee was born—that is, Lee Harvey Oswald—I never could say the name Lee because my husband was always called Lee. Am I making it plain?"

(No, but go on.)

"He was really named after the General, so I kept the watch for Lee. I had it all those years and then I gave it to Lee when he returned from Russia. I feel like these things are mine and I want them, but I have been very unsuccessful in getting them back. Also, there is a little navy blue wool suit that the three boys wore and I have carried that around for over twenty-six years and it didn't even have a moth hole in it. It was an adorable little suit. Lee's picture in *Life*—'Evolution of an Assassin'—at six months has the suit on, and I gave it to my daughter-in-law, Robert's wife, just about three months before the assassination because I was nursing and moving around and I asked her to keep it for me. And that has not been returned to me. Actually, I have suffered a great deal."

The refrain, annunciating travail, came off with her customary unwavering matter-of-factness.

Among her souvenirs of Lee, Mrs. Oswald did still have a "little replica of a Magnus organ that I bought him while we were in New York for Christmas, 1953. I paid, let's see, I paid approximately $39.95 for it." This and other properties to whose sentimental value had been added a historic dimension, she kept in storage.

She spoke of letters she had written to prominent people when Lee was in Russia. "Here is a young boy, and let's say he was adventurous or anything about him, but anyhow he was in Russia trying to renounce his citizenship. Instead of blasting him on the front pages, why didn't they get together and see that he came home to his native land? I sent a telegram to the Mayor of Fort Worth, but I didn't receive an answer. I wrote to Sam Rayburn and to Christian Herter—I wonder what became of those letters? I also wrote to Mr. Khrushchev, July 19, 1960. I stated that Lee had gone to Russia in September of 1959 and that I had one letter from him in January, but my letter to him was returned and I never heard from him again. I asked Mr. Khrushchev to supply me with any information about his whereabouts, if he was working and so on and so forth, I said that I was much worried and deeply concerned as a mother would be.

"Now I did not receive an answer from Mr. Khrushchev, and this brings up another interesting aspect of the case. The letter to Christian Herter and the letter to Sam Rayburn and the letter to Congressman Jim White all expressed the same thing. I said from what I had read in the newspaper, my son said that he wanted to live in a Communist country, in a working man's country because of the Communists here and hate and racial discrimination and everything. And I made it perfectly plain that as an individual, even though he was young, he had served in the Marines and he had become an adult, not in age but in maturity because of his hitch in the Marines, and as an individual, if this was what he wanted to do I in no way wanted to influence him because I thought he had a right to his own life, and this I believe. Yet Representative Ford had a big article in *Life* magazine about 'Mother's Myth, Son an Agent,' and he must have—or he *should* have known that I in no way wanted to influence my son to come home. He said that I went to Washington in 1961, which I did, when I was in dire need, which I was, but I went to petition President Kennedy to get my son to come home in order to support and help me, *not* to influence him. What an injustice to a mother!"

In the most abrupt and perfunctory parenthesis possible, she said that it was time for more iced tea, and, raising her voice above the chattering of the ice cubes as she briskly stirred our glasses of strange brew, she lectured and invoked and apostrophized without transition and with a grand if confounding disregard for chronology. Immediately after she had served up Representative Ford's head on a platter, she took the Secret Service to task.

"The Secret Service would not let me get near my daughter-in-law. I fought and fought like a wild animal. I called the head of the Secret Service I guess every day, begging to see my daughter-in-law, and they wouldn't let me get near her. So she changed her testimony. First it was, 'Lee was good man, Lee no do nothing, Lee no kill nobody.' And then I was pushed out, absolutely pushed out, and Marina Oswald's husband was a louse. Now I arrived in Dallas on March the ninth at the height of the Ruby trial and was told by reporters, and I can verify this, that Mrs. Paine was in Marina's house, but the point I'm going to make and make strongly is that I do not think it was fair that Mrs. Paine spoke with Marina Oswald before Mrs. Paine herself testified. Now I didn't have that opportunity, or my sons. I had never talked to John Edward or Robert or Marina or vice versa, so no one in the close family knew what each other was going to say. And this is very sad because we could have understood each other a little better, rather than bog each other down, as it came out some time. But Mrs. Paine did have that privilege to talk to my daughter-in-law, and this I don't like. This I don't like one bit. Why do the Secret Service let this strange woman see my daughter-in-law, and not me? But the Secret Service never questioned me, nor the FBI either. The Secret Service and the FBI never came near me."

"But you *have* been interviewed?" I said because there had

flashed before my inward eye newspaper stories about her without number.

"Oh, yes, yes, of course I've been interviewed by the newspapers, if that's what you mean," she said crossly, still put out by having been given the cold shoulder by the FBI and the Secret Service. "I've been interviewed by *them* by the galore. Now let me give you an instance of how I hold a lot of these cards that will show up the inaccuracies and the errors. About the diary—you asked about that."

I had not asked about the diary; in fact, I had forgotten its existence. Possibly the question had come from someone nearer the front of the house.

"It has never been verified how the diary was leaked. It said in one article that no one knew where the diary came from, but a certain reporter in Dallas interviewed the widow, Mrs. Marina, quite often, so it implied that this is where the diary came from. And he refused to release where it came from. But she and her attorney expressed indignation about the release of the diary and so on, and they sent telegrams to the Warren Commission saying they didn't think it was right, and the Warren Commission was going to investigate, and the FBI. So I just sat and waited. I smile inwardly quite a bit when I read about myself. I smile and say, 'Oh, goodness, how can you be so wrong?' Only way I can survive, to have a little sense of humor.

"So I was smiling and waiting—this is good—all this the FBI's going to check, you know. I'm waiting and waiting, but no one came, so after the third day I called the FBI, which is in Dallas, and I forget the man's name and I told him who I was and I said, 'You know I have been waiting for someone to come over and question me about the release of the so-called diary. And nobody has.' And he said, 'Well, do you have the diary, Miz Oswald?' And I said, 'No, I don't, but I just can't imagine all the fuss about the diary and not coming and asking if I released the diary.' He said, 'They didn't come because they knew you didn't have it.' And I said, 'Yes, they know I didn't have it because *they* released it *themelves*!' Now do you get an idea of what I'm talking about? Why, I mean, this just insults my intelligence."

For one second I was carried back in time to a winter when I had been a student at the University of Heidelberg. One afternoon an American friend and I were moseying through Woolworth's on the Hauptstrasse (we found this a good way to pick up the German words for miscellaneous hardware) when we saw a Japanese student at the stationery counter having a plainly fruitless conversation with the clerk. My friend Hightower (now a distinguished sinologist at Harvard) had a smattering of Japanese and was as much impelled, I think, to show it off as he was to do a good turn. The Japanese was grateful—he had wanted gummed reinforcements for his loose-leaf notebook—and we fell into a ridiculous conversation. All of us had a little German, the Japanese had a few snippets of English, about as many as Hightower had of Japanese. Our communication for some reason seemed to us worthy and charming, and we continued it out to the street and into a *Konditorei*, where we became fast friends before we had finished our coffee. After that, for several months, Herr Hai, Hightower, and I met once or twice a week and together we read *Ulysses*, holding the text in three languages. At any rate it *seems* to me we did; I daresay we tried it once and gave up. Somehow the snap went all out of Joyce's puns when we tried them on in German and Japanese. What little German we had, diminished and grew deformed, and we began to forget our own languages; we remained friends, but I think that when we met for coffee, we read to ourselves and simply smiled at one another from time to time.

Mrs. Oswald's conversation with the FBI man about the diary left me in just about as deep water as I had been in when I had tried to understand Hightower's elucidation in German of Joyce's play on "metempsychosis" to Hai.

"You see, they have never questioned me about one thing," she went on. "What I'm trying to say is that the normal thing is they should have been at my door right away. I *could* have had the diary. It was my son's diary. But I was never questioned. So the proof of the pudding is that they knew it was absolutely leaked, and they let it die down—you didn't hear any more about it. You see, this is a good example because *I could have had the diary*. If they were sincere, they could have come to me, let's face it. One and one just don't make two. My book is going to be called *One and One Don't Make Two* or *This and That*. They're concerned about the diary, and everybody's investigating, but nobody comes and asks this old mother if she had the diary and she released it. So I never believed that it was my son's diary."

I grew increasingly muddled as she escorted me down cul-de-sacs and through woods which, significantly she felt, could not be seen for the trees. As various as the terrae incognitae were the points of time at which we traversed them. Sometimes I was in New Orleans listening to Lee as he sang "Silent Night" with a "nice little voice," but at the next moment I was at the Six Flags Motel with the Mesdames Marguerite and Marina Oswald after the boy's murder, and johnny-on-the-spot *Life* magazine was there infiltrating the ranks of cops. I examined the contents of Lee's sea bag when he came back from Formosa—he carried with him a book of Christmas carols and a Christmas card from his mother which she had sent him in 1956. I went to Washington with her to the hearings before the Warren Commission and stayed in a suite of rooms the size of a house—dining room, grand piano, everything; I was haunted by the spectral figures of unnamed Secret Service men with a lot of accounting to do, by FBI men who had stayed away from her door, "high officials" who blew their tops when Mrs. Oswald asked them direct questions. I saw a copy of the letter written to Khrushchev (she keeps a copy of everything she writes), I saw a Mother's Day card signed "Lee" that had come from Russia in 1960, and I saw the subpoena requiring her to appear instanter at the Ruby trial. (Sheer perseverance had won her this peremptory invitation: she had been barred from the courtroom.)

The tapes were finally used up and the ashtray beside me was full of cigarette stubs. We stood up and both of us stretched like women who had done a hard day's work cleaning out the cellar and putting up rhubarb. The room was disheveled with exhibits, and the furniture was still out of place where we had moved it to accommodate the tape recorders. I offered to help Mrs. Oswald tidy up, but she said, "No, no, I don't have another thing to do. I was hoping I could give you a bite of supper, but I suppose you can't stay."

"No, I can't," I said. "I'm sorry."

She laughed. "If you cahn't, you cahn't," she said, parodying a broad "a" that does not exist in my speech. "You go on back to Dallas now, and you be fresh for tomorrow because we've still got a lot to talk about, hear? Tomorrow!" She was struck with a numbing thought. "Tomorrow is Mother's Day and I will go to Lee Harvey Oswald's grave, but I will be a mother alone, a mother in history alone on Mother's Day."

A vaporing cloak of wistfulness enveloped her for no longer than the twinkling of an eye. Resourceful woman, she found a dandy solution to her dilemma, and gaily, as if she were planning a picnic or a frisk through an amusement park, she said, "I know! I'll take *you*!"

III

INFERNAL thunderclaps shocked me awake on Mother's Day, and the rain on my windows sounded like kettledrums being belted by a gang of lunatics. A dolorous gloaming hung in my air-conditioned room, where the temperature was always that of a meat cooler (the windows, of course, could not be opened, so that even on a warm day I had gooseflesh if I took off my sweater), and the rushing wetness outside was a palpable ectoplasm within. My impulse was to eliminate the day by taking a sleeping pill, but I was committed; I must go with Mrs. Oswald to her son's grave.

For a long time I lay abed dawdling over a great pot of coffee and the Dallas *News*. Pitching and tossing through the dispatches from South Vietnam and the Dominican Republic, I had the dislocating feeling that I was not reading about the culmination of crises today that would be annulled by different ones tomorrow, but that I was trying to get into my head the complicated background and causes of a *fait accompli* for a history examination. The living, current, and inexplicable chaos was not happening plangently in South Asia or in the West Indies; it was not political upheaval and war. It was the assassination of President Kennedy that had taken place only hours—or even minutes—ago.

Probably the storm through which we drove to Fort Worth was not the very worst I had ever seen, but at the time I could not recall another to equal its infuriated lightning and its dooming detonations and the niagaras that roared down on us from four directions, baffling the windshields. It sounded like catastrophe, and I was sorry to be in alien corn. But by the time we got to Mrs. Oswald's street, the fulminations began to peter out and the malevolent splendor was replaced by a sniffling nastiness, the kind of mess that causes angleworms to materialize, mauve and visceral, on sidewalks.

Somewhere in the neighborhood a voice, much amplified, was blaring. I thought at first it was coming from the sound truck of a political candidate on a mobile stump or from one advertising an American Legion carnival, but as I got out of the car, I realized that it was pouring out of Mrs. Oswald's house and that the voice belonged to her. I knocked, unheard, several times. The tulips, I saw, had been decapitated by the wind and their stems were limp among the stiff spears of the everlasting humbug heather.

"What an injustice to a mother!" shouted Mrs. Oswald's disembodied voice. "If this was true, the facts couldn't hurt me so deeply, or I would say, 'Consider the source.' But this quote, along with many others, has gone all over the world and I have been attacked publicly as a mother by television commentators. They said I was going from place to place speaking in behalf of my son. Was it because I wanted to vindicate myself as a mother? What an awful thing! I have taken this with all the composure I know how, but inwardly I have seethed."

The door was open, but the screen was latched. The tape recorders were on the floor, where we had left them yesterday, and I could see the discs of both revolving as they released a hundred and eighty words a minute. I knocked again more loudly and called out. In a moment, Mrs. Oswald appeared. I had interrupted her in the middle of her lunch, and she continued to chew through her welcoming smile as she opened the screen. She was behindhand, she explained, because she thought I might be delayed by the storm—she herself thought nothing of these funny old Texas storms and loved driving through them, but she didn't know how people from Massachusetts took to Wild West weather. (As I have said, I had come down from Connecticut and she had my address there. But this kind of minutia did not concern her. From time to time she had advised me to look something up in the Warren Report, and she would preface this by saying alternately, "When you get back to New York," or "When you get back to Boston." Once, experimentally, I said that I would soon have to return to my post at Austin, and this news had no effect at all.)

I made out her observations about the comical Ole Wild West storms largely by reading her lips, since her recorded voice drowned out her current one. She let me in and turned the volume down and invited me to join her in a snack. I thanked her and refused and asked if I might put my soaked umbrella in the bathroom.

The living room was even more disordered than it had been

when I left it the day before. The coffee table was piled high with newspaper clippings and pamphlets and Xeroxed documents; the lids of the tape recorders lay on the floor, and their canvas covers were wadded up as if someone had meant to throw them out but hadn't got around to it. Evidently Mrs. Oswald had been so busy in my absence that she had let her nest go hang.

The bedroom, however, was as neat as if no one had ever slept or dressed in it, and in the ascetic, antiseptic bathroom, besides the towels imprinted with unlikely anemones, the only things I saw were a bottle of hand lotion named "To a Wild Rose" and an ornamental bar of soap embossed with sharp golden lilies. If Mrs. Oswald suffered from dyspepsia or conjunctivitis, she did not tell the world about it by leaving her medicaments on view.

In the living room, the affirmative voice went on: "I understand that Mr. William Manchester was commissioned by the Kennedy family to rewrite the events of the three days and his book will be out on November 22, 1968. Mr. Manchester is the author of *Profiles in Courage*."

(She had told me this earlier, and when I had diffidently suggested that perhaps she had the title confused with Manchester's book called *Portrait of a President*, she indicated that the confusion resided in my addlepate. Today she went on record.)

"I would like to say now, unless Mr. William Manchester discusses my life and my son's life personally with me, this book will also be inaccurate. He came to see me, but he was here no more than ten or fifteen minutes. However, there was one very important question he asked: and I will tell you the question. He asked me what a certain party looked like, and did I have a picture of this certain party. I didn't ask any questions, and he just stayed about ten minutes in my home. I say he will make the same mistakes as the Commission members unless he cooperates with me about my life and my son's life. This is why there's so many distortions in the Warren Report. They spoke to outsiders and they questioned my boys about age six and seven that couldn't remember things, and they didn't have the courtesy to come to me and verify these facts. They printed whatever they were told. And so I state here and now to the American people that if Mr. Manchester does not spend at least four days with me, the Kennedy book will also be inaccurate. Because I feel like I, Mrs. Marguerite Oswald, is the only one that can rectify some of the inaccuracies. I am the mother of this boy. The other two boys were in the service, they don't know about a lot of our life and it has to come from me.

"Many of the readers are wondering, 'Well, why doesn't Mrs. Oswald put all of this into one book so that we can get some of the true story?' It is impossible, dear reader. To begin with, this book would have to be researched for about a year or so. And no one has come to my aid—no publisher with the money, or a writer to do this type work. So until that time and money are afforded me, I will do the best I can. I will admit it is not enough, but as a mother I am doing the best I can."

I looked at myself in the mirror over the washbasin and stuck out my tongue and then went back to the living room. Mrs. Oswald was at her dining table, proceeding with her plentiful lunch. She got up and shut off the machines, and she explained, "I'll start this over from the beginning for you. You see, when I got up this morning, I thought I'd just put something on the tape all on my own. We can erase it if you don't like it, but I really and truly think I have some good instances here for you. I've got some real dynamite and some real exclusives."

I was not pleased, by any means. I had brought no other tapes and there were several questions I wanted to ask her, but erasing all that yardage scared me because I was sure we would botch it and there would be nothing left; so I managed an accepting smile and sat down, prepared to listen.

"Can you do more than one thing at a time?" she asked. "I mean, can you listen and read and so on and so forth, all at once? I can. I can cook and look at TV and clean house and this and that—busy, busy, busy. Some one of the reporters wrote me up as 'The Unsinkable Mrs. Oswald.' Because if you can, I want you to look at these scrapbooks and some other things. I'll just go on and finish my dinner."

In point of fact, I cannot easily assign my attention to two foci simultaneously, and it sets my teeth on edge to hear Scarlatti on a phonograph while cocktail conversation is going on; I can be seduced to attitudes I despise if a symphony is the background to a discussion of zoning laws. But Mrs. Oswald sat me down before a pile of albums and then went to fool with the tape recorders and recited excerpts of her litany to the American way of life, and I had no choice but to divide myself into several receptacles.

There were four big green albums of newspaper clippings, one devoted to Lee, one to Marina, one to Ruby, and one to herself. They were kept meticulously; each clipping adhered to the page in precise relation to the edges, and all were protected by jackets of thick cellophane. Once I was arrested by surprise and a fleeting pity: in the album about herself (the headlines read "Mrs. Oswald Continues Talkathon in Washington," "Mother of Kennedy Assassin Arrives Here to Talk"), I found a small pressed flower, a cluster of trailing arbutus perhaps, or a star of Bethlehem.

Nothing in the memory books was news to me, and so, although I dutifully turned the pages, I was not reading but was listening to Mrs. Oswald's Mother's Day Epistle.

It began serenely: "Upon waking up this morning, and it being Mother's Day, I've decided that in defense of myself and my son, Lee Harvey Oswald, I would put a little something on the tape. I sincerely hope that you will find it newsworthy and print it. Here again, I know you want just a casual interview and you want to keep away from the Warren Commission Report, but because it is involved in my personal life and that of my son, I will have to go back to it from time to time.

"Now they talked about me working as an insurance lady. Here on page 378 of the Warren Commission Report they say, 'She would sometimes take Lee with her, apparently leaving him alone in the car while she transacted her business. Once she worked during the school year. Lee had to leave an empty house in the morning and return to it for lunch and again at night. His mother having trained him to do that rather than to play with other children.' What an injustice! Anybody who ever sold insurance, and there are many, many insurance men that are going to read this and listen to me and know, a person like I was selling insurance and didn't want to make a killing, we could go out in one hour's time and collect thirty dollars. And so I was home most of the time with my boy Lee. I was usually with him unless I had a definite appointment. I always tried to make my appointments later on, when both the man and the woman were at home, because I found in the beginning when I started to sell and I talked to the woman I was asked to come back to discuss it with the husband. Well, then I would be immediately rejected at the door, and the simple reason for that was that the wife had discussed what I said with the husband, and of course she didn't know as much about it as I did and she didn't present a good case. So I would have definite appointments instead, and usually, out of the four or five calls, I would sell something.

"Now about did he play with other children. When Lee was eleven years old, he visited my sister in New Orleans, Louisiana, which is five hundred and twenty-five miles from Fort Worth. I put him on a train and alone he went. I did caution him to be very careful and not go with strangers or talk with any men who might want to make his acquaintance, and there again I am proud that I thought about these things. This is motherhood. Yet I was criticized in the Warren Report. My sister told the story that I told Lee not to talk to anyone, and it was taken up quite a bit—I think about a page long. That this is what I taught Lee in life, to be by himself. No, no, this is not the case at all. This was a particular instance. And I also told him when he went to school not to go in a car with a stranger, and isn't this what we teach our children? In defense of motherhood also, Lee stayed at my sister's home for two weeks, and that was the arrangement. My sister remarks in her testimony that while he was there he refused to play with any other children. She went into great detail that they tried to get him out of the house and play with the children. Let's understand things a little bit! Here was a perfect stranger, a visitor, he hadn't lived in New Orleans since he was five years old. Now he's eleven and he knew no one in the neighborhood. How do you get an eleven-year-old boy a girl, who in this day and age is almost at maturity? I have to smile because the whole thing is so ridiculous."

I glanced over at the diner, who smiled in confirmation, and I believe I smiled, too.

"Did she bring any eleven- or twelve-year-olds into the home for Lee to meet? And did he refuse to meet them and go off and play with them? Ah! That would be different, but, no, no, she didn't like him in the house listening to television or reading comic books. She wanted him to go out and play with other children. What other children were there for Lee to play with? So again, let's have defense of Lee Harvey Oswald.

"Another thing I objected to in my sister's testimony, when Mr. Jenner asked if any of her boys sold newspapers, and she said, oh, yes, her son Gene did, and she wanted them to know that he saved his money and bought war bonds with it. Well, this is a remarkable and admirable thing for a boy to do. And Mr. Jenner asked if she ever knew that Lee sold papers and she said no, and there was other people questioned about that. There again, I go in defense of my son. Lee traveled with me and Mr. Eckdahl, and when he did go to school he was at an age where he couldn't even be hired to sell newspapers. The boys in the newspaper business were fifteen and sixteen years old, which is the trend today. My own newspaper boy is about seventeen years old, and these boys are working their way through college. Now, we're talking about a young boy, because this was before age thirteen, before the New York episode. But you see, I'm proud of my sister's boys. I think she has a nice family, but let's go a little deeper into an understanding. She remarked very proudly that her boy bought war bonds. *Her* boy had a father who was in the bookmaking business and had a very large income—they own their own home. He was very liberal with his money, and even though Gene did have a newspaper route, he did not contribute to the household. As a matter of fact, his father gave him lunch money besides. So you see this is the difference, let's face it. This is where the human element comes in. This is where I have been persecuted. I have shed many a tear."

My brains were scrambled eggs. I was reminded, as I tossed in the sponge and gave up trying to proceed from *a* to *b* to *c*, of one of those games in which you are meant to direct a blob of mercury, by clever twists of the wrist, through a maze so that it fetches up, all of a piece, in a central zone. Sometimes the blob sprawls out like an amoeba and at other times it multiplies itself by twenty so that there are tiny beads all over the place; sometimes the integer remains but takes a wayward route and lodges far from the goal. Such a plaything (*soi-disant*) can lead to temper tantrums in the middle-aged. I could get no foothold in Mrs. Oswald's reminiscences, and yet, while my mind roved aimlessly every which way, it remained here in this room and on this day. I tried, during the sporadic bursts of thunder and short-lived, violent spates, to transport myself to a ship my husband and I had once taken from the Piraeus to New York in November, when the seas were the kind that had wrecked the *Hesperus*; but I couldn't pay heed to the memory. Usually when I am totally bewildered (this happens to me often at the opera and ninety-two percent of the time when I am listening to a learned paper or a political speech) I can get my bearings by reciting the names of the states or by declining a *stark männlich* noun (I use *der Stuhl*) and then a *schwach weiblich* one (*die Frau*) and a *gemischt sächlich* one (*das Ohr* is as good a castrato as any); but today I couldn't summon up more than a score of states, and German declensions were quite out of the question. So I went back to following the leader on my great leaden clodhoppers.

". . . And these are the things I have the ability of noticing. Why? Because it's affecting me personally and I'm this type person. Lee was this type person, he had wisdom. He didn't have—well, he finished his high school education in the Marines, and I wouldn't say he was an uneducated man, knowing Russian like he did and a little Spanish and German, just a young boy. You know, Russian's a very hard language. But a formal education, he did not have. He had the know-how. I myself don't have a high school education and I know I speak very bad English, but a ten thousand dollar a year engineering man begged me to marry him. I made him wait a year, and he was a Harvard man. I've been on television with the highest caliber of people and held my own, so I don't think I do so bad in that department. I'm uneducated, but very versatile.

"I think it's a natural thing, it isn't anything that I've studied or learned, it's just doing things that come naturally, as the phrase goes, and Lee had it. Believe me, Lee Harvey Oswald had this natural wisdom. Some people with a formal education are so dull that really and truly I find them stupid. All they know is what's in the books, and that's that."

I gave up counting on the disclosure of the "exclusives" she had hinted at; the dynamite did not go off.

"I didn't date," I heard her tell dear reader. "My son John said before the commission, 'She didn't have any friends.' Of course I didn't have any friends. Why? Because I was a *mother*, *a working mother*! When I came home, I had to take care of the house and the groceries and make sure that my children had clean clothes, so what time did I have for friends? I think this is in my favor, that I didn't run around with men and drink and deprive my children. I devoted my life to you boys!"

Throughout the soliloquy, the performer herself sat rapt, her elbows among her lunch dishes. Although her house was temporarily a fright, she was not. She was wearing a trim green linen suit with a smart white blouse. I had the feeling that, except when she was in bed, she was never *en déshabillé*, but was always dressed ready to receive anyone who wished to have the scales removed from his eyes, and that in one of her bureau drawers there was a pile of clean white gloves. It was evident that she knew and cared about clothes; I had heard that she occasionally went into Neiman-Marcus to try on coats and dresses. She was one of those women whose eye can go directly to the one appropriate thing on a rack of cheap clothes, who can shop triumphantly in a bargain basement, an outlet store, or a thrift shop. This is an urban gift, but if she had been a country woman, she could have made unerring selections from a mail-order catalogue or run up her wardrobe on a sewing machine with professional results. She would never make the mistake of going in for conspicuous novelty; if she wore costume jewelry, it would not be gauche. If she were to travel with those bands of women that you see in the summer in Europe, her drip-drys would do what they are advertised to do and not dissolve or come out irremediably wadded up.

"And let me tell you this, if you research the life of Jesus Christ, you find that you never did hear anything more about the mother of Jesus, Mary, after He was crucified. And really nobody has worried about my welfare. Now when I say I get letters, I mean they are from the public and they are the only thing that keep me going and I bless them for it. But I'm talking about my children, my sister. No one, when my son was murdered, no member of the family, no immediate friend came to me and gave me consolation. They didn't want to be involved, you see. You say, 'Your nieces and nephews couldn't send a telegram or a note? Your own sons and their wives?' But I'm gonna be honest with you—not a soul . . ."

The tape ended abruptly; the coda was a metallic squawk.

"How's that?" said Mrs. Oswald, poised, gratified by the ovation she was receiving from beyond the footlights. "Oh, how I wish there was more time! I have stories and coincidences by the galore, and things that I can prove are not according to Hoyle. If we just had the time, we could write them up and become millionairesses. The first book in the series would be *One and One Make Two*."

She had suggested this title in our first interview, and in the second had revised it to *One and One Don't Make Two*. Possibly they were to be in sequel, two volumes, boxed.

As she talked, she unplugged the recorders and removed the tapes, but replacing the covers flummoxed her and she laughed. "Let's get our Yankee mechanical genius to work," she said, and made a flirtatious *moue*. "Hurry on, now. I want you to see the grave by daylight."

I restored the covers and put the canvas overcoats on the machines while Mrs. Oswald went to get my umbrella and her purse. She locked the bedroom door after her, and she double-locked the outer door. "Of course I don't dare keep the really valuable things in the house. They're in storage, insured, but even so, there's plenty here that interested parties could steal, and I can't run the risk."

Her Buick Skylark was blue and new and dapper, as lovingly tended as Whistler's "Mother." "My money from *Esquire* paid for this," she said. "I could have got a lot more for those letters from Lee if I'd held out, but I felt it was my duty to the American people to release them when I did."

Her garage was narrow and her uphill driveway was muddy and the turn at the top was awkward; she maneuvered the obstacles with skill and aplomb and drove off through the wet streets as if the car were a friend whose company she liked better than any other in the world. I do not drive and I am an edgy passenger and I sense incompetence immediately, but I felt safe with this able woman: she respected her property and her person too much to get us into any trouble. I had been wondering from the beginning what she would do with money if a windfall showered her out of the blue, and now I knew at least one place a chunk of it would go, and that would be into the purchase of a high-class automobile with all the fixings. My driver's black limousine was lubberly behind us.

Mrs. Oswald said she would like to stop at the post office because quite often she got a good deal of mail on Sunday. "Oh, the letters I got at the beginning! People writing to ask for my autograph, and of course at that time I was just a novice and didn't know any better and would give it. But now I don't. Hemingway always said, 'All right, you can have my autograph if you pay for it,' and I take the same stand."

I am in luck. I have a note from her and it is signed "Marguerite Oswald, Mother of Lee Harvey Oswald." The "O" is shaped like a heart with a scimitar through it.

She came back from the post office empty-handed, but said that Mother's Day might have something to do with the fact that she had got no letters. "I certainly do want to take the opportunity to thank all the people that write me," she said. "They write me in connection with what I am doing, and they are the ones that give me the courage to continue in what I believe is right. Our American way of life is my theme."

"Yes, I know," I said. "Did you like New York?"

"Oh, I liked New York. I went there because John Edward was there and he was in the Coast Guard at that particular time. He was stationed at Staten Island and never moved around, so he and his wife were kind of stable. Of course I didn't expect to live with my daughter-in-law, but that's where I did go when I first got to New York, until I could find a place and housing— you know there's housing in New York."

I agreed, even though by now I knew that she was not interested in any response of any sort to anything.

"Then through some friends of my daughter-in-law's they found me an apartment and I was delighted. It was five blocks from my son's house, but when I went to pay them the man said, well, you'll have to give a hundred dollars under the table. Coming from Texas and not having housing regulations, I didn't even know what he was talking about. He said, well, apartments were very scarce and in order to get this one you'll have to pay a hundred dollars under the table. Of course I'll never do anything like this. I hurt myself rather than do something like this—it's the principle, let's say. Most people would have thought, I'll just go ahead and pay and be glad to have an apartment, but not me. I think it's just wrong. But then I did get an apartment, and this brings up, did I like New York or didn't I like New York. Yes, I liked New York just fine. I had to leave because of Lee. He couldn't adjust to New York. It was so different—apartment-house living, and such a mixture of different people, and he was a young boy. He was in these segregated schools and they called him a rebel and he was talking about them as a Yankee. I mean, this is a regular trend and nothing abnormal.

"Every Sunday we would go visit the Museum of Natural History or the Planetarium and we'd have dinner at Rockefeller Center, and when I would go to work on Monday, they'd say, 'Well, Oswald, tell us New Yorkers what you found out about New York.' I may go to New York one of these days. I like to travel, just like Lee. He was in the Philippines, he was in Corregidor, he was in Formosa, he was in Japan, so he's been all over besides Russia. That boy was being trained. Let me give you an instance of some of the work I've done on him being trained as an agent. I received this letter from him on November 8, 1961. And on the back of the letter it said, 'Name, Address, Male, Occupation,' and then something I couldn't make out. It looked like a '4' and a '1' and then it had a post-office box, 703 in Washington, D.C. When I received this letter, I wrote asking them to tell me about my son because he was in Russia, and I said that on the back of his letter was this post-office box number. Do you know my letter was not answered or returned to me? Now this is *significant*: that box number has that letter to this day. And do you know who the box number is? Veterans of Foreign Wars, in Washington, D.C.! So this is just a little part of my research of Lee."

The sun was fully out, and on either side of the broad highway, a wavering effluvium rose from the flat fields. Herds of Hereford whitefaces grazed in the pastures between archipelagoes of oil drums; the scene looked like a photograph for a geography book in a chapter on "Principal Industries of the States."

"And here's another thing I just can't swallow. Lee *said* he was a Marxist. He went to Russia with all the publicity, he had a Russian wife, we know all these facts, and he was giving out

Fair Play for Cuba literature. I don't know, they say it was, it could have been any kind of literature. Someone said to me, 'Miz Oswald, you're just too easy, how do you know it was Fair Play for Cuba literature?' Well, now since I read the Warren Commission Report, I will admit it probably was Fair Play for literature."

(Her slips of the tongue and elisions, though arresting, did not, I think, have any oblique meaning; they happened, most of them at any rate, simply because she talked so fast.)

"So there's nothing to show he did anything shady. He was on a television program, on WDSU, in New Orleans, and he said he was a Marxist, not a Communist, a Marxist. There was a difference and Marina said there was a difference. I don't know about that. But you do have a higher up and you do have an extrasensory perception, and the truth, I think, always prevails. Tomorrow I will show you a picture that will just show how wrong they were in Washington."

"I won't be here tomorrow," I said.

"Oh, yes, I keep forgetting, you have to go back to Boston."

She stopped for a light, and when it had changed and we sailed on, she said, "I have enough material for at least five books. I could write one just on Mrs. Paine alone—her testimony is really something to break down. And books, I don't know *how* many books I could write about Lee and the way things happened to him all his life. Now here is a good instance. When we came to Texas from New Orleans, he entered Arlington High School. He entered in the end of September, when school opens, and then he joined the service on October 17th. So approximately he was in school four weeks. Yet there are *three* pictures of my son and one that has him laughing and turning around in the classroom for the yearbook. Now why pick out Lee Harvey Oswald? You'll say, 'Miz Oswald, I don't get the point.' Now the point is how it goes on and on and on and on. Lee Harvey Oswald's picture was taken three times at Arlington High School, out of all the boys there. Why? It doesn't make sense, and since I'm not the only one finding these circumstances, I have to wonder."

I looked out my window, and to the fumy fields I mouthed the words, "Miz Oswald, I don't get the point."

"Now this material of mine, we could run it for two or three years every month in a big national magazine, and after that as a sort of a soap opera on radio or even on TV. And then there'd be the paperbacks and the foreign translations and so on and so forth. Couldn't you take the summer off and come on down and rent the other side of the house so we could write it all up? I mean, I would give of my time and voice and let you see the work I've done and we could split the proceeds."

She had at no time expressed the slightest curiosity about me, and I wondered what she thought I was going to take the summer off *from*: from living in Boston, perhaps. I feel quite sure that if one day I had turned up wearing a beard she would have paid no attention.

For some time I had been aware that a cat was lurking nearby, ready to pounce and get my tongue, and at this invitation he succeeded and took it far away. I could do no more than stammer like a schoolgirl, "I don't know."

"I know a discount house where you could get a hot plate cheap, and you could use my icebox," she said, the practical planner working hand in hand with the dreamer. "There's that back porch, so we could wander back and forth, very informal and relaxed, in our housecoats if the weather got hot. We could set up all my exhibits on what-you-call-'ems—sawhorses is what I mean. And buy a couple of tape recorders, and we'd be in business."

"Mmm."

"I don't care about the money. I say money is only good to its use, but I want history to be straightened out. Of course there is the money too. I gave up my job to come to the rescue and I only have twenty-three hundred dollars to my name. I tell you we could make millions and you could become quite well known."

Now we had reached the gates of the cemetery and she changed her tack.

In the voice of a tourist guide, she said, "Like everything else in life, this is divided up into classes. There is the section for the rich people, and some very fine people are buried there, and there is the one for the poor people, and then there is the one for the middle class. Lee Harvey Oswald is buried in the middle-class section, as it should be according to his station in life."

The graveyard was deserted; we met no other car and we saw no mourners as we spiraled up between granite lambs and marble cherubim, and Mrs. Oswald plaintively remarked on this. "If it had been a sunny day, you'd have seen the cars lined up clear up to the gates, people coming to see where my son is buried."

Then, in a moment, round a bend, we did see a car ahead of us at the top of a slight rise. "Now, there!" she said. "There's somebody after all, even though it isn't such a nice day, and they're coming to see Lee."

We stopped directly behind a car, which, apple green where it was not besmirched by mud or scabbed with rust, could not have been less than twenty years old; it was long and broad and uncommonly tall, and its rear window was a high, narrow oval through which no human eye could see. It looked as if, when it had been new and probably black, it had been used as a getaway car. Its occupants were slogging through the mud across the road as we opened our doors. They were five boys in their late teens, all rangy and simianly long-armed and all wearing dirty dungarees, dirty T-shirts, dirty sneakers, shaggy, dirty hair.

"They're heading straight for Lee," whispered Mrs. Oswald. "Now it's that age I want to reach with my books. The young people. I want to write it all in a way they will understand and know the truth of history."

She moved purposefully forward, bowing on either side to her vassals and her audience, and halted at a grave at the edge of the road. The vile boys stepped back and she beamed on them beneficently. They quickly fanned out among other graves higher up the slope, but I was conscious of their eyes on us.

The small granite stone that marks Lee Harvey Oswald's grave bears only his name and the dates of his birth and his death. Surrounding it today were half-drowned yellow pansies. Beside it, resting against a wire bracket, was a pale green cross made of styrofoam, the arms of which were wreathed with artificial freesias. A young weeping willow tree grew at the head of the grave, its vulnerable leaves touched quietly by the light, damp breeze. Plastic philodendron, as glossy as a grass snake, wound up its trunk.

Mrs. Oswald plucked a weed from among the pansies, bent the pliable freesias into a more becoming embrace around the cross, brushed off her hands, and gave me one of them to shake. Her mission was efficiently completed.

"It turned out to be a right nice Mother's Day after all," she said. "But on some Mother's Day, I think it would be wonderful for the United States to come out and say my son was an agent. It would be wonderful if they would come out in behalf of his family and his mother and say he died in the service of his country. They're not all-powerful, and not everything they do is right. I love my United States, but I don't think just because I was born in it, that we're perfect. And I feel that my son Lee Harvey Oswald felt the same way. If he learned those truths .from me, I didn't teach him, but if he sensed that was the way I felt, I make no apology for that either. We are not always right and I feel sure that as Americans we know this and we will admit it some day. Let's have a little defense of Lee Harvey Oswald! On Mother's Day, let's come out and say that he died in the service of his country."

"Is that what you mean by your statement on the little scroll?" I asked.

"No comment," said Mrs. Oswald. "I do not comment on my statement." She was curtly official, putting the multiplied me (I was a rude mob of impertinent reporters) in my place; but immediately she was friendly again, perhaps thinking of me as her future collaborator lounging around at ease in my housecoat.

"Now you think about what I said about coming on down here for the summer. I'll be happy to cooperate with you. It would be a big deal."

She dismissed her troops and got into her car, waved absent-mindedly and drove off. As soon as she was gone, the five sightseers converged upon the grave, and my driver, as he opened the door for me, said, "I don't like the looka them. They had a guard on the grave up until a while back. I reckon they figure nobody cares about it no more."

We were silent for several miles, and then he said, "The day it happened I was hauling some folks from Love. Prettiest day you ever did see, and all of a sudden we heard it on the radio that the President was dead. I took this party to their hotel and then I went out in the country and set by myself. I never reported back to work till next morning."

Today as we drove over the road where the motorcade had been hideously halted, bringing the whole world abruptly to a stop, and past the Book Depository whence the bullets had been fired, I observed, as I had done on each of my trips to and from Fort Worth by this same route, that the physical site did not accentuate my recollected woe. Indeed, I was instead returned to my own apartment in New York, where, quite by accident, I had turned on the radio and had heard the first inconclusive bulletins. At other times in my life I have stood on memorable ground and have directly apprehended experience that heretofore had been once removed because I had only read about it: once when I drove inland from the Normandy beaches, I knew for the first time with uncluttered pain what the invasion had been, and the deaths, along those pretty lanes and within those pretty groves of trees, of my friends and kinsmen became more than abstractions.

But John Kennedy died everywhere, not more in Dallas than in Paris or Calcutta or in my apartment in New York City.

Epilogue

I LEFT Dallas the next day in a preposterous storm, five times as rip-roaring as the one the day before. Even for Baron von Munchausen it was laid on too thick. The rain, much wetter than any other I had ever been soaked by, came down hell bent for election, and the lightning was a stretch on the imagination. My plane was two hours late getting in from El Paso and then for another hour, after it did get in, it sat on the field unopened. One of the men at the gate told me, "They can't open the doors. If they did, those passengers would get blown right back to the border." He laughed as he said it, with regional pride.

We were finally allowed to board, escorted by men in nor'westers and hip boots, carrying bumbershoots the size of umbrella trees. One of these turned inside out and the poor fellow who had been handling it was almost lifted off his feet; I would not have been surprised if he'd been swept aloft and had vanished from view, as Sinbad was carried away from the valley of diamonds by the Roc. I thought of a joke one of my drivers had told me. A Texan, visiting Niagara Falls, was asked if there was anything like that in the Lone Star State and he replied, "No, but we've got a plumber in Houston that can fix it." Just about anything can happen in Texas; while I was in Dallas, I heard of a curriculum for pre-pre-school children that included a course in "Remedial Creeping and Crawling."

Once we were off the ground, the commotion died down, and as Texas receded, the firmament grew pure. My flight to New York was as smooth as sleep. But no matter how gentle an airplane ride is, no matter how consolingly cloudless the empyrean, no matter how reassuring the look of the crew, when I am in the sky I meditate on life and death. And now in minute particular I relived the day in 1963 when the random element in the universe went hog-wild. Within half an hour of the final awful bulletin from Parkland Memorial Hospital, New York City was as still as a ghost town. The streets were all but deserted; traffic was nearly at a standstill. I tried without success to telephone my husband at *The New Yorker* office—all the telephone lines were jammed, as sometimes they are in a great blizzard.

My husband was ill and had been for a long time and his illness had generated a deep depression. But in the last couple of weeks, he had been sanguine and nearly himself again and we had resumed the life we'd lived before, of having friends in to dinner or going out to his favorite restaurants. The night before, we had made a pub crawl to our familiar saloons, to Bleeck's and P. J. Moriarity's and Tim Costello's and we'd had a good time; tonight, Friday, we planned to go to a fight at the Garden. I can't remember who was fighting that night but it seems to me it may have been Dick Tiger; in any case it was someone Joe thought had talent. Everything, of course, was cancelled. I recall being shocked, I really don't know why, when I heard that some people went ahead and had the dinner parties they'd planned.

It was late in the afternoon when Joe got through to me, and his voice was more despairing than it had been at any other time since he'd been sick. I think I had counted on him to tell me that the news I'd heard on the radio wasn't true, that it was some monstrous hoax, and that a whole world of possibilities still lay open to Kennedy. None of us could believe it. I slept very poorly that night, waking often to the knowledge that something dreadful had happened, and not being able at first to remember what it was, and then remembering. Twice during the night I went in to Joe's room, where he was sleeping lightly too, but he could not tell me that I had only been having a nightmare of stupendous violation.

For days we all went about our business like somnambulists.

After Joe died, a few weeks later, as I was clearing out his office I got rid of pounds and pounds of newspapers that he was using in writing his "Wayward Press" piece, and the headlines freshly flabbergasted me and my rage came back. Suddenly death was larger than life and suddenly it was terrifyingly twice as natural.

APPENDICES

M RS. OSWALD claims that the famous picture of Lee Harvey with his guns was fabricated, and she said, "Well, actually, my son has never been indicted for the murder of President Kennedy, Officer Tippit, or the shots at General Walker. This is their evaluation. Now I expect to evaluate their findings a little differently as prior testimony I have been showing the inaccuracies. But since this is the twentieth century, I would hope that pictures would do it. I have many pictures in my possession which prove that things are not according to Hoyle. And the main picture I have is a picture of my son, Lee Harvey Oswald, exploited in the February issue of *Life* magazine, 1964, as the assassin and killer of Tippit, and the gun. This picture is a fake. I have many, many articles, many books saying it's a fake. It was told that it was a fake before the Warren Commission and they go into great detail about this picture and finally come up with the conclusion that the magazines and newspapers that had this particular photograph admitted that they inadvertently removed some of the parts of the gun from the picture. Now we have three or four pages on this and it's very official, and it looks like it's really the truth. I'm sure they were honest about it and they believe it. I'm going to ask one question and answer it myself. Mrs. Oswald, what gives you the authority, just a laywoman, to contradict the Warren Report findings where they had experts testing the negatives and the photographs? Well, I went about it in just a little different way.

"The exact date in April that this photograph was supposed to have been made at 214 Neeley Street, down in West Texas, and taken by my daughter-in-law, Marina Oswald. I took a picture with the same camera. I have proved in 1964 that this picture cannot be taken because of the foliage. I went back in December, 1964, and I took the yard again, which showed the same background of the picture in *Life* magazine. Now in 1965, April, just a few weeks ago, I went back to 214 Neeley Street, and I took photographs again. I'm in the picture each time. You can see only my face because of the foliage, which has to prove that this picture was taken right before the assassination as a plant or immediately after, which would be in the month of November, when this foliage wouldn't be like it would be in April. Now I have these pictures and I would like someone to call my hand on this, some official. Let's get that ball a-rolling."

She showed me the photographs of herself amid shrubbery beside a house, but because my recollection of the background in the photograph of Lee was shadowy, I could not be amazed except at the ingenuity and perseverance of her research.

The day before, in her excoriation of Mrs. Paine, she had said, "And one thing that insults my intelligence, the morning after when we had left, Marina and I had left with the *Life* representative at ten thirty that morning, it says that the police came back to the house later on, so she went to the grocery store and told them to go ahead and search the house. Now I don't know, I just don't swallow some of these things, particularly when they go on and on and on. I don't say it isn't possible that a woman would give the police, invite 'em in, and say, 'You go in the house, I'm going to the grocery store.'

"Well, this was the time they found the pictures! This was the time the police found the pictures that were in the garage, when Mrs. Paine wasn't home and *she* didn't know anything about the pictures. It's proved in the Warren Commission Report that the Dallas police called that night and asked Mr. Paine to come to the station to identify the *pictures*! And told them that they found the *pictures* in his garage. Well, there's much, much more to this, but this will just give you an idea of the many lies."

Her voice was at its most impassioned and her face at its pinkest with indignation when she talked of the pictures, but the enigma is beyond my elucidation.

II

John Edward Pic, in fact, lived on 92nd Street between First and Second Avenues. Bear in mind that he was stationed on Staten Island, a distance of nearly fifteen miles. Mrs. Oswald had an apartment in the Bronx, but one of the jobs she had took her daily to 42nd Street in Manhattan, and at another time she worked at Martin's department store in the downtown section of Brooklyn, so that she must have traveled almost an hour by subway, surely the least agreeable means of transportation in the world. Why did she not get a job nearer her apartment or an apartment nearer her job?

When she released her son's letters from Russia, she said in her explanatory notes that the reason Lee Harvey had written to her at so many different addresses was that she was a practical nurse and moved from place to place as her services were required. But she was not always a practical nurse, and the Warren Report, as I have indicated, shows that in both New Orleans and Fort Worth she moved continually. Since the assassination, she has had at least three different addresses.

III

One day after I had been to Dallas I was lunching in New York with a psychoanalyst friend of mine and mentioned Mrs. Oswald's saying that Freud had said that if there were no persecution there would be no persecution complex. He told me that Freud had, indeed, written something in the essay *Certain Neurotic Mechanisms in Jealousy, Paranoia and Homosexuality* that could be so construed through either, on the one hand, a superficial reading or, on the other, a very attentive one. I have looked at the essay, but I am altogether out of my depth and leave the interpretation to the doctors. What interests me and what interested my friend is how Mrs. Oswald came by this esoterism.

IV

According to a story that appeared in the New York newspapers, a gun collector named John King claimed that he paid Oswald's widow $10,000 for the Italian army rifle that killed the President and the .38 that killed Officer Tippit, and he was suing the government for them. They had been in Washington, together with all the other evidence accumulated by the Warren Commission, but had then been returned to Dallas, where they were in the custody of the FBI. The Justice Department, in its quite understandable effort to keep the weapons, was being assisted, curiously enough, by the Internal Revenue Service, whose argument was that Oswald falsified papers in buying the guns and they might thereby be confiscated under the Alcohol and Tobacco Tax Unit. The technicality applies to items for which less than $2,500 was paid, and while King said that he paid $10,000, Oswald is said to have bought the rifle and sniperscope for $19.95 and the pistol for $29.95.

On November 2, 1965, President Johnson signed a bill authorizing the federal government to take ownership of the rifle that killed President Kennedy. The new legislation authorizes the attorney general to designate as federal property items of evidence collected by the Warren Commission.

SELECTED ESSAYS

The Psychological Novel*

M Y title sounds in these days like a cliché and in all days it
is, I think, a tautology; a cliché because for so long now
there has been so much talk about Freud and his fellows and
their literary uses—a great deal of it talk through an old hat—
and a tautology because the novel does not exist that is not psychological, is not concerned with emotional motivations and
their intellectual resolutions, with instincts and impulses and
conflicts and behavior, with the convolutions and complexities
of human relationships, with the crucifixions and the solaces of
being alive. I am in danger, to be sure, of keeling over on this
tack and saying that all fiction is actually fact, that novels *are*
psychology, and if I should [   ] be nothing more for me to
say and in my traumatic embarrassment, I should be obliged to
spend my forthcoming honorarium on a visit to a psychologist
who would not, I am very sure, be content with a copy of one
of my books as payment of his fee in kind.

But lately we have come to assign a special meaning to the
word "psychological" and we use it to label a sort of writing
which we distinguish from the "historical" novel or the novel
of adventure or of uncomplicated romantic love. It involves a
subjective scrutiny of the human heart and mind, usually the
author's own heart and mind, often in a sort of imagined removal from the everyday and active world, and more often than
not communicated by a method that is not inhibited by the
restrictions of traditional rules. One thinks at once of Proust's
painstaking and loving examination of his past experience, his
patient exploration of his relationships with his mother and his
grandmother and his lovers and his friends and his servants,
and the effect of gardens upon him, and of the sea, and of
conversation, and of the remembered taste of tea-cakes. One
knows that his diagnostic methods cannot be entirely different
from those of the psychoanalyst who rejects no part of his
patient's reflections. Similarly, the stream-of-consciousness of
James Joyce resembles the method of free association, and the

*A paper read at the Bard College *Conference on the Novel*.

ordered interior monologue of Mrs. Dalloway, a modification of this. Because Proust is an artist, his novel transcends its technique and is a novel and does not smell of the clinic; but unfortunately few writers can use so subjective a system and remain as objective as he does, and his imitators seem generally to fetch up in a morass of inartistic and embarrassingly personal soul-searching which is not any newer and not any less sentimental than *The Sorrows of Werther*.

There is the tendency to think that psychological fiction must find its matter in the vile or the strange or the perverse and this can only mean that we are confounding "psychology" with "abnormal psychology" or with psychiatry or even with teratology, which is the study of monsters. And along with this misconception has gone the fad of borrowing the vocabulary of psychology rather than its methods of analysis and deduction; and it is fashionable to be forthrightly and ungraciously autobiographical as if Freud had come as the emancipator of the skeleton in the closet. The skeleton remains a skeleton and one skeleton does not look very much different from another. It would be hard to count the novels of recent years which have been strip-tease acts in the psychiatric ward or on the psychoanalyst's couch; when the last garment is flung off, there is again the familiar set of bones whose only claim to being unusual is that some of them are out of joint: but "out of joint" is synonymous with "inarticulate."

There can be no question that we are deeply in Freud's debt. He has made our moral attitudes more humane and he has modified our habits of observation, making us more alert to our conduct and to the patterns and symbols of our experience, enriching our insights, sharpening our sense of meaning. And he has done all this even though few of us have actually read him and even fewer have read him well. We know about the Oedipus complex almost as soon as we know about the American Revolution and we tend to know about it not through reference to Sophocles but to Freud. Words like "masochism" and "sadism" and "sublimation" and "compulsion" are the property of everyone; and we all know that our dreams are not what they seem but are the disguised symbols of our subconscious desires; and we know that our characters began to form in our plagued infancy; and it is no longer possible to accept our families nor the world about us without a sort of shrewd mistrust. But it is all too easy to acquire the notion that what Freud discovered was new, that these abstract words denote something peculiar to our times, to imagine that the emotions are the product of the 20th Century, invented to occupy the time and fill the pockets of psychiatrists, a breed that emerged suddenly and somehow adventitiously. It is possible, in this infatuation, to forget that Shakespeare knew as much about people as Freud did and that he said it all very much better. People have been losing their week ends from the beginning of time and if they have only just recently been ending up in Bellevue, they have ended up in other places just as interesting. Dickens' little man in *Bleak House* went up in spontaneous combustion from drinking too much gin, and Huckleberry Finn's father, no slouch when it came to the bottle, died dead drunk. This is not a criticism of Mr. Jackson's book but only a reminder that booze has been going to the heads of characters in books for a long time and that we do not need science to tell us what happens to them then. We do not make a drunk any drunker by calling him a dipsomaniac nor do we alter the alcoholic content of whiskey by calling it a substitute for love. In general, I think, the writers who steal the doctors' thunder get only second-hand thunder that the doctors stole from them in the first place.

Henry James is no more Freudian than Freud is Jamesian and I am offended by Mr. Clifton Fadiman's remarks on "The Jolly Corner" which he has included in his collection of James's short stories; he says that this story is really a psychoanalysis in which the author is at once the patient and the doctor. This strikes me as a rather foolish sort of literary criticism and, in a sense, an impertinent sort since it lowers the story from its great stature as an imagined and constructed work of literature to the level of a dressed-up case-history, a public exhibition of James's private life. I do not say that Fadiman is altogether wrong but that he is not precise, for certainly James could not have imagined that he was addressing an audience of psychiatrists, and for literary purposes, it is more to the point to investigate his artistic intention than the medical by-product of his result. And what more, really, is Fadiman saying than that James is so dedicated to telling the truth about reality that even science cannot tell it better? The implication in this sort of criticism is that writers like James have been the prophets of the new scientists instead of their teachers. Edmund Wilson brilliantly disposed of the idea that *The Turn of the Screw* was a ghost story, arguing in a thoroughly convincing way that the ghosts were not seen by the children nor by anyone else save the neurasthenic governess and were, therefore, only the hallucinatory projections of her emotional deformities. But now James's notebooks have been published and in them James says that *The Turn of the Screw* is a ghost story and it seems to me that he is in a better position to judge what he meant than Wilson unless he is prophetically pulling the wool over Wilson's eyes.

Recently I got in the mail a prodigious sample of this confusion of a science with an art and this delight in ambulatory madness. A person from the middle west wrote to me introducing himself as the editor of a new quarterly to be called "Neurotica" and this is what he said:

> The rebels against boredom, dullness and security, whether they be artists, writers, scientists or dilettantes, have one token they share in common; the farewell slap given by the inane majority.
>
> The slap takes many forms, but the one that is flung with the word "neurotic" is the challenge to a new magazine . . . NEUROTICA.
>
> The editors of NEUROTICA would like you to be among its growing list of contributors. Enclosed is an arbitrary listing of possible article headings and gists of ideas meant only to suggest a mood, indicate a spirit. More important is: new material that we hope will make its way to our offices to help in the cultivation of a side street in the publishing field, a magazine that explores, in both fiction and non-fiction the problems, interests, and tastes of the neurotic personality. Particularly we are interested in securing original works that have the potency, beauty, strangeness of interest to penetrate the lethargy of the jaded.
>
> Since our payment is small, the main compensation comes from having helped to create the written bric-a-brac that builds the cenotaph to those named and nameless who sought a cheap elixir to postpone madness.

I do not find this prose crystal-clear and so perhaps my reaction to the letter is frivolous; there may be something worthwhile here that I am too loutishly well-adjusted to perceive. I cannot tell what connotation the word "cheap" has in the last unusual clause, "a cheap elixir to postpone madness," so that I do not know whether my audience is going to be vulgar or impoverished or, possibly, stingy. I would not have any idea of how to go about creating a piece of written bric-a-brac (I can only think of polychrome) to make a tomb for some people who have names and some who have not and who, since they only "postponed madness" by drinking the stuff, perhaps went mad after they died.

When I looked at the "arbitrary listing of article headings" which were intended to "suggest a mood, indicate a spirit," I wondered if this were a leg-pull administered by one of my friends or by a frolicsome Freshman at Harvard. For these were some of the subjects toward which I, as a writer of fiction, might like to direct my talent:

> The Castration Complex in Animals
> Aspects of Midwest Baudelaireism
> Touches in Hollywood Films that only a Neurotic Would
> Spot
> Some Strange Turns of Apperception in Isomorphic
> Symbolism
> Can You Slap Your Mother: a Semantic Problem
> The Drive to Be a Misfit and Its Reward

The mood that is suggested to me is black and the spirit indicated is a quick elixir in a shot glass. The question presents itself: what person in me is the letter-writer addressing? The novelist or the neurotic who he assumes, *a priori*, I am? Does he think that I am a neurotic because I am a novelist or a novelist because I am a neurotic? And does he think that because I am a neurotic novelist, I am therefore equipped to write a literary essay on "The Castration Complex in Animals," or "Some Strange Turns of Apperception in Isomorphic Symbolism," a subject to which I have never given a moment's thought in my whole life, partly, I suppose, because until a few days ago I did not know what "isomorphic" meant and I only looked it up then because I did not want to seem an illiterate boob. I found that isomorphism is "superficial similarity in organisms that are phylogenetically different, resulting from convergence." The information did not inspire me to look up those other words. I was much more interested in a picture on the same page of the dictionary of a being called an "isopod" who is described as "any of a large order of small sessile-eyed crustaceans in which the body is composed of seven free thoracic segments each bearing a pair of legs typically alike in size and direction." I think that if I were pressed very much and offered a sum, I might be able to write a story about an isopod who, through some hideous misfortune, was born with legs that did *not* all go in the same direction so that all its life it did not know where it was and was destroyed at last by a lobster from Maine with which it identified itself out of a complicated neurosis, one symptom of which was a psychosomatic disorder of its sessile eyes. In fairness to Mr. X of NEUROTICA, I suppose I must believe that this subject was not meant for me but for a learned critic; that "The Castration Complex in Animals" was intended for a neurotic veterinarian who is also invited to this bric-a-brac bee; and "Aspects of Midwest Baudelaireism" was probably intended for a poet—perhaps for Paul Engle who lives in Iowa City—or for the Drs. Menninger who cure alcoholics in Kansas. But let me look for a minute at a subject that was meant as much for me as for the other people whose unstable company I now theoretically keep: "The Drive to Be a Misfit and Its Reward." Since for the sake of argument, I am a rebel against security, it is natural—indeed, it is *normal*—for me to have a powerful drive toward being a misfit, but I do not know what my reward is going to be: you have seen my isopod murdered in cold blood by a lobster from down east and you already know without my telling you any details of the plot that this uncomfortable and certainly unrewarding end comes to him not because he is a successful rebel against security but because he is a victim of insecurity. I do not mean that his unfitness to survive makes him ineligible to be the protagonist of my story—on the contrary, I have grown very fond of him and see in him a world of possibilities—but that I must not let my affection for him run away with me; I must not be so charitable that I try to persuade you that his deformed legs are attractive or that his life has been a desirable one that you should strive to imitate. I, the author, and you, the reader, must be objective and not envy the isopod nor wholly identify ourselves with him as the poor isopod has identified himself with the lobster. I cannot possibly pretend that his demise was a reward that he was glad to get, and therefore I do not feel that I am qualified to write for NEUROTICA. I do not argue, you understand, for happy endings but only for true endings based upon true premises, for that detachment from our characters' eccentricities and misadventures that prevents us from making them into improbable prodigies but that, on the contrary, enables us to be psychologically sound. There is no subject that is not fit for fiction, but if we use skullduggery to deceive our readers and, by the same token, ourselves, we will be either bores or villains, and naturally I go on the assumption that I am in the society of people who want to be charming and who want to be good. I would never have forgiven Evelyn Waugh if he had convinced me in *A Handful of Dust* that what happened to Tony Last was not only dramatic but was fun as well and I had got myself captured by a loony in the jungles who, for the rest of my life, made me read Dickens aloud to him, beginning with *Little Dorrit*.

I must apologize for being unsporting, for I have shot at and I hope I have killed a sitting bird. Unfortunately, most of the game is not so easy and one is led astray, while hunting it, by the will-o'-the-wisp of fashion which, from a distance, looks like the real thing. But if we are not headlong, we will eventually bag what is useful and leave behind what is not.

To be writers, then, we must be psychologists and to be good writers we must be good psychologists, and this is only another way of saying that we must be experts in the study of reality and cool judges of our own natures. We are not doctors, whose task is to cure, nor are we courts of law whose task is to condemn. If we assume either of these roles and are wanting in irony and are the servants of our pride and prejudice rather than of our sense and sensibility, we may bog down in self-pity or we may distort our personal misfortune into polemic or our idiosyncrasy into gospel. This is the error into which have fallen the people whose best-selling novels are described in the advertisements as "important social documents." These are the sermons, embedded in stories, that bear a message, that are preached in language that can be understood by that famous

man of our times, the man in the street; they are the works
that are called "scathing indictments" and "fearless exposés."
I do not know what would have been the professions of these
writers in another age; some of them would have been essayists
and some would have been evangelists and a few might have
been martyrs and many would have been hangmen and a lot of
them would have been the man in the street; but almost none
of them would have been novelists and, in point of fact, almost
none of them are novelists now. I read the novel called *The
Snake Pit*, which gave an account of the nervous collapse and
the incarceration in a state mental institution and recovery there
of a sensitive lady writer. It was difficult to determine what the
book was about, whether it was a prolonged joke about nervous
breakdowns, whether it was an attempt to prove that suffering
will cease in spite of the nosy interference of medicine, whether
it was an attack on the conditions to be found in state hospitals,
or whether it was only a pastoral yarn on the theme that the
course of true love never does run smooth. Subsequently, I was
set straight on this point by advertisements that told me it was
an attack on the hospitals. I was given the further information
that this was a "true" story and the reason it was true was that
the author had actually been in a state mental institution and
therefore knew what she was talking about. The publication of
her novel was followed shortly by some articles on the same
subject which paraphrased, in non-fiction, her fictionalized
account. I thought about the book again, and while I was very
sorry indeed that the hospitals are so badly understaffed and so
shockingly mismanaged and so dirty and that the patients do
not even have any decent playing cards, it did not really give
me pause. It might have done if I had believed in the story, if,
in the first place, I had been persuaded to feel and see and have
faith in these causes and the nature of the heroine's tragedy; a
sensitive lady writer is not the most agreeable protagonist in
the world anyhow because she always tends to write the book
herself, and I did not like this one and I did not believe in her
for a minute; if I had, I daresay it would have followed that I
would have been convinced by all her adventures in the asylum
and, at last, by her cure and the story's staggeringly happy
ending. But as it was, her calamity and her bravery seemed
very much fixed up and very much beside the point of my own

life; such implausible things, I thought, really do only happen to implausible people in books and there is nothing for me, a lady writer not in a book, to be afraid of.

But there is a story by Chekhov called "Ward No. 6" which does badly scare me, and I know, because Chekhov has never tricked me, that what he is telling me is true, that it is hideous to be mad, that madhouses are the most awful places in the world and that I must do everything I possibly can to keep from going mad even though I might be lucky enough to lose my mind in a clean, well-lighted bin. Perhaps I am showing myself to be selfish and ingrown, addicted to interpreting what I read in the light of what I want for myself and not what I want for the world in general; but I have an idea that I am not very much different from other readers, and I wonder how much good these do-good books do. One hears it said that while they may fail as novels, they are still important and useful as tracts—and besides, they all make splendid movies now that Hollywood has suddenly discovered the human mind and race prejudice and alcoholism and juvenile delinquency. But I submit that this isn't enough, that a good novel must stand without crutches and that any novelist must be willing to be judged in the terms of his craft and not in those of other crafts. I would not take my business to a lawyer who knew no law but who played the fiddle well, and I would not study Latin under a teacher whose Latin was faulty but whose botany was first-rate. And similarly, I want to read novels by novelists and not by cranks—whether they are popular best sellers or obscurantist axe-grinders like Henry Miller and Kenneth Patchen—who blackmail me into violent attitudes by hollering at me that such and such is so whether I believe it or not.

It is true that if we ignore the horrifying wounds of our society, we will be irresponsible, but we will be equally irresponsible if we do nothing but angrily probe them to make them hurt all the more, and we will not heal them by scolding like magpies. As human beings, and therefore as writers, we are confronted by wars and the wickedness that makes them, and the famine and disease and spiritual mutilations that follow them, by the shipwreck of our manners and our morality, by an almost universal sickness of heart. And the most romantic writer and the most diligently lighthearted clown of a writer cannot fail to be touched by the massive mood that lies upon the whole world. Still, we are not entitled to be slovenly and hysterical because the world is a mess nor to be incoherent because governments do not make sense; intolerance hardly seems the weapon most effective to fight intolerance, and fanaticism has no place in literature unless it is embodied in a character or a situation to serve a literary, not a missionary, purpose. Humphrey Slater's recent book, *The Heretics*, deals gravely and well with the brutal persecutions of the Albigensians in the Middle Ages which brought about the pathetic Children's Crusade, but Slater is not himself brutal, and tragic as his story is, it does not leave one's feelings in disarray.

Our essential problem, bad as our world is, is not different from that of serious writers at any other time in history, and this is true even in spite of the atomic bomb. For the problem is how to tell the story so persuasively and vividly that our readers are taken in and are made to believe that the tale is true, that these events have happened and could happen again and do happen everywhere and all the time. This was Dostoievsky's problem when he wrote about a crime of passion and the reasons why it was committed and the effect of it upon the criminal; it was Jane Austen's problem when she wrote about the manners in bourgeois drawing rooms where young ladies schemed to get themselves married; and it was Flaubert's when he wrote *Madame Bovary* and told the story of what today we would call a "neurotic" woman. *Crime and Punishment* and *Pride and Prejudice* and *Madame Bovary* can all be called psychological novels since they investigate motives and they report, not through exposition but through credible action, the causes of events and the influence of these events on the lives of their characters. And like all good psychologists, Dostoievsky, Jane Austen, and Flaubert remain impartial and do not sit in moral judgment upon their created people but allow the reader to draw his own conclusions. Sinclair Lewis, probably a man of very considerable ability, does not grant this privilege to his reader but demands that he despise characters who are not really despicable but are only foolish and to sympathize with others who are not really likeable but are only pitiable. *Main Street* could have been a very good book if Lewis had presented the facts and let it go at that; but, unfortunately he all but froths at the mouth in his defense of sensibility against the outrages of small-town midwestern insensibility, and because of the obtrusion of his personal passion he obscures the universal issues and writes of such specific and contemporary affronts that the book seems as meaningless as old slang twenty years after its publication. If he had been a sound psychologist, he would have known that Carol Kennicott's really interesting misfortune was not that she was forced to be acquainted with people who read Edgar Guest and spoke like barbarians but that she went so completely to pieces over these and similar trifles. Unlike Emma Bovary's disintegration, hers seems to be one that could have taken place only in a particular part of America and at a particular time. And thus Lewis has failed to tell anything but the most ephemeral and local sort of truth.

I have concluded that probably the reason writing is the most backbreaking of all professions is that it is so very difficult to tell the truth. Even though we may know certainly that our perceptions are accurate and that only one set of conclusions can be drawn from them, we are still faced with how to communicate the findings perceptively and conclusively. The language seems at times inadequate to convey exactly what we have seen and what we have deduced from it and much too often writers shirk their responsibility and take refuge in rhetoric—as the preaching novelists do—or in snobbish, esoteric reference, as Henry Miller and his followers do, in samples of language other than their own and in jargon, and in elaborate approximations that almost but do not quite say what they mean. But the language is quite able to take care of any of our needs if we are only affectionate and respectful toward it and, above all, patient with ourselves: patient, not only in our hunt for the proper words themselves, but patient in waiting for our observations to mature in us, to lose their confused immediacy so that their timelessness will emerge and their meaning will become available to our reader and applicable to him as well as to ourselves. The towering example in our times of creative impatience is the work of Thomas Wolfe, whose enormous energy drove him like a lunatic to write passages of great power and intensity but, much more often, to beat drearily about the bush for page after page in a sort of banal delirium which communicated nothing but the vague feeling that a genius was in the vicinity but was loafing on the job. It was his habit as a writer seldom to leave the crowded, noisy chambers of his own mind, and in consequence his books are mostly raw, boyish emotion and almost no grown-up thought; in his extraordinary, humorless narcissism, he spent the language as prodigally as if it grew on trees. One turns with relief from such a muddled, spendthrift pool-gazer as Wolfe to a pinchpenny like Hemingway at his best, in, for example, *The Killers* in which, without ever resorting to psychological exegesis, he produces a small work of permanent wisdom, a psychologically accurate portrait of sentimental toughs.

I do not think it matters what one writes about nor what method one selects to use; one may be altogether autobiographical or use none of one's own experience; it is equally good to innovate and to stick to the traditional rules; one may employ an omniscient observer or tell the tale without a guide. None of this matters if the eye and the ear, and therefore the pen, remain loyal to reality. Like the psychiatrist, the novelist must see his characters at once as individuals and as members of the human race; like him, the novelist must determine why they speak as they do and why they behave as they do and what in their nature causes them to react as they do to the situations into which he, their omnipotent sponsor, puts them.

The first chapter of *Pride and Prejudice* contains as sound psychology as it is possible to find. It might, indeed, have been more titillating if Jane Austen had read psychology, for there is possibly a sinister undertone that hints at incest in Mr. Bennet's preference for his daughter Lizzy; and Mr. Bennet is even something of a sadist in taking with such tormenting calm the news, that so inspires his wife, of the arrival in the neighborhood of a bachelor of large fortune; and Mrs. Bennet is a possessive mother and she does not understand her husband at all and she has attacks of nerves which doubtless stem from all sorts of hidden frustrations and resentments.

But while all the implications are there and could be made much of, there is no doctoring in Jane Austen's tone: there is psychology and there is truth and there is the calm acceptance of the vagaries and the vanities and the self-defeats of all people at all times; she knows that men are different from women and that while Mr. Bennet and his wife are individuals with individual problems, they are not any different from anyone else in their fundamental architecture of feeling and of conduct. Examples could endlessly be multiplied and they could be taken from every writer we are accustomed to think of as a "great" writer, from Hawthorne, or Melville, or Tolstoi, or Hardy or Thackeray, and even from Dickens when he is not being a goose. But it is not necessary if you agree with my original premise that a psychological novel is the same thing as a novel.

Truth and the Novelist

THERE are certain questions that nonwriters cannot resist putting to writers. At the beginning of the conversation, the nonwriter, having been warned by his hostess of the business of his interlocutor, says, "Do you write under your own name?" as if the profession, especially for women, were even now regarded as daring and disreputable as in the days when Edith Wharton, still known as Pussy Jones, shocked all of Newport by publishing a book of poems at almost the same time that she was presented to society. The question, to be sure, is asked because the nonwriter has never heard of the writer and hopes for a clue, but one is tempted sometimes to reply, "No, I call myself Charles Dickens." I myself have been taken several times for a Miss Stafford who writes a newspaper column on matters pertaining to health and for another Miss Stafford who is an analyst of handwriting, and many people have thrilled to meet me as the Miss Stafford who sings and whom they never dreamed wrote novels as well. It is usually established next whether one writes poetry or prose and afterward the nonwriter inquires, "And what kind of novels are they? Are they love stories or whodunits?" This question has always flummoxed me, and I have never found a satisfactory answer to it since I do not know what hard and fast category into which to put myself. I sidle out of that one and then am confronted with, "Where do you get your plots? Do you make them up or do you take them from real life?" Or I am posed this favorite, "Doesn't everyone clam up when you come into a room for fear you'll put 'em in a book?" For it is generally felt that the writer of fiction is a clever and deadly enemy, armed with the most treacherous of weapons and ready to lampoon his friends and relatives at the slightest provocation; some people, as a result, do genuinely fear and hate us, but more, while protesting the opposite, long to find themselves masquerading in our make-believe. And we are often invited to expose the secrets of a life whose owner, for reasons of security, cannot expose himself. Not long ago, I had a letter from a woman in Michigan who, stating perfunctorily that she had read one of my books, went on to say,

"I've always wanted to write a book but haven't the knack. However, I do have a plot that someone could make into a wonderful book if you would like to write a book that has real spice. I have lots of reason for not wanting anyone to know that it is my life but I was once really attractive to men and always had at least three in love with me at once. Now I've settled down and am living a quiet life. I have seven children. People who know only a few of the real facts have told me a book of my life would sell like fury. If you are interested I will sell it to you and make arrangements to see you if you could come here and I'd have to have your word for it no one would know it was my story. You could make a fortune and become really famous. I can tell you in one day and night all the real facts."

And in a postscript she added pressingly, "I'll only be at this address for one month so please let me know right away if interested. If not, I'll write someone else who may take this deal."

Her imminent decampment for parts unknown—though she had professed to be settled down and living quietly with her brood of seven—together with the word *deal* which I mistrust except as it is used in a game of cards, gave me the uneasy impression that she had been hawking her wares for years and had had to move on periodically like the unlicensed sellers of walking dolls and hand-painted neckties on the streets of New York. I did not accept the invitation to travel to Michigan and there to listen for twenty-four hours to the roll call of her old flames, feeling, perhaps unreasonably, that this would not be my style, just as Eudora Welty once refused an opportunity to listen to one hundred fishing anecdotes, the repertory of someone else who didn't have the knack. I have no doubt that the sweetheart of Michigan *had* spent an interesting life—clearly it had been a busy one—but to the imaginative writer, nearly all lives are interesting, all are raw material for fiction; so I saved the train fare and worried along with some other "real spice" that I had on hand.

The most interesting lives of all, of course, are our own and there is nothing egomaniacal nor unmannerly in our being keenly concerned with what happens to us; if we did not firmly believe that ours are the most absorbing experiences and the most acute perceptions, and the most compelling human involvements, we would be no writers at all and we would, as well, be very dull company. But it is not fair to buttonhole our reader with an exegesis of ourselves if there is the slightest risk of his being bored or embarrassed or offended; and while I have no objection to the use of autobiography—for in a sense all writing is of necessity autobiographical—I should counsel any beginner to winnow carefully and to add a good portion of lies, the bigger the better. Too great an addiction to the truth is a hindrance to any writer, and I think with terrible pity of a minor lady poet in Ohio who is not capable of so much as a fib. In a long narrative poem called *A Trek Through Florida*, which recounts a trip she made by Greyhound bus with her sister, she says that they set forth one evening to see the planes take off at Pensacola; but after the reader has danced a while with excitement in his anticipation of the spectacle, he is dismayed to find that because of bad weather, there is no activity on the flying field at all and he has to get right back in the bus. This is to me the most frustrating poem in the English language, even worse than the couplet composed by the same puritanical truth-teller,

> Then why should I not love him,
>   my father and my chum?
> I don't think there's more just like
>   him, but there may be some.

When I was young, I had the fortune and the pleasure of talking from time to time with Ford Madox Ford who, with the generosity that made him beloved of his pupils, read and commented on my aimless and plotless short stories and on inchoate chapters of novels that were destined to die unborn. One time, in appraising a character he found disproportionately unsympathetic, he asked me how closely I had drawn the portrait from life, and when I replied that I had been as sedulous as I knew how, he said, "That's impolite and it's not fiction." He went on to observe then that the better one knows one's characters in life, the harder it is to limn them in fiction because one has too much material, there are too many facets to tell the truth about, there are whole worlds of inconsistencies and variants, and objectivity will fade when one's personal attitude is permitted excessive prominence. It is the business of the reader, not of the author, to sit in judgment; the author is not allowed to say, "This man is a villain and you must believe me because I have known him all my life." Unless you show forth his iniquities, the reader may not find him iniquitous at all, not knowing that he sent the author a nasty comic valentine in the fourth grade.

I took Ford's advice very much to heart and subsequently I found that I could transform experience into artistic substance by the simplest expedients: by shifting the scene from the North to the South or from the East to the West, by changing the occupation of a character or the color of his hair or the fit of his clothes. In his mythical environment and with his new lineaments and his unfamiliar wardrobe, my acquaintance was presently easy to handle.

And then, after years of attacking from ambush and throwing up smoke screens, I made the same tactical error I had made in the beginning, and did so unconsciously. It is my intention to tell you about this, a problem completely autobiographical. I am no teacher and I could not teach anyone the first thing about writing; the most I can do is to seek my own creed in the conclusions I hope to draw from this rather depressing and instructive story. The creed is different from the one I held ten years ago and I dare say it is different from the one I shall hold ten years hence. All the imponderables that play upon us, the state of the world, the intellectual fashions of our times, our personal triumphs and misfortunes, our reading and our writing itself slowly shift the emphasis of our beliefs. But one of the greatest blessings of all to a fiction writer is that he may change his mind and never be called a turncoat.

My story begins in Cambridge, Massachusetts, one evening in 1946 when two poets and I were exchanging memories of life in the thirties. We were coevals and we had had the same frame of reference. I told them an intricate tale of an act of violence in which I had been peripherally involved when I was in college; I had been witness to a suicide that had come at the end of a spectacularly ugly life, but one so illustrative of the middle years of the decade that my description of it sounded like an old lecture on the manners and the morals of those days. The actions were motivated by the dislocations of the twenties that had still not been set right, by the depression, by the end of prohibition, by the New Deal. It involved that famous song of our times "Gloomy Sunday" that was said to have started an epidemic of suicide amongst college students all over the world; the game Monopoly figured in it and the Young Communist League, *Ulysses*, the undergraduate vogue of swallowing goldfish and the world-wide furore caused by the birth of the Dionne quintuplets. It concerned a boy who had sat next to me in Latin Comedy and had made a tolerable sum of pocket money for himself by renting out, at a dollar and a half a day, an unexpurgated copy of *Lady Chatterley's Lover* which he had smuggled in from France on a tramp steamer. Because in that region there was still local option and our town was dry, there was, in my story, a bootlegger who kept his pints of filmy booze hidden from the revenue officers under a manure pile in his back yard. There were medical students who went on ether jags, chemistry students who stole grain alcohol from the laboratory and made bathtub gin in milk bottles for consumption at the Junior Prom; professors who were open advocates of the U.S.S.R. and were neither questioned nor shunned; sophomore firebrands who were later to go to the Spanish Revolution with the International Brigade; and German exchange students who created incidents in classes in political economy. Just as important were the omissions: anti-Semitism was not yet a major issue nor had the Catholic Church begun to attract intellectual converts in any number; a postgraduate year in Germany was still the ambition of many; and the vocabulary of psychiatry was not universal. (How the times have changed! Not long ago a taxi driver in New York, transporting me a mortally long distance, told me in meticulous detail all he had discussed that morning with his analyst. He assured me that he was not a nut but if he were, he would be diagnosed as a manic-depressive.)

But in addition to its being typical of our generation, my story had universal elements and an urgent drama and compelling implications. And when I had finished with my recital, my friends said that I must write it down, that it was obviously my next novel and that it was, so to speak, ready-made. I should write it, they said, just as I had told it to them. I was then close to the end of my second book and was casting about for a new subject; and since I respected the taste and the wisdom of the poets, I decided to follow their suggestion and a few months later began my novel about college life in the thirties and the shocking event that had altered the whole course of my existence and had loitered horridly as a nightmare for eleven years. At this point I should say that five years before that evening in Cambridge and six years after I had seen a life go up in gun-smoke, I had written the whole thing down in a long story which was a failure since I did not know what it was about and had no idea what my own feeling toward the characters in it was. But in 1946 I believed that by this time the emotional experience had sunk deeply enough to rise again as literary experience, and now that the immediacy was removed, I could examine its components judiciously and disclose its meanings. I had been so out of touch with all the people who had been involved that I was certain I could create them out of whole cloth.

But from the very start I faced more perplexing problems than ever before in my life. They stemmed partly from the fact that I had told the story and that afterward, in many conversations with my friends, I talked still more of it. This was an infraction of what should be one of the cardinal rules of writing: keep your mouth shut about work-in-progress. But my troubles went deeper: the matter was extremely personal and interior and was, I discovered, quite as painful in recollection as it had been in its genesis when I watched the death throes of a tormented human being. I found that I had, after all, *not* forgotten the people I had known then, and I reproduced all the miseries of those days with pitiless accuracy. I am reminded here of another occasion on which I wrote directly out of my own life; I wrote a story about an automobile accident I had been in, in which my skull had been fractured and my nose had been smashed to smithereens. In describing the pain that assailed my heroine, I so perfectly revived my own old pain that each time I sat down at my typewriter I acquired a shattering headache that no amount of aspirin could cure. But that was only a physical distress, and the canvas I had set out to cover was not a large one.

I fancy that in the next three and a half years, as I worked on the suicide story, I accumulated twenty pounds of manuscript and destroyed an equal amount. I completed two versions, one in the first person and one in the third; I tried and rejected the omniscient observer; I made an effort to imitate Dostoevski's method in *The Brothers Karamazov*, the use of a fellow citizen to record the lives of the principals. By actual count, I wrote twenty-three versions of the first chapter with twenty-three different accentuations. But the book continued to be a mess, heavy, flat, oppressively factual and cumbrously emotional. Something ailed my prose and all my rhythms were off; it was as if I had been cut off from language and from tone and mood and from the understanding of the simplest methods of composition. I was writing about people I knew as well as I knew myself, about a setting that was as immediately before my senses as the room in which I sat at my typewriter, about a sequence of events that I had thought about and talked about a hundred times. And even so, every page, every sentence, bore the signature of a prevaricator. I told lies right and left not only about my characters but about humanity in general, but they were not good lies; they were pedestrian, malicious and transparent.

The clever reasons why I could not progress in the book varied as I thought them up: college was too remote from me, I claimed, so I went for some months to Columbia to study botany, and I became so absorbed by what I saw under my microscope that I arrived at the laboratory bright and early every morning and came home at sundown. I was persuaded that my study would have a double function; not only would I redeem the sense of campus life but I might acquire the levelheaded objectivity of a scientist. But I saw no students. I was instructed by a geneticist in his own laboratory, and I saw him and his companions who were breeding mice with tails like bolts of lightning and mice that danced in circles counter-clockwise. I learned a good deal about botany and something about genetics and about the jokes that make scientists laugh, but these acquisitions did not further the project on my desk at home.

I hit upon another explanation: the fault lay in my residence in New York, an improbable place for a writer; and although this I do believe is true, moving out of the city would not have solved the problem; anyhow, at that time, it was impossible. However, this gave me an excuse to study brochures issued by real estate brokers advertising country properties and to acquaint myself thoroughly with the rural regions of Ireland described for me in exuberant guidebooks. To escape the noise of my apartment building where, below me, there was a music school for children who ceaselessly practiced the piccolo obbligato from "The Stars and Stripes Forever," I used to go with my notebooks to a small private library, thinking that in the luxurious quiet there I would come to terms with the book. But I tended rather to come to terms with the books Mrs. Wharton had written than with the one I had not. Occasionally I spent whole mornings at the zoo in Central Park communing with Joe the chimpanzee who smokes cigars and sometimes strolls in a sailor suit, hand in hand with his keeper. Frequently I walked across Brooklyn Bridge and I closely studied the motley buildings of Welfare Island from a bench on the East River Drive; I took sight-seeing boats around the island of Manhattan and I lunched one Saturday in Hoboken where, in a single block, I counted twenty-two saloons. In the worst periods of guilt I consoled myself by saying that all this was grist to the mill and that in time I would make use of the sights and sounds and smells in these byways of the city. There were sometimes stretches when I wrote for ten hours a day, but these were followed by long intervals when I avoided the sight of the manuscripts on my desk as if they were the source of a physical pain and I fled my rooms, seeking a fresh affection but firmly convinced that I was really looking for a way to write this novel which had been scheduled for publication numerous times. I set deadlines for myself and I had my publisher set deadlines for me. The light at my desk was bad, so I had lengthy consultations with people who might remedy it. I was distracted by the piccolos, by dogs that barked and babies that howled, by the cocktail parties I went to and the ones I did not go to but heard about. Probably the most ingenious of my escapes was this: I declined an advance from my publisher and therefore, in order to live, I was obliged to write short stories and articles which naturally consumed my time and claimed my attention. Then my apartment began to depress and confine me, and I moved to another so much costlier that I had to spend even longer hours on earning my bread and butter. Pervading all these troubled months was the deep sense that whatever gift I once had had was gone forever.

A few days before last Christmas, on an afternoon after a

morning when I started on page one again for the twenty-fourth time, the reason I could not write the novel dawned upon me. It was ever so simple: I hated my material. The years I had elected to write about had not been happy ones for me nor for any of my characters and we emerged, in my merciless pages, unappealing to a degree in our melancholy; humorless, morbid, self-seeking, unworthy of any but the dreary fates I meted out to us. I had used my old tricks: had elongated people who in real life were short, had turned men into women and professors into priests, had stricken hale men with heart disease and had invested imbeciles with erudition. But while the disguises might have fooled my readers, they did not take me in for a minute; and behind the fake mustaches and the plaster noses, the wigs, the wooden legs and bogus passports, I saw my friends and foes and kinsmen. But most of all, I saw my own ubiquitous self, practicing ventriloquism to no purpose. I was everywhere hampered by my irrational feeling that I must not alter the facts, that I must tell the truth and, moreover, tell nothing *but* the truth, that every act must come in its proper chronological order, as the poets had said; it was as if I were making a confession to a jury upon which my very life depended. I riffled through the enormous pile of typewritten paper and concluded that every page of it was bad. Whether the architecture of the book and the prose of it and its conception were really as bad as I judged them to be, I shall probably never know, but my own dislike of it was sufficient; I realized that I would never publish it no matter how I treated it in its final version.

In this conviction on that bright day I burned it up, leaving no word of it behind. As the last feather of smoke curled up my chimney, I underwent a severe shock that lasted for several days. But when it had passed, I knew from the joyous state of my mind that I had performed one of the most sensible acts of my life. There came to me the realization that for all these fruitless months I had been the victim of a delusion; I had believed that because the events of my story had been important to me and had enormously influenced my thought and my behavior, they were therefore of literary use and significance. I had felt that I *must* write it down, that I *must* make this explanation of myself as a specimen of my generation in the formative years. There is a belief held by many that every novelist has in him one book that is more particularly *his* book than any other, that in it he will reveal the quintessence of his talent. *The Sun Also Rises* is probably Hemingway's and *The Great Gatsby* is Fitzgerald's. This may be true for every writer and it may not be, but of one thing I am certain: that book evolves as naturally as does any other and it is not possible to say, as the poets urged me to say before I started to compose, "This is my testament. Here will be the crystallization of what I, as a writer, want to say." And further, I do not believe that this book must necessarily be the most autobiographical. I remembered, as I glanced once at the pile of ashes in my grate, that twice before I had destroyed completed novels. They, too, had dealt with signal happenings in my life and they, too, had been seen unclearly through a cloud of emotion; I had destroyed them for the same reason, that I had disliked my data, had been more personally omnipresent than coolly omniscient, and that in failing to please myself I failed equally to please my reader. As it happens those books, written a good many years ago, were predicated on principles and prejudices that I have long since repudiated, and I am frank to admit that I would be ashamed if they existed now between a publisher's terribly durable covers. The ending of this story is a very happy one. About a week after the fire, I began to write a brand new novel, one that had been at the back of my mind, tantalizing me all the time that I had been hagridden by the other. It deals with people I have never met and with a permutation of circumstances that has no counterpart in my own life, and it is set in a part of the world that bewitches me. (I had always quarreled with the landscape of the other.) I am not required to resuscitate any black humors and therefore to suffer them again; and because my protagonist is not myself, I am kindly and uninhibited. I have no need to settle scores with any of my characters and therefore have no fear of hurting anyone's feelings if I make him base when it suits my purpose, or absurd when it suits my mood. Above all, I am freed of the crippling tendency to tell the truth; I'll make those planes take off at Pensacola even if there is a hurricane and every last one of the pilots is dead drunk.

I do not advocate the rejection of experience, for if I did, and practiced what I preached, I would have to stop writing tomorrow. But I do argue long and loud against the case history, and particularly the case history that is long on psychological analysis and short on action and plot. I don't like to read intimate facts that are none of my business, and I blush darkly in the presence of a flagellant who whips himself for his private sins with the terms he borrows from the doctors. There are times when I wish we might return to the reticence of my parents' era when people kept their secrets; sinners might beat their breasts and scream out their trespasses at revival meetings, but one didn't meet those people socially; now, they are on hand at every cocktail party, fresh from the analyst's couch. It was perhaps ridiculous and I dare say it was sometimes unkind to hide away relatives of unsound mind in upper bedrooms, but still that seems to me more becoming than to brag in public about the lunatic heritage that can explain our own misdeeds.

You could justly accuse me of disobeying my own rules, for certainly I have revealed myself to you in a very private dilemma; and you know how much time I have wasted and you know that I idle in the primate house and have a predilection for amassing useless information about saloons in Hoboken. The small advice I offer is this: take with a grain of salt the cliché that it is possible to rid oneself of a grief or a guilt or an ugly memory by writing of it; if you write of yourself, write with compassion and lay the blame for setting the house on fire on someone else. If the story is intolerable to you or boring or disgusting, the chances are that is how it will strike your reader. Don't talk your story away, not even to a publisher who gives you a long expensive lunch at the Ritz. And unless you thought of it first, don't let anyone, not even a brace of poets, tell you what to write. But above all, if you have committed every folly and broken every rule in the book, don't be afraid to give up. When the labors of three years and a half went up the chimney and out to mingle with the atmosphere of New York, I felt in control of my own bailiwick again now that the intruder, that rabid devotee of truth, was banished.

An Etiquette for Writers

B EING here in this room on this campus in this town that
confronts these particular mountains and these queer Flat-
irons is no simple or perfunctory act for me. I speak of more
than my habitual and crippling stage-fright and of more than
my normal writer's queasiness whenever I am far away from
my typewriter and my work-in-progress. I speak of an additional—and a more disabling—impediment. Here and now I
am hobbled by sentiment and I am beset at every turn by a multitude of associations; for in returning to Boulder after many
years, I have returned to scenes and landmarks that are more
familiar to me than any later ones can ever be, more acutely
meaningful since it was amongst them that, for all practical
purposes, my history had its beginnings. The churches of the
town, its graveyards, the junctions of its streets, the buildings
of the University, the gullies of the foothills, all these are rel-
iquaries crammed with mementoes of finished enthusiasms,
heartbreaks, astonishments, intrigues, revelations, shames and
terrors. For I lived here through crucial years, from the time
that I was ten and wore a hideous haircut and was tearfully
inept in Palmer Method at the University Hill School and still
believed in the spanking machine, until I was twenty one and,
after many humiliating failures to do so, finally passed enough
hours of Physical Education to entitle me to receive a diploma
in Macky Auditorium.

Those are years when the palates of our faculties are clean
and vernal and we urgently and directly take in the shape
and the color, the sound and the smell and the feeling of the
physical world and can, without groping for the word, name
the name of our sensation or emotion. They are not the richest
years, for the greenhorn intellect is still tactless and unequivocal
and cannot yet recognize ambiguity or nuance or paradox
or overtone or continuity. Nor can the heart, rigid with the
puritan righteousness of youth, distinguish clearly between the
vexatious and the unforgivable or between the pleasant and the
adorable. It is not a tolerant time of life, but it is a time of rather
great and reckless integrity; we have gone headlong to the roots

of the matter if we have not yet discovered the heart of it. The helmets and the masks, the arms and the armor that we take on later protect and socialize us but they also disguise; and with such cumbersome paraphernalia, our route is necessarily roundabout. I look back upon those years of my own life with certain admiration and with certain embarrassment and with no desire whatever to live them over again. I am glad that I was once obliged to be intransigent, but I am even more glad that I am now mollified and slowed down by the obliquities of middle age. But if I could, I would recapture the faith that I had then.

I was in Connecticut when I got the invitation to come to this conference, three quarters of a continent away from Boulder and the University and even more distantly removed in time from my childhood and girlhood and studenthood. But feeling is not dislocated by dislocation and the years can only partly censor memory, and ever since I wrote saying that I would come, I have been attended by a vivid and vocal entourage of past experience, impressions, gratitudes, satisfactions and regrets. Each time I considered some useful and objective subject on which to speak tonight, I was deflected by the backwash of memory on which I would then drift waywardly and will-lessly, my mind's eye blind to the domesticated landscape of New England and able only to see these fierce peaks and lonely plains. Transported from this year of Ike and Mamie Eisenhower and England's new queen and Willy Sutton and Ingrid Bergman's twins and Whittaker Chambers, I was often returned in my reflections to a summer fifteen years ago when, instead of standing behind a lectern, I sat out there, listening, on different evenings, to John Crowe Ransom, and Ford Madox Ford and John Peale Bishop and Sherwood Anderson. I was nervous to think of the change in my role from pupil to teacher, and if I had remembered what any of those writers had said, I would have cribbed shamelessly from them. But I remembered only the way they had looked and remembered the headiness of being in the presence of the practitioners of the art I had always honored above all else in life. In Connecticut, with my cat on my lap, I shivered and shook to contemplate my effrontery in coming here to state my creed, and I blushed darkly to think that in my audience there might be some of my former teachers who would still see and hear in me the gawky, wobbly, sloppy student I had been. I writhed so much I scared my cat when pitilessly I reminded myself of horrible gaffes I had made on final examinations and of bone-headed attitudes I had not had the sense to conceal.

But I could not dwell in any year or any mood for long; at one moment I saw myself in the stacks of the library lip-reading eleventh century religious poems and taking notes for my master's thesis, each page of which was to bear at the bottom a dense frieze of *op cits* and *ibids* intended to convey an air of erudition; but the next moment I was eleven years old and was learning how to shuffle cards under the tutelage of a gifted friend who knew six different kinds of solitaire. There might abruptly stand before me isolated, out of its context, the fact that the Earl of Oxford had once called Sir Philip Sidney a puppy, but before I could detain this interesting piece of gossip and learn why I had preserved it all these years, it was obliterated and replaced by the razzmatazz of an early Hallowe'en party when I was thrillingly frightened out of seven years' growth by a bird from the ninth grade, dressed up to represent a mummy, who shook my hand with a chamois glove filled with wet corn meal. Or again, on the heels of my recollection of the first Shakespeare play I ever saw when the Ben Greet players came to town in *Macbeth*, there came, with almost equal interest, the image of a yellow trolley car that used to proceed carefully down from the top of Mapleton Hill and up University Hill until it reached the Chautauqua and there it paused, exhausted, for a long and silent time while the conductor and the passengers got out and ritualistically drank at the water fountain in the shelter house as if this were a spa and they had taken a trolley ride to a cure.

Thinking, then, of Boulder and of my sources here—the book-learning all mixed up with beefsteak fries and famous snowstorms, the scandals of the town and gown confused— thinking thus of Boulder, I felt a commingling of affection and revulsion, emotions that did not cancel one another out but coexisted in a disharmony so intense and so exhilarating and so burdened with my own early and late history, that I concluded at last it would be impossible for me to speak here with academic detachment of the art of the novel, or the state of the novel, or the future of the novel, or the novelist and society, or the novelist and psychoanalysis. I knew that I should be able to do little more than peregrinate amongst personal meanders. At first this seemed a cheat, for my audience presumably would come to learn how to write and publish books and not to listen to my reminiscences. But still, these are the pastures where my imagination feeds and since I believe that memory is one of the writer's most useful tools, perhaps I can extend and shape some of my souvenirs into precepts. Anyhow, I could not in Boulder or anywhere else, give a recipe for writing a novel because there is none; I have heard that there are now on sale such things as "plot dictionaries" which must surely be supplemented by "character directories" and "setting atlases" and "mood guides." I have also heard of machines that not only compute difficult sums and do square root but in addition can compose musical themes; I have no doubt that they will eventually carry their impertinence to the point of parsing sentences and from there it will be no step at all to writing fiction. But I trust that these automatic Quiz Kids will remain a minority group and that their work will be nothing more than a flash in the pan, and that most of the writing we will read will still be home-made and will come from people who learn how to write through a less arithmetical kind of trial and error and who, through their striving toward an excellence and an originality of expression, will dedicate themselves honestly and with love and in faith to the tradition of English letters.

I do not remember a time, after I learned the alphabet, when I did not want to write. I had no axes to grind and no crusades to lead when I was six, but I pledged allegiance to the English language at about that time and my chauvinism has been steadfast ever since. My education is abysmally defective for I could never learn to do a single thing but read and write, partly, I suppose, because it never occurred to me that anything else was of the slightest consequence. By the time I did see that other matters were integral to the perpetuation of the world, it was too late: my nervous patterns were all used up and against almost all other branches of learning, I had a pathogenic and ineradicable phobia.

I do not think that in the beginning I looked on writing as a "profession," and certainly I did not think of it as "work." I wrote for my own amusement—as Miss Kathleen Winsor was recently adjudged in court to have written *Forever Amber*, making her thus eligible for an income-tax refund on the grounds that her revenue had derived from play, not work. I did, however, require an audience and when I could not get a human member of my family to listen to me read aloud my plays and ballads and my short, short, short stories, I read them to our patient dog who loved me. I believe I must have imagined a writing career to be a perpetually happy state of mind or a serene *modus vivendi*, lived out on a high, pure Olympus whose summit was reached on wings. I had not heard of Sisyphus then nor did I know that nine tenths of one's travel is by shank's mare. When I began my first novel in the seventh grade, a thriller set in the British Museum, I was not yet concerned with the economics of my calling and the thought of publication never crossed my mind: my intentions, in this book, from its first page to its twelfth and final page, was absolutely chaste and uncommercial. I typed it all out in upper case letters on the biggest and oldest and loudest typewriter ever seen which came into my possession briefly in some way I have now forgotten. I filled in the punctuation by hand with colored pencils and I bound the manuscript with cardboard and tied it with white rick-rack. For a long time I read it over at least once a day with undiminishing reverence. I am under the impression that someone else—besides the dog—read it and said at the time that I had talent, but I am not at all sure that I was not my own discoverer.

For at least the first half of my life, I was unaware that writing was a "business," as big and complicated and ramified as the automobile or the movie industries. Nor that its society was as stratified as that of ancient Rome. Nor did I have the faintest inkling that before I was to reach the age of franchise, the "cacoethes scribendi" which even early in the eighteenth century Addison had described as being "as epidemical as the small pox," was, in our century, to be as common as the common cold. As I began to learn about starvation among writers and cold attics, consumption, debtor's prisons, dope, drink, madness, I began to suspect that writers' lives were not automatically all fun and games. But I made no personal application of my suspicion and I went on being ignorant that throughout this enormous nation, hundreds upon hundreds of my coevals in situations similar to mine were plotting novels and plotting their lives exactly as I was doing. Not knowing that I was entering a business, I did not ever dream that competition was going to be so fierce. Once I strayed for a few minutes into the thought of being an acrobatic dancer because I had learned to turn a third-rate handspring, but I abandoned the idea because I naively imagined that the field was overcrowded.

I went on never having heard of Madison Avenue, called "Ulcer Gulch" by cynical underlings in publishing houses, called, sometimes, by the more sanguine and higher salaried officers, "the Street." I did not know about the importance of having or of not having an agent—a condition that is debated until the cows come home at literary cocktail parties and on the commuting trains to Westchester and Fairfield counties. I had never heard of an option or a contract, of Scandinavian rights or west-coast representatives or clipping bureaus or promotion campaigns or book-and-author lunches. For a long time, of course, I thought that all writers were dead but even after I discovered that they were not, I did not think they were ever on view. The first writer I ever saw was Robert Frost and I saw him up close in the dining room of a small lodge in Boulder Canyon where I had been hired as a maid-of-all-works the summer I was twelve. He ordered a glass of milk to drink with his lunch and I was so light-headed that when I was cutting a lemon for his companion's iced tea, I nicked my finger nastily and a drop of my blood fell into the poet's glass. I gave it to him just as it was—it didn't show much and this romantic transfusion gave me something to think about when I was kept awake at night by pack-rats gallivanting through the attic over my head.

Perhaps my most innocent notion was that when writers talked "shop," they talked of writing, for by the time I had got to college and had gravitated toward others of my persuasion, this is what we did.

In my last year at the university, I was a member of a small group who wrote and hoped eventually *really* to write and who, making no bones about it, called ourselves "the intelligensia." We had no sponsorship and no organization and our meetings were sporadic. But once every week or so we gathered together on the mezzanine of a melancholy sandwich-and-beer establishment on 13th Street, long since replaced by something smarter, where, for the Mermaid Tavern's hock or sack, we substituted attenuated and legal three point two. Occasionally we read aloud from our own work, but for the most part we read from the writers we had just discovered: Joyce, Proust, Pound, Eliot, Lawrence, Gide, Hemingway, Faulkner. Our prejudices were vitriolic and our admirations were rhapsodic; we were possessive, denying to anyone outside our circle the right to enjoy or to understand *The Wasteland* or *Swann's Way* or *A Portrait of an Artist as a Young Man*. We were clumsy and arrogant and imitative, relentlessly snobbish and hopelessly undiscriminating. We did not know where we were at but wherever it was, we heard the thunderous music of the spheres. It made no difference at all that we were for the most part tone-deaf. Perhaps I do my friends an injustice and they were less befuddled than I, so I shall speak only for myself when I say that I was so moonstruck by the world of modern writing that had opened up before me that I saw no difference at all in the intentions of Thomas Wolfe and Marcel Proust or those of James Joyce and Thomas Mann: all of them were godly and inviolable. Contemporaneity was our principal but not our only concern: for we had also taken up Flaubert, Stendhal, Conrad, Heine, Swift, all the Russians, the English metaphysical poets, Goethe, St. Augustine, Defoe and Nietzsche. We longed as much for other centuries as we identified ourselves with our own and we existed in a state of dichotomy: the ivory tower (a phrase that did not seem tarnished to us) that we occupied was being ceaselessly assailed by the Zeitgeist (another term we found fresh and apt). In spite of our airs and posturings and greed, we were serious and we knew that ours was no golden, carefree age: we had been reared in the Depression and our sensibilities had taken on the complexion of the national dilemma; we were dependent on NYA and the FERA jobs for our books and laboratory fees; in a sense we were living on borrowed time because we knew that after our graduation we were going to have more than a spectator's knowledge of unemployment. Along with *Walden* and *Culture and Anarchy*, we read *The Theory of the Leisure Class* and Trotsky's *Autobiography*. We began to hear of anti-semitism; Hitler began to show that he was more than a nut; and presently the Spanish revolution was to begin, giving us the foretaste of the sanguinary confusion that has deformed the world for thirteen years.

But hope and energy and political illiteracy safeguarded us against any real emotional involvement with these issues and while we heard the Zeitgeist wail and rattle our windowpanes, we stayed snug a while in that mild, crepuscular saloon and quoted *Sweeney among the Nightingales.* So long as there are students, so long as there are writers-in-the-making, there will be these microcosms, varying according to the wars that are being fought and the intellectual vogues that are in style. We cut our baby teeth on the repercussions of the Sacco and Vanzetti trial as a new generation has cut its on Alger Hiss.

Although we, the intelligentsia of the University of Colorado, occasionally talked of the responsibility of the writer to his society and debated whether he was ethically obliged to mirror his times, we did not think in ulterior terms of reform or revolution or restoration. We were incontrovertibly single-minded and thought only in terms of writing. The play was the thing, or the poem was or the novel or the story. And because we did not yet know anything much about psychoanalysis beyond a smattering of its vocabulary, we did not investigate the morbid reasons for our impulses to write; we would have been shocked and disbelieving if anyone had even jokingly suggested that we were disinterring and exposing derangements and unwholesome desires. We may often have doubted our talent and despaired of our ability to perform, but our motives for writing never came into question. It is to the luxury and freedom of that immediate, unrealistic and simple fervor that I look back with such longing. A fervor that cools, willy-nilly, when the practical ends of writing come to subordinate the aims of it.

The Zeitgeist at last blows the tree too hard and down comes cradle and baby and all. Eight years after I left Boulder, a propitious wind knocked me down to earth where I landed on my feet in clover and if, later on, I found that the clover was an ersatz wartime substitute for the real thing, it served me for a time. For luckily my first book came out in 1944, a halcyon year for the purveyors of anything and everything since the whole nation was on a spending spree, buying everything that was on sale, including novels. In comparison to other books that came out at that time, mine had a feeble career, but from the periphery, I could see the workings of the "book business" in which it was sometimes difficult to tell whether writing was its raison d'etre or was, on the contrary, its product or commodity. For example, once at a cocktail party I met a literary agent who maintained a stable of impressively thriving novelists and who had been told by our host that I had been published in a few magazines that operated on budgets that were modest almost to the vanishing point. He looked coldly at me and coldly said, "A writer has to make a lot of money to interest an agent."

The writer seemed to exist for the sake of the publishing house and not the other way around: I would hear that "So and So is writing a book for Macmillan," Macmillan assuming thereby a role rather like that of patron. I was to learn of the sly and shameless practice among publishers of "stealing" authors from each other; these larcenies sometimes took weeks to accomplish and involved litigation, bribes, slander, fist-fights, terrible hangovers and many of the emotions one associates with the divorce courts. I was to be made acquainted with the power of the bookseller and of the newspaper critic, with the relative weight borne by the daily and Sunday reviews, with the danger of getting into bad odor with the capricious Mr. Orville Prescott of the *Times* and with the back-of-the-book editors at *Time Magazine*. Writers were often schooled and trained and groomed as if for a presentation at court before their first books came out. Recall the publication of *Forever Amber* by Miss Kathleen Winsor; her name and face were so familiar by the time her huge book was on the stands that one felt she had always been with us, legendary but substantial like Uncle Sam. I do not clearly remember the details of her publisher's campaign and actually I recall only one anecdote preceding Macmillan's biggest day since the release of *Gone with the Wind*. The story was current that Macmillan at Number 60 Fifth Avenue and Sheed and Ward, the Catholic publishers at Number 63, used the same printer and that galleys for the Right Reverend Monseignor Ronald Knox's translation of the New Testament were delayed for an unconscionable time because plates from *Forever Amber* had been mixed with some for the Gospel according to Saint Matthew. If this frolicsome error had not been discovered in time, Sheed and Ward might very well have hit a jackpot as gratifying as their neighbors did.

I was more concerned with the private-made-public life of someone else at the time Miss Winsor made her debut and I failed, also, to read her book. But a few months ago, I read her second and also very large book, *Star Money*. The protagonist of the novel is a young woman of extraordinary beauty and clothes-sense who writes a historical novel and overnight is sky-rocketed to fame, fortune and intolerable heart-ache. In the introduction to the French edition M. Andre Maurois says, "The heroine, Shireen . . . writes, as did Kathleen Winsor, an historical novel in which Janetta, the heroine, is a parallel of the author, just as she would have liked to have been herself." This reminds one of the girl on the cornflakes box holding a box of cornflakes with a girl on it holding a box of cornflakes. A consistently interesting aspect of this book—or this continuum—about a writer writing a book is that the reader never catches either the flesh-and-blood author or the fictional author in the act of writing. In a recent profile of him in *Life Magazine*, Mr. Mickey Spillane, progenitor of a detective named Mike Hammer who uses a Luger freely and has been known to use sherry as a chaser for Bourbon, emphatically wants it understood that he is no author, he is a writer, a proclamation that I construe to mean that he wants no one to mistake him for a high-brow or long-hair or finicking esthete; he is a straight-talking, hard-drinking, down-to-earth working man, twice as tough as nails. For all his ruggedness, Mr. Spillane has made a fundamental error in his self-analysis, for the fact is that whether he likes it or not, he is an author and he is not a writer; he has created something—he has, to use one of the most odious neologistic verbs in the language, "authored" something but so far he has not written anything. Miss Kathleen Winsor and/or Miss Shireen Delaney are also authors in *Star Money*. At the opening of the book, Kathleen's Amber and Shireen's Janetta are already between hard covers and on the market, and we proceed now to the results of the fait accompli. We watch the harvest of a bumper crop of jewels by Van Cleef and Arpels, shoes by Delman, hats by Mr. John, maquillage by Elizabeth Arden, escorts by the Ivy League. The product, that is, the book, is swamped and completely lost to sight under these myriad, gleaming, high-priced by-products. The adornments so completely hide the Christmas tree that they appear to dangle of their own accord in midair, immune to the law of gravity. It is clear that once Shireen has seen Ulcer

Gulch they'll never be able to get her back down on the farm again.

I am not preaching a sermon against venality and I do not want to sound catty; there is almost nothing I like better than money and I get a great deal of real pleasure out of reading about it. I am only using this highly informative and probably quite accurate document to illustrate a phenomenon of our times in which the writing of fiction and particularly of novels has come to be a means to an end and the end is something that belongs more properly to the world of entertainment or of politics.

For writing is a private, an almost secret enterprise carried on within the heart and mind in a room whose doors are closed; the shock is staggering when the doors are flung open and the eyes of strangers are trained on the naked and newborn; one's doubts and misgivings and fears should be allowed to rest in sick-room quiet for a while. The experts may proceed to the examination but the parent should not be asked to make any further contribution. Let me quote again from M. Maurois to show what happened to Miss Winsor: "Success was swift and spectacular. Kathleen Winsor was sent out by her publishers on an autographing tour of America, attended banquets, spoke over the radio and became a target for newsmen everywhere. They weren't always favorable. Unwisely she confessed that she had written for fame and money. Byron had learned the costly lesson that one doesn't get away with such remarks, even when true. Kathleen Winsor, it should be noted, had many other reasons for writing a novel. Among them were two: a deep-seated inferiority complex, and a painful need of public expression. These, though, she avoided mentioning. They were kept well hidden within her. But whenever she heard a vicious joke about Amber, she was likely to cry." I will elide this generous Frenchman's avuncular psychiatry only pausing to observe that I cannot believe Miss Winsor's inferiority complex will be cured by his announcement and that the "painful need for public expression" can hardly be called singular in a writer or, indeed, in any specimen of *homo sapiens.* Now chivalrous as his exegesis is, it is an exegesis of the creator and not of the creation and this putting of the cart before the horse is symptomatic of what is wrong today in this wide-spread vulgarization and personalization of writing, this confounding of it with another kind of activity altogether. In recent years we have seen the birth and flourishing of literary reputations months and sometimes even years before the writers to whom they belong ever appear in print. They have acquired a solid status on the strength of their intention, on their charm and their wit and their presentableness at dinner parties; in some cases, it seems almost superfluous for them to publish at all. I know of a man who has been called a writer all his life—and he is nearing sixty—who has, neverthless published nothing except an excerpt from his "forthcoming novel" in an obscure and ephemeral magazine. On hearing that he had gone to the country to finish his book, a canard that began at least twenty years ago, a friend of mine said, "Oh, really? What is he reading?" It is a full-time job to be a non-practicing writer and I suppose that it is an honorable enough profession but it should get itself a new name. The tunes one sings for one's supper must be neither sour nor stale; the news in the gossip columns is short-lived and must therefore continually be replenished and this necessitates ever widening one's social orbit, continually revealing just enough and not too much of what is significant in one or what is original and appealing. It is quite as profitable to appear in *Town and Country* in a photograph that includes Mrs. Harrison Williams or the Duchess of Windsor as it is to be noticed favorably in the book pages.

I do not mean to imply that I disapprove of the praise and the petting of writers nor that we should not get the same worldly rewards that people in other professions do, but I object to our being treated—and our allowing ourselves to be treated—as performers and being transferred from our bailiwick into an element in which we cannot possibly be at home. It does not follow that because we can write, we can also speak over the radio or that we will "televise" well. Nor does it follow that because I can write a book about an unhappy woman reared in the twentieth century I am therefore qualified to make a five-hundred word statement for a symposium in a women's magazine on why modern women are more unhappy than those of the nineteenth century.

As I talk, I realize that my viewpoint is probably parochial and that beyond the borders of New York's narcissistic pool, readers do not bother much about the private opinions and the private habits of the writers they read. Still I have been asked, in Bloomington, Indiana, in Greensboro, North Carolina, in Wiscasset, Maine whether I write in long-hand or on the typewriter, whether writing is easy or hard for me, what it is in my spiritual composition that makes it impossible for me to write happy stories. And it was from Texas that there came to me a lengthy questionnaire drawn up by someone who was compiling statistics on the feeding and working habits of free-lance writers in preparation for a college thesis. On the first page, I was peremptorily asked to give my age, birthplace and the details of my education. I was then asked whether I managed just to eke out a living, whether I lived well or whether I lived luxuriously and could afford to take trips. Was I married? If so, what did my husband do? Did I contribute to his support? Could I afford a secretary? What, exactly, was my income? What had it been when I started out? Did I write at home or where? During the day or night? Morning or afternoon? Did I smoke while writing? What did I smoke? Drink while writing? What did I drink? Did I think best lying down, sitting down or on my feet? Did I need a snack during each break to give me energy to go on? If so, what did I eat? Did I prefer to write in a large room or in a small area? How much in 1951 did I deduct from income taxes for expenses? How many rejections per story or article did I usually have before placing it? Was I glad I was a free-lance writer?

I did not return the questionnaire but saved it in a file marked "Frights" but if I had I would have given this nosy Parker something to put in his pipe and smoke. I could have told him that my royalty statement from Houghton Mifflin in 1951 for a story appearing in one of the O'Brien collections was one fifteenth of a cent. I could have made him sit up and take notice by saying that I always write in my bare feet, that I am a mouth-breather during composition and that I do my best work immediately after my hair has been washed. These facts, I think, are quite as pertinent to the process of writing as the time of day I sit down at my typewriter.

None of it has anything to do with writing. I have been asked whether I think radio appearances and autographing parties and book-and-author luncheons do one any good: I take this to mean do they quicken the sale of one's book, for I cannot think of any other *good* that could possibly derive from them, except in a purely accidental way. I don't know the answer for anyone but myself: for me it is a categorical *no*. Last spring, my publishers had conclusively demonstrated to them that I was one of their writers to be kept under wraps if my books were not to be boycotted by potential buyers who saw me in the flesh. Always before I had remained discreetly in the country during publication week, but there had been changes in the firm and all the publicity people were new when my third book came out last spring. They arranged three appearances for me: one of them was very pleasant since it involved nothing but a comfortable journey to Boston on a pretty day and an agreeable meeting with half a dozen genial reviewers; and one of them was a diverting lunch in Washington at which my fellow-speakers were Mr. Francis Biddle and Senator Taft, a trinity consciously contrived for laughs. Having had a very good time indeed on both of these occasions in cities of which I am fond and where I have friends, I agreed, at the height of my euphoria and not really paying attention, to go to a book-and-author lunch in a city in Connecticut where culture-fever is on the rampage. Such was my well-being at the time and such my absentmindedness that I did not fully take in the fact that the lunch was to be held in a large department store and that I was being sent up quite literally as a salesman for my own book. I did not get a proper briefing from the publicity department and from the start, everything went wrong. In the first place, I arrived alone and grubbily by day-coach. I should have been in a parlor-and-breakfast car with my fellow-speakers and I should have been attended, as they were, by someone from the publishing house to act as buffer and claque. At the station I found a taxi with difficulty and learned later that if I had played my cards right, I would have been met by the company limousine. When I got to the store, I went to the book-department though I should have been taken directly to the president's suite of rooms at the top of the building; a clerk who was about to go to lunch grumpily took me up in the freight elevator. For some time the four authors made conversation with the store executives and a few newspaper reporters; one of the authors, by her own profession, wrote "self improvement" books; one was a professional Irishman with a prodigious store of anecdotes told in brogue about ghosts and the wee folk; and the other, besides myself, was a woman who writes non-fictionally on numerous subjects and whose manner I much admired that day. Happily we did not lunch with our audience but we sat down, twenty in all, in the private dining room. I was seated on the left of the president and this meant that I was served last and served like a stepchild; I got no butter for my baked potato and I was left altogether out of the dessert. I was addressed once by my hostess: she said, "Running a department store is so much different from writing a book," a statement I found absolutely irrefutable and one that left me speechless. When lunch was over, we were led into an auditorium where five hundred ladies in hats were waiting for us. The self-improvement writer spoke first and went straight to their hearts: she told them that she was sure they were going to like this book the best of all she had written because it was her own favorite although she was still fond of her early books as she knew, by its warm response to their reissues the reading public was. She talked affectionately and easily and it was evident, from the ladies' faces, that her plug for self-improvement was doing its job. The next speaker was the woman I liked who stated straight off that she was not kidding herself nor any member of her audience: she was not talking to them for the love of it—in fact she loathed this sort of thing—but was here frankly and solely to sell her book; she could live on a hundred dollars a month but she would appreciate it if the ladies would help her raise her standard of living. She urged them to buy many copies of her new book. The rough treatment was just as effective as the smooth and the ladies were in a fine receptive mood by the time I was announced.

I had written out a five minute speech which I thought quite amusing and appropriate, starting out with a tried and tested anecdote about Gibbon. But I knew, the moment I opened my mouth, that no one in that vast hall was going to like it, that not many had ever heard of Gibbon and that certainly no one had ever heard of me until that very day. I cannot speak extemporaneously and could not ad lib and I sickly continued to the end of my speech which now sounded in my own ears intellectual and rarefied and snobby. During it, the faces which had first been thoughtful and then mirthful, turned to stone.

They hated me; they thought I was stuck-up; and the worst of it was that I could not retreat after my failure but had to sit there on the platform while the Irishman won their hearts with his County Mayo drolleries that lasted for thirty-five minutes.

The final part of this jollification took place in an even bigger room where our books were piled on counters and where tea and green cakes were being dispensed and where we, the authors, were situated behind a long table, rather like a slave block, with sample copies of our books and a fountain pen in front of us. The listening-public which had now become the buying-public were to buy our books and bring them to us to be autographed. The Irishman's $12.00 book on spooks indigenous to the ruined castles of the west of Ireland sold like hot-cakes; the self-improvement lady developed writer's cramp; the woman I liked was mobbed. But no one, not even an employee in the disguise of a customer, bought a copy of my book and I felt exactly the same feverish humiliation I had felt in grammar school when the Valentines were handed out and I either got none or a scurrilous comic one from my worst enemy. A sympathetic young photographer from a local paper hovered around me, trying to take a picture of me in the act of signing a copy of my book and his embarrassment added horribly to my own. Several ladies thumbed through my book and said they would wait until it came to the lending library. And one in a hat apparently constructed of crushed black beetles, after telling the self-improvement one that she wished they were next door neighbors, asked me to agree with her that it was a waste of money to buy novels since you only read them once and after that they did nothing but clutter up the house. I believe a gong finally rang or perhaps a store executive told us we could go; I took the fountain pen only to discover that it was no good and could not have cost more than a quarter to begin with. I did, however, collect my trainfare from my publishers and made a small profit by pretending that I had travelled Pullman both ways.

No serious writer takes any of this seriously. There is no need at all to expose oneself; keeping oneself before the public eye is, I think, totally unessential: we do not get forgotten so quickly nor so completely as actors and orators do and since our media are not remotely similar, we should not try to compete with them. Writers should write and their books should be read, but on the whole they should not be seen.

And I would be practicing what I am preaching if it had not seemed to me time to come back to Boulder to review the scenes of my origin and to thank my teachers for nourishing the better aspects of my character.

CHRONOLOGY

NOTE ON THE TEXTS

NOTES

Chronology

1915   Born Jean Wilson Stafford on July 1 in Covina, California, the fourth child of John Richard Stafford and Ethel McKillop Stafford. (Father, born 1874 in Atchison County, Missouri, was the son of a successful cattle rancher. After graduating from Amity College in College Springs, Iowa, he worked as a journalist in Chicago and New York City and for the telephone company in Tarkio, Missouri. Mother, born 1876 in Rock Port, Missouri, was the daughter of an attorney. She attended Tarkio College and taught school in Rock Port and Salida, Colorado. Parents married in Tarkio in 1907 and had three children: Mary Lee, born 1908, Marjorie, born 1909, and Richard [Dick], born 1911. Father published novel *When Cattle Kingdom Fell* in 1910 and later wrote Western stories for pulp magazines under the names Jack Wonder, Ben Delight, and O. B. Miles. Family moved in 1912 to Covina, where father used his inheritance to purchase a ten-acre walnut ranch and build an eight-room house at 831 Lark Ellen Avenue.)

1920   Father sells walnut ranch and moves family to San Diego, where he speculates in stocks. Stafford enters kindergarten.

1921   Father loses proceeds from sale of the Covina ranch along with much of his inheritance in the stock market. Family travels by car to Colorado in summer and moves into rented house in Ivywild neighborhood of Colorado Springs. Stafford enters first grade. Father borrows money from his mother and continues writing.

1923   Family moves to Stratton Park area of Colorado Springs.

1925   Family moves to house on Arapahoe Street in Boulder so that Mary Lee can live at home while attending the University of Colorado. Stafford begins attending University Hill school.

1928   Family moves to house at 1112 University Avenue. Mother begins taking in female students as boarders. Father

859

remains unemployed while working on treatise on government finance and debt (book is never completed).

1929   Mary Lee graduates from University of Colorado and begins teaching in Hayden, Colorado. Stafford enters State Preparatory School as sophomore.

1930   Marjorie graduates from University of Colorado. Stafford begins working during summers as a waitress and maid at a dude ranch in Ward, Colorado.

1931–32   Wins statewide student essay contest for "Disenchantment," account of her family's move from California to Colorado. Marjorie begins teaching in Tahlequah, Oklahoma. Stafford becomes features editor of *Prep Owl*, her high school newspaper. Family moves to house at 631 University Avenue. Stafford graduates from high school in June 1932.

1932–34   Enters University of Colorado on scholarship that covers her tuition fees. Studies philosophy, Latin, and the history of science. Majors in English and takes courses in Victorian literature, Middle English, and Anglo-Saxon taught by Professor Irene McKeehan, who becomes her academic mentor. Writes stories and short plays for creative writing course taught by John McLucas. Dick graduates from Colorado A&M in Fort Collins in 1933 and becomes forest ranger in Oregon. Stafford earns money for expenses in series of campus jobs, including posing as nude model for art classes.

1934–35   Leaves home and moves into boardinghouse at 1001 Tenth Street. Becomes friends with Lucy McKee Cooke and Andrew Cooke, married law students at the center of social circle known for heavy drinking and sexual experimentation. Moves in with the Cookes.

1935–36   Becomes friends with Robert Hightower, a premed student with literary interests. On the evening of November 9, 1935, Lucy McKee Cooke returns home in an agitated state, quarrels with her husband, and then fatally shoots herself while Stafford is telephoning a physician for assistance. Stafford's parents move to Denver. Forms lifelong friendship with Paul Thompson, an instructor in the English department, and Dorothy Thompson, his wife. Writes senior thesis "Profane and Divine Love in English Literature of the Thirteenth Century." Awarded scholarship to study Anglo-Saxon at the University of Heidelberg for one year; Hightower also receives a scholarship at Heidelberg. Writes one-act play about the death of Beethoven, *Tomorrow in Vienna*, that is performed by the University of Colorado drama club in April 1936. Awarded BA and MA degrees in English in June. Attends summer writers' conference at the University, where she meets Whit Burnett and Martha Foley, editors of *Story* magazine and the Story Press, and Robert Penn Warren. Lands in Cuxhaven, Germany, on September 18 and joins Hightower in Heidelberg. Struggles with spoken German and stops attending lectures in November.

1937   Visits Munich and Paris before returning to the United States in April. Falls ill with infection caused by ovarian cysts and is hospitalized for three weeks in Brooklyn and Manhattan. (Stafford will suffer from ill health for much of her adult life, exacerbated by heavy drinking, heavy smoking, and poor eating.) Spends much of the summer on ranch in Hayden owned by Mary Lee and her husband, Harry Frichtel. Attends the University of Colorado writers' conference, where she meets the novelists Ford Madox Ford, Evelyn Scott, and Caroline Gordon, the poet and critic Allen Tate (who is married to Gordon), and Robert Lowell (born 1917), an aspiring poet from a socially prominent Boston family. Begins teaching composition at Stephens College, a women's college in Columbia, Missouri, in the fall, but quickly comes to dislike the college and her students. Works on novel "Which No Vicissitude" and corresponds with both Hightower, who is studying East Asian languages at Harvard, and Lowell, an undergraduate at Kenyon College.

1938   Whit Burnett of the Story Press rejects "Which No Vicissitude." Begins writing "Neville," novel inspired by her experiences at Stephens. College declines to renew her contract. Meets Hightower in Albany, New York, in June, and travels with him to Colorado before going to Oswego, Oregon, where her parents now live. Begins teaching composition at the University of Iowa in September. Leaves Iowa City in November and travels to Cambridge, where she moves in with Hightower. Sees Lowell when he visits Boston at Thanksgiving. Moves to rented room in house at 2 Monument Street in Concord.

Atlantic Monthly Press rejects "Neville" but pays her $250 for an option on her new novel "Autumn Festival," about an affair between an American student in Germany and a Nazi aviator. On December 21 Stafford and an intoxicated Lowell are driving through Cambridge when Lowell turns down a dead-end lane and hits a wall. Stafford suffers a smashed nose and fractures to her jaw, right cheekbone, and skull that keep her in the hospital for almost a month.

1939   Undergoes five facial operations from late winter through early spring (will have breathing problems and suffer from headaches for the rest of her life). Sues Lowell's insurance company for $25,000. Submits "Autumn Festival" to Atlantic Monthly Press in late summer. Spends two months in fall at Mary Lee's ranch in Hayden. Atlantic Monthly Press rejects "Autumn Festival." Short story "And Lots of Solid Color" published in November *American Prefaces* magazine. Moves into Cambridge apartment with two roommates. Receives $4,000 settlement from Lowell's insurance company, which she uses to pay debts. Writes to Hightower in December that she is engaged to Lowell.

1940   Marries Lowell at St. Mark's Episcopal Church in New York City, April 2. Spends spring at ranch in Hayden while Lowell finishes senior year at Kenyon. Hightower marries Florence (Bunny) Cole, one of Stafford's Cambridge roommates. (After surviving Japanese internment in China, Hightower becomes a professor of Chinese literature at Harvard.) Attends Lowell's graduation from Kenyon on June 9. Stafford and Lowell spend several weeks in Memphis at home of Lowell's classmate, the writer Peter Taylor, who becomes her lifelong friend. In the summer they move to Baton Rouge, where Lowell has a fellowship at Louisiana State University. Stafford becomes office manager of the *Southern Review*, literary magazine edited by Cleanth Brooks and Robert Penn Warren. During trip to New Orleans in October Lowell strikes Stafford during a quarrel and breaks her nose.

1941   Lowell is received into the Roman Catholic Church in late March. Stafford also joins the Church, and at Lowell's insistence, they are remarried in Catholic ceremony. Suffering from recurring fevers and respiratory

problems, she spends most of the spring at her sister's
ranch in Hayden. Moves in the summer with Lowell to
New York City, where they rent apartment at 63 West
11th Street. Becomes part-time secretary to Frank Sheed
of the Catholic publishing firm Sheed & Ward. Works on
new novel "The Outskirts."

1942   Meets Robert Giroux, an editor at Harcourt, Brace and
Company, after he reads manuscript of "The Outskirts."
Signs contract with Giroux on April 30 for its publication
by Harcourt, Brace in return for $500 advance. In the
summer Stafford and Lowell move to Monteagle, Tennessee, where they live in a large house with Allen Tate
and Caroline Gordon.

1943   Sends manuscript of "The Outskirts" to Harcourt, Brace
in February. Begins cutting and revising the novel in
response to comments by editor Lambert Davis (Giroux
is serving in the navy) as well as criticism from Tate and
Gordon. Spends July and August at the Yaddo artists'
colony in Saratoga Springs, New York. Joins Lowell in
New York City in early September and learns that he
has decided to resist induction into the armed services.
Lowell sends public letter to President Franklin Roosevelt on September 7, refusing to serve as a protest
against the Allied bombing of Germany and the policy of
unconditional surrender; on October 13 he is sentenced
to serve one year and one day in prison. Stafford rents
apartment on East 17th Street. Visits Lowell in federal
prison at Danbury, Connecticut. Becomes friends with
writer Delmore Schwartz.

1944   Submits revised version of manuscript to Harcourt, Brace
in January (the novel is retitled *Boston Adventure* by the
publisher). Story "The Darkening Moon" published
in January *Harper's Bazaar*. After Lowell is paroled
in March and assigned to work as a hospital janitor in
Bridgeport, Connecticut, Stafford finds apartment for
them in the Black Rock district of Bridgeport. Story
"The Lippia Lawn" appears in Spring *Kenyon Review*.
Stafford is visited in July by her brother Dick, now a
second lieutenant in the 95th Infantry Division. *Land
of Unlikeness*, Lowell's first book of poetry, is published
September 18 in edition of 250 copies. *Boston Adventure* published September 21 in first printing of 22,000

copies. It receives favorable reviews and becomes a best seller (Harcourt, Brace edition sells 35,000 copies by May 1945, in addition to 199,000 copies sold by the Book League of America and 144,000 copies of a condensed Armed Services edition). Learns in October that Dick was killed on September 18 in a jeep accident shortly after his division landed in France. Visits parents and sisters in Oregon. Moves with Lowell to rented house on nine acres of land in rural area of Westport, Connecticut. Story "A Reunion" published in Fall *Partisan Review*.

1945   Commutes to New York one day a week to teach course in short story writing at Queens College. Hires Marian Ives as her literary agent. Awarded Guggenheim Fellowship in April. Works on novella that becomes novel *The Mountain Lion*. Story "The Home Front" published in Spring *Partisan Review*; "Between the Porch and the Altar" appears in June *Harper's*. After Westport house is sold by its owner, Stafford uses earnings from *Boston Adventure* to buy house in Damariscotta Mills, Maine, and moves there with Lowell in August.

1946   Signs contract with Harcourt, Brace for publication of *The Mountain Lion*. Stafford and Lowell leave Damariscotta Mills in late January and stay with Delmore Schwartz in Cambridge for several weeks. Story "The Present" (later retitled "The Captain's Gift") published in April *Sewanee Review*. Completes final version of *The Mountain Lion* in Damariscotta Mills in late April. Hosts series of visitors, June–August, including John Berryman and Eileen Simpson, Peter Taylor, Robert Hightower, Robert Giroux, Philip and Nathalie Rahv, and the painter Frank Parker. In September Stafford and Lowell go to New York City, where they soon separate. Stafford drinks heavily. On a psychiatrist's advice she enters a sanitarium in Detroit, but soon leaves and goes to Denver, where she sees Mary Lee for a few days before returning to New York. Stays in series of hotels in New York and Connecticut and continues to drink while rarely eating. Learns that Lowell has abandoned Catholicism and is seeking a divorce. In late November Stafford enters the Payne Whitney Psychiatric Clinic at New York Hospital, where she is treated by Dr. Mary

Jane Sherfey. Story "The Interior Castle" is published in the November–December *Partisan Review*.

1947 Story "The Hope Chest" is published in January *Harper's* and "A Slight Maneuver" appears in the February *Mademoiselle*. Stafford learns that her mother is dying of malignant melanoma and is granted emergency leave from the hospital. Arrives in Oregon after her mother's death on February 3. *The Mountain Lion* is published by Harcourt, Brace on March 1; it receives enthusiastic reviews but sells poorly. *Lord Weary's Castle*, Lowell's second volume of poetry, is awarded Pulitzer Prize in May. Stafford sells house in Damariscotta Mills. "My Sleep Grew Shy of Me," essay about her insomnia, published in *Vogue*, October 15. Released from Payne Whitney in November. Continues to see Dr. Sherfey (will remain in therapy with her until the late 1950s). Rents apartment at 27 West 75th Street. Delivers lecture on "The Psychological Novel" at Bard College literary conference (published in *Kenyon Review*, Spring 1948). Signs contract with Harcourt, Brace in late November for novel "In the Snowfall," inspired by her friendship with Lucy McKee Cooke, and receives $4,000 advance. Fires Marian Ives as her agent (will represent herself for the next seven years).

1948 Story "Children Are Bored on Sundays" appears in the February 21 issue of *The New Yorker*, the first of twenty-four stories Stafford will publish in the magazine. Becomes friends with Katharine White, her fiction editor at *The New Yorker*. Meets President Harry S. Truman in Washington, D.C., when she receives National Press Club award on April 3. Awarded second Guggenheim Fellowship. Spends six weeks in U.S. Virgin Islands obtaining divorce from Lowell. Forms lasting friendship with the writers Nancy and Robert Gibney, who own a home on St. John. Stafford receives onetime payment of $6,500 when divorce becomes final on June 14. "Profiles: American Town," article about Newport, Rhode Island, appears in August 28 issue of *The New Yorker*. Story "The Bleeding Heart" published in the September *Partisan Review*, and "A Summer Day" appears in the September 11 issue of *The New Yorker*.

1949   Three of her stories appear in *The New Yorker* during
        the year: "The Cavalier" (February 12), "Pax Vobis-
        cum" (later retitled "A Modest Proposal," July 23), and
        "Polite Conversation" (August 20). Learns in April that
        Lowell has suffered a severe mental collapse and has been
        hospitalized. (Stafford and Lowell will occasionally see
        each other until his death.) Visits Great Britain, Ireland,
        France, and Germany during summer. Publishes articles
        in *The New Yorker* about the Edinburgh Festival (Sep-
        tember 17) and returning to Heidelberg (December 3).
        Meets Oliver Jensen (born 1914), an editor at *Life*, in the
        fall.

1950   Marries Oliver Jensen on January 28 at Christ Church
        Methodist in New York City. They honeymoon in Haiti
        and Jamaica, then move into Jensen's apartment at 222
        East 71st Street. Delivers lecture "Observations on the
        Uses of Autobiography in Fiction" at Wellesley College
        on April 17 (published as "Truth and the Novelist" in
        Harper's Bazaar, August 1951). Article "Enchanted
        Island," written in Jamaica, appears in May *Mademoiselle*.
        Publishes three stories in *The New Yorker*, "A Country
        Love Story" (May 6), "The Maiden" (July 29), and "The
        Nemesis" (later retitled "The Echo and the Nemesis,"
        December 16), as well as "Old Flaming Youth," which
        appears in the December *Harper's Bazaar*. Moves with
        Jensen into house on Long Lots Road in Westport, Con-
        necticut. Sets aside "In the Snowfall" in December and
        begins novel *The Catherine Wheel*.

1951   Becomes friends with the writer Peter De Vries, a neigh-
        bor in Westport. Story "The Healthiest Girl in Town"
        published in *The New Yorker* April 7. Visits Mary Lee
        in Colorado during summer and sees father for the
        last time. Completes *The Catherine Wheel* in the fall.
        Article "Home for Christmas" appears in December
        Mademoiselle.

1952   *The Catherine Wheel* is published by Harcourt, Brace on
        January 14 and receives mixed reviews; it sells 12,000
        copies in three months. Serves on jury that gives the
        National Book Award for Fiction to James Jones for
        From Here to Eternity. Drinks heavily as marriage to
        Jensen becomes increasingly strained. During the year
        publishes articles "The Art of Accepting Oneself"

(*Vogue*, February 1) and "It's Good to Be Back" (*Mademoiselle*, July) and stories "The Violet Rock" (*The New Yorker*, April 26), "Life Is No Abyss" (*Sewanee Review*, July), "I Love Someone" (*Colorado Quarterly*, Summer), and "The Connoisseurs" (*Harper's Bazaar*, October). Attends University of Colorado writers' conference in Boulder, where she delivers lecture "An Etiquette for Writers" on July 22. Leaves Westport home in early November and moves to Hotel Irving on Gramercy Park South in New York City. Undergoes hysterectomy to remove fibroid tumors at New York Hospital. Travels to U.S. Virgin Islands in late December to obtain divorce.

1953   Publishes three stories in *The New Yorker* during the year: "The Shorn Lamb" (later retitled "Cops and Robbers," January 24), "The Liberation" (May 30), and "In the Zoo" (September 19). Divorce from Jensen granted on February 20. Elected to the Cosmopolitan Club, New York City club for professional women. *Children Are Bored on Sunday*, collection of ten stories, published by Harcourt, Brace in May. Stafford breaks with Harcourt, Brace in dispute over the English publication of the story collection. Signs contract with Random House on October 23, receiving $7,000 advance for a novel and volume of short stories. Moves to apartment in house at 24 Elm Street in Westport.

1954   Novella *A Winter's Tale*, adapted from her unfinished novel "Autumn Festival," is included in *New Short Novels*, edited by Mary Louise Aswell and published in paperback by Ballantine in February. "New England Winter" appears in February issue of travel magazine *Holiday*. Story "Bad Characters" published in *The New Yorker*, December 4.

1955   Publishes three stories in *The New Yorker* during the year: "Beatrice Trueblood's Story" (February 26), "Maggie Meriwether's Rich Experience" (June 25), and "The Warlock" (December 24). Travels to England in late summer, but cuts trip short and returns home because of financial worries.

1956   During the year Stafford publishes three stories in *The New Yorker*, "The End of a Career" (January 21), "A Reading Problem" (June 30), and "The Mountain Day"

(August 18), as well as "The Matchmaker" (later retitled "Caveat Emptor") in *Mademoiselle* (May). Hires James Oliver Brown as her new literary agent. Sails to England in June and rents flat at 20 Chesham Place in the Belgravia district of London. Begins friendship with Eve Auchincloss, an editor at *Harper's Bazaar*, who will help her obtain magazine writing assignments. Meets and begins affair with A. J. (Joe) Liebling (born 1904), a writer for *The New Yorker* since 1935 who is separated from his second wife and living in Europe for tax reasons. Visits Belgium in September after Liebling goes to Algeria on assignment. Returns to Westport in early autumn.

1957   Sees Liebling when he visits New York City for two weeks in January. Moves to apartment at 18 East 80th Street. Publishes stories "My Blithe, Sad Bird" (April 6) and "A Reasonable Facsimile" (August 3) in *The New Yorker*. Travels to England in early September to see Liebling. They visit Paris together before returning in November to New York, where they move into separate rooms at the Fifth Avenue Hotel in Greenwich Village.

1958   Finds it difficult to sell stories to *The New Yorker* after Katharine White retires as a fiction editor. Story "The Reluctant Gambler" appears in *Saturday Evening Post*, October 4. Publishes two articles in *Harper's Bazaar*: "Divorce: Journey Through Crisis" (November) and "New York Is a Daisy" (December).

1959   Interviews Isak Dinesen for *Horizon* magazine (article appears in September). Liebling reaches divorce settlement with his wife, Lucille Spectorsky. Stafford and Liebling marry at New York City Hall on April 3 and move into apartment at 43 Fifth Avenue; they also spend time at house Liebling owns at 929 Fireplace Road in the Springs section of East Hampton, New York. Story "The Scarlet Letter" appears in July *Mademoiselle*. Travels in July to Louisiana, where Liebling covers election campaign of Governor Earl Long (Stafford had suggested that he write about Long). Sails to England in late August. Visits Isle of Arran off the west coast of Scotland, the ancestral home of her mother's family, while Liebling covers British general election. In October they travel to

Greece and the Aegean and then go on Mediterranean cruise before returning to New York in late November.

1960   "Souvenirs of Survival: The Thirties Revisited," memoir of her college years, appears in *Mademoiselle* in February. Sent by *Harper's Bazaar* to Reno, Nevada, to cover production of the film *The Misfits*, starring Marilyn Monroe, directed by John Huston and written by Arthur Miller. Writes article that is rejected by the magazine. Publishes six film reviews in *Horizon*, September 1960–May 1961, including pieces on Satyajit Ray, Italian neorealism, and Akira Kurosawa.

1961   "The Ardent Quintessences," article on whiskey and cocktails, appears in April *Harper's Bazaar*. Moves with Liebling in fall to apartment at 45 West 10th Street.

1962   Serves on jury that gives National Book Award in fiction to Walker Percy for *The Moviegoer*. Leaves Random House and signs contract with Robert Giroux, now an editor at Farrar, Straus and Cudahy, for a novel, a collection of stories, and a book about Arran and the Greek island of Samothrace. Receives $12,000, of which $7,000 is used to repay her Random House advance. *The Lion and the Carpenter and Other Tales from the Arabian Nights* published by Macmillan as part of its "Marvelous Tales" series of children's books. *Elephi, the Cat with the High IQ*, children's book about one of the many cats Stafford kept during her lifetime, published in September by Farrar, Straus and Cudahy.

1963   Travels with Liebling to Normandy, the Loire Valley, and Paris in July and August. Visits American military cemetery above Omaha Beach where her brother Dick is buried, but is unable to find his grave. Goes to London before returning to New York in September. Begins seeing internist Dr. Thomas Roberts, who will be her primary physician for the rest of her life. Liebling is hospitalized with viral pneumonia on December 21 and dies from heart and renal failure on December 28.

1964   Collapses from heavy drinking in January and spends sixteen days recovering in New York Hospital. Begins writing book reviews for *The New York Review of Books* and for *Vogue* (will publish fifty-two reviews in the magazine from January 1964 to March 1974). Story "The Tea Time of Stouthearted Ladies" published in the Winter *Kenyon Review*. Suffers heart attack in early April and is hospitalized for five weeks, but does not quit smoking. Moves to Long Island country house in the Springs that she inherited from Liebling, which sits on thirty acres of meadowland. Maintains active social life despite not knowing how to drive. Story "The Ordeal of Conrad Pardee" appears in the July *Ladies' Home Journal*. Spends 1964–65 academic year as Fellow at the Center for Advanced Studies at Wesleyan University. *Bad Characters*, collecting nine stories and novella "A Winter's Tale," published by Farrar, Straus and Co., October 12. Resumes heavy drinking by the end of the year.

1965   Travels to Fort Worth, Texas, in May to interview Marguerite Oswald, mother of Lee Harvey Oswald, the accused assassin of President John F. Kennedy. Receives $6,000 grant from the Rockefeller Foundation to work on her novel. Article "The Strange World of Marguerite Oswald" published in the October *McCall's*.

1966   Father dies on January 9 in Lake Oswego, Oregon. *A Mother in History*, expanded version of her profile of Marguerite Oswald, published February 25 by Farrar, Straus and Giroux; it receives mixed reviews and sells 10,000 copies in three months. Article "Truth in Fiction," a revised version of "Truth and the Novelist," published in the October 1 *Library Journal*.

1967   Accepts two-year appointment as adjunct professor in the writing program of Columbia University's School of the Arts. Rents apartment at 11 East 87th Street and teaches class on the short story that meets once a week.

1968   Dislikes students and is unhappy with political turmoil on campus. Signs new contract with Farrar, Straus and Giroux on June 27 for volume of collected stories and her novel in progress, now titled "The Parliament of Women." Story "The Philosophy Lesson" appears in *The New Yorker*, November 16. Resigns teaching position after fall semester.

1969   *The Collected Stories of Jean Stafford* is published February 17 by Farrar, Straus and Giroux and receives favorable reviews. Stafford becomes regular contributor to the *Washington Post Book World* (publishes forty-four reviews in the newspaper from March 1969 through October 1976). Writes lengthy Christmas roundup of children's books for *The New Yorker* (continues to write this feature annually through 1975).

1970   Stafford is elected to the American Academy and Institute of Arts and Letters in January. Serves as writer in residence for two weeks at Pennsylvania State University. Publishes articles "My (Ugh!) Sensitivity Training" in *Horizon* (Spring) and "Love Among the Rattlesnakes," about Charles Manson and his followers, in *McCall's* (March). *The Collected Stories of Jean Stafford* awarded Pulitzer Prize for Fiction on May 4.

1971   Delivers series of five lectures on "Tradition and Dissent" at Barnard College in March. Writes introduction for *The American Coast*, picture book published by Scribner's. Publishes articles "Suffering Summering Houseguests" in *Vogue* (August 15) and "Intimation of Hope" in *McCall's* (December).

1972   *The Mountain Lion* is reissued in hardcover by Farrar, Straus and Giroux in April with a new preface by Stafford. Awarded honorary LittD degree by the University of Colorado at Boulder on May 24. Gives talk at Norlin Library in which she pays tribute to her mentor Irene McKeehan (published as "Miss McKeehan's Pocketbook" in Spring 1976 *Colorado Quarterly*). Suffers from worsening respiratory problems. Becomes regular contributor to *Vogue* (will publish nine feature articles in the magazine through June 1975, including profiles of newspaper publisher Katharine Graham and Representative Millicent Fenwick). Receives additional $3,000 advance for "The Parliament of Women."

1973–74   Delivers commencement address at Southampton College in June 1973. Continues to support herself through freelance journalism, publishing reviews and articles in *The New York Times*, *The New York Times Book Review*, *McCall's*, and *Esquire*.

1975   Fires James Oliver Brown as her literary agent and replaces him with Timothy Seldes of Russell & Volkening. Serves on jury that awards Pulitzer Prize for Fiction to Michael Shaara for *The Killer Angels*. Diagnosed with chronic obstructive pulmonary disease. Begins writing monthly book review column for *Esquire* in October (last review appears in October 1976).

1976   Suffers ischemic stroke on November 8, which causes severe aphasia and leaves her unable to write or speak intelligibly.

1977   Robert Lowell dies of heart attack on September 12. Stafford lessens her financial worries by selling her thirty acres of meadowland for $114,000 in December.

1978   "An Influx of Poets," story extracted by Giroux from the manuscript for "The Parliament of Women," published in *The New Yorker* on November 6. ("Woden's Day," another extract from "The Parliament of Women," is published posthumously in *Shenandoah* in Autumn 1979.) Makes new will that leaves most of her estate to Josephine Monsell, her longtime housekeeper in Springs.

1979   Admitted to New York Hospital February 20 with advanced pulmonary disease. Transferred on March 20 to Burke Rehabilitation Center in White Plains, New York, where she dies from cardiac arrest March 26. Her ashes are interred next to Liebling on April 10 after graveside service in the Green River Cemetery, East Hampton, New York.

Note on the Texts

This volume contains the thirty stories included in *The Collected Stories of Jean Stafford* (1969), along with sixteen other stories; *A Mother in History* (1966), Jean Stafford's journalistic profile of Marguerite Oswald; and three literary essays published from 1948 to 1952.

Jean Stafford signed a contract with Farrar, Straus and Giroux on June 27, 1968, for publication of a volume of collected stories, receiving a $2,500 advance. Stafford chose thirty stories for inclusion in the collection. All of them had previously been published in periodical form, and nineteen of the stories had also been included by Stafford in earlier collections of her short fiction. Nine of the stories were collected in *Children Are Bored on Sunday* (1953); five stories were collected in *Stories* (1956), an anthology of work by Stafford, John Cheever, Daniel Fuchs, and William Maxwell; and five stories were collected for the first time in *Bad Characters* (1964), a volume that also included three stories that had appeared in *Stories*. (*Selected Stories of Jean Stafford*, published in paperback by New American Library in 1966, collected sixteen stories that had previously appeared in both periodical and book form.) Stafford grouped the stories she had chosen for the new collection into four sections based on their geographic setting and wrote a short "Author's Note" that appeared as a preface. *The Collected Stories of Jean Stafford* was published in New York by Farrar, Straus and Giroux on February 17, 1969, and was awarded the Pulitzer Prize for Fiction. An English printing was published in London by Chatto & Windus in April 1970. Stafford is not known to have made any changes for the English publication. This volume prints the text of the 1969 Farrar, Straus and Giroux edition of *The Collected Stories of Jean Stafford*, but corrects six typesetting errors that appeared in that edition: at 147.5, 152.25, 155.11, 162.5, and 165.26, "Sewell" becomes "Sewall," and at 374.30, "Leahy" becomes "Lahey."

The list below provides periodical and first book publication for each of the stories, keyed to the following abbreviations:

CAB   *Children Are Bored on Sunday* (New York: Harcourt, Brace and Company, 1953)
ST   *Stories* by Jean Stafford, John Cheever, Daniel Fuchs, and William Maxwell (New York: Farrar, Straus & Cudahy, 1956)
BC   *Bad Characters* (New York: Farrar, Straus & Company, 1964)

Maggie Meriwether's Rich Experience. *The New Yorker*, June 25, 1955. ST.

The Children's Game. *Saturday Evening Post*, October 4, 1958 (as "The Reluctant Gambler").

The Echo and the Nemesis. *The New Yorker*, December 16, 1950 (as "The Nemesis"). CAB (as "The Echo and the Nemesis").

The Maiden. *The New Yorker*, July 29, 1950. CAB.

A Modest Proposal. *The New Yorker*, July 23, 1949 (as "Pax Vobiscum"). CAB (as "A Modest Proposal").

Caveat Emptor. *Mademoiselle*, May 1956 (as "The Matchmakers"). BC (as "Caveat Emptor").

Life Is No Abyss. *Sewanee Review*, July 1952.

The Hope Chest. *Harper's Magazine*, January 1947.

Polite Conversation. *The New Yorker*, August 20, 1949.

A Country Love Story. *The New Yorker*, May 6, 1950. CAB.

The Bleeding Heart. *Partisan Review*, September 1948. CAB.

The Lippia Lawn. *Kenyon Review*, Spring 1944 (signed "Phoebe Lowell").

The Interior Castle. *Partisan Review*, November–December 1946. CAB.

The Healthiest Girl in Town. *The New Yorker*, April 7, 1951.

The Tea Time of Stouthearted Ladies. *Kenyon Review*, Winter 1964.

The Mountain Day. *The New Yorker*, August 18, 1956.

The Darkening Moon. *Harper's Bazaar*, January 1944.

Bad Characters. *The New Yorker*, December 4, 1954. ST.

In the Zoo. *The New Yorker*, September 19, 1953. ST.

The Liberation. *The New Yorker*, May 30, 1953. ST.

A Reading Problem. *The New Yorker*, June 30, 1956. BC.

A Summer Day. *The New Yorker*, September 11, 1948. CAB.

The Philosophy Lesson. *The New Yorker*, November 16, 1968.

Children Are Bored on Sunday. *The New Yorker*, February 21, 1948. CAB.

Beatrice Trueblood's Story. *The New Yorker*, February 26, 1955. ST.

Between the Porch and the Altar. *Harper's Magazine*, June 1945. CAB.

I Love Someone. *Colorado Quarterly*, Summer 1952.

Cops and Robbers. *The New Yorker*, January 24, 1953 (as "The Shorn Lamb"). BC (as "Cops and Robbers").

The Captain's Gift. *Sewanee Review*, April 1946 (as "The Present"). BC (as "The Captain's Gift").

The End of a Career. *The New Yorker*, January 21, 1956. BC.

The section of this volume titled "Other Stories" presents fourteen stories that were not included in *The Collected Stories of Jean Stafford*, plus two stories that were published after 1969. Thirteen of the stories appeared in periodical form from 1939 to 1964, while "A Winter's

Tale" was first published in *New Short Novels* (1954), an anthology edited by Mary Louise Aswell that included work by Stafford, Shelby Foote, Elizabeth Etnier, and Clyde Miller. Three of the stories were also collected by Stafford in book form; one story appeared in *Children Are Bored on Sunday* (1953) and two stories were included in *Bad Characters* (1964).

Stafford signed a contract with Farrar, Straus and Giroux in 1968 for "The Parliament of Women," a novel she had already been working on for several years. The novel was still unfinished when Stafford suffered an ischemic stroke in 1976 that caused severe aphasia and left her unable to write. After reading the manuscript of "The Parliament of Women," her longtime editor Robert Giroux extracted two sections that he believed "could, with minor emendations, stand alone as stories." Despite her aphasia, Giroux wrote, "Jean was able to go over both stories with me in the summer of 1978" and agreed to their publication. "An Influx of Poets" was published in *The New Yorker* in the fall of 1978, and "Woden's Day" appeared posthumously in *Shenandoah* in the fall of 1979.

The list below provides the sources for the texts presented in the "Other Stories" section of this volume, keyed to the same abbreviations used above:

And Lots of Solid Color. *American Prefaces*, November 1939.

A Reunion. *Partisan Review*, Fall 1944.

The Home Front. CAB. First published in *Partisan Review*, Spring 1945.

A Slight Maneuver. *Mademoiselle*, February 1947.

The Cavalier. *The New Yorker*, February 12, 1949.

Old Flaming Youth. *Harper's Bazaar*, December 1950.

The Violet Rock. *The New Yorker*, April 26, 1952.

The Connoisseurs. *Harper's Bazaar*, October 1952.

A Winter's Tale. BC. First published in *New Short Novels*, ed. Mary Louise Aswell (New York: Ballantine Books, 1954).

The Warlock. *The New Yorker*, December 24, 1955.

My Blithe, Sad Bird. *The New Yorker*, April 6, 1957.

A Reasonable Facsimile. BC. First published in *The New Yorker*, August 3, 1957.

The Scarlet Letter. *Mademoiselle*, July 1959.

The Ordeal of Conrad Pardee. *Ladies' Home Journal*, July 1964.

An Influx of Poets. *The New Yorker*, November 6, 1978.

Woden's Day. *Shenandoah*, vol. XXX, no. 3 (1979).

Six typesetting errors that appeared in the source texts used in the "Other Stories" section have been corrected in this volume: at 468.38

and 469.4, "*Badmeister*" becomes "*Bademeister*," and at 574.5, 574.6, 575.5, and 576.14, "Schnaaps" becomes "Schnapps."

In March 1965 Barbara Lawrence, an editor at *McCall's*, offered Stafford $2,500 to write a profile of Marguerite Oswald, mother of Lee Harvey Oswald, the accused assassin of President John F. Kennedy. Stafford accepted her offer, and traveled to Fort Worth, Texas, in May to interview Oswald. "The Strange World of Marguerite Oswald" appeared in the October 1965 number of *McCall's* and attracted considerable public attention, leading to an agreement between Stafford and Farrar, Straus and Giroux for the publication of an expanded version of the article. *A Mother in History* was published in New York by Farrar, Straus and Giroux on February 25, 1966, and sold 10,000 copies in three months. Stafford is not known to have made any changes in the English edition that was published in London by Chatto & Windus in September 1966. This volume prints the text of the 1966 Farrar, Straus and Giroux edition of *A Mother in History*, but corrects a typesetting error in that edition: at 784.7, "let you give me" becomes "let me give you."

The section of this volume titled "Selected Essays" presents three essays published by Stafford from 1948 to 1952. "The Psychological Novel" was delivered as a paper at a conference on the novel held at Bard College on November 7–8, 1947, and published in the Spring 1948 number of *Kenyon Review*. This volume prints the text that appeared in *Kenyon Review*, but corrects a typesetting error. At 815.12–13, "be nothing more for me to say and in my traumatic embarrassment," was printed twice on two repeated lines. This volume omits the repetition and prints a bracketed two-em space, i.e., [   ] at 815.12 to indicate where several words were apparently omitted from the *Kenyon Review* text as a result of the error. "Truth and the Novelist" was based on "Observations on the Uses of Autobiography in Fiction," a lecture delivered at Wellesley College on April 17, 1950. It appeared in the August 1951 number of *Harper's Bazaar*, and the text printed here is taken from *Harper's Bazaar*. "An Etiquette for Writers" was delivered as a lecture on July 22, 1952, at the Writers' Conference in the Rocky Mountains, an annual event held at the University of Colorado, Boulder, Stafford's alma mater. It was issued as a typescript by the University of Colorado in 1952. The text printed in this volume is taken from a photocopy of the typescript in the Beinecke Rare Book and Manuscript Library, of the Yale University Library, Za St13 +952E.

This volume presents the texts of the original printings chosen for inclusion here, but it does not attempt to reproduce nontextual features of their typographic design. The texts are presented without change, except for the correction of typographical errors. Spelling, punctuation, and capitalization are often expressive features and are not altered, even when inconsistent or irregular. The following is a list of typographical errors corrected, cited by page and line number: 11.15, Weriwether; 67.8, gunwhales; 104.18, freize; 110.8, rambuctious; 198.34, wand.; 219.1, Renaisrance; 274.17, Schmalz,; 303.10, Poly; 304.17, as it; 330.13–17, 126 Belleview; 335.11, mover; 343.34, ask; 387.5, hygenic; 388.5, entrace; 449.13, dessicated; 451.22, houshold; 452.5, live Berlin; 464.29, Bunner; 486,12, Late,; 517.17, saxaphone; 563.11, acceped; 563.2, Konditoreien; 564.32, Peris; 565.34, skiied;; 585.12, hands,; 588.25, off); 613.16, Kimball was; 725.28–29, Sheepscott; 732.34, Year's; 746.29, and this; 747.2, inadmissable; 756.22, asked.; 782.19, become; 782.27, became; 788.22, had had; 795.13, as a good; 797.24, intertested; 798.25, staple; 802.37, philodrendron; 805.20, Start; 829.1, nack.; 839.18, intriques,; 840.18, gratitudes satisfaction; 841.12, abruply; 842.1, perigrinate; 842.21, arithemetical; 842.40, adjuged; 843.33, pox"; 844.14, Scandanavian; 844.35, intelligensia; 845.8, *The*; 845.11, werever; 845.20, Stendahl,; 845.22, Nietzche; 845.35, Walden; 845.35, Culture and Anarchy,; 845.35–36, The Theory of the Leisure Class; 845.36, Autobiography; 846.11, intelligensia; 846.11–12, Colorado occasionally; 846.22, derangments; 847.31, 63 used; 847.40, Windor; 848.14, flesh-and-blood-; 849.38, exigesis; 850.23, Town and Country; 850.24, Winsor; 850.40, narcissustic; 851.6, compostion; 851.31, collection; 853.34, mouth that; 854.4, thirty five.

Notes

In the notes below, the reference numbers denote page and line of this volume (the line count includes headings). No note is made for material included in the eleventh edition of *Merriam-Webster's Collegiate Dictionary*. Biblical quotations are keyed to the King James Version. Quotations from Shakespeare are keyed to *The Riverside Shakespeare*, ed. G. Blakemore Evans (Boston: Houghton Mifflin, 1974). For further biographical background and references to other studies see David Roberts, *Jean Stafford: A Biography* (Boston: Little, Brown, 1988); Charlotte Margolis Goodman, *Jean Stafford: The Savage Heart* (Austin: University of Texas Press, 1990); and Ann Hulbert, *The Interior Castle: The Art and Life of Jean Stafford* (New York: Alfred A. Knopf, 1992).

THE COLLECTED STORIES OF JEAN STAFFORD

2.1   *For Katharine S. White*] White (1892–1977) was Jean Stafford's fiction editor at *The New Yorker* from 1948 to 1958.

3.2–5   my father . . . *When Cattle Kingdom Fell*] Novel (1910) by John Richard Stafford (1874–1966). See Chronology in this volume.

3.8–9   Margaret Lynn . . . *A Stepdaughter of the Prairie*] Lynn (1869–1958), a professor of English at the University of Kansas, published her memoir in 1914.

3.11–12   cacoëthes scribendi] Latin phrase for an incurable compulsion to write.

5.1   THE INNOCENTS ABROAD] Travel book (1869) by Mark Twain (Samuel Clemens, 1835–1910), recounting his trip to Europe and the Holy Land in 1867.

7.30   Koh-i-noor] "Mountain of light," the Persian name for a 191-carat diamond acquired by the British East India Company when it annexed Punjab in 1849. The diamond was presented to Queen Victoria, recut to 105.6 carats, and is now part of the Crown Jewels.

8.6   *fête champêtre*] Outdoor festival, garden party.

8.8   Longchamp] Racecourse in the Bois de Boulogne in Paris.

8.20   Sweet Briar] Private women's college in Sweet Briar, Virginia, founded in 1901.

8.32   Orient Express] Passenger train service that operated between Paris and Istanbul from 1889 to 1977, with interruptions during the two world wars.

9.8   Eton] An elite boarding school for boys, founded in 1440 near Windsor, England.

9.9–10   Maxim's . . . Le Grand Seigneur] Fashionable Parisian restaurants.

10.5   tweeny] A "between maid," i.e., a maidservant who works under the direction of other domestic staff.

11.32   *tilleul*] Herbal tea made from the flowers of a lime or linden tree.

14.18   Herdwick] A breed of domestic sheep.

16.12   *cinq heures*] Five o'clock in the afternoon.

17.3   medical school of Vanderbilt University] The university is located in Nashville, Tennessee.

17.28   Harrow] An elite boarding school for boys, founded in 1572 in what is now a borough in northwest London.

19.40   Marshall Plan] The European Recovery Program, established in 1948 and known as the Marshall Plan after George C. Marshall (1880–1959), U.S. secretary of state, 1947–49.

20.6   the Duchess of Kent] Princess Marina, Duchess of Kent (1906–1968), widow of Prince George, Duke of Kent (1902–1942), younger brother of Edward VIII and George VI and an uncle of Elizabeth II.

20.39   *pneumatique*] A letter delivered via the network of pneumatic tubes used by the Parisian postal system from 1866 to 1984.

21.6   Tidewater] The coastal region of Virginia.

22.31–33   *"Messieurs . . . va plus,"*] "Gentlemen, ladies, place your bets!; Nothing goes, i.e., no more bets."

23.26   Knokke-le-Zoute] A coastal resort in northeast Belgium located between Zeebrugge and the Dutch border.

25.34   Canfield] Solitaire card game.

26.14–15   La Scala] Opera house in Milan, Italy.

26.35   Albany] A mansion off Piccadilly, London, built in 1771–76, that was divided into a series of separate apartments in 1803. Its residents have included numerous writers, artists, performers, politicians, and society figures.

26.39   Kerry blues] A blue terrier breed developed in County Kerry, Ireland.

28.2   Romney] George Romney (1734–1802), fashionable English portrait painter.

29.7   *digue*] Dike.

31.15   *plage*] Beach.

31.37   teratoid] Malformed, monstrous.

32.12   Happy Hooligan's hat] An unlucky but good-natured hobo, Happy

Hooligan was the main character in a newspaper comic strip (1900–32) written and drawn by Frederick Burr Opper (1857–1937).

34.31 *râteau*] Rake.

34.35 played *en plein*] Placed a bet on a single number.

36.13–14 in alien corn] Cf. John Keats (1795–1821), "Ode to a Nightingale" (1819): "Through the sad heart of Ruth, when, sick for home, / She stood in tears amid the alien corn."

37.33 Layamon's *Brut*] A Middle English poem chronicling the history of Britain, composed early in the thirteenth century by a priest in the Midlands. Half of the poem's 16,000 lines are devoted to legends of King Arthur.

38.12 *Wilhelm Tell*] *Guillaume Tell* (1829), opera with music by Gioachino Rossini (1792–1868) and a libretto by Étienne de Jouy (1764–1846) and Hippolyte Louis Florent Bis (1789–1855), based on the play (1804) by Friedrich Schiller (1759–1805) about the legendary fighter for Swiss independence.

38.29 *Friseur*] Hairstylist.

39.24 *Speculum*] An American quarterly journal of medieval studies, founded in 1926.

40.6 "Minuet in G"] Probably a reference to the Minuet in G Major by the German composer Christian Petzold (1677–1733), a work that was attributed to Johann Sebastian Bach (1685–1750) until the 1970s.

40.14 Brown Shirts] Members of the *Sturmabteilung* (Storm Division), the paramilitary arm of the Nazi Party.

41.19 San Bernardino] A mountain resort in southern Switzerland.

46.40 Walther von der Vogelweide's] Vogelweide was a German lyric poet (c.1170– c. 1230).

47.11–12 *villeggiatura*] A holiday in the country.

50.2 *Bierstuben*] Taverns.

57.31 Theater] U.S. Forces, European Theater, official designation of the American forces serving in Europe, 1945–47.

59.22 *Karaffen*] Carafes, decanters.

61.21 Philosophenweg,] Philosopher's Walk, a footpath in Heidelberg overlooking the Neckar.

62.26 *Salome*] Opera (1905) by Richard Strauss (1864–1949) that used as its libretto the translation by Hedwig Lachmann (1865–1918) of the play (1893) by Oscar Wilde (1854–1900).

65.16 *Totentanz*] Dance of the dead.

70.20–21   island of Jost Van Dykes] One of the British Virgin Islands.

76.1   *Caveat Emptor*] Let the buyer beware.

79.17   *Finnegans Wake*] Novel (1939) by James Joyce (1882–1941).

79.19   Edward Bok, whose *Americanization of*] *The Americanization of Edward Bok* (1920), an autobiography by the Dutch-American magazine editor and social reformer Edward Bok (1863–1930).

80.16   *Lohengrin*] Opera (1850) composed and written by Richard Wagner (1813–1883).

81.19–20   Dauphin . . . son of Louis XVI] The younger son of Louis XVI and Marie Antoinette, Louis Charles (1785–1795) became the Dauphin (heir apparent) of France on the death of his brother in 1789. He was proclaimed Louis XVII by French monarchists after the execution of his father in 1793, but was never crowned and died in prison. It was rumored that he had escaped from captivity, and dozens of pretenders claiming to be "the lost Dauphin" came forward during the nineteenth century.

82.24   Kodachrome] A brand of color still film manufactured by Kodak from 1935 to 2009.

82.27–28   Barney Google] Character in syndicated comic strip *Take Barney Google, F'rinstance*, created in 1919 by Billy DeBeck (1890–1942) and later renamed *Barney Google and Snuffy Smith*. The strip was continued after DeBeck's death by Fred Lasswell (1916–2001).

82.39   Benares vase] A brass vase made in Benares (Varanasi) in northern India.

83.26   Whitehead-Russell *Principia Mathematica*] Three-volume work (1910–13) on mathematical logic by Alfred North Whitehead (1891–1947) and Bertrand Russell (1872–1970).

84.22   *"Quel tapage."*] "What a fuss."

87.5   Mr. Toad] Eccentric character in *The Wind in the Willows* (1908), a novel for children by Kenneth Grahame (1859–1932).

88.33–34   Fuller Brush man] A door-to-door salesman for the Fuller Brush Company.

89.17–18   *"Allons donc! Quelle sottise!"*] "Come now! What foolishness!"

89.29   the Dauphin] See note 81.19–20.

90.12   *'Je ne sais pas.'*] 'I don't know.'

93.1–3   THE BOSTONIANS . . . THE AMERICAN SCENE] *The Bostonians* (1886), novel by Henry James (1843–1916); *The American Scene* (1907), travel book by James.

96.27   Mount Auburn Cemetery] A cemetery in Cambridge, Massachusetts, founded in 1831.

97.10   Patriots' Day] A Massachusetts holiday commemorating the Revolutionary War battles of Lexington and Concord. It was observed on April 19 from 1894, when the holiday was established, until 1969, when the date was changed to the third Monday in April.

97.39   Fala's neck] Fala (1940–1952), a Scottish terrier, was President Franklin D. Roosevelt's dog.

98.1   Jamaica Pond] A pond in the Jamaica Plain neighborhood of Boston.

102.15   *McCall's*] A monthly women's magazine published from 1897 to 2002.

104.33   "Hold 'em Hootie."] Instrumental recording released in 1941 by Kansas City jazz pianist and bandleader Jay McShann (1916–2006).

105.18   'Bluebird of Happiness'] Song (1934) with music by Sandor Harmati (1892–1936) and lyrics by Edward Heyman (1907–1981) and Harry Parr-Davies (1914–1955).

114.29   *Bowdoin College*] A liberal arts college for men in Brunswick, Maine. (The college became coeducational in 1971.)

114.32–33   *Mrs. Gaskell . . .* Cranford] Novel (1853) by Elizabeth Gaskell (1810–1865).

118.13   *Trianon*] The Grand and the Petit Trianon are palaces in the gardens of the main Palace of Versailles.

120.22   the "Jupiter"] Mozart's Symphony no. 41 in C Major (K. 551) became known as the "Jupiter symphony" early in the nineteenth century.

121.26   Moxie] A carbonated soft drink.

123.15   a Vic] An RCA Victrola record player, also used as a general term for a phonograph.

126.26–27   Saint-Simon . . . Dictionary] Louis de Rouvroy, Duc de Saint-Simon (1675–1755), French statesman whose memoirs of the court of Versailles were first published posthumously in 1829–30. *A New English Dictionary*, published by Oxford University Press from 1888 to 1928, was reissued as the *Oxford English Dictionary* in 1933.

127.19   *A Tree Grows in Brooklyn*] Novel (1943) by Betty Smith (1896–1972), made into a film in 1945.

127.34–35   'Town Meeting of the Air'] *America's Town Meeting of the Air* was a popular public affairs radio program that was broadcast on the NBC Blue network, 1935–43, and on ABC Radio, 1943–56.

128.14   'Quiz Kids'] Radio quiz show featuring child contestants that was broadcast on NBC from 1940 to 1953.

132.8   Castine] A town on Penobscot Bay in eastern Maine.

137.14–15   Henry Ford's Wayside Inn] Located in Sudbury, Massachusetts, the inn opened in 1716 as Howe's Tavern. It was made famous by Henry Wadsworth Longfellow in his verse collection *Tales of a Wayside Inn* (1863). Henry Ford purchased the inn and the surrounding land in 1923 and partially developed the site as a historical village before selling the property in 1945.

146.31   Radcliffe] Harvard undergraduate college for women, founded in 1879 as the Harvard Annex and chartered as Radcliffe College in 1894.

146.36   Canfield] See note 25.34.

147.5   Samuel Sewall] Massachusetts jurist and diarist (1662–1730) who was one of the judges in the Salem witch trials.

147.20–21   Pavlov's submissive dog] Ivan Pavlov (1849–1936), Russian physiologist whose research included experiments in creating a conditioned response in dogs.

148.20–21   This inn . . . Henry Ford on it] See note 137.14–15.

148.25   King Philip] English name of Metacom (1638–1676), a Wampanoag sachem whose resistance to colonial encroachments on Native lands and sovereignty led in the summer of 1675 to the outbreak of the conflict in New England known as King Philip's War. The fighting ended in Massachusetts soon after colonial forces killed Metacom in August 1676, while continuing in present-day Maine until 1678.

150.23   Currier and Ives prints] Nathaniel Currier (1813–1888) established a lithographic printmaking firm in New York City in 1835 and formed a partnership with James Merritt Ives (1824–1895) in 1857.

154.4–5   "Juanita" and "Valencia"] "Juanita," a love ballad (1853) with lyrics by the English writer and social reformer Caroline Norton (1808–1877) and music arranged by T. G. May; "Valencia" (1924), song by Spanish composer José Padilla (1889–1960).

154.8   *Sweetheart Stories*] Pulp romance magazine published from 1925 to 1943.

154.21–22   *Self Reliance*] "Self-Reliance," essay by Ralph Waldo Emerson (1803–1882) initially published in *Essays: First Series* (1841).

155.6–7   shooting Cowboy at the pool hall] Cowboy is a pool game derived from English billiards that uses four balls and is played to 101 points.

156.5   "We Three Kings"] Christmas carol composed in 1857 by John Henry Hopkins, Jr. (1820–1891) and first published in 1863.

156.18   tuberculosis seal] A charitable holiday seal sold to raise funds for the treatment of tuberculosis. They were first introduced in the United States in 1907.

158.24 Neccos] Candy wafers sold by the New England Confectionary Company.

164.5 Patriots' Day] See note 97.10.

166.31 Rosie O'Grady] "Sweet Rosie O'Grady," song (1896) with music and lyrics by vaudeville singer and composer Maude Nugent (c. 1874–1958).

170.6 Schmierkäse] Cheese spread.

171.22 *tilleul*] See note 11.32.

179.14–15 at Saranac reading *Lalla Rookh*] Saranac Lake, New York, a resort area in the Adirondacks where numerous sanatoriums and "cure cottages" for tuberculosis patients seeking rest and fresh air were established in the late nineteenth and early twentieth centuries. *Lalla Rookh, an Oriental romance* (1817), narrative poem by Irish poet, journalist, and composer Thomas Moore (1779–1852).

180.12 Katherine Mansfield] Pen name of the New Zealand–born English writer Katherine Mansfield Beauchamp Murry (1888–1923), whose works include the story "The Garden Party" (1922).

186.27 Jacob's ladder] See Genesis 28:12.

191.2 MAGIC MOUNTAINS] *The Magic Mountain* (1925), novel by Thomas Mann (1875–1955) set in a Swiss sanatorium for tuberculosis patients.

193.28 pom-pom-pulla-way] A tag game.

194.30 cowboy pool] See note 155.6–7.

196.23 Russian bank] A card game for two players derived from solitaire.

196.40–197.1 advanced degree from Radcliffe] Radcliffe (see note 146.31) began awarding advanced degrees in 1894 to women taking graduate courses of study at Harvard. The practice continued until 1962, when women were permitted to formally enroll in the Harvard Graduate School of Arts and Sciences.

198.7–8 crack-the-whip] Children's game where the players hold hands and are pulled by their leader until the line breaks.

199.10 Hitchcock] Connecticut furniture manufacturer Lambert Hitchcock (1795–1852).

199.34 Victrola] See note 123.15.

200.4 *Rebecca of Sunnybrook Farm*] American children's novel (1903) by Kate Douglas Wiggin (1856–1923).

200.27 *Scholastic* magazine] Billed as "The National High School Bi-Weekly," the magazine debuted in 1922.

200.30 Governor Bradford] William Bradford (1590–1657), a passenger on the *Mayflower*, served as governor of Plymouth colony, 1621–33, 1635–36, 1637–38, 1639–44, and 1645–57. His history of the colony, *Of Plimoth Plantation*, written between 1630 and 1651, was first published in 1856.

200.39–201.1 Professor Kittredge] George Lyman Kittredge (1860–1941) taught English literature at Harvard University from 1888 to 1936.

201.18 Huntley & Palmers] Firm of British biscuit makers founded in Reading in 1822 by Joseph Huntley (1775–1857). In 1841 George Palmer (1818–1897) became a partner in the firm and guided its expansion into a global business famous for packaging its products in elaborately decorated tins.

201.19 S. S. Pierce] Boston grocery firm founded by Samuel Stillman Pierce (1807–1881) in 1831.

202.31 *Diagnostics of Internal Medicine*] Medical treatise (1901) by Glentworth Reeve Butler (1855–1926), a physician at Methodist Episcopal Hospital in Brooklyn, New York.

203.16 Unguentine] A topical antiseptic ointment introduced in 1893.

204.2 *tour jeté*] Turning leap in ballet.

204.32 the movie Ben Hur] *Ben-Hur: A Tale of the Christ* (1925), silent film directed by Fred Niblo (1874–1948) and starring Ramon Navarro (1899–1968), adapted from the novel (1880) by Lew Wallace (1827–1905).

206.16–17 Glenwood range] A line of kitchen ranges manufactured by the Weir Stove Company in Taunton, Massachusetts.

207.20 interurban] An electric railway linking cities or towns.

208.6 'The Cameo Girl.'] Musical (1921) with book by Myrta Bel Gallier and Neil Twomey, lyrics by Grant Clarke (1891–1931) and Ballard Macdonald (1882–1935), and music by Gallier and James V. Monaco (1885–1945).

213.9 Victrola] See note 123.15.

215.16 Hoosier cabinet] A freestanding kitchen cabinet with a countertop workspace.

216.27 got a con] A conditional failing grade that allows a student to retake the final examination.

217.5 Studebaker] Automobile company based in South Bend, Indiana, that manufactured gasoline-powered cars from 1904 to 1966.

218.29 ATOs] Alpha Tau Omegas.

219.2–4 Donne . . . *Divine Poems*] Series of nineteen devotional sonnets by John Donne (1572–1631) published posthumously in 1633.

219.10 "I Wonder Who's Kissing Her Now,"] Song (1909) with music by

Harold Orlob (1883–1982) and lyrics by Will M. Hough (1883–1963) and Frank R. Adams (1882–1962).

220.25   pukka sahib] Hindi term for "excellent fellow," often used to address British colonial officials in India.

221.9   trade rats] Pack rats.

222.2   *De Amicitia*] Treatise on friendship by Marcus Tullius Cicero (106–43 B.C.E.), written in 44 B.C.E.

223.14–15   three point two] Beer containing 3.2 percent alcohol by weight. Under the liquor code adopted in Colorado after the end of Prohibition, 3.2 percent beer was available for purchase in "dry" jurisdictions that prohibited the sale of stronger alcoholic beverages, and could be legally bought by persons from the age of eighteen to twenty-one.

223.27   Sen-Sen] A brand of licorice-flavored breath freshener.

224.24–25   *The Well-Tempered Clavichord*] *The Well-Tempered Clavier*, collection (book I, 1722; book II, 1742) of keyboard preludes and fugues by Johann Sebastian Bach (1685–1750).

224.25–26   "The Object of My Affection"] Song (1934) written by Truman Virgil "Pinky" Tomlin (1907–1987).

224.28   "The Stein Song."] The University of Maine school song, also known as the "Maine Stein Song," with music (1901) by E. A. Fenstad and lyrics (1902) by Lincoln Colcord (1883–1947). It was first published in 1910 and made popular in 1930 by the singer Rudy Vallee (1901–1986).

226.13   Bryn Mawr] Liberal arts college for women in Bryn Mawr, Pennsylvania, founded in 1885.

226.33–34   opening night at Central City] The Colorado town is home to a summer opera festival founded in 1932.

227.9   Kadota figs] A variety of green fig.

229.30–31   *War and Peace*] Novel (1865–69) by Leo Tolstoy (1828–1910).

233.26–27   striped apache jersey] A horizontally striped jersey, after the style associated with *les Apaches*, a street gang subculture that flourished in Paris in the early 1900s.

235.16   Vassar] A liberal arts college for women (now coeducational) in Poughkeepsie, New York, founded in 1861.

240.21   Bach's "Sheep May Safely Graze."] "Schafe können sicher weiden," soprano aria from the cantata (1713) *Was mir behagt, ist nur die muntre Jagd* (The lively hunt is all my heart's desire), BWV 208, with a libretto by Salomon Franck (1659–1725).

248.20–21 San Quentin bacon] Meat from poached game, after the state prison in California.

252.24–25 Coleman lamps] Kerosene lamps that provide unusually bright light.

253.25 kalsomine] Calcimine, a white or pale wash used on walls.

256.1 *Bad Characters*] In the "Author's Note" to her collection of stories *Bad Characters* (1964), Stafford wrote:

I do not look on all the characters in these stories as bad; some of them do have wicked hearts, but as many of them are victims. Emily Vanderpool, who narrates the title story and who acknowledges that she has a bad character, is someone I knew well as a child; indeed, I often occupied her skin and, looking back, I think that while she was notional and stubborn and a trial to her kin, her talent for iniquity was feeble—she wanted to be a road-agent but she hadn't a chance. Her troubles stemmed from the low company she kept, but she did not seek these parties out: they found her. It is a widespread human experience. The strenuous young man in "A Reasonable Facsimile" is not bad, he is merely poisonous and the sociologist in "Caveat Emptor" is, by reason of his calling, awful and to be avoided at all cost but he isn't bad. The personification of rectitude, Judge Bay, who appears in several of the stories, and Landlady Placer in "In the Zoo" go on my black list which is headed by the name of Frau Professor Galt in the short novel, "A Winter's Tale."

(For "A Reasonable Facsimile," see pp. 643–64 in this volume; "Caveat Emptor," pp. 76–92; "In the Zoo," pp. 276–96; "A Winter's Tale," pp. 560–96.)

256.8 Tenderfoot Scout] The second rank achieved in the Boy Scouts.

256.12 Russian bank] See note 196.23.

257.24 Canon City] The Colorado Territorial Penitentiary was built in Cañon City in 1871. It became the state penitentiary in 1876 and housed a small number of female inmates until 1935.

258.39 Andy-I-Over] Tag game using a ball; also called Annie-Annie Over and Ante Over.

259.27–28 "The Blue Danube."] Waltz (1866) by the younger Johann Strauss (1825–1899).

259.35 jackstones] Stones or other objects used to play jacks.

260.3 Frisco] St. Louis–San Francisco Railway, a railroad company that did not operate farther west than Texas, Oklahoma, and Colorado.

262.11 "Ish ka bibble!] Slang for "I should care!"

263.32 *weltschmerzlich*] Adjective form for *weltschmerz*.

265.31 *Black Beauty*] Children's novel (1877) by Anna Sewell (1820–1878) about the life of a horse in nineteenth-century England.

266.38–39 Eastern Star] Masonic organization open to both women and men.

268.26 Piggly Wiggly] A grocery store chain founded in 1916.

268.36 Katzenjammer Kids] Popular comic strip created by Rudolph Dirks (1877–1968) in 1897 that was drawn by Harold Knerr (1882–1949) from 1914 to 1949.

270.19–20 Kresge's and Woolworth's] Chain of discount stores founded in 1899 by S. S. Kresge (1867–1966); discount store chain founded in 1879 by Frank W. Woolworth (1852–1919).

271.5 Garden of the Gods] Public park in Colorado Springs famous for its red sandstone formations.

271.19–20 Woolworth's golden-and-vermilion bedlam.] Woolworth's store signs used gold lettering on a vermilion background.

272.5–6 Miss Fagin] Fagin is a thief and fence who teaches children to steal in *Oliver Twist* (1838) by Charles Dickens (1812–1870).

274.17 Emmy Schmalz] The landlady in *Moon Mullins*, a comic strip created by Frank Willard (1893–1958) in 1923.

277.31 Burlington] The Chicago, Burlington and Quincy Railroad.

281.29 black Irish] An American term for people of Irish origin with black hair and dark eyes, sometimes used to refer disparagingly to lower-class Irish-Americans.

283.38 Fuller Brush men] See note 88.33–34.

285.37 the Sorosis] An independent women's club with local chapters across the United States, founded in New York City in 1868 by the journalist Jane Cunningham Croly (1829–1901).

298.8 *Immensee*] Novella (1851) by Theodor Woldsen Storm (1817–1888).

299.12 *The Heart of Midlothian*] Historical novel (1818) by Walter Scott (1771–1832).

315.13–14 Paul Pry] A meddling busybody, after the main character in the English comedy *Paul Pry* (1825) by John Poole (1786–1872).

317.9 Mountain Jim Nugent] James Nugent, known as "Rocky Mountain Jim," was a mountain guide who settled at Muggins Gulch near Estes Park, Colorado, around 1868. He lost an eye in a grizzly bear attack in 1869 and was fatally shot by persons unknown in 1874.

317.12 *Hans Brinker*] *Hans Brinker; or, The Silver Skates* (1865), children's novel by Mary Mapes Dodge (1831–1905).

318.32   Sax Rohmer] Pseudonym of English novelist Arthur Sarsfield Ward (1883–1959), a prolific writer of horror and crime stories best known as the creator of the criminal mastermind Dr. Fu Manchu.

319.11–12   *Rebecca of Sunnybrook Farm*] See note 200.4.

319.12   *Misunderstood Betsy*] Possibly a reference to *Understood Betsy* (1917), children's novel by Dorothy Canfield Fisher (1879–1958).

319.25   *Tom Sawyer Abroad*] Novel (1894) by Mark Twain (Samuel Clemens, 1835–1910).

319.39–40   Volstead Act] Common name for the National Prohibition Act, after its sponsor, Minnesota Republican congressman Andrew J. Volstead (1860–1947). Passed over President Wilson's veto on October 28, 1919, the act enforced the Eighteenth Amendment by making illegal the manufacture, transport, and sale (but not the possession) of intoxicating liquor.

320.39   Model T] Automobile mass-produced by the Ford Motor Company, 1908–27.

321.39   'A little child shall lead them,'] Isaiah 11:6.

322.22   A.E.F.] American Expeditionary Forces, the U.S. Army in Europe in World War I.

324.18   Wonder State] The official state nickname of Arkansas, 1923–53.

324.23–24   Mrs. O'Leary's cow] The fire that devastated Chicago on October 8, 1871, began in the West Side barn of Patrick and Catherine O'Leary, allegedly when their cow kicked over a lantern.

325.13   "Holy, Holy, Holy."] Hymn (1826) by the Anglican cleric Reginald Heber (1783–1826) that was set to music in 1861 by John Bacchus Dykes (1823–1876).

334.10   cast my bread upon the waters] Cf. Ecclesiastes 11:1.

335.23   Butterick patterns] Sewing patterns sold by the company founded in 1867 by Ebenezer Butterick (1826–1903).

339.15–16   Volstead Act] See note 319.39–40.

340.28   INDIAN SERVICE] Name commonly used for the Office of Indian Affairs, established within the War Department in 1824 and transferred to the Department of the Interior in 1849. The agency was renamed the Bureau of Indian Affairs in 1947.

345.4–5   "The Battle Hymn of the Republic"] Song (1862) with words by Julia Ward Howe (1819–1910), written to the music of the soldiers' song "John Brown's Body," based on the folk hymn "Say, brothers, will you meet us?"

345.34   Honest Harold] Harold L. Ickes (1874–1952) served as secretary of the interior, 1933–46.

346.23 Eversharp] Brand name of a mechanical pencil patented in 1913 by Charles Rood Keeran (1883–1948).

348.10 Clyde Barrow's] Barrow (1909–1934) led an armed robbery gang that included his partner Bonnie Parker (1910–1934) on a crime spree in the Southwest and Midwest from 1932 to 1934. The gang murdered nine law officers and four civilians before Barrow and Parker were killed in a police ambush in Bienville Parish, Louisiana.

350.20 Kayo] The younger brother of Moon Mullins in the eponymous comic strip; see note 274.17.

352.11 Clara Bow] Bow (1905–1965) was an American silent film star, known as the "It" Girl after her starring role in It (1927).

354.19 jackstones] See note 259.35.

354.22 22] A rifle firing .22-caliber ammunition.

356.7 *The Ode on Intimations of Immortality*] "Ode: Intimations of Immortality from Recollections of Early Childhood" (written 1802–4, published 1807) by William Wordsworth (1770–1850).

356.18 *Framley Parsonage*] Novel (1861) by Anthony Trollope (1815–1882), part of the Chronicles of Barsetshire series.

357.13–14 Cord town car] A luxury automobile manufactured by the Auburn Automotive Company, 1929–32 and 1936–37.

358.15 SAE] Sigma Alpha Epsilon, a college fraternity.

363.1 *Children Are Bored on Sunday*] Stafford included this note in her story collection *Children Are Bored on Sunday* (1953): "The title of this book is borrowed, with many thanks, from the title of the song '*Les enfants s'ennuient le dimanche*' by Mr. Charles Trenet." Trenet (1913–2001) wrote and recorded the song in 1939.

363.4 "The Three Miracles of Zenobius,"] Painting by Sandro Botticelli (1445–1510) in the Metropolitan Museum of Art in New York City.

364.22 Wallace] Henry A. Wallace (1888–1965) was secretary of agriculture, 1933–40, vice president of the United States, 1941–45, secretary of commerce, 1945–46, and a left-wing third-party candidate for president in 1948.

364.23 Monsignor Sheen] Fulton J. Sheen (1895–1979) taught theology and philosophy at Catholic University, 1926–50, and was the host of *The Catholic Hour* radio program, 1930–52. Sheen later served as auxiliary bishop of New York, 1951–66, and as bishop of Rochester, 1966–69, and was the host of several television programs, including *Life Is Worth Living*, 1952–57.

365.4 Jamesian] Referring to the literary style of Henry James.

365.7 'tis a pity she's a whore] Cf. *'Tis Pity She's a Whore* (1633), tragedy by John Ford (1586–c. 1639).

368.15–16 Crivelli Madonna] Painting of Madonna and Child (c. 1480) by Italian painter Carlo Crivelli (c. 1430–1495) in the Metropolitan Museum of Art.

368.17–19 Goya's little red boy . . . plump cat] Portrait of Manuel Osorio Manrique de Zúñiga by Francisco Goya (1746–1828) in the Metropolitan Museum of Art. In the painting the boy's pet bird is being watched by three cats.

368.21 bounty jumper] Civil War term for a person who volunteers for military service, collects an enlistment bounty, and then deserts.

368.38–369.1 Ezra Pound . . . "Cantos."] *The Cantos*, long poem by Ezra Pound (1885–1972) published in parts from 1917 to 1962.

369.22–23 Rembrandt's . . . "The Noble Slav"] *Man in an Oriental Costume*, also known as *Man in a Turban*, painting (1632) by Rembrandt van Rijn (1606–1669).

369.34 the Sun] *The Sun*, daily newspaper published in New York City from 1833 to 1950, when it merged with the *New York World-Telegram*.

370.35 two Holbeins] Portraits by German painter Hans Holbein the Younger (c. 1497–1543).

371.32 Van Eyck diptych] *The Crucifixion; The Last Judgment* by Jan van Eyck (c. 1390–1441).

371.35–36 Jo Davidson's . . . Jules Bache] Painted terra-cotta sculpture (1936) by Jo Davidson (1883–1952) of the head of banker and philanthropist Jules Semon Bache (1861–1944).

374.30 the Presbyterian, the Lahey Clinic] Presbyterian Hospital in New York City and the Lahey Clinic in Boston.

375.8 Alcatraz] Alcatraz Island in San Francisco Bay, the site of a federal maximum-security penitentiary, 1934–63.

383.25–27 "It sounds like . . . Ichabod Crane] See "Rip Van Winkle" and "The Legend of Sleepy Hollow" by Washington Irving (1783–1859), first published in *The Sketch Book of Geoffrey Crayon, Gent.* (1819–1820).

398.3–6 *Lay up to yourselves . . . heart also.*] Matthew 6:20–21.

398.10 tower of ivory . . . house of gold] Invocations from the Litany of the Blessed Virgin Mary, also known as the Litany of Loreto, approved by Pope Sixtus V in 1587.

401.12 *South Pacific*] Musical (1949) composed by Richard Rodgers (1902–1979), with lyrics by Oscar Hammerstein II (1895–1960) and book by Hammerstein and Joshua Logan (1908–1988), based on *Tales of the South Pacific* (1947) by James Michener (1907–1997).

403.23   the Frick] The Frick Collection, art museum in Manhattan.

404.37–38   *cogitant, ergo sum*] They think, therefore I am.

412.33   Gestapo] From *Geheime Staatspolizei* (Secret State Police), the political police in Nazi Germany.

417.2   *Studentenmensur*] A duel fought between students at a German university.

421.24–25   St. Marks-in-the-Bouwerie] Episcopal church located at Second Avenue and East 10th Street. Built from 1795 to 1799, it is the second oldest church in Manhattan.

423.30   her first Assembly] The Assembly Balls were exclusive New York society events, inaugurated in 1882.

424.25   V-mail] Victory Mail, lightweight letter forms used for overseas military correspondence during World War II.

425.11   Anzio] Allied troops landed at Anzio, south of Rome, on January 22, 1944, establishing a beachhead that would be the scene of heavy fighting until the Allied breakout on May 23.

425.15–16   mistakes of Versailles] The terms of the Treaty of Versailles, signed by Germany and the Allies on June 28, 1919.

425.28   "the four freedoms"] In his State of the Union address to Congress on January 6, 1941, President Franklin D. Roosevelt spoke of "four essential human freedoms": freedom of speech, freedom of worship, freedom from want, and freedom from fear.

427.18–19   Pitti Palace] Palace in Florence, used as an art museum.

428.5   *moules marinières*] Marinated mussels.

428.11–12   Helena Rubinstein] An immigrant from Poland, Rubinstein (1872–1965) founded her highly successful cosmetics business in New York City in 1915.

435.28   Lady Chatterley's lover] Oliver Mellors, a gamekeeper who becomes the lover of Lady Constance Chatterley in the novel *Lady Chatterley's Lover* (1928) by D. H. Lawrence (1885–1930).

435.38   *fêtes champêtres*] See note 8.6.

438.14   "The Faerie Queene"] Epic poem (1590–96) by Edmund Spenser (c. 1552–1599).

OTHER STORIES

450.35 Packard] American company that manufactured luxury automobiles, 1899–1958.

451.6 Indian service] See note 340.28.

451.7 *Honest Harold*] See note 345.34.

451.16 *Mommsen's History of Rome*] German scholar Theodor Mommsen (1817–1903) published his history of the Roman republic in three volumes, 1854–56.

452.38 *Das Kapital*] Three-volume critique of capitalism by Karl Marx (1818–1883), published in 1867, 1885, and 1894; the second and third volumes were edited and completed by Friedrich Engels, using Marx's notes.

452.38–39 *Saturday Review of Literature*] Weekly magazine founded in 1924 that was renamed *Saturday Review* in 1952.

453.13–14 Shirley Temple . . . nation's culture] Child actor Shirley Temple (1928–2014) had starring roles in nineteen films released from 1934 to 1939. An annual poll of movie exhibitors named her as the top moneymaking star in Hollywood from 1935 to 1938.

453.32 *The Past Recaptured*] Title of the first English translation (1931) of *Le Temps retrouvé* (1927) by Marcel Proust (1871–1922), the seventh and final volume of *À la recherche du temps perdu*. The novel has also been translated as *Time Regained*.

463.14 the Sound] Long Island Sound.

464.9–10 BULLARD WORKER] An employee of the Bullard Machine Tool Company of Bridgeport, Connecticut.

464.25–31 Sikorsky . . . Chance Vought] Sikorsky, Remington Arms, Brunner-Ritter, and Chance Vought were all defense contractors with plants located in or near Bridgeport, Connecticut.

467.10–11 *Buddenbrooks . . . The Charterhouse of Parma*] *Buddenbrooks*, novel (1901) by Thomas Mann (1875–1955); *Crime and Punishment* (1866), novel by Fyodor Dostoevsky (1821–1881); *The Charterhouse of Parma* (1839), novel by Stendhal (Henri Beyle, 1783–1842).

467.13–14 *For Whom the Bell Tolls . . . The Story of San Michele*] *For Whom the Bell Tolls* (1940), novel by Ernest Hemingway (1899–1961); *The Late George Apley* (1937), novel by John Marquand (1893–1960); *The Golden Treasury* (1861), anthology of songs and lyrical poems edited by Francis Palgrave (1824–1897); *The Story of San Michele* (1929), memoir by the Swedish physician Axel Munthe (1857–1949).

467.24 Mensa] Cafeteria.

467.33 Schmierkäse] See note 170.6.

468.5 *Rotwein*] Red wine.

468.19 *Konditorei*] Pastry shop.

468.38 *Bademeister*] Bath attendant.

473.35 "*Gut' Mahlzeit.*"] "Enjoy your meal."

475.6 "Philosophen Weg,"] See note 61.21.

482.23–24 that book by the doctor of Hitler] Possibly a reference to *I Was Hitler's Doctor* (1943), a memoir credited to "Dr. Karl Krueger" first published in 1941 as *Inside Hitler*. The book was fabricated by its publisher, Samuel Roth (1893–1974), and his ghostwriter, David George Plotkin (1899–1968).

484.19–20 "*Und er geht . . . wunderbar.*"] "And he goes so and so and so!" "'Twas unbelievably wonderful."

487.23 *The House of Mirth*] Novel (1905) by Edith Wharton (1862–1937).

493.1 Rogers Peet] Men's clothier founded in New York City in 1874.

496.7 *Lead, Kindly Light*] Hymn (1833) by John Henry Newman (1801–1890), based on Exodus 13:21–22.

497.13 *altes Gebäude*] Old building, the main university building, dating from 1712–28.

497.16 *deutsches Mädel*] German girl.

499.24 Reichswehr] Name for the German military from 1919 to 1935, when it was renamed as the Wehrmacht.

500.3 Brown Shirts and Black Shirts] Respectively, members of the *Sturmabteilung* (see note 40.14) and the SS (*Schutzstaffel*, Protection Detachment). Originally Hitler's Nazi Party bodyguard, the SS became the main instrument of state terror in the Third Reich, gaining control of the police, the secret police, and the concentration camps, and forming its own military force.

500.34 "Widsith"] Old English poem, probably from the seventh century, that was preserved in the late tenth century.

501.7 "*Bitte, mein Herr,*"] "Please, sir."

501.20 the Königstuhl] A hill overlooking Heidelberg.

501.26 Walther von der Vogelweide] See note 46.40.

501.39 *Bierstuben*] See note 50.2.

502.7 "The Owl and the Nightingale."] Middle English poem, written in the twelfth or thirteenth century, in the form of a verse debate between the title creatures.

504.2   Volksschule] Free state-mandated primary school.

510.13–14   Storm Troopers] Members of the *Sturmabteilung* (SA), the paramilitary arm of the Nazi Party.

510.25–26   *Konditoreien*] See note 468.19.

511.11   *"Guten Abend"*] "Good evening."

511.36   "Horst Wessel" song] Horst Wessel (1907–1930), a Berlin SA (Storm Division) leader, wrote "Die Fahne Hoch" ("The Flag Up High") in 1929 and set it to the melody of a German sailors' song. After Wessel was fatally shot by Communist militants he was made into a martyr by Nazi propaganda chief Joseph Goebbels, and his song became the party anthem and, after 1933, the second national anthem of the Third Reich.

517.29   Love Nest] A brand of candy bar.

517.30   Hippolyte] A brand of marshmallow crème.

517.35   Victrola] See note 123.15.

518.24   Jean Harlow hair] American film actress Jean Harlow (1911–1937) was known as the "Blonde Bombshell" for her platinum blonde hair.

519.1   Girls' Friendly] An Episcopal social organization for girls and young women, founded in England in 1875 and in the United States in 1877.

524.26–27   "Show Me the Way . . . "Sleepy Time Gal"] "Show Me the Way to Go Home," song (1925) by James Campbell (1903–1967) and Reginald Connelly (1895–1963), writing as Irving King. "Sleepy Time Gal," song (1925) with music by Richard A. Whiting (1891–1938) and Ange Lorenzo (1894–1971), lyrics by Joseph Alden and Raymond B. Egan (1890–1952).

525.12   Faith Baldwin's books] Baldwin (1893–1978) was a prolific and popular American writer of romance fiction whose novels often had working women as their protagonists.

526.6   Fabrikoid] Trade name for artificial leather made from cotton cloth coated with nitrocellulose.

526.24–25   "I wandered lonely as a cloud"] First line of lyric poem (1807) by William Wordsworth (1770–1850).

527.38   penitentiary in Canon City] See note 257.24.

528.30   "John Gilpin's Ride,"] "The Diverting History of John Gilpin," comic ballad (1782) by English poet William Cowper (1731–1800) about the rider of a runaway horse.

535.29   Nucoa] A brand of margarine.

544.26   Rob Roy] Rob Roy MacGregor (1671–1734), Scottish Highland outlaw and subject of Walter Scott's novel *Rob Roy* (1817).

547.31 Broadfirth] Breidafjordur, a large bay on the west coast of Iceland.

548.27 *The Shepheardes Calendar*] Series of twelve pastoral poems, one for each month, published in 1579 by Edmund Spenser (c. 1552–1599).

552.26 the Danieli] A hotel in Venice.

553.28 *Middlemarch*] Novel (1872) by George Eliot (Mary Ann Evans, 1819–1880).

553.38 Sacco and Vanzetti trial] Nicola Sacco (1891–1927) and Bartolomeo Vanzetti (1888–1927) were sentenced to death in 1921 for the murder of two men during a payroll robbery in South Braintree, Massachusetts, the previous year. Their case became an international cause célèbre, with their defenders arguing that the two men had been unfairly convicted because of their Italian immigrant backgrounds and anarchist beliefs. Sacco and Vanzetti were denied clemency after a special commission reported that they had received a fair trial and were guilty beyond a reasonable doubt, and they were electrocuted on August 23, 1927.

557.32 Breach Candy] A neighborhood in South Mumbai.

563.2 Konditoreien] See note 468.19.

563.9 Philosophenweg] See note 61.21.

564.18 co-operative society at Antigonish] Beginning in the 1920s, St. Francis Xavier University in Antigonish developed a series of cooperative social, economic, and educational programs in rural Nova Scotia.

565.29 Chilton Club] A Boston women's club founded in 1910.

565.31 Winsor School] A private school for girls founded in Boston in 1886.

566.1 Bossuet] Jacques-Bénigne Bossuet (1627–1704), French bishop, theologian, and orator.

566.3 Ronald Knox] Knox (1888–1957) was an English Catholic priest, theologian, and writer of detective fiction.

566.4 the Adlon] A luxury hotel in Berlin that opened in 1907.

566.38 Altesgebäude . . . S. S. Pierce] See notes 497.13 and 201.19.

568.10 *sous cloche*] Under a bell.

568.17 the Little Flower] Saint Thérèse of Lisieux (1873–1897), a French Carmelite nun.

568.21 "Sistine Madonna"] Painting by Raphael (1483–1520), commissioned by Pope Julius II (1443–1513) in 1512.

569.20–21 *Ich möchte ein Bad, bitte."*] I would like a bath, please.

571.38 Stormtroopers and Blackshirts] Stormtroopers, members of the SA; Blackshirts, members of the SS, after their black uniforms.

576.28–29 *Guten abend! Aufwiedersehen! Danke schön!*] Good evening! Goodbye! Thank you very much!

578.14 Blackwood] A bridge bidding convention developed by Easley Blackwood (1903–1992).

578.29–30 Walther von der Vogelweide] See note 46.40.

579.8 von Ribbentrop] Joachim von Ribbentrop (1893–1946) served as Hitler's personal diplomatic representative, 1935–36, German ambassador to the United Kingdom, 1936–38, and foreign minister of Nazi Germany, 1938–45. He was sentenced to death by the Nuremburg international war crimes tribunal and hanged.

580.13 *The Student Prince*] Operetta (1924) with music by Sigmund Romberg (1887–1951) and lyrics by Dorothy Donnelly (1876–1928), based on *Old Heidelberg* (1901), a play by Wilhelm Meyer-Förster (1862–1934).

580.29 Hitler Jugend] Hitler Youth, Nazi youth organization established in 1926. By 1936 it had almost 5.5 million members, representing more than 60 percent of the German population age ten to eighteen.

586.5 *Deus te amo*] God, I love you.

586.26 Bierstuben] See note 50.2.

587.17–18 on their way . . . war in Spain] Nazi Germany supported the Nationalist rebels in the Spanish Civil War, 1936–39, sending arms, transport, and troops. The German "Condor Legion" eventually numbered 10,000 men, including a strong air force contingent.

593.2 *Bergbahn*] Mountain railway.

595.17 *"Lebewohl."*] "Farewell."

598.40 Groton] An Episcopal boarding school for boys, founded in Groton, Massachusetts, in 1884.

601.38 Jack Rose] A cocktail made with apple brandy, lemon, and grenadine.

612.6–7 comic book of "Nancy,"] Comic strip created in 1938 by Ernie Bushmiller (1905–1982), who first introduced the "Nancy" character in the *Fritzi Ritz* comic in 1933.

612.39–40 sinking of the Titanic] The British ocean liner *Titanic* sank in the North Atlantic on April 15, 1912, with the loss of some 1,500 lives after hitting an iceberg.

614.36 Canfield] See note 25.34.

614.37 beating Sol] Winning at solitaire.

617.34   "St. Louis Blues"] Song (1914) by W. C. Handy (1873–1958).

624.21   peau de soie] Paduasoy, a corded silk fabric.

624.38   Brown Shirt] See note 40.14.

625.3   kino] Cinema.

625.36   pfeffernuesse] Small spiced cookies.

626.8   La Scala] Opera house in Milan, Italy.

626.10   university of Ruprecht-Karl] The university is officially named Ruprecht Karl University of Heidelberg, after Ruprecht I (1309–1390), Count Palatine of the Rhine, who founded the university in 1386, and Karl Friedrich (1728–1811), Grand Duke of Baden, who reestablished it as a state institution in 1803.

626.11–12   Studentenlokale] Student taverns.

626.16   "Noch einmal"] "One more time."

627.5   "Gaudeamus Igitur"] "So Let Us Rejoice," traditional university song dating to at least the eighteenth century.

628.8   Abinger] A parish in south Surrey.

628.21   sehr rot] Very red.

631.31   Philosophenweg] See note 61.21.

632.6   Dienstmädchen] Maid.

633.5   "Die Entführung aus dem Serail"] The Abduction from the Seraglio (1782), opera by Wolfgang Amadeus Mozart (1756–1791) with libretto by Gottlieb Stephanie (1741–1800).

633.13   kalte Ente . . . Abendsonnenschein] Cold Duck at my place, in the true German evening sunshine.

634.40   Bierstuben] See note 50.2.

639.12   Information Service] A division of the American military government that administered the postwar occupation of Germany.

644.31   dunkles Bier] Dark beer.

646.16   the Hibbert Journal] An English quarterly review of religion, theology, and philosophy, published 1902–68.

646.35   Goren and Culbertson] American contract bridge players Charles Goren (1901–1991) and Ely Culbertson (1891–1955).

647.30–31   "Gaudeamus Igitur"] See note 627.5.

650.2   CARE packages] Parcels of food supplies distributed by the nongovernmental relief organization Cooperative for American Remittances to

Europe, founded in 1945. The organization later was renamed Cooperative for American Remittances to Everywhere (1953), Cooperative for American Relief Everywhere (1959), and Cooperative for Assistance and Relief Everywhere (1993).

650.16   *cacoëthes scribendi*] See note 3.11–12.

650.40   Hudson-River-Bracketed] Architectural style originated by Alexander Jackson Davis (1803–1892).

651.16   Sydenham] Thomas Sydenham (1624–1689), English physician and author of *Observations Medicae* (1676), considered a founder of clinical medicine.

651.17   René Théophile Hyacinthe Laënnec] French physician (1781–1826) who invented the stethoscope.

653.2   Holthausen's glossary . . . Klaeber's] Ferdinand Holthausen (1860–1956), a professor at Kiel University, published his edition of *Beowulf* in 1905. Frederick Klaeber (1863–1954), a German-American professor at the University of Minnesota, published his first edition of the poem in 1922 and subsequently revised it in 1928, 1936, and 1950.

656.15   Bernkasteler Doktor] A vineyard in the Mosel Valley famous for its Riesling wine.

656.26   *Bowle*] Punch.

657.29   the Lincoln Highway] Transcontinental highway route running from New York to San Francisco that was dedicated by the private Lincoln Highway Association in 1913. The "Colorado Loop" of the Lincoln Highway ran southwest from Big Springs, Nebraska, to Denver, and then north to Cheyenne, Wyoming.

657.31   Croce] Benedetto Croce (1866–1952), Italian philosopher, historian, and politician.

657.38   "Voyage of the 'Beagle,'"] *Journal of Researches into the Geology and Natural History of the various countries visited by H.M.S. Beagle* (1839, revised 1845), account by Charles Darwin (1809–1882) of his work as a naturalist during the around-the-world voyage of H.M.S. *Beagle* from 1831 to 1836.

658.5   Whitehead and Russell] See note 83.26.

658.12–13   "Diary of William Dunlap"] Dunlap (1766–1839) was a New York theater producer, dramatist, painter, and historian of American art and theater. His diary was published in 1930.

658.21–22   'The Rape of the Lock.'] Mock-heroic poem (1712, expanded 1714) by Alexander Pope (1688–1744).

658.25–27   *manille . . . ponto*] In ombre, *manille* is the second highest trump card, *basto* the third, and, if the trump suit is red, *ponto* the fourth.

661.13   Piesporter] A German white wine from the Mosel region.

661.21–22   Breisgau] The region around the city of Freiburg in southwest Germany.

667.15   Ingersoll] A brand of pocket watch.

668.8   interurban] See note 207.20.

668.28   Mr. Tambo–Mr. Bones dialogues] Stock characters in blackface minstrel shows who exchanged jokes.

669.40   bounty-jumping] See note 368.21.

671.5   Canon City] See note 257.24.

672.23   King Philip] See note 148.25.

672.31   a His Master's Voice dog] Nipper, a part-terrier mixed breed, was depicted listening to a phonograph in *His Master's Voice* (1898), a painting by English artist Francis Barraud (1856–1924). The painting became the basis for a trademark used in England by the Gramophone Company and in the United States by the Victor Company and, later, RCA.

673.7   Victoria and Albert Museum] London museum of decorative art and design, founded in 1852.

674.14   fought at Murfreesboro] Civil War battle, also known as Stones River, fought in Tennessee, December 31, 1862–January 2, 1863, that ended in a Union victory.

674.19   the Teapot Dome] Wyoming oil field, named after a nearby rock formation, that became notorious as the focus of a bribery scandal during the Harding administration.

682.38   Palmer Method] A method of penmanship developed by Austin Palmer (1860–1927).

684.32   Spink's] Spink & Son, London firm dealing in coins, medals, and art, founded in 1666.

685.3   *pensées*] Literary reflections, aphorisms.

685.12   Rumpelmayer's] A popular café located in the Hotel St. Moritz on Central Park South in Manhattan.

685.36   this gentil, parfit Knyght] Cf. "The Knight's Tale" in *The Canterbury Tales* (1387–1400) by Geoffrey Chaucer (c. 1342/43–1400): "a verray, parfit, gentil knyght."

686.29   Winston Churchill] American novelist Winston Churchill (1871–1947), whose works include *Richard Carvel* (1899), *The Crisis* (1901), and *The Crossing* (1904), moved to Cornish, New Hampshire, in 1899.

688.21   Ward McAllister] A wealthy attorney, McAllister (1827–1895) helped

Caroline Schermerhorn Astor (1830–1908) select the members of the New York social elite known as "the Four Hundred." His influence was resented by other society figures who accused him of self-promotion.

691.20   Childe Harold in the Juras] See Lord Byron (1788–1824), *Childe Harold's Pilgrimage*, Canto III (1816), stanzas 86–93.

693.17   *bal masqué*] Masked ball.

698.11   *Decodon verticillatus*] Swamp loosestrife.

698.38   *Trifolium repens*] White clover.

701.35   *Pride and Prejudice*] Novel (1813) by Jane Austen (1775–1817).

704.26–27   Foxe's "Book of the Martyrs,"] *Acts and Monuments of These Later and Perilous Days* (1563) by John Foxe (1517–87), popularly known as *The Book of Martyrs*, which recorded the persecution of English Protestants.

705.10   Piper Cub] American single-engine, two-seat, high-wing monoplane manufactured from 1938 to 1947.

706.27   the East Wind] A passenger train that ran in the summer from Washington, D.C., to Portland, Maine.

710.20   Anna Livia Plurabelle] The principal female character in *Finnegans Wake* (1939) by James Joyce (1882–1941).

711.11   Quimper pitcher] Pottery from Quimper, a city in Brittany, France.

711.40–712.1   "Over the sea to Skye,"] From "The Skye Boat Song" (1884), with lyrics by Sir Harold Boulton (1859–1935), set to a traditional Scottish air. The song tells of the escape of Bonnie Prince Charlie after his defeat at the battle of Culloden in 1746.

712.2   block-flöte] Recorder.

712.31–32   Aucassin . . . Blanchefleur] *Aucassin et Nicolette*, French romance in prose and verse from the early thirteenth century; *Floris and Blanchefleur*, Middle English verse romance from the thirteenth century, based on a twelfth-century French original.

713.5–6   Virginia City . . . Beebe's printer's devil] An anachronistic reference to Lucius Beebe (1902–1966), a New York society journalist who moved in 1950 to Virginia City, Nevada, where he later revived the *Territorial Enterprise*, a newspaper Mark Twain had written for in the 1860s.

713.13–14   Coleman lamps] See note 252.24–25.

713.37   shoe-peg corn] White sweet corn.

714.16   *"Mea maxima culpa"*] "Through my most grievous fault." The phrase is used in the confessional prayer recited at the beginning of the traditional Latin Mass.

715.2   Teresa's "Interior Castle,"] *El Castillo Interior*, mystical spiritual guide written in 1577 by Saint Teresa of Ávila (1515–1582), a Carmelite nun.

715.25–26   Dauber & Pine] Used bookstore in Manhattan, 1922–83.

716.12–15   "A Little Street in Delft" . . . "Thomas More."] *The Little Street* by Johannes Vermeer (1632–1675), painted in 1657–58; *A Sunday Afternoon on the Island of La Grand Jatte* by Georges Seurat (1859–1891), painted in 1884–86; *St. Francis in Ecstasy* by Giovanni Bellini (c. 1430–1516), painted 1475–80; the portrait of Sir Thomas More by Hans Holbein the Younger (c. 1497–1543) was commissioned in 1527.

717.4–5   Scollay Square . . . Widner] Scollay Square in downtown Boston, now the site of the Government Center; Widener Library, the main library on the Harvard campus.

717.21–22   Boston *Evening Transcript* . . . poem] Daily newspaper (except Sunday) published 1830–1941, the subject of a comic poem ("The readers of the *Boston Evening Transcript* / Sway in the wind like a field of ripe corn") by T. S. Eliot (1888–1965), first published in *Poetry* in 1915 and later included in his collection *Poems* (1920).

719.7–8   Sandwich tumblers] Glassware produced in the vicinity of Sandwich, Massachusetts.

720.7   Pepperpot Bridge] Informal name for the Longfellow Bridge connecting Cambridge and Boston across the Charles River, inspired by the shape of its four central towers.

721.14   Locke-Ober] A French restaurant in Boston.

722.9   Filene's] Boston department store.

723.14–15   like Paolo and Francesca] In Canto V of Dante's *Inferno*, where they are condemned to the Second Circle of Hell.

726.1   Loeb "Confessions of St. Augustine,"] The Loeb Classical Library edition (1912) of the *Confessions* of Saint Augustine (354–430) printed the Latin text along with a translation by William Watts (c. 1590–1649) first published in 1631.

726.5   Monica's death] Augustine wrote about the death of Monica, his mother, in Book IX of the *Confessions*.

726.34   the Sorosis] See note 285.37.

728.20   the Wilson range] Mount Wilson (14,246 feet) is the highest point in the San Miguel Mountains in southwest Colorado.

728.28   Amity College] Four-year institution in College Springs, Iowa, that opened in 1872 and closed in 1913. Stafford's father was an Amity graduate.

730.8   Zweites Frühstück] Second breakfast.

730.11–12   *Der Liebling Vogel*] The darling bird.

730.37   little Lords and Ladies Fauntleroy] Young aristocrats, after *Little Lord Fauntleroy*, children's novel (1886) by Frances Hodgson Burnett (1849–1924).

731.10–11   Tammany lion's tail] Tammany Hall, the Democratic political machine in Manhattan, was usually depicted in cartoon form as a voracious tiger.

731.22   Arrian] Greek historian and Stoic philosopher (c. 86– c. 160).

732.34–35   Seven Years' War] Conflict (1756–63) fought on a global scale by Britain, Prussia, and Portugal against France, Austria, Russia, Spain, and Sweden. The war ended in a victory for the Anglo-Prussian coalition.

733.8   antigodlin] Lopsided, askew.

735.34   *Century* magazine] *The Century Magazine* was launched in 1881 and ceased publication in 1930.

736.19   Sabbitarian] A person who strictly observes the Sabbath.

738.6–7   Marshall Field's] Chicago department store (1881–2006).

739.4–5   Mommsen] See note 451.16.

739.7   *Madame Butterfly*] Opera (1904) by Giacomo Puccini (1858–1924) with libretto by Luigi Illica (1857–1919) and Giuseppe Giacosa (1847–1906).

739.33   *Science and Health*] Book (1875) by Mary Baker Eddy (1821–1910), a central text of Christian Science. It was retitled *Science and Health with Key to the Scriptures* in 1886.

741.10   Graymalkin] A gray cat, and the name of the familiar called upon by the First Witch in *Macbeth*, I.i.8.

742.13–14   *very* rotten in the state of Denmark] See *Hamlet*, I.iv.90.

742.17   Haviland] American importer of porcelain made in Limoges, France.

742.20   didies] Diapers.

742.33   Hupmobile] Automobile manufactured by the Hupp Motor Car Company of Detroit, 1909–39.

743.21–22   Christian Endeavor] Young People's Society of Christian Endeavor, an interdominational evangelical movement founded in Portland, Maine, in 1881 by Francis Edward Clark (1851–1927).

745.5   gowk] Cuckoo.

745.18   *The Book of the Martyrs*] See note 704.26–27.

745.22–35   "Therefore the Lord . . . Thy men] Isaiah 3:17–25.

747.30   Pierce Arrow] Luxury automobile manufactured by the Pierce-Arrow Motor Car Company of Buffalo, New York, 1904–38.

748.17   "There were . . . in a tree"] From the Scottish folk song "The Twa Corbies."

A MOTHER IN HISTORY

751.10   arrest and murder . . . Oswald] Lee Harvey Oswald (1939–63), a former U.S. Marine who had defected to the Soviet Union and then returned, was arrested in Dallas on the afternoon of November 22, 1963, and charged with the murders of President John F. Kennedy (1917–1963) and police officer J. D. Tippit (1924–1963). Oswald was fatally shot in the basement of police headquarters on November 24 by Jack Ruby (Jacob Rubenstein, 1911–1967), a Dallas nightclub owner.

751.26–27   Warren Commission . . . assassination] President Lyndon B. Johnson appointed the seven-member commission by executive order on November 29, 1963. The commission, headed by Chief Justice Earl Warren (1891–1974), submitted its findings to Johnson on September 24, 1964, and its 888-page report was released on September 27.

752.4   his father died . . . later married] Robert Edward Lee Oswald (1896–1939) died of a heart attack in New Orleans on August 19, 1939, two months before the birth of his son Lee Harvey Oswald on October 18. Marguerite Oswald (1907–1981) married Edwin Ekdahl in 1945; they were divorced in 1948.

753.3–4   the testimony . . . for seventy-five years] On November 26, 1964, the Warren Commission published twenty-six volumes of testimony and exhibits as a supplement to its previously released report. The unpublished records of the commission were then transferred to the National Archives to remain under seal for seventy-five years, but almost all of them have now been released as the result of subsequent legislation.

753.32   a young boy . . . at twenty] Oswald defected to the Soviet Union in October 1959. He returned to the United States in June 1962 with Marina, his Russian wife, and their daughter June.

753.38–754.1   A. J. Liebling, once described . . . taken refuge."] In his book *The Earl of Louisiana* (1961). Abbott Joseph Liebling (1904–1963) was a staff writer for *The New Yorker* from 1935 until his death. He and Stafford were married in 1959.

753.40   Al Smith] Alfred E. Smith (1873–1944), a native of the Lower East Side of Manhattan, served as governor of New York, 1923–28, and was the Democratic candidate for president in 1928.

754.29   *The Wounded Land*] *The Wounded Land: Journey Through a Divided*

America (1964), translation of *Der Tod in Texas: Ein amerikanische Tragödie* by the Hungarian-born journalist and novelist Hans Habe (1911–1977).

754.34   Whistler's "Mother."] Portrait of Anna McNeill Whistler (1804–1881) painted in 1871 by her son James Abbott McNeill Whistler (1834–1903), who titled it *Arrangement in Grey and Black No. 1*.

755.2   Paul Pry] See note 315.13–14.

755.4   Ben Casey] Hour-long television medical drama (1961–65) starring Vince Edwards (1928–96) as an idealistic neurosurgeon.

756.38   Neiman-Marcus] Dallas department store.

757.32–33   rumored . . . President had Addison's disease] John F. Kennedy was diagnosed with Addison's disease in 1947 and treated with corticosteroids for the remainder of his life. When supporters of Lyndon B. Johnson told the press in July 1960 that Kennedy suffered from the disease, Robert F. Kennedy responded that his brother had never had "an ailment described classically as Addison's Disease, which is a tuberculose destruction of the adrenal gland," but had suffered from "some adrenal insufficiency" in the postwar period.

758.2   Texas Book Depository] The Texas School Book Depository building in downtown Dallas. Lee Harvey Oswald shot President Kennedy from the window of a sixth-story storeroom in the depository, where he had been working as a shipping clerk since October 16, 1963.

758.17–19   quote Mrs. Kennedy . . . my Jack,'] The Warren Commission quoted Jacqueline Kennedy (1929–1994) as saying "Oh, my God, they have shot my husband. I love you, Jack" after the President suffered his fatal head wound.

758.22   Governor Connally] John Connally (1917–1993), the Democratic governor of Texas, 1963–69, was seated in front of the President in his limousine. The Warren Commission quoted him as saying "My God, they are going to kill us all" after he was seriously wounded by a bullet that passed through the President's neck.

758.25   derangements in the Dominican Republic] Fighting broke out in the Dominican Republic on April 24, 1965, between military supporters of the elected former president Juan Bosch (1909–2001), who had been ousted in a coup in 1963, and troops loyal to the ruling junta. Concerned that the violence could lead to a Communist takeover, President Johnson ordered a major U.S. military intervention that succeeded in imposing a cease-fire. U.S. troops remained in the Dominican Republic as part of an inter-American peacekeeping force until after Bosch's defeat by Joaquín Balaguer (1906–2002) in the July 1966 presidential election.

758.34–35   Warren had tears . . . commission?] Chief Justice Warren initially declined to head up the investigating commission, believing it would be incompatible with his judicial role, but agreed to serve after meeting with

President Johnson on November 29, 1963. The press reported that the chief justice had tears in his eyes after the President appealed to his patriotism and referred to his army service in World War I. (Warren later wrote in his memoirs that Johnson had also warned him that allegations of Communist involvement in the assassination, if left unchecked, could lead to a nuclear war in which 40 million Americans might be killed.)

759.32   Norman Vincent Peale] Peale (1898–1993) was the Reformed Protestant pastor at Marble Collegiate Church in New York City, 1932–84, and author of the best-selling *The Power of Positive Thinking* (1952).

760.20   brother, John Edward] His half brother, John Edward Pic (1932–2000).

761.9   Mayor Wagner's] Robert F. Wagner (1910–1991) was the Democratic mayor of New York City, 1954–65.

762.30   twenty-six volumes . . . Report] See note 753.3–4.

763.10   her first son by him] Robert Edward Lee Oswald, Jr. (1934–2017).

764.12   joined the Marines] Oswald enlisted in the Marines in October 1956 and was honorably discharged from active duty in September 1959.

767.2   Marina] Marina Nikolayevna Prusakova (b. 1941), a pharmacist, married Oswald in Minsk on April 30, 1961. They had two daughters, June, born February 15, 1962, and Rachel, born October 20, 1963.

768.5   Mrs. Paine] Marina Oswald and her children were living with her friend Ruth Hyde Paine (b. 1932) in Irving, Texas, when President Kennedy was assassinated.

769.7–8   Blenheim Castle? . . . Marion Davies' house?] Blenheim Palace in Oxfordshire, England, home of the Dukes of Marlborough and the birthplace of Winston Churchill. Ocean House, also known as Beach House, was a large mansion in Santa Monica, California, built in 1929 by William Randolph Hearst for his mistress, the film actress Marion Davies (1897–1961). Davies sold the estate in 1947, and the house was demolished in 1956.

769.39–770.1   paperback . . . Kerry Thornley] *Oswald* (1965) by Kerry Thornley (1938–1998), who had served with Oswald in California and Japan. Thornley testified before the Warren Commission and gave its staff the manuscript of *The Idle Warriors*, an unpublished novel he had written before the assassination about a Marine who defects to the Soviet Union. (The novel was published in 1991.)

770.23   Birchers] Members of an extreme right-wing political organization founded in Indiana in 1958 by Robert Welch (1899–1985) and named after John Birch (1918–45), an American intelligence officer killed by the Chinese Communists at the end of World War II.

771.6–7   Mark Lane . . . *The Defenders*' man] Mark Lane (1927–2016), an attorney in New York City, published an article questioning Oswald's guilt in the *National Guardian* on December 19, 1963, and was engaged by Marguerite Oswald to represent her son's interests before the Warren Commission. Lane appeared before the commission twice to challenge the evidence against Oswald and became an outspoken critic of its final report. His book *Rush to Judgment*, published in August 1966, was a best seller. Perry Mason, a fictitious Los Angeles defense attorney created by mystery novelist Erle Stanley Gardner (1889–1970), was played on television (1957–66) by Raymond Burr (1917–1993). Melvin Belli (1907–1996) was an attorney who defended Jack Ruby at his trial in 1964. *The Defenders* was an hour-long television legal drama (1961–65) starring E. G. Marshall (1914–1998) and Robert Reed (1932–1992) as a father-and-son team of defense attorneys.

773.31 Mr. Martin] James Martin was the manager of the Six Flags motel in Arlington, Texas, where Marina and her children stayed under Secret Service protection after Oswald's murder. She later lived with the Martin family for several weeks in the early winter of 1964, during which time Martin served as her business manager.

773.32 put her on television] Marina Oswald gave her first television interview to Eddie Barker (1927–2012), the news director of KRLD-TV in Dallas, on January 27, 1964. The interview was broadcast nationally on the *CBS Evening News*.

774.9 Veronica in *The Cranes Are Flying*] Tatyana Samoylova (1934–2014) played Veronika, the heroine of *The Cranes Are Flying* (1957), a World War II drama written by Viktor Rozov (1913–2004) and directed by Mikhail Kalatozov (1903–2004). The film was released in the United States in 1960.

774.13–14 Lisa in *Pique Dame* . . . the Neva] In the opera *Pique Dame* (1890), also known as *The Queen of Spades*, composed by Pyotr Tchaikovsky (1840–1893) with a libretto by his brother Modest Tchaikovsky (1850–1916). The opera was based on the novella (1834) by Alexander Pushkin (1799–1837), in which the character of Liza does not die.

774.15 Masha, . . . three sisters] The middle sister in *Three Sisters* (1901), play by Anton Chekhov (1860–1904).

775.15 my sister] Lillian Murret (1900–1989).

776.38–777.40 Mrs. Tippit . . . wealthy woman] Marie Frances Tippit, nee Gasway (b. 1928), the widow of J. D. Tippit. Oswald shot and killed Tippit when the patrolman stopped him for questioning about forty-five minutes after the President was shot. In September 1965 the Associated Press reported that the family had received $647,579 in donations from the public, half of which went to a trust fund for the three Tippit children.

777.11–12 television interview with Belli] Marguerite Oswald and Melvin Belli (see note 771.6–7) were interviewed together on August 5, 1964, by Les Crane (1933–2008) on his late-night ABC talk program.

778.5–7 all bruised up . . . a scuffle.'] Oswald scuffled with Dallas police officers when he was apprehended in a movie theater at approximately 1:45 P.M. on November 22.

779.5–6 Castle Rackrent] Novel (1800) by Maria Edgeworth (1768–1849) about the decline of an Anglo-Irish landowning family.

779.37 my sister] See note 775.15.

781.38–39 Lee's picture in *Life* . . . at six months] The photograph appeared in *Life* on February 21, 1964, as part of a feature titled "The Evolution of an Assassin." Its caption identified the picture as having been taken in 1941 when Oswald was two.

782.7 Magnus organ] An electronic chord organ. (The Magnus Corporation began manufacturing organs in 1958; the first chord organ was introduced by Hammond in 1950.)

782.19 Sam Rayburn . . . Christian Herter] Rayburn (1882–1961), a Democrat from Texas, served in the U.S. House of Representatives, 1913–61, and was Speaker of the House, 1940–47, 1949–53, and 1955–61. Christian Herter (1895–1966) served as secretary of state, 1959–61.

782.20 Khrushchev] Soviet leader Nikita Khrushchev (1894–1971), first secretary of the Communist Party, 1953–64, and premier, 1958–64.

782.31 Congressman Jim White] No person named "White" served in the Eighty-sixth Congress (1959–61).

783.1–2 Representative Ford . . . an Agent,'] Gerald R. Ford (1913–2006), a member of the Warren Commission, published an inside account of its work, "Piecing Together the Evidence," in *Life* on October 2, 1964; "Mother's Myth: Oswald was a Paid U.S. Agent" was one of the page headings used in the article. Ford was a Republican representative from Michigan, 1949–73, vice president, 1973–74, and president of the United States, 1974–77.

783.25 the Ruby trial] Dallas nightclub owner Jack Ruby (1911–1967) was convicted of murder and sentenced to death on March 14, 1964. His conviction was overturned on appeal in October 1966 on the grounds that his confession was improperly admitted into evidence and that he should have been granted a change of venue. Ruby died in custody of lung cancer while awaiting a new trial.

784.9–15 the diary . . . reporter in Dallas] Oswald's "Historic Diary" of his time in the Soviet Union, with entries from October 16, 1959, to March 27, 1962. Its existence was revealed in the *Dallas Morning News* on June 27, 1964, by Hugh Aynesworth (b. 1931), who did not disclose how he had obtained the diary.

785.6 Hightower] James Hightower (1915–2006), professor of Chinese literature at Harvard University, 1948–81. For Stafford's relationship with Hightower, see Chronology, 1935–40.

785.14 *Konditorei*] See note 468.19.

785.17 *Ulysses*] Modernist novel (1922) by James Joyce (1882–1941) set in Dublin, Ireland, on June 16, 1904.

786.7 "Silent Night"] Austrian Christmas carol (1818), with words by Joseph Mohr (1792–1848) and music by Franz Xaver Gruber (1787–1863).

788.12–13 Dallas *News* . . . Dominican Republic] On May 9, 1965, the *Dallas Morning News* carried Associated Press dispatches reporting the heaviest U.S. air strikes yet against North Vietnam and violations of the cease-fire in the Dominican Republic by anti-junta rebels (see note 758.25).

788.28 in alien corn] See note 36.13–14.

790.16–22 William Manchester . . . *Portrait of a President*] Manchester (1922–2004) was the author of *Portrait of a President: John F. Kennedy in Profile* (1962). His book *The Death of a President: November 20–November 25, 1963* was published in April 1967 after Manchester made a series of deletions at the insistence of Jacqueline Kennedy and Robert F. Kennedy, who had sought to block its publication after initially authorizing the project. John F. Kennedy received the Pulitzer Prize for Biography for his book *Profiles in Courage* (1956).

794.5 Mr. Jenner] Albert E. Jenner, Jr. (1907–1988), a prominent Chicago attorney, served as an assistant counsel to the Warren Commission.

794.22 father . . . bookmaking business] Charles "Dutz" Murret (1901–1964), a bookie and boxing promoter associated with New Orleans underworld figure Sam Saia (1900–1965).

795.6–7 the seas were . . . *Hesperus*] "The Wreck of the Hesperus" (1802), narrative poem by Henry Wadsworth Longfellow (1807–1882).

795.11–13 *stark männlich* . . . *Das Ohr*] *Stark männlich*, strong masculine; *der Stuhl*, the chair; *schwach weiblich*, weak feminine; *die Frau*, the woman; *gemischt sächlich*, mixed neuter; *das Ohr*, the ear.

797.27–29 money from *Esquire* . . . letters from Lee] "Lee Oswald's Letters to His Mother" appeared in the May 1964 issue of *Esquire*, presenting in facsimile sixteen handwritten letters Oswald had sent from the Soviet Union, 1959–62, along with annotation by Marguerite Oswald and a portrait of her taken by photographer Diane Arbus (1923–1971). She received $4,000 from the magazine for the letters.

800.1 Fair Play for Cuba] The Fair Play for Cuba Committee, a pro-Castro group organized in New York City in 1960.

800.11 television program . . . in New Orleans] Oswald was briefly interviewed on WDSU-TV on August 21, 1963, after he had participated in a WDSU radio program on Cuba.

803.36 from Love] Love Field, the main Dallas airport from 1927 to 1974.

805.3–4 Baron von Munchausen] Karl Friedrich Hieronymus von Münch-hausen (1720–1797), German soldier and hunter famous for telling implausible and absurd tales of his exploits. A number of stories attributed to him were compiled and embellished by Rudolph Erich Raspe (1737–1794) in *Baron Munchausen's Narrative of his Marvellous Travels and Campaigns in Russia*, published in London in 1785.

805.32 Parkland Memorial Hospital] In Dallas, where President Kennedy was pronounced dead.

806.13–15 fight at the Garden . . . Dick Tiger] The cancelled fight was a light heavyweight match between Johnny Persol (b. 1940) and Allen Thomas (b. 1941). Dick Tiger (Richard Ihetu, 1929–1971), a Nigerian boxer, held the middleweight championship, 1962–63 and 1965–66, and the light heavyweight championship, 1966–68.

809.2–3 famous picture . . . his guns] The photograph showed Oswald standing in his backyard, wearing a holstered revolver and holding a rifle in one hand and copies of *The Worker* and *The Militant* newspapers in the other. (*The Worker* was published by the Communist Party of the United States, while *The Militant* was aligned with the Trotskyist Socialist Workers Party.)

809.6 General Walker] Major General Edwin Walker (1909–1993) resigned his commission in the U.S. army in 1961 after being officially admonished for distributing right-wing literature to his troops and for publicly describing Harry S. Truman, Eleanor Roosevelt, and Dean Acheson as "definitely pink." An advocate of the invasion of Cuba and opponent of the civil rights movement, Walker was arrested, but not indicted, for inciting violent resistance to the integration of the University of Mississippi in 1962. On April 10, 1963, a bullet fired into Walker's home in Dallas narrowly missed him as he sat at his desk. The Warren Commission concluded that Oswald had fired the shot, using the same rifle later used to kill President Kennedy.

809.12 February issue of *Life*] The photograph appeared in *Life* on February 21, 1964.

809.27 exact date in April] The Warren Commission concluded that the photograph was probably taken on March 31, 1963.

809.28 down in West Texas] 214 Neeley Street is an address in the Oak Cliff neighborhood in west Dallas.

810.19 the police . . . the garage] The photographs were found during a search of the Paine home in Irving, Texas, on November 23, 1963.

811.16–17 Freud . . . *Paranoia and Homosexuality*] The essay was first published in German in 1922 and in English a year later.

SELECTED ESSAYS

815.12   should [   ] be] The bracketed space indicates where several words were apparently omitted from the text printed in the Spring 1948 *Kenyon Review*.

815.35   Bard College *Conference on the Novel*] Participants in the conference, held on November 7–8, 1947, included the literary critics F. W. Dupee (1904–1979) and Lionel Trilling (1905–1975).

816.1   Mrs. Dalloway] The eponymous protagonist of the novel (1925) by Virginia Woolf (1882–1941).

816.8   *The Sorrows of Werther*] *The Sorrows of Young Werther*, novel (1774) by Johann Wolfgang von Goethe (1749–1832).

817.13   Dickens' little man in *Bleak House*] Krook, a rag-and-bone dealer in the novel (1852–53).

817.16   Mr. Jackson's novel] *The Lost Weekend* (1944), novel about an alcoholic writer by Charles Jackson (1903–1968).

817.26–27   Mr. Clifton Fadiman's . . . "The Jolly Corner"] Fadiman (1904–1999), an essayist, critic, and editor, included "The Jolly Corner" (1908) in *The Short Stories of Henry James* (1945), a selection published by the Modern Library.

818.3–4   Edmund Wilson . . . *Turn of the Screw*] Wilson (1895–1972) wrote about James's novella *The Turn of the Screw* (1898) in his essay "The Ambiguity of Henry James" (1934).

818.8–9   James's notebooks have been published] In *The Notebooks of Henry James* (1947), edited by F. O. Matthiessen (1902–1950) and Kenneth B. Murdock (1895–1975).

820.19   Paul Engle] Engle (1908–1991) was director of the Iowa Writers' Workshop, 1941–65.

820.20–21   Drs. Menninger . . . Kansas] Charles Menninger (1862–1953) and his son Karl Menninger (1893–1990) cofounded the Menninger Clinic, a psychiatric facility in Topeka, Kansas, in 1919. Another son, William Menninger (1899–1966), joined the clinic in 1927.

821.14–18   Evelyn Waugh . . . read Dickens aloud] In the novel *A Handful of Dust* (1934) by Evelyn Waugh (1903–1966), the protagonist Tony Last is held captive in the Amazon jungle by the illiterate Mr. Todd, who requires that Last read the works of Dickens to him aloud.

821.19   *Little Dorrit*] The novel was published serially in 1855–57.

822.9–10   *The Snake Pit*] Novel (1946) by Mary Jane Ward (1905–1981) based on her experiences in a psychiatric hospital.

823.4   Chekhov . . . "Ward No. 6"] The story, set in a provincial mental asylum, was first published in 1892.

823.28   Kenneth Patchen] An American experimental poet, Patchen (1911–1972) was the author of the novels *The Journal of Albion Moonlight* (1941) and *Memoirs of a Shy Pornographer* (1945).

824.7–8   Humphrey Slater's . . . *The Heretics*] Novel (1946) by the English writer and painter Humphrey Slater (1906–1958).

824.25–27   *Madame Bovary . . . Pride and Prejudice*] Novel (1857) by Gustave Flaubert (1821–1880); novel (1866) by Fyodor Dostoyevsky (1821–1881); novel (1813) by Jane Austen (1775–1817).

825.7   Carol Kennicott's] Protagonist of the novel *Main Street* (1920) by Sinclair Lewis (1885–1951).

825.9   Edgar Guest] British-born American poet (1881–1959) known for his sentimental, optimistic verse.

826.7–8   Hemingway . . . *The Killers*] The story was first published in *Scribner's Magazine* in March 1927.

828.8–10   Edith Wharton . . . to society] *Verses*, a collection of twenty-nine poems by Edith Newbold Jones, was privately printed in 1878. She made her social debut the following year at age seventeen.

828.16   the Miss Stafford who sings] American popular singer Jo Stafford (1917–2008).

830.26   Ford Madox Ford] English writer, born Ford Hermann Hueffer (1873–1939), author of *The Good Soldier* (1915) and the *Parade's End* tetralogy (1924–1928). Stafford met Ford in Boulder at the 1937 University of Colorado writers' conference.

831.35   witness to a suicide] See Chronology, 1934–36.

832.2   "Gloomy Sunday"] Hungarian song (1933) with music by Rezső Seress (1899–1968) and lyrics by László Jávor (1903–1992). An English version was published in 1936 with lyrics by Sam M. Lewis (1885–1959).

832.7   Dionne quintuplets] Annette, Cécile, Yvonne, Marie, and Émilie were born on May 28, 1934, in Callander, Ontario. All five sisters survived to adulthood.

832.10   *Lady Chatterley's Lover*] See note 435.28. The first unexpurgated American edition of the novel was published in 1959.

832.21   International Brigade] Foreign volunteers who fought for the Republic against the Nationalists in the Spanish Civil War (1936–1939).

833.29   I wrote . . . automobile accident] "The Interior Castle," pp. 176–90 in this volume. For Stafford's own accident, see Chronology, 1938–39.

833.37–38   as I worked . . . suicide story] See Chronology, 1947 and 1950.

834.1–2   Dostoevski's . . . *The Brothers Karamazov*] The novel was serially published in 1879–80.

835.3–4   piccolo . . . "The Stars and Stripes Forever"] March (1897) by John Philip Sousa (1854–1932).

835.13   Welfare Island] Now Roosevelt Island.

837.2–3   *The Sun Also Rises* . . . *The Great Gatsby*] Novel (1926) by Ernest Hemingway (1899–1961); novel (1925) by F. Scott Fitzgerald (1896–1940).

837.23   a brand new novel] *The Catherine Wheel* (1952).

839.2–3   Flatirons] A series of sandstone rock formations in the foothills west of Boulder, Colorado.

839.21   Palmer Method] See note 682.38.

840.25–26   Willy Sutton . . . Whittaker Chambers] Willie Sutton (1901–1980), a notorious armed bank robber and escaped convict, was arrested in Brooklyn on February 18, 1952, and sentenced in May to thirty years to life in prison; he was released in 1969. Arnold Schuster, the young salesman who had recognized Sutton on the subway and identified him to the police, was murdered on March 8, 1952, reportedly by New York underworld figures angered by the favorable publicity he had received. Film actor Ingrid Bergman (1915–1982), then married to director Roberto Rossellini (1906–1971), gave birth to twin girls, Isotta Ingrid and Isabella, on June 18, 1952. Whittaker Chambers (1901–1961), a member of the Communist Party from 1925 to 1938, testified before the House Committee on Un-American Activities in 1948 that former State Department official Alger Hiss had been a Soviet intelligence agent in the 1930s. Chambers published his best-selling autobiography *Witness* in May 1952.

840.29–30   Ransom . . . Anderson] John Crowe Ransom (1888–1974), poet, literary critic, and founding editor of *Kenyon Review*; Ford Madox Ford, see note 830.26   ; John Peale Bishop (1892–1944), poet, critic, and novelist; Sherwood Anderson (1876–1941), novelist and short story writer.

841.13–14   Earl of Oxford . . . a puppy] Edward de Vere, Earl of Oxford (1550–1604) quarreled in 1579 with his literary and political rival Sir Philip Sidney (1554–1586) on a tennis court, probably at Greenwich Palace. When Oxford demanded that Sidney leave the court, Sidney refused, and Oxford angrily called him a "puppy." Sidney gave Oxford the lie by replying "in respect all the world knows puppies are gotten by dogs and children by men," and then withdrew. A duel between the two men was prevented by the intercession of Queen Elizabeth.

841.22   Ben Greet players] English acting company founded by Ben Greet (Sir Philip Barling Greet, 1857–1936).

842.17   Quiz Kids] See note 128.14.

842.39–843.1 Kathleen Winsor . . . income-tax refund] *Forever Amber* (1944), a best-selling historical romance set in seventeenth-century England, was the debut novel of Kathleen Winsor (1919–2003). The U.S. Court of Claims ruled on June 3, 1952, that because Winsor had written the manuscript primarily for her own amusement the $195,000 net proceeds she received for the sale of the film rights should have been taxed as capital gains rather than ordinary income. Winsor was awarded a $26,358.72 refund.

843.31 "cacoethes scribendi"] See note 3.11–12.

843.32–33 Addison . . . small pox"] Joseph Addison (1672–1719) in *The Spectator*, No. 582, August 18, 1714.

844.40 Mermaid Tavern's] London tavern whose patrons in the early seventeenth century included the writers Ben Jonson (1572–1637), John Donne (1572–1631), John Fletcher (1579–1625), and Francis Beaumont (1584–1616).

845.1 three point two] See note 223.14–15.

845.7–8 *The Wasteland . . . Young Man*] *The Waste Land*, poem by T. S. Eliot; *Swann's Way* (1913), novel by Marcel Proust, the first volume of *In Search of Lost Time*; *A Portrait of the Artist as a Young Man* (1916), novel by James Joyce.

845.31 NYA and the FERA jobs] The National Youth Administration (1935–43) and Federal Emergency Relief Administration (1933–35), New Deal agencies.

845.35–36 *Walden . . . Autobiography*] *Walden; or, Life in the Woods* (1854) by Henry David Thoreau (1817–1862); *Culture and Anarchy* (1869) by Matthew Arnold (1822–1888); *The Theory of the Leisure Class: An Economic Study of Institutions* (1899) by Thorstein Veblen (1857–1929); *My Life* (1930) by Leon Trotsky (1879–1940).

846.5 *Sweeney among the Nightingales*] Poem (1919) by T. S. Eliot.

846.9–10 Sacco and Vanzetti] See note 553.38.

846.10 Alger Hiss] Alger Hiss] Hiss (1904–1992), an official in the State Department from 1936 to 1946, was accused in 1948 of espionage for the Soviet Union by Whittaker Chambers (see note 840.25–26) and convicted of perjury in 1950. (He was not prosecuted for espionage because the statute of limitations had expired.) Although he maintained his innocence for the remainder of his life, documents made public in the 1990s, including decoded cable messages, strongly indicate that Hiss served as a Soviet intelligence agent.

847.19–20 Orville Prescott] Prescott (1907–1996) was the principal book reviewer for *The New York Times*, 1942–66.

847.29 *Gone with the Wind*] Novel (1936) by Margaret Mitchell (1900–1949).

847.33 Ronald Knox] See note 566.3.

848.2 *Star Money*] The novel was published in 1950.

848.15–16   recent profile . . . Mickey Spillane] Spillane (1918–2006) was profiled in *Life* on June 23, 1952.

848.17   Luger] German semiautomatic pistol.

850.24   Mrs Harrison Williams . . . Winsor] American socialite and fashion icon Mona von Bismarck, born Mona Strader (1897–1983), was married from 1926 to 1953 to the wealthy utilities financier Harrison Charles Williams (1873–1953). American-born Wallis Simpson (1896–1986) became Duchess of Windsor in 1937 when she married the former Edward VIII six months after his abdication.

851.31   O'Brien collections] Edward J. O'Brien (1890–1941) was the founder and editor (1915–41) of *The Best American Short Stories* series. He was succeeded as series editor (1941–77) by Martha Foley (1897–1977).

852.16   Francis Biddle . . . Senator Taft] Francis Biddle (1886–1968), U.S. attorney general, 1941–45, and chairman of the liberal Americans for Democratic Action, 1950–53; Robert A. Taft (1889–1953), conservative Republican senator from Ohio, 1939–53.

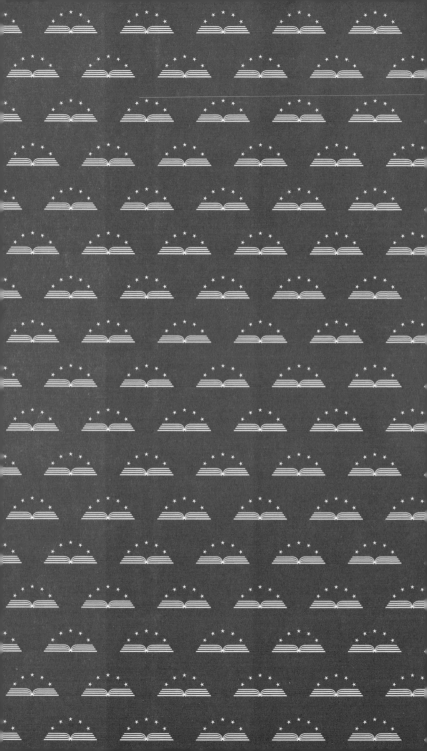